To Love a Duchess

By Karen Ranney

To Love a Duchess

 AN ALL FOR LOVE NOVEL

KAREN RANNEY

AVONBOOKS

An Imprint of HarperCollins*Publishers*

TO LOVE A DUCHESS. Copyright © 2018 by Karen Ranney LLC. All rights reserved. Printed in the United States of America. No part of this book may be used or reproduced in any manner whatsoever without written permission except in the case of brief quotations embodied in critical articles and reviews. For information, address HarperCollins Publishers, 195 Broadway, New York, NY 10007.

First Avon Books mass market printing: August 2018
First Avon Books hardcover printing: July 2018

Print Edition ISBN: 978-0-06-284872-7

Digital Edition ISBN: 978-0-06-284105-6

Avon, Avon & logo, and Avon Books & logo are registered trademarks of HarperCollins Publishers in the United States of America and other countries.

HarperCollins is a registered trademark of HarperCollins Publishers in the United States of America and other countries.

FIRST EDITION

18 19 20 21 22   LSC   10 9 8 7 6 5 4 3 2 1

To Love a Duchess

Chapter One

September 1864
Marsley House
London, England

*H*e felt the duke's stare on him the minute he walked into the room.

Adam Drummond closed the double doors behind him quietly so as not to alert the men at the front door. Tonight Thomas was training one of the young lads new to the house. If they were alerted to his presence in the library, they would investigate.

He had a story prepared for that eventuality. He couldn't sleep, which wasn't far from the truth. Nightmares often kept him from resting more than a few hours at a time. A good thing he had years of practice getting by with little sleep.

He'd left his suite attired only in a collarless white shirt and black trousers. Another fact for which he'd have to find an explanation. As the majordomo of Marsley House, he was expected to wear the full uniform of his position at all times, even in the middle of the night. Perhaps not donning the white waistcoat, cravat, and coat was an act of rebellion.

Strange, since he'd never been a rebel before. It was this place, this house, this assignment that was affecting him.

For the first time in seven years he hadn't borrowed a name or a history carefully concocted by the War Office. He'd taken the position as himself, Adam Drummond, Scot and former soldier with Her Majesty's army. The staff knew his real name. Some even knew parts of his true history. The housekeeper called him Adam, knew he was a widower, was even aware of his birthdate.

He felt exposed, an uncomfortable position for a man who'd worked in the shadows for years.

He lit one of the lamps hanging from a chain fixed to the ceiling. The oil was perfumed, the scent reminiscent of jasmine. The world of the Whitcombs was unique, separated from the proletariat by two things: the peerage and wealth.

The pale yellow light revealed only the area near the desk. The rest of the huge room was in shadow. The library was *ostentatious,* a word he'd heard one of the maids try to pronounce.

"And what does it mean, I'm asking you?" She'd been talking to one of the cook's helpers, but he'd interjected.

"It means *fancy.*"

She'd made a face before saying, "Well, why couldn't they just say *fancy,* then?"

Because everything about Marsley House was ostentatious.

This library certainly qualified. The room had three floors connected by a circular black iron staircase. The third floor was slightly larger than the second, making it possible for a dozen lamps to hang from chains affixed to each level at different heights. If he'd lit them all it would have been bright as day in here, illuminating thousands of books.

He didn't think the Whitcomb family had read every one of the volumes. Some of them looked as if they were new, the dark green leather and gold spines no doubt as shiny as when they'd arrived from the booksellers. Others were so well worn that he couldn't tell what the titles were until he pulled them from the shelves and opened them. There were a great many books on military history and he suspected that was the late duke's doing.

He turned to look at the portrait over the mantel. George Whitcomb, Tenth Duke of Marsley, was wearing his full military uniform, the scarlet jacket so bright a shade that Adam's eyes almost watered. The duke's medals gleamed as if the sun had come out from behind the artist's window to shine directly on such an exalted personage. He wore a sword tied at his waist and his head was turned slightly to the right, his gaze one that Adam remembered. Contempt shone in his eyes, as if everything the duke witnessed was beneath him, be it people, circumstances, or the scenery of India.

Adam was surprised that the man had allowed himself to be painted with graying hair. Even his muttonchop whiskers were gray and brown. In India, Whitcomb had three native servants whose sole duties were to ensure the duke's sartorial perfection at all times. He was clipped and coiffed and brushed and shined so that he could parade before his men as the ultimate authority of British might.

His eyes burned out from the portrait, so dark brown that they appeared almost black, narrowed and penetrating.

"Damn fine soldiers, every single one of them. All mongrels, of course, but fighting men."

At least the voice—surprisingly higher in pitch than Adam had expected—was silent now. He didn't have to hear himself being called a mongrel again. Whitcomb had been talking about the British regiments assigned to guard the East India Company settlements. He could well imagine the man's comments about native soldiers.

What a damned shame Whitcomb had been killed in a carriage accident. He deserved a firing squad at the very least. He wished the duke to Hell as he had ever since learning of the man's death. The approaching storm with its growling thunder seemed to approve of the sentiment.

As if to further remind him of India, his shoulder began to throb. Every time it rained the scar announced its presence, the bullet wound just one more memory to be expunged. It was this house. It brought to mind everything he'd tried to forget for years.

Adam turned away from the portrait, his attention on the massive, heavily tooled mahogany desk. This, too, was larger than it needed to be, raised on a dais, more a throne than a place a man might work. A perfect reflection of the Duke of Marsley's arrogance.

The maids assigned this room had left the curtains open. If he had been a proper majordomo he would no doubt chastise them for their oversight. But because he'd been a leader of men, not of maids, he decided not to mention it.

Lightning flashed nearby, the strike followed by another shot of thunder. The glass shivered in the mullioned panes.

Maybe the duke's ghost was annoyed that he was here in the library again.

The careening of the wind around this portion of Marsley House sounded almost like a warning. Adam disregarded it as he glanced up to the third floor. He would have to be looking for a journal. That was tantamount to searching for a piece of coal in a mine or a grain of sand on the beach.

This assignment had been difficult from the beginning. He'd been tasked to find evidence of the duke's treason. While he believed the man to be responsible for the deaths of hundreds of people, finding the proof had been time consuming and unsuccessful to this point.

He wasn't going to give up, however. This was more than an assignment for him. It was personal.

One of the double doors opened, startling him.

"Sir?"

Daniel, the newest footman, stood there. The lad was tall, as were all of the young men hired at Marsley House. His shock of red hair was accompanied by a splattering of freckles across his face, almost as if God had wielded a can of paint and tripped when approaching Daniel. His eyes were a clear blue and direct as only the innocent could look.

Adam always felt old and damaged in Daniel's presence.

"Is there anything I can do for you, sir?" the young footman asked.

"I've come to find something to read." There, as an excuse it should bear scrutiny. He could always claim that he was about to examine the Marsley House ledgers, even though he normally performed that task in his own suite.

"Yes, sir."

"I think we had a prowler the other night," Adam said, improvising. "One of the maids mentioned her concern."

"Sir?"

Daniel was a good lad, the kind who wouldn't question a direct order.

"I'd like you to watch the outer door to the Tudor garden."

"Yes, sir," Daniel said, nodding.

"Tell Thomas that I need you there."

"Yes, sir," the young man said again, still nodding.

Once he, too, had been new to a position. In his case, Her Majesty's army. Yet he'd never been as innocent as Daniel. Still, he remembered feeling uncertain and worried in those first few months, concerned that he wasn't as competent at his tasks as he should be. For that reason he stopped the young man before he left the library.

"I've heard good reports about you, Daniel."

The young man's face reddened. "Thank you, sir."

"I think you'll fit in well at Marsley House."

"Thank you, Mr. Drummond."

A moment later, Daniel was gone, the door closed once again. Adam watched for a minute before turning and staring up at the third floor.

The assignment he'd been given was to find one particular journal. Unfortunately, that was proving to be more difficult than originally thought. The Duke of Marsley had written in a journal since he was a boy. The result was that there were hundreds of books Adam needed to read.

After climbing the circular stairs, he grabbed the next two journals to be examined and brought them back to the first floor. He doubted if the duke would approve of him sitting at his desk, which was why Adam did so, opening the cover of one of the journals and forcing himself to concentrate on the duke's overly ornate handwriting.

He didn't look over at the portrait again, but it still seemed as if the duke watched as he read.

At first Adam thought it was the sound of the storm before realizing that thunder didn't speak in a female voice. He stood and extinguished the lamp, but the darkness wasn't absolute. The lightning sent bright flashes of light into the library.

Moving to the doors, he opened one of them slightly, expecting to find a maid standing there, or perhaps a footman with his lover. He knew about three dalliances taking place among the staff, but he wasn't going to reprimand any of them. As long as they did their jobs—which meant that he didn't garner any attention for the way he did his—he wasn't concerned about their behavior in their off hours.

It wasn't a footman or a maid engaged in a forbidden embrace. Instead, it was Marble Marsley, the widowed duchess. She'd recently returned from her house in the country, and he'd expected to be summoned to her presence as the newest servant on the staff and one of the most important. She hadn't sent for him. She hadn't addressed him.

He had to hand it to the duke; he'd chosen his duchess well. Suzanne Whitcomb, Duchess of Marsley, was at least thirty years younger than the duke and a beautiful woman. Tonight her dark brown hair was arranged in an upswept style, revealing jet-black earrings adorned with diamonds. Her face was perfect, from the shape to the arrangement of her features. Her mouth was generous, her blue-gray eyes the color of a Scottish winter sky. Her high cheekbones suited her aristocratic manner, and her perfect form was evident even in her many-tiered black cape the footman was removing.

Did she mourn the bastard? Is that why she'd remained in her country home for the past several months?

From his vantage point behind the door, he watched as she removed her gloves and handed them to the footman, shook the skirts of her black silk gown, and walked toward him with an almost ethereal grace.

He stared at her, startled. The duchess was crying. Perfect tears fell down her face as silently as if she were a statue. He waited until she passed, heading for the staircase that swooped like a swallow's wing through the center of Marsley House, before opening the door a little more.

Glancing toward the vestibule, he was satisfied that Thomas, stationed at the front door, couldn't see him. He took a few steps toward the staircase, watching.

The duchess placed her hand on the banister and, looking upward, ascended the first flight of steps.

He had a well-developed sense of danger. It had saved his life in India more than once. But he wasn't at war now. There weren't bullets flying and, although the thunder might sound like cannon, the only ones were probably at the Tower of London or perhaps Buckingham Palace.

Then why was he getting a prickly feeling on the back of his neck? Why did he suddenly think that the duchess was up to something? She didn't stop at the second floor landing or walk down the corridor to her suite of rooms. Instead, she took one step after another in a measured way, still looking upward as if she were listening to the summons of an angel.

He glanced over at the doorway, but the footman wasn't looking in his direction. When he glanced back at the staircase, Adam was momentarily confused because he couldn't see her. At the top of the staircase, the structure twisted onto itself and then disappeared into the shadows. There were only two places she could have gone: to the attic, a storage area that encompassed this entire wing of Marsley House. Or to the roof.

He no longer cared if Thomas saw him or not. Adam began to run.

Where the hell was the daft woman?

Adam raced up the first flight of stairs, then the second, wondering if he was wrong about Marble Marsley. He'd overheard members of the staff calling her that and had assumed she'd gotten the label because she was cold and pitiless. A woman who never said a kind word to anyone. Someone who didn't care about another human being.

In that, she and her husband were a perfect pair.

But marble didn't weep.

He followed the scent of her perfume, a flowery, spicy aroma reminding him of India. At the top of the staircase, he turned to the left, heading for an inconspicuous door, one normally kept closed. It was open now, the wind blowing the rain down the ten steps to lash him in the face.

He'd been here only once, on a tour he'd done to familiarize himself with the place. Marsley House was a sprawling estate on the edge of London, the largest house in the area and one famous enough to get its share of carriages driving by filled with gawping Londoners out for a jaunt among their betters.

Not that the Marsley family was better than anyone else, no matter what they thought. They had their secrets and their sins, just like any other family.

He kept the door to the roof open behind him, grateful for the lightning illuminating his way. If only the rain would stop, but it was too late to wish for that. He was already drenched.

In a bit of whimsy, the builder of Marsley House had created a small balcony between two sharply pitched gables. Chairs had been placed there, no doubt for watching the sunset over the roofs of London.

No one in their right mind would be there in the middle of a storm. As if agreeing with him, thunder roared above them.

The duchess was gripping the balcony railing with both hands as she raised one leg, balancing herself like a graceful bird about to swoop down from the top of a tree.

People didn't swoop. They fell.

What the hell?

He began to run, catching himself when he would have fallen on the slippery roof.

"You daft woman," he shouted as he reached her.

She turned her face to him, her features limned by lightning.

He didn't see what he saw. At least that's what he told himself. No one could look at the Duchess of Marsley and not be witness to her agony.

He grabbed one of her arms, pulling her to him and nearly toppling in the process. For a moment he thought her rain-soaked dress was heavy enough to take them both over the railing.

Then the daft duchess began to hit him.

He let fly a few oaths in Gaelic while trying to defend himself from the duchess's nails as she went for his eyes. Her mouth was open and for a curious moment, it almost looked like she was a goddess of the storm, speaking in thunder.

He stumbled backward, pulling her on top of him when she would have wrenched free. He had both hands on each of her arms now, holding her.

She was screaming at him, but he couldn't tell what she was saying. He thought she was still crying, but it might be the rain.

He pushed away from the railing with both feet. He'd feel a damn sight better if they were farther away from the edge. As determined as she was, he didn't doubt that she would take a running leap the minute she got free.

The storm was directly overhead now, as if God himself dwelt in the clouds and was refereeing this fight to the death. Not his, but hers.

He was a few feet away from the railing now, still being pummeled by the rain. Twice she got a hand free and struck him. Once he thought she was going to make it to her feet. He grabbed the sodden bodice of her dress and jerked her back down. She could die on another night, but he was damned if he was going to let her do it now.

He made it to his knees and she tried, once more, to pull away.

She got one arm free and then the second. Just like he imagined, she made for the railing again. He grabbed her skirt as he stood. When she turned and went for his eyes again, he jerked the fabric with both hands, desperate to get her away from the edge.

The duchess stumbled and dropped like a rock.

He stood there being pelted by rain that felt like miniature pebbles, but the duchess didn't move. Her cheek lay against the roof; her eyes were closed, and rain washed her face clean of tears.

He bent and scooped her up into his arms and headed for the door, wondering how in hell he was going to explain that he'd felled the Duchess of Marsley.

Chapter Two

*A*dam's luck ran out on the family floor. He nodded to the footman stationed outside the duchess's suite, wondering what kind of training the man had received from the previous majordomo. The young man's eyes didn't reveal any emotion at the sight of Adam carrying an unconscious duchess, both of them dripping on the crimson runner. All he did was open one of the doors and step aside to reveal the sitting room.

The lamps had been left lit inside the room. Adam expected the duchess's maid to greet him. No one did.

The scent of the duchess's perfume was even stronger in the sitting room. He stood there uncertain, glancing over his shoulder only when the door closed softly behind him.

He had never been in the duchess's chambers before. The sitting room alone looked as if it took up half this wing. The walls were covered in a pale ivory silk patterned with embroidered branches complete with birds of different colors.

Two sofas sat perpendicular to the white marble fireplace on the far wall. They, too, were covered in ivory silk. The crimson-and-ivory rug was woven in a pattern similar to the silk on the walls. The furniture was mahogany and crafted with feminine touches, like curved legs ending in delicate paws.

The tenement in Glasgow where he'd been born and raised could be put inside this room and still have space left over. The cost of the ivory silk curtains alone could probably have fed his family for a year.

The duchess lay like a black cloud in his arms, her head lolling against his chest. Her cheek still bore a red mark where she'd struck the roof.

Should he attempt to apologize? Or explain? Or simply hope that she'd forget the entire incident?

Why had she tried to throw herself off the roof? Had she loved the bastard that much? The Duke of Marsley didn't deserve her devotion, especially two years after his death.

He wanted to give instructions to the footman to keep her inside her suite, but doubted that would work. The duchess was their employer, the goddess in this little kingdom of Marsley House. None of the servants would go against her for fear they would be dismissed.

Maybe the duchess's maid was close enough to the duchess to be able to alter her behavior. She might have some influence. If she didn't, maybe she'd know someone who would.

But the maid wasn't here, even though she should have been waiting for the duchess to return.

He strode across the room, uncaring that his shoes squished on the expensive carpet or that the duchess's skirt dripped a path to her bedroom.

This chamber was as richly furnished as the sitting room. The bed was easily four times the size of his in the servants' quarters and, no doubt, four times as comfortable.

Here the ivory color was featured again, in the bed coverings and the curtains on the floor-to-ceiling windows. Even the vanity was swathed in ivory silk.

He glanced at the silver brushes and assortment of jars. His late wife, Rebecca, or his sister would have loved this room. He could almost imagine each woman sitting there, delight sparkling in their eyes as they used the downy powder puff or that pink stuff. What did women call it? Pomade? He really didn't know.

He pushed the ghosts of his past away and walked to the bed, depositing the duchess on the spread before stepping back.

He'd thought she was marble, but it was all too clear she wasn't. Not with that agony in her eyes.

She'd wanted to die.

He stretched out one hand and pulled the bell rope beside the bed. A night maid, in addition to a night footman, was on duty in the kitchen, ready to serve the duchess if she required anything. This time she didn't need tea or digestive biscuits. Only Ella, the lady's maid who should have been here.

She wasn't his responsibility, thankfully, but was disciplined by the duchess or Mrs. Thigpen, the housekeeper, if the duchess preferred.

After opening the chest at the end of the bed, he found a blanket, which he draped over the duchess. She needed to be undressed, and quickly, before she caught a chill. But he wasn't about to compound his sins of the evening by attempting that.

Her lashes were incredibly long, brushing her cheeks. Her face was as pale as any of those poor souls they'd found at Manipora. Death, or almost death in the case of the duchess, had bestowed a marble purity to their faces. The duchess's lips were nearly blue, and he found himself wanting to warm them, to bring back some color. If for no other reason than to prove that she wasn't dead after all.

At least she hadn't died tonight, but what would happen tomorrow? Would she succeed in her aim?

When the night maid arrived, he had her send for Ella. The girl was a gossip, but one quick glance at him froze any future words she might have spoken. If anyone talked about him standing in the duchess's bedroom, or her looking nearly like a corpse, he knew where to go. The young maid knew it, too, if the wide-eyed stare she gave him was any indication.

She nearly flew from the room to fetch Ella, leaving him alone with the duchess once more.

He didn't move from his stance beside the bed. *Stand easy* was a pose he'd learned as barely more than a boy in the army. He assumed it now, his hands interlocked behind his back, his legs spread a foot or so apart. His gaze didn't move from the woman on the bed. If he'd looked away, he would have missed the fluttering of her lashes.

"It's awake you are," he said.

He cleared his throat, annoyed at himself. When he was tired, or under the effect of strong emotion, he sometimes fell into the Glaswegian accent of his youth, the same cadence of speech he'd been at pains to alter once he'd left Scotland. It returned now, as did his accent, belying the twenty years or so since he last set foot on Scottish soil.

She appeared to still be unconscious, but he wasn't fooled. The duchess was playacting.

Should he apologize or simply pretend that the incident on the roof hadn't happened?

If he didn't appease her, he'd probably be dismissed on the spot, and he'd have to go back and admit that he'd failed spectacularly at his mission.

That was not going to happen.

She turned her head slowly, her eyes opening reluctantly.

He felt a jolt when she pinned him with her stare.

"Who are you?"

He'd been introduced to her when she arrived back in London a few days earlier. She hadn't looked up from her task of removing her gloves, one finger at a time. He hadn't even warranted a quick glance. He'd opened the door for her on two other occasions and she'd sailed past like a schooner in full wind.

This was the first time she actually looked at him. He didn't move from his stance, but he allowed himself a small, cool smile.

"I am your new majordomo, Your Grace," he said. "Your solicitor hired me two months ago."

She closed her eyes again and turned her head once more.

"Go away," she said softly, her voice sounding as if it held unshed tears.

"I've sent for your maid," he said. "She should be here any moment."

"I don't want her here, either," she said.

He knew hell all about a woman's relationship with her maid, but he suspected it must be a close one. After all, the latter helped the former dress, cared for her clothing, fixed her hair, and was no doubt the recipient of confidences. Evidently, the Duchess of Marsley and her lady's maid didn't share that bond.

He wasn't going to send Ella away. In fact, he would feel much better if Her Grace had a companion at all times, especially if she got a yen to throw herself off the roof.

She didn't say anything further. Nor did he. Instead, they were separated only by a few feet, two silent people in different poses and in vastly different roles in society. They might as well have been on different sides of the world.

He brought his feet together, released his arms, and took a deep breath. Walking to the opposite wall, he used a finger to lift one of the curtain panels, then stared out at the night. The rain was still falling steadily. The lightning was giving a show in the distant sky, but the thunder had been muted. Here, in this room, in this house, the silence was almost absolute but for the plaintive cry of a cat.

The duchess didn't have any pets, so he reasoned it was probably a stray cat that had taken up residence somewhere close by and wasn't happy about the rain. When he finished with the duchess, he would go find the poor animal and give it some shelter. No creature deserved to be cold, wet, and probably hungry.

The door opened, then closed. Footsteps heralded Ella's arrival. A moment later she stood in the doorway to the sitting room, her attention first on the duchess and then on him.

Ella was of an uncertain age, past the first blush of youth and slightly older than the duchess. She always appeared to be judging something, most often standing rigid with her hands clutched tight to each other at her midriff. She rarely smiled and although he'd heard other members of the staff laugh on numerous occasions, he'd never heard Ella. He didn't think she was capable of it.

The word *dour* had been invented to describe people like Ella.

He didn't like the maid, an instant judgment he'd made the third day after the duchess had arrived from the country. He and Ella had passed each other on the servants' stairs and she'd given him a contemptuous look.

He'd wanted to stop her right then and ask her why she thought she was so much better than the other staff. Was it because she served a duchess? Did she somehow believe that she possessed some power because she'd laundered a member of the peerage's unmentionables? Or did her hair?

As a real majordomo, he needed to be familiar with the various hierarchies in the world of servants. He wasn't since he'd never employed a servant. Nor had he grown up around them, so he'd needed to do some research.

A lady's maid was a position that required some skill and experience. One needed to know—according to a book he'd found in the library—how to care for her employer's clothing. She was to direct the staff that would care for her employer's belongings, such as the maids who would clean the duchess's suite. She ordered items of clothing, gifts, and other necessities as dictated by her employer.

In Ella's case, another one of her duties was to be as insufferable as possible.

The maid's expression was continually haughty. She didn't dine with the rest of the staff, but planned her meals so that when everyone was finished she could eat in relative privacy in the small dining room set aside for the servants. No doubt she would've preferred to have a sitting room attached to her bedroom, but those two suites on the third floor had been set aside for the housekeeper and the majordomo.

"Her Grace needs your assistance," he said to Ella.

The fact that he didn't explain any further earned him a glance from the duchess.

When he returned her look she closed her eyes, but not before giving him a quick impression of gratitude, which didn't make any sense.

Ella removed the blanket from the duchess. She shook her head when realizing the state of the younger woman's attire. He didn't know if the black silk dress was ruined and he didn't care, but the duchess needed to change as quickly as possible and get warm.

So did he, for that matter.

"I don't understand," Ella said. "What happened?"

He had a feeling that nothing would satisfy Ella but the absolute truth. However, she wasn't going to get it from him. Let the duchess tell her maid whatever she wanted.

He moved toward the doorway, wanting his bed and his solitude.

"*Airson caoidh fear gun onair a tha gòrach,*" he said to the duchess before making his way out of her suite.

He was rewarded with a frown from both women.

Chapter Three

"What happened, Your Grace? Why are you wet?"

She really wished Ella wasn't here. She could have done for herself quite well if the room wasn't suddenly spinning. She needed to compose herself and take a few minutes to blink back the dizziness, but Ella had an arm around her back and was insisting that she sit up.

"What happened?"

Suzanne swallowed against the sudden sourness on her tongue. She still tasted the wine she'd drunk at her father's dinner. Too much wine. How many glasses had she consumed? Too many if she couldn't remember.

"Your Grace, why are your clothes sodden?"

Here she needed to be careful. Drummond had surprised her by not revealing the entire story. But if she wasn't cautious now, Ella would summon her father to Marsley House and Suzanne would be forced to endure his scrutiny and lectures.

She opened her eyes. Ella looked even more angry tonight than she normally did.

"The storm was spectacular. I went on the roof to see it."

"The roof?" Ella said.

"I wanted to see the display of lightning."

There, that was plausible enough. In addition, it sounded slightly idiotic, which wouldn't disappoint either Ella or her father.

"But on the roof, Your Grace?" the maid asked, her voice conveying some degree of skepticism.

"The rain had momentarily stopped," she said.

"Your dress is wet, Your Grace."

"It started to rain again," she answered as Ella began unfastening her clothes. She was wet and the cold was finally beginning to penetrate the gray fog that always surrounded her.

"Where is your other hair clip?" Ella asked.

"My hair clip?"

"Yes, Your Grace," Ella said, her voice just this side of rude. "Your hair clip. One of two that you inherited from your mother. The ones that look like leaves, Your Grace, and are filled with diamonds."

Suzanne kept her eyes closed. She really didn't want to see the maid right now. She didn't want to see anything at all. How odd that she could still see the newly hired majordomo standing there in his militaristic way, his eyes heated with fury. How very strange to be hated by one's servants.

"Where is the hair clip?" Ella asked.

Suzanne raised her right hand. Georgie's mourning ring was still on her third finger. That, and her mourning brooch, were the only pieces of jewelry she cared about right now.

No doubt Ella would inform her father of her laxity. The maid was fawning but only toward her father. Not a foolish thing to be, all in all. Had he encouraged her to spy on Suzanne? Sometimes she felt herself being observed by Ella, as if the maid were making mental notes of what to write at a later date. Did she journal as assiduously as her late husband, George?

How odd that she didn't know. Nor did she care. If she could have, she would have dispensed with Ella entirely, but her father would no doubt hire someone else in her stead.

Ella was extremely proficient at her position. She hadn't lost a collar, cuff, or corset cover since Ella had come to Marsley House six months ago. All of her lace was laundered to perfection. Her unmentionables were darned when necessary and replaced other-

wise. A summons from Ella would bring all manner of tradesmen, seamstresses, and jewelers, each one of them eager to be
recognized as providing trade to the Duchess of Marsley.

If she cared about any of those things, she'd be quite content
with Ella's execution of her duties. Since she didn't, Suzanne felt
apathetic and wished she could feel the same about Ella.

She didn't like the maid, and that feeling seemed to be growing
every day. How very odd. She hadn't objected to Ella at the beginning, but then she hadn't felt much of anything. Now the only
emotion she felt was antipathy.

She looked at Ella, trying to figure out what it was about the
other woman that was sparking so much sudden feeling.

Ella's hair was much lighter than Suzanne's own dark brown.
Instead, it was almost the color of honey and seemed to have a will
of its own, one of constant disobedience, frizzing when it rained.
The maid's eyes were brown, almost the color of whiskey. Her lips
were thin, the better to disappear in her face when she was in a
critical mood, and her nose was slightly askew, as if it had been
broken once. Or perhaps the Almighty, having seen Ella's character as an adult, had tweaked it in remonstration.

She'd never asked Ella about her parentage, her childhood, her
wishes or wants, or anything remotely personal. She hadn't asked
if the other woman liked chocolate or had a dog as a child, or
what kind of weather she preferred. She knew as little about the
other woman as she could and only wished that she could say
the same about Ella's knowledge of her.

She kept her thoughts to herself. At least Ella could not invade
them. She never willingly confided in Ella. Instead, she watched
every comment she uttered in the maid's presence, which meant
that she hadn't spoken freely for months.

Her majordomo hadn't been as constrained, had he? What had
Drummond said to her? Had it been Gaelic? How strange that her
solicitor would hire a Scotsman, especially since her father didn't
like Scotland or its people. She'd often heard him complain about

them for some reason or another. Either they were too penurious or they had a tendency to speak their thoughts too honestly.

One did not challenge Edward Hackney without paying a dear price.

"Your Grace?"

She met Ella's eyes.

"The hairpin?"

She didn't know where the hairpin was. She didn't care. But if she said such a thing, Ella would tell her father and she'd receive an involved speech about treasuring the possessions of her dear departed mother. As if she needed a lecture.

How many times in the past two years had she wished her mother had survived the cancer that had taken her life? How many times had she spoken to her in the quiet of the night, as if praying more to her mother than to God Himself?

"Why was Drummond in your bedroom?"

She didn't remember that part. When she remained silent, Ella continued.

"You returned from the dinner early, Your Grace."

Was the woman going to challenge everything she did? Yes, if Ella proved faithful to her past.

Suzanne was so tired, almost too tired to care that she was wet and had probably soaked the mattress. Her head hung down, her hair plastered against her cheeks. She didn't bother removing it.

She stood, finally, a little wobbly and using the mattress behind her as a bulwark. Each separate garment was stripped from her, Ella's ministrations not requiring any thought. All she needed to do was stand as straight as she was able, given that the room was spinning again, and obey her maid's commands. *Lift that foot, then that one. Raise your arm. Lower it, Your Grace.*

Ella led her into the bathing chamber, handed her a cloth to wash her face as she washed and dried the rest of Suzanne's body. In earlier days, before Ella, she would have dismissed her maid and bathed in the polished marble tub across the room.

If she hadn't been so tired. If she had cared a bit more. If it hadn't been beyond her.

She raised her arms again when Ella dressed her in a voluminous silk nightgown. Once attired for the night, with all her other needs taken care of, she was led to the vanity, where Ella removed the rest of her hairpins and began to dry her hair with a thick towel.

"I've looked through your garments, Your Grace, and I can't find it."

She stared at Ella's reflection in the mirror, uncertain what the other woman was talking about.

"Your hairpin. Your mother's hairpin."

Did she truly need to care about her mother's hairpin? Would her mother mind if it was lost? Did angels care about such things?

She was so very tired, but she tried to remember what had happened tonight. Her father had been displeased. She'd taken too many glasses of wine from the footmen circulating in the public rooms. She'd dared to look unimpressed at some official's title. Or perhaps she'd done something else for which she'd been summarily banished.

Earlier, however, she'd pretended attentiveness as she was introduced to her father's newest protégé. She'd answered the questions put to her with a half smile on her face. She'd endured the endless conversations swirling around her.

Now she just wanted to be left alone.

No one seemed to understand that. Not Ella. Certainly not her father. Not even her Scottish majordomo.

She opened her eyes and stared at her image in the mirror. There was a red mark on her cheek. When had that happened? She suddenly remembered. She'd fallen and he'd picked her up as if she'd weighed no more than a feather.

Abruptly, Ella thrust a glass in front of her.

Without looking she knew what the glass contained. A green liquid that smelled of grass and promised oblivion.

"I don't need it," she said. The wine had dulled her wits, numbing her to everything.

"I'm instructed to give it to you, Your Grace."

Her father's orders. *Keep Suzanne in a half-dazed state both day and night. She's more amenable that way. She smiles more. She will agree to almost anything.*

She took the glass, but didn't drink it.

Ella didn't move. She would remain where she was until Suzanne downed the contents. Part of her didn't want to drink it. Another part, more the coward, craved the stupor that would come over her when she did.

To forget, that was the aim. To pretend that nothing had ever happened. To live in a perpetual dream. If only she could. If only she didn't have to wake every day.

"You can leave, Ella. I'll drink it later."

How strange that it hurt to talk. She pressed her fingers to her cheek.

"If you don't mind, Your Grace, I'll stay until you finish the draught."

Leave me. Words she didn't say. What difference did it make, in the end? She would take the potion and sleep. Tomorrow would be the same as today. *Dress, Suzanne. Be pretty, if vacuous. Smile when commanded. Turn this way, then that. Nod or shake your head, depending on the situation or the dictate.* She was only a body, not unlike those marionettes she'd once seen at Covent Garden. No one cared what she felt or thought. Why shouldn't she live in the gray beyond?

She downed the contents of the glass and handed it back to Ella, who smiled. Was that triumph she saw in the other woman's eyes? She didn't care about that, either.

Chapter Four

*A*dam took one of the Marsley carriages to Schomberg House in central London, but he made a quick side trip first.

Mrs. Ross, a widow and his landlady, had begun taking in boarders of a certain type to stave off loneliness, a fact she shared with him when he'd first arrived in London.

"I'm partial to military men, myself," she'd said. "They can handle themselves, and they're handy to have around. They know what's what."

He'd only nodded at the time, but she'd called on him over the years. He'd fixed a broken table leg, escorted a boarder who hadn't paid her for three weeks back over the threshold, examined an oil lamp and declared it inoperable, moved countless pieces of furniture, and had been as helpful as he could be when he was there.

Whenever he announced that he'd be away for a few weeks, she only nodded and asked him if he knew when he'd return. On some occasions, he'd been able to give her an answer. Most of the time he could only give her a general idea, but he always paid his rent ahead of time so she'd keep his rooms and dust and tidy up as needed.

She'd taken one look at the scrawny black kitten he'd found trapped outside the duchess's sitting room and welcomed him into her home.

The poor thing had been shivering and terrified when he'd finally found it. Somehow it had crawled under an outcropping, a bit of decorative brickwork where there was some shelter from the storm. He'd wrapped it in a towel, warmed it, and managed to feed it some of his breakfast before bringing it to Mrs. Ross.

"Oh my, yes, what a little darling. Of course he can be our mouser."

She'd welcomed him back to England with the same generosity of spirit. He'd been ill on the ship, suffering the effects of a lingering fever, and Mrs. Ross had nursed him back to health. He didn't have any doubt that she'd treat the kitten with the same kindness.

Some people in the world were generous and caring. Mrs. Ross was one of those.

What type of person was the duchess?

He hadn't been able to stop thinking of her, and that both annoyed and concerned him. If she attempted to end her life again, would someone be there to prevent it?

The carriage rolled to a stop in front of Schomberg House. The place was rumored to have once been a gambling den and a brothel. Now the redbrick-and-stone four-story building housed the organization for which he worked. They were housed here almost as an afterthought, but close enough to the War Office in Cumberland House, like misbehaving children under an adult's stern guidance.

The quarters were nothing like the site of the new Foreign Office building on King Charles Street that, along with the India Office, was going to be an example of Palladian architecture gone amok. Evidently, anyone visiting the buildings was supposed to come away impressed at the empire's use of columns, decorative molding, and polished marble.

The building he entered was devoid of columns or marble floors. Instead, there were hallways with doors, none of them marked save for a number. He took the first turn to the left and walked down a hallway tinted yellow by the sunlight spilling in through a far window.

He might have been walking through a deserted building for all the sounds that reached him. The silence was profound, broken only by the muffled noise of a door closing on the second floor and the footfalls on the nearby stairs.

The place smelled of dust and something else: strong black tea. Behind these doors were no doubt small braziers with kettles bubbling away. He was, after all, in the middle of a government building.

Seven years ago, when he'd left the army, Sir Richard Wells had made him a proposition. "Come and work for me. It's a new branch of the War Office. Something that might interest you."

Despite his questions, he'd only been given a cursory explanation of exactly what kind of branch it was, to whom they reported, and why. After a few dozen assignments, he had a better idea.

What he was doing wasn't officially sanctioned, but it benefitted the empire. He'd become a member of a group Sir Richard called the Silent Service, men who might never be recognized for their actions, but who were—one assignment at a time—making the empire safer.

Adam stopped before a room bearing a thirty on the plaque and placed his hand on the wooden knob. When he opened the door, his first sight was of Oliver Cater sitting at his desk in the outer office. He'd been a corporal in their regiment, a young man with a subdued personality and a terror of loud noises. Roger had been his protector of sorts, making sure that Oliver wasn't taunted for his lack of courage. The younger man had reciprocated by being intensely loyal.

Adam hadn't been surprised that Oliver had followed Roger to the War Office.

He glanced up as Adam entered, his bushy eyebrows drawing together. When he got older, Oliver's eyebrows would probably turn gray, get longer, and act like a forest in front of his small brown eyes. Adam couldn't help but wonder what age would do to the moles that dotted Oliver's face.

He pulled out the handkerchief from his pocket, unwrapped it, and placed the candy on Oliver's desk.

"Grace's licorice?" Oliver asked.

Adam nodded. Grace, the cook at Marsley House, had a sweet tooth and kept several treats around for herself and the other servants as well. Adam always took a few from the jar when he was reporting to Roger and gave them to Oliver.

He glanced toward the closed door. "Is he in?"

After selecting one of the candies and popping it into his mouth, Oliver nodded. "He's waiting for you."

Adam entered the office, closed the door behind him, and turned.

Roger was his age, a little shorter and heavier, but possessed of an affable smile that he often used. He was smiling now, an expression that was lost on Adam. He always looked at a man's eyes and he never missed the calculating glint in Roger's, as if he were measuring the worth of someone even as he was convincing them to throw in with one of his schemes.

The outside corners of Roger's eyes turned down, giving him the appearance of a bloodhound. A very trustworthy, kind, and loyal bloodhound.

Appearances could often be deceiving, however.

If anyone could find an easy way to do something, it was Roger. In India he'd gotten a reputation for being able to procure those items a soldier wanted and was willing to pay for. The East India Company had been an unwieldy bureaucracy. The talk had always been that if you needed something found, Roger Mount was your man. Roger had gotten a reputation for finding things that couldn't be found, for obtaining the unobtainable, and for making things happen.

Until he'd been sent to Lucknow, a neighboring garrison, Roger had been making a tidy sum for himself.

When they'd met again a few years ago, Adam hadn't been surprised that Roger had achieved some of his goals. He was no longer just a former soldier, but had risen to the rank of Assistant Undersecretary for Foreign Affairs, a position that allowed him to act as a liaison to the Foreign Office. He didn't doubt that Roger's promotion was due in part to the other man's ability to recognize a

fortuitous circumstance when it appeared. The advantageous marriage he'd made had also helped. Roger was, simply put, ambitious.

"I'm not right for this assignment," Adam said, taking the chair
in front of Roger's desk. "I haven't found the damn journal and
I'm probably on my way out."

Roger Mount sat back in his desk chair, steepled his fingers,
and regarded Adam as if he were much older and wiser. The pose
was a wasted gesture. He and Roger had fought together in India.
He knew the other man's peccadilloes and failings. Nor was he
impressed by this large office or the desk that looked as if it had
cost a family's yearly wages.

"What makes you think you're wrong for the position?"

He debated telling Roger about his actions of the night before,
then decided against it. For some odd reason, he didn't want to
divulge the duchess's suicidal intentions to anyone. He couldn't
rid himself of the image of her face lit by lightning and the agony
he'd seen in her eyes.

"I just know I am," Adam said.

A muscle in Roger's cheek clenched and released several times
before the other man spoke again.

"You're the best I've got for the position," Roger finally said.
The words were uttered calmly and spaced apart to give them
more weight.

"Why, because I'm a Scot?"

Dispensable, in other words. Easily explained away. *Oh, yes,
Drummond. Good man, but he was a Scot, you know.*

They stared at each other. They'd had this discussion many
times in the past and here it was again.

"No, not because you're a Scot, damn it. You're good at fitting
in. People like you."

"I'm a lousy majordomo."

"On the contrary. I've heard very good reports about you."

Adam didn't say anything for a moment. When he did speak,
his voice was tight. "Do you have someone else at Marsley House?
Someone spying on me?"

Roger leaned forward, all earnestness and honesty. Adam wasn't fooled by that pose, either.

"You didn't want to be a servant, Adam. Do you blame me? I had to protect the mission. It's important."

"Who is it?"

Roger shook his head.

He wasn't unduly surprised that Roger had sent someone in to check on him. Roger was capable of smiling to his face and saying something snide about him the minute Adam was out of his office.

He'd never had any delusions that he and Roger were friends, not like Roger pretended. They hadn't been friends in India and they weren't friends now, especially since fate decreed that he had to report to the other man, albeit temporarily. He'd much rather have had his original boss, Sir Richard Wells, but Sir Richard had agreed with Roger that Adam would be best on this assignment. It had been Roger's idea from the beginning to send someone into Marsley House.

"I'm not sure I can find the damn thing."

"You'll find it. If you don't give up," Roger said. There was a look in his eyes that dared Adam to argue.

"The man wrote in a journal every day of his life. I've found journals that began from his boyhood."

"But nothing from India?"

"I've found some from India, too, but they haven't revealed anything."

He'd never failed before and he didn't like the idea of failing now. But there were times—and he was very much afraid that this was one of those—when circumstances were arrayed against him.

"I need you there," Roger said.

He'd heard that same sort of speech two months ago when he'd first been sent to Marsley House.

Adam rolled his shoulders and angled himself in the uncomfortable chair.

"You have to go back and find the damn journal. We can't afford a scandal like that being made public. The Foreign Office is making amends in India, Adam. We're trying to atone for the mistakes we made there. Can you imagine what would happen if it got out that the Duke of Marsley betrayed his own men? The world would see that whole business of Manipora in a different light."

"God help us," Adam said dryly.

He doubted that anyone would ever discover the duke's confession. Most of the journals he'd read looked as if they hadn't been moved since first being placed on the third floor of the library. However, it wasn't his place to argue with a superior and for this assignment, that's what Roger was.

"Who the hell confesses to treason in a journal?" Adam asked.

"Perhaps someone who wants to justify the action," Roger said. "Or feels a sense of guilt?"

He wasn't familiar with questioning his superiors, but in this instance he couldn't bite back his curiosity.

"How do you know he wrote about Manipora? Or about what he did?"

"The information was passed to us from a person very close to the duke," Roger said.

"Who?"

He was coming close to insubordination, but he didn't pull back the question. Instead, he waited, anticipating that Roger would tell him it wasn't any of his business.

"A member of his staff, someone who was very concerned about what he'd learned."

In other words, he wasn't going to get an identity of the informant.

"I know you disliked the duke," Roger said.

"The man was an idiot," Adam said, stretching out one foot and tapping it on the bottom of the desk in front of him.

The duke was not, contrary to his own estimation, a military genius. He'd been arrogant but also impulsive, a deadly combination. He hadn't thought it necessary to solicit the advice or opinions of others, several of whom knew significantly more than he. Consequently, he'd often gone off without the whole story, leading his men into skirmishes that had proved deadly.

Adam had lost his share of friends, not to the glory of the British Empire as much as the stupidity of one of its peers.

"You've never let your personal opinions blind you on an assignment, Adam. Don't do it on this one."

Roger let that comment linger in the air for a moment or two before sitting back, smiling, and offering tea.

Adam didn't want tea; he wanted answers, but he knew Roger wasn't going to be forthcoming. He might get one piece of the puzzle. Another operative would get a second piece. The only person who could put the entire puzzle together was the man heading the assignment. As an operative, Adam wasn't supposed to know every reason and rationale. He was only supposed to be a good civil servant and obey his directives.

Most of the time he didn't have a problem with that. This assignment was different. Of course his personal opinions were going to surface.

Roger rang a bell on the corner of his desk, and a few minutes later Oliver came through the door with a tray containing a teapot, two cups and saucers, a small pitcher filled with milk, and a bowl of sugar.

"I hear the duchess has returned to London," Roger said after preparing his cup and taking a sip. "What is she like?"

Adam did the same, more to give himself time to think than because he wanted tea, especially something that was yellow, smelled of flowers, and reminded him of India. He threw in a teaspoon or two of sugar to make it palatable and managed a sip. He preferred coffee, but that was tantamount to treason here in this War Office warren.

What was the duchess like?

Sad, for one. Intriguing, for another. He wanted to ask her questions he had no business asking. Why had she married the duke? Why did she mourn the man with such ferocity two years after his death?

He couldn't banish the memory of that look in her eyes.

"Maybe the duchess knows where the journal is," Roger said. "Perhaps you could wheedle the information out of her."

He doubted that was ever going to happen, especially after the events of the previous night.

"Someone else would be better in this position," Adam said.

"You're doing fine," Roger said. "You're one of the Service's most trusted operatives. No one else could do better than you, Adam."

If that was true, why had Roger sent another agent in to Marsley House?

He stood, knowing that they were about to go into a circular argument. Nothing he said was going to make any difference to Roger. Either Adam would have to walk away from his position at the War Office or he'd have to go back to Marsley House.

"Make a friend of her," Roger suggested. "Be a confidant. You might even hint that you knew her husband in India. That could form a bond between the two of you."

He doubted the duchess had much to do with her husband's prior military career. The fact, and it disturbed him to admit it even to himself, was that he didn't want to return to Marsley House, not even to submit his resignation and pack his belongings. He didn't want to see the duchess again. He didn't want to explain how resentful he felt about her grief. He didn't want to feel a surge of compassion for her. Nor did he want to have this odd compulsion to explain that he was trying to find proof that the Duke of Marsley had been a son of a bitch and responsible for the deaths of hundreds of people.

The duchess wouldn't mourn the bastard if she knew the truth.

Chapter Five

"I have been unable to find the hairpin, Your Grace."

It wasn't fair that she had to wake to Ella's complaints. If she put the pillow over her face would that silence the woman? Suzanne doubted it.

"I'm certain it will turn up," she said, blinking open her eyes.

Staring up at the sunburst pattern of silk over the bed didn't banish the sound of Ella's voice. Had it always been this grating?

"It is not among your things, Your Grace. And I've had the coachman check the carriage. Could you have left it at the dinner party?"

The dinner party had been a political event, a way of advancing another young man's career. She'd gone because it had been a command from her father, only to discover that there were a great many people in attendance, more than could be adequately seated at her father's expansive dining table. Instead of offering his guests service à la Russe, the dinner courses were arranged on the sideboards in the dining room, with the guests free to mill about or return to the food of their choice.

Had anyone else dared to entertain in such a fashion, the result would probably have been chaotic, but of course it wasn't. Her father left nothing to chance. A bevy of footmen wandered among the guests, ready to take plates or glasses or to offer more wine.

"Your Grace?"

Suzanne opened her eyes and turned her head to find Ella standing beside the bed as she did most mornings. At least the woman retired to her own chamber at night, giving Suzanne some much needed solitude.

If she had her way, she wouldn't have a lady's maid at all. But George had insisted. She'd quite liked Lily, the maid who'd abruptly quit six months ago. Ella had come to Marsley House then, recommended by her solicitor. Her father had also approved of the woman, and it had just been easier to keep Ella on after that.

Ignoring what was around her, be it people or things, made life so much simpler. What did anything matter, after all? It was easier to close her eyes and pretend she was somewhere else, a special place in her mind where she was alone and not bothered by anyone's questions or concerns.

He was suddenly there, in her mind like a storm god. A Scot wreathed in a blinding flash of lightning. Who did he think he was, speaking to her with such contempt in his voice? She'd had to endure a great deal in the last six years, but he had gone over the line. She was not going to be spoken to in such a way or be physically assaulted.

Perhaps her irritation at the majordomo was the reason she waved Ella away now.

"I don't need your help this morning," she said.

Ella ignored her. "Would you like to wear the silk with the ruching or the gathered skirt?"

Did it matter what she wore? That was not a comment she made to Ella. If she had said something so improvident to her maid, the woman would've responded with a lecture on mourning. She had passed two years, so technically she could don lavender if she wished or another subdued shade. But the color of her garments didn't matter. She would carry around a hole in her heart for the rest of her life.

"You have a visitor, Your Grace."

She looked at Ella in surprise. "A visitor? What time is it?"

"Nine thirty, Your Grace."

No one called at that hour in the morning. To do so was the height of rudeness, especially when she wasn't expecting them.

"Who is it?"

"A Mrs. Noreen Armbruster."

"Tell her I'm not receiving visitors. Tell her I'm away. Tell her anything."

"I would have done so ordinarily, Your Grace, but she said that you told her to call this morning, that the two of you talked last evening and specifically made an appointment. Nor does she look the type to leave without getting her way."

Ella sniffed, which was her way of expressing disgust. Evidently Mrs. Armbruster had annoyed the maid. For that alone, Suzanne should make the effort to visit with the woman.

She didn't remember a Mrs. Armbruster, but she didn't say so to Ella. Nor did she confide that the night before had been a blur.

No wonder her father had insisted that she depart for home. She had probably embarrassed him in some way, but then she often did simply by being herself.

Once she would've cared. Once, years ago, she would've felt bad that they clashed so often. She would have felt that she'd let her mother down in some way.

"He doesn't mean to be a hard man, Suzanne," her mother had often told her. "It's just that he wants to accomplish a great deal in his life and the rest of us are slower and get in his way."

Edward Hackney had already accomplished a great deal. Was it enough for him? She didn't know and she'd never ask. They didn't have that kind of relationship. Not one of true thoughts and honest answers. Instead, he told her what he wanted her to do and she, for the most part, acceded without much clamor or fuss.

"Be kind to your father, my dearest Suzanne," her mother had said. "Try to understand him. If something happens to me it will just be the two of you." Had her mother known that her words would be prophetic? She'd died less than a month later.

At least her father hadn't married again. Was that because he'd truly loved her mother and mourned her still? Or because of expediency? He couldn't take the time or the energy to court another woman?

Another instance of never knowing.

She chose the silk with the ruching on the top of the bodice. She added a small black mourning cameo of a mother and child at the base of her throat.

"I'll get your tonic," Ella said.

"Not this morning."

She stared at herself in the mirror. She was too pale. Once she might have cared more about her appearance. Now all that mattered was that she was clean and presentable.

"Your tonic, Your Grace," Ella said.

Suzanne stood, moved away from the vanity, and headed for the sitting room door. She wasn't going to take that vile stuff this morning. Perhaps after her meeting with the majordomo. Until then, she needed to keep her wits about her and it was difficult to do that after ingesting the green potion.

Ella trailed after her instead of remaining behind and straightening up her chambers. Ella insisted on doing the cleaning herself, rather than allowing one of the upstairs maids into the suite. Suzanne knew exactly why she did that. It was yet another way she could maintain control.

The same reason the maid was now following her down the grand staircase.

At the bottom, Suzanne turned and faced Ella, uncaring that there were at least three footmen who could overhear their conversation. She had ceased having any privacy the day she moved into Marsley House. Over the years, she'd gradually become accustomed to the fact that she would always have people listening or watching her. In a sense, the green potion had helped with that, too.

This morning, however, she was herself, albeit with a headache. "That will be all," she said.

Her look defied the other woman to argue with her. It was probably the fact that there were witnesses that made Ella simply nod in response.

"That will be all," she repeated.

Ella nodded once more, but this time she turned and began ascending the staircase.

Mrs. Armbruster had been put into the Persian room. George's grandfather had named this parlor after all the artifacts he'd collected from Persia and the Far East.

Suzanne hesitated in the doorway, realizing that it had been months since she'd been in this room. Thankfully, Mrs. Thigpen was an excellent housekeeper and didn't require daily monitoring. She felt a surge of gratitude toward the woman as well as the staff. There was no dust anywhere. The floors were swept and polished. The brass gleamed. The windows sparkled.

If only she were as well kept as her house.

Someone had had the good sense to offer Mrs. Armbruster refreshments, and the woman was sitting in the pasha's chair next to the window. George's grandfather claimed the chair was a throne used by a ruler of one of the disparate tribes in Persia. Its upholstery was crimson, and its arms and legs ended in lion's paws. A gilded wooden crown in a pattern that no doubt meant something to someone of Persian descent stretched four feet above the back of the chair. The morning sun danced on the gold, then came to rest on Mrs. Armbruster's bright red hair.

It was the hair Suzanne remembered more than Mrs. Armbruster's doughy, kind face. The woman had sparkling blue eyes that seemed amused as she placed her teacup on the table beside her.

They had indeed spoken last night, but Suzanne could not remember one single thing either of them had said.

"Mrs. Armbruster," she said. "I'm so sorry to make you wait."

"Your Grace, it's no bother at all. I have spent the time admiring this surprising room."

Suzanne glanced around at the shelves and the hundreds of knickknacks.

A crimson sofa sat in front of the fireplace and a primarily crimson carpet was underfoot. Even the wall covering was crimson, patterned in France and no doubt extraordinarily expensive.

She always thought of blood when she entered this room and from the history of Persia, she thought it was an apt comparison.

"It was an interest of my husband's grandfather," she said.

The man had a great many interests. One of them wasn't fodder for polite conversation.

Infidelity had been a hobby among the Whitcomb men.

"I'm very much afraid I don't have an apron, Your Grace."

Suzanne looked at the other woman. "I don't understand, Mrs. Armbruster."

"That lovely dress might be ruined."

She still didn't understand.

Mrs. Armbruster stood.

The woman was formidable, a presence in the room. It had nothing to do with her height, which was considerable, or her girth, or even the jutting of her bosom that made her look like the figurehead of a clipper ship. No, Mrs. Armbruster had something else, a quality that reminded Suzanne, oddly enough, of her father.

He, too, could quell anyone's comments or rebellion with a glance.

"Shall we go?" Mrs. Armbruster asked, heading for the parlor door.

"I beg your pardon? Where?"

The older woman glanced over her shoulder at Suzanne. "To the hospital, of course. We discussed it last night. We most desperately need your patronage, Your Grace."

She was marshaling her arguments as to why she couldn't possibly leave Marsley House when Mrs. Armbruster came to stand in front of her.

"You promised, Your Grace."

She'd never willingly broken a promise, even during these ghastly past years. Her mother had been her example in that.

"A woman's word is as good as a man's, Suzanne. Men aren't the only ones to live by a code of honor."

She wanted to ask her mother, then, if her father had a code of honor. But her mother had been ill and she hadn't. There were some questions that could never be asked and some answers that would never be given.

Mrs. Armbruster placed her hand on Suzanne's arm. That's how they left the Persian Parlor and headed for the front of Marsley House: Mrs. Armbruster sailing through the corridors and Suzanne feeling like she was being towed after the woman.

At the door, the footman furnished Mrs. Armbruster with her shawl while another servant fetched Suzanne's cloak.

"Where is that fascinating majordomo of yours, Your Grace? He's a military man, isn't he? You can always tell. They have a certain air about them. Not to mention that yours is a phenomenally handsome creature."

She focused on what Mrs. Armbruster was saying. "You've met my majordomo?"

"Indeed I have. You may not realize this, my dear, but I came to see you a month ago, not realizing that you were at your country home. It was only the very best of circumstances that my husband and I were invited to your father's dinner party. Such a fascinating man, your father."

She didn't know which comment to respond to first. Thankfully, Mrs. Armbruster didn't seem to expect a response.

"It's a beautifully sunny day, my dear. You shan't need that," the older woman said, eyeing Suzanne's black wool cloak. "However, it might serve as an apron of sorts, especially when we get to the nursery."

Her hands froze in the act of putting on her gloves. "Nursery?" Her feet felt embedded in the marble of the foyer. They wouldn't move. For the love of all that was holy, she couldn't visit a nursery.

Mrs. Armbruster glanced at her.

"Trust me, Your Grace. Please."

"I can't," she said.

"You must."

Suzanne shook her head. She didn't care how insistent the other woman was, she couldn't.

Chapter Six

$\mathcal{A}$dam arrived back at Marsley House in time to see a carriage pull away from the front entrance. He gave the signal to the driver to halt for a moment as it passed. Her Grace, the Duchess of Marsley, turned a white face toward him. He had the curious sensation that she needed assistance and that he was the only person who could help her. Their eyes met. Hers widened just for a moment before she composed herself once more, facing forward.

She'd been on his mind ever since last night, but the fact that no gossip had surfaced about the duchess being ill reassured him somewhat.

After the carriage passed he gave the signal for his driver to take him around the back of the house to the stables. The encounter, brief as it was, disturbed him. This assignment had been difficult from the beginning, but she was at the root of his sudden wish to be gone from Marsley House.

Until last night, he hadn't been excessively impatient with the slow pace of his investigation, knowing that it could take some time to find proof of the duke's treason. Now he wanted it done, completed, and over.

He hadn't wanted to come back to the house, but he'd done so because *duty* was a word that meant something to him. He'd been a dutiful soldier in India despite the stupidity of the orders he'd been given. Now he was a dutiful servant of the War Office and the Silent Service. Duty, however, sometimes required a sacrificial commitment. He'd learned that at Manipora.

He'd been a boy when he entered the army and it had molded and shaped him. Growing up in the tenements of Glasgow, he'd been concerned with elemental things like eating and keeping warm. It was only later, after comparing himself to his fellow soldiers, that he'd realized how much he was missing.

He could read, thanks to his mother, who'd died early of a lingering cough, but not before she had instilled some knowledge in her son and daughter. It was Mary, his sister, who had insisted on him learning his numbers and practicing his reading. After enlisting in the army, he'd begun to procure books, spending his hard-earned wages on a volume that he carried around in his knapsack. He would sometimes trade with another soldier. One of the wives at the British Legation in India had given him two books. He still had them at his lodgings and they were among his most treasured possessions.

A book, to him, was like a portable school. A book, unlike a headmaster, didn't care in what area of Glasgow he'd been raised, or whether he'd had the time or the energy to haul a bucketful of water up three flights of stairs so that he could wash. A book didn't offer judgment about his accent or his profanity. But the words, assimilated at his own pace, taught him.

So did his fellow soldiers. He emulated those men who'd purchased their commissions for a lark. He learned to eat with manners, figured out which words were insulting and not to be used often. Over time he softened his Glaswegian accent so that people didn't have any trouble understanding him.

"You're like a hawk," one of the women at the garrison once said to him. "You watch everything, Drummond, but you rarely speak. Why is that?"

He hadn't been able to explain it to her. Thankfully, she'd turned away so he was spared the necessity of trying to be polite.

His early years had been like barren soil. Only two flowers had brightened the landscape: his mother and his sister. They'd both been gone too soon, leaving him nothing but a brown-and-gray existence. Ever since being sent to India, however, he'd gradually begun to realize that life—for most people—was a flower garden.

They took for granted that they would be healthy and, for the most part, happy. They smiled and laughed, rejoiced in their children, good food, and companionship.

He had wanted that and he'd cultivated it for himself. At the same time, he decided that he would never willingly go back to that barren world of barely existing, of drawing breath but resenting even that because nothingness was so much more preferable to his current life.

He read philosophy and poetry and, like the Duke of Marsley, military theory. A few times, he even read novels, although in some cases he found the prose overblown and the dialogue ridiculously dramatic.

Nor was he like any of the heroes portrayed in some of those books. He might have been considered brooding, but that was only because he believed in thinking more than speaking.

But he certainly wasn't a duke or a count or a mysterious owner of a deserted castle. He was only himself, and while he might be proud of some of his accomplishments, he doubted that they would be of interest to any woman like the heroines in some of those novels.

He made his way upstairs. From the information he'd acquired from Mrs. Thigpen, he knew that Marsley House was one of the largest private homes in London. He couldn't help but wonder if the builder, the third duke, had wanted to rival a palace. He'd come close to doing exactly that with the building's seventy-eight rooms. No wonder the staff was almost as large as a company.

In addition to all the bedchambers there were rooms to polish shoes and rooms to trim lamps and rooms to clean cutlery, press the newspapers, store the common dishes, and dry the dish towels. There was even a room that was set up with a broad oak table, stools, and a wooden clock over the door. On a shelf was a book on the peerage and one on etiquette. He'd taken that to be where the newest members of staff were educated on their duties. He'd had more than one peek at both of those books, but had found even more information in the library.

When Adam had first arrived, there were additional footmen assigned night duty—one for each of the wings and one outside the duke and duchess's quarters.

He'd gradually limited the number of personnel assigned to night duty. One of the reasons was simple logistics. He couldn't explore the library—and any of the other rooms—if he had to avoid eleven footmen. The second reason was that they didn't need all those footmen whose sole duty was to stand there and try not to fall asleep.

Because of his position Adam had a corner suite on the third floor with a bedroom, a sitting room that had been converted into an office, and a bathing chamber. He returned to his rooms now and spent several moments changing. He'd become accustomed to a uniform in the army, but a majordomo was supposed to dress in formal attire day and night. He wore black trousers, well-shined black shoes, a black tailcoat over a white shirt that had been starched to the point it could almost stand alone, a white waistcoat, and a white tie.

Once dressed, he walked into the office. The room was plain, devoid of any furnishings but his desk and one straight-backed chair. Someone had tried to add a touch of color to the room in the draperies, a crimson-and-beige stripe that looked as if it had been taken from one of the downstairs parlors.

He had not, despite the length of this assignment, attempted to personalize the space. Depending on who he was supposed to be, he often furnished personal items: a picture of a wife, or a sweetheart, a book or two, a watch inscribed with the name he was using at the time. They all went toward corroborating his false persona.

At Marsley House, his bedroom and office had been left bare. Perhaps because he had a more personal connection to this assignment.

For a few hours he occupied himself with the tasks of his role. The sheer volume of documents he needed to read, approve, sign, or forward to the family solicitor seemed to increase every day.

He arranged for the alterations to the uniforms of two fast-growing footmen. After writing down a recipe for silver polish, he tucked it into his pocket to give to the head footman who was responsible for making it, showing how it was to be applied, and supervising the staff in its application. Adam would inspect the silver later and arrange for it to be returned to its place in the pantry. It was his responsibility to count the damn stuff every night and make sure that one of the staff hadn't made off with a fork or spoon. At least he wasn't required to sleep next to the pantry, although Mrs. Thigpen had informed him that such had been the arrangement for years. That's why there was a room across the hall now used for extra china and stemware.

Before coming to Marsley House, he'd always thought that a housekeeper was responsible for everything that happened in an establishment. His assumption was incorrect, at least here. Adam was tasked with Marsley House running smoothly, which meant that if the roof needed retiling he had to ensure it was done. The same went for filling the pavement in front of the house. Last week he had the bother of getting one of the wrought iron gates at the front of the drive repaired.

He'd replaced an elderly majordomo, one Mrs. Thigpen called Old Franklin.

"The poor man became so forgetful and hard of hearing that he needed help with his tasks," Mrs. Thigpen had told him. "Sankara helped him a great deal. Sankara Bora. He was the duke's secretary and handled a great many details about the house. And Fairhaven, the family's house in the country."

Adam had found that Mrs. Thigpen was a font of knowledge. He went back to the well now, finding the housekeeper in her office beside the kitchen. The room smelled of cinnamon, but all of Marsley House was perfumed in some way. One maid was assigned to exchange the potpourri in all the rooms on a weekly basis. The scent was different depending on the chamber.

Mrs. Thigpen—or Olivia, as she insisted he call her—was eating what looked to be a raisin biscuit and passed the plate to him.

He smiled his thanks, sat on the chair next to her desk, and took one of the biscuits. Like anything Grace cooked, it was delicious.

Olivia had a long thin face with a broad nose, an appearance that made him unfortunately think of a horse. She had a similarly horsey laugh and large teeth. In addition, she had a curious gait. Not a limp exactly, but she tended to list a little to the right side when she walked.

He'd wanted to ask if she'd had a childhood accident that affected her, but it was too personal a question. However, he tried to ease her burden whenever he could, giving orders to all the footmen to assist her if they saw Olivia carrying anything.

"Have you any idea where the duchess has gone?" he asked after spending a few minutes in pleasantries. He helped himself to two additional biscuits, which only prompted Olivia's smile.

"Has she gone somewhere? Not very usual of her, Adam. I don't know. Shall I ring for her maid? Ella will probably know. She doesn't share much about the duchess, however."

"Never mind," he said. "It isn't important. I merely saw her on my way in."

"She may have gone visiting," Olivia offered. "The new duke is a second cousin of the late duke. They socialized some. Perhaps she's gone to see him."

Was she even considered a duchess if there was a new duke? He didn't know. Nor was he comfortable in sharing his ignorance with Olivia.

A good deal of the time he had to hide his lack of knowledge from the rest of the staff. To do that, he had to appear standoffish, demonstrating a haughty kind of arrogance that always irritated him when he had to face it in another individual. He'd managed to frighten a good percentage of the maids, most of whom did a curious little curtsy when they saw him. It wasn't until Olivia said something that he understood why.

"You're new," she said. "A great many of the staff are frightened of you, Adam. You could let anyone go at any time."

"I have no intention of letting anyone go, Olivia," he'd said.

"Well, if you don't mind, Adam, I shall convey that to the rest of the staff. I know it would reassure everyone."

Now whenever he encountered one of the frightened maids, he went out of his way to smile. They still acted nervous, but if they'd come from a background similar to his, he could understand their fear. Being a servant helped them escape from grinding poverty. Of course, nowadays, there were other avenues as well. A girl could find work in the shops or the factories. They didn't have to go into service. But it seemed to him that working at Marsley House wasn't a bad plan for making your way in the world.

He advised Olivia that he was ordering another two bolts of cloth for uniforms and was sending the monthly expenditures to Mr. Barney, the family solicitor. She nodded and said she'd tell the seamstress who made most of her living sewing livery for the Marsley House staff. She informed him that one of the maids had tearfully left their employ this morning, citing homesickness. He would be responsible for hiring a replacement.

He thanked Olivia for the biscuits and headed for the library, specifically to the third floor and the shelves containing the duke's journals.

When he'd first begun his assignment, he'd started with the duke's years in India. None of those books had furnished the proof that he needed. Then he took the last book and moved backward through time. A gap existed between that journal and the date of the duke's death, but there had been other times when the duke had simply stopped writing for a while. Adam had finally started over at the beginning, giving himself the chore of reading all of the Duke of Marsley's self-indulgent writings. So far he'd learned a great deal about the duke and most of it was boring.

This week he'd reached the man's early twenties. George Whitcomb had written extensively about his conquest of the ladies. On more than one occasion he'd seemed to delve into self-examination and said something cogent like, "It is my title, I am sure, that brings them like bees buzzing around the garden." Then he'd added a comment that made Adam realize he wasn't aware of himself at all. "But it is my title, after all. It is part of me. My heritage. I was reared to be the Duke of Marsley. And as such, I will accept any bounty that my title delivers to me."

The duke had had the same attitude in India, the same self-glorification. It was as if, when he spoke, he simply amazed himself and had to spend several minutes in silent awe of his own brilliance. Of course, his aides and the other men surrounding him acted as impressed as George no doubt felt.

Beware a man who holds power with no one to check it. One of the many lessons Adam had learned in the army.

He grabbed two of the journals and returned to the desk on the first floor. It would be better if he could examine the books without the possibility of being interrupted by a maid. However, he didn't want to change the schedule and therefore incite curiosity. The less attention he attracted, the better.

At least there was no threat of the duchess coming into the library.

Where had the duchess gone and why had he gotten the feeling that she needed to be rescued?

The sooner he found the proof he needed, the better. He wanted to be gone from Marsley House and its duchess in all possible haste.

Chapter Seven

*S*uzanne had no idea how she'd been manipulated into entering Mrs. Armbruster's carriage. She hadn't had much of a choice. Her only alternative had been to strike the older woman. Or perhaps scream at the top of her lungs.

She'd been impotent in the face of the older woman's implacable determination.

The vehicle was not as luxurious as her own, but then, her carriage had been a gift from her husband on their second anniversary. As if a vehicle was enough of an inducement to ignore George's straying from the marital bed. She'd pretended not to notice and, later, not to care. The terrible thing about pretense was that sometimes it became real.

Her hand on the bottom of the window was warm even through her gloves. The sun was insistent about brightening the day. She pulled her hand down and placed one atop the other at her waist.

"It's not just money we're after," the older woman said. "These poor babies need more than that. Food first, it's true, but they also need kindness. They need someone to care for them, Your Grace, and you struck me as the type of person who would care."

"You don't know me, Mrs. Armbruster. Nor did you when you first came to see me. What gave you the notion I would be interested in a hospital?"

The other woman shook her head. "No, Your Grace, not just a hospital. It's called Haven Foundling Hospital."

She was going to be sick. She couldn't possibly visit such a place, but she had the inkling that whatever she said would be countered by this most insistent woman. She had to do something, anything, to get Mrs. Armbruster to turn the carriage around and take her home. She just wanted—desperately needed—an end to this. Hopefully before anything more terrible happened.

"Recently we took a few babies from St. Pancras Workhouse," Mrs. Armbruster was saying. "That despicable place stank of sewage, Your Grace. Flies were allowed to breed everywhere and the poor infants had been left to lie for hours in their own waste."

Suzanne closed her eyes and wished that the woman would stop talking. She and God had an arrangement. He would no longer punish her and she wouldn't pray. She was not going to betray their truce now by slipping and praying that He would do something to quiet Mrs. Armbruster. Not that God would listen. He hadn't been listening for two years.

"I realize that Spitalfields is a terrible place, Your Grace. Father Gilbert and the Sisters of Mercy have recently opened a refuge on Providence Row. It's a place where destitute women and children can find a meal and a bed at night. But we know there is always more of a need than there is an answer to that need."

She'd heard of Spitalfields at one of her father's innumerable political dinners. Someone had described it as Hell on earth and had then apologized profusely to the assembled guests.

She mutely nodded, turning to the window again.

In the past few minutes the merry sun had vanished. Houses leaned together, obscuring the view of the sky. The crowded London streets had altered as well. The color of the pavement was darker and had a slick and slimy look to it. An odor came to her then of an open sewer or the Thames in previous summers. She held her handkerchief to her nose and wondered if Mrs. Armbruster came this way every day. Or was this journey only to impress upon Suzanne the dire conditions of the people living in Spitalfields?

Only a few people were visible. The women who stood on the street corners had stark white faces with pale mouths and dark shadowed eyes. How odd to realize that she and a woman of the streets had the same lack of hope, the same disinterested view of the world.

The men were thin, startled easily, and glanced around nervously before their eyes settled on the passing carriage. Their looks were hungry and not simply for food. They wanted what she had without knowing the price she'd paid for it.

"Why?" Suzanne asked, turning to Mrs. Armbruster.

"Why you?" The woman smiled brightly again.

Suzanne shook her head. "No. Why you?"

For the first time, Mrs. Armbruster looked taken aback. Suzanne could see that she was formulating an answer. No doubt something that sounded good but was far from honest.

She pressed her advantage. "Why you, Mrs. Armbruster? What about the situation inspired you, particularly, to do something? To raise money? To attempt to change the conditions of these children?"

The other woman's gaze settled on her hands. Although Mrs. Armbruster wore gloves, Suzanne could tell that her knuckles were swollen and her thumbs disfigured from arthritis.

"I had a maid," she finally said. "A good girl. Tenny was her name. She came from Ireland and was as bright a soul as you could ever meet. She and I looked like mother and daughter with our red hair. But Tenny's eyes were as green as the hills of Ireland."

Suzanne didn't interrupt the woman, even though she was certain the tale didn't end well.

"She left my employ, I'm sorry to say, but at the time I was happy for her. She benefitted herself by taking up service in a wealthy merchant's home." Mrs. Armbruster took a deep breath, let it out, and continued Tenny's story. "It wasn't an advancement at all, poor thing. Instead, she got herself with child and was dismissed."

The older woman stared out at the sight of Spitalfields.

"She didn't come to me, and I wish she had. I would have spared her the agony of her actions. She put her child in the care of a woman who promised to look after it while Tenny worked. The infant died only three weeks later and Tenny was beside herself. She passed not long after and although the physician said she died of natural causes, I think it was a broken heart, myself."

She turned to look at Suzanne. "Had she placed the infant with an orphanage or a workhouse, the effect would have been the same. The child would probably still have died. Most infants do in those circumstances."

A band tightened around Suzanne's chest, keeping her heart from bursting. She could barely breathe, but somehow she asked a question of the older woman. "But they don't with your organization?"

"No," Mrs. Armbruster said flatly. "They don't. We give each baby individual care and pride ourselves on the fact that each thrives under it. Yet we have a list of nearly five hundred women and their children who desperately need help. I don't know how many of them are still alive, Your Grace. I do know that we could have saved most of them."

"Have they no place to go?" she asked.

"One would think their families would take them in, but that isn't the case, regrettably. They've shamed their relatives and they want nothing to do with them."

"Not even for the sake of the child?"

"Unfortunately, the child is seen as expendable." Mrs. Armbruster's voice was dull. Gone was her bright smile, and tears pooled in her eyes. "That's why, Your Grace, I'm appealing to you."

She didn't want to help. She didn't want anything to do with Mrs. Armbruster and her Foundling Hospital. She wanted to be returned to Marsley House now, as swiftly as the horses could carry her. She wanted to retreat to her suite, bolt the door behind her, and take some of Ella's tonic, the better to forget everything.

"We exist not only to save those poor children, Your Grace, but to give their mothers a chance once more to enter society. We teach them to read, do sums, and write. We train them in various positions so that they are able to support their children. When the children get older, we provide a school for them."

"All of which sounds exceedingly virtuous, Mrs. Armbruster. If you'll return me home I'll communicate with my solicitor and ensure you are given a generous sum."

"But that's not enough, Your Grace."

It was assuredly going to have to be. She could not tolerate much more. Her hands were clammy. Her heart was beating entirely too fast. Her stomach was churning. She was going to be deathly sick in front of the woman, in front of all of London, but she didn't care as much about that as the feeling that she was breaking in two.

What had she said to the woman to give the impression that she was interested in this cause? She suspected that she'd said almost anything in order to keep the woman from going on and on about her charity. People normally didn't mention children around her. They knew enough to keep silent on that topic. She doubted that Mrs. Armbruster had been as tactful and now she was trapped in a carriage with the woman.

Any moment now and her heart was going to spill out of her chest. It would go tumbling down over her bodice, her skirt, and throw itself out the door of the carriage, there to be run over by the wide wheels.

What did she need with a heart, anyway? Hers had been dead for years.

She closed her eyes and leaned her head back against the seat.

"Please, Mrs. Armbruster. I'm feeling unwell. I need to return home."

"But Your Grace, we're here. We'll get you a bracing cup of tea and all will be well, you'll see."

Chapter Eight

❧

Mrs. Armbruster didn't offer her tea. Instead, she led Suzanne to the main part of the hospital.

Suzanne didn't know what she expected, but it wasn't a neat row of cribs, each sitting next to an iron cot with a thin mattress. Every cot had a small table next to it with a lamp and a Bible and a small trunk at its foot.

Only five of the twenty beds and cribs were currently occupied.

"They've just given birth," Mrs. Armbruster whispered. "The girl at the end, the one with the short black hair, is our newest patient. Amy was found in the ocean. It was thought that she tried to drown herself, but she was rescued by a kindhearted sailor and brought here. I shudder to think what would've happened to her if she'd been taken anywhere else."

"Where are the rest of the girls?" she asked.

"Some might be with the physician. Others might be in the garden. We have a small yard in the back. We want them to take their babies with them, of course. There will be plenty of time for them to be separated. Now it's important that they get to know each other."

She turned and walked with Mrs. Armbruster as they headed down a wide corridor with windows at each end, flooding the space with light. Everything was painted white, but instead of giving it a sterile look, the absence of color merely brightened the space and allowed the sun to tinge everything a pale yellow.

Mrs. Armbruster opened a door at the end of the hall to reveal a room with a wall of windows. The space was bright and sunny, and the yellow, green, blue, and pink cribs added color to the space. Here there were no cots, only cribs, each one of them occupied.

There was a curious sweetness to the air, as if there were flowers somewhere nearby. Was the Foundling Hospital normally this clean or had it been straightened for her arrival?

Suzanne froze in the doorway, watching as three girls went from crib to crib, caring for the infants.

One girl went to the crib closest to Suzanne and lifted an infant from it.

"Henry, what have you done so soon? You just want to make sure I can't sit down for a moment, don't you?"

The baby drooled happily down the shoulder of her dress, reached out, and batted her nose with his clenched fist. The girl laughed as if it was a game they had played many times before.

"Come, my dear," Mrs. Armbruster said.

The woman grabbed Suzanne's arm and nearly hauled her into the room, making a sweeping gesture with her free hand to encompass all the cribs.

"These are our foundlings, Your Grace. These poor babies have either lost their mothers or they were found on our doorstep."

She couldn't imagine anything more terrible, having to give up a child in order to ensure its life. Would she have done that? Yes, in a heartbeat.

The young girl assigned to care for Henry turned and walked toward them.

To her absolute horror, the young girl thrust Henry at her.

"Would you like to hold him?"

Suzanne broke free of Mrs. Armbruster's grip and stepped backward, away from the infant, and kept going until she hit the far wall.

Henry didn't like being held with hands beneath his arms and began to wail. The young girl pulled him back into her embrace, cradling him until he was calm. Mrs. Armbruster nodded at the girl, and she took Henry to the changing table and replaced his diaper.

Suzanne crossed her arms in front of her, expecting a lecture, a verbal treatise on the joy of caring for an innocent child. At the very least, she anticipated a solicitation for funds.

Instead, Mrs. Armbruster approached her slowly, almost as if Suzanne were a rabid dog or a fox that had been cornered and was now snarling and threatening to bite.

The woman reached out and touched her arm again.

"I know, Your Grace. I know."

That's all she said before dropping her hand.

No one ever said a word. No one offered condolences or sympathy. Not one person had, in these last two years, ever come to her and said, *I am sorry, Suzanne.*

Yet Mrs. Armbruster had done more than that.

There were tears in the older woman's eyes. Suzanne closed her own eyes, kept her arms folded, the better to prevent herself from shattering.

The silence lengthened and strengthened, creating a bubble around them. No doubt one of the babies cried. Or was soothed by one of its minders. Perhaps someone even spoke or crooned or laughed. But here, in a room set aside for orphaned infants, neither of them spoke.

Words were beyond Suzanne. Nor would she have been able to listen to anything Mrs. Armbruster had to say.

Finally, when she could bear the silence no longer, the other woman said, "We should return to Marsley House, Your Grace."

Suzanne only nodded, so grateful she nearly wept.

Suzanne walked swiftly back to the entrance, nodding to the driver, who dismounted from his perch and opened the carriage door. Once inside, she settled herself in the corner of the seat.

Mrs. Armbruster remained silent for long moments.

Suzanne studied the passing scenery. Not that there was anything to admire about what she saw. The darkness, the grayness of the very air pushed down on her. She pressed her handkerchief to her nose in an effort to tolerate the stench.

"I'm sorry, Your Grace," Mrs. Armbruster finally said. "I should not have taken you there. But I'd heard that you were a kind woman and thought you might be able to help. Those poor babies need someone to care."

Suzanne didn't respond. At least she hadn't burst out wailing in front of Mrs. Armbruster. For a good many months she had done that, to the shock of the servants. That's why she'd finally gone to their country house, where there were fewer witnesses to her grief.

"You expect too much from me."

"Yes," Mrs. Armbruster said, surprising her. "I have, Your Grace, and that is my failing. I sometimes push too hard, and I ask your forgiveness."

Her hand curled below the window, the knuckles showing white. When the carriage turned left, an errant beam of sunlight danced along her skin. She pulled her hand back and buried it in her cloak. She wasn't dead, but sometimes she felt guilty for being alive. Why should she feel the sun when he didn't?

"What will happen to them? All those infants?"

"There aren't that many," Mrs. Armbruster said, a touch of defensiveness in her voice. Suzanne wanted to tell her she wasn't being critical, merely curious.

"That's why we keep our numbers down, Your Grace. We want to ensure a favorable outcome for each child we take in."

"Is there a reason for the different colored cribs?"

She glanced over at Mrs. Armbruster. The other woman had tilted her head slightly, reminding her of an inquisitive bird.

"The pink, blue, yellow, and green," Suzanne said. "Is there a reason for those colors?"

Mrs. Armbruster shook her head. "No, but how wise of you, my dear. Perhaps we should make it mean something. An infant below six months could go in a blue crib. One below three months might go in the yellow. That sort of thing. We don't do that now, but it's definitely an idea."

"And the girls, assigned to care for the babies," Suzanne said. "You might have them wearing a different colored smock depending on what age they are assigned to."

Mrs. Armbruster smiled slightly as she nodded.

"To answer your earlier question, Your Grace, some of the infants will be sent to foster homes until they're four or five years old. At that time, they'll come back to the hospital to live. In a different section, of course, but there all the same."

"Isn't that cruel? To pull them away from the only family they'd ever known?"

"Most foster families are not equipped to raise a child, but they're willing to help one get past infancy."

"And the girls? The girls who stay with their children? Is there a favorable outcome for them?"

Mrs. Armbruster gave her a look that she couldn't interpret. It was almost as if the older woman didn't wish to speak any further. As if Suzanne had asked her an intimate question, one that was rude by its very nature.

"Your Grace, does it matter? You've already given me the impression that you prefer to have nothing to do with the hospital. I can certainly understand why."

Suzanne wanted to explain, to offer some kind of justification. But what would she say? She didn't expose her grief. She didn't parade it, unveil it, and hold it aloft for other people to see. It was hers and perhaps some would say that she had breathed life into it, that she'd made it substantial and real. Perhaps she had, but who could blame her?

Perhaps little Henry.

"I know what you're feeling, Your Grace. You think that if you put aside your grief, even for a moment, it means you didn't love him. But I can assure you that caring about something else will not mean that you love him any less. Or that you've ceased to mourn him."

She glanced at the other woman to find Mrs. Armbruster regarding her with kind eyes.

She'd gone along with the woman practically kidnapping her, thrusting her into a carriage, and taking her to the Foundling Hospital. She'd endured a tour, and then, when it was too much, demanded to be returned home. She would not tolerate being lectured on grief.

What did the woman expect? That she would want to hold each and every one of those infants? That she would kiss a downy head and smile at an infant's grin? That she would put out a finger to have a chubby fist grip it?

The ache was back, but then it had never truly gone away. It sat there, waiting, for something to unfurl it. A sight, a sound, a thought was all it needed and then the ache became a very real pain.

She was not given to being direct in her speech, but it seemed as if Mrs. Armbruster was demanding it of her. Whatever happened to tact or a little reticence in manner? The woman had said it herself. She pushed too hard. Perhaps she deserved Suzanne pushing back in turn.

"What is it you want from me, Mrs. Armbruster?"

"I didn't have the opportunity to show you our other project, Your Grace. The Institute. We're taking in girls who have gotten themselves in trouble. That is not the proper way to call it, of course. They did not do it to themselves, but the law does not see that as correct. Society punishes only the female in this case."

Mrs. Armbruster turned a little so that she was facing Suzanne.

"Until they give birth, they have a home and a roof over their heads. They are fed and kept warm and out of the elements. I want you to meet some of them. They aren't terrible girls, Your Grace. They might have been foolish. They might have listened to the blandishments of young men. Some of them were even taken advantage of by their employers.

"In addition, I would like to name the Institute after you, Your Grace. That is, if you wanted to become one of our patrons."

She looked at Mrs. Armbruster, stunned. She hadn't agreed to any kind of financial backing. In fact, she didn't have the kind of funds the other woman evidently hoped she'd donate.

The only money George had left her was what remained of the huge amount her father had settled on him at their marriage. A dowry, if one was kind. Payment for taking her as his bride if one was more realistic. While her husband hadn't been profligate, he hadn't been a miser, either. No doubt he'd purchased a few baubles for his mistresses. She knew, from his bragging, that he'd bet on more than one horse.

But to sponsor—and fund—an organization the size of Mrs. Armbruster's? No, she didn't have the ability to do that.

What on earth was she supposed to say?

Thankfully, the carriage was turning into the drive, through the wrought iron gates, up the slight incline to the circular approach to Marsley House.

Mrs. Armbruster was still looking at her.

The carriage rolled to a stop and the footman was opening the carriage door.

Suzanne murmured something about speaking with her solicitor and said her farewells as quickly as politeness dictated before descending from the carriage. She climbed the steps faster than she could ever remember doing and entered the door with a sigh of relief. After she removed her hat and gloves and placed both on the sideboard, the footman helped her off with her cloak.

Where was Drummond?

Another irritant—this one, at least, she could do something about.

Chapter Nine

$\mathcal{D}$rummond was nowhere to be found. The annoying man was not in the pantry supervising the polishing of the silver. Nor was he in his office—and she'd sent a maid to fetch him.

"He's often in the library, Your Grace," one of the footmen said, bowing slightly to her.

Why on earth would he be in the library? He hadn't struck her as being particularly scholarly the night before.

He wasn't there, either.

Rather than send the entirety of the staff looking for him—and causing a great deal of speculation, not to mention gossip—she sublimated her irritation and set herself on another course, that of finding her mother's hair clip.

The roof was bathed by sunlight. There were only a few tiny puddles here and there as proof of the storm the night before. A cool wind brushed the tendrils of hair away from her cheeks. The air smelled fresh with no tinge of decay. The sky was a brilliant blue and from here, atop Marsley House, she could see the skyline of London stretching out before her. No hint of Spitalfields was visible.

Although the house boasted a formal Tudor garden, she missed the valleys and fertile fields of the country. Summer seemed to last so much longer there until, at last, autumn reluctantly arrived, turning the leaves brown and scattering them across the lanes.

Standing here she might have been a princess in a castle, one elevated away from the masses. Instead, she knew she wasn't royalty. Nor was she exempt from the emotions any other person felt.

At the moment it was anger. Anger at Mrs. Armbruster, at her father, at Drummond. Some of that anger—perhaps most of it—was set aside for herself. She should have been stronger. She should have refused to go to the Foundling Hospital. She should have stayed in the country.

Perhaps she should only be angry at circumstances. Fate had decreed her life, altered her destiny, and changed her future.

She walked to the edge of the roof, putting her hands on the banister, and looked down at the gravel approach below her. The height made her dizzy and more than a little nauseous. Cautiously, she stepped back.

A sparkle caught her attention. Something was lodged not far from the railing, an object gleaming in the afternoon sun. She was bending to retrieve it when she was suddenly grabbed about the waist and jerked back a few feet.

"Och, you daft woman," an accented voice said.

"Let me go!"

"Why, so you can try to throw yourself from the roof again? Not on my watch."

She tried to wrench herself away, but Drummond had a good grip on her. His arms were wrapped around her midriff and were pressing upward on her breasts. She hadn't been touched like that by a man for years. She had certainly never been assaulted by one.

She tried to use her elbows to punch him but he didn't release her. Instead, he pulled her backward until the heels of her shoes were grinding into the surface of the roof.

"Let me go, you idiot. I wasn't going to throw myself off the roof. I was looking for something."

"And is that what you were trying to do last night, you daft woman?"

"Would you stop calling me that," she said. She'd never been talked to in such a manner. Who did he think he was? "Let me go," she said, calming herself so she could speak. Her heart was racing and she could barely breathe. "I didn't. It was a mistake. You misinterpreted everything."

"Did I misinterpret you crawling over the railing last night?"

"Did I really do that?" she asked, startled.

"Aye, you did, and very determined you were."

"I had too much wine," she said, embarrassed to be making such a confession to someone she didn't know. Someone who was in her employ, at least for now.

"I've had my share of nights like that, Duchess. I never once tried to end my life."

She didn't have anything to say in defense of herself. Was there a defense she could offer? Not one word came to mind. Prior to last night she couldn't remember ever being on the roof.

"How did you know where I was?" she asked.

"I was told you were looking for me when I got back from the stables."

"And you naturally came here to see if I was intent on throwing myself to my death again?"

"Something like that," he said, not relaxing his hold.

"You can let me go," she said. "I can assure you that I have no intention of ending my life."

In the past few minutes she'd allowed herself to relax in his grip. She lay her head back against his chest. Anyone looking at them might think they were lovers who'd slipped up to the roof for a few moments alone and now stood there, captivated by the sight of London lit by the sun.

No one would think that the two of them were antagonists.

"I don't know what came over me," she said, compelled to say something. "I don't remember wanting to end my life. I'm glad you stopped me."

"He isn't worth it, you know. Not all your grieving."

Anger suddenly bubbled up from where it had been hiding. She pulled free of him and turned.

"How could you say such a hideous thing?"

"Because it's the truth."

She hadn't meant to cry. She really hadn't. Especially not in front of him. But she couldn't hold back the reservoir of tears, all that weeping she wouldn't permit herself to do at the hospital. She took a step back, but he wouldn't allow her that. Instead, he reached out and grabbed her wrist and pulled her to him. Only then did she realize that she'd been backing up to the edge.

For some reason, that made her cry harder. Then he was holding her again. His arms were around her back, his hands flat against her cloak. She couldn't reach up and brush her face, so she had no other choice but to lay her cheek against his jacket and let it soak up her tears.

He said something in Gaelic to her, some barely whispered words in a voice that sounded reluctant and ill at ease.

When she tried to move away, he shushed her and pulled her close once again.

"I'm sorry," he said. "I had no right to speak of your husband that way. Of course you mourn him. That's what wives do, don't they?"

She held herself still, closing her eyes against her tears. He thought she was crying for George. He thought her grief was for a man she'd never truly understood, for a stranger with whom she lived for six years.

She moved her arm up and placed her hand against Drummond's chest. His heart thundered against her palm.

"*Gabh mo leisgeul*," he said. "I didn't mean to ridicule your pain."

"What are you saying?"

"I'm sorry. It's Gaelic for *I'm sorry*, and I am."

He confused her. What kind of man was this Scottish major-domo? On one hand, he was vicious in his speech, yet he'd tried to save her not once but twice.

She pushed free finally, taking a step back and keeping her gaze on the surface of the roof. She couldn't look at him. She couldn't acknowledge this moment of intimacy. He was the first man who'd touched her or attempted to comfort her for years.

Also, he was the only man who'd ever apologized for his actions.

"I was going to release you from my service the minute I saw you today," she said, her voice low. "I was going to demand that you leave Marsley House within the hour, without recommendation or reference. I was going to tell you how much I detested your speaking to me in that way and that I considered you a despicable creature."

She dared herself to look up at him.

Mrs. Armbruster was right.

Why hadn't she noticed how handsome he was until this exact second? His eyes were a soft green. His hair was thick and black, and he had a dimple on the left side of his mouth. His was a strong, square face, one that would probably be transformed by a smile. Now it was stern and somber and a little daunting.

"But I can't do any of those things now, Drummond. Not after coming to the conclusion that you saved me from myself. That was last night, however. Today I only came here to find something."

He didn't look as if he believed her and she regretted that.

"I do not mourn my husband," she said, giving him the truth as a gift, a payment for his protection of her. "God forgive me, but all I felt was relief at his death."

She turned and headed for the door to the third floor. How odd that she could feel his eyes on her all the way down the stairs.

*A*DAM WALKED TO the edge of the roof, stood where the duchess had been, and looked around. It took him a moment, but he saw what she'd been reaching for, a leaf-shaped diamond brooch. He bent and picked it up. The brooch rested in his palm, the diamonds glittering and sparkling like fire was in their depths.

What kind of woman treated this bauble with such disdain? The kind who had been, no doubt, raised with no fear. Not like his mother, who worried about each meal or if the landlord was coming before she'd earned the rest of the rent. He'd been twelve when she died of a cough that had consumed her.

If she'd still been alive or if Mary had lived, he would've stayed behind in Glasgow. He would've made his way, somehow, maybe at the foundry or one of the cotton mills. He'd have been determined to support them. But that was water into the Clyde, wasn't it? They hadn't lived and there'd been no reason for him to stay there.

He pushed the thoughts of his past down deep. What good was it to dwell on something he couldn't change?

He closed his fist around the brooch so tightly that he could feel the diamonds pressing into his skin. Marble Marsley—hardly that, though, was she?

Whom did she mourn? He hadn't asked Mrs. Thigpen enough questions about the Duchess of Marsley, and he was determined to correct that oversight as quickly as possible.

First, however, he had an obligation to return to his pose as majordomo and then to his assignment. Along the way, if he could forget the surprising duchess, all the better.

Chapter Ten

*S*he really should have dismissed Drummond on the spot. Instead, she'd allowed him to comfort her. She wasn't acting anything like a duchess, was she? First going to the Foundling Hospital and then being embraced by a servant.

Perhaps she'd simply needed to be held. For those few minutes when he'd put his arms around her she'd allowed herself to weaken. In that short space of time she didn't have to be the Duchess of Marsley. She didn't have to be possessed of poise and reserve. She didn't have to be strong.

Drummond hadn't told her that she should get over her loss. He didn't say that she needed to put her past behind her. Not once had he uttered those despicable words: *Sometimes things happen. We need to get beyond them.*

What was the recipe for getting beyond this? What, exactly, did she do? Did she burn a certain herb? Did she utter an incantation? Did she memorize a certain verse or a whole book from the Bible? Did she prostrate herself on the chapel floor? Did she summon a wise woman or a physician? Did she consult the most learned men in London?

She would've done all of those things eagerly, but nothing would have altered the reality of her life. Nothing would have ended the cavernous emptiness she felt.

Instead of entering her suite she hesitated at the door, unwilling to go inside and face Ella. The fact that she was hiding from her maid was yet another embarrassment. When would she cease being a person subject to the whims of others?

She walked to the end of the corridor where George's rooms were located. Slowly, giving herself time to reconsider, she opened his sitting room door and slid inside.

The smell of beeswax permeated the room, an indication that the maid had been diligent. Although he'd been gone two years, his suite was dusted every day. Every morning the curtains were opened as if someone might wish to witness the view of the approach to Marsley House. Once a week the windows were polished, as were the mirrors. The cushions on the yellow-and-brown-striped sofa and chairs were fluffed. The pale yellow carpet with its brown frame was brushed once a month and twice a year taken outside to be beaten.

Yet no one would ever return to take up residence in this suite again.

She went to the small desk between the two floor-to-ceiling windows and extracted the key from the center drawer. It never used to be here, but she kept it in this place for safekeeping. Her life was not her own and any semblance of privacy was laughable with Ella going through her pockets, reticule, and anything else she wished on the premise that she was caring for Suzanne's belongings.

The one thing Ella hadn't yet done was prowl through the duke's suite.

Suzanne pocketed the key, turned, and surveyed the room. She would have to commend Mrs. Thigpen for assigning a conscientious maid to the suite. Whoever had been in charge had done an admirable job. Even George couldn't have faulted the girl. Even though he would have tried, unless she was pretty enough to seduce.

She opened the door to the duke's suite slowly, looking down the hallway to ensure that Ella wasn't coming or going. When she saw no one in the corridor, she slipped out of the room and closed the door quietly behind her.

Although the servants' stairs would have been closer to the room she sought, she took the main staircase to the third floor. The chances of encountering one of the maids were greater in the afternoon. They worked from seven until eleven and then again from one until dark, going through Marsley House from the first floor to the third, with the public rooms rotated on Mrs. Thigpen's schedule.

No one, however, ever entered the room that was her destination. She'd given orders that it was to be considered sacrosanct. No one was to dust or rearrange anything. Everything was to be left exactly as it had been that day. That terrible day. The day that essentially ended her life.

She didn't allow herself to come here often, because the temptation would be to remain in here, cloistered, with memories of happiness like bubbles surrounding her. She might have turned insane in this room from longing or grief.

She stood outside the door with her hand gripping the key as she willed her heart to slow its frantic beating and her lungs to fill with air. After the events of this morning, she needed to remind herself of things gone and over, but never forgotten.

Sadness felt sentient, reaching out with a clawlike grip and holding on to her soul.

Slowly she inserted the key in the lock and turned it, hearing the click as loud as a gunshot. Here, in this quiet corridor, every sound was magnified.

She turned the latch and stepped inside, then closed the door swiftly behind her. As it was most times, the room was shadowed and still. Because she knew the space so well, she didn't need light to see her way to the windows. She opened one set of curtains and then another, turning and surveying the room in the bright sunlight.

She could feel the warmth of the sun on her shoulders. How strange that she felt so cold inside, as if she could never truly be warm again.

The wind sighed against the windows, promising the chill of

winter soon to come. Winter was the dead season when every-thing, perhaps even life itself, went dormant.

There, in the corner, was the crib he was so proud to have out-grown. Next to it was the small bed with its pillow and bright blue coverlet. At three years old he had been his own person with his father's arrogance and her humor.

The silence in the nursery still shocked her. It grated on her, reminding her at the same time it enshrouded her. There were no soft giggles. No remonstrances from the nurse. No excited, "Up, up," demands from Georgie. Nothing but an eternal quiet that must mimic the grave.

Here, in this room, she remembered happiness and joy. Here, as in no other space on the earth, she remembered a small voice asking innumerable questions and demanding that the world slow and stop for him.

She walked toward the crib, reached out, and put her hand on the ornate carving of the spindles. The crib was an heirloom, like most of the furniture at Marsley House. George had used it, but there would never be another child to use the crib. Memories would have to be enough. Georgie bouncing up and down, im-patient to be about the investigation of his day. Her raising him up in her arms as he grinned at her.

He had been just like Henry in his optimism and joy.

Henry had few chances in life, while Georgie had had the world spread out before him. Whatever he'd wanted to do, however he'd wanted to accomplish it, both his mother and father would have moved mountains to ensure he could have done it.

In their love for their child she and George were united. It was in everything else they were separate.

She sat on the end of Georgie's bed, staring at the far wall where all his toys were arranged. His toy soldiers would never again fight imaginary battles. His stuffed rabbit would never be clutched to his chest as he fought sleep. A wooden horse on wheels sat next to a wagon filled with blocks, all waiting patiently for their owner to return and play with them.

For the first time in two years, her tears were manageable. She wasn't assaulted by the strength of her grief. Because she had already wept in her majordomo's arms? Or had she begun to realize, finally, inexorably, that she might wish it and will it and pray for it but she was never going to see her darling child again. He would forever be three years old and she would forever be his grieving mother.

Henry didn't have a mother. She pushed that thought away but it surfaced again. None of those babies at the Foundling Hospital had a mother to care for them. They'd been made artificial orphans because of shame. Those poor children would always be known as foundlings. They'd go through life with that stigma, being branded as a child even their own mother hadn't wanted.

Life was sometimes cruel; she knew that only too well. Was that why she'd tried to scale the railing and fall from the roof? She couldn't honestly remember wanting to end her life. She couldn't imagine doing that despite everything.

Had the wine dulled her wits? Or had it merely allowed her true wishes to come out?

She clasped her arms around her waist, feeling cold. She hadn't known the pastor who'd officiated at her husband and son's service. He'd been an acquaintance of George's and had pontificated at length on her husband's glorious military history. He'd offered a dozen platitudes in the guise of comfort, none of which had penetrated her gray haze. Something about God never making mistakes and reuniting under faith and other sayings that made absolutely no sense.

Nothing made sense in her life right now. Suddenly she was feeling a myriad of emotions—anger, curiosity, rebellion—added to the grief she almost always felt. Yet this sadness was different and it took her a moment to isolate why. She felt as if she were mourning not only her son, but the fate of Henry and those other babies.

Mrs. Armbruster had a great deal to answer for.

Chapter Eleven

The duchess hid for a week. At least, that's what it felt like to Adam. She didn't go anywhere. Nor did she entertain visitors. No one came to call.

After his last encounter with the duchess he'd gone to Mrs. Thigpen, knowing that the woman would know the answer to his question.

She insisted on him joining her for lunch, and since the meal was a beef-and-pork pie, he wasn't adverse. When he finished and he put his fork down, he complimented Mrs. Thigpen on the talents of the cook. For a few minutes he listened as she detailed all the dishes in which Grace excelled. When the housekeeper was done he leaned forward and dropped his voice. Although there was no one else in the staff dining room, he didn't want his question overheard by anyone passing in the corridor.

"Olivia, I have a favor to ask. I realize that what I'm asking is somewhat intrusive, and I apologize for that. My curiosity, however, demands an answer."

"Of course, Adam. What do you want to know?"

"Who does the duchess mourn?"

She sat back in the chair and regarded him solemnly. Had he overstepped? For several moments he thought she wouldn't answer him, but then she sighed.

"Georgie," she said. "Her son."

When he didn't say anything, she continued. "We didn't think the poor dear would survive it," Mrs. Thigpen said, dabbing at the corners of her eyes with a lace-trimmed handkerchief. "It was such a terrible dark time. She doted on Georgie. I think he was the light in her life."

She didn't add, and he was probably wrong in assuming, but he wondered if her son was the only bright spot in the duchess's life. He could only assume what marriage to the duke had been like.

He'd gotten to the duke's thirties and had to read page after page of the man's bragging about his conquests. The duke had been proud of his sword—as he'd called it—and the wide swath he'd cut through the female population. From what Adam had read, he hadn't limited his swordplay to London, but had taken advantage of more than one young girl who'd come to work at Marsley House.

He hadn't respected the man in India, a feeling that had led to loathing soon enough. His memory summoned up images of the duke ordering the rebels to be blown from cannons, reason enough to despise the man. The more journals he read, the more his opinion was reinforced. The Duke of Marsley was morally bankrupt and ethically challenged.

"The darling died in the accident, of course," Olivia said. "Drowned, poor mite. I can still hear the duchess's scream when she was told."

She shook her head, her attention on the tabletop, but Adam could see that she was reliving that moment.

"Why does no one ever mention his name? Or say anything about him?"

Mrs. Thigpen glanced at him. "It wasn't for lack of love for Georgie. We all loved him as well. But it was out of respect for the duchess. Poor thing, to lose her husband and her son in the same accident. We all decided—the previous majordomo, the stable master, the land steward, and me—not to mention the child. And we gave the order that the staff was not to speak of either of them, for her sake."

He only nodded in response. He didn't have a thing to say.

As the days passed he started to look for her. She hadn't come to any of the public rooms. He'd even unbent enough to ask Ella where the duchess was.

"Why would you want to know?" she asked, giving him a narrow-eyed look.

"I need to speak with her about a matter."

"I'll tell her you need to see her," she said, but he didn't believe her.

If it suited her purposes, Ella would say something. If not, she'd remain silent. It wasn't loyalty to the duchess as much as it was power. People like Ella hoarded information because it might prove valuable to them in the future.

Nor was the Silent Service forthcoming with information. He was never told more than he absolutely needed to know. The temptation was to do the same in return, to keep back a few details to protect oneself. He'd run into those kinds of people, too.

"Where is she?" he asked, a mistake the minute the words came out of his mouth.

"Is that any of your concern?"

The tone of Ella's voice was one of disdain, as icy as the duchess.

Except that the duchess hadn't seemed cold a week ago.

He watched as the maid sauntered off without another word. Too bad he didn't have the power to dismiss Ella.

Over the past two months he'd established a pattern of behavior for himself as majordomo. The week was filled with approving expenditures or meeting with the upper staff or interviewing the maids and footmen. He believed in information filtering up the chain of command. He was also able to head off any misunderstandings about new rules and regulations that he'd initiated.

Every morning he inspected the staff along with Mrs. Thigpen. That was another change—he wanted to ensure that the staff knew that the housekeeper was well respected and someone they could go to if they had a problem.

Unless there was a visitor expected—which rarely happened at Marsley House—he did not man the door. Instead, a senior footman was assigned that position along with a junior footman in training. Adam was a stickler for training, and no doubt it was because of his time in the army. He never wanted to be surprised. Instead, he believed in preparing for every contingency.

He'd been woefully unprepared for the duchess. Nor had he counted on her father.

Chapter Twelve

"What do you mean she doesn't want to see me?"

The man's voice carried to the third floor of the library, where Adam was starting to read the duke's confessions about his forties. He'd had to wait until late afternoon, when the three maids assigned to the room had finished dusting it. At the slow pace he was going, a few more midnight visits were in order. Few people bothered him in the middle of the night.

He bit back an oath, stood, and straightened his jacket before descending the staircase and heading toward the front door.

The junior footman in training looked terrified, a strange sight since he towered over the man being refused admittance. The senior footman, on the other hand, was trying to appear conciliatory. Adam counted three bows from Thomas by the time he made it to the front door.

"What's going on, Thomas?" Adam asked.

"I'll tell you what's going on," the visitor said. "This damn fool is keeping me from my daughter."

Evidently, the short man with the voice of a giant was Edward Hackney. Adam had heard of the man in India. Hackney had been one of the directors of the British East India Company, making a fortune over the years.

He wondered if it was just a coincidence that both the late duke and Hackney had deep ties to India. So did he, since he'd been in the country at the same time.

Hackney's head seemed oddly out of proportion to the rest of his body, as if God had created a man of small stature and then had only large heads left over. Nothing matched. His nose was long, his mouth almost too broad for his face. His neck was a little squat, giving the impression that his shoulders were too close to his ears.

What he lacked in physical presence, however, Hackney made up for in sheer determination.

"You will take me to my daughter this instant."

Adam glanced at Thomas. "Have you let the duchess know that she has a visitor?"

"Not just a visitor, damn it," Hackney said. "I'm her father."

"Her Grace is not receiving, sir," Thomas said, his expression deadpan while Daniel still looked terrified. It couldn't have been easy to refuse Hackney.

At Thomas's words, Hackney grew even more belligerent.

"Like hell. Where is she?"

Daniel looked at Adam. "She's in the conservatory, sir."

When Hackney would have pushed past both the footmen and strode into the house, Adam held up his hand.

"If you'll wait a moment, sir, I will inquire of Her Grace if she wishes to see you."

He'd been in command of hundreds of men. He knew just what kind of tone to employ to a recalcitrant soldier or an idiot general. In this case he chose something halfway between either extreme, but that left Hackney no doubt that he wasn't going to enter Marsley House.

"Who the hell do you think you are?"

"A member of your daughter's staff, sir," he said. "I will ask the duchess what she wishes to do."

As he turned and left, Adam thought the older man might be on the verge of apoplexy.

At least the duchess had come out of her room.

According to Mrs. Thigpen, the conservatory was one of the duchess's favorite rooms, and he could well imagine why. It was one of the brightest rooms at Marsley House in a building that had hundreds of windows to let in the light. Here the windows jutted out and met at the ceiling to form a roof of sorts. He'd been in this room during a storm once. Nature had surrounded him, the sound of the rain against the windows like a giant drum.

He stood in the doorway, admiring the various kinds of plants for a few seconds. He knew nothing about growing things. In Glasgow, they'd never been close to a garden. In India, he had been too busy to learn about the native flora and fauna.

There was a small enclosed area to the left with a table and two chairs against the window. The Duchess of Marsley was seated there, her hands clasped together on the tabletop, her face turned not toward the conservatory, but toward the back of the house and the kitchen garden.

At his appearance, she turned her head and regarded him with a steady look. He fingered her brooch in his pocket and thought about returning it now.

Instead he said, "Your father is here to see you."

"I know." Her voice was calm, almost too calm. "I can hear him."

He took a few steps toward her. "He seems intent upon seeing you, Your Grace."

"Does he?"

She didn't say anything else. Nor did she look away. She blinked slowly, as if she were half-awake.

"Some people always get what they want. Have you ever noticed that, Drummond?"

"I have," he said, wondering if he should summon some tea for her. Something strong to wake her. Or had she been drinking?

"My father always gets his way. He demands it."

"He doesn't have to in this case, Your Grace."

"Oh, Drummond, you must take my word for it. He will never accept no. Not from me. Not from anyone. He can be quite ferocious."

She smiled lightly, but it wasn't an expression of amusement.

"Would you like me to send him away, Your Grace?"

"I should like that very much, Drummond, but I'm afraid it will not work."

She looked almost fragile sitting there in the sunlight in her black dress. Her blue-gray eyes seemed to see down into his soul. No doubt it was only his guilty conscience that made him think that. Why the hell should he be feeling guilty? It was her husband who was the traitor.

"What did you say to me?"

He frowned, not understanding.

"The other night, on the roof. And then in my bedroom. You said something to me. In Gaelic, I think. What was it?"

He toyed with the idea of lying to her. It hadn't been the most polite of expressions.

"What the hell are you doing hiding out in this place, Suzanne? You're the Duchess of Marsley. Act like it. You don't need to go to ground like a damn fox."

They both turned to see Hackney pushing his way into the conservatory, the two footmen following. Short of physically accosting the man, there was nothing they could have done. A determined bully could outmaneuver a servant trained in tact and politeness any day.

Adam was slightly different.

He caught the duchess's flinch and saw her face pale slightly.

Turning, he stood between her and Hackney. He braced himself with his feet apart, his arms crossed in front of him.

"The duchess is not at home," he said, parroting an expression he'd been taught. The art of lying was specific among the upper class. You didn't actually come out and say that you didn't want to see someone. Instead, you implied that you weren't there, even though everyone knew you were.

"Get out of my way, you damn fool," Hackney said.

He outweighed the man by at least fifty pounds and a good six inches. Plus, he wasn't a normal majordomo. He'd been a soldier in Her Majesty's army, with experience in the Sepoy Rebellion, and countless skirmishes before and after. He'd been wounded twice and promoted for his stubbornness.

He didn't back down easily.

"The duchess is not at home," he repeated, more than willing to act as a human bulwark against Hackney and his daughter.

He felt her hand on his shoulder and smelled her perfume as she came to stand beside him. The scent was different from what she'd worn that night on the roof. Light yet lingering and suiting her better.

She trailed her hand over his sleeve to rest at his elbow.

"That's all right, Drummond," she said. Her voice was calm, as if he were a wild animal and she his trainer. "I'll see my father."

Without a word she left them, leading the way, evidently, because Hackney followed her. Adam wanted to as well, but remained in the conservatory with the two footmen.

"She could have made our job a damn sight easier, sir, if she'd agreed to see the man in the first place."

Adam looked at Daniel. "That is the last time I'll hear criticism of the duchess, do you understand? If you value your place here."

To his credit, Daniel looked a little abashed. He nodded. "I understand, sir. It won't happen again."

Adam dismissed them and as they went back to their post, he turned and looked at the view the duchess had found so interesting.

What was wrong with her? And why did he care?

Chapter Thirteen

"You look worse than you did the other night," her father said. "You're not going to be of any use to me, Suzanne, if you don't at least look the part. People are impressed to meet a duchess, but not if she looks like a chambermaid."

She had heard it all before. Countless times, as a matter of fact. On so many occasions that whenever her father started on this tirade, she stopped listening.

Instead, she chose to think about Drummond. Drummond had protected her. He'd stood there, defying her father in a way no one else ever had. How odd that she could see him in a kilt, perhaps with a broadsword strapped across his chest.

She led her father into one of his favorite rooms, the Green Parlor, so called because of the predominant color. A mural of a forest had been painted on three walls, with the fourth wall being given over to three ceiling-to-floor windows. Despite the sensation of openness, she always felt closed in when she came here.

He hadn't come to Marsley House to comment upon her appearance. Nor to criticize her in other ways, although that would surely come. No, her father wanted something.

Planning was what separated the successful man from the failure. Her father had imparted that bit of wisdom to her when she was a child. After she'd married, he'd used that axiom with George on numerous occasions. Although he hadn't considered

George a planner. More a quintessential example of failure, which of course he was.

George hadn't added to the family coffers. Every attempt at investing had ended in ruin. Even his military career was speckled with rumors. Other men had been singled out for their courage or their brilliant tactical minds. Sometimes, George had been invited to those functions, only to return and pepper the air with oaths and questions she couldn't possibly answer.

Didn't the fools know what I did in India? I defeated the damn rebels, didn't I? Did I ever get any credit for it?

Occasionally, they would get visitors, men who'd once reported to George. He would be in his element, the magnanimous duke in command of the troops. For days a glow would seem to surround him.

Her father sometimes had that same effect on George, his flattery not the least bit subtle. Yet George had been an easy pawn to manipulate, someone who could be called upon to attend any dinner or ball, thereby granting to her wealthy father the social standing he craved.

Since George's death and after a suitable period of mourning—according to her father's decree more than society's—she'd been expected to attend all of her father's gatherings as a hostess of sorts. In actuality, she was not permitted to do more than smile and make a few inane comments. She wandered from room to room in the palatial home her father had built, ensuring that people saw her and knew that she was the Duchess of Marsley. In other words, she was her father's placard, an advertisement as glaring as those men who marched up and down the street selling something.

"Are you ailing?" her father asked now. "If so, I have an excellent physician you should see."

"I'm fine, Father. Truly."

He didn't say anything out of any concern for her, not really. She'd always realized what kind of man he was. He wasn't cruel as much as unaware. He was so driven that he didn't understand that other people might not possess the same ambition or need.

She'd never liked riding, but as a child she'd been forced to learn because her father believed all proper gentlewomen were also good with horses. Once her mount had gotten spooked and raced down the lane at a terrifying speed. Everything was a blur until the mare finally stopped. Suzanne imagined that's how her father went through life, at such a fast pace that he saw other people only as indistinguishable patterns.

She didn't know anything about his past. He'd never discussed his childhood and refused to answer questions. She always thought it was because his upbringing embarrassed him, but that wasn't a comment she'd ever make. If her father had his way, everyone would believe that he'd just appeared on the earth one day, fully formed and grown.

To the best of her knowledge she didn't have any paternal grand-parents. She didn't know if he had any other relatives. Whenever she asked, which hadn't been for years, he changed the subject. For that reason, she'd always suspected that he came from poor, if not desperate, conditions. He'd made himself wealthy, a fact that should have been an object of pride instead of shame.

After selling his shares of the East India Company, yet another topic she wasn't supposed to discuss, he'd delved into politics, of all things. Her father had no political ambition for himself. In this he wasn't lacking in self-knowledge. She'd once overheard him discussing the matter with one of his secretaries and his frankness had so surprised her that she hadn't been able to forget his words.

"I'm too blunt," he'd said. "I have a way of speaking that puts people off. And I don't look the part. I'm too short and I'm not a pretty boy. It's best if I become the power behind a candidate instead of being the candidate. That way we can win."

Her father's motives had always been shrouded in mystery, but she couldn't help but wonder, after hearing his words, if the reason he was doing this—and had become so wealthy—was to prove to the world that he was just as good as anyone else.

That was another subject she could never discuss with him. He didn't require her understanding, only her presence at the gatherings he arranged. Each one was designed to introduce one of his protégés, men he was sponsoring for public office.

He liked taking an ambitious young man, grooming him, ensuring that he became known, and doing everything within his power to help that individual win his first election.

So far he'd done that three times and, as his successes mounted, so did his resolve. Now he was concentrating his efforts on potential members of Parliament.

His power base might be growing, but Suzanne wished he would keep out of her life.

"I'm having a luncheon," he said now. "Several highly placed personages will be there."

She only nodded. He didn't ask if she would attend. He merely informed her what time and what event and she was expected to dress accordingly and be there.

"I'm getting tired of seeing you in black, Suzanne. I think you should give some thought to another color."

This was a conversation they had every time they met. Normally she remained silent, allowing him to rant without her participation. Today, however, she felt compelled to answer.

"It wouldn't be proper, Father," she said, moving to the end of the couch. As he did every time he came into this room, he chose the opposite chair. "People would talk."

"I don't think so. I've consulted experts on the subject, Suzanne. They concur with me. Two years is long enough for you to wear black."

She shouldn't have said anything, but silence was getting more difficult. She was not going to wear lavender simply because he didn't want to remember. He'd done the same with her mother. Two weeks after her death he'd begun to distribute her belongings to her friends and the servants. He was so determined to erase every trace of her that it was as if she'd never existed.

"I don't need trinkets," he'd said when she confronted him about his actions. "I'll never forget your mother. She'll always remain in my heart."

She wasn't entirely certain her father had a heart, but maybe he'd been telling the truth. In the last ten years he hadn't found another woman to take her mother's place. To the best of her knowledge—and thanks to information parlayed by chatty servants—he didn't entertain on his own. Every dinner party, every social event, was a result of a calculation. Who should attend? Who should be singled out for attention? Who was more valuable?

"I expect you to be there," he said. "You need to get past your sorrow, not wallow in it."

She stared at him. "Wallow in it?"

He nodded. "You need to devote yourself to a few good causes. If you like, I'll have Martin send you a list of acceptable activities."

She stood and looked down at her father. Anger surged through her, banishing the last of the gray haze from Ella's tonic.

"How could you say such a thing?"

"Sit down, Suzanne. We have a great deal more to discuss."

"No, we don't," she said. "I'm not one of your political cronies. I'm not a pawn on your chessboard."

She was not going to stay here and listen to him berate her. Instead, she walked out of the room. Let him condemn her for being rude; she didn't care.

Chapter Fourteen

$\mathcal{A}$dam made his way back to the library, trying to dismiss the image of the duchess leaving the conservatory with her father. There was something about the set of her shoulders that disturbed him. Almost as if she were curving into herself.

Edward Hackney was one of those men who saw nothing wrong with browbeating someone in his employ or the women in his life.

Adam knew quite well that the man was rich, but he didn't give a flying farthing. Men with that kind of wealth were as arrogant as the peerage, thinking that they were better than other people.

They weren't, but the problem was that no one had the nerve to tell them. Most of the time they were allowed to get away with their arrogance. They'd been born and one day would die like everyone else. Between those two dates it seemed to be important for them to let everyone know exactly who they were and what they possessed.

A title might be bestowed upon a man at his birth, but Adam doubted that Saint Peter would be reading out the name of the Duke of Marsley. Instead, it would be George Whitcomb who stood there, waiting to be judged.

As for himself, Adam was all too aware of his own sins as well as his failings.

It would be better to quickly finish up this assignment and get back to his lodgings. He wanted to stop worrying about whether he fit the majordomo template or how to handle personnel problems.

Granted, he would miss Mrs. Thigpen, who turned out to have a surprising sense of humor and a practical grasp of life itself. He would miss several of the footmen who looked to him as an older brother.

He wanted an assignment that was more professional and less personal. Perhaps without a woman who sparked his protective instincts. Or made him think, even once, how beautiful she was.

Being at Marsley House was not good for him, and it didn't matter how many times Roger implied that this assignment could easily advance his career. Roger had been guilty of promising too much and delivering too little before. He'd be a fool to take him at his word.

Adam made his way back to the third floor, staring at the shelves filled with the duke's journals. He had a suspicion that they had not originally been stored up here. He couldn't imagine, given the duke's character, that he would want his personal journals so far from hand.

The duke had been remarkably thin-skinned. When he perceived an insult, he recorded the slight along with the name of the infringing individual, the situation, and the date—the better to remember. It was a good thing that he hadn't been able to read the minds of the men under his command. There weren't enough journals in the world to record all those comments.

Adam reached for the fourteenth volume on the third shelf from the bottom, knowing that he probably wasn't going to get anything of substance from this book, either. Chronologically, Whitcomb had just arrived in India. Four years would elapse before the Sepoy Rebellion. Until then, the duke would have enough time to make a complete ass of himself and reveal the depth of his incompetence.

The man's appointment had been a royal favor and one that had surprised a great many people. It was entirely possible that Whitcomb, as the Duke of Marsley and the heir to a distinguished family, had some sort of relationship with the Queen. If he did, Adam doubted if the information would ever be passed along to him, a Scot from Glasgow, and the poor part of Glasgow, at that.

He heard the library door open and swore beneath his breath. He should have taken one of the journals back to his office to read the duke's increasingly indecipherable handwriting at his leisure.

Silently, he made his way to where the circular staircase ended, peering down into the cavernous first floor. To his surprise, the duchess stood there, her fists clamped on the black skirt of her dress, her lips thinned.

A second later Hackney entered the room, nearly slamming the door behind him.

"Have you lost your mind, Suzanne? Or all semblance of manners?"

"You would push yourself into my home, Father, and then lecture me on manners?" she asked, turning to face him.

"What's gotten into you?"

"I didn't feel like having a visitor," the duchess said. "Yet you didn't feel it necessary to respect my wishes."

"Are you drinking, Suzanne?" Hackney put both fists on his hips and glared at his daughter.

"You needn't be insulting, Father."

"And you needn't walk away when I'm trying to talk to you."

"You're not talking to me. You were beginning to lecture me again. I don't need to be lectured."

"Evidently you do, or you would've behaved much better than you have today."

Hackney's florid face was made even redder by his irritation. There was no doubt that he was furious with his daughter.

Adam couldn't see the duchess's face from here because her back was to him. However, she didn't sound as dazed as she had earlier. Whatever she'd taken or drunk had evidently worn off.

"You've changed, daughter, and it isn't becoming."

"I've changed?"

"Your grief has turned you into a harridan."

The duchess took a few quick steps back, almost as if Hackney had announced that he carried the plague.

"Behave like the widow of a duke, daughter. Georgie's dead and the sooner you come to that realization and accept the permanence of it, Suzanne, the better you will be."

She took another step back, her fingers now pressed to her mouth.

Hackney, to his credit, looked as if he realized how damaging his words had been. He reached out one hand then dropped it when she took another step back.

"I think you should leave," she said, her voice tight. "I really don't want to see you right now."

"I think that's a good idea," Hackney said. "I'll send you notice of the luncheon. I expect you to be there."

Hackney didn't say anything else as he turned and left the room.

She was weeping again, the sound like a spear to Adam's chest. He wanted to pummel Hackney.

What kind of father talked to his daughter that way?

Adam waited a few minutes until he was certain that the man wasn't returning. He left the journal flat on the bookshelf and was descending the staircase to talk to the duchess when she left the library.

Was she going back to the roof?

He understood her grief now, in a way he hadn't before.

Adam caught sight of the edge of her black skirt as she made it to the second floor landing. She wasn't going to the roof, but to her own suite.

He went up the stairs anyway, just in time to see her enter the duke's sitting room. He was descending the stairs when she came out again. He pretended to be testing to see if there was dust on the wainscoting just in case she interrogated him as to his actions. But the duchess didn't come to the first floor. Instead, she headed for the third.

He followed her, hoping to God she wasn't going to the roof after all. Once again, however, she confused him, turning left toward a part of the wing that wasn't used for servants' quarters. Nor was it near the entrance to the roof.

A door closing behind her was the only clue to where she'd gone.

Adam remained at the end of the hall, watching. A few minutes passed and she didn't emerge.

He walked to the door and stood in front of it. Twice he raised his hand, debating about whether to knock. Twice he lowered it. Should he interrupt her? Should he offer his condolences?

What the hell should he do about the Duchess of Marsley? He couldn't, in all good conscience, call her Marble Marsley anymore.

Perception was based on perspective, another lesson he'd learned in the army, but not from his superiors. He'd watched as one indignity after another was dealt out to the native population by the British East India Company. He hadn't been able to understand how an organization as expansive and all-consuming had been so blind to its own actions. They had no inkling that a great many of their policies were insulting to the populace, like the idiotic decision to use beef tallow to grease the cartridges for the new Enfield rifles. By doing so, they managed to offend the Hindu population, for whom the eating of cows was forbidden.

He'd been as blind about the Duchess of Marsley, judging her by his own personal prejudices and biases.

At least he'd tried to comfort her. He could still feel her standing close to him, her arms around his waist, her cheek against his chest. He felt her tears against his knuckles, and more than once he looked at his hand as if to see evidence of them still there.

He, too, knew what grief was. It was a cruel emotion, one that sapped your energy and gave nothing in return. Anger sometimes brought wisdom. Fear encouraged caution. Love? Love was perfect in its own sense. But grief? All it brought was anguish and despair and the pitiless certainty that you would always feel it in some degree.

Rebecca's death still weighed heavily on him, as well as the loss of his mother and sister. He'd had friends he'd watched die for no more reason than they were serving in the army. He knew grief only too well.

If the duchess was cold, if she held herself stiff and aloof from others, it could be that she was like Mrs. Anderson in India. The poor woman had watched two of her children die of fever. He'd been assigned to take her to the ship bound for England. She'd barely spoken, but when she had, he could hear the despair in her voice. He'd wanted to say something then, too, but what words could possibly ease someone trying to cope with that kind of loss?

He didn't have anything to say now, either, so he turned and walked away.

Chapter Fifteen

$\mathscr{T}$wo days later Adam entered the housekeeper's office, only to be informed that the duchess wished to see him. Mrs. Thigpen looked worried, which was not a good sign. The housekeeper normally remained calm and unmoved even in the worst of crises.

"Do you know why?" he asked her. "Have I done something wrong?"

That was always a possibility. He had navigated many roles in the previous seven years, but this stint as a majordomo had been the most difficult one of all.

"I don't know," Mrs. Thigpen said, sighing. "She does seem in a mood, which is strange. The duchess is normally very sweet and unassuming."

He hadn't seen that side of the duchess yet, but he wisely kept silent.

"I do wish her father would not come and visit," Mrs. Thigpen said, surprising him. "She's always so agitated after he leaves."

"The duchess doesn't seem to be very much like him."

"She doesn't, does she? From the very first moment she moved into Marsley House, I liked her. She never put on airs and she always treated every member of the staff with kindness. She went out of her way to say please and thank you, which is more than I can say about Mr. Hackney. Or the duke, for that matter."

"He was in India, wasn't he?" Adam asked, trying to sound as nonchalant as he could. He'd never considered that Mrs. Thigpen might be a source of information about India, but the woman had been employed at Marsley House for two decades. The duke might have said something to her about Manipora.

"That he was, and very enthusiastic about the prospect. At least, that's what his valet told me. Of course, Paul didn't last long in his employ. Once he got to India, His Grace replaced him."

The duke had been surrounded by a coterie of people who either protected him from others or the rest of the world from George.

She glanced at the clock. "Best be off, then, before she rings again."

He entered the library, closed the door behind him, and walked to the desk where the duchess was sitting. She kept him standing there while she pretended to be interested in the account books in front of her. He saw those once a month when they were sent from the solicitor. He was expected to make comments and notations, and enter in any unexpected expenses that hadn't been otherwise listed. The books were then sent back to the solicitor for evaluation. He hadn't realized a step in the process was that the duchess reviewed them as well.

She finally looked up, her face wiped of any expression, and said to him, "Your penmanship leaves a great deal to be desired, Drummond."

He bit back a smile. If that's all she could find fault with, then he was in no danger of being dismissed.

"I apologize, Your Grace," he said, bowing slightly. "I will attempt to do better."

She glanced away and then back at him. "See that you do."

He nodded, moved to stand at parade rest position, his legs slightly apart, his hands clasped behind him. He could stand for hours if need be. At least the sun wasn't beating down on his head and shoulders. Plus, he'd had a good breakfast, so he was prepared to remain here for as long as she kept him.

Somehow, he'd annoyed her. No doubt protecting her from her father had been one of his sins. Another might be that he'd held her in his arms. Was she going to call him out on that, too? If so, he was tempted to tell her that, if he'd known about Georgie, he would have done even more. He would have embraced her fully, let her cry as long as she wanted, knowing exactly how she felt.

"You've spent entirely too much on the conservatory," she said.

"Two of the window panes were broken, Your Grace. With the winter coming on, I didn't want the damage to go unrepaired. Otherwise, the plants would've suffered, resulting in an even greater expenditure."

She looked annoyed at his answer.

She was evidently fishing for something to complain about or some reason to have him stand in front of the desk like a suppli-cant. Very well, he would play this game. While she was looking for some reason to upbraid him, he would admire the picture she made, framed by the windows behind her, with the sun dancing on her dark brown hair.

Her nose was perfect for her face, neither too large nor too narrow and aristocratic. A woman's mouth was a fascinating thing. Hers was perfect. The upper and bottom lip were exactly the same size. Both full, but not overly so. Nor was it too small for her face. It was another perfect feature, as were her eyes. He couldn't remember ever seeing that shade of blue before. It was almost as if God couldn't decide whether to give her gray eyes or blue and combined the two.

Her long and slender fingers trailed down the notations he'd made, one by one, as if seeking an error.

He much preferred her as she was now, annoyed and deter-mined, than how she'd been that day in the conservatory.

She looked up then and said, "You've never been a majordomo before, have you, Drummond?"

He forced a smile to his face. "Why would you ask that, Your Grace?"

"For the simple reason that I desired an answer, Drummond."

Her eyes were narrowed and that beautiful mouth of hers thinned. He might not be able to charm her with his answer, but he had every intention of doing the very best he could.

"Your Grace, I was a sergeant in the army for many years. I was responsible for a hundred men, their welfare, their deportment, and whatever was needed to ensure their well-being. I was promoted to lieutenant, which meant that my responsibilities increased. Instead of simply a hundred men it was ten times that. When I gave your solicitor my qualifications, he thought that I would serve the position and Your Grace well. Have I not done so?"

They exchanged a glance. He almost dared her to tell him where he had not done his best in this position. If he'd erred, and they both knew it, it was in being too familiar with her.

He would not apologize for that.

After a moment, she stared down at the account book. "You may go, Drummond."

That was all. Not an explanation of why he'd been called into the library. Not an apology for wasting his time or insulting him. Nothing. Just a dismissal by a duchess.

He stood there wrestling with himself. He needed to finish his assignment. He didn't need to cause any more conflict between the two of them. That was not his mission. The man he was, however, separate and apart from being a member of the Silent Service, wanted to ask what she'd objected to the most, that he'd treated her like a woman or that he had no intention of changing his behavior?

Instead, he did a smart about-face and left the room, feeling that a great many things had been left unsaid.

SUZANNE WATCHED THE library door close behind Drummond before sitting back. She gripped the arms of the chair tightly with both hands, her fingers resting on the indentations of the lion's paws.

Why had she summoned him? She hadn't seen him for two days. Two days in which she'd heard his voice from time to time. He had a low laugh, one that captured her attention. His instructions to the staff were done in a no-nonsense kind of voice as if he would brook no disobedience.

He'd stared down her father. For that alone, he should be rewarded.

The man was entirely too attractive, however. Dressed in his majordomo uniform he almost looked like a prince leaving for a night of revelry. He moved as if he were comfortable with himself. She doubted if his hands ever trembled. Or if he ever looked uncertain.

He was entirely too intriguing.

Was that why she'd summoned him?

He hadn't looked afraid. Instead, there had been a look in his green eyes that was almost insulting. No, not insulting. Challenging, perhaps. Almost as if he'd been daring her. To do what? Dismiss him? He was an excellent majordomo. Even the account books indicated that. He actually requested bids from several tradesmen instead of paying anything they demanded like Old Franklin had. In addition, he'd questioned several expenditures they'd normally always paid with the result that they were saving money at the greengrocers and the butcher.

Besides, he was excellent at protecting her.

Was that why she'd summoned him?

Had she felt the need to be protected? Perhaps she had, but how absolutely idiotic of her to think of her majordomo. He was a member of her staff. He was in her employ. She paid his wages.

She really shouldn't have any curiosity about the man. Still, it had been nice to see him. He was looking well, fit and hardy. It was important to ensure the well-being of her staff. That's the only reason she'd summoned him, of course.

She shook her head at that thought. She wasn't given to lying to herself and she didn't intend to start now.

For some reason, he made her feel safe. He inspired something within her, some kind of admiration she hadn't often felt. He hadn't sought her out in the past two days, reason enough to send for him.

She missed him. There, the truth, as idiotic as it was.

Chapter Sixteen

$\mathcal{A}$dam was almost to the grand staircase on his way to the library when he saw the light beneath the mysterious door. He didn't think. He didn't consider the matter before putting his hand on the latch and pushing the door open.

He didn't know what he expected, but it wasn't what he saw. The Duchess of Marsley was sitting on the side of a small bed. In her lap was a well-worn floppy yellow rabbit with one eye slightly askew. When the door opened, she looked up.

What surprised him was her silence. She didn't demand that he leave or close the door behind him. She didn't say a word.

He should have respected her privacy. At the least he should have realized that he'd erred in opening the door. Overriding that was a curious and instinctive response to the picture of her sitting there, her eyes filled with tears. He didn't want to leave her alone.

After entering the room he closed the door behind him.

The walls of the nursery were painted a soft blue. Some shelves on two walls were filled with toys and some with books. He'd never imagined that one child could have so many possessions, but Georgie had been the heir to a dukedom. A child feted from the moment he'd drawn breath.

He had the feeling that rank hadn't mattered to the Duchess of Marsley. She would have cherished her child regardless. His own mother had been like that, making no secret of her love for him and Mary. She told him often, cupping her hand against his cheek, smiling into his eyes.

"I love you, *mo mhac*. Never forget that, my lad."

Only later, when he'd been far away from Glasgow, had he realized how rare that devotion had been.

Georgie had been loved the same way, he suspected, not in poverty but plenty.

He came and, no doubt in defiance of every kind of etiquette, sat next to her on the bed. She looked startled for a moment, but she didn't move away.

The room smelled of cloves and oil from the lamp mixed with the duchess's perfume. For a few moments they didn't speak, sitting in companionable silence with Marsley House quieting around them.

He turned his head to look at her. The duchess had a beautiful face, but the angle of her chin seemed too sharp. Was she eating enough?

"Are you hungry, Suzanne? Can I bring you anything? Some pastries, biscuits? Cook made a roast and I know she'd be pleased if you had some."

"It's nearly midnight, Drummond, and you're offering to feed me?" she asked, brushing away one lone tear from her cheek.

"Have you eaten lately?"

"Now you're my nanny?"

He didn't answer, merely watched her.

"I had quite a lovely dinner, as a matter of fact," she said.

He was somewhat satisfied, but he would alert Mrs. Thigpen as well. Perhaps the duchess had some favorite dishes that Grace could make to tempt her appetite.

"How old was he?" he finally asked.

She blinked at him. That was all. For a moment he didn't think she was going to answer, but then she did, the words filled with tears.

"Georgie was three," she said.

"*Gabh mo leisgeul.*"

"You've said that before. *I'm sorry.* Is that what it means?"

He nodded.

Her gaze went back to the stuffed animal on her lap. "Thank you."

"What happened?" he asked.

"I had a cold," she said, brushing the fur on the floppy-eared rabbit. "Isn't that odd? I haven't had a cold since."

She didn't speak for a moment and he didn't urge her to continue, content to sit and wait.

"George was impatient with sickness. George was impatient about most things. He was all for visiting his second cousin," she added after several minutes. "He's the current Duke of Marsley. Poor man never expected to be duke and was shocked by it, I think. He married an heiress, which is a good thing because there's no money to go with the title."

She looked at the ceiling and the walls of the nursery as if to encompass the whole of Marsley House. "This is an expensive place to maintain. You might call it the price of George's bachelorhood. My father bought him for me. He'd always wanted to be connected to the peerage and now he has a duchess for a daughter."

She smiled slightly, but the expression had no humor in it.

"That day, George wanted to take Georgie and his nurse with him. I asked him to wait, but he wouldn't. I told him that it was too cold, that the weather would warm in a few days, but he didn't listen. No one could get George to do something he didn't want to do. So I waved them goodbye from the front steps. I expected them back by nightfall and when they didn't return, I knew. I knew something terrible had happened, although I didn't learn exactly what until the next day."

She lifted her eyes to him. In them was the same expression he had seen that first night, endless grief.

"The bridge collapsed. Who expects a bridge to collapse? But it did and the carriage plunged into the water. The coachman was saved and the nurse, but not Georgie or his father."

She arranged the rabbit on her lap and took a deep breath before continuing. "I've often thought of them together in those last moments. George would hold Georgie in the freezing water and reassure him. He wouldn't let Georgie be afraid, of that I'm certain."

He didn't know what to say to comfort her. He suspected that mere words wouldn't help.

"I didn't really wish to throw myself off the roof that night," she said. "At least, I don't think I did." She glanced over at him. "I had too much wine and that's never happened before."

"I've known a great many men who swear that they wouldn't have done something if they hadn't been intoxicated."

Her smile was barely a curve of her lips. "There is that, I suppose. I think it would be wise for me to avoid spirits of any kind from now on."

"That might be a good decision."

The room was shadowed, lit only by a small lamp beside the bed. Ever since he'd entered, they'd spoken as contemporaries. He hadn't called her *Your Grace* and she hadn't banished him from the room.

He was loath to leave, even though it would've been the right thing to do so.

"I should have known you were in the military," she said.

The statement surprised him. "Why?"

"You have a military bearing. An acquaintance of mine mentioned it."

"Do I? No doubt it's from hours of standing at attention."

"Why did you leave? My husband used to say that only failures leave the army. Good men stay and retire."

He didn't give a damn about what her husband used to say, but he tried to answer her without revealing his contempt for the duke.

"I found myself at odds with the aims of the army," he said.

Her smile made an appearance again. "Then the army's loss is our gain."

He had expected her to question him further, but she only cradled the bunny against her chest, pressing her chin against the stuffed animal's head.

"This was Georgie's favorite toy," she said. "He didn't take it with him that last day. His father didn't approve of toys." She looked at the rabbit and then at Adam as if introducing them. "His name is Babbit because he couldn't say rabbit."

He looked around him, at the evidence of a child who had been loved and cherished.

"Do you come here often?"

Had he dared too much with his question? He thought so when she didn't answer him.

"Less now than I once did," she finally said. "I used to find some comfort here. I pretended that Georgie was with his nurse and that he'd return in a little while." She didn't say anything for a moment, and when she spoke again, there were tears once more in her voice. "Now it's almost too painful. I can't pretend anymore and this is just a reminder of everything that was, but will never be again. I've finally realized that nothing will be the same. He isn't coming back. He won't ever be older than three."

She didn't say anything further.

He remembered the cruel comment her father had made.

"You will always be his mother," he said. "He'll always be alive in your heart."

She took a deep breath and looked at him again. "How wise you are, Drummond. Do you often counsel the grieving? Or do you mourn a loss of your own?"

"A great many people."

She surprised him by reaching over and placing her hand on his wrist. Her hand was warm, the connection something he hadn't expected.

"Who?"

He hadn't thought of the duchess as being determined, but the steady look in her eyes indicated that he had underestimated the strength of her will. She wanted an answer. Very well, he would give it to her.

"My mother, first," he said. "And then my sister. Friends, men I knew in the army." He hesitated for a moment. "My wife, Rebecca."

Her hand closed around his wrist as if she measured his pulse or wanted to keep him seated there.

"Tell me about her."

He smiled, but it was an effort. He rarely talked about Rebecca. Doing so filled him with regret. He couldn't alter the events of the past, but it didn't stop him from wanting to do so.

"Please," she said.

Because there were still tears in her eyes, he began to speak.

"When I think of Rebecca I think of sunshine," he said. "She had light blond hair and a bright smile and a laugh that could make you laugh along with her. She was the sister of one of my lieutenants and had come out to India with a few of her friends."

He stared down at where Suzanne's hand rested on his wrist, remembering.

"We've come to find husbands," Rebecca had said when he'd been introduced to her. *"At the end of six months, if we haven't succeeded, we're going back to England."*

She was like that, without guile or shame or even embarrassment. Yet she was so charming and pretty that most people forgave her any gaffe she might have uttered.

He and Rebecca had married five days before she was due to return to England.

"What is your name?" the duchess asked now.

He glanced at her.

"Your given name," she said.

"Adam."

"Thank you, Adam."

She stood and went to the door, opening it. He stood as well, knowing that he was being politely invited to leave. She surprised him, however, by going to the bedside table and extinguishing the light, then joining him in the corridor. She closed and locked the door before pocketing the key.

He wanted to say something to her. A caution along the lines of, *Don't come here that often. Don't punish yourself.* Instead, he looked down at her, standing in the shadows.

He took a step toward her, unable to bear the anguish in her eyes.

"Suzanne."

She only nodded. When he went to her and pulled her into his arms, a space that she seemed to fill so perfectly, she sighed deeply again and sagged against him.

They stood like that for several moments.

"Some people cling to grief," he said. "As a way to keep their loved one close." He wanted to tell her that it didn't work. It didn't make the passage through anguish any easier. Nor did it bring a loved one back.

She stepped away, keeping her head down. Had he angered her? Perhaps that would be better than her sorrow.

"Good night, Suzanne."

Only after he left her, heading back toward his room, did he remember that he hadn't given her the brooch in his pocket. He didn't call out to her, merely watched as she descended the staircase to the second floor. He would see her tomorrow and give it to her then.

The anticipation of that moment was a warning. He'd go back down to the library in a few minutes and start searching again. Once he'd found that damn journal he'd leave Marsley House and its surprising duchess behind.

That day couldn't come fast enough.

Chapter Seventeen

"Where have you been, Your Grace?"

At her entrance into the sitting room, Ella stood. She'd been occupying Suzanne's favorite wing chair in front of the fire. A cup of tea sat on the table beside her. Where was the footstool and a pillow, perhaps, for her back? Suzanne was only surprised that her maid hadn't ordered a tray of cake and biscuits.

But Ella had always made herself at home in the duchess's suite, hadn't she?

As she walked into the bedroom, Suzanne held up her hand. "I really don't need your help tonight, Ella," she said.

She wanted to be alone, to think about the surprising events that had just transpired. Tonight, she'd acquired a friend. A strange and unexpected friend in her majordomo. His words had been so welcome and his understanding so complete that she couldn't help but be grateful.

She turned to see Ella standing in the doorway. Evidently, she was not going to get rid of the maid until she performed her duties.

"I still haven't found your hair clip, Your Grace. I've gone through both armoires and the carriage and I haven't been able to find it. It's very valuable, Your Grace. Your father will not be happy that it's missing."

"Then we don't need to tell him, do we, Ella? Unless, of course, you insist on reporting to him every week. Or is it more often than that? I noticed a flurry of correspondence leaving the country for London. Do you write him every day?"

Ella didn't wilt under her questions. Instead, the maid got a mulish look on her face: flat eyes, clenched lips, and a silence that dared Suzanne to question her further.

"Tell him what you want," she said. "I don't care. Tell him I threw it in the Thames. Or out the carriage window."

"I should have accompanied you, Your Grace. I think I should do so in the future."

"That won't be necessary," she said, walking into the bedroom.

She began to unbutton the bodice of her dress. Ella came to stand in front of her, but Suzanne turned.

"You're dismissed," she said. "I don't need help undressing."

"Of course you do," Ella said, coming to stand in front of her once more. She pushed Suzanne's hands out of the way and finished unfastening the row of buttons.

When had she lost all authority? Or had she ever possessed it? She stepped back, away from Ella.

"Will you please leave me?"

"Your Grace, don't be unreasonable. Let's get you ready for bed, shall we?"

The maid picked up the nightgown draped across the end of the bed. "We don't need to have an argument about this, do we?"

"No, we don't," Suzanne said.

Grabbing the nightgown, she walked into the bathing chamber and closed the door. Tomorrow she would ask Drummond—Adam—to have someone install a lock on this door. Ella had never disturbed her privacy here, but she didn't have any faith that the maid would continue to leave her alone.

She undressed, unfastening the busk of her corset, her shift, and the rest of her undergarments before washing and brushing her teeth. After removing her hairpins, she threaded her fingers through her hair before braiding it loosely. George had always liked her hair long, and maybe it was for that reason that she now kept it trimmed to just below her shoulders. He wouldn't have approved, but George was no longer here to issue his pronounce-ments.

She couldn't help but wonder what he would have thought about Ella.

Her previous maid had been from India, coming to England with George and several other people who were added to the staff at Marsley House.

Her father hadn't approved.

"They're damn sly, Suzanne," her father had said. "Always plot-ting and planning."

Although she didn't agree with her father's words, she under-stood why he said them. He'd been horrified at the rebellion in India. Because of that, he'd pulled out of the East India Company, severing both financial and personal ties with men with whom he'd done business for decades.

It was in India that he'd met George, a penurious duke who had been giving some vague thoughts to marrying and produc-ing a legitimate heir. At last count George had seven children scattered around London and India. He hadn't cared enough to learn their names, but at least he'd known whether they were sons or daughters.

She had never imagined anyone like George. He was proud of his libertine nature. He made no apologies for the fact that he liked women and had no intentions whatsoever of remain-ing true to his marital vows. The very thought of having to lash himself to one woman for the rest of his days was an idiotic notion. Once, he'd even gone so far as to attempt to explain his philosophy to her.

"You might think of me as a stallion, my dear. Would a stallion be restricted to one paddock and a single mare? Of course not. He would be given freedom to roam and attract any likely mate."

She could recall the exact moment of his stallion soliloquy. She'd been sitting in the Blue Parlor on the second floor. It had been a spring evening and the windows had been open to let in the air, cooled from an earlier rainstorm. A moth had found its way in to circle the lamp on the table to her left. She'd been reading, a fascinating lurid novel that would have been forbidden to her a few years earlier.

George had come into the room to say good-night. The carriage was waiting. No doubt his fellow revelers were also becoming impatient, waiting for him to arrive. When he'd finished speaking, he had looked at her expectantly, almost as if he wished her approval, which was ludicrous. George required no one's approval, not even God's.

She hadn't been surprised at his words. What had startled her was the fact that he thought it important enough—that he thought *her* important enough—to hear his personal philosophy. Of course, it might have been because she was the mother of his heir. Georgie was only a few months old at the time.

She'd returned to her book without speaking and he'd left a moment later. That night was a turning point, something she'd realized looking back. Once Georgie had been born, his father absolved himself of any further marital responsibility. The stallion speech was just a formal announcement of that fact.

For the great honor of becoming a duchess she was supposed to ignore George's peccadilloes and be a supportive and silent wife. Since their marriage had never been based on mutual affection she'd pushed any thoughts of developing respect for her husband out of her mind and kept quiet about his various women.

She and George had lived separate lives. The only times they were together were when her father invited them to one of his innumerable gatherings.

When she left the bathroom, she encountered Ella standing there, holding the tonic out for her to drink.

The detestable tonic, something her father and Ella decided was important for her to drink. She loathed the taste and the effects.

"No," she said. "I won't take it."

"You must, Your Grace." There was that implacable tone in Ella's voice.

"Why, Ella? Because you say so?"

"It's good for you, Your Grace."

"No."

That's all she said. Just no. She didn't argue or take the glass. Instead, she skirted Ella and climbed the steps to her bed, bending over to extinguish the lamp.

"You can stand there until dawn, Ella. I'm not taking your bloody tonic."

Ella gasped. Was she shocked because of Suzanne's profanity? Or simply because she'd refused and this time she hadn't backed down?

When she heard the sound of the door closing behind the maid, she took a deep breath and banished any thoughts of Ella. Instead, she was thinking of Drummond and his revelations. Or how she'd felt when he'd so gently taken her into his arms.

Chapter Eighteen

Adam slept late, something he'd rarely done. In his childhood if he was abed instead of out at first light, it meant that he lost a job with one of the hawkers. He was relegated to selling broadsides for a penny, working eight hours for a pittance. He had to make money every day or they didn't eat. In the army, he would have been cashiered out if he'd acted like a slug.

His night had been filled with wild dreams, things that didn't make any sense in the way of dreams. The duke had featured prominently as well as the duchess. Adam had heard her crying and had been trying to reach her, swimming through icy water to get to her side.

When he finally woke, his first thought was of her. He allowed himself to recall the sight of her profile, the sweet dawning of her smile, and the ballet of her hands.

He needed to be gone from here before too much more time passed.

After dressing in his majordomo uniform and brushing his hair, he descended the staircase to the first floor.

"It's a glorious day, Adam," Mrs. Thigpen said, greeting him when he entered the staff dining room.

To his relief, the housekeeper didn't say anything about his late start to the morning. That was the difference between being a servant and being a majordomo, evidently. Instead, she smiled brightly at him when he asked if he could share her table.

"Please," she said, waving him to a chair opposite her. "There are clouds on the eastern horizon, however. My late husband used to say that if you see clouds before nine o'clock, it means that there will be a storm before seven. He was a great watcher of clouds."

"We called those *banff bailies* in Scotland," he said, sitting. "Big white clouds that promise rain."

"You've been away from your home for a great many years, haven't you, Adam?"

He nodded. "Twenty or so," he said.

"Have you not thought of going back?"

"I've no one there, Olivia, and that's the reason to return, isn't it?"

She left him before he finished his breakfast, allowing him to contemplate his duties for the day. Today was earmarked for interviewing footmen and maids. He staggered the meetings so that he saw each member of the staff at least once a month. That way, he could hear any complaints or suggestions himself rather than allowing them to fester unheard. He also was able to keep personnel disagreements at a minimum. If someone made a remark about another staff member, he disconcerted both of them by having them meet in his office and air out any grievances. In that way, he sent out an unmistakable message: he didn't approve of petty annoyances or disagreements. If someone had an issue with someone else, it was in their best interest to solve the problem before it was escalated to him.

Last week he had the disagreeable task of having to let one of the scullery maids go. She was with child and had kept it a secret until Mrs. Thigpen discovered it one morning. At least, in the maid's case, she had a family to turn to, just as his sister, Mary, had. Hopefully, she would survive childbirth.

"You can always come back here after you have your child, Constance," he told the girl.

She hadn't met his eyes, choosing to stare down at her reddened fingers instead. But she'd nodded her understanding. He'd wanted to know who the father was, but he hadn't asked. Some things he didn't have to know in his post as majordomo. At least she hadn't been impregnated by the duke.

From the records left by Old Franklin, the Duke of Marsley had managed to make himself known to a great many female staff members. Three maids had quit unexpectedly in a one-month period. Two had been dismissed for being with child. Adam had read that an extraordinary measure had been taken to protect the women employed at Marsley House—locks had been installed on all the doors on the third floor.

He was almost to the staircase when he heard Ella. She had a particularly annoying voice, one that grated on him. Something he realized as he listened: the angrier Ella was, the more annoying her voice became.

"It's not proper that you go without me, Your Grace," she was saying.

"Are you implying that I am not a proper companion? How utterly cheeky of you, young woman."

He knew that voice. He stepped into the foyer. The woman who turned and glanced at him before her expression melted into a smile had come to Marsley House once before. He couldn't remember her name, but she'd been pleasant and polite.

Evidently, Ella had the capacity for bringing out the worst in everyone.

The duchess was standing close to the door, her hand on the latch as if she wanted to escape the scene. She glanced at him and to his surprise, her face flushed. Was she remembering their embrace from the night before? He hadn't been able to forget it, either.

Her eyes were clear, her look direct. She was dressed as she'd been since he knew her: in black silk. The meaning for it struck him more today, for some reason. He wanted to go to her, tilt her chin up with his hand, and look into her face. He wanted to ask if she was all right. Had she slept well? Had she eaten? What were her plans for today?

None of those questions would have been proper. Nor was this feeling, this novel and unexpected sensation in his stomach, as if it were suddenly buoyant.

It took a few seconds for him to identify what he was feeling. When he did, he almost stepped back, retreating from the foyer, the sight of her, and his own dismaying happiness.

She'd made his day brighter just by seeing her. She'd caused his pulse to race and his spirit to soar.

Good God, had he gone daft?

"I must insist, Your Grace."

His attention was recaptured by Ella's whine. He stepped forward, putting himself between the stranger and the maid.

"May I be of service?"

"Mr. Drummond," the woman said, "how very nice to see you again."

He bowed slightly, wishing he could remember her name. What had her calling card said? Bruiser? Bullister? He didn't remember names as well as he did facts like geographical details, dates, and troop strength.

"You evidently have enough time on your hands, Ella," the duchess said. "Perhaps Drummond can give you something to do."

That was hardly fair, giving him the task of dealing with the prickly maid.

"Of course, Your Grace," he said, bowing slightly.

He glanced at Suzanne and then away. It wouldn't do to look at her. She was particularly attractive today and he didn't want the temptation.

"Mrs. Armbruster, shall we go?" the duchess said.

Armbruster, that was it. That was the name of the woman.

He nodded to Daniel, who was being put in a difficult position by the duchess's stance. She was gripping the door latch herself, which was a task normally performed by the footman. The young man stood there looking helpless.

Adam walked to the duchess's side and put his hand over hers. You would have thought it was scalding by how quickly she jerked her hand back. Her color grew even deeper as she stood aside, allowing him to open the door for her.

She was wearing a different perfume today, a scent that was spicy yet not overpowering. He'd never been affected by a woman's perfume, but he was by hers. Did she wear it behind her ear? On her neck?

Even as he lectured himself, even as part of him felt as if he stood outside his body and stared in disbelief at his own actions, he wanted to bend closer and breathe deeply. Or take her into his arms and hold her tenderly for a few hours.

He was losing his mind, his determination, and his sense of duty. All because a beautiful woman smelled good.

"I'm certain I can find something for Ella to do," he said, stepping back.

She only nodded, not looking at him.

"Thank you, Drummond," she said as she descended the steps, leaving him staring after her.

Mrs. Armbruster leaned close on her way out the door. "You have the most charming smile, Mr. Drummond," she said. "It's really quite lovely."

He didn't know what the hell to say to that, so he gave her one of his lovely smiles.

When the door closed he was left with the footman and the view of Ella stomping down the corridor on the way to the back of the house. Good, the last thing he wanted—or needed—was to have to deal with a petulant maid.

"Where are they going?" he asked, but Daniel only shook his head.

"I don't know, sir. They didn't say."

Another mystery to solve, but not as important as his tasks for the day. He nodded and headed to his office, all the while attempting to push the thought of the Duchess of Marsley from his mind.

Chapter Nineteen

"I was very surprised, Your Grace, that you agreed to this outing, and very pleased as well," Mrs. Armbruster said.

"I'm looking forward to seeing your Institute," Suzanne said.

When she'd received the woman's note this morning, it seemed like an excellent way to get out of Marsley House. She needed to be away, just in case her father called on her again. Plus, she was growing exceedingly tired of Ella and wanted to escape the woman's frowns and snide remarks.

Why had she tolerated the woman all this time? The fact that Ella had been in her employ six months seemed impossible now. But then, she'd been taking Ella's tonic and it had numbed everything.

Evidently, it had also stolen her reason.

Without the tonic, it had taken her longer to fall asleep last night. Her thoughts had been scattered, but they'd kept returning to Drummond. He was an exceedingly handsome man. In addition, he'd been kind and understanding.

People didn't seem to comprehend that it was easier to be alone than to try to pretend that everything was normal, that the world went on, and life still happened.

Drummond—Adam—had seemed to know that. No doubt because he'd his own share of grief with the death of his wife.

Had she said anything comforting to him? She couldn't remember, which made her think that she'd been immersed in her own sorrow. He hadn't been as selfish. He'd wanted to know about Georgie. He'd sat there and listened as she talked.

How natural it had felt to allow him to comfort her.

In those moments in the nursery she'd come to a startling realization. She wasn't numb to all feeling. She noted the strength of a man's embrace, the way he smelled—of bay rum and starch and a faint hint of the potpourri Mrs. Thigpen added to all the drawers. Had the housekeeper made a special recipe for Adam?

She liked the way he spoke, a Scottish accent that was flattened down just a little, as if he'd spent more time away from Scotland than in it.

She also noted the expression in his green eyes. Instead of the almost apathetic look in some higher-ranked servants—as if they'd seen it all and couldn't be bothered to deal further with the vagaries of human nature—Adam's gaze was always interested and curious. And kind. He'd said two words to her—*I'm sorry*—and it had touched her deeply.

"The girls at the Institute are from all kinds of backgrounds," Mrs. Armbruster was saying. "They have each been visited by circumstances that the rest of society deems unfit to contemplate."

"Ignoring something doesn't make it go away," Suzanne said.

Mrs. Armbruster gave her a bright, toothy smile. "How right you are, my dear." She placed her gloved hand on Suzanne's arm and leaned close. "You don't mind if I call you that, do you? You remind me so much of my own dear Diane. It's been four years since she and her husband emigrated to Queensland and I do miss her so."

"Of course not," Suzanne said.

Few people had treated her as if she were human in the past six years. Six years a duchess. Except for having had Georgie, she would much rather have gone back to being Suzanne Hackney. Her father would never have been satisfied with that, however. She was a commodity and he'd made a good bargain, at least according to him.

The Institute was also located in Spitalfields, a place that did not brighten with familiarity. Nor was the smell of it any more acceptable the second time she was here. How did Mrs. Armbruster tolerate it? For that matter, how did the inhabitants of the Foundling Hospital and the Institute?

The carriage halted in front of a two-story redbrick building. The entrance was a single door in the wall.

"We do not advertise what we do here, Your Grace," Mrs. Armbruster said. "There are some groups, unfortunately some that are religious in nature, who take umbrage at the fact that we are encouraging sin, in their words."

"Are you?" Suzanne asked, accepting the coachman's hand as she exited the carriage.

"I suppose that there are some people who think that, but what we do is rescue young women who have gotten themselves into trouble with the help of young men."

Suzanne didn't have a rejoinder to that, so she merely followed the older woman into the building.

Everything about the Institute was bland and neutral. The walls were beige. The wooden floors were covered with a beige runner. The rooms they passed were also beige, as if the entire building had been designed to be as nondescript as possible.

Mrs. Armbruster strode on ahead as if determined to reach a certain point. Suzanne had no choice but to follow her, removing her gloves as she did so and wishing she could dispense of her hat as easily.

The corridor smelled of onions and something sweet, apples. Onions and apples—what a curious combination. The kitchen to their left was filled with women milling about or seated at the long wooden table in the center of the room. Mrs. Armbruster only waved in passing.

The next doorway led to a music room, which surprised Suzanne because she hadn't thought of music as something that might be taught in such conditions. When she said as much to Mrs. Armbruster, the woman smiled.

"Many of these girls are frightened, Your Grace. Music, we've found, is a great equalizer. If you can get a few girls to sing a song they all know together, it eases them, and makes them less afraid."

Mrs. Armbruster finally stopped, turned to the right, and entered a beige room, this one a parlor. Impressively large, the room had two fireplaces on opposite walls. A selection of couches, chairs, tables, and lamps were scattered about the room. Nothing seemed to match and Suzanne couldn't help but wonder if every item in the parlor was a castoff from someone's home.

A great many of the couches and chairs were occupied, all by girls who seemed much too young to be in their condition. All of them were with child. Some looked to be due to give birth at any moment, while others probably had a few months left.

"Do they have no families?" Suzanne asked in a low voice.

Mrs. Armbruster turned to her, her doughy face softened into lines of compassion. For her naïveté? Or for the girls who surrounded them?

"The very sad fact, Your Grace, is that most of them do have families. But their families have thrown them out or locked the doors and banished them for their great sin. You will note, however, that the young men who helped them get into this condition are never punished in any way. Not by reputation. Not by the law. Not even financially."

She'd been sick for the first three months with Georgie, but after that, the entire time until his birth had been one of joy and anticipation. What must it be like to be with child and have no home, no family, no shelter, or anyone to care?

"Is there nothing that can be done?" she asked.

She had so much and they had so little. No, they had nothing except themselves and Mrs. Armbruster, a woman whose zeal was the match of any politician.

"Some brave men in Parliament are attempting to pass laws to effect change, but those are slow measures. In the meantime, we have young women who would suffer without assistance. Everyone is foolish from time to time, my dear. Each one of us has done something we regret. A bad decision, a choice made in the heat of the moment should not result in tragedy." Mrs. Armbruster cleared her throat. "In addition, Your Grace, there are some girls who had no choice in the matter. No choice at all."

Her voice took on a practical tone. "We need to help them provide for themselves. We have classes," she added. "We train them in various skills that an employer might wish to have. A great many of our girls have gone into service. Some work as milliners, some as seamstresses, and a few at nearby factories."

"Surely not when they're with child?"

The older woman nodded. "If they are healthy, yes, Your Grace. We've found that some occupation is harmful for neither the mother nor the child. A girl will remain here until her baby is born. Then she'll stay until she can find employment. We'll give her whatever education she wishes. Several of our girls have gone on to be quite successful, I'm proud to say."

The woman beamed at her. "We have plans to charge the girls a small amount each month to live here after their child is born. Only if they've acquired a position, that is." Mrs. Armbruster leaned close. "It's my fervent wish never to deny a girl a place here, Your Grace. They've already lost so much. I would hate for them to lose this haven as well. But there are those who will disobey our tenets. And some, I regret to say, who have abandoned their babies and left."

Suzanne couldn't imagine such a thing, but she had never been in a similar situation as these girls.

Before she could ask any further questions, Mrs. Armbruster walked to the middle of the room and called for attention.

"Girls, I have a very important visitor to introduce to you."

Suzanne felt her stomach drop and wished that Mrs. Armbruster had warned her prior to the announcement.

"I'd like to present Her Grace, the Duchess of Marsley. Please welcome her to the Institute."

She was startled to be suddenly surrounded by the occupants of the parlor, most of them wishing to talk to her. Some girls just reached out a hand to touch her shoulder or her arm, almost as if she were an icon of some sort.

Mrs. Armbruster didn't do a thing other than smile toothily at her and leave her there, surrounded and awash in a sea of conversation.

"What's it like being a duchess?"

"Did you marry a prince?"

"Not a prince, a duke. She'd have to marry a duke."

"Are you rich?"

"Of course she's rich. She wouldn't be a duchess without being rich."

"Where's your crown? Why didn't you wear it today?"

"They don't wear crowns. Do they?"

One by one she tried to answer as many questions tossed to her as she could. She had one of her own after glancing at Mrs. Armbruster, who was still grinning at her.

What else was the woman planning?

Chapter Twenty

*A*dam's first interview of the day was with Daniel. He spoke to the junior footman about his family. Daniel wasn't married. Nor did he have a sweetheart. He did, however, have a mother and five sisters, which probably went far in explaining why Daniel was grateful to have a room in the servant's wing.

"Have I done something wrong, sir?" Daniel finally asked.

Adam wasn't the least surprised to see high color on the young man's cheekbones. Daniel was one of those people who would always reveal what they were feeling on their face.

Adam crossed his arms. "What do you think you've done wrong?" he asked. He always got more information from men under his command when he asked questions than when he made pronouncements.

"I can't think of anything, sir," Daniel said. "I did all my duties today, just like before. Before I went on the door, that is."

"Who did you relieve?" Adam asked.

"Patrick, sir. He takes the early watch."

Adam sat back in his chair and studied the young man. Even though Daniel was one of two men hired in the previous quarter, Adam doubted he was the spy.

He decided to show the young man some mercy. "I don't know anything that you've done incorrectly, Daniel. In fact, I've heard many good comments about you.

"If you don't mind sending Nathan in," he said, standing and extending his hand.

Daniel looked a little surprised as they shook hands. Adam didn't know if it was something that a majordomo normally did. If it wasn't, perhaps it should have been.

This role was playacting. Granted, there were times in his life—and other roles—when he'd felt the same. Being Rebecca's husband had felt odd to him, a confession he hadn't made to himself until a few years after Manipora. Being considered a hero when he'd only been lucky was another role that hadn't fit. He didn't know what other people thought a hero was, but he had his own definition. A hero was a man who didn't want to die so much that he was willing to do stupid things. For that, the British Army had rewarded him with a lieutenancy and a medal.

Daniel went out the door and Nathan came into the office.

"Close the door," he said, sitting. He indicated with one hand where Nathan should sit, in the straight chair in front of his desk.

Nathan was assigned to the south wing, an area that Adam didn't visit all that much, which meant he didn't know the young man well despite Nathan being a fellow Scot.

The footman was tall and as scrawny as a tree in winter. His neck was long, his chin pronounced, and his ears stuck out on either side of his head like handles.

"How do you like working at Marsley House?" Adam asked the young man as he sat on the chair in front of the desk.

Nathan nodded several times. Adam waited, but that was evidently the only answer he was going to get.

"How do you find London?"

Let Nathan try to answer that question with a nod or shake of his head.

"Crowded."

"And the food at Marsley House?"

"Good."

If Nathan was his spy, then he doubted Roger was getting more than a monosyllabic report.

Adam wasn't an expert at ferreting out confidence men and tricksters, but he did tend to listen to that small voice within, the same one that was now telling him that Nathan wasn't his man. He dismissed the footman after a few more questions and equally short answers.

It was entirely possible that Roger had installed someone at Marsley House before giving Adam his assignment. If that were the case, he would have to go further back and start interviewing staff hired months before he arrived.

That thought had the effect of souring his mood even more. Just add that mystery to another—where had the Duchess of Marsley gone?

Adam continued his planned interviews, which resulted in two surprises. One, that he suspected that one of the upper maids was with child. She'd been tearful throughout the entire meeting and unable to verbalize to him what the problem was.

The second surprise was that there was a Don Juan on the staff. This revelation had been made by yet another maid, one evidently feeling spurned by the man in question. He turned out to be Walter Lyle, who went by the name of Wals to his friends, of which he apparently had many at Marsley House.

The young man was personable, with a ready wit and a quick smile. His flashing brown eyes were probably attractive to women. There was something about Wals that disturbed Adam, however, and it wasn't related to possibly being Roger's spy. There was a calculating look in the footman's eyes, as if he were measuring the vulnerabilities of those he met. In addition, Wals had a propensity for cologne and now smelled like a curious combination of lemon, orange, and lavender.

He didn't know if the footman was responsible for the upper maid's predicament, but he intended to find out. He would have, too, if he hadn't been interrupted by Thomas, who knocked on the office door, then peered inside.

"Sir, Her Grace is asking to see you."

The duchess had returned.

The anticipation he felt was ill-timed, incorrect, and out of place. He was her majordomo. She was his employer. He couldn't forget the role he was playing.

He dismissed Wals with an admonition that they would meet again soon.

"Go back to your room and do a quick wash," he told the footman. "This time don't douse yourself with scent."

Wals looked at him in surprise—evidently, most people didn't comment on his lemon/orange/lavender odor.

Adam followed Thomas downstairs to find the duchess standing in the foyer accompanied by two young women he'd never seen. Mrs. Thigpen was also there, and the older woman was twisting her hands nervously, something she rarely did.

"Your Grace," he said, bowing slightly.

"Drummond," she responded, tilting up her chin at him. "These are your new staff members. I understand from Mrs. Thigpen that you are solely responsible for hiring new staff."

He exchanged a quick glance with the housekeeper. "Yes, Your Grace."

"Ruby and Hortense are to be given light duty only," she said, gesturing to the two young women. "Both of them are with child."

Once again, he and Mrs. Thigpen exchanged a look. Didn't the duchess understand that such a condition was grounds for dismissal?

The look in the duchess's eyes wasn't one of grief. More like resolution, or a steely kind of determination he'd seen before.

Of all the subjects in all the world, he'd never thought to discuss a woman being with child with the Duchess of Marsley.

"There's an upper maid that I suspect is in that condition, Your Grace. She was going to lose her position. Should I reconsider and keep her on?"

She merely blinked at him for a moment, her color steadily rising. In anyone else he might have thought them about to suffer from apoplexy, but he suspected the duchess's courage was hard-won and that she was as embarrassed as he to be discussing this topic in the foyer.

"Would you like to adjourn to the library, Your Grace?"

She nodded, preceding him down the hall and through the double doors.

"I really must insist that you make room for them, Drummond," she said, the minute she entered the room. She whirled and faced him. "It's my home, after all."

"Yes, Your Grace."

"And to dismiss a girl simply because she's in trouble . . . That's not very compassionate."

"No, Your Grace."

"You weren't really going to do that, were you?"

He nodded.

"Why?"

"Each of the girls knows the conditions of her employment."

"That hardly seems fair, Drummond. Do you do the same for the men in that situation?"

"No, but I think we should."

She looked surprised at that.

"They are hardly virgin births, Your Grace," he said, hoping she'd forgive him his plain speaking. "It does take a male and a female."

Her complexion grew pinker.

"I do think she should be allowed to stay on as long as she can," the duchess said. "Does she have any family who will take her in?"

"I don't know," he said.

She looked surprised again. "Well, you should, Drummond."

He nodded once more. "You're right, Your Grace."

Her eyes narrowed. "You're being very agreeable about this, Drummond. Are you just saying what you think I want to hear to humor me?"

He smiled, the expression genuine. "I am not."

"Then you won't dismiss the upstairs maid," she said.

"Not if you don't wish it, Your Grace."

"And the new girls, they'll be welcome?"

"As much as it is in my power to ensure, Your Grace."

"What exactly does that mean, Drummond?"

She had called him Adam last night.

"Human beings sometimes don't act in ways that we would wish them to," he said. "They may be accepted by the rest of the staff. Or not."

"I will not have them called names," she said.

"Of that I can guarantee you," he answered.

His own sister had been called a whore for loving a peer who'd taken advantage of her. He'd do everything in his power to ensure that no one said anything about the two new maids, but he couldn't manage anyone's thoughts.

People were occasionally stodgy in their thinking. They might espouse a more advanced attitude, but they often fell back on tried and true ways. A girl in trouble was not an object of pity as much as derision, especially from other women. He couldn't help but wonder if, behind their criticism, was the thought, *There but for the grace of God go I.*

"Do you disapprove, Drummond?"

"It's not my place to approve or disapprove, Your Grace. As you stated, it's your home."

She regarded him steadily for more than a minute. He returned her look, thinking that she was surprising him again. She wasn't as fragile as he'd thought. Instead, he had the startling notion that the Duchess of Marsley could give as much as she got.

She was, after all, Edward Hackney's daughter. He shouldn't forget that.

"I had to do something," she said finally. "Mrs. Armbruster is one of those people who overwhelms you with good deeds. She's started a Foundling Hospital and an Institute for Women. I couldn't become her patron, so I had to make some gesture. It seemed a good idea to employ two of the girls who were new to the Institute."

He could understand a compassionate gesture gone awry. How many times in his past had he tried to do a good thing only for the outcome to be less than what he'd desired?

"Your Grace," he said, wanting to make her feel better, "it was a very kind thing that you did. I will let the upper maid know that you would like her to stay on for a few more weeks or months. I will find out if she has a family to go to and if she doesn't, we'll make some arrangement for her. As for the other girls, I'm certain that they will work out fine."

"Do you really think so, Drummond?"

He wasn't, no, but he didn't want to disappoint her, so he only smiled in response.

"It's best if I'm not at home when Mrs. Armbruster calls again," she said, her tone one of wry resignation. "Heaven knows how many other maids I'll come home with if I visit with her again."

He wanted to do exactly what he'd done last night, pull her into his arms and hold her there for a moment. Enough time, perhaps, for them to become acquainted with the shape and the warmth of each other. He wanted to breathe in the scent of her hair and feel her breasts pressing against his chest.

He should remember his mission, his assignment, and nothing more.

Stepping to the side, he opened the library door, and bowed slightly to her before leaving. Would she realize how much he wanted to stay?

Chapter Twenty-One

$\mathcal{T}$he morning was beautiful, a perfect autumn morning without a hint of clouds in the sky. Suzanne stood at the open window of her sitting room, staring out at the day. The breeze was brisk, carrying a hint of the chill that the night would bring.

The formal Italian garden to the front of the house didn't look any different in autumn than it did in spring. No blowsy, untidy flowers were allowed to bloom here. Nothing but clipped hedges and crushed granite paths.

Everything about Marsley House was manicured for presentation. She'd often felt that way about herself, delivered unto George coiffed and attired, trained and schooled—a *fait accompli*—the perfect duchess.

The trees below her were bathed in the sun, one side of their leaves tinted gold. An errant leaf had escaped the attention of the gardeners and it tumbled across the lawn in a joyous demonstration of freedom.

She wanted to be like that leaf. To throw off her role and race over the grass. The habits of a lifetime were difficult to break, however. Yet wouldn't it be lovely to be someone other than who she was, if only for a few hours?

Who would that be? An image came to her then, a day from her childhood. She and her governess, Miss Moore, had gone on a picnic. Miss Moore believed in a variety of learning locations, and her mother hadn't disapproved. On that day, they'd spread out a blanket beneath a tree. The land had sloped down to a gurgling brook. The passage of time had no doubt painted the scene with perfection. A breeze had blown the glorious perfume of lilacs to her. She could remember laughing, but not the reason.

She'd been ten years old, racing out of childhood with abandon. She wanted to know everything. Why did the bees skip certain flowers? What made the clouds go skidding across the sky? Why had the Egyptians made the pyramids the way they had? Miss Moore answered every eager question, even the ones about India, where her father spent so much of his time.

How strange that she would never feel quite that free again. On his return from India, her father had dismissed Miss Moore, replacing her with a narrow-eyed harridan who reminded her of Ella.

Gone was the appreciation for her childish curiosity. Instead, she'd been stuffed full of information, dates, names, and locations. If she dared to ask a question she only received a frown in return.

Was that child still inside her? Did she have the ability to turn an eager face to the world? She had wanted that for Georgie. She had wanted to show him that there were wonders and marvels to see and share.

Part of her died the day he did. She'd felt as if everything inside had shriveled and burned, leaving nothing but ashes in its wake. Yet now she had the oddest thought. Could something of that young girl still exist?

She was not acting like herself, or at least the person she'd been for so very long. Ever since that night on the roof, she'd changed. She'd refused, again last night, to take the tonic. Granted, it was harder to fall asleep, but she'd occupied herself with thoughts of Adam.

There was something about the way he'd said his wife's name. *Rebecca.* It was spoken in such a gentle tone, almost as if he cradled the word in his hand to mark on its uniqueness.

He hadn't said how his wife had died and she found herself awash in curiosity. Everything about the man sparked her interest.

Why had he gone from being in the army to being a majordomo? He hadn't liked that comment she made, repeating something that George had often said—that a man only left the army if he was a failure. Adam's eyes had taken on a flat look and his mouth had thinned.

A proper majordomo, perhaps one without military experience, would have moderated his expression and hidden what he was feeling. Adam hadn't done that.

A month ago she would never have spent significant time wondering about a male in her employ. Yet a month ago she would never have gone to the Foundling Hospital or the Institute. Nor would she have returned to Marsley House with two new servants in tow.

Yes, she was most definitely changing.

She should go and check to see how the new girls were settling in. While she was at it, she would find Adam and finally get an answer from him about something else. What exactly had he said that night he'd brought her back to her room?

She avoided the bedroom because Ella was going through her wardrobe and sighing in disapproval. Evidently Suzanne had spilled something on a bodice or stained a cuff or dirtied her hem.

She stopped and surveyed herself in the mirror on the wall. She patted her hair into place, practiced a benevolent smile, and straightened the cameo at her neck. Without a word to Ella, she left her suite in search of Adam. How very odd to feel such anticipation.

Her majordomo was flat on his back in the middle of the library.

"Drummond?" she said at the door. "Are you all right?" She flew to his side and stared down at him. "What's wrong?"

"Nothing, Your Grace."

"You haven't fallen?"

"No, I haven't. Nor fainted."

"Then what are you doing on the floor?" she asked.

"Looking at the roof, Your Grace."

She glanced up. "It's not a roof," she said. "It's a cupola."

"Very well," he said agreeably. "The cupola. I'm trying to make out the patterns of the stained glass and I've found that it's much easier to be in this position than bending my neck that far back."

She looked up at the ceiling and realized that she had rarely noticed the stained glass windows.

"What does it signify?" he asked. "I thought, at first, that the windows were religious in nature, that they depicted a scene from the Bible. After studying them for a while, I don't think so."

"All I know is that George had them redone after he returned from India."

He glanced at her. "Did he?"

She nodded.

"How odd if they're Hindu."

"I don't think it would be any more odd than the Persian Parlor or the Chinese Room or the Egyptian Room."

"You have a point," he said. He stretched his hand toward her. "Would you care to join me, Your Grace?"

"I'm the Duchess of Marsley. I don't get on the floor."

Sitting up, he smiled at her. "You look horrified at the idea."

"I am," she said, fingering the cameo at her throat. "I couldn't imagine what the staff might say if one of them saw me."

"Perhaps they'd call you daft," he said. "Or eccentric. 'Did you hear what the Duchess of Marsley did? She was seen on the floor of the library staring up at the cupola. Have you ever heard of anything more ludicrous?'"

"Are you a spy, Adam?"

She'd never seen anyone's face change so quickly. In one instant, there was humor in his eyes and his mouth was curved in a teasing smile. In the next second, his face lost all expression.

He didn't answer her. He got to his feet, brushed off his trousers and the sleeves of his jacket, paying close attention to his cuffs.

"There isn't that much dust on the floor, Adam," she finally said.

She folded her arms in front of her, trying to push down the odd combination of feelings rising up from her stomach. She'd rarely felt anger and fear at the same time, but she did now.

"Are you a spy?" she asked again.

"A spy?"

He was stalling for time, but she'd much prefer if he would just be honest with her.

She nodded. "For my father. Is that why you're in my household? To report back to him? To tell him when I've done anything untoward? Is that why he didn't immediately order me to dismiss you?"

The idea was new, but it made a great deal of sense.

She didn't say anything further, only turned and went to stand behind the desk, studying the view from the sparkling windows. This room reminded her too much of George, especially with the portrait of him in his military uniform hanging over the fireplace. He'd been especially proud of that painting. When it had been completed, he'd invited hundreds of people to the house to marvel at how distinguished and handsome he'd looked.

It felt like he was watching her now in that way of his, as if he were half amused by her youthful naïveté and half bored senseless. She'd been too young for him, too unschooled in certain ways.

"I never met your father until the other day," he said. "I'm not spying for him. Nor am I reporting back to him about anything."

"If you're not," she said, still not turning, "then you would be unusual. Ella is one of his spies."

"Is she? I knew there was a reason I didn't like the woman."

She glanced at him over her shoulder and then back at the view.

"Why do you keep her on?" he asked.

It had been easier to simply endure Ella than to change the situation. What else was she simply enduring? She didn't know, but perhaps it was time she found out.

She turned, finally, to find that he was standing much too close. She should have stepped back, but the window was there. She put her hands on his chest to push him away, but then she looked up at his face.

His green eyes were much too attractive and much too intent.

He brushed his knuckles against her cheek. She didn't retreat. Nor did she tell him that he mustn't touch her. She was inviolate, his employer, the Duchess of Marsley. What would anyone say to see him touch her so? What comment would they make if they noticed that his gaze was particularly tender?

She didn't care.

She shouldn't smile at her majordomo. Or feel as if a rusty door had been opened in her chest. She shouldn't spread her fingers wide against the fabric of his jacket, feeling the pounding of his heart as rapid as her own.

When he lowered his head slowly, she measured the seconds in held breaths. He didn't rush. He didn't pressure her. Instead, he gave her a chance to protest. Or to caution him. Or to pull away. Or, finally, to act shocked and disapproving.

She should have said something like, *You're dismissed, Adam. Leave this moment and I will have your belongings sent to you.*

She remained silent, even as he reached out and cupped her face with both hands now, studying her with intent eyes. Did he wish to remember what she looked like forever? She felt bemused and bathed in confusion.

When his lips touched hers, it was an explosion of feeling. Disbelief banished in the presence of bright sprinkles of delight.

One of the maids had been brushing a threadbare rug from the servants' quarters one day. Suzanne had seen her at her task in the back garden, noting that the sun's rays shone through the worn fibers. She felt like that now, as if her soul, pitted and frayed in places, was being illuminated somehow.

His hands cupped her shoulders and then reached around to her back, slowly bringing her forward, closer to him. Her hands joined behind his neck.

Her mouth opened and he inhaled her breath and gave her back some of his. He tasted of coffee and iced cinnamon buns.

His lips were warm, tender, and capable of inducing all sorts of strange and fascinating sensations.

Shivers traveled down her body, seemed to wrap around her stomach, and made their way up to her breasts. Her feet tingled. It was difficult to breathe, to concentrate, and to make sense of what she was doing.

Had he stolen her reason completely with a kiss?

She didn't want to move. She didn't want to become a duchess again. Instead, she wanted to be who she had once been, the young girl about whom she'd wondered earlier.

That Suzanne would have wholeheartedly joined in this kiss. She would've stood on tiptoe as she was doing right now, to deepen it. She would have delighted at the fact that her heart was racing and her body felt as if it were warming from the inside out.

Somehow that girl had taken over, pushing the duchess aside.

Chapter Twenty-Two

$\mathcal{R}$eason surfaced gradually, penetrating the haze of pleasure surrounding Adam. What the hell was he doing?

He was jeopardizing everything, his position of majordomo, his assignment, not to mention his honor.

Shame should have suffused him as he stepped back. He should have immediately apologized, explained that it had been a while since he'd kissed a woman. Since he'd even wanted to kiss anyone.

Instead, he shook his head, the gesture substituting for all the words he couldn't say.

She was a duchess and he was as far from the peerage as anyone could be.

She was going to say the words to dismiss him. He waited for them as the seconds ticked past. Instead, she stood there, her fingers pressed to her lips, looking at him as if she had never before seen a man.

"Why did you kiss me?" she asked.

"Do I need a reason?"

"Why, Adam?"

Very well, if she insisted on the truth, he would give it to her.

"Because you're a beautiful woman," he said. "And you're very kissable." As if that weren't bad enough, he decided to give her another layer of honesty. "I've thought about doing it for days now."

If she was going to dismiss him, let it be for cause.

"Have you?"

Her cheeks were turning pink again, a barometer of her emotions. He couldn't tell, however, if she was feeling embarrassment or anger.

He reached out with both hands, gripped her shoulders, and pulled her gently to him.

"I have," he said and bent to kiss her again. In for a penny, in for a pound.

She didn't pull away. She didn't strike him with her fists. She wrapped her arms around his waist as if afraid that he would leave her.

He had no intention of doing that. His thoughts were swirled and jumbled things. All he knew was that he needed to hold her, needed to kiss her, in a way that was elemental. His life depended on it.

Her palms were suddenly flat against his chest and she was pulling away.

He didn't want to let her go, but he dropped his hands. His breathing was erratic, and every thought was centered not on his assignment or his role or even how he would explain to Mount why he'd been summarily dismissed. He was thinking about the pleasure she'd so effortlessly given him.

The image of her in his bed, her hair tousled, her lips swollen from his kisses, wouldn't leave him. He wanted to disrobe her slowly. Were her breasts as large as they felt pressed against his chest? He imagined her long and perfectly formed legs wrapped around his waist.

He wanted to feel her, stroke her skin without layers of clothing between them. He wanted her hands all over him, her breath against his throat.

Staring down at the carpet was easier than looking at her. He couldn't apologize and was as far from being sorry as he was from respecting the Duke of Marsley. He would be able to recall her in his arms for years, if not forever. That startled catch in her breath when he first kissed her would be something he'd always remember. How could he possibly regret kissing Suzanne?

She took another step back and he wanted to tell her that he wasn't going to ravish her, at least not without her consent. She had nothing to fear from him, never mind that he'd kissed her. That was as far as his efforts of seduction would go. Not because of his assignment. Nor because she would surely dismiss him any second now, but because any relationship they had must be on equal footing. He didn't want to overwhelm her. He didn't want to seduce her. He wanted her, but he also hoped she wanted him.

That night in her bedroom, when he'd looked into her eyes and seen only anguish, the need had been born in him to give her comfort. But this, what he felt now, was different. He ached to lose himself in her, quiet all the memories swirling around in his head. For a few moments, the past had disappeared. When he held Suzanne all he'd been conscious of was her, him, and pleasure.

He thrust his hand into his jacket pocket, retrieved the brooch, and held out his hand, palm up.

"I found your brooch," he said. "It's what you were looking for the other day, wasn't it?"

His voice didn't sound like himself, almost as if it were difficult to speak.

She reached out and took the piece of jewelry, holding it between two fingers.

"It's not a brooch," she said, sounding different as well. Thankfully, however, there was no evidence of tears in her voice. "It's a hair clip. You see?" She turned the brooch on its back and opened a clasp. "It slides onto my hair like that."

"I am somewhat lacking in my knowledge of diamond hairpins, Your Grace."

How effortlessly he had fallen back into his role. He was her servant. She was his employer. They should not forget such things. In addition, he was someone else. Someone she didn't know about.

Standing there, however, he felt closer to his real self than he had for quite some time. Had a single kiss rendered him defenseless? Very well, two kisses. And more if she had allowed him.

Perhaps it was a good thing that the portrait of her dead husband watched them.

She was staring at him, her eyes steady. Her color was still high. He concentrated on her lips. Those lips made him want to kiss her again.

"Do you want an apology?" he asked. "Shall I confess to my animalistic nature?"

"Do you have one?"

"Around you, evidently," he said.

"The maids are safe, then?"

"Assuredly, Your Grace."

"And me, Drummond? Am I safe?"

"Honesty compels me to say that I'm not entirely certain."

Her eyebrows rose.

She probably thought he was teasing her, but he was being deadly serious.

"Then I should avoid you at all costs," she said.

"It would probably be the best advice I could give you."

"So if you came upon me in a parlor, for example, I should scream for assistance? If nothing else, I should ring for a maid?"

"Or perhaps you should have a chaperone at all times, Your Grace."

"Strictly to prevent you from demonstrating your animalistic nature, is that correct?"

"Yes."

"Drummond, you can't say such things. I am no great beauty. Surely not someone to inspire a man like you to do wicked things."

"Not wicked, Your Grace. Simply human nature. You have lips I want to kiss. And a form it gives me great pleasure to hold. As to your beauty, if you want compliments, I will endeavor to come up with a few. You should know your own attributes, however."

"Drummond, you are the most extraordinary man and this has been the most extraordinary conversation."

He only smiled at her.

"I don't require an apology," she said.

"Then any time you would wish to duplicate the experience, Your Grace, I stand ready to serve."

They exchanged a very long look. He wasn't entirely certain what she was thinking, but her smile was once more in evidence. If he wasn't mistaken, there was a glint of humor in her eyes.

Good. Marble Marsley needed to be shattered until the woman within was revealed.

She nodded at him, just once, grabbed her skirt with both hands, and, with chin tilted up slightly, left the library.

She'd given him a bad turn when she'd asked if he was a spy. What kind of man set his daughter's servants to watching her?

The more he learned about Edward Hackney, the more he thought that the ex-director of the East India Company bore watching as well.

He stared at the closed door for several minutes before he, too, left the room.

Chapter Twenty-Three

*H*e'd kissed her.

He'd kissed her and she'd let him.

No, she hadn't lied to him. She'd wholeheartedly participated.

She shouldn't have. She shouldn't have allowed him to touch her. Or hold her. Or kiss her.

If she were a true duchess, she should have dismissed him on the spot. He was her majordomo. He was on the staff of Marsley House. He was her servant. She should have banished him immediately. At the very least she should have been embarrassed and ashamed.

What was she doing?

She was betraying everything she'd been reared to believe was right, proper, and just. She was behaving like a harlot. Yet she felt alive when she was around him. He challenged her, annoyed her, and intrigued her. Plus, he'd protected and defended her.

He'd kissed her.

What was she going to do about Drummond?

She really should avoid him at all costs, but she didn't want to barricade herself in her room with only Ella as company again.

She'd forgotten to ask about the maids. She would have to talk to him soon. If she began to feel the least bit of anticipation about that meeting, she should squelch that feeling immediately. Perhaps it would be better if she acquired another maid as a chaperone.

Someone to shadow her as she went from room to room in case she and Drummond encountered each other.

How, though, was she supposed to forget those kisses?

No, she really should have dismissed him this time, but she knew she wasn't going to do anything of the sort.

Maybe she wasn't a true duchess at all.

Suzanne realized she was heading back to her suite and then stopped herself. She didn't want to encounter Ella right now, especially when she was feeling . . . Her thoughts stuttered to a halt. How, exactly, was she feeling?

The hard knot of tension wasn't there in her chest. Nor did she feel like a huge hole existed in her stomach.

She abruptly sat on the bench just past the landing on the second floor. From here she could see part of the staircase and to the end of the corridor.

What exactly was she feeling? A curious excitement, something she hadn't experienced in a great many . . . Her thoughts stopped again. It hadn't been months since she'd felt this way. It had been years.

For a while after Georgie's death, she'd willed herself to die. That's what it had felt like. She hadn't been able to eat or sleep well. It was as if her body was shutting down in stages so that she might be with her son. She hadn't died, though. She'd survived. She'd gotten through those endless months. Somehow, she counted one month, then two, then six, then a year. She'd gotten through that year and more, existing and enduring.

What was it that Mrs. Armbruster had said?

"I know what you're feeling, Your Grace. You think that if you put aside your grief, even for a moment, it means you didn't love him."

She'd wanted to ask Mrs. Armbruster if such wisdom had been acquired through her own loss, but she hadn't.

Learning of someone else's pain didn't ease her grief one whit. All it did was make her feel uncomfortable because she hadn't known.

Had she been that selfish? Yes, for two years she had been.

"Your Grace, you haven't taken your tonic."

She looked up to see Ella standing there. In her hands was a cup no doubt containing the green, noxious brew Suzanne hated. How had she missed the maid's approach? The other woman crept about on cat feet. Sometimes Suzanne thought she did so in order to startle her.

"You didn't take your tonic last night, Your Grace," she said, thrusting the cup at Suzanne. "Nor did you have it this morning."

"I don't want it," she said.

Taking the tonic might render her nights dreamless, but it rendered her days fog-like. More than once she'd found herself sitting in the same chair for hours. Nor could she remember people or events well.

These past two days, when she hadn't taken the tonic, she'd felt more like herself.

"I don't want it," she repeated.

"Your father won't be pleased."

Neither was Ella, if the expression on her face was any indication. The maid's mouth was pinched and the lines at the corners of her eyes were more prevalent this morning, almost as if she had practiced frowning for a good while before coming to find Suzanne.

"He will just have to be displeased with me, Ella," she said. "I'm not taking it. I don't like how I feel when I've had it."

"You know you need it," Ella said, once more thrusting the cup at her. "It's helped you handle your sadness, Your Grace. Without it, I'm certain that life will be so much more difficult for you."

Suzanne pushed the cup away, silenced by surprise. While it was true that she didn't like the other woman, Ella had always behaved properly up until now. The maid had never before talked to her with such contempt in her voice.

She said the words quite carefully, so there would be no misunderstanding. "I'm not going to take the tonic anymore, Ella. I don't care what you tell my father. I'm not taking it."

For the third time, Ella shoved the cup in her face, some of the liquid almost sloshing over the rim. The smell was as bad as it had always been, like grass that had begun to rot.

"Take it, Your Grace."

Suzanne stood, moving a little distance away from the maid.

"Evidently you've forgotten your place, Ella."

"My place is to ensure that you're doing what you should do, Your Grace. That includes taking your tonic. Everyone agrees that it's the best thing for you. You wouldn't want to suffer the effects of not taking it, would you?"

That was a scary question, one she'd not considered. She'd taken the tonic ever since Ella had come to Marsley House six months ago. Was there some sort of deleterious effect if she didn't drink it?

She would just have to find out, wouldn't she?

"No," she said, turning and heading for the staircase.

Ella was undeterred.

She followed Suzanne all the way down to the first floor, talking the entire time.

"You'll be sick, Your Grace. You'll get hideous headaches. You'll be subjected to uncontrollable weeping."

At the base of the stairs, Suzanne turned to face her maid.

"It sounds ghastly, Ella."

The other woman's face was triumphant as she pushed the cup toward Suzanne.

"So ghastly," Suzanne said, grabbing the cup, "that I can assure you I am never going to drink it again."

She marched some distance to the foyer, where Thomas was pretending not to overhear her discussion with Ella. She handed him the cup and he took it, looking somewhat bemused.

"Get rid of this, Thomas," she said.

Ella still didn't cease. "You can't do that, Your Grace. I'm only acting in your best interest."

Suzanne really didn't like being lectured. First by her father and now her maid. Had she always seemed so malleable and desirous of direction? She took a deep breath and, for good measure, said a quick prayer. Surely God would understand her need to do this. God might, but her father wouldn't. Well, she would have to solve that problem as well.

One mountain at a time, however.

"I'm afraid we don't suit, Ella. I think it would be best if you find other employment. I will, of course, give you a letter of recommendation, but I would appreciate it very much if you would leave Marsley House within the hour. We'll be more than happy to send your trunk after you."

She turned and was heading down the corridor when Ella grabbed her by the arm, jerking her so hard that she nearly fell.

"You can't just dismiss me like that," Ella said.

"I can, and I just have." She looked beyond Ella to where Thomas was standing, his eyes wide.

"Go find Drummond," she said.

Ella leaned close.

"If you dismiss me, I'll tell everyone that you've been acting oddly and how worried I am about you. You're inconsolable. Poor thing, you've been made mad by grief."

She tried to free herself from Ella's grip, but the other woman only held her tighter.

"Tell him you changed your mind," Ella said, her tight-lipped smile disconcerting.

Why hadn't she dismissed the woman months ago? The answer shamed her. Perhaps she'd become a little too dependent on Ella's tonic. Perhaps she'd wanted dreamless sleep and formless days. Perhaps she'd even needed the tonic once. She didn't need it now.

"Let me go," Suzanne said.

"You heard her," Adam said, coming up behind the maid.

Suzanne had never been so happy to see anyone.

"The duchess is not herself, Drummond," Ella said without looking at him. "This doesn't concern you."

At least she wasn't the only one being targeted by Ella's venomous rage and contempt.

"I think it does."

Drummond glanced at her and seemed to take in the situation immediately. He frowned when he saw that Ella was still gripping her arm. He came to Suzanne's side, reached out and peeled the other woman's hand away.

"What would you like me to do, Your Grace?"

"Escort Ella to the door, if you would, please. I've dismissed her, but she's refusing to leave."

"The duchess is deranged," Ella said, still standing too close. "She's lost her wits. She's gone mad. You shouldn't listen to anything she says. They're the ramblings of an idiot."

"Let's go," Drummond said, reaching out and grabbing Ella's arm.

"Can't you see she's not in her right mind? The entire staff knows it. They laugh behind her back. The Duchess of Marsley, simpleton."

"Now, Ella," Drummond said.

"How protective you are," Ella said, eyeing Drummond up and down. "What an interesting development. I'm sure her father would want to know."

He didn't say a word, merely took Ella to the door. She truly didn't have a choice, because Drummond was so much larger and more determined.

Suzanne watched as Thomas opened the door and Drummond unceremoniously escorted the woman down the steps before directing the footman to close the door in her face.

It might have been amusing but for the insults Ella was shouting. She sincerely hoped that the other servants weren't listening, but that was almost too much to hope for. Was the staff really laughing at her behind her back?

Drummond returned to her side, took her arm in a grip that was a great deal gentler than the one he'd used on Ella, and walked her into the closest parlor.

Here George's great-grandfather's acquisitions from Egypt were displayed against sand-colored walls. She'd always liked this room because it seemed to transport her to a different place and time. Unfortunately, she didn't feel that same sensation now, looking at all the canopic jars and intricately carved chests.

She couldn't stop herself from trembling and that both concerned and annoyed her.

Ella had been vicious. She hadn't expected that. Nor had she anticipated seeing herself in the maid's eyes. Had she truly appeared that distraught, insensible, and weak?

Drummond released her to close the door, then turned back to her.

She looked up at him. "Did you tell her? Did you tell her about that night on the roof?"

"No, of course I didn't," he said.

"Did you tell anyone?"

He pulled her into his arms. She really should have stepped away, but she was so cold and she hadn't stopped trembling.

"No, Suzanne, I didn't tell anyone."

"I am not deranged."

"I never thought you were."

"I'm not a simpleton," she said.

"No, you aren't."

She pulled back and looked up into his face. "Do you mean that?"

He nodded.

"Ella told me that I would suffer if I didn't take the tonic. Why would she say that?"

"Would you like me to find out what's in it?"

"Could you do that?"

"I could," he said.

"You are a magical majordomo, Drummond. Is there no lack of things you can do?"

He didn't respond to that comment. Evidently, he was modest as well.

She pressed her forehead against his chest and wished her trembling would stop.

"Are they all laughing at me?"

"No," he said.

She wanted to know what he was thinking. When had she come to value his opinion so much?

"Do you think I'm disordered in my thoughts? Or that my actions have been odd?"

"I think you've been suffering from a great loss," he said. "And that you've been alone with it. You don't have to be alone anymore, Suzanne."

She grabbed his jacket with both her fists, feeling as if he was the only steady person in the universe.

"What happened on the roof was odd behavior, Drummond. Kissing you was odd. Always wanting to talk to you is odd. I have a feeling that most people would see my recent behavior as strange."

"Sometimes you need to ignore what other people say."

He wrapped his arms around her, and rocked slightly from one side to the other, almost as if she were a fractious babe.

"Surround yourself with the right kind of people. Be very selective of who you speak with and who you listen to."

She felt the first stirrings of amusement. "You mean like you, of course."

"Of course," he said, his voice holding a tinge of humor.

She sighed. "I really don't need to be hugged, Drummond."

He only tightened his embrace.

"I should dismiss you, too," she said.

"You can't dismiss me. Just today I approved the purchase of a dozen spoons. And as many bowls for Cook. I am in the process of looking over designs for the expansion of the kitchen garden. I'm much too important to dismiss."

"Is that where you were just now, the kitchen?"

"No. I was in the library."

"On your back again?" she asked, pulling away to look up into his face. "Were you studying the stained glass windows again?"

"I was not. I was actually looking for a book on herbs."

"Herbs? For the kitchen garden?"

He nodded.

"You're always in the library, Drummond."

"I don't always sleep well, Your Grace. It helps to find a book to read."

She stepped back. He dropped his arms, his faint smile fading as he looked at her.

"She won't be allowed inside Marsley House again, Your Grace. You needn't worry about that."

How easily they went from first names back to their proper roles. She preferred to be called Suzanne. What would Ella say to that? No doubt that she'd lost her mind. Perhaps she had. If so, she preferred this existence to the one she'd been living for so long.

"Where does she keep the tonic?" he asked.

"I don't know," she said. "I've never seen it around my rooms."

"Then, with your permission, I'll go search Ella's."

She nodded.

"Would you like to accompany me?"

She would, but not for reasons she wanted to explain. She didn't want to be alone at the moment and if that made her sound defenseless and weak, she didn't care.

Chapter Twenty-Four

$\mathcal{A}$dam decided that he really needed to finish his assignment and leave Marsley House. More than ever now. He shouldn't have been so honest with her. He shouldn't have kissed Suzanne earlier and comforted her a moment ago. He was almost as much a lecher as Whitcomb. Had she known about her husband's character? Had she cared that the duke hadn't been faithful? A strange thought as he accompanied her up the grand staircase to the third floor.

Placing his hand at the small of her back, he guided her toward the servants' quarters. He caught her glancing to the left, toward the corridor where the nursery was located. Had she been back to the room since they'd talked that night?

He had too much curiosity about Suzanne.

A tendril of her hair had come loose from her severe bun and he wanted to push it back into place. He kept his hands to himself.

"We need to find you another maid," he said. There, a good enough distraction and one that might occupy his thoughts for a few moments.

She only nodded.

"Is there anyone on staff you would like to promote?"

She shook her head.

He wished she would speak and wondered why she was suddenly so silent. Was it due to the proximity of the nursery? Or did it have something to do with the fact that she'd dismissed

Ella? Although she was walking with her hands folded in front of her, he could tell that she was still trembling.

"The woman needed to be dismissed," he said, his voice rough.

She glanced over at him.

"You didn't like her," she said.

"No, I didn't."

She didn't say anything to his admission.

"I don't know if any of the maids would like to have Ella's position," she said. "It does come with a significant increase in wages, does it not?"

He nodded. Since he'd recently reviewed the quarterly expenditures he was aware of what was paid to every person. Mrs. Thigpen and the cook earned substantially more than the rest of the staff, but that was because of their positions and their longevity. His salary as majordomo was the equivalent of what was paid to five footmen.

"Do you think Ella told them I was mad?"

He glanced at her. "I don't think Ella communicated with the other maids at all," he said. "She considered herself above them."

"Perhaps Mrs. Thigpen might have a recommendation," she said when he stopped in front of Ella's door. "Someone not like Ella in any way."

"I don't think that's a difficult requirement. Ella was unique in her disagreeableness."

After opening the door, he stepped aside for her to enter first.

Ella's room was larger than a normal maid's quarters, but not as spacious as his rooms or those assigned to Mrs. Thigpen. The hierarchy in the servants' ranks at Marsley House was as pronounced as that of the army. A lady's maid was below the rank of governess or majordomo but higher than those maids assigned to the family quarters. They, in turn, were above the public room maids, who were over the scullery maids. Stable boys figured somewhere in the mix, but Adam was damned if he knew exactly where.

He looked around him, wondering if the duchess had the same impression he was getting. Ella didn't reveal who she was with her personal possessions. The single bed was neatly made; the pillow looked as if it had been fluffed before being placed at the head of the bed in the middle of the mattress. Her clothes were hung on the hooks arranged on the far wall in militaristic precision by color. The only item on the small bedside table was an oil lamp with a gold shade.

A vanity had been provided, topped with a mirror. Here there was only a utilitarian brush, a comb, and a small tortoiseshell-topped box of hairpins.

No perfume scented the room. Instead, there was a curious herbal odor, almost as if Ella had kept plants on the windowsill.

He began opening the drawers of the small bureau below the window. He intensely disliked going through a woman's unmentionables, be it this assignment or another, but he couldn't pick and choose. You couldn't falter in your mission just because you didn't like certain parts of it.

He found the bottle in the bottom drawer, tucked beneath Ella's nightgowns.

Holding up the brown bottle stoppered with a cork, he asked, "Is this it?"

She nodded. "Are the contents green?"

He uncorked the bottle, upended it on the tip of his finger, and nodded. "It's green." He tasted it, immediately identifying the main ingredient. "It's also opium," he said.

"Opium?"

"Did you know?" he asked as he put the cork back in the bottle.

"Of course not," she said.

She still stood at the door, her hands fisted at her waist. The tautness of her demeanor made him think that she could easily explode into anger. Or tears. Of the two, he preferred anger. It was certainly justified.

Why was Ella giving Suzanne opium?

"She always said my father told her to do it."

That didn't make any sense. "Why would your father want you drugged?"

She shrugged, which wasn't an answer, at least one he wanted. He didn't push her to explain, however. Sometimes, it was better to wait until someone was ready to talk.

He closed the drawer, looked around, and decided he'd found everything there was to find.

The duchess still hadn't spoken. He abandoned patience for a more direct approach.

"Suzanne."

She glanced at him wide eyed, but didn't correct him. Nor did she fix an imperious stare on him and demand that he remember her rank. They'd gone beyond that, hadn't they?

"Why would your father want you drugged?"

"Do you know anything about my father?" she asked.

"A little. He was with the East India Company."

"A director," she said. "He's a man who's never seen an obstacle. He doesn't abide them."

That still wasn't an answer.

She sat on the ladder-back chair beside the bed, taking some time to arrange her skirt. She was playing for time and he knew it.

Just as he was at the point of asking again, she looked up at him.

"It's very important for him to be able to dictate the outcome of events. At least those over which he has some control."

He didn't comment. Hackney was a bully, which was a less polite way of saying the same thing.

She looked at the bottle still in his hand and then away, blinking rapidly. If she cried, he'd simply gather her up in his arms and comfort her again.

"He thought he could control you," he said.

"Evidently." Her voice was dull.

He tossed the bottle onto the bed and went to her, drawing her up in his arms. This was getting to be a habit.

"Suzanne," he began, looking down at her face.

He wanted to kiss her again. Yet he wasn't the type of man to be dominated by his impulses. He was disciplined, set on his course, dedicated to his duty. She was a detriment to that, a temptation he couldn't obey. That's what he told himself even as he bent his head to kiss her again.

Ella's room was a strange place for a forbidden embrace. Still, he didn't move even after he lifted his mouth from hers. Instead, he brushed his lips against her heated cheek, then each closed eyelid, tasting her tears.

"You shouldn't cry," he said. "You should be enraged, not sad."

She blinked open her eyes and looked up at him. He stepped back, dropping his arms when all he really wanted to do was keep holding her.

"I have more experience with sorrow than I do with rage, Adam."

"You shouldn't," he said. "Not in this case. You deserve better than to be treated like a puppet, Suzanne. No one has that right."

She didn't answer, merely began moving toward the door. Glancing over her shoulder at him, she said, "At least I don't have to deal with Ella anymore."

He didn't respond. Sooner or later he was going to finish his assignment, and there would be no further reason to remain at Marsley House. No reason whatsoever to try to protect the Duchess of Marsley.

The thought was accompanied by an unsurprising amount of regret.

Chapter Twenty-Five

Suzanne couldn't sleep. Now that she knew what the tonic contained, there wasn't any doubt in her mind why she hadn't had a problem with insomnia since Ella had started in her employ. Opium.

She'd read newspaper accounts of opium dens in the East End. More than once she'd been solicited by various individuals and asked to contribute to campaigns against the opium trade. The most influential group had been represented at one of her father's dinners and it was a cause he purported to espouse.

She had never understood her father and time had not imbued her with any more insight. For some reason he'd thought it necessary for her to take Ella's tonic. Did he mean for it to soften her grief? Or was it just a way to control her? When it came to her father's motives, either was possible.

Adam hadn't told her if she should worry about any ill effects from discontinuing the tonic. Other than being unable to sleep, were there any other symptoms? Or had Ella lied about that? She didn't doubt that Ella used truth like a weapon.

A little after midnight Suzanne gave up the pretense of sleeping, got up, and slipped on her dressing gown. Of thick, gold-colored quilted flannel, it had a corded belt with a large tassel at each end. A similar cord, without tassels, tied the neck closed. Most of her garments were black, but not her nightgowns and dressing gowns. The dye the laundress used had not only made her skin itch but the color had bled onto the sheets, ruining them. When that had happened, she'd decided not to wear mourning to bed.

Her new maid was a young girl Mrs. Thigpen had recommended. Emily was a sweet person, if a bit cloying. She'd been promoted from her position as one of the upstairs maids and was eager to perform her new duties. Suzanne didn't think that her wardrobe had ever been so assiduously cared for or her hair done as well.

"Is there anything else I can do for you, Your Grace?" If Emily had asked her once, she'd done so five hundred times in the past two days. Suzanne had assured the girl that she needed nothing further, that Emily was performing every task perfectly, and that she was certain the two of them would deal very well together. Above all, Emily did not try to make her take opium every morning and every evening. That alone would make her well disposed toward the girl.

Suzanne glanced at herself in the pier glass. She'd plaited her hair for night and now wrapped the plait around the top of her head, securing it with pins and a short length of black ribbon. Picking up the atomizer, she sprayed a little of her favorite perfume on her neck, then ridiculed herself for doing so. The scent lingered in the air, reminiscent of early blooming roses.

Ella had always spritzed her with the perfume George had bought her, something spicy that smelled of India, he'd said. After dismissing Ella, she'd taken the bottle and put it in the rubbish, uncaring that only half of it was gone. She'd always disliked it but her wishes had never been consulted.

The fact that her father also liked the perfume brought another issue to the forefront of her mind. She was going to have to handle the matter of Ella but she didn't know quite how right now. She wasn't sure what explanation for Ella's actions her father would give her, if he gave one at all. When she'd confronted him in the past, he'd sometimes answered her questions and just as often blustered that he knew what he was doing and she shouldn't question him. All she had now were questions. She wasn't certain she would be able to believe him regardless of what he said.

She closed the door of the sitting room quietly so as not to alert the footman stationed at the end of the corridor. He sat on a chair she insisted he use. Standing at attention—something George had demanded—seemed ludicrous, especially in the middle of the night. She didn't mind if the footmen dozed. Their presence was to alert the family in case of fire or the unlikely event of a stranger entering Marsley House. Of the two, fire was much more likely.

October was still comfortable during the day although the nights were chilly, making her grateful for the flannel gown. This month the skies would start to become overcast and it seemed to her that they would stay that way throughout the winter, only brightening when spring arrived.

The flame on the enormous gasolier over the grand staircase was lowered at night, creating pools of shadows that were illuminated only by the newel posts with their gas lamps. She was more familiar with going up the stairs to the third floor and the nursery than going down to the library.

She didn't want to go to Georgie's room right now. She didn't need to sit and look at the array of his toys in order to recall her son. She could feel his body snuggled up against her, his head on her chest. She could still feel her fingers smoothing back his silky blond hair. She could hear his voice, and there were still moments when she swore she heard his laughter. He'd been a happy child, a healthy little boy. She'd been so thankful for that. She'd never anticipated something might happen to him.

She didn't need to be in the nursery in order to remember him. He would live in her heart forever.

What was it Drummond had said? Something about clinging to her grief in order to keep Georgie close. She'd been irritated at his comment, but over the past several days she'd been wondering if he wasn't correct. Perhaps grief could be as addictive as opium.

She got to the bottom of the staircase, then turned and walked down the long corridor to the library. The room had always been George's domain, and she'd avoided it for the most part in the past two years. Adam, however, seemed to gravitate toward it. He'd mentioned that he often found it difficult to sleep and chose a book to read. Would he consider her outrageous for hoping that was the case tonight?

She'd never been around anyone like him. Adam didn't seem to wish anything from her—not influence, or money. In every situation in which they'd been together, he'd acted protectively. She couldn't remember the last time—if ever—that a man had been so solicitous of her or cared about her welfare.

She might have considered him her contemporary but for his faint Scottish accent and his tendency to speak in Gaelic from time to time. He made her think improbable thoughts, such as what her life would have been like if she hadn't married George. Their relationship had been strained from the beginning. After all, he was almost thirty years her senior, a duke her father insisted that she marry simply because he was titled.

She'd always been a docile, obedient daughter, but she didn't feel a bit docile or obedient at the moment.

The sameness of her life and the emptiness of it had stretched out before her, punctuated only by her father's demands. The day she'd banished him from Marsley House had been a turning point. At first she'd thought she was acting unlike herself. In the past few days she realized that she was behaving like the person she'd once been, the courageous young girl who hadn't been beaten down by circumstance and tragedy.

She liked that Suzanne. Once reborn, she hoped that woman wouldn't disappear. She didn't want to be subservient to anyone, a leaf to someone else's wind.

The library doors stood like a barrier before her. She hadn't seen Adam for two days. She'd asked about him a few times, and on each occasion he'd either been with one of the other staff members or in a meeting with the stable master or occupied with some task. It was as if he was avoiding her.

Perhaps he regretted kissing her.

She didn't regret kissing him.

If he admitted that it was unwise for him to do so, she'd tell him how she felt. If he cautioned her to remember her title, she'd tell him that her title had never brought her happiness, but that the kiss they'd shared had. She would be blunt and daring and truthful.

Perhaps she'd tell him how sorry she was about his wife and how much she wished he hadn't had to go through that type of grief. When you lost someone you loved, it changed you. It made you more conscious that nothing was really permanent. Life was more than sometimes unfair. It could be cruel.

She hoped he had someone to comfort him in that time, but she doubted it. It was sometimes easier to withdraw from the world—like she had—than to confess that she felt like she had to rebuild herself from the inside out. She suspected that Adam had been like her in that respect, both of them isolated in their grief.

She didn't feel so alone now and it was because of him. She wanted to tell him that. They'd talked about everything in the past week. She'd shared stories of her childhood while he talked of Scotland. For the first time in a long time she greeted each day with eagerness. For that she needed to thank him. If that was foolish, it didn't matter. The Suzanne she had once been and wanted to be again was brave enough to say such a thing.

There was a possibility that she was courting scandal. If anyone saw them here together it would mean gossip throughout Marsley House. *Did you hear that the duchess was found in a compromising situation with Drummond? She has no shame. Or she simply doesn't care.*

The latter would be closer to the truth. All her life she'd been the epitome of everything right and proper and all it had earned her was the privilege of being a hermit in a cold behemoth of a house.

Perhaps she had no shame. Perhaps she should be chastised. How odd that she didn't care.

If she opened the doors and saw that the paraffin lamps were lit, that would mean he was in the library. If the room was dark, he wouldn't be there. All she had to do was to grab the handle of the door and open it. Nothing more than that.

Tonight she didn't want to be the Duchess of Marsley. Tonight she simply wanted to be Suzanne.

She grabbed the handle, then released it and took a few steps back, staring at the door as if it were the yawning maw of a monster from her opium-induced nightmares.

He'd held her. He had kissed her. When he'd drawn back the other day, his hands had trembled the faintest bit as if he were as moved as she. Surely he wouldn't make fun of her for seeking him out. Even if it was after midnight. Even if she did have a title and he was a servant.

She stepped toward the door again, grabbed the handle, and without giving herself time to think, opened one of the doors.

The room was dark. The gas sconce in the corridor allowed her to see well enough to step inside. At first, she thought that the entire library was dark, but then she caught a shadow flickering on the third floor.

The silence constrained her from announcing her presence. How would she explain herself? That she was lonely and of all the people sleeping beneath the roof of Marsley House, he was the only one she sought? Could she possibly be that honest?

Grabbing the skirt of her dressing gown with one hand and the banister with the other, she began to climb the curved iron stairs. Perhaps by the time she got to the third floor, the proper words, the right words would occur to her. Her dressing gown was as thick as a coat and would have been proper to wear to entertain had she been ill. Perhaps, however, she should have changed into a day dress.

At the second floor landing, she looked up. The shadows were no longer flickering. Instead, there was only darkness above her.

The faint light from the hallway sconce was not enough to illuminate the steps. Had she been mistaken after all? Had she only seen
what she wanted to see?

   She was taking a hesitant step upward when she heard a sound.
She looked up as a black shape suddenly descended, pushing
and shoving against her. She lost her grip on the banister as she
tumbled backward. She had the curious thought that the world
had been upended. When she landed her head struck something
sharp. Her mind registered the pain for one instant and then
thought was lost in the nothingness.

Chapter Twenty-Six

𝒜dam had learned a valuable lesson about sleep in the army—take advantage of every opportunity. It might be a while until he got another. That he couldn't sleep tonight annoyed him, but he knew exactly why he couldn't and that irritated him even more.

He sat up, swung his legs over the bed, and lit the lamp on his bedside table. When he reached out for the brooch, he remembered that he'd returned it to Suzanne. When had the damn thing become a talisman? It hadn't looked like something she would choose to wear. She needed a curved bit of gold with one single diamond instead of that gaudy hairpin.

He was like a lovesick boy.

He should remember his mission, the reason he was here at Marsley House, instead of thinking about the duchess.

He dressed but wore only a shirt and trousers, not the uniform of his position. It was nearly two in the morning. The only people who would see him were the footmen assigned to night duty. All good men he trusted. They would ensure the duchess was safe even after he was gone. Not that she knew she was in danger, but if word ever got out that the duke's actions had resulted in the massacre at Manipora, the people of England might well take matters into their own hands. Hell, he'd even given thought to destroying the portrait of the bastard that showed him smugly smiling.

He couldn't imagine any man, especially a peer of the English realm, betraying his own countrymen. According to Roger, that's exactly what had happened. The duke had communicated with the rebel leader, giving him information about the fortifications at Manipora so they could be easily overrun.

He didn't allow himself to think of India very often. There were times, however, when he couldn't help but remember Rebecca. Late at night when he couldn't sleep or when he'd imbibed too much whiskey. Or when he'd been caught up in someone else's conversation and their talk turned to wives. Mostly he tried to avoid situations like those, but there were times when he couldn't.

Their marriage might have been one of convenience, but Rebecca had begun to charm him. She had a delightful laugh and the enthusiasm of a child for new things and experiences. Perhaps he hadn't loved her in the beginning, but he'd given her his loyalty and his growing affection.

He nodded to the footman stationed on the third floor. Instead of heading toward the servants' stairs he walked to the main staircase. His position as majordomo meant that he was in a gray zone: neither truly a servant and definitely not one of the family. However, due to the level of responsibility given him, he was also accorded the great honor of being visible. He did not, unlike the other servants, have to duck into one of the closets accessed through the paneling rather than be seen by the duchess.

He hesitated before descending the staircase, looking down the corridor at the nursery. He couldn't see a light beneath the door. Hopefully, Suzanne was asleep, a more natural sleep now that she wasn't being given opium.

What the hell had Hackney been doing? Why had he conspired with Suzanne's maid?

He hadn't seen Suzanne for days, yet he was conjuring her up from memory, down to the smell of her perfume as he entered the library. That, if nothing else, was a sign that he needed to get the hell away from Marsley House.

After lighting the paraffin lamp closest to the desk, he turned, intent on mounting the stairs to the third level. Only then did he see her.

Suzanne was sprawled on the floor, her dressing gown open, the belt tossed up to her neck, the tassel wicking up the blood beneath her head.

For one frozen second, he couldn't move. His brain didn't function, either. He couldn't think what to do or how to even call for help. Thankfully, his inactivity didn't last. He ran to the base of the steps where Suzanne lay, got to his knees and placed a hand on her neck, his fingers feeling for a pulse. He let out a breath when he found one. Every instance he'd observed in his army career, every single bit of advice he'd gotten on how to treat the injured swirled through his mind. None of it was valuable at the moment.

Her cheek was cold, her face pale. How long had she been like this? Damn it, that was something else he didn't know.

He stood, went to the door, and called for the footman there. When the man arrived, he ordered him to summon Mrs. Thigpen, another footman, and a cot from the storeroom.

"And hurry," he added. The latter wasn't necessary since the young man had taken a look at the figure of the duchess on the floor and blanched.

Mrs. Thigpen, thank God and all the angels, had some experience in wounds. He was sending another one of the footmen to summon the duchess's physician when the housekeeper turned Suzanne's head gently, showing him the blood-matted hair.

"Poor thing must have struck her head on one of those metal steps, Adam. See this gash?"

She parted Suzanne's hair, showing him a two-inch wound still bleeding. He'd never been affected by the sight of blood until this moment. Nor had he ever considered himself a coward, but something clenched in his stomach and it felt too damn much like fear.

He wanted to ask Mrs. Thigpen if Suzanne would be all right, but he remained silent. It wouldn't do for a majordomo to express undue concern about the mistress of the house. Still, he followed the two footmen carrying Suzanne up the stairs on the cot that was doubling as a stretcher. The housekeeper and another maid bearing a large handled basket accompanied them. Evidently, Mrs. Thigpen was prepared for any emergency, including one that made no sense.

What had Suzanne been doing in the library at this hour? None of the lamps had been lit when he entered the room, which meant that she must've been going up the stairs in the darkness.

Most of the books on the second floor dealt with military history and tactics along with obscure philosophical volumes, and he couldn't see the duchess wanting to read one of those. This side of the third floor was given over to the duke's journals.

Had she been going to the second or the third level? Had she wanted to read one of her husband's journals?

The events of tonight reminded him that he'd allowed himself to take his mind off his assignment. He couldn't afford to feel compassion, empathy, or any other emotion for the Duchess of Marsley.

She was just another person he needed to fool until he found what he needed.

At least, that's what he tried to tell himself.

Chapter Twenty-Seven

$\mathcal{S}$uzanne awoke to find Dr. Gregson poking a needle in her thumb.

"Can you feel that?" he asked, his smile nearly obscured by the gray beard covering his face. He had been a kindly figure to her all her life, at least until this moment.

"Yes!" she said, jerking back her hand.

He pulled out the covers from the bottom of the bed and did the very same thing to her big toe.

"And that?"

"Yes!" she said, drawing her foot away.

He wasn't the only person doing odd things to her. Mrs. Thigpen was placing a wet cloth on her forehead and Emily was standing there looking terrified while fanning her the whole time.

Even Adam was involved, keeping vigil at the door with his arms crossed, looking as fierce as one of those statues in the Egyptian parlor.

"Have you any pain anywhere, my dear?" Dr. Gregson asked. "Any pain at all?"

She couldn't imagine why he was asking her that question. Then it slowly came back to her. She'd gotten out of bed, put on her dressing gown, gone downstairs, and entered the library. How very odd that she couldn't remember anything after that.

"My head hurts," she said, and would've put her hand exactly on that spot except that the back of her head was covered up with a substantial bandage.

"What happened?"

She looked from one to the other, but none of the people in her bedroom seemed to know any more than she did.

"I went into the library," she said. "But that's all I remember."

"Drummond found you at the base of the stairs, Your Grace," Mrs. Thigpen said. "Did you fall?"

She couldn't remember. When she said as much, Dr. Gregson nodded.

"It happens that way sometimes," he said.

"Will she ever remember what happened?"

She looked up at Adam. She had wanted to ask the same question, but he was faster.

Dr. Gregson came and sat on the chair someone had moved beside the bed. Once there, he took her wrist in his hand, felt for her pulse, and then nodded approvingly before speaking.

"Sometimes," he said. "Sometimes not. It all is determined by the circumstances."

She didn't have the slightest idea what he meant, but decided that it would be a waste of time to inquire further. In other words, Dr. Gregson didn't know.

She closed her eyes, tried to remember, but all she got was darkness. She wasn't comfortable with the idea that something had happened and yet she had no inkling of it. Was the memory simply gone forever? Or would it pop up unexpectedly like a word she couldn't recall and that suddenly—when her mind was no longer on it—appeared before her as if it were written on the air?

"We will let you rest," Dr. Gregson said. "I've left a tonic for you with Mrs. Thigpen."

Her eyes flew open. "No tonic. No preparation. No potion. Nothing, Dr. Gregson."

He frowned at her. His beard didn't obscure his disapproval.

"Your head will begin to throb, my dear. You will need something for the pain."

"I will take my mind off it or occupy myself in other ways, Dr. Gregson. I will not be taking anything."

He looked at Mrs. Thigpen. "Nonetheless, my good woman, I will leave the tonic in your hands. Perhaps you can convince my patient to do what is best."

She was not going to take anyone's tonic, a fact that Adam alone seemed to understand. When she glanced at him he nodded. At least she had one ally in the room.

"Emily will sit with you for a while," Mrs. Thigpen said. "I think it best that she have someone with her, do you not agree, Dr. Gregson?"

He nodded emphatically. "That I do. I will return tomorrow. I do not expect you to be out of this bed. I don't expect any further complications, but you must take care not to overdo."

She doubted that anyone would let her do anything. She started to nod, but the throbbing at the base of her neck stopped her.

"Very well, Dr. Gregson, I shall be a model patient."

He shook his head, his way of saying that he strongly doubted that fact, and left the room, followed by Mrs. Thigpen.

"What time is it?" she asked, looking at Adam, who'd moved to the end of the bed.

"Nearly dawn."

Only a few hours had passed since she'd entered the library, then. She suddenly got the impression of darkness, something swooping down on top of her.

"Would it be possible to have some tea?" she asked, turning to Emily.

The young girl jumped up from the chair she'd taken when the physician left the room and nodded.

"Of course, Your Grace. I'll be right back."

"You've remembered something," Adam said the moment the door closed behind Emily.

"I don't know if I have or not."

Before she could say another word, the door opened again.

Mrs. Thigpen entered, bearing a brown bottle. They were going to go to war if the woman thought she was going to take another dose of laudanum or opium or anything designed to strip her wits from her. To her surprise, however, the housekeeper merely held up the bottle.

"Will you reconsider, Your Grace?"

Suzanne managed a smile for the woman, who had always been a dear to her and Georgie. She didn't deserve a show of temper.

"No, Mrs. Thigpen, I will not."

The housekeeper nodded and tucked the bottle back into her dressing gown pocket. "I told the physician that you were set in your mind, but he would insist."

"He's a stubborn old goat," Adam said.

Mrs. Thigpen looked like she was biting back a smile.

If they'd been alone, she would have told Adam what she'd remembered, but she didn't want to speak in front of the housekeeper. There were times when Mrs. Thigpen became a trifle histrionic. She expanded on things and used hyperbole when none was necessary. Several threads of gossip had originated with the housekeeper. If she hadn't been so exemplary at her job, her enjoyment of a good story might have been cause for dismissal.

Consequently, Suzanne remained silent.

Nor did it look like the housekeeper was going to leave, not as long as Adam was standing there.

"Thank you," Suzanne said. "I understand you found me."

He nodded.

He looked straight at her, almost as if he were examining her. Did he know how handsome he was, with his green eyes and freshly shaved face? He didn't wear a mustache or a goatee. She had an inkling that he would be as handsome with both, but she was strangely glad he had gone against fashion.

"A good thing," Mrs. Thigpen said. "Otherwise, it might have been morning until one of the maids discovered you."

Left hanging in the air was the question—what had either of them been doing in the library at that hour?

Adam bowed slightly. "I will say good-night, Your Grace."

She smiled in return. A very cold and frosty smile that she'd perfected in the years of being married to George. It was a reserved expression, one he'd approved of, that gave no hint of true favor toward the recipient.

She watched him leave the room and instantly felt the difference.

Mrs. Thigpen took the chair beside her bed, reached out, and patted the mattress beside Suzanne's hand.

"A most unusual man," the housekeeper said, as if expecting a confidence. "At first all the maids were afraid of him. Now they just act silly around him."

So did she. A thought she was definitely not going to share with the housekeeper.

Chapter Twenty-Eight

Adam wasn't able to see Suzanne again for a few more hours. He did so on the pretense of taking her a luncheon tray, a duty that was not strictly in his list of responsibilities. He needed to see the duchess in order to learn what had happened the night before. That was in keeping with his mission, more important than being a majordomo at Marsley House.

He made his way up the grand staircase with a large tray containing a teapot, a cup and saucer, Suzanne's lunch that was covered with a lid but smelled of roast beef, and a small vase with one of the flowers from the conservatory. This one had a bright yellow center with pink petals. He knew nothing about flowers and couldn't have named it if pressed, but it was a cheerful little thing that bobbed as he went up the stairs.

He set the tray on the table beside the double doors and knocked lightly. When Emily opened the door, he refused to surrender the tray to her. Instead, he asked that she open the second door for him.

"It's very heavy," he said in explanation as he stepped inside the sitting room.

She smiled in thanks and led the way to Suzanne's bedroom, standing aside as he entered.

The duchess was awake, sitting up against both pillows. He wasn't surprised to note that her hair had been artfully arranged around the bandage to conceal it. He wouldn't consider her vain, but she was careful with her appearance.

What did startle him, however, was the fact that she had dark circles beneath her eyes. He wondered if it was the effect of the head wound.

"Are you feeling well, Your Grace?" he asked, genuinely concerned.

"I have a beastly headache, Drummond," she said, smiling. "Other than that, I'm fine."

"Mrs. Thigpen has some karpura." He glanced at Emily and then back at the duchess. "Camphor," he added. "If you massage it into your temples, it should ease your headache."

"That sounds lovely. Emily, would you mind fetching some for me?"

The young maid looked torn at the prospect of leaving the duchess alone with him. Thankfully, Suzanne eased her conflict by saying, "Thank you, Emily," and adding a smile.

Emily finally nodded and excused herself.

Once they heard the sitting room door close, he moved toward the bed. She pushed herself up with both hands. He steadied the tray as she moved the pillow behind her back.

"Are you going to tell me what you remembered?" he asked, sitting beside the bed.

"How did you know?"

He only smiled.

"Very well," she said, somewhat crossly. "I did remember something, but I'm not sure what it was. Or who it was."

He sat beside the bed, knowing he had some time before Emily and Mrs. Thigpen found the camphor where he'd hidden it. He'd taken the metal box containing the white, waxy camphor and hidden it behind the sack of flour in the pantry.

"I was climbing the stairs," she said. "At first I thought something had fallen on me, but then I realized whoever was there was wearing a cloak or something black. They pushed me."

"You're saying someone was in the library?"

"Yes. On the third level. At first I thought it was you."

"Is that why you went to the library? To find me?" That was

probably the most improvident question he could have asked and he wanted to immediately call it back.

Her cheeks turned pink as he watched. The metamorphosis from haughty duchess to embarrassed woman fascinated him. He told himself to look away, to give her some privacy, but he didn't.

In the next breath, she turned the tables on him.

"Tell me about your wife, Adam. Has she been gone long?"

No one asked about his wife. No one who knew about India ever spoke about it. Suzanne's ignorance was a shield, yet her curiosity was a spear.

"Seven years," he said.

"Have you had no desire to remarry in all that time?"

"No."

He could only give her that one-word answer and nothing further. However, he had the feeling that his monosyllabic response would not be enough for the Duchess of Marsley. He was beginning to think that she was her father's daughter, as stubborn and determined as Hackney.

"Did you love her very much?"

He reached for the teapot, their fingers meeting. He didn't remove his hand immediately and neither did she. Their eyes met and something seemed to flow between them, an emotion he didn't want to analyze at the moment. She finally pulled her hand away.

"I thought her smile engaging," he said. "And she was very kindhearted."

She didn't say anything for a moment.

"It sounds like you're describing a woman you've just met. Or maybe a friend about which you wish to say nothing detrimental."

He couldn't fault her insight.

"Rebecca needed to be married. It was suggested that I should marry as well. She was killed at Manipora."

The words were spoken with infinite calm, almost as if they carried little import. Still, they lingered in the air between them.

He never spoke about Rebecca. Until that night in the nursery, he hadn't said her name aloud for a good year, maybe more.

"India," she said. "George told the story often. It was an example, he said, of the treachery of the people."

He didn't say anything. He couldn't talk about the Duke of Marsley without wanting to add a few profanities and she didn't deserve that.

"Did you know my husband?"

"I knew him. I served under him."

"You never said."

"The topic did not come up, Your Grace."

"I much prefer it when you call me Suzanne."

He looked away, unwilling to let her see his confusion. Ever since the night on the roof she'd befuddled him. She was unlike any of the peerage he'd met. She didn't hold herself above others. She didn't consider herself better than her servants. If she had been perceived as distant, he suspected it had been because of her grief. Now, tucked up in bed, with her pink cheeks and her troubled eyes, she wanted him to call her Suzanne.

It would be so much better if he remembered his place, his role, and his mission. Everything else was ancillary and unimportant.

The confusion he felt was his problem, not hers.

"Did you wear a kilt in the army?"

He shook his head, grateful that she had changed the subject.

"I don't even own one anymore," he said. But he didn't tell her what he thought, that it wasn't the clothes that made the Scot. Nor was it the accent. Instead, it was his heart, his mind, and his soul. He was a creature of independence, someone who had willingly yoked himself to the British Army first and now to the Silent Service. Neither organization should ever take his loyalty for granted and so far neither had.

"You didn't like my husband, did you, Adam?"

He looked at her, wondering if he should tell her the truth. In the end, he didn't have a choice. The truth donned wings and flew from his mouth.

"I despised him, Suzanne."

"Why?"

"Because he was responsible for the death of my wife."

She looked stricken. The moment he'd spoken the words he wanted to call them back. Not because they were untrue. He believed the Duke of Marsley was guilty of treason.

Yet Suzanne was innocent of her husband's sins. At this exact moment, however, she looked as if he'd accused her.

Reaching out, he poured her some of the tea Mrs. Thigpen had brewed. The smell of it, something strong and spicy, reminded him of India. That's probably why the floodgates had opened up on his memory, and emotions spilled out.

"Forgive me," he said.

"Why?" she asked again. "For saying what you felt?"

"Yes. Some things should not be given voice."

She didn't say anything for a long moment, merely took the cup and saucer from him, careful not to let her hand touch his.

"Tell me about it," she said. "Tell me about Manipora."

That was the very last thing he wanted to do. He glanced at her and then away. How could anyone refuse to grant Suzanne whatever she wished when her eyes were filled with such compassion?

Chapter Twenty-Nine

"We lived at Manipora," he said, then cleared his throat.

She should have interrupted and told him it wasn't necessary that he tell her the story, but the truth was that she very much wanted to know. Everything about him incited her curiosity.

"By June the rebellion had spread, getting closer to Manipora. General Wheeler, however, thought the locals would remain loyal. After all, he'd married an Indian woman and he'd learned the local language. He was so convinced of that fact that he sent most of the soldiers assigned to Manipora to help Lucknow."

"Leaving Manipora without defenses?" she asked.

"Not entirely," he said. "Some military men were left as well as a significant number of businessmen." He stared at the far wall for a moment, almost as if he was viewing Manipora seven years ago.

"The rebels attacked the entrenchment. Their forces numbered over twelve thousand men, but we held on for three weeks."

She asked the next question softly, wondering if she should. "Your wife was at Manipora. Were you there, too?"

He nodded, leaving Suzanne to wonder if she should stop him now. There was an expression on his face that wasn't hard to interpret. The tale of Manipora wouldn't be easy for him to relate.

"On June twenty-six," Adam continued, "we were overrun. Somehow, the rebels learned of our defenses and entered the entrenchment. Wheeler surrendered and accepted the offer of safe passage to Allahabad. The next day we headed for the Ganges and the forty boats arranged to take us there. Safe passage evidently didn't mean the same to the rebels as it did to Wheeler because we were shot at after we boarded the boats and left the dock. Two boats got away. I was in one of them. The boats holding the women and children were brought by the Indians back to Manipora."

Her meal forgotten, she was caught up in Adam's story, relayed in such a calm tone that it might seem, to a casual listener, that he felt nothing about the circumstances. Yet emotion was there in the timbre of his voice, in the way he kept having to stop as if to guard his words, and the deep breaths he took. She couldn't help but wonder if it was the first time he'd ever discussed Manipora with anyone.

"The women and children were moved from the entrenchment to another house in the city," he said. "The plan was to use them for bargaining with the East India Company. Unfortunately, that didn't happen." He took another deep breath.

"Where were you?"

"I'd been assigned to General Wheeler's boat. We led a charge against the rebel soldiers and were able to get away. We decided to take refuge in a shrine, but we were overrun by a crowd of villagers with clubs. We finally reached the river again and began swimming downstream. I didn't realize, until much later, that the women had been taken prisoner."

"How much later?"

"Several weeks," he said in that same dull voice. "I'd been shot. We were rescued by men who worked for Raja Singh, who was still loyal to the British, but by the time I was able to make it back to Manipora, word had already come of what had happened."

George had told her about Manipora and she'd read the horrible details in the newspaper. The rebels had been alerted that British troops were headed for Manipora to rescue the women and children. In those last days, one hundred twenty-four children and seventy-three women had been killed, their bodies thrown down a well. Soldiers had reached Manipora the day after the killings.

Incensed by what they saw, they'd retaliated with violence against the population of the city.

She didn't know what to say or what kind of comfort to offer Adam. Words were just noise that echoed against the wall you'd built around yourself.

What people said sometimes didn't make any sense. *Time heals all wounds. God never gives us anything we can't handle.* One intrepid soul had the temerity to tell her, "God evidently wanted Georgie to be one of his angels." Someone—and she couldn't remember who—had stepped between her and that woman as if afraid that Suzanne would say something cutting. They needn't have worried. She'd been so shocked by that announcement that she'd been unable to speak.

Now she had nothing to say to Adam. All she had to offer him was her empathy, compassion, and tears. None of those things, however, were worthwhile in the face of his loss.

She stretched out her hand, kept it in the air until he clasped it and brought their joined hands down to the mattress.

Her other hand wiped her tears away from her cheeks.

"I've made you cry. I'm sorry."

"Don't be. It's a daily occurrence. I've gotten quite used to it."

She smiled at him and he surprised her by returning the expression.

They didn't have the opportunity to speak further because the door to the sitting room opened. Adam dropped her hand and stood as Emily rushed into the room, breathless.

"I'm so sorry, Your Grace. I apologize. We couldn't find the camphor so I had to go to the stables and get some from the stable master."

"That was very responsible of you, Emily. Thank you. And thank you, Drummond," she said. "For bringing me my tray."

He only bowed slightly, his faint smile still in evidence.

When he was gone, she explained to Emily that her tears were due to the pain in her head, no doubt leaving the young maid thinking that she was weak and infirm. Better that than what she was truly feeling, anguish for Adam. For the first time in a very long time she was not immersed in her own pain. She was not the only one to have suffered a loss. At least she'd not had to fight for her life on top of everything else.

In the newspaper accounts of Manipora she'd learned that only four men had survived the attack. Evidently, Adam was one of the four.

Her majordomo was a hero. A survivor who'd managed to escape being killed not once but countless times under monumental odds. Upon his return to England he'd avoided the attention the press would have lavished on him. Now here he was, at Marsley House.

George thankfully rarely spoke about India because his command there had happened before their marriage. On one occasion, however, he'd talked about General Wheeler and his idiocy in not guarding his magazine.

She'd listened attentively, said something supportive when George hesitated, and tried to be a good wife. All in all, her husband's account of Manipora had been remarkably different from Adam's.

The more she knew of Adam, the more she admired him. Yet in addition to that admiration was another emotion, one that startled her. She liked him. She liked the way he looked at the world.

She'd become frozen in time while Adam had kept moving through his life. She'd never heard him say anything that would make her think he was mired in sadness. Instead, he struck her as a man who had his eyes focused on the future, not the past.

She liked him and even more. He attracted her, intrigued her, and charmed her down to her toes.

He hadn't asked her why she had been in the library. Would she have told him the truth?

I wanted a kiss, Adam.

No, perhaps that wouldn't have been the wisest course.

Chapter Thirty

$\mathcal{F}$or the next week, Adam stayed close to Suzanne. He didn't care if the maids gave him quick glances as he prowled the corridor outside the duchess's suite. Or if the footmen looked as if they wanted to ask questions when he assigned two of them to guard her door.

Every morning he checked on her without a single coherent reason for doing so. He didn't even bother coming up with a pretense.

His greeting to the duchess was the same in case anyone was within earshot.

"Everything was calm last night, Your Grace. How are you feeling?"

She would answer in the same manner, her voice holding that tone he'd come to expect of the peerage: haughty, almost cold. However, she always had a twinkle in her eyes.

"I'm feeling well, Drummond. Thank you for asking."

Each morning he would simply nod and leave, relieved.

Every afternoon he would bring her tea. Emily would join him in setting up the tray for the duchess, offering her a selection of tarts or biscuits Grace had made. Conscious of the maid's presence, he would tell Suzanne what was happening in the house, including any repairs that were ongoing. He found himself discussing matters pertaining to the staff, none of which he'd ever communicated to her.

She, in turn, asked questions about Scotland. He found himself telling her stories of his childhood and she reciprocated, making him think that the two children they'd been weren't that far apart in their dreams and wishes.

She even asked about Wals, which made Emily's cheeks turn a bright red. Evidently the footman had made inroads there. Adam was torn between wanting to warn Emily that the young footman had no sense of decorum and wasn't loyal to one female and simply allowing nature to take its course.

Suzanne was the one who cautioned her maid, surprising him again.

"Wals is a reprobate." She glanced at Adam and said, "I've met him once. He was exceedingly charming. Too much so for my peace of mind." Her attention turned to Emily again. "I do hope that you don't allow your heart to be involved. If he isn't yet, he's well on his way to becoming a lecher, a despoiler of innocents. I'd be truly concerned if you were involved with him."

Emily only curtsied, mumbled something in agreement, and left the room.

He and Suzanne looked at each other. Unspoken was the certainty that Emily had already been wooed by Wals.

In the evening, after Emily was dismissed for the night, he visited the duchess again. Their conversations were always more personal at that hour. He found himself anticipating their nightly talks, learning a great deal about Suzanne Hackney and her life as a wealthy man's daughter.

It was an upbringing that, strangely enough, mirrored his in some ways. She didn't have to worry about where her next meal was coming from, but with her father so often in India, she was essentially an orphan for most of the time. Without any siblings, Suzanne had learned to be comfortable with being alone, just as he had.

The drawback with that kind of attitude was that he didn't make friends easily. Neither did she. When he came to see her on Wednesday afternoon, she was entertaining Mrs. Armbruster.

The older woman was telling a tale that made Suzanne laugh. He'd left the room annoyed and it wasn't difficult for him to figure out why.

He had made her smile, but he'd never made the duchess laugh. Mrs. Armbruster had. In addition, she'd stolen his time with Suzanne.

Thursday morning was the same familiar regimen, but by the afternoon Suzanne had been given permission to leave her bed for the sitting room. Sunday she was pronounced healthy enough to go anywhere in the house, which meant that it would have looked odd for him to call on her in her suite.

He'd spent a great many hours in the past week trying to figure out who the other operative was at Marsley House. The minute Suzanne had said something, he'd known that the second man had also been given the task of finding the duke's journal. There was no other reason for him to be on the third floor of the library.

With the help of two footmen, Adam had checked the locks on all the windows. Three of them were found to be broken, with the entrance point being the laundry.

He added lookouts, stationing two stable boys at the rear, between the kitchen garden and the stables. Two footmen were added to the front, assigned to the gate area. Any of the men were to report to him if they saw something amiss. For a week nothing had happened which, paired with Suzanne's recuperation, allowed him to concentrate on other matters: namely, confronting Roger Mount.

On Monday Adam decided it was time to pay a call on Roger. He wasn't going to send advance notice of his arrival. If the other man was busy, then Roger would need to rearrange his schedule. If he was gone, Adam would wait for Roger to return. They were going to talk and this time the conversation was going to provide Adam the information he needed.

Traffic through London was congested as it always was. He tapped impatiently on the fabric below the window, grateful that it was only an overcast day and not raining.

He'd rarely allowed himself the luxury of rage, but he felt it now. He wanted to throttle Roger.

It was one thing to put a man in danger if he knew the odds and the risk. Suzanne didn't deserve to be treated that way. She'd done nothing other than bow to her father's pressure and marry the Duke of Marsley.

He wished he'd known her back then, but she probably would have had nothing to do with him. He hadn't smoothed all his rough edges. Not that he lacked his share of them now. Put him in a fancy dinner party—and thankfully he'd only one experience with all those forks and knives and spoons—and he was out of his element. He'd much rather be given a sword and be in hand-to-hand combat with an enraged Sepoy.

What the hell had Roger been thinking? What would make him pit two operatives against each other? It wasn't as if Adam hadn't proven his worth to the Crown. He'd received commendations on more than one assignment.

Whoever had been installed at Marsley House had made a tactical error. The man should not have endangered Suzanne. Roger had been an idiot not to make that perfectly clear. He had to pull Adam's shadow out of Marsley House. Today.

When the carriage finally reached the War Office, Adam told the driver that he wouldn't be long. He bounded up the steps two at a time and made his way to Roger's office.

He'd forgotten Oliver's aversion to loud noises, and the man reacted to the slamming of the outer door by jumping nearly a foot. Adam waved Oliver back into his chair.

"Is he here?"

"He is, but he can't be disturbed."

He strode across the room, surprised when Oliver sprang up from his chair, rounded the desk, and put out an arm. As if that would stop him.

In India, Oliver had been pale and sweating almost continually. It wasn't just the heat and the humidity that had affected him. Oliver had spent the majority of his time in India genuinely frightened.

The man looked the same now.

"Step away," Adam told him. "I don't care how busy he is. I'm going to see him now."

"He has someone with him, Drummond. You can't interrupt. It's a very important meeting."

"Then he's just going to have to reschedule it," he said. He didn't care if the Queen was in Roger's office.

Oliver was no match for him and he pushed the secretary out of the way and opened the door, only to stand there speechless.

Edward Hackney sat in the comfortable chair in front of Roger's desk, his feet up on a needlepoint stool, a cup of tea in his right hand, the saucer in his left. Roger's pose was as indolent, slumped back in his chair, an affable smile on his face.

Thoughts cascaded into Adam's mind like a fusillade of bullets. This was a meeting of men who knew each other well. Roger had never mentioned that he was acquainted with Suzanne's father. What the hell was Hackney doing at the War Office? Did he know of Adam's assignment? If he didn't, the man wouldn't lose any time informing his daughter of the fact that he'd seen Adam here, a thought that was reinforced by Hackney's expression as he turned.

The two of them exchanged a look.

Roger stood, his smile fading into a frown. "What are you doing here?"

He had too many questions and absolutely no answers, so Adam didn't even try to respond. Instead, he turned on his heel and left Roger's office, intent on getting back to Marsley House at all possible speed.

SUZANNE WAS READING in the Grecian Parlor, a restful place due to its colors of beige and tan and the fact that it was away from most of the activities midday. None of the maids came here after eleven and the footmen weren't stationed in this corridor until after dark. Consequently, few people interrupted her unless she rang.

"Suzanne."

She was startled to hear Adam call her name. She looked up to find him framed in the doorway. He wasn't wearing his usual majordomo attire. Instead, he was dressed only in a white shirt and black trousers beneath a long topcoat. In his hands he held her cloak.

"Will you come with me?" he said.

"Will I come with you?"

He nodded. "Will you come with me?"

What a silly conversation they were having, but Adam evidently didn't feel that way. There was a look in his eyes, the same expression that had been there when he was talking about India. Serious and somber, with another emotion she couldn't decipher.

"Where?" she asked.

"Somewhere safe," he said. "Where we can talk."

She should have countered that Marsley House was safe. That there were hundreds of rooms they could occupy that would be private enough, but something in his voice or in his eyes kept her silent.

"Yes," she said, surprising herself.

She stood, placed her book on the sofa cushion beside her, and approached him.

Instead of offering his arm, he grabbed her hand. He walked quickly down the corridor of the north wing, and turned left and then right to a rear door that was not often used.

"Adam? Is something wrong?"

"Yes," he said. "But I can't talk about it until we're away from here."

She stopped and when he would have pulled her to him, she shook her head.

"Is it my father?" she asked. "Has he been hurt? Has there been another accident?"

He put his arm around her shoulders, drew her close, and looked down into her face. "Your father is fine, Suzanne. I promise you that. There is something wrong, but give me a few minutes and I will explain everything."

There were dozens and dozens of servants around Marsley House, but they only encountered one maid. She glanced at their joined hands and then away, trying to hide her smile but being unable to do so successfully.

Suzanne realized she was probably going to be the subject of gossip in the servants' quarters. Why wasn't she more concerned?

She would think about that later.

Perhaps she was wrong to trust Adam. She, who had lost trust in nearly everything. Yet for some reason she did. Perhaps it was because they'd each known anguish. Adam knew how she felt, what she'd gone through, and he was possibly the only person she'd met who did. They'd each experienced the worst of what life could deliver. Or maybe she trusted him because he'd always sought to protect her.

She squeezed his hand and nodded, assent in a gesture.

He helped her with her cloak, and together they left Marsley House.

Chapter Thirty-One

$\mathcal{A}$dam didn't know why he was doing what he was doing. Or, rather, he knew exactly why he was doing it. He just couldn't believe he was actually going through with it.

His duty was to the Crown. The army had saved him, had fed him, had trained him. He'd transferred his allegiance from the army to the War Office and it was as strong as ever.

Yet he was skirting dangerously close to violating his duty at the moment.

He wasn't sure that he had a clear picture about anything, and that lack of understanding made him both frustrated and angry. It wasn't just seeing Hackney at the War Office. It was Roger putting a second operative at Marsley House. It was the sensation he'd always had that he was being manipulated.

What the hell had Hackney been doing in Roger's office? Why had Roger been entertaining a wealthy former East India Company director?

Had Hackney always known who Adam was? The look on the older man's face had been one of surprise, so it was possible he hadn't.

The one thing Adam was certain of in this entire fiasco was that he wanted to tell Suzanne who he was before Hackney had a chance to mention their encounter this morning. He didn't want her to think that he'd violated her trust or taken advantage of her. Although how she could think anything else, he didn't know.

The truth was always best. He would just have to tell her who he was and let fate decide what happened after that.

He gave the driver the address to his lodgings, normally twenty minutes away in good traffic. It took them twice as long to reach the house he'd considered home for the past six and a half years.

He and Suzanne talked of inconsequential things, like the weather or the new maids at Marsley House. Both of them were settling in well and performing their tasks admirably. In fact, Mrs. Thigpen had asked if there was any way that the two girls could come back to work after the birth of their children.

"What do you think?" he asked now, desperate for any subject other than why he was taking her away from Marsley House. If he began his explanation too soon, she could easily command the driver to turn the carriage around and take her home.

"I think it would be a wonderful idea. And the babies can come and stay, too."

He glanced at her in surprise.

"We've all those rooms, Adam. It seems to me that the infants would be better there than at the Institute or the Foundling Hospital. The girls don't seem willing to abandon their children, thank heavens. Their babies need to be somewhere safe, just like them."

She stared up at the ceiling of the carriage. "We could turn one of the rooms on the third floor into a nursery. Maybe Mrs. Armbruster knows of a young girl who could come and watch the babies during the day."

"You realize that the girls are unwed?"

For the first time since he'd spirited her away from Marsley House, she looked annoyed.

"And they're women of ill repute, little more than prostitutes, isn't that what people say? Harlots." She shook her head. "If you ask either of them, Adam, they were in love. They made a mistake, true, but must they be severely punished for it?"

She stared out at the street a moment before returning her gaze to him. "And another thing. Where are the men? Where are the men that they fell in love with? Have you noticed that they're no-where around? Nor does the law compel them to provide for their children."

Only one time had he seen her so fierce and that's when she'd fired Ella.

"Tell me about the Foundling Hospital," he said. "And the Institute."

She frowned at him. "Are you really interested?"

He nodded.

"It's Mrs. Armbruster's project. Hers and her husband. She didn't say, but I suspect that their efforts began in the church. A great many charities are run by the church for sinners. Only you can't be too much of a sinner."

That comment surprised him, but he didn't speak.

"You can be a fallen woman, but if you also have an illegitimate child, there aren't many places where you can get help. People like the Armbrusters step in and offer a solution. Otherwise, these poor girls would have nowhere to go. They would be living on the streets with their children." She leaned back against the seat. "It's not an ideal situation," she added, describing the layout of the Institute and the Foundling Hospital. "But at least those poor babies aren't doomed to die a terrible death."

He suddenly understood why she was more than willing to open up Marsley House to the two girls and their infants. Her need to help, to rescue those girls, had at its roots her inability to have prevented Georgie's death.

The carriage slowed. A glance out the window showed him that they were in Pimlico and nearing his lodgings.

He hadn't seen Mrs. Ross since he'd brought the kitten to her. The kitten, strangely enough, was the first to greet him when he jumped down from the carriage and held out his hand to help Suzanne.

The kitten jumped from an overhanging branch to land on the top of the carriage roof. He gave Adam a quick once-over, then calmly settled in to wash himself.

Adam chuckled.

"A friend of yours?" Suzanne asked, smiling up at the kitten.

"I'd say he was a friend of yours," he corrected her. "I found him at Marsley House. Outside your bedroom window, as a matter of fact."

"And you brought him here?" she asked, looking up and down the avenue.

"It's where I live."

On one side, terraced houses lined the street, the hedges pruned to militaristic precision in front of each home. Steeply pitched slate roofs sheltered each identical-looking house, the bay windows acting like eyes on their neighbors. On the other side of the street sat detached houses, one of which belonged to Mrs. Ross. The white stucco structure had been built only twenty years ago when her husband died.

"I lost a husband and gained a house," she was fond of saying.

The residence, with its four classical columns, was a sprawling structure consisting of four floors and a substantial basement. His lodgings opened up to the garden, an overgrown hodgepodge of colorful blooms and out-of-control greenery. When he'd first seen it, Adam had smiled, realizing that Mrs. Ross's garden represented England to him. An England that had remained the same for centuries and would likely resist change.

He offered Suzanne his arm and they proceeded up the curved walk. Mrs. Ross, who had acute hearing, opened the front door, smiling a greeting.

"Mr. Drummond, how lovely to see you again."

She looked from him to Suzanne, an expectant expression on her face and curiosity in her eyes. He glanced at Suzanne, then at his landlady.

"Mrs. Ross, I'd like you to meet Suzanne Hackney. My cousin." Both women looked at him.

"Your cousin?" Mrs. Ross said. "I thought you had no family in London, Mr. Drummond."

"I've only recently returned," Suzanne said. "I was living in Sussex."

At least she'd managed not to lie on that point, which was more than he could say for himself.

He'd known that he'd have to appease Mrs. Ross. He hadn't planned on lying to her, but at the last moment he hadn't been willing to divulge Suzanne's identity. Mrs. Ross was not above a little gossip over the hedges. What he didn't want was for Suzanne to be the topic of the week.

"Then welcome, Miss Hackney. Any family member of Mr. Drummond's is welcome here," Mrs. Ross said, turning and holding the door open.

"Actually, it's Mrs.," Suzanne said as Adam stepped aside and let Suzanne precede him inside the house.

As usual, it smelled of cinnamon and oranges and something else that reminded him of pepper. He'd rarely tasted Mrs. Ross's cooking, preferring to do for himself, but occasionally he'd shared meals with the other two lodgers. After the first experience, he'd learned to decline a meal whenever Mrs. Ross was making something fancy. She was good with roasts and fish but tended to odd flavors in her stews and casseroles.

"I noticed the kitten outside," he said.

"The best mouser I've ever seen," Mrs. Ross replied, straightening her apron. "Can I do anything for you, Mr. Drummond? Or your cousin?"

"We don't require anything, Mrs. Ross, but thank you."

"You'll let me know?"

He smiled. "Indeed I will."

He led the way down the hallway, turned to the left, and inserted his key in the lock. Mrs. Ross stood behind them, even as he put his hand on the small of Suzanne's back and urged her inside.

Once more he turned to his landlady and smiled. "Thank you, Mrs. Ross."

"Mr. Drummond," she said, nodding.

She glanced once more at Suzanne, taking in her black silk dress.

He closed the door in his landlady's face, wondering how long she was going to remain in the hall.

Moving into the sitting room he stood in front of the now cold fireplace. The day wasn't chilly enough to build a fire. Yet it would have given him something to do rather than stand here and wonder how to begin this conversation.

"Why did you lie?" he asked, removing his coat and tossing it onto the back of the chair.

"Why did you?" she said when he took her cloak from her and placed it beside his coat.

Time had run out. He needed to tell her the truth now.

Suzanne walked slowly into the room, looking around. The rebels had burned everything they'd owned at Manipora. There was nothing of his life with Rebecca here. No traces of his life in India or anything to indicate that he'd spent a substantial amount of his life there.

Instead, the room was furnished with Mrs. Ross's castoffs: a comfortable sofa upholstered in a faded blue fabric, a chair with a flower print beside the fire, two tables, each equipped with a lamp. A few bits of statuary, a faded blue-and-red carpet on the wood floor. Shabby yet welcoming. Nothing pretentious or costing a fortune, just a few places to sit and talk or read.

He had arrived back in England with a valise and two changes of clothing. That's all. He'd acquired some additional clothes, but he hadn't made any substantial purchases for his rooms. Without much effort he could walk out the door and leave little trace of himself behind.

He glanced toward her, then away. The moment the words were spoken, things would change between them. The friendship that had grown in the past few weeks, the easy camaraderie they enjoyed, all that would vanish.

He'd be left only with the longing.

Chapter Thirty-Two

Ever since leaving Marsley House, Suzanne felt as if she were living a different life. She wasn't the Duchess of Marsley at the moment, but someone else. Perhaps she was just Suzanne Hackney, the girl she'd wondered about a few days earlier.

No noise penetrated the heavy door to the corridor. She couldn't hear anyone else in the house. It was as if the world faded away.

Adam didn't answer her, but strode through the sitting room, leaving her to follow.

The room she entered was flooded by light from the six windows facing a garden. She watched as Adam opened two of the windows on either side of a door. The day was chilly, but the air was fresh, laden with the scent of flowers.

A rectangular table was against the far wall with a stool beneath it. A large metal-rimmed bowl for washing up was stacked next to a few dishes and cups. The opposite wall held a fireplace with a curious stove in the middle of it, something that looked as if it could be used not only to heat the room but also to cook.

The closest she could come to labeling this space was to think of it as half kitchen, half conservatory. Granted, the plants were on the outside, but it would be difficult to ignore the blowsy beauty of the late-blooming flowers. The yellow wallpaper, in a geometric pattern, brightened the space even more.

"These are your lodgings?" she asked as he went to the round table in the middle of the room and pulled out a chair for her.

"They are."

"Yet you live at Marsley House."

"Only recently," he said.

"But you felt it necessary to keep lodgings elsewhere?"

"There's something I have to tell you, Your Grace."

He called her that—Your Grace—when he wanted to distance himself from her. She got the hint, but it annoyed her nonetheless.

"What is it, Adam?"

Her use of his first name was deliberate. He might want to distance himself from her, but she had kissed him. More than once. Their kisses had been wondrous, something she'd never before experienced.

She'd confided in him. He had confided in her. Did he think their conversations were everyday occurrences? She'd never shared her pain with anyone else and now he was calling her Your Grace?

She sat, placing her hands atop the table. She hadn't worn her hat or her gloves. Or brought her reticule. No wonder Mrs. Ross had looked at her oddly. What kind of woman went somewhere without being properly dressed?

Someone flooded with curiosity. Someone fascinated and interested and too emotional right at the moment.

He sat opposite her, and stretched out his hands. For a moment she didn't understand, but then he grabbed her hands and held them beneath his. She wanted to pull free, but she didn't. She wanted the ache in her chest to disappear, but that didn't happen, either.

"Why do you live here, Adam, when you should be living at Marsley House?" She wished her voice didn't sound so plaintive. She cleared her throat. "I think I deserve an explanation, don't you?"

He nodded, but didn't speak for a moment.

"Would you like some tea?" he asked.

"No."

One of his eyebrows arched. "Brandy?"

"No."

"Is there anything you'd like?"

"An explanation. Why did you tell Mrs. Ross I was your cousin?"

"I couldn't very well come out and tell her that I'd spirited the Duchess of Marsley to my rooms."

She moved her gaze from their hands to his face. His cheeks were bronzed.

"I saw your father this morning," he said.

She hadn't expected that.

"Did you?"

He nodded. "At the War Office."

She frowned at him. "That isn't unusual. He has several political protégés who work in the government."

"Does he? Do you know their names?" he asked.

She knew them very well since she'd attended every event to introduce the three men to potential campaign donors. "Harry Taylor, Roger Mount, and James Parker. Those are the ones he's working with this year."

"Roger Mount?"

She nodded. "What were you doing at the War Office, Adam?"

"Meeting with the man who sent me to Marsley House."

She held herself very still. For some reason it was important for her to remain calm and composed.

"I don't understand," she said. There, her voice didn't sound plaintive at all.

"I'm not a majordomo, Suzanne."

"Then why are you working at Marsley House?"

"Being at Marsley House is one of my assignments," he said.

"One of your assignments." She pulled her hands free.

How odd that she'd become a magpie in the past few minutes. She could only repeat what he was saying, which didn't aid in curing her confusion.

"Yes."

"You're not a majordomo. But you took the position."

"For another reason," he said.

"Another reason? Are you telling me that you are spying for my father?"

"No."

"Is your name really Adam Drummond?"

"Yes."

"And Rebecca? Was she real?"

"I wouldn't lie about her."

"Were you really in the army?"

"Yes."

"What other reason, Adam?"

He didn't say anything, only stood and walked to the door leading to the garden. For a moment he remained there, staring out at the plants and flowers, his back to her.

"Would you be content to know that it was important?" he finally asked.

"No."

He turned and came back to the table, taking a seat opposite her. This time he didn't grab her hands. She had the feeling he was not only physically distancing himself from her but emotionally as well.

"I was spying, but not for your father. I'm a member of a group of men who work for the government," he said. "We find and keep secrets. We protect and guard."

"That sounds very patriotic," she said. "And as clear as London fog."

His smile was rueful; his glance quick and shuttered.

"The Duke of Marsley was a traitor," he said. "My mission was to find evidence to prove it."

She stared at him, shocked. "You can't be serious."

"I've never had a mission that was more serious, Suzanne."

She shook her head. "My husband was a great many things, Adam—a libertine, grossly unfaithful—but no one could fault his loyalty to the army or the Crown."

"I have it on good authority that he wasn't all that loyal."

"Then whoever your authority was, he's lying to you."

"And my own experiences, Suzanne? Are they false, too?"

She felt cold in a way that had nothing to do with the weather. "What do you mean?"

"There were rumors at Manipora that someone betrayed us. One of the reasons the rebels didn't overpower us at first is that we commanded cannon to the east side of our barricade. They also thought we had trenches filled with explosives surrounding the entrenchment. Someone let the rebel leader know that it had been a carefully planted lie. Someone gave him the plans of the entrenchment. Someone intimately familiar with Manipora."

"He was no traitor, Adam. George always said that his time in the army, in India, was among his favorite memories. Men who used to serve under him would visit Marsley House every month. They seemed to love him."

"Or they were looking for financial help," Adam said, his tone dry.

"What kind of evidence were you searching for?"

"A journal," he said. "Specifically from his time in India."

She stared at him, suddenly understanding. "That's why you're always in the library," she said.

Her voice had taken on a sharp tone, the same one she'd used with Ella. She didn't try to soften it or ease her words in any way. He'd betrayed her and yet he would probably never understand why.

She hadn't opened her heart since Georgie. She hadn't stretched out a hand to another person. Even her faint attempts with Mrs. Armbruster were just that, attempts. With Adam—Drummond—she'd revealed herself completely. She'd hidden nothing from him, and all this time he'd been as transparent as a piece of slate.

He'd lied to her.

It wasn't disappointment she felt. No, it was more than that. Something crucial and necessary had broken inside her.

Chapter Thirty-Three

*S*uzanne moved her hands to her lap and clasped them together. She felt sick, but it wasn't a physical feeling as much as a soul-deep one. No wonder he had brought her here, someplace where she was stranded, cut off from everything she knew as familiar. She couldn't summon one of the footmen to take him away. She couldn't ring for a maid or send for her solicitor. Instead, she was trapped here, forced to listen to his notions about George.

"I will be the first to admit that George was a horrible husband. Or at least, the kind of husband I didn't want. But he took great pride in his duties for the army."

"I will wager that he enjoyed putting on his pretty red uniform jacket with all its polished metals and looking like a general."

She would not gaze up at him or in any way acknowledge that his words were unfortunately correct. Sometimes she'd caught George standing in front of his portrait in the library, his chest puffed out and his chin lifted, almost as if he were inspecting the man portrayed in his finery.

"Did your father know your husband in India?"

She nodded. "They never discussed India, at least in my presence."

But, then, they didn't talk about much around her. Their last argument, two nights before George's death, had been so loud that she could hear them from the second-floor sitting room.

"Spend your money on my daughter or my grandson. Not your mistresses and bastards."

For his part, George had hated the fact that her father didn't have to worry about money and had enough to finance the careers of various young men who craved power.

A thought occurred to her and it was so discomfiting that she pushed it away for a moment, but it kept returning. Would George have engaged in treason if it would have profited him to do so? If the rebel leader—and she wasn't sure exactly who Adam had been speaking about—had promised him a king's ransom, would George have succumbed? Surely not. He was the Duke of Marsley, the tenth in a long line of distinguished men.

Unfortunately, those same men had done what they could to dissipate the family coffers.

Yet if George had engaged in treason, why would he have agreed to marry her? Or had the lure of even more money been too much to ignore?

Wasn't it telling that she didn't know the exact nature of George's character despite having been married to him for six years?

Another thought occurred to her, one that was just as unsettling. She could guarantee that Adam would never have betrayed his men or his country.

"As horrible as George was, Drummond, I didn't hate him. But I want, very much, to hate you."

If she hadn't been watching him so closely, she wouldn't have seen the way his eyes changed, became flat and expressionless.

"And do you?"

His question was a whip, a cat of nine tails against her raw and bleeding emotions.

It would have been easier if she could have hated Adam instead of understanding. He wanted to be able to blame his wife's death on someone and George was an available scapegoat. She would have felt the same if it could be proved that someone was culpable for Georgie's death.

She pounded her fist on the table, just once. Adam's eyes widened. Good. She wanted to startle him. Let him feel just a portion of what she was experiencing right now.

"How dare you do that to me. How dare you come into Marsley House and be charming and comforting and protective? How dare you make me think certain things, Drummond. How dare you kiss me." That last was said in a lower voice. She should have been ashamed, not him. He had only ventured to kiss her. She had allowed it. No, she had gone on to encourage it. That night in the library, she'd sought it.

"Were you the one who pushed me down the stairs? In the library, was it you?"

His face changed again, became set in stone. "You would think that of me?" Even his voice was rough.

"I wish I did," she said, shaking her head. "I truly do."

They were exchanging too many truths. Honesty was causing a bloodletting. During those six years with George, she'd craved an end to the lies. Why, then, was she feeling the opposite now?

Adam confused her. He had from the very beginning.

"The fool mourns an idiot."

"What does that mean?"

"You wanted to know what I said to you that night on the roof. That's what it was. In Gaelic."

"So even then you were warning me about George, is that it?"

"No," he said. "Even then I was calling you an idiot for grieving for him. *Gabh mo leisgeul.* I hadn't gotten to know you."

"Did you kiss me because it was part of your assignment?" she asked, surprised at her own daring. Was she truly brave enough to hear the truth? Wasn't it better, though, than always wondering?

"I kissed you because I wanted to," he said. "It wasn't the wisest thing to do and it was definitely in violation of my assignment. You weren't the only fool in this, Suzanne."

"Kissing me was acting the fool?"

"Yes," he said. "Because I wanted to do it again, constantly. Or take you to my bed and keep you there for a day or two."

She was no longer cold. In fact, her body was becoming strangely heated. Her heart, however, felt like it was breaking. She needn't have worried about causing any scandal. The Duchess of Marsley and her majordomo. Not true. The Duchess of Marsley and a man of mystery. Suzanne and a fraud, a liar, and a spy.

She tried, she really did, but the tears couldn't be stopped. She hadn't brought her reticule, either, which meant that now she had no handkerchief, nothing.

"Suzanne."

"Go away," she said.

"I can't."

"You have to. I insist upon it. I demand it."

"How like a duchess you sound," he said. "Quite like Marble Marsley."

"What?" She glanced over at him to find him holding out a pristine white handkerchief.

"That's what they called you. The staff at Marsley House. At least, they did. I haven't heard that name for a while now."

"Marble?" she asked, dabbing at her tears.

"As in cold, unaffected."

"Or like a crypt," she said. "Like the crypt at Fairhaven."

He looked startled.

She didn't expect the knock on the outer door.

Adam strode through the room. She followed him, just in case it was her driver asking for instructions. If it was, she'd tell him that she very much wanted to return to Marsley House. Now, please.

"I brought you some biscuits," Mrs. Ross said, extending a tray toward Adam. "I remember how much you liked my Scotch shortbread. You said it was just like what you could find in Glasgow."

She shot a quick look toward Suzanne. "Are you from Scotland, too?"

Suzanne shook her head.

Mrs. Ross gave her a once-over, the look not so much rude as it was comprehensive.

"You've been crying," the older woman said. She glanced at

Adam for confirmation, but he didn't say anything, leaving it to Suzanne to explain as best she could.

"We have just been talking about my poor dead George," she said. "My husband."

"It's sorry I am," Mrs. Ross said. "It's a hard thing we widows face, doing without the men we love."

Suzanne nodded.

Mrs. Ross startled her by entering the room, reaching out, and patting Suzanne on the upper arm, a gesture of comfort and one she'd never before received. Had that been because she was a duchess? Most people were intimidated by her title. Or had she appeared cold and unaffected, like marble?

"Thank you, Mrs. Ross."

The two of them looked at each other and nodded, a wordless communication that had nothing to do with Adam, who still stood there with a tray of biscuits, glancing from one to the other.

In the next moment, the landlady turned and left the sitting room. Adam closed the door behind her and retreated to the kitchen, placing the tray of biscuits in the middle of the circular table before going to a cupboard against the far wall. A minute later he returned with a bottle of wine that he uncorked and sat beside the biscuits.

"Mrs. Ross really does make excellent shortbread," he said.

"It's the middle of the afternoon," she said. "Surely tea would be better."

"I might not ever have you in my rooms again, Your Grace. I think it's a momentous occasion and needs to be celebrated."

Perhaps he was right. Besides, she'd followed rules all her life, all the ones laid down by her governesses, her father, George, plus all the ones that society decreed. On this one occasion, on this singular day, with a man who wasn't a majordomo after all, but a hero and a spy, she would defy every convention. It was better than her tears. Or her anger. She'd drink a glass of wine and have a piece of Scottish shortbread and try to hate him.

"Why now?" she asked. "Why tell me the truth now?"

He didn't meet her eyes, a clue she'd noticed when Adam didn't want to answer. He also blew out a breath from time to time, as if the effort to hold back his words was too much.

She'd evidently been studying him assiduously to notice those traits. Or the fact that he could sometimes hold his face just so, as if refusing to reveal any of his thoughts or emotions.

She was content to wait for an answer as she sipped her wine. She hadn't had any spirits since attending her father's dinner weeks ago. At least now she wasn't taking that hideous tonic. If she did something improvident it would be difficult to blame it on anything else other than her own wishes and wants.

He took a sip of his wine and placed the glass on the table before meeting her gaze.

"Because I thought it was possible that your father would tell you first."

That was a surprise.

"Why did you care? Is that the only reason for your honesty, Adam? Because you thought you'd be found out?"

He looked away and she had a feeling that he wasn't going to answer.

She sipped at her wine and waited.

Chapter Thirty-Four

"Being at Marsley House was my duty," he said.

"Do you always do your duty, Adam?"

"Yes."

He was determined to give her the truth, even if it was harsh or difficult to hear.

She nodded and that simple gesture had the effect of disturbing him greatly. He wanted to know her thoughts, but Suzanne was like an ornate puzzle box. Brute force would not open it. Instead you needed to use a deft touch and patience.

He topped off his glass then held it aloft.

"*Firinn*," he said. "To truth."

She finally raised her own glass and clinked it with his.

Her look was directing and unflinching. He could get lost in her eyes.

Marble Marsley. He'd never considered that the staff might have been talking about her grief, and he should have. The appellation wasn't an unkind one as much as one of understanding.

"To truth," she finally said.

They each took a sip of wine.

"Why do you think George was responsible for the massacre at Manipora?" she asked.

She had mastered the art of ensuring that her voice gave nothing away. She sounded perfectly calm, entirely reasonable. If he hadn't seen her fingers trembling, he would have thought her unmoved by the question.

"Because he was the most logical person. He met with the rebel leader twice. He knew Manipora well. He'd made foolish decisions in the past that had resulted in casualties. He might have thought that trying to end the siege was wise. Or he might have given out the information accidentally."

"Do you think him that much of an idiot?"

"Yes," he said, making no apologies for his bluntness.

She took another sip of her wine, then carefully placed the glass down on the table. She stared at the crystal pattern for a moment before asking, "Did you take these goblets from Marsley House?"

He sat back in his chair, his gaze not veering from her. He was beginning to understand Suzanne Hackney Whitcomb. She used words as bricks, not only to pummel her opponent, but to build a wall between her and anyone else. Insinuating that he'd stolen something was one way to anger him. Added to that was the hint that he couldn't have afforded his own crystal goblets. Or that he was too much a member of the hoi polloi to drink his wine from a glass.

"You know I didn't," he finally said.

She glanced at him and then away.

"Yes. No, I mean—" She looked at him again. "No, of course you wouldn't have. Forgive me."

"Anything."

She took a deep breath then released it. "It makes no sense, Adam. Let's say you're right and that George did have something to do with what happened at Manipora. Why would he make a record of it? Why would he write anything down? He had a secretary who was privy to everything George did. Why put a secret like that into words so Sankara could read it? Or anyone else, for that matter?"

"For the same reason that anyone writes about his triumphs and his tribulations. To be heard. To let someone else know what he did. To be praised or lauded, perhaps. To be judged in future years. I don't know, Suzanne, but then, I don't know why Whitcomb kept journals since he was twelve."

He took another sip of his wine. "Answer a question for me. Why demonstrate such loyalty to him now?"

Her faint smile surprised him, as did her next words. "George considered himself a great shot, but he was abysmal at hunting. He thought he was a marvelous equestrian, but he had a very poor seat. He believed himself quite well versed in the amatory arts, as he called it, but the truth was . . ." Her voice trailed off and her blush intensified. "I had thought that being in the army, commanding men, was the one skill he possessed in truth. I never heard different from anyone. I thought in this thing, alone, he might have been adept."

Standing, she went to one of the windows overlooking the garden, taking the same pose Adam had earlier.

The wind had calmed, preparing for nightfall. The glow cast by the setting sun made the plants appear touched by gold. The sky was indigo, that shade just before darkness.

The air was sweet here in this secluded garden in the middle of London. Instead of a hint of the odiferous Thames, there was the scent of grass and soon-to-go-dormant riotous plants. He always felt at peace looking at Mrs. Ross's garden.

"After Georgie died, I hated this time of day," she said. "It always reminded me of when I joined Georgie's nurse and we'd ready him for bed." She took a deep breath. "He fussed about it. I used to sit in his room and rock him until he fell asleep." She placed her fingertips on the window as if wanting to touch the plants in the garden before the shadows obscured them. "I can still feel the linen of his nightshirt against my fingers."

He understood, perhaps more than she knew.

"My roughest time was morning. Rebecca was an early riser and loved to greet the dawn. I hated mornings for a long time."

"How did the feeling go away?" she asked, turning.

"It's been replaced. I deliberately changed my life so that I wouldn't be reminded of things I couldn't alter. I came back to

England. I became a member of the Silent Service. I obtained new lodgings." He met her gaze. "You live in the same house. You see the same people you used to see when Georgie was alive. You visit his room. No wonder you're still in pain."

She looked taken aback, almost as if he'd insulted her.

"Do you think going to Georgie's nursery is a terrible thing for me to do?"

He thought about the best way to say the words. "I think that we hold on to pain as a way of keeping those we lost close. If we suffer it means we care more. That isn't really true, but it's what we feel."

She didn't say anything for a moment, merely studied him in that way of hers.

"So you think I should raze Marsley House," she said. "And dismiss all the staff."

He shook his head. "I think you should move from Marsley House," he said. "Take the staff with you, but find a new home."

She looked startled.

"Or, if you won't do that, get rid of Georgie's nursery. It serves him no purpose and it only keeps your heart bleeding. You don't need physical things around you to remind you of your son."

She blinked several times, and he was prepared for her tears. When they came, he reached for the handkerchief she'd left on the table and took it to her.

"You are forever doing things like that, Drummond."

"Yes, I know, Your Grace."

"I do dislike you intensely at times."

"The feeling has been mutual, Your Grace."

She surprised him by smiling through her tears. All he could do was answer her smile with one of his own.

"Do you hate me?" he asked.

She sighed. "No."

"Do you still want to?"

"No."

He stood close, too close for propriety, but when had that ever mattered to him, especially around her?

He smoothed his fingers over her cheek, feeling the warm softness of her skin. A blush followed his touch, almost as if he had the power to summon her embarrassment. Tenderness was not something he felt often, but Suzanne had always drawn emotion from him in ways that no other woman had, even Rebecca.

In the next moments it felt as if his heart slowed, each beat important, profound in a way he couldn't explain.

They were united in loss. With each other they'd shared both their greatest sorrows and their most touching recollections.

Grief, however strong, however powerful, was not their foundation. Life connected him to Suzanne. He knew her as he'd known no other person. He accepted her, expecting her to be nothing more than what she was, because that was enough.

He bent down, brushed a kiss against her forehead, ridiculing himself as he did so. He was acting like he'd never touched a woman or kissed one. She was not a saint and yet he didn't feel unlike a supplicant. The room was silent, only the breeze outside blowing the green fronds of one of Mrs. Ross's plants against the window. A gentle tap, then another, as if to recall him to himself.

He felt more himself than he had for years.

He grinned at her. "If the cat is away, the mice play."

She looked startled. He only gave her a second to think about what he said before he took her hand and led her into his bedroom.

Chapter Thirty-Five

*A*dam held her hand as they entered his bedroom. She could have easily pulled away. When he dropped her hand to close the door behind them, she could have turned and demanded that he let her out. At any moment she could have demurred, claiming propriety, or a fear of scandal, or a half dozen other excuses.

She didn't have to stand there mute and still.

The room was shadowed, the pieces of furniture gray squares or rectangles except for the bed with its pale spread.

He came to stand in front of her and unfastened the cameo at her neck. When he was done he handed it to her, almost as if it were a gesture of sorts. The brooch represented her status, her title, perhaps even her persona, the Duchess of Marsley, the role she'd held for the past six years.

By handing it to her it felt almost as if he was giving her a choice, a final option. She walked a few feet away to the table beside his bed and gently placed it there before returning once more to him.

If she were castigated for this moment then let it be for the truth of it. She had not been overpowered. Nor had she been convinced. She was in his bedroom of her own free will. It was her choice fueled by the emotions racing through her. This was passion. This was desire. This was tenderness. This heat that felt like hot oil flowing through her body was caused by the way he touched her and kissed her and looked at her.

She reached out and flattened her hands against his chest. Not to push him away, but simply to feel him. He placed his hands on her upper arms, drawing her closer. Time crawled, slowing almost to a stop. Each separate movement they made felt as if it had happened before, that they had practiced on endless occasions for just this moment. How else could he so perfectly unfasten all the buttons on her bodice, help her to remove her dress, her hoop, the corset, until she stood there in front of him attired in only her shift and stockings?

She stripped him of his shirt, pushing it off his shoulders, before unbuttoning the placket of his trousers. Never before had she thought to undress a man and yet her fingers worked with expert precision.

Pressing her palms against his skin she marveled at the feel of him. Everything was firm and warm. Her fingers stroked over his chest, through the hair and down to the open waistband of his trousers. The heels of her hands measured the shape of the muscles of his stomach.

"Suzanne."

She even liked his voice, low and holding the first hint of urgency.

The rhythm of her breathing increased as if to keep pace.

She had never felt like this before, growing heated with a heavy feeling deep in the core of her, as if her body knew that something wonderful, different, and amazing was about to happen. If they stopped right now, if she donned all her clothes and escaped from this lovely home, she would still not forget this day or the promise of this night. Or the sheer joy of this moment standing before him exposed and vulnerable yet not feeling either.

She had the curious notion that she was supposed to be here. In this exact spot with her hands exploring the body of a man who'd touched her heart. It was right and fitting that she offered her body to him not in sacrifice, but in wonder.

He toed off his shoes and then his trousers. In seconds, the rest of his clothing was gone and he stood before her, naked in the gray shadows. What a pity there wasn't sunlight to see him.

He lifted the hem of her shift. She stood silently as he pulled the garment up and off. He surprised her by kneeling, helping her remove her shoes and then rolling down her stockings one by one.

A voice that sounded too much like her governess made its way to the forefront of her mind. *You should be embarrassed. Or ashamed. Or certainly you should be feeling fear. What would the world say to see you here, Suzanne Hackney Whitcomb?*

The world would be scandalized. No doubt everyone she knew would be horrified. She would certainly be pilloried. Why should she listen to anyone? She was strong enough and brave enough to choose her own path, even if the world decried it. And the path she chose at the moment was to be with Adam, the one man who could break her heart, spur her to rage, and then drive her to passion.

He stood, dropping her stockings on the same chair where the rest of her clothing lay.

Wordlessly, he put his hands on her waist and gently pulled her forward until her breasts grazed his chest, her nipples sensitive against the soft hair there, the rigid part of him insistent and startlingly impressive against her.

"I want to light a lamp to see you," he said, mirroring her earlier thought. "Or maybe study you by firelight. I knew you would be as beautiful as you are."

She was filled with so much happiness, almost as if she were a sparkling wine. She wound her arms up and around his neck.

"How can you tell?" she asked, a smile in her voice.

"I can feel you," he said.

Both his hands palmed her breasts, his thumbs gently flicking her nipples. He bent his head and mouthed one, sucking gently. She could feel the sensation deep inside her.

Her hands cupped the back of his head as he lifted her, carrying her to his bed.

At another time she might've felt the chill in the air, but not now. His body warmed her, covered her, and sheltered her. His hands stroked over her skin, memorizing the shape of her legs, the curve of her hips, the indentation of her waist. Then they were back at her breasts, measuring them, holding them for his lips. His fingers were teasing and tender, gentle and exploring. One hand went to cup her derriere, turning her slightly toward him. He inserted a leg between both of hers, his thigh pressing up against her. She responded by undulating against him, wanting the touch.

His fingers were suddenly there, stroking through the moisture. He made a sound in the back of his throat. A hungry growl that echoed her own sudden ferocious need.

The serenity she'd felt earlier was abruptly gone, replaced by her body's dictates. Sliding out from under him she rose up, demanding in a way she had never been. She wanted to feel him. Her abdomen rode against his hip, slid down to his upper thigh and over the rigid tumescence jutting out like a sword.

A friendly sword, one that responded to her hand. She had never touched a man there, never felt curiosity or compulsion. Never wanted to make him groan as Adam did when her fingers slid over that intriguing shaft.

When had she become so adventurous? When had this act become so imbued with joy?

She didn't have time to wonder because she was suddenly tumbled onto her back.

Chapter Thirty-Six

*A*dam entered her slowly, conscious of the fact that it had been a while for her, as well as for him.

He didn't want completion as much as he wanted to indulge in the act of love with Suzanne. He wanted to feel her around him and to bring her pleasure. Above all, he wanted to ensure that she would remember this, remember them, of all the memories she held in her heart.

His movements were slow, deliberate, elongating the seconds as he gently pulled out of her.

He propped himself up on his arms, brushed light kisses across her mouth until her hands reached out, locked at the back of his head, and pulled him down for a deeper kiss.

If he was mutely counseling himself to slow the moments, she was doing the exact opposite. Her heart beat so rapidly it was like a frightened bird's.

His lips traced a path between her breasts and to each nipple in turn. Her hands slid to his neck and then to his shoulders, her nails gripping him, commanding without words.

He smiled as he sucked on a nipple. A moment later he kissed his way down to her abdomen. Her indrawn breath gave him a clue that she'd never been touched like this before.

He'd learned some things in India and he was all for using his education.

Sitting in front of her, he pulled her up to her knees and then moved her so that she sat on his lap. Her eyes were wide, her mouth curved.

"Adam?"

"You're not a duchess here. Not in my bed."

She only shook her head. He wished he had lit the lamp to see her.

He sat cross-legged, placed each of her legs on either side of his waist and then lifted her derriere into position. Her eyes widened even further as he entered her again.

Passion could be fun and experimental, engrossing and stirring. Passion could make you feel as if you were turned inside out, like you had never truly lived until that moment of bliss. He had the feeling that Suzanne had never felt that, never been powerless and adrift in wonder.

He bent his head and bit at her neck where it joined her shoulder. She gasped.

"Drummond."

"How very duchess-like you sound," he said. "If I were truly your servant I would be quivering in my boots."

"If you were truly my servant I would dismiss you right now."

"Would you?"

He moved one of his hands from her bottom to her breast, his thumb flicking an erect nipple, then lifting it for his mouth. He paid attention to that one nipple, and when he raised his eyes to her, Suzanne's head was back, her eyes were closed, and she was biting her lip.

"I am so very sorry, Your Grace. I will never do it again."

Her eyes flew open. "Now that's a pity, Drummond."

"I wouldn't want to be dismissed."

"I shall take your employment under advisement," she said, her voice trembling slightly. "I may reconsider, but only if you promise to be very, very good. But it shall be on a probationary basis only."

"How can I possibly convince you of my rehabilitation?" he asked, returning both hands to her derriere, lifting her up a little and then letting her slide back down on him.

She was biting her lip again.

He reached out and with his thumb pulled her lip free. If anyone was going to bite her mouth, it was going to be him. He matched the action to the thought, and would have smiled at the sound she made, helpless and needy, had he not been caught up in the same sensation.

It felt as if they were in the middle of a vortex, some wild waterspout of feeling. He wanted to laugh and bring her pleasure right then and there. He wanted to end it yet elongate the moments. His breath was harsh and fast. His heart was beating like he was running a race, and perhaps he was.

He put his hands on her waist, placed his cheek against hers and forced himself to take several deep breaths.

It didn't work. He still wanted her. He still wanted to feel her shudder around him. He wanted to taste her and mouth her and teach her all those things he knew, but he hadn't counted on his own weakness and need.

"Adam."

When had his name become an aphrodisiac? Or was it her voice, soft and tremulous?

He lowered his mouth over hers.

"Suzanne," he said softly. Had anyone ever felt free enough to call her something different? A derivative of Suzanne or some sweet nickname?

He wanted to light the lamp again to see her. Was her face rosy? Did her eyes glitter with passion? Were the centers of them black and deep like an ocean whirlpool?

He lifted her up again and lowered her once more before placing one hand on the small of her back and the other behind him to give him leverage. He raised his hips.

"Oh, Adam."

"Am I doing something wrong again?"

This time she didn't answer him, only moaned.

He couldn't wait. He wanted her to come in his arms. He wanted to feel her gripping him.

Moving his hand, he trailed his fingers through her soft folds, down to where they joined. She gasped again and the sound spurred him on.

He wanted her. He didn't think he'd ever desired anything more than Suzanne finding pleasure in his arms. He lifted her up and when she opened her eyes and would've protested further, he merely kissed her silent.

"In a moment," he said, rolling her to her stomach and pulling her up to her knees.

He entered her quickly, so deep inside he almost came right at that moment. She gripped the sheets with both hands. She might have been unfamiliar with this position, but she acclimated herself in mere seconds, pushing back against him with her beautiful derriere.

He slid his hands up to her waist then to her breasts.

She pushed back against him again, impatient and autocratic once more.

"In a moment, duchess," he said, his voice sounding harsh.

"Now, Drummond."

The one thing bad about this position was that he couldn't kiss her, couldn't nibble on those full lips.

He pulled back until he was nearly out of her and then slid back in again, slowly. She pushed back against him as if encouraging him or demanding him to finish.

"In good time, duchess," he said.

He pulled at her nipples, then trapped each one between his fingers, palming her breasts.

Once more he withdrew. Suzanne arched her back.

She was perfect in every way, from her breasts, to her derriere, to her long legs, to the curve of her waist. He would not have changed one single thing about her. The fact that she was eager and impatient was just one more delight.

She leaned forward, bracing herself on her forearms, her cheek against the mattress. Each time he slid forward she moaned, a soft appeal that had the effect of making him even harder, even more desperate for completion. He moved his hands from her breasts to her hips, pulling her tighter against him even as he felt her begin to shudder.

Her body trapped him, cradled him, imprisoned him in a demanding grip. He was powerless to control himself. No words on earth, no will, nothing could have stopped him from joining her in that next moment. Bliss overcame him, nearly felled him, and for long minutes he was in the center of a maelstrom, awash in a storm of sensation.

When it was over, with aftershocks still thundering through his frame, he collapsed on the bed, holding her. His rational mind surfaced, told him to release her and move away. Instead, he wrapped his arms around Suzanne's waist, his lips against her neck, needing her as much now as he had a moment earlier.

Reason enough, perhaps, to feel the dagger points of warning.

Chapter Thirty-Seven

Suzanne lay awake, listening to the wind howling around Mrs. Ross's house. Nature had brought them a storm overnight. Perhaps she'd been aware of the thunder and the lightning in a vague way. Adam had interested her more.

The rain came down in a thunderous volley and then seemed to stop for a little while, a curiously calming rhythm.

Her arm was extended toward Adam, who was still asleep. Her hand was curled, her knuckles resting against his bare chest. For some reason, it was important to her that they touch and maintain a connection.

He'd loved her again in the predawn hours before the world woke. This had been a silent joining, one without a word spoken. Their dance had been perfectly choreographed from the beginning of time. A strong and muscular male paired with a curvy, soft female. The only sounds they'd made were those of pleasure. The only requests were done with a kiss or a tender touch.

They had probably scandalized Mrs. Ross. Had their driver waited outside all night? Was Michael sitting, even now, in the rain? Adam had left his rooms for a few minutes last night. Had it been to make arrangements?

How very irresponsible of her not to have thought of Michael before now. She was not like George in that regard. He'd thought anyone in his employ should endure any sort of ill treatment. The privilege of working for the Duke of Marsley was enough, in his mind, to make up for any discomfort.

Yet she'd acted as selfishly last night, hadn't she? She'd forgotten about anything but Adam.

If Michael had returned to Marsley House, had it been with a tale that he couldn't wait to share with the rest of the staff? Surely she should be more concerned about her reputation? How very odd that it didn't matter to her one whit. She just didn't care.

The wind howled at the window as if to chastise her.

What did she care about the opinions of others? They hadn't sat with her during the long, dark, endless nights. Not one of them had inquired as to her pain. None of them had even mentioned Georgie in all this time. As if the loss of her child was something unmentionable like her corset or shift.

She turned her head toward the window. Dawn had been overpowered by the storm, the rainbow of colors on the eastern sky muted by black clouds. Shadows lingered in this bedroom, draped Adam, and shielded both of them.

They would whisper about her behavior, that she wasn't acting the role of duchess but one of a strumpet. What did she care about her title? It had never brought her happiness or belonging or a true home. If Georgie had lived she would have tolerated George without a word spoken in protest. If her son hadn't perished, she would have endured her life, grateful for the gift of being a mother. Now?

She stared at the shadowed ceiling.

A thought was beginning to penetrate the haze of grief surrounding her for the past two years. Living didn't mean that she loved Georgie any less. In the back of sadness, pushing forward inexorably was another emotion: hope. It had no actual reason for being. It wasn't tied to anything tangible. It simply existed like the sunrise and the sunset, ephemeral and constant.

Georgie's death had taught her that her world, the world that was familiar and normal, would be forever different. Nothing would be the same. Yet her life needn't be over. She could still feel. Last night had proven that.

Adam's hand touched her cheek gently before he rose up and kissed her softly.

"Have you been awake long?"

"Only a few minutes," she said, rolling over to face him. She was naked beneath the sheet, but she didn't feel awkward or self-conscious. Instead, she felt free in ways she never had before. The Daring Duchess. She much preferred that to Marble Marsley.

His fingers pushed the hair behind her ear. She was going to have a terrible time brushing it later. She would have to borrow his brush because she hadn't left Marsley House with her reticule and didn't have a comb.

When she returned home, everyone would know what she'd been doing. She hadn't taken a great deal of care with her clothing last night. No doubt it was wrinkled, but the black silk didn't show much abuse. Perhaps she could get away with it.

"What excuse shall we give when we return to Marsley House?" she asked.

"Why must we return?"

Now that was an idea, one she hadn't considered. Perhaps she could run away completely from her role and that enormous house. Georgie had been the only bright light in an otherwise dull and dark existence.

She reached out, her fingers trailing over Adam's bristly cheek and then tracing the shape of his lips. What a truly handsome man he was. Her hero. Her man of mystery. What had he called it? Not the War Office, but something else. The Silent Service.

She placed her hand gently over the scar on his shoulder. "How did you get this?" she asked.

"I was shot."

"At Manipora," she said.

He nodded.

Horrified, she stared at that small mark. A few inches lower and it would have struck his heart. He would have died in India and she would never have known him.

She pressed both hands against his chest.

"Oh, Adam," she said, unable to tell him what she felt. She was both terrified and grateful. He must take greater care. He could still be injured.

What would she do without him?

The question shocked her. He wasn't her majordomo. He wasn't her servant. He owed her no loyalty or devotion. After today she would probably never see him again.

"Sankara," she said, the name suddenly occurring to her.

"The duke's secretary?"

She nodded. "He came home from India with George. I sometimes think Sankara was George's only friend. If anyone would know where that journal is, it's Sankara."

"He left after your husband died, didn't he?"

"I was all for him staying on, but I think he was lost without George."

He leaned over to kiss her again.

"Fair enough," he said, several delightful moments later. "I'll send word to him."

She shook her head. "Sankara won't come. He's a man of great pride, Adam."

"Then I'll go see him."

She curved her palm against his cheek. "Not without me. I absolutely insist upon it."

"Are you back to being a duchess, Your Grace?"

"I am, Drummond, and I also insist that you kiss me again. Consider it a command."

"Very well, but only because I always do my duty."

And much more than that.

Chapter Thirty-Eight

❧

𝒜 few hours later they dressed. He was more fortunate than Suzanne. What wardrobe he kept at his lodgings was assiduously cared for by Mrs. Ross. He had a snowy-white recently laundered and ironed shirt, and trousers to wear. He considered suggesting that Mrs. Ross might be willing to put an iron to Suzanne's wrinkled dress, then immediately thought better of the idea.

Like it or not, his landlady was protective of him. You might even say that she was possessive to a certain degree. He had not, up until now, done anything to dissuade her. It had been pleasant to have someone fuss over him.

However, now it might prove to be a problem.

He shaved and finished dressing, then entered the kitchen to find the windows misted over. The day was a wet one, the view of the sky promising even more rain. After having lived in India for so many years, he liked the smell of an English rainy day. Something in the air tingled his nose and made his lungs want to expand even farther. Rain cleansed and wiped the dust off nature.

"However do you make tea?" Suzanne asked.

He turned from his examination of the garden to see her standing there barefoot in her wrinkled black dress.

He smiled and wondered how long it had been since amusement had cut through his thoughts and lightened his heart.

"Is the duchess about to be a serving girl?" he asked.

She sent him a look over her shoulder. "I've been known to do some extraordinary things from time to time," she said, contemplating the small stove set into the room's fireplace with a frown.

"Normally, Mrs. Ross brings me tea."

She sent him another look. "I don't think that's a good idea, Drummond."

"Neither do I, Your Grace."

They smiled at each other in perfect accord.

He hadn't been able to get the sight of her out of his mind. He'd always remember her in his bed, the down pillows behind her, her rosy and flushed skin against the backdrop of his sheets. The covers had been rumpled, the counterpane fanned to the bottom of the bed.

He walked to the table, grabbed the neck of the wine bottle and held it aloft.

"'A jug of wine, a loaf of bread, and thou beside me singing in the wilderness.'"

"Are you quoting, Drummond?"

"Indeed I am," he said. "I, too, have been known to do some extraordinary things from time to time. It's from the *Rubáiyát of Omar Khayyám*. A Persian poet."

"Must I sing?" she asked with a smile. "And where is this loaf of bread you claim? I'm starving."

"Regretfully, I don't have any bread, either."

"Only wine," she said. "I'll get silly at breakfast."

"Something I should very much like to encourage," he said. "I'll get silly along with you."

She tilted her head slightly, regarding him in the same manner he used to inspect the footmen.

"I cannot think of anyone else with whom I'd rather be silly, Drummond."

"Nor I, Your Grace."

She walked to him, took the bottle, and startled him by uncorking it and taking a swig. Then she stood on tiptoe and kissed him.

Kissing Suzanne's wine-flavored lips was a treat, one he duplicated often in the next few minutes.

He was about to suggest that they adjourn to the bedroom once again. Or, if she preferred, he could easily throw down a blanket on the floor and they could make love in view of the rain-tossed garden. The only problem was that Mrs. Ross was almost as protective of her plants as she was of him. He wouldn't be surprised to see her peering in the window with her umbrella in one hand and her flower basket in another.

"Where is our driver?" Suzanne asked, banishing his thought of making love for the whole of the morning.

"I sent Michael back to Marsley House last night."

She nodded, as if she'd expected that information.

"And you asked him to come back this morning, didn't you?"

It was his turn to nod.

"We are so very scandalous, Drummond."

"No, we aren't, Your Grace. You were visited by a violent headache. Mrs. Ross, who, incidentally, is an old friend of yours, settled you into a guest bedroom. I slept on a downstairs sofa."

"You're doing it again," she said. "You're protecting me when no one asked you to do so."

Her words rankled him. "A man should not have to be asked to protect the woman he . . ." His words trailed off. What the hell was he about to say?

They stared at each other.

"I apologize, Suzanne," he finally said. "It's a natural response to want to care for someone."

She still didn't say anything, and it was probably the first time in his life when silence was acutely disturbing. Should he tell her that he hadn't known the words he was about to utter until he heard them? That made him sound like a simpleton, didn't it? Unfortunately, it was the truth.

"I'll go and check if Michael is here," he said.

Anything but stand there and try to figure out what, exactly, he was feeling. He didn't have any problems analyzing obscure patterns, deciphering codes, or understanding the people he'd been assigned to watch. But emotions? That was entirely different and out of his range of expertise. Could anyone claim to be an expert? God knew he couldn't, especially now.

Michael was in the carriage in front of the house. Adam spoke with him for a few minutes.

"Begging your pardon, Mr. Drummond, but is Her Grace all right?"

"She's fine," he said. "Her headache seems much better this morning."

Michael nodded, evidently satisfied.

An hour later he and Suzanne managed to exit the house without encountering Mrs. Ross. No doubt she was watching them from one of her many windows. He didn't turn and look.

Mrs. Ross had, up until now, showed a remarkable lack of curiosity as to his movements. He couldn't help but wonder if she was part of the growing network of War Office operatives. He tried to remember how he'd first learned of her all those years ago, but he couldn't recall. For some reason, however, he thought she'd been recommended to him by someone at the War Office.

If that was true, it made him uncomfortable. The woman's caring and concern could mask an assignment—to keep an eye on him.

When had he become so watchful and questioning of everyone around him? Since he learned that Roger had put another operative at Marsley House. Since he'd started examining every single one of Roger's motivations.

Reaching out, he placed his hand on the small of Suzanne's back, walking with her to the carriage. Once he'd given Michael their destination, they arranged themselves inside the vehicle.

He had an idea and it wasn't sitting well with him. Instead of Hackney supporting Roger in his ambitious run for Parliament, maybe their relationship was more complex.

Was Roger working on Hackney's behalf? Was this whole assignment merely to hide the fact that Hackney had something to do with Manipora? After all, Hackney had been in India at the time.

In return for Roger's protecting Hackney—and in gratitude—Hackney would be Roger's financial backer during his run for Parliament.

Another thing that had been bothering him ever since that first meeting with Roger—how had the man come by his knowledge of the journal? He'd mentioned that someone—an informant—had been close to the duke. Was it his former secretary?

Adam's suspicions of Hackney, coupled with Suzanne's vehement denials of the duke's treason, were making him seriously question his conclusions, something he'd never before done.

"What's wrong, Adam?"

He glanced at Suzanne. Her eyes were filled with worry. Not grief. Not pain. Only worry, but he wanted to see her as she was this morning with a grin on her face and amusement in her eyes. She deserved to be happy.

He was determined to give that to her.

"Nothing," he said, smiling at her.

He wouldn't say anything to her yet. Not until his ideas were more fully formed.

Chapter Thirty-Nine

*Sankara Bora lived in a detached house in a fashionable part of London, exactly opposite from where Adam had thought he would live. Evidently, being the secretary to the Duke of Marsley had been a profitable venture.

"Sankara married after George died," Suzanne said, almost as if she'd heard his thoughts. "She is the daughter of a prince, I'm told."

There had been stranger pairings. That of a War Office operative and a duchess, for example.

The double bay windows looked like eyes staring at them. The black wrought iron fence contained two green squares intersected by a pathway leading to a red painted front door. He had the impression, as they walked up to the house, that they were being watched. It could just be that his senses were on high alert and he was seeing enemies where there were none. After the events of the past weeks, he could be excused for eyeing the world around him somewhat skeptically.

He used the brass knocker in the shape of a lotus blossom and waited.

"I don't have my reticule," Suzanne said. "Or my calling cards."

He wasn't familiar with the niceties of society, so he couldn't offer any suggestions. Surely you could call on someone without announcing yourself? Whether or not it was proper, it was what they were going to have to do.

The door was opened by a young maid in a black uniform with a spotless white apron. He shouldn't have been surprised by the fact that she was Indian. No doubt the rest of Sankara's staff was of his nationality. In the same fashion, English servants had been highly desired by English families in India.

"I should very much like to see Mr. Bora, if he's available," Suzanne said, before he could speak. "If you would, please, tell him that the Duchess of Marsley is calling."

The young girl's eyes widened, she hurriedly curtsied, and she stepped aside for them to enter the house.

Being with a duchess could be helpful.

They were led into a formal parlor, one that could rival Marsley House for the richness of its decor. The room was crowded with furniture, all of it overstuffed, fringed, and dark brown in color. Even the draperies hanging at the bay window were brown. Adam immediately felt as if he was entombed in a trench. Even the air smelled dusty, but that was no doubt from the collection of stuffed birds in their glass domes. Six ferns hung in front of the window, further darkening the space.

He preferred the congestion of the London streets to this room.

After Suzanne sat at the end of one of the uncomfortable-looking sofas he took up a position in one of the wing chairs opposite. Neither he nor Suzanne said a word. Even conversation was choked to death in this parlor.

Thankfully, they didn't have long to wait until the duke's secretary made his appearance.

Sankara Bora was a tall, stick figure of a man, with an elongated neck and a prominent Adam's apple. His hawk-like nose looked as if it had been stretched to match the length of his face. His large mouth, now smiling, was his only softening feature. Even his brown eyes were hard, like clods of earth in a drought.

"Sankara," Suzanne said, smiling. "Thank you for seeing us."

"On the contrary, Your Grace. Thank you for coming to see me. I have few visitors these days and none who bring me memories of happier times."

"I would like you to meet a friend of mine. Adam is from the War Office, and he has some questions about George."

Her words surprised him, but they shouldn't have. She wouldn't have continued with his masquerade, although he wasn't quite ready to give it up. They needed Sankara, however, and perhaps the best way to approach him was with directness and honesty.

The two men sat in the matching wing chairs opposite Suzanne.

"You are the majordomo at Marsley House," Sankara finally said. "Or you have pretended to be."

Again, Adam shouldn't have been surprised, but he was.

"You have friends on the staff," he said.

Sankara nodded. "I bring Mrs. Thigpen some spices for her cook from time to time as well."

He couldn't remember having seen such a distinctive man before. When he said as much, Sankara smiled once more.

"I have found that it is better to be unnoticed than it is to be singled out."

The secretary struck him as the type of man who would avoid a direct answer and use words as a wall. Therefore, Adam used a frontal attack.

"I was the majordomo," he said. "I was placed there by people who believed that the Duke of Marsley acted contrary to England's interests when he was in India. Do you have any knowledge of that?"

"You have come here to prove that the duke has done such a thing?" Sankara asked, looking at Suzanne.

"On the contrary," she said. "I've come to have you help me prove George was not a traitor."

They were silenced by the arrival of a maid carrying a heavily laden tray. Adam wanted answers, not tea, but he buried his impatience after Suzanne's quick look. Refusing Sankara's offer of refreshments would be an insult.

There were more rules on how to treat people socially than all the regulations in the army.

After Suzanne had been served, he accepted the cup of tea as

well as two sugary biscuits. They would have to suffice for breakfast and maybe lunch if he couldn't speed this meeting along.

For a few minutes, Suzanne and Sankara discussed matters of
mutual interest: the cook's new curry recipe, Mrs. Thigpen's interest in the stable master at Fairhaven, the contents of the kitchen
garden. Adam ate another two biscuits, drank the tea that smelled
and tasted of citrus and cinnamon, and listened to them talk.

Finally, during a lull in their conversation, he turned to the
former secretary. "I believe that the duke gave information to the
rebels about Manipora," he said. If he didn't get to the heart of the
matter, they would be here all day, being polite and oh, so proper.

"Who has given you this information?" Sankara asked.

He was violating all sorts of rules and had, ever since yesterday. But seeing Hackney in Roger's office had also alerted him
that he might have gotten everything wrong.

"An undersecretary at the War Office," he said. "His name is
Roger Mount. He says that the Duke was a traitor and the information is in a journal that the duke kept."

Sankara didn't say anything for a long moment. "You have
looked for this journal?"

Adam nodded. He decided to tell the other man the truth. "I'm
not the only one," he said. "I believe there's another operative
at Marsley House, someone who injured the duchess the other
night."

He sent a quick glance to Suzanne, hoping she understood why
he hadn't mentioned his suspicions to her earlier.

She gave him a look that made him certain they were going to
discuss this omission later.

"I have seen his journals," Sankara said. "Before the duke's
death, he required me to write in them." He gave Suzanne an
apologetic look. "Forgive me, Your Grace, for speaking of such
personal things, but the duke was not well."

"In what way?" Suzanne asked, sounding surprised. "He never
mentioned his ill health to me, Sankara."

"This I can understand," the secretary said. "His Grace was a proud man, but his vision was not what it had been. He was finding it difficult to read."

Adam exchanged a glance with Sankara. If the duke had been as much of a lecher as he'd written about for years, it was entirely possible he had been suffering from the end stages of syphilis. Adam knew the signs only because some men in his regiment had been unwise in their choice of partners.

"An *aadmi* came to see the duke not long before his death."

"I don't know what that means, Sankara," Suzanne said.

"A man," Adam translated.

"You speak Hindi?" Sankara asked.

He nodded. "I lived in India for a number of years. It's a fascinating country."

"That it is. Almost as intriguing as your England. And Scotland, if I do not mistake your accent."

Adam inclined his head.

"You say a man," Adam said. "Who was he?"

"A soldier. One from a native regiment that reported to His Grace."

A Sepoy, in other words. Nearly eighty percent of the Sepoys had participated in the rebellion of 1857. Those who hadn't had proved invaluable to understanding what had started the open resistance to British rule.

Had the one who'd visited the duke also come bearing information?

Sankara was a man comfortable with formalities. Being direct with him hadn't helped. Adam had a feeling they would continue to circle the issue until the man felt more at ease. Either that, or he needed something to cut through to Sankara, some knowledge that would jolt the man. It was entirely possible that the secretary had been privy to the duke's secrets. Whether he would reveal any of them was the question.

"I lost my wife at Manipora," Adam said. It was a story he didn't often tell, yet here he was divulging it again.

The secretary looked at him, his eyes intent.

"You have my deepest condolences, Mr. Drummond. Is it vengeance you seek?"

"In a sense," Adam said, giving the other man the truth. "I want the person who betrayed us punished."

"Vengeance does not restore our loved ones to us, however."

"No, it doesn't. But perhaps it allows those of us left behind a little peace, knowing that justice has been served."

Sankara contemplated the contents of his teacup. Adam bit back his irritation.

"I can understand why you would want to protect his memory, Sankara," Suzanne said. "Especially if he was guilty of such a terrible deed. But if he was not, if he is innocent, will you help me prove that?"

"Silence is a shroud we should wrap around our heroes," Sankara said.

Adam could feel his temper ratchet up a few notches. Hero? What the hell had the Duke of Marsley ever done to deserve that label?

"Not if it conceals the truth," Suzanne said. "What is the truth, Sankara?"

He lifted his eyes and exchanged a glance with Suzanne. "You do not know what you are asking me, Your Grace. I was the duke's faithful servant. I was his confidant, if you wish."

"I don't care about his women, Sankara. If you think to keep that knowledge from me, then you're too late. I know and I've always known."

"And I don't care about his personal life," Adam said. "All I care about is whether he betrayed us. Did he?"

He and Sankara exchanged a long look.

"If I give you proof of his innocence, will you use it to ensure His Grace isn't portrayed as a traitor?"

"If it's really proof," Adam said.

The secretary abruptly stood and left the room. He and Suzanne glanced at each other. What proof was Sankara going to bring them?

Chapter Forty

"Do you think he's coming back?" Suzanne asked.

She hoped Sankara was, for Adam's sake. He looked as if he wanted to pummel the absent secretary.

She couldn't blame him. Were she Adam, she'd probably feel the same way. If the person who was responsible for the bridge's collapse was before her now, she doubted if she would be understanding. Instead, she'd want some kind of justice for Georgie.

The problem was that she honestly didn't believe George had been a traitor. From what he said, nothing else in his life had meant as much to him as his position in the army. He loved his medals and being able to inspect the troops. He loved being thought of as a general. She assumed it was because he hadn't done anything to be the Duke of Marsley. Being awarded a position of leadership had required that he convince others he was worthy of the honor.

It was the one thing he'd done on his own.

Granted, he might have been as inept at command as he had been other things. But a traitor? He was related, albeit by some distance, to the Queen. The relationship mattered to him and she couldn't see him betraying the crown.

However, Sankara's reluctance bothered her.

Who decreed that nothing bad should ever be said about the dead? Was it just one of those rules in society that everyone agreed to obey? The minute you died a halo surrounded you or, as Sankara said, a shroud of silence.

She would hate if George's honor was tainted and his reputation suffered, but if he was guilty of what Adam believed, then it would be the price he needed to pay for his treason even posthumously.

Standing, she smoothed down her skirt. She'd worn her at-home hoop only the day before, and the dress was one of her favorites with lace on the shoulders and down the bodice. Still, she was in no condition to be calling on anyone.

She'd worked diligently on her hair using Adam's military brushes, but she'd been missing a few of her pins and the style was more casual than she normally wore.

Nor was she going to think about the fact that her lips still looked swollen and there was a pink spot on her chin—a mark from Adam's night beard.

What had Sankara thought of her appearance? The secretary had always been a proper individual and it was quite obvious that she hadn't been all that proper recently. Surely she should be feeling more ashamed of her behavior? At the very least she should be chastising herself.

How very odd that she wasn't.

In fact, and it was a confession that she didn't feel comfortable saying aloud, she didn't want to return to Marsley House all that much. The house had become a prison of sorts. While she was within it, she was expected to act in a certain way, to be a certain person. She couldn't be the Suzanne of her youth, but must always be the Duchess of Marsley.

"I never wanted to be a duchess," she said, moving to the window.

The room was quite oppressive and all these ferns in front of the glass blocked the view.

She hadn't meant to say that, but now that she had, she turned and faced Adam.

"My father was all for having a title in the family. What was a great deal of wealth, after all, if you couldn't buy your way into the peerage?"

He didn't say anything, but his look wasn't condemnatory. Instead, she saw warmth in his eyes, the same look he'd had this morning in his bed. She smiled at him, suddenly absurdly happy despite the seriousness of their errand.

"The Whitcombs were on the edge of poverty. They had an ancient family name. They had enormous credit, which they used to live on. By the time George came around, the credit was used up and the money was gone. So my father bought me a duke and George got a fortune in return."

Adam still hadn't said anything.

"It's the way of the world, I was told. The law of supply and demand. There aren't that many dukes, all in all. They cost a pretty penny. I don't know how much my father paid George, but it was evidently enough."

"Do you think it was worth it for him?"

"For my father or for George?" she asked.

"Either or both," he said, smiling.

"I don't think George cared all that much. I think he was content enough to have his second cousin assume the title at his death. When Georgie came along, everything changed. He was devoted to Georgie. As for my father, his investment hasn't ended. George might be dead, but he still has a duchess for a daughter. I'm a commodity he trots out whenever he can. I think he was annoyed the first year of my mourning because he couldn't present me at his dinner parties and gatherings. It would've shocked society. But it's been two years now and he's all for getting me out of black and parading me around." She shook her head.

"What if you had fallen in love?" Adam asked. "Would he have allowed you to marry the man of your choice?"

"Only if the union could benefit him in some way." She turned back to the window, fingering one of the fern leaves. "My father is desperate to be accepted," she said. "I never realized that when I was a child. Or even when I married George. It was only in the last few years that I've become aware of it."

He didn't say anything in response. How tactful Adam could be at times.

"As for love, I don't think I'm that brave."

"Is love something you need courage for?"

She nodded. "I think that when you love someone, you also invite pain into your heart. You tell it to come in, but sit in the back, because it isn't needed right now. Then one day, maybe sooner, maybe later, you summon it forward and you tell it, 'It's your turn.'"

"That doesn't always happen, Suzanne," he said.

"It has for the two of us."

He stood and walked to her, grabbing one of her hands and holding it between his.

"That doesn't mean it would happen again."

"What about you, Adam? Are you ready to marry? To fall in love again?"

He didn't get a chance to answer, because Sankara entered the room, hesitating at the doorway.

They turned to face him.

Suddenly, Suzanne felt a sense of dread that she had to keep swallowing down.

In his arms he cradled a large volume, one of the journals that George had used to chronicle his days. She'd never known why he had documented everything so assiduously, especially since some of his actions had not been especially laudable. She'd never read any of the journals, unwilling to be privy to his intimate thoughts, especially those dating from the years of their marriage. There were some things she didn't need—or want—to know.

"I have guarded the duke's secrets as if they were my own," Sankara said. "Some of which are detailed here. Even more important, however, there is proof of his innocence."

Adam strode toward him, but Sankara shook his head. Instead, he approached her and extended the journal with both hands.

"Your Grace, I know you to be an honorable woman. For the friendship and affection I held for His Grace, I beg you to read this with kindness. Do not fault him for his failings. He was, after all, no greater than the rest of us."

She didn't quite know what Sankara wanted from her, but she took the journal, and said, "He was my husband and Georgie's father. For that alone, he gets my loyalty, Sankara. I will leave it up to God to judge George."

He relinquished the book and stepped back, bowing slightly. "That is as much as I can expect, Your Grace."

"Why did you take it?" Adam asked.

"To protect George," Suzanne said. "Did he have another mistress, Sankara?"

The secretary bowed his head before meeting her eyes. "And another child, Your Grace."

Her stomach clenched. "What does that make? Eight?"

"I believe so, Your Grace."

She wrapped her arms around the oversized journal, nodded to Sankara, and looked at Adam.

He startled her by addressing Sankara again.

"Did you speak to anyone at the War Office, Sankara?"

Sankara didn't answer him, merely regarded Adam as if he'd suddenly sprouted a horn in the middle of his forehead.

"I was told that their informant was someone close to the duke, someone who was disturbed by learning of the duke's treachery."

"I know of no treachery, sir. His Grace was not a perfect man, but he was no traitor."

Adam didn't answer, only nodded once.

Soon enough, they said their thanks and their farewells, hopefully masking the fact that she was desperate to leave Sankara's home as quickly as possible. Once they were in the carriage, she clutched George's journal to her chest and sat back against the seat.

Reason enough, perhaps, to succumb to tears.

Chapter Forty-One

$Adam$ decided that he could go for a very long time without seeing Suzanne in tears again. At least this time, he had not caused them. Or perhaps he had, by insisting that the Duke of Marsley was guilty of treason.

He pulled the journal from her grasp, placed it on the seat, and moved to sit beside her. Putting his arm around her, he encouraged her to place her head on his shoulder. When she finally did, he held her as she wept, thinking that he would rather face a hundred rebelling Sepoys than her tears.

Her crying affected him in an odd way. A cavernous space opened up in his chest, almost as if he had been shot. Right at the moment it was preferable to this.

He wished he had the capacity to take the pain from her.

Some part of himself, probably more intuitive and less practical, understood that what he was feeling was something he hadn't expected. It was part of that moment at his lodgings when he'd been about to confess emotions he'd not yet admitted to himself.

His other hand went to her far shoulder, cocooning her in his embrace. He heard himself say things he'd rarely said, bits of Gaelic he'd once spoken. Words from his childhood when his mother was well and Mary existed only to bedevil him.

The vibration of the carriage wheels over the cobblestones was jarring and he wanted to spare Suzanne that, also. Did he want to wrap her in cotton bunting and protect her from the world?

Yes. The answer was so fast that he startled himself. Yes. He wanted to ensure that she was never injured, that no one ever said anything unkind to her. He wanted to take away her grief, even though that was something he couldn't do, any more than she could strip him of his. Instead, perhaps, they could ease each other, mitigate the anguish when it emerged from time to time, coax it to shrink again. Perhaps they could learn to live with the holes in their hearts and patch them up with other, better, sweeter memories.

Yes, he did want to smooth her way, make her laugh, and hear her indrawn breath of wonder like he had last night. He wanted to repeat that over and over again on as many days as God granted him.

That's what he'd started to say this morning.

"He isn't worth your tears," he said. "Or your loyalty."

She placed her hand on his jacket before sliding it against his shirt. He could feel the warmth of her fingers on his skin just as he had last night.

"I'm not crying for George," she said. A moment later she shook her head. "Oh, maybe I am. I'm crying for everything, Adam. Everything and nothing. Doesn't that make me sound foolish?"

"No," he said. "Just human."

Too soon they entered the gates of Marsley House. Adam withdrew his arms, moving to sit on the opposite seat. He blessed the fact that he'd grabbed two handkerchiefs this morning and passed one to Suzanne.

She blotted at her face, then shook her head.

"I must look a fright," she said, her voice low.

"If I didn't know better, I would think you were soliciting for compliments. Some women do not cry well. With some, tears only seem to increase their allure."

She smiled. "If I didn't know better, Drummond, I would think you were hinting at an increase in salary."

He was glad she'd brought it up.

"I need to retain my role of majordomo for a little while," he said. "At least until I find out who was in the library that night."

She nodded, then looked away at the sight of Marsley House growing nearer.

"Do you think it was your father?" he asked, a question he'd been considering for a while. Hackney had acted like a bully with Suzanne. Had he deliberately injured his daughter?

She glanced at him. "I don't know. How would he have gotten in?"

"Perhaps he had a contact within the staff."

She reached over and grabbed the journal, holding it close to her chest.

"I have the feeling that things are happening around me. Things I need to know."

"I have the same feeling," he said.

She didn't say anything. Nor did he speak further. What could he say, after all?

The door opened, but before she exited the carriage, Suzanne handed him the journal.

"Perhaps I'm a coward, Adam, but I don't want to read George's words. My life was almost idyllic back then. I concentrated on Georgie and that was all. Perhaps it wasn't fair to George, but I don't think he wanted it any other way."

He took the book from her. "If you're sure."

She nodded. "Keep what you learn about me to yourself, if you would. Or about any of George's women. I don't want to learn about his children, either. I do not wish them ill, Adam, but neither do I want to know that they're well and happy and have bright futures. I'm not that much of an angel."

"And if I discover that he is a traitor? Do you want to know that?"

She nodded.

He was prevented from saying anything else by the opening of the carriage door.

THEY HAD BEEN gone a day and a half with no explanation. The story Adam had concocted had been received by Olivia with no indication that she disbelieved him. After all, he was in the company of the Duchess of Marsley, whose reputation was heretofore sacrosanct. He trusted the housekeeper to disseminate the tale as well as she did most gossip. He would continue on with the premise that he had nothing to hide.

In other words, bluster worked when all else failed.

As for Suzanne, her new maid was so awed by working for a duchess that she'd never question her.

He tended to those details that couldn't wait due to his absence before returning to his office. He brought himself a pot of tea, to the surprise of one of the upstairs maids. He was not supposed to serve himself, but allow the staff to do for him. Under normal conditions he would've agreed. It was important to keep boundaries as they were and traditions as they always had been. His role as majordomo would end soon and he didn't want to upset the status quo.

However, these were not normal conditions. He didn't want to be alone with a maid. She might ask him questions about their absence from Marsley House. He didn't want to talk about Suzanne. First of all, she didn't deserve being an object of gossip. Second, he was afraid that what he felt for her might inadvertently be revealed.

Not that it mattered. Nothing could come of their relationship, such as it was.

He placed the journal on the surface of the desk, lit the lamp, poured himself a cup of tea, and settled in to read. Within a few minutes he began to understand why Sankara had been so reluctant to turn over the journal.

While it was true that the duke had a mistress and she had delivered him another child, somewhere along the way the man had become more and more intrigued with the woman under his own roof. Whole chapters of the journal were devoted to Suzanne. How she walked and spoke, the way she tended to Georgie, refusing to give over the whole of his care to his nurse. Everything about her seemed to fascinate the duke, and it was all too obvious what was happening. The Duke of Marsley was falling in love with his wife.

Four hours later he stopped and stared. There, in Sankara's distinctive flowing handwriting, was the information he'd been looking for all these months.

I was visited on April 13th by a soldier from India who recounted a story I found disheartening to believe. It seemed that there was a traitor in our midst, someone who traded with the Sepoy rebels.

He moved on to the second page, impatient with the duke's flowery explanation of how his visitor looked, what he wore, and the refreshments he'd been served. It wasn't until the fourth page that the secret was finally revealed.

When the name *Manipora* was mentioned he hesitated, forcing himself to read slowly. When he finished, he stared at the far wall for a few minutes, unwilling, or perhaps even unable, to believe what he had read.

His forearms rested on the desk, on either side of the ledger. His hands clenched into fists. He forced them to relax, splayed his fingers on the wood of the desk. If he concentrated on anything other than the words, he could allow himself to process what they truly meant.

Everything he'd believed had been a lie.

Rebecca's face came into his mind, the memory of the last time he'd seen her perfectly etched in his memory. Her eyes had been filled with fear as he'd tried to reassure her.

"They've given us safe passage," he'd said. "We'll be together soon enough."

"Are you certain?" she'd asked, her voice thin.

He'd hugged her then, taking a minute from his duties to comfort his wife. He'd seen her into the boat with the other women and children before heading for the barge carrying the rest of the garrison.

Standing, he circled the desk, unable to calm his sudden restlessness. His mind was racing, his thoughts first jumbled and then arranging themselves into an almost militaristic order.

Someone had betrayed them. That's why they'd been forced to negotiate with the rebel leader. The information of the compound and all their fortifications could only have come from someone who'd either lived at Manipora or had knowledge of the defenses.

That's why he'd always thought the Duke of Marsley culpable. The man had a command role. It was to him that the head of the entrenchment had pleaded for reinforcements. It was the duke who'd sent half their garrison to Lucknow to help stifle the rebellion there.

That was another mistake Adam had made—not seeing the intent behind the massacre. It hadn't been stupidity. Instead, it had been greed.

He'd never entertained the idea that the Duke of Marsley might be innocent. Instead, he'd been intent on finding proof that the man was guilty of treason. He'd had tunnel vision and that was never a good trait to possess in the War Office. He'd believed everything he'd been told like a gullible puppet. All along, his instincts had been shouting at him to pay attention, and it wasn't until he'd seen Edward Hackney in Roger's office that he'd listened.

He rang for Thomas and when the footman appeared, he apologized for the lateness of the hour.

"It's a sensitive errand I'm sending you on, Thomas, and I'd appreciate your tact."

The younger man nodded. "Of course, sir," he said, as proper as an English sergeant.

He gave the senior footman the envelope with instructions. "You must wait for an answer," he said.

Inside the envelope were two questions: *Did the Duke of Marsley confront the traitor with the truth? Did he tell him about the journal?*

Chapter Forty-Two

When Suzanne returned to her room, she bathed and then changed into another dress, black silk with ruffles on the bodice and sleeves. Now she quickly surveyed herself in the mirror, put on her mourning ring, and forced a smile to her face for Emily's sake.

"Are you sure you're feeling well, Your Grace?" Emily asked. "I was so sad to hear that you were ill. I should have been with you. Was it because of the accident, do you think?"

Suzanne met her maid's eyes in the mirror and held up another hairpin. Emily was exceedingly talented at doing her hair. The girl was skilled in a great many things, plus she was much more amenable than Ella.

"You mustn't worry, Emily," she said. "I'm feeling much better, thank you. Mrs. Ross is very kind."

No one was to know that Adam maintained lodgings outside of his role as majordomo. That would require too much explanation. Thankfully, Emily didn't continue to question her. Nor did anyone look at her, point their finger, and declare that she was now a fallen woman, one of those despicable creatures who engaged in sin.

Not that it felt like sin. She could still remember every bit of last night. She couldn't get over how wonderful making love was with Adam. Despite his many women, it was entirely possible that George had been bad at that skill, too. Or it could be that she and George hadn't suited at all, in any way.

She and Adam certainly did. She liked talking to him. Or discussing things, even arguing with him.

". . . told him that I'm certain you would be fine."

She met Emily's eyes in the mirror. Whatever had her maid been talking about? She could feel her face warm. She'd been thinking of other things.

"Oh, I am," she said. "I'm feeling absolutely wonderful," she added, so brightly that Emily's eyes widened in surprise.

Had she never sounded happy before? Evidently not. She'd not only been grieving, but in the past six months she'd been drugged, too. She must have been like a gray cloud moving through Marsley House, ready to rain on anyone who said a word to her.

"How long have you been working here, Emily?"

"Since I was fourteen, Your Grace. It's been six years now."

Six years. Six years and she couldn't remember seeing Emily in the past. In fact, she'd thought that Emily had been recently hired. What did that say about her?

"So you knew Georgie," she said.

"Oh, yes, Your Grace. Such a beautiful little boy and such a tragedy. We were so sad about him. And for you, too."

Another thing that she hadn't noticed. She'd been so immersed in her own anguish that she hadn't seen anything beyond her own pain.

Don't neglect today in your longing for yesterday. Had Adam said that?

She had given up today, hadn't she? She'd been determined to be a martyr to grief. Perhaps she'd been Marble Marsley after all. A creature who was cold and hard and entombed in her own emotional grave.

Could she be as strong as Adam? He'd remade his life. No, she didn't have his strength. Yet the minute she had that thought, something within her rebelled. She'd endured being married to

George. She'd never let anyone know how much she'd disliked her husband. She'd also recently stood up to her father.

Maybe she was stronger than she once believed herself to be. Maybe even strong enough to live in the present.

"There, Your Grace," Emily said.

The maid stepped back as Suzanne looked at herself in the mirror again. "You've given me a new hairstyle," she said.

"I thought it would favor your face, Your Grace. But I can change it back if you don't like it."

"I do like it," she said, surprised.

She looked a little different. Her hair was drawn up on both sides, pinned back and tucked up into an assortment of curls.

"I really do. How did you become so skilled?"

"I used to practice, Your Grace. With the other maids."

She could almost imagine those nightly events, a few girls in one room giggling and talking.

"I think your practicing paid off well. Thank you, Emily."

The young girl looked surprised again. Had she not thanked members of the staff before now? Surely that wasn't right. She had the horrible thought that that was exactly what she'd done. She couldn't blame her actions on Ella's potion. For five out of the six months she hadn't fought against taking it. Had she wanted to escape the grayness of her life? Or had she wanted to escape herself?

"Oh, Your Grace, I forgot." Emily rushed into the sitting room and returned a moment later holding an envelope. "This came for you yesterday by messenger."

She recognized the handwriting of one of her father's two secretaries and wanted to refuse to take the envelope. Emily didn't deserve her sudden irritation so she opened it, reading the invitation that was a barely masked summons to her father's next luncheon.

She abruptly stood, stuffing the invitation into her skirt pocket.

"Thank you, Emily," she said, leaving her bedroom for the sitting room. If she followed her usual routine, she would go down to dinner, taken in the family dining room. Her meal would be attended by a plethora of people, from the footman stationed behind her chair to the maids who would offer her a selection of courses.

Most of the time she motioned for all of them to leave. She remained at the foot of the long mahogany table in the room designed to show off the lineage of generations of Whitcombs. The walls were adorned with a portrait gallery of previous dukes, all of them looking prosperous and more than a little portly. They stared down at her from their framed perches in studied disapproval. A lone woman dining in stately and aloof elegance.

She wished she was free enough to seek Adam out. They would talk as they had today. Or last night cuddled together in bed. She'd told him secrets she'd never divulged to another soul and he had reassured her that she wasn't terrible for hating the life foisted upon her. Or that it was natural to think that she sometimes heard Georgie call her name.

So much had happened in the past four weeks that her head whirled when she thought of it. She had changed since that night on the roof. Perhaps she hadn't grown or altered her life until now because there had been no impetus to do so. All it had taken was a man of mystery. Someone who'd dared to question her actions, give her advice, and challenge her.

She'd taken him as her lover. *Her lover.* Even the words were scandalous.

Rather than worry Mrs. Thigpen and Grace, she went ahead and ate a quick dinner, but instead of dismissing the staff, she conversed with them. She learned that one of the girls had been born in Wales, another had a married sister due to make her an aunt any day, and one of the footmen had a talent for mimicry. Afterward, she thanked Grace for a lovely meal before finally going in search of Adam.

She couldn't go to his rooms. Marsley House was settling down for the night. Half of the staff was retiring to the third floor and would see her. Nor could she send a footman to him with a note.

Her only hope was that he would come to the library. If he didn't she'd simply brazen it out and go to him.

She hadn't wanted to read George's journal, but she needed to know the answer to the mystery. That was not, however, the only reason she wanted to see Adam. She liked being around him. She liked herself when she was with him. Besides, she missed him. Even a few hours without him made her want to seek him out, speak to him for a moment or two.

She loved him.

Love made her feel silly and foolish and youthful and filled with joy, all at the same time.

She needed to tell him. He would no doubt counter with reasons why they couldn't be together. He would say that she was the Duchess of Marsley, the chatelaine of one of the largest houses in London. She would just have to marshal her arguments, explain that she would gladly trade having a title for being with him.

He wasn't exactly her servant. She wasn't exactly his employer. Those were just roles they had to play for a little while. When it was over he would be Adam Drummond and she would be Suzanne Whitcomb.

Titles didn't matter one little bit. Hers certainly hadn't made her life easier. Nor had it bestowed on her great happiness.

They would be free to spend as much time together as they wanted. They could discuss anything they wished for as long as they wished without worry as to appearance or staff gossip. She could share her life with him and he could confide in her. They would laugh about silly things and counter the sadness that had enveloped both of them for so long.

She could hold him and tell him how sorry she was about Rebecca. She would tell him that her death wasn't his fault. He'd never said, but she knew he felt that way. People like Adam took on the responsibility that others sometimes shirked.

Adam, with his military background, had been pressed into a mold as rigid as the one used to form her. If they stepped outside of the person they had been reared and trained to be, would the world collapse? Would society take a deep breath and suddenly vanish? Would London crumble around them?

No one would notice. No one had noted the death of an innocent child and an unwise duke. The world had gone on as if nothing had happened, as if there hadn't been a rending in the fabric of her life. The world had barely noticed when hundreds of women and children had been killed in a senseless massacre.

Now she pressed her hand against the library door. The last time she'd entered this room she'd encountered someone who wished her harm. Perhaps it had been a stranger. Or even worse, it had been someone living at Marsley House.

Until now she'd never been all that brave. Or perhaps she'd never been in circumstances in which she needed courage. The double library doors loomed as a test.

Pushing open one of the doors, she stepped inside. The moonlit night was the only illumination as she made her way to the desk and lit the hanging lamp. The silence surrounding her should have been absolute, but it was accompanied by memories.

She could almost hear George pontificating on some subject, correcting a member of the staff guilty of an infraction, or commanding the servants as if they were a battalion. Georgie's laughter sounded faintly from those times when she'd brought him to see his father. George had always spared the time to hold his son, bounce him on one knee, and admire how fast Georgie was growing.

The faint light from the lamp illuminated only the surface of the desk. She glanced up to the third floor. Again, her courage was being tested. All her life she'd been protected, guarded, and cosseted. Even her grief had been sheltered.

Until Adam. Until she was forced to realize that her loss wasn't special or unique, that there were other people who had suffered in their lives, too.

She took one step up the curved iron staircase and then another, her hand clamped to the banister. At the second floor landing she hesitated. The shadows were deeper here, the darkness absolute. The faint light from the desk surrendered to the moonlight for dominance.

One more flight and she was on the third floor. She couldn't remember the last time she'd been here. If she recalled correctly, a small reading nook was at the end of this row of shelves. Beside the love seat was a table and lamp. She reached out with her right hand against the books, her breath shallow as she made her way even farther into the darkness.

When she lit the lamp, she blew out a breath filled with relief. Nothing greeted her but rows and rows of books. No, not books. Journals. George's journals that he'd kept since he was a child. She walked to the end of the row. Each one was marked with a notation, but it wasn't a date. She selected one of the journals at random and took it with her to the love seat.

Did she really want to read George's words? She never had before. Even this afternoon she'd given Adam the journal, unwilling to learn about George's children.

Courage again, that's what she needed.

Sitting, she opened the journal to the first page, beginning to read.

Chapter Forty-Three

"What are you doing here?" Adam asked, his head appearing as he climbed the circular iron stairs.

Suzanne looked up. A month ago she would have responded with a very cold and rather autocratic remark. *Who are you to question me, Drummond?* However, a great deal had happened since then, and Adam had been involved in most of it. He'd kissed her, held her while she cried, saved her life, and been her lover.

For that reason and even a greater one—that she wished to be a better person than she had been—she gave him the truth.

"I came looking for you," she said. "Then I dared myself to come up here. I don't like feeling afraid and I didn't want to feel that way every time I came into the library."

She was prepared for him to lecture her, but he didn't. Instead, he came to her side and sat down on the love seat beside her. Only then did she realize that he carried the journal Sankara had given them.

"We were both reading George's journals," she said, glancing down at the book on her lap. "I was reading about the time before he was sent to India. It was startling to see his handwriting."

Adam held her hand and squeezed it gently.

She opened the journal to the part that had almost made her cry.

"'I am hoping to be given a commission, one that will allow me to place the Whitcomb name in glory again. I have not done a good job of it to date and would have shamed my father and grandfather by my inaction. Yet I believe I am destined for greatness, a feeling that has been in my heart since my boyhood. As duke I will lead men to valor and be the epitome of all that is good and right and just about England.'"

She slowly closed the book and put it on the table.

"But he didn't, did he? I think he knew what a failure he was. I think he didn't want to come out and say the words, but I think he knew."

Adam only squeezed her hand again.

"Perhaps he was a traitor, after all," she said. "If he thought it might bring him glory or respect or fame, it's possible that he might have done something terrible for a good reason."

"He wasn't a traitor, Suzanne," he said.

She turned her head to look at him. "Did you find something?"

He nodded.

"What?"

He looked like he was debating with himself.

"Do you know who it was?" she asked.

He nodded.

If he thought she was content to remain in ignorance, he was badly mistaken.

"Who is it, Adam?"

"Roger," he said. "Roger Mount."

"Your friend at the War Office?"

"Hardly that," he said dryly. "Roger doesn't have any friends, just people he uses."

"And he's the traitor?"

He nodded.

"Why?"

"Why does anyone betray his country? Maybe money, for one. The rebel leader was the adopted son of a prince. He had a fortune at his disposal. Enough to pay any amount of money for information. Revenge? Roger was sent to Lucknow because he didn't get along with the commander at Manipora. He always thought rules and regulations applied to everyone else, but not him."

He handed her the journal. "I think you should read it."

She took the book but didn't open it. "I really don't want to read about George's women," she said. She tried to give him back the journal, but he wouldn't take it.

"That's not what he wrote. You need to read it, Suzanne."

She studied him for a moment. He didn't look away.

Biting back a sigh, she opened the book.

*F*ROM TIME TO time he glanced over at Suzanne. He knew what she was reading. Part of him wanted to spare her any hurt those pages might cause. Yet it wouldn't have been right to hide the information from her.

He wanted to ask her forgiveness for a great many things, none of which she'd had any part in, but for which he'd judged her. She hadn't known that his sister had been taken advantage of by a young lord who'd only laughed at her excited announcement that she was going to have his child. Adam hadn't bothered to let the man know that Mary had died in childbirth and that his son had perished as well. At least the Duke of Marsley had cared for his bastards. Mary's lover hadn't been interested in anything beyond taking her innocence.

Nor did Suzanne know that the tenement in which he'd been born and reared was a slapdash of three-story buildings leaning against each other, owned by a peer who'd raised the rents every year with careless disregard for any of his tenants.

Whatever contempt he felt for the aristocracy, it was not fair to visit it upon Suzanne.

She turned the pages quickly, evidently more familiar with Sankara's formal handwriting than he had been.

He glanced toward the rows of journals. Something didn't look right. He knew these books well since he'd haunted the library in the past months.

"Did you mix up the journals?" he asked.

"No. Why?"

"The middle section is out of place," he said.

He went and stood in front of the bookcase in question, finger-ing the volumes that had been moved. He'd come to the library after Suzanne had been injured. The books weren't out of place then. Nor were they out of order two days ago.

"Someone was in the library last night," he said.

"How do you know?"

"Because this book," he said, pulling it out, "should be in that section." He pointed to the journals on the next shelf.

"It might've been one of the maids," she said.

"No. I think it was the same person who pushed you down the stairs." He glanced at her. "You should go back to your suite, Suzanne."

"Why?"

"Because I think someone is going to come to the library to-night to look for the journal."

She folded her arms and frowned at him, an expression he'd seen on Edward Hackney's face. He had a feeling he was about to encounter the same obstinacy in his daughter.

"I'm not moving, Adam. I should very much like to push him down the stairs myself and see how he likes it."

He bit back his smile. The situation wasn't amusing.

"I'm going to sit in the dark and wait for him, Suzanne. I assure you it will be exceedingly boring."

"I have nothing more pressing to do, Adam. I shall enjoy the experience."

From the look on her face, lips tight, eyes narrowed, it didn't seem that she was going to descend the stairs and leave the library.

"Then I'm going to extinguish the light," he said. "I don't want our visitor to know that we're here."

He went down the stairs, turning the key on the lamp before

making his way back up to the third floor. Once he sat beside her again he blew out the lamp on the table next to the love seat, plunging them into darkness.

"Do you really think someone is still looking for this journal?" she asked.

He turned to her. "If we're lying in wait for someone, it's important that we're quiet."

"Not until you tell me who you think it is."

Yes, she was most definitely stubborn.

"I haven't the slightest idea," he said. "Only that he was assigned here by Roger."

He sat in the darkness holding her hand. A month ago, no more than that, he'd been a different person. His world had narrowed to become his work and only that. When he thought about those things that mattered in his life there was a huge black spot where the smiling faces of loved ones used to be. His mother, Mary, Rebecca, and long lost friends. Whatever the reason, he'd been left alone and he'd adjusted in his way.

He hadn't expected Suzanne. Nor had he anticipated that she'd make him feel whole again.

Passion linked them, true. He desired her right at the moment. Something else, however, formed a bridge between them. Not mutual loss as much as trust, a growing friendship, and more. He knew that he could tell her almost anything and she would accept it. If she judged him it would be fairly. She was also loyal, somewhat to a fault in the case of the Duke of Marsley.

The fact was that their time together was coming to an end. Now that he had the journal, there was no need for him to remain at Marsley House. His assignment was over. He didn't even need to discover the identity of the second operative. The man would be recalled to the War Office soon enough, but Adam wanted the pleasure of punching the idiot in the nose first for hurting Suzanne.

Reaching over, he put his arm behind her back. She leaned against him, placing her head on his shoulder.

She would never be the Duchess of Marsley to him again. Instead, when he allowed himself to think of Suzanne, it would be with a surprising amount of regret. Not for what had happened between them, but for a future that would never be theirs.

Chapter Forty-Four

❧

The minutes ticked by uneventfully. About an hour later, from Adam's estimation, he heard a noise, a muffled click. He knew that sound. He'd made it himself, entering the library in the darkest hours of the night. He withdrew his arm from Suzanne, his body tensing.

He stood and walked halfway to the stairs, then pressed himself back against the bookcases. None of the lamps were lit, which made Adam think that the intruder was familiar with the library. No doubt he knew there was another lamp next to the love seat.

He could hear steps on the metal stairs.

A black shape appeared at the landing. Adam forced himself to wait. The shadow began walking toward the bookcase.

Suzanne gasped, the sound faint but enough to stop the man in his tracks.

So much for the element of surprise. Adam launched himself, only to encounter a softer form than he'd expected, one that felt pillowy.

"What the . . . ?"

He didn't have a chance to say anything further before he was bitten on the wrist. It was one thing to restrain a man, but he'd never encountered one who used his teeth as a weapon.

Suddenly, the light blazed in the corner. He stared at the person he'd pinned to the shelf.

Ella glared back at him. The hood of the black cloak she wore tumbled from her head, revealing hair frizzing about her face.

He stared at her uncomprehendingly for a moment before all the pieces of the puzzle fit into place.

He'd been right in thinking that Roger had placed an operative at Marsley House before him. He hadn't gone back far enough. Ella had been here four months before he arrived. Another mistake he'd made and one he wouldn't make again—not considering that Roger would use a woman. Female agents were new to the War Office.

"What are you doing here?" Suzanne said, standing and approaching them.

"She's Roger's other operative," he said. "And the person who threw you down the stairs."

"That was an accident," Ella said, spitting the words out.

"You failed," he said. "We found the journal."

She stopped struggling in his grip. "Then I haven't failed," she said. "The assignment was to find the journal. It didn't matter who accomplished it."

He would've thought the same thing a while ago, at least until he'd discovered the identity of the traitor.

"How did you get in?" Suzanne asked.

Ella didn't answer. If the look she sent Suzanne was any indication, Ella detested her former employer.

"I believe Ella is playing coy, Your Grace," he said, smiling at Suzanne. "If you would precede me down the stairs, and inform the footman on duty to summon the authorities, we'll rid ourselves of her."

"You can't do that," Ella said when Suzanne edged past them for the stairs. "You know I was working for the War Office."

"I know that you're guilty of burglary. Not to mention bodily harm."

She twisted in his grasp. "You can't do this, Drummond."

Her face was contorted with barely controlled rage. Perhaps in another circumstance he could have ignored her actions, knowing that she was a member of the Silent Service. But she'd harmed Suzanne and for that she needed to be held accountable. Let the War Office explain her actions. He wasn't going to shield her.

Ella tried to free herself again. It must have infuriated her that he could keep her pinned with his hands. Just in case, he kept himself carefully out of range of her teeth.

He held her wrists tight as they descended the steps. If she fell it would be because of her own behavior. She seemed to realize that, and didn't try to pull away from him.

"Roger isn't going to be happy," she said.

"Strangely enough, that isn't one of my concerns."

By the time he and Ella got to the front door, a crowd had gathered. Thomas had evidently not retired for the night, and as the head footman he'd summoned an additional man. Mrs. Thigpen was there, attired in a dressing gown with her hair done up in rags. The night maid stood beside her, eyes wide as she looked at him holding Ella. He didn't doubt that stories would fly around Marsley House by morning.

Suzanne stood apart from the rest, the duke's journal clutched to her chest.

He wanted to go to her. Instead, he spoke to Thomas, explaining that Ella had entered Marsley House in order to steal. She'd been here before, at least twice, he suspected, after she'd been dismissed. When the authorities arrived, she was to be surrendered to them.

Thomas nodded, looking as fierce as a young man could. "Yes, Mr. Drummond. I'll see that it's done."

He didn't have any doubt that Thomas would do exactly as he said. "I would take the precaution of tying her hands and perhaps her feet," he added.

Although Thomas looked surprised, he nodded. The footman glanced over at Mrs. Thigpen, who immediately sent the night maid after some sturdy rope.

"Roger will hear about this," Ella said.

He didn't bother telling her that Roger was going to face his own justice shortly.

"He's not a fancy majordomo," Ella said, addressing Thomas, then glancing at the housekeeper. "He's not a servant at all. He's a member of the Silent Service. A spy."

Mrs. Thigpen glanced at him, but instead of wearing an expression of shock on her face, she looked pleased. Almost satisfied, as if Ella had proven her right about something.

He walked to where Suzanne stood.

"Your Grace, thank you for your assistance this evening."

They had an audience of curious people who were not trying to hide their interest. Anything he said at this moment would be enhanced and speculated on by the entire staff, especially since Ella had divulged his identity. Tonight would be his last night at Marsley House.

He didn't want to leave Suzanne yet. Above all, he didn't want her to be standing there alone. She needed to be surrounded, not by servants, but by people who cared about her, who loved her. People who admired her for who she was, not the title she bore.

She nodded to him, a gesture that was definitely duchess-like.

"Thank you, Drummond. We wouldn't have discovered the identity of the burglar without your investigation."

He bowed slightly and left them. The sheer fact that he hadn't countered Ella's words was an admission. Perhaps they would ask for clarification from Suzanne. Or perhaps he would be confronted before he left tomorrow morning.

At least he had lodgings, even though he was certain that he was going to have to soothe Mrs. Ross's feathers when he returned. Suzanne's perfume would still be in his rooms. Her scent would be on his sheets.

He climbed the stairs slowly, entered the shadowed office he would leave tomorrow, and lit the lamp. He sat heavily, staring off into space, filled with a sudden and surprising feeling of hopelessness.

That wasn't like him.

He pushed the feeling away and concentrated on examining each of the ledgers that were his responsibility. He entered the rest of the expenses that had been furnished to him, made notes about the staff, and finalized the entries that would be sent to the solicitor. He wanted everything to be perfect for the next major-domo. He might have been playing a part, but he didn't want anyone to say that he had neglected the job.

A few hours later he put away the books for the last time and locked the drawer, putting the key on the top of the desk.

When someone knocked he stood and walked to the door, expecting it to be Thomas. Instead, Suzanne stood there, the journal clutched in her arms.

Chapter Forty-Five

Suzanne didn't say anything, only went to his desk and put the journal on it, opening the book to the pages revealing the traitor.

"You and I really should not be here alone," he said. "It was one thing in my lodgings, but here gossip spreads quickly."

"I don't care."

"Well, I do, for your sake. Don't be foolish, Suzanne."

She looked at him. "We have more important things to discuss, Adam, than whether the staff is talking about us."

He motioned her to the chair in front of his desk and closed the door. She sat, staring at the journal. She'd read it straight through.

Adam finally sat and faced her.

"You've been crying," he said.

"How do you know?" She'd examined herself in the mirror before leaving her sitting room.

"Your eyes look luminous when you've been crying."

She didn't admit to her tears, but he was right.

"I didn't love George, but I could have dealt well with him for the rest of my life. He was my husband, after all. But I think he was lonely, and for that I'm sorry I didn't feel more for him. I've known what it was like to be lonely surrounded by dozens of people. It's not an emotion I would wish on anyone." She looked down at the journal. "All he had to do was to give me a little notion of what he was feeling and everything could have changed. But he didn't."

"Some men can't," he said. "They're content to worship from afar. Or they're afraid that their affections will be rebuffed. I read a poet not too long ago and the last lines were, 'For of all sad words of tongue and pen, the saddest are these: it might have been!'"

"Do you ever wonder what your life would have been like if Rebecca had lived?"

"Not anymore. In the first year I did, but I think it was partly because I refused to believe that Manipora had really happened. Time gives you a finality as nothing else can."

He reached over and placed his hand on hers.

She cleared her throat before speaking. "What are you going to do about Roger? And don't tell me it's War Office business, please."

She'd been shocked at the words she'd read, but probably not as much as Adam.

There was no doubt, in my mind at least, that what my visitor said was the truth. It made perfect sense that Roger Mount might be the one who conspired with the rebels to overrun Manipora. He had been familiar with the rebel leader, having done business with him in the past. A sorrowful thing, but one that must be addressed.

She was certain he was about to speak when there was a knock on the door. She quickly stood.

He pointed toward his bedroom and she nodded, slipping into the room and pressing herself close to the door, listening.

"Mr. Bora didn't look surprised to see me, sir," Thomas said. "In fact, it was like he was expecting me."

"Did you get the answer?"

"He wrote it down right away, sir, and sealed it up."

Adam thanked Thomas. A moment later she heard the door close.

She peered into the room to see Adam tearing open an envelope. She opened the door fully and he turned to her, his face a mask.

"What is it, Adam?"

He handed her the envelope. There, in Sankara's swooping handwriting, were the words: *His Grace visited the War Office.*

Adam's face was expressionless, but there was a look in his eyes that she'd seen in her own mirror: disbelief mixed with a feeling of betrayal. The same look she'd worn when first learning that her husband was not interested in maintaining his marriage vows.

"You didn't want George to be right, did you?" she asked.

He smiled faintly. "No, I didn't."

She understood that feeling—when everything you'd based your life on crumbled into dust. Or when you realized that you'd been hopelessly ignorant until that moment.

"What does it mean, Adam?"

Hopefully he wouldn't treat her like George had, preferring to put his thoughts and feelings on paper instead of voicing them.

"Evidently, the duke visited Roger, no doubt to let him know what he'd learned."

She stared at him. "Why would he do something like that?"

Adam looked at her. In his eyes was an expression she'd seen before, something close to pity but warmer.

"Perhaps he thought that Roger would confess to his actions and that he'd be lauded for capturing a traitor. It's a bit naive, if not dangerous. Any man who was willing to sacrifice the people of Manipora wouldn't hesitate to silence your husband. The duke probably told Roger that he'd written it all down, thinking that would keep him safe."

She turned and walked, stiff-legged, back into Adam's bedroom.

He was very neat, no doubt a result of his army background. The coverlet on the narrow bed was squared. The sheets were pulled tight. Even the pillow was aligned just so on the mattress.

A bowl of potpourri smelling of sage sat next to two silver-backed brushes atop the dresser. The wardrobe was closed, but even from here she could smell the cedar shavings in the bottom. He was probably very organized there, too, his shirts and jackets in militaristic order.

She sat heavily, staring at the painting on the wall. She'd seen it before. It had hung in the hallway in the north wing once. Nothing was ever lost at Marsley House. They circulated furniture and artwork throughout the rooms. Up until this moment she hadn't known that some of the works found their way to the third floor. She was glad, though. Someone else should enjoy the depiction of rust-colored flowers against a brighter background.

All she had to do was keep looking at the porcelain vase in the painting and she would be able to keep her emotions together. That's all. A simple task, really.

"Suzanne?"

No, not now. She really couldn't answer any questions right now. That would shatter her. Speaking would ruin this false poise.

"Suzanne."

He was determined, wasn't he? The same persistence had no doubt made him a hero after Manipora. Yet he hadn't been able to save all those women and children. All those young, innocent lives. His determination hadn't meant anything then, had it? Was that why he'd pursued George with such insistence?

He came and picked her up as if she weighed no more than a feather, then sat again, with her on his lap. She'd never sat on anyone's lap in her entire life. At another time, it would have been a novel experience. Right at the moment she couldn't concentrate on anything but the refrain repeating in her mind.

She was so cold that it felt like January in this third-floor room. January without a fire going in the nearby grate. January and she was standing atop the roof again.

"The accident. The bridge. It wasn't an accident, was it? Is it because of what George knew?"

"I don't know." But the knowledge was there in the tone of his voice and the fact that the pity in his eyes had warmed to something else.

She felt like her insides were being crushed by a weight heavier than anything she'd ever known.

He pressed her cheek against his chest. His heart was beating loudly, proof that he was alive. She needed life at the moment, especially when she felt so cold and nearly dead.

Survival and stubbornness, that was Adam. He'd fought her and challenged her and now at this, another dark hour, he was with her, warming her, holding her when she felt like she was going to split into a thousand pieces.

"We may never know, Suzanne. I doubt it's something that Roger will admit to doing."

She nodded. "Would it be something he'd do to protect himself?"

For the longest time she didn't think he would answer her, but finally he did, the one word so soft and low and so horrible that she almost asked him to repeat it.

"Yes."

She closed her eyes and concentrated on breathing. It shouldn't matter if it had been an accident that had taken Georgie's life or an intentional act. The result was the same. Her darling son had died. But it did matter. When she said as much to Adam, he nodded.

"What are you going to do?" she asked.

"Confront him. We have the journal as proof and Sankara might be willing to give a sworn statement as well."

"Would that be enough?"

"Yes." This time the word was strong and assertive.

"I want to go with you."

"I don't think that would be a good idea, Suzanne."

"I'm the Duchess of Marsley," she said. "The title opens some doors, Adam. Even at the War Office."

"I'm certain that you're right, but I don't think it's going to matter in this case. Besides, it might be dangerous. He's not a man to underestimate."

"Please."

She couldn't remember the last time she'd begged someone for something. It might have been as a child. She'd learned that it was better to keep silent than to allow herself to appear vulnerable or needy. Now, however, she had no qualms about letting Adam see exactly how she felt.

"I want to see his face when you ask him about the bridge."

"Suzanne."

"I'll know," she said. She pressed her hand against his chest. "I'll know if he's lying."

He didn't say anything, but she wasn't foolish enough to think she'd won this battle. Adam was capable of simply leaving Marsley House without any notice and carrying out his mission without her.

She pulled back and looked at him. "I have to do this. For Georgie. For George. Just like you had to come after George for your wife. Not vindication, Adam. Justice."

"There's every possibility that Roger would look you in the face and lie."

"I'd know if he was lying," she said again, feeling a certainty she couldn't explain.

"All right."

She nodded, allowed herself to sink back into his embrace, putting her head on his shoulder.

Tomorrow, then. All she had to do was get through the night.

Chapter Forty-Six

"It's late, Suzanne."

One of his hands was at her hip, the other smoothed from her shoulder to her elbow and back again.

"You should return to your suite," he said.

"I should."

"Emily will be waiting for you."

"I dismissed her for the night," she said.

He didn't say anything for a moment. She wanted to ask him what he was thinking but decided that it would probably be more prudent to keep her curiosity to herself.

"I don't want to leave," she said. There, a little more honesty for him. "I could always invite you to my bed, but then it would be difficult to hide you from Emily. Or pretend that I've been virtuous."

"Suzanne."

There was a note in his voice she couldn't identify. Did he object to her staying?

"Do you lie?"

"What?"

"You intimated that Roger was skilled in lying. Is that a function of being in the Silent Service? Have you ever lied to me?"

The seconds ticked along ponderously.

"I don't think so," he said.

She pulled back to look at him. "Why do you sound so surprised?"

There was an expression in his beautiful green eyes she couldn't decipher. Bemusement, perhaps.

"It never felt right to lie to you, Suzanne."

She sank back against his chest, feeling a lightness streaming through her like sunlight. It didn't banish the darkness completely, but made it gray more than black.

"I don't want to leave," she said, giving him the truth. "I don't want to."

He said something half under his breath, a word that was so startling she rose up to look at him again.

"Do you truly want me to leave, Adam?" Did he know how difficult a question that was to ask?

She was so worried about his response that she didn't anticipate the kiss. Was it possible for the top of your head to simply float off and vanish? Every part of her body welcomed him, wanted his touch and the magic that he brought her. She'd never before considered herself a sensual person or one motivated by her baser instincts. Such things were for people who were lax in their morals or hadn't been trained to be proper. At least, that's what she'd always been taught. But what if everything she'd learned up until now was wrong? What if you could be entirely decorous and yet love with abandon?

She sat up, never losing contact with Adam's lips, and wound her arms around his neck.

He breathed her name against her mouth. No doubt it was an admonition of some sort.

Was he cautioning her about her own behavior? Or was it his lack of control he was warning her about? Either way, she didn't care. Let them both be profligate and unwise and wild.

She thought she heard him say her name again, but she was concentrating on kissing her way across his face and down his throat. He had a beautiful neck. She had never noticed a man's neck until now.

His hands were holding her shoulders in a tight grip, but she noticed he didn't push her away. If she wanted to leave, now was the time.

Why would she choose lying in her solitary bed, staring up at the ceiling, in exchange for being with Adam? Kissing him and anticipating what they would do together? She might have been foolish at times in her life, but she learned from her mistakes quite quickly.

She was not leaving.

Delight was threading through her body, making her aware of muscles and nerves and sensations she had never truly noticed until this moment.

She nibbled on his ear, smiling when he muttered something under his breath.

"I'm not leaving," she said. "I don't want to."

"Heaven forbid I make you do something you don't want, Your Grace."

She leaned back, smiling at him, happiness rushing through her. She shouldn't have been so filled with joy at that moment. He was teasing her again and no one ever had. His eyes were intent as they studied her, and there was something in the depths of them that made her heart soar.

"Thank you, Drummond."

He frowned. "What for?"

"For liking me," she said.

He shook his head. "Sometimes, Suzanne, you say the most ridiculous things. Who wouldn't like you? Who wouldn't cherish you? And love you?"

She was going to cry again and it had nothing to do with grief or sorrow. Her heart was so full that she couldn't bear it.

All she could do was frame his face with her hands and kiss him gently and tenderly. "And you, Adam? Who wouldn't love you? And cherish you? And admire you and respect you?"

He abruptly stood and carried her to the end of his bed. It was smaller than hers, the mattress thinner and the sheets not the quality designed for a duchess. Yet she wouldn't be anywhere else, because it didn't matter. Nothing mattered but the look in his eyes as he slowly unbuttoned her bodice, giving her time to protest or refuse or stay his hands.

Instead, she reached up and began to unbutton his shirt, freeing him from his clothes with sudden talented fingers. When had she become so adept at undressing a man?

He had been her tutor in passion, and now the pupil was impatient to demonstrate everything she'd learned from him.

"You are wearing entirely too many clothes," he said a moment later.

"I would say the same about you." They smiled at each other.

Fingers flew as well as buttons. Laces were loosened and then a corset was tossed across the room. She stood to rid herself of her dress. Her cameo was placed on his bedside table, but she had no idea where one stocking had gone. Its mate was draped over the chair where they had earlier sat. And her shift? It was the last garment to be dispensed with and she stood there before him, naked and as vulnerable as she had ever been in her life.

She should have covered herself with her hands. She should have grabbed the blanket at the end of his bed and draped it over herself. She should have done something other than just stand there and let him look his fill. The light on the desk in the other room was sufficient to expose her. Unlike last night, she had no shield of darkness. Nor did she want one.

He was bare-chested and had removed his shoes, but his trousers were still on. She approached him and began to unfasten the placket.

He reached out and smoothed his hands down her arms, and then he pressed his palms to her nipples and cupped her breasts. She had never realized how sensitive her breasts were until Adam touched her. She closed her eyes at the sensation.

She blocked out the past and the future and concentrated only on this, the present with him.

He bent to kiss her, but she shook her head.

"Not until you're undressed. It's only fair. If I'm naked, you should be naked."

She'd always been modest. She hadn't liked being completely naked even in front of her maid. Why was she being so brazen now? She thought it was because of the look in his eyes again, that same intensity that warmed her from the inside out.

Or could it be that desire was heating her body, turning her into someone else? The Suzanne she'd always wanted to be. The girl who reveled in her freedom. Being naked in front of him, unafraid, untouched by modesty was the greatest demonstration of freedom she could imagine.

They tumbled onto the bed, the mattress sinking in the middle, almost creating a well around them and causing her to laugh. They didn't wait. Instead, he entered her and she widened her legs, first wrapping her feet around his calves and then his waist. They were so close, so wound together that their heartbeats seemed to match, their breathing in tandem.

This was different from before. Before when he'd loved her, it had been sensual and erotic, then gentle and sweet. This was a maelstrom, fury and fire. She'd wanted wildness and abandon and he gave it to her and demanded, with each movement, that she come with him and experience the wholeness of passion with him.

It was Adam, so she put her trust in him, wrapping her arms around his neck, lost in his kisses. His thrusts and withdrawal teased and pleasured her at the same time. His mouth left hers to gently bite at the base of her neck, a gesture of capture, a demand for surrender. Then his lips were pulling at her nipples, saying her name against her breasts.

Her body shuddered, clamped around him with a demand of its own. She saw darkness and sparkles behind her eyelids as if the heavens had exploded in a black night sky.

For a moment, she wasn't Suzanne. She was simply a being, a creature of pleasure insensate but for bliss. Her hips thrust up to implore him to return. Her arms clung to him as his back arched.

Her body responded so perfectly to him, with him, as if they were destined to love each other. Nor was it simply her physical body that was involved, but her mind as well. She'd given him trust and he'd returned it. They'd revealed secrets to each other. With him she didn't have to be anybody but herself. Not a woman with a title. Not the daughter of the fantastically wealthy Edward Hackney.

She held him as he shuddered in her arms a few minutes later, his body reaching completion. She realized that in this, too, they were alike. Each needed the other, not only for pleasure but for holding in the aftermath, to treasure that small window of time when it was acceptable to be so open and vulnerable, to be weak.

She didn't try to hide her tears. She doubted she could have if she'd wanted to. This weeping came from another place entirely. Not grief exactly, but something similar. Anticipatory loss, perhaps. Seeing something troubling ahead and being unable to stop it.

He collapsed beside her, the sound of her name now coated with wonder.

She wanted him to stay, to remain with her. Sometimes being a duchess didn't matter at all.

Tomorrow they would go and label a man a traitor.

Yet tonight was hers and she wasn't going to give a second back to the world.

Chapter Forty-Seven

Suzanne woke at dawn, stretched, and ran the ball of her foot down a masculine, hairy leg. What a delightful pleasure it was to wake up with someone beside you. You began your morning feeling as if you weren't alone, that whatever happened during the day, their thoughts would occasionally be on you, that they would smile in remembrance. Or that they would hurry to be back in your company.

"I have to leave," he said.

That simple comment was like a spear to her chest. For a little while she'd pretended that reality wasn't real, that he didn't have to assume his rightful place in the world. As did she.

She would miss him. She would miss him much more than she should. But then, she didn't wake up in the bed of just any man. He was the only man. George's visits to her bed had been perfunctory things, a few hours here and there and then gone. He'd never slept beside her. She had never awakened with a smile on her face at the sound of his snoring. Not once in the middle of the night had she ever placed her hand on his naked back just to touch him.

"I will have to replace you," she said, her eyes still closed. There, her voice sounded quite calm, didn't it? "As the senior footman, Thomas would be next in line for your position, wouldn't he? Is he up to it?"

"I would take him rather than bringing someone else in, someone new."

"I think I shall dismiss my solicitor," she said, blinking open her eyes. "After all, he was the one who recommended you. He did the same with Ella. What do you think his relationship is with your Mr. Mount?"

"He's not my Mr. Mount," Adam said, rising up on his forearms. He reached out one hand and trailed a finger down her nose, then pressed it against her lips just once. "I think there is some cooperation going on between them, but I'm not sure why just yet."

"You're going to find out, aren't you?"

"I hate a mystery that hasn't been solved," he said.

"That sounds like you still have questions."

He smiled. "Let's just say I have a certain degree of curiosity."

"And a sense of justice," she said. "I think it's probably your quest for justice that fuels most of your actions, Adam."

"You make me sound much more virtuous than I am."

"Must you leave?" she asked, even though she knew the answer.

What she was really asking—and she couldn't help but wonder if he knew—was, *Must you leave me?*

Yesterday, she'd wondered if she was brave enough to love again. Now she knew it didn't matter what she decided or if she was courageous enough. Love had come to her without her participation, without inviting it into her heart. He might cause her pain. He might grant her anguish. She had no choice in the matter. She loved him and would do anything for him. And to keep him with her she might even beg.

She swung her legs over the side of the bed, the sheet still draped in front of her. She didn't want to seem needy or weepy. She wanted to be strong and resolute, someone like Mrs. Armbruster, perhaps. A woman who knew exactly what she wanted from life and had no qualms about demanding it.

Perhaps she should emulate that determined lady.

She stood and gathered up her clothing, wishing she had the courage to ask him not to watch her so closely. Did he expect her to dress in front of him? Evidently, because when she glanced at him he didn't look away.

Very well, if she was going to be strong and resolute she would begin right this moment. She dropped the sheet and reached for her shift, standing and pulling it on, hoping to appear nonchalant. The truth was she was acutely conscious of his gaze on her.

"You will be dressing in front of me, won't you?" she asked. "It's only fair."

"I'm not nearly as beautiful as you are."

She pulled the shift into place, pushed her hair back, and looked at him. "You underestimate yourself, Drummond. You're quite the most beautiful man I've ever seen."

If she'd had the time she would have sat on his chair and watched him for long moments, absolutely fascinated by the fact that his cheeks were turning bronze. Had she embarrassed him? The idea was both charming and amusing.

She pulled on her pantaloons and then her corset, fastening the busk with a little more difficulty than she'd anticipated. Since she had to go down only one flight of stairs to reach her suite, she decided that it was not sufficiently important to put on her stockings. She slipped her feet inside her shoes and tied the laces before putting on her dress. She was not in any way properly attired, but it would be enough to get to her rooms and slip beneath the covers before Emily arrived.

"You haven't forgotten, have you?" she asked, standing and grabbing her stockings. "You will let me go with you when you confront him?"

"I'm afraid that will have to wait," he said. "He won't be at work today and I don't think it wise to confront him at his house. I'll go and see Sir Richard first."

"No," she said, reaching into her pocket for the invitation Emily had given her, now a little worse for wear, and handed it to him. "He'll be at my father's house."

One of his eyebrows arched as he read.

"It's one of my father's political luncheons."

"Honoring his protégés?" he asked.

She nodded.

"Your father isn't going to be pleased if we make a scene. Does that bother you?"

"Not in the least," she said.

"I've never been to a political luncheon. What's it like?"

"A great many important people commenting on the food and the wine," she said. "And talking about and over each other. Sometimes they want to be overheard. At other times, not."

"It sounds like any War Office gathering. Or any social function after I became lieutenant."

She studied him. "I'll bet you were exceedingly handsome in your uniform," she said.

"It was less complicated than what I had to wear as your major-domo."

"I've noticed that you don't wear a hat, though."

"I detest them," he said. "I only wear them when I have to, which isn't often, thank heavens."

"I should very much like to dispense with hats. And corsets. And stockings."

He chuckled. "Why stockings?"

"They're never seen. You only wear them because of your shoes. But sometimes they are bothersome. If you don't tie the garter tight enough, they slip down. If you tie the garter too tight, they chafe."

"But they're delightful to remove," he said, smiling.

She hesitated at his door, wanting to say something else but uncertain what it should be. If she said thank you it wouldn't be just for the pleasure he'd given her last night, but for his kindness and concern, his tenderness and gentleness, as well as the laughter he'd summoned from some dark place. He had been like sunlight in the dark cave in which she'd lived for so long, and she would never forget that. She'd never forget him, either. But she didn't want to have to remember him. She didn't want to have to summon memories. She didn't want him to leave.

How could she say all that in just a few words in parting? She couldn't. Her plea would have to wait until later. She did have one last question, though.

"Why?" she asked. "Why try to prove that the traitor was George, even after his death? The War Office couldn't punish him. All that you could do was harm his reputation."

"I was told that the Foreign Office was trying to make amends in India, making up for the mistakes made during those years, and that they didn't want any further embarrassments to surface now." He swung his legs to the side of the bed. "That's the story I was given. And I took it in, every lying word. The truth? A traitor didn't want to be discovered."

They shared a long look before she finally nodded.

"Until noon," she said before opening the door, looking both ways and slipping out of his room.

Suzanne reached her chambers without being seen—at least, she hoped so. There was a possibility that the footman stationed at the end of the corridor saw her, but he'd been chosen for that duty not only because of his trustworthiness, but his devotion to tact. If he'd seen her, she doubted he would tell the tale of the duchess who crept through Marsley House before dawn with her hair askew and clutching her stockings in one hand.

She opened her sitting room door and, relieved, leaned back against it.

At least until Emily stood, scaring her into a gasp.

"Begging your pardon, Your Grace, but I was worried about you and decided to check on you early."

How very commendable of Emily. Unfortunately, she couldn't think of a thing to say to her maid.

"He's a very attractive man, Your Grace," Emily said.

There was no unkindness in the remark. No cruelty in Emily's eyes. Instead, there was only a slight bit of humor, if she wasn't mistaken. All in all, it seemed as if she had an ally in her maid.

Suzanne didn't quite know how to respond. She could, of course, retreat behind the icy demeanor that kept people away.

They didn't bother her when she was being the Duchess of Marsley. They didn't intrude. They wouldn't even think of asking her a personal question or being brash.

Emily was new to the position and no doubt would understand being chastised for her impudence. Yet something stopped Suzanne. The younger her, the person she longed to be, stepped forward and said, "Emily, I have been very sinful. I know I should feel terrible, but I don't. Is that horrible?"

Emily waved one hand in the air. "The minister would say yes, Your Grace, but the rest of us would understand. I guess that's why sin is sin, if you'll pardon me for saying so. If it didn't feel good, why would we do it?"

She couldn't help but laugh. Emily was going to be good for her, she could tell.

"Then if you don't mind," she said, "it will be our secret."

"I'll paint my lips blue if I say something bad about you."

Suzanne smiled. "What's that from?"

"It's what my brothers and sisters say. It's almost a family vow."

She found herself interested in Emily's family, questioning how many brothers and sisters she had—five—where they lived and what her parents were like. From the girl's conversation, it was evident that Emily had been one of the fortunate ones, growing up in a family that truly loved each other, even as adults.

"Help me dress," she said striding toward the bedroom and one of her two armoires. "I need to look very much like a duchess today," she added, glancing at Emily over her shoulder. "And I will need your talents with my hair."

Neither of them mentioned that she hadn't worn a braid the night before and that it would take some time to brush her hair free of tangles and tame it into shape.

That was the price one paid for love and perhaps even lust.

But, oh, it was worth it.

Chapter Forty-Eight

They didn't speak for long moments after leaving Marsley House. Adam's two valises were in the back of the carriage. He'd said his goodbyes to those friends he'd made, a little surprised at how many there were. Even those members of staff with whom he'd had disagreements or issues came to wish him well and see him off.

Mrs. Thigpen—Olivia—had been the more difficult of partings. He'd wanted to explain to her why he'd engaged in deception, but found that the words wouldn't come. He hadn't wanted to take advantage of her. He had genuinely appreciated their friendship. At least he got that part out.

"I understand, Adam. Truly I do. It's the rest that flummoxes me."

"The rest?"

"It's Her Grace, Adam. She's not the type to trifle with, and it's sad I am that you've taken advantage of her."

He hadn't said anything in response. Not one word had come to mind.

"You aren't wearing mourning," he said to Suzanne now.

He'd never seen Suzanne wearing anything but black. The color had suited her, but this lavender shade was even more attractive. It made her blue-gray eyes appear more piercing, and enhanced her creamy complexion. He admitted to himself that he could spend a great deal of time simply looking at Suzanne. Her beauty was understated, elegant, and everything about her made you want to study her more.

"It's half mourning," she said.

There was something about her voice, too. Low-pitched, it seemed to travel up and down his spine. It was a hell of a thing to find himself aroused by the sound of her voice. She could recite the list of the scullery maids' duties and he'd still find himself captivated.

He wanted to ask her if there was a reason why she had gone to half mourning now. He wasn't all that versed on society and every one of its rules, especially the ones about grieving. Had she done it because of him? The arrogance of that thought kept him silent.

"Does it matter what color clothing you wear?" she asked after a moment. "You don't wear a black armband, but it doesn't dictate your thoughts or the feelings in your heart."

He'd never talked about how he felt about Rebecca. Yet he found himself doing so often with Suzanne. It was a strange catharsis, discussing his lost wife with a woman who'd gone through her own anguish. Another point of comparison: she'd made no secret of the fact that she hadn't loved George. Nor had he been reticent about telling her that Rebecca had become his wife more out of convenience than emotion.

"No," he said. "It doesn't matter what you wear. Nothing will change what you think or feel. Time numbs the pain a little, but it never changes the facts."

"Do you ever get used to that? Or the bitterness?"

He smiled at her. "Bitterness is only anger unvoiced, I think. You can rid yourself of anger by expressing it in some way."

"Most people don't want to hear what you feel," she said.

He nodded. "You can tell me, Suzanne."

How long had he lived without love? Seven years? He could manage as long as he had a task, a goal, something to accomplish. He'd kept frenetically busy, one of the few operatives who could be put to work without regard to family obligations, holidays, or a personal life, for that matter. He didn't have people pulling on him, demanding that he share his attention with them. Damn it.

He didn't want to live that life any longer, a realization only weeks old, ever since meeting Suzanne.

She'd taught him, without words, that it was important to care about someone. To feel that his day was complete if he shared his life with her. To worry about someone else more than he did himself. He wanted to ask her thoughts, protect her from being hurt, and help her heal. He wanted to ask her opinion, share laughter with her, kiss her until they both lost the idea of time or place. He wanted to hold her when grief overwhelmed her, share his own sorrows with her and let her soothe him. He wanted the two of them to face the world together as a couple, a pair.

Yet that simple wish was a ludicrous and insane one. A dream dreamt by an idiot.

That thought kept him silent as they drove through London.

Adam had never been to Edward Hackney's house and had not once considered that it might be only slightly smaller than Marsley House. The evidence of wealth was there not only in the Palladian architecture, but the sheer expanse of lawn that surrounded the home, protected by a tall brick wall.

The British Royal family had nothing on Hackney when it came to a palace. Adam was only surprised that Hackney hadn't purchased a grand estate away from London so the man could hold political country house weekends.

A line of carriages was parked on the far left side of the road some distance away from the house. It took them nearly a half hour to make the approach and pull into the circular drive. Once the door was opened by a liveried footman, Adam left the carriage and helped Suzanne navigate the steps.

He didn't know how women did it with all that material and flouncy skirt. He much preferred her naked, a comment that he might have made in another circumstance. He'd always been circumspect, but it seemed like his entire nature was changing.

"Your Grace," the footman said. "Would you like me to send word to your father that you've arrived?"

"That's not necessary," she said. "I'm certain he knew the moment we entered the gate." She glanced up at Adam. "My father knows everything that happens almost before it does."

That comment concerned him. It made him wonder if Hackney knew about Roger's actions in India. If Hackney was sponsoring Roger for Parliament, it seemed not only possible but probable that he'd been informed about everything in Roger's past. He'd want to know about any scandal or anything embarrassing that might hamper Roger's rise to power. Nor would Hackney want to be associated with anyone who could ultimately detrimentally affect his own reputation.

If Hackney had known about India, did that also make him a traitor?

Knowledge of a crime as well as the identity of the perpetrator should be shared with the proper authorities. The fact that Hackney hadn't done so made him guilty, but to a lesser degree. His actions hadn't caused the death of good soldiers and the massacre of women and children.

For that, Roger should be punished and Adam was going to make certain he was.

Chapter Forty-Nine

*S*uzanne was dressed in lavender, which her father had coaxed her to do. No doubt he'd think she had done so because of him. She was here, when she'd announced her intention not to attend. She was attired in a dress that was fashionable in its way and her hat, while not as large—or as outlandish as some, she noticed—had been designed by a famous London milliner. All in all, her father wouldn't be displeased by her appearance.

On the other hand, he was bound to become apoplectic when he saw Adam with her. When he realized why they were here he would be enraged.

How very odd that she was looking forward to angering her father.

Most of her life, she'd done everything in her power to be a peacemaker. She had acceded to his most unreasonable requests. She had been conciliatory and understanding. More than once, she'd sublimated her own wishes for his. She'd married a man she hadn't loved because he'd dictated it.

No more. Not again. Not one more time was she going to be the obedient, dutiful daughter. That behavior had garnered her nothing. Her father hadn't been more approving. He hadn't said anything kinder or nicer to her. Granted, her life had changed, but she couldn't say that it had improved.

Marsley House was a colossus. It didn't matter how many rooms it had. She could enter only one at a time. None of the objects, knickknacks, and belongings collected by the previous dukes added to her life in any way.

Nor did she care how many dresses she owned or how many hats, pairs of gloves, or shoes.

Money, possessions, and a title had never brought her joy. Only Georgie had.

If an angel appeared before her and said, "Suzanne Hackney Whitcomb, I give you a choice. All the money your father has given you, all the power and the prestige that your husband granted you, would you trade everything for the ability to see your son again? Choose."

She would have spoken before the angel finished. She'd have given anything—any amount of possessions or trinkets or even her life—for a moment with her son. To be able to tell him how much she loved him. To be able to hold him in her arms for just a few minutes.

She blinked rapidly. Now was neither the time nor the place to lose her composure. Adam reached out his hand and grabbed hers. He was watching her with a look of concern.

People did not hold hands at London luncheons. They did not gaze into each other's eyes the way the two of them were doing. She could tell that their behavior was eliciting curiosity and more than a few speculative glances.

What the rest of the world didn't understand was that Adam was her lifeline right now. He added to her strength. He knew what she was feeling and realized how close she was to tears.

They entered her father's house, a place she'd never felt that she belonged. It hadn't been her home any more than Marsley House was hers. She held no affection for the stately architecture, the wide foyer with its stark white columns or the pink-and-gray-veined marble floor.

There were two dining rooms. One was small and accommodated a dozen diners. The other was much larger, given to occasions such as this, when thirty or more people would sit down to a meal lasting at least two hours. There, the grand mahogany table, a design her father had ordered and which had taken nearly a year to complete, would be arrayed with a king's ransom in silver, gold, and crystal. The three chandeliers above the table would be lit despite the brightness of the day, illuminating the emerald green of the wallpaper and the curtains that mimicked the lush growth of the gardens surrounding the house.

Everyone would come away from a Hackney luncheon with praise for the food, the company, the ambiance, and their surroundings.

For now, the guests milled about the public rooms, a drawing room decorated in white and gold, and the library now open to visitors as it was never normally.

Her father was evidently attempting to make an impression on the various dignitaries in attendance.

Adam suddenly stiffened. She followed his gaze to see a man surrounded by a group of other men, some accompanied by their wives. When the crowd parted slightly, she recognized him as Roger Mount. She recalled meeting him at the last dinner party. He'd been almost obsequious to her, an annoying man she dismissed almost as soon as they'd been introduced. His wife, she remembered, was the opposite. She'd insisted on telling Suzanne who her father was and then describing her garden in excruciating detail.

Roger was shorter than Adam, a stocky man equipped with a perpetual smile. He looked entirely normal if a little self-serving but, then, she had met a great many political men who were just the same. Had he been responsible for her son and George's death? He didn't look evil, but did evil have an appearance? Perhaps innocuous-seeming people were the most dangerous.

She would have approached him if Adam had relinquished her hand. She glanced at him again to see him studying her.

"That isn't wise," he said.

She didn't want to be particularly wise, but the chance to say that was gone when Adam squeezed her hand in warning.

"Daughter, you're looking lovely."

She glanced to her left to see her father standing there, flanked by his two secretaries, Jerome and Martin. She nodded to the men before greeting her father, turning her head slightly so that he could kiss her cheek, as was his habit.

This time he added a glare to the kiss. "Drummond."

Adam smiled. "Hackney."

"We need to talk. I believe you aren't who you're pretending to be."

"I know exactly who he is, Father," she said.

He stared at their joined hands. Any other time, she would've released Adam's hand, but now she clung to it almost out of rebellion.

"Are you in the habit of demonstrating affection in public, Suzanne?"

"Are you in the habit of consorting with traitors, Father? Or even worse, being friends with the man who was responsible for your grandson's death?"

"What are you talking about?"

"Ask Roger Mount," she said. "Demand that he tell you the truth, unless you already know it."

Her father looked at Adam.

"He betrayed the East India Company, Hackney," Adam said. "And the regiment stationed there, not to mention hundreds of women and children. He sold information about the entrenchment to the rebel leader."

"That isn't possible," her father said.

"That's what I said when I discovered that my maid was poisoning me," Suzanne said. "On your orders."

"I don't understand." The look of confusion on her father's face was almost convincing.

"Do you deny that you gave Ella opium to give to me?"

"Of course I do. Why would I do that?" His brows drew together and his eyes narrowed. When her father was angry, the world knew it, and he was getting to that stage. Even his secretaries took a step back, ever so tactfully.

"You and I have had our differences, but you're my daughter. I'd never do anything to harm you."

She glanced at Adam.

"It's entirely possible that Ella was giving you the drug to control you on her own," he said. "The better to give her time to find the journal."

"You two aren't making any sense," her father said. "Opium? Journal? Explain yourselves. Especially the part about how Mount's a traitor. What's your proof?"

"One of the soldiers who served under the duke in India came to see him," Adam said. "I was attached to Manipora," he added. "We all suspected that someone betrayed us to the rebels. He identified Roger."

Roger was excusing himself from his coterie and beginning to walk toward them. He stopped some distance away, almost as if he sensed the tenor of the conversation about him.

"He's responsible for hundreds of deaths at Manipora," Adam said. "In addition, the duke confronted Mount with what he knew."

Her father stared at Adam for a long moment. "Was he responsible for the accident?" he finally asked.

"I don't know," Adam said. "One thing I do know is the extent of Mount's ambition. He didn't give a thought to the deaths of a few hundred people. A few more wouldn't concern him."

"I hope you're wrong," her father said. "But I'm damn well going to find out." Without another word, he started to walk toward Roger.

Chapter Fifty

Hackney approached Roger, stopping in front of the younger man. His expression must have warned Roger's admirers. One by one they began to move back, almost as if they were afraid the encounter was going to result in violence.

There was every possibility it would.

"Did you have the duke killed?" Hackney asked.

Adam had to hand it to Hackney. What he lacked in tact he made up for in fury. There was no doubt in anyone's mind that he was enraged.

Everyone in earshot—which was everyone he could see—was watching.

Roger said something in response, too low for Adam to hear. He released Suzanne's hand and made his way to the two men.

"I found the journal, Roger," Adam said in a low voice.

Up until then Roger had ignored his approach, but the moment Adam spoke, the other man turned to him.

He'd never seen a man's face change so quickly. It was like one side of Roger's nature flipped to reveal another, truer self. Something in the depths of his eyes flickered. His face stilled and became almost painted on.

"There never was an informant, was there?" Adam said. "The duke himself told you what he knew. He also told you he'd recorded the truth. No wonder you've been looking for the journal ever since he died." He asked another question, one that had occurred to him when he'd read the duke's words. "And me? I was dispensable, too. You probably had plans for me after I found the journal."

"I don't know what you're talking about."

There was no way this was going to end well. If nothing else, he needed to get Roger to another room, somewhere their conversation wouldn't be overheard. He'd spotted a former general and the Lord Mayor of London among the guests. The last thing the Silent Service needed was to have their mission or this assignment publicly known. He'd already said too much and Hackney didn't look like he was going to keep silent.

Suzanne approached, halting when she reached Roger. "You killed my son, didn't you? And my husband."

"Of course I didn't, Your Grace," Roger said. He didn't get a chance to explain—or prevaricate.

"You damn bastard!"

Edward Hackney pulled his fist back and struck Roger so hard that his nose became a geyser of blood. Roger stumbled, fell to his knees, and was hit again before he could right himself. Hackney looked as if he'd continue pummeling the younger man if Adam hadn't pulled him back.

"Let me go! That bastard killed my grandson. He deserves everything he gets."

"I agree, but now is not the time. Nor is it the place."

Hackney was wild-eyed, his face florid, his hands still balled into fists.

There wasn't a doubt in Adam's mind that Hackney wanted to hit him, too. If he did, he'd be hard-pressed not to return the blow despite the man's age. Maybe there was something in his face that indicated he wouldn't be as easy a target as Roger, because Hackney dropped his fists.

"Is it true?" Hackney asked. For the first time, he sounded his age. "Did he kill Georgie, Suzanne?"

She went to her father and grabbed his arm. Adam saw the minute her anger fled to be replaced by sadness.

Hackney looked tired and defeated. "I didn't know, Suzanne. I didn't know."

She nodded in response, patting his arm.

"You're one of his operatives, aren't you?" Hackney asked, glancing at Adam.

"No," Adam said, determined to clear up that point. "I was just attached to this operation."

He was acutely aware that he was broadcasting his role in the War Office to any interested party. He wasn't going to say anything else.

Bending down, Adam grabbed Roger under the arm, and hauled him upright. He gestured for one of the servants and sent him after their driver. He didn't trust Hackney's staff, but he knew Michael. He would help Adam get Roger to the authorities.

"What are you going to do with him?" Hackney asked. "He should be bloody well shot at dawn. Or blown from cannon."

Adam didn't say anything, but he wanted to ask if the former East India Company director had ever seen that particular death sentence carried out. It had been a favorite of the duke's. A man had to see it only once before deciding that he would do anything rather than view it again.

Suzanne still had his arm and was regarding her father with some concern. As well she should. Hackney's florid face had become nearly white.

Something caught his attention, movement on the edge of the crowd that had formed around them. He turned a dazed Roger over to Michael and stepped away, ignoring the questions that followed him.

It had been too easy.

Roger's capture, the knowledge that he was the spy, had all been too easy. Granted, searching for the journal had been a trial, but everything else? Something wasn't right and the feeling was only minutes old.

The man walking swiftly toward the door told Adam that his instincts were spot-on.

He began to push himself through the crowd. Just when he thought he'd lost him, Adam caught sight of Oliver sliding out the front door, heading for the iron gate.

He began to run.

Catching up to him just before he hit the street, Adam grabbed the other man's arm and whirled him around.

"You're the traitor. Not Roger. You."

Oliver didn't have Roger's ability to smooth his face of all expression. It wasn't difficult to see the sudden hatred in his eyes.

"But Roger knew, didn't he?"

"He didn't know," Oliver said. "He didn't know anything."

"But he figured it out soon enough, I'll wager. When? After the duke visited him? All his ambitions would go up in a puff of smoke if someone learned his secretary was guilty of treason. Nobody would believe that he hadn't known, too."

Oliver's only response was a smirk.

Roger had cautioned him about letting his personal opinion color his judgment on this assignment, yet that's exactly what he hoped Adam would do. He'd counted on Adam's dislike of the duke to blind him to the truth. He depended on Adam's thirst for some kind of justice to keep him focused.

It had almost succeeded. But for Suzanne, it might have.

Oliver didn't fight him as Adam dragged him back to Hackney's house. For good measure, he solicited the help of two of Hackney's burly footmen, but Oliver didn't struggle. He was one of those snake-like creatures who preferred operating in the shadows than being overt.

"Why did you do it?" Adam asked. "Was it the money?"

He half expected Oliver to remain silent, but the other man surprised him by answering.

"I wanted to go home."

He stared at Oliver in disbelief. "You wanted to go home?"

Oliver nodded.

"You were at Lucknow with Roger," Adam said. "You weren't even at Manipora."

"I wanted to come back to England. I didn't want to fight anymore. I wanted it to be all over."

Adam was left without a response. It was over, for all the men, women, and children who'd died that day.

Hackney broke through the crowd, Suzanne following.

"He's the real traitor," Adam said, glancing at Oliver. "He's the one who betrayed us at Manipora."

"And Roger?" Hackney asked.

"He's the murderer," Adam said. "I'm taking them both to Sir Richard. He'll know what to do with them."

Adam exchanged a look with Suzanne. He wanted to tell her goodbye and perhaps say something else. The moment wasn't one for intimacies. He had two traitors to bring to justice.

All he could do was smile at her, and say goodbye in Gaelic: *"Mar sin leat."*

Chapter Fifty-One

"Neither Mount nor Cater are saying that much," Sir Richard told Adam a week later.

They sat in Sir Richard's large paneled office in the War Office building. The windows were lightly etched to prevent anyone from seeing in, but done in such a manner that plenty of light entered the space.

The chair in which Adam sat was upholstered in material that felt like a tapestry. He guessed that the chair itself was an antique like Sir Richard's desk, the globe on a stand, and the replica of the ship that rested in the middle of the fireplace mantel.

The room was furnished more like a parlor than an office, with a comfortable-looking couch in the corner, a table with a lamp and chairs that were less old and softer than where he sat. The scent of leather and pipe tobacco seemed to cling to the walls, perfuming the air.

Sir Richard looked down at the stacks of papers on his desk before glancing at him.

"I think we can concur that they were both to blame. Cater for treason and Mount for trying to cover it up."

"And the accident, sir? Was it truly an accident?"

Sir Richard sighed. "We may never know." He met Adam's look. "I have my own ideas, of course, about that damnable business. I think it a bit too coincidental that the duke died when he did, after threatening to expose Mount. But I've no proof, Adam."

"Another instance of never knowing for sure, sir?"

"Exactly, Adam. It's the type of job we do. You've shown great discretion in this matter. Under difficult circumstances, I might add."

"Thank you, sir," he said.

His superior studied him for another few minutes. Adam knew better than to say anything until Sir Richard was ready for further conversation. The older man was not averse to silencing his subordinates with a hand gesture or a terse, "Be still."

Sir Richard Wells was a man of indeterminate years who never seemed to age, at least not since Adam had first met him seven years ago. His shock of thick white hair was always perfectly coiffed. His black suits never showed a speck of lint. He was the perfect representation of a senior government official with his craggy face and the lines that had been put there by concern and worry. A tall man, he had a habit of bending forward at the shoulders as if he'd been taught as a child that it was rude to tower over people. His dark blue eyes were shielded by bushy white brows that resembled two caterpillars crawling across his face.

They were currently meeting above his nose in a ferocious frown.

"I'd like you to consider taking a new position. One of a supervisory nature. It would mean that you weren't out in the field, of course, but we could use a man of your discretion and experience. Sometimes decisions are made without any input. Your presence would mean that we'd get the view from the other side, so to speak."

He had reported to Sir Richard for every one of his assignments except this last one. The man had always treated him well, respected his concerns, and communicated honestly and fairly with him. On this occasion, however, he thought that there might be something else Sir Richard wasn't saying.

His promotion might be masquerading as something else.

"In other words, Sir Richard, if I remain quiet about the massacre at Manipora, I'll get an office, title, and a promotion. Is that it?"

The other man leaned back in his chair, steepled his fingers, and regarded Adam with his usual somber look. Sir Richard didn't smile very often, and when he did it was mostly in recognition of some irony that amused him. He wasn't given to joviality or even a lightness of speech. Instead, he acted as if the weight of the world—or the Commonwealth's presence in it—was on his shoulders. It just might have been.

"Speaking out about Manipora now wouldn't be wise. Divulging Cater's or Mount's role in it wouldn't serve any purpose. Nor would the morale of the army be buoyed in learning that two of their own betrayed them. But to answer your question, no, this offer is not a bribe or an inducement to silence. Tell the story if you wish. I can't stop you, but I see no point in it. It will not resurrect the dead." Sir Richard looked away for a moment before redirecting his attention to Adam. "Although I can understand why you would wish it otherwise. Damned awful business."

Sir Richard had a capacity for understatement.

"I have no intention of saying anything, Sir Richard. I owe the army and you my life."

The older man shook his head. "A fortuitous arrangement in my case, Adam. You have shown yourself to be a great patriot all these years."

Adam bit back a smile. *Patriot* was another word like *hero* that was regularly bandied about. They both came down to doing what was right at any particular time. Choosing not the easiest course, but the correct one.

"I want you for this post, Adam. Not because of what happened in the past, but what is coming around the corner for us. I think you'd be the right man in the position."

"Then I accept, Sir Richard, and I thank you."

He wasn't a fool, however and Sir Richard knew it. They would butt heads in the future. If he took this position he wouldn't be an operative as much as a politician, and he was most definitely not a politician.

The older man stood, extended his hand. "It is we who should thank you, Adam. This promotion will make a change for you. Are you prepared for that?"

He nodded as he shook Sir Richard's hand. "I am, sir."

A few minutes later he took his leave, entering the hired cab for a ride back to his lodgings.

A week had passed since the scene at Edward Hackney's home. A week since he'd seen Suzanne. A miserable week in which he had been beset by insomnia, an inability to think straight, and a general dissatisfaction. He was in a deplorable mood according to Mrs. Ross, who'd labeled him dour. He couldn't argue with her.

He'd had various assignments in the course of the past seven years. None of them had been like the one at Marsley House, where he had been required to form friendships of a sort.

Surprisingly, he missed a great many of those people.

Mrs. Thigpen with her love of gossip and condemnation of the same. She'd never realized what a paradox she was. Thomas, earnest and brave, up for any adventure. He would have made an excellent soldier. He liked Daniel as well and would miss the young man.

He'd isolated himself over the years, and it was only after he'd left Marsley House that he realized how much.

He gave some thought to returning to Glasgow before his new position began, just to reacquaint himself with his roots. If nothing else, seeing Glasgow might center him, give him some appreciation for how far he'd come. His life hadn't been a straight trajectory. It had ebbed and flowed like a burn tumbling over rocks. At the moment it was ebbing and it irritated him.

Maybe the change of job was just what he needed. He'd be busy, his time and thoughts occupied so that he could forget a certain duchess. Or maybe he'd never be able to forget Suzanne.

The new position would mean that he would not have to go out into the field. He wouldn't have to pretend to be different people at different times with different goals and motivations. He would be a guide, possibly a mentor, certainly a boss over other men who would be doing the job that he'd been doing for seven years. In the army he'd been successful leading men and it had been almost natural for him. He didn't have a problem with the new position. It was the rest of his life that was up in the air.

Suzanne arrived at Adam's lodgings, thanked Michael, and walked up the path to Mrs. Ross's front door with some trepidation. She'd never done what she was about to do.

She hadn't loved George; she hadn't even liked him very much. Loving her son, loving Georgie, had made her feel whole. When he'd died, she'd lost that feeling because he'd taken part of her heart with him. She would never get that part back and it was right and fitting that it was missing. Yet she could still love and still live.

That's what Adam had taught her.

She'd seen the worst of life. She'd been in the darkness too long and was grateful for any faint flicker of light. Adam was a candle, a bright flame that promised to keep burning.

Now all she had to do was take the greatest risk of her life.

Chapter Fifty-Two

The carriage Adam had hired slowed to a stop in front of Mrs. Ross's house. As he left the vehicle and paid the driver, he noticed another, much more expensive carriage parked across the street. Michael tipped his hat to him.

Adam stood there for a moment, frozen. Suzanne was here. Suzanne was here.

He almost got back into the carriage and commanded the man to drive around London for a few hours, anything but have to encounter the Duchess of Marsley.

They'd parted amicably enough, but she should have known it was final. The idyll had come to an end.

Now she was here.

He would have to say goodbye and leave no uncertainty in her mind.

He'd never before been a coward, but it was the hardest walk he ever made up to Mrs. Ross's front door. He didn't even get a chance to open the door before the woman herself opened it, frowning at him.

"It's an explanation I'm due, Mr. Drummond. You never said your cousin was the Duchess of Marsley. A duchess! I would have brought out my best china. And shortbread? I only served her shortbread!"

He didn't know what to say first, so he let his landlady's words wash over him. Mrs. Ross scolded him for a good five minutes before he could make his way into the foyer.

"I put Her Grace in the visitors' parlor."

Not only did he have to encounter Suzanne, but he had to have a witness in doing so.

He was going to refuse his promotion. Instead, he was going to return to Scotland. He was going to wander among the sparsely populated Highlands. He was going to keep sheep as company. Not people. He might get a dog, but that was it.

He found himself guided into the parlor by Mrs. Ross's insistent hand on his elbow. He glanced at her, but she wasn't looking at him. Instead, she had a half smile on her face and an expression of determination in her eyes. He had the thought that he was being paid back for keeping Suzanne in his rooms overnight. He wouldn't put it past Mrs. Ross to dole out her own brand of societal chastisement.

"Thank you, Mrs. Ross," he said, pulling free. "You've been very kind."

There was enough firmness in his voice that she finally looked at him.

"Thank you," he said again. He entered the parlor, turned, and closed the door in her face. No doubt he would have to pay for that rudeness, too, but not right now. Instead, he had a greater problem: facing Suzanne.

She sat on the excruciatingly uncomfortable horsehair-stuffed sofa. Most of the furniture in this parlor—that none of the lodgers were allowed to use unless they had important guests—was in a particular shade of green. Unfortunately, not all the greens matched. He always thought of it as the bile parlor. Mrs. Ross, on the other hand, adored her furniture and considered the room to be the height of fashion.

The room smelled of Mrs. Ross's perfume, an odor of musk and woods that always made him want to sneeze. Today was no exception. He almost used that as an excuse for leaving.

Suzanne had already removed her hat and gloves, which were beside her on the sofa. There was no sign of her cloak, and the day was chilly enough to have called for one. No doubt it had been taken by Mrs. Ross and put in a safe place.

The kitten sat on her lap, eyes half-closed, his smile tinted with bliss. Adam didn't have any doubt that the cat was purring. Or that he resented the interruption. Adam was the recipient of a baleful feline stare before the cat jumped down from Suzanne's lap and disappeared behind the sofa.

Suzanne was as beautiful as she'd ever been, but there were signs of fatigue on her face. The shadows beneath her eyes were too dark and her face was too pale.

Had she been ill? He felt a spurt of fear that wouldn't dissipate no matter how much he told himself that her health was none of his concern.

"My father has agreed to fund Mrs. Armbruster's Institute and Foundling Hospital," she said, in lieu of a greeting. "Isn't that wonderful news?"

"Yes."

Success—he'd uttered one word. Surely other words were just as easy. Why, then, did it seem almost impossible to say anything?

He couldn't help but wonder how she'd managed the feat of getting Hackney to support two projects that could potentially be scandalous. Perhaps Suzanne had threatened to go public with the story of Roger Mount. Would she have done such a thing? Or was it the older man's way of reparation?

"Why?" There, one more word.

She smiled at him, one of those duchess smiles she'd given him at the beginning. An expression that really didn't mean anything since it was merely a momentary lifting of the lips.

"Does it matter? As long as good deeds are done?"

"Did you blackmail him?" He congratulated himself for speaking an entire sentence.

Both her eyebrows arched at him and her smile became genuine. "Do you really think I could do such a thing?"

"Why does the idea seem to please you?"

"Because it sounds utterly daring. Although, I must admit, I feel utterly daring right now. No, I didn't blackmail him. I did my best to convince him."

"Why?" Good lord, was he back to monosyllables?

"Because of a little baby by the name of Henry," she said. "I couldn't stop thinking about Henry. Any more than I could stop thinking about you."

He hadn't expected that.

"You didn't come to see me," she said, leveling a stern look at him. "I waited, but you didn't come. Neither that night nor the next day. Not for a week. Then, Adam, I realized you weren't going to come back to see me. I was part of your mission and your assignment was over."

Hardly that, but he didn't correct her.

"I don't think it's very fair that you've ignored me."

How the hell could anyone ignore her?

"I'm selling Marsley House," she added. "I'm taking your advice. I'm looking at property not far from here and I need your input, Drummond."

"Have you forgotten, Your Grace, that I'm no longer employed by you? I'm no longer your majordomo."

"Oh, do let's be serious, Drummond. You were never just my majordomo. You were my savior." Her voice changed, softened. "My rescuer. My lover."

What did she want from him?

"The sale of Marsley House will enable me to buy another house. I want a place of my own. Some place I've chosen that feels like home."

"Congratulations, Your Grace."

She startled him by looking up at the ceiling, then shaking her head.

"You're not going to make this easy on me, are you?"

"Make what easy?"

"I do not wish to live without you, Drummond."

He felt almost like he had when he'd been shot. He was in a state of shock, as if it was happening to someone else. Or like he was observing the emotions but not quite able to feel them.

"I don't wish to live without you," she repeated.

He stared at her. "You're a duchess."

"Do you hold that against me? I would gladly change my past if I could. But I can't."

"You're a duchess."

She rolled her eyes. She actually rolled her eyes at him.

"On this, Drummond, you must allow me some authority. I realize I'm a duchess." She spoke slowly as if he weren't capable of understanding her words. "There's nothing I can do about it. Nor do I seem to be able to alter my feelings about you."

He was incapable of speaking again. He'd never had this problem before, but she stripped every word from his brain.

She shook her head, stood, and circumvented the furniture to reach him still standing with his back to the door. Reaching up, she framed his face with her hands.

"I love you, Adam. I've been miserable away from you. I want to sleep next to you at night. I want to love you whenever I wish. I want to hold you when sorrow overtakes you. I want you to comfort me, too, but I also want to laugh with you and tell you silly things."

"Suzanne."

"I love you."

He had a feeling she was going to keep saying that until he responded in some way.

"Suzanne." He took a step to the right. She followed him.

"Do you not feel the same?"

"I was raised in a tenement in Glasgow," he said, letting his accent fall heavy on his words. "I made something of myself in the army, but I've not the fortune of your father. Or a title like George."

"So?"

She was the most stubborn woman.

"I can't give you anything, Suzanne. Not like you've lived. Not what you've known. I have a new position, but it still won't mean that I can give you what you're used to."

She smiled softly. "Are you married, Adam?"

"You know I'm not."

"Are you spoken for?" she asked.

"No."

"Then you can give me what I most value," she said. "You."

He closed his eyes and reached for her.

"This isn't wise," he said, just before kissing her.

Long moments later she said, "Oh, Adam, it's the wisest, most intelligent decision either of us has ever made."

He had to kiss her again after that.

He didn't know when he started saying the words, but they seemed to flow from him without conscious thought.

"I love you," he said as he kissed the tip of her nose. "I love you," he repeated when he trailed kisses from one cheek to the other with a stop at her lips. "I love you. I love you. I love you. *Tha gaol agam ort.*"

He enfolded her in his arms and rocked with her, the moment punctuated by silence and a sense of awe. This beautiful woman with her strong heart loved him. He must have done something right in his life to deserve her.

When he said as much to Suzanne, she only kissed him again.

He led her back to the sofa, moved her hat and gloves, and sat beside her. Only then did he notice she'd removed the ancestral ring that had been hers by right of marriage to the Duke of Marsley.

"I don't have any heirlooms," he said, picking up her hand.

The mourning ring was still in place, but he knew it represented Georgie, not her husband.

"I don't need any heirlooms."

"I haven't a title to offer you."

"There's only one I want, Adam."

He smiled, the first time since he'd entered this room. His life had not been what he'd expected. Circumstances and situations had challenged him and nearly destroyed him at times. Yet here watching him with a smile on her lips and joy in her beautiful eyes was the reward for every difficulty he'd ever faced and every dark night.

"Then be my wife, Suzanne. We'll be foolish together."

There was a slight noise at the door. He glanced at it, then back at Suzanne. No doubt Mrs. Ross was standing there with her ear to the door, ensuring herself of their propriety. Perhaps she had reason to be suspicious of the two of them alone.

If they were anywhere else more private, he might have given her grounds to be horrified.

"Come and see the house I've found," she said, standing. "It's just large enough, but not too large. Mrs. Thigpen says it's infinitely manageable and Grace is thrilled with the kitchen."

She held out her hand for him.

A new position. A new home. More importantly, a new life with a woman he loved and admired. Granted, that meant Hackney would be his father-in-law, but he could manage.

Standing, he pulled her to him. The house could wait for a few moments. Long enough for another dozen kisses at the very least.

Author's Note

$\mathcal{M}$rs. Armbruster's Institute and Foundling Hospital was located in Spitalfields, an area of London where many philanthropic ventures began. For example, the American philanthropist George Peabody began a foundation on Commercial Street in 1864 to improve the living conditions of the working poor.

St. Pancras Workhouse existed and is now St. Pancras Hospital. Unfortunately, the poor hygiene in the infant ward was so appalling that many babies died during their stay or after returning from foster care. Charles Dickens wrote about such parish treatment in *Oliver Twist*.

In the Victorian era it was possible to easily purchase cocaine, laudanum, opium, and arsenic. In the 1860s the publication of information about London's East End opium dens inspired various organizations to begin campaigns against the importation of opium. In 1868 the Pharmacy Act limited the sale of dangerous drugs to those registered to dispense them. However, few people ever spoke up about the addictive powers of those drugs during the nineteenth century.

Manipora was loosely based on the Massacre of Cawnpore (1857) now known as Kanpur.

Being a spy was not considered a gentlemanly occupation in the nineteenth century and was relegated to the middle classes, often former military men. Although the Secret Service Bureau wasn't formed until 1903, I imagined the frustration of military men, especially after the Crimean War and the Sepoy Rebellion.

In 1855 the Board of Ordnance had been dissolved and all duties transferred to the War Office. Both the Secretary of State for War and the Commander-in-Chief of the Army held equal responsibilities. Prince George, Second Duke of Cambridge, took on the job of Commander-in-Chief in 1856. Unfortunately, he was heavily resistant to any kinds of reform.

When you were stopped at the top, you developed other ways to get things done. In this case, I envisioned a loose grouping of men—the Silent Service—who worked for the empire with the tacit approval of men who would probably not support them if their actions ever became public.

The Schomberg House was divided into three sections in 1769. The three units were, at various times, homes for artists, a high-class bordello, a haberdashery, a fashionable textile store, a bookshop, and a gambling den. All three units were purchased by the British government in 1859 for use by the War Office, but were largely demolished in 1956. Only the facades remain.

The next book in

Karen Ranney's

ALL FOR LOVE
series,

To Wed an

Heiress,

goes on sale Spring 2019.
Preorder your copy now!

CASSANDRA BEFORE PRIAM

FROM A POMPEIAN WALL PAINTING

THE BIMILLENNIAL VIRGIL

VIRGIL
AND OTHER
LATIN POETS

EDITED BY J. B. GREENOUGH

G. L. KITTREDGE

THORNTON JENKINS

GINN AND COMPANY

GINN AND COMPANY

BOSTON · NEW YORK · CHICAGO · LONDON
ATLANTA · DALLAS · COLUMBUS · SAN FRANCISCO

PREFACE

In this new edition, which is offered as a modest tribute on the bimillennial anniversary of Virgil's birth, Part One contains Books I–VI of the Æneid, followed by a full summary of Books VII–XII.

In response to many requests from teachers and in accordance with the recommendations in the Report of the Classical Investigation, the Second Part includes not only about four hundred lines from Ovid's *Metamorphoses* but also some of the best passages in the *Fasti* and the *Tristia*, as well as one extract from the *Epistles from Pontus* and two from the *Heroides*. Some of these selections embody famous tales from mythology and the legendary history of Rome; others contain important biographical matter. Several lively extracts from Catullus are also included and a number of the most celebrated odes of Horace.

Thus those teachers who wish to complete the first six books of the Æneid have a wide choice for reading at sight or for additional illustrative study, and those also who prefer to substitute other Latin poetry for one or two books of the Æneid will find abundant and varied material at their disposal. It is believed that the opportunity to compare different poetical treatments of the same theme will be welcomed by teachers and pupils alike. Thus the myth of Cacus as told by Ovid will be found along with Virgil's account of the same monster; the story of Orpheus and Eurydice is given in both Virgil's words (in his Georgics) and in Ovid's; Ovid's account of his ship stands by the side of the poem which Catullus dedicated to his favorite yacht; for the Golden Mean the pupil has a chance to compare Horace and Ovid; for the Golden Age he may read both Ovid and Tibullus.

The Grammatical Summary in the Introduction enables the editors to simplify the references in the Notes. References to this Summary are made in the Notes by the abbreviation "Introd." (as, "Introd. § 66"). The grammars cited are those of Allen and Greenough (A.), D'Ooge (D.), Bennett (B.), and Gildersleeve (G.). At the suggestion of teachers, the notes for certain selections in Part Two are sparse.

The illustrations have been carefully studied. Many of them are reproduced from ancient statues, wall paintings, and other works of art. Such pictures represent objects or ideas which were familiar to the Latin poets and their contemporaries, and thus serve as graphic notes, as it were, to the passages which they illustrate. In addition, however, there have been included a considerable number of illustrations from the pen of Mr. Rodney Thomson, whose skill in revivifying the days of old is well known. Such pictures undoubtedly serve to stimulate the imagination of pupils and thus to make the subject matter real and appealing. The editors wish to express their gratitude to Dr. George A. Plimpton for allowing them to present a facsimile of one of the Virgil manuscripts in his collection (see p. 265). This is especially interesting as showing the form in which a poet like Chaucer read his classics.

G. L. KITTREDGE
THORNTON JENKINS

CONTENTS

PART I. VIRGIL

PART II. OVID AND OTHER POETS

LIST OF ILLUSTRATIONS

IN THE TEXT

IN THE NOTES

I

P. VERGILI MARONIS
AENEIS

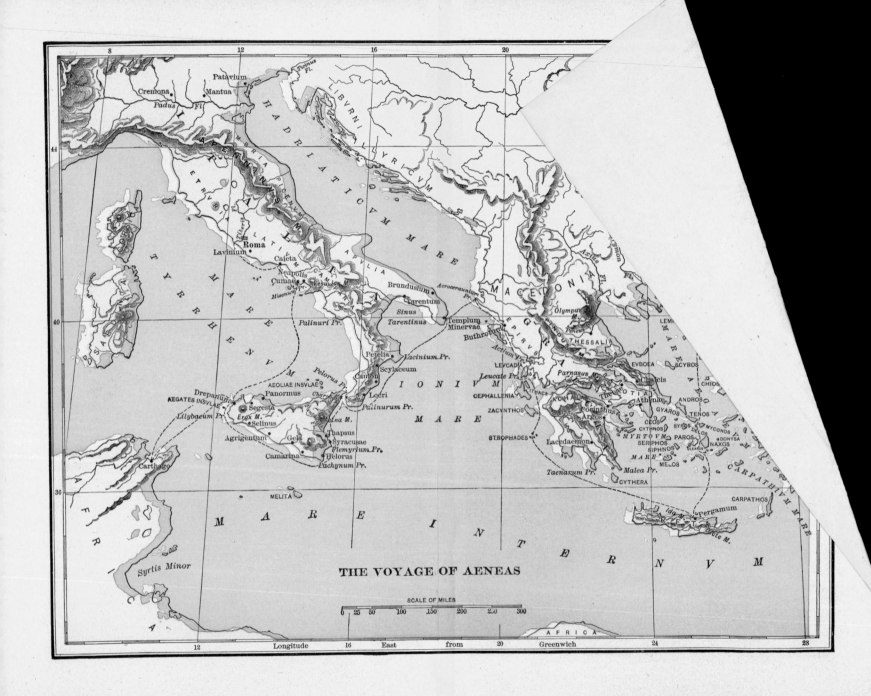

THE VOYAGE OF AENEAS

SCALE OF MILES

0   25   50   100   150   200   250   300

INTRODUCTION

VIRGIL'S Æneid is not merely the noblest expression of the Roman mind in poetry: it is also one of the greatest achievements in the literature of the world. For some two thousand years it has been an accepted model for epic or heroic poetry, and modern literature is full of echoes or imitations of its phrases, its ideas, its situations, and its incidents. It still serves as a standard of chaste and self-restrained poetic art, by which, consciously or unconsciously, we judge all works in the grand style. Thus, familiarity with the Æneid is not only valuable in itself, but also enriches and intensifies our appreciation of poetry in general. The works and the spirit of Virgil are a part of the intellectual and artistic inheritance of our race.

THE AUGUSTAN AGE

Augustus and his times. The time of Virgil, the so-called Augustan Age, was the most flourishing period of Latin literature. It extended from the death of Julius Cæsar (44 B.C.) to the death of Augustus (A.D. 14). For generations the Romans had studied and imitated the works of the Greeks, and in the first century B.C. we find a long list of eminent writers—Varro, Lucretius, Catullus, Cicero, Gallus, Cæsar, and Sallust; but not until the Augustan Age was literature recognized as a profession apart from law and politics. Augustus was wise enough to see that the encouragement of letters would help powerfully in establishing sound government and in securing his own position as head of the State. He was himself a cultivated man who took an active interest in art and literature, and the nobles of his court followed his example. His reign was, after 30 B.C., an interval of peace after the long and exhausting struggle of the civil wars. Literature became fashionable, and everybody of any consequence aspired to be a writer, or at least a critic. A class of men arose to whom literature was the serious business of life, not an amusement or a mere adjunct to a political career.

3

Influence of Alexandria. But probably the greatest stimulus came from the gradual introduction of the literature of Alexandria, which had begun in the last half of the second century B.C. The seeds of Greek culture, scattered far and wide by the overthrow of Grecian liberty, had been particularly fruitful in that city. Here two great libraries were established, and a long line of scholars, critics, and authors flourished for centuries. There was a great revival of learning, and writers tried their hand at almost every form of composition — learned treatise, history, epic, lyric, elegiac, didactic poetry, epigram, and satire. The study of this great body of literature could not but excite the Romans to imitation.

VIRGIL'S LIFE

Birth and education. By general consent, Virgil (*Publius Vergilius Maro*)[1] stands first among the writers of the Augustan Age.

Virgil was born 70 B.C. at Andes, in the municipality of Mantua, in North Italy. His father was doubtless a Roman citizen, probably of old Italian stock, and seems to have been a well-to-do landholder. He gave his son an excellent education, with a view to a political career. Virgil studied at Cremona and Milan, and afterwards, at about the age of seventeen (53 B.C.), went to Rome to complete his training. There he seems to have studied rhetoric under Epidius, who was also the tutor of the boy Octavius (afterwards Augustus). But Virgil's tastes and his uncertain health led him to abandon politics and the law. He is said to have appeared once, and once only, as an advocate.

Study of philosophy at Naples. How long Virgil remained in Rome we do not know, but about 48 B.C. he went to Naples to devote himself to the Epicurean philosophy as a pupil of Siron, the most popular professor of the time. Naples, originally a colony from Greece, was still largely a Greek city; and the poet's acquaintance with Greek literature, which he had of course begun to study as a boy, must have become extensive and intimate during these years of early manhood. His Georgics are permeated with the scientific theories of Epicurus.

---

[1] The form *Virgil* (instead of *Vergil*) is derived from the mistaken spelling *Virgilius*, but has for centuries been the accepted English form of the poet's name.

Seizure of Virgil's estate. The year 41 B.C. marks a crisis in Virgil's life. In the civil war that followed the assassination of Julius Cæsar in 44 B.C., the city of Cremona, forty miles from the poet's birthplace, took the side of the Republican party led by Brutus and Cassius. After their defeat at Philippi (42 B.C.), the territory of Cremona, with a part of that of Mantua, was confiscated and assigned to the victorious soldiery of the Triumvirs — Octavius, Mark Antony, and Lepidus. The estate of Virgil's father, who was still living, was seized among the rest, or at least was in danger of seizure. Virgil may have been at home at the time. At all events, his acquaintance with men of influence at Rome saved the property. Asinius Pollio, who had been military governor in North Italy, took a warm interest in the young poet. Cornelius Gallus and Alfenus Varus, both probably Virgil's former fellow students, appear to have interceded in his favor. He went to Rome and appealed to Octavius, who assured him of peaceable possession. His First Eclogue expresses his gratitude.

Somewhat later, perhaps, Virgil was involved in a boundary dispute, in which (according to the usual story) his life was threatened; the claimant chased him, sword in hand, and he was forced to swim across the Mincius to escape. These occurrences, however, are doubtful, depending upon an interpretation of the Ninth Eclogue that is not undisputed. The whole subject of Virgil's experiences with these lands is obscure and confused. We know that he received a villa and estate at Nola in Campania, and these may have been granted him in lieu of his ancestral property.

Virgil becomes famous. At about this time Virgil wrote his Eclogues, which were finished by 40 B.C. and published soon after. These instantly made him famous at Rome, and he joined the circle of Mæcenas, one of the chief advisers of Augustus and a noted patron of literature. He received a house in the city on the Esquiline Hill, but his favorite residence, after the year 37 B.C. (aet. 33), was in the neighborhood of Naples. The next few years were spent in the composition of the Georgics, — four books on husbandry, — the most finished and elaborate of all his poems. These were probably written at the request of Mæcenas, who desired by all means to restore the old Roman virtues of thrift, industry, and fondness for rustic life.

The Æneid. It was after the defeat of Antony at Actium, and the settlement of the empire under the rule of Augustus (30 B.C.), that Virgil began the composition of the Æneid. Reports and great expectations soon began to spread as to the coming work, as testified in the celebrated couplet of Propertius (ii. 34. 65, 66):

> Cedite, Romani scriptores; cedite, Grai:
> Nescio quid maius nascitur Iliade.

A few years later, Virgil consented to read portions of the new poem to Augustus and his sister Octavia, who had lately lost her son, the young Marcellus. In compliment to her, Virgil had inserted the beautiful lines (vi. 868–886) in allusion to her loss. As he recited these verses with great power and pathos, — for among his accomplishments he was a most effective reader, — Octavia swooned away; and when she recovered, she ordered 10,000 sesterces (about $500) to be paid to the poet for each of the memorial lines.

Visit to Greece. When the Æneid was brought to a close, — though unfinished in detail, — Virgil set out (19 B.C.) on a journey to Greece, that he might give the leisure of a few years to its careful revision, and then devote the remainder of his life to philosophy.

Death of Virgil. Augustus, arriving soon after at Athens from the East, prevailed on Virgil to go back with him to Italy. This journey proved fatal to him. His delicate lungs suffered from the harsh air of the coast, while his frame was racked with seasickness and worn with the fatigue of a visit to Megara on the homeward voyage. He barely lived to reach Italy, and died at Brundisium on September 21, 19 B.C., aged not quite fifty-one. He had left instructions, we are told, that the Æneid should be burned, since it lacked the finishing touches; but the command of Augustus saved it.

His tomb. Virgil was buried, by his own desire, near Naples. At the crest of the rock that overhangs the grotto of Posilipo, beneath a low ivy-grown roof of stone, was formerly said to be the modest epitaph:

> MANTVA ME GENVIT: CALABRI RAPVERE: TENET NVNC
> PARTHENOPE[1]: CECINI PASCVA RVRA DVCES

no doubt of a later date. The exact place of his burial is uncertain and may be now covered by the waters of the Bay of Naples.

[1] The old name of Naples.

VIRGIL'S WORKS

THE MINOR POEMS

Authorship. Certain minor poems, ascribed to Virgil in ancient times, have been regarded by many modern scholars as spurious. These are *Catalepton* (or *Catalepta*), *Culex*, *Ciris*, *Aetna*, *Copa*, and *Dirae*, to which may be added *Moretum*. Except for *Moretum*, there seems to be no strong reason for rejecting these pieces, which may well be the product of Virgil's literary apprenticeship.

Catalepton. The *Catalepton* or *Catalepta* ("Trifles") is a collection of epigrams and other short poems in various metres and of various dates, mostly early. Some of them, if genuine, have much autobiographical interest.

Culex. The *Culex* ("Gnat") is said to have been written when Virgil was only sixteen. It is a sportive mock-epic of 414 lines. A sleeping shepherd is about to be bitten by a serpent when a friendly gnat awakes him with its sting. Still half-asleep, he slaps at the insect and kills it. That night the ghost of the gnat appears, reproaches the shepherd for his ingratitude, and tells a long story of its adventures in the world of the dead. The poem was freely translated by Spenser under the title of "Virgil's Gnat."

Ciris. The *Ciris*, probably begun in 48 B.C. and finished somewhat later, reads like an episode from Ovid's *Metamorphoses*. Nisus, king of Megara, has a crimson lock of hair. So long as this is not cut off, he is unconquerable. He is besieged by Minos, king of Crete. Scylla, his daughter, falls in love with Minos and shears the charmed lock. The city is captured and Nisus and Scylla are enslaved, but are changed to birds by the gods — Nisus to a sparrow-hawk and Scylla to the bird called a *ciris*.

Aetna. The *Aetna*, commonly regarded as not Virgilian, deals with the cause of volcanic eruptions. It may have been written about 50 B.C.

Moretum and *Copa*. The *Moretum* (translated by Cowper) describes the preparation of the *moretum*, a kind of rustic salad. In the *Copa* a dancing tavern-maid (*copa*) sings a song inviting travellers to rest and take refreshment in the garden of her wayside inn.

Dirae. In the *Dirae* ("Curses") a shepherd prays that his little farm may be laid waste by fire and flood and poisoned by pestilential air, so as to be useless to the soldier who has robbed him of it. In the conclusion, apparently a separate poem, he bids farewell to his home and his beloved Lydia. If genuine, these two pieces were written shortly before the Eclogues.

THE ECLOGUES

Subject and form. The *Eclogues* ("Selections") are ten short pastoral poems which treat of the loves and occupations of herdsmen (Greek βουκόλοι, *boukoloi*) and hence are called *Bucolics.* In form they are chiefly imitations of the Greek pastoral poets. The scenes, however, are largely Italian, and the subjects refer often to the history of the time and even to incidents in Virgil's own life, such as the attempted seizure of his father's estate.

The Greek pastoral poets. In any highly artificial state of civilization, men are prone to dwell with imaginative longing on the simplicity of country life and to play at farming and to fancy themselves shepherds or herdsmen. This tendency was especially marked in Sicily about 275–250 B.C., and found expression in the Idyls or "picture poems" of Theocritus, Bion, Moschus, and other writers of the same Greek school. Some forty of these poems have come down to us.

Reputation of the Eclogues. Virgil's Eclogues, which adapted Greek models with skill and taste to Italian conditions of life, became instantly popular at Rome. Their perfection of form, delicacy of treatment, and charm of language have maintained for them ever since a place of high distinction in pastoral literature.

THE GEORGICS

Character of the Georgics. These four books on husbandry belong to Virgil's second period. The work was published in 29 B.C. It is universally regarded as the greatest of all didactic (i.e. "teaching") poems.

The original aim of didactic poetry was to embody in a metrical form the rules of some art or science, so as more easily to fix them in the memory. The somewhat dry precepts of the Greek *Works and Days* attributed to Hesiod bear this stamp. This object had, however, been more or less lost sight of in the later Greek didactic poetry, which sought to give a higher literary form and a more elegant dress to subjects which might as well have been treated in prose if the object had been merely instruction.

Object of the poem. Virgil's object, then, was not to write a text-book for practical farmers. It was rather to give pleasure by idealizing an art that his readers were already acquainted with, and to encourage the pursuit of the art among the great landed proprietors. The subject may well have been suggested by Mæcenas, who felt the need of fostering agriculture after the waste and desolation of the civil wars.

Treatment of the subject. In the Georgics Virgil does not attempt to give intelligible directions as to the complete management of land or animals. He picks out here and there topics which he finds suitable for poetry. The value of the work consists in the fine poetic feeling with which he treats natural phenomena and man's relation to the powers which he can engage in his service, or with which he has to contend for his life and subsistence.

THE ÆNEID

Epic poetry. The Æneid has stood for many centuries as a model of epic poetry. Properly speaking, however, an epic consists of a body of immemorial tradition, which has taken form in the mind and language of a people, and which, while the traditions were yet living and believed in, has been worked up in a single poem, or group of poems, whose antiquity and national character have made them, in some sense, sacred books. This is what the poems of Homer were to the Greeks, the Mahabharata and Ramayana to the Hindoos, and the Nibelungen to the Germans. Such epics usually contain an element of the supernatural. The gods may intervene to thwart or assist the hero, or may otherwise take a share or manifest an interest in the action. Such divine actors are technically called the *machines* (or, collectively, the *machinery*) of the poem.

Heroic ballads. The genesis of the epic is somewhat as follows. Among the popular songs of primitive peoples are always a consider-able number in narrative form which deal with heroic figures —

THE ÆNEID

legendary warriors, old kings or chiefs. Such poems may be called *ballads*, though this term includes much more than the special kind of ballads that here concern us. The essentials of a genuine ballad are that it should tell a story, should be meant for singing, and should have no author. To discuss this last requirement would be to open the whole question of popular (i.e. folk) literature. Here it is enough to define the having no author as meaning that the ballad must have been handed down by oral tradition, and must in some fashion have taken its origin from the life, the belief, the traditions of the people. It is not, and cannot be, the conscious artistic work of a literary class or a literary man.

Development of the epic. A number of such ballads as this, each dealing with an episode in the life of a legendary character (whether originally historical or not) may become associated into a sort of cycle. This cycle is, in a sense, already an epic; but it is an epic loosely constructed, and ready at any minute to fall to pieces into parts roughly corresponding to the ballads of which it is made up, or to combine with other similar cycles in making up a larger poem approaching still nearer to the finished epic. After a sufficient number of syntheses, dissolvings, and recombinations (which, in any given case, become so complicated, if there is any long period of time to consider, that it is impossible to trace them in detail), an epic is the result.

Influence of art. At almost any stage in this development, conscious art, as represented by the professional minstrel, may intervene; and, in most cases, before the popular epics assume a form sufficiently definite to reach civilized ears or to be written down, literature, in the person of the combiner and codifier, has exercised its artificial influence on them. Some of these processes may be seen in that little epic, the old English *Gest of Robin Hood*. This was put into its present form by some minstrel or writer of the fifteenth century who had a genuine feeling for the ballad. The materials with which he worked were narrative songs about Robin Hood, which had already begun to gather into cycles, attaching themselves to various places where the legendary outlaw had been celebrated. The combiner has stitched his materials together loosely, but has unified the style to some extent, and has left a work which cannot very easily be resolved into its elements, in fact, an epic. A more modern instance is that of the so-called Finnish epic — the Kalevala. The scholar Lönnrot, in the last century, took down from actual recitation a vast number of heroic songs, and these he combined, with considerable skill, into a single long poem of an epic character, without, as he asserted, adding a line of his own. This illustrates the adaptability of such legendary material to combinative literary treatment, and gives some idea of what has actually been done in the case of older epics.

The Æneid as an epic. The Æneid is an epic in a very different sense, — in what, for the sake of distinction, may be called the literary sense. Though it has the foundation of traditions and all the divine machinery of the true epic, yet the traditions are no longer living; the divine machinery is no longer a matter of belief. The traditions are dug out by antiquarian research. The machinery is manufactured to order, as it were, in a modern workshop. Many of the incidents are labored invention, while the whole is written with a definite purpose, as a work of art. These things put it in a widely different class from the Iliad and Odyssey, which served as its models, and with which it has been oftenest compared. But still it is an imitation of the popular epic, rests on similar traditions, has like formulæ of phrase and conventionalities of treatment, and assumes the same mythical character.

Purpose of the Æneid. Further, the purpose for which the Æneid was written distinguishes it from other artificial epics. It is the product of patriotic sentiment and of belief in the divine origin and high destiny of the Roman State. It is said that the poem was written at the request of Augustus; but it is no mere flattery of a reigning house. The supremacy of the Julian family was identified in the mind of the poet and his readers with the culmination of the Roman State in victory and peace.

Subject of the Æneid. The subject of the Æneid is the destruction of Troy, the seven years' wandering of Æneas, and his settlement in Italy, with the wars raised against him by the native princes. All of these events, according to Virgil's view, led up, by fate and the divine will, to the establishment of the city of Rome.

The Trojan War. Hecuba, wife of the Trojan king, Priam, had dreamed that she bore a firebrand. Accordingly, when her son Paris was born, he was left to perish on Mount Ida. Being rescued, he lived as a shepherd on the mountain, where he was visited by the three great goddesses — Hera (*Juno*), Pallas, and Aphrodite (*Venus*) — to award the prize of beauty among them, the golden apple of discord. His reward for bestowing the prize on Venus was to have the most beautiful of women for his bride. This was Helen, wife of Menelaus, king of Sparta, daughter of Zeus (*Jupiter*) and Leda ; and a wrong to her was to be revenged by all the heroes and chiefs of Greece, who had been her suitors. Paris visited Sparta, won the love of Helen, and carried her away to Troy. Hence the famous ten years' siege and the destruction of the sacred city.

The Tale of Troy. About the Tale of Troy had gathered a vast body of legendary adventure, contained in the "Cyclic Poets," the festal Odes, the Attic Tragedies, and, above all, in the great Homeric poems, the Iliad and Odyssey. The Iliad deals with an episode of the war. It tells the disasters which befell the Grecian army from the wrath of Achilles, its most famous champion, against Agamemnon, brother of Menelaus, and leader of the host. The poem ends with the death and burial of Hector, the noblest champion of Troy, who is slain by Achilles in revenge for the death of his friend Patroclus. The return of Ulysses to Ithaca, after his long wanderings, is the subject of the Odyssey, which contains also the story of the capture of Troy by the stratagem of the wooden horse, and of the fate of several other Grecian chiefs beside Ulysses.

Tradition used by Virgil. Among the various traditions, there was a story that Æneas, after escaping from the sack of Troy, had taken refuge in Italy. How old this tradition was, and whence it was derived, is uncertain. It is not found in any Greek form. The story, including the episode of Dido, was treated by Nævius (235 B.C.), who could hardly have invented it. It was alluded to by Ennius (born 239 B.C.), and had been adopted as a favorite theory before the time of Augustus. Virgil supplements it with details drawn from local tradition, and with many of his own manufacture ; and in this way he has connected the imperial times with the age of gods and heroes.

Summary of the Æneid. The first six books of the Æneid deal with the wanderings of Æneas in his voyage from Troy to the Tiber, and are modelled in general on the Odyssey. The last six books resemble the Iliad. since they are largely concerned with the combats of various heroes in the struggle between the Trojan settlers and the Italian chiefs. A brief outline is given below; fuller summaries of the first half of the poem are prefixed to the several books. Book vi is followed by an abstract of Books vii–xii.

Book i. Æneas and his fleet, on their long voyage from Troy to Italy, are buffeted by a storm but reach the coast of Africa, where Queen Dido from Tyre has recently founded Carthage. Dido receives the Trojans hospitably and requests of Æneas the story of their wanderings.

Book ii. Æneas tells of the fall and sack of Troy and of his escape from the burning city with his father Anchises, his little son Ascanius, and a band of Trojans.

Book iii. Æneas' tale concluded: after a futile settlement in Crete and a visit to Helenus and Andromache in Epirus, the Trojans reach Sicily and land at Drepanum, where Anchises dies; thence they have come to Carthage.

Book iv. Dido falls in love with Æneas and takes him for her husband. Warned by Mercury, Æneas sets sail for Italy. Dido kills herself in despair.

Book v. Threatened by a storm, Æneas lands in Sicily, where he is welcomed by Acestes. Funeral games are held in honor of the dead Anchises. Æneas sets sail for Latium.

Book vi. Arriving at Cumæ, Æneas visits the World Below, guided by the Sibyl. The shade of Anchises prophesies the glories of Rome. The exiles reach the harbor of Cajeta.

Book vii. Æneas reaches the Tiber and is well received by King Latinus of Latium, who offers him his daughter Lavinia in marriage. But war breaks out between the Italians and Æneas.

Book viii. Æneas secures the alliance of Evander. Vulcan forges arms for Æneas.

Book ix. Turnus, a brave Rutulian hero, who had been betrothed to Lavinia, attacks the fleet in the absence of Æneas. Exploits of Nisus and Euryalus. The course of the fight.

Book x. Further incidents of the battle. Combat between Turnus and Æneas, etc.

Book xi. The course of the war. Camilla comes to the aid of Turnus. The Rutulians are besieged by Æneas.

Book xii. A treaty is made, providing that the war shall be settled by a single combat between Turnus and Æneas. The treaty is broken by Juturna, sister of Turnus, and both parties rush to arms. Turnus is slain and despoiled by Æneas.

Virgil's Fame

Virgil's early fame. Even before the composition of the Æneid, Virgil had gained a place among the first in Roman literature. The fame of the Æneid began before the work was completed, and after his death Virgil speedily became, next to Homer, the great poet of antiquity. His influence shows itself in all succeeding Latin literature, as well in prose as in poetry. Almost every writer refers to him as the great genius of the nation. His writings became one of the chief instruments of a liberal education. The interest in his works survived the decay of classical learning. They preserved the spark that at the revival of letters was to burst out into a flame to light and warm the world.

Virgil's later fame. Though Ovid was the favorite Latin poet of the Middle Ages, yet Virgil was never wholly neglected. The Æneid was held in high esteem not so much for its artistic perfection as for the information which it furnished concerning the " matter of Troy," one of the main branches of mediæval romantic material. The fact that some of the leading nations of Western Europe thought themselves descended from the Trojans assured the Æneid of an interested reading wherever there was culture enough to understand it. In the twelfth century the story was worked over into the old French " Romance of Æneas," which, though it seems to us like a parody, enjoyed considerable popularity, and was not without influence on European literature.

Virgil in the Middle Ages. Virgil himself was transformed by the ignorance of the Middle Ages into a mythical person. He became a wonderful magician, who used his art for the defence of the city of Rome. On the strength of the Fourth Eclogue he was regarded as a prophet of the coming of Christ. The Æneid was interpreted as an allegory. Bernard of Chartres, a famous teacher of the twelfth century, declares that Virgil " describes human life under the guise of the history of Æneas, who is the symbol of the soul." Dante calls Virgil " the sea of all knowledge " and " the sage who knew all things."

It was this belief in Virgil as a philosopher and prophet, as well as admiration for his art, that made Dante select him for his guide through the world below.

Virgil and Chaucer. From the time of Chaucer (1340?–1400) the influence of Virgil on English literature has been almost continuous. Chaucer, who was a student of Dante and an admirer of Petrarch and Boccaccio, the leaders of the revival of learning in Italy, is outspoken in his admiration for Virgil. He summarizes a large part of the Æneid at the beginning of his *House of Fame.* In his *Legend of Good Women* he tells the story of Dido, treating it in true mediæval fashion as an episode of faithless chivalric love. The perfection of form and sense of artistic restraint which distinguish the best poetry of Chaucer are doubtless in some measure due to his enthusiastic study of Virgil.

Virgil in the Elizabethan Age. The second period of Italian influence in our literature shows the influence of Virgil in the most signal manner. The Earl of Surrey (1517?–1547) translated Books ii and iv of the Æneid into blank verse (an early specimen of this metre), and throughout the Elizabethan Age the greatness of Virgil was never questioned. His influence was exerted both directly and also indirectly through the medium of the Italians of the Renaissance. Spenser (1552–1599), who was in many ways a marked contrast to Virgil, but who resembled him in the seriousness of his moral and religious purpose and in the purity of his ideals, not only imitated his Eclogues (in the *Shepherds' Calendar*), but continually reproduces bits of the Æneid in his *Faery Queen.* The heroic and the bucolic poets of the seventeenth century, much affected by the Italians and by Spenser, acknowledged Virgil as their master. Even the unsuccessful attempt to reconstruct English metre on classical models testifies to the reverence in which he was held. This attempt (with which the names of Gabriel Harvey and Sir Philip Sidney are inseparably associated) reached the acme of absurdity in Stanihurst's translation of a part of the Æneid in hexameters. The great epic of Milton was composed according to principles drawn from the Æneid, though Milton was also a careful student of Homer.

Later influence of Virgil. In the Restoration period Dryden (1631–1700) not only translated Virgil, but imitated him often. It was the sanity of Virgil's art, the finish of his versification, the precision and felicity of his diction that affected Dryden, rather than any higher qualities of artistic and moral earnestness or of imagination. The same qualities that appealed to Dryden made Virgil rather than Homer the favorite poet of the English Augustan Age — the age of Addison and Pope and Swift. The artificiality of the time took peculiar pleasure in his Pastorals — a kind of poetry in which highly conventionalized states of society have often delighted.

Influence in recent times. The Romantic Revival, beginning obscurely in imitations of Spenser and of Milton's minor poems, and gaining strength from the unique genius of Gray (1716–1771), prepared the way for the great Romantic movement of the early nineteenth century. This movement was so revolutionary that it would not have been strange if, in the passionate repudiation of other eighteenth-century ideals, Virgil too had been neglected. But his position still remains secure as, next to Homer, the greatest of epic poets.

THE GRAMMAR AND STYLE OF THE ÆNEID

1. *The diction of poetry.* One who begins the Æneid after reading the Gallic War of Cæsar and the Orations of Cicero is at once aware that the style and grammar are not the same as those of Latin prose. Thus, the separation of **Trōiae** (i. 1) from the word it modifies shows that the order of words of poetry is different from that of prose; the omission of a preposition with **Ītaliam** (i. 2) shows a difference in syntax, and the genitive plural **superum** (i. 4) a difference in the forms of words. The main points of difference between the diction of the Æneid and that of Cæsar and Cicero are described in the sections that follow.

I. SYNTAX

2. *General character of the syntax.* The syntax of the Æneid is in general much easier and simpler than that of prose, and there are few difficulties of grammar except where the ellipsis of words produces obscurity, or where a specially poetical construction is used. More is demanded of the cases in poetry than in prose. Constructions of the cases are therefore relatively more varied and constructions of subordinate clauses less varied than in prose.

3. *Poetical constructions.* Of the unfamiliar constructions in the Æneid, some are archaisms (or old expressions), retained because poetry is fond of ancient usage; some are imitations of Greek idioms; some are a combination of the two.

USE OF CASES

Nominative

4. *As subject.* The subject of a finite verb is in the nominative (A. 339; D. 316; B. 166; G. 203).

Tyriī tenuēre **colōnī**, *Tyrian colonists inhabited* [*it*], i. 12.

5. *As subject of the historical infinitive.* The nominative is used as the subject of the historical infinitive (A. 463; D. 320; B. 335; G. 647).

hinc **Ulixēs** terrēre, *from this time Ulysses frightened* [*me*], ii. 97.

6. *In exclamations.* The nominative may be used in exclamations (A. 339, *a*; D. 319).

ēn **dextra fidēs**que, *lo, the faith and plighted word!* iv. 597.

Genitive

7. *Possessive.* The possessive genitive denotes the person or thing to which an object, quality, feeling, or action belongs (A. 343; D. 328; B. 198; G. 362).

Trōiae ab ōrīs, *from the shores of Troy*, i. 1.
vī **superum**, *by the power of the gods*, i. 4.

8. *Subjective.* The possessive genitive may denote the person or thing that possesses the feeling or quality, or does the act, denoted by the noun on which it depends (A. 343, N.[1]; D. 326, I; B. 199; G. 363, 1).

clāmor **virum** strīdorque **rudentum**, *the shouting of the men and the creaking of the ropes*, i. 87.

9. *Predicate.* The possessive genitive often stands in the predicate, connected with its noun by a verb (A. 343, *b, c*; D. 330; B. 198, 2; G. 366).

grātēs persolvere dignās nōn **opis** est **nostrae**, *to render worthy thanks is not within our power*, i. 600.

10. *Appositional.* A limiting genitive is sometimes used instead of a noun in apposition (A. 343, *d*; D. 335; B. 202: G. 361).

urbem **Patavī**, *the city of Patavium*, i. 247.

11. *Material.* The genitive may denote the substance or material of which a thing consists (A. 344; D. 348; B. 197).

aquae mōns, *a mountain of water*, i. 105.

12. *Quality.* The genitive is used to denote quality, but only when the quality is modified by an adjective (A. 345; D. 338; B. 203; G. 365).

> **tantae mōlis** erat Rōmānam condere gentem, [*a task*] *of so great toil it was to found the Roman race*, i. 33.

13. *Partitive.* Words denoting a part are followed by the genitive of the whole to which the part belongs (A. 346; D. 342; B. 201; G. 367).

quārum pulcherrima, *the fairest of whom*, i. 72.

14. *Objective.* Nouns of *action, agency,* and *feeling* govern the genitive of the object (A. 348; D. 354; B. 200; G. 363, 2).

studiīs **bellī**, *in its passion for war*, i. 14.

15. *Indefinite value.* Certain adjectives of quantity are used in the genitive to denote indefinite value (A. 417; D. 341; B. 203, 3; G. 379).

tantī, *of such account*, iii. 453.

16. *With adjectives.* The genitive is used with adjectives of *desire, knowledge, memory, fulness, power, sharing, guilt,* and their opposites; also with participles in **-ns**, when they are used as adjectives, and (in poetry and late prose) with verbals in **-āx** (A. 349, *a–c*; D. 357; B. 204; G. 374, 375).

> **veteris** memor **bellī**, *mindful of the former war*, i. 23.
> servantissimus **aequī**, *most observant of justice*, ii. 427.
> **fictī** tenāx, *persistent in what is false*, iv. 188.

17. *Specification.* The genitive is used in poetry with almost any adjective to denote that *with reference to which* the quality exists (A. 349, *d*; D. 356; B. 204, 4; G. 374, N.⁶).

fessī **rērum**, *weary of toil*, i. 178.

18. *With verbs of remembering and forgetting.* Verbs of *remembering* and *forgetting* take either the accusative or the genitive of the object.

Meminī takes the accusative when it has the literal sense of *retaining in the mind* what one has seen, heard, or learned; so **oblīviscor** in the opposite sense, — to *forget* literally.

Meminī takes the genitive when it means to *be mindful* or *regardful of* a person or thing; so **oblīviscor** in the opposite sense, — *to disregard* (A. 350; D. 358; B. 206; G. 376).

> oblīviscere **Grāiōs**, *forget the Greeks* (banish them from your mind, as if you had never known them), ii. 148.
>
> nostrōs **huius** meminisse minōrēs, [*grant that*] *our descendants may be mindful of this day,* i. 733.

19. *With verbs of accusing, condemning, and acquitting.* Verbs of *accusing, condemning,* and *acquitting* take the genitive of the charge or penalty (A. 352; D. 336, 337; B. 208; G. 378).

> damnātī **mortis**, *doomed to death,* vi. 430.

20. *With verbs of pity.* Verbs of *pity,* as **misereor** and **miserēscō**, take the genitive (A. 354, *a*; D. 365; B. 209, 2; G. 377).

> miserēre **labōrum**, *pity my sufferings,* ii. 143.

21. *With impersonals.* As impersonals, **miseret, paenitet, piget, pudet, taedet** (or **pertaesum est**), take the genitive of the *cause of the feeling* and the accusative of the *person affected* (A. 354, *b*; D. 363; B. 209, 1; G. 377).

> piget [eās] inceptī, *they loathe the undertaking,* v. 678.

22. *With verbs of plenty and want.* Verbs of *plenty* and *want* sometimes govern the genitive (A. 356; D. 349; B. 212; G. 383).

> implentur **veteris Bacchī** pinguisque **ferīnae**, *they fill themselves with old wine and fat venison,* i. 215.

23. *Peculiar genitives.* The genitive is used with **ergō**, *because of,* **instar**, *like,* and **tenus**, *as far as* (A. 359, *b*; D. 331; G. 373 and 417, 14).

> illius ergō, *on his account,* vi. 670.
>
> equus īnstar **montis**, *a horse as huge as a mountain* (*like a mountain*), ii. 15.

Dative

24. *Indirect object of a transitive verb.* The dative of the indirect object with the accusative of the direct may be used with any transitive verb whose meaning allows (A. 362 ; D. 371; B. 187, I ; G. 345).

mihī causās memorā, *tell me the reasons*, i. 8.

25. *Indirect object of an intransitive verb.* The dative of the indirect object may be used with any intransitive verb whose meaning allows (A. 366 ; D. 376 ; B. 187, II ; G. 346).

quīs (= quibus) contigit, *whom it befell*, i. 95.

26. *Indirect object of special verbs.* Many verbs signifying to *favor, help, please, trust,* and their contraries ; also to *believe, persuade, command, obey, serve, resist, envy, threaten, pardon,* and *spare* take the dative (A. 367 ; D. 376 ; B. 187, II, *a* ; G. 346).

parce metū, *spare your fears*, i. 257.

27. *Indirect object with compound verbs.* Many verbs compounded with ad, ante, con, in, inter, ob, post, prae, prō, sub, super, and some with circum admit the dative of the indirect object (A. 370 ; D. 382 ; B. 187, III ; G. 347).

illum scopulō īnfīxit, *she impaled him on a rock*, i. 45.

28. *With certain verbs.* Misceō, iungō, verbs of *contending,* and some others may take the dative in poetry instead of a noun with a preposition (A. 368, 3, N., and *a* ; 413, *a*, N.; D. 381; B. 358, 3 ; G. 346, N.[6]).

furit aestus harēnīs, *the seething flood rages with the sands*, i. 107.

29. *Possession.* The dative is used with esse and similar words to denote possession (A. 373 ; D. 390 ; B. 190 ; G. 349).

tantaene animīs caelestibus īrae [sunt], *have heavenly minds such wrath ?* i. 11.

30. *Agent.* The dative of the agent is used with the passive periphrastic conjugation, and, in poetry, with almost any passive form A. 374, 375 ; D. 392 ; B. 189 ; G. 354).

quippe vetor fātīs, *to be sure, I am forbidden by the fates*, i. 39.

The ablative of agent (§ 53) is rarely used in the Æneid.

31. *Reference.* The dative is used to denote the person (or, rarely, the thing) affected by the action or situation expressed by the verb (A. 376, 378; D. 385; B. 188; G. 350).

   rēgnum **gentibus** esse, *to be a seat of royal power for the nations*, i. 17.

The so-called ethical dative of the personal pronouns is really a faded variety of the dative of reference. It is used to show a certain interest felt by the person indicated (A. 380; D. 388; B. 188, 2, *b*; G. 351).

   tibi bellum geret, *he shall wage war for you*, i. 261.

32. *Separation.* Many verbs of *taking away* and the like take the dative (especially of a *person*) instead of the ablative of separation. Such are compounds of **ab**, **dē**, **ex**, and a few of **ad** (A. 381; D. 389; B. 188, 2, *d*; G. 345, R.[1]).

   silicī scintillam excūdit, *he strikes a spark from flint*, i. 174.

33. *Purpose.* The dative is used to denote the purpose or end, often with another dative of the person or thing affected (*double dative construction*) (A. 382; D. 395; B. 191; G. 356).

   populum ventūrum **excidiō Libyae**, *a people would come for the ruin of Libya*, i. 22.

34. *Place to which.* In poetry the *place to which* is often expressed by the dative (A. 428, *h*; D. 367; B. 193; G. 358).

   īnferret deōs **Latiō**, *bring the gods to Latium*, i. 6.

This poetical construction occurs more than sixty times in Books i–vi of the Æneid.

35. *With adjectives.* The dative is used with adjectives of *fitness, nearness, likeness, service, inclination*, and their opposites (A. 384; D. 397, *a*; B. 192, 1; G. 359).

   gēns inimīca **mihī**, *a nation hostile to me*, i. 67.

ACCUSATIVE

36. *Direct object.* The direct object of a transitive verb is put in the accusative (A. 387; D. 404; B. 172, 174; G. 330).

   videt **classem**, *he sees the fleet*, i. 128.

37. *Cognate.* An intransitive verb often takes the accusative of a noun of kindred meaning. This construction is loosely used by the poets (A. 390; D. 408; B. 176, 4; G. 332, 333).

arma virumque canō, *I sing [a song of] arms and the hero*, i. 1.

38. *Predicate accusative.* An accusative in the predicate referring to the same person or thing as the direct object, but not in apposition with it, is called a predicate accusative (A. 392; D. 416; B. 177; G. 340).

39. *With verbs of naming, etc.* Verbs of *naming, choosing, appointing, making, esteeming, showing,* and the like, may take a predicate accusative along with the direct object (A. 393; D. 417; B. 177, 1; G. 340).

faciat tē **parentem**, *make thee a parent*, i. 75.

40. *With verbs of asking, etc.* Some verbs of *asking* and *teaching* may take two accusatives, one of the person (*direct object*) asked, and the other of the thing (*secondary object*) (A. 396; D. 413; B. 178, 1, a–c; G. 339).

quōs illī **poenās** reposcent, *of whom they will exact the penalty*, ii. 139. Cf. iv. 50, and vi. 759.

41. *Adverbial.* The accusative, especially of certain adjectives, is used adverbially (A. 397, *a*; D. 438; B. 176, 3; G. 333, 1).

multum iactātus, *much tossed about*, i. 3.

42. *Specification.* In poetry the accusative is often used with an adjective or a verb to denote the part affected (A. 397, *b*; D. 427; B. 180; G. 338).

nūda **genū**, *with knee bare (bare as to the knee)*, i. 320.

This construction is borrowed from the Greek and is often called the synecdochical or Greek accusative.

43. *Direct object of a verb in the middle voice.* In poetry the accusative is sometimes used as the direct object of a passive verb that has the character of a Greek verb in the middle voice. This construction is most common with verbs meaning *clothe* (A. 397, *c*; D. 406, *d*;

B. 175, 2, *d*; G. 338, N.[2] For the middle voice see A. 156, *a*; D. 406, *d*, footnote; B. 256; G. 212, R.).

inūtile ferrum cingitur, *he girds on the useless steel*, ii. 510.

44. *In exclamations.* The accusative is used in exclamations (A. 397, *d*; D. 436; B. 183; G. 343, 1).

īnfandum, *O horror!* i. 251.

45. *Subject of an infinitive.* The subject of an infinitive is in the accusative (A. 397, *e*; D. 419; B. 184; G. 343, 2).

tē dare iūra loquuntur, *they say that you define (give) the rights*, i. 731.

46. *Time and space.* Duration of time and extent of space are expressed by the accusative (A. 423, 425; D. 420; B. 181, 1; G. 334–336).

tot annōs bella gerō, *I have been waging war so many years*, i. 47.

47. *Place to which.* Place *to which* is regularly expressed by the accusative with **ad** or **in**, except in names of towns, small islands, and **domus** and **rūs**, where the preposition is omitted. In poetry, too, the preposition is often omitted (A. 426, 2; 427; 428, *g*; D. 428, 430, 434; B. 182; G. 337).

in altum vēla dabant, *they were setting sail to the deep*, i. 34.
Ītaliam vēnit, *he came to Italy*, i. 2.

48. *With prepositions.* Certain prepositions are used with the accusative (A. 220, *a*, *c*; D. 276, 278; B. 141, 143; G. 416, 418).

Iūnōnis ob īram, *on account of the wrath of Juno*, i. 4.

ABLATIVE

49. *Separation.* Verbs meaning to *remove, set free, be absent, deprive*, and *want* take the ablative (sometimes with **ab** or **ex**) (A. 401; D. 440; B. 214; G. 390).

Trōas arcēbat longē **Latiō**, *she was keeping the Trojans far from Latium*, i. 31.

50. *Source.* The ablative (usually with a preposition) is used to denote the source from which anything is derived (A. 403; D. 451; B. 215; G. 395).

prōgeniem **Trōiānō ā sanguine** dūcī, *a race was springing from Trojan blood*, i. 19.

51. *Material.* The ablative is used to denote the material of which anything consists (A. 403, 2; D. 452; B. 224, 3; G. 396).

ātrō **sanguine** guttae, *drops of dark blood*, iii. 28.

52. *Cause.* The ablative is used to express cause (A. 404; D. 462; B. 219; G. 408).

īnsignem **pietāte** virum, *a man distinguished for his piety*, i. 10.

53. *Agent.* The voluntary agent after a passive verb is expressed by the ablative with **ā** or **ab** (A. 405; D. 453; B. 216; G. 401).

ab Eurōō flūctū curvātus, *curved by the eastern wave*, iii. 533.

The only other instances of this construction in Books i–vi are iv. 356 and 377. The dative (§ 30) is common.

54. *Comparison.* The comparative degree is often followed by the ablative signifying *than* (A. 406; D. 446; B. 217; G. 398).

terrīs magis **omnibus** coluisse, *to have cherished more than all lands*, i. 15.

55. *Means.* The ablative is used to denote the means or instrument of an action (A. 409; D. 468; B. 218; G. 401).

hīs accēnsa, *inflamed by these things*, i. 29.

The ablative of the *way by which* is a variety of the ablative of means (A. 429, *a*; D. 474; B. 218, 9; G. 389).

prōvehimur **pelagō**, *we sail forth over the sea*, iii. 506.

56. *With deponent verbs.* The deponents ūtor, fruor, fungor, **potior**, and **vēscor**, with several of their compounds, govern the ablative (A. 410; D. 469, *a*; B. 218, 1; G. 407).

hīs vōcibus ūsa est, *she spoke thus* (*used these words*), i. 64.

57. *With* **opus** *and* **ūsus.** **Opus** and **ūsus**, signifying *need*, take the ablative (A. 411; D. 469, *b*; B. 218, 2; G. 406).

animīs opus [est], *there is need of courage*, vi. 261.

58. *Manner.* The manner of an action is denoted by the ablative; usually with **cum** unless a limiting adjective is used with the noun.

In poetry the preposition is often omitted, even when there is no adjective in the phrase (A. 412; D. 459, 460; B. 220; G. 399).

> **magnō cum murmure**, *with great rumbling*, i. 55.
> **turbine** perflant, *they blow in a whirlwind*, i. 83.

59. *Accompaniment.* Accompaniment is denoted by the ablative, regularly with **cum** (A. 413; D. 456; B. 222; G. 392).

> haec **sēcum** [dīcit], *thus she soliloquizes* (*she says these things with herself*), i. 37.

60. *Degree of difference.* With comparatives and words implying comparison the ablative is used to denote the degree of difference (A. 414; D. 475; B. 223; G. 403).

> **multō** tremendum magis, *much more to be shuddered at*, ii. 199.

61. *Quality.* The quality of a thing is denoted by the ablative with an adjective or genitive modifier (A. 415; D. 466; B. 224; G. 400).

> **praestantī** corpore nymphae, *nymphs of surpassing beauty*, i. 71.

62. *Price.* The price of a thing is put in the ablative (A. 416; D. 470; B. 225; G. 404).

> **aurō** corpus vēndēbat, *he was selling the body for gold*, i. 484.

The other instances of this construction in Books i–vi are ii. 104; vi. 621; vi. 622.

63. *Specification.* The ablative of specification denotes that *in respect to which* something is or is done (A. 418; D. 478; B. 226; G. 397).

> **studiīs** asperrima bellī, *very violent in its passion for war*, i. 14.

64. *Accordance.* The ablative is used to express that *in accordance with which* anything is or is done (A. 418, *a*; D. 458; B. 226; G. 397).

> **foedere certō**, *under fixed conditions*, i. 62.

This is a variety of the ablative of specification.

65. *Absolute.* A noun or pronoun, with a participle in agreement, may be put in the ablative to define the *time* or *circumstances* of an action (A. 419; D. 480; B. 227; G. 409).

> **nūmine laesō**, *purpose having been thwarted*, i. 8.

66. *With adjectives.* The ablative is used with the adjectives **dignus**, **indignus**, **frētus**, **contentus**, and **laetus**, also with adjectives of *filling*

and *abounding*, *freedom* and *want* (A. 431, *a*; 418, *b*; 409, *a*; 402, *a*; D. 479; 469, *c*, *d*; 440; B. 226, 2; 218, 3; 219, 1; 218, 8; 214, *d*; G. 397, N.²; 401, N.⁶; 405, N.⁸).

> **hāc galeā** contentus, *content with this helmet*, v. 314.
> **illā** frētus, *relying on this*, iv. 245.
> **tegmine** laetus, *exulting in the skin*, i. 275.
> fēta **austrīs**, *teeming with winds*, i. 51.

67. *Place where* (*locative ablative*). Place *where* is regularly expressed by the ablative with **in**; but in poetry the preposition is often omitted (A. 426, 3; 429, 4; D. 485 and N.; B. 228 and *d*; G. 385 and N.¹).

> **summō in fluctū**, *on the crest of the wave*, i. 106.
> **terrīs et altō**, *on land and sea*, i. 3.

68. *Place whence.* Place *from which* is regularly expressed by the ablative with **ā (ab)**, **dē**, **ē (ex)**, except in names of towns, small islands, and **domus** and **rūs**, where the preposition is omitted. In poetry, too, the preposition is often omitted with other words (A. 426, 1; 427; 428, *g*; D. 441, 442, 444; B. 229 and 1; G. 390, 391 and N.).

> ab **ōrīs**, *from the shores*, i. 1.
> dētrūdunt nāvīs **scopulō**, *they shove off the ships from the rock*, i. 145.

69. *With prepositions.* The ablative is used with certain prepositions (A. 220, *b*, *c*; D. 277, 278; B. 142, 143; G. 417, 418).

> ē **cōnspectū**, *out of sight*, i. 34.

70. *Time.* Time *when*, or *within which*, is expressed by the ablative (A. 423; D. 492; B. 230, 231; G. 393).

> **aestāte novā**, *in the early summer*, i. 430.

VOCATIVE

71. *Direct address.* The vocative is the case of direct address (A. 340; D. 321; B. 171; G. 23, 5; 201, R.¹).

> **Mūsa**, *O Muse!* i. 8.
> **Ō** ter beātī, *O thrice happy*, i. 94.

LOCATIVE

72. *Place where.* The locative is used to express *place where* with names of towns and small islands, and in the forms **domī** (from **domus**), **rūrī** (from **rūs**), **humī** (from **humus**), and a few others:

> **humī**, *on the ground*, i. 193.

Virgil sometimes uses the locative of names of large islands or countries (A. 427, 3 and *a*; D. 486–488; B. 232; G. 411).

> **Crētae**, *in Crete*, iii. 162.

USES OF THE INFINITIVE

73. *As subject of* **est** *and of impersonal verbs.* The infinitive may be used as the subject of **est** and of many impersonal verbs or passive verbs used impersonally (A. 452, 1; 454; D. 833, 834; B. 327, 330; G. 422).

> tantae mōlis erat Rōmānam **condere** gentem, *so great a task it was to found the Roman race*, i. 33.
> quīs contigit **oppetere** [mortem], *to whom it befell to meet death*, i. 96.
> cūr **iungere** nōn datur, *why is it not permitted to join?* i. 408.

74. *In apposition, etc.* The infinitive may be used in apposition with the subject or as a predicate nominative (A. 452, 2, 3; D. 835; B. 326; G. 424).

> ūna salūs [est] victīs, nūllam **spērāre** salūtem, *the vanquished have one safety only, to hope for no safety*, ii. 354.

75. *As complement of verbs denoting "be able," etc.* The infinitive is used as the complement of verbs denoting *to be able, dare, undertake, remember, forget, be accustomed, begin, continue, cease, hesitate, learn, know how, fear*, and the like (A. 456; D. 836, 837; B. 328, 1; G. 423).

> nec posse Teucrōrum **āvertere** rēgem, *and to be unable to turn aside the king of the Trojans*, i. 38.

76. *With other verbs.* In general, the poets use the infinitive freely with verbs that in prose require a subjunctive clause. Some verbs of the same meanings, however, take (or may take) an infinitive in prose. The details must be learned by practice or from a complete grammar.

77. *As complement of verbs denoting willingness, etc.* Many verbs take either a subjunctive clause or a complementary infinitive, without difference of meaning. Such are verbs signifying *willingness, necessity, propriety, resolve, command, prohibition, effort,* and the like.

The infinitive is much more freely used with verbs of *willingness,* etc., in poetry than in prose (A. 457; D. 836, 837; B. 328; G. 423).

> coniungere dextrās ārdēbant, *they were eager to join right hands,* i. 514.
> parce **scelerāre** manūs, *forbear to defile your hands,* iii. 42.

78. *With verbs denoting "admonish," etc.* Virgil uses the infinitive with verbs meaning *to admonish, ask, bargain, command, decree, determine, permit, persuade, resolve, urge,* and *wish.* In prose, a substantive clause of purpose with **ut** is the regular construction with most of these verbs (A. 563 and N.; D. 720, I and *d*; B. 295 and N.; G. 546 and N.[3]).

> hortāmur **fārī**, *we urge* [*him*] *to speak,* ii. 74.
> **celerāre** fugam suādet, *he urges* [*her*] *to hasten flight,* i. 357.

79. *As object.* The infinitive with subject accusative is used as the object of **volō, nōlō, iubeō, cupiō,** and **patior**: also of verbs of *determining, decreeing, resolving,* and *bargaining* (A. 563, *a–d*; D. 839 *b–d*; B. 331, II–IV; 295, N.; G. 532).

> tot **volvere** cāsūs virum impulerit, *forced a man to run the round of so many misfortunes,* i. 9.

80. *As main verb in indirect discourse.* The infinitive with subject accusative is used in indirect statements with verbs of *knowing, thinking, telling,* and *perceiving* (A. 579, 582; D. 839, *a*; B. 314, 1; G. 650).

> prōgeniem **dūcī** audierat, *she had heard that a people was springing,* i. 19.
> quam Iūnō fertur **coluisse,** *which Juno is said to have cherished,* i. 15.

81. *With adjectives.* Virgil occasionally uses the infinitive with an adjective or a participle:

> certa **morī,** *bent on death,* iv. 564.

Thus the infinitive is used once with **certus,** once with **parātus,** once with **dignus,** once with **magnus,** and twice with **praestantior** (A. 460, *b*; 461; D. 841 and *a*; B. 333; G. 421, N.[1], *c*; 428, N.[3]; 552, R.[2]).

82. *Historical.* The infinitive is often used for the imperfect indicative in narration, and takes a subject in the nominative (A. 463; D. 844; B. 335; G. 647).

hinc Ulixēs **terrēre**, *from this time Ulysses frightened* [*me*], ii. 97.

83. *In exclamations.* The infinitive, with subject accusative, may be used in exclamations (A. 462; D. 843; B. 334; G. 534).

mēne inceptō **dēsistere**, *what! I desist from my purpose!* i. 37.

84. *To express purpose.* Virgil uses the infinitive to express purpose:

nōn nōs **populāre** vēnimus, *we have not come to lay waste*, i. 527.

This construction occurs nine times with **dō** in Books i–vi and once each with **instituō**, **vacō**, and **veniō** (A. 460, *c*; D. 842; B. 326, N.; G. 421, notes).

USES OF THE IMPERATIVE

85. *In commands (second person).* The imperative is used in commands and entreaties (A. 448, 449; D. 689; B. 281; G. 266).

mihī causās **memorā**, *tell me the reasons*, i. 8.

86. *In commands (third person).* In poetry the third person of the imperative is sometimes used (A. 448, *a*; D. 690, *b*; B. 281, 1; G. 267).

nec foedera **suntō**, *there shall be no treaties*, iv. 624.

87. *In prohibitions.* The poet sometimes uses **nē** and the imperative or the present subjunctive in a prohibition. The customary prose construction is **nōlī** and an infinitive (A. 450 and notes; D. 690, N.; 675; 676, *a*; B. 276; 281, 2; G. 263, 2; 270).

equō **nē crēdite**, *do not trust the horse*, ii. 48.

II. ORDER OF WORDS

88. *The order of words in the Æneid.* In prose there is a recognized normal order of words in the sentence. Variations from this order emphasize the word or words removed from the normal position. In the Æneid wider variations of order are found than would be permissible in prose. These variations sometimes arise from metrical

convenience. At other times they arise from the desire to obtain emphasis or poetical effect. Observance of the case-endings and of the rules of syntax will usually obviate any difficulty caused by unusual order of words.

89. *Variations from the order of words in prose.* The following variations from the normal order of words in prose are noticeable in the Æneid:

a. A genitive may be separated from its noun:

> Trōiae . . . ōrīs, i. 1.
> studiīs . . . bellī, i. 14.

b. An attributive adjective may be separated from its noun:

> Lāvīnia . . . lītora, i. 2.
> saevae . . . Iūnōnis, i. 4.

c. Words associated in thought may be separated:

> et terrīs . . . et altō, i. 3.
> posthabitā . . . Samō, i. 16.

d. A preposition may follow its noun:

> Ītaliam contrā, i. 13.
> maria omnia circum, i. 32.

e. A verb may be placed at the beginning of a verse — a position of especial emphasis in poetry — regardless of its relation to the other words in the clause:

> īnferret, i. 6.
> exciderant, i. 26.

f. A conjunction or relative pronoun is often not the first word in its clause or phrase:

> Trōiae quī, i. 1.
> Tyriās ōlim quae, i. 20.
> omnīs ut, i. 74.

III. Unusual Forms of Words

90. *Unusual forms.* The new forms of words which the pupil meets in the Æneid are of two classes: (1) *archaisms*, that is, forms that had once been in use but that were not common in Latin prose at

the time when Virgil was writing; and (2) *Greek forms*, that is, Greek case-endings retained for words that had been brought over into Latin from the Greek, especially proper names.

91. *Archaisms.* The following peculiar forms (mostly archaisms) are found in the Æneid:

a. -**āī** for -**ae** of the genitive singular of the first declension:

aulāī, iii. 354.

b. -**um** for -**ārum** of the genitive plural of the first declension:

Aeneadum, i. 565.

c. -**um** or -**om** for -**ōrum** of the genitive plural of the second declension:

superum, i. 4.

d. -**ū** for -**uī** of the dative singular of the fourth declension:

currū, i. 156.

e. -**um** for -**uum** of the genitive plural of the fourth declension:

currum, vi. 653.

f. ollī for illī, and ollīs for illīs: i. 254; vi. 730.
g. quīs for quibus: i. 95.
h. mī for mihi: vi. 104.
i. ast for at: i. 46.
j. nī for nisi: i. 58.
k. -**ier** for -**ī** of the present infinitive passive:

accingier, iv. 493.

l. -**ēre** for -**ērunt** of the perfect indicative active:

tenuēre, i. 12.

m. -**ībat**, -**ībant**, for -**iēbat**, -**iēbant**, of the imperfect of the fourth conjugation:

lēnībat, vi. 468.

n. Shortened (syncopated) forms of the perfect and pluperfect:

accestis = accessistis, i. 201.
exstīnxtī = exstīnxistī, iv. 682.
exstīnxem = exstīnxissem, iv. 606.
trāxe = trāxisse, v. 786.
Cf. repostum = repositum, i. 26.

o. Syncopated forms of nouns :

> vinclīs for vinculīs, i. 54.
> perīclum for perīculum, ii. 709.
> ōrāclum for ōrāculum, iii. 143.

p. Archaic forms of nouns :

> Karthāgō for Carthāgō, i. 13.
> honōs for honor, i. 609.
> diī for diēī, i. 636.

92. *Greek forms.* Virgil uses the ending **-a** for the accusative singular and the ending **-as** for the accusative plural of certain nouns of the third declension that were borrowed from the Greek :

> āera, i. 300.
> lebētas, iii. 466.

93. *Greek forms of proper names.* Many of the proper names of the Æneid are originally Greek. Some of these nouns are entirely Latinized. Others, however, retain certain Greek case-endings.

For Greek nouns of the first declension (as **Andromachē, Aenēās, Anchīsēs**), see A. 44 ; D. 81 ; B. 22 ; G. 65 ; of the second (as **Tityus** or **Tityos, Androgeōs, Dēlos**), see A. 52 ; D. 89 ; B. 27 ; G. 65 ; of the third (as **Orphēus, Orontēs, Ulixēs, Paris, Capys, Dīdō**), A. 82, 83 ; D. 112 ; B. 47 ; G. 65.

IV. Miscellaneous Differences

94. *The passive as a middle voice.* The Greek language has a middle voice, as well as an active and a passive voice. A verb in the Greek middle voice represents the subject as acting on himself, and is therefore like an English or Latin verb with a reflexive pronoun (as **sē accingunt**, *they gird themselves*, i. 210).

In Latin the passive voice is often used in the manner of the Greek middle voice, especially in poetry (A. 156, *a*, N. ; D. 406, *d* ; B. 175, 2, *d* ; 256 ; G. 218).

> Aeneadae Libyae **vertuntur** ad ōrās. *the followers of Æneas turn (themselves) toward the shores of Libya,* i. 158.
> **implentur** veteris Bacchī, *they fill themselves with old wine,* i. 215.

95. *The perfect passive participle as a present.* In prose the perfect participle of a few deponent verbs (as **veritus** and **arbitrātus**) is used with the sense of a present. In poetry the perfect participle of other verbs is occasionally used in this way (A. 491; D. 848; B. 336, 5; G. 282, N.).

> caelō **invectus** apertō, *riding under a clear sky*, i. 155.
> **tūnsae** pectora, *beating their breasts*, i. 481.

96. *The plural of a noun instead of the singular.* The poets often use a plural noun where a singular form might be expected. The plural of abstract nouns is used to denote repeated instances of the quality :

> īrae, *wrath*, i. 11 (cf. i. 25).
> furiās, *mad deed*, i. 41.

The plural of words denoting places is found :

> ōstia, *mouth*, i. 14.
> Pergama, *Troy*, i. 466.

Sometimes the plural appears to be used for metrical reasons :

> montīs, i. 61.
> silentia, i. 730.

Other words have a plural form at the whim of the poet (A. 100, *c*; 101, N.[2]; D. 126, *c*; 127, N.; B. 55, 4, *c*; G. 204, N.[5] and N.[6]).

> scēptra, *sceptre*, i. 57.
> puppibus, *ship*, i. 183.
> vīna, *wine*, i. 195.

97. *Adjectives and participles used as nouns.* Adjectives and participles are used more freely as nouns in poetry than in prose, especially in the neuter gender :

> altō, *the sea*, i. 3 (cf. i. 34).
> inceptō, *purpose*, i. 37.
> meritīs, *services*, i. 74.
> brevia, *shoals*, i. 111.

98. *Variety of names for the same thing.* In order to avoid monotony Virgil uses a variety of names for the same thing. For instance, the

sea is so often mentioned that, for variety, a large number of names are necessary. Thus, **altum, alta, aequor, aequora, maris aequor, mare, maria, aestus, sāl, salum, fluctus** (sing. and plur.), **pontus, unda, undae, pelagus, freta, vada** (salsa), **vortex, gurges,** are all used in essentially the same meaning. The Trojans are called **Trōes, Teucrī, Dardanī, Dardanidae, Aeneadae**; and the Greeks, **Grāī, Danaī, Argīvī, Achīvī, Pelasgī.**

Variety is often secured by the use of *patronymics,* — nouns indicating descent or relationship (A. 244; D. 282, *g*; B. 148, 6; G. 182, 11).

> **Tȳdīdēs,** *son of Tydeus* (for Diomedes), i. 97.
> **Aeacidēs,** *grandson of Æacus* (for Achilles), i. 99.
> **Othryadēs,** *son of Othrys* (for Panthus), ii. 336.
> **Tyndaris,** *daughter of Tyndarus* (for Helen), ii. 569.

99. *Omitted words.* The omission of words necessary to the grammatical structure of the sentence is very common in poetry. Such ellipsis of pronouns and of forms of **esse** is especially frequent:

> tantaene [sunt] animīs caelestibus īrae, *have heavenly minds such anger?* i. 11.
> [eam] tenuēre colōnī, *settlers inhabited it,* i. 12.

100. *Metonymy.* The poets are fond of metonymy ("change of name"), — a figure of speech by which one calls a thing by the name of something else that is related to that thing or suggests it: as *the sword* for *warfare, forces* for *soldiery* or *army, sail* for *ships.*

Examples from the Æneid are

> **sāl,** *salt* (for the *sea*), i. 35.
> **puppēs,** *sterns* (for *ships*), i. 69.
> **scĕptra,** *sceptre* (for *royal power*), i. 78.
> **pontus,** *sea* (for *wave*), i. 114.
> **Cerēs** for *grain,* i. 177.
> **Bacchus** for *wine,* i. 215.

THE VERSIFICATION OF THE ÆNEID

101. *Latin poetry quantitative.* Latin poetry depends for its rhythm not on accent, but on quantity. In distinction from English poetry, which produces its effect by a succession of accented and unaccented syllables, Latin poetry gets its effect from a certain succession of long and short syllables, depending on the metre employed in the poem.

102. *Long and short syllables.* A syllable in Latin poetry is *long* (1) if it contains a long vowel or a diphthong, or (2) if it contains a short vowel followed by two consonants (one of which may be at the beginning of the following word). Otherwise, it is *short.* But a syllable containing a short vowel followed by a mute (*p, b, t, d, c, g*) and a liquid (*l, r*) may be either long or short, according to the needs of the verse: thus in **patris** the **a** is short, but the first syllable is common, i.e. it may be either long or short.

103. *Feet: dactyl, spondee.* A combination of syllables forms what is known as a *foot.* In the metre in which the Æneid is written two kinds of foot are used: a long syllable and two short syllables (‿ ◡ ◡, **conderet**), called a *dactyl*; and two long syllables (‿ ‿, **ōrīs**), called a *spondee.* The rules of the metre exclude many words from the Æneid: all, for example, in which a single short syllable comes between two long ones (as in all the cases of **aēquĭtās** and similar words); many forms of verb inflection, as **fēcĕrant**; and all forms where more than two short syllables come together, as in **fŭĕrĭmŭs, ĭtĭnĕrĭs**. The first syllable of the dactyl and the spondee is always accented: this accent is called the *ictus.* The accented part of a foot is known as the *thesis*; the unaccented part, as the *arsis.*

104. *Dactylic hexameter.* The metre of the Æneid is known as *dactylic hexameter.* It is called *hexameter* because each line, or verse, contains six feet; and it is called *dactylic* because the dactyls are more numerous than the spondees. The first four feet of the hexameter may be either dactyls or spondees. The fifth foot is usually a dactyl. A verse having a spondee in the fifth foot is called *spondaic.* The sixth foot is always a spondee. The last syllable of a verse may be short in itself; if it is short, it is regarded as long, because a spondee is necessary in the last foot. Such a syllable is known as the *syllaba* *anceps* (the doubtful syllable). The metrical scheme of the dactylic hexameter is as follows:

$$\underset{\underset{or}{\underline{}\ \_}}{\overset{\underline{/}\ \cup\ \cup}{}} \bigg| \underset{\underset{or}{\underline{}\ \_}}{\overset{\underline{/}\ \cup\ \cup}{}} \bigg| \underset{\underset{or}{\underline{}\ \_}}{\overset{\underline{/}\ \cup\ \cup}{}} \bigg| \underset{\underset{or}{\underline{}\ \_}}{\overset{\underline{/}\ \cup\ \cup}{}} \bigg| \underset{or,\ occasionally,}{\overset{\underline{/}\ \cup\ \cup}{\underline{}\ \_}} \bigg| \overset{\underline{/}\ \underset{\smile}{}}{} \bigg|$$

Ar-ma vi | rum-que ca | no, Tro | iae qui | pri-mus ab | o-ris (i. 1).[1]

Mu-sa, mi | hi cau | sas me-mo | ra, quo | nu-mi-ne | lae-so (i. 8).

The verses which are most light and rapid and agreeable to the ear are those in which dactyls are more numerous, or alternate with spondees; when there are many spondees — especially when the verse is spondaic — a slow and labored movement is given to the line, which is, however, often very expressive (see ii. 251, 463-466).

105. *Cæsura*. An examination of the lines marked out in the preceding paragraph shows that words often end within a foot: | Ar-ma vi | ; | no Tro |. The ending of a word within a foot is called *cæsura*. In Virgil's time it was considered as absolutely necessary for an agreeable cadence. If there is a cæsura at the end of some principal word or phrase or at some pause in the sense, it is called *the cæsura*. This main cæsura is often a great help to the sense and must always be observed in the reading of the verse. It may occur after the thesis (*masculine cæsura*), or in the arsis of a dactyl (*feminine cæsura*). The masculine cæsura is more common than the feminine. The place of *the cæsura* is oftenest in the *third* foot, less often in the *fourth*; in the latter case there is sometimes another cæsura in the second foot, dividing the verse into three parts instead of two.

Ar-ma vi | rum-que ca | no, ‖ Tro | iae qui | pri-mus ab | o-ris (i. 1).
　　　　　　　　the cæsura

[1] The long-quantity marks here indicate long syllables, not necessarily long vowels.

$$\text{Mu-sa,} \quad \text{mi}|\text{hi} \quad \text{cau}|\text{sas} \quad \text{me-mo}|\text{ra,} \parallel \text{quo} \mid \text{nu-mi-ne} \mid \text{lae-so} \quad \text{(i. 8).}$$

the cæsura

The ending of a word with the end of a foot is called *diæresis*, as in **numine**, above.

106. *Elision, ecthlipsis.* A vowel at the end of a word is usually not pronounced when the next word begins with a vowel or *h*; this is called *elision*. A vowel and *m* at the end of a word are also elided when the next word begins with a vowel or *h*; this is called *ecthlipsis*.

$$\text{li-to-ra,} \mid \text{mul-t}^{\text{um}} \text{ il} \Big\| \text{l}^{\text{e}} \text{ et ter}|\text{ris iac}|\text{ta-tus et} \mid \text{al-to} \quad \text{(i. 3).}$$

It is not known with certainty just how elided syllables were treated by the Romans in reading. They may have been entirely omitted, or they may have been only slurred.

107. *Metrical licenses.* Virgil does not always adhere rigidly to the general rules of hexameter verse. The metrical licenses which he permits himself follow:

108. *Hiatus.* Sometimes, especially before the principal cæsura or at a pause in the verse or between proper names, a final vowel is not elided: this is *hiatus*. In the following verse there is hiatus before the cæsura:

$$\text{post-ha-bi}|\text{ta co-lu}|\text{is-se Sa}|\text{mo;} \parallel \text{hic} \mid \text{il-li-us} \mid \text{ar-ma} \quad \text{(i. 16).}$$

109. *Semi-hiatus.* In several lines of the Æneid a long vowel or diphthong is made short before a word beginning with a vowel: this is called *semi-hiatus*. So in the following verse at the end of the first foot:

$$\text{in-su-lae} \mid \text{I-o-ni}^{\text{o}} \mid \text{in mag}|\text{no,} \parallel \text{quas} \mid \text{di-ra Ce}|\text{lae-no} \quad \text{(iii. 211).}$$

110. *Diastole.* Often a short syllable is treated as long: this change is known as *diastole*:

> **vidēt**, i. 308.
> **pulvīs**, i. 478.
> **iactetūr**, i. 668.
> **peterēt**, i. 651.
> **-quē**, iii. 91.

111. *Systole.* Occasionally a long syllable is treated as short. This is called *systole.*

> stetĕrunt, ii. 774.
> constitĕrunt, iii. 681.

112. *I and u as consonants.* Virgil sometimes treats the vowels *i* and *u* as consonants. When so treated these letters may help to make the preceding syllable long by position. This is called *synæresis.*

> ābiĕtĕ, ii. 16.
> gēnuă, v. 432.
> ōmniă, vi. 33.

113. *Proper names.* The quantity of vowels in certain proper names varies:

> Lāvīnia, i. 2, but Lăvīnī, i. 258.
> Sȳchaeus, i. 343, but Sȳchaeum, i. 348.

114. *Synapheia.* Sometimes a verse ends in a syllable which is elided before the initial vowel of the following verse. Such verses are known as *hypermetric*, and the elision is known as *synapheia.* All hypermetric verses in Books i–vi of the Æneid end in -que: i. 332; i. 448; ii. 745.

115. *Synizesis.* Two vowels belonging to different syllables are sometimes to be pronounced together as one syllable: this combination of syllables is called *synizesis.* Instances are Oīleī, i. 41; Īlioneī, i. 120; aureā, i. 698; sciō, iii. 602; aureīs, v. 352; alveō, vi. 412; dehinc, i. 131; deinde, i. 195.

116. *Directions for marking the quantity of verses.* In marking the quantity of verses the pupil will be aided if he proceeds in the following manner:

1. Mark the last foot: it is always a spondee.
2. Mark the fifth foot: it is generally a dactyl.
3. Mark the first syllable of the verse long.
4. Elide syllables wherever elision, or ecthlipsis, is possible.
5. Mark throughout the verse those vowels that are long by position, i.e. vowels that are followed by two consonants. Remember the exception (§ 102), and remember that one consonant may be the initial letter of the following word.
6. Mark diphthongs long.

7. Mark the final syllable of words declined by cases.

8. Mark short those vowels followed by another vowel or *h*. Remember that *u* after *q* is not marked, and look out for the quantity of vowels in Greek nouns.

9. Finally mark the remaining syllables according to the needs of the various feet. The quantity of these syllables is to be explained either by the authority of the Vocabulary, or by the rules for the increments of declension and conjugation, or by exceptions to the general rules for quantity.

117. *Monosyllabic ending of the verse.* Sixty verses in Books i–vi end in a monosyllabic word. In more than half of these verses the last word is **est**, and there is elision before the monosyllabic word: **ūsa est**, i. 64. In twelve verses the next to the last word also is a monosyllable: **fās est**, i. 77. Certain expressions recur at the end of the verse: **necesse est**, iii. 478, iv. 613; vi. 514, 737; **locūta est**, i. 614; iii. 320; vi. 189. Sometimes Virgil may have been aiming at a particular poetical effect: **aquae mōns**, i. 105; **humī bōs**, v. 481.

THE ELEGIAC STANZA

The elegiac stanza consists of two verses,— a hexameter followed by a pentameter.

The pentameter is the same as the hexameter, except that it omits the last half of the third foot and of the sixth foot:

$$\acute{}\cup\cup \mid \acute{}\cup\cup \mid \acute{}\bar{\wedge} \Vert \acute{}\cup\cup \mid \acute{}\cup\cup \mid \acute{}\bar{\wedge}$$

or $\acute{}\_$ *or* $\acute{}\_$

The pentameter verse is therefore to be scanned as two half-verses, the second of which always consists of two dactyls followed by a single syllable.

The elegiac stanza is a favorite with Ovid. An example follows (from *Fasti*, ii. 83–84):

Quod ma-re | non no|vit, ‖ quae | ne-scit A|rī-o-na | tel-lus?

Car-mi-ne | cur-ren|tēs ‖ il-le te|nē-bat a‖quās.

The elegiac stanza has been imitated in English:

Ín the hex|ámeter | ríses ‖ the | foúntain's | sílvery | cólumn;

Ín the pen|támeter | áye ‖ fálling in | mélody | báck.

P. VERGILI MARONIS AENEIDOS

LIBER I

THE LANDING IN AFRICA

The wrath of Juno, jealous for the glory of Carthage, compels the long wanderings of Æneas, and detains the Trojan exiles from destined Italy (1–33). She beholds them on their voyage from Sicily, and, angry because they have so long escaped destruction, she solicits Æolus, god of winds, to overwhelm them with a tempest: the storm bursts forth (34–101). The Trojan fleet is scattered and in peril: but Neptune lifts his head and stills the waves (102–156). Æneas, with seven ships, reaches the coast of Africa, where he finds food and rest (157–222). Venus appeals to Jupiter, reminds him of his promises with regard to the Trojans, and begs him to help Æneas. Jupiter comforts Venus by promise of the coming glories of Rome, and sends Mercury to move the Tyrian colonists to hospitality (223–304). Æneas, while exploring the country with Achates, is met by Venus in the guise of a huntress, who tells him of Dido's flight from Tyre and her founding of the city of Carthage on the African shore. She tells him that his missing ships are safe and bids him go to Carthage, first making him and Achates invisible by a miraculous mist (305–417). Æneas admires the new city; sees in the temple of Juno the pictured story of the Trojan

War; and at length (still unseen) beholds Queen Dido, attended by
some of his own companions whom he thought lost, who come as envoys from the scattered ships (418–519). The appeal of the shipwrecked men moves the compassion of Dido, and she offers to receive
them as her subjects: upon which the mist dissolves, and Æneas appears before the queen (520–593). He declares himself, expresses his
gratitude to the queen, and greets his restored companions. Dido receives him to royal hospitality in her halls, and sends gifts to the sailors
(594–642). Achates is despatched to the fleet for the young Ascanius.
Venus, however, fears that the Carthaginians may prove treacherous
and appeals for help to her son, Cupid. By a stratagem of the goddess,
Cupid is disguised in the likeness of Ascanius and comes to Dido's court
instead of the young prince. At the banquet Cupid inspires in the queen
a fatal passion for Æneas (643–722). The evening passes in feasting
and song, when Dido requests of Æneas the connected story of his
wanderings (723–756).

The poet tells his theme and invokes the Muse

ARMA virumque canō, Trōiae quī prīmus ab ōrīs
 Ītaliam, fātō profugus, Lāvīniaque vēnit
 lītora, multum ille et terrīs iactātus et altō
vī superum saevae memorem Iūnōnis ob īram;
multa quoque et bellō passus, dum conderet urbem, 5
īnferretque deōs Latiō, genus unde Latīnum,
Albānīque patrēs, atque altae moenia Rōmae.

Mūsa, mihī causās memorā, quō nūmine laesō,
quidve dolēns, rēgīna deum tot volvere cāsūs
īnsignem pietāte virum, tot adīre labōrēs   10
impulerit. Tantaene animīs caelestibus īrae?

Juno loves Carthage, but hates the Trojans

Urbs antīqua fuit, Tyriī tenuēre colōnī,
Karthāgō, Ītaliam contrā Tiberīnaque longē
ōstia, dīves opum studiīsque asperrima bellī;
quam Iūnō fertur terrīs magis omnibus ūnam   15

posthabitā coluisse Samō; hīc illius arma,
hīc currus fuit; hoc rēgnum dea gentibus esse,
sī quā fāta sinant, iam tum tenditque fovetque.
Prōgeniem sed enim Trōiānō ā sanguine dūcī
audierat, Tyriās ōlim quae verteret arcēs;   20

THE FATES WITH MINERVA ·

hinc populum lātē rēgem bellōque superbum
ventūrum excidiō Libyae: sīc volvere Parcās.
Id metuēns, veterisque memor Sāturnia bellī,
prīma quod ad Trōiam prō cārīs gesserat Argīs—
necdum etiam causae īrārum saevīque dolōrēs   25
exciderant animō: manet altā mente repostum
iūdicium Paridis sprētaeque iniūria fōrmae,
et genus invīsum, et raptī Ganymēdis honōrēs—
hīs accēnsa super, iactātōs aequore tōtō
Trōas, rēliquiās Danaum atque immītis Achillī,   30
arcēbat longē Latiō, multōsque per annōs
errābant, āctī fātīs, maria omnia circum.
Tantae mōlis erat Rōmānam condere gentem!

Juno is angry because Æneas and his companions have escaped destruction

Vix ē cōnspectū Siculae tellūris in altum
vēla dabant laetī, et spūmās salis aere ruēbant,   35
cum Iūnō, aeternum servāns sub pectore volnus,
haec sēcum: 'Mēne inceptō dēsistere victam,
nec posse Ītaliā Teucrōrum āvertere rēgem?
Quippe vetor fātīs. Pallasne exūrere classem
Argīvum atque ipsōs potuit submergere pontō,   40
ūnius ob noxam et furiās Āiācis Oīleī?
Ipsa, Iovis rapidum iaculāta ē nūbibus ignem,
disiēcitque ratēs ēvertitque aequora ventīs,
illum exspīrantem trānsfīxō pectore flammās
turbine corripuit scopulōque īnfīxit acūtō.   45
Ast ego, quae dīvum incēdō rēgīna, Iovisque
et soror et coniūnx, ūnā cum gente tot annōs
bella gerō! Et quisquam nūmen Iūnōnis adōret
praetereā, aut supplex ārīs impōnet honōrem?'

Juno persuades Æolus, god of the winds, to help her

Tālia flammātō sēcum dea corde volūtāns   50
nimbōrum in patriam, loca fēta furentibus austrīs,
Aeoliam venit. Hīc vāstō rēx Aeolus antrō
luctantīs ventōs tempestātēsque sonōrās
imperiō premit ac vinclīs et carcere frēnat.
Illī indignantēs magnō cum murmure montis   55
circum claustra fremunt; celsā sedet Aeolus arce
scēptra tenēns, mollitque animōs et temperat īrās.
Nī faciat, maria ac terrās caelumque profundum
quippe ferant rapidī sēcum verrantque per aurās.
Sed pater omnipotēns spēluncīs abdidit ātrīs,   60
hoc metuēns, mōlemque et montīs īnsuper altōs
imposuit, rēgemque dedit, quī foedere certō

et premere et laxās scīret dare iussus habēnās.
Ad quem tum Iūnō supplex hīs vōcibus ūsa est:
  'Aeole,—namque tibī dīvum pater atque hominum rēx
et mulcēre dedit fluctūs et tollere ventō,—   66
gēns inimīca mihī Tyrrhēnum nāvigat aequor,
Īlium in Ītaliam portāns victōsque penātīs:
incute vim ventīs submersāsque obrue puppīs,
aut age dīversōs et disice corpora pontō.   70
Sunt mihi bis septem praestantī corpore nymphae,
quārum quae fōrmā pulcherrima Dēïopēa,
cōnūbiō iungam stabilī propriamque dicābō,
omnīs ut tēcum meritīs prō tālibus annōs
exigat, et pulchrā faciat tē prōle parentem.'   75
  Aeolus haec contrā: 'Tuus, Ō rēgīna, quid optēs
explōrāre labor; mihi iussa capessere fās est.
Tū mihi, quodcumque hoc rēgnī, tū scēptra Iovemque
conciliās, tū dās epulīs accumbere dīvum,
nimbōrumque facis tempestātumque potentem.'   80

Æolus lets loose the winds

  Haec ubi dicta, cavum conversā cuspide montem
impulit in latus: ac ventī, velut agmine factō,
quā data porta, ruunt et terrās turbine perflant.
Incubuēre marī, tōtumque ā sēdibus īmīs
ūnā Eurusque Notusque ruunt crēberque procellīs   85
Āfricus, et vāstōs volvunt ad lītora fluctūs.
Īnsequitur clāmorque virum strīdorque rudentum.
Ēripiunt subitō nūbēs caelumque diemque
Teucrōrum ex oculīs; pontō nox incubat ātra.
Intonuēre polī, et crēbrīs micat ignibus aethēr,   90
praesentemque virīs intentant omnia mortem.
  Extemplō Aenēae solvuntur frīgore membra:
ingemit, et duplicīs tendēns ad sīdera palmās

tālia vōce refert: 'Ō terque quaterque beātī,
quīs ante ōra patrum Trōiae sub moenibus altīs   95
contigit oppetere! Ō Danaum fortissime gentis
Tȳdīdē! Mēne Īliacīs occumbere campīs
nōn potuisse, tuāque animam hanc effundere dextrā,
saevus ubi Aeacidae tēlō iacet Hector, ubi ingēns
Sarpēdōn, ubi tot Simoīs correpta sub undīs   100
scūta virum galeāsque et fortia corpora volvit?'

The fleet of Æneas is in danger of destruction

Tālia iactantī strīdēns Aquilōne procella
vēlum adversa ferit, fluctūsque ad sīdera tollit.
Franguntur rēmī; tum prōra āvertit, et undīs
dat latus; īnsequitur cumulō praeruptus aquae mōns.   105
Hī summō in fluctū pendent; hīs unda dehīscēns
terram inter fluctūs aperit; furit aestus harēnīs.
Trīs Notus abreptās in saxa latentia torquet
(saxa vocant Italī mediīs quae in fluctibus ārās,
dorsum immāne marī summō); trīs Eurus ab altō   110
in brevia et syrtīs urguet, miserābile vīsū,
inlīditque vadīs atque aggere cingit harēnae.
Ūnam, quae Lyciōs fīdumque vehēbat Orontēn,
ipsius ante oculōs ingēns ā vertice pontus
in puppim ferit: excutitur prōnusque magister   115
volvitur in caput; ast illam ter fluctus ibīdem
torquet agēns circum, et rapidus vorat aequore vortex.
Appārent rārī nantēs in gurgite vāstō,
arma virum, tabulaeque, et Trōïa gaza per undās.
Iam validam Īlioneī nāvem, iam fortis Achātae,   120
et quā vectus Abās, et quā grandaevus Alētēs,
vīcit hiems; laxīs laterum compāgibus omnēs
accipiunt inimīcum imbrem, rīmīsque fatīscunt.

Neptune intervenes and ends the storm

Intereā magnō miscērī murmure pontum,
ēmissamque hiemem sēnsit Neptūnus, et īmīs   125
stāgna refūsa vadīs, graviter commōtus; et altō
prōspiciēns, summā placidum caput extulit undā.
Disiectam Aenēae tōtō videt aequore classem,
īluctibus oppressōs Trōas caelīque ruīnā,
nec latuēre dolī frātrem Iūnōnis et īrae.   130
Eurum ad sē Zephyrumque vocat, dehinc tālia fātur:
' Tantane vōs generis tenuit fīdūcia vestrī?
Iam caelum terramque meō sine nūmine, ventī,
miscēre, et tantās audētis tollere mōlēs?
Quōs ego—sed mōtōs praestat compōnere fluctūs.   135
Post mihi nōn similī poenā commissa luētis.
Mātūrāte fugam, rēgīque haec dīcite vestrō:
nōn illī imperium pelagī saevumque tridentem,
sed mihi sorte datum. Tenet ille immānia saxa,
vestrās, Eure, domōs; illā sē iactet in aulā   140
Aeolus, et clausō ventōrum carcere rēgnet.'
    Sīc ait, et dictō citius tumida aequora plācat,
collēctāsque fugat nūbēs, sōlemque redūcit.
Cȳmothoē simul et Trītōn adnīxus acūtō
dētrūdunt nāvīs scopulō, levat ipse tridentī,   145
et vāstās aperit syrtīs et temperat aequor,
atque rotīs summās levibus perlābitur undās.
Ac velutī magnō in populō cum saepe coörta est
sēditiō, saevitque animīs ignōbile volgus,
iamque facēs et saxa volant, furor arma ministrat,   150
tum, pietāte gravem ac meritīs sī forte virum quem
cōnspexēre, silent, arrēctīsque auribus adstant;
ille regit dictīs animōs, et pectora mulcet:
sīc cūnctus pelagī cecidit fragor, aequora postquam
prōspiciēns genitor caelōque invectus apertō   155
flectit equōs, currūque volāns dat lōra secundō.

*The Trojans, with seven ships, land in Africa and prepare
for a meal*

Dēfessī Aeneadae, quae proxima lītora, cursū
contendunt petere, et Libyae vertuntur ad ōrās.
Est in sēcessū longō locus: īnsula portum
efficit obiectū laterum, quibus omnis ab altō   160
frangitur inque sinūs scindit sēsē unda reductōs.
Hinc atque hinc vāstae rūpēs geminīque minantur
in caelum scopulī, quōrum sub vertice lātē
aequora tūta silent; tum silvīs scaena coruscīs
dēsuper horrentīque ātrum nemus imminet umbrā.   165
Fronte sub adversā scopulīs pendentibus antrum,
intus aquae dulcēs vīvōque sedīlia saxō,
nymphārum domus: hīc fessās nōn vincula nāvīs
ūlla tenent, uncō nōn alligat ancora morsū.
Hūc septem Aenēās collēctīs nāvibus omnī   170
ex numerō subit; ac magnō tellūris amōre
ēgressī optātā potiuntur Trōes harēnā,
et sale tābentīs artūs in lītore pōnunt.
Ac prīmum silicī scintillam excūdit Achātēs,
suscēpitque ignem foliīs, atque ārida circum   175
nūtrīmenta dedit, rapuitque in fōmite flammam.
Tum Cererem corruptam undīs Cereāliaque arma
expediunt fessī rērum, frūgēsque receptās
et torrēre parant flammīs et frangere saxō.

Æneas kills seven deer and bids his companions take courage

Aenēās scopulum intereā cōnscendit, et omnem   180
prōspectum lātē pelagō petit, Anthea sī quem
iactātum ventō videat Phrygiāsque birēmīs,
aut Capyn, aut celsīs in puppibus arma Caīcī.
Nāvem in cōnspectū nūllam, trīs lītore cervōs
prōspicit errantīs; hōs tōta armenta sequuntur   185

NEPTUNE

ā tergō, et longum per vallīs pāscitur agmen.
Cōnstitit hīc, arcumque manū celerīsque sagittās
corripuit, fīdus quae tēla gerēbat Achātēs ;
ductōrēsque ipsōs prīmum, capita alta ferentīs
cornibus arboreīs, sternit, tum volgus, et omnem   190
miscet agēns tēlīs nemora inter frondea turbam
nec prius absistit, quam septem ingentia victor
corpora fundat humī, et numerum cum nāvibus aequet.
Hinc portum petit, et sociōs partītur in omnīs.
Vīna bonus quae deinde cadīs onerārat Acestēs   195
lītore Trīnacriō dederatque abeuntibus hērōs,
dīvidit, et dictīs maerentia pectora mulcet :
  ꞌŌ sociī—neque enim ignārī sumus ante malōrum—
Ō passī graviōra, dabit deus hīs quoque fīnem.
Vōs et Scyllaeam rabiem penitusque sonantīs   200
accestis scopulōs, vōs et Cyclōpia saxa
expertī : revocāte animōs, maestumque timōrem
mittite : forsan et haec ōlim meminisse iuvābit.
Per variōs cāsūs, per tot discrīmina rērum
tendimus in Latium ; sēdēs ubi fāta quiētās   205
ostendunt ; illīc fās rēgna resurgere Trōiae.
Dūrāte, et vōsmet rēbus servāte secundīs.'

The Trojans feast, and mourn for their missing companions

  Tālia vōce refert, cūrīsque ingentibus aeger
spem voltū simulat, premit altum corde dolōrem.
Illī sē praedae accingunt dapibusque futūrīs ;   210
tergora dēripiunt costīs et vīscera nūdant ;
pars in frūsta secant veribusque trementia fīgunt ;
lītore aēna locant aliī, flammāsque ministrant.
Tum vīctū revocant vīrīs, fūsīque per herbam
implentur veteris Bacchī pinguisque ferīnae.   215
Postquam exēmpta famēs epulīs mēnsaeque remōtae,
āmissōs longō sociōs sermōne requīrunt,

spemque metumque inter dubiī, seu vīvere crēdant,
sīve extrēma patī nec iam exaudīre vocātōs.
Praecipuē pius Aenēās nunc ācris Orontī, 220
nunc Amycī cāsum gemit et crūdēlia sēcum
fāta Lycī, fortemque Gyān, fortemque Cloanthum.

R. H. FRANKENBERG

Venus appeals to Jupiter to help the Trojans

Et iam fīnis erat, cum Iuppiter aethere summō
dēspiciēns mare vēlivolum terrāsque iacentīs
lītoraque et lātōs populōs, sīc vertice caelī 225
cōnstitit, et Libyae dēfīxit lūmina rēgnīs.
Atque illum tālīs iactantem pectore cūrās
trīstior et lacrimīs oculōs suffūsa nitentīs
adloquitur Venus: ' Ō quī rēs hominumque deumque
aeternīs regis imperiīs, et fulmine terrēs, 230
quid meus Aenēās in tē committere tantum,
quid Trōes potuēre, quibus, tot fūnera passīs,
cūnctus ob Ītaliam terrārum clauditur orbis?
Certē hinc Rōmānōs ōlim, volventibus annīs,
hinc fore ductōrēs, revocātō ā sanguine Teucrī, 235
quī mare, quī terrās omnī diciōne tenērent,
pollicitus: quae tē, genitor, sententia vertit?
Hōc equidem occāsum Trōiae trīstīsque ruīnās
sōlābar, fātīs contrāria fāta rependēns;
nunc eadem fortūna virōs tot cāsibus āctōs 240
īnsequitur. Quem dās fīnem, rēx magne, labōrum?
Antēnor potuit, mediīs ēlāpsus Achīvīs,
Illyricōs penetrāre sinūs, atque intima tūtus
rēgna Liburnōrum, et fontem superāre Timāvī,
unde per ōra novem vāstō cum murmure montis 245
it mare prōruptum et pelagō premit arva sonantī.
Hīc tamen ille urbem Patavī sēdēsque locāvit
Teucrōrum, et gentī nōmen dedit, armaque fīxit
Trōïa; nunc placidā compostus pāce quiēscit:

nōs, tua prōgeniēs, caelī quibus adnuis arcem, 250
nāvibus (īnfandum!) āmissīs, ūnīus ob īram
prōdimur atque Italīs longē disiungimur ōrīs.
Hic pietātis honōs? Sīc nōs in scēptra repōnis?'

*Jupiter comforts Venus and foretells the glory
of the Trojan race*

Ollī subrīdēns hominum sator atque deōrum,
voltū quō caelum tempestātēsque serēnat, 255
ōscula lībāvit nātae, dehinc tālia fātur:
' Parce metū, Cytherēa: manent immōta tuōrum
fāta tibī; cernēs urbem et prōmissa Lavīnī
moenia, sublīmemque ferēs ad sīdera caelī
magnanimum Aenēān; neque mē sententia vertit. 260
Hic tibi (fābor enim, quandō haec tē cūra remordet,
longius et volvēns fātōrum arcāna movēbō)
bellum ingēns geret Ītaliā, populōsque ferōcēs
contundet, mōrēsque virīs et moenia pōnet,
tertia dum Latiō rēgnantem vīderit aestās, 265
ternaque trānsierint Rutulīs hīberna subāctīs.
At puer Ascanius, cui nunc cognōmen Iūlō
additur,—Īlus erat, dum rēs stetit Īlia rēgnō,—
trīgintā magnōs volvendīs mēnsibus orbīs
imperiō explēbit, rēgnumque ab sēde Lavīnī 270
trānsferet, et longam multā vī mūniet Albam.
Hīc iam ter centum tōtōs rēgnābitur annōs
gente sub Hectoreā, dōnec rēgīna sacerdōs,
Mārte gravis, geminam partū dabit Īlia prōlem.
Inde lupae fulvō nūtrīcis tegmine laetus 275
Rōmulus excipiet gentem, et Māvortia condet
moenia, Rōmānōsque suō dē nōmine dīcet.
Hīs ego nec mētās rērum nec tempora pōnō;
imperium sine fīne dedī. Quīn aspera Iūnō,
quae mare nunc terrāsque metū caelumque fatīgat, 280

cōnsilia in melius referet, mēcumque fovēbit
Rōmānōs rērum dominōs gentemque togātam:
sīc placitum. Veniet lūstrīs lābentibus aetās,
cum domus Assaracī Phthīam clārāsque Mycēnās
servitiō premet, ac victīs dominābitur Argīs.   285
Nāscētur pulchrā Trōiānus orīgine Caesar,
imperium Ōceanō, fāmam quī terminet astrīs,—
Iūlius, ā magnō dēmissum nōmen Iūlō.
Hunc tū ōlim caelō, spoliīs Orientis onustum,
accipiēs sēcūra; vocābitur hic quoque vōtīs.   290
Aspera tum positīs mītēscent saecula bellīs;
cāna Fidēs, et Vesta, Remō cum frātre Quirīnus,
iūra dabunt; dīrae ferrō et compāgibus artīs
claudentur Bellī portae; Furor impius intus,
saeva sedēns super arma, et centum vīnctus aēnīs   295
post tergum nōdīs, fremet horridus ōre cruentō.'

*Jupiter sends Mercury to inspire the Carthaginians
with friendly feelings*

Haec ait, et Māiā genitum dēmittit ab altō,
ut terrae, utque novae pateant Karthāginis arcēs
hospitiō Teucrīs, nē fātī nescia Dīdō
fīnibus arcēret: volat ille per āera magnum   300
rēmigiō ālārum, ac Libyae citus adstitit ōrīs.
Et iam iussa facit, pōnuntque ferōcia Poenī
corda volente deō; in prīmīs rēgīna quiētum
accipit in Teucrōs animum mentemque benignam.

*Æneas, while exploring the country, meets Venus disguised
as a huntress*

At pius Aenēās, per noctem plūrima volvēns,   305
ut prīmum lūx alma data est, exīre locōsque
explōrāre novōs, quās ventō accesserit ōrās,

quī teneant, nam inculta vidēt, hominēsne feraene,
quaerere cōnstituit, sociīsque exācta referre.
Classem in convexō nemorum sub rūpe cavātā   310
arboribus clausam circum atque horrentibus umbrīs
occulit; ipse ūnō graditur comitātus Achātē,
bīna manū lātō crīspāns hastīlia ferrō.

MERCURY

Cui māter mediā sēsē tulit obvia silvā
virginis ōs habitumque gerēns, et virginis arma   315
Spartānae, vel quālis equōs Thrēissa fatīgat
Harpalycē, volucremque fugā praevertitur Hebrum.
Namque umerīs dē mōre habilem suspenderat arcum
vēnātrīx, dederatque comam diffundere ventīs,
nūda genū, nōdōque sinūs collēcta fluentīs.   320
Ac prior, 'Heus,' inquit, 'iuvenēs, mōnstrāte meārum
vīdistis sī quam hīc errantem forte sorōrum,
succīnctam pharetrā et maculōsae tegmine lyncis,
aut spūmantis aprī cursum clāmōre prementem.'

ÆNEAS AND VENUS (AS HUNTRESS)

Sīc Venus; et Veneris contrā sīc fīlius ōrsus: 325
'Nŭlla tuārum audīta mihī neque vīsa sorōrum—
Ō quam tē memorem, virgō? Namque haud tibi voltus
mortālis, nec vōx hominem sonat: Ō, dea certē—
an Phoebī soror? an nymphārum sanguinis ūna?—
sīs fēlīx, nostrumque levēs, quaecumque, labōrem,   330
et, quŏ sub caelō tandem, quibus orbis in ōrīs
iactēmur, doceās. Ignārī hominumque locōrumque
errāmus, ventō hūc vāstīs et fluctibus āctī:
multa tibi ante ārās nostrā cadet hostia dextrā.'

Venus tells the story of Dido's flight

Tum Venus: 'Haud equidem tālī mē dignor honōre; 335
virginibus Tyriīs mōs est gestāre pharetram,
purpureōque altē sūrās vincīre cothurnō.
Pūnica rēgna vidēs, Tyriōs et Agēnoris urbem;
sed fīnēs Libycī, genus intrāctābile bellō.
Imperium Dīdō Tyriā regit urbe profecta,   340
germānum fugiēns. Longa est iniūria, longae
ambāgēs; sed summa sequar fastīgia rērum.
'Huic coniūnx Sȳchaeus erat, dītissimus agrī
Phoenīcum, et magnō miserae dīlēctus amōre,
cui pater intāctam dederat, prīmīsque iugārat   345
ōminibus. Sed rēgna Tyrī germānus habēbat
Pygmaliōn, scelere ante aliōs immānior omnīs.
Quōs inter medius vēnit furor. Ille Sychaeum
impius ante ārās, atque aurī caecus amōre,
clam ferrō incautum superat, sēcūrus amōrum   350
germānae; factumque diū cēlāvit, et aegram,
multa malus simulāns, vānā spē lūsit amantem.
Ipsa sed in somnīs inhumātī vēnit imāgō
coniugis, ōra modīs attollēns pallida mīrīs,
crūdēlīs ārās trāiectaque pectora ferrō   355

nūdāvit, caecumque domūs scelus omne retēxit.
Tum celerāre fugam patriāque excēdere suādet,
auxiliumque viae veterēs tellūre reclūdit
thēsaurōs, ignōtum argentī pondus et aurī.
Hīs commōta fugam Dīdō sociōsque parābat: 360
conveniunt, quibus aut odium crūdēle tyrannī
aut metus ācer erat; nāvīs, quae forte parātae,
corripiunt, onerantque aurō: portantur avārī
Pygmaliōnis opēs pelagō; dux fēmina factī.
Dēvēnēre locōs, ubi nunc ingentia cernēs   365
moenia surgentemque novae Karthāginis arcem,
mercātīque solum, factī dē nōmine Byrsam,
taurīnō quantum possent circumdare tergō.
Sed vōs quī tandem, quibus aut vēnistis ab ōrīs,
quōve tenētis iter?' Quaerentī tālibus ille   370
suspīrāns, īmōque trahēns ā pectore vōcem:

Æneas tells Venus of his misfortunes

'Ō dea, sī prīmā repetēns ab orīgine pergam,
et vacet annālīs nostrōrum audīre labōrum,
ante diem clausō compōnat Vesper Olympō.
Nōs Trōiā antīquā, sī vestrās forte per aurīs   375
Trōiae nōmen iit, dīversa per aequora vectōs
forte suā Libycīs tempestās appulit ōrīs.
Sum pius Aenēās, raptōs quī ex hoste penātīs
classe vehō mēcum, fāmā super aethera nōtus.
Ītaliam quaerō patriam et genus ab Iove summō.   380
Bis dēnīs Phrygium cōnscendī nāvibus aequor,
mātre deā mōnstrante viam, data fāta secūtus;
vix septem convolsae undīs Eurōque supersunt.
Ipse ignōtus, egēns, Libyae dēserta peragrō,
Eurōpā atque Asiā pulsus.' Nec plūra querentem   385
passa Venus mediō sīc interfāta dolōre est:

Venus assures Æneas that his companions are safe

' Quisquis es, haud, crēdō, invīsus caelestibus aurās
vītālīs carpis, Tyriam quī advēneris urbem.
Perge modo, atque hinc tē rēgīnae ad līmina perfer.
Namque tibī reducēs sociōs classemque relātam   390
nūntiō, et in tūtum versīs aquilōnibus āctam,
nī frūstrā augurium vānī docuēre parentēs.
Aspice bis sēnōs laetantīs agmine cycnōs,
aetheriā quōs lāpsa plagā Iovis āles apertō
turbābat caelō; nunc terrās ōrdine longō   395
aut capere, aut captās iam dēspectāre videntur:
ut reducēs illī lūdunt strīdentibus ālīs,
et coetū cīnxēre polum, cantūsque dedēre,
haud aliter puppēsque tuae pūbēsque tuōrum
aut portum tenet aut plēnō subit ōstia vēlō.   400
Perge modo, et, quā tē dūcit via, dīrige gressum.'

Venus reveals herself to Æneas

Dīxit, et āvertēns roseā cervīce refulsit,
ambrosiaeque comae dīvīnum vertice odōrem
spīrāvēre, pedēs vestis dēflūxit ad īmōs,
et vēra incessū patuit dea. Ille ubi mātrem   405
agnōvit, tālī fugientem est vōce secūtus:
' Quid nātum totiēns, crūdēlis tū quoque, falsīs
lūdis imāginibus? Cūr dextrae iungere dextram
nōn datur, ac vērās audīre et reddere vōcēs?'

Æneas and Achates are veiled in a cloud

Tālibus incūsat, gressumque ad moenia tendit: 410
at Venus obscūrō gradientīs āere saepsit,
et multō nebulae circum dea fūdit amictū,
cernere nē quis eōs, neu quis contingere posset,
mōlīrīve moram, aut veniendī poscere causās.

Īpsa Paphum sublīmis abit, sēdēsque revīsit 415
laeta suās, ubi templum illī, centumque Sabaeō
tūre calent ārae, sertīsque recentibus hālant.

Æneas and Achates get their first view of Carthage,
and enter the city

Corripuēre viam intereā, quā sēmita mōnstrat.
Iamque ascendēbant collem, quī plūrimus urbī
imminet, adversāsque aspectat dēsuper arcēs. 420
Mīrātur mōlem Aenēās, māgālia quondam,
mīrātur portās strepitumque et strāta viārum.
Īnstant ārdentēs Tyriī, pars dūcere mūrōs,
mōlīrīque arcem et manibus subvolvere saxa,
pars optāre locum tēctō et conclūdere sulcō; 425
iūra magistrātūsque legunt sānctumque senātum;
hīc portūs aliī effodiunt; hīc alta theātrī
fundāmenta locant aliī, immānīsque columnās
rūpibus excīdunt, scaenīs decora alta futūrīs.
Quālis apēs aestāte novā per flōrea rūra 430
exercet sub sōle labor, cum gentis adultōs
ēdūcunt fētūs, aut cum līquentia mella
stīpant et dulcī distendunt nectare cellās,
aut onera accipiunt venientum, aut agmine factō
ignāvum fūcōs pecus ā praesaepibus arcent: 435
fervet opus, redolentque thymō frāgrantia mella.
'Ō fortūnātī, quōrum iam moenia surgunt!'
Aenēās ait, et fastīgia suspicit urbis.
Īnfert sē saeptus nebulā, mīrābile dictū,
per mediōs, miscetque virīs, neque cernitur ūllī. 440

Æneas views the temple of Juno

Lūcus in urbe fuit mediā, laetissimus umbrae,
quō prīmum iactātī undīs et turbine Poenī
effōdēre locō signum, quod rēgia Iūnō

mōnstrārat, caput ācris equī; sīc nam fore bellō
ēgregiam et facilem vīctū per saecula gentem.   445
Hīc templum Iūnōnī ingēns Sīdōnia Dīdō
condēbat, dōnīs opulentum et nūmine dīvae,
aerea cui gradibus surgēbant līmina, nexaeque
aere trabēs, foribus cardō strīdēbat aēnīs.
Hōc prīmum in lūcō nova rēs oblāta timōrem   450
lēniit, hīc prīmum Aenēās spērāre salūtem
ausus, et adflīctīs melius cōnfīdere rēbus.
Namque sub ingentī lūstrat dum singula templō,
rēgīnam opperiēns, dum, quae fortūna sit urbī,
artificumque manūs inter sē operumque labōrem   455
mīrātur, videt Īliacās ex ōrdine pugnās,
bellaque iam fāmā tōtum volgāta per orbem,
Atrīdās, Priamumque, et saevum ambōbus Achillem.
Cōnstitit, et lacrimāns, 'Quis iam locus,' inquit, 'Achātē,
quae regiō in terrīs nostrī nōn plēna labōris?   460
Ēn Priamus! Sunt hīc etiam sua praemia laudī;
sunt lacrimae rērum et mentem mortālia tangunt.
Solve metūs; feret haec aliquam tibi fāma salūtem.'
Sīc ait, atque animum pictūrā pāscit inānī,
multa gemēns, largōque ūmectat flūmine voltum.   465

*Æneas looks at scenes from the Trojan War painted on the
temple walls*

Namque vidēbat utī bellantēs Pergama circum
hāc fugerent Grāī, premeret Trōiāna iuventūs,
hāc Phryges, īnstāret currū cristātus Achillēs.
Nec procul hinc Rhēsī niveīs tentōria vēlīs
agnōscit lacrimāns, prīmō quae prōdita somnō   470
Tȳdīdēs multā vāstābat caede cruentus,
ārdentīsque āvertit equōs in castra, priusquam
pābula gustāssent Trōiae Xanthumque bibissent.
Parte aliā fugiēns āmissīs Trōilus armīs,

īnfēlīx puer atque impār congressus Achillī,   475
fertur equīs, currūque haeret resupīnus inānī,
lōra tenēns tamen; huic cervīxque comaeque trahuntur
per terram, et versā pulvīs īnscrībitur hastā.
Intereā ad templum nōn aequae Palladis ībant
crīnibus Īliades passīs, peplumque ferēbant,   48c
suppliciter trīstēs et tūnsae pectora palmīs;
dīva solō fīxōs oculōs āversa tenēbat.
Ter circum Īliacōs raptāverat Hectora mūrōs,
exanimumque aurō corpus vēndēbat Achillēs.
Tum vērō ingentem gemitum dat pectore ab īmō   485
ut spolia, ut currūs, utque ipsum corpus amīcī,
tendentemque manūs Priamum cōnspexit inermīs.
Sē quoque prīncipibus permixtum agnōvit Achīvīs,
Ēōāsque aciēs et nigrī Memnonis arma.
Dūcit Amāzonidum lūnātīs agmina peltīs   490
Penthesilēa furēns, mediīsque in mīlibus ārdet,
aurea subnectēns exsertae cingula mammae,
bellātrīx, audetque virīs concurrere virgō.

*Æneas sees Dido enter the temple, and his missing
companions come up*

Haec dum Dardaniō Aenēae mīranda videntur,
dum stupet, obtūtūque haeret dēfīxus in ūnō,   495
rēgīna ad templum, fōrmā pulcherrima Dīdō,
incessit magnā iuvenum stīpante catervā.
Quālis in Eurōtae rīpīs aut per iuga Cynthī
exercet Diāna chorōs, quam mīlle secūtae
hinc atque hinc glomerantur Orēades; illa pharetram   500
fert umerō, gradiēnsque deās superēminet omnīs:
Lātōnae tacitum pertemptant gaudia pectus:
tālis erat Dīdō, tālem sē laeta ferēbat
per mediōs, īnstāns operī rēgnīsque futūrīs.
Tum foribus dīvae, mediā testūdine templī,   505

saepta armīs, soliōque altē subnīxa resēdit.
Iūra dabat lēgēsque virīs, operumque labōrem
partibus aequābat iūstīs, aut sorte trahēbat:

THRONE

cum subitō Aenēās concursū accēdere magnō
Anthea Sergestumque videt fortemque Cloanthum,   510
Teucrōrumque aliōs, āter quōs aequore turbō
dispulerat penitusque aliās āvexerat ōrās.
Obstipuit simul ipse simul percussus Achātēs
laetitiāque metūque; avidī coniungere dextrās

ārdēbant; sed rēs animōs incognita turbat.   515
Dissimulant, et nūbe cavā speculantur amictī,
quae fortūna virīs, classem quō lītore linquant,
quid veniant; cūnctīs nam lēctī nāvibus ībant,
ōrantēs veniam, et templum clāmōre petēbant.

Ilioneus addresses Dido in behalf of the Trojans

Postquam intrōgressī et cōram data cōpia fandī,   520
maximus Īlioneus placidō sīc pectore coepit:
' Ō rēgīna, novam cui condere Iuppiter urbem
iūstitiāque dedit gentīs frēnāre superbās,
Trōes tē miserī, ventīs maria omnia vectī,
ōrāmus, prohibē īnfandōs ā nāvibus ignīs,   525
parce piō generī, et propius rēs aspice nostrās.
Nōn nōs aut ferrō Libycōs populāre penātīs
vēnimus, aut raptās ad lītora vertere praedās;
nōn ea vīs animō, nec tanta superbia victīs.
Est locus, Hesperiam Grāī cognōmine dīcunt,   530
terra antīqua, potēns armīs atque ūbere glaebae;
Oenōtrī coluēre virī; nunc fāma minōrēs
Ītaliam dīxisse ducis dē nōmine gentem.
Hic cursus fuit:
cum subitō adsurgēns fluctū nimbōsus Orīōn   535
in vada caeca tulit, penitusque procācibus austrīs
perque undās, superante salō, perque invia saxa
dispulit; hūc paucī vestrīs adnāvimus ōrīs.
Quod genus hoc hominum? Quaeve hunc tam barbara mōren
permittit patria? Hospitiō prohibēmur harēnae;   540
bella cient, prīmāque vetant cōnsistere terrā.
Sī genus hūmānum et mortālia temnitis arma,
at spērāte deōs memorēs fandī atque nefandī.
' Rēx erat Aenēās nōbīs, quō iūstior alter
nec pietāte fuit, nec bellō maior et armīs.   545
Quem sī fāta virum servant, sī vēscitur aurā

aetheriā, neque adhūc crūdēlibus occubat umbrīs,
nōn metus; officiō nec tē certāsse priōrem
paeniteat. Sunt et Siculīs regiōnibus urbēs
arvaque, Trōiānōque ā sanguine clārus Acestēs.   550
Quassātam ventīs liceat subdūcere classem,
et silvīs aptāre trabēs et stringere rēmōs:
sī datur Ītaliam, sociīs et rēge receptō,
tendere, ut Ītaliam laetī Latiumque petāmus;
sīn absūmpta salūs, et tē, pater optime Teucrum,   555
pontus habet Libyae, nec spēs iam restat Iūlī,
at freta Sīcaniae saltem sēdēsque parātās,
unde hūc advectī, rēgemque petāmus Acestēn.'
    Tālibus Īlioneus; cūnctī simul ōre fremēbant
Dardanidae.   560

Dido assures Ilioneus that the Trojans are welcome

Tum breviter Dīdō, voltum dēmissa, profātur:
'Solvite corde metum, Teucrī, sēclūdite cūrās.
Rēs dūra et rēgnī novitās mē tālia cōgunt
mōlīrī, et lātē fīnīs custōde tuērī.
Quis genus Aeneadum, quis Trōiae nesciat urbem,   565
virtūtēsque virōsque, aut tantī incendia bellī?
Nōn obtūsa adeō gestāmus pectora Poenī,
nec tam āversus equōs Tyriā Sōl iungit ab urbe.
Seu vōs Hesperiam magnam Sāturniaque arva,
sīve Erycis fīnīs rēgemque optātis Acestēn,   570
auxiliō tūtōs dīmittam, opibusque iuvābō.
Voltis et hīs mēcum pariter cōnsīdere rēgnīs;
urbem quam statuō vestra est, subdūcite nāvīs;
Trōs Tyriusque mihī nūllō discrīmine agētur.
Atque utinam rēx ipse Notō compulsus eōdem   575
adforet Aenēās! Equidem per lītora certōs
dīmittam et Libyae lūstrāre extrēma iubēbō,
sī quibus ēiectus silvīs aut urbibus errat.'

Æneas is disclosed

Hīs animum arrēctī dictīs et fortis Achātēs
et pater Aenēās iamdūdum ērumpere nūbem   580
ārdēbant. Prior Aenēān compellat Achātēs:
'Nāte deā, quae nunc animō sententia surgit?
Omnia tūta vidēs, classem sociōsque receptōs.
Ūnus abest, mediō in fluctū quem vīdimus ipsī
submersum; dictīs respondent cētera mātris.'   585
   Vix ea fātus erat, cum circumfūsa repente
scindit sē nūbēs et in aethera pūrgat apertum.
Restitit Aenēās clārāque in lūce refulsit,
ōs umerōsque deō similis; namque ipsa decōram
caesariem nātō genetrīx lūmenque iuventae   590
purpureum et laetōs oculīs adflārat honōrēs:
quāle manūs addunt eborī decus, aut ubi flāvō
argentum Pariusve lapis circumdatur aurō.

Æneas thanks Dido for her hospitality

   Tum sīc rēgīnam adloquitur, cūnctīsque repente
imprōvīsus ait: 'Cōram, quem quaeritis, adsum,   595
Trōïus Aenēās, Libycīs ēreptus ab undīs.
Ō sōla īnfandōs Trōiae miserāta labōrēs,
quae nōs, rēliquiās Danaùm, terraeque marisque
omnibus exhaustōs iam cāsibus, omnium egēnōs,
urbe, domō sociās, grātēs persolvere dignās   600
nōn opis est nostrae, Dīdō, nec quicquid ubīque est
gentis Dardaniae, magnum quae sparsa per orbem.
Dī tibi, sī qua piōs respectant nūmina, sī quid
usquam iūstitia est et mēns sibi cōnscia rēctī,
praemia digna ferant. Quae tē tam laeta tulērunt   605
saecula? Quī tantī tālem genuēre parentēs?
In freta dum fluviī current, dum montibus umbrae
lūstrābunt convexa, polus dum sīdera pāscet,

semper honōs nōmenque tuum laudēsque manēbunt,
quae mē cumque vocant terrae.' Sīc fātus, amīcum   610
Īlionēa petit dextrā, laevāque Serestum,
post aliōs, fortemque Gyān fortemque Cloanthum.

Dido welcomes Æneas

Obstipuit prīmō aspectū Sīdōnia Dīdō,
cāsū deinde virī tantō, et sīc ōre locūta est:
' Quis tē, nāte deā, per tanta perīcula cāsus   615
īnsequitur? Quae vīs immānibus applicat ōrīs?
Tūne ille Aenēās, quem Dardaniō Anchīsae
alma Venus Phrygiī genuit Simoëntis ad undam?
Atque equidem Teucrum meminī Sīdōna venīre
fīnibus expulsum patriīs, nova rēgna petentem   620
auxiliō Bēlī; genitor tum Bēlus opīmam
vāstābat Cyprum, et victor diciōne tenēbat.
Tempore iam ex illō cāsus mihi cognitus urbis
Trōiānae nōmenque tuum rēgēsque Pelasgī.
Ipse hostis Teucrōs īnsignī laude ferēbat,   625
sēque ortum antīquā Teucrōrum ab stirpe volēbat.
Quārē agite, Ō tēctīs, iuvenēs, succēdite nostrīs.
Mē quoque per multōs similis fortūna labōrēs
iactātam hāc dēmum voluit cōnsistere terrā.
Nōn ignāra malī, miserīs succurrere discō.'   630

The Trojans are royally entertained

Sīc memorat; simul Aenēān in rēgia dūcit
tēcta, simul dīvum templīs indīcit honōrem.
Nec minus intereā sociīs ad lītora mittit
vīgintī taurōs, magnōrum horrentia centum
terga suum, pinguīs centum cum mātribus agnōs,   635
mūnera laetitiamque diī.
At domus interior rēgālī splendida lūxū
īnstruitur, mediīsque parant convīvia tēctīs:

arte labōrātae vestēs ostrōque superbō,
ingēns argentum mēnsīs, caelātaque in aurō 640
fortia facta patrum, seriēs longissima rērum
per tot ducta virōs antīquā ab orīgine gentis.

*Achates is sent to the fleet to bring Ascanius and gifts
for the queen*

Aenēās (neque enim patrius cōnsistere mentem
passus amor) rapidum ad nāvīs praemittit Achātēn,
Ascaniō ferat haec, ipsumque ad moenia dūcat; 645
omnis in Ascaniō cārī stat cūra parentis.
Mūnera praetereā, Īliacīs ērepta ruīnīs,
ferre iubet, pallam signīs aurōque rigentem,
et circumtextum croceō vēlāmen acanthō,
ōrnātūs Argīvae Helenae, quōs illa Mycēnīs, 650
Pergama cum peterēt inconcessōsque hymenaeōs,
extulerat, mātris Lēdae mīrābile dōnum:
praetereā scēptrum, Īlionē quod gesserat ōlim,
maxima nātārum Priamī, collōque monīle
bācātum, et duplicem gemmīs aurōque corōnam. 655
Haec celerāns iter ad nāvīs tendēbat Achātēs.

Venus still fears for the safety of the Trojans

At Cytherēa novās artēs, nova pectore versat
cōnsilia, ut faciem mūtātus et ōra Cupīdō
prō dulcī Ascaniō veniat, dōnīsque furentem
incendat rēgīnam, atque ossibus implicet ignem; 660
quippe domum timet ambiguam Tyriōsque bilinguīs;
ūrit atrōx Iūnō, et sub noctem cūra recursat.
Ergō hīs āligerum dictīs adfātur Amōrem:

Venus appeals to Cupid for aid in a new plot

'Nāte, meae vīrēs, mea magna potentia sōlus,
nāte, patris summī quī tēla Typhōïa temnis, 665
ad tē cōnfugiō et supplex tua nūmina poscō.

Frāter ut Aenēās pelagō tuus omnia circum
lītora iactētūr odiīs Iūnōnis inīquae,
nōta tibi, et nostrō doluistī saepe dolōre.
Hunc Phoenīssa tenet Dīdō blandīsque morātur   670
vōcibus; et vereor, quō sē Iūnōnia vertant
hospitia; haud tantō cessābit cardine rērum.
Quōcircā capere ante dolīs et cingere flammā
rēgīnam meditor, nē quō sē nūmine mūtet,
sed magnō Aenēae mēcum teneātur amōre.   675
Quā facere id possīs, nostram nunc accipe mentem.
Rēgius accītū cārī genitōris ad urbem
Sīdoniam puer īre parat, mea maxima cūra,
dōna ferēns, pelagō et flammīs restantia Trōiae:
hunc ego sōpītum somnō super alta Cythēra   680
aut super Īdalium sacrātā sēde recondam,
nē quā scīre dolōs mediusve occurrere possit.
Tū faciem illīus noctem nōn amplius ūnam
falle dolō, et nōtōs puerī puer indue voltūs,
ut, cum tē gremiō accipiet laetissima Dīdō   685
rēgālīs inter mēnsās laticemque Lyaeum,
cum dabit amplexūs atque ōscula dulcia fīget,
occultum īnspīrēs ignem fallāsque venēnō.'

Cupid visits Dido's palace in the form of Ascanius

Pāret Amor dictīs cārae genetrīcis, et ālās
exuit, et gressū gaudēns incēdit Iūlī.   690
At Venus Ascaniō placidam per membra quiētem
inrigat, et fōtum gremiō dea tollit in altōs
Īdaliae lūcōs, ubi mollis amāracus illum
flōribus et dulcī adspīrāns complectitur umbrā.

The grand banquet to the Trojans begins

Iamque ībat dictō pārēns et dōna Cupīdō   695
rēgia portābat Tyriīs, duce laetus Achātē.
Cum venit, aulaeīs iam sē rēgīna superbīs

aureā composuit spondā mediamque locāvit.
Iam pater Aenēās et iam Trōiāna iuventūs
conveniunt, strātōque super discumbitur ostrō.   700
Dant manibus famulī lymphās, Cereremque canistrīs
expediunt, tōnsīsque ferunt mantēlia villīs.
Quīnquāgintā intus famulae, quibus ōrdine longō
cūra penum struere, et flammīs adolēre penātīs;
centum aliae totidemque parēs aetāte ministrī,   705
quī dapibus mēnsās onerent et pōcula pōnant.
Nec nōn et Tyriī per līmina laeta frequentēs
convēnēre, torīs iussī discumbere pictīs.
Mīrantur dōna Aenēae, mīrantur Iūlum
flagrantīsque deī voltūs simulātaque verba   710
[pallamque et pictum croceō vēlāmen acanthō].

Cupid inspires Dido with love for Æneas

Praecipuē īnfēlīx, pestī dēvōta futūrae,
explērī mentem nequit ārdēscitque tuendō
Phoenīssa, et pariter puerō dōnīsque movētur.
Ille ubi complexū Aenēae collōque pependit   715
et magnum falsī implēvit genitōris amōrem,
rēgīnam petit: haec oculīs, haec pectore tōtō
haeret et interdum gremiō fovet, īnscia Dīdō
īnsīdat quantus miserae deus; at memor ille
mātris Acīdaliae paulātim abolēre Sychaeum   720
incipit, et vīvō temptat praevertere amōre
iam prīdem residēs animōs dēsuētaque corda.

The evening is spent in feasting

Postquam prīma quiēs epulīs, mēnsaeque remōtae,
crātēras magnōs statuunt et vīna corōnant.
Fit strepitus tēctīs, vōcemque per ampla volūtant   725
ātria; dēpendent lychnī laqueāribus aureīs
incēnsī, et noctem flammīs fūnālia vincunt.

Hīc rēgīna gravem gemmīs aurōque poposcit
implēvitque merō pateram, quam Bēlus et omnēs
ä Bēlō solitī ; tum facta silentia tēctīs : 730
' Iuppiter, hospitibus nam tē dare iūra loquuntur,
hunc laetum Tyriīsque diem Trōiāque profectīs
esse velīs, nostrōsque huius meminisse minōrēs.
Adsit laetitiae Bacchus dator, et bona Iūnō ;
et vōs, Ō, coetum, Tyriī, celebrāte faventēs.' 735
Dīxit, et in mēnsam laticum lībāvit honōrem,
prīmaque, lībātō, summō tenus attigit ōre ;
tum Bitiae dedit increpitāns ; ille impiger hausit
spūmantem pateram, et plēnō sē prōluit aurō ;
post aliī procerēs. Citharā crīnītus Iōpās 740
personat aurātā, docuit quem maximus Atlās.
Hic canit errantem lūnam sōlisque labōrēs ;
unde hominum genus et pecudēs ; unde imber et ignēs ;
Arctūrum pluviāsque Hyadas geminōsque Triōnēs ;
quid tantum Ōceanō properent sē tinguere sōlēs 745
hībernī, vel quae tardīs mora noctibus obstet.
Ingeminant plausū Tyriī, Trōesque sequuntur.

*Dido invites Æneas to tell the story of the fall of Troy and of
his wanderings*

Nec nōn et variō noctem sermōne trahēbat
īnfēlīx Dīdō, longumque bibēbat amōrem,
multa super Priamō rogitāns, super Hectore multa ; 750
nunc quibus Aurōrae vēnisset fīlius armīs,
nunc quālēs Diomēdis equī, nunc quantus Achillēs.
' Immō age, et ā prīmā dīc, hospes, orīgine nōbīs
īnsidiās,' inquit, 'Danaum, cāsūsque tuōrum,
errōrēsque tuōs ; nam tē iam septima portat 755
omnibus errantem terrīs et fluctibus aestās.'

LIBER II

THE TALE OF TROY

Æneas begins the tale. The Greeks, discouraged, had withdrawn to Tenedos, leaving the wooden horse, in which chosen warriors were hidden (1–39). Laocoön in vain protests against receiving it within the walls : meanwhile Sinon, pretending to have fled from the Greeks, is received in confidence by Priam, whom he persuades that the horse is a sacred offering to Minerva (40–198). Laocoön and his sons are destroyed by two monstrous serpents : the horse is brought with rejoicing into the city, and at night Sinon sets free the Grecian chiefs (199–267). The ghost of Hector appears to Æneas, and warns him to flee. The city is seen in flames : Æneas and his companions take arms (268–369). Victorious encounter with a party of Greeks : a disastrous conflict follows, and they come to Priam's palace (370–452). Defence and storming of the palace : the fate of Priam, slain by Pyrrhus, while vainly attempting to protect his son (453–558). Æneas returns to his own house—first meeting Helen, whom Venus warns him not to slay —and beholds in a vision the divinities who preside at the destruction of Troy (559–663). Anchises at first refuses to fly, but is encouraged by a divine omen (664–704). Æneas, bearing his father, and attended by his wife Creüsa, and his son, seeks escape ; but, confused by a sudden alarm, loses Creüsa on the way (705–751). He seeks her in vain at his palace, which is now filled with the armed enemy ; but she meets him in a vision and comforts him by assurance of her own deliverance from hostile hands. At dawn, he finds a numerous company escaped from the city, with whom he seeks the shelter of Mount Ida (752–804).

Æneas begins his story

CONTICUERE omnes, intentique ora tenebant.
Inde toro pater Aeneas sic orsus ab alto :
Infandum, regina, iubes renovare dolorem,
Troianas ut opes et lamentabile regnum
eruerint Danai ; quaeque ipse miserrima vidi,   5

et quorum pars magna fui. Quis talia fando
Myrmidonum Dolopumve aut duri miles Ulixi
temperet a lacrimis? Et iam nox umida caelo
praecipitat, suadentque cadentia sidera somnos.
Sed si tantus amor casus cognoscere nostros   10
et breviter Troiae supremum audire laborem,
quamquam animus meminisse horret, luctuque refugit,
incipiam.

The Greeks build a huge wooden horse, fill it with soldiers, and sail away to Tenedos

Fracti bello fatisque repulsi
ductores Danaum, tot iam labentibus annis,
instar montis equum divina Palladis arte   15
aedificant, sectaque intexunt abiete costas:
votum pro reditu simulant; ea fama vagatur.
Huc delecta virum sortiti corpora furtim
includunt caeco lateri, penitusque cavernas
ingentis uterumque armato milite complent.   20
Est in conspectu Tenedos, notissima fama
insula, dives opum, Priami dum regna manebant,
nunc tantum sinus et statio male fida carinis:
huc se provecti deserto in litore condunt.

The Trojans debate what they are to do with the horse

Nos abiisse rati et vento petiisse Mycenas: 25
ergo omnis longo solvit se Teucria luctu;
panduntur portae; iuvat ire et Dorica castra   •
desertosque videre locos litusque relictum.
Hic Dolopum manus, hic saevus tendebat Achilles;
classibus hic locus; hic acie certare solebant.   30
Pars stupet innuptae donum exitiale Minervae,
et molem mirantur equi; primusque Thymoetes
duci intra muros hortatur et arce locari,

THE TROJAN HORSE

sive dolo, seu iam Troiae sic fata ferebant.
At Capys, et quorum melior sententia menti,   35
aut pelago Danaum insidias suspectaque dona
praecipitare iubent, subiectisque urere flammis,
aut terebrare cavas uteri et temptare latebras.
Scinditur incertum studia in contraria volgus.

Laocoön warns the Trojans

Primus ibi ante omnis, magna comitante caterva,   40
Laocoön ardens summa decurrit ab arce,
et procul: 'O miseri, quae tanta insania, cives?
Creditis avectos hostis? Aut ulla putatis
dona carere dolis Danaum? Sic notus Ulixes?
Aut hoc inclusi ligno occultantur Achivi,   45
aut haec in nostros fabricata est machina muros
inspectura domos venturaque desuper urbi,
aut aliquis latet error; equo ne credite, Teucri.
Quicquid id est, timeo Danaos et dona ferentis.'
Sic fatus, validis ingentem viribus hastam   50

in latus inque feri curvam compagibus alvum
contorsit: stetit illa tremens, uteroque recusso
insonuere cavae gemitumque dedere cavernae.
Et, si fata deum, si mens non laeva fuisset,
impulerat ferro Argolicas foedare latebras,   55
Troiaque nunc staret, Priamique arx alta, maneres.

Sinon, a Greek, is brought in as a willing prisoner

Ecce, manus iuvenem interea post terga revinctum
pastores magno ad regem clamore trahebant
Dardanidae, qui se ignotum venientibus ultro,
hoc ipsum ut strueret Troiamque aperiret Achivis,   60
obtulerat, fidens animi atque in utrumque paratus,
seu versare dolos, seu certae occumbere morti.
Undique visendi studio Troiana iuventus
circumfusa ruit, certantque inludere capto.
Accipe nunc Danaum insidias, et crimine ab uno   65
disce omnes.

Namque ut conspectu in medio turbatus, inermis
constitit atque oculis Phrygia agmina circumspexit:
'Heu, quae nunc tellus,' inquit, 'quae me aequora possunt
accipere? Aut quid iam misero mihi denique restat, 70
cui neque apud Danaos usquam locus, et super ipsi
Dardanidae infensi poenas cum sanguine poscunt?'
Quo gemitu conversi animi, compressus et omnis
impetus. Hortamur fari; quo sanguine cretus,
quidve ferat, memoret, quae sit fiducia capto.   75
Ille haec, deposita tandem formidine, fatur:

Sinon pretends that Ulysses was his enemy

'Cuncta equidem tibi, rex, fuerit quodcumque, fatebor
vera,' inquit, 'neque me Argolica de gente negabo:
hoc primum; nec, si miserum Fortuna Sinonem
finxit, vanum etiam mendacemque improba finget.   80

Fando aliquod si forte tuas pervenit ad auris
Belídae nomen Palamedis et incluta fama
gloria,—quem falsa sub proditione Pelasgi
insontem infando indicio, quia bella vetabat,
demisere neci, nunc cassum lumine lugent,—   85
illi me comitem et consanguinitate propinquum
pauper in arma pater primis huc misit ab annis,
dum stabat regno incolumis regumque vigebat
consiliis, et nos aliquod nomenque decusque
gessimus. Invidia postquam pellacis Ulixi—   90
haud ignota loquor—superis concessit ab oris,
adflictus vitam in tenebris luctuque trahebam,
et casum insontis mecum indignabar amici.
Nec tacui demens, et me, fors si qua tulisset,
si patrios umquam remeassem victor ad Argos,   95
promisi ultorem, et verbis odia aspera movi.
Hinc mihi prima mali labes, hinc semper Ulixes
criminibus terrere novis, hinc spargere voces
in volgum ambiguas, et quaerere conscius arma.
Nec requievit enim, donec, Calchante ministro—   100
sed quid ego haec autem nequiquam ingrata revolvo?
Quidve moror, si omnis uno ordine habetis Achivos,
idque audire sat est? Iamdudum sumite poenas;
hoc Ithacus velit, et magno mercentur Atridae.'

Sinon pretends that the Greeks were about to sacrifice him

Tum vero ardemus scitari et quaerere causas,   105
ignari scelerum tantorum artisque Pelasgae.
Prosequitur pavitans, et ficto pectore fatur:
'Saepe fugam Danai Troia cupiere relicta
moliri, et longo fessi discedere bello;
fecissentque utinam! Saepe illos aspera ponti   110
interclusit hiems, et terruit Auster euntis.

Praecipue, cum iam hic trabibus contextus acernis
staret equus, toto sonuerunt aethere nimbi.
Suspensi Eurypylum scitantem oracula Phoebi
mittimus, isque adytis haec tristia dicta reportat: 115
Sanguine placastis ventos et virgine caesa,
cum primum Iliacas, Danai, venistis ad oras;
sanguine quaerendi reditus, animaque litandum
Argolica. Volgi quae vox ut venit ad auris,
obstipuere animi, gelidusque per ima cucurrit   120
ossa tremor, cui fata parent, quem poscat Apollo.

   'Hic Ithacus vatem magno Calchanta tumultu
protrahit in medios; quae sint ea numina divum,
flagitat; et mihi iam multi crudele canebant
artificis scelus, et taciti ventura videbant.   125
Bis quinos silet ille dies, tectusque recusat
prodere voce sua quemquam aut opponere morti.
Vix tandem, magnis Ithaci clamoribus actus,
composito rumpit vocem, et me destinat arae.
Adsensere omnes, et, quae sibi quisque timebat,   130
unius in miseri exitium conversa tulere.
Iamque dies infanda aderat; mihi sacra parari,
et salsae fruges, et circum tempora vittae:
eripui, fateor, leto me, et vincula rupi,
limosoque lacu per noctem obscurus in ulva   135
delitui, dum vela darent, si forte dedissent.
Nec mihi iam patriam antiquam spes ulla videndi,
nec dulcis natos exoptatumque parentem;
quos illi fors et poenas ob nostra reposcent
effugia, et culpam hanc miserorum morte piabunt.   140
Quod te per superos et conscia numina veri,
per si qua est quae restet adhuc mortalibus usquam
intemerata fides, oro, miserere laborum
tantorum, miserere animi non digna ferentis.'

*The Trojans take pity on Sinon. He tells them that the horse
is an offering to Minerva, and that they will conquer the
Greeks if they receive it into the city*

His lacrimis vitam damus, et miserescimus ultro.   145
Ipse viro primus manicas atque arta levari
vincla iubet Priamus, dictisque ita fatur amicis:
'Quisquis es, amissos hinc iam obliviscere Graios;
noster eris, mihique haec edissere vera roganti: 149
Quo molem hanc immanis equi statuere? Quis auctor?
Quidve petunt? Quae religio, aut quae machina belli?'
Dixerat. Ille, dolis instructus et arte Pelasga,
sustulit exutas vinclis ad sidera palmas:
  'Vos, aeterni ignes, et non violabile vestrum
testor numen,' ait, 'vos, arae ensesque nefandi,   155
quos fugi, vittaeque deum, quas hostia gessi:
fas mihi Graiorum sacrata resolvere iura,
fas odisse viros, atque omnia ferre sub auras,
si qua tegunt; teneor patriae nec legibus ullis.
Tu modo promissis maneas, servataque serves,   160
Troia, fidem, si vera feram, si magna rependam.
  'Omnis spes Danaum et coepti fiducia belli
Palladis auxiliis semper stetit. Impius ex quo
Tydides sed enim scelerumque inventor Ulixes,
fatale adgressi sacrato avellere templo   165
Palladium, caesis summae custodibus arcis,
corripuere sacram effigiem, manibusque cruentis
virgineas ausi divae contingere vittas;
ex illo fluere ac retro sublapsa referri
spes Danaum, fractae vires, aversa deae mens.   170
Nec dubiis ea signa dedit Tritonia monstris.
Vix positum castris simulacrum, arsere coruscae
luminibus flammae arrectis, salsusque per artus
sudor iit, terque ipsa solo—mirabile dictu—
emicuit, parmamque ferens hastamque trementem.   175

THE PALLADIUM

'Extemplo temptanda fuga canit aequora Calchas,
nec posse Argolicis exscindi Pergama telis,
omina ni repetant Argis, numenque reducant
quod pelago et curvis secum avexere carinis.
Et nunc, quod patrias vento petiere Mycenas,   180
arma deosque parant comites, pelagoque remenso
improvisi aderunt: ita digerit omina Calchas.
Hanc pro Palladio moniti, pro numine laeso
effigiem statuere, nefas quae triste piaret.
Hanc tamen immensam Calchas attollere molem   185
roboribus textis caeloque educere iussit,
ne recipi portis, aut duci in moenia possit,
neu populum antiqua sub religione tueri.
Nam si vestra manus violasset dona Minervae,
tum magnum exitium (quod di prius omen in ipsum   190
convertant!) Priami imperio Phrygibusque futurum;
sin manibus vestris vestram ascendisset in urbem,
ultro Asiam magno Pelopea ad moenia bello
venturam, et nostros ea fata manere nepotes.'

Talibus insidiis periurique arte Sinonis   195
credita res, captique dolis lacrimisque coactis,
quos neque Tydides, nec Larissaeus Achilles,
non anni domuere decem, non mille carinae.

Laocoön and his sons are slain by serpents

Hic aliud maius miseris multoque tremendum
obicitur magis, atque improvida pectora turbat.   200
Laocoön, ductus Neptuno sorte sacerdos,
sollemnis taurum ingentem mactabat ad aras.
Ecce autem gemini a Tenedo tranquilla per alta—
horresco referens—immensis orbibus angues
incumbunt pelago, pariterque ad litora tendunt;   205
pectora quorum inter fluctus arrecta iubaeque
sanguineae superant undas; pars cetera pontum
pone legit, sinuatque immensa volumine terga.
Fit sonitus spumante salo; iamque arva tenebant,
ardentisque oculos suffecti sanguine et igni,   210
sibila lambebant linguis vibrantibus ora.
Diffugimus visu exsangues: illi agmine certo
Laocoönta petunt; et primum parva duorum
corpora natorum serpens amplexus uterque
implicat, et miseros morsu depascitur artus;   215
post ipsum auxilio subeuntem ac tela ferentem
corripiunt, spirisque ligant ingentibus; et iam
bis medium amplexi, bis collo squamea circum
terga dati, superant capite et cervicibus altis.
Ille simul manibus tendit divellere nodos,   220
perfusus sanie vittas atroque veneno,
clamores simul horrendos ad sidera tollit:
quales mugitus, fugit cum saucius aram
taurus, et incertam excussit cervice securim.

At gemini lapsu delubra ad summa dracones   225
effugiunt saevaeque petunt Tritonidis arcem,
sub pedibusque deae clipeique sub orbe teguntur.
Tum vero tremefacta novus per pectora cunctis
insinuat pavor, et scelus expendisse merentem
Laocoönta ferunt, sacrum qui cuspide robur   230
laeserit, et tergo sceleratam intorserit hastam.
Ducendum ad sedes simulacrum orandaque divae
numina conclamant.

The horse is brought into Troy

Dividimus muros et moenia pandimus urbis.
Accingunt omnes operi, pedibusque rotarum   235
subiciunt lapsus, et stuppea vincula collo
intendunt: scandit fatalis machina muros,
feta armis.   Pueri circum innuptaeque puellae
sacra canunt, funemque manu contingere gaudent.
Illa subit, mediaeque minans inlabitur urbi.   240
O patria, O divum domus Ilium, et incluta bello
moenia Dardanidum, quater ipso in limine portae
substitit, atque utero sonitum quater arma dedere:
instamus tamen immemores caecique furore,
et monstrum infelix sacrata sistimus arce.   245
Tunc etiam fatis aperit Cassandra futuris
ora, dei iussu non umquam credita Teucris.
Nos delubra deum miseri, quibus ultimus esset
ille dies, festa velamus fronde per urbem.

That night the Greeks return and enter the city, aided by Sinon; they are joined by those concealed in the horse

Vertitur interea caelum et ruit Oceano nox,   250
involvens umbra magna terramque polumque
Myrmidonumque dolos; fusi per moenia Teucri
conticuere, sopor fessos complectitur artus:

LAOCOÖN

et iam Argiva phalanx instructis navibus ibat
a Tenedo tacitae per amica silentia lunae   255
litora nota petens, flammas cum regia puppis
extulerat, fatisque deum defensus iniquis
inclusos utero Danaos et pinea furtim
laxat claustra Sinon. Illos patefactus ad auras
reddit equus, laetique cavo se robore promunt   260
Thessandrus Sthenelusque duces, et dirus Ulixes,
demissum lapsi per funem, Acamasque, Thoasque,
Pelidesque Neoptolemus, primusque Machaon,
et Menelaus, et ipse doli fabricator Epeos.
Invadunt urbem somno vinoque sepultam;   265
caeduntur vigiles, portisque patentibus omnis
accipiunt socios atque agmina conscia iungunt.

Hector appears in a dream to Æneas and bids him leave Troy

Tempus erat, quo prima quies mortalibus aegris
incipit, et dono divum gratissima serpit.
In somnis, ecce, ante oculos maestissimus Hector   270
visus adesse mihi, largosque effundere fletus,
raptatus bigis, ut quondam, aterque cruento
pulvere, perque pedes traiectus lora tumentis.
Ei mihi, qualis erat, quantum mutatus ab illo
Hectore, qui redit exuvias indutus Achilli,   275
vel Danaum Phrygios iaculatus puppibus ignis,
squalentem barbam et concretos sanguine crinis
volneraque illa gerens, quae circum plurima muros
accepit patrios. Ultro flens ipse videbar
compellare virum et maestas expromere voces: 280
'O lux Dardaniae, spes O fidissima Teucrum,
quae tantae tenuere morae? Quibus Hector ab oris
exspectate venis? Ut te post multa tuorum
funera, post varios hominumque urbisque labores

HECTOR'S GHOST WARNING ÆNEAS

defessi aspicimus! Quae causa indigna serenos   285
foedavit voltus? Aut cur haec volnera cerno?'
   Ille nihil, nec me quaerentem vana moratur,
sed graviter gemitus imo de pectore ducens,
'Heu fuge, nate dea, teque his,' ait, 'eripe flammis.
Hostis habet muros; ruit alto a culmine Troia.   290
Sat patriae Priamoque datum: si Pergama dextra
defendi possent, etiam hac defensa fuissent.
Sacra suosque tibi commendat Troia penatis:
hos cape fatorum comites, his moenia quaere
magna, pererrato statues quae denique ponto.'   295
Sic ait, et manibus vittas Vestamque potentem
aeternumque adytis effert penetralibus ignem.

*Æneas awakes and finds Troy in flames; he decides to get together
a band of men and to fight to the death*

   Diverso interea miscentur moenia luctu,
et magis atque magis, quamquam secreta parentis
Anchisae domus arboribusque obtecta recessit,   300
clarescunt sonitus, armorumque ingruit horror.
Excutior somno, et summi fastigia tecti
ascensu supero, atque arrectis auribus adsto:
in segetem veluti cum flamma furentibus Austris
incidit, aut rapidus montano flumine torrens   305
sternit agros, sternit sata laeta boumque labores,
praecipitesque trahit silvas, stupet inscius alto
accipiens sonitum saxi de vertice pastor.
Tum vero manifesta fides, Danaumque patescunt
insidiae. Iam Deiphobi dedit ampla ruinam   310
Volcano superante domus; iam proximus ardet
Ucalegon; Sigea igni freta lata relucent.
Exoritur clamorque virum clangorque tubarum.
Arma amens capio; nec sat rationis in armis,

sed glomerare manum bello et concurrere in arcem 315
cum sociis ardent animi; furor iraque mentem
praecipitant, pulchrumque mori succurrit in armis.

Æneas meets Panthus, who tells him that the Greeks are masters
of the city

Ecce autem telis Panthus elapsus Achivum,
Panthus Othryades, arcis Phoebique sacerdos;
sacra manu victosque deos parvumque nepotem 320
ipse trahit, cursuque amens ad limina tendit.
'Quo res summa loco, Panthu? Quam prendimus arcem?'
Vix ea fatus eram, gemitu cum talia reddit:
'Venit summa dies et ineluctabile tempus
Dardaniae: fuimus Troes, fuit Ilium et ingens 325
gloria Teucrorum; ferus omnia Iuppiter Argos
transtulit; incensa Danai dominantur in urbe.
Arduus armatos mediis in moenibus adstans
fundit equus, victorque Sinon incendia miscet
insultans; portis alii bipatentibus adsunt, 330
milia quot magnis umquam venere Mycenis;
obsedere alii telis angusta viarum
oppositis; stat ferri acies mucrone corusco
stricta, parata neci; vix primi proelia temptant
portarum vigiles, et caeco Marte resistunt.' 335

Æneas and his comrades make a desperate rally

Talibus Othryadae dictis et numine divum
in flammas et in arma feror, quo tristis Erinys,
quo fremitus vocat et sublatus ad aethera clamor.
Addunt se socios Ripheus et maximus armis
Epytus oblati per lunam Hypanisque Dymasque, 340
et lateri adglomerant nostro, iuvenisque Coroebus,
Mygdonides: illis ad Troiam forte diebus

venerat, insano Cassandrae incensus amore,
et gener auxilium Priamo Phrygibusque ferebat,
infelix, qui non sponsae praecepta furentis   345
audierit.

Quos ubi confertos audere in proelia vidi,
incipio super his: 'Iuvenes, fortissima frustra
pectora, si vobis audentem extrema cupido
certa sequi, quae sit rebus fortuna videtis: 350
excessere omnes, adytis arisque relictis,
di, quibus imperium hoc steterat; succurritis urbi
incensae; moriamur et in media arma ruamus.
Una salus victis, nullam sperare salutem.'

Sic animis iuvenum furor additus: inde, lupi ceu   355
raptores atra in nebula, quos improba ventris
exegit caecos rabies, catulique relicti
faucibus exspectant siccis, per tela, per hostis
vadimus haud dubiam in mortem, mediaeque tenemus
urbis iter; nox atra cava circumvolat umbra.   360
Quis cladem illius noctis, quis funera fando
explicet, aut possit lacrimis aequare labores?
Urbs antiqua ruit, multos dominata per annos;
plurima perque vias sternuntur inertia passim
corpora, perque domos et religiosa deorum   365
limina. Nec soli poenas dant sanguine Teucri;
quondam etiam victis redit in praecordia virtus
victoresque cadunt Danai: crudelis ubique
luctus, ubique pavor, et plurima mortis imago.

Androgeos mistakes Æneas and his followers for Greeks

Primus se, Danaum magna comitante caterva,   370
Androgeos offert nobis, socia agmina credens
inscius, atque ultro verbis compellat amicis:
'Festinate, viri: nam quae tam sera moratur

segnities? Alii rapiunt incensa feruntque
Pergama; vos celsis nunc primum a navibus itis?'   375
Dixit, et extemplo, neque enim responsa dabantur
fida satis, sensit medios delapsus in hostis.
Obstipuit, retroque pedem cum voce repressit:
improvisum aspris veluti qui sentibus anguem
pressit humi nitens, trepidusque repente refugit   380
attollentem iras et caerula colla tumentem;
haud secus Androgeos visu tremefactus abibat.
Inruimus, densis et circumfundimur armis,
ignarosque loci passim et formidine captos
sternimus: adspirat primo fortuna labori.   385

*The Trojans disguise themselves in Greek armor and are
successful for the moment*

Atque hic successu exsultans animisque Coroebus,
'O socii, qua prima,' inquit, 'fortuna salutis
monstrat iter, quaque ostendit se dextra, sequamur;
mutemus clipeos, Danaumque insignia nobis
aptemus: dolus an virtus, quis in hoste requirat?   390
Arma dabunt ipsi.' Sic fatus, deinde comantem
Androgei galeam clipeique insigne decorum
induitur, laterique Argivum accommodat ensem.
Hoc Ripheus, hoc ipse Dymas omnisque iuventus
laeta facit; spoliis se quisque recentibus armat.   395
Vadimus immixti Danais haud numine nostro,
multaque per caecam congressi proelia noctem
conserimus, multos Danaum demittimus Orco.
Diffugiunt alii ad navis, et litora cursu
fida petunt: pars ingentem formidine turpi   400
scandunt rursus equum et nota conduntur in alvo.

CASSANDRA

The Trojans attempt to rescue Cassandra

Heu nihil invitis fas quemquam fidere divis!
Ecce trahebatur passis Priameïa virgo
crinibus a templo Cassandra adytisque Minervae,
ad caelum tendens ardentia lumina frustra,—   405
lumina, nam teneras arcebant vincula palmas.
Non tulit hanc speciem furiata mente Coroebus,
et sese medium iniecit periturus in agmen.
Consequimur cuncti et densis incurrimus armis.

The Trojans are assailed by their friends

Hic primum ex alto delubri culmine telis   410
nostrorum obruimur, oriturque miserrima caedes
armorum facie et Graiarum errore iubarum.
Tum Danai gemitu atque ereptae virginis ira
undique collecti invadunt, acerrimus Aiax,
et gemini Atridae, Dolopumque exercitus omnis;   415
adversi rupto ceu quondam turbine venti
confligunt, Zephyrusque Notusque et laetus Eois

Eurus equis; stridunt silvae, saevitque tridenti
spumeus atque imo Nereus ciet aequora fundo.
Illi etiam, si quos obscura nocte per umbram 420
fudimus insidiis totaque agitavimus urbe,
apparent; primi clipeos mentitaque tela
agnoscunt, atque ora sono discordia signant.
Ilicet obruimur numero; primusque Coroebus
Peneleï dextra divae armipotentis ad aram 425
procumbit; cadit et Ripheus, iustissimus unus
qui fuit in Teucris et servantissimus aequi:
dis aliter visum; pereunt Hypanisque Dymasque
confixi a sociis; nec te tua plurima, Panthu,
labentem pietas nec Apollinis infula texit. 430
Iliaci cineres et flamma extrema meorum,
testor, in occasu vestro nec tela nec ullas
vitavisse vices Danaum, et, si fata fuissent
ut caderem, meruisse manu. Divellimur inde,
Iphitus et Pelias mecum, quorum Iphitus aevo 435
iam gravior, Pelias et volnere tardus Ulixi,
protinus ad sedes Priami clamore vocati.

The fighting is desperate at Priam's palace

Hic vero ingentem pugnam, ceu cetera nusquam
bella forent, nulli tota morerentur in urbe,
sic Martem indomitum, Danaosque ad tecta ruentis 440
cernimus, obsessumque acta testudine limen.
Haerent parietibus scalae, postisque sub ipsos
nituntur gradibus, clipeosque ad tela sinistris
protecti obiciunt, prensant fastigia dextris.
Dardanidae contra turris ac tota domorum 445
culmina convellunt; his se, quando ultima cernunt,
extrema iam in morte parant defendere telis;
auratasque trabes, veterum decora alta parentum
devolvunt; alii strictis mucronibus imas

obsedere fores; has servant agmine denso.   450
Instaurati animi, regis succurrere tectis,
auxilioque levare viros, vimque addere victis.

Æneàs defends the palace roof against the Greeks

Limen erat caecaeque fores et pervius usus
tectorum inter se Priami, postesque relicti
a tergo, infelix qua se, dum regna manebant,   455
saepius Andromache ferre incomitata solebat
ad soceros, et avo puerum Astyanacta trahebat.
Evado ad summi fastigia culminis, unde
tela manu miseri iactabant inrita Teucri.
Turrim in praecipiti stantem summisque sub astra   460
eductam tectis, unde omnis Troia videri
et Danaum solitae naves et Achaïa castra,
adgressi ferro circum, qua summa labantis
iuncturas tabulata dabant, convellimus altis
sedibus, impulimusque; ea lapsa repente ruinam   465
cum sonitu trahit et Danaum super agmina late
incidit: ast alii subeunt, nec saxa, nec ullum
telorum interea cessat genus.

Pyrrhus forces an entrance into Priam's palace

Vestibulum ante ipsum primoque in limine Pyrrhus
exsultat, telis et luce coruscus aëna;   470
qualis ubi in lucem coluber mala gramina pastus
frigida sub terra tumidum quem bruma tegebat,
nunc, positis novus exuviis nitidusque iuventa,
lubrica convolvit sublato pectore terga
arduus ad solem, et linguis micat ore trisulcis.   475
Una ingens Periphas et equorum agitator Achillis,
armiger Automedon, una omnis Scyria pubes
succedunt tecto, et flammas ad culmina iactant.
Ipse inter primos correpta dura bipenni

limina perrumpit, postisque a cardine vellit 480
aeratos; iamque excisa trabe firma cavavit
robora, et ingentem lato dedit ore fenestram.
Apparet domus intus, et atria longa patescunt;
apparent Priami et veterum penetralia regum,
armatosque vident stantis in limine primo. 485

The terror within the palace as the Greeks enter

At domus interior gemitu miseroque tumultu
miscetur, penitusque cavae plangoribus aedes
femineis ululant; ferit aurea sidera clamor.
Tum pavidae tectis matres ingentibus errant,
amplexaeque tenent postis atque oscula figunt. 490
Instat vi patria Pyrrhus; nec claustra, neque ipsi
custodes sufferre valent; labat ariete crebro
ianua, et emoti procumbunt cardine postes.
Fit via vi; rumpunt aditus, primosque trucidant
immissi Danai, et late loca milite complent. 495
Non sic, aggeribus ruptis cum spumeus amnis
exiit, oppositasque evicit gurgite moles,
fertur in arva furens cumulo, camposque per omnis
cum stabulis armenta trahit. Vidi ipse furentem
caede Neoptolemum geminosque in limine Atridas; 500
vidi Hecubam centumque nurus, Priamumque per aras
sanguine foedantem, quos ipse sacraverat, ignis.
Quinquaginta illi thalami, spes tanta nepotum,
barbarico postes auro spoliisque superbi,
procubuere; tenent Danai, qua deficit ignis. 505

The fate of Priam

Forsitan et Priami fuerint quae fata requiras.
Urbis uti captae casum convolsaque vidit
limina tectorum et medium in penetralibus hostem,
arma diu senior desueta trementibus aevo

circumdat nequiquam umeris, et inutile ferrum   510
cingitur, ac densos fertur moriturus in hostis.
Aedibus in mediis nudoque sub aetheris axe
ingens ara fuit iuxtaque veterrima laurus,
incumbens arae atque umbra complexa penatis.
Hic Hecuba et natae nequiquam altaria circum,   515
praecipites atra ceu tempestate columbae,
condensae et divum amplexae simulacra sedebant.
Ipsum autem sumptis Priamum iuvenalibus armis
ut vidit, 'Quae mens tam dira, miserrime coniunx,
impulit his cingi telis? Aut quo ruis?' inquit;   520
'Non tali auxilio nec defensoribus istis
tempus eget; non, si ipse meus nunc adforet Hector.
Huc tandem concede; haec ara tuebitur omnis,
aut moriere simul.' Sic ore effata recepit
ad sese et sacra longaevum in sede locavit.   525
     Ecce autem elapsus Pyrrhi de caede Polites,
unus natorum Priami, per tela, per hostis
porticibus longis fugit, et vacua atria lustrat
saucius: illum ardens infesto volnere Pyrrhus
insequitur, iam iamque manu tenet et premit hasta.   530
Ut tandem ante oculos evasit et ora parentum,
concidit, ac multo vitam cum sanguine fudit.
Hic Priamus, quamquam in media iam morte tenetur,
non tamen abstinuit, nec voci iraeque pepercit:
'At tibi pro scelere,' exclamat, 'pro talibus ausis,   535
di, si qua est caelo pietas, quae talia curet,
persolvant grates dignas et praemia reddant
debita, qui nati coram me cernere letum
fecisti et patrios foedasti funere voltus.
At non ille, satum quo te mentiris, Achilles   540
talis in hoste fuit Priamo; sed iura fidemque
supplicis erubuit, corpusque exsangue sepulcro
reddidit Hectoreum, meque in mea regna remisit.'

HELEN IN HIDING

Sic fatus senior, telumque imbelle sine ictu
coniecit, rauco quod protinus aere repulsum   545
e summo clipei nequiquam umbone pependit.
Cui Pyrrhus: 'Referes ergo haec et nuntius ibis
Pelidae genitori; illi mea tristia facta
degeneremque Neoptolemum narrare memento.
Nunc morere.' Hoc dicens altaria ad ipsa trementem   550
traxit et in multo lapsantem sanguine nati,
implicuitque comam laeva, dextraque coruscum
extulit, ac lateri capulo tenus abdidit ensem.
Haec finis Priami fatorum; hic exitus illum
sorte tulit, Troiam incensam et prolapsa videntem   555
Pergama, tot quondam populis terrisque superbum
regnatorem Asiae. Iacet ingens litore truncus,
avolsumque umeris caput, et sine nomine corpus.

The death of Priam reminds Æneas of his own family

At me tum primum saevus circumstetit horror.
Obstipui; subiit cari genitoris imago,   560
ut regem aequaevum crudeli volnere vidi
vitam exhalantem; subiit deserta Creüsa,
et direpta domus, et parvi casus Iuli.
Respicio, et quae sit me circum copia lustro.
Deseruere omnes defessi, et corpora saltu   565
ad terram misere aut ignibus aegra dedere.

Æneas meets Helen, and is tempted to slay her

Iamque adeo super unus eram, cum limina Vestae
servantem et tacitam secreta in sede latentem
Tyndarida aspicio: dant clara incendia lucem
erranti passimque oculos per cuncta ferenti.   570
Illa sibi infestos eversa ob Pergama Teucros
et poenas Danaum et deserti coniugis iras

praemetuens, Troiae et patriae communis Erinys,
abdiderat sese atque aris invisa sedebat.
Exarsere ignes animo; subit ira cadentem 575
ulcisci patriam et sceleratas sumere poenas.
'Scilicet haec Spartam incolumis patriasque Mycenas
aspiciet, partoque ibit regina triumpho,
coniugiumque, domumque, patres, natosque videbit,
Iliadum turba et Phrygiis comitata ministris? 580
Occiderit ferro Priamus? Troia arserit igni?
Dardanium totiens sudarit sanguine litus?
Non ita: namque etsi nullum memorabile nomen
feminea in poena est, nec habet victoria laudem,
exstinxisse nefas tamen et sumpsisse merentis 585
laudabor poenas, animumque explesse iuvabit
ultricis flammae, et cineres satiasse meorum.'

Venus bids Æneas spare Helen, and reveals to him
the gods who are destroying the city

Talia iactabam, et furiata mente ferebar
cum mihi se, non ante oculis tam clara, videndam
obtulit et pura per noctem in luce refulsit 590
alma parens, confessa deam qualisque videri
caelicolis et quanta solet, dextraque prehensum
continuit, roseoque haec insuper addidit ore:
'Nate, quis indomitas tantus dolor excitat iras?
Quid furis, aut quonam nostri tibi cura recessit? 595
Non prius aspicies ubi fessum aetate parentem
liqueris Anchisen; superet coniunxne Creüsa,
Ascaniusque puer? Quos omnis undique Graiae
circum errant acies, et, ni mea cura resistat,
iam flammae tulerint inimicus et hauserit ensis. 600
Non tibi Tyndaridis facies invisa Lacaenae
culpatusve Paris: divum inclementia, divum,
has evertit opes sternitque a culmine Troiam.

Aspice—namque omnem, quae nunc obducta tuenti
mortalis hebetat visus tibi et umida circum   605
caligat, nubem eripiam; tu ne qua parentis
iussa time, neu praeceptis parere recusa:—
hic, ubi disiectas moles avolsaque saxis
saxa vides mixtoque undantem pulvere fumum,
Neptunus muros magnoque emota tridenti   610
fundamenta quatit, totamque a sedibus urbem
eruit; hic Iuno Scaeas saevissima portas
prima tenet, sociumque furens a navibus agmen
ferro accincta vocat.

Iam summas arces Tritonia, respice, Pallas   615
insedit, nimbo effulgens et Gorgone saeva.
Ipse pater Danais animos virisque secundas
sufficit, ipse deos in Dardana suscitat arma.
Eripe, nate, fugam, finemque impone labori.
Nusquam abero, et tutum patrio te limine sistam.'   620
Dixerat, et spissis noctis se condidit umbris.

Æneas sees that Troy is doomed and hastens to his own house

Apparent dirae facies inimicaque Troiae
numina magna deum.
Tum vero omne mihi visum considere in ignis
Ilium et ex imo verti Neptunia Troia;   625
ac veluti summis antiquam in montibus ornum
cum ferro accisam crebrisque bipennibus instant
eruere agricolae certatim,—illa usque minatur
et tremefacta comam concusso vertice nutat,
volneribus donec paulatim evicta supremum   630
congemuit, traxitque iugis avolsa ruinam.
Descendo, ac ducente deo flammam inter et hostis
expedior; dant tela locum, flammaeque recedunt.

Anchises stubbornly refuses to leave Troy

Atque ubi iam patriae perventum ad limina sedis
antiquasque domos, genitor, quem tollere in altos   635
optabam primum montis primumque petebam,
abnegat excisa vitam producere Troia
exsiliumque pati. 'Vos O, quibus integer aevi
sanguis,' ait, 'solidaeque suo stant robore vires,
vos agitate fugam: 640
me si caelicolae voluissent ducere vitam,
has mihi servassent sedes. Satis una superque
vidimus excidia et captae superavimus urbi.
Sic O sic positum adfati discedite corpus.
Ipse manu mortem inveniam; miserebitur hostis   645
exuviasque petet; facilis iactura sepulcri.
Iam pridem invisus divis et inutilis annos
demoror, ex quo me divum pater atque hominum rex
fulminis adflavit ventis et contigit igni.'
   Talia perstabat memorans, fixusque manebat.   650
Nos contra effusi lacrimis, coniunxque Creüsa
Ascaniusque omnisque domus, ne vertere secum
cuncta pater fatoque urguenti incumbere vellet.
Abnegat, inceptoque et sedibus haeret in isdem.
Rursus in arma feror, mortemque miserrimus opto: 655
nam quod consilium aut quae iam fortuna dabatur?
'Mene efferre pedem, genitor, te posse relicto
sperasti, tantumque nefas patrio excidit ore?
Si nihil ex tanta superis placet urbe relinqui,
et sedet hoc animo, perituraeque addere Troiae   660
teque tuosque iuvat, patet isti ianua leto,
iamque aderit multo Priami de sanguine Pyrrhus,
natum ante ora patris, patrem qui obtruncat ad aras.
Hoc erat, alma parens, quod me per tela, per ignis
eripis, ut mediis hostem in penetralibus, utque   665

Ascanium patremque meum iuxtaque Creüsam
alterum in alterius mactatos sanguine cernam?
Arma, viri, ferte arma; vocat lux ultima victos.
Reddite me Danais; sinite instaurata revisam
proelia. Numquam omnes hodie moriemur inulti.'   670

Creüsa implores Æneas to protect his family

Hinc ferro accingor rursus clipeoque sinistram
insertabam aptans, meque extra tecta ferebam.
Ecce autem complexa pedes in limine coniunx
haerebat, parvumque patri tendebat Iulum:
'Si periturus abis, et nos rape in omnia tecum;   675
sin aliquam expertus sumptis spem ponis in armis,
hanc primum tutare domum. Cui parvus Iulus,
cui pater et coniunx quondam tua dicta relinquor?'

A sign from the gods makes Anchises give way

Talia vociferans gemitu tectum omne replebat,
cum subitum dictuque oritur mirabile monstrum.   680
Namque manus inter maestorumque ora parentum
ecce levis summo de vertice visus Iuli
fundere lumen apex, tactuque innoxia mollis
lambere flamma comas et circum tempora pasci.
Nos pavidi trepidare metu, crinemque flagrantem   685
excutere et sanctos restinguere fontibus ignis.
At pater Anchises oculos ad sidera laetus
extulit, et caelo palmas cum voce tetendit:
    'Iuppiter omnipotens, precibus si flecteris ullis,
aspice nos; hoc tantum, et, si pietate meremur,   690
da deinde auxilium, pater, atque haec omina firma.'
Vix ea fatus erat senior, subitoque fragore
intonuit laevum, et de caelo lapsa per umbras
stella facem ducens multa cum luce cucurrit.

THE SIGN FROM HEAVEN

Illam, summa super labentem culmina tecti,   695
cernimus Idaea claram se condere silva
signantemque vias; tum longo limite sulcus
dat lucem, et late circum loca sulpure fumant.
Hic vero victus genitor se tollit ad auras,
adfaturque deos et sanctum sidus adorat.   700
'Iam iam nulla mora est; sequor et qua ducitis adsum.
Di patrii, servate domum, servate nepotem.
Vestrum hoc augurium, vestroque in numine Troia est.
Cedo equidem, nec, nate, tibi comes ire recuso.'

Æneas gives directions for flight

Dixerat ille; et iam per moenia clarior ignis   705
auditur, propiusque aestus incendia volvunt.
'Ergo age, care pater, cervici imponere nostrae;
ipse subibo umeris, nec me labor iste gravabit;
quo res cumque cadent, unum et commune periclum,
una salus ambobus erit. Mihi parvus Iulus   710
sit comes, et longe servet vestigia coniunx:
vos, famuli, quae dicam, animis advertite vestris.
Est urbe egressis tumulus templumque vetustum
desertae Cereris, iuxtaque antiqua cupressus
religione patrum multos servata per annos.   715
Hanc ex diverso sedem veniemus in unam.
Tu, genitor, cape sacra manu patriosque penatis;
me, bello e tanto digressum et caede recenti,
attrectare nefas, donec me flumine vivo
abluero.'   720
Haec fatus, latos umeros subiectaque colla
veste super fulvique insternor pelle leonis,
succedoque oneri; dextrae se parvus Iulus
implicuit sequiturque patrem non passibus aéquis;
pone subit coniunx: ferimur per opaca locorum;   725
et me, quem dudum non ulla iniecta movebant

tela neque adverso glomerati ex agmine Grai,
nunc omnes terrent aurae, sonus excitat omnis
suspensum et pariter comitique onerique timentem.

Iamque propinquabam portis, omnemque videbar   730
evasisse viam, subito cum creber ad auris
visus adesse pedum sonitus, genitorque per umbram
prospiciens, 'Nate,' exclamat, 'fuge, nate, propinquant!
Ardentis clipeos atque aera micantia cerno!'

Æneas, with Anchises and Ascanius, reaches the temple of
Ceres outside the city; but Creüsa has disappeared

Hic mihi nescio quod trepido male numen amicum   735
confusam eripuit mentem. Namque avia cursu
dum sequor, et nota excedo regione viarum,
heu, misero coniunx fatone erepta Creüsa
substitit, erravitne via, seu lassa resedit,
incertum; nec post oculis est reddita nostris.   740
Nec prius amissam respexi animumque reflexi,
quam tumulum antiquae Cereris sedemque sacratam
venimus; hic demum collectis omnibus una
defuit, et comites natumque virumque fefellit.

Æneas, in despair, returns into the city to look for Creüsa

Quem non incusavi amens hominumque deorumque,   745
aut quid in eversa vidi crudelius urbe?
Ascanium Anchisenque patrem Teucrosque penatis
commendo sociis et curva valle recondo;
ipse urbem repeto et cingor fulgentibus armis.
Stat casus renovare omnis, omnemque reverti   750
per Troiam, et rursus caput obiectare periclis.

Principio muros obscuraque limina portae,
qua gressum extuleram, repeto, et vestigia retro
observata sequor per noctem et lumine lustro.

Horror ubique animo, simul ipsa silentia terrent.   755
Inde domum, si forte pedem, si forte tulisset,
me refero: inruerant Danai, et tectum omne tenebant.
Ilicet ignis edax summa ad fastigia vento
volvitur; exsuperant flammae, furit aestus ad auras.
Procedo et Priami sedes arcemque reviso.   760
Et iam porticibus vacuis Iunonis asylo
custodes lecti Phoenix et dirus Ulixes
praedam adservabant. Huc undique Troïa gaza
incensis erepta adytis, mensaeque deorum,
crateresque auro solidi, captivaque vestis   765
congeritur; pueri et pavidae longo ordine matres
stant circum.

The phantom of Creüsa appears to Æneas with words of comfort and prophecy

Ausus quin etiam voces iactare per umbram
implevi clamore vias maestusque Creüsam
nequiquam ingeminans iterumque iterumque vocavi.   770
Quaerenti et tectis urbis sine fine furenti
infelix simulacrum atque ipsius umbra Creüsae
visa mihi ante oculos et nota maior imago.
Obstipui, steteruntque comae et vox faucibus haesit.
Tum sic adfari et curas his demere dictis: 775
'Quid tantum insano iuvat indulgere dolori,
O dulcis coniunx? Non haec sine numine divum
eveniunt; nec te comitem hinc portare Creüsam
fas, aut ille sinit superi regnator Olympi.
Longa tibi exsilia, et vastum maris aequor arandum,   780
et terram Hesperiam venies, ubi Lydius arva
inter opima virum leni fluit agmine Thybris;
illic res laetae regnumque et regia coniunx
parta tibi. Lacrimas dilectae pelle Creüsae.

Non ego Myrmidonum sedes Dolopumve superbas 785
aspiciam, aut Grais servitum matribus ibo,
Dardanis, et divae Veneris nurus.
Sed me magna deum genetrix his detinet oris:
iamque vale, et nati serva communis amorem.'
Haec ubi dicta dedit, lacrimantem et multa volentem 790
dicere deseruit, tenuisque recessit in auras.
Ter conatus ibi collo dare bracchia circum:
ter frustra comprensa manus effugit imago,
par levibus ventis volucrique simillima somno.

*Æneas returns to his companions and they all take refuge in
the mountains near Troy*

Sic demum socios consumpta nocte reviso. 795
Atque hic ingentem comitum adfluxisse novorum
invenio admirans numerum, matresque virosque,
collectam exsilio pubem, miserabile volgus.
Undique convenere, animis opibusque parati,
in quascumque velim pelago deducere terras. 800
Iamque iugis summae surgebat Lucifer Idae
ducebatque diem, Danaique obsessa tenebant
limina portarum, nec spes opis ulla dabatur;
cessi, et sublato montis genitore petivi.

LIBER III

THE WANDERINGS OF ÆNEAS

The exiles sail in early summer, and arrive at Thrace, but are alarmed by the prodigy of a bleeding thicket over Polydorus's grave (1–68). At Delos they consult Apollo, and (misunderstanding his oracle) settle in Crete, whence they are driven by a pestilence (69–146). Æneas is warned in a vision that Italy is the destined land: they set sail, but are overtaken by a storm (147–208). Seeking shelter at the Strophades, they are driven thence by the Harpies, and follow the coast as far as Epirus (209–293). Here they find Helenus and Andromache, who joyfully receive them in hospitality (294–355). The prophecy of Helenus: they depart, laden with gifts (356–505). They hail the coast of Italy, and proceed till they near Sicily and the residence of the Cyclops: the spectacle of Mount Ætna (506–587). Here they rescue one of the companions of Ulysses. The monster Polyphemus is seen approaching the shore: his cries summon his companions (588–681). Retracing their course, to avoid Scylla and Charybdis, they land at the port of Drepanum: the death of Anchises (682–718).

The Trojans build a fleet and embark

POSTQUAM res Asiae Priamique evertere gentem
   immeritam visum superis, ceciditque superbum
   Ilium, et omnis humo fumat Neptunia Troia,
diversa exsilia et desertas quaerere terras
auguriis agimur divum, classemque sub ipsa   5
Antandro et Phrygiae molimur montibus Idae,
incerti, quo fata ferant, ubi sistere detur,
contrahimusque viros. Vix prima inceperat aestas,
et pater Anchises dare fatis vela iubebat,
litora cum patriae lacrimans portusque relinquo   10
et campos, ubi Troia fuit: feror exsul in altum
cum sociis natoque penatibus et magnis dis.

The Trojans land in Thrace and begin to build a town

Terra procul vastis colitur Mavortia campis,
Thraces arant, acri quondam regnata Lycurgo,
hospitium antiquum Troiae sociique penates,   15
dum fortuna fuit. Feror huc, et litore curvo
moenia prima loco, fatis ingressus iniquis,
Aeneadasque meo nomen de nomine fingo.

A voice from the tomb of murdered Polydorus urges Æneas
to leave Thrace

Sacra Dionaeae matri divisque ferebam
auspicibus coeptorum operum, superoque nitentem   20
caelicolum regi mactabam in litore taurum.
Forte fuit iuxta tumulus, quo cornea summo
virgulta et densis hastilibus horrida myrtus.
Accessi, viridemque ab humo convellere silvam
conatus, ramis tegerem ut frondentibus aras,   25
horrendum et dictu video mirabile monstrum.
Nam, quae prima solo ruptis radicibus arbos
vellitur, huic atro liquuntur sanguine guttae,
et terram tabo maculant. Mihi frigidus horror
membra quatit, gelidusque coit formidine sanguis.   30
Rursus et alterius lentum convellere vimen
insequor, et causas penitus temptare latentis:
ater et alterius sequitur de cortice sanguis.
Multa movens animo nymphas venerabar agrestis
Gradivumque patrem, Geticis qui praesidet arvis,   35
rite secundarent visus omenque levarent.
Tertia sed postquam maiore hastilia nisu
adgredior, genibusque adversae obluctor harenae—
eloquar, an sileam?—gemitus lacrimabilis imo
auditur tumulo, et vox reddita fertur ad auris: 40
'Quid miserum, Aenea, laceras? Iam parce sepulto;

parce pias scelerare manus. Non me tibi Troia
externum tulit, aut cruor hic de stipite manat.
Heu, fuge crudelis terras, fuge litus avarum:
nam Polydorus ego; hic confixum ferrea texit   45
telorum seges et iaculis increvit acutis.'
Tum vero ancipiti mentem formidine pressus
obstipui, steteruntque comae et vox faucibus haesit.

The story of Polydorus

Hunc Polydorum auri quondam cum pondere magno
infelix Priamus furtim mandarat alendum   50
Threicio regi, cum iam diffideret armis
Dardaniae, cingique urbem obsidione videret.
Ille, ut opes fractae Teucrum, et fortuna recessit,
res Agamemnonias victriciaque arma secutus,
fas omne abrumpit; Polydorum obtruncat, et auro   55
vi potitur. Quid non mortalia pectora cogis,
auri sacra fames? Postquam pavor ossa reliquit,
delectos populi ad proceres primumque parentem
monstra deum refero, et quae sit sententia posco.
Omnibus idem animus, scelerata excedere terra,   60
linqui pollutum hospitium, et dare classibus austros.
Ergo instauramus Polydoro funus, et ingens
aggeritur tumulo tellus; stant Manibus arae,
caeruleis maestae vittis atraque cupresso,
et circum Iliades crinem de more solutae;   65
inferimus tepido spumantia cymbia lacte
sanguinis et sacri pateras, animamque sepulcro
condimus, et magna supremum voce ciemus.

The Trojans arrive in Delos, and consult the oracle

Inde, ubi prima fides pelago, placataque venti
dant maria et lenis crepitans vocat Auster in altum,   70
deducunt socii navis et litora complent:

POLYDORUS

provehimur portu, terraeque urbesque recedunt.
Sacra mari colitur medio gratissima tellus
Nereïdum matri et Neptuno Aegaeo,
quam pius Arcitenens oras et litora circum   75
errantem Mycono e celsa Gyaroque revinxit,
immotamque coli dedit et contemnere ventos.
Huc feror; haec fessos tuto placidissima portu
accipit; egressi veneramur Apollinis urbem.
Rex Anius, rex idem hominum Phoebique sacerdos,   80
vittis et sacra redimitus tempora lauro,
occurrit; veterem Anchisen agnoscit amicum.
Iungimus hospitio dextras, et tecta subimus.

Templa dei saxo venerabar structa vetusto:
'Da propriam, Thymbraee, domum; da moenia fessis   85
et genus et mansuram urbem; serva altera Troiae
Pergama, reliquias Danaum atque immitis Achilli.
Quem sequimur? Quove ire iubes, ubi ponere sedes?
Da, pater, augurium, atque animis inlabere nostris.'

The oracle seems to command Æneas to seek a home in Crete

Vix ea fatus eram: tremere omnia visa repente,   90
liminaque laurusque dei, totusque moveri
mons circum, et mugire adytis cortina reclusis.
Submissi petimus terram, et vox fertur ad auris:
'Dardanidae duri, quae vos a stirpe parentum
prima tulit tellus, eadem vos ubere laeto   95
accipiet reduces. Antiquam exquirite matrem:
hic domus Aeneae cunctis dominabitur oris,
et nati natorum, et qui nascentur ab illis.'

Haec Phoebus; mixtoque ingens exorta tumultu
laetitia, et cuncti quae sint ea moenia quaerunt,   100
quo Phoebus vocet errantis iubeatque reverti?
Tum genitor, veterum volvens monumenta virorum,
'Audite, O proceres,' ait, 'et spes discite vestras:

Creta Iovis magni medio iacet insula ponto;
mons Idaeus ubi, et gentis cunabula nostrae.   105
Centum urbes habitant magnas, uberrima regna;
maximus unde pater, si rite audita recordor,
Teucrus Rhoeteas primum est advectus in oras,
optavitque locum regno. Nondum Ilium et arces
Pergameae steterant; habitabant vallibus imis.   110
Hinc mater cultrix Cybelae Corybantiaque aera
Idaeumque nemus; hinc fida silentia sacris,
et iuncti currum dominae subiere leones.
Ergo agite, et, divum ducunt qua iussa, sequamur;
placemus ventos et Gnosia regna petamus.   115
Nec longo distant cursu; modo Iuppiter adsit,
tertia lux classem Cretaeis sistet in oris.'
Sic fatus, meritos aris mactavit honores,
taurum Neptuno, taurum tibi, pulcher Apollo,
nigram Hiemi pecudem, Zephyris felicibus albam.   120

The Trojans settle in Crete, where a pestilence befalls them

　Fama volat pulsum regnis cessisse paternis
Idomenea ducem, desertaque litora Cretae,
hoste vacare domos, sedesque adstare relictas.
Linquimus Ortygiae portus, pelagoque volamus,
bacchatamque iugis Naxon viridemque Donusam,   125
Olearon, niveamque Paron, sparsasque per aequor
Cycladas, et crebris legimus freta concita terris.
Nauticus exoritur vario certamine clamor;
hortantur socii: 'Cretam proavosque petamus!'
Prosequitur surgens a puppi ventus euntis   130
et tandem antiquis Curetum adlabimur oris.
Ergo avidus muros optatae molior urbis,
Pergameamque voco, et laetam cognomine gentem
hortor amare focos arcemque attollere tectis.

Iamque fere sicco subductae litore puppes;   135
conubiis arvisque novis operata iuventus;
iura domosque dabam: subito cum tabida membris,
corrupto caeli tractu, miserandaque venit
arboribusque satisque lues et letifer annus.
Linquebant dulcis animas, aut aegra trahebant   140
corpora; tum sterilis exurere Sirius agros;
arebant herbae, et victum seges aegra negabat.
Rursus ad oraclum Ortygiae Phoebumque remenso
hortatur pater ire mari, veniamque precari:
quam fessis finem rebus ferat; unde laborum   145
temptare auxilium iubeat; quo vertere cursus.

In a vision Æneas is bidden by the penates to seek Italy

Nox erat, et terris animalia somnus habebat:
effigies sacrae divum Phrygiique penates,
quos mecum a Troia mediisque ex ignibus urbis
extuleram, visi ante oculos adstare iacentis   150
in somnis, multo manifesti lumine, qua se
plena per insertas fundebat luna fenestras;
tum sic adfari et curas his demere dictis:
'Quod tibi delato Ortygiam dicturus Apollo est,
hic canit, et tua nos en ultro ad limina mittit.   155
Nos te, Dardania incensa, tuaque arma secuti,
nos tumidum sub te permensi classibus aequor,
idem venturos tollemus in astra nepotes,
imperiumque urbi dabimus; tu moenia magnis
magna para, longumque fugae ne linque laborem.   160
Mutandae sedes: non haec tibi litora suasit
Delius, aut Cretae iussit considere Apollo.
Est locus, Hesperiam Grai cognomine dicunt,
terra antiqua, potens armis atque ubere glaebae;
Oenotri coluere viri; nunc fama minores   165

Italiam dixisse ducis de nomine gentem:
hae nobis propriae sedes; hinc Dardanus ortus,
Iasiusque pater, genus a quo principe nostrum.
Surge age, et haec laetus longaevo dicta parenti
haud dubitanda refer: Corythum terrasque requirat   170
Ausonias; Dictaea negat tibi Iuppiter arva.'

Æneas obeys the penates and sails away from Crete

Talibus attonitus visis et voce deorum—
nec sopor illud erat, sed coram agnoscere voltus
velatasque comas praesentiaque ora videbar;
tum gelidus toto manabat corpore sudor—   175
corripio e stratis corpus, tendoque supinas
ad caelum cum voce manus, et munera libo
intemerata focis.   Perfecto laetus honore
Anchisen facio certum, remque ordine pando.
Agnovit prolem ambiguam geminosque parentes,   180
seque novo veterum deceptum errore locorum.
Tum memorat: 'Nate, Iliacis exercite fatis,
sola mihi talis casus Cassandra canebat.
Nunc repeto haec generi portendere debita nostro,
et saepe Hesperiam, saepe Itala regna vocare.   185
Sed quis ad Hesperiae venturos litora Teucros
crederet, aut quem tum vates Cassandra moveret?
Cedamus Phoebo, et moniti meliora sequamur.'
Sic ait, et cuncti dicto paremus ovantes.
Hanc quoque deserimus sedem, paucisque relictis   190
vela damus, vastumque cava trabe currimus aequor.

A storm arises

Postquam altum tenuere rates, nec iam amplius ullae
apparent terrae, caelum undique et undique pontus,
tum mihi caeruleus supra caput adstitit imber.

noctem hiememque ferens, et inhorruit unda tenebris. 195
Continuo venti volvunt mare, magnaque surgunt
aequora; dispersi iactamur gurgite vasto;
involvere diem nimbi, et nox umida caelum
abstulit; ingeminant abruptis nubibus ignes.
Excutimur cursu, et caecis erramus in undis. 200
Ipse diem noctemque negat discernere caelo
nec meminisse viae media Palinurus in unda.
Tris adeo incertos caeca caligine soles
erramus pelago, totidem sine sidere noctes.
Quarto terra die primum se attollere tandem 205
visa, aperire procul montis, ac volvere fumum.
Vela cadunt, remis insurgimus; haud mora, nautae
adnixi torquent spumas et caerula verrunt.

The Trojans make a landing at the Strophades, and are attacked by the Harpies

Servatum ex undis Strophadum me litora primum
accipiunt; Strophades Graio stant nomine dictae, 210
insulae Ionio in magno, quas dira Celaeno
Harpyiaeque colunt aliae, Phineïa postquam
clausa domus, mensasque metu liquere priores.
Tristius haud illis monstrum, nec saevior ulla
pestis et ira deum Stygiis sese extulit undis. 215
Virginei volucrum voltus, foedissima ventris
proluvies, uncaeque manus, et pallida semper
ora fame.
Huc ubi delati portus intravimus, ecce
laeta boum passim campis armenta videmus, 220
caprigenumque pecus nullo custode per herbas.
Inruimus ferro, et divos ipsumque vocamus
in partem praedamque Iovem; tum litore curvo
exstruimusque toros, dapibusque epulamur opimis.

At subitae horrifico lapsu de montibus adsunt   225
Harpyiae, et magnis quatiunt clangoribus alas,
diripiuntque dapes, contactuque omnia foedant
immundo; tum vox taetrum dira inter odorem.
Rursum in secessu longo sub rupe cavata,
arboribus clausi circum atque horrentibus umbris,   230
instruimus mensas arisque reponimus ignem:
rursum ex diverso caeli caecisque latebris
turba sonans praedam pedibus circumvolat uncis,
polluit ore dapes. Sociis tunc, arma capessant,
edico, et dira bellum cum gente gerendum.   235
Haud secus ac iussi faciunt, tectosque per herbam
disponunt ensis et scuta latentia condunt.
Ergo ubi delapsae sonitum per curva dedere
litora, dat signum specula Misenus ab alta
aere cavo. Invadunt socii, et nova proelia temptant,   240
obscenas pelagi ferro foedare volucres:
sed neque vim plumis ullam nec volnera tergo
accipiunt, celerique fuga sub sidera lapsae
semesam praedam et vestigia foeda relinquunt.

The evil prophecy of Celæno

Una in praecelsa consedit rupe Celaeno,   245
infelix vates, rumpitque hanc pectore vocem:
'Bellum etiam pro caede boum stratisque iuvencis,
Laomedontiadae, bellumne inferre paratis,
et patrio Harpyias insontis pellere regno?
Accipite ergo animis atque haec mea figite dicta,   250
quae Phoebo pater omnipotens, mihi Phoebus Apollo
praedixit, vobis Furiarum ego maxima pando.
Italiam cursu petitis, ventisque vocatis
ibitis Italiam, portusque intrare licebit;
sed non ante datam cingetis moenibus urbem,   255

quam vos dira fames nostraeque iniuria caedis
ambesas subigat malis absumere mensas.'
Dixit, et in silvam pinnis ablata refugit.

At sociis subita gelidus formidine sanguis
deriguit; cecidere animi, nec iam amplius armis,   260
sed votis precibusque iubent exposcere pacem,
sive deae, seu sint dirae obscenaeque volucres.
Et pater Anchises passis de litore palmis
numina magna vocat, meritosque indicit honores:
'Di, prohibete minas; di, talem avertite casum,   265
et placidi servate pios!'

The Trojans sail to Actium and thence to Buthrotum

                              Tum litore funem
deripere, excussosque iubet laxare rudentis.
Tendunt vela Noti; fugimus spumantibus undis,
qua cursum ventusque gubernatorque vocabat.
Iam medio apparet fluctu nemorosa Zacynthos   270
Dulichiumque Sameque et Neritos ardua saxis.
Effugimus scopulos Ithacae, Laërtia regna,
et terram altricem saevi exsecramur Ulixi.
Mox et Leucatae nimbosa cacumina montis
et formidatus nautis aperitur Apollo.   275
Hunc petimus fessi et parvae succedimus urbi;
ancora de prora iacitur, stant litore puppes.
Ergo insperata tandem tellure potiti,
lustramurque Iovi votisque incendimus aras,
Actiaque Iliacis celebramus litora ludis.   280
Exercent patrias oleo labente palaestras
nudati socii; iuvat evasisse tot urbes
Argolicas, mediosque fugam tenuisse per hostis.
Interea magnum sol circumvolvitur annum,
et glacialis hiems aquilonibus asperat undas.   285

Aere cavo clipeum, magni gestamen Abantis,
postibus adversis figo, et rem carmine signo:
AENEAS HAEC DE DANAIS VICTORIBUS ARMA.
Linquere tum portus iubeo et considere transtris:
certatim socii feriunt mare et aequora verrunt.   290
Protinus aërias Phaeacum abscondimus arces,
litoraque Epiri legimus portuque subimus
Chaonio, et celsam Buthroti accedimus urbem.

At Buthrotum Æneas finds Andromache and Helenus

Hic incredibilis rerum fama occupat auris,
Priamiden Helenum Graias regnare per urbes,   295
coniugio Aeacidae Pyrrhi sceptrisque potitum,
et patrio Andromachen iterum cessisse marito.
Obstipui, miroque incensum pectus amore,
compellare virum et casus cognoscere tantos.
Progredior portu, classis et litora linquens,   300
sollemnis cum forte dapes et tristia dona
ante urbem in luco falsi Simoëntis ad undam
libabat cineri Andromache, Manisque vocabat
Hectoreum ad tumulum, viridi quem caespite inanem
et geminas, causam lacrimis, sacraverat aras.   305
Ut me conspexit venientem et Troïa circum
arma amens vidit, magnis exterrita monstris
deriguit visu in medio, calor ossa reliquit;
labitur, et longo vix tandem tempore fatur:
'Verane te facies, verus mihi nuntius adfers,   310
nate dea? Vivisne, aut, si lux alma recessit,
Hector ubi est?' Dixit, lacrimasque effudit et omnem
implevit clamore locum. Vix pauca furenti
subicio, et raris turbatus vocibus hisco:
'Vivo equidem, vitamque extrema per omnia duco;   315
ne dubita, nam vera vides.

Heu, quis te casus deiectam coniuge tanto
excipit, aut quae digna satis fortuna revisit
Hectoris Andromachen?   Pyrrhin' conubia servas?'
　　Deiecit voltum et demissa voce locuta est: 320
'O felix una ante alias Priameïa virgo,
hostilem ad tumulum Troiae sub moenibus altis
iussa mori, quae sortitus non pertulit ullos,
nec victoris eri tetigit captiva cubile!
Nos, patria incensa, diversa per aequora vectae,   325
stirpis Achilleae fastus iuvenemque superbum,
servitio enixae, tulimus: qui deinde, secutus
Ledaeam Hermionen Lacedaemoniosque hymenaeos,
me famulo famulamque Heleno transmisit habendam.
Ast illum, ereptae magno inflammatus amore   330
coniugis et scelerum Furiis agitatus, Orestes
excipit incautum patriasque obtruncat ad aras.
Morte Neoptolemi regnorum reddita cessit
pars Heleno, qui Chaonios cognomine campos
Chaoniamque omnem Troiano a Chaone dixit,   335
Pergamaque Iliacamque iugis hanc addidit arcem.
Sed tibi qui cursum venti, quae fata dedere?
Aut quisnam ignarum nostris deus appulit oris?
Quid puer Ascanius? superatne et vescitur aura,
quem tibi iam Troia—   340
Ecqua tamen puero est amissae cura parentis?
Ecquid in antiquam virtutem animosque virilis
et pater Aeneas et avunculus excitat Hector?'
　　Talia fundebat lacrimans longosque ciebat
incassum fletus, cum sese a moenibus heros   345
Priamides multis Helenus comitantibus adfert,
agnoscitque suos, laetusque ad limina ducit,
et multum lacrimas verba inter singula fundit.
Procedo, et parvam Troiam simulataque magnis
Pergama, et arentem Xanthi cognomine rivum   350

HELENUS AND ÆNEAS

agnosco, Scaeaeque amplector limina portae.
Nec non et Teucri socia simul urbe fruuntur:
illos porticibus rex accipiebat in amplis;
aulaï medio libabant pocula Bacchi,
impositis auro dapibus, paterasque tenebant.   355

Æneas consults the seer Helenus about his future course

Iamque dies alterque dies processit, et aurae
vela vocant tumidoque inflatur carbasus austro.
His vatem adgredior dictis ac talia quaeso:
'Troiugena, interpres divum, qui numina Phoebi,
qui tripodas, Clarii laurus, qui sidera sentis,   360
et volucrum linguas et praepetis omina pinnae,
fare age—namque omnem cursum mihi prospera dixit
religio, et cuncti suaserunt numine divi
Italiam petere et terras temptare repostas:
sola novum dictuque nefas Harpyia Celaeno   365
prodigium canit, et tristis denuntiat iras,
obscenamque famem—quae prima pericula vito?
Quidve sequens tantos possim superare labores?'

Reply of Helenus: 'Your Italian home is afar off'

Hic Helenus, caesis primum de more iuvencis,
exorat pacem divum, vittasque resolvit   370
sacrati capitis, meque ad tua limina, Phoebe,
ipse manu multo suspensum numine ducit,
atque haec deinde canit divino ex ore sacerdos:
'Nate dea,—nam te maioribus ire per altum
auspiciis manifesta fides: sic fata deum rex   375
sortitur, volvitque vices; is vertitur ordo—
pauca tibi e multis, quo tutior hospita lustres
aequora et Ausonio possis considere portu,
expediam dictis; prohibent nam cetera Parcae

scire Helenum farique vetat Saturnia Iuno.   380
Principio Italiam, quam tu iam rere propinquam
vicinosque, ignare, paras invadere portus,
longa procul longis via dividit invia terris.
Ante et Trinacria lentandus remus in unda,
et salis Ausonii lustrandum navibus aequor,   385
infernique lacus, Aeaeaeque insula Circae,
quam tuta possis urbem componere terra:
signa tibi dicam, tu condita mente teneto:
cum tibi sollicito secreti ad fluminis undam
litoreis ingens inventa sub ilicibus sus   390
triginta capitum fetus enixa iacebit,
alba, solo recubans, albi circum ubera nati,
is locus urbis erit, requies ea certa laborum.
Nec tu mensarum morsus horresce futuros:
fata viam invenient, aderitque vocatus Apollo.   395

'Shun the eastern shore'

'Has autem terras, Italique hanc litoris oram,
proxima quae nostri perfunditur aequoris aestu,
effuge; cuncta malis habitantur moenia Grais.
Hic et Narycii posuerunt moenia Locri,
et Sallentinos obsedit milite campos   400
Lyctius Idomeneus; hic illa ducis Meliboei
parva Philoctetae subnixa Petelia muro.
Quin, ubi transmissae steterint trans aequora classes,
et positis aris iam vota in litore solves,
purpureo velare comas adopertus amictu,   405
ne qua inter sanctos ignis in honore deorum
hostilis facies occurrat et omina turbet.
Hunc socii morem sacrorum, hunc ipse teneto:
hac casti maneant in religione nepotes.

Avoid Scylla and Charybdis and sail round Sicily'

'Ast ubi digressum Siculae te admoverit orae   **410**
ventus, et angusti rarescent claustra Pelori,
laeva tibi tellus et longo laeva petantur

SCYLLA

aequora circuitu: dextrum fuge litus et undas.
Haec loca vi quondam et vasta convolsa ruina—
tantum aevi longinqua valet mutare vetustas—   **415**
dissiluisse ferunt, cum protinus utraque tellus
una foret; venit medio vi pontus et undis
Hesperium Siculo latus abscidit, arvaque et urbes

litore diductas angusto interluit aestu.
Dextrum Scylla latus, laevum implacata Charybdis   420
obsidet, atque imo barathri ter gurgite vastos
sorbet in abruptum fluctus rursusque sub auras
erigit alternos et sidera verberat unda.
At Scyllam caecis cohibet spelunca latebris,
ora exsertantem et navis in saxa trahentem.   425
Prima hominis facies et pulchro pectore virgo
pube tenus, postrema immani corpore pistrix,
delphinum caudas utero commissa luporum.
Praestat Trinacrii metas lustrare Pachyni
cessantem, longos et circumflectere cursus,   430
quam semel informem vasto vidisse sub antro
Scyllam, et caeruleis canibus resonantia saxa.

'Appease Juno'

'Praeterea, si qua est Heleno prudentia, vati
si qua fides, animum si veris implet Apollo,
unum illud tibi, nate dea, proque omnibus unum   435
praedicam, et repetens iterumque iterumque monebo:
Iunonis magnae primum prece numen adora;
Iunoni cane vota libens, dominamque potentem
supplicibus supera donis: sic denique victor
Trinacria finis Italos mittere relicta.   440

'Consult the Sibyl at Cumæ'

'Huc ubi delatus Cumaeam accesseris urbem,
divinosque lacus, et Averna sonantia silvis,
insanam vatem aspicies, quae rupe sub ima
fata canit, foliisque notas et nomina mandat.
Quaecumque in foliis descripsit carmina virgo,   445
digerit in numerum, atque antro seclusa relinquit.
Illa manent immota locis, neque ab ordine cedunt;

verum eadem, verso tenuis cum cardine ventus
impulit et teneras turbavit ianua frondes,
numquam deinde cavo volitantia prendere saxo,   450
nec revocare situs aut iungere carmina curat:
inconsulti abeunt, sedemque odere Sibyllae.
Hic tibi ne qua morae fuerint dispendia tanti,—
quamvis increpitent socii, et vi cursus in altum
vela vocet, possisque sinus implere secundos,—   455
quin adeas vatem precibusque oracula poscas
ipsa canat, vocemque volens atque ora resolvat.
Illa tibi Italiae populos venturaque bella,
et quo quemque modo fugiasque ferasque laborem
expediet, cursusque dabit venerata secundos.   460
Haec sunt, quae nostra liceat te voce moneri.
Vade age, et ingentem factis fer ad aethera Troiam.'

The Trojans bid farewell to Helenus and Andromache

Quae postquam vates sic ore effatus amico est,
dona dehinc auro gravia sectoque elephanto
imperat ad navis ferri, stipatque carinis   465
ingens argentum, Dodonaeosque lebetas,
loricam consertam hamis auroque trilicem,
et conum insignis galeae cristasque comantis,
arma Neoptolemi; sunt et sua dona parenti.
Addit equos, additque duces;   47c
remigium supplet; socios simul instruit armis.
Interea classem velis aptare iubebat
Anchises, fieret vento mora ne qua ferenti.
Quem Phoebi interpres multo compellat honore:
'Coniugio, Anchisa, Veneris dignate superbo,   475
cura deum, bis Pergameis erepte ruinis,
ecce tibi Ausoniae tellus; hanc arripe velis.
Et tamen hanc pelago praeterlabare necesse est;

Ausoniae pars illa procul, quam pandit Apollo.
Vade,' ait, 'O felix nati pietate. Quid ultra   480
provehor, et fando surgentis demoror austros?'
  Nec minus Andromache digressu maesta supremo
fert picturatas auri subtemine vestes
et Phrygiam Ascanio chlamydem (nec cedit honore),
textilibusque onerat donis, ac talia fatur: 485
'Accipe et haec, manuum tibi quae monumenta mearum
sint, puer, et longum Andromachae testentur amorem,
coniugis Hectoreae. Cape dona extrema tuorum,
O mihi sola mei super Astyanactis imago:
sic oculos, sic ille manus, sic ora ferebat;   490
et nunc aequali tecum pubesceret aevo.'
  Hos ego digrediens lacrimis adfabar obortis:
'Vivite felices, quibus est fortuna peracta
iam sua; nos alia ex aliis in fata vocamur.
Vobis parta quies; nullum maris aequor arandum,   495
arva neque Ausoniae semper cedentia retro
quaerenda: effigiem Xanthi Troiamque videtis,
quam vestrae fecere manus, melioribus, opto,
auspiciis, et quae fuerit minus obvia Grais.
Si quando Thybrim vicinaque Thybridis arva   500
intraro, gentique meae data moenia cernam,
cognatas urbes olim populosque propinquos,
Epiro, Hesperia, quibus idem Dardanus auctor
atque idem casus, unam faciemus utramque
Troiam animis; maneat nostros ea cura nepotes.'   505

The Trojans set sail from Epirus

  Provehimur pelago vicina Ceraunia iuxta,
unde iter Italiam cursusque brevissimus undis.
Sol ruit interea et montes umbrantur opaci;
sternimur optatae gremio telluris ad undam,
sortiti remos, passimque in litore sicco   510

corpora curamus; fessos sopor irrigat artus.
Necdum orbem medium Nox horis acta subibat:
haud segnis strato surgit Palinurus et omnis
explorat ventos, atque auribus aëra captat;
sidera cuncta notat tacito labentia caelo,   515
Arcturum pluviasque Hyadas geminosque Triones,
armatumque auro circumspicit Oriona.
Postquam cuncta videt caelo constare sereno,
dat clarum e puppi signum; nos castra movemus,
temptamusque viam et velorum pandimus alas.   520

The Trojans land in Italy

Iamque rubescebat stellis Aurora fugatis,
cum procul obscuros collis humilemque videmus
Italiam. *Italiam* primus conclamat Achates,
Italiam laeto socii clamore salutant.
Tum pater Anchises magnum cratera corona   525
induit, implevitque mero, divosque vocavit
stans celsa in puppi:
'Di maris et terrae tempestatumque potentes,
ferte viam vento facilem et spirate secundi.'
Crebrescunt optatae aurae, portusque patescit   530
iam propior, templumque apparet in arce Minervae.
Vela legunt socii, et proras ad litora torquent.
Portus ab Euroo fluctu curvatus in arcum;
obiectae salsa spumant aspargine cautes;
ipse latet; gemino demittunt bracchia muro   535
turriti scopuli, refugitque ab litore templum.

The omen of the horses threatens war

Quattuor hic, primum omen, equos in gramine vidi
tondentis campum late, candore nivali.
Et pater Anchises: 'Bellum, O terra hospita, portas;

THE OMEN OF THE HORSES

bello armantur equi, bellum haec armenta minantur.   540
Sed tamen idem olim curru succedere sueti
quadrupedes, et frena iugo concordia ferre;
spes et pacis,' ait. Tum numina sancta precamur
Palladis armisonae, quae prima accepit ovantis,
et capita ante aras Phrygio velamur amictu;   545
praeceptisque Heleni, dederat quae maxima, rite
Iunoni Argivae iussos adolemus honores.

*The Trojans sail along the southern coast of Italy past Scylla
and Charybdis*

Haud mora, continuo perfectis ordine votis,
cornua velatarum obvertimus antemnarum,
Graiugenumque domos suspectaque linquimus arva.   550
Hinc sinus Herculei (si vera est fama) Tarenti
cernitur; attollit se diva Lacinia contra,
Caulonisque arces et navifragum Scylaceum.
Tum procul e fluctu Trinacria cernitur Aetna,
et gemitum ingentem pelagi pulsataque saxa   555
audimus longe fractasque ad litora voces,
exsultantque vada, atque aestu miscentur harenae.
Et pater Anchises: 'Nimirum haec illa Charybdis:
hos Helenus scopulos, haec saxa horrenda canebat.
Eripite, O socii, pariterque insurgite remis!'   560
Haud minus ac iussi faciunt, primusque rudentem
contorsit laevas proram Palinurus ad undas:
laevam cuncta cohors remis ventisque petivit.
Tollimur in caelum curvato gurgite, et idem
subducta ad Manis imos desedimus unda.   565
Ter scopuli clamorem inter cava saxa dedere:
ter spumam elisam et rorantia vidimus astra.
Interea fessos ventus cum sole reliquit,
ignarique viae Cyclopum adlabimur oris.

The Trojans land in Sicily and spend a terrible night
near Ætna

Portus ab accessu ventorum immotus et ingens   570
ipse; sed horrificis iuxta tonat Aetna ruinis;
interdumque atram prorumpit ad aethera nubem,
turbine fumantem piceo et candente favilla,
attollitque globos flammarum et sidera lambit;
interdum scopulos avolsaque viscera montis   575
erigit eructans, liquefactaque saxa sub auras
cum gemitu glomerat, fundoque exaestuat imo.
Fama est Enceladi semustum fulmine corpus
urgueri mole hac, ingentemque insuper Aetnam
impositam ruptis flammam exspirare caminis;   580
et fessum quotiens mutet latus, intremere omnem
murmure Trinacriam, et caelum subtexere fumo.
Noctem illam tecti silvis immania monstra
perferimus, nec quae sonitum det causa videmus.
Nam neque erant astrorum ignes, nec lucidus aethra   585
siderea polus, obscuro sed nubila caelo,
et lunam in nimbo nox intempesta tenebat.

A deserted Greek, Achœmenides, begs aid of Æneas

Postera iamque dies primo surgebat Eoo
umentemque Aurora polo dimoverat umbram:
cum subito e silvis, macie confecta suprema,   590
ignoti nova forma viri miserandaque cultu
procedit, supplexque manus ad litora tendit.
Respicimus: dira inluvies immissaque barba,
consertum tegumen spinis; at cetera Graius,
[et quondam patriis ad Troiam missus in armis.]   595
Isque ubi Dardanios habitus et Troïa vidit
arma procul, paulum aspectu conterritus haesit,
continuitque gradum; mox sese ad litora praeceps

cum fletu precibusque tulit : 'Per sidera testor,
per superos atque hoc caeli spirabile lumen,   600
tollite me, Teucri; quascumque abducite terras;
hoc sat erit. Scio me Danais e classibus unum,
et bello Iliacos fateor petiisse penatis ;
pro quo, si sceleris tanta est iniuria nostri,
spargite me in fluctus, vastoque immergite ponto.   605
Si pereo, hominum manibus periisse iuvabit.'
Dixerat, et genua amplexus genibusque volutans
haerebat. Qui sit, fari, quo sanguine cretus,
hortamur; quae deinde agitet fortuna, fateri.
Ipse pater dextram Anchises, haud multa moratus,   610
dat iuveni, atque animum praesenti pignore firmat.

Achæmenides tells the Trojans about Polyphemus, the Cyclops

Ille haec, deposita tandem formidine, fatur :
'Sum patria ex Ithaca, comes infelicis Ulixi,
nomine Achaemenides, Troiam genitore Adamasto
paupere—mansissetque utinam fortuna!—profectus.   615
Hic me, dum trepidi crudelia limina linquunt,
immemores socii vasto Cyclopis in antro,
deseruere. Domus sanie dapibusque cruentis,
intus opaca, ingens; ipse arduus, altaque pulsat
sidera—Di, talem terris avertite pestem;—   620
nec visu facilis nec dictu adfabilis ulli.
Visceribus miserorum et sanguine vescitur atro.
Vidi egomet, duo de numero cum corpora nostro
prensa manu magna, medio resupinus in antro,
frangeret ad saxum, sanieque aspersa natarent   625
limina; vidi atro cum membra fluentia tabo
manderet, et tepidi tremerent sub dentibus artus.
Haud impune quidem; nec talia passus Ulixes,
oblitusve sui est Ithacus discrimine tanto.

Nam simul expletus dapibus vinoque sepultus   630
cervicem inflexam posuit, iacuitque per antrum
immensus, saniem eructans et frusta cruento
per somnum commixta mero, nos magna precati
numina sortitique vices, una undique circum
fundimur, et telo lumen terebramus acuto,—   635
ingens, quod torva solum sub fronte latebat,
Argolici clipei aut Phoebeae lampadis instar,—
et tandem laeti sociorum ulciscimur umbras.
Sed fugite, O miseri, fugite, atque ab litore funem
rumpite.   640
Nam qualis quantusque cavo Polyphemus in antro
lanigeras claudit pecudes atque ubera pressat,
centum alii curva haec habitant ad litora volgo
infandi Cyclopes, et altis montibus errant.
Tertia iam lunae se cornua lumine complent,   645
cum vitam in silvis inter deserta ferarum
lustra domosque traho, vastosque ab rupe Cyclopas
prospicio, sonitumque pedum vocemque tremesco.
Victum infelicem, bacas lapidosaque corna,
dant rami, et volsis pascunt radicibus herbae.   650
Omnia conlustrans, hanc primum ad litora classem
prospexi venientem. Huic me, quaecumque fuisset,
addixi: satis est gentem effugisse nefandam.
Vos animam hanc potius quocumque absumite leto.'

Polyphemus is seen on the shore

Vix ea fatus erat, summo cum monte videmus   655
ipsum inter pecudes vasta se mole moventem
pastorem Polyphemum et litora nota petentem,
monstrum horrendum, informe, ingens, cui lumen ademptum
Trunca manu pinus regit et vestigia firmat;

lanigerae comitantur oves—ea sola voluptas 660
solamenque mali.
Postquam altos tetigit fluctus et ad aequora venit,
luminis effossi fluidum lavit inde cruorem,
dentibus infrendens gemitu, graditurque per aequor
iam medium, necdum fluctus latera ardua tinxit. 665
Nos procul inde fugam trepidi celerare, recepto
supplice sic merito, tacitique incidere funem;
verrimus et proni certantibus aequora remis.
Sensit, et ad sonitum vocis vestigia torsit;
verum ubi nulla datur dextra adfectare potestas, 670
nec potis Ionios fluctus aequare sequendo,
clamorem immensum tollit, quo pontus et omnes
contremuere undae, penitusque exterrita tellus
Italiae, curvisque immugiit Aetna cavernis.

In terror the Trojans put to sea and sail along the south of Sicily

At genus e silvis Cyclopum et montibus altis 675
excitum ruit ad portus et litora complent.
Cernimus adstantis nequiquam lumine torvo
Aetnaeos fratres, caelo capita alta ferentis,
concilium horrendum: quales cum vertice celso
aëriae quercus, aut coniferae cyparissi 680
constiterunt, silva alta Iovis, lucusve Dianae.
Praecipites metus acer agit quocumque rudentis
excutere, et ventis intendere vela secundis.
Contra iussa monent Heleni Scyllam atque Charybdim
inter, utramque viam leti discrimine parvo, 685
ni teneant cursus; certum est dare lintea retro.
Ecce autem Boreas angusta ab sede Pelori
missus adest. Vivo praetervehor ostia saxo

Pantagiae Megarosque sinus Thapsumque iacentem.
Talia monstrabat relegens errata retrorsus   690
litora Achaemenides, comes infelicis Ulixi.
  Sicanio praetenta sinu iacet insula contra
Plemyrium undosum; nomen dixere priores
Ortygiam. Alpheum fama est huc Elidis amnem
occultas egisse vias subter mare; qui nunc   695
ore, Arethusa, tuo Siculis confunditur undis.
Iussi numina magna loci veneramur; et inde
exsupero praepingue solum stagnantis Helori.
Hinc altas cautes proiectaque saxa Pachyni
radimus et fatis numquam concessa moveri   700
apparet Camerina procul campique Geloï,
immanisque Gela fluvii cognomine dicta.
Arduus inde Acragas ostentat maxima longe
moenia, magnanimum quondam generator equorum;
teque datis linquo ventis, palmosa Selinus,   705
et vada dura lego saxis Lilybeïa caecis.

The landing at Drepanum, and the death of Anchises

  Hinc Drepani me portus et inlaetabilis ora
accipit. Hic, pelagi tot tempestatibus actus,
heu genitorem, omnis curae casusque levamen,
amitto Anchisen: hic me, pater optime, fessum   710
deseris, heu, tantis nequiquam erepte periclis!
Nec vates Helenus, cum multa horrenda moneret,
hos mihi praedixit luctus, non dira Celaeno.
Hic labor extremus, longarum haec meta viarum.
Hinc me digressum vestris deus appulit oris.   715
  Sic pater Aeneas intentis omnibus unus
fata renarrabat divum, cursusque docebat.
Conticuit tandem, factoque hic fine quievit.

LIBER IV

DIDO AND ÆNEAS

Dido converses with her sister Anna of her love for Æneas (1–53), which she betrays also by other tokens (54–89). Juno concerts with Venus a device for uniting them in marriage (90–128). A hunting party is formed for the queen and her guests: Dido and Æneas are driven by the divine plot to take shelter in a cave (129–172). Fame reports their alliance: jealous wrath of Iarbas (173–217). Jupiter sends Mercury to command the departure of Æneas, whom he finds laying the foundations of the citadel (218–278). Æneas summons his companions: Dido reproaches him with his intended flight (279–392). The fleet is made ready: he listens unmoved to the entreaties of Dido and Anna (393–449). The queen, maddened, resolves on death, first seeking magic incantations (450–521). Sleepless, at night, she exclaims against Trojan perfidy. Meanwhile Mercury in a vision again warns Æneas to flee: he hastens the departure of the fleet (522–583). Despair of Dido at his flight: she invokes curses upon the fugitive and his posterity (584–629). Simulating religious rites, she causes her chamber to be prepared, and slays herself, after a last appeal to her sister (630–692). Juno, by embassy of Iris, releases her tormented spirit (693–705).

Dido tells her sister Anna of her love for Æneas

AT regina gravi iamdudum saucia cura
    volnus alit venis, et caeco carpitur igni.
        Multa viri virtus animo, multusque recursat
gentis honos; haerent infixi pectore voltus
verbaque, nec placidam membris dat cura quietem.   5
    Postera Phoebea lustrabat lampade terras,
umentemque Aurora polo dimoverat umbram,
cum sic unanimam adloquitur male sana sororem:
'Anna soror, quae me suspensam insomnia terrent!

Quis novus hic nostris successit sedibus hospes,   10
quem sese ore ferens, quam forti pectore et armis!
Credo equidem, nec vana fides, genus esse deorum:
degeneres animos timor arguit.   Heu, quibus ille
iactatus fatis! quae bella exhausta canebat!
Si mihi non animo fixum immotumque sederet,   15
ne cui me vinclo vellem sociare iugali,
postquam primus amor deceptam morte fefellit;
si non pertaesum thalami taedaeque fuisset,
huic uni forsan potui succumbere culpae.
Anna, fatebor enim, miseri post fata Sychaei   20
coniugis et sparsos fraterna caede penatis,
solus hic inflexit sensus, animumque labantem
impulit: agnosco veteris vestigia flammae.
Sed mihi vel tellus optem prius ima dehiscat,
vel Pater omnipotens adigat me fulmine ad umbras,   25
pallentis umbras Erebi noctemque profundam,
ante, Pudor, quam te violo, aut tua iura resolvo.
Ille meos, primus qui me sibi iunxit, amores
abstulit; ille habeat secum servetque sepulcro.'
Sic effata sinum lacrimis implevit obortis.   30

Anna encourages Dido in her love

Anna refert: 'O luce magis dilecta sorori,
solane perpetua maerens carpere iuventa,
nec dulcis natos, Veneris nec praemia noris?
Id cinerem aut Manis credis curare sepultos?
Esto: aegram nulli quondam flexere mariti,   35
non Libyae, non ante Tyro; despectus Iarbas
ductoresque alii, quos Africa terra triumphis
dives alit: placitone etiam pugnabis amori?
Nec venit in mentem, quorum consederis arvis?
Hinc Gaetulae urbes, genus insuperabile bello,   40
et Numidae infreni cingunt et inhospita syrtis;

hinc deserta siti regio, lateque furentes
Barcaei. Quid bella Tyro surgentia dicam,
germanique minas?
Dis equidem auspicibus reor et Iunone secunda   45
hunc cursum Iliacas vento tenuisse carinas.
Quam tu urbem, soror, hanc cernes, quae surgere regna
coniugio tali!   Teucrum comitantibus armis
Punica se quantis attollet gloria rebus!
Tu modo posce deos veniam, sacrisque litatis   50
indulge hospitio, causasque innecte morandi,
dum pelago desaevit hiems et aquosus Orion,
quassataeque rates, dum non tractabile caelum.'
    His dictis incensum animum inflammavit amore,
spemque dedit dubiae menti, solvitque pudorem.   55
Principio delubra adeunt, pacemque per aras
exquirunt; mactant lectas de more bidentis
legiferae Cereri Phoeboque patrique Lyaeo,
Iunoni ante omnis, cui vincla iugalia curae.
Ipsa, tenens dextra pateram, pulcherrima Dido   60
candentis vaccae media inter cornua fundit,
aut ante ora deum pinguis spatiatur ad aras,
instauratque diem donis, pecudumque reclusis
pectoribus inhians spirantia consulit exta.

Dido's passion increases

    Heu vatum ignarae mentes! quid vota furentem,   65
quid delubra iuvant? Est mollis flamma medullas
interea, et tacitum vivit sub pectore volnus.
Uritur infelix Dido, totaque vagatur
urbe furens, qualis coniecta cerva sagitta,
quam procul incautam nemora inter Cresia fixit   70
pastor agens telis, liquitque volatile ferrum
nescius; illa fuga silvas saltusque peragrat
Dictaeos; haeret lateri letalis harundo.

DIDO'S SACRIFICE

Nunc media Aenean secum per moenia ducit,
Sidoniasque ostentat opes urbemque paratam;   75
incipit effari, mediaque in voce resistit;
nunc eadem labente die convivia quaerit,
Iliacosque iterum demens audire labores
exposcit, pendetque iterum narrantis ab ore.
Post, ubi digressi, lumenque obscura vicissim   80
luna premit suadentque cadentia sidera somnos,
sola domo maeret vacua, stratisque relictis
incubat, illum absens absentem auditque videtque;
aut gremio Ascanium, genitoris imagine capta,
detinet, infandum si fallere possit amorem.   85
Non coeptae adsurgunt turres, non arma iuventus
exercet, portusve aut propugnacula bello
tuta parant; pendent opera interrupta, minaeque
murorum ingentes aequataque machina caelo.

Juno craftily suggests to Venus the marriage of Dido and Æneas

Quam simul ac tali persensit peste teneri   90
cara Iovis coniunx, nec famam obstare furori,
talibus adgreditur Venerem Saturnia dictis:
'Egregiam vero laudem et spolia ampla refertis
tuque puerque tuus, magnum et memorabile numen,
una dolo divum si femina victa duorum est!   95
Nec me adeo fallit veritam te moenia nostra
suspectas habuisse domos Karthaginis altae.
Sed quis erit modus, aut quo nunc certamine tanto?
Quin potius pacem aeternam pactosque hymenaeos
exercemus? Habes, tota quod mente petisti: 100
ardet amans Dido, traxitque per ossa furorem.
Communem hunc ergo populum paribusque regamus
auspiciis; liceat Phrygio servire marito,
dotalisque tuae Tyrios permittere dextrae.'

Venus assents to Juno's scheme

Olli—sensit enim simulata mente locutam,   105
quo regnum Italiae Libycas averteret oras—
sic contra est ingressa Venus: 'Quis talia demens
abnuat, aut tecum malit contendere bello,
si modo, quod memoras, factum fortuna sequatur?
Sed fatis incerta feror, si Iuppiter unam   110
esse velit Tyriis urbem Troiaque profectis,
miscerive probet populos, aut foedera iungi.
Tu coniunx: tibi fas animum temptare precando.
Perge; sequar.' Tum sic excepit regia Iuno:
'Mecum erit iste labor: nunc qua ratione quod instat   115
confieri possit, paucis, adverte, docebo.
Venatum Aeneas unaque miserrima Dido
in nemus ire parant, ubi primos crastinus ortus
extulerit Titan, radiisque retexerit orbem.
His ego nigrantem commixta grandine nimbum,   120
dum trepidant alae, saltusque indagine cingunt,
desuper infundam, et tonitru caelum omne ciebo.
Diffugient comites et nocte tegentur opaca:
speluncam Dido dux et Troianus eandem
devenient; adero, et, tua si mihi certa voluntas,   125
[conubio iungam stabili propriamque dicabo.]
hic hymenaeus erit.'—Non adversata petenti
adnuit, atque dolis risit Cytherea repertis.

Dido and Æneas go hunting

Oceanum interea surgens Aurora reliquit.
It portis iubare exorto delecta iuventus;   130
retia rara, plagae, lato venabula ferro,
Massylique ruunt equites et odora canum vis.
Reginam thalamo cunctantem ad limina primi
Poenorum exspectant, ostroque insignis et auro

stat sonipes, ac frena ferox spumantia mandit.   135
Tandem progreditur, magna stipante caterva,
Sidoniam picto chlamydem circumdata limbo.
Cui pharetra ex auro, crines nodantur in aurum,
aurea purpuream subnectit fibula vestem.
Nec non et Phrygii comites et laetus Iulus   140
incedunt. Ipse ante alios pulcherrimus omnis
infert se socium Aeneas atque agmina iungit.
Qualis ubi hibernam Lyciam Xanthique fluenta
deserit ac Delum maternam invisit Apollo,
instauratque choros, mixtique altaria circum   145
Cretesque Dryopesque fremunt pictique Agathyrsi;
ipse iugis Cynthi graditur, mollique fluentem
fronde premit crinem fingens atque implicat auro;
tela sonant umeris: haud illo segnior ibat
Aeneas; tantum egregio decus enitet ore.   150
Postquam altos ventum in montis atque invia lustra,
ecce ferae, saxi deiectae vertice, caprae
decurrere iugis; alia de parte patentis
transmittunt cursu campos atque agmina cervi
pulverulenta fuga glomerant montisque relinquunt.   155
At puer Ascanius mediis in vallibus acri
gaudet equo, iamque hos cursu, iam praeterit illos,
spumantemque dari pecora inter inertia votis
optat aprum, aut fulvum descendere monte leonem.

A sudden storm forces Dido and Æneas to seek shelter in
a cave

Interea magno misceri murmure caelum   160
incipit; insequitur commixta grandine nimbus;
et Tyrii comites passim et Troiana iuventus
Dardaniusque nepos Veneris diversa per agros
tecta metu petiere; ruunt de montibus amnes.
Speluncam Dido dux et Troianus eandem   165

deveniunt: prima et Tellus et pronuba Iuno
dant signum; fulsere ignes et conscius aether
conubiis, summoque ulularunt vertice nymphae.
Ille dies primus leti primusque malorum

ROMAN MARRIAGE

causa fuit; neque enim specie famave movetur,   170
nec iam furtivum Dido meditatur amorem:
coniugium vocat; hoc praetexit nomine culpam.

Rumor spreads the story of Æneas and Dido

Extemplo Libyae magnas it Fama per urbes—
Fama, malum qua non aliud velocius ullum;
mobilitate viget, virisque adquirit eundo,   175
parva metu primo, mox sese attollit in auras,
ingrediturque solo, et caput inter nubila condit.

Illam Terra parens, ira inritata deorum,
extremam (ut perhibent) Coeo Enceladoque sororem
progenuit, pedibus celerem et pernicibus alis,   180
monstrum horrendum, ingens, cui, quot sunt corpore plumae,
tot vigiles oculi subter, mirabile dictu,
tot linguae, totidem ora sonant, tot subrigit auris.
Nocte volat caeli medio terraeque per umbram,
stridens, nec dulci declinat lumina somno ;   185
luce sedet custos aut summi culmine tecti,
turribus aut altis, et magnas territat urbes ;
tam ficti pravique tenax, quam nuntia veri.

Haec tum multiplici populos sermone replebat
gaudens, et pariter facta atque infecta canebat :   190
venisse Aenean, Troiano sanguine cretum,
cui se pulchra viro dignetur iungere Dido ;
nunc hiemem inter se luxu, quam longa, fovere
regnorum immemores turpique cupidine captos.
Haec passim dea foeda virum diffundit in ora.   195
Protinus ad regem cursus detorquet Iarban,
incenditque animum dictis atque aggerat iras.

*Iarbas, a rejected suitor of Dido, is enraged and appeals to
his father, Jupiter Ammon*

Hic Hammone satus, rapta Garamantide nympha,
templa Iovi centum latis immania regnis,
centum aras posuit, vigilemque sacraverat ignem,   200
excubias divum aeternas, pecudumque cruore
pingue solum et variis florentia limina sertis.
Isque amens animi et rumore accensus amaro
dicitur ante aras media inter numina divum
multa Iovem manibus supplex orasse supinis :   205
    'Iuppiter omnipotens, cui nunc Maurusia pictis
gens epulata toris Lenaeum libat honorem,
aspicis haec, an te, genitor, cum fulmina torques,

nequiquam horremus, caecique in nubibus ignes
terrificant animos et inania murmura miscent? 210
Femina, quae nostris errans in finibus urbem
exiguam pretio posuit, cui litus arandum
cuique loci leges dedimus, conubia nostra
reppulit, ac dominum Aenean in regna recepit.
Et nunc ille Paris cum semiviro comitatu, 215
Maeonia mentum mitra crinemque madentem
subnixus, rapto potitur; nos munera templis
quippe tuis ferimus, famamque fovemus inanem.'

*Jupiter despatches Mercury to warn Æneas not to dally
at Carthage*

Talibus orantem dictis arasque tenentem
audiit omnipotens, oculosque ad moenia torsit 220
regia et oblitos famae melioris amantis.
Tum sic Mercurium adloquitur ac talia mandat:
'Vade age, nate, voca Zephyros et labere pinnis,
Dardaniumque ducem, Tyria Karthagine qui nunc
exspectat, fatisque datas non respicit urbes, 225
adloquere, et celeris defer mea dicta per auras.
Non illum nobis genetrix pulcherrima talem
promisit, Graiumque ideo bis vindicat armis;
sed fore, qui gravidam imperiis belloque frementem
Italiam regeret, genus alto a sanguine Teucri 230
proderet, ac totum sub leges mitteret orbem.
Si nulla accendit tantarum gloria rerum,
nec super ipse sua molitur laude laborem,
Ascanione pater Romanas invidet arces?
Quid struit, aut qua spe inimica in gente moratur, 235
nec prolem Ausoniam et Lavinia respicit arva?
Naviget; haec summa est; hic nostri nuntius esto.'
Dixerat. Ille patris magni parere parabat
imperio; et primum pedibus talaria nectit

MERCURY WITH CADUCEUS

aurea, quae sublimem alis sive aequora supra   240
seu terram rapido pariter cum flamine portant;
tum virgam capit: hac animas ille evocat Orco
pallentis, alias sub Tartara tristia mittit,
dat somnos adimitque, et lumina morte resignat.
Illa fretus agit ventos, et turbida tranat   245
nubila; iamque volans apicem et latera ardua cernit
Atlantis duri, caelum qui vertice fulcit,
Atlantis, cinctum adsidue cui nubibus atris
piniferum caput et vento pulsatur et imbri;
nix umeros infusa tegit; tum flumina mento   250
praecipitant senis, et glacie riget horrida barba.
Hic primum paribus nitens Cyllenius alis
constitit; hinc toto praeceps se corpore ad undas
misit, avi similis, quae circum litora, circum
piscosos scopulos humilis volat aequora iuxta.   255
Haud aliter terras inter caelumque volabat
litus harenosum ad Libyae ventosque secabat
materno veniens ab avo Cyllenia proles.

Mercury warns Æneas to flee

Ut primum alatis tetigit magalia plantis,
Aenean fundantem arces ac tecta novantem   260
conspicit; atque illi stellatus iaspide fulva
ensis erat, Tyrioque ardebat murice laena
demissa ex umeris, dives quae munera Dido
fecerat, et tenui telas discreverat auro.
Continuo invadit: 'Tu nunc Karthaginis altae   265
fundamenta locas, pulchramque uxorius urbem
exstruis, heu regni rerumque oblite tuarum?
Ipse deum tibi me claro demittit Olympo
regnator, caelum ac terras qui numine torquet;
ipse haec ferre iubet celeris mandata per auras: 270
Quid struis, aut qua spe Libycis teris otia terris?
Si te nulla movet tantarum gloria rerum,
[nec super ipse tua moliris laude laborem,]
Ascanium surgentem et spes heredis Iuli
respice, cui regnum Italiae Romanaque tellus   275
debentur.' Tali Cyllenius ore locutus
mortalis visus medio sermone reliquit,
et procul in tenuem ex oculis evanuit auram.

Æneas is perplexed, but decides to leave Carthage secretly

At vero Aeneas aspectu obmutuit amens,
arrectaeque horrore comae, et vox faucibus haesit.   280
Ardet abire fuga dulcisque relinquere terras,
attonitus tanto monitu imperioque deorum.
Heu quid agat? Quo nunc reginam ambire furentem
audeat adfatu? Quae prima exordia sumat?
Atque animum nunc huc celerem, nunc dividit illuc,   285
in partisque rapit varias perque omnia versat.
Haec alternanti potior sententia visa est:

Mnesthea Sergestumque vocat fortemque Serestum,
classem aptent taciti sociosque ad litora cogant,
arma parent, et quae rebus sit causa novandis   290
dissimulent; sese interea, quando optima Dido
nesciat et tantos rumpi non speret amores,
temptaturum aditus, et quae mollissima fandi
tempora, quis rebus dexter modus. Ocius omnes
imperio laeti parent ac iussa facessunt.   295

Dido suspects Æneas' purpose of flight

At regina dolos—quis fallere possit amantem?—
praesensit, motusque excepit prima futuros,
omnia tuta timens. Eadem impia Fama furenti
detulit armari classem cursumque parari.
Saevit inops animi, totamque incensa per urbem   300
bacchatur, qualis commotis excita sacris
Thyias, ubi audito stimulant trieterica Baccho
orgia, nocturnusque vocat clamore Cithaeron.
Tandem his Aenean compellat vocibus ultro:

Dido reproaches Æneas

'Dissimulare etiam sperasti, perfide, tantum   305
posse nefas tacitusque mea decedere terra?
Nec te noster amor, nec te data dextera quondam,
nec moritura tenet crudeli funere Dido?
Quin etiam hiberno moliris sidere classem,
et mediis properas aquilonibus ire per altum,   310
crudelis? Quid, si non arva aliena domosque
ignotas peteres, sed Troia antiqua maneret,
Troia per undosum peteretur classibus aequor?
Mene fugis? Per ego has lacrimas dextramque tuam te
(quando aliud mihi iam miserae nihil ipsa reliqui),   315
per conubia nostra, per inceptos hymenaeos,
si bene quid de te merui, fuit aut tibi quicquam

dulce meum, miserere domus labentis, et istam—
oro, si quis adhuc precibus locus—exue mentem.
Te propter Libycae gentes Nomadumque tyranni   320
odere, infensi Tyrii; te propter eundem
exstinctus pudor, et, qua sola sidera adibam,
fama prior. Cui me moribundam deseris, hospes?
hoc solum nomen quoniam de coniuge restat.
Quid moror? An mea Pygmalion dum moenia frater   325
destruat, aut captam ducat Gaetulus Iarbas?
Saltem si qua mihi de te suscepta fuisset
ante fugam suboles, si quis mihi parvulus aula
luderet Aeneas, qui te tamen ore referret,
non equidem omnino capta ac deserta viderer.'   330

Æneas declares that duty forces him to seek Italy

Dixerat. Ille Iovis monitis immota tenebat
lumina, et obnixus curam sub corde premebat.
Tandem pauca refert: 'Ego te, quae plurima fando
enumerare vales, numquam, regina, negabo
promeritam; nec me meminisse pigebit Elissae,   335
dum memor ipse mei, dum spiritus hos regit artus.
Pro re pauca loquar. Neque ego hanc abscondere furto
speravi—ne finge—fugam, nec coniugis umquam
praetendi taedas, aut haec in foedera veni.
Me si fata meis paterentur ducere vitam   340
auspiciis et sponte mea componere curas,
urbem Troianam primum dulcisque meorum
reliquias colerem, Priami tecta alta manerent,
et recidiva manu posuissem Pergama victis.
Sed nunc Italiam magnam Gryneus Apollo,   345
Italiam Lyciae iussere capessere sortes:
hic amor, haec patria est. Si te Karthaginis arces,
Phoenissam, Libycaeque aspectus detinet urbis,
quae tandem, Ausonia Teucros considere terra,

invidia est? Et nos fas extera quaerere regna. 350
Me patris Anchisae, quotiens umentibus umbris
nox operit terras, quotiens astra ignea surgunt,
admonet in somnis et turbida terret imago;
me puer Ascanius capitisque iniuria cari,
quem regno Hesperiae fraudo et fatalibus arvis. 355
Nunc etiam interpres divum, Iove missus ab ipso—
testor utrumque caput—celeris mandata per auras
detulit; ipse deum manifesto in lumine vidi
intrantem muros, vocemque his auribus hausi.
Desine meque tuis incendere teque querelis; 360
Italiam non sponte sequor.'

Dido curses Æneas in her frenzy

Talia dicentem iamdudum aversa tuetur,
huc illuc volvens oculos, totumque pererrat
luminibus tacitis, et sic accensa profatur:
'Nec tibi diva parens, generis nec Dardanus auctor, 365
perfide; sed duris genuit te cautibus horrens
Caucasus, Hyrcanaeque admorunt ubera tigres.
Nam quid dissimulo, aut quae me ad maiora reservo?
Num fletu ingemuit nostro? Num lumina flexit?
Num lacrimas victus dedit, aut miseratus amantem est? 370
Quae quibus anteferam? Iam iam nec maxima Iuno,
nec Saturnius haec oculis pater aspicit aequis.
Nusquam tuta fides. Eiectum litore, egentem
excepi, et regni demens in parte locavi;
amissam classem, socios a morte reduxi. 375
Heu furiis incensa feror! Nunc augur Apollo,
nunc Lyciae sortes, nunc et Iove missus ab ipso
interpres divum fert horrida iussa per auras.
Scilicet is superis labor est, ea cura quietos
sollicitat. Neque te teneo, neque dicta refello. 380
I, sequere Italiam ventis, pete regna per undas.

Spero equidem mediis, si quid pia numina possunt,
supplicia hausurum scopulis, et nomine Dido
saepe vocaturum. Sequar atris ignibus absens,
et cum frigida mors anima seduxerit artus, 385
omnibus umbra locis adero. Dabis, improbe, poenas.
Audiam, et haec Manis veniet mihi fama sub imos.'
His medium dictis sermonem abrumpit, et auras
aegra fugit, seque ex oculis avertit et aufert,
linquens multa metu cunctantem et multa parantem 390
dicere. Suscipiunt famulae, conlapsaque membra
marmoreo referunt thalamo stratisque reponunt.

The Trojans prepare to depart

At pius Aeneas, quamquam lenire dolentem
solando cupit et dictis avertere curas,
multa gemens magnoque animum labefactus amore, 395
iussa tamen divum exsequitur, classemque revisit.
Tum vero Teucri incumbunt, et litore celsas
deducunt toto navis; natat uncta carina;
frondentisque ferunt remos et robora silvis
infabricata, fugae studio. 400
Migrantis cernas, totaque ex urbe ruentis.
Ac velut ingentem formicae farris acervum
cum populant, hiemis memores, tectoque reponunt;
it nigrum campis agmen, praedamque per herbas
convectant calle angusto; pars grandia trudunt 405
obnixae frumenta umeris; pars agmina cogunt
castigantque moras; opere omnis semita fervet.

Dido makes a last appeal to Æneas

Quis tibi tum, Dido, cernenti talia sensus?
quosve dabas gemitus, cum litora fervere late
prospiceres arce ex summa, totumque videres 410
misceri ante oculos tantis clamoribus aequor?

Improbe Amor, quid non mortalia pectora cogis?
Ire iterum in lacrimas, iterum temptare precando
cogitur, et supplex animos submittere amori,
ne quid inexpertum frustra moritura relinquat.   415
    'Anna, vides toto properari litore; circum
undique convenere; vocat iam carbasus auras,
puppibus et laeti nautae imposuere coronas.
Hunc ego si potui tantum sperare dolorem,
et perferre, soror, potero. Miserae hoc tamen unum   420
exsequere, Anna, mihi. Solam nam perfidus ille
te colere, arcanos etiam tibi credere sensus;
sola viri mollis aditus et tempora noras.
I, soror, atque hostem supplex adfare superbum:
non ego cum Danais Troianam exscindere gentem   425
Aulide iuravi, classemve ad Pergama misi,
nec patris Anchisae cineres Manisve revelli;
cur mea dicta negat duras demittere in auris?
Quo ruit? Extremum hoc miserae det munus amanti:
exspectet facilemque fugam ventosque ferentis.   430
Non iam coniugium antiquum, quod prodidit, oro,
nec pulchro ut Latio careat regnumque relinquat:
tempus inane peto, requiem spatiumque furori,
dum mea me victam doceat fortuna dolere.
Extremam hanc oro veniam—miserere sororis—   435
quam mihi cum dederit, cumulatam morte remittam.'

Æneas is firm

    Talibus orabat, talisque miserrima fletus
fertque refertque soror: sed nullis ille movetur
fletibus, aut voces ullas tractabilis audit;
fata obstant, placidasque viri deus obstruit auris.   440
Ac, velut annoso validam cum robore quercum
Alpini Boreae nunc hinc nunc flatibus illinc

eruere inter se certant; it stridor, et altae
consternunt terram concusso stipite frondes;
ipsa haeret scopulis, et, quantum vertice ad auras   445
aetherias, tantum radice in Tartara tendit:
haud secus adsiduis hinc atque hinc vocibus heros
tunditur, et magno persentit pectore curas;
mens immota manet; lacrimae volvuntur inanes.

Dido, haunted by visions, longs for death

Tum vero infelix fatis exterrita Dido   450
mortem orat; taedet caeli convexa tueri.
Quo magis inceptum peragat lucemque relinquat,
vidit, turicremis cum dona imponeret aris,
horrendum dictu, latices nigrescere sacros,
fusaque in obscenum se vertere vina cruorem.   455
Hoc visum nulli, non ipsi effata sorori.
Praeterea fuit in tectis de marmore templum
coniugis antiqui, miro quod honore colebat,
velleribus niveis et festa fronde revinctum:
hinc exaudiri voces et verba vocantis   460
visa viri, nox cum terras obscura teneret;
solaque culminibus ferali carmine bubo
saepe queri et longas in fletum ducere voces;
multaque praeterea vatum praedicta priorum
terribili monitu horrificant. Agit ipse furentem   465
in somnis ferus Aeneas; semperque relinqui
sola sibi, semper longam incomitata videtur
ire viam, et Tyrios deserta quaerere terra.
Eumenidum veluti demens videt agmina Pentheus,
et solem geminum et duplicis se ostendere Thebas; 470
aut Agamemnonius scaenis agitatus Orestes
armatam facibus matrem et serpentibus atris
cum fugit, ultricesque sedent in limine Dirae.

ORESTES AND THE FURIES

Dido has a funeral pyre built

Ergo ubi concepit furias evicta dolore
decrevitque mori, tempus secum ipsa modumque   475
exigit, et, maestam dictis adgressa sororem,
consilium voltu tegit, ac spem fronte serenat:
   'Inveni, germana, viam—gratare sorori—
quae mihi reddat eum, vel eo me solvat amantem.
Oceani finem iuxta solemque cadentem   480
ultimus Aethiopum locus est, ubi maximus Atlas
axem umero torquet stellis ardentibus aptum:
hinc mihi Massylae gentis monstrata sacerdos,
Hesperidum templi custos, epulasque draconi
quae dabat, et sacros servabat in arbore ramos,   485
spargens umida mella soporiferumque papaver.
Haec se carminibus promittit solvere mentes
quas velit, ast aliis duras immittere curas,
sistere aquam fluviis, et vertere sidera retro;
nocturnosque movet Manis; mugire videbis   490
sub pedibus terram, et descendere montibus ornos.

Testor, cara, deos et te, germana, tuumque
dulce caput, magicas invitam accingier artes.
Tu secreta pyram tecto interiore sub auras
erige, et arma viri, thalamo quae fixa reliquit   495
impius, exuviasque omnis, lectumque iugalem,
quo perii, superimponas: abolere nefandi
cuncta viri monumenta iuvat, monstratque sacerdos.'
Haec effata silet; pallor simul occupat ora.
Non tamen Anna novis praetexere funera sacris   500
germanam credit, nec tantos mente furores
concipit, aut graviora timet, quam morte Sychaei:
ergo iussa parat.

R. H. FRANKENBERG

Dido, concealing her purpose of suicide, performs a sacrifice
to the gods below

At regina, pyra penetrali in sede sub auras
erecta ingenti taedis atque ilice secta,   505
intenditque locum sertis, et fronde coronat
funerea; super exuvias ensemque relictum
effigiemque toro locat, haud ignara futuri.
Stant arae circum, et crinis effusa sacerdos
ter centum tonat ore deos, Erebumque Chaosque,   510
tergeminamque Hecaten, tria virginis ora Dianae.
Sparserat et latices simulatos fontis Averni,
falcibus et messae ad lunam quaeruntur aënis
pubentes herbae nigri cum lacte veneni;
quaeritur et nascentis equi de fronte revolsus   515
et matri praereptus amor.
Ipsa mola manibusque piis altaria iuxta,
unum exuta pedem vinclis, in veste recincta,
testatur moritura deos et conscia fati
sidera; tum, si quod non aequo foedere amantis   520
curae numen habet iustumque memorque, precatur.

In despair Dido laments her fate

Nox erat, et placidum carpebant fessa soporem
corpora per terras, silvaeque et saeva quierant
aequora: cum medio volvuntur sidera lapsu,
cum tacet omnis ager, pecudes pictaeque volucres,   525
quaeque lacus late liquidos, quaeque aspera dumis
rura tenent, somno positae sub nocte silenti
[lenibant curas, et corda oblita laborum].
At non infelix animi Phoenissa, nec umquam
solvitur in somnos, oculisve aut pectore noctem   530
accipit: ingeminant curae, rursusque resurgens
saevit amor, magnoque irarum fluctuat aestu.
Sic adeo insistit, secumque ita corde volutat:

'En, quid ago? Rursusne procos inrisa priores
experiar, Nomadumque petam conubia supplex,   535
quos ego sim totiens iam dedignata maritos?
Iliacas igitur classis atque ultima Teucrum
iussa sequar? Quiane auxilio iuvat ante levatos,
et bene apud memores veteris stat gratia facti?
Quis me autem, fac velle, sinet, ratibusve superbis   540
invisam accipiet? Nescis heu, perdita, necdum
Laomedonteae sentis periuria gentis?
Quid tum, sola fuga nautas comitabor ovantis,
an Tyriis omnique manu stipata meorum
inferar, et, quos Sidonia vix urbe revelli,   545
rursus agam pelago, et ventis dare vela iubebo?
Quin morere, ut merita es, ferroque averte dolorem.
Tu lacrimis evicta meis, tu prima furentem
his, germana, malis oneras atque obicis hosti.
Non licuit thalami expertem sine crimine vitam   550
degere, more ferae, talis nec tangere curas!
Non servata fides cineri promissa Sychaeo!'
Tantos illa suo rumpebat pectore questus.

HECATE

Æneas is urged by Mercury not to delay

Aeneas celsa in puppi, iam certus eundi,
carpebat somnos, rebus iam rite paratis.   555
Huic se forma dei voltu redeuntis eodem
obtulit in somnis, rursusque ita visa monere est—
omnia Mercurio similis, vocemque coloremque
et crinis flavos et membra decora iuventa:
'Nate dea, potes hoc sub casu ducere somnos,   560
nec, quae te circum stent deinde pericula, cernis,
demens, nec Zephyros audis spirare secundos?
Illa dolos dirumque nefas in pectore versat,
certa mori, varioque irarum fluctuat aestu.
Non fugis hinc praeceps, dum praecipitare potestas?   565
Iam mare turbari trabibus, saevasque videbis
conlucere faces, iam fervere litora flammis,
si te his attigerit terris Aurora morantem.
Heia age, rumpe moras. Varium et mutabile semper
femina.' Sic fatus nocti se immiscuit atrae.   570

The Trojans depart in haste

Tum vero Aeneas, subitis exterritus umbris,
corripit e somno corpus, sociosque fatigat:
'Praecipites vigilate, viri, et considite transtris;
solvite vela citi. Deus aethere missus ab alto
festinare fugam tortosque incidere funis   575
ecce iterum instimulat. Sequimur te, sancte deorum,
quisquis es, imperioque iterum paremus ovantes.
Adsis O placidusque iuves, et sidera caelo
dextra feras.' Dixit, vaginaque eripit ensem
fulmineum, strictoque ferit retinacula ferro.   580
Idem omnis simul ardor habet, rapiuntque ruuntque;
litora deseruere; latet sub classibus aequor;
adnixi torquent spumas et caerula verrunt.

Dido sees the Trojans sail away

Et iam prima novo spargebat lumine terras
Tithoni croceum linquens Aurora cubile.   585
Regina e speculis ut primum albescere lucem
vidit, et aequatis classem procedere velis,
litoraque et vacuos sensit sine remige portus,
terque quaterque manu pectus percussa decorum,
flaventisque abscissa comas, 'Pro Iuppiter, ibit   590
hic,' ait, 'et nostris inluserit advena regnis?
Non arma expedient, totaque ex urbe sequentur,
deripientque rates alii navalibus? Ite,
ferte citi flammas, date vela, impellite remos!—
Quid loquor, aut ubi sum? Quae mentem insania mutat? 595
Infelix Dido, nunc te facta impia tangunt.
Tum decuit, cum sceptra dabas.—En dextra fidesque,
quem secum patrios aiunt portare penatis,
quem subiisse umeris confectum aetate parentem!
Non potui abreptum divellere corpus, et undis   600
spargere? Non socios, non ipsum absumere ferro
Ascanium, patriisque epulandum ponere mensis?—
Verum anceps pugnae fuerat fortuna:—fuisset.
Quem metui moritura? Faces in castra tulissem,
implessemque foros flammis, natumque patremque   605
cum genere exstinxem, memet super ipsa dedissem.

Dido curses the Trojans and their descendants

'Sol, qui terrarum flammis opera omnia lustras,
tuque harum interpres curarum et conscia Iuno,
nocturnisque Hecate triviis ululata per urbes,
et Dirae ultrices, et di morientis Elissae,   610
accipite haec, meritumque malis advertite numen,
et nostras audite preces. Si tangere portus
infandum caput ac terris adnare necesse est,

et sic fata Iovis poscunt, hic terminus haeret:
at bello audacis populi vexatus et armis, 615
finibus extorris, complexu avolsus Iuli,
auxilium imploret, videatque indigna suorum
funera; nec, cum se sub leges pacis iniquae
tradiderit, regno aut optata luce fruatur,
sed cadat ante diem, mediaque inhumatus harena. 620
Haec precor, hanc vocem extremam cum sanguine fundo.
Tum vos, O Tyrii, stirpem et genus omne futurum
exercete odiis, cinerique haec mittite nostro
munera. Nullus amor populis, nec foedera sunto.
Exoriare aliquis nostris ex ossibus ultor, 625
qui face Dardanios ferroque sequare colonos,
nunc, olim, quocumque dabunt se tempore vires.
Litora litoribus contraria, fluctibus undas
imprecor, arma armis; pugnent ipsique nepotesque.'

The death of Dido

Haec ait, et partis animum versabat in omnis, 630
invisam quaerens quam primum abrumpere lucem.
Tum breviter Barcen nutricem adfata Sychaei;
namque suam patria antiqua cinis ater habebat:
'Annam cara mihi nutrix huc siste sororem;
dic corpus properet fluviali spargere lympha, 635
et pecudes secum et monstrata piacula ducat;
sic veniat; tuque ipsa pia tege tempora vitta.
Sacra Iovi Stygio, quae rite incepta paravi,
perficere est animus, finemque imponere curis,
Dardaniique rogum capitis permittere flammae.' 640
Sic ait: illa gradum studio celerabat anili.
At trepida, et coeptis immanibus effera Dido,
sanguineam volvens aciem, maculisque trementis
interfusa genas, et pallida morte futura,
interiora domus inrumpit limina, et altos 645

conscendit furibunda rogos, ensemque recludit
Dardanium, non hos quaesitum munus in usus.
Hic, postquam Iliacas vestes notumque cubile
conspexit, paulum lacrimis et mente morata,
incubuitque toro, dixitque novissima verba: 650
    'Dulces exuviae, dum fata deusque sinebat,
accipite hanc animam, meque his exsolvite curis.
Vixi, et, quem dederat cursum fortuna, peregi,
et nunc magna mei sub terras ibit imago.
Urbem praeclaram statui; mea moenia vidi;   655
ulta virum, poenas inimico a fratre recepi;
felix, heu nimium felix, si litora tantum
numquam Dardaniae tetigissent nostra carinae!'
    ·Dixit, et os impressa toro, 'Moriemur inultae,
sed moriamur,' ait. 'Sic, sic iuvat ire sub umbras.   660
Hauriat hunc oculis ignem crudelis ab alto
Dardanus, et nostrae secum ferat omina mortis.'
Dixerat; atque illam media inter talia ferro
conlapsam aspiciunt comites, ensemque cruore
spumantem, sparsasque manus. It clamor ad alta   665
atria; concussam bacchatur Fama per urbem.
Lamentis gemituque et femineo ululatu
tecta fremunt; resonat magnis plangoribus aether,
non aliter quam si immissis ruat hostibus omnis
Karthago aut antiqua Tyros, flammaeque furentes   670
culmina perque hominum volvantur perque deorum.

Anna's lament for her dying sister

    Audiit exanimis, trepidoque exterrita cursu
unguibus ora soror foedans et pectora pugnis
per medios ruit, ac morientem nomine clamat:
'Hoc illud, germana, fuit? Me fraude petebas?   675
Hoc rogus iste mihi, hoc ignes araeque parabant?
Quid primum deserta querar? Comitemne sororem

sprevisti moriens? Eadem me ad fata vocasses;
idem ambas ferro dolor, atque eadem hora tulisset.
His etiam struxi manibus, patriosque vocavi   680
voce deos, sic te ut posita crudelis abessem?
Exstinxti te meque, soror, populumque patresque
Sidonios urbemque tuam. Date volnera lymphis
abluam, et extremus si quis super halitus errat,
ore legam.' Sic fata, gradus evaserat altos,   685
semianimemque sinu germanam amplexa fovebat
cum gemitu, atque atros siccabat veste cruores.
Illa, gravis oculos conata attollere, rursus
deficit; infixum stridit sub pectore volnus.
Ter sese attollens cubitoque adnixa levavit;   690
ter revoluta toro est, oculisque errantibus alto
quaesivit caelo lucem, ingemuitque reperta.

Iris releases the spirit of Dido

Tum Iuno omnipotens, longum miserata dolorem
difficilisque obitus, Irim demisit Olympo,
quae luctantem animam nexosque resolveret artus.   695
Nam quia nec fato, merita nec morte peribat,
sed misera ante diem, subitoque accensa furore,
nondum illi flavum Proserpina vertice crinem
abstulerat, Stygioque caput damnaverat Orco.
Ergo Iris croceis per caelum roscida pinnis,   700
mille trahens varios adverso sole colores,
devolat, et supra caput adstitit: 'Hunc ego Diti
sacrum iussa fero, teque isto corpore solvo.'
Sic ait, et dextra crinem secat: omnis et una
dilapsus calor, atque in ventos vita recessit.   705

LIBER V

THE FUNERAL GAMES

Æneas, departing, sees the blaze of Dido's funeral pile. A storm threatens, and he turns his course towards Sicily, where he is received with welcome by Acestes (1–41). He prepares to celebrate with sacrifice and funeral games the anniversary of his father's death (42–103). First contest, race of four Galleys; incidents of the race: the first prize is won by Cloanthus (104–285). Second contest, Foot race: Nisus and Euryalus (286–361). Third contest, the Cestus: Dares and Entellus; the gigantic strength of the latter, who wields the gauntlets of Eryx (362–484). Fourth contest, Archery; the dove shot in mid-air by Eurytion; the fiery flight of Acestes' arrow (485–544). The Equestrian game, *Troianus*, led by Ascanius in skilful evolutions (545–603). Juno moves the Trojan women to repining at their long wandering; led by Pyrgo, they set fire to the fleet: the flames cannot be stayed, until Jupiter sends a timely rain, by which all the ships but four are rescued (604–699). Æneas purposes to found a colony in Sicily; but is warned in a vision by Anchises to proceed with his stoutest followers to Latium: those who desire remain behind under protection of Acestes; the rest set sail (700–778). At the entreaty of Venus, Neptune, with the Tritons and sea-nymphs, attends his course. The fleet passes safe upon the waters, with the loss of the pilot Palinurus alone, who, overcome by the god of sleep, falls into the sea and perishes (779–871).

A storm forces the Trojans to seek harbor in Sicily

INTEREA medium Aeneas iam classe tenebat
　certus iter, fluctusque atros Aquilone secabat,
　moenia respiciens, quae iam infelicis Elissae
conlucent flammis. Quae tantum accenderit ignem,
causa latet; duri magno sed amore dolores　　　　　　5
polluto, notumque furens quid femina possit,
triste per augurium Teucrorum pectora ducunt.

Ut pelagus tenuere rates, nec iam amplius ulla
occurrit tellus, maria undique et undique caelum,
olli caeruleus supra caput adstitit imber,   10
noctem hiememque ferens, et inhorruit unda tenebris.
Ipse gubernator puppi Palinurus ab alta:
'Heu! quianam tanti cinxerunt aethera nimbi?
Quidve, pater Neptune, paras?' Sic deinde locutus
colligere arma iubet validisque incumbere remis,   15
obliquatque sinus in ventum, ac talia fatur:
'Magnanime Aenea, non, si mihi Iuppiter auctor
spondeat, hoc sperem Italiam contingere caelo.
Mutati transversa fremunt et vespere ab atro
consurgunt venti, atque in nubem cogitur aër.   20
Nec nos obniti contra, nec tendere tantum
sufficimus. Superat quoniam Fortuna, sequamur,
quoque vocat, vertamus iter. Nec litora longe
fida reor fraterna Erycis portusque Sicanos,
si modo rite memor servata remetior astra.'   25
    Tum pius Aeneas: 'Equidem sic poscere ventos
iamdudum et frustra cerno te tendere contra:
flecte viam velis. An sit mihi gratior ulla,
quove magis fessas optem demittere navis,
quam quae Dardanium tellus mihi servat Acesten,   30
et patris Anchisae gremio complectitur ossa?'
Haec ubi dicta, petunt portus, et vela secundi
intendunt Zephyri; fertur cita gurgite classis,
et tandem laeti notae advertuntur harenae.

The Trojans are welcomed at Segesta by Acestes

    At procul ex celso miratus vertice montis   35
adventum sociasque rates, occurrit Acestes,
horridus in iaculis et pelle Libystidis ursae,

Troïa Criniso conceptum flumine mater
quem genuit: veterum non immemor ille parentum
gratatur reduces, et gaza laetus agresti 40
excipit, ac fessos opibus solatur amicis.

Æneas proclaims games in honor of Anchises

Postera cum primo stellas Oriente fugarat
clara dies, socios in coetum litore ab omni
advocat Aeneas, tumulique ex aggere fatur:
'Dardanidae magni, genus alto a sanguine divum, 45
annuus exactis completur mensibus orbis,
ex quo reliquias divinique ossa parentis
condidimus terra maestasque sacravimus aras.
Iamque dies, nisi fallor, adest, quem semper acerbum,
semper honoratum—sic di voluistis—habebo. 50
Hunc ego Gaetulis agerem si syrtibus exsul,
Argolicove mari deprensus et urbe Mycenae,
annua vota tamen sollemnisque ordine pompas
exsequerer, strueremque suis altaria donis.
Nunc ultro ad cineres ipsius et ossa parentis, 55
haud equidem sine mente reor, sine numine divum,
adsumus et portus delati intramus amicos.
Ergo agite, et laetum cuncti celebremus honorem;
poscamus ventos; atque haec me sacra quotannis
urbe velit posita templis sibi ferre dicatis. 60
Bina boum vobis Troia generatus Acestes
dat numero capita in navis; adhibete penatis
et patrios epulis et quos colit hospes Acestes.
Praeterea, si nona diem mortalibus almum
Aurora extulerit radiisque retexerit orbem, 65
prima citae Teucris ponam certamina classis;
quique pedum cursu valet, et qui viribus audax

aut iaculo incedit melior levibusque sagittis,
seu crudo fidit pugnam committere caestu,
cuncti adsint, meritaeque exspectent praemia palmae.   70
Ore favete omnes, et cingite tempora ramis.'

Funeral rites are performed at the tomb of Anchises

Sic fatus, velat materna tempora myrto;
hoc Helymus facit, hoc aevi maturus Acestes,
hoc puer Ascanius, sequitur quos cetera pubes.
Ille e concilio multis cum milibus ibat   75
ad tumulum, magna medius comitante caterva.
Hic duo rite mero libans carchesia Baccho
fundit humi, duo lacte novo, duo sanguine sacro,
purpureosque iacit flores, ac talia fatur:
'Salve, sancte parens: iterum salvete, recepti   80
nequiquam cineres, animaeque umbraeque paternae.
Non licuit finis Italos fataliaque arva,
nec tecum Ausonium (quicumque est) quaerere Thybrim.'
Dixerat haec, adytis cum lubricus anguis ab imis
septem ingens gyros, septena volumina traxit,   85
amplexus placide tumulum lapsusque per aras,
caeruleae cui terga notae, maculosus et auro
squamam incendebat fulgor, ceu nubibus arcus
mille iacit varios adverso sole colores.
Obstipuit visu Aeneas. Ille agmine longo   90
tandem inter pateras et levia pocula serpens
libavitque dapes, rursusque innoxius imo
successit tumulo, et depasta altaria liquit.
Hoc magis inceptos genitori instaurat honores,
incertus, geniumne loci famulumne parentis   95
esse putet: caedit binas de more bidentis,
totque sues, totidem nigrantis terga iuvencos;
vinaque fundebat pateris, animamque vocabat

Anchisae magni Manisque Acheronte remissos.
Nec non et socii, quae cuique est copia, laeti   100
dona ferunt, onerant aras, mactantque iuvencos;
ordine aëna locant alii, fusique per herbam
subiciunt veribus prunas et viscera torrent.

SERPENT TASTING THE SACRIFICE

The spectators gather for the games; the prizes are displayed

Exspectata dies aderat, nonamque serena
Auroram Phaëthontis equi iam luce vehebant,   105
famaque finitimos et clari nomen Acestae
excierat; laeto complerant litora coetu,
visuri Aeneadas, pars et certare parati.
Munera principio ante oculos circoque locantur
in medio, sacri tripodes viridesque coronae,   110
et palmae pretium victoribus, armaque et ostro
perfusae vestes, argenti aurique talenta;
et tuba commissos medio canit aggere ludos.

The boat race

Prima pares ineunt gravibus certamina remis
quattuor ex omni delectae classe carinae.   115
Velocem Mnestheus agit acri remige Pristim,
mox Italus Mnestheus, genus a quo nomine Memmi;
ingentemque Gyas ingenti mole Chimaeram,
urbis opus, triplici pubes quam Dardana versu
impellunt, terno consurgunt ordine remi;   120
Sergestusque, domus tenet a quo Sergia nomen,
Centauro invehitur magna, Scyllaque Cloanthus
caerulea, genus unde tibi, Romane Cluenti.

Est procul in pelago saxum spumantia contra
litora, quod tumidis submersum tunditur olim   125
fluctibus, hiberni condunt ubi sidera cori;
tranquillo silet, immotaque attollitur unda
campus, et apricis statio gratissima mergis.
Hic viridem Aeneas frondenti ex ilice metam
constituit signum nautis pater, unde reverti   130
scirent, et longos ubi circumflectere cursus.
Tum loca sorte legunt, ipsique in puppibus auro
ductores longe effulgent ostroque decori;
cetera populea velatur fronde iuventus,
nudatosque umeros oleo perfusa nitescit.   135
Considunt transtris, intentaque bracchia remis;
intenti exspectant signum, exsultantiaque haurit
corda pavor pulsans, laudumque arrecta cupido.

The start

Inde, ubi clara dedit sonitum tuba, finibus omnes,
haud mora, prosiluere suis; ferit aethera clamor   140
nauticus, adductis spumant freta versa lacertis.
Infindunt pariter sulcos totumque dehiscit
convolsum remis rostrisque tridentibus aequor.

Non tam praecipites biiugo certamine campum
corripuere, ruuntque effusi carcere currus,   145
nec sic immissis aurigae undantia lora
concussere iugis pronique in verbera pendent.
Tum plausu fremituque virum studiisque faventum
consonat omne nemus, vocemque inclusa volutant
litora, pulsati colles clamore resultant.   150

Gyas and Cloanthus struggle for the lead. Gyas throws his
pilot overboard

Effugit ante alios primisque elabitur undis
turbam inter fremitumque Gyas; quem deinde Cloanthus
consequitur, melior remis, sed pondere pinus
tarda tenet. Post hos aequo discrimine Pristis
Centaurusque locum tendunt superare priorem;   155
et nunc Pristis habet, nunc victam praeterit ingens
Centaurus, nunc una ambae iunctisque feruntur
frontibus, et longa sulcant vada salsa carina.
Iamque propinquabant scopulo metamque tenebant,
cum princeps medioque Gyas in gurgite victor   160
rectorem navis compellat voce Menoeten:
'Quo tantum mihi dexter abis? Huc dirige gressum;
litus ama, et laevas stringat sine palmula cautes;
altum alii teneant.' Dixit; sed caeca Menoetes
saxa timens proram pelagi detorquet ad undas.   165
'Quo diversus abis?' iterum 'Pete saxa, Menoete!'
cum clamore Gyas revocabat; et ecce Cloanthum
respicit instantem tergo, et propiora tenentem.
Ille inter navemque Gyae scopulosque sonantis
radit iter laevum interior, subitoque priorem   170
praeterit, et metis tenet aequora tuta relictis.
Tum vero exarsit iuveni dolor ossibus ingens,
nec lacrimis caruere genae, segnemque Menoeten,

GALLEY

oblitus decorisque sui sociumque salutis,
in mare praecipitem puppi deturbat ab alta;   175
ipse gubernaclo rector subit, ipse magister,
hortaturque viros, clavumque ad litora torquet.
At gravis ut fundo vix tandem redditus imo est,
iam senior madidaque fluens in veste Menoetes
summa petit scopuli siccaque in rupe resedit.   180
Illum et labentem Teucri et risere natantem,
et salsos rident revomentem pectore fluctus.

*Sergestus tries to overtake Gyas, but runs the Centaur on
the rocks*

Hic laeta extremis spes est accensa duobus,
Sergesto Mnestheique, Gyan superare morantem.
Sergestus capit ante locum scopuloque propinquat,   185
nec tota tamen ille prior praeëunte carina;
parte prior, partem rostro premit aemula Pristis.

At media socios incedens nave per ipsos
hortatur Mnestheus: 'Nunc, nunc insurgite remis,
Hectorei socii, Troiae quos sorte suprema 190
delegi comites; nunc illas promite viris,
nunc animos, quibus in Gaetulis syrtibus usi,
Ionioque mari Maleaeque sequacibus undis.
Non iam prima peto Mnestheus, neque vincere certo;
quamquam O!—sed superent, quibus hoc, Neptune, dedisti;
extremos pudeat rediisse; hoc vincite, cives, 196
et prohibete nefas.' Olli certamine summo
procumbunt; vastis tremit ictibus aerea puppis,
subtrahiturque solum; tum creber anhelitus artus
aridaque ora quatit, sudor fluit undique rivis. 200
 Attulit ipse viris optatum casus honorem.
Namque furens animi dum proram ad saxa suburget
interior, spatioque subit Sergestus iniquo,
infelix saxis in procurrentibus haesit.
Concussae cautes, et acuto in murice remi 205
obnixi crepuere, inlisaque prora pependit.
Consurgunt nautae et magno clamore morantur,
ferratasque trudes et acuta cuspide contos
expediunt, fractosque legunt in gurgite remos.

Mnestheus passes Sergestus and Gyas

 At laetus Mnestheus successuque acrior ipso 210
agmine remorum celeri ventisque vocatis
prona petit maria et pelago decurrit aperto.
Qualis spelunca subito commota columba,
cui domus et dulces latebroso in pumice nidi,
fertur in arva volans, plausumque exterrita pinnis 215
dat tecto ingentem, mox aëre lapsa quieto
radit iter liquidum, celeres neque commovet alas:
sic Mnestheus, sic ipsa fuga secat ultima Pristis
aequora, sic illam fert impetus ipse volantem.

Cloanthus wins the boat race

Et primum in scopulo luctantem deserit alto   220
Sergestum brevibusque vadis, frustraque vocantem
auxilia, et fractis discentem currere remis.
Inde Gyan ipsamque ingenti mole Chimaeram
consequitur; cedit, quoniam spoliata magistro est.
Solus iamque ipso superest in fine Cloanthus: 225
quem petit, et summis adnixus viribus urget.
Tum vero ingeminat clamor, cunctique sequentem
instigant studiis, resonatque fragoribus aether.
Hi proprium decus et partum indignantur honorem
ni teneant, vitamque volunt pro laude pacisci;   230
hos successus alit: possunt, quia posse videntur.
Et fors aequatis cepissent praemia rostris
ni palmas ponto tendens utrasque Cloanthus
fudissetque preces, divosque in vota vocasset:
'Di, quibus imperium est pelagi, quorum aequora curro,   235
vobis laetus ego hoc candentem in litore taurum
constituam ante aras, voti reus, extaque salsos
porriciam in fluctus et vina liquentia fundam.'
Dixit, eumque imis sub fluctibus audiit omnis
Nereidum Phorcique chorus Panopeaque virgo,   240
et pater ipse manu magna Portunus euntem
impulit; illa Noto citius volucrique sagitta
ad terram fugit, et portu se condidit alto.

Æneas gives out the prizes

Tum satus Anchisa, cunctis ex more vocatis,
victorem magna praeconis voce Cloanthum   245
declarat, viridique advelat tempora lauro,
muneraque in navis ternos optare iuvencos,
vinaque et argenti magnum dat ferre talentum.
Ipsis praecipuos ductoribus addit honores:

THE WRECK

victori chlamydem auratam, quam plurima circum   250
purpura maeandro duplici Meliboea cucurrit,
intextusque puer frondosa regius Ida
velocis iaculo cervos cursuque fatigat,
acer, anhelanti similis, quem praepes ab Ida
sublimem pedibus rapuit Iovis armiger uncis;   255
longaevi palmas nequiquam ad sidera tendunt
custodes, saevitque canum latratus in auras.
At qui deinde locum tenuit virtute secundum,
levibus huic hamis consertam auroque trilicem
loricam, quam Demoleo detraxerat ipse   260
victor apud rapidum Simoënta sub Ilio alto,
donat habere viro, decus et tutamen in armis.
Vix illam famuli Phegeus Sagarisque ferebant
multiplicem, conixi umeris; indutus at olim
Demoleos cursu palantis Troas agebat.   265
Tertia dona facit geminos ex aere lebetas,
cymbiaque argento perfecta atque aspera signis.

The return of the Centaur

Iamque adeo donati omnes opibusque superbi
puniceis ibant evincti tempora taenis,
cum saevo e scopulo multa vix arte revolsus,   270
amissis remis atque ordine debilis uno,
inrisam sine honore ratem Sergestus agebat.
Qualis saepe viae deprensus in aggere serpens,
aerea quem obliquum rota transiit, aut gravis ictu
seminecem liquit saxo lacerumque viator;   275
nequiquam longos fugiens dat corpore tortus,
parte ferox, ardensque oculis, et sibila colla
arduus attollens, pars volnere clauda retentat
nixantem nodis seque in sua membra plicantem:
tali remigio navis se tarda movebat;   280

vela facit tamen, et velis subit ostia plenis.
Sergestum Aeneas promisso munere donat,
servatam ob navem laetus sociosque reductos.
Olli serva datur, operum haud ignara Minervae,
Cressa genus, Pholoë, geminique sub ubere nati.   285

The foot race: Æneas announces the prizes

Hoc pius Aeneas misso certamine tendit
gramineum in campum, quem collibus undique curvis
cingebant silvae, mediaque in valle theatri
circus erat; quo se multis cum milibus heros
consessu medium tulit exstructoque resedit.   290
Hic, qui forte velint rapido contendere cursu,
invitat pretiis animos, et praemia ponit.
Undique conveniunt Teucri mixtique Sicani,
Nisus et Euryalus primi,
Euryalus forma insignis viridique iuventa,   295
Nisus amore pio pueri; quos deinde secutus
regius egregia Priami de stirpe Diores;
hunc Salius simul et Patron, quorum alter Acarnan,
alter ab Arcadio Tegeaeae sanguine gentis;
tum duo Trinacrii iuvenes, Helymus Panopesque,   300
adsueti silvis, comites senioris Acestae;
multi praeterea, quos fama obscura recondit.
Aeneas quibus in mediis sic deinde locutus:
'Accipite haec animis, laetasque advertite mentes:
nemo ex hoc numero mihi non donatus abibit;   305
Gnosia bina dabo levato lucida ferro
spicula caelatamque argento ferre bipennem,
omnibus hic erit unus honos. Tres praemia primi
accipient, flavaque caput nectentur oliva.
Primus equum phaleris insignem victor habeto;   310
alter Amazoniam pharetram plenamque sagittis

HORSE WITH TRAPPINGS

Threiciis, lato quam circum amplectitur auro
balteus, et tereti subnectit fibula gemma;
tertius Argolica hac galea contentus abito.'

Euryalus wins by the aid of Nisus

Haec ubi dicta, locum capiunt, signoque repente   315
corripiunt spatia audito, limenque relinquunt,
effusi nimbo similes, simul ultima signant.
Primus abit longeque ante omnia corpora Nisus
emicat, et ventis et fulminis ocior alis;
proximus huic, longo sed proximus intervallo,   320
insequitur Salius; spatio post deinde relicto
tertius Euryalus;
Euryalumque Helymus sequitur; quo deinde sub ipso
ecce volat calcemque terit iam calce Diores,
incumbens umero, spatia et si plura supersint,   325
transeat elapsus prior, ambiguumve relinquat.

Iamque fere spatio extremo fessique sub ipsam
finem adventabant, levi cum sanguine Nisus
labitur infelix, caesis ut forte iuvencis
fusus humum viridisque super madefecerat herbas.   330
Hic iuvenis iam victor ovans vestigia presso
haud tenuit titubata solo, sed pronus in ipso
concidit immundoque fimo sacroque cruore.
Non tamen Euryali, non ille oblitus amorum;
nam sese opposuit Salio per lubrica surgens;   335
ille autem spissa iacuit revolutus harena.
Emicat Euryalus, et munere victor amici
prima tenet, plausuque volat fremituque secundo.
Post Helymus subit, et nunc tertia palma Diores.

Salius vainly protests that he was fouled

Hic totum caveae consessum ingentis et ora   340
prima patrum magnis Salius clamoribus implet,
ereptumque dolo reddi sibi poscit honorem.
Tutatur favor Euryalum, lacrimaeque decorae,
gratior et pulchro veniens in corpore virtus.
Adiuvat et magna proclamat voce Diores,   345
qui subiit palmae, frustraque ad praemia venit
ultima, si primi Salio reddantur honores.

Æneas awards the prizes, and gives presents to Salius and Nisus

Tum pater Aeneas, 'Vestra,' inquit, 'munera vobis
certa manent, pueri, et palmam movet ordine nemo;
me liceat casus miserari insontis amici.'   350
Sic fatus, tergum Gaetuli immane leonis
dat Salio, villis onerosum atque unguibus aureis.
Hic Nisus, 'Si tanta,' inquit, 'sunt praemia victis,
et te lapsorum miseret, quae munera Niso

digna dabis, primam merui qui laude coronam,   355
ni me, quae Salium, fortuna inimica tulisset?'
Et simul his dictis faciem ostentabat et udo
turpia membra fimo. Risit pater optimus olli,
et clipeum efferri iussit, Didymaonis artem,
Neptuni sacro Danais de poste refixum.   360
Hoc iuvenem egregium praestanti munere donat.

The boxing match: Dares is the only contestant

Post, ubi confecti cursus, et dona peregit:
'Nunc si cui virtus animusque in pectore praesens,
adsit, et evinctis attollat bracchia palmis.'
Sic ait, et geminum pugnae proponit honorem,   365
victori velatum auro vittisque iuvencum,
ensem atque insignem galeam solacia victo.
Nec mora: continuo vastis cum viribus effert
ora Dares, magnoque virum se murmure tollit;
solus qui Paridem solitus contendere contra,   370
idemque ad tumulum, quo maximus occubat Hector,
victorem Buten, immani corpore qui se
Bebrycia veniens Amyci de gente ferebat,
perculit, et fulva moribundum extendit harena.
Talis prima Dares caput altum in proelia tollit,   375
ostenditque umeros latos, alternaque iactat
bracchia protendens, et verberat ictibus auras.
Quaeritur huic alius; nec quisquam ex agmine tanto
audet adire virum manibusque inducere caestus.
Ergo alacris, cunctosque putans excedere palma,   380
Aeneae stetit ante pedes, nec plura moratus
tum laeva taurum cornu tenet, atque ita fatur:
'Nate dea, si nemo audet se credere pugnae,
quae finis standi? Quo me decet usque teneri?
Ducere dona iube.' Cuncti simul ore fremebant   385
Dardanidae, reddique viro promissa iubebant.

The aged Entellus is induced by Acestes to meet Dares

Hic gravis Entellum dictis castigat Acestes,
proximus ut viridante toro consederat herbae:
'Entelle, heroum quondam fortissime frustra,
tantane tam patiens nullo certamine tolli   390
dona sines? Ubi nunc nobis deus ille magister
nequiquam memoratus Eryx? Ubi fama per omnem
Trinacriam, et spolia illa tuis pendentia tectis?'
Ille sub haec: 'Non laudis amor, nec gloria cessit
pulsa metu; sed enim gelidus tardante senecta   395
sanguis hebet, frigentque effetae in corpore vires.
Si mihi, quae quondam fuerat, quaque improbus iste
exsultat fidens, si nunc foret illa iuventas,
haud equidem pretio inductus pulchroque iuvenco
venissem, nec dona moror.' Sic deinde locutus   400
in medium geminos immani pondere caestus
proiecit quibus acer Eryx in proelia suetus
ferre manum, duroque intendere bracchia tergo.
Obstipuere animi: tantorum ingentia septem
terga boum plumbo insuto ferroque rigebant.   405
    Ante omnis stupet ipse Dares, longeque recusat;
magnanimusque Anchisiades et pondus et ipsa
huc illuc vinclorum immensa volumina versat.
Tum senior talis referebat pectore voces:
    'Quid, si quis caestus ipsius et Herculis arma 410
vidisset, tristemque hoc ipso in litore pugnam?
Haec germanus Eryx quondam tuus arma gerebat,—
sanguine cernis adhuc sparsoque infecta cerebro,—
his magnum Alciden contra stetit; his ego suetus,
dum melior viris sanguis dabat, aemula necdum   415
temporibus geminis canebat sparsa senectus.
Sed si nostra Dares haec Troïus arma recusat,
idque pio sedet Aeneae, probat auctor Acestes,

DARES AND ENTELLUS

aequemus pugnas. Erycis tibi terga remitto;
solve metus; et tu Troianos exue caestus.'   420
Haec fatus, duplicem ex umeris reiecit amictum,
et magnos membrorum artus, magna ossa lacertosque
exuit, atque ingens media consistit harena.

The boxing match begins. Entellus falls

Tum satus Anchisa caestus pater extulit aequos,
et paribus palmas amborum innexuit armis.   425
Constitit in digitos extemplo arrectus uterque,
bracchiaque ad superas interritus extulit auras.
Abduxere retro longe capita ardua ab ictu,
immiscentque manus manibus, pugnamque lacessunt.
Ille pedum melior motu, fretusque iuventa;   430
hic membris et mole valens, sed tarda trementi
genua labant, vastos quatit aeger anhelitus artus.
Multa viri nequiquam inter se volnera iactant,
multa cavo lateri ingeminant, et pectore vastos
dant sonitus, erratque auris et tempora circum   435
crebra manus, duro crepitant sub volnere malae.

Stat gravis Entellus nisuque immotus eodem,
corpore tela modo atque oculis vigilantibus exit.
Ille, velut celsam oppugnat qui molibus urbem,
aut montana sedet circum castella sub armis,   440
nunc hos, nunc illos aditus, omnemque pererrat
arte locum, et variis adsultibus inritus urget.
Ostendit dextram insurgens Entellus, et alte
extulit : ille ictum venientem a vertice velox
praevidit, celerique elapsus corpore cessit.   445
Entellus viris in ventum effudit, et ultro
ipse gravis graviterque ad terram pondere vasto
concidit, ut quondam cava concidit aut Erymantho,
aut Ida in magna, radicibus eruta pinus.
Consurgunt studiis Teucri et Trinacria pubes ;   450
it clamor caelo, primusque accurrit Acestes,
aequaevumque ab humo miserans attollit amicum.
At non tardatus casu neque territus heros
acrior ad pugnam redit, ac vim suscitat ira.

Entellus defeats Dares ; then, to show his strength, he brains
the bull which he won as a prize

Tum pudor incendit viris et conscia virtus,   455
praecipitemque Daren ardens agit aequore toto,
nunc dextra ingeminans ictus, nunc ille sinistra ;
nec mora, nec requies ; quam multa grandine nimbi
culminibus crepitant, sic densis ictibus heros
creber utraque manu pulsat versatque Dareta.   460
Tum pater Aeneas procedere longius iras
et saevire animis Entellum haud passus acerbis ;
sed finem imposuit pugnae, fessumque Dareta
eripuit, mulcens dictis, ac talia fatur :
'Infelix, quae tanta animum dementia cepit ?   465
Non viris alias conversaque numina sentis ?
Cede deo.' Dixitque et proelia voce diremit.

Ast illum fidi aequales, genua aegra trahentem,
iactantemque utroque caput, crassumque cruorem
ore eiectantem mixtosque in sanguine dentes,   470
ducunt ad navis; galeamque ensemque vocati
accipiunt; palmam Entello taurumque relinquunt.
Hic victor, superans animis tauroque superbus:
     'Nate dea, vosque haec,' inquit, 'cognoscite, Teucri,
et mihi quae fuerint iuvenali in corpore vires,   475
et qua servetis revocatum a morte Dareta.'
Dixit, et adversi contra stetit ora iuvenci,
qui donum adstabat pugnae, durosque reducta
libravit dextra media inter cornua caestus,
arduus, effractoque inlisit in ossa cerebro.   480
Sternitur exanimisque tremens procumbit humi bos.
Ille super talis effundit pectore voces:
'Hanc tibi, Eryx, meliorem animam pro morte Daretis
persolvo; hic victor caestus artemque repono.'

The contest in archery

     Protinus Aeneas celeri certare sagitta   485
invitat qui forte velint, et praemia ponit,
ingentique manu malum de nave Seresti
erigit, et volucrem traiecto in fune columbam
quo tendant ferrum, malo suspendit ab alto.
Convenere viri, deiectamque aerea sortem   490
accepit galea; et primus clamore secundo
Hyrtacidae ante omnis exit locus Hippocoöntis;
quem modo navali Mnestheus certamine victor
consequitur, viridi Mnestheus evinctus oliva.
Tertius Eurytion, tuus, O clarissime, frater,   495
Pandare, qui quondam, iussus confundere foedus,
in medios telum torsisti primus Achivos.
Extremus galeaque ima subsedit Acestes,
ausus et ipse manu iuvenum temptare laborem.

Tum validis flexos incurvant viribus arcus 500
pro se quisque viri, et depromunt tela pharetris.
Primaque per caelum, nervo stridente, sagitta
Hyrtacidae iuvenis volucris diverberat auras;
et venit, adversique infigitur arbore mali.
Intremuit malus, timuitque exterrita pinnis 505
ales, et ingenti sonuerunt omnia plausu.
Post acer Mnestheus adducto constitit arcu,
alta petens, pariterque oculos telumque tetendit.
Ast ipsam miserandus avem contingere ferro
non valuit; nodos et vincula linea rupit, 510
quis innexa pedem malo pendebat ab alto:
illa notos atque atra volans in nubila fugit.
Tum rapidus, iamdudum arcu contenta parato
tela tenens, fratrem Eurytion in vota vocavit,
iam vacuo laetam caelo speculatus, et alis 515
plaudentem nigra figit sub nube columbam.
Decidit exanimis, vitamque reliquit in astris
aetheriis, fixamque refert delapsa sagittam.

The arrow of Acestes takes fire in the sky: he is awarded
a special prize

Amissa solus palma superabat Acestes;
qui tamen aërias telum contendit in auras, 520
ostentans artemque pater arcumque sonantem.
Hic oculis subito obicitur magnoque futurum
augurio monstrum; docuit post exitus ingens,
seraque terrifici cecinerunt omina vates.
Namque volans liquidis in nubibus arsit harundo, 525
signavitque viam flammis, tenuisque recessit
consumpta in ventos; caelo ceu saepe refixa
transcurrunt crinemque volantia sidera ducunt.
Attonitis haesere animis, superosque precati
Trinacrii Teucrique viri; nec maximus omen 530

abnuit Aeneas; sed laetum amplexus Acesten
muneribus cumulat magnis, ac talia fatur:
'Sume, pater; nam te voluit rex magnus Olympi
talibus auspiciis exsortem ducere honores.
Ipsius Anchisae longaevi hoc munus habebis,   535
cratera impressum signis, quem Thracius olim
Anchisae genitori in magno munere Cisseus
ferre sui dederat monumentum et pignus amoris.'
Sic fatus cingit viridanti tempora lauro,
et primum ante omnis victorem appellat Acesten.   54o
Nec bonus Eurytion praelato invidit honori,
quamvis solus avem caelo deiecit ab alto.
Proximus ingreditur donis, qui vincula rupit;
extremus, volucri qui fixit harundine malum.

An equestrian game is performed by Ascanius and other boys

At pater Aeneas, nondum certamine misso,   545
custodem ad sese comitemque impubis Iuli
Epytiden vocat, et fidam sic fatur ad aurem:
'Vade age, et Ascanio, si iam puerile paratum
agmen habet secum cursusque instruxit equorum,
ducat avo turmas et sese ostendat in armis   550
dic,' ait. Ipse omnem longo decedere circo
infusum populum, et campos iubet esse patentis.

Incedunt pueri, pariterque ante ora parentum
frenatis lucent in equis, quos omnis euntis
Trinacriae mirata fremit Troiaeque iuventus.   555
Omnibus in morem tonsa coma pressa corona:
cornea bina ferunt praefixa hastilia ferro:
pars levis umero pharetras; it pectore summo
flexilis obtorti per collum circulus auri.
Tres equitum numero turmae ternique vagantur   560
ductores: pueri bis seni quemque secuti
agmine partito fulgent paribusque magistris.

Una acies iuvenum, ducit quam parvus ovantem
nomen avi referens Priamus,—tua clara, Polite,
progenies, auctura Italos,—quem Thracius albis   565
portat equus bicolor maculis, vestigia primi
alba pedis frontemque ostentans arduus albam.
Alter Atys, genus unde Atii duxere Latini,
parvus Atys, pueroque puer dilectus Iulo.
Extremus, formaque ante omnis pulcher, Iulus   570
Sidonio est invectus equo quem candida Dido
esse sui dederat monumentum et pignus amoris.
Cetera Trinacriis pubes senioris Acestae
fertur equis.

 Excipiunt plausu pavidos, gaudentque tuentes   575
Dardanidae, veterumque agnoscunt ora parentum.
Postquam omnem laeti consessum oculosque suorum
lustravere in equis, signum clamore paratis
Epytides longe dedit insonuitque flagello.

 Olli discurrere pares, atque agmina terni   580
diductis solvere choris, rursusque vocati
convertere vias infestaque tela tulere.
Inde alios ineunt cursus aliosque recursus
adversi spatiis, alternosque orbibus orbis
impediunt, pugnaeque cient simulacra sub armis;   585
et nunc terga fuga nudant, nunc spicula vertunt
infensi, facta pariter nunc pace feruntur.
Ut quondam Creta fertur Labyrinthus in alta
parietibus textum caecis iter, ancipitemque
mille viis habuisse dolum, qua signa sequendi   590
falleret indeprensus et inremeabilis error;
haud alio Teucrum nati vestigia cursu
impediunt, texuntque fugas et proelia ludo,
delphinum similes, qui per maria umida nando
Carpathium Libycumque secant luduntque per undas.   595
Hunc morem cursus atque haec certamina primus

Ascanius, Longam muris cum cingeret Albam,
rettulit, et priscos docuit celebrare Latinos,
quo puer ipse modo, secum quo Troïa pubes;
Albani docuere suos; hinc maxima porro   600
accepit Roma, et patrium servavit honorem;
*Troia*que nunc pueri, *Troianum* dicitur agmen.
Hac celebrata tenus sancto certamina patri.

Iris, sent by Juno, rouses the Trojan women to set fire to
the ships and so end their wanderings

Hic primum fortuna fidem mutata novavit.
Dum variis tumulo referunt sollemnia ludis,   605
Irim de caelo misit Saturnia Iuno
Iliacam ad classem, ventosque adspirat eunti
multa movens, necdum antiquum saturata dolorem.
Illa, viam celerans per mille coloribus arcum,
nulli visa cito decurrit tramite virgo.   610
Conspicit ingentem concursum, et litora lustrat,
desertosque videt portus classemque relictam.
At procul in sola secretae Troades acta
amissum Anchisen flebant, cunctaeque profundum
pontum aspectabant flentes. 'Heu tot vada fessis   615
et tantum superesse maris!' vox omnibus una.
Urbem orant; taedet pelagi perferre laborem.
Ergo inter medias sese haud ignara nocendi
conicit, et faciemque deae vestemque reponit;
fit Beroë, Tmarii coniunx longaeva Dorycli,   620
cui genus et quondam nomen natique fuissent;
ac sic Dardanidum mediam se matribus infert:

'O miserae, quas non manus,' inquit, 'Achaïca bello
traxerit ad letum patriae sub moenibus! O gens
infelix, cui te exitio Fortuna reservat?   625
Septima post Troiae excidium iam vertitur aestas,
cum freta, cum terras omnis, tot inhospita saxa

IRIS

sideraque emensae ferimur, dum per mare magnum
Italiam sequimur fugientem, et volvimur undis.
Hic Erycis fines fraterni, atque hospes Acestes: 630
quis prohibet muros iacere et dare civibus urbem?
O patria et rapti nequiquam ex hoste penates,
nullane iam Troiae dicentur moenia? Nusquam
Hectoreos amnis, Xanthum et Simoënta, videbo?
Quin agite et mecum infaustas exurite puppis.   635
Nam mihi Cassandrae per somnum vatis imago
ardentis dare visa faces: *Hic quaerite Troiam;*
hic domus est, inquit, *vobis*. Iam tempus agi res,
nec tantis mora prodigiis. En quattuor arae
Neptuno; deus ipse faces animumque ministrat.'   640

The women fire the ships

Haec memorans, prima infensum vi corripit ignem,
sublataque procul dextra conixa coruscat,
et iacit: arrectae mentes stupefactaque corda
Iliadum. Hic una e multis, quae maxima natu,
Pyrgo, tot Priami natorum regia nutrix: 645
'Non Beroë vobis, non haec Rhoeteïa, matres,
est Dorycli coniunx; divini signa decoris
ardentisque notate oculos; qui spiritus illi,
qui voltus, vocisque sonus, vel gressus eunti.
Ipsa egomet dudum Beroën digressa reliqui   650
aegram, indignantem, tali quod sola careret
munere, nec meritos Anchisae inferret honores.'
Haec effata.

At matres primo ancipites, oculisque malignis
ambiguae spectare rates miserum inter amorem   655
praesentis terrae fatisque vocantia regna,
cum dea se paribus per caelum sustulit alis,
ingentemque fuga secuit sub nubibus arcum.

Tum vero attonitae monstris actaeque furore
conclamant, rapiuntque focis penetralibus ignem;   660
pars spoliant aras, frondem ac virgulta facesque
coniciunt. Furit immissis Volcanus habenis
transtra per et remos et pictas abiete puppis.

Ascanius appeals to the matrons

Nuntius Anchisae ad tumulum cuneosque theatri
incensas perfert navis Eumelus, et ipsi   665
respiciunt atram in nimbo volitare favillam.
Primus et Ascanius, cursus ut laetus equestris
ducebat, sic acer equo turbata petivit
castra, nec exanimes possunt retinere magistri.
'Quis furor iste novus? Quo nunc, quo tenditis,' inquit, 670
'heu, miserae cives? Non hostem inimicaque castra
Argivum, vestras spes uritis. En, ego vester
Ascanius!' Galeam ante pedes proiecit inanem,
qua ludo indutus belli simulacra ciebat;
accelerat simul Aeneas, simul agmina Teucrum.   675
Ast illae diversa metu per litora passim
diffugiunt, silvasque et sicubi concava furtim
saxa petunt; piget incepti lucisque, suosque
mutatae agnoscunt, excussaque pectore Iuno est.
Sed non idcirco flammae atque incendia viris   680
indomitas posuere; udo sub robore vivit
stuppa vomens tardum fumum, lentusque carinas
est vapor, et toto descendit corpore pestis,
nec vires heroum infusaque flumina prosunt.

Æneas prays to Jupiter, and the flames are stayed

Tum pius Aeneas umeris abscindere vestem,   685
auxilioque vocare deos, et tendere palmas:
'Iuppiter omnipotens, si nondum exosus ad unum
Troianos, si quid pietas antiqua labores

respicit humanos, da flammam evadere classi
nunc, Pater, et tenuis Teucrum res eripe leto.   690
Vel tu,—quod superest,—infesto fulmine morti,
si mereor, demitte, tuaque hic obrue dextra.'
Vix haec ediderat, cum effusis imbribus atra
tempestas sine more furit, tonitruque tremescunt
ardua terrarum et campi ; ruit aethere toto   695
turbidus imber aqua densisque nigerrimus austris ;
implenturque super puppes ; semusta madescunt
robora ; restinctus donec vapor omnis, et omnes,
quattuor amissis, servatae a peste carinae.

*Æneas is advised by Nautes to leave a part of his company
to settle in Sicily*

At pater Aeneas, casu concussus acerbo,   700
nunc huc ingentis, nunc illuc pectore curas
mutabat versans, Siculisne resideret arvis,
oblitus fatorum, Italasne capesseret oras.
Tum senior Nautes, unum Tritonia Pallas
quem docuit multaque insignem reddidit arte,   705
haec responsa dabat, vel quae portenderet ira
magna deum, vel quae fatorum posceret ordo,
isque his Aenean solatus vocibus infit :
    'Nate dea, quo fata trahunt retrahuntque, sequamur ;
quidquid erit, superanda omnis fortuna ferendo est.   710
Est tibi Dardanius divinae stirpis Acestes :
hunc cape consiliis socium et coniunge volentem ;
huic trade, amissis superant qui navibus, et quos
pertaesum magni incepti rerumque tuarum est ;
longaevosque senes ac fessas aequore matres,   715
et quidquid tecum invalidum metuensque pericli est,
delige, et his habeant terris sine moenia fessi :
urbem appellabunt permisso nomine Acestam.'

Anchises, in a vision, bids Æneas follow the counsel of Nautes

Talibus incensus dictis senioris amici,
tum vero in curas animo diducitur omnis.   720
Et nox atra polum bigis subvecta tenebat:
visa dehinc caelo facies delapsa parentis
Anchisae subito talis effundere voces:
'Nate, mihi vita quondam, dum vita manebat,
care magis, nate, Iliacis exercite fatis,   725
imperio Iovis huc venio, qui classibus ignem
depulit et caelo tandem miseratus ab alto est.
Consiliis pare, quae nunc pulcherrima Nautes
dat senior; lectos iuvenes, fortissima corda,
defer in Italiam. Gens dura atque aspera cultu   730
debellanda tibi Latio est.

Anchises urges Æneas to visit the Lower World

                Ditis tamen ante
infernas accede domos, et Averna per alta
congressus pete, nate, meos. Non me impia namque
Tartara habent, tristes umbrae, sed amoena piorum
concilia Elysiumque colo. Huc casta Sibylla   735
nigrarum multo pecudum te sanguine ducet:
tum genus omne tuum, et quae dentur moenia, disces.
Iamque vale: torquet medios Nox umida cursus,
et me saevus equis Oriens adflavit anhelis.'
Dixerat, et tenuis fugit, ceu fumus, in auras.   740
Aeneas, 'Quo deinde ruis, quo proripis?' inquit,
'Quem fugis, aut quis te nostris complexibus arcet?'
Haec memorans cinerem et sopitos suscitat ignis,
Pergameumque Larem et canae penetralia Vestae
farre pio et plena supplex veneratur acerra.   745

*The feeble are left in Sicily, and the other Trojans sail
sadly away*

Extemplo socios primumque arcessit Acesten,
et Iovis imperium et cari praecepta parentis
edocet, et quae nunc animo sententia constet.
Haud mora consiliis, nec iussa recusat Acestes.
Transcribunt urbi matres, populumque volentem   750
deponunt, animos nil magnae laudis egentis.
Ipsi transtra novant, flammisque ambesa reponunt
robora navigiis, aptant remosque rudentisque,
exigui numero, sed bello vivida virtus.
Interea Aeneas urbem designat aratro   755
sortiturque domos; hoc Ilium et haec loca Troiam
esse iubet. Gaudet regno Troianus Acestes,
indicitque forum et patribus dat iura vocatis.
Tum vicina astris, Erycino in vertice sedes
fundatur Veneri Idaliae, tumuloque sacerdos   760
ac lucus late sacer additur Anchiseo.

  Iamque dies epulata novem gens omnis, et aris
factus honos: placidi straverunt aequora venti,
creber et adspirans rursus vocat Auster in altum.
Exoritur procurva ingens per litora fletus;   765
complexi inter se noctemque diemque morantur.
Ipsae iam matres, ipsi, quibus aspera quondam
visa maris facies et non tolerabile nomen,
ire volunt, omnemque fugae perferre laborem.
Quos bonus Aeneas dictis solatur amicis,   770
et consanguineo lacrimans commendat Acestae.
Tris Eryci vitulos et Tempestatibus agnam
caedere deinde iubet, solvique ex ordine funem.
Ipse, caput tonsae foliis evinctus olivae,
stans procul in prora pateram tenet, extaque salsos   775

porricit in fluctus ac vina liquentia fundit.
Prosequitur surgens a puppi ventus euntis.
Certatim socii feriunt mare et aequora verrunt.

Venus appeals to Neptune for a safe voyage for the Trojans

At Venus interea Neptunum exercita curis
adloquitur, talisque effundit pectore questus: 780
'Iunonis gravis ira nec exsaturabile pectus
cogunt me, Neptune, preces descendere in omnis;
quam nec longa dies, pietas nec mitigat ulla,
nec Iovis imperio fatisque infracta quiescit.
Non media de gente Phrygum exedisse nefandis   785
urbem odiis satis est, nec poenam traxe per omnem:
reliquias Troiae, cineres atque ossa peremptae
insequitur: causas tanti sciat illa furoris.
Ipse mihi nuper Libycis tu testis in undis
quam molem subito excierit: maria omnia caelo   790
miscuit, Aeoliis nequiquam freta procellis,
in regnis hoc ausa tuis.
Per scelus ecce etiam Troianis matribus actis
exussit foede puppis, et classe subegit
amissa socios ignotae linquere terrae.   795
Quod superest, oro, liceat dare tuta per undas
vela tibi, liceat Laurentem attingere Thybrim,—
si concessa peto, si dant ea moenia Parcae.'

*Neptune promises that the Trojans shall reach Italy, and
calms the sea*

Tum Saturnius haec domitor maris edidit alti:
'Fas omne est, Cytherea, meis te fidere regnis,   800
unde genus ducis: merui quoque; saepe furores
compressi et rabiem tantam caelique marisque.

Nec minor in terris, Xanthum Simoëntaque testor,
Aeneae mihi cura tui. Cum Troïa Achilles
exanimata sequens impingeret agmina muris,   805
milia multa daret leto, gemerentque repleti
amnes, nec reperire viam atque evolvere posset
in mare se Xanthus, Pelidae tunc ego forti
congressum Aenean nec dis nec viribus aequis
nube cava rapui, cuperem cum vertere ab imo   810
structa meis manibus periurae moenia Troiae.
Nunc quoque mens eadem perstat mihi; pelle timores.
Tutus. quos optas, portus accedet Averni.
Unus erit tantum, amissum quem gurgite quaeres;
unum pro multis dabitur caput.'   815

His ubi laeta deae permulsit pectora dictis,
iungit equos auro Genitor, spumantiaque addit
frena feris, manibusque omnis effundit habenas.
Caeruleo per summa levis volat aequora curru;
subsidunt undae, tumidumque sub axe tonanti   820
sternitur aequor aquis; fugiunt vasto aethere nimbi.
Tum variae comitum facies, immania cete,
et senior Glauci chorus, Inousque Palaemon,
Tritonesque citi, Phorcique exercitus omnis;
laeva tenet Thetis, et Melite, Panopeaque virgo,   825
Nisaee, Spioque, Thaliaque, Cymodoceque.

Hic patris Aeneae suspensam blanda vicissim
gaudia pertemptant mentem: iubet ocius omnis
attolli malos, intendi bracchia velis.
Una omnes fecere pedem, pariterque sinistros,   830
nunc dextros solvere sinus; una ardua torquent
cornua detorquentque; ferunt sua flamina classem.
Princeps ante omnis densum Palinurus agebat
agmen; ad hunc alii cursum contendere iussi.

*Palinurus, pilot of the fleet, is cast into the sea by the
god of sleep*

Iamque fere mediam caeli nox umida metam   835
contigerat; placida laxabant membra quiete
sub remis fusi per dura sedilia nautae:
cum levis aetheriis delapsus Somnus ab astris
aëra dimovit tenebrosum et dispulit umbras,
te, Palinure, petens, tibi somnia tristia portans   840
insonti; puppique deus consedit in alta,
Phorbanti similis, funditque has ore loquelas:
'Iaside Palinure, ferunt ipsa aequora classem;
aequatae spirant aurae; datur hora quieti.
Pone caput, fessosque oculos furare labori: 845
ipse ego paulisper pro te tua munera inibo.'
Cui vix attollens Palinurus lumina fatur:
'Mene salis placidi voltum fluctusque quietos
ignorare iubes? Mene huic confidere monstro?
Aenean credam quid enim fallacibus auris,   850
et caeli totiens deceptus fraude sereni?'
    Talia dicta dabat, clavumque adfixus et haerens
nusquam amittebat, oculosque sub astra tenebat.
Ecce deus ramum Lethaeo rore madentem,
vique soporatum Stygia, super utraque quassat   855
tempora, cunctantique natantia lumina solvit.
Vix primos inopina quies laxaverat artus,
et super incumbens cum puppis parte revolsa,
cumque gubernaclo, liquidas proiecit in undas
praecipitem ac socios nequiquam saepe vocantem;   860
ipse volans tenuis se sustulit ales ad auras.
Currit iter tutum non setius aequore classis,
promissisque patris Neptuni interrita fertur.

Iamque adeo scopulos Sirenum advecta subibat,
difficilis quondam multorumque ossibus albos,   865
tum rauca adsiduo longe sale saxa sonabant:
cum pater amisso fluitantem errare magistro
sensit, et ipse ratem nocturnis rexit in undis,
multa gemens, casuque animum concussus amici:
'O nimium caelo et pelago confise sereno,   870
nudus in ignota, Palinure, iacebis harena!'

LIBER VI

THE WORLD BELOW

Æneas arrives at Cumæ, and seeks the Sibyl's cave: the temple of Phœbus, constructed by Dædalus (1–41). Inspiration of the Sibyl: she prophesies war (42–97). Æneas solicits that he may enter the abode of Hades: the required gift to Proserpine of the Golden Bough (98–155). Death of Misenus. While the trees are felled for his funeral pile, Æneas, guided by doves to the mouth of Acheron, finds the sacred bough: the funeral rites (156–235). After due rites have been paid, he follows the Sibyl to the world of shadows: apparitions of horror at its entrance; Charon and his skiff (236–336). Shade of Palinurus on the hither side (337–381). The passage of the Styx: Cerberus, and the judge Minos. The abode of suicides and unhappy lovers: the angry shade of Dido (382–476). Shades of fallen heroes. Deiphobus accosts Æneas, but is checked by the Sibyl (477–547). Phlegethon, and the fiery dungeons of the damned: the judge Rhadamanthus; the Giants, Tityos, Ixion, Theseus (548–627). The branch is fixed at the entrance of the palace of Dis: the Elysian Fields; ancient heroes of Troy (628–678). The shade of Anchises is met in a secluded vale: he explains the system and divine life of things (679–755). Anchises unfolds the heroic story and future glories of Rome (756–854). Vision of the young Marcellus: the two Gates of Sleep (855–901).

Æneas arrives at Cumæ and visits the temple of Apollo

SIC fatur lacrimans, classique immittit habenas,
 et tandem Euboïcis Cumarum adlabitur oris.
  Obvertunt pelago proras; tum dente tenaci
ancora fundabat navis, et litora curvae
praetexunt puppes. Iuvenum manus emicat ardens   5
litus in Hesperium; quaerit pars semina flammae
abstrusa in venis silicis, pars densa ferarum
tecta rapit silvas, inventaque flumina monstrat.

At pius Aeneas arces, quibus altus Apollo
praesidet, horrendaeque procul secreta Sibyllae   10
antrum immane petit, magnam cui mentem animumque
Delius inspirat vates, aperitque futura.
Iam subeunt Triviae lucos atque aurea tecta.

The doors of the temple, the work of Dædalus, are described

Daedalus, ut fama est, fugiens Minoïa regna,
praepetibus pinnis ausus se credere caelo,   15
insuetum per iter gelidas enavit ad Arctos,
Chalcidicaque levis tandem super adstitit arce.
Redditus his primum terris, tibi, Phoebe, sacravit
remigium alarum, posuitque immania templa.
In foribus letum Androgeo: tum pendere poenas   20
Cecropidae iussi—miserum!—septena quotannis
corpora natorum; stat ductis sortibus urna.
Contra elata mari respondet Gnosia tellus:
hic crudelis amor tauri, suppostaque furto
Pasiphaë, mixtumque genus prolesque biformis   25
Minotaurus inest, Veneris monumenta nefandae;
hic labor ille domus et inextricabilis error;
magnum reginae sed enim miseratus amorem
Daedalus ipse dolos tecti ambagesque resolvit,
caeca regens filo vestigia. Tu quoque magnam   30
partem opere in tanto, sineret dolor, Icare, haberes.
Bis conatus erat casus effingere in auro;
bis patriae cecidere manus.

The Cumœan Sibyl greets Æneas

                              Quin protinus omnia
perlegerent oculis, ni iam praemissus Achates
adforet, atque una Phoebi Triviaeque sacerdos,   35
Deiphobe Glauci, fatur quae talia regi:

'Non hoc ista sibi tempus spectacula poscit;
nunc grege de intacto septem mactare iuvencos
praestiterit, totidem lectas de more bidentis.'
Talibus adfata Aenean (nec sacra morantur   40
iussa viri), Teucros vocat alta in templa sacerdos.

THESEUS AND THE MINOTAUR

*Æneas is made aware of the presence of Apollo and
offers prayer*

Excisum Euboïcae latus ingens rupis in antrum,
quo lati ducunt aditus centum, ostia centum;
unde ruunt totidem voces, responsa Sibyllae.
Ventum erat ad limen, cum virgo, 'Poscere fata   45

tempus,' ait; 'deus, ecce, deus!' Cui talia fanti
ante foris subito non voltus, non color unus,
non comptae mansere comae; sed pectus anhelum,
et rabie fera corda tument; maiorque videri,
nec mortale sonans, adflata est numine quando   50
iam propiore dei. 'Cessas in vota precesque,
Tros,' ait, 'Aenea? Cessas? Neque enim ante dehiscent
attonitae magna ora domus.' Et talia fata
conticuit. Gelidus Teucris per dura cucurrit
ossa tremor, funditque preces rex pectore ab imo: 55

*The prayer of Æneas: he beseeches Phœbus to continue his
favor and begs the Sibyl to utter a prophecy*

'Phoebe, gravis Troiae semper miserate labores,
Dardana qui Paridis direxti tela manusque
corpus in Aeacidae, magnas obeuntia terras
tot maria intravi duce te, penitusque repostas
Massylum gentis praetentaque syrtibus arva,   60
iam tandem Italiae fugientis prendimus oras;
hac Troiana tenus fuerit Fortuna secuta.
Vos quoque Pergameae iam fas est parcere genti,
dique deaeque omnes quibus obstitit Ilium et ingens
gloria Dardaniae. Tuque, O sanctissima vates,   65
praescia venturi, da, non indebita posco
regna meis fatis, Latio considere Teucros
errantisque deos agitataque numina Troiae.
Tum Phoebo et Triviae solido de marmore templum
instituam, festosque dies de nomine Phoebi.   70
Te quoque magna manent regnis penetralia nostris:
hic ego namque tuas sortes arcanaque fata,
dicta meae genti, ponam, lectosque sacrabo,
alma, viros. Foliis tantum ne carmina manda,
ne turbata volent rapidis ludibria ventis;   75
ipsa canas oro.' Finem dedit ore loquendi.

The Sibyl prophesies wars in Italy for the Trojans

At, Phoebi nondum patiens, immanis in antro
bacchatur vates, magnum si pectore possit
excussisse deum; tanto magis ille fatigat
os rabidum, fera corda domans, fingitque premendo. 80
Ostia iamque domus patuere ingentia centum
sponte sua, vatisque ferunt responsa per auras:
'O tandem magnis pelagi defuncte periclis!
Sed terrae graviora manent. In regna Lavini
Dardanidae venient; mitte hanc de pectore curam; 85
sed non et venisse volent. Bella, horrida bella,
et Thybrim multo spumantem sanguine cerno.
Non Simoïs tibi, nec Xanthus, nec Dorica castra
defuerint; alius Latio iam partus Achilles,
natus et ipse dea; nec Teucris addita Iuno 90
usquam aberit; cum tu supplex in rebus egenis
quas gentis Italum aut quas non oraveris urbes!
Causa mali tanti coniunx iterum hospita Teucris
externique iterum thalami.
Tu ne cede malis, sed contra audentior ito, 95
qua tua te Fortuna sinet. Via prima salutis,
quod minime reris, Graia pandetur ab urbe.'

Talibus ex adyto dictis Cumaea Sibylla
horrendas canit ambages antroque remugit,
obscuris vera involvens: ea frena furenti 100
concutit, et stimulos sub pectore vertit Apollo.

Æneas begs the Sibyl to guide him to his father in the
Lower World

Ut primum cessit furor et rabida ora quierunt,
incipit Aeneas heros: 'Non ulla laborum,
O virgo, nova mi facies inopinave surgit;
omnia praecepi atque animo mecum ante peregi. 105

Unum oro: quando hic inferni ianua regis
dicitur, et tenebrosa palus Acheronte refuso,
ire ad conspectum cari genitoris et ora
contingat; doceas iter et sacra ostia pandas.
Illum ego per flammas et mille sequentia tela   110
eripui his umeris, medioque ex hoste recepi;
ille meum comitatus iter, maria omnia mecum
atque omnis pelagique minas caelique ferebat,
invalidus, viris ultra sortemque senectae.
Quin, ut te supplex peterem et tua limina adirem,   115
idem orans mandata dabat. Gnatique patrisque,
alma, precor, miserere;—potes namque omnia, nec te
nequiquam lucis Hecate praefecit Avernis;—
si potuit Manis arcessere coniugis Orpheus,
Threïcia fretus cithara fidibusque canoris,   120
si fratrem Pollux alterna morte redemit,
itque reditque viam totiens. Quid Thesea, magnum
quid memorem Alciden? Et mi genus ab Iove summo.'

The Sibyl directs Æneas to find the Golden Bough as an offering to Proserpine

Talibus orabat dictis, arasque tenebat,
cum sic orsa loqui vates: 'Sate sanguine divum,   125
Tros Anchisiade, facilis descensus Averno;
noctes atque dies patet atri ianua Ditis;
sed revocare gradum superasque evadere ad auras,
hoc opus, hic labor est. Pauci, quos aequus amavit
Iuppiter, aut ardens evexit ad aethera virtus,   130
dis geniti potuere. Tenent media omnia silvae,
Cocytusque sinu labens circumvenit atro.
Quod si tantus amor menti, si tanta cupido,
bis Stygios innare lacus, bis nigra videre
Tartara, et insano iuvat indulgere labori,   135

accipe, quae peragenda prius. Latet arbore opaca
aureus et foliis et lento vimine ramus,
Iunoni infernae dictus sacer ; hunc tegit omnis
lucus, et obscuris claudunt convallibus umbrae.
Sed non ante datur telluris operta subire,   140
auricomos quam quis decerpserit arbore fetus.
Hoc sibi pulchra suum ferri Proserpina munus
instituit. Primo avolso non deficit alter
aureus, et simili frondescit virga metallo.
Ergo alte vestiga oculis, et rite repertum   145
carpe manu ; namque ipse volens facilisque sequetur,
si te fata vocant ; aliter non viribus ullis
vincere, nec duro poteris convellere ferro.
Praeterea iacet exanimum tibi corpus amici—
heu nescis—totamque incestat funere classem,   150
dum consulta petis nostroque in limine pendes.
Sedibus hunc refer ante suis et conde sepulcro.
Duc nigras pecudes ; ea prima piacula sunto :
sic demum lucos Stygis et regna invia vivis
aspicies.' Dixit, pressoque obmutuit ore.   155

*Æneas finds the body of Misenus on the shore, and the
Trojans prepare for its burial*

Aeneas maesto defixus lumina voltu
ingreditur, linquens antrum, caecosque volutat
eventus animo secum. Cui fidus Achates
it comes, et paribus curis vestigia figit.
Multa inter sese vario sermone serebant,   160
quem socium exanimem vates, quod corpus humandum
diceret. Atque illi Misenum in litore sicco,
ut venere, vident indigna morte peremptum,
Misenum Aeoliden, quo non praestantior alter
aere ciere viros, Martemque accendere cantu.   165

Hectoris hic magni fuerat comes, Hectora circum
et lituo pugnas insignis obibat et hasta:
postquam illum vita victor spoliavit Achilles,
Dardanio Aeneae sese fortissimus heros
addiderat socium, non inferiora secutus.   170
Sed tum, forte cava dum personat aequora concha,
demens, et cantu vocat in certamina divos,
aemulus exceptum Triton, si credere dignum est,
inter saxa virum spumosa immerserat unda.

Ergo omnes magno circum clamore fremebant,   175
praecipue pius Aeneas. Tum iussa Sibyllae,
haud mora, festinant flentes, aramque sepulcri
congerere arboribus caeloque educere certant.
Itur in antiquam silvam, stabula alta ferarum;
procumbunt piceae, sonat icta securibus ilex,   180
fraxineaeque trabes cuneis et fissile robur
scinditur, advolvunt ingentis montibus ornos.
Nec non Aeneas opera inter talia primus
hortatur socios, paribusque accingitur armis.

Doves guide Æneas in his search for the Golden Bough

Atque haec ipse suo tristi cum corde volutat,   185
aspectans silvam immensam, et sic forte precatur:
'Si nunc se nobis ille aureus arbore ramus
ostendat nemore in tanto, quando omnia vere
heu nimium de te vates, Misene, locuta est.'
Vix ea fatus erat, geminae cum forte columbae   190
ipsa sub ora viri caelo venere volantes,
et viridi sedere solo. Tum maximus heros
maternas agnoscit aves, laetusque precatur:
'Este duces, O, si qua via est, cursumque per auras
dirigite in lucos, ubi pinguem dives opacat   195
ramus humum. Tuque, O, dubiis ne defice rebus,

diva parens.' Sic effatus vestigia pressit,
observans quae signa ferant, quo tendere pergant.
Pascentes illae tantum prodire volando,
quantum acie possent oculi servare sequentum.   200
Inde ubi venere ad fauces grave olentis Averni,
tollunt se celeres, liquidumque per aëra lapsae
sedibus optatis geminae super arbore sidunt,
discolor unde auri per ramos aura refulsit.
Quale solet silvis brumali frigore viscum   205
fronde virere nova, quod non sua seminat arbos,
et croceo fetu teretis circumdare truncos,
talis erat species auri frondentis opaca
ilice, sic leni crepitabat brattea vento.
Corripit Aeneas extemplo avidusque refringit   210
cunctantem, et vatis portat sub tecta Sibyllae.

R. H. FRANKENBERG

The funeral of Misenus is held on the shore

Nec minus interea Misenum in litore Teucri
flebant, et cineri ingrato suprema ferebant.
Principio pinguem taedis et robore secto
ingentem struxere pyram, cui frondibus atris   215
intexunt latera, et feralis ante cupressos
constituunt, decorantque super fulgentibus armis.
Pars calidos latices et aëna undantia flammis
expediunt, corpusque lavant frigentis et unguunt.
Fit gemitus. Tum membra toro defleta reponunt,   220
purpureasque super vestes, velamina nota,
coniciunt. Pars ingenti subiere feretro,
triste ministerium, et subiectam more parentum
aversi tenuere facem. Congesta cremantur
turea dona, dapes, fuso crateres olivo.   225
Postquam conlapsi cineres et flamma quievit,
reliquias vino et bibulam lavere favillam,

ossaque lecta cado texit Corynaeus aëno.
Idem ter socios pura circumtulit unda,
spargens rore levi et ramo felicis olivae,   230
lustravitque viros, dixitque novissima verba.
At pius Aeneas ingenti mole sepulcrum
imponit, suaque arma viro, remumque tubamque,
monte sub aërio, qui nunc Misenus ab illo
dicitur, aeternumque tenet per saecula nomen.   235

Æneas sacrifices to the gods of the Lower World

His actis, propere exsequitur praecepta Sibyllae.
Spelunca alta fuit vastoque immanis hiatu,
scrupea, tuta lacu nigro nemorumque tenebris,
quam super haud ullae poterant impune volantes
tendere iter pinnis—talis sese halitus atris   240
faucibus effundens supera ad convexa ferebat:
unde locum Grai dixerunt nomine Aornon.
Quattuor hic primum nigrantis terga iuvencos
constituit, frontique invergit vina sacerdos;
et summas carpens media inter cornua saetas   245
ignibus imponit sacris, libamina prima,
voce vocans Hecaten, Caeloque Ereboque potentem.
Supponunt alii cultros, tepidumque cruorem
suscipiunt pateris. Ipse atri velleris agnam
Aeneas matri Eumenidum magnaeque sorori   250
ense ferit, sterilemque tibi, Proserpina, vaccam.
Tum Stygio regi nocturnas incohat aras,
et solida imponit taurorum viscera flammis,
pingue super oleum fundens ardentibus extis.
Ecce autem, primi sub lumina solis et ortus,   255
sub pedibus mugire solum, et iuga coepta moveri
silvarum, visaeque canes ululare per umbram,
adventante dea. 'Procul, O procul este, profani,'

conclamat vates, 'totoque absistite luco;
tuque invade viam, vaginaque eripe ferrum: 260
nunc animis opus, Aenea, nunc pectore firmo.'

Æneas and the Sibyl begin the descent to the Lower World

Tantum effata, furens antro se immisit aperto;
ille ducem haud timidis vadentem passibus aequat.

Di, quibus imperium est animarum, umbraeque silentes,
et Chaos, et Phlegethon, loca nocte tacentia late, 265
sit mihi fas audita loqui; sit numine vestro
pandere res alta terra et caligine mersas!

Ibant obscuri sola sub nocte per umbram,
perque domos Ditis vacuas et inania regna:
quale per incertam lunam sub luce maligna 270
est iter in silvis, ubi caelum condidit umbra
Iuppiter, et rebus nox abstulit atra colorem.

The dire shapes at the entrance

Vestibulum ante ipsum, primisque in faucibus Orci,
Luctus et ultrices posuere cubilia Curae;
pallentesque habitant Morbi, tristisque Senectus, 275
et Metus, et malesuada Fames, ac turpis Egestas,
terribiles visu formae: Letumque, Labosque;
tum consanguineus Leti Sopor, et mala mentis
Gaudia, mortiferumque adverso in limine Bellum,
ferreique Eumenidum thalami, et Discordia demens, 280
vipereum crinem vittis innexa cruentis.

In medio ramos annosaque bracchia pandit
ulmus opaca, ingens, quam sedem Somnia volgo
vana tenere ferunt, foliisque sub omnibus haerent.
Multaque praeterea variarum monstra ferarum: 285
Centauri in foribus stabulant, Scyllaeque biformes,
et centumgeminus Briareus, ac belua Lernae

horrendum stridens, flammisque armata Chimaera,
Gorgones Harpyiaeque et forma tricorporis umbrae.
Corripit hic subita trepidus formidine ferrum   290
Aeneas, strictamque aciem venientibus offert,
et, ni docta comes tenuis sine corpore vitas
admoneat volitare cava sub imagine formae,
inruat, et frustra ferro diverberet umbras.

*Æneas and the Sibyl reach the Styx, where many ghosts
are waiting for Charon to ferry them across*

Hinc via, Tartarei quae fert Acherontis ad undas.   295
Turbidus hic caeno vastaque voragine gurges
aestuat, atque omnem Cocyto eructat harenam.
Portitor has horrendus aquas et flumina servat
terribili squalore Charon, cui plurima mento
canities inculta iacet; stant lumina flamma,   300
sordidus ex umeris nodo dependet amictus.
Ipse ratem conto subigit, velisque ministrat,
et ferruginea subvectat corpora cymba,
iam senior, sed cruda deo viridisque senectus.

Huc omnis turba ad ripas effusa ruebat,   305
matres atque viri, defunctaque corpora vita
magnanimum heroum, pueri innuptaeque puellae,
impositique rogis iuvenes ante ora parentum:
quam multa in silvis autumni frigore primo
lapsa cadunt folia, aut ad terram gurgite ab alto   310
quam multae glomerantur aves, ubi frigidus annus
trans pontum fugat, et terris immittit apricis.
Stabant orantes primi transmittere cursum,
tendebantque manus ripae ulterioris amore.
Navita sed tristis nunc hos nunc accipit illos,   315
ast alios longe submotos arcet harena.

Aeneas, miratus enim motusque tumultu,
'Dic,' ait, 'O virgo, quid volt concursus ad amnem?

Quidve petunt animae, vel quo discrimine ripas
hae linquunt, illae remis vada livida verrunt?' 320
Olli sic breviter fata est longaeva sacerdos:
'Anchisa generate, deum certissima proles,

CHARON

Cocyti stagna alta vides Stygiamque paludem,
di cuius iurare timent et fallere numen.
Haec omnis, quam cernis, inops inhumataque turba est;
portitor ille Charon; hi, quos vehit unda, sepulti. 326
Nec ripas datur horrendas et rauca fluenta
transportare prius quam sedibus ossa quierunt.
Centum errant annos volitantque haec litora circum;
tum demum admissi stagna exoptata revisunt.' 330

Constitit Anchisa satus et vestigia pressit,
multa putans, sortemque animi miseratus iniquam.
Cernit ibi maestos et mortis honore carentis
Leucaspim et Lyciae ductorem classis Oronten,
quos, simul a Troia ventosa per aequora vectos,   335
obruit Auster, aqua involvens navemque virosque.

The ghost of Palinurus tells the story of his death

Ecce gubernator sese Palinurus agebat,
qui Libyco nuper cursu, dum sidera servat,
exciderat puppi mediis effusus in undis.
Hunc ubi vix multa maestum cognovit in umbra,   340
sic prior adloquitur : 'Quis te, Palinure, deorum
eripuit nobis, medioque sub aequore mersit?
Dic age. Namque, mihi fallax haud ante repertus,
hoc uno responso animum delusit Apollo,
qui fore te ponto incolumem, finisque canebat   345
venturum Ausonios. En haec promissa fides est?'
Ille autem : 'Neque te Phoebi cortina fefellit,
dux Anchisiade, nec me deus aequore mersit.
Namque gubernaclum multa vi forte revolsum,
cui datus haerebam custos cursusque regebam,   350
praecipitans traxi mecum. Maria aspera iuro
non ullum pro me tantum cepisse timorem,
quam tua ne, spoliata armis, excussa magistro,
deficeret tantis navis surgentibus undis.
Tris Notus hibernas immensa per aequora noctes   355
vexit me violentus aqua ; vix lumine quarto
prospexi Italiam summa sublimis ab unda.
Paulatim adnabam terrae ; iam tuta tenebam,
ni gens crudelis madida cum veste gravatum
prensantemque uncis manibus capita aspera montis   360
ferro invasisset, praedamque ignara putasset.

Nunc me fluctus habet, versantque in litore venti.
Quod te per caeli iucundum lumen et auras,
per genitorem oro, per spes surgentis Iuli,
eripe me his, invicte, malis : aut tu mihi terram   365
inice, namque potes, portusque require Velinos ;
aut tu, si qua via est, si quam tibi diva creatrix
ostendit—neque enim, credo, sine numine divum
flumina tanta paras Stygiamque innare paludem—
da dextram misero, et tecum me tolle per undas,   370
sedibus ut saltem placidis in morte quiescam.'
    Talia fatus erat, coepit cum talia vates :
'Unde haec, O Palinure, tibi tam dira cupido?
Tu Stygias inhumatus aquas amnemque severum
Eumenidum aspicies, ripamve iniussus adibis?   375
Desine fata deum flecti sperare precando.
Sed cape dicta memor, duri solacia casus.
Nam tua finitimi, longe lateque per urbes
prodigiis acti caelestibus, ossa piabunt,
et statuent tumulum, et tumulo sollemnia mittent,   380
aeternumque locus Palinuri nomen habebit.'
His dictis curae emotae, pulsusque parumper
corde dolor tristi : gaudet cognomine terrae.

Charon refuses to take Æneas and the Sibyl across the Styx,
but consents on seeing the Golden Bough

    Ergo iter inceptum peragunt fluvioque propinquant.
Navita quos iam inde ut Stygia prospexit ab unda   385
per tacitum nemus ire pedemque advertere ripae,
sic prior adgreditur dictis, atque increpat ultro :
'Quisquis es, armatus qui nostra ad flumina tendis,
fare age, quid venias, iam istinc, et comprime gressum.
Umbrarum hic locus est, somni noctisque soporae ;   390
corpora viva nefas Stygia vectare carina.

Nec vero Alciden me sum laetatus euntem
accepisse lacu, nec Thesea Pirithoumque,
dis quamquam geniti atque invicti viribus essent.
Tartareum ille manu custodem in vincla petivit,   395
ipsius a solio regis, traxitque trementem;
hi dominam Ditis thalamo deducere adorti.'
　　Quae contra breviter fata est Amphrysia vates:
'Nullae hic insidiae tales; absiste moveri;
nec vim tela ferunt; licet ingens ianitor antro   400
aeternum latrans exsanguis terreat umbras,
casta licet patrui servet Proserpina limen.
Troïus Aeneas, pietate insignis et armis,
ad genitorem imas Erebi descendit ad umbras.
Si te nulla movet tantae pietatis imago,   405
at ramum hunc' (aperit ramum, qui veste latebat)
'agnoscas.' Tumida ex ira tum corda residunt.
Nec plura his. Ille admirans venerabile donum
fatalis virgae, longo post tempore visum,
caeruleam advertit puppim, ripaeque propinquat.   410
Inde alias animas, quae per iuga longa sedebant,
deturbat, laxatque foros; simul accipit alveo
ingentem Aenean. Gemuit sub pondere cymba
sutilis, et multam accepit rimosa paludem.
Tandem trans fluvium incolumis vatemque virumque   415
informi limo glaucaque exponit in ulva.

The Sibyl drugs Cerberus

Cerberus haec ingens latratu regna trifauci
personat, adverso recubans immanis in antro.
Cui vates, horrere videns iam colla colubris,
melle soporatam et medicatis frugibus offam   420
obicit. Ille fame rabida tria guttura pandens
corripit obiectam, atque immania terga resolvit

fusus humi, totoque ingens extenditur antro.
Occupat Aeneas aditum custode sepulto,
evaditque celer ripam inremeabilis undae.   425

Æneas sees the ghosts of the untimely dead

Continuo auditae voces, vagitus et ingens,
infantumque animae flentes in limine primo,
quos dulcis vitae exsortis et ab ubere raptos
abstulit atra dies et funere mersit acerbo.
Hos iuxta falso damnati crimine mortis.   430
Nec vero hae sine sorte datae, sine iudice, sedes:
quaesitor Minos urnam movet; ille silentum
conciliumque vocat vitasque et crimina discit.
Proxima deinde tenent maesti loca, qui sibi letum
insontes peperere manu, lucemque perosi   435
proiecere animas. Quam vellent aethere in alto
nunc et pauperiem et duros perferre labores!
Fas obstat, tristique palus inamabilis unda
alligat, et noviens Styx interfusa coërcet.

The fields of mourning

Nec procul hinc partem fusi monstrantur in omnem   440
lugentes campi: sic illos nomine dicunt.
Hic, quos durus amor crudeli tabe peredit,
secreti celant calles et myrtea circum
silva tegit; curae non ipsa in morte relinquunt.
His Phaedram Procrimque locis, maestamque Eriphylen   445
crudelis nati monstrantem volnera, cernit,
Euadnenque et Pasiphaën; his Laodamia
it comes, et iuvenis quondam, nunc femina, Caeneus,
rursus et in veterem fato revoluta figuram.

The shade of Dido

Inter quas Phoenissa recens a volnere Dido   450
errabat silva in magna; quam Troïus heros
ut primum iuxta stetit agnovitque per umbras
obscuram, qualem primo qui surgere mense
aut videt, aut vidisse putat, per nubila lunam,
demisit lacrimas, dulcique adfatus amore est: 455
    'Infelix Dido, verus mihi nuntius ergo
venerat exstinctam, ferroque extrema secutam?
Funeris heu tibi causa fui? Per sidera iuro,
per superos, et si qua fides tellure sub ima est,
invitus, regina, tuo de litore cessi.   460
Sed me iussa deum, quae nunc has ire per umbras,
per loca senta situ cogunt noctemque profundam,
imperiis egere suis; nec credere quivi
hunc tantum tibi me discessu ferre dolorem.
Siste gradum, teque aspectu ne subtrahe nostro.   465
Quem fugis? Extremum fato, quod te adloquor, hoc est.'
    Talibus Aeneas ardentem et torva tuentem
lenibat dictis animum, lacrimasque ciebat.
Illa solo fixos oculos aversa tenebat,
nec magis incepto voltum sermone movetur,   470
quam si dura silex aut stet Marpesia cautes.
Tandem corripuit sese, atque inimica refugit
in nemus umbriferum, coniunx ubi pristinus illi
respondet curis aequatque Sychaeus amorem.
Nec minus Aeneas, casu concussus iniquo,   475
prosequitur lacrimis longe, et miseratur euntem.

Æneas meets the shades of dead warriors, Trojan and Greek

Inde datum molitur iter. Iamque arva tenebant
ultima, quae bello clari secreta frequentant.
Hic illi occurrit Tydeus, hic inclutus armis

Parthenopaeus et Adrasti pallentis imago;   480
hic multum fleti ad superos belloque caduci
Dardanidae, quos ille omnis longo ordine cernens
ingemuit, Glaucumque Medontaque Thersilochumque,
tris Antenoridas, Cererique sacrum Polyboeten,
Idaeumque, etiam currus, etiam arma tenentem.   485
Circumstant animae dextra laevaque frequentes;
nec vidisse semel satis est; iuvat usque morari,
et conferre gradum, et veniendi discere causas.
At Danaum proceres Agamemnoniaeque phalanges
ut videre virum fulgentiaque arma per umbras,   490
ingenti trepidare metu; pars vertere terga,
ceu quondam petiere rates; pars tollere vocem
exiguam, inceptus clamor frustratur hiantis.

Æneas listens to the story of Deiphobus

Atque hic Priamiden laniatum corpore toto
Deiphobum videt et lacerum crudeliter ora,   495
ora manusque ambas, populataque tempora raptis
auribus, et truncas inhonesto volnere naris.
Vix adeo agnovit pavitantem et dira tegentem
supplicia, et notis compellat vocibus ultro:
'Deiphobe armipotens, genus alto a sanguine Teucri,   500
quis tam crudelis optavit sumere poenas?
Cui tantum de te licuit? Mihi fama suprema
nocte tulit fessum vasta te caede Pelasgum
procubuisse super confusae stragis acervum.
Tunc egomet tumulum Rhoeteo litore inanem   505
constitui, et magna Manis ter voce vocavi.
Nomen et arma locum servant; te, amice, nequivi
conspicere, et patria decedens ponere terra.'
Ad quae Priamides: 'Nihil O tibi amice relictum;
omnia Deiphobo solvisti et funeris umbris.   510
Sed me fata mea et scelus exitiale Lacaenae

his mersere malis; illa haec monumenta reliquit.
Namque ut supremam falsa inter gaudia noctem
egerimus, nosti; et nimium meminisse necesse est.
Cum fatalis equus saltu super ardua venit   515
Pergama, et armatum peditem gravis attulit alvo,
illa, chorum simulans, euhantis orgia circum
ducebat Phrygias; flammam media ipsa tenebat
ingentem, et summa Danaos ex arce vocabat.
Tum me, confectum curis somnoque gravatum,   520
infelix habuit thalamus, pressitque iacentem
dulcis et alta quies placidaeque simillima morti.
Egregia interea coniunx arma omnia tectis
amovet, et fidum capiti subduxerat ensem;
intra tecta vocat Menelaum, et limina pandit,   525
scilicet id magnum sperans fore munus amanti,
et famam exstingui veterum sic posse malorum.
Quid moror? Inrumpunt thalamo; comes additur una
hortator scelerum Aeolides. Di, talia Grais
instaurate, pio si poenas ore reposco!   530
Sed te qui vivum casus, age, fare vicissim,
attulerint. Pelagine venis erroribus actus,
an monitu divum? An quae te fortuna fatigat,
ut tristis sine sole domos, loca turbida, adires?'

   Hac vice sermonum roseis Aurora quadrigis   535
iam medium aetherio cursu traiecerat axem;
et fors omne datum traherent per talia tempus;
sed comes admonuit, breviterque adfata Sibylla est:
'Nox ruit, Aenea; nos flendo ducimus horas.
Hic locus est, partis ubi se via findit in ambas: 540
dextera quae Ditis magni sub moenia tendit,
hac iter Elysium nobis; at laeva malorum
exercet poenas, et ad impia Tartara mittit.'
Deiphobus contra: 'Ne saevi, magna sacerdos;

discedam, explebo numerum, reddarque tenebris.   545
I decus, i, nostrum; melioribus utere fatis!'
Tantum effatus, et in verbo vestigia torsit.

*Æneas beholds Tartarus, and its horrors are described
by the Sibyl*

Respicit Aeneas subito, et sub rupe sinistra
moenia lata videt, triplici circumdata muro,
quae rapidus flammis ambit torrentibus amnis,   550
Tartareus Phlegethon, torquetque sonantia saxa.
Porta adversa ingens, solidoque adamante columnae,
vis ut nulla virum, non ipsi exscindere bello
caelicolae valeant; stat ferrea turris ad auras,
Tisiphoneque sedens, palla succincta cruenta,   555
vestibulum exsomnis servat noctesque diesque.
Hinc exaudiri gemitus, et saeva sonare
verbera; tum stridor ferri, tractaeque catenae.
Constitit Aeneas, strepituque exterritus hausit.
'Quae scelerum facies, O virgo, effare; quibusve   560
urgentur poenis? Quis tantus plangor ad auras?'
Tum vates sic orsa loqui: 'Dux inclute Teucrum,
nulli fas casto sceleratum insistere limen;
sed me cum lucis Hecate praefecit Avernis,
ipsa deum poenas docuit, perque omnia duxit.   565
Gnosius haec Rhadamanthus habet, durissima regna,
castigatque auditque dolos, subigitque fateri,
quae quis apud superos, furto laetatus inani,
distulit in seram commissa piacula mortem.
Continuo sontis ultrix accincta flagello   570
Tisiphone quatit insultans, torvosque sinistra
intentans anguis vocat agmina saeva sororum.
Tum demum horrisono stridentes cardine sacrae
panduntur portae. Cernis custodia qualis

TANTALUS, IXION, AND SISYPHUS

vestibulo sedeat, facies quae limina servet?   575
Quinquaginta atris immanis hiatibus Hydra
saevior intus habet sedem. Tum Tartarus ipse
bis patet in praeceps tantum tenditque sub umbras,
quantus ad aetherium caeli suspectus Olympum.

Famous evildoers

'Hic genus antiquum Terrae, Titania pubes,   580
fulmine deiecti fundo volvuntur in imo.
Hic et Aloïdas geminos immania vidi
corpora, qui manibus magnum rescindere caelum
adgressi, superisque Iovem detrudere regnis.
Vidi et crudelis dantem Salmonea poenas,   585
dum flammas Iovis et sonitus imitatur Olympi.
Quattuor hic invectus equis et lampada quassans
per Graium populos mediaeque per Elidis urbem

ibat ovans, divumque sibi poscebat honorem,
demens, qui nimbos et non imitabile fulmen   590
aere et cornipedum pulsu simularet equorum.
At pater omnipotens densa inter nubila telum
contorsit, non ille faces nec fumea taedis
lumina, praecipitemque immani turbine adegit.
Nec non et Tityon, Terrae omniparentis alumnum,   595
cernere erat, per tota novem cui iugera corpus
porrigitur, rostroque immanis voltur obunco
immortale iecur tondens fecundaque poenis
viscera, rimaturque epulis, habitatque sub alto
pectore, nec fibris requies datur ulla renatis.   600
Quid memorem Lapithas, Ixiona Pirithoumque?—
quos super atra silex iam iam lapsura cadentique
imminet adsimilis; lucent genialibus altis
aurea fulcra toris, epulaeque ante ora paratae
regifico luxu; Furiarum maxima iuxta   605
accubat, et manibus prohibet contingere mensas,
exsurgitque facem attollens, atque intonat ore.

Punishments of the impious

'Hic, quibus invisi fratres, dum vita manebat,
pulsatusve parens, et fraus innexa clienti,
aut qui divitiis soli incubuere repertis,   610
nec partem posuere suis (quae maxima turba est),
quique ob adulterium caesi, quique arma secuti
impia nec veriti dominorum fallere dextras,
inclusi poenam exspectant. Ne quaere doceri
quam poenam, aut quae forma viros fortunave mersit.   615
Saxum ingens volvunt alii, radiisque rotarum
districti pendent; sedet, aeternumque sedebit,
infelix Theseus; Phlegyasque miserrimus omnis
admonet, et magna testatur voce per umbras:

Discite iustitiam moniti, et non temnere divos.   620
Vendidit hic auro patriam, dominumque potentem
imposuit; fixit leges pretio atque refixit;
hic thalamum invasit natae vetitosque hymenaeos;
ausi omnes immane nefas, ausoque potiti.
Non, mihi si linguae centum sint oraque centum,   625
ferrea vox, omnis scelerum comprendere formas,
omnia poenarum percurrere nomina possim.'

Æneas and the Sibyl reach the palace of Pluto, where Æneas deposits the Golden Bough

Haec ubi dicta dedit Phoebi longaeva sacerdos:
'Sed iam age, carpe viam et susceptum perfice munus;
acceleremus,' ait; 'Cyclopum educta caminis   630
moenia conspicio atque adverso fornice portas,
haec ubi nos praecepta iubent deponere dona.'
Dixerat, et pariter, gressi per opaca viarum,
corripiunt spatium medium, foribusque propinquant.
Occupat Aeneas aditum, corpusque recenti   635
spargit aqua, ramumque adverso in limine figit.

Æneas views the Elysian Fields

His demum exactis, perfecto munere divae,
devenere locos laetos et amoena virecta
fortunatorum nemorum sedesque beatas.
Largior hic campos aether et lumine vestit   640
purpureo, solemque suum, sua sidera norunt.
Pars in gramineis exercent membra palaestris,
contendunt ludo et fulva luctantur harena;
pars pedibus plaudunt choreas et carmina dicunt.
Nec non Threïcius longa cum veste sacerdos   645
obloquitur numeris septem discrimina vocum,
iamque eadem digitis, iam pectine pulsat eburno.

Hic genus antiquum Teucri, pulcherrima proles,
magnanimi heroes, nati melioribus annis,
Ilusque Assaracusque et Troiae Dardanus auctor.   650
Arma procul currusque virum miratur inanis.
Stant terra defixae hastae, passimque soluti
per campum pascuntur equi. Quae gratia currum
armorumque fuit vivis, quae cura nitentis
pascere equos, eadem sequitur tellure repostos.'   655
    Conspicit, ecce, alios dextra laevaque per herbam
vescentis, laetumque choro paeana canentis
inter odoratum lauri nemus, unde superne
plurimus Eridani per silvam volvitur amnis.
Hic manus ob patriam pugnando volnera passi,   660
quique sacerdotes casti, dum vita manebat,
quique pii vates et Phoebo digna locuti,
inventas aut qui vitam excoluere per artis,
quique sui memores aliquos fecere merendo,
omnibus his nivea cinguntur tempora vitta.   665

Musæus conducts Æneas to Anchises

    Quos circumfusos sic est adfata Sibylla,
Musaeum ante omnis, medium nam plurima turba
hunc habet, atque umeris exstantem suspicit altis:
'Dicite, felices animae, tuque, optime vates,
quae regio Anchisen, quis habet locus? Illius ergo   670
venimus, et magnos Erebi tranavimus amnis.'
Atque huic responsum paucis ita reddidit heros:
'Nulli certa domus; lucis habitamus opacis,
riparumque toros et prata recentia rivis
incolimus. Sed vos, si fert ita corde voluntas,   675
hoc superate iugum; et facili iam tramite sistam.'
Dixit, et ante tulit gressum, camposque nitentis
desuper ostentat; dehinc summa cacumina linquunt

Æneas meets his father

At pater Anchises penitus convalle virenti
inclusas animas superumque ad lumen ituras   680
lustrabat studio recolens, omnemque suorum
forte recensebat numerum carosque nepotes,
fataque fortunasque virum moresque manusque.
Isque ubi tendentem adversum per gramina vidit
Aenean, alacris palmas utrasque tetendit,   685
effusaeque genis lacrimae, et vox excidit ore:
     'Venisti tandem, tuaque exspectata parenti
vicit iter durum pietas? Datur ora tueri,
nate, tua, et notas audire et reddere voces?
Sic equidem ducebam animo rebarque futurum,   690
tempora dinumerans, nec me mea cura fefellit.
Quas ego te terras et quanta per aequora vectum
accipio! quantis iactatum, nate, periclis!
Quam metui, ne quid Libyae tibi regna nocerent!'
Ille autem: 'Tua me, genitor, tua tristis imago,   695
saepius occurrens, haec limina tendere adegit:
stant sale Tyrrheno classes. Da iungere dextram,
da, genitor, teque amplexu ne subtrahe nostro.'
Sic memorans, largo fletu simul ora rigabat.
Ter conatus ibi collo dare bracchia circum,   700
ter frustra comprensa manus effugit imago,
par levibus ventis volucrique simillima somno.

At the river Lethe Æneas sees the souls of those who are to live again in the Upper World

Interea videt Aeneas in valle reducta
seclusum nemus et virgulta sonantia silvae,
Lethaeumque, domos placidas qui praenatat, amnem.   705
Hunc circum innumerae gentes populique volabant;
ac—velut in pratis ubi apes aestate serena

ÆNEAS AND ANCHISES

floribus insidunt variis, et candida circum
lilia funduntur—strepit omnis murmure campus.
Horrescit visu subito, causasque requirit   710
inscius Aeneas, quae sint ea flumina porro,
quive viri tanto complerint agmine ripas.

Tum pater Anchises: 'Animae, quibus altera fato
corpora debentur, Lethaei ad fluminis undam
securos latices et longa oblivia potant.   715
Has equidem memorare tibi atque ostendere coram,
iam pridem hanc prolem cupio enumerare meorum,
quo magis Italia mecum laetere reperta.'
'O pater, anne aliquas ad caelum hinc ire putandum est
sublimis animas, iterumque ad tarda reverti   720
corpora? Quae lucis miseris tam dira cupido?'
'Dicam equidem, nec te suspensum, nate, tenebo,'
suscipit Anchises, atque ordine singula pandit.

*Anchises discourses of the nature of the soul, and of its
purification after death*

'Principio caelum ac terras camposque liquentis
lucentemque globum Lunae Titaniaque astra   725
spiritus intus alit, totamque infusa per artus
mens agitat molem et magno se corpore miscet.
Inde hominum pecudumque genus, vitaeque volantum,
et quae marmoreo fert monstra sub aequore pontus.
Igneus est ollis vigor et caelestis origo   730
seminibus, quantum non noxia corpora tardant,
terrenique hebetant artus moribundaque membra.
Hinc metuunt cupiuntque, dolent gaudentque, neque auras
dispiciunt clausae tenebris et carcere caeco.
Quin et supremo cum lumine vita reliquit,   735
non tamen omne malum miseris nec funditus omnes
corporeae excedunt pestes, penitusque necesse est

multa diu concreta modis inolescere miris.
Ergo exercentur poenis, veterumque malorum
supplicia expendunt: aliae panduntur inanes   740
suspensae ad ventos; aliis sub gurgite vasto
infectum eluitur scelus, aut exuritur igni;
quisque suos patimur Manis; exinde per amplum
mittimur Elysium, et pauci laeta arva tenemus;
donec longa dies, perfecto temporis orbe,   745
concretam exemit labem, purumque relinquit
aetherium sensum atque auraï simplicis ignem.
Has omnis, ubi mille rotam volvere per annos,
Lethaeum ad fluvium deus evocat agmine magno,
scilicet immemores supera ut convexa revisant,   750
rursus et incipiant in corpora velle reverti.'

Anchises points out to Æneas the Alban kings and Romulus

Dixerat Anchises, natumque unaque Sibyllam
conventus trahit in medios turbamque sonantem,
et tumulum capit, unde omnis longo ordine possit
adversos legere, et venientum discere voltus.   755
  'Nunc age, Dardaniam prolem quae deinde sequatur
gloria, qui maneant Itala de gente nepotes,
inlustris animas nostrumque in nomen ituras,
expediam dictis, et te tua fata docebo.
Ille, vides, pura iuvenis qui nititur hasta,   760
proxima sorte tenet lucis loca, primus ad auras
aetherias Italo commixtus sanguine surget,
Silvius, Albanum nomen, tua postuma proles,
quem tibi longaevo serum Lavinia coniunx
educet silvis regem regumque parentem,   765
unde genus Longa nostrum dominabitur Alba.
  'Proximus ille Procas, Troianae gloria gentis,
et Capys, et Numitor, et qui te nomine reddet

Silvius Aeneas, pariter pietate vel armis
egregius, si umquam regnandam acceperit Albam.   770
Qui iuvenes! Quantas ostentant, aspice, viris,
atque umbrata gerunt civili tempora quercu!
Hi tibi Nomentum et Gabios urbemque Fidenam,
hi Collatinas imponent montibus arces,
Pometios Castrumque Inui Bolamque Coramque.   775
Haec tum nomina erunt, nunc sunt sine nomine terrae.

  'Quin et avo comitem sese Mavortius addet
Romulus, Assaraci quem sanguinis Ilia mater
educet. Viden, ut geminae stant vertice cristae,
et pater ipse suo superum iam signat honore?   780
En, huius, nate, auspiciis illa incluta Roma
imperium terris, animos aequabit Olympo,
septemque una sibi muro circumdabit arces,
felix prole virum: qualis Berecyntia mater
invehitur curru Phrygias turrita per urbes,   785
laeta deum partu, centum complexa nepotes,
omnis caelicolas, omnis supera alta tenentis.

Anchises points out the descendants of Iulus (the Julian Line), among them Augustus

  'Huc geminas nunc flecte acies, hanc aspice gentem
Romanosque tuos. Hic Caesar et omnis Iuli
progenies, magnum caeli ventura sub axem.   790
Hic vir, hic est, tibi quem promitti saepius audis,
Augustus Caesar, Divi genus, aurea condet
saecula qui rursus Latio regnata per arva
Saturno quondam, super et Garamantas et Indos
proferet imperium: iacet extra sidera tellus,   795
extra anni solisque vias, ubi caelifer Atlas
axem umero torquet stellis ardentibus aptum.
Huius in adventum iam nunc et Caspia regna
responsis horrent divum et Maeotia tellus,

et septemgemini turbant trepida ostia Nili. 800
Nec vero Alcides tantum telluris obivit,
fixerit aeripedem cervam licet, aut Erymanthi
pacarit nemora, et Lernam tremefecerit arcu;
nec, qui pampineis victor iuga flectit habenis,
Liber, agens celso Nysae de vertice tigris. 805
Et dubitamus adhuc virtutem extendere factis,
aut metus Ausonia prohibet consistere terra?

The Roman kings and the heroes of the early republic are seen

'Quis procul ille autem ramis insignis olivae
sacra ferens? Nosco crinis incanaque menta
regis Romani, primum qui legibus urbem 810
fundabit, Curibus parvis et paupere terra
missus in imperium magnum. Cui deinde subibit,
otia qui rumpet patriae residesque movebit
Tullus in arma viros et iam desueta triumphis
agmina. Quem iuxta sequitur iactantior Ancus, 815
nunc quoque iam nimium gaudens popularibus auris.
Vis et Tarquinios reges, animamque superbam
ultoris Bruti, fascesque videre receptos?
Consulis imperium hic primus saevasque secures
accipiet, natosque pater nova bella moventis 820
ad poenam pulchra pro libertate vocabit—
infelix, utcumque ferent ea facta minores:
vincet amor patriae laudumque immensa cupido.
Quin Decios Drusosque procul saevumque securi
aspice Torquatum et referentem signa Camillum. 825

The spirits of Cæsar and Pompey come into view

'Illae autem, paribus quas fulgere cernis in armis,
concordes animae nunc et dum nocte premuntur,
heu quantum inter se bellum, si lumina vitae

attigerint, quantas acies stragemque ciebunt!
Aggeribus socer Alpinis atque arce Monoeci   830
descendens, gener adversis instructus Eoïs.
Ne, pueri, ne tanta animis adsuescite bella,

POMPEY

neu patriae validas in viscera vertite viris;
tuque prior, tu parce, genus qui ducis Olympo,
proice tela manu, sanguis meus! —   835

*Æneas sees other heroes of the republic and is told the
mission of Rome*

'Ille triumphata Capitolia ad alta Corintho
victor aget currum, caesis insignis Achivis.
Eruet ille Argos Agamemnoniasque Mycenas,
ipsumque Aeaciden, genus armipotentis Achilli,
ultus avos Troiae, templa et temerata Minervae.   840
Quis te, magne Cato, tacitum, aut te, Cosse, relinquat?

Quis Gracchi genus, aut geminos, duo fulmina belli,
Scipiadas, cladem Libyae, parvoque potentem
Fabricium vel te sulco, Serrane, serentem?
Quo fessum rapitis, Fabii? Tu Maximus ille es, 845
unus qui nobis cunctando restituis rem.
Excudent alii spirantia mollius aera,
credo equidem, vivos ducent de marmore voltus,
orabunt causas melius, caelique meatus
describent radio, et surgentia sidera dicent: 850
tu regere imperio populos, Romane, memento;
hae tibi erunt artes; pacique imponere morem,
parcere subiectis, et debellare superbos.'

Æneas sees the young Marcellus and hears of his sad fate

Sic pater Anchises, atque haec mirantibus addit:
'Aspice, ut insignis spoliis Marcellus opimis 855
ingreditur, victorque viros supereminet omnis!
Hic rem Romanam, magno turbante tumultu,
sistet, eques sternet Poenos Gallumque rebellem,
tertiaque arma patri suspendet capta Quirino.'
Atque hic Aeneas,—una namque ire videbat 860
egregium forma iuvenem et fulgentibus armis,
sed frons laeta parum, et deiecto lumina voltu:
'Quis, pater, ille, virum qui sic comitatur euntem?
Filius, anne aliquis magna de stirpe nepotum?
Qui strepitus circa comitum! Quantum instar in ipso! 865
Sed nox atra caput tristi circumvolat umbra.'
Tum pater Anchises lacrimis ingressus obortis:
'O gnate, ingentem luctum ne quaere tuorum;
ostendent terris hunc tantum fata, neque ultra
esse sinent. Nimium vobis Romana propago 870
visa potens, Superi, propria haec si dona fuissent.
Quantos ille virum magnam Mavortis ad urbem
campus aget gemitus, vel quae, Tiberine, videbis

funera, cum tumulum praeterlabere recentem!
Nec puer Iliaca quisquam de gente Latinos   875
in tantum spe tollet avos, nec Romula quondam
ullo se tantum tellus iactabit alumno.
Heu pietas, heu prisca fides, invictaque bello
dextera! Non illi se quisquam impune tulisset
obvius armato, seu cum pedes iret in hostem,   880
seu spumantis equi foderet calcaribus armos.
Heu, miserande puer, si qua fata aspera rumpas,
tu Marcellus eris. Manibus date lilia plenis,
purpureos spargam flores, animamque nepotis
his saltem accumulem donis, et fungar inani   885
munere.'—Sic tota passim regione vagantur
aëris in campis latis, atque omnia lustrant.
Quae postquam Anchises natum per singula duxit,
incenditque animum famae venientis amore,
exin bella viro memorat quae deinde gerenda,   890
Laurentisque docet populos urbemque Latini,
et quo quemque modo fugiatque feratque laborem.

Through the gates of sleep Æneas and the Sibyl return to the Upper World

Sunt geminae Somni portae, quarum altera fertur
cornea, qua veris facilis datur exitus umbris;
altera candenti perfecta nitens elephanto,   895
sed falsa ad caelum mittunt insomnia Manes.
His ubi tum natum Anchises unaque Sibyllam
prosequitur dictis, portaque emittit eburna,
ille viam secat ad navis sociosque revisit:
tum se ad Caietae recto fert litore portum.   900
Ancora de prora iacitur, stant litore puppes.

ÆNEAS AND THE SIBYL

SUMMARY OF THE ÆNEID,
BOOKS VII–XII

BOOK VII

ÆNEAS LANDS IN ITALY AND WAR BREAKS OUT WITH THE INHABITANTS

Leaving the harbor of Caieta, Æneas sails northward along the coast of Italy, passing so close to the realm of Circe the enchantress that he can hear the howls of the men whom she has transformed into wild beasts by her magic arts. Next morning his fleet enters the River Tiber, and the Trojans land on the bank.

At that time this region (Latium) was governed by an aged king, Latinus, whose wife was named Amata. They had but one child—a daughter, Lavinia, whom many princes sought in marriage. Chief among them was Turnus, the brave young king of the Rutulians, a neighboring tribe. He was favored by Queen Amata, but Latinus hesitated, for signs and omens had shown the purpose of the gods that Lavinia should marry some foreign hero, and this had also been plainly revealed by the voice of the god Faunus, father of King Latinus, speaking an oracle from his sacred grove. This oracle had become known throughout the neighboring cities by the time that Æneas landed.

Æneas and his companions prepare a scanty meal, using flat cakes for lack of plates. These cakes they afterwards eat, thus fulfilling the prophecy of the Harpy Celæno (iii. 245–257) that they should "devour their tables" before they could settle in Italy. Their wanderings, then, are finished, and next day they build and fortify a camp.

An embassy is sent to Latinus. He receives them well, tells them that he has heard that their ancestor Dardanus was of Italian origin, and asks what they desire. Ilioneus, in reply, requests the king's permission to settle in his realm. Latinus accepts their friendship and offers Lavinia to Æneas in marriage, according to the omens that assigned her a husband from a distant land.

Meantime Juno, angry at the failure of her efforts to keep the Trojans away from Italy, summons the Fury Allecto from the infernal regions and despatches her to stir up discord. Allecto drives Amata frantic and then visits Turnus, inciting him to make war upon the strangers.

While Turnus is calling the Rutulians to arms, Allecto visits the Trojans, and contrives that Iulus, while hunting, shall kill a pet stag, belonging to the daughter of King Latinus' chief herdsman. An affray follows, and the shepherds appeal to the king. Turnus urges Latinus to make war on the Trojans. He consents reluctantly, and shuts himself up in his house in despair. The gates of war in the Temple of Janus are opened by Juno.

The poet enumerates the Italian tribes that combine against Æneas and describes their chieftains. Among those who come to the aid of the Latins is the warlike Volscian maiden Camilla.

BOOK VIII

PREPARATIONS FOR WAR. ALLIANCE OF ÆNEAS WITH EVANDER. THE ARMS OF ÆNEAS

Turnus gives the signal for war. The chieftains muster their forces and send to Apulia to ask help from Diomedes, the Grecian hero, who had settled there since the end of the Trojan War. Father Tiber appears to Æneas in a dream, bids him be of good courage, and tells him to seek aid from Evander, an Arcadian, who had founded a city called Pallanteum on what was afterwards the site of Rome.

Next morning Evander suggests to Æneas an alliance with the Etruscans, who have revolted against Mezentius, their cruel king. Mezentius has taken refuge at the court of Turnus, and the Etruscans, eager to get him into their power, are awaiting a foreign leader foretold by one of their prophets. Evander himself is too old for warfare but offers his son Pallas to Æneas as companion and ally. Prompted by an omen from Venus, Æneas accepts, sends part of his followers back to the camp, and sets out for Etruria with Pallas and certain picked men.

When near the camp of the insurgent Etruscans, Æneas and his companions stop to rest in a grove, and Venus appears, bringing the arms which Vulcan has made. The shield is embossed with scenes from the future history of Rome, from the time of Romulus to the triumph of Augustus after the Battle of Actium.

BOOK IX

THE WAR WITH THE ITALIANS

Juno sends her messenger Iris to urge Turnus to attack the Trojans before Æneas returns. The Trojans see the dust of the approaching army and shut themselves up in camp as Æneas had ordered, though their impulse is to meet the foe in the open field. Turnus, astonished at their inaction, prepares to set fire to the ships, which are anchored by the side of the camp. His purpose is to induce the Trojans to come out of their shelter. The ships are saved by a miracle: Jupiter, at the prayer of Cybele, causes them to break their moorings and sail out into deep water, where they are transformed into nymphs.

Turnus, nothing daunted, addresses his troops, declaring that this prodigy is unfavorable to the Trojans, who cannot now escape. He stations guards to blockade the camp by land and draws off his army for a night's rest.

Nisus, a Trojan hero, proposes to his friend Euryalus to make their way through the besiegers' camp in the darkness and carry the news of the attack to Æneas. The Trojan commanders approve, and the two set out on their desperate attempt. They pass through the enemy's lines in safety. They slaughter many of their sleeping foes and take booty, but are surprised at the last moment by a troop of Latins who are on their way to join the besiegers. Nisus escapes, but, missing his companion, turns back to seek him, and both are killed, fighting bravely.

At dawn Turnus attacks the camp anew, and the Trojans recognize the heads of Nisus and Euryalus carried on spear-points. The mother of Euryalus laments his fall.

The camp is stoutly defended, and many fall on both sides. The Trojans make a sally. Turnus rushes in at the open gate and is shut in. Single-handed he almost causes a panic among the Trojans, but they rally and he is forced back. He escapes by swimming the Tiber.

BOOK X

THE BATTLE CONTINUES

Jupiter calls a council of the gods. "Why," he asks, "is this battle going on when I have forbidden war between the Italians and the Trojans?" Venus blames Turnus and his Rutulians; Juno retorts with spirit, and both goddesses have their partisans among the divinities. Jupiter decides that the fight must continue, but declares that the fates will find a way to be fulfilled in the outcome.

The battle still rages. The Rutulians strive to take the camp by storm, and the Trojans defend it with difficulty.

Meanwhile Æneas has formed an alliance with Tarchon, leader of the Etruscan insurgents, and, accompanied by him and other chiefs of Etruria, is sailing down the river in the night. He is met by the sea-nymphs—the transformed ships—and one of them, Cymodocea, warns him of the perilous situation of the camp and the danger to Ascanius.

Æneas reaches the camp at daybreak, but Turnus resists his landing. In the fight that follows, Pallas is slain and despoiled by Turnus, who proudly decks himself with the young hero's splendid girdle. Æneas rages in the conflict like the hundred-armed giant Ægæon when he attempted to scale the heavens and defied the thunderbolts of Jupiter. The siege of the Trojan camp is broken, and Ascanius makes a sally with his companions.

Juno beseeches Jupiter to allow her to save Turnus. He consents, but warns her that the destined result of the war cannot be changed. She sends a shade or phantom in the shape of Æneas. This Turnus pursues. It takes refuge in one of the ships. Turnus follows, but no sooner has he leapt on board than Juno unmoors the ship and he is swept away from the scene of the struggle, sorely against his will. Thrice Turnus tries to kill himself with his own sword, thrice to plunge into the river and swim back, but the goddess prevents.

Æneas wounds Mezentius, who is rescued by his son Lausus, but Lausus is slain. Mezentius returns to the fight to avenge his son and also meets his death at the hands of Æneas.

BOOK XI

A TRUCE FOR BURIAL OF THE DEAD. THE WAR RESUMED AFTER THE TRUCE

Æneas erects a trophy of the arms of Mezentius, encourages his men, and mourns for Pallas. The body of Pallas is carried to his father's city, escorted by a thousand soldiers.

Ambassadors arrive from King Latinus, asking for a truce for burial of the dead. Æneas grants their request. He declares that he has none

but friendly feelings toward the Latins, and that he should have preferred to decide his quarrel with Turnus by single combat. The envoys
admire the justice and moderation of Æneas and express their wish for
an alliance. The truce is to last for twelve days. Evander receives the
corpse of his son Pallas and laments his death. Both Trojans and Italians
build pyres near the Tiber, and the bodies of the slain are burned with
funeral rites.

There is mourning in the city of King Latinus. Drances, one of the
ambassadors who had been sent to ask for the truce, declares that
Turnus alone is to blame. Others take Turnus' part, and the influence
of Queen Amata works in his favor. In the midst of the tumult, the
envoys return from the city of Diomedes and bring word of his refusal
to join the Latins against Æneas. A council is held. Latinus wishes to
make peace. Drances, always an opponent of Turnus, advises that
Lavinia be given to Æneas in marriage, or, at all events, that Turnus
accept the challenge of Æneas to end the war by single combat. Turnus
replies with vigor: he is not afraid to meet Æneas man to man, but
urges the Latins not to give up the struggle.

In the midst of the debate, word comes that Æneas is advancing with
his host, the truce having expired. The Latins and Rutulians rush to
arms, and Turnus once more takes command. At the city gates he is
met by the warrior-maiden Camilla with her Volscian horsemen, who
offers to encounter the forces of Æneas while Turnus protects the city
with his infantry. He directs her to oppose the enemy's cavalry, who
have been sent ahead, while he himself lays an ambush for the main
body of Æneas' army in a mountain pass near-by.

The poet tells the story of Camilla. Her father Metabus, driven from
his Volscian kingdom when she was an infant, carried her in his arms.
In his flight he came to the river Amasenus, then in high flood. The
pursuers were close at hand. Tying the baby to the shaft of his spear,
he hurled the weapon to the farther bank, with a vow to Diana that
Camilla should be her maiden if her life were saved. The spear remained
fixed in the ground across the river, and Metabus swam the stream and
carried off his little daughter in triumph. Camilla was reared in the
forest and was trained in warfare from her early youth, refusing all
offers of marriage and remaining Diana's votaress. And now Diana,
seeing her about to fight with the Trojans, sends the nymph Opis to slay
with an arrow whoever shall harm the maiden, be it Trojan or Italian.

Meantime the Trojan and Etruscan cavalry approach. In the battle
that follows, Camilla performs heroic exploits, but is killed with a

javelin by Arruns, an Etruscan, who falls in his turn by the avenging arrow of Opis. The cavalry of Camilla and of the Rutulians are routed and take refuge in the city, but many are shut out in the confusion, and there is great slaughter.

Turnus, learning of the disaster, abandons his ambuscade and hastens to the town. Thus Æneas and the main body of his troops approach without opposition. Night comes on, and both Turnus and Æneas encamp outside the walls.

BOOK XII

END OF THE WAR. VICTORY OF ÆNEAS AND DEATH OF TURNUS

Turnus, seeing that the fortune of war has been unfavorable to the Italians, addresses King Latinus, offering to meet Æneas in single combat. Latinus begs him to renounce his claim to Lavinia and allow Æneas to marry her, since that is the manifest will of the gods ; but he refuses. Queen Amata beseeches Turnus to yield, but he insists on the combat. A solemn treaty is made : if Turnus is victorious, the Trojans shall give up the contest ; if Æneas conquers, he is to marry Lavinia, and Trojans and Latins shall form one people forever.

Turnus has a sister named Juturna, a water-nymph, who—fearing that her brother is no match for Æneas, and prompted by Juno, the inveterate foe of the Trojans—takes the form of an Italian warrior and urges the Rutulians to renew the fight. A sign from heaven, caused by Juturna, adds to their zeal: an eagle seizes a swan in his talons, but, pursued by the rest of the flock, drops his prey and takes to flight. Tolumnius, a Rutulian augur, interprets this as a favorable omen and violates the treaty by throwing a spear, which strikes down one of Æneas' allies.

Both sides rush to arms. Æneas does his best to restore peace, but is wounded by an arrow from an unknown hand and forced to retire. During his absence Turnus works havoc among the Trojans, none of whom can stand against him. The surgeon Iapyx tries in vain to extract the arrow, and a complete rout seems imminent. But Venus, concealed in a cloud, heals the wound, and Æneas returns to the fray, followed by a host of heroes. The Rutulians are put to flight. Æneas seeks everywhere for Turnus, but Juturna takes the shape of Turnus' charioteer, Metiscus, and always guides his horses in some other direction. At length Æneas resolves to storm the city.

Queen Amata, terrified by the assault on the town, and believing that Turnus has been killed, hangs herself in despair. A wounded horseman makes his way through the host and summons Turnus to the aid of the city, which is about to fall into the hands of the Trojans. Turnus leaps from his chariot and forces his way through the combatants to the place where Æneas is attacking the wall. Æneas turns to meet him, and both armies cease fighting as the two leaders join at last in single combat.

Jupiter bids Juno give up her enmity to the Trojans. She consents, on condition that the Trojan race shall be absorbed in that of the Latins.

Turnus is struck down. Æneas is moved to spare his life, but he sees the belt of the slain Pallas, which Turnus is wearing, and he slays him in wrath and grief as an atoning sacrifice for Pallas' death.

II

SELECTIONS FROM OVID AND OTHER LATIN POETS

ORPHEUS AND THE BEASTS

FROM A POMPEIAN WALL PAINTING

INTRODUCTION

OVID'S LIFE

OVID (*Publius Ovidius Naso*) was born in 43 B.C. at Sulmo (now Sulmona) in Central Italy. The family was wealthy and had for generations belonged to the Equestrian Order. Like Virgil, Ovid was designed for the legal profession; and, with that in view, he received a thorough training in rhetoric and oratory at Rome and, as part of his education, visited Athens and Asia Minor. Unlike Virgil, however, Ovid did not immediately abandon a professional career : he practised law in Rome and held a number of judicial offices. But he was too rich and too easy-going to be politically ambitious, and he found society and literature more to his taste than the courts. We are told that he was a " good speaker " (*bonus declamator*), but that he " disliked argument."

Ovid at Rome. Ovid soon became a prime favorite in the brilliant and dissolute society of his time. He was witty and accomplished, his fortune was ample, and he was by nature amiable and generous, appreciative of merit in others, and free from jealousy and pettiness. Though fond of ease and pleasure, there is no reason to believe that he was given to dissipation. He had an unrivalled talent for fluent, elegant, and melodious expression in verse. " His oratory," it is said, " was like a prose song," and he himself tells us that " whatever he undertook to say, took form in verse " — *Quidquid tentabam dicere versus erat.* He had published several works and was in the full tide of literary and social success when suddenly, at the age of fifty (A.D. 8), he was banished by the emperor, Augustus.

Banishment. The alleged reason for Ovid's banishment was the immorality of one of his works, but this must have been a mere pretext. The poem in question (*Ars Amatoria*) had been before the public for about ten years. Ovid himself mentions (besides the poem) some " error " on his own part. This word *error* is intentionally ambiguous; but Ovid insists, again and again, that he had not been

237

guilty of any crime (*scelus*), though he admits that the emperor was justly offended. Probably the poet was somehow involved in a scandal affecting the imperial family. No evidence is available, however, and the whole affair must always remain a mystery.

Place of exile. The place to which Ovid was banished was Tomis or Tomi, an insignificant port in Mœsia on the Black Sea (*Pontus Euxinus*) near the modern Kustendje. He was not an exile (*exsul*) in the full Roman sense of the term, for he was allowed to retain his property. Thus he cannot have suffered actual hardship. Still, his situation was disagreeable enough. Rome was to Ovid what Paris is to a Parisian. He was separated from his wife and daughter, from his literary and personal friends, who were many, and from all that made life worth living to a man of his tastes and habits. The climate seemed to him unendurably harsh and cold, and the rude inhabitants of the district were a poor substitute for the aristocratic society of the metropolis. The townsfolk of Tomis were largely Getæ, with some intermixture of the descendants of Greek colonists. Outside the walls, the country was swept clean by periodical raids of the native barbarians, whose "poisoned darts" were especially feared. These bands, indeed, sometimes attacked the town itself.

Life at Tomis. Neither by nature nor by training was Ovid enabled to bear adversity with fortitude. He poured forth constant laments in verse, with humble petitions for pardon and restoration, or at least for a less disagreeable place of exile. His complaints often sound unmanly to us, and his flattery of Augustus seems downright slavish. In that regard, however, one should make allowance for the manners of an age when even Virgil had not scrupled to style the emperor the offspring of the gods (*Æneid*, vi. 792). Though Ovid's spirit was broken, his temper was not soured. He made friends with his Getic neighbors, learned to speak and write their language, and even composed a Getic poem in praise of Augustus, which is unfortunately lost.

Death of Ovid. Ovid had lived in banishment between five and six years when Augustus died (A.D. 14). There is some reason to believe that he was beginning to relent. At least, Ovid thought so, and he continued his appeals to the succeeding emperor, Tiberius. But all was in vain, and Ovid died at Tomis A.D. 17 or 18 and was buried near-by.

OVID'S WORKS

The Metamorphoses. Ovid's masterpiece, the *Metamorphoses*, extends to fifteen books. It had occupied his leisure for some years before his exile, and it was substantially complete, though lacking a final revision, when disaster overtook him. In his despair, he burnt the manuscript just before setting out for Tomis, but other copies were in existence.

Plan of the Metamorphoses. The design of the poem is to tell of *Transformations* — of "forms changed into new bodies" — in an unbroken narrative from the Creation to the time of the author.

> In nova fert animus mutatas dicere formas
> corpora. Di, coeptis (nam vos mutastis et illas)
> adspirate meis, primaque ab origine mundi
> ad mea perpetuum deducite tempora carmen!

He begins, accordingly, with primeval Chaos and the moulding of the universe out of the four elements, describes the Four Ages (of Gold, Silver, Bronze, and Iron), and the Destruction of the Giants, the Deluge, and the repeopling of the earth. Then, one after another, woven into a continuous narrative with marvellous ease and skill, Ovid tells scores of the best stories of Greek mythology — grave and gay, romantic and tragic, in infinite variety. In the fourteenth book he passes over to the myths of Italy, and in the fifteenth he closes the series with the Apotheosis of Julius Cæsar, whose soul ascends to heaven in the shape of a comet. He concludes with a justifiable expression of confidence in his own literary immortality: "And now I have finished a work which neither Jove's wrath nor fire, neither iron nor devouring time, can ever destroy. . . . Throughout the conquered earth, as far as the dominion of Rome extends, I shall be read by the people and shall live through all ages in fame."

> Iamque opus exegi quod nec Iovis ira nec ignis
> nec poterit ferrum nec edax abolere vetustas.
> Cum volet, illa dies, quae nil nisi corporis huius
> ius habet, incerti spatium mihi finiat aevi;
> parte tamen meliore mei super alta perennis
> astra ferar, nomenque erit indelebile nostrum.
> Quaque patet domitis Romana potentia terris,
> ore legar populi, perque omnia saecula fama,
> si quid habent veri vatum praesagia, vivam.

Style of the Metamorphoses. The style and metre of the Metamorphoses are easy, flexible, fluent, and expressive. Now and then the author's uncanny cleverness at turning phrases may run away with him for a line or two, but even in such cases the cleverness is undeniable, and we should beware of taking the poet too seriously. Matter and manner are well suited to each other. The variety of expression is marvellous and matches the variety of subject and of treatment. There is no suggestion of monotony. Subtle and delicate touches in description and narration abound. The characters stand out clearly. The scenery is vivid. The zest of the author never fails and the reader's interest never flags.

Object of the Metamorphoses. The object of the Metamorphoses is that of all good story-telling — *to entertain.* And there is no more entertaining book in the world, just as Ovid has no superior as a story-teller. In the opinion of Dryden — the most competent and least prejudiced of critics — he divides the palm with Chaucer alone. The Metamorphoses is the world's Wonder Book. It has enjoyed an uninterrupted and well-deserved popularity from the moment of its publication to the present day.

OVID'S OTHER WORKS

Besides the Metamorphoses, Ovid wrote the following poems:

Amores, three books of love elegies; *De Medicamine Faciei*, "On the Treatment of the Complexion," a poem on cosmetics; *Heroides*, "The Heroines," a collection of letters in verse, most of them supposed to be written by Penelope, Dido, Medea, and other ladies of the heroic age to their faithless or absent lovers or husbands; *Ars Amatoria*, "The Art of Love," and *Remedia Amoris*, "Remedies for Love," two mock didactic poems; *Medea*, a tragedy (lost); *Fasti*, "The Calendar," an account of the festivals, etc., of the Roman year, arranged by months (planned for twelve books, but only half finished); *Tristia*, "Sorrows," in five books, and *Epistulae ex Ponto*, "Letters from Pontus," in four, — both written in exile, — consisting of laments, petitions to the emperor, messages to his wife and friends at Rome, etc.; *Ibis*, a fierce attack on some enemy at Rome; *Halieutica*, "Fishing," a fragmentary didactic poem; lost poems in honor of Augustus and Tiberius, one of them in the Getic language.

CATULLUS

Catullus (*C. Valerius Catullus*) was born about 84 B.C. at Verona. His family was well-to-do, and, though he occasionally complains of an empty purse, we are not to suppose that he was ever in serious difficulties in this regard. At all events, he possessed a residence on the lovely promontory of Sirmio and an estate near Tibur, and he was the owner of a fast yacht which he celebrates in one of his most delightful poems. He went to Rome in early manhood and, like Ovid, played a lively part in the gay society of the metropolis. Near the end of his life he visited Bithynia in the train of the prætor Memmius, probably in the hope of improving his fortunes, but a year's experience with this provincial governor was quite enough, and he was glad to return to his home at Sirmio. He died soon after, when about thirty years of age, in or about the year 54 B. C.

Catullus is regarded as the greatest of Roman lyric poets. Though he wrote under the influence of the Greeks of the Alexandrian school, he shows marked originality. He has left us a collection of a hundred and sixteen poems — most of them very short — many of them the vivid expression (serious or sportive) of emotions of the moment. We have love lyrics, affectionate or humorous addresses to friends, satirical epigrams (often frankly abusive, though the abuse is not always to be taken seriously), and "occasional poems" in great variety. His love poems, addressed to Lesbia (who is thought to have been really the beautiful and dissolute Clodia, sister of Clodius the demagogue) appear to be the genuine record of an unhappy passion. Larger pieces are two marriage odes ; *Attis*, which deals with the orgies of Cybele ; and *The Marriage of Peleus and Thetis* (408 lines), which introduces the episode of Ariadne and Theseus with Ariadne's Lament.

HORACE

Horace (*Q. Horatius Flaccus*) was born on December 8, 65 B.C., at Venusia (now Venosa) on the Apulian border. His father had been a slave but had been freed before Horace was born, and, like many freedmen (*libertini*), enjoyed a respectable position in society, though he was neither rich nor distinguished. He gave his clever son every possible advantage, taking him to Rome at about the age of twelve and attending carefully to his education and behavior. In his eighteenth year — his father having died in the meantime — Horace went to Athens (as students now visit a foreign university) to finish his training in literature and philosophy.

Civil war broke out on the assassination of Julius Cæsar in 44 B.C., and Horace became an officer in the Republican army of Brutus. Two years later, the Republican cause collapsed at the Battle of Philippi. Horace fled from the field, as he tells us himself, but there is no evidence that he played a coward's part. The victory of Octavius (afterwards known as Augustus) and Antony was decisive, and Horace merely shared in the general rout. He made his peace with the victors and returned to Rome, a ruined man, for his inherited estate at Venusia was confiscated. He obtained a small office, however, and managed to live on the income until his talents attracted the attention of Mæcenas, one of Octavius's ministers and a generous patron of literature. Mæcenas presented him with a farm in the Sabine territory, which, with occasional gifts, enabled him to live comfortably thereafter. He often visited Rome and soon came to enjoy the favor of the Emperor Augustus. The poets Virgil and Tibullus were among his personal friends. He died suddenly in November, 8 B. C.

The chief works of Horace are his *Odes*, his *Satires*, and his *Epistles*. His *Odes*, which follow the best Greek models, reach a high degree of perfection as works of art, though they can hardly claim to be the expression of a master spirit in lyric poetry. His *Satires* are far more original. These concern themselves rather with the follies and weaknesses than with the sins of mankind. His aim, he tells us, is to correct men's foibles by humorous and friendly raillery. His subjects are discontent, vulgar display, avarice, legacy-hunting, and so on; and he does not spare himself in his criticism of his neighbors. Some of the pieces are not satire at all in our modern sense. As a whole the collection has been well compared to what we call "the comedy of manners." Horace shows himself throughout a keen observer of social conditions, and he writes with amazing vivacity, wit, humor, and urbanity.

In the *Epistles*, Horace's masterpiece, these qualities are even more remarkable. These poems deal, like the *Satires*, with the manners of the time, and present a philosophy of life which is marked by common sense and practical wisdom. Some of them deal with literature, and here Horace takes high rank as a literary critic. The *Satires* and *Epistles* have exercised a powerful influence upon English authors. This is especially evident in the eighteenth century, and most of all in the *Imitations of Horace*, by Alexander Pope.

METRE

1. A trochee consists of a long accented syllable followed by a short unaccented syllable, as **rḗgĭs**.

2. An iambus consists of a short unaccented syllable followed by a long accented syllable, as **fĕrṓ-cis**.

3. Substitutes for the trochee are the irrational spondee ($\angle$ >) and the cyclic dactyl ($\overset{\frown}{\angle}\cup\cup$).

The irrational spondee ($\angle$ > or > $\angle$) consists of two long syllables, but occupies only the time of one long and one short syllable. The symbol > denotes a long syllable shortened.

The cyclic dactyl ($\overset{\frown}{\angle}\cup\cup$) consists of one long and two short syllables, but occupies only the time of one long and one short syllable.

Thus each of these two feet is equivalent in time to a trochee, and the irrational spondee (in the form > $\angle$) may be equivalent to an iambus ($\cup$ $\angle$).

4. A single long syllable may be so prolonged as to occupy the time of one long and one short syllable. Such prolongation is indicated by the symbol $\llcorner$.

5. One or more syllables placed before the proper beginning of the measure are called an *anacrusis* (that is, a prelude).

6. A verse lacking a syllable at the end is called *catalectic*, that is, having a pause to fill the measure. Such a pause may be represented by the sign $\wedge$.

7. Four of the extracts from Catullus (iii, xiii, xlvi, xlix) are in *hendecasyllabics* (that is, verses of eleven syllables). There are five feet. The movement is trochaic. Thus (iii),

$$\underset{\text{Lū-gē-t}^{e},}{\angle \quad >} \Big| \underset{\text{Ō Ve-ne}}{\overset{\frown}{\angle}\cup\cup} \Big| \underset{\text{rēs}}{\angle} \quad \underset{\text{Cu}}{\cup} \Big| \underset{\text{pī-di}}{\angle\cup} \Big| \underset{\text{nēs-que.}}{\angle \quad \cup}$$

The first foot is usually an irrational spondee ($\angle$ >), equivalent to a trochee ($\angle$ $\cup$), but may be a regular trochee ($\angle$ $\cup$, as in iii. **7**, **ipsă**) or an iambus (‿ _́, as in iii. 17, **tuā**). The second foot is a cyclic dactyl (‿́‿ ‿), equivalent in time to a trochee. The third, fourth, and fifth feet are trochees. The last syllable in the verse may be long in itself (as in iii. 3), but is treated as short (*syllaba anceps*).

This metre is also called *Phalæcean*.

The general effect of hendecasyllabic verse has been imitated in English by Tennyson :

> Ó you | chórus of | índo|lént re|víewers.
>
> . . . . . .
>
> Lóok, I | cóme to the | tést, a | tíny | póem,
> Áll com|pósed in a | métre | óf Ca|túllus.

8. Catullus, iv, is in the *iambic trimeter*. Every verse consists of two measures, each consisting of two iambi. Thus,

$$\text{‿ }_́\text{ ‿ }_́\text{|‿ } \| \text{ }_́\text{ ‿}_́\text{|‿ }_́\text{ ‿ }_́$$
Pha-sel-lus il|le ‖ quem vi-dē|tis ho-spi-tēs.

The last syllable may, of course, be short (*syllaba anceps*).

9. Catullus, xxxi, is in the so-called *choliambic* verse. Thus,

$$> \ \vdots \ _́\text{‿}|_́ > \ | \ _́ \text{‿} \ | _́\text{‿}|_́ \ _́ \ \text{‿}$$
Pae-nᵉ ⋮ īn-su|lā-rum, | Sir-miᵒ, | īn-su|lā|rum-que.

The movement is trochaic with anacrusis. The anacrusis may consist of a short syllable (‿) or of a long syllable shortened (>). Note the irrational spondee (_́ >), equivalent to a trochee, in the second foot, and the prolonged long syllable (L_́), equivalent to a trochee, in the fifth foot. The second foot may be a trochee, as in *v.* 8.

10. Three of the extracts from Horace (i. 2, i. 22, and ii. 10) are in the *Sapphic* stanza. Thus (i. 2),

$$_́ \text{‿}|_́ >|_́\!\!\!\!\text{‿} \text{‿}|_́ \text{‿}|L_́|_́ \wedge$$
Iam sa|tis ter|rīs ‖ ni-vis | at-que | dī|rae

$$_́ \text{‿}|_́ >|_́\!\!\!\!\text{‿} \text{‿}|_́ \text{‿}|L_́|\overset{\smile}{\text{‿}} \wedge$$
gran-di|nis mī|sit ‖ pa-ter, | et ru|ben|te

$$_́ \text{‿}|_́ >|_́\!\!\!\!\text{‿} \text{‿}|_́ \text{‿} \ | L_́|_́ \wedge$$
dex-te|rā sa|crās ‖ ia-cu|lā-tus | ar|cīs

$$_́\!\!\!\!\text{‿} \text{‿} \ | _́ \text{‿}$$
ter-ru-it | ur-bem.

The first three verses are alike. Each consists of six feet in a trochaic movement. Note the irrational spondee ($\perp$ >) in the second foot, the cyclic dactyl ($\overset{\frown}{\perp}\smile \smile$) in the third foot, and the prolonged monosyllable ($\llcorner\perp$) in the fifth. These three verses are catalectic.

The fourth verse consists of a cyclic dactyl followed by a trochee.

The last syllable of each verse may be either long or short (*syllaba anceps*).

11. Three of the extracts from Horace (i. 34, iii. 2, and iii. 5) are in the *Alcaic* stanza. Thus (i. 34),

$$> \;\vdots\; \perp \;\smile \mid \perp \; > \;\Vert\; \overset{\frown}{\smile} \smile \mid \perp \;\smile \mid \; \perp \;\wedge$$
Par : cus de | ō-rum ‖ cul-tor et | in-fre | quēns,

$$> \vdots \perp \smile \mid \perp \; > \; \Vert \; \overset{\frown}{\smile} \smile \mid \perp \smile \mid \perp \; \wedge$$
in : sā-ni | en-tis ‖ dum sa-pi | en-ti | ae

$$> \;\vdots\; \perp \;\smile \mid \perp \; > \mid \perp \;\smile \mid \perp \;\smile$$
cōn : sul-tus | er-rō, | nunc re | tror-sum

$$\overset{\frown}{\smile} \smile \mid \overset{\frown}{}\smile \; \smile \mid \perp \smile \mid \perp \; —$$
vē-la da | re at-que i-te | rā-re | cur-sūs.

The first and the second verse begin with a monosyllabic anacrusis (which may be a short syllable or a long syllable shortened) and continue with five feet in a trochaic movement. Note the irrational spondee ($\perp$ >) in the second foot and the cyclic dactyl ($\overset{\frown}{\perp}\smile \smile$) in the third. The final foot is an incomplete trochee. Thus the verse is catalectic. The final syllable may be short in itself (as in i. 34. 9), but counts as long (*syllaba anceps*).

The third verse begins, like the first two, with anacrusis, and continues with four feet in a trochaic movement. Note the irrational spondee ($\perp$ >) in the second foot.

The fourth verse consists of two cyclic dactyls ($\overset{\frown}{\smile}\smile$) and two trochees ($\perp \smile$). The final syllable may be either long or short, but counts as short (*syllaba anceps*).

12. Two of the extracts from Horace (i. 14 and iii. 13) are in the *Third Asclepiadean* stanza. Thus (i. 14),

$$\perp \; > \mid \overset{\frown}{\smile} \smile \mid \llcorner\perp \; \Vert \; \overset{\frown}{\smile} \smile \mid \perp \;\smile \mid \perp \; \wedge$$
Ō nā | vis, re-fe | rent ‖ in ma-re | tē no | vī

$$\perp \; > \mid \overset{\frown}{\smile} \smile \mid \llcorner\perp \; \Vert \; \overset{\frown}{\smile} \smile \mid \perp \;\smile \mid \perp \; \wedge$$
fluc-tūs ! | Ō quid a | gis? ‖ For-ti-ter | oc-cu | pā

$$\acute{} \; > \;\Big|\; \overline{\acute{}\smile}\;\smile\Big|\underline{}\acute{}\;\Big|\;\underline{\smallsmile}\;\wedge$$
por-tum! | Nōn-ne vi|dēs | ut

$$\acute{} \; > \;\Big|\; \overline{\acute{}\smile}\;\smile\Big|\underline{}\acute{}\smile\Big|\underline{\smallsmile}\;\wedge$$
nū-dum | rē-mi-gi|ō la|tus.

The first and the second verse consist of six feet in a trochaic movement. In the third foot one long syllable is prolonged (⌐́) so as to occupy the time of one long and one short (´ ⌣). Note the cyclic dactyls (⌢́ ⌣) in the second and the fourth foot   The verses are catalectic.

The third verse consists of four feet in a trochaic movement. Note the prolonged syllable in the third foot (⌐́). The verse is catalectic.

The fourth verse (also catalectic) consists of four feet in a trochaic movement. Note the cyclic dactyl (⌢́ ⌣) in the second foot.

The last syllable of every verse is counted as long, even if it is short in itself (*syllaba anceps*).

13. One of the extracts from Horace (ii. 18) alternates a catalectic verse consisting of two trochaic measures (each consisting of two trochaic feet) with a verse consisting of three iambic measures (each consisting of two iambic feet). Thus,

$$\underline{} \;\smile\; \acute{} \;\smile\;\Big|\; \acute{} \;\smile\; \underline{\smallsmile} \;\wedge$$
Nōn e-bur ne-qu^e | au-re-um

$$\smile\; \acute{} \;\smile\; \acute{}\Big|\smile\;\Big\|\; \acute{} \;\smile\; \acute{} \;\Big|\smile\underline{}\acute{}\;\underline{\smallsmile}$$
me-ā re-nī|det ‖ in do-mō | la-cū-nar.

In the first verse, the last trochee is incomplete, consisting of a single syllable. This, though either long or short in itself, counts as long (*syllaba anceps*).

In the second verse note that the last measure (equivalent to two iambi) consists of a short syllable, followed by a prolonged long syllable (⌐́ equivalent to ´ ⌣) and by a syllable which may be either long or short but is scanned as long (*syllaba anceps*). The first iambus may be replaced by an irrational spondee (> ´), as in *vv.* 6, 34. 1.

This second verse may be scanned as catalectic trochaic with anacrusis. Thus,

$$\smile\;\vdots\;\acute{}\smile\;\acute{}\;\smile\;\Big\|\;\acute{}\;\smile\;\acute{}\;\smile\Big|\underline{}\acute{}\;\underline{\smallsmile}\;\wedge$$
me:ā re-nī-det ‖ in do-mō la|cū-nar.

PYRAMUS AND THISBE

Pyramus and Thisbe, who live at Babylon in adjacent houses, fall in love, but their parents forbid their marriage. They discover a cleft in the wall between the houses and through this exchange their vows. At last they arrange to meet at the tomb of Ninus, outside the city. Thisbe arrives first, but is frightened by a lioness and hides in a cave near-by. She drops her mantle, which is torn by the lioness. Pyramus finds it stained with blood, and, thinking that Thisbe has been devoured, kills himself. Thisbe returns and kills herself with Pyramus' sword (*Metamorphoses*, iv. 55–166). See Gayley, *Classic Myths*, pp. 147–149.

The story of Pyramus and Thisbe is retold by Chaucer in *The Legend of Good Women* and forms the plot of the play presented before Theseus by the Athenian artisans in *A Midsummer Night's Dream*.

PYRAMUS et Thisbe, iuvenum pulcherrimus alter,
altera quas oriens habuit praelata puellis,   56
contiguas tenuere domos, ubi dicitur altam
coctilibus muris cinxisse Semiramis urbem.
Notitiam primosque gradus vicinia fecit;
tempore crevit amor. Taedae quoque iure coissent,   60
sed vetuere patres: quod non potuere vetare,
ex aequo captis ardebant mentibus ambo.
Conscius omnis abest: nutu signisque loquuntur;
quoque magis tegitur, tectus magis aestuat ignis.
Fissus erat tenui rima, quam duxerat olim   65
cum fieret, paries domui communis utrique.
Id vitium nulli per saecula longa notatum—
quid non sentit amor?—primi vidistis amantes,
et vocis fecistis iter; tutaeque per illud
murmure blanditiae minimo transire solebant.   70
Saepe, ubi constiterant hinc Thisbe, Pyramus illinc,
inque vices fuerat captatus anhelitus oris,

'Invide,' dicebant, 'paries, quid amantibus obstas?
Quantum erat, ut sineres toto nos corpore iungi,
aut, hoc si nimium, vel ad oscula danda pateres?   75
Nec sumus ingrati: tibi nos debere fatemur
quod datus est verbis ad amicas transitus aures.'
Talia diversa nequiquam sede locuti,
sub noctem dixere 'Vale,' partique dedere
oscula quisque suae non pervenientia contra.   80
    Postera nocturnos aurora removerat ignes,
solque pruinosas radiis siccaverat herbas:
ad solitum coiere locum. Tum murmure parvo
multa prius questi, statuunt ut nocte silenti
fallere custodes foribusque excedere temptent,   85
cumque domo exierint, urbis quoque tecta relinquant;
neve sit errandum lato spatiantibus arvo,
conveniant ad busta Nini lateantque sub umbra
arboris. Arbor ibi niveis uberrima pomis
ardua morus erat, gelido contermina fonti.   90
Pacta placent; et lux, tarde discedere visa,
praecipitatur aquis, et aquis nox exit ab isdem.
Callida per tenebras, versato cardine, Thisbe
egreditur fallitque suos, adopertaque vultum
pervenit ad tumulum dictaque sub arbore sedit.   95
Audacem faciebat amor. Venit ecce recenti
caede leaena boum spumantes oblita rictus,
depositura sitim vicini fontis in unda.
Quam procul ad lunae radios Babylonia Thisbe
vidit, et obscurum trepido pede fugit in antrum,   100
dumque fugit, tergo velamina lapsa reliquit.
Ut lea saeva sitim multa compescuit unda,
dum redit in silvas, inventos forte sine ipsa
ore cruentato tenues laniavit amictus.
    Serius egressus, vestigia vidit in alto   105
pulvere certa ferae totoque expalluit ore

Pyramus. Ut vero vestem quoque sanguine tinctam
repperit, 'Una duos,' inquit, 'nox perdet amantes;
e quibus illa fuit longa dignissima vita,
nostra nocens anima est. Ego te, miseranda, peremi,   110
in loca plena metus qui iussi nocte venires,
nec prior huc veni. Nostrum divellite corpus,
et scelerata fero consumite viscera morsu,
O quicumque sub hac habitatis rupe leones!
Sed timidi est optare necem.' Velamina Thisbes   115
tollit et ad pactae secum fert arboris umbram;
utque dedit notae lacrimas, dedit oscula vesti,
'Accipe nunc,' inquit, 'nostri quoque sanguinis haustus!'
Quoque erat accinctus, demisit in ilia ferrum;
nec mora, ferventi moriens e vulnere traxit   120
et iacuit resupinus humo. Cruor emicat alte,
non aliter quam cum vitiato fistula plumbo
scinditur, et tenui stridente foramine longas
eiaculatur aquas atque ictibus aëra rumpit.
Arborei fetus adspergine caedis in atram   125
vertuntur faciem, madefactaque sanguine radix
purpureo tingit pendentia mora colore.

Ecce, metu nondum posito, ne fallat amantem,
illa redit iuvenemque oculis animoque requirit,
quantaque vitarit narrare pericula gestit.   130
Utque locum et visa cognoscit in arbore formam,
sic facit incertam pomi color: haeret an haec sit.
Dum dubitat, tremebunda videt pulsare cruentum
membra solum, retroque pedem tulit, oraque buxo
pallidiora gerens exhorruit aequoris instar,   135
quod tremit, exigua cum summum stringitur aura.
Sed postquam remorata suos cognovit amores,
percutit indignos claro plangore lacertos,
et laniata comas amplexaque corpus amatum
vulnera supplevit lacrimis, fletumque cruori   140

miscuit, et gelidis in vultibus oscula figens,
'Pyrame,' clamavit, 'quis te mihi casus ademit?
Pyrame, responde! tua te carissima Thisbe
nominat: exaudi vultusque attolle iacentes!'
Ad nomen Thisbes oculos a morte gravatos   145
Pyramus erexit, visaque recondidit illa.
Quae postquam vestemque suam cognovit et ense
vidit ebur vacuum, 'Tua te manus,' inquit, 'amorque
perdidit, infelix! Est et mihi fortis in unum
hoc manus; est et amor: dabit hic in vulnera vires.   150
Persequar exstinctum, letique miserrima dicar
causa comesque tui. Quique a me morte revelli
heu sola poteras, poteris nec morte revelli.
Hoc tamen amborum verbis estote rogati,
O multum miseri, meus illiusque parentes,   155
ut quos certus amor, quos hora novissima iunxit,
componi tumulo non invideatis eodem.
At tu, quae ramis arbor miserabile corpus
nunc tegis unius, mox es tectura duorum,
signa tene caedis, pullosque et luctibus aptos   160
semper habe fetus, gemini monimenta cruoris.'
Dixit, et aptato pectus mucrone sub imum,
incubuit ferro, quod adhuc a caede tepebat.
Vota tamen tetigere deos, tetigere parentes;
nam color in pomo est, ubi permaturuit, ater,   165
quodque rogis superest, una requiescit in urna.

PERSEUS AND ANDROMEDA

Cassiopeia, the wife of the Æthiopian king Cepheus, had boasted that she was more beautiful than the sea-nymphs. As a punishment, a sea-monster had laid waste the coast region. To put an end to his ravages, Andromeda, the king's daughter, is bound to a rock on the shore (in obedience to an oracle of Ammon), to be devoured by the monster. Perseus slays the monster and wins Andromeda as his bride (*Metamorphoses*, iv. 662–763). See Gayley, *Classic Myths*, pp. 211–213.

CLAUSERAT Hippotades aeterno carcere ventos,
    admonitorque operum caelo clarissimus alto
    Lucifer ortus erat: pennis ligat ille resumptis
parte ab utraque pedes teloque accingitur unco,   665
et liquidum motis talaribus aëra findit.
Gentibus innumeris circumque infraque relictis,
Aethiopum populos Cepheaque conspicit arva.
Illic immeritam maternae pendere linguae
Andromedan poenas iniustus iusserat Hammon.   670
Quam simul ad duras religatam bracchia cautes
vidit Abantiades (nisi quod levis aura capillos
moverat, et tepido manabant lumina fletu,
marmoreum ratus esset opus), trahit inscius ignes,
et stupet, et visae correptus imagine formae   675
paene suas quatere est oblitus in aëre pennas.
Ut stetit, 'O,' dixit, 'non istis digna catenis,
sed quibus inter se cupidi iunguntur amantes,
pande requirenti nomen terraeque tuumque,
et cur vincla geras.' Primo silet illa nec audet   680
appellare virum virgo; manibusque modestos
celasset vultus, si non religata fuisset.
Lumina, quod potuit, lacrimis implevit obortis.
Saepius instanti, sua ne delicta fateri
nolle videretur, nomen terraeque suumque,   685
quantaque maternae fuerit fiducia formae,

indicat. Et, nondum memoratis omnibus, unda
insonuit, veniensque immenso belua ponto
imminet et latum sub pectore possidet aequor.
Conclamat virgo. Genitor lugubris et una   690
mater adest, ambo miseri, sed iustius illa;
nec secum auxilium, sed dignos tempore fletus
plangoremque ferunt, vinctoque in corpore adhaerent,
cum sic hospes ait: 'Lacrimarum longa manere
tempora vos poterunt; ad opem brevis hora ferendam est.
Hanc ego si peterem Perseus, Iove natus . . .,   696
Gorgonis anguicomae Perseus superator, et alis
aetherias ausus iactatis ire per auras,
praeferrer cunctis certe gener. Addere tantis   700
dotibus et meritum, faveant modo numina, tempto.
Ut mea sit, servata mea virtute, paciscor.'
Accipiunt legem (quis enim dubitaret?) et orant
promittuntque super regnum dotale parentes.

Ecce velut navis praefixo concita rostro   705
sulcat aquas, iuvenum sudantibus acta lacertis,
sic fera, dimotis impulsu pectoris undis,
tantum aberat scopulis quantum Balearica torto
funda potest plumbo medii transmittere caeli,
cum subito iuvenis, pedibus tellure repulsa,   710
arduus in nubes abiit. Ut in aequore summo
umbra viri visa est, visam fera saevit in umbram;
utque Iovis praepes, vacuo cum vidit in arvo
praebentem Phoebo liventia terga draconem,
occupat aversum, neu saeva retorqueat ora,   715
squamigeris avidos figit cervicibus ungues,
sic, celeri missus praeceps per inane volatu,
terga ferae pressit, dextroque frementis in armo
Inachides ferrum curvo tenus abdidit hamo.
Vulnere laesa gravi modo se sublimis in auras   720
attollit, modo subdit aquis, modo more ferocis

PERSEUS FREEING ANDROMEDA

versat apri quem turba canum circumsona terret.
Ille avidos morsus velocibus effugit alis;
quaque patet, nunc terga cavis super obsita conchis,
nunc laterum costas, nunc qua tenuissima cauda   725
desinit in piscem, falcato vulnerat ense.
Belua puniceo mixtos cum sanguine fluctus

MEDUSA

ore vomit: maduere graves adspergine pennae.
Nec bibulis ultra Perseus talaribus ausus
credere conspexit scopulum, qui vertice summo   730
stantibus exstat aquis, operitur ab aequore moto.
Nixus eo, rupisque tenens iuga prima sinistra,
ter quater exegit repetita per ilia ferrum.
Litora cum plausu clamor superasque deorum
implevere domos. Gaudent generumque salutant   735
auxiliumque domus servatoremque fatentur
Cassiope Cepheusque pater. Resoluta catenis
incedit virgo, pretiumque et causa laboris.

Ipse manus hausta victrices abluit unda;
anguiferumque caput dura ne laedat harena,   740
mollit humum foliis, natasque sub aequore virgas
sternit et imponit Phorcynidos ora Medusae.
Virga recens bibulaque etiam nunc viva medulla
vim rapuit monstri, tactuque induruit huius,
percepitque novum ramis et fronde rigorem.   745
At pelagi nymphae factum mirabile temptant
pluribus in virgis, et idem contingere gaudent,
seminaque ex illis iterant iactata per undas;
nunc quoque curaliis eadem natura remansit,
duritiam tacto capiant ut ab aëre, quodque   750
vimen in aequore erat, fiat super aequora saxum.

  Dis tribus ille focos totidem de caespite ponit,
laevum Mercurio, dextrum tibi, bellica virgo;
ara Iovis media est. Mactatur vacca Minervae,
alipedi vitulus, taurus tibi, summe deorum.   755
Protinus Andromedan et tanti praemia facti
indotata rapit. Taedas Hymenaeus Amorque
praecutiunt, largis satiantur odoribus ignes,
sertaque dependent tectis, et ubique lyraeque
tibiaque et cantus, animi felicia laeti   760
argumenta, sonant. Reseratis aurea valvis
atria tota patent, pulchroque instructa paratu
Cepheni proceres ineunt convivia regis.

DÆDALUS AND ICARUS

Minos, king of Crete, had employed Dædalus, a skilful Athenian, to construct the famous Labyrinth in which the Minotaur (afterwards killed by Theseus) was confined. To escape from Crete—since Minos would not let him go and had seized all the ships—Dædalus made wings for himself and his young son Icarus. As they flew through the sky, Icarus approached too near the sun, which melted the wax that fastened the feathers, and, falling into the sea, he was drowned (*Metamorphoses*, viii. 183–235). See Gayley, *Classic Myths*, pp. 246–248. For Theseus and the Minotaur see p. 301.

DAEDALUS interea, Creten longumque perosus
  exsilium tactusque loci natalis amore,
  clausus erat pelago. 'Terras licet,' inquit, 'et undas
obstruat, at caelum certe patet: ibimus illac.   186
Omnia possideat, non possidet aëra Minos.'
Dixit, et ignotas animum dimittit in artes,
naturamque novat. Nam ponit in ordine pennas,
a minima coeptas, longam breviore sequente,   190
ut clivo crevisse putes. Sic rustica quondam
fistula disparibus paulatim surgit avenis.
Tum lino medias et ceris adligat imas,
atque ita compositas parvo curvamine flectit,
ut veras imitetur aves. Puer Icarus una   195
stabat et, ignarus sua se tractare pericla,
ore renidenti modo quas vaga moverat aura
captabat plumas, flavam modo pollice ceram
mollibat, lusuque suo mirabile patris
impediebat opus. Postquam manus ultima coepto   200
imposita est, geminas opifex libravit in alas
ipse suum corpus, motaque pependit in aura.
  Instruit et natum, 'Medio'que 'ut limite curras,
Icare,' ait, 'moneo, ne, si demissior ibis,
unda gravet pennas, si celsior, ignis adurat.   205

Inter utrumque vola; nec te spectare Boöten
aut Helicen iubeo strictumque Orionis ensem.
Me duce carpe viam.' Pariter praecepta volandi
tradit et ignotas umeris accommodat alas.

DÆDALUS AT WORK

Inter opus monitusque genae maduere seniles,   21 ₦
et patriae tremuere manus. Dedit oscula nato
(non iterum repetenda) suo, pennisque levatus
ante volat comitique timet, velut ales, ab alto
quae teneram prolem produxit in aëra nido;
hortaturque sequi damnosasque erudit artes,   21ʃ
et movet ipse suas et nati respicit alas.
Hos aliquis, tremula dum captat harundine pisces,

aut pastor baculo stivave innixus arator,
vidit et obstipuit, quique aethera carpere possent
credidit esse deos. Et iam Iunonia laeva   220
parte Samos (fuerant Delosque Parosque relictae),
dextra Lebinthos erat fecundaque melle Calymne,
cum puer audaci coepit gaudere volatu,
deseruitque ducem, caelique cupidine tactus
altius egit iter. Rapidi vicinia solis   225
mollit odoratas, pennarum vincula, ceras.
Tabuerant cerae: nudos quatit ille lacertos,
remigioque carens non ullas percipit auras;
oraque caerulea patrium clamantia nomen
excipiuntur aqua, quae nomen traxit ab illo.   230
At pater infelix, nec iam pater, 'Icare,' dixit,
'Icare,' dixit, 'ubi es? qua te regione requiram?
Icare,' dicebat. Pennas adspexit in undis;
devovitque suas artes, corpusque sepulcro
condidit; et tellus a nomine dicta sepulti.   235

ORPHEUS AND EURYDICE

Orpheus, best of musicians, had married Eurydice, whom he tenderly loved. Soon after, Eurydice was bitten by a serpent and died. Orpheus descended to Hades, made his way into the presence of Pluto and Proserpine, king and queen of the World of Shades, and sang a song of petition, begging that his wife might be restored to him. His prayer was granted, on condition that he should not look back at Eurydice as she followed him on the path to the world of the living. When they had almost reached this world, Orpheus, in love and longing, stole one glance at his wife, and Eurydice vanished, never to return (*Metamorphoses*, x. 1–77). See Gayley, *Classic Myths*, pp. 165–168.

INDE per immensum, croceo velatus amictu,
    aethera digreditur Ciconumque Hymenaeus ad oras
    tendit, et Orphea nequiquam voce vocatur.
Adfuit ille quidem, sed nec sollemnia verba
nec laetos vultus nec felix attulit omen. 5
Fax quoque quam tenuit lacrimoso stridula fumo
usque fuit, nullosque invenit motibus ignes.
Exitus auspicio gravior. Nam nupta per herbas
dum nova Naïadum turba comitata vagatur,
occidit, in talum serpentis dente recepto. 10
    Quam satis ad superas postquam Rhodopeïus auras
deflevit vates, ne non temptaret et umbras,
ad Styga Taenaria est ausus descendere porta,
perque leves populos simulacraque functa sepulcro
Persephonen adiit inamoenaque regna tenentem 15
umbrarum dominum; pulsisque ad carmina nervis
sic ait: 'O positi sub terra numina mundi,
in quem reccidimus, quicquid mortale creamur!
si licet et, falsi positis ambagibus oris,
vera loqui sinitis, non huc, ut opaca viderem 20
Tartara, descendi, nec uti villosa colubris
terna Medusaei vincirem guttura monstri.

Causa viae est coniunx, in quam calcata venenum
vipera diffudit, crescentesque abstulit annos.
Posse pati volui, nec me temptasse negabo: 25
vicit Amor. Supera deus hic bene notus in ora est:
an sit et hic, dubito. Sed et hic tamen auguror esse;
famaque si veteris non est mentita rapinae,
vos quoque iunxit Amor. Per ego haec loca plena timoris,
per Chaos hoc ingens vastique silentia regni,   30
Eurydices, oro, properata retexite fata!
Omnia debemus vobis, paulumque morati,
serius aut citius sedem properamus ad unam.
Tendimus huc omnes, haec est domus ultima; vosque
humani generis longissima regna tenetis.   35
Haec quoque, cum iustos matura peregerit annos,
iuris erit vestri: pro munere poscimus usum.
Quod si fata negant veniam pro coniuge, certum est
nolle redire mihi: leto gaudete duorum.'

Talia dicentem nervosque ad verba moventem   40
exsangues flebant animae; nec Tantalus undam
captavit refugam, iacuitque Ixionis orbis,
nec carpsere iecur volucres, urnisque vacarunt
Belides, inque tuo sedisti, Sisyphe, saxo.
Tunc primum lacrimis victarum carmine fama est   45
Eumenidum maduisse genas. Nec regia coniunx
sustinet oranti, nec qui regit ima, negare;
Eurydicenque vocant. Umbras erat illa recentes
inter, et incessit passu de vulnere tardo.
Hanc simul et legem Rhodopeïus accipit Orpheus,   50
ne flectat retro sua lumina, donec Avernas
exierit valles: aut irrita dona futura.

Carpitur adclivis per muta silentia trames,
arduus, obscurus, caligine densus opaca.
Nec procul afuerunt telluris margine summae: 55
hic, ne deficeret metuens, avidusque videndi,

ORPHEUS AND EURYDICE

MERCURY, HERCULES, AND CERBERUS

flexit amans oculos—et protinus illa relapsa est.
Bracchiaque intendens prendique et prendere captans,
nil nisi cedentes infelix arripit auras.
Iamque iterum moriens non est de coniuge quicquam   60
questa suo: quid enim nisi se quereretur amatam?
supremumque vale, quod iam vix auribus ille
acciperet, dixit, revolutaque rursus eodem est.
    Non aliter stupuit gemina nece coniugis Orpheus
quam tria qui timidus, medio portante catenas,   65
colla canis vidit, quem non pavor ante reliquit
quam natura prior, saxo per corpus oborto;
quique in se crimen traxit voluitque videri
Olenos esse nocens; tuque, O confisa figurae,
infelix Lethaea, tuae, iunctissima quondam   70
pectora, nunc lapides, quos umida sustinet Ide.
    Orantem frustraque iterum transire volentem
portitor arcuerat. Septem tamen ille diebus
squalidus in ripa Cereris sine munere sedit:

cura dolorque animi lacrimaeque alimenta fuere.   75
Esse deos Erebi crudeles questus, in altam
se recipit Rhodopen pulsumque aquilonibus Haemum.

Virgil tells the story in his Georgics, iv. 454–527.

MAGNA luis commissa: tibi has miserabilis Orpheus
     haudquaquam ad meritum poenas, ni fata resistant,
     suscitat, et rapta graviter pro coniuge saevit.   456
Illa quidem, dum te fugeret per flumina praeceps,
immanem ante pedes hydrum moritura puella
servantem ripas alta non vidit in herba.
At chorus aequalis Dryadum clamore supremos   460
implerunt montis; flerunt Rhodopeïae arces
altaque Pangaea et Rhesi Mavortia tellus
atque Getae atque Hebrus et Actias Orithyia.
Ipse, cava solans aegrum testudine amorem,
te, dulcis coniunx, te solo in litore secum,   465
te veniente die, te decedente canebat.
Taenarias etiam fauces, alta ostia Ditis,
et caligantem nigra formidine lucum
ingressus, Manisque adiit regemque tremendum,
nesciaque humanis precibus mansuescere corda.   470
At cantu commotae Erebi de sedibus imis
umbrae ibant tenues simulacraque luce carentum,
quam multa in foliis avium se milia condunt
vesper ubi aut hibernus agit de montibus imber,—
matres atque viri defunctaque corpora vita   475
magnanimum heroum, pueri innuptaeque puellae
impositique rogis iuvenes ante ora parentum;
quos circum limus niger et deformis harundo
Cocyti tardaque palus inamabilis unda
alligat, et noviens Styx interfusa coercet.   480
Quin ipsae stupuere domus atque intima Leti

Tartara caeruleosque implexae crinibus anguis
Eumenides, tenuitque inhians tria Cerberus ora,
atque Ixionii vento rota constitit orbis.
Iamque pedem referens casus evaserat omnis, 485
redditaque Eurydice superas veniebat ad auras,
pone sequens (namque hanc dederat Proserpina legem),
cum subita incautum dementia cepit amantem,
ignoscenda quidem, scirent si ignoscere Manes:
restitit, Eurydicenque suam, iam luce sub ipsa, 490
immemor (heu!) victusque animi, respexit. Ibi omnis
effusus labor atque immitis rupta tyranni
foedera, terque fragor stagnis auditus Avernis.
Illa, 'Quis et me,' inquit, 'miseram et te perdidit, Orpheu,
quis tantus furor? En iterum crudelia retro 495
fata vocant, conditque natantia lumina somnus.
Iamque vale! Feror ingenti circumdata nocte,
invalidasque tibi tendens (heu non tua!) palmas.'
Dixit, et ex oculis subito, ceu fumus in auras
commixtus tenuis, fugit diversa, neque illum, 500
prensantem nequiquam umbras et multa volentem
dicere, praeterea vidit; nec portitor Orci
amplius obiectam passus transire paludem.
Quid faceret? Quo se rapta bis coniuge ferret?
Quo fletu Manis, qua numina voce moveret? 505
Illa quidem Stygia nabat iam frigida cymba.
   Septem illum totos perhibent ex ordine menses,
rupe sub aëria deserti ad Strymonis undam,
flevisse et gelidis haec evolvisse sub antris,
mulcentem tigris et agentem carmine quercus; 510
qualis populea maerens philomela sub umbra
amissos queritur fetus, quos durus arator
observans nido inplumis detraxit; at illa
flet noctem, ramoque sedens miserabile carmen
integrat, et maestis late loca questibus implet. 515

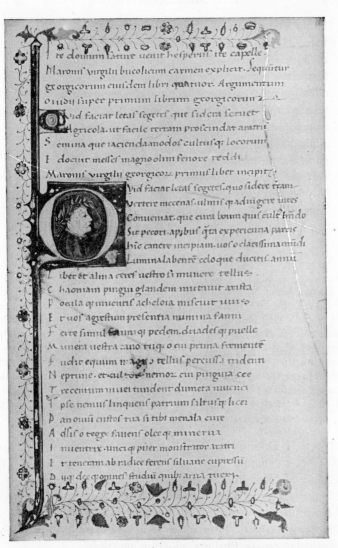

A MEDIÆVAL MANUSCRIPT OF VIRGIL

(Courtesy of George A. Plimpton)

Nulla Venus, non ulli animum flexere hymenaei.
Solus Hyperboreas glacies Tanaimque nivalem
arvaque Riphaeis numquam viduata pruinis
lustrabat, raptam Eurydicen atque inrita Ditis
dona querens; spretae Ciconum quo munere matres   520
inter sacra deum nocturnique orgia Bacchi
discerptum latos iuvenem sparsere per agros.
Tum quoque marmorea caput a cervice revulsum
gurgite cum medio portans Oeagrius Hebrus
volveret, 'Eurydicen' vox ipsa et frigida lingua,   525
'A miseram Eurydicen!' anima fugiente vocabat;
'Eurydicen' toto referebant flumine ripae.

MIDAS AND THE GOLDEN TOUCH

Silenus, foster father of Bacchus, is found by Phrygian peasants while he is wandering aimlessly about, and is conducted to their king Midas, an old friend. Midas entertains him hospitably and restores him to his foster son. In gratitude, Bacchus gives Midas his choice of gifts. Midas asks that whatever he touches may turn to gold. The boon proves a curse, for even his food and drink become gold under his magic touch. Midas prays for release. Bacchus bids him bathe in the source of the River Pactolus. The wondrous gift passes from the king to the river, which ever since has rolled down golden sands (*Metamorphoses*, xi. 85-145). See Gayley, *Classic Myths*, pp. 157-158.

NEC satis hoc Baccho est: ipsos quoque deserit agros
cumque choro meliore sui vineta Timoli   86
Pactolonque petit, quamvis non aureus illo
tempore nec caris erat invidiosus harenis.
Hunc adsueta cohors, Satyri Bacchaeque, frequentant,
at Silenus abest. Titubantem annisque meroque   90
ruricolae cepere Phryges, vinctumque coronis
ad regem duxere Midan, cui Thracius Orpheus
orgia tradiderat cum Cecropio Eumolpo.

MIDAS

Qui simul agnovit socium comitemque sacrorum,
hospitis adventu festum genialiter egit 95
per bis quinque dies et iunctas ordine noctes.
Et iam stellarum sublime coegerat agmen
Lucifer undecimus, Lydos cum laetus in agros
rex venit, et iuveni Silenum reddit alumno.
    Huic deus optandi gratum, sed inutile, fecit 100
muneris arbitrium, gaudens altore recepto.
Ille, male usurus donis, ait, 'Effice quicquid
corpore contigero fulvum vertatur in aurum.'
Adnuit optatis nocituraque munera solvit
Liber, et indoluit quod non meliora petisset. 105
    Laetus abit gaudetque malo Berecyntius heros;
pollicitique fidem tangendo singula temptat.
Vixque sibi credens, non alta fronde virentem
ilice detraxit virgam: virga aurea facta est.
Tollit humo saxum: saxum quoque palluit auro. 110
Contigit et glaebam: contactu glaeba potenti
massa fit. Arentes Cereris decerpsit aristas:
aurea messis erat. Demptum tenet arbore pomum:
Hesperidas donasse putes. Si postibus altis
admovit digitos, postes radiare videntur. 115
Ille etiam liquidis palmas ubi laverat undis,
unda fluens palmis Danaën eludere posset.
Vix spes ipse suas animo capit, aurea fingens
omnia. Gaudenti mensas posuere ministri
exstructas dapibus nec tostae frugis egentes. 120
Tum vero, sive ille sua Cerealia dextra
munera contigerat, Cerealia dona rigebant;
sive dapes avido convellere dente parabat,
lamina fulva dapes admoto dente premebat.
Miscuerat puris auctorem muneris undis: 125
fusile per rictus aurum fluitare videres.

Attonitus novitate mali, divesque miserque,
effugere optat opes, et quae modo voverat, odit.
Copia nulla famem relevat; sitis arida guttur
urit, et inviso meritus torquetur ab auro.   130
Ad caelumque manus et splendida bracchia tollens,
'Da veniam, Lenaee pater! Peccavimus,' inquit,
'sed miserere, precor, speciosoque eripe damno!'
Mite deum numen Bacchus peccasse fatentem
restituit; factique fide data munera solvit.   135
'Neve male optato maneas circumlitus auro,
vade,' ait, 'ad magnis vicinum Sardibus amnem,
perque iugum ripae labentibus obvius undis
carpe viam, donec venias ad fluminis ortus;
spumigeroque tuum fonti, qua plurimus exit,   140
subde caput corpusque simul, simul elue crimen.'
    Rex iussae succedit aquae. Vis aurea tinxit
flumen, et humano de corpore cessit in amnem.
Nunc quoque iam veteris percepto semine venae
arva rigent auro madidis pallentia glaebis.   145

THE DESTRUCTION OF CACUS

One of the tasks imposed on Hercules by Eurystheus was to capture the oxen of Geryon, a three-headed monster who dwelt in the island of Erythia off the coast of Spain. While returning with the cattle, Hercules spent a night in Latium, where Evander, an Arcadian, had established a city called Pallanteum on the site of what was afterwards Rome. There some of the cattle were stolen by Cacus, a fire-breathing giant who lived in a cave on the Aventine Mount. The story of the theft and of the destruction of Cacus by Hercules is found in both Virgil and Ovid. In Virgil (Æneid, viii. 190–267), Evander tells the tale to Æneas, as follows:

IAM primum saxis suspensam hanc aspice rupem,   190
   disiectae procul ut moles desertaque montis
   stat domus et scopuli ingentem traxere ruinam.
Hic spelunca fuit, vasto summota recessu,
semihominis Caci facies quam dira tenebat,
solis inaccessam radiis; semperque recenti   195
caede tepebat humus, foribusque adfixa superbis
ora virum tristi pendebant pallida tabo.
Huic monstro Volcanus erat pater: illius atros
ore vomens ignis magna se mole ferebat.
Attulit et nobis aliquando optantibus aetas   200
auxilium adventumque dei. Nam maximus ultor,
tergemini nece Geryonae spoliisque superbus,
Alcides aderat taurosque hac victor agebat
ingentis, vallemque boves amnemque tenebant.

At furiis Caci mens effera, ne quid inausum   205
aut intractatum scelerisve dolive fuisset,
quattuor a stabulis praestanti corpore tauros
avertit, totidem forma superante iuvencas;
atque hos, ne qua forent pedibus vestigia rectis,
cauda in speluncam tractos versisque viarum   210
indiciis raptos saxo occultabat opaco:
quaerenti nulla ad speluncam signa ferebant.

Interea, cum iam stabulis saturata moveret
Amphitryoniades armenta abitumque pararet,
discessu mugire boves atque omne querelis   215
impleri nemus et colles clamore relinqui.
Reddidit una boum vocem vastoque sub antro
mugiit et Caci spem custodita fefellit.
Hic vero Alcidae furiis exarserat atro
felle dolor: rapit arma manu nodisque gravatum   220
robur et aërii cursu petit ardua montis.

  Tum primum nostri Cacum videre timentem
turbatumque oculis: fugit ilicet ocior Euro
speluncamque petit, pedibus timor addidit alas.
Ut sese inclusit ruptisque immane catenis   225
deiecit saxum, ferro quod et arte paterna
pendebat, fultosque emuniit obice postis,
ecce furens animis aderat Tirynthius omnemque
accessum lustrans huc ora ferebat et illuc,
dentibus infrendens. Ter totum fervidus ira   230
lustrat Aventini montem, ter saxea temptat
limina nequiquam, ter fessus valle resedit.

  Stabat acuta silex, praecisis undique saxis
speluncae dorso insurgens, altissima visu,
dirarum nidis domus opportuna volucrum.   235
Hanc, ut prona iugo laevum incumbebat in amnem,
dexter in adversum nitens concussit et imis
avolsam solvit radicibus; inde repente
impulit, impulsu quo maximus intonat aether,
dissultant ripae refluitque exterritus amnis.   240
At specus et Caci detecta apparuit ingens
regia, et umbrosae penitus patuere cavernae:
non secus ac si qua penitus vi terra dehiscens
infernas reseret sedes et regna recludat
pallida, dis invisa, superque immane barathrum   245
cernatur, trepident immisso lumine Manes.

Ergo insperata deprensum luce repente
inclusumque cavo saxo atque insueta rudentem
desuper Alcides telis premit omniaque arma
advocat et ramis vastisque molaribus instat.   250
Ille autem, neque enim fuga iam super ulla pericli,
faucibus ingentem fumum (mirabile dictu)
evomit involvitque domum caligine caeca,

HERCULES AND THE LION

prospectum eripiens oculis, glomeratque sub antro
fumiferam noctem commixtis igne tenebris.   255
Non tulit Alcides animis seque ipse per ignem
praecipiti iecit saltu, qua plurimus undam
fumus agit nebulaque ingens specus aestuat atra.
Hic Cacum in tenebris incendia vana vomentem
corripit in nodum complexus et angit inhaerens   260
elisos oculos et siccum sanguine guttur.
    Panditur extemplo foribus domus atra revolsis,
abstractaeque boves abiurataeque rapinae

caelo ostenduntur, pedibusque informe cadaver
protrahitur. Nequeunt expleri corda tuendo 265
terribilis oculos, voltum villosaque saetis
pectora semiferi atque exstinctos faucibus ignis.

Ovid (*Fasti*, i. 543–582) gives this account of the death of
Cacus:

ECCE boves illuc Erytheïdas applicat heros
emensus longi claviger orbis iter.
Dumque huic hospitium domus est Tegeaea, vagantur
incustoditae lata per arva boves. 546
Mane erat: excussus somno Tirynthius actor
de numero tauros sentit abesse duos.
Nulla videt quaerens taciti vestigia furti.
Traxerat aversos Cacus in antra ferox, 550
Cacus, Aventinae timor atque infamia silvae,
non leve finitimis hospitibusque malum.
Dira viro facies, vires pro corpore, corpus
grande (pater monstri Mulciber huius erat),
proque domo longis spelunca recessibus ingens, 555
abdita, vix ipsis invenienda feris.
Ora super postes adfixaque bracchia pendent,
squalidaque humanis ossibus albet humus.
Servata male parte boum Iove natus abibat:
mugitum rauco furta dedere sono. 560
'Accipio revocamen,' ait, vocemque secutus
impia per silvas ultor ad antra venit.
Ille aditum fracti praestruxerat obice montis:
vix iuga movissent quinque bis illud opus.
Nititur hic umeris (caelum quoque sederat illis) 565
et vastum motu conlabefactat onus.
Quod simul eversum est, fragor aethera terruit ipsum,
ictaque subsedit pondere molis humus.

Prima movet Cacus collata proelia dextra
 remque ferox saxis stipitibusque gerit. 570
Quis ubi nil agitur, patrias male fortis ad artes
 confugit et flammas ore sonante vomit.
Quas quotiens proflat, spirare Typhoëa credas
 et rapidum Aetnaeo fulgur ab igne iaci.
Occupat Alcides, adductaque clava trinodis 575
 ter quater adverso sedit in ore viri.
Ille cadit mixtosque vomit cum sanguine fumos
 et lato moriens pectore plangit humum.
Immolat ex illis taurum tibi, Iuppiter, unum
 victor et Euandrum ruricolasque vocat 580
constituitque sibi, quae Maxima dicitur, aram,
 hic ubi pars urbis de bove nomen habet.

ARION AND THE DOLPHIN

Arion, a musician and lyric poet of Lesbos, sang so sweetly to the
accompaniment of his harp that, like Orpheus, he charmed birds and
beasts and running water. Once, as Ovid tells in the following verses
(*Fasti*, ii. 83–118), when threatened with death by sailors who wished
to rob him, Arion arrayed himself in his singing robes, played as it were
his swan-song, and leaped overboard. A dolphin, charmed by the music,
bore him to safety on its back.

QUOD mare non novit, quae nescit Ariona tellus?
 Carmine currentes ille tenebat aquas.
 Saepe sequens agnam lupus est a voce retentus;
 saepe avidum fugiens restitit agna lupum; 86
saepe canes leporesque umbra iacuere sub una,
 et stetit in saxo proxima cerva leae;
et sine lite loquax cum Palladis alite cornix
 sedit, et accipitri iuncta columba fuit. 90
Cynthia saepe tuis fertur, vocalis Arion,
 tamquam fraternis obstipuisse modis.

ARION AND THE DOLPHIN

Nomen Arionium Siculas impleverat urbes,
    captaque erat lyricis Ausonis ora sonis.
Inde, domum repetens, puppem conscendit Arion   95
    atque ita quaesitas arte ferebat opes.
Forsitan, infelix, ventos undasque timebas?
    At tibi nave tua tutius aequor erat.
Namque gubernator destricto constitit ense
    ceteraque armata conscia turba manu.   100
Quid tibi cum gladio? Dubiam rege, navita, puppem!
    Non haec sunt digitis arma tenenda tuis.
Ille metu vacuus, 'Mortem non deprecor,' inquit,
    'sed liceat sumpta pauca referre lyra.'
Dant veniam ridentque moram. Capit ille coronam,   105
    quae possit crines, Phoebe, decere tuos;
induerat Tyrio bis tinctam murice pallam;
    reddidit icta suos pollice chorda sonos,
flebilibus numeris veluti canentia dura
    traiectus pinna tempora cantat olor.   110
Protinus in medias ornatus desilit undas;
    spargitur impulsa caerula puppis aqua.
Inde—fide maius—tergo delphina recurvo
    se memorant oneri supposuisse novo.
Ille sedens citharamque tenet, pretiumque vehendi,   115
    cantat et aequoreas carmine mulcet aquas.
Di pia facta vident. Astris delphina recepit
    Iuppiter et stellas iussit habere novem.

JANUS

THE PATRIOTISM OF THE FABII

Once, when the Romans were at war, they had much trouble with the people of Veii, who made raids along the frontier. The noble family of the Fabii undertook to check the raiders, so that the Roman army might operate elsewhere; but they were caught in a trap set by the enemy, and were all slain. Ovid tells the story in the following verses (*Fasti*, ii. 195–242):

HAEC fuit illa dies in qua Veientibus armis   195
    ter centum Fabii, ter cecidere duo.
  Una domus vires et onus susceperat urbis:
  sumunt gentiles arma professa manus.
Egreditur castris miles generosus ab isdem,
  e quis dux fieri quilibet aptus erat.   200
Carmentis portae dextro est via proxima Iano:
  Ire per hanc noli, quisquis es: omen habet.
Illa fama refert Fabios exisse trecentos.
  Porta vacat culpa; sed tamen omen habet.

Ut celeri passus Cremeram tetigere rapacem,— 205
    turbidus hibernis ille fluebat aquis,—
castra loco ponunt; destrictis ensibus ipsi
    Tyrrhenum valido Marte per agmen eunt,
non aliter quam cum Libyca de gente leones
    invadunt sparsos lata per arva greges. 210
Diffugiunt hostes inhonestaque volnera tergo
    accipiunt; Tusco sanguine terra rubet.
Sic iterum, sic saepe cadunt. Ubi vincere aperte
    non datur, insidias armaque tecta parant.
Campus erat: campi claudebant ultima colles 215
    silvaque montanas occulere apta feras.
In medio paucos armentaque rara relinquunt,
    cetera virgultis abdita turba latet.
Ecce velut torrens, undis pluvialibus auctus
    aut nive quae zephyro victa tepente fluit, 220
per sata perque vias fertur, nec, ut ante solebat,
    riparum clausas margine finit aquas:
sic Fabii vallem latis discursibus implent,
    quodque vident, sternunt; nec metus alter inest.
Quo ruitis, generosa domus? Male creditis hosti! 225
    Simplex nobilitas, perfida tela cave!
Fraude perit virtus. In apertos undique campos
    prosiliunt hostes et latus omne tenent.
Quid faciant pauci contra tot milia fortes?
    Quidve, quod in misero tempore restet, adest? 230
Sicut aper longe fulvis latrantibus actus
    fulmineo celeres dissipat ore canes,
mox tamen ipse perit: sic non moriuntur inulti
    volneraque alterna dantque feruntque manu.
Una dies Fabios ad bellum miserat omnes; 235
    ad bellum miseros perdidit una dies.
Ut tamen Herculeae superessent semina gentis,
    credibile est ipsos consuluisse deos.

Nam puer impubes at adhuc non utilis armis
    unus de Fabia gente relictus erat: 240
scilicet ut posses olim tu, Maxime, nasci,
    cui res cunctando restituenda foret.

THE DEIFICATION OF ROMULUS

After a reign of almost forty years, one day, while Romulus was ad-
ministering the laws, a storm scattered the people. When they returned,
he had disappeared. His father, Mars, had taken him up to heaven.
Henceforth the Romans worshipped him as the god Quirinus (Ovid,
Fasti, ii. 491–512).

EST locus, antiqui Capreae dixere Paludem.
    Forte tuis illic, Romule, iura dabas.
    Sol fugit, et removent subeuntia nubila caelum,
    et gravis effusis decidit imber aquis.
Hinc tonat, hinc missis abrumpitur ignibus aether.   495
    Fit fuga. Rex patriis astra petebat equis.
Luctus erat, falsaeque patres in crimine caedis;
    haesissetque animis forsitan illa fides;
sed Proculus Longa veniebat Iulius Alba,
    lunaque fulgebat, nec facis usus erat,   500
cum subito motu saepes tremuere sinistrae.
    Rettulit ille gradus, horrueruntque comae.
Pulcher et humano maior trabeaque decorus
    Romulus in media visus adesse via
et dixisse simul, 'Prohibe lugere Quirites,   505
    nec violent lacrimis numina nostra suis.
Tura ferant placentque novum pia turba Quirinum
    et patrias artes militiamque colant.'
Iussit, et in tenues oculis evanuit auras.
    Convocat hic populos iussaque verba refert.   510
Templa deo fiunt, collis quoque dictus ab illo est,
    et referunt certi sacra paterna dies.

KING NUMA RECEIVES THE ANCILE

In response to King Numa's appeals to Jupiter, an oval shield, called
an ancile, was dropped from heaven and came into the possession of the
king. This shield was regarded as a pledge of Roman power and its
preservation as necessary for the prosperity of Rome. Numa had
eleven other shields exactly like it made, that the genuine shield might
not be stolen. Every March the twelve shields were carried in procession through the streets of the city by priests called Salii, and were then
restored to their place in the Temple of Mars. Ovid gives an account of
the reception of the ancile (*Fasti*, iii. 285–382).

ECCE deum genitor rutilas per nubila flammas   285
     spargit et effusis aethera siccat aquis.
  Non alias missi cecidere frequentius ignes.
  Rex pavet, et volgi pectora terror habet.
Cui dea 'Ne nimium terrere! Piabile fulmen
  est,' ait, 'et saevi flectitur ira Iovis.   290
Sed poterunt ritum Picus Faunusque piandi
  tradere, Romani numen utrumque soli.
Nec sine vi tradent: adhibeto vincula captis.'
  Atque ita, qua possint erudit arte capi.
Lucus Aventino suberat niger ilicis umbra,   295
  quo posses viso dicere, 'Numen inest!'
In medio gramen muscoque adoperta virenti
  manabat saxo vena perennis aquae.
Inde fere soli Faunus Picusque bibebant.
  Huc venit et fonti rex Numa mactat ovem   300
plenaque odorati disponit pocula Bacchi,
  cumque suis antro conditus ipse latet.
Ad solitos veniunt silvestria numina fontes
  et relevant multo pectora sicca mero.
Vina quies sequitur. Gelido Numa prodit ab antro,   305
  vinclaque sopitas addit in arta manus.
Somnus ut abscessit, pugnando vincula temptant
  rumpere: pugnantes fortius illa tenent.

JUPITER

Tunc Numa: 'Di nemorum, factis ignoscite nostris,
    si scelus ingenio scitis abesse meo;   310
quoque modo possit fulmen monstrate piari.'
    Sic Numa; sic quatiens cornua Faunus ait:
'Magna petis, nec quae monitu tibi discere nostro
    fas sit. Habent finis numina nostra suos.
Di sumus agrestes, et qui dominemur in altis   315
    montibus: arbitrium est in sua tela Iovi.
Hunc tu non poteris per te deducere caelo;
    at poteris nostra forsitan usus ope.'
Dixerat haec Faunus; par est sententia Pici.
    'Deme tamen nobis vincula,' Picus ait.   320
'Iuppiter huc veniet, valida perductus ab arte.
    Nubila promissi Styx mihi testis erit.'
Emissi laqueis quid agant, quae carmina dicant
    quaque trahant superis sedibus arte Iovem,
scire nefas homini. Nobis concessa canentur,   325
    quaeque pio dici vatis ab ore licet.
Eliciunt caelo te, Iuppiter. Unde minores
    nunc quoque te celebrant Eliciumque vocant.
Constat Aventinae tremuisse cacumina silvae,
    terraque subsedit pondere pressa Iovis.   330
Corda micant regis, totoque e corpore sanguis
    fugit, et hirsutae deriguere comae.
Ut rediit animus, 'Da certa piamina,' dixit,
    'fulminis, altorum rexque paterque deum,
si tua contigimus manibus donaria puris,—   335
    hoc quoque, quod petitur, si pia lingua rogat.'
Adnuit oranti; sed verum ambage remota
    abdidit et dubio terruit ore virum.
'Caede caput' dixit. Cui rex 'Parebimus' inquit:
    'caedenda est hortis eruta cepa meis.'   340
Addidit hic 'Hominis.' 'Summos,' ait ille, 'capillos.'
    Postulat hic animam; cui Numa 'Piscis' ait.

THE CHARIOT OF THE SUN

Risit et 'His,' inquit, 'facito mea tela procures,
　　O vir colloquio non abigende deum.
Sed tibi, protulerit cum totum crastinus orbem　　　345
　　Cynthius, imperii pignora certa dabo.'
Dixit, et ingenti tonitru super aethera motum
　　fertur, adorantem destituitque Numam.
Ille redit laetus memoratque Quiritibus acta.
　　Tarda venit dictis difficilisque fides.　　　350
'At certe credemur,' ait, 'si verba sequetur
　　exitus. En audi crastina, quisquis ades.
Protulerit terris cum totum Cynthius orbem,
　　Iuppiter imperii pignora certa dabit.'
Discedunt dubii, promissaque tarda videntur,　　　355
　　dependetque fides a veniente die.
Mollis erat tellus rorata mane pruina;
　　ante sui populus limina regis adest.
Prodit, et in solio medius consedit acerno:
　　innumeri circa stantque silentque viri.　　　360

Ortus erat summo tantummodo margine Phoebus:
    sollicitae mentes speque metuque pavent.
Constitit atque, caput niveo velatus amictu,
    iam bene dis notas sustulit ille manus
atque ita, 'Tempus adest promissi muneris,' inquit: 365
    'pollicitam dictis, Iuppiter, adde fidem.'
Dum loquitur, totum iam sol emoverat orbem,
    et gravis aetherio venit ab axe fragor.
Ter tonuit sine nube deus, tria fulmina misit.
    Credite dicenti: mira, sed acta, loquor.   370
A media caelum regione dehiscere coepit;
    summisere oculos cum duce turba suo.
Ecce levi scutum versatum leniter aura
    decidit. A populo clamor ad astra venit.
Tollit humo munus, caesa prius ille iuvenca   375
    quae dederat nulli colla premenda iugo;
atque ancile vocat, quod ab omni parte recisum est,
    quaque notes oculis, angulus omnis abest.
Tunc, memor imperii sortem consistere in illo,
    consilium multae calliditatis init: 380
plura iubet fieri simili caelata figura,
    error ut ante oculos insidiantis eat.

TRIPTOLEMUS

While Ceres was seeking her lost daughter, Proserpine, who had been carried down to the Lower World by Pluto to be his queen, she traversed the whole earth. At last in her wanderings she came to the place in Greece where afterwards was the city Eleusis. Here, worn out, she sat down on a stone and for nine days and nights remained there in the open air without sleep or food. Near-by was the humble home of an old man named Celeus, whose son Triptolemus lay sick of a fever. Celeus and his daughter took pity on the tired woman (for they did not know she was a goddess) and persuaded her to come into their cottage. Ovid (*Fasti*, iv. 507–562) tells how Ceres saved the life of Triptolemus, how she tried in vain to make him immortal, and how she promised that he should teach men to plow, to sow, and to harvest their crops. See Gayley, *Classic Myths*, pp. 159–161.

FORS sua cuique loco est. Quo nunc Cerealis Eleusin,
 dicitur hoc Celei rura fuisse senis.
 Ille domum glandes excussaque mora rubetis
portat et arsuris arida ligna focis.   510
Filia parva duas redigebat monte capellas,
 et tener in cunis filius aeger erat.
'Mater!' ait virgo—mota est dea nomine matris—
 'Quid facis in solis incomitata locis?'
Restitit et senior, quamvis onus urget, et orat,   515
 tecta suae subeat quantulacumque casae.
Illa negat. Simularat anum, mitraque capillos
 presserat. Instanti talia dicta refert:
'Sospes eas semperque parens! Mihi filia rapta est.
 Heu, melior quanto sors tua sorte mea est!'   520
Dixit et, ut lacrimae (neque enim lacrimare deorum est),
 decidit in tepidos lucida gutta sinus.
Flent pariter molles animis virgoque senexque;
 e quibus haec iusti verba fuere senis:

'Sic tibi, quam raptam quereris, sit filia sospes: 525
   surge nec exiguae despice tecta casae!'
Cui dea 'Duc' inquit. 'Scisti qua cogere posses.'
   Seque levat saxo subsequiturque senem.
Dux comiti narrat quam sit sibi filius aeger,
   nec capiat somnos invigiletque malis.   530
Illa soporiferum, parvos initura penates,
   colligit agresti lene papaver humo.
Dum legit, oblito fertur gustasse palato
   longamque imprudens exsoluisse famem.
Quae quia principio posuit ieiunia noctis,   535
   tempus habent mystae sidera visa cibi.
Limen ut intravit, luctus videt omnia plena;
   iam spes in puero nulla salutis erat.
Matre salutata—mater Metanira vocatur—
   iungere dignata est os puerile suo.   540
Pallor abit, subitasque vident in corpore vires:
   tantus caelesti venit ab ore vigor.
Tota domus laeta est (hoc est, materque paterque
   nataque: tres illi tota fuere domus).
Mox epulas ponunt, liquefacta coagula lacte   545
   pomaque et in ceris aurea mella suis.
Abstinet alma Ceres, somnique papavera causas
   dat tibi cum tepido lacte bibenda, puer.
Noctis erat medium placidique silentia somni:
   Triptolemum gremio sustulit illa suo   550
terque manu permulsit eum; tria carmina dixit,
   carmina mortali non referenda sono,
inque foco corpus pueri vivente favilla
   obruit, humanum purget ut ignis onus.
Excutitur somno stulte pia mater, et amens,   555
   'Quid facis?' exclamat membraque ab igne rapit.
Cui dea, 'Dum non es,' dixit, 'scelerata fuisti:
   inrita materno sunt mea dona metu.

CERES

Iste quidem mortalis erit, sed primus arabit
  et seret et culta praemia tollet humo.'   560
Dixit, et egrediens nubem trahit inque dracones
  transit et alifero tollitur axe Ceres.

THE FOUNDING OF ROME AND THE DEATH
OF REMUS

Romulus and Remus were the grandsons of Numitor, whose kingdom
had been stolen from him by his brother Amulius. When they grew up,
they put Amulius to death and restored the kingdom to their grandfather. Later it became necessary to build a new city for the growing
number of shepherds and farmers under the rule of the two brothers.
A question arose as to which of the brothers should have the honor of
founding the city. The consultation of the omens by Romulus and
Remus; the building of the city wall by Romulus; and the death of
Remus, who had leaped over the low wall in derision at its apparent weakness, are described by Ovid in the following verses (*Fasti*, iv. 809–852):

IAM luerat poenas frater Numitoris, et omne
  pastorum gemino sub duce volgus erat.   810
  Contrahere agrestes et moenia ponere utrique
  convenit; ambigitur moenia ponat uter.
'Nil opus est,' dixit 'certamine' Romulus 'ullo:
  magna fides avium est. Experiamur aves.'
Res placet. Alter adit nemorosi saxa Palati,   815
  alter Aventinum mane cacumen init.
Sex Remus, hic volucres bis sex videt ordine. Pacto
  statur, et arbitrium Romulus urbis habet.
Apta dies legitur, qua moenia signet aratro.
  Sacra Palis suberant; inde movetur opus.   820
Fossa fit ad solidum; fruges iaciuntur in ima
  et de vicino terra petita solo.
Fossa repletur humo, plenaeque imponitur ara,
  et novus accenso fungitur igne focus.

VESTA

Inde premens stivam designat moenia sulco: 825
  alba iugum niveo cum bove vacca tulit.
Vox fuit haec regis: 'Condenti, Iuppiter, urbem,
  et genitor Mavors Vestaque mater, ades!
Quosque pium est adhibere deos, advertite cuncti!
  Auspicibus vobis hoc mihi surgat opus.   830
Longa sit huic aetas dominaeque potentia terrae,
  sitque sub hac oriens occiduusque dies!'
Ille precabatur. Tonitru dedit omina laevo
  Iuppiter, et laevo fulmina missa polo.
Augurio laeti iaciunt fundamina cives,   835
  et novus exiguo tempore murus erat.
Hoc Celer urget opus, quem Romulus ipse vocarat,
  'Sint'que, 'Celer, curae' dixerat 'ista tuae.
Neve quis aut muros aut factam vomere fossam
  transeat, audentem talia dede neci.'   840
Quod Remus ignorans humiles contemnere muros
  coepit et 'His populus' dicere 'tutus erit?'
Nec mora, transiluit. Rutro Celer occupat ausum.
  Ille premit duram sanguinulentus humum.
Haec ubi rex didicit, lacrimas introrsus obortas   845
  devorat et clausum pectore volnus habet.
Flere palam non volt exemplaque fortia servat,
  'Sic'que 'meos muros transeat hostis!' ait.
Dat tamen exsequias; nec iam suspendere fletum
  sustinet, et pietas dissimulata patet.   850
Osculaque applicuit posito suprema feretro
  atque ait, 'Invito frater adempte, vale!'

FLORA'S DELIGHT IN THE SPRING

Ovid makes Flora, goddess of the flowers, delight especially in the Spring (*Fasti*, v. 207–220).

VERE fruor semper: vere est nitidissimus annus,
    arbor habet frondes, pabula semper humus.
    Est mihi fecundus dotalibus hortus in agris:
aura fovet, liquidae fonte rigatur
    aquae.   210
Hunc meus implevit generoso flore
    maritus
    atque ait, 'Arbitrium tu, dea,
    floris habe.'
Saepe ego digestos volui numerare
    colores
    nec potui: numero copia maior
    erat.
Roscida cum primum foliis excussa
    pruina est,   215
    et variae radiis intepuere comae,
conveniunt pictis incinctae vestibus
    Horae
    inque leves calathos munera nos-
    tra legunt.
Protinus accedunt Charites nec-
    tuntque coronas
    sertaque caelestes implicitura
    comas.   220

FLORA

IPHIGENIA AMONG THE TAURIANS

When the Greeks were gathered at Aulis, ready to set out for Troy, no fair wind filled the sails of their ships. Calchas, a priest, explained the continued calm as due to the anger of Diana, who was offended because Agamemnon, leader of the Greek host, had killed a stag sacred to her. He also declared that the only way to appease the goddess was to offer Agamemnon's own daughter, Iphigenia, as a sacrifice. Agamemnon finally yielded, and preparations were made for the horrible rite. At the last moment, however, Diana was moved to pity. She carried away Iphigenia in a cloud to a distant place on the Black Sea and there made her a priestess in her temple among the barbarous Taurians. Ovid, in one of his Epistles from Pontus (iii. 2. 35–100), recounts an incident that happened while Iphigenia was a priestess of the Tauric Diana. See Gayley, *Classic Myths*, pp. 280–281, 316.

VOS etiam seri laudabunt saepe nepotes,   35
    claraque erit scriptis gloria vestra meis.
      Hic quoque Sauromatae iam vos novere Getaeque,
  et tales animos barbara turba probat.
Cumque ego de vestra nuper probitate referrem
    (nam didici Getice Sarmaticeque loqui),   40
forte senex quidam, coetu cum staret in illo,
  reddidit ad nostros talia verba sonos:
'Nos quoque amicitiae nomen, bone, novimus, hospes,
  quos procul a vobis Pontus et Hister habet.
Est locus in Scythia (Tauros dixere priores)   45
  qui Getica longe non ita distat humo;
hac ego sum terra (patriae nec paenitet) ortus.
  Consortem Phoebi gens colit illa deam.
Templa manent hodie vastis innixa columnis,
  perque quater denos itur in illa gradus.   50
Fama refert illic signum caeleste fuisse:
  quoque minus dubites, stat basis orba dea;
araque, quae fuerat natura candida saxi,
  decolor adfuso tincta cruore rubet.

DIANA

Femina sacra facit taedae non nota iugali,   55
    quae superat Scythicas nobilitate nurus.
Sacrifici genus est (sic instituere parentes)
    advena virgineo caesus ut ense cadat.
Regna Thoans habuit Maeotide clarus in ora,
    nec fuit Euxinis notior alter aquis.   60

ORESTES AND THE TAURIANS

Sceptra tenente illo, liquidas fecisse per auras
    nescio quam dicunt Iphigenian iter,
quam levibus ventis sub nube per aethera vectam
    creditur his Phoebe deposuisse locis.
Praefuerat templo multos ea rite per annos,   65
    invita peragens tristia sacra manu;
cum duo velifera iuvenes venere carina
    presseruntque suo litora nostra pede.
Par fuit his aetas et amor; quorum alter Orestes,
    ast Pylades alter: nomina fama tenet.   70
Protinus immitem Triviae ducuntur ad aram,
    evincti geminas ad sua terga manus.
Spargit aqua captos lustrali Graia sacerdos,
    ambiit ut fulvas infula longa comas.

IPHIGENIA

Dumque parat sacrum, dum velat tempora vittis,   75
  dum tardae causas invenit ipsa morae,
"Non ego crudelis, iuvenes. Ignoscite!" dixit,
  "Sacra suo facio barbariora loco.
Ritus is est gentis. Qua vos tamen urbe venitis?
  quodve parum fausta puppe petistis iter?"   80
Dixit. Et audito patriae pia nomine virgo
  consortes urbis comperit esse suae.
"Alteruter votis," inquit, "cadat hostia sacris;
  ad patrias sedes nuntius alter eat."
Ire iubet Pylades carum periturus Oresten;   85
  hic negat, inque vices pugnat uterque mori.
Exstitit hoc unum quo non convenerit illis;
  cetera par concors et sine lite fuit.
Dum peragunt iuvenes pulchri certamen amoris,
  ad fratrem scriptas exarat illa notas.   90
Ad fratrem mandata dabat; cuique illa dabantur
  (humanos casus aspice!) frater erat.
Nec mora: de templo rapiunt simulacra Dianae
  clamque per immensas puppe feruntur aquas.
Mirus amor iuvenum, quamvis abiere tot anni,   95
  in Scythia magnum nunc quoque nomen habet.'
Fabula narrata est postquam volgaris ab illo,
  laudarunt omnes facta piamque fidem.
Scilicet hac etiam, qua nulla ferocior ora est,
  nomen amicitiae barbara corda movet.   100

PENELOPE TO ULYSSES

In the first letter of the *Heroides* (*vv.* 25–84), Ovid makes Penelope chide her husband Ulysses for his long delay in returning home to Ithaca after the fall of Troy. See Gayley, *Classic Myths*, pp. 338–344.

ARGOLICI rediere duces, altaria fumant,   25
    ponitur ad patrios barbara praeda deos.
    Grata ferunt nymphae pro salvis dona maritis;
illi victa suis Troïca fata canunt.
Mirantur iustique senes trepidaeque puellae;
    narrantis coniunx pendet ab ore viri.   30
Atque aliquis posita monstrat fera proelia mensa,
    pingit et exiguo Pergama tota mero:
'Hac ibat Simois, hac est Sigeia tellus,
    hic steterat Priami regia celsa senis;
illic Aeacides, illic tendebat Ulixes,   35
    hic alacer missos terruit Hector equos.'
Omnia namque tuo senior, te quaerere misso,
    rettulerat nato Nestor, at ille mihi.
Rettulit et ferro Rhesumque Dolonaque caesos,
    utque sit hic somno proditus, ille dolo.   40
Ausus es, O nimium nimiumque oblite tuorum,
    Thracia nocturno tangere castra dolo
totque simul mactare viros, adiutus ab uno!
    At bene cautus eras et memor ante mei?
Usque metu micuere sinus, dum victor amicum   45
    dictus es Ismariis isse per agmen equis.
Sed mihi quid prodest vestris disiecta lacertis
    Ilios, et murus quod fuit, esse solum,
si maneo qualis Troia durante manebam,
    virque mihi dempto fine carendus abest?   50
Diruta sunt aliis, uni mihi Pergama restant,
    incola captivo quae bove victor arat.

Iam seges est ubi Troia fuit, resecandaque falce
  luxuriat Phrygio sanguine pinguis humus;
semisepulta virum curvis feriuntur aratris   55
  ossa; ruinosas occulit herba domos.
Victor abes; nec scire mihi quae causa morandi,
  aut in quo lateas ferreus orbe licet.
Quisquis ad haec vertit peregrinam litora puppim,
  ille mihi de te multa rogatus abit;   60
quamque tibi reddat, si te modo viderit usquam,
  traditur huic digitis charta novata meis.
Nos Pylon, antiqui Neleïa Nestoris arva,
  misimus: incerta est fama remissa Pylo.
Misimus et Sparten: Sparte quoque nescia veri.   65
  Quas habitas terras, aut ubi lentus abes?
Utilius starent etiam nunc moenia Phoebi
  (irascor votis heu levis ipsa meis!):
scirem ubi pugnares, et tantum bella timerem,
  et mea cum multis iuncta querella foret.   70
Quid timeam ignoro; timeo tamen omnia demens,
  et patet in curas area lata meas.
Quaecumque aequor habet, quaecumque pericula tellus,
  tam longae causas suspicor esse morae.
Haec ego dum stulte metuo, quae vestra libido est,   75
  esse peregrino captus amore potes.
Forsitan et narres quam sit tibi rustica coniunx,
  quae tantum lanas non sinat esse rudes.
Fallar, et hoc crimen tenues vanescat in auras,
  neve, revertendi liber, abesse velis!   80
Me pater Icarius viduo discedere lecto
  cogit et immensas increpat usque moras.
Increpet usque licet! Tua sum, tua dicar oportet:
  Penelope coniunx semper Ulixis ero.

PENELOPE AND ULYSSES

DIDO

DIDO TO ÆNEAS

In the seventh letter of the *Heroides* of Ovid, Dido closes her appeal
to the departing Æneas (*vv.* 181–194). Cf. Æneid, iv. 296 ff.

ASPICIAS utinam quae sit scribentis imago!
    Scribimus, et gremio Troïcus ensis adest;
    perque genas lacrimae strictum labuntur in ensem,
qui iam pro lacrimis sanguine tinctus erit.
Quam bene conveniunt fato tua munera nostro!   185
    Instruis impensa nostra sepulcra brevi.
Nec mea nunc primum feriuntur pectora telo:
    ille locus saevi volnus Amoris habet.
Anna soror! soror Anna! meae male conscia culpae,
    iam dabis in cineres ultima dona meos.   190

Nec consumpta rogis inscribar 'Elissa Sychaei,'
  hoc tamen in tumuli marmore carmen erit:
'Praebuit Aeneas et causam mortis et ensem.
  Ipsa sua Dido concidit usa manu.'

ARIADNE FALLS IN LOVE WITH THESEUS

King Minos of Crete had a son Androgeos, a champion wrestler, who
was murdered by the Athenians, envious of his triumphs. To avenge the
murder, Minos forced the Athenians to pay him yearly tribute, consisting of seven young men and seven young women, whom he shut up in
the Cretan Labyrinth to be destroyed by the Minotaur, a horrible
monster, half-man and half-bull.

Theseus, son of the Athenian king Ægeus, resolved to put an end
to the tribute and sailed to Crete to slay the Minotaur. The king's
daughter, Ariadne, fell in love with Theseus. She gave him a ball of
twine, bidding him unwind the twine as he entered the Labyrinth, so that
he might have something to guide him out of the maze. When Theseus
left Crete, after slaying the Minotaur, he took Ariadne with him; but
he deserted her in the island of Naxos. See Gayley, *Classic Myths*, pp.
252–257. Catullus (lxiv. 76–102) thus describes the coming of Theseus
to Crete and Ariadne's love for him:

R. H. FRANKENBERG

NAM perhibent olim, crudeli peste coactam
      Androgeoneae poenas exsolvere caedis,
      electos iuvenes simul et decus innuptarum
Cecropiam solitam esse dapem dare Minotauro.
Quis angusta malis cum moenia vexarentur,   80
ipse suum Theseus pro caris corpus Athenis
proicere optavit, potius quam talia Cretam
funera Cecropiae, nec funera, portarentur;
atque ita, nave levi nitens ac lenibus auris,
magnanimum ad Minoa venit sedesque superbas.   85
Hunc simul ac cupido conspexit lumine virgo
regia,—quam suavis exspirans castus odores
lectulus in molli complexu matris alebat,

quales Eurotae progignunt flumina myrtos
aurave distinctos educit verna colores,— 90
non prius ex illo flagrantia declinavit
lumina quam cuncto concepit corpore flammam
funditus atque imis exarsit tota medullis.
Heu! misere exagitans immiti corde furores,
sancte puer, curis hominum qui gaudia misces, 95
quaeque regis Golgos quaeque Idalium frondosum,
qualibus incensam iactastis mente puellam
fluctibus in flavo saepe hospite suspirantem!
Quantos illa tulit languenti corde timores!
Quanto saepe magis fulgore expalluit auri, 100
cum, saevum cupiens contra contendere monstrum,
aut mortem appeteret Theseus aut praemia laudis.

ARIADNE'S LAMENT

Ariadne, deserted by Theseus on the island of Naxos, complains of
her desertion (Catullus, lxiv. 132–201).

SICINE me patriis avectam, perfide, ab aris,
perfide, deserto liquisti in litore, Theseu?
Sicine discedens, neglecto numine divum,
immemor ah! devota domum periuria portas? 135
Nullane res potuit crudelis flectere mentis
consilium? Tibi nulla fuit clementia praesto
immite ut nostri vellet miserescere pectus?
At non haec quondam blanda promissa dedisti
voce mihi, non haec miserae sperare iubebas, 140
sed conubia laeta, sed optatos hymenaeos:
quae cuncta aerii discerpunt inrita venti.
Nunc iam nulla viro iuranti femina credat,
nulla viri speret sermones esse fideles,
quis dum aliquid cupiens animus praegestit apisci, 145

ARIADNE DESERTED

nil metuunt iurare, nihil promittere parcunt;
sed simul ac cupidae mentis satiata libido est,
dicta nihil meminere, nihil periuria curant.
Certe ego te, in medio versantem turbine leti,
eripui, et potius germanum amittere crevi 150
quam tibi fallaci supremo in tempore deessem;

SCYLLA

pro quo dilaceranda feris dabor alitibusque
praeda, neque iniecta tumulabor mortua terra.
Quaenam te genuit sola sub rupe leaena?
Quod mare conceptum spumantibus exspuit undis, 155
quae Syrtis, quae Scylla rapax, quae vasta Charybdis,
talia qui reddis pro dulci praemia vita?
Si tibi non cordi fuerant conubia nostra,
saeva quod horrebas prisci praecepta parentis,
at tamen in vestras potuisti ducere sedes, 160

quae tibi iucundo famularer serva labore,
candida permulcens liquidis vestigia lymphis,
purpureave tuum consternens veste cubile.
Sed quid ego ignaris nequiquam conqueror auris,
exsternata malo, quae, nullis sensibus auctae, 165
nec missas audire queunt nec reddere voces?
Ille autem prope iam mediis versatur in undis,
nec quisquam apparet vacua mortalis in alga.
Sic, nimis insultans extremo tempore, saeva
Fors etiam nostris invidit questibus auris. 170
Iuppiter omnipotens, utinam ne tempore primo
Gnosia Cecropiae tetigissent litora puppes,
indomito nec dira ferens stipendia tauro
perfidus in Creta religasset navita funem,
nec malus hic, celans dulci crudelia forma 175
consilia, in nostris requiesset sedibus hospes!
Nam quo me referam? Quali spe perdita nitor?
Idaeosne petam montes,—ah! gurgite lato
discernens ponti truculentum ubi dividit aequor?
An patris auxilium sperem, quemne ipsa reliqui 180
respersum iuvenem fraterna caede secuta?
Coniugis an fido consoler memet amore,
quine fugit lentos incurvans gurgite remos?
Praeterea nullo litus, sola insula, tecto,
nec patet egressus pelagi cingentibus undis; 185
nulla fugae ratio, nulla spes; omnia muta,
omnia sunt deserta; ostentant omnia letum.
Non tamen ante mihi languescent lumina morte,
nec prius a fesso secedent corpore sensus,
quam iustam a divis exposcam prodita multam 190
caelestumque fidem postrema comprecer hora.
Quare, facta virum multantes vindice poena
Eumenides, quibus anguino redimita capillo
frons exspirantis praeportat pectoris iras,

huc, huc adventate, meas audite querelas,   195
quas ego (vae miserae!) extremis proferre medullis
cogor inops, ardens, amenti caeca furore.
Quae quoniam verae nascuntur pectore ab imo,
vos nolite pati nostrum vanescere luctum;
sed, quali solam Theseus me mente reliquit,   200
tali mente, deae, funestet seque suosque!

OVID'S AUTOBIOGRAPHY

In one of his poems Ovid left to posterity an account of his life
(*Tristia*, iv. 10). An extract follows.

ILLE ego qui fuerim, tenerorum lusor amorum
    quem legis, ut noris, accipe, posteritas.
    Sulmo mihi patria est, gelidis uberrimus undis,
milia qui novies distat ab urbe decem.
Editus hinc ego sum; nec non ut tempora noris,   5
    cum cecidit fato consul uterque pari.
Si quid id est, usque a proavis vetus ordinis heres,
    non sum fortunae munere factus eques.
Nec stirps prima fui. Genito sum fratre creatus,
    qui tribus ante quater mensibus ortus erat.   10
Lucifer amborum natalibus adfuit idem:
    una celebrata est per duo liba dies.
Haec est armiferae festis de quinque Minervae,
    quae fieri pugna prima cruenta solet.
Protinus excolimur teneri, curaque parentis   15
    imus ad insignes urbis ab arte viros.
Frater ad eloquium viridi tendebat ab aevo,
    fortia verbosi natus ad arma fori;
at mihi iam parvo caelestia sacra placebant,
    inque suum furtim Musa trahebat opus.   20

Saepe pater dixit, 'Studium quid inutile temptas?
  Maeonides nullas ipse reliquit opes.'
Motus eram dictis totoque Helicone relicto
  scribere conabar verba soluta modis:
sponte sua carmen numeros veniebat ad aptos;   25
  quicquid temptabam dicere, versus erat.
Interea, tacito passu labentibus annis,
  liberior fratri sumpta mihique toga est,
induiturque umeris cum lato purpura clavo,
  et studium nobis, quod ante fuit, manet.   30
Iamque decem frater vitae geminaverat annos,
  cum perit, et coepi parte carere mei.
Cepimus et tenerae primos aetatis honores,
  deque viris quondam pars tribus una fui.
Curia restabat; clavi mensura coacta est;   35
  maius erat nostris viribus illud onus;
nec patiens corpus, nec mens fuit apta labori,
  sollicitaeque fugax ambitionis eram.
Et petere Aoniae suadebant tuta sorores
  otia, iudicio semper amata meo.   40
Temporis illius colui fovique poetas,
  quotque aderant vates, rebar adesse deos.
Saepe suas volucres legit mihi grandior aevo,
  quaeque necet serpens, quae iuvet herba, Macer.
Saepe suos solitus recitare Propertius ignes,   45
  iure sodalicii qui mihi iunctus erat.
Ponticus heroo, Bassus quoque clarus iambis
  dulcia convictus membra fuere mei.
Detinuit nostras numerosus Horatius aures,
  dum ferit Ausonia carmina culta lyra.   50
Vergilium vidi tantum; nec amara Tibullo
  tempus amicitiae fata dedere meae.
Successor fuit hic tibi, Galle; Propertius illi;
  quartus ab his serie temporis ipse fui.

Utque ego maiores, sic me coluere minores,　55
　notaque non tarde facta Thalia mea est.
Carmina cum primum populo iuvenalia legi,
　barba resecta mihi bisve semelve fuit.

OVID'S LAST NIGHT IN ROME

In the *Tristia* (i. 3. 1–62) Ovid describes the last night he spent in
Rome before leaving the city for his place of exile on the Black Sea.

CUM subit illius tristissima noctis imago
　　qua mihi supremum tempus in urbe fuit,
　cum repeto noctem qua tot mihi cara reliqui,
labitur ex oculis nunc quoque gutta meis.
Iam prope lux aderat qua me discedere Caesar　5
　finibus extremae iusserat Ausoniae.
Nec spatium fuerat, nec mens satis apta parandi:
　torpuerant longa pectora nostra mora.
Non mihi servorum, comites non cura legendi,
　non aptae profugo vestis opisve fuit.　10
Non aliter stupui quam qui Iovis ignibus ictus
　vivit et est vitae nescius ipse suae.
Ut tamen hanc animi nubem dolor ipse removit,
　ut tandem sensus convaluere mei,
adloquor extremum maestos abiturus amicos,　15
　qui modo de multis unus et alter erant.
Uxor amans flentem flens acrius ipsa tenebat,
　imbre per indignas usque cadente genas.
Nata procul Libycis aberat diversa sub oris:
　non poterat fati certior esse mei.　20
Quocumque aspiceres, luctus gemitusque sonabant,
　formaque non taciti funeris intus erat.
Femina virque meo, pueri quoque, funere maerent;
　inque domo lacrimas angulus omnis habet.

Si licet exemplis in parvo grandibus uti, 25
  haec facies Troiae, cum caperetur, erat.
Iamque quiescebant voces hominumque canumque,
  Lunaque nocturnos alta regebat equos.
Hanc ego suspiciens et ab hac Capitolia cernens,
  quae nostro frustra iuncta fuere Lari, 30
'Numina vicinis habitantia sedibus,' inquam,
  'iamque oculis numquam templa videnda meis,
dique relinquendi, quos urbs habet alta Quirini,
  este salutati tempus in omne mihi!
Et quamquam sero clipeum post volnera sumo, 35
  attamen hanc odiis exonerate fugam,
caelestique viro, quis me deceperit error
  dicite, pro culpa ne scelus esse putet,
ut quod vos scitis, poenae quoque sentiat auctor:
  placato possum non miser esse deo.' 40
Hac prece adoravi superos ego: pluribus uxor,
  singultu medios impediente sonos.
Illa etiam ante Lares sparsis astrata capillis
  contigit exstinctos ore tremente focos,
multaque in adversos effudit verba Penates 45
  pro deplorato non valitura viro.
Iamque morae spatium nox praecipitata negabat,
  versaque ab axe suo Parrhasis Arctos erat.
Quid facerem? Blando patriae retinebar amore;
  ultima sed iussae nox erat illa fugae. 50
A! quotiens aliquo dixi properante, 'Quid urges?
  Vel quo festines ire, vel unde, vide!'
A! quotiens certam me sum mentitus habere
  horam, propositae quae foret apta viae.
Ter limen tetigi, ter sum revocatus, et ipse 55
  indulgens animo pes mihi tardus erat.
Saepe 'Vale' dicto, rursus sum plura locutus,
  et quasi discedens oscula multa dedi.

Saepe eadem mandata dedi meque ipse fefelli,
    respiciens oculis pignora cara meis.   60
Denique 'Quid propero? Scythia est quo mittimur,' inquam:
    'Roma relinquenda est. Utraque iusta mora est.'

OVID'S SHIP

Ovid praises his ship, and prays that it may carry him safely to the
place of his exile on the Black Sea (*Tristia*, i. 10. 1–14).

EST mihi (sitque, precor!) flavae tutela Minervae,
    navis, et a picta casside nomen habet.
    Sive opus est velis, minimam bene currit ad auram;
    sive opus est remo, remige carpit iter.
Nec comites volucri contenta est vincere cursu,   5
    occupat egressas quamlibet ante rates;
et patitur fluctus fertque assilientia longe
    aequora, nec saevis icta fatiscit aquis.
Illa, Corinthiacis primum mihi cognita Cenchreis,
    fida manet trepidae duxque comesque fugae,   10
perque tot eventus et iniquis concita ventis
    aequora Palladio numine tuta fuit.
Nunc quoque tuta, precor, vasti secet ostia Ponti,
    quasque petit, Getici litoris intret aquas.

THAT YACHT OF MINE!

On his return to Sirmio from Bithynia, Catullus hung up as an offering in a shrine at his villa a model of the ship that had brought him safely home. The poem which follows (iv) seems to have been a dedicatory inscription for the offering.

PHASELLUS ille quem videtis, hospites,
 ait fuisse navium celerrimus,
 neque ullius natantis impetum trabis
nequisse praeterire, sive palmulis
opus foret volare sive linteo.   5
Et hoc negat, minacis Hadriatici
negare litus insulasve Cycladas
Rhodumque nobilem horridamque Thraciam
Propontida trucemve Ponticum sinum,
ubi iste post phasellus antea fuit   10
comata silva: nam Cytorio in iugo
loquente saepe sibilum edidit coma.
Amastri Pontica et Cytore buxifer,
tibi haec fuisse et esse cognitissima
ait phasellus; ultima ex origine   15
tuo stetisse dicit in cacumine,
tuo imbuisse palmulas in aequore,
et inde tot per impotentia freta
erum tulisse, laeva sive dextera
vocaret aura, sive utrumque Iuppiter 20
simul secundus incidisset in pedem;
neque ulla vota litoralibus diis
sibi esse facta, cum veniret a mari
novissimo hunc ad usque limpidum lacum.
Sed haec prius fuere: nunc recondita 25
senet quiete seque dedicat tibi,
gemelle Castor et gemelle Castoris.

A HOMESICK POET

In his homesick moments Ovid wrote the following poem from his
place of banishment on the Black Sea (*Tristia*, iii. 8).

NUNC ego Triptolemi cuperem conscendere currus,
    misit in ignotam qui rude semen humum;
nunc ego Medeae vellem frenare dracones,
    quos habuit fugiens arce, Corinthe, tua;
nunc ego iactandas optarem sumere pinnas,   5
    sive tuas, Perseu, Daedale, sive tuas:
ut, tenera nostris cedente volatibus aura,
    aspicerem patriae dulce repente solum,
desertaeque domus vultus, memoresque sodales
    caraque praecipue coniugis ora meae!   10
Stulte, quid haec frustra votis puerilibus optas,
    quae non ulla tibi fertque feretque dies?
Si semel optandum est, Augustum numen adora,
    et quem sensisti, rite precare, deum.
Ille potest pinnasque tibi currusque volucres   15
    tradere. Det reditum: protinus ales eris.
Si precer haec (neque enim possum maiora precari),
    ne mea sint timeo vota modesta parum.
Forsitan hoc olim, cum iam satiaverit iram,
    tunc quoque sollicita mente rogandus erit.   20
Quod minus interea est, instar mihi muneris ampli,—
    ex his me iubeat quolibet ire locis.
Nec caelum nec aquae faciunt nec terra nec aurae.
    Ei mihi! perpetuus corpora languor habet,
seu vitiant artus aegrae contagia mentis,   25
    sive mei causa est in regione mali.
Ut tetigi Pontum, vexant insomnia, vixque
    ossa tegit macies nec iuvat ora cibus.

Quique per autumnum percussis frigore primo
    est color in foliis, quae nova laesit hiems,   30
is mea membra tenet; nec viribus adlevor ullis,
    et numquam queruli causa doloris abest.
Nec melius valeo, quam corpore, mente; sed aegra est
    utraque pars aeque, binaque damna fero.
Haeret et ante oculos veluti spectabile corpus   35
    astat fortunae forma legenda meae;
cumque locum moresque hominum cultusque sonumque
    cernimus, et quid sim quid fuerimque subit,
tantus amor necis est, querar ut cum Caesaris ira
    quod non offensas vindicet ense suas.   40
At quoniam semel est odio civiliter usus,
    mutato levior sit fuga nostra loco.

WINTER IN THRACE

    Ovid thus describes the cold and gloom of Thrace in winter (*Tristia*,
iii. 10. 1–40).

SI quis adhuc istic meminit Nasonis adempti
    et superest sine me nomen in urbe meum,
    suppositum stellis numquam tangentibus aequor
me sciat in media vivere barbarie.
Sauromatae cingunt, fera gens, Bessique Getaeque,   5
    quam non ingenio nomina digna meo!
Dum tamen aura tepet, medio defendimur Histro;
    ille suis liquidus bella repellit aquis.
At cum tristis Hiems squalentia protulit ora,
    terraque marmoreo candida facta gelu est,   10
dum vetat et boreas et nix habitare sub Arcto,
    tum liquet has gentes axe tremente premi.
Nix iacet, et iactam nec sol pluviaeque resolvunt,
    indurat boreas perpetuamque facit.

Ergo ubi deliciut nondum prior, altera venit,   15
   et solet in multis bima manere locis.
Tantaque commoti vis est aquilonis ut altas
   aequet humo turres tectaque rapta ferat.
Pellibus et sutis arcent mala frigora bracis,
   oraque de toto corpore sola patent.   20
Saepe sonant moti glacie pendente capilli,
   et nitet inducto candida barba gelu.
Nudaque consistunt, formam servantia testae,
   vina; nec hausta meri, sed data frusta bibunt.
Quid loquar ut vincti concrescant frigore rivi,   25
   deque lacu fragiles effodiantur aquae?
Ipse, papyrifero qui non angustior amne
   miscetur vasto multa per ora freto,
caeruleos ventis latices durantibus Hister
   congelat et tectis in mare serpit aquis.   30
Quaque rates ierant, pedibus nunc itur, et undas
   frigore concretas ungula pulsat equi;
perque novos pontes, subter labentibus undis,
   ducunt Sarmatici barbara plaustra boves.
Vix equidem credar; sed cum sint praemia falsi   35
   nulla, ratam debet testis habere fidem:
vidimus ingentem glacie consistere pontum,
   lubricaque immotas testa premebat aquas.
Nec vidisse sat est: durum calcavimus aequor,
   undaque non udo sub pede summa fuit.   40

UPON THE DEATH OF MY LADY'S SPARROW

Catullus (iii) mourns the death of a pet sparrow that had belonged
to his sweetheart Clodia, whom he calls Lesbia. With this poem may be
compared Burns's poem 'To a Mouse, on turning her up with his plough.'

LUGETE, O Veneres Cupidinesque
    et quantum est hominum venustiorum!
    Passer mortuus est meae puellae,
passer, deliciae meae puellae,
quem plus illa oculis suis amabat;   5
nam mellitus erat, suamque norat
ipsa tam bene quam puella matrem;
nec sese a gremio illius movebat,
sed, circumsiliens modo huc modo illuc,
ad solam dominam usque pipiabat.   10
Qui nunc it per iter tenebricosum
illuc unde negant redire quemquam.
At vobis male sit, malae tenebrae
Orci, quae omnia bella devoratis:
tam bellum mihi passerem abstulistis.   15
Vae factum male! Vae miselle passer!
Tua nunc opera meae puellae
flendo turgiduli rubent ocelli.

AN INVITATION TO DINNER

Catullus (xiii) invites Fabullus to dinner, but tells him that he must
furnish the meal himself.

CENABIS bene, mi Fabulle, apud me
    paucis, si tibi di favent, diebus,
    si tecum attuleris bonam atque magnam
cenam, non sine candida puella
et vino et sale et omnibus cachinnis.   5

Haec si, inquam, attuleris, venuste noster,
cenabis bene; nam tui Catulli
plenus sacculus est aranearum.
Sed contra accipies meros amores
seu quid suavius elegantiusve est;   10
nam unguentum dabo quod meae puellae
donarunt Veneres Cupidinesque,
quod tu cum olfacies, deos rogabis
totum ut te faciant, Fabulle, nasum.

HOME AGAIN!

Catullus (xxxi) expresses his joy at returning to his villa at Sirmio
after a year in Bithynia.

PAENE insularum, Sirmio, insularumque
ocelle, quascumque in liquentibus stagnis
marique vasto fert uterque Neptunus,
quam te libenter quamque laetus inviso,
vix mi ipse credens Thyniam atque Bithynos   5
liquisse campos et videre te in tuto!
O quid solutis est beatius curis,
cum mens onus reponit, ac peregrino
labore fessi venimus larem ad nostrum
desideratoque adquiescimus lecto?   10
Hoc est quod unum est pro laboribus tantis.
Salve, O venusta Sirmio, atque ero gaude!
Gaudete vosque, O Lydiae lacus undae!
Ridete, quidquid est domi cachinnorum!

FAREWELL TO BITHYNIA!

Out of pure joy at the prospect of leaving Bithynia on his homeward journey Catullus wrote the following poem (xlvi).

IAM ver egelidos refert tepores;
   iam caeli furor aequinoctialis
   iucundis Zephyri silescit auris.
Linquantur Phrygii, Catulle, campi,
Nicaeaeque ager uber aestuosae;   5
ad claras Asiae volemus urbes.
Iam mens praetrepidans avet vagari;
iam laeti studio pedes vigescunt.
O dulces comitum valete coetus,
longe quos simul a domo profectos   10
diversae variae viae reportant!

AT THE TOMB OF A BROTHER

While in Asia Minor, Catullus made funeral offerings at the tomb of his brother, who had died and been buried in the Troad some time before. In connection with the offering he wrote verses of farewell (ci).

MULTAS per gentes et multa per aequora vectus
   advenio has miseras, frater, ad inferias,
   ut te postremo donarem munere mortis
et mutam nequiquam adloquerer cinerem,
quandoquidem fortuna mihi tete abstulit ipsum,   5
   heu miser indigne frater adempte mihi!
Nunc tamen interea haec, prisco quae more parentum
   tradita sunt tristi munere ad inferias,
accipe fraterno multum manantia fletu,
   atque in perpetuum, frater, ave atque vale!   10

THANKS TO CICERO

Cicero on some unknown occasion gave Catullus assistance, either at law or in the Forum. Catullus expresses his thanks in these verses (xlix).

DISERTISSIME Romuli nepotum,
    quot sunt quotque fuere, Marce Tulli,
    quotque post aliis erunt in annis,
gratias tibi maximas Catullus
agit, pessimus omnium poeta,   5
tanto pessimus omnium poeta
quanto tu optimus omnium patronus.

ODE TO AUGUSTUS

An ode addressed by Horace to the Emperor Augustus, praying that he may live long as the guide and guardian of the Roman state (*Odes*, i. 2).

IAM satis terris nivis atque dirae
    grandinis misit pater, et rubente
    dextera sacras iaculatus arcis
        terruit urbem,

terruit gentis, grave ne rediret   5
saeculum Pyrrhae nova monstra questae,
omne cum Proteus pecus egit altos
        visere montis,

piscium et summa genus haesit ulmo,
nota quae sedes fuerat columbis,   10
et superiecto pavidae natarunt
        aequore dammae.

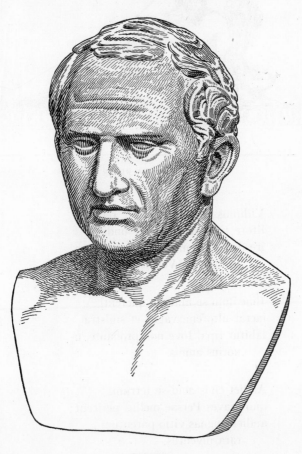

CICERO

THE TIBER AS A RIVER GOD

Vidimus flavum Tiberim, retortis
litore Etrusco violenter undis,
ire deiectum monumenta regis   15
    templaque Vestae,

Iliae dum se nimium querenti
iactat ultorem, vagus et sinistra
labitur ripa, Iove non probante, u-
    xorius amnis.   20

Audiet civis acuisse ferrum,
quo graves Persae melius perirent;
audiet pugnas vitio parentum
    rara iuventus.

Quem vocet divum populus ruentis   25
imperi rebus? Prece qua fatigent
virgines sanctae minus audientem
    carmina Vestam?

AUGUSTUS

Cui dabit partis scelus expiandi
Iuppiter? Tandem venias precamur, 30
nube candentis umeros amictus,
　　　augur Apollo;

sive tu mavis, Erycina ridens,
quam Iocus circum volat et Cupido;
sive neglectum genus et nepotes 35
　　　respicis, auctor,

heu! nimis longo satiate ludo,
quem iuvat clamor galeaeque leves
acer et Marsi peditis cruentum
　　　voltus in hostem; 40

sive mutata iuvenem figura
ales in terris imitaris almae
filius Maiae, patiens vocari
　　　Caesaris ultor:

serus in caelum redeas diuque 45
laetus intersis populo Quirini,
neve te nostris vitiis iniquum
　　　ocior aura

tollat; hic magnos potius triumphos,
hic ames dici pater atque princeps, 50
neu sinas Medos equitare inultos
　　　te duce, Caesar!

THE SHIP OF STATE

The ship of state is shattered by the civil wars and cannot weather another storm. Let her seek safety in harbor and there rest in peace (*Odes*, i. 14).

O NAVIS, referent in mare te novi
  fluctus! O quid agis? Fortiter occupa
   portum! Nonne vides ut
 nudum remigio latus

et malus celeri saucius Africo   5
antemnaeque gemant ac sine funibus
 vix durare carinae
  possint imperiosius

aequor? Non tibi sunt integra lintea,
non di quos iterum pressa voces malo.   10
 Quamvis Pontica pinus,
  silvae filia nobilis,

iactes et genus et nomen inutile,
nil pictis timidus navita puppibus
 fidit. Tu nisi ventis   15
  debes ludibrium, cave.

Nuper sollicitum quae mihi taedium,
nunc desiderium curaque non levis,
 interfusa nitentis
  vites aequora Cycladas!   20

INTEGER VITAE

Horace declares that an innocent and victorious man need fear no
dangers (*Odes*, i. 22). Cf. Milton, *Comus*, 589–590:

> Virtue may be assailed, but never hurt,
> Surprised by unjust force, but not enthralled.

INTEGER vitae scelerisque purus
  non eget Mauris iaculis neque arcu
  nec venenatis gravida sagittis,
    Fusce, pharetra,

sive per Syrtis iter aestuosas   5
sive facturus per inhospitalem
Caucasum vel quae loca fabulosus
    lambit Hydaspes.

Namque me silva lupus in Sabina,
dum meam canto Lalagen et ultra   10
terminum curis vagor expeditis,
    fugit inermem,—

quale portentum neque militaris
Daunias latis alit aesculetis
nec Iubae tellus generat, leonum   15
    arida nutrix.

Pone me pigris ubi nulla campis
arbor aestiva recreatur aura,
quod latus mundi nebulae malusque
    Iuppiter urget;   2)

pone sub curru nimium propinqui
solis, in terra domibus negata:
dulce ridentem Lalagen amabo,
    dulce loquentem.

DIVINE PROVIDENCE

For a time Horace believed, with the Epicureans, that the gods, if
they exist at all, do not manifest themselves to mortals or concern themselves with human affairs, but live apart in

> The lucid interspace of world and world,
> Where never creeps a cloud or moves a wind . . .
> Nor sound of human sorrow mounts to mar
> Their everlasting calm.

In the following ode, however, he tells us that his confidence in that
senseless creed (*insanientis sapientiae*) has become shaken; for he has
heard something that the Epicureans declare to be a physical impossibil-
ity but that the common people accept as a voice of God, namely,
thunder out of a clear sky (*Odes*, i. 34).

PARCUS deorum cultor et infrequens,
   insanientis dum sapientiae
      consultus erro, nunc retrorsum
   vela dare atque iterare cursus

cogor relictos. Namque Diespiter,   5
igni corusco nubila dividens
   plerumque, per purum tonantis
      egit equos volucremque currum,

quo bruta tellus et vaga flumina,
quo Styx et invisi horrida Taenari   10
   sedes Atlanteusque finis
      concutitur. Valet ima summis

mutare et insignem attenuat deus,
obscura promens. Hinc apicem rapax
   Fortuna cum stridore acuto   15
     sustulit; hic posuisse gaudet.

THE GOLDEN MEAN

   In this ode, one of the most famous and finished of his poems, Horace sets forth his favorite doctrine of the golden mean, or moderation in all things, as the best guide for conduct (*Odes*, ii. 10).

RECTIUS vives, Licini, neque altum
     semper urgendo neque, dum procellas
     cautus horrescis, nimium premendo
  litus iniquum.

Auream quisquis mediocritatem   5
diligit, tutus caret obsoleti
sordibus tecti, caret invidenda
    sobrius aula.

Saepius ventis agitatur ingens
pinus, et celsae graviore casu   10
decidunt turres, feriuntque summos
    fulgura montis.

Sperat infestis, metuit secundis
alteram sortem bene praeparatum
pectus. Informis hiemes reducit   15
    Iuppiter; idem

submovet. Non, si male nunc, et olim
sic erit. Quondam cithara tacentem
suscitat musam neque semper arcum
    tendit Apollo.   20

ATLAS

Rebus angustis animosus atque
fortis appare; sapienter idem
contrahes vento nimium secundo
    turgida vela.

EVER THE GOLDEN MEAN

Horace, happy and contented in his small property and in the possession of good character and good friends, contrasts his own lot with
that of some unnamed person who is never satisfied with what he has
acquired but goes on adding to his property and constructing buildings,
forgetting that death ends all both for the poor and for the rich (*Odes*,
ii. 18).

NON ebur neque aureum
        mea renidet in domo lacunar;
        non trabes Hymettiae
    premunt columnas ultima recisas
Africa; neque Attali   5
    ignotus heres regiam occupavi,
nec Laconicas mihi
    trahunt honestae purpuras clientae:
at fides et ingeni
    benigna vena est, pauperemque dives   10
me petit. Nihil supra
    deos lacesso nec potentem amicum
largiora flagito,
    satis beatus unicis Sabinis.
Truditur dies die   15
    novaeque pergunt interire lunae:
tu secanda marmora
    locas sub ipsum funus, et sepulcri
immemor struis domos,
    marisque Bais obstrepentis urges   20

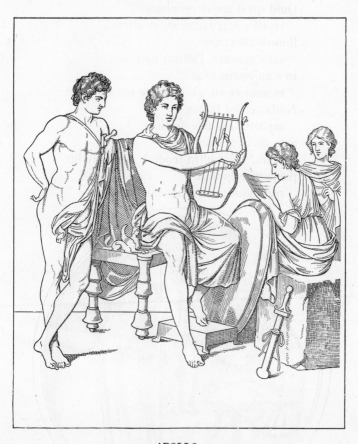

APOLLO

submovere litora,
   parum locuples continente ripa.
Quid quod usque proximos
   revellis agri terminos et ultra
limites clientium   25
   salis avarus? Pellitur paternos
in sinu ferens deos
   et uxor et vir sordidosque natos.
Nulla certior tamen
   rapacis Orci fine destinata   30
aula divitem manet
   erum. Quid ultra tendis? Aequa tellus
pauperi recluditur
   regumque pueris, nec satelles Orci

PROMETHEUS AND HIS IMAGE

PLUTO

callidum Promethea   35
   revexit auro captus. Hic superbum
Tantalum atque Tantali
   genus coercet; hic, levare functum
pauperem laboribus
   vocatus atque non vocatus, audit.   40

THE GOLDEN MEAN IN LIFE

In one of the poems of the *Tristia* (iii. 4. 1–34), Ovid, out of his own
experience, advises a friend that there is a golden mean which will bring
peace and comfort in life.

O MIHI care quidem semper, sed tempore duro
     cognite, res postquam procubuere meae:
    usibus edocto si quicquam credis amico,
   vive tibi et longe nomina magna fuge.
Vive tibi, quantumque potes, praelustria vita: 5
   saevum praelustri fulmen ab igne venit.
Nam quamquam soli possunt prodesse potentes,
   non prosit potius, si quis obesse potest.
Effugit hibernas demissa antemna procellas,
   lataque plus parvis vela timoris habent.   10
Aspicis ut summa cortex levis innatet unda
   cum grave nexa simul retia mergat onus?
Haec ego si monitor monitus prius ipse fuissem,
   in qua debebam forsitan urbe forem.
Dum tecum vixi, dum me levis aura ferebat,   15
   haec mea per placidas cumba cucurrit aquas.
Qui cadit in plano (vix hoc tamen evenit ipsum),
   sic cadit ut tacta surgere possit humo;
at miser Elpenor, tecto delapsus ab alto,
   occurrit regi debilis umbra suo.   20

Quid fuit ut tutas agitaret Daedalus alas,
  Icarus immensas nomine signet aquas?
Nempe quod hic alte, demissius ille volabat;
  nam pennas ambo non habuere suas.
Crede mihi: bene qui latuit, bene vixit, et intra   25
  fortunam debet quisque manere suam.
Non foret Eumedes orbus, si filius eius
  stultus Achilleos non adamasset equos;
non natum in flamma vidisset, in arbore natas,
  cepisset genitor si Phaëthonta Merops.   30
Tu quoque formida nimium sublimia semper,
  propositique, precor, contrahe vela tui.
Nam pede inoffenso spatium decurrere vitae
  dignus es et fato candidiore frui.

TRUE MANLINESS

In this ode Horace declares that to cultivate the characteristic Roman
virtues of manly courage and loyalty (*virtus* and *fides*) is the best object that a young man can have as he sets out in life (*Odes*, iii. 2).

ANGUSTAM amice pauperiem pati
    robustus acri militia puer
      condiscat, et Parthos ferocis
  vexet eques metuendus hasta,

vitamque sub divo et trepidis agat   5
in rebus. Illum ex moenibus hosticis
    matrona bellantis tyranni
      prospiciens et adulta virgo

suspiret (eheu!) ne rudis agminum
sponsus lacessat regius asperum   10
    tactu leonem, quem cruenta
      per medias rapit ira caedes.

Dulce et decorum est pro patria mori.
Mors et fugacem persequitur virum,
   nec parcit imbellis iuventae   15
     poplitibus timidoque tergo.

Virtus, repulsae nescia sordidae,
intaminatis fulget honoribus,
   nec sumit aut ponit securis
     arbitrio popularis aurae.   20

Virtus, recludens immeritis mori
caelum, negata temptat iter via,
   coetusque volgaris et udam
     spernit humum fugiente penna.

Est et fideli tuta silentio   25
merces. Vetabo qui Cereris sacrum
   volgarit arcanae sub isdem
     sit trabibus fragilemque mecum

solvat phaselon. Saepe Diespiter
neglectus incesto addidit integrum;   30
   raro antecedentem scelestum
     deseruit pede Poena claudo.

REGULUS

The Romans always pointed to Regulus as a man of honor and a true patriot. While in command of an army in Africa in the First Punic War, he was defeated by the Carthaginians and captured. They sent him to Rome with an embassy to ask for an exchange of prisoners. He gave his word that he would return if the exchange were not effected. On arriving in Italy, he refused to kiss his wife and children, because, being a prisoner, he was no longer a Roman citizen and was unfit to associate with his family or friends. He persuaded the senate to refuse the exchange, and went back to suffer torture and death. Horace celebrates Regulus in one of his *Odes* (iii. 5. 41–56).

FERTUR pudicae coniugis osculum
    parvosque natos, ut capitis minor,
        ab se removisse et virilem
           torvus humi posuisse voltum,

donec labantis consilio patres   45
    firmaret auctor numquam alias dato,
        interque maerentis amicos
           egregius properaret exsul.

Atqui sciebat quae sibi barbarus
    tortor pararet. Non aliter tamen   50
        dimovit obstantis propinquos
           et populum reditus morantem

quam si clientum longa negotia,
    diiudicata lite, relinqueret,
        tendens Venafranos in agros   55
           aut Lacedaemonium Tarentum.

TO THE SPRING OF BANDUSIA

An ode (iii. 13) written by Horace to a spring that was very dear to
him. Perhaps it was near his birthplace at Venusia, perhaps on his own
Sabine farm.

O FONS Bandusiae, splendidior vitro,
    dulci digne mero non sine floribus,
       cras donaberis haedo,
    cui frons turgida cornibus

primis et venerem et proelia destinat: 5
frustra; nam gelidos inficiet tibi
    rubro sanguine rivos,
       lascivi suboles gregis.

Te flagrantis atrox hora Caniculae
nescit tangere, tu frigus amabile   10
    fessis vomere tauris
       praebes et pecori vago.

Fies nobilium tu quoque fontium,
me dicente cavis impositam ilicem
    saxis unde loquaces   15
       lymphae desiliunt tuae.

AN ANCIENT OXCART

THE GOLDEN AGE

In the Golden Age, when Saturn reigned, there were no roads for travel, and men lived happily in their native homes. There were no ships either, and therefore no foreign trade. All was peace and plenty. But now, under Jupiter's rule, there is war, there is seafaring, there are countless ways of sudden death (Tibullus, i. 3. 35–50).

QUAM bene Saturno vivebant rege, priusquam 35
    tellus in longas est patefacta vias!
Nondum caeruleas pinus contempserat undas,
    effusum ventis praebueratque sinum,
nec vagus, ignotis repetens compendia terris,
    presserat externa navita merce ratem. 40
Illo non validus subiit iuga tempore taurus;
    non domito frenos ore momordit equus;
non domus ulla fores habuit; non fixus in agris,
    qui regeret certis finibus arva, lapis.

Ipsae mella dabant quercus, ultroque ferebant   45
  obvia securis ubera lactis oves.
Non acies, non ira fuit, non bella, nec ensem
  immiti saevus duxerat arte faber.
Nunc Iove sub domino caedes et volnera semper,
  nunc mare, nunc leti mille repente viae.   50

Ovid gives a similar description of the Golden Age in his *Meta-morphoses*, i. 89–112.

AUREA prima sata est aetas, quae vindice nullo,
   sponte sua, sine lege fidem rectumque colebat;   90
   poena metusque aberant, nec verba minacia fixo
aere legebantur, nec supplex turba timebat
iudice ora sui, sed erant sine iudice tuti.
Nondum caesa suis, peregrinum ut viseret orbem,
montibus in liquidas pinus descenderat undas,   95
nullaque mortales praeter sua litora norant.
Nondum praecipites cingebant oppida fossae.
Non tuba directi, non aeris cornua flexi,
non galeae, non ensis erant: sine militis usu
mollia securae peragebant otia gentes.   100
Ipsa quoque immunis rastroque intacta, nec ullis
saucia vomeribus, per se dabat omnia tellus;
contentique cibis nullo cogente creatis,
arbuteos fetus montanaque fraga legebant,
cornaque et in duris haerentia mora rubetis,   105
et quae deciderant patula Iovis arbore glandes.
Ver erat aeternum, placidique tepentibus auris
mulcebant zephyri natos sine semine flores.
Mox etiam fruges tellus inarata ferebat,
nec renovatus ager gravidis canebat aristis;   110
flumina iam lactis, iam flumina nectaris ibant,
flavaque de viridi stillabant ilice mella.

SATURN

SATURN.

NOTES

I. THE ÆNEID

BOOK I

1. Arma virumque: this is the theme of the Æneid, — the *conflicts* attending the settlement of the Trojans in Italy, and the adventures of the *hero* (first named in *v.* 92) who led the expedition from Troy. The wars in Italy are described in Books vii–xii, and the adventures in Books i–vi. For construction see Introd. § 37. — **Troiae:** see the account of the Trojan War, Introd., pp. 11–12. — **primus venit:** the Trojan Antenor came to northern Italy before Æneas (*v.* 242); but Virgil here disregards his arrival, perhaps because northern Italy (Cisalpine Gaul) was not until 42 B.C. regarded as belonging to Italy proper.

2. Italiam: acc. of place to which, with the preposition omitted (Introd. § 47). — **fato:** abl. of means with *profugus* (Introd. § 55). — **profugus:** Æneas was not a mere adventurer, but was driven from his home by fate; the verbal adjective is equivalent to a perf. participle, *exiled.* — **Lavinia litora:** i. e. the shores of Latium. Lavinium, an ancient town in Latium, was thought to have been the original Trojan settlement in Italy, and to have been named after Lavinia (daughter of Latinus, king of the Latins), whom Æneas married. *Lavinia* is pronounced in three syllables, the last *i* having the sound of *y*, and being treated as a consonant (Introd. § 112).

3. multum: adv. acc. with the participle *iactatus* (Introd. § 41). — **ille:** repeats the subject (*qui, v.* 1) with emphasis, *the man* [*who was*] *long* (lit. *much*) *tossed about.* — **terris, alto:** abl. of place where, with preposition omitted (Introd. § 67).

4. vi: the immediate cause, while *ob iram* is the more remote cause. — **superum:** gen. pl. m. (Introd. § 91, *c*). — **memorem,** *ever-mindful:* this adj. logically belongs with *Iunonis,* but it is poetically transferred to *iram.* Juno is represented as filled with a relentless hatred of Troy, which does not stop at the destruction of the city but pursues Æneas into his distant exile.

NOTE. The grammars cited are those of Allen and Greenough (A.), D'Ooge (D.), Bennett (B.), and Gildersleeve and Lodge (G.) References with *Introd.* and the mark § are to the Grammatical Summary in the Introduction.

5. multa quoque et bello passus, *and who likewise suffered much in war also.* The participle *passus, having suffered,* may be translated by a relative clause. — **quoque** connects *multa passus* with *multum iactatus*: Æneas' sufferings did not end with his arrival, but continued in the subsequent wars. — **bello :** for case see Introd. § 67. — **dum conderet,** *until he could found*: the clause denotes purpose (A. 553; D. 765; B. 293, III, 2; G. 572); although the gods thwarted him to please Juno, yet they meant that he should succeed in the end. — **urbem :** Lavinium.

6. deos, *his gods*: i.e. the penates, or household gods, statues of whom Æneas carried with him (*v.* 68). From ii. 717–720 they appear to be the special gods of Æneas' household, but other passages treat them as gods of the Trojan state (so ii. 293). — **Latio :** dat. after *inferret* (Introd. § 27). — **genus Latinum :** Æneas, having married Lavinia and founded the town Lavinium, succeeded Latinus as king and united the Trojans and Latins into one people.

7. Albani patres . . . Romae : Ascanius, son of Æneas, founded Alba Longa, from which city Romulus and Remus came to found Rome. Virgil has in mind, also, great senatorial families of his time, which traced their descent from Alba Longa, and so back to Troy.

8. Musa, etc.: Virgil follows the regular epic method, invoking the Muse, and referring all the plot to the gods. — **mihi :** final *i* of this word may be either long or short; A. 604, *f*, exc.; D. 961; B. 363, 3; G. 707, 4, exc. 4. — **quo numine laeso,** *what divine purpose* [of Juno] *having been thwarted*: abl. abs. (Introd. § 65).

9. quid, *feeling pain at what*; *doleo* is often transitive. — **regina deum :** i.e. Juno, wife of Jupiter, identified with the Greek Hera as the enemy of the Trojans, and with the Phœnician Astarte as the patroness of Carthage. — **deum :** see n. on *superum, v.* 4. — **volvere,** *to run the round of* (as if the misfortunes were a circle arranged by destiny). For inf. see Introd. § 79.

10. pietate includes the devotion of Æneas to his father as well as his reverence for the gods. The gods could pursue with vengeance even a pious man, either because under the power of Fate he thwarted their purposes, or because his ancestors had committed crimes. For case see Introd. § 52.

11. impulerit : indir. question; A. 574; D. 812; B. 300, 1; G. 467. — **animis :** dat. of possessor; supply *sunt* (Introd. § 29). — **irae,** *wrath*; for use of plur. see Introd. § 96.

12. antiqua : i.e. in reference to Virgil's time. Carthage was founded by Phœnicians from Tyre about three centuries later than the date (1184 B.C.) traditionally assumed for the fall of Troy. — **tenuere :** for form see Introd. § 91, *l*; *eam* is to be supplied. Such omission of words is common in poetry.

13. longe : modifying *contra*.

14. ostia : for plur. see Introd. § 96. — **opum :** gen. of specification with *dives*, a poetical construction (Introd. § 17). — **studiis,** *in its passion* *for*: abl. of specification (Introd. § 63). Virgil had in mind the experience of Rome in the Punic Wars. — **belli**: obj. gen. with *studiis* (Introd. § 14).

15. quam . . . coluisse, *which Juno is said to have cherished*: Introd. § 80. The gods were supposed to be especially fond of the places where

Fig. 1

they were most worshipped, or whence their worship first came. — **terris omnibus**: abl. of comparison (Introd. § 54); *omnibus = ceteris.* — **unam**: often used with superlatives for emphasis; here *magis omnibus* = a superlative.

16. posthabita Samo, *holding* [*even*] *Samos in less regard*: abl. abs. (Introd. § 65). Juno had an old and famous temple at Samos. See Fig. 1 (from a coin). — **Samo; hic**: hiatus (Introd. § 108). — **illīus**: note the short *i* (Introd. § 111). — **arma, currus**: Juno is sometimes represented with shield and spear; see Fig. 2 (from coins). The reference here is probably to some arms long preserved as relics in her temple.

17. hoc refers to Carthage but takes the gender of *regnum*: A. 296, *a*; B. 246, 5; G. 211, R.[5] — **tenditque fovetque,** *this the goddess — if by any means the fates permit — already aims and fondly hopes to make the seat of royal power for the nations.* — **gentibus**: dat. of reference (Introd. § 31). — **esse**: cf. the inf. with *impulerit*, *v.* 9.

18. fata: even the gods must yield to the fates. — **sinant**: fut. protasis, of which the apodosis is absorbed in *tendit esse*, etc. — **iam tum,** *even then*, while Carthage was in its infancy and before Rome was founded.

Fig. 2

19. sed enim, *but* [*she feared for Carthage*] *for*, etc., referring to the doubt implied in *si . . . sinant*: the context easily suggests the words omitted in such an ellipsis. — **duci**: pres. tense, because Æneas, the founder of the race, was still living.

20. Tyrias: i. e. Carthaginian (cf. *v.* 12). — **quae verteret,** *which was to overthrow*: rel. clause of purpose; A. 531; D. 715; B. 282, 2; G. 630.

21. populum late regem, *a people widely ruling.* The noun *regem* is used as an adj., and so may be modified by the adv. *late*: A. 321, *c*; D. 506, *b*; G. 288, R. — **bello**: see Introd. § 63. Cf. Milton, *Comus*, 33: "An old and haughty nation, proud in arms."

22. excidio Libyae : double dative (Introd. § 33). Libya, the name of a district in northern Africa, is here used for all of Africa under Carthaginian rule. — **sic volvere Parcas,** *so the Fates spin* [the thread of destiny]. Three Parcae, or Destinies, are conceived as spinning the threads of human fate : Clotho holds a spindle ; Lachĕsis draws the thread, and Atrŏpos cuts it off. Notice that Fate, or the Fates, have now been mentioned three times.

23. veteris belli: the Trojan War (Introd., p. 11). — **Saturnia,** *daughter of Saturn,* is subj. of *arcebat, v.* 31. Saturnus was an ancient Italian divinity of agriculture, identified with the Greek Cronos and thus regarded as the father of Jupiter (*Zeus*), Juno (*Hera*), Ceres, Neptune, and Pluto. His reign in Italy was regarded as a Golden Age of peace and plenty.

24. prima, *as chief* : Juno had taken the lead in helping the Greeks. — **ad Troiam,** *round Troy* : A. 428, *d* ; D. 431 ; B. 182, 3 ; G. 386, R.² — **pro caris Argis :** Juno (*Hera*) was worshipped with especial veneration at Argos, where she had a great temple. Argos is here put for all Greece.

25. necdum etiam, *nor even now.* — **irarum :** plur., referring to the many manifestations of her wrath (Introd. § 96).

26. animo : Introd. § 68. — **alta mente,** etc., *laid away deep in her mind* (Introd. § 67). — **repostum** for *repositum* : Virgil sometimes uses forms from which a syllable has been omitted (cf. i. 249 ; ii. 379) ; such forms are called *syncopated* (Introd. § 91, *n*).

27. iudicium Paridis : Introd., p. 12. Tennyson's *Œnone* tells the story. — **spretae iniuria formae,** *the insult to* (lit. *of*) *her slighted beauty* ; i. e. the disparagement shown to her beauty in the decision of Paris. For construction see A. 497 ; D. 866 ; B. 337, 6.

28. genus invisum : Juno hated the Trojans also from jealousy, since Dardanus, the founder of the Trojan race, was son of Jupiter and Electra. — **rapti Ganymedis honores :** the selection of Ganymede, Priam's brother, to be cupbearer of the gods in place of Juno's daughter, Hebe, was a third reason for Juno's hatred of the Trojans. Ganymede was carried off to Olympus by an eagle.

29. his accensa, *inflamed by these things,* i. e. what has been told in the foregoing verses : for case of *his* see Introd. § 55. — **super** (= *insuper*), *besides,* i. e. in addition to her anxiety for Carthage. — **aequore :** Introd. § 67.

30. Troas : Greek acc. plur. of *Trōs* (Introd. § 92). — **reliquias Danaum,** *those left by the Greeks,* i. e. those who escaped from them. For *Danaum* see Introd. §§ 91, *c* ; 8. — **Achilli :** a Greek noun (Introd. § 93).

31. Latio : abl. of separation (Introd. § 49).

32. errabant, *had wandered* (and still were wandering) ; A. 471, *b* ; D. 654 ; B. 260, 4 ; G. 234. — **circum :** for position of preposition see Introd. § 89, *d*.

33. tantae molis, [*a task*] *of so great toil it was* : gen. of quality in the predicate, limiting *condere,* subj. of *erat* (Introd. § 12).

34. Here begins the account of the wanderings of the Trojans. The story is begun in the middle. The Trojans have passed in Sicily the sixth winter of their wanderings, have just left Drepanum (iii. 707), and are now sailing away for Italy, as they hope. The earlier adventures are told by the hero himself (books ii and iii). This is a natural device to rouse interest (as in many modern novels). Cf. *Paradise Lost*, which, as Milton himself says, "hastes into the midst of things, presenting Satan with his angels now fallen into hell" (i. 50), the story of their fall not being fully told until *v.* 563 ff.

35. dabant, *they* (the Trojans) *were spreading.* — **laeti :** they thought that the end of their wanderings was near. — **salis,** *of the sea* (lit. *salt*): Introd. §§ 98, 99. — **aere,** *bronze beaks* (of the ships). The most ancient metal work was made of bronze, an alloy of copper and tin, much easier to melt than pure copper, as well as harder. — **ruebant,** *were ploughing up*; *ruo = eruo.*

36. cum Iuno . . . secum, sc. *loquitur.* The construction with "*cum* inverse" would require the omitted verb in the indic.: A. 546, *a*; D. 751; B. 288, 2; G. 581. — **sub pectore,** *in her heart.*

37. mene . . . desistere, *what! I desist!* (Introd. § 83). — **incepto :** Introd. § 49.

38. nec posse, *and be unable.* — **Italia :** for construction cf. *Latio, v.* 31. — **Teucrorum,** *of the Trojans,* often called *Teucri* from their earliest (mythical) king, Teucer. See Introd. § 98.

39. quippe, *to be sure* (expressing indignation by giving an ironical explanation of the facts). — **Pallasne . . . potuit :** i.e. could Pallas do this while I, the queen of the gods, am baffled in my efforts? This is a reply to the ironical suggestion of *vetor.*

40. Argivum : for form see Introd. § 91, *c*. Pallas destroyed the fleet of Ajax Oïleus when the Greeks were returning from Troy. — **ipsos,** *the men themselves.* — **ponto :** either means, or place where.

41. unius : opposed to *classem,* — a whole fleet for one man's crime. — **furias,** *madness* (Introd. § 96). The great crimes of antiquity were thought to have been committed in a frenzy induced by the Furies, the agents of divine wrath. Hence *furiae* is often used of ungovernable passion. Ajax, son of Oïleus (a hero less distinguished than Ajax, son of Telamon), is said to have offered violence to Cassandra, daughter of Priam and priestess of Pallas, and that, too, at the altar of the goddess. — **Oïleï :** trisyllabic; *ei* is read as one syllable (*synizesis* : Introd. § 115).

42. ipsa iaculata, *hurling with her own hands.* Pallas was the only deity except Jupiter who might wield the thunderbolt. See Fig. 3 (from a coin).

43. que . . . que, *both . . . and* (or simply *and*).

44. illum : Ajax. — **pectore :** abl. of separation (Introd. § 49).

45. turbine: abl. of means (Introd. § 55).— **infixit,** *impaled.*— **scopulo:** either dat. (Introd. § 27) or abl. (§ 67). Cf. *Paradise Lost,* ii. 178 ff. :

> While we, perhaps,
> Designing or exhorting glorious war,
> Caught in a fiery tempest, shall be hurl'd
> Each on his rock transfix'd, the sport and prey
> Of racking whirlwinds.

46. ast: old form of *at.* — **incedo,** *move :* the word suggests dignity by mentioning the gait at all when there is no need of it. The gait (*incessus*)

of the gods was supposed to be an even, gliding movement, not the mere human act of walking. Cf. Gray, *Progress of Poesy* (of Venus): " In gliding state she wins her easy way."

47. annos: Introd. § 46.

48. gero, *have been* (and still am) *waging;* A. 466; D. 650; B. 259, 4; G. 230: cf. n. on *errabant, v.* 32. — **quisquam :** implying a negative; A. 311; D. 573; B. 252, 4; G. 317. — **adoret :** deliberative subjunc.; A. 444; D. 678; B. 277; G. 466.

Fig. 3

49. praeterea, *any more,* or *hereafter.*— **aris:** dat. (Introd. § 27). — **imponet:** the future in this usage differs little from the deliberative subjunctive. — **honorem,** *an offering.*

50. corde: Introd. § 67.

51. patriam, luctantis, indignantes : since these words belong strictly only to persons, their use makes a lively personification of the winds. — **austris :** one of the most violent winds used for them all (Introd. § 66).

52. Aeoliam : one of the Lipari Islands, northeast of Sicily. — **Aeolus :** god of the winds. Ulysses was said to have visited his island and to have received from him — to ensure good weather — the winds tied up in a bag; but the sailors, thinking the bag contained treasure, untied it, and a storm was the result (Odyssey). — **antro :** Introd. § 67.

54. imperio: Introd. § 55.— **vinclis :** syncopated form of *vinculis* (Introd. § 91, *o*). — **frenat,** *curbs :* as if the winds were horses; cf. *premere et laxas dare habenas, v.* 63.

55. magno cum murmure : abl. of manner (Introd. § 58). Observe the alliteration : A. 641; B. 375, 3.

56. arce : a lofty seat or citadel within the cave or beside it, not the mountain itself.

57. sceptra : the plur. is here used for metrical reasons (Introd. § 96). — **animos,** *passions ;* regular in the plural for the *feelings,* especially *pride.*

58. ni : this old form of *nisi* is retained in laws, religious formulas, and poetry. — **ni faciat . . . ferant . . . verrant :** the pres. subjunc. instead of the imperf. is found in poetry in present conditions contrary to fact (A. 517, *e*; D. 799; G. 596, R.¹). Here the present is more vivid than the imperf., as suggesting what would happen if Æolus should ever neglect his duty.

59. quippe, *doubtless they would bear away*; not ironical as in *v.* 39. — **verrant,** *sweep*.

60. pater omnipotens: Jupiter.

61. molem et montis, *a mass of lofty mountains.* The use of two nouns connected by a conjunction instead of one modified noun is known as *hendiadys*; A. 640; D. 944; B. 374, 4; G. 698. — **insuper,** *above them*.

62. foedere certo, *under fixed conditions*: abl. of accordance (Introd. § 64). Æolus is to release the winds only when ordered.

63. sciret, etc., *should know, when bidden, both how to check and how to give loose rein.* — **sciret:** subjunc. in a rel. clause of purpose; A. 531, 2; D. 715; B. 282, 2; G. 630. — **premere,** from the motion of the hand in drawing the reins, is opposed to *laxas dare*; *habenas* is object of both verbs. For the use of the infin. see Introd. § 75. — **iussus:** A. 496; D. 861; B. 337, 2; G. 664.

64. vocibus: Introd. § 56. — **usa est:** elide, reading *usa'st*; A. 13, N.; D. 982; G. 719, exc. For the monosyllabic word at the end of the verse see Introd. § 117.

65. namque introduces the reason of her coming to him. — **rex:** Introd. § 117.

66. mulcere, tollere: objects of *dedit*; in prose *ut mulceas, tollas* would be used (Introd. § 77). — **vento:** the winds were thought to calm as well as raise the sea.

67. Tyrrhenum aequor: south and west of Italy. — **aequor:** a kind of cognate acc. (Introd. § 37).

68. Ilium: they "carried Ilium" because they were on their way to found a new city to continue the old race. — **victos:** as the old home of the penates was destroyed, they might be called *conquered.* — **penatis:** the penates were the Roman household gods, under whose protection were the food and the store-room of the house and the material prosperity of the family. Associated with the penates as guardian deities of the household were the *lares*, spirits of the dead who hovered round the dwelling they had inhabited in life, and watched over its safety (see n. on v. 744). The images of the lares and penates were placed near the hearth, where offerings of food and drink were made to them at each meal. The Roman state, as well as the private family, had its lares and penates, for whom a fire was always kept burning in the temple of Vesta. So old was the worship of these deities that the Romans were pleased to believe that Æneas brought the penates with him from Troy.

69. incute vim ventis, *give force to the winds,* as it were by a blow of the sceptre. — **submersas obrue,** *overwhelm so that they will be sunk,* or *overwhelm and sink.* This use of a word in a clause preceding the one where it would naturally appear is called *prolepsis* (i.e. *anticipation*): A. 640; B. 374, 5.

70. age diversos, *drive them* (the men) *scattered*; cf. n. on *submersas*, *v.* 69. — **disice:** the first syllable is long; A. 11, *e*; D. 968, N.; B. 9, 3.

71. mihi: Introd. § 29. — **praestanti corpore:** abl. of quality (Introd. § 61).

72. quarum: Introd. § 13. — **formā:** Introd. § 63. — **Deïopea,** instead of being in the acc. as object of *iungam*, is attracted into the case of the relative *quae*.

73. conubio: *i* is treated as a consonant and the word is pronounced in three syllables (Introd. § 112). — **iungam:** sc. *tibi.* Juno bribes him because the act is beyond his lawful province. — **propriam dicabo,** *will assign* [*her*] *to you as your own.*

74. meritis, *services.*

75. exigat: purpose; A. 531, 1; D. 713; B. 282, 1; G. 545. — **faciat te parentem:** two accusatives (Introd. § 39). — **prole:** abl. of means with *faciat.*

76. haec: sc. *dicit* (Introd. § 99). — **tuus . . . explorare,** *yours* [*is*] *the task to determine what you will have* (Introd. § 73). — **optes:** indir. question; A. 574; D. 812; B. 300, 1; G. 467.

77. mihi: dat. of reference (Introd. § 31). — **capessere:** for kind of verb see A. 263, 2, *b*; D. 290, *b*, 1; G. 191, 5.

78. tu mihi . . . concilias, *you win for me whatever rule I have,* implying that it is small. — **hoc:** sc. *est.* — **regni:** partitive gen. with *quodcumque* (Introd. § 13). — **sceptra Iovemque,** *the sceptre* (i.e. power) *from Jove:* hendiadys; cf. n. to *v.* 61.

79. accumbere: see n. on *mulcere, v.* 66. The Romans reclined at meals, and Virgil attributes the same custom to earlier nations and to the gods, though in fact the Greeks sat, as we do.

80. nimborum: obj. gen. (Introd. § 14). — **facis:** sc. *me.*

81. dicta: sc. *sunt.* — **conversa cuspide,** *with spear-point turned.*

82. impulit in latus, *he struck on its side.* — **velut agmine facto** (abl. abs.), *like an assaulting column:* a brief simile. Simile and metaphor, the two most important figures of speech, are especially common in poetry. Both are founded on *comparison.* A simile expresses a figurative resemblance between two objects, actions, or ideas in the form of a definite comparison, usually with *like* or *as.* A metaphor indicates the resemblance by applying to one of the objects, actions, or ideas a word that literally designates the other. Thus, in the present case, *in an assaulting column* (without *like*) would be a metaphor.

83. qua, *where.* — **data:** sc. *est.* — **turbine:** abl. of manner (Introd. § 58).

84. incubuere: the perf. suddenly shifts the point of view to indicate the swiftness of the act; *and now they have fallen upon the sea, and are ploughing up.* — **mari:** dat. (Introd. § 27). — **totum:** sc. *mare*.

85. una: adv. — **Eurusque,** etc.· the winds from all quarters are conceived as let loose together and, by their simultaneous action in opposite directions, causing the storm. — **ruunt** = *eruunt.* — **procellis,** *gusts:* abl. of means with *creber* (Introd. § 55).

86. Africus: the southwest wind, blowing hot from Africa, is often one of the most violent on the Italian coast.

87. virum: cf. *superum, v.* 4.

90. intonuere poli, *the heavens thunder:* see n. on *incubuere, v.* 84. — **micat,** *flashes.*

92. solvuntur, etc., *his limbs are paralyzed by the chill of terror.* The ancients betrayed their emotions in a far more lively way than would be allowable in a modern hero. Æneas is here mentioned by name for the first time.

93. duplicis palmas, *both his hands.* The ancient attitude of prayer was not with clasped hands, but with the palms spread upward, as if to receive the blessing.

94. talia voce refert, *thus he speaks.* — **O terque quaterque beati:** Introd. § 71.

95. quîs = *quibus:* dat. with *contigit* (Introd. § 91, *g*); for case see Introd. § 25. — **ante ora:** a happy lot, because their friends were witnesses of their deeds and glorious death.

96. contigit, *befell:* usually said of good fortune, as here. — **oppetere:** sc. *mortem,* hence, *to die.*

97. Tydide, *the son of Tydeus,* Diomedes, who met Æneas in single combat, and would have killed him had he not been saved by Venus, his mother. *Tydide* is a patronymic: Introd. § 98; A. 244; D. 282, *g*; B. 148, 6; G. 182, 11. — **mene . . . potuisse,** *to think that I could not have,* etc.: cf. *v.* 37. — **campis:** abl. of place where.

98. dextra: abl. of means.

99. saevus, *stern,* not sparing the foe. -- **Aeacidae:** Achilles, grandson of Æacus. For case form see A. 44; D. 81; B. 22; G. 65. — **telo iacet,** *lies slain by the spear.*

100. Sarpedon: a Lycian prince, son of Jupiter, and an ally of the Trojans. In Homer his body is said to have been borne home by Sleep and Death, but Virgil does not care for this detail. — **Simois,** etc., *the Simois rolls the shields, and helmets, and stalwart forms of so many heroes carried away beneath its waves;* grammatically *tot* belongs to all the accusatives. The Simois was a small river near Troy.

102. iactanti, *as he utters:* dat. of reference, sc. *ei* (Introd. § 31). — **stridens Aquilone procella,** *a hurricane howling with the north wind.* For the case of *Aquilone* see Introd. § 55.

103. velum adversa ferit, *strikes the sail in front*; *adversa* (adj. with *procella*) is equivalent to an adverb. The ancient ship had a square sail, suspended from a yard. The ship of Æneas is sailing before a southerly wind, when suddenly a north wind strikes the sail from an opposite quarter, swinging the vessel round broadside to the waves (cf. *v.* 104). — **ad sidera tollit:** exaggerated language, such as this, is known as *hyperbole.* This particular passage set a literary fashion which lasted for about two thousand years. Cf. Shakspere, *Othello,* ii. 1. 11 ff.:

> For do but stand upon the foaming shore,
> The chidden billow seems to pelt the clouds;
> The wind-shaked surge, with high and monstrous mane,
> Seems to cast water on the burning Bear
> And quench the guards of the ever-fixed pole:
> I never did like molestation view
> On the enchafed flood.

104. remi: oars as well as sails were used on the ancient ship. — **prora** is subj. both of *avertit* and *dat.* — **avertit** [*se*], *swings round* (lit. *turns away*).

105. cumulo: abl. of manner. — **mons:** Introd. § 117.

106. his: dat. of reference.

107. terram . . . aperit: Virgil continues his hyperbole. — **furit aestus harenis,** *the seething flood rages with the sands.* They are approaching the syrtes (*v.* 111).

108. tris: sc. *navis.* — **Notus:** a north wind would appear to be needed to drive the ships from west of Sicily to the coast of Africa, but Virgil here mentions the various winds without much regard to their direction. — **abreptas torquet,** *seizes and hurls.* — **latentia,** *hidden* by the roaring waves; in calm weather they are visible (*dorsum immane, v.* 110) at the surface. These reefs are supposed to lie just outside the Bay of Carthage.

109. Parenthetical: *rocks like what, in midwater, the Italians call* "*altars,*" — not necessarily this particular group, which they probably knew nothing about.

111. in brevia et syrtis, *on the shoals and sandbanks:* i.e., probably, the shoals of the great syrtis, though these are east of Carthage. Poetry pays little attention to geographical accuracy. — **visu:** A. 510; D. 882, II; B. 340, 2; G. 436.

112. vadis: Introd. § 34. — **aggere,** *embankment.*

114. ipsius, *the leader himself* (Æneas). For *ĭ* cf. *illĭus, v.* 16. — **ingens pontus:** like our phrase "a heavy sea." — **a vertice,** *from above:* the prepositional phrase belongs grammatically with *ferit,* but in sense serves as an adj. with *pontus.*

115. puppim: A. 75, *b*; D. 102, *c*; B. 38, 1; G. 57. — **excutitur,** *is washed overboard.* — **pronus volvitur in caput,** *is thrown* (lit. *rolled*) *headlong.*

THE ÆNEID. BOOK I

11

116. illam, *her*: the ship, in distinction from the helmsman.

117. torquet agens circum, *whirls round* (lit. *whirls, driving her round*). — **rapidus,** *greedy* (cf. *rapio, seize*). — **aequore :** locative abl.

118. rari, *scattered here and there.* — **gurgite,** *the sea* (Introd. § 98).

119. arma : the shields, for instance, would float visibly for a while, but the word may refer to any of their equipments.

120. Ilionei : *ei* is pronounced as one syllable (Introd. § 115).

121. quā, *that in which*: properly abl. of instrument (Introd. § 55); the antecedent (*eam*) is implied.

122. laxis compagibus, *with loosened joints*: instrumental abl.

123. imbrem : properly *rain-flood*; but here *water* in general. — **rimis :** abl. of manner; cf. *vv.* 83, 105.

124. murmure : abl. of manner. Observe the alliteration.

125. emissam : sc. *esse.* — **Neptunus :** Neptune, god of the ocean, was a brother of Jupiter. His palace was in the depths of the sea ; but he made his home on Olympus when he chose. The symbol of his power was the trident, or three-pronged spear, with which he could shatter rocks, call forth or subdue storms, and shake the shores. He created the horse and was the patron of horse races. His own steeds were brazen-hoofed and golden-maned. They drew his chariot over the sea, which became smooth before him, while dolphins and other monsters of the deep gamboled about his path. In his honor black and white bulls, white boars, and rams were sacrificed (Gayley).

126. stagna refusa, *that the still waters had been forced up* (lit. *poured back*) *from the lowest depths.* — **vadis :** abl. of separation (Introd. § 49). — **commotus,** *disturbed* (in mind); but as a god he must be represented with *placidum caput.* — **alto prospiciens,** *looking forth over the deep* ; *alto* is locative abl.

127. unda : abl. of separation.

128. aequore : locative abl.

129. caeli ruina, *the wreck of the sky*: the violent rain is regarded as an actual downfall of the sky itself.

130. fratrem : obj. of *latuere, were hidden from*; A. 396, *c* ; D. 406, *c.* — **doli, irae :** her *craft* (known to him as her brother), and the *wrath* which led to its exercise.

131. dehinc : here monosyllabic by synizesis (Introd. § 115).

132. generis fiducia vestri, *confidence in your origin*: the winds were the sons of Aurora and the Titan Astræus ; and so on the one side of divine origin, and on the other sprung from the rivals of the gods.

133. iam, *at length.* — **caelum,** etc.: cf. *Paradise Lost,* iv. 452–453:

> I heard the wrack,
> As earth and sky would mingle.

134. miscere: Introd. § 75. — **tantas moles,** *such huge waves.*

135. quos ego: he leaves his unfinished threat to their imagination; he can spare no time for words. Such a break is called *aposiopēsis* (i.e. a sudden silence): A. 641; D. 941; G. 691. — **praestat,** *it is better.* — **componere:** Introd. § 73.

136. post, *hereafter.* — **commissa,** *your misdeeds.* — **non simili poena** (abl. of instrument), *by no penalty like this* (i.e. by a punishment greater than the offence): *litotes*; see A. 641; D. 947; B. 375, 1; G. 700. — **luetis,** *you shall atone for.*

138. non illi, *not to* HIM (emphatic).

139. sorte datum: sc. *esse.* Jupiter, Neptune, and Pluto were said to have chosen their realms by lot when they divided the universe which had been ruled by their father Saturn.

140. vestras: though addressing Eurus, he includes them all.— **se iactet,** *let him play the king* (lit. *vaunt himself*). — **aula:** as a king, he must have his *court* somewhere.

141. clauso: i.e. reign over the imprisoned winds, without power to let them loose.

142. dicto citius, *quicker than the word:* abl. of comparison; A. 406, *a*; D. 446, *b*; cf. B. 217, 3; G. 398, N.[1]

144. Cymothoë, a sea nymph, and *Triton,* Neptune's trumpeter, blowing a conch shell, are mentioned to suggest all the minor sea divinities. — **adnixus,** *pushing against* the ships.

145. navis: the three ships mentioned, *v.* 108. — **scopulo:** abl. of separation. — **levat:** using the trident as a lever.

146. aperit, *clears a passage through.* — **syrtis:** the sandbanks piled against the ships; cf. *v.* 112.

147. lĕvibus, *light,* skimming the surface. See Fig. 4 (from a gem). — **rotis:** abl. of manner.

148. veluti, *just as:* introducing one of the most celebrated of Virgil's similes (see n. on *v.* 82). The ferocity of a mob and the power of an eloquent speaker were things very familiar to the Romans. Cf. the opening scene of Shakspere's *Coriolanus.* — **magno in populo:** the greater the crowd, the more striking the effect of the speaker. — **saepe** belongs properly to the whole idea, and so is equivalent to *as often happens.*

149. seditio, *riot,* lit. *a going apart* (= *se-itio*). — **animis** (abl. of manner), *with passion:* cf. *v.* 57, n. — **ignobile,** *mean* or *obscure.* — **volgus:** for declension see A. 48, *a*; D. 87; B. 26, 2; G. 34.

150. iam: see n. on *v.* 133. — **faces,** *firebrands.* Rome, then largely built of wood, was very vulnerable to this favorite weapon of the mob.

151. tum: correlative with *cum, v.* 148. — **gravem,** *of weight* or *influence.* — **meritis,** *services* (to the state). — **si quem** belongs with *virum*; *quem, some, any,* is the usual indefinite pronoun with *si.*

152. conspexere: plur. because here the individuals are thought of, though a collective noun (*volgus*) is used before. — **arrectis auribus adstant,** *stand by with listening ears.*

153. regit . . . animos, *sways their minds by words* (addressed to their reason); *pectora mulcet, calms their passion* (whose seat was supposed to be in the breast). — **mulcet:** used originally of the *stroking* of an animal, and so of *soothing* the blind passion of the crowd.

154. sic: correlative with *veluti, v.* 148. — **pelagi:** for declension see A. 48, *a*; D. 87; B. 26, 2. — **fragor,** *crash* of the breakers. — **aequora prospiciens,** *looking forth on the waters.*

155. caelo aperto, *under a clear sky:* locative abl. — **invectus,** *riding* (Introd. § 95). See Fig. 4 (from an ancient gem).

156. curru: dat. (Introd. § 91, *d*). — **secundo,** *smoothly gliding* (lit. *following*).

157. Aeneadae, *companions of Æneas* (Introd. § 98). — **quae proxima** (sc. *erant*), *the nearest.*

158. vertuntur, *turn:* used in the reflexive or middle sense (Introd. § 94).

159. insula, etc., *an island makes a harbor by the opposition of its sides* [like a breakwater],

Fig. 4

against which every billow from the deep breaks (lit. *is broken*) *and divides into receding waves* (lit. *into drawn-back curves*).

160. quibus: abl. of instrument with *scinditur.* — **ab alto:** cf. n. to *a vertice, v.* 114.

162. hinc atque hinc, *on this side and that* (i.e. on both sides of the harbor, at each of the two entrances). — **rupes,** *cliffs:* the shore in general was rocky. — **gemini . . . scopuli,** *twin peaks* or *headlands* (one on each side).

164, 165. silvis, etc., *like a scene with waving woods, a dark forest with bristling shade* (referring to the forms of the firs, etc.) *juts over from above.* Literally *scaena* and *nemus* (referring to the same thing, though connected by *et*) are subjects of *imminet.* — **silvis:** abl. of quality (Introd. § 61). — **scaena** is properly the decorated wall at the back of the stage in Roman theatres (see Fig. 5): here, the background of wooded hills as seen from the shore. — **umbra:** abl. of manner. Cf. Milton, *Comus,* 37–39:

> This drear wood,
> The nodding horror of whose shady brows
> Threats the forlorn and wandering passenger.

166. fronte sub adversa, *under the opposite cliff,* i.e. the cliff at the far end of the harbor as one looked in from the entrance. — **scopulis pendentibus,** *of overhanging rocks*: abl. of quality.

167. aquae dulces, *fresh springs.* — **vivo saxo,** *of living rock,* i.e. rock in its natural state: abl. of material (Introd. § 51).

168. nympharum domus: the ancient imagination associated nymphs with any beautiful or romantic spots in the natural world (woods, lakes, etc.).

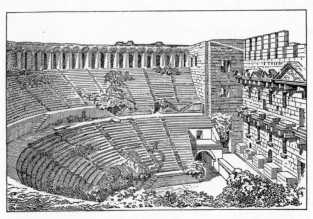

Fig. 5

170. omni ex numero: there had been twenty in all (*v.* 381); one was lost; twelve were scattered but afterwards came to shore (*v.* 393).

171. amore: abl. of manner.

172. harena: Introd. § 56.

173. sale tabentis, *dripping with the brine*: abl. of means.

174. silici, *from flint* (Introd. § 32).

175. suscepit, *caught.* — **foliis,** dry *leaves,* used as tinder (Introd. § 55). — **circum** goes with *dedit.* This separation of the parts of a compound verb is called *tmesis* ("cutting"). It is really the poetical retention of an earlier form of expression, when the preposition (originally adv.) had not become united with the verb. A. 640; D. 992; B. 367, 7; G. 726.

176. nutrimenta: anything that would keep the spark alive, — chips, stubble, etc. — **rapuit,** etc., *he kindled a blaze in dry fuel.*

177. Cererem, *corn*: identified with the goddess herself by the so-called figure *metonymy* (Introd. § 100). Ceres (the Greek Demeter) was goddess of the growing grain and hence of agriculture in general. She was daughter

of Saturn and mother of Proserpina (Pluto's wife). — **corruptam,** *damaged.*
— **Cerealia arma,** *utensils of Ceres,* or *cooking utensils*: such as a mortar
and pestle, baking-pans, etc.

178. expediunt: i.e. from the ships. — **fessi rerum,** *weary of toil*:
gen. of specification (Introd. § 17). — **fruges receptas,** *the grain that was
recovered* (from the sea).

179. torrere, *to parch,* before grinding (*frangere*).

180, 181. omnem prospectum . . . petit, *surveys* (lit. *seeks*) *the whole
view, far and wide over the sea.* — **pelago**: locative abl. — **Anthea si
quem videat,** [*to see*] *if he can see anything of Antheus* (lìt. *any Antheus*):
indir. quest.; A. 576, *a*; D. 814, *c*; B. 300, 3; G. 460, *b*. — **Anthea**: for
form see A. 81; D. 112; B. 47, 1; G. 65.

182. Phrygias, *Trojan.*

183. Capyn: for form see A. 82; D. 112. — **puppibus**: Introd. § 96. —
arma, *shields,* perhaps arranged in order along the quarter.

184. navem nullam, tris cervos: an example of *chiasmus*: A. 598,
f and N.; D. 934, *f*; B. 350, 11, *c*; G. 682 and R.

187. hic: adverb.

188. tela: attracted into the relative clause; A. 307, *e*; D. 559; B. 251,
4; G. 616, 2.

190. cornibus arboreis: abl. of quality. — **volgus,** *the herd.* — **omnem
. . . turbam,** *driving them with his weapons, he scatters the whole mass
among the leafy woods*: i.e. he breaks up the herd (which had been an
orderly *agmen*) and disperses it among the trees so that trees and deer are
in a manner mixed.

193. fundat, aequet: A. 551, *c*; D. 759 and N.²; cf. B. 292; G. 577.
— **humi**: locative (Introd. § 72).

194. partitur: sc. *cervos.* — **in** = *inter, among.*

195. deinde: dissyllabic (Introd. § 115). — **cadis onerarat,** *had laden in
jars*; *cadis* is dat.: A. 364; D. 374; B. 187, I, *a*; G. 348. — **Acestes**: a
king of Sicily whose hospitable court the Trojans had just left. This is not
distinctly stated here, though implied in *v.* 34, because Æneas is to stop in
Sicily again on his later voyage (Book v).

196. litore Trinacrio: Sicily, so called because of its three promontories
and triangular shape. — **heros**: Acestes.

198. neque practically = *non.* — **ignari,** *without knowledge.* — **ante**:
adv. equivalent to an adj. qualifying *malorum,* which is itself used as a noun.

199. O passi graviora, *ye who have suffered heavier woes.* — **deus,**
some god.

200. Scyllaeam = *Scyllae, of Scylla.* She was a six-headed monster,
destructive to mariners, who lived in a cave on the Italian side of the Strait
of Messina. The Trojans had been warned not to sail through this strait

(iii. 410 ff.), and when they came to this point they had turned south round Sicily (iii. 555 ff.). — **rabiem,** *madness,* especially of animals: appropriate of Scylla, who was surrounded by dogs or wolves (iii. 424–432). — **penitus sonantis scopulos,** *rocks resounding far within* (i.e. with the barking of Scylla's dogs, which represents the breaking waves).

201. accestis = *accessistis:* Introd. § 91, *n.* — **Cyclopia saxa:** i.e. the caves of the Cyclopes on the eastern side of Sicily. During their landing in this part of Sicily, the Trojans had had an exciting encounter with Polyphemus, one of these giants (iii. 655 ff.).

202. experti: sc. *estis.*

203. mittite = *dimittite.* — **et,** *even.* — **meminisse:** Introd. § 73.

204. discrimina rerum, *crises,* or *doubts and dangers.*

205. tendimus (sc. *iter*), *we are making our way.*

206. regna: Introd. § 96.

207. vosmet = *vos* + the emphatic particle *-met:* A. 143, *d*; D. 180, *a*; B. 84, 2; G. 102, N.² — **rebus secundis,** *for happier days* (Introd. § 24).

208. curis: abl. of cause. — **aeger,** *though sick at heart.*

209. spem simulat, premit dolorem: chiasmus; cf. n. on *v.* 184. — **voltu:** abl. of means. — **altum corde,** *deep in his heart.*

210. se praedae accingunt, *they gird themselves for their prey,* i.e. to prepare the feast: the loose-hanging clothes of the ancients had to be buckled up for any active work. — **praedae:** dat. of purpose (Introd. § 33).

211. tergora, *skin.* — **costis:** abl. of separation. — **viscera,** *the flesh.*

212. pars secant: plur. verb with a collective noun; the object is still *viscera.* — **veribus:** abl. of instrument.

214. fusi, *reclining:* cf. n. on *vertuntur, v.* 158.

215. implentur: Introd. § 94. — **Bacchi, ferinae:** Introd. § 22; cf. n. on *Cererem, v.* 177, for the metonymy.

216. exempta [*est*], *when their hunger had been satisfied* (lit. *taken away*): A. 543; D. 745; B. 287, 1; G. 561. — **mensae remotae** [*sunt*], *when the meal was ended,* lit. *when the tables were removed.* The phrase comes from the Roman custom of removing the table at the end of a meal.

217. requirunt, *ask after:* i.e. they question one another as to the probable fate of each of their missing comrades.

218. spem inter = *inter spem.* — **seu credant:** indir. quest. depending on *dubii, wavering.* The direct question would have been deliberative, *credamus? shall we believe?* A. 575, *b*; D. 816; B. 300, 2; G. 467.

219. extrema, *the last extremity,* i.e. death. — **nec iam exaudire,** *and no longer hear from afar.* Virgil alludes to the custom of calling the dead (*conclamatio*) as a part of the funeral rites.

221. secum, *in his own breast* (lit. *with himself*) — so as not to dishearten his companions (see *v.* 209).

223. finis: of their sad conversation, as night fell.

223–225. Cf. Milton, *Paradise Lost*, iii. 56 ff.:

> Now had th' Almighty Father from above,
> From the pure empyrean where he sits
> High thron'd above all highth, bent down his eye,
> His own works and their works at once to view.

224. despiciens, *looking down upon.* — **velivolum,** *winged with sails.* — **iacentis,** *low-lying* (as they appear when seen from on high).

225. sic: i.e. looking down. — **vertice caeli,** *at the summit of the heavens.*

226. regnis: abl. of place where.

227. iactantem, *revolving,* or *pondering,* properly shifting his cares about like a heavy load. — **talis curas,** *such cares* as became the ruler of the world, indicated by *despiciens,* etc.

228. tristior, *sadder than her wont.* Sorrow is unusual with her. See A. 291, *a*; D. 154, N.; B. 240, 1; G. 297. — **oculos suffusa nitentis,** *her bright eyes filled with tears*; *oculos* is acc. of specification (Introd. § 42) with *suffusa.*

229. Venus (the Greek Aphrodite), goddess of love and beauty, was daughter of Jupiter and mother of Cupid and Æneas. According to one myth, she arose from the foam of the sea near the island of Cythera (see *v.* 257). The rose and the myrtle were sacred to her and she was borne through the air in a chariot drawn by doves, her sacred birds. — **O qui,** *O thou who.* — **-que . . . -que,** *both . . . and.*

231. quid . . . tantum, *what offence so great can my Æneas have committed against you?*

232. quibus: dat. of reference. — **tot funera passis,** *having suffered so many losses,* particularly in the fall of Troy.

233. ob Italiam: i.e. on account of Juno's unwillingness for them to reach Italy. — **terrarum orbis:** *the whole earth* (lit. *the circle of the lands*).

234. hinc: from him and his race. — **Romanos . . . fore:** indir. disc. depending on *pollicitus*; A. 579; D. 884; B. 314, 1; G. 650. — **volventibus annis,** *as the years roll by.*

235. revocato a sanguine, *from the restored race* (lit. *recalled,* i.e. from destruction). — **Teucri:** cf. n. on *v.* 38.

236. tenerent, *shall hold*: imperf. by sequence of tenses for the fut. of direct discourse; A. 585; D. 889; B. 318; G. 654.

237. pollicitus: sc. *es.* — **sententia,** *purpose.*

238. hoc (abl. of means), *with this,* i.e. the promised glory of the Trojan race. — **equidem,** *at least.*

239. fatis . . . rependens, *compensating adverse fates with fate,* i.e. with the hope of a happier fate. — **fatis:** abl. of means.

240. nunc: opposed to the time indicated by *solabar*; *I used to find comfort for the fall of Troy; but now* I find that hope was vain.

242. Antenor: cf. n. on *primus, v.* 1. — **elapsus Achivis:** i.e. at the fall of Troy.

243. intima regna Liburnorum, *the realms of the Liburni far within,* i.e. far up the Adriatic. — **tutus,** *in safety*: he had escaped the perils of the Adriatic as well as the danger from a hostile people.

244. superare, *pass beyond* (with the suggestion also of surmounting difficulties).

245. per ora novem: the Timavus is a small river and bay, or creek, at the head of the Adriatic, where several springs — the actual number is seven — flow by underground channels in the limestone into the salt water. When the waters are forced back by a storm, the salt water finds its way through these crevices, so as to disgorge " with roaring flood " through the springs upon the land, —*pelago premit arva sonanti.* — **vasto . . . montis:** the noise of the water rushing forth is reëchoed by the mountain.

246. it mare proruptum, *it bursts forth, a raging sea*: the river is called a sea because it overflows the fields. — **pelago sonanti,** *with roaring flood.*

247. urbem Patavi: Introd. § 10.

248. arma fixit: i.e. in the temples, in gratitude for the peace which made them useless. This refers to an ancient custom by which the implement of an abandoned vocation was made a votive offering.

249. compostus = *compositus, undisturbed* (lit. *settled to rest* after the turmoils of his former wars).

250. nos, *yet we.* — **tua progenies:** Venus was a daughter of Jupiter, and Æneas was the son of Venus. — **caeli arcem,** *the height of heaven,* i.e. deification for Æneas. — **adnuis,** *dost promise* (by thy nod).

251. infandum, *O horror* (lit. *unspeakable thing*): Introd. § 44. — **unius:** Juno.

253. hic, etc., *is this the honor shown to piety ? Hic* refers to the previously stated facts, but agrees in gender with *honos.* — **sic . . . reponis,** *is it thus that you restore us to our rule ?* i.e. give to us that which is already ours by your promise.

254. olli: old form for *illi*; dat. with *subridens* (Introd. § 27).

255. voltu, *look,* i.e. *expression* (of countenance).

256. oscula (diminutive of *os*), *the pretty lips*: A. 243 ; D. 282, *a*; B. 148, 1; G. 181, 12. — **libavit,** *gently kissed.* — **debinc:** one syllable (Introd. § 115).

257. parce metu, *spare your fears*: for form of *metu* cf. *curru, v.* 156; for case see Introd. § 26. — **Cytherea:** Venus is called *Cytherea* from the island of Cythera, south of the Peloponnesus, near which she was said to have been born from the foam of the sea.

258. tibi: dat. of reference (Introd. § 31). — **Lăvini:** cf. *Lāvinia, v.* 2 ; freedom in the quantity of vowels in proper names is permissible in poetry.

259. sublimem, *on high*: referring again to the deification of Æneas (cf. *v.* 250).

260. neque . . . vertit: a reply to the question of Venus in *v.* 237.

261. tibi: ethical dat. (Introd. § 31).

262. longius et volvens, *and unrolling farther* (the scroll of fate). See Fig. 6. — **arcana:** with *volvens* and *movebo.* — **movebo,** *will disclose.* Observe that Jupiter himself must obey the fates.

263. bellum: the war with Turnus, recounted in the last six books of the Æneid. — **Italia:** abl. of place where (Introd. § 67).

264. mores, *institutions.* — **ponet,** *shall establish.*

265. tertia aestas: he shall live to reign three years in peace. — **dum . . . viderit:** A. 553, N.[2]; D. 765, N.; B. 293, III, 1; G. 571.

266. terna . . . hiberna, *three winters*: the distributive is used instead of a cardinal when a noun plural in form but usually singular in meaning is used in a plural sense. — **Rutulis subactis,** *after the Rutulians have been subdued*: dat. of reference. The Rutulians were a Volscian people who, under the

Fig. 6

leadership of their king, Turnus, were the chief antagonists of Æneas in his settlement in Italy (see Book vii).

267. at: though Æneas' reign shall be short, *yet*, etc. — **puer Ascanius:** son of Æneas. — **Iülo:** attracted from the nom. to the dat. to agree with *cui*; A. 373, *a*; D. 390, *a*; B. 190, 1; G. 349, R.[5] Virgil reminds his readers that the Julian family, of which Augustus was a member, claimed descent from Ascanius (Iülus).

268. res . . . Ilia, *the Ilian* (= Trojan) *state.* — **stetit . . . regno,** *stood firm in regal power*; *regno* is abl. of specification.

269. volvendis mensibus (abl. of quality with *orbis*), *cycles* (years) *of revolving months.* — **volvendis:** the gerundive is here equivalent to a present participle (*volventibus*).

271. Alba Longa was about fifteen miles southeast of Rome.

272. hic: at Alba. — **iam,** *in turn*, i.e. after the transfer. — **totos, unbroken.** — **regnabitur,** *the dynasty shall last*, impers.: A. 208, *d*; D. 266, *b*; B. 256, 3; G. 208, 2.

273. Hectorea: the Trojan race is so called after its greatest hero, Hector, son of Priam.— **regina sacerdos,** *a priestess of royal blood.* She was daughter of King Numitor and priestess of Vesta.

274. Marte gravis, *pregnant by Mars.* Mars (the Greek Ares), son of Jupiter and Juno, was god of war. Battle and slaughter were his delight. He was armed with spear, plumed helmet, and shield. He fought on foot or in a four-horse chariot.— **geminam . . . prolem,** *shall give birth to twin children* (Romulus and Remus).— **Ilia:** i.e. of the house of Ilus; she is commonly called Rhea Silvia.

275. lupae: a she-wolf was nursing Romulus and Remus when they were found by Faustulus, a shepherd.— **tegmine:** Introd. § 66. Romulus was no doubt represented in pictures, etc., as clad in a wolf's skin.— **laetus,** *exulting.*

276. excipiet, *shall next receive.*— **Mavortia moenia,** *the walls sacred to Mars,* i.e. Rome. Mars was the patron deity of Rome.

277. Romanos . . . dicet, *shall call them Romans. Roma* was fancifully supposed to be derived from the name *Romulus.*

278. metas . . . tempora, *neither boundaries for their state nor limits of time:* *rerum* goes in sense with both accusatives.

280. metu: abl. of means.— **fatigat,** *harasses.*

281. consilia . . . referet, *shall change her plans for the better.*

282. rerum dominos, *lords of affairs* (practically = *lords of the world*). — **togatam:** the toga was the peculiar garb of the Romans, and was required to be worn on all state occasions. As it was the robe of peace, the phrase here alludes to their civil greatness, while *rerum dominos* indicates their military dominion.

283. placitum: sc. *est.*— **lustris labentibus** (abl. abs.), *as the years glide by:* a *lustrum* is the period between two successive public purifications,— in theory four years, but in later practice five: here the word is used indefinitely.

284. domus Assaraci: i.e. the Trojan race. Ilus and Assaracus, sons of Tros, were the founders of the two royal families of Troy.— **Phthia** (the home of Achilles, in Thessaly), *Mycenae* (the royal city of Agamemnon, in Argolis), and *Argos* (the home of Diomedes, in Argolis) represent all Greece, which was made subject to Rome 146 B.C.

285. Argis: dative (Introd. § 28).

286. Caesar: i.e. Augustus.

287. Oceano: abl. of means. The ancients supposed that a great river, Oceanus, flowed round the earth.— **terminet:** rel. clause of purpose; A. 531, 2; D. 715; B. 282, 2; G. 630. Cf. *Paradise Lost,* xii. 369-371:

> He shall ascend
> The throne hereditary, and bound his reign
> With earth's wide bounds, his glory with the heavens.

288. Iulius: i.e. Augustus (C. Julius Cæsar Octavianus Augustus).

289. caelo: abl. of place where. Augustus was honored as a divinity even before his death. — **spoliis . . . onustum:** the allusion is to the surrender by the Parthians of the standards taken from Crassus in 53 B.C., as well as to the victory of Augustus at Actium in 31 B.C.

290. vocabitur . . . votis: another allusion to the deification or Augustus. — **hic quoque,** *he too,* as well as Æneas.

291. aspera . . . mitescent saecula: in this verse and the following verses the return of the Golden Age is prophesied, in which there shall be a restoration of good faith, simple homely virtues, brotherly love, and peace both private and public. See *Eclogue* iv and Pope's adaptation of it in his *Messiah.*

292. cana Fides, *venerable Faith* (lit. *white-haired*). — **Vesta:** goddess of the Hearth; here used for the dignity and sanctity of domestic life. See Vocabulary. — **Remo cum fratre Quirinus:** here Romulus (called *Quirinus* after his death) is represented as ruling with his brother, not as having slain him according to the common legend.

293. ferro . . . artis, *with close-fitting joints of iron* (hendiadys): abl. of means with *claudentur.*

Fig. 7

294. Belli portae: i.e. the gates of the temple of Janus, which were open in time of war and closed in peace. They were closed by Augustus for the first time after two hundred years (and the third time in Roman history) in 29 B.C. and again in 25 B.C. For the temple see Fig. 7 (from a coin). Janus was the ancient Italian god of entrances (cf. *ianua, gate, door*) and of beginnings. He is represented with two faces, "looking before and after." The first month of the year was named after him *Ianuarius.* — **Furor impius:** alluding to civil war, called *impius* because it is a conflict between persons bound together by a common kindred and religion. Note the personification of *Furor.* Personification is a figure of speech which represents (1) a lifeless object, (2) one of the lower animals, or (3) an idea, quality, or other abstraction, *as a person,* i.e. as capable of thought, feeling, or speech. Cf. *v.* 55, where the Winds are personified.

295. vinctus, *with his hands bound.*

296. horridus (adj.) may be translated by an adv., *horribly.* — **ore:** abl. of instrument with *fremet.*

297. Maia genitum, *the son of Maia,* Mercury (Introd. § 50).

298. novae: modifies *Karthaginis.* — **pateant, arceret:** the historical present (*demittit*) is followed by primary sequence, which changes to secondary in *v.* 300 (*arceret*); A. 485, *e*; D. 700; B. 268, 3; G. 511. R.[1]

299. hospitio, *in hospitality*: abl. of manner.

300. aëra : for form see Introd. § 92.

301. remigio alarum, *by the oarage of his wings.* The winged cap of Mercury (*petăsus*) and the winged sandals (*talaria*) are compared to a ship's banks of oars. This figure of speech is called *metonymy* (Introd. § 100). — **adstitit,** *has alighted*: see note on *incubuere, v.* 84.

302. -que, *and accordingly.*

303. quietum animum, *calm feelings*, i.e. free from alarm, which might lead her to oppose their coming.

304. mentem benignam, *friendly thoughts*, implying active good will and help.

306. lux alma, *the kindly light.* — **exire :** depends on *constituit, v.* 309.

307. quas . . . oras : indir. question, object of *quaerere, v.* 309.

308. qui teneant, sc. *eas* : indir. question, object of *quaerere.* — **nam :** introduces the reason of his doubt. He sees they are not cultivated, but he is in doubt whether they are the waste lands of a people, or absolutely wild. — **inculta,** *wilderness*: adj. used as a noun (Introd. § 97). — **vidĕt :** the older quantity is here retained in the final syllable. — **-ne . . . -ne** = *utrum . . . an,* in a double question, sometimes occurs in poetry.

309. exacta, *his discoveries* (lit. *things found out*).

310. convexo, *a hollow*: cf. *vv.* 164–165.

312. comitatus : the perf. participle of a deponent verb sometimes has a passive sense, as here. — **Achate :** abl. of means.

313. bina : because usually borne in pairs. — **lato ferro,** *with broad iron head*: abl. of quality. — **crispans,** *brandishing.*

314. cui sese tulit obvia, *came to meet him*: for the case of *cui* see A. 370, *c*; D. 384; cf. B. 192, 1; G. 359.

315. virginis : to address a mortal, a divinity must take mortal shape; here, that of a huntress maid is appropriate to the locality. — **habitum,** *appearance.* — **gerens,** *having,* or *with.* — **arma :** loosely used of dress as well as the equipments.

316. Spartanae : used as if in apposition with *virginis,* i.e. *either of a Spartan maid, or such a one as Thracian Harpalyce when she tires,* etc.

317. Harpalyce : a female warrior of Thrace. — **Hebrum :** to ancient poets rivers are a type of swiftness. Virgil seems unaware that the Hebrus (a river in Thrace) is not swift.

318. umeris : abl. of place from which. — **de more,** *after the manner* of hunters. — **habilem,** *light* (for handling).

319. venatrix, *as a huntress.* — **diffundere :** infinitive of purpose (Introd. § 84).

320. genu : acc. of specification (Introd. § 42). — **nodo . . . fluentis,** *having the flowing folds [of her garment] gathered in a knot,* to aid her in her movements. *Sinus* is acc. with *collecta*, a participle used in a middle sense. See Fig. 8 (from a statuette of Diana).

321. prior: she was the first to speak. — **monstrate,** *tell me* (lit. *show*) *if you have seen*, etc.

322. errantem, *ranging* (in quest of game); **prementem,** *pressing close in pursuit*, and so following a long distance: in either case they might lose their way.

323. succinctam, *girt with*; cf. *gerens, v.* 315.

325. Venus, Veneris filius : brought together, to put more sharply the fact that they do not meet as mother and son.

326. mihi : dat. of agent (Introd. § 30).

327. memorem : deliberative subjunctive; A. 444; D. 678; B. 277; G. 265. The question takes the place of a name. In addressing a divinity it was thought to be important to use the correct name; otherwise the god might not regard the prayer. — **namque** gives the reason for the doubt implied by the question. — **tibi :** sc. *est* (Introd. § 29).

328. nec, etc., *nor does your voice sound like a mortal's.* — **hominem :** cogn. acc. (Introd. § 37).

329. Phoebi soror (sc. *es*): Diana, as he judges from her dress. Diana, goddess of hunting, and Phœbus Apollo were the children of Latona. They were born on the island of Delos. Diana is a maiden goddess, the ideal of modesty, grace, and maidenly vigor. She is associated with her brother, the prince of archery, in nearly all his adventures, and in attributes she is his feminine

Fig. 8

counterpart. As he is identified with sunlight, so is she, his fair-tressed sister, with the chaste brilliance of the moon. Despising the weakness of love, Diana imposed upon her nymphs vows of perpetual maidenhood, any violation of which she was swift and severe to punish. Graceful in form and free of movement, equipped for the chase, and surrounded by a bevy of fair companions, the swift-rushing goddess was wont to scour hill, valley, forest, and plain (Gayley). — **sanguinis :** partitive genitive (Introd. § 13).

330. sis felix, *grant me favor* (lit. *may you be gracious*): optative subjunctive; A. 441; D. 681, I; B. 279, 1; G. 260. — **quaecumque :** sc. *es*.

331. tandem, *I pray.*

332. locorumque : *-que* is elided before *erramus* in the next verse (Introd. § 114).

334. multa hostia, *many a victim*, in case you grant my prayer. — **nostra . . . dextrā :** abl. of means.

335. equidem, *it is true.* — **honore :** for case see A. 418, *b*, N.[1]; D. 479, N.; B. 226, 2 ; G. 397, N.[2]

336. virginibus : dat. of possession. — **Tyriis :** Carthaginian ; cf. note on *v.* 12. — **mos est :** this is only the usual dress of Carthaginian maidens, and does not indicate a goddess, as you suppose.

337. purpureo : the purple (or crimson) dye of Tyre was famous. — **cothurno :** the high-laced boot was a part of the hunting dress.

338. Punica : a word kindred with *Phœnician.* — **Tyrios, Agenoris :** added to explain *Punica*, of which Æneas could be expected to know nothing, as well as to indicate a civilized race ; hence *sed* in the next verse. Agenor was founder of Sidon, the metropolis of Tyre. The *lands*, however, are not Phœnician, but Libyan.

339. genus : in apposition with the noun implied in *Libyci.*

340. imperium regit, *holds the sovereignty.*

341. fugiens : present in reference to *profecta.* — **longa est :** it would be a long story to recount the wrongs.

342. ambages, *details.* — **fastigia,** *the main points.*

343. huic . . . erat, *she once had.* — **ditissimus,** etc., *richest of the Phœnicians in land* (Introd. § 17).

344. miserae (dat. of agent), *by his unhappy wife* : why *unhappy*, she goes on to tell.

345. intactam, *a maid.* — **primis ominibus,** *in her first marriage* (abl. of means) : the ritual of consulting omens (used in all important matters, and especially in marriage) is put for marriage rites in general. — **iugarat :** a syncopated form (Introd. § 91, *n*).

347. ante alios omnis, *than all others.* Virgil combines two phrases : *ante omnis alios immanis* and *aliis omnibus immanior.* — **scelere :** abl. of specification.

348. quos . . . furor, *in the midst between them came a feud.* — **medius** = an adv. — **Sychaeum :** the *y* is here short, though long in *v.* 343.

349. impius ante aras, clam ferro incautum : the arrangement of the words heightens the impiety and treachery of the act. Pygmalion's crime was impious both because it violated the sanctity of the family and especially because he committed the murder at the altars of the household gods — the penates (iv. 20–21).

350. amorum is gen. with *securus = immemor* (Introd. § 16), *heedless of the love of his sister* for her husband.

352. multa simulans, *devising many falsehoods* (lit. *pretending many things*). — **malus,** *wickedly.* — **amantem :** translate with *aegram, the loving wife, sick at heart.*

353. ipsa sed : Pygmalion's false stories to account for the disappearance of Sychæus were in vain, for the ghost of Sychæus came and revealed the crime. — **inhumati,** *unburied* : the ancients believed that the spirit of a murdered man haunted the place of the crime, especially if the body had not been buried with due rites.

355. aras, pectora : the plurals have no real force (Introd. § 96).

356. nudavit, *laid bare* the altars as the scene, and his breast as the evidence of the crime: *zeugma*; A. 640; D. 950, *h*; B. 374, 2, *a*; G. 690. — **caecum,** *hidden.* — **retexit,** *uncovered :* cf. *recludit, v.* 358.

357. celerare : cf. n. on *mulcere, v.* 66; sc. *ei (her).*

358. auxilium viae, *as an aid for her journey.* — **veteres,** *old,* and so not discovered by Pygmalion.

359. ignotum, *unknown :* i. e. kept secret, apart from his other wealth.

360. his commota : i. e. the crime produces fear; the treasures give hope of escape. — **parabat,** *began to make ready :* zeugma; cf. n. on *v.* 356.

361. conveniunt, *those gather, in whom,* etc. — **quibus :** dat. (Introd. § 29). — **odium crudele,** *fierce hatred* for past wrongs. — **tyranni :** obj. gen. (Introd. § 14).

362. metus acer : i. e. for wrongs to come. The contrast with *odium crudele* is indicated by placing the two pairs in the same order. This arrangement is called *anaphora :* A. 598, *f*; D. 939; B. 350, 11, *b*; G. 682.

363. avari, etc.: his greed is contrasted with the distance to which his treasures are gone.

364. pelago, *over the sea :* A. 429, *a*; D. 474; B. 218, 9; G. 389.

365. devenere locos, *they landed at the spot* (lit. *came down to the places*): for case of *locos* see Introd. § 47.

367. mercati : sc. *sunt.* — **Byrsam,** *called Byrsa from the name of the deed.* The colonists, according to the story, bought as much land as they could cover with a bull's hide. By cutting the hide into strips, they were able to enclose a generous site for their town. The legend probably arose from a confusion of the Phœnician *bursa,* "citadel," with the Greek word βύρσα (*bursa*), "hide."

368. possent : subjunctive in indir. disc. depending on the verb of *saying* implied in *mercati.*

369. vos : expressed for emphasis on account of the change of subject. — **qui :** sc. *estis.*

370. talibus [sc. *verbis*], *as follows :* sc. *respondit.*

371. imo : A. 293; D. 510; B. 241, 1; G. 291, R.[2]

372. dea : Æneas still believes her a goddess. — **repetens,** *going back.* — **pergam,** *I should continue on,* i. e. give the whole story in detail from the very beginning. For condition see A. 516, *b*; D. 789; B. 303; G. 596.

373. vacet (impersonal), *if you should have time* (i. e. empty time, leisure).

374. ante . . . Olympo, *before I should finish, Vesper would bring the day to an end, closing [the gate of] Olympus.* Mount Olympus in Thessaly, the residence of the gods, had come to be the conventional poetic term for *heaven.*

375. Troia: abl. of place from which with *vectos*. — **vestras:** instead of *tuas*, because Æneas includes her fellow Carthaginians.

377. forte sua, *by its own chance*, or *by mere chance:* i.e. the Trojans had not come intentionally and therefore had no hostile designs. — **oris:** cf. *Latio, v.* 6.

378. pius: properly so called on account of his filial piety in carrying his father: however, the word was probably not restricted to that, but indicates Virgil's whole idea of his character; cf. n. on *pietate, v.* 10. — **ex,** *from the midst of.*

379. fama . . . notus: a boast quite in keeping with ancient notions. Modesty, real or assumed, is a late growth of civilization. — **aethera:** Introd. § 92.

380. patriam: because the founder of the Trojan race, Dardanus (son of Jupiter and Electra), came originally from Italy.

381. bis denis: the distributive is used in place of a cardinal, because ten are counted each time. — **Phrygium conscendi aequor,** *I climbed the Phrygian sea,* because the sea seems to rise as it recedes; or, abandoning the figure, translate by *embarked upon.* — **navibus,** Introd. § 55.

382. data fata: Æneas speaks of himself as guided by the fates, which have been *spoken* (*data*) to him at various times (see ii. 771 ff.; iii. 94 ff., 154 ff.). — **secutus:** present in sense (Introd. § 95).

383. vix septem, *barely seven:* i.e. only seven have been saved and these with difficulty.

384. ipse: opposed to the ships. — **ignotus:** his person is unknown, though his fame has spread (cf. *fama notus, v.* 379). — **Libyae:** Africa is the only continent left, for he has been driven from Asia (Troy) and Europe (Thrace, iii. 13–68), and is still forbidden to reach Italy.

385. plura: cognate acc. — **querentem:** the prose construction with *passa* would be *eum queri.*

387. haud invisus caelestibus, *not hateful to the gods* (litotes; cf. n. on *v.* 136), for it is by the favor of heaven that you have arrived in this hospitable land. — **auras vitalis carpis,** *you breathe the breath of life.*

388. adveneris: subjunctive in a rel. clause of cause; A. 535, *e*; D. 730, I; B. 283, 3; G. 633.

389. perge modo, *only go on,* and you will find good fortune.

390. tibi, etc., *I report to you your companions returned and your fleet brought back.* It is not necessary to supply *esse: reduces* (adj.) and *relatam* serve as pred. acc. with *nuntio;* A. 393, N.; D. 417, *a*; B. 177, 2; G. 340.

391. in tutum, *into a safe harbor.* — **versis aquilonibus** (abl. abs.), *by a change in the winds.*

392. vani, *falsely,* not implying intentional deceit on the parents' part. —- **docuere:** sc. *me;* then the verb has two objects (Introd. § 40). — **parentes:** Venus still pretends she is a mortal.

393. aspice, etc.: the swans are in two groups, one alighting (*terras capere*), the other looking down on the place where the first has alighted (*terras captas*), and preparing to join them. These groups are again described, the former as *reduces*, the latter in *cinxere* etc. in *v.* 398. The ships correspond to the two groups: those already in the harbor (*portum tenet*), to the former, and those just coming in (*subit ostia*), to the latter. — **senos:** cf. n. on *denis, v.* 381. Observe that the number is that of the missing ships. — **laetantis agmine,** *flying joyously in a flock* (lit. *rejoicing in a flock*): they have escaped the eagle. — **cycnos:** sacred to Venus.

394. lapsa, *swooping down* on the swans, which flew low like most other waterfowl. — **plaga:** abl. of place from which. — **Iovis ales:** the eagle. — **aperto caelo:** where they were exposed, as were the ships on the open sea.

395. turbabat, *of late was scattering; but now* (*nunc*), etc. — **ordine:** they are reunited after their dispersion.

396. captas [*terras*] **iam despectare,** *to be looking down on the place already covered* (by the birds that have alighted).

397. ut, *as.*

398. coetu (abl. of manner) **cinxere polum,** *have encircled the sky in a flock.* — **cantus:** showing their freedom from alarm. This picture of security is a good omen for the ships.

399. haud aliter, *just so* (lit. *not otherwise*). — **pubes tuorum,** *the band of your youths* (lit. *the youth of yours*).

400. subit ostia, *are making the entrance.*

402. avertens, *as she turned away,* and not till then, she allowed her divine nature to appear.

403. ambrosiae, *ambrosial* (properly, *immortal*). Most commonly applied to the food of the gods; but the gods used ambrosia also for ointment and perfume.

404. vestis defluxit: all the goddesses except Diana (*v.* 329) had flowing garments. — **imos:** see n. on *v.* 371.

405. patuit (used in a kind of passive sense), *was manifest a goddess:* cf. n. on *incedo, v.* 46; *dea* is pred. nominative. — **dea ille:** note the hiatus (Introd. § 108).

407. natum, *your* [true] *son:* emphatic by its position. — **tu quoque:** i.e. as well as the other divinities.

408. dextrae: *iungo* may have an abl. of accompaniment or, in poetry, a dat., as here (Introd. § 28). — **iungere:** infin. as subject (Introd. § 73).

409. veras: i.e. in our true character, as mother and son.

410. talibus: sc. *verbis.*

411. obscuro aere, *a dark mist* (i.e. one that concealed them). Such concealment by a supernatural mist is very common in epic poetry and in old tradition. — **gradientis:** sc. *eos.*

412. circum ... fudit: tmesis; cf. n. on *v.* 175. — **multo ... amictu,** *with the ample folds of a cloud.*

415. Paphum: Paphos, in Cyprus, the seat of the most noted temple and worship of Venus. — **sublimis,** *on high,* or *through the air.*

416. laeta: cf. *tristior, v.* 228. She is now more confident about the well-being of the Trojans. — **illi:** dat. of possession; sc. *est.* — **Sabaeo:** Saba was a town in Arabia famous, among other things, for its spices. Cf. *Paradise Lost,* iv. 162:

> Sabæan odors, from the spicy shore
> Of Araby the blest.

417. ture, sertis: no blood was shed on the altars of Venus. The garland had a prominent part in religious and other rites. The manufacture of garlands as an article of trade is shown in Fig. 9.

Fig. 9

418. corripuere viam, *they sped on their way.*

419. ascendebant, *they were now climbing* (descriptive imperf., as the poet here takes a new point of view). — **plurimus,** *high above,* i.e. so large that much of its bulk was above the city.

420. adversas arces, *the towers opposite.*

421. molem: *the mass* (of buildings). — **magalia quondam,** *but now* (i.e. shortly before) *a cluster of huts.*

422. miratur ... viarum: he wonders at these signs of a great city in what he thought a desert. — **strata** (*pavements*) **viarum** = *stratas vias, the paved streets.*

423. pars ... pars, *some to ... some to*: in appos. with *Tyrii.* — **ducere:** complementary with *instant* (Introd. § 75).

424. subvolvere, *to roll up* (by putting levers, etc., under).

425. tecto, *for a group of buildings*: dat. of purpose (Introd. § 33).

426. iura . . . legunt: zeugma, *they make laws and select magistrates*; see n. on *v.* 356. Mention of the government is out of place at this point and the verse seems inconsistent with *v.* 507; consequently it is regarded as spurious.

427. alta, *deep.* — **theatri:** Virgil is thinking of his own time rather than of primitive Carthage. Even Rome had no permanent theatre until 58 B.C., and none of stone until 55 B.C. To the poet, however, a great theatre was a matter of course in a great city.

429. rupibus: abl. of place from which. — **scaenis . . . futuris,** *lofty decorations for the future stage*: cf. n. on *v.* 164.

430. qualis . . . labor: *talis,* the antecedent of *qualis,* is omitted; *such toil was theirs as busies the bees.* A celebrated simile, often imitated (as by Milton in *Paradise Lost,* i. 768–775); cf. n. on *v.* 82. The fourth book of Virgil's *Georgics* is about bees, from which this description is repeated here (iv. 162–169). — **aestate nova:** abl. of time (Introd. § 70).

434. venientum: poetical form of genitive; A. 121, *b,* 2; D. 149, N.; B. 70, 7; G. 83, N.²

435. ignavum, *lazy,* or *inefficient* for lack of skill. — **pecus:** in app. with *fucos.*

436. fervet, *is all alive*: a figure derived from the agitation of boiling.

437. O . . . surgunt: Æneas, who knows that he is destined to found a city, is impressed by the good fortune of those whose city is already founded.

438. suspicit, *looks up to.* He has now come down the hill and approached the walls.

440. miscet: sc. *se.* — **viris:** dat. (Introd. § 28). — **ulli:** dat. of agent (Introd. § 30).

441. umbrae: Introd. § 17.

442. quo . . . loco = *ubi, the spot where.* — **primum . . . effodere . . . signum,** *dug up the first token* (of rest and security).

444. monstrarat, *had told of.* — **caput equi:** a horse or horse's head as a symbol of the city, was common on Carthaginian coins. — **acris,** *spirited*: an omen of their energy and warlike disposition. The adjective is, as often in poetry, a descriptive epithet, not denoting an individual, but expressing a general characteristic, as we should say "the cruel tiger." — **sic:** i.e. if they dug up the head and built the city on that spot. — **fore:** a continuation of the omen, in indir. disc. dependent on *monstrarat; for thus,* [she said,] *the race should be,* etc.

445. facilem victu, *easily subsisting*: A. 510; D. 882, II; B. 340, 2; G. 436. The horse is represented as an omen both of prosperity in peace and success in war.

446. Sidonia, *Phœnician* (Introd. § 98); see n. on *v.* 338.

447. donis opulentum et numine divae, *rich in gifts* (i.e. offerings) *and in the divine presence of the goddess.*

448. cui . . . limina, *a bronze threshold crowned its steps* (lit. *rose on the steps*): *cui* is dat. of reference (Introd. § 31). — **nexaeque . . . trabes,** *beams cased with bronze.* The abundance of metal work shows the costliness and splendor of the structure. — -**que** is elided before *aere* in the next verse : see *v.* 332 (Introd. § 114).

449. foribus: dat. of reference. — **cardo stridebat :** Roman doors (which were usually double ; hence the plur. *foribus*) were hung upon pivots, one of which fitted into the lintel, the other into the sill. See Fig. 22, p. 68.

450. hoc primum, etc.: the temple gives the first hint of Dido's interest in his fortunes (see the description that follows). — **nova res oblata,** *an unexpected sight which presented itself.*

452. rebus: abl. with *confidere*: A. 431; D. 376, N.²; B. 219, 1; G. 401, N.⁶

453. sub : Æneas and Achates have entered the temple. — **lustrat dum,** *as he surveys*; A. 556; D. 763; B. 293, 1; G. 229, R. — **singula,** *various objects in turn* (one by one).

454. reginam opperiens : Æneas takes it for granted that Dido will visit the temple for a morning sacrifice. — **quae . . . sit :** *miratur* has as objects a noun clause (indir. quest.) and two nouns.

455. artificum manus, *the artists' skill.* — **inter se,** *comparing them with each other.* — **operum laborem,** *the toil of the work,* i.e. the toilsome work. There is nothing to indicate that the temple was unfinished.

456. pugnas : probably painted in the vestibule or colonnade. These pictures could have no significance for the Phœnicians. Virgil here transfers to this nation the arts and customs of the Greeks and Romans, who constantly made use of mural paintings.

457. iam, *by this time.*

458. Atridas : Agamemnon and Menelaus, sons of Atreus, were leaders among the Greeks. — **saevum ambobus :** enraged against Agamemnon as well as hostile to Troy. His quarrel with Agamemnon, in consequence of which he withdrew from the fighting, caused severe losses to the Greeks. It is the subject of the Iliad.

459. lacrimans : cf. n. on *v.* 92.

460. nostri laboris, *of our suffering* (Introd. § 16).

461. en Priamus : probably in the scene of the ransom of Hector's body (*v.* 484). See Fig. 10 (from a vase painting). — **sunt sua praemia laudi,** *merit has its fit reward* : dat. of possession. — **sua :** the reflexive, instead of referring back to the grammatical subject, refers to *laudi* (the subject of the thought); A. 301, *b*; D. 523; B. 244, 4; G. 309, 2.

462. rerum, *for trials* : objective genitive (Introd. § 14).

463. aliquam salutem, *some [degree of] safety.* — **haec fama,** *this renown* (of Troy).

464. inani, *lifeless* (lit. *empty, without reality*).

465. multa : cognate acc. (Introd. § 37).

466. uti, *how*: introducing the indirect questions. Most of the scenes are taken from the Iliad. — **circum :** Introd. § 89, *d*.

467. hac, *here* (in *this* picture). — **premeret** (sc. *eos*), *were in close pursuit*. Note that the omission of the conjunction between *fugerent* and *premeret* (asyndeton) sharpens the contrast: A. 323, *b*; D. 619; B. 346; G. 474, N.

468. hac : in another picture. — **Phryges :** sc. *fugerent.* — **cristatus :** the helmet of the Homeric warrior was decorated with waving plumes.

469. nec procul hinc : i.e. in the next picture. — **Rhesi :** Rhesus was a Thracian king who came to the aid of the Trojans. An oracle had foretold

Fig. 10

that Troy would not be taken by the Greeks if the horses of Rhesus should eat the grass of Troy or drink the water of the Trojan river Xanthus. He was killed and his horses seized by Ulysses and Diomedes (*Tydides*) on the night of his arrival. — **niveis velis :** an anachronism; huts thatched with straw were used in the Homeric period.

470. primo somno : abl. of time.

471. vastabat : imperf. describing the scene shown by the picture.

472. avertit : perf. because Virgil is narrating a fact about Diomedes, and not merely describing something shown by the picture. — **priusquam . . . gustassent,** *before they should taste*: subjunctive as showing the motive; A. 551, *b*, N.[1]; D. 759, N.[1]; B. 292, 1, *b*; G. 577.

474. parte alia : in still another picture. — **Troilus :** the youngest son of Priam, slain by Achilles.

475. infelix . . . Achilli, *luckless youth, no match for Achilles in combat* (lit. *having encountered Achilles unequal*). — **Achilli :** poetical dat. with a verb of contending (Introd. § 28).

476. fertur, haeret : the pres. tense describes the picture; cf. *vastabat, v.* 471. — **curru :** abl. with *haeret.* — **resupinus :** on his back, and feet foremost.

477. huic: dat. of reference.

478. versa . . . hasta, *with his spear-shaft* (lit. *his turned spear*). — **pulvīs:** *ī* is possibly the original quantity retained.

479. interea: another picture. — **non aequae** (= *iniquae*), *unfriendly* (to the Trojans).

480. crinibus passis (*pando*), *with dishevelled hair* (lit. *spread loosely* over their shoulders); a sign of mourning, especially of women, which is closely connected with supplication in all ages. — **peplum:** as an offering to the goddess. The peplum was the outside garment of the Grecian women. Virgil has in mind the costly robe, adorned with the great deeds of the goddess, which the Athenians bore to the temple of Pallas yearly in the Panathenaic festival.

Fig. 11

481. tunsae pectora, *beating their breasts* (Introd. § 43). The participle has the meaning of a present, like *secutus* in *v.* 382 (Introd. § 95).

482. solo: abl. of place where (Introd. § 67).

483, 484. raptaverat . . . vendebat: the scene is that of the ransom of Hector's body by Priam at Achilles' tent after Achilles had dragged it about the walls of Troy (see Fig. 10, vase painting). — **auro:** abl. of price (Introd. § 62).

485. tum dat: the common historical present; the preceding verbs have been present because descriptive of the actual pictures. — **vero:** introducing as usual the most important moment of the narrative.

486. currus: plur. for metrical reasons (Introd. § 96).

487. tendentem manus: in supplication.

488. se quoque: i.e. in another battle scene. — **principibus:** cf. n. on *viris, v.* 440.

489. Eoas, Memnonis: Memnon, son of Tithonus and Aurora, led the Æthiopian allies of Troy. The myth, however, places Æthiopia in the East; hence *Eoas*. Memnon was killed by Achilles.

490. Amazonidum: the Amazons were a nation dominated by warlike women. It was their custom to bring up only the female children, whom they hardened by martial discipline; the boys were either dispatched to the neighboring nations or put to death. In the Trojan War Penthesilea, queen of the Amazons, came with a band of her warriors to the aid of Troy. Having slain many of the bravest Greeks, she was at last slain by Achilles,

But when the hero bent over his fallen foe and contemplated her beauty, youth, and valor he bitterly regretted his victory (Gayley). See Fig. 11 (from a statue in the Vatican). — **lunatis**, *crescent* (in form). — **peltis**, abl. of quality (Introd. § 61).

491. mediis, *in the midst.*

492. aurea . . . cingula (acc. plur.), *a golden girdle bound beneath* (lit. *binding a golden girdle beneath*). — **exsertae**, *uncovered.*

493. bellatrix, virgo : the contrast suggested in these words is heightened by their position as first and last in the verse. — **viris :** cf. n. on *Achilli, v.* 475.

494. Dardanio, *Trojan* (and therefore particularly interested in these pictures). — **miranda :** pred. after *videntur*; *seem marvellous.*

497. stipante, *thronging about,* an almost technical word for *escorting* a gɪeat personage.

498. qualis: correlative with *talis, v.* 503. — **Eurotae,** the *Eurotas,* a river of Sparta; here Diana was

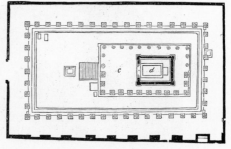

Fig. 12

worshipped. — **Cynthi :** Mount Cynthus on Delos was also a favorite haunt of Diana.

499. Dīana : notice the *ī*; elsewhere in the Æneid it is short. — **choros,** *the dancing bands.*

500. glomerantur, *gather :* used in a middle sense (Introd. § 94). — **Oreades :** nymphs of the mountains. — **illa,** *she.*

501. deas : the Oreads.

502. Latonae : mother of Diana and Apollo. Notice with what effect the human element is introduced, the mother's pride heightening the daughter's glory.

504. instans, *intent upon.*

505. foribus divae, *in the doorway of the goddess.* — **media testudine templi** (abl. of place where), *in the middle of the vaulted temple.* In the front part of a temple was a porch, beyond which began the *cella,* or interior temple. It was at the entrance to this inner part that Dido took her place. The temple had a vaulted roof (called *testudo,* as resembling the shell of a tortoise). See Figs. 12 (plan of the Temple of Venus at Pompeii) and 13 (vaulted chamber in the Baths at Pompeii).

506. armis : i.e. by armed men (*metonymy,* see Introd. § 100). — **alte subnixa,** *sitting on high.*

507. iura dabat : a Roman picture. From the close relation of government and religion in Rome, temples were used for all public purposes : the senate met, the treasury was kept, and courts were held in temples. — **iura legesque,** *laws and decrees* : i. e. she acted both as judge and lawgiver.

508. aequabat, trahebat : she makes the shares as equal as possible, or assigns them by lot, — as the Romans divided provinces, etc., among their magistrates.

509. cum subito : Dido was thus occupied *when suddenly*, etc. — **concursu,** *a crowd* that had flocked about them as strangers.

Fig. 13

510. videt : indicative with "*cum* inverse"; A. 546, *a*; D. 751 ; B. 288, 2 ; G. 581.

511. aequore : abl. of place where.

512. penitus, *far away*, i.e. far out of their course. — **oras :** acc. of place to which ; cf. *Italiam, v.* 2.

514. coniungere : depends on *ardebant* (as if *volebant*) ; Introd. § 77.

515. res incognita, *their uncertain situation* : they are puzzled by this embassy from the ships and uncertain how they themselves may be received by Dido.

516. dissimulant, *they remain hidden* (they *conceal* something, that is, their presence). — **speculantur,** *they watch to see*.

517. quae fortuna [*sit*] : the indir. questions are objects of *speculantur*.

518. lecti, *picked men* (as envoys).

519. orantes veniam, *begging for mercy* (or *favor*). — **clamore :** abl. of manner (Introd. § 58). They are protesting loudly against their treatment when they landed ; cf. *vv.* 539–541.

520. coram fandi, *of speaking* [*to the queen*] *in person.*

521. maximus [sc. *natu*], *the eldest,* and so first in rank. — **placido . . . pectore,** *with calm breast*: as suited his age and dignity (contrasted with *clamore* in *v.* 519).

522. condere : object of *dedit*; cf. n. on *v.* 66.

523. iustitia, *with just restraint,* as representing a superior civilization among the savage tribes of Africa (*gentis superbas*). In reality, Dido had built her city only by sufferance; but this address might properly be spiced with flattery.

524. ventis . . . vecti, *carried by the winds over every sea.*

525. infandos, *inhuman,* as violating the right of peaceful strangers.

526. propius . . . nostras, *look more closely at our condition* : though coming in an armed fleet, we have no hostile purposes.

527. populare : poetical infin. of purpose (Introd. § 84). — **penatis,** *homes.*

528. vertere, *to drive away* (as booty).

529. non ea vis, etc.: i.e. we have no such thought of violence : conquered men are of course capable of no such insolence. — **animo, victis :** dat. of possession ; sc. *est.*

530. Hesperiam : i.e. "the Western Land," a name for Italy borrowed from the Greeks.

532. Oenotri : Œnotria means "Land of Vines" (which were much cultivated in Italy). — **nunc:** this implies that Œnotria was its former name. — **fama :** sc. *est.* — **minores,** *descendants.*

533. ducis : according to this account the name *Italia* (which is really akin to *vitulus, a bull,* and means "land of herds ") is derived from Italus, a leader of the Œnotrians.

534. hic cursus fuit, *this* (namely, to this land) *was our voyage.* This is the first of the many incomplete verses found in the Æneid, evidences of the unfinished state in which the poem was left by Virgil's untimely death.

535. cum subito, *when suddenly* (as in *v.* 509). — **adsurgens fluctu,** *rising over the wave*; *fluctu* is abl. — **nimbosus Orion :** the rising of Orion near sunrise, which occurred about midsummer, and the setting, which was the beginning of winter, were times of stormy weather for the peoples about the Mediterranean.

536. tulit : sc. *nos.* — **penitus,** *far.* — **austris** (abl. of means): one wind put generally for all.

537. superante salo (abl. abs.), *while the sea dashed over us.*

538. pauci, *only a few of us.* — **oris :** dat. of place to which (Introd. § 34).

539. tam barbara, i.e. *is so barbarous as to,* etc.

541. prima terra : *the very margin of the land* (the beach).

543. at sperate, *at least expect.* — **deos :** sc. *esse.* — **fandi, nefandi,** *right, wrong*: for gen. see Introd. § 16.

544. erat: he does not know that Æneas is still alive. — **quo,** etc., *than whom no other man was,* etc.

545. pietate: abl. of specification with *iustior*; i.e. scrupulous in performing his duties to the gods.

546. vescitur, *breathes* (lit. *feeds on,* air being as necessary to life as food). — **aura:** Introd. § 56.

547. aetheria, *of heaven,* as opposed to the Lower World. — **neque . . . occubat,** *and does not yet lie low.* — **crudelibus . . . umbris:** abl. of place where; the Lower World, the place of the shades, is meant.

548. non metus, *you need have no fear,* for Æneas will repay the obligation. Some translate *we have no fear* (supplying *est nobis*); but this makes poor connection with what follows. — **officio . . . paeniteat,** *and do not regret to have been first in the rivalry of kind deeds,* i.e. by making Æneas your debtor in receiving us hospitably. — **officio:** abl. of specification. — **certasse** = *certavisse.*

549. paeniteat: A. 439; D. 674; B. 275, 1; G. 263, 3. — **sunt et,** etc.: i.e. in the event of his death (which Ilioneus, to avoid the omen of speaking of such a calamity, does not mention), the cities and fields (*arva*) of Sicily will be our refuge, and you will have the friendship of Acestes to repay your kindness to us.

551. liceat subducere, *let it be allowed us to haul up our storm-racked ships:* hortatory or jussive subjunctive; cf. note on *v.* 549.

552. silvis: abl. of place where. — **aptare,** *to hew out* (lit. *to fit, adjust*): the beams would have to be hewed and fitted. — **stringere,** *to fashion* (lit. *to trim*): the oars, hardly more than saplings, would only need to be stripped and slightly trimmed.

553. si . . . tendere: translate after *ut . . . petamus.* — **tendere** [sc. *iter*], *to hold our course to Italy.*

554. ut . . . petamus: expresses the purpose of *subducere.*

555. sin, *but if* (on the other hand). — **salus,** *hope of safety.* — **Teucrum:** gen. plur. (Introd. § 91, *c*).

556. nec . . . iam, *and no longer.* — **Iuli:** obj. gen. (Introd. § 14).

557. freta, *seas.* — **sedes paratas:** i.e. the cities of Acestes, in contrast to those they hoped to build themselves.

559. ore fremebant, *murmured their applause.*

561. voltum demissa, *with downcast face* (in womanly modesty): for case of *voltum* see Introd. § 42.

563. res dura, *my hard situation.* — **talia:** i.e. the attack on the Trojans as they attempted to land (*v.* 541). This is Dido's apology for the inhospitable conduct of her subjects.

564. late tueri: for fear of Pygmalion she cannot safely allow strangers even to land.

565. Aeneadum (gen. plur.), *the Trojans* generally, but with a courteous reference to their chief. For form see Introd. § 91, *b.* — **Troiae :** Introd. § 10. — **quis . . . nesciat,** *who can be ignorant ?* deliberative subjunctive; A. 444 ; D. 678 ; B. 277 ; G. 265.

566. virtutesque virosque (hendiadys), *the brave deeds of its heroic men.* — **tanti,** *that great.*

567. obtusa adeo, *so blunted* or *dulled* by our own misfortunes as to be ignorant of the Trojans.

568. nec . . . urbe, *nor does the Sun harness his horses so far away from the Tyrian city :* i.e. their hearts are not chilled by unkindly skies, as men's might be in cold regions, far from the sun's course.

569. Saturnia arva : i.e. Italy, where Saturn was supposed to have ruled as king in the Golden Age.

570. Erycis finis : i.e. Sicily. Eryx, a son of Butes and Venus, gave his name to a mountain in the west of Sicily, where was a celebrated temple of Venus. He is mentioned later in the Æneid as a famous pugilist (v. 392).

571. auxilio : men and arms. — **opibus :** supplies of food, money, etc.

572. voltis et = *et si voltis, and again if you wish.*

573. urbem quam statuo : more commonly the relative would precede the noun, and a demonstrative (*ea*) would stand in the antecedent clause ; as, *quam urbem statuo, ea vestra est.*

574. mihi : dat. of agent (Introd. § 30). — **agetur,** *shall be dealt with.*

575. Noto = *vento :* cf. *austris, v.* 536.

576. adforet, *were* [now] *here :* A. 441, 442 ; D. 680, 681, II ; B. 279, 1, 2 ; G. 260, 261. — **equidem,** *in fact :* I will even go so far as to send in search of him. — **certos,** *trustworthy men.*

578. si, *in case.* — **eiectus,** *shipwrecked.*

579. animum : acc. of specification (Introd. § 42).

580. iamdudum . . . ardebant, *had long been eager :* A. 471, *b* ; D. 654 ; B. 260, 4 ; G. 234.

582. dea : abl. of source (Introd. § 50). — **sententia,** *purpose.*

584. unus abest, *one only is missing :* Orontes (*v.* 113).

585. dictis matris : *vv.* 390–400.

586. circumfusa, *surrounding* (lit. *poured about* them).

587. scindit se . . . purgat, *breaks and clears.*

588. restitit, *stood forth.*

589. os umerosque : i.e. in face, form, and build (acc. of specification). — **ipsa,** *herself,* the goddess of beauty.

590. nato : dat. with *adflarat* (= *adflaverat*). — **lumen . . . purpureum,** *the ruddy glow.*

591. laetos . . . honores, *joyous charms ;* of the sparkling of the eyes in joy.

592. quale . . . decus, *such beauty as art gives to ivory* (i.e. by inlaying or setting it in gold): strictly there would be an antecedent, *tale decus*, in app. with the objects of *adflarat*.

593. Parius lapis: the white marble from the island of Paros in the Ægean was famous.

594. cunctis improvisus, *unexpectedly to all*; *cunctis* is dat. of agent with *improvisus*.

595. coram adsum, *am here before you*.

597. O sola miserata, *O you who alone have had pity!* (i.e. the only stranger to show pity). Acestes had helped them (*vv.* 195–196), but he was a kinsman.

598. quae . . . socias, *who make us sharers in your city and home.* — **reliquias Danaum:** see n. on *v.* 30.

599. omnium: Introd. § 16.

600. urbe, domo: abl. of place where. Note the omission of the conjunction (*asyndeton*): A. 323, *b*; D. 619; B. 346; G. 474, N.

601. non opis est nostrae, *it is not within our power* (Introd. § 9). — **nec quicquid,** *nor* [within that of] *whatever exists of the Trojan race anywhere.*

602. sparsa: there were settlements of Trojan exiles in Crete, Epirus, and Sicily, which Æneas and his comrades had visited.

603. di . . . ferant, *may the gods repay*: optative subjunctive; A. 441; D. 681, I; B. 279 and 1; G. 260. — **si quid,** etc., *if justice is of any account.*

604. sibi: dat. of reference. — **recti:** Introd. § 16.

605. quae te, etc., *what age has been so blest as to,* etc.

606. tanti, (so) *illustrious.* — **talem,** *such a daughter.*

607. montibus: dat. of reference for a gen. modifying *convexa.*

608. convexa, *the rounded masses.* — **polus pascet,** *the sky feeds*: the æther of the sky was thought to feed the perpetual fire of the stars.

609. honos, an old form of *honor.* — **manebunt,** *shall abide with us.*

610. quae me cumque: tmesis; see n. on *v.* 175.

612. post = *postea.*

613. primo modifies *aspectu*, but is to be translated as an adv.: first Dido's feeling was astonishment at the sudden appearance of Æneas; then her interest was awakened by the strange fate (*casu*) which had brought him.

615. quis . . . casus, *what destiny*: the usual adj. form is *qui.*

616. vis: not merely power but *violence*, as usual in the singular. — **immanibus oris,** *these wild shores*, as inhabited by the barbarous African tribes: dat. of place to which.

617. Dardanio Anchisae: hiatus (Introd. § 108). The verse is spondaic (Introd. § 104).

618. alma, *fostering*, a regular epithet of Venus.

619. atque equidem, *and in fact*: now I think of it, I do remember. — **Teucrum:** this Teucer was a son of Telamon, king of Salamis, and a nephew of Priam. He fought against the Trojans. Upon his return from the Trojan War, he was driven from home by his father because he did not bring back his brother Ajax, and sought a home in Cyprus, where he built a second Salamis. He is here represented as stopping on the way at Sidon, apparently to make terms with Belus, who was then master of Cyprus. — **venire:** A. 584, *a* and N.; D. 830; G. 281, N.

621. Beli: father of Dido.

623. iam, *even*.

624. Pelasgi, *Grecian*: properly, the race inhabiting Greece before the Hellenic.

625. ipse, emphasizing *hostis, though an enemy*. — **ferebat,** *extolled*.

626. volebat, *would have it that*. His mother, Hesione, was a daughter of Laomedon, king of Troy.

627. agite, *come !* — **tectis:** Introd. § 34.

630. mali, miseris: observe the effect of the juxtaposition of these words and of the alliteration. — **disco,** *I learn how*, etc. This is one of the most famous verses of the Æneid.

> Who, by the art of known and feeling sorrows,
> Am pregnant to good pity. *King Lear*, iv. 6. 226.

> What sorrow was, thou bad'st her know,
> And from her own she learned to melt at others' woe.
> GRAY, *Hymn to Adversity*, vv. 15–16.

632. templis: abl. of place where. — **indicit honorem,** *proclaims a sacrifice of thanksgiving*.

633. nec minus, *moreover*: the two negatives counteract each other.

634. magnorum . . . suum, *a hundred bristling carcasses of great swine*: **terga,** *backs*, is used for the whole body ("the part for the whole"); see Introd. § 100.

635. suum: gen. plur. of *sus*.

636. munera, laetitiam: in app. with *tauros, terga, agnos*; translate *gifts for the enjoyment of the day*. These gifts were as well the usual marks of hospitality (*munera*) as a means to enable the Trojans to join in the festivities (*laetitiam*). — **dii:** archaic form of *diei*.

637. domus interior, *the interior of the house*: A. 293; cf. D. 510; B. 241, 1; G. 291, R.[2] — **splendida,** *magnificently*.

638. instruitur, *is decked*, temporarily, for the occasion. — **mediis tectis:** not in the ordinary dining room (*triclinium*), but in the great state apartment (*atrium*).

639. arte laboratae, *skilfully embroidered*. — **vestes:** the *robes* which were thrown over the couches. — **ostro superbo,** *of gorgeous purple*,

precious on account of the royal and costly dye: abl. of quality. There
were both embroidered and plain coverlets.

640. ingens argentum, *a vast amount of silver plate.* — **auro :** instead
of directly mentioning the golden goblets and vases, Virgil speaks of the
heroic figures chased and embossed (*caelata*) upon them.

Fig. 14

642. ducta, *brought down* (i.e. continued in unbroken series).

643. neque, *not.* — **patrius amor,**
fatherly love.

644. rapidum, *in haste :* adj. for adv.

645. ferat, ducat : subjunctives without *ut* after the idea of *commanding* in
praemittit; A. 565, *a*; D. 720, *d*; B.
295, 8; G. 546, R.²

646. cari, *fond.* — **stat,** *centres.*

647. munera : the guest also was expected to offer gifts. — **ruinis :** dat. of
separation (Introd. § 32).

648. pallam : a rectangular mantle of
wool reaching to the feet. Cf. Milton, *Il
Penseroso, v. 97*: "Gorgeous Tragedy, in
sceptred pall." — **signis auroque rigentem,** *stiff with figures of gold*: hendiadys;
see n. on *v.* 61. For an ornamented robe
see Fig. 14; for other articles of apparel
mentioned, see Fig. 15.

649. velamen : in Homer the various
articles of headdress, especially the veils,
are treated as most important points of
feminine apparel: hence the veil is a suitable gift to Dido. — **acantho :** the
acanthus leaf was often used in art by the Greeks.

650. Argivae Helenae, Mycenis : Helen was the wife of Menelaus,
king of Sparta. Argos and Mycenæ were cities of Agamemnon, his
brother, the latter being Agamemnon's capital. The names are poetically
used to indicate that part of Greece where the brothers held sway. The
objects are of all the more value from their associations.

651. Pergama : i.e. Troy (properly, the citadel of Troy). — **peterēt :** for the
quantity of the last syllable see note on *v.* 308. — **hymenaeos :** i.e. with Paris.

652. Ledae : Helen was the daughter of Jupiter and Leda.

653. Ilione : Priam's eldest daughter, wife of Polymestor, king of Thrace.

654. maxima [sc. *natu*], *eldest.* — **collo monile,** *a necklace* (lit. *a necklace for the neck*): *collo* is an unusual instance of the dat. of purpose without a verb; cf. A. 382, 2; D. 395, *a*; G. 356, N.³

655. duplicem . . . coronam: a coronet of two rings, one set with jewels and the other of gold. — **gemmis, auro:** abl. of manner.

656. haec celerans, *speeding these commands.*

657. Cytherea: see n. on *v.* 257.

658. consilia: Venus is making plans to circumvent Juno; see *v.* 674. — **ut:** the clauses which follow are substantive clauses of purpose, in app. with *consilia.* — **faciem . . . et ora,** *form and features:* see n. on *oculos, v.* 228. — **Cupido:** Cupid, the god of love, was the son of Venus, and her constant companion. He was often represented with eyes covered because of the blindness of his actions. With his bow and arrows, he shot the darts of desire into the bosoms of gods and men (Gayley).

659. furentem . . . reginam, *inflame the queen to madness* (proleptic use of the adjective; cf. *v.* 69).

660. ossibus, *in her frame:* dat. (Introd. § 27). — **ignem,** *the fire of love.*

661. quippe, *for, in truth.* — **domum ambiguam,** *the treacherous house,* as described in *vv.* 348–368. — **bilinguis,** *deceitful:* saying one thing and meaning another. The bad faith of the Carthaginians (*Punica fides*) was proverbial, at least among their enemies the Romans.

Fig. 15

662. urit atrox Iuno, *the thought of cruel Juno inflames her* with anxiety.

663. Amorem: Cupid.

664. solus: i.e. *who alone art;* nom., as if it were in a rel. clause, and not vocative though in apposition with *nate;* A. 340, *a;* D. 323; B. 171, 2; G. 201, R.[2]

665. patris summi: Jupiter. — **tela Typhoïa:** i.e. thunderbolts, the weapons with which Jupiter killed the giant Typhoeus. The idea that Cupid scorned the thunderbolts of Jupiter was a favorite one with the ancients, who sometimes even represented him as wielding the thunderbolts, an indication of the resistless force of love.

666. numina: i.e. the exercise of your power.

667. frater ut iactetur, *how thy brother is tossed*: indir. question, subj. of *nota [sunt]*.

668. iactetūr : the last syllable is long (Introd. § 110).

669. nota [sc. *sunt*], *are things known to you.* — **nostro,** *my.*

671. vereor quo, *I am anxious as to what turn Juno's hospitality may take* (lit. *whither*, etc.); *quo* introduces an indirect question. — **Iunonia :** since Carthage is especially devoted to Juno as its protecting goddess, Venus fears that Dido is acting under Juno's influence.

672. cessabit : sc. *Iuno.* — **cardine,** *crisis* (lit. *hinge* or *turning point*) : Introd. § 70.

673. capere, cingere : military phrases. The infinitives are complementary with *meditor.* — **ante,** *in advance.* — **flamma :** the flames of love, but still with an allusion to military operations.

674. ne quo numine, *lest by the influence of some divinity* (i.e. Juno).

675. mecum teneatur, *and that she may be bound to me* : sc. *ut.*

676. qua . . . possis, *in what way you may* : an indir. question depending on the idea of thought implied in *mentem.*

677. accitu, *at the summons* : abl. of cause.

678. cura, *object of care.*

679. pelago . . . restantia, *remaining from the sea and the flames* : Introd. § 49.

680. sopitum somno, *slumbering in sleep* (abl. of manner). This alliterative use of words from the same root is common in poetry. — **Cythera :** see n. to *v.* 257.

681. Idalium : a town and grove in Cyprus where Venus was worshipped.

682. medius occurrere [sc. *dolis*], *to come in to interrupt them* ; *medius* is adverbial in sense.

683. noctem non amplius unam, *one night, no more* : A. 407, *c* ; D. 450 ; B. 217, 2 ; G. 296, R.⁴

684. falle, *counterfeit* or *assume.* — **puer,** *boy that you are* : as Cupid is also a boy the disguise will be easy.

686. regalis . . . Lyaeum, *at the royal table when the wine is flowing* (lit. *in the midst of the royal tables and the wine of Bacchus*). *Lyaeus* (used here as an adjective) is a name of Bacchus.

688. inspires (with *ut, v.* 685) : purpose of *indue* (*v.* 684). — **ignem :** see n. on *v.* 660. — **fallas veneno :** i.e. poison her unnoticed, the same idea as in *occultum ignem.*

690. gaudens incedit : he practises his steps with a mischievous delight in the masquerading trick.

691. Ascanio : dat. of reference.

692. inrigat, *sheds like dew.* — **fotum gremio,** *fondled in her embrace.*

693. Idaliae : the same as Idalium (*v.* 681).

694. floribus, umbra: ablatives of means with *complectitur.*—**adspirans,** *breathing its fragrance.*

696. duce Achate, *rejoicing to be guided by Achates* (lit. *rejoicing in his guide Achates*): he imitates the feeling and action which Ascanius would naturally have shown (different from the mischief implied in *v.* 690).

697. venit: historical present. — **aulaeis superbis,** *among the gorgeous hangings* (of the banqueting hall).

698. aurea: i.e. adorned with gold; contracted into two syllables (Introd. § 115). — **mediam locavit,** *placed herself in the midst,* i.e. at the middle place of the middle couch, with Æneas on her left and Bitias (*v.* 738) on her right, with the rest on the side couches.

700. strato ostro, *on the purple coverlets* (lit. *on the outspread purple*). — **discumbitur,** *they recline* (in their several places): the passive verb is impersonal; A. 208, *d*; D. 266, *b*; B. 138, IV; G. 208, 2; cf. *regnabitur* in *v.* 272.

701. dant lymphas: this washing of hands was usual at ancient banquets. — **manibus:** dat. of reference. — **Cererem,** *bread:* cf. n. on *v.* 177. **canistris,** *from baskets.*

702. tonsis villis, *with the nap clipped close* (abl. of quality).

703. intus: i.e. in the rooms where the food was prepared. — **quibus . . . cura . . . struere,** *whose care it was to set forth:* sc. *est* with *cura*; *quibus* is dat. of possession. — **ordine . . . penum:** *the banquet in long array* (consisting of many courses).

704. flammis . . . penatis, *to sacrifice to the penates with flames:* a poetical way of saying *to keep the fires burning in the kitchen.* The kitchen, the place of the hearth, was sacred to the household gods.

706. qui . . . onerent: rel. clause of purpose; A. 531, 2; D. 715; B. 282, 2; G. 630.

707. nec non et, *and the Carthaginians too.* — **limina laeta,** *the glad doorways,* as if they shared the joy of the feasters.— **frequentes,** *in throngs.*

708. pictis, *embroidered* (lit. *painted*).

710. flagrantis, *ruddy as flame,* i.e. of more than human beauty.

712. pesti, *ruin:* i.e. her love for Æneas with its consequences, ruinous to herself.

713. expleri mentem, *satisfy her heart:* for case of *mentem* see Introd. § 42. — **tuendo,** *with gazing:* abl. of means.

715. complexu . . . colloque, *on the neck of Æneas and in his embrace:* ablatives of place where.

717. oculis, pectore: abl. of means.

718. Dido: the repetition of the subject gives added pathos, as if it were "alas, poor Dido!"

719. insidat, *is clinging to her:* indirect question.

720. matris Acidaliae: Venus, so called from a fountain (Acidalius) in Bœotia, sacred to Venus and the Graces.

721. praevertere, *turn away,* i.e. from Sychæus to a new object.—**vivo amore** (abl. of means): as opposed to the dead Sychæus.

722. iam pridem resides (plur. of *reses*), *long at rest.*—**desueta corda,** *her heart disused* to love.

Fig. 16

723. postquam: sc. *est* or *fuit*; A. 543; D. 745; B. 287; G. 561. The wine was not brought in till after the feast. — **epulis:** dat. of possession. — **mensae remotae:** cf. n. on *v.* 216.

724. craterăs: for form see Introd. § 92. The *crater* was a large bowl in which the wine and water were mixed. — **coronant,** *wreathe* with a garland.

725. fit, *then arises.*—**strepitus:** i.e. of conversation. — **tectis,** *through the hall.*

726. atria: see n. on *v.* 638. — **dependent:** night has come on before they finish. — **lychni:** see Fig. 16. — **laquearibus:** the panels between the cross-beams of the ceiling were decorated with gilding, an arrangement often imitated in modern buildings. — **aureis:** two syllables (*synizesis:* Introd. § 115).

727. funalia, *torches,* in which a stout cord (*funis*) did service as wicking.

728. hic, *hereupon.*

729. pateram: a shallow bowl or saucer used for libations, here an heirloom in the royal house; it is brought out to honor the guest. See Fig. 17. — **Belus:** obviously a remote ancestor of Dido, not her father (*v.* 621). — **et omnes a Belo,** *and all the descendants of Belus.*

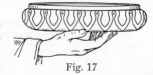

Fig. 17

730. soliti: sc. *erant* and *implere.*— **silentia:** the first bringing in of the wine had a sacred character, and, before the drinking began, a small quantity was always poured out as a libation.

731. Iuppiter: as the god of hospitality. — **hospitibus,** *hosts and guests:* the word includes both meanings. — **dare iura,** *define the rights.*

732. Tyriis: dat. after *laetum* (Introd. § 35).— **Troia:** abl. of place from which.

733. velis, *grant:* A. 439 and *a*; D. 674, *a*; B. 275, 2; G. 263, 2, *a.* — **huius** [sc. *diei*]: Introd. § 18.

734. Iuno: Juno's favor is invoked along with that of Bacchus, since she is the protecting divinity of Carthage.

735. coetum . . . celebrate, *throng the assembly.* — **faventes,** *with joyous mien* : they were to attend with expressions of joy, and without wrangling to disturb the hallowed rites. Ill-omened words, among which were reckoned all expressions of hatred or sorrow, were supposed to mar the effect of religious observances.

736. in mensam : on the table as on an altar sacred to hospitality. — **laticum honorem,** *an offering of wine.*

737. prima, *she first,* as the first in rank. — **libato** (impersonal), *when the libation had been made* : A. 419, *c* ; D. 483 ; G. 410, N.⁴ — **summo tenus . . . ore,** *with* (lit. *as far as*) *the tips of her lips.* As hostess Dido must go through the form of drinking, but she keeps the feminine proprieties.

738. Bitiae : a Carthaginian noble. — **increpitans,** *with a challenge* (to drink deep). — **impiger,** *nothing loath,* contrasted with Dido's *summo ore.*

739. se proluit, *took a deep draught.*

740. cithara, *on his lyre,* abl. of means. — **crinitus :** ancient bards, as well as Apollo, the god of song, were represented with flowing hair.

741. personat, *plays* (lit. *resounds*). — **Atlas :** Atlas, fabled to have been the earliest astronomer, was identified with Mount Atlas in north-western Africa, which bounded the western horizon of the ancients. So here, Iopas, coming from the same vicinity, is represented as a Numidian taught by Atlas. The subject of his song was common matter for poetical treatment among the ancients.

742. labores, *the eclipses* : literally *the toils* or *struggles,* since the sun was regarded as in difficulties during an eclipse.

743. unde [sc. *sint* or *sit*]: indir. question. — **ignes,** *lightnings.*

744. Arcturum, Hyadas, Triones : these constellations are mentioned for the stars in general. — **pluvias Hyadas :** a group of seven stars, whose rising with the sun was accompanied by rainy weather. — **geminos Triones,** *the two Bears* (the Great and the Little Bear). Each of these constellations consists of seven stars which the Romans called *Triones, plough-oxen,* or *Septentriones, the seven plough-oxen.*

745. quid . . . properent : i.e. why the days are so short in winter.

746. quae . . . obstet : *what delay retards the lingering nights,* i.e. the long nights of winter. Night was thought to have its course through the heavens as well as day.

747. ingeminant plausu, *redouble their applause* (lit. *with applause* ; abl. of means).

748. nec non et, *so also,* as another part of the entertainment ; cf. *v.* 707.

749. longum . . . amorem, *long draughts of love.*

750. Priamo : abl. with *super, concerning, about.*

751. quibus armis : his arms, which were famous, had been made by Vulcan. — **Aurorae filius :** Memnon, the Æthiopian king who came to the aid of Troy (*v.* 489).

752. quantus, *how tall,* or *how mighty.*

753. immo, *nay rather* (always with a negative force). Here it intro-duces the request for a complete narration from the beginning (*a prima origine*), as contrasted with the preceding separate details. — **age:** cf. *agite, v.* 627.

BOOK II

Æneas' tale to Dido takes up Books ii and iii and brings the story of the poem down to the point at which Book i opens.

1. conticuere: perf. indicating a momentary act; *were hushed.* — **intenti ora tenebant:** imperf. of continued action; *looked toward him with eager attention* (lit. *were holding their faces,* etc.).

2. toro: *the couch* on which he reclined at table.

3. infandum: emphatic because of its position. The effect may be pro-duced in English by translating, ' Unspeakable, O queen, is the sorrow that you bid me renew.'

4. ut eruerint: indir. quest. depending on the verb " to tell " implied in *dolorem renovare*; *how the Greeks utterly destroyed,* etc.

5. quae, etc.: *distressful things which*; this clause and that in the next verse are in app. with *dolorem.* — **que . . . et:** *both . . . and.*

6. et quorum, etc.: may be translated literally. — **fando,** *in speaking*; compare *tuendo,* i. 713.

7. Myrmidonum Dolopumve: Thessalian soldiers of Achilles. — **Ulixi:** genitive, see Introd. § 93.

8. temperet a lacrimis: *could refrain from tears.* Deliberative sub-junctive; A. 444; D. 678; B. 277; G. 466. — **caelo:** *from the sky.*

9. praecipitat: night is regarded as running its course through the heaven in the same way as the day or the sun. — **cadentia:** *setting*: indicating the approach of morning.

10. cognoscere: complem. inf. with *amor* [*est*], which is equivalent to a verb of wishing; Introd. §§ 76, 77. *Cognoscendi* would be the prose con-struction: A. 504; D. 874; B. 338, 1; G. 428.

11. supremum laborem: *the last agony*; *labor* implies suffering as well as struggle.

12. meminisse horret: *shudders to recall.* Verbs of fearing regularly take the infinitive in this sense, though usually only *vereor* is in fact so used; A. 456; D. 837; B. 328, 1; G. 550, N.[5] — **luctu refūgit,** *shrinks* (lit. *has shrunk*) *back from the grief.*

14. Danaum: gen. plur.; Introd. § 91. — **labentibus** (abl. abs.): i. e. having passed and still continuing to glide away; it was the tenth year of the war.

15. instar montis, *huge as a mountain*: *instar* (lit. *the image*) is really an indecl. noun in appos. with *equum* (Introd. § 23). — **Palladis:** Minerva was the patroness of all kinds of handicraft.

16. aedificant, *build*, indicating the size by the very use of a word which is used of houses. — **intexunt abiete costas,** *line the ribs with hewn fir*, i.e. with strips running across the ribs. — **abiete:** trisyllable $\_ \cup \cup$; for the *synaeresis* see Introd. § 112.

17. reditu: i.e. to Greece.

18. huc includunt, *they shut up in it* (lit. *hither*). — **delecta corpora:** since only the bravest chiefs were to dare the perilous ambuscade.

19. lateri: dat., in a sort of apposition with *huc*, but governed by *includunt*; Introd. § 27. — **penitus,** *deep within*: another hint at the immense size.

20. milite (collective), *soldiery*.

21. est, *there is.* — **Tenedos:** about four miles from the coast of Troy.

22. opum: Introd. § 17.

23. tantum sinus, *a mere bay.* — **male fida,** *ill-faithful*, i.e. *treacherous.* — **male** has with adjs. expressing good qualities a negative force; with those expressing bad, an intensive force (cf. iv. 8).

24. condunt: i.e. the Greeks.

25. abiisse rati [*sumus*], *supposed they had gone*: the subject of *abiisse* (*eos*) is omitted; A. 581, N.[1]; D. 887, I, *a*; B. 314, 5; G. 527, R.[3] — **Mycenas:** a very ancient city near Argos, and the home of Agamemnon. Its remains, in a very archaic style of art, are among the most interesting in Greece. Here used for all *Greece* generally (Introd. § 98).

26. luctu: abl. of separation (Introd. § 49).

27. Dorica, *Grecian*: see Introd. § 98.

29–30. Quoted as specimens of the remarks of the Trojans. — **tendebat,** *had his camp* (lit. *used to spread* (his tents)).

30. classibus: dat. of reference (Introd. § 31); the fleet had been hauled up on the shore. — **acie:** abl. of manner (Introd. § 58).

31. stupet: as equivalent to a strong *miratur*, here governs an acc. — **exitiale,** *fatal* (to the Trojans). — **Minervae:** obj. gen.; the horse, according to the lying story told to the Trojans by Sinon (ii. 162 ff.), was intended to take the place of the Palladium, which the Greeks had stolen from the citadel of Troy, thereby offending Minerva.

33. duci [sc. *equum*]: in prose a substantive clause of purpose would be used (Introd. § 78).

34. dolo, *treachery.* According to an oracle, a child born on a certain day was to be the destruction of Troy. Both Paris and a son of Thymœtes were born on that day, and Priam put to death the son of Thymœtes. — **iam:** i.e. the time had now come for this destiny. — **ferebant,** *ordained*.

35. quorum . . . menti, *those in whose mind was a better* (i.e. wiser) *thought*: dat. of possession (Introd. § 29).

36. pelago: dative of place to which (Introd. § 34).

37. -que, *or*.

38. **cavas :** agreeing with *latebras*,

39. **studia,** *parties* (more lit. *party feelings*).

40. **primus ante omnīs :** i. e. taking the lead in his eager partisanship. — **ibi,** *at this moment.*

41. **ab arce :** where he had been occupied as priest.

42. **quae,** etc., *what madness is this ?* Such use of *tam, talis,* and *tantus* in nearly the sense of our simple demonstratives is very common.

43. **avectos :** sc. *esse.*

44. **dolis :** ablative of separation. — **Danaum :** modifies *dona.*

47. **inspectura, ventura,** *to look down on our houses,* etc.: fut. part. of purpose; A. 499, 2; D. 868; B. 337, 4; G. 438, N. One of the common means of siege was to build towers overtopping the walls, and move them forward on wheels. The huge horse is suspected to be such an *engine of war.* — **urbi :** dat. of place to which.

48. **error,** *trick.* — **ne credite :** Introd. § 87; in prose, *nolite credere.*

49. **et,** *even.* — **ferentīs :** acc. plural. Cf. *Paradise Lost,* ii. 391 : "And count thy specious gifts no gifts, but guiles."

51. **inque feri,** etc., *against the belly of the monster rounded with jointed framework.* — **compagibus :** abl. of manner or means.

52. **stetit,** *stuck there.* — **illa,** *the spear.* — **utero recusso,** *the belly of the horse reëchoing* (lit. of the sound, *struck back*): abl. abs.

53. **insonuere,** etc.: cf. *Paradise Lost,* ii. 788, 789 :

> Hell trembled at the hideous name, and sigh'd
> From all her caves, and back resounded *Death !*

54–56. **si fata,** etc.: a condition cont. to fact, with past prot. (*fuisset*) and mixed apod. (*impulerat, staret, maneres*). — **impulerat :** used for *impulisset* for metrical reasons.

54. **mens,** *our minds.* — **laeva,** as applied to *the fates,* means *unpropitious*; as applied to *minds,* it means *dull, blinded.* The first meaning is derived from the language of augury. An appearance on the left was inauspicious (cf. *sinister*) among the Greeks, whom Virgil here follows, though originally the left was the fortunate quarter among the Romans. The second meaning comes from the awkwardness (*gaucherie*) of the left hand. Such uses of words in a double sense are avoided in modern style, and in the classics we explain them by the so-called rhetorical figure *zeugma*; but they probably seemed neither irregular nor objectionable to the ancients.

55. **Argolicas,** *of the Greeks.* The Latin uses an adj. of possession when it can, often where English prefers *of.* — **foedare :** infinitive instead of a substantive clause with *ut* (as in *v.* 33).

56. **arx :** vocative.

57. **manūs :** Greek acc. with *revinctum,* which agrees with *iuvenem* (Introd. § 42).

59. Dardanidae: in apposition with *pastores.*—**qui:** subject of *obtulerat.*—**venientibus,** *to them* (the shepherds) *as they came*: dat. with *obtulerat.*

60. hoc . . . aperiret, *to contrive this very thing, that is, to open,* etc.: the subjunc. *aperiret* explains *hoc ipsum.*

61. fidens animi, *confident in heart*: A. 358; D. 357, N.²; B. 232, 3; G. 374, N.⁷

62. versare dolos, *to practise wiles* (if he should succeed) or to die if discovered: the infinitives are in apposition with *utrumque.*

64. circumfusa ruit, *gather about him.* — **certant:** the number changes because they *vie with each other* individually, though they *gather* in a body.

65. accipe, *learn.*

66. disce omnes: i. e. the nature of all the Greeks.

67. turbatus: although *fidens animi,* he is frightened when he finds himself in the midst of his enemies.

68. A spondaic verse: Introd. § 104.

70. iam, *any longer.*

71. cui neque locus, etc., *who have no place anywhere among the Greeks, and besides even the Trojans,* etc.: *cui* is dat. of possession.

72. poenas poscunt, *demand my punishment by a bloody death* (as he infers from their fierce looks: cf. also *v.* 64).

73. animi, *feelings.*

74. fari: inf. instead of a substantive clause; sc. *eum.*— **cretus:** sc. *sit.*

75. quidve ferat, *or what news he brings*: indir. question. — **memoret,** *let him tell* = *tell us* (we say): in indir. disc. for imperative of direct; A. 588; D. 887, III; B. 316; G. 652. — **quae . . . capto,** *on what is his reliance as a captive* (lit. *what reliance is to him captured*): dat. of possession (sc. *ei* with *capto*).

76. formidine, pavitans (*v.* 107): the embarrassment was genuine and natural; not enough to destroy his presence of mind and so spoil his scheme, but enough to make a favorable impression on his captors.

77. equidem: makes the whole expression more forcible, like our " I will, indeed I will." — **fuerit quodcumque,** *whatever shall come of it*: fut. perf.

78. vera, *truly.* — **me:** sc. *esse.* — **Argolica:** in answer to the question in *v.* 74.

79. hoc primum, *this first!* i. e. let this compromising fact be stated once for all: sc. *dictum esto.* — **miserum:** pred. adj.

80. improba, *malicious goddess that she is.*

81. fando, *by report*: abl. of means; A. 507; D. 879; B. 338, 4, *a*; G. 431. — **aliquod . . . Palamedis,** *if perchance any such name as Palamedes,* etc. (lit. *any name of Palamedes*).

82. Belidae, *descendant of Belus*: this Belus was king of Egypt. — **Palamedis:** Ulysses, to avoid joining in the Trojan expedition, feigned madness, yoking together a horse and a bull, ploughing a field with this team, and sowing it with salt. Palamedes laid Telemachus in the furrow. Ulysses turned out, and being thus proved sane, was held to the service. In revenge he procured the death of Palamedes in the way hinted at in the text. — **incluta famā gloria**, *his renown made famous by the speech of men.* — **famā :** i. e. the talk about his renown. — **gloria :** the renown itself.

83. falsa sub, etc., *under a false and treacherous accusation.*

84. indicio, *charge :* to prove treachery, Ulysses hid money and a forged letter from Priam in the tent of Palamedes. — **vetabat,** *tried to stop :* conative imperf.; A. 471, *c*; D. 653; B. 260, 3; G. 233.

85. nunc cassum lumine, *now when he is dead* (lit. *deprived of light*): abl. of separation.

86. illi : dat. of reference.

87. pauper : his poverty was his reason for sending the boy, as war was with the ancients a regular means of gaining wealth. — **primis ab annis :** i. e. at an early age — as soon as he was old enough to serve.

88. stabat : the subject is Palamedes. — **regno :** locative abl.

89. consiliis : locative abl.

90. invidia : abl. of cause or means.

91. haud ignota : to win confidence, he weaves in well-known facts. — **superis ab oris,** *from the world above* (this world).

92. trahebam, tacui : notice the change of tense.

93. mecum, *alone by myself.*

94-96. me . . . ultorem : indir. disc. dependent on *promisi. Me . . . ultorem* (to which *promisi* gives a future sense) = *me ulturum* [*esse*]. Thus it stands for a fut. apod. (dir. disc.: *ultor ero = ulciscar*); the prot. is *tulisset, remeassem* (dir. disc.: *tulerit, remeavero*). — **tulisset,** *should allow.*

95. Argos : used for Greece in general. Sinon's home was in Eubœa.

97. mihi : dat. of reference.

98. terrere, spargere, quaerere : historical infinitives (Introd. § 82). Cf. *Paradise Lost, v.* 702–703 :

> Tells the suggested cause, and casts between
> Ambiguous words and jealousies.

99. volgum : masc. here, but usually neut. — **quaerere,** etc., *conscious of his guilt, he began to seek arms* of defence against him who might be his accuser.

100. nec enim (the negative of *etenim*, in which the force of *et* is lost), *for he did not rest,* etc., referring back to *prima labes.* — **donec :** Sinon artfully breaks off just when he has roused the keenest curiosity. — **Calchante ministro :** abl. abs. Calchas was a soothsayer who came to Troy with the Greeks.

101. sed autem = merely *but*; the repetition is pleonastic and colloquial. — **haec ingrata,** *this thankless story*: i. e. unpleasant and useless for me to tell and uninteresting for you to hear.

102. quidve moror, *or why do I delay you?* — **uno ordine** (abl. of manner): in one degree of estimation, i.e. *as all alike.*

103. id: i.e. the fact that I am a Greek. — **iamdudum sumite poenas,** *inflict* (lit. *take*) *the punishment long since due*, i. e. which you have long been eager to inflict. — **sumite:** punishment is regularly looked on as a fine or forfeit which the inflicter takes (hence *sumere*, ' to inflict ') and the sufferer gives (hence *dare*, ' to suffer ').

104. Ithacus: Ulysses; his home was on the island of Ithaca. — **velit,** *would like it*: apodosis for fut. less vivid condition, of which the protasis is omitted: so also *mercentur*; A. 516, *b*; D. 789; B. 303; G. 596. — **magno:** abl. of price (Introd. § 62). — **Atridae:** Agamemnon and Menelaus, sons of Atreus.

105. tum vero, *then more than ever.* Notice that these words regularly introduce the most important point or the decisive moment in the narrative. — **ardemus:** i. e., before we were *eager*, but now we *long*.

107. prosequitur, *proceeds* with his tale.

108. Troia relicta: abl. abs.

109. bello: to be taken with both *fessi* and *discedere*; they were wearied *with* the war, and anxious to depart *from* it.

110. fecissent: optative subjunctive; A. 441, 442; D. 680, 681, II; B. 279; G. 260, 261.

111. euntis, *as they were just going.*

112. praecipue: the previous occurrences were omens forbidding departure, and now still more were there signs of divine wrath. — **cum iam,** *when now.* — **acernis:** cf. *v.* 16, where the construction is said to be of fir. This variety is merely an epic convention, not a blunder; compare the use of various names for the Greeks, etc. (Introd. § 98).

114. scitantem, *to inquire*: pres. part. expressing purpose; A. 490. 3; G. 670, 3, N. — **oracula,** *the responses* (the proper meaning of the word); the most famous oracles of Apollo were at Delphi and Delos.

116. sanguine: i.e. the sacrifice of Iphigenia at Aulis (on the Eubœan Strait), where the Greek fleet mustered for the Trojan expedition, and where it was detained by head winds until Agamemnon consented to the sacrifice of his daughter to Diana. See Tennyson's *Dream of Fair Women*, sts. 25–30. Fig. 18 (from an ancient wall painting) represents the scene. — **placastis:** syncopated form of *placavistis.*

118. reditus: plur. because the Greeks would return to their homes in various parts of Greece. — **anima:** abl. of means (a regular construction for the thing sacrificed). — **litandum** [*est*], *expiation must be made*: impersonal.

120. gelidusque . . . cucurrit : cf. *Paradise Lost*, ix. 888–890 :

> Adam . . . amaz'd,
> Astonied stood, and blank, while horror chill
> Ran through his veins, and all his joints relax'd.

121. cui fata parent, [*in doubt*] *for whom the fates are preparing* (such a destiny): an indir. question depending on the doubt implied in *tremor*,

Fig. 18

etc. The response itself is supposed to be a preliminary arrangement for the death of some one. The cause of the agitation of the people is explained by *v.* 130.

122. hic, *at this moment.*

123. numina : i.e. expressions of the divine will.

124. flagitat : implies violence or insistence. — **iam canebant,** *began to foretell* (prophecies being usually given in verse).

125. artificis, *the trickster :* i.e. Ulysses. — **taciti :** i.e. some also saw, but were silent. — **ventura,** *what would happen.*

126. quinos: the distributive is regularly used with numeral adverbs; cf. i. 381, note. — **ille:** Calchas. — **tectus,** *hiding his thoughts.*

128. vix tandem, *at length reluctantly:* i.e. with pretended reluctance, as *composito* shows.

129. composito, *according to compact,* strictly an impersonal ablative absolute; cf. i. 737, note. — **rumpit,** *breaks his silence; rumpit* is in a manner causative: he makes his voice break the bands that held it.

130. quae . . . tulere, *what each dreaded for himself, they bore* (i.e. permitted) *when turned to one wretch's ruin.* The emphatic position of *unius* and *tulere* suggests this as the best interpretation.

132. sacra: arrangements for the sacrifice. — **parari:** hist. inf.

133. salsae fruges: coarse meal mixed with salt (called also *mola*) was regularly sprinkled on the victim's head before a sacrifice. — **vittae,** *fillets:* bands which were wound round the victim's head.

134. fateor: it was sacrilege to escape, for he was already devoted (*sacer*) to the god. — **leto:** dative of separation (Introd. § 32). — **vincula rupi:** i.e. escaped from confinement.

136. darent: A. 553; D. 765; B. 293, III, 2; G. 572. — **dedissent:** subjunctive of integral part; the pluperfect is used by sequence of tenses for fut. perf.: A. 593; D. 907; B. 324, 1; G. 663, 1.

137. nec iam, *no longer.* — **mihi:** dat. of possession; sc. *est.*

139. quos poenas reposcent, *of whom they, perchance, will exact the penalty for my escape:* Introd. § 40.

141. quod, *therefore* (lit. *as to which*): acc. of specification. The word regularly introduces adjurations. — **te:** Sinon is speaking to Priam. — **veri:** Introd. § 16.

142. per [sc. *eam fidem*], *by whatever inviolate truth yet remains to mortals anywhere.* — **si qua est:** the perfidy of the Greeks makes him doubt if good faith anywhere exists. — **restet:** rel. cl. of characteristic; A. 535, *a*; D. 726; B. 283, 2; G. 631, 2.

143. laborum: Introd. § 20.

144. non digna, *undeserved misfortunes.*

145. lacrimis: dat., a bold *synecdoche*; what is given *to him* on account of the tears is said to be given *to the tears* themselves: A. 641; G. 695. — **ultro,** *besides* (lit. *beyond* his asking, which was only for his life).

146. viro: dat. of reference; translate as if genitive modifying *manicas.*

147. dictis: abl. of manner.

148. hinc iam, *from henceforth.* — **Graios:** for case see Introd. § 18.

149. noster, *one of us.*

150. quo, *to what end?* — **quis auctor:** i.e., by whose counsel?

151. quae religio, *what religious vow* (or *offering*)? The repeated questions in various forms show the old man's eager curiosity as well as his doubt.

153. vīnclīs = *vīncŭlīs*, which would be impossible in hexameter. — **ad sidera,** *toward the stars* (including all the heavenly bodies).

154. non violabile : i.e. an oath by these divine powers must not be broken.

156. deum (gen. plur.): i.e. worn in honor of the gods. — **quas hostia gessi :** and hence so much the more sacred an oath to him.

157. fas : sc. *est.* — **sacrata,** *consecrated* by religious obligation, like the oath of enlistment of the Roman soldier. — **resolvere,** *to break* (lit. *to unbind,* that is, to loose the obligation): infinitive used as subject (Introd. § 73). — **iura,** i.e. *iura iuranda, oaths.*

158. ferre sub auras, *bring out to light* (lit. *to air*) from their hiding-place.

159. si qua tegunt, *whatever they* (the Greeks) *conceal.*

160. promissis : locative abl. — **maneas :** *abide by your promises :* poetical use of hortatory (jussive) subjunc.; A. 439, *a*; D. 674, *a*; B. 275, 2; G. 263, 2, *a*.

161. Troia : an appeal to the holy city itself, more impressive than one to the king alone. — **magna rependam,** *greatly repay :* the protasis of a fut. more vivid condition, of which the apodosis is found in *maneas* and *serves.*

162. belli : obj. gen.

163. auxiliis stetit, *depended on the help :* abl. of place where. — **ex quo,** *ever since.*

164. sed enim, *but* [*their hopes began to fail*] *for,* etc. For the ellipsis see n. to i. 19.

165. fatale Palladium (Greek dimin. of *Pallas*): a small wooden image of the goddess. As long as it remained in the city Troy could not be captured. It was polluted by the touch of the bloodstained hands of Diomedes and Ulysses, Sinon says, and hence the goddess was offended.

168. virgineas divae vittas, *the fillets of the maiden goddess .* these seem to have differed in form from those of matrons.

169. ex illo, *since then :* correl. to *ex quo.* — **fluere,** *ebb :* historical infinitive; so also *referri.*

170. fractae : sc. *sunt.* — **aversa :** sc. *est.*

171. ea signa, *signs of this* (i.e. of her hostility). — **Tritonia :** a name of Pallas, of uncertain origin. — **monstris** (*moneo*), *warnings.*

173. luminibus arrectis, *staring eyes :* abl. of separation.

174. ipsa, *the goddess herself* (more amazing than the other warnings).

175. trementem : the agitation of the goddess is indicated more vividly by the rattling of her arms.

176. canit : see note, *v.* 124. — **temptanda** [*esse*]: indir. disc.

178. omina : Virgil here transfers a Roman custom to the Homeric Greeks. The Romans undertook no expedition without the direction of the gods, who were supposed to dwell in the city, and were consulted by auspices before setting out. If the event was unsuccessful, the auspices had to be taken again in the city, and the whole enterprise be begun anew. The term for this was *repetere auspicia*, of which *repetere omina* is here a variation. — **repetant :** fut. prot. in indir. disc. — **Argis,** *from Argos.* — **numen,** *the favoring presence* of the gods, as shown by renewed favorable auspices.

179. quod . . . avexere : i.e. the divine favor which they brought with them when they came from Greece. — **pelago,** *by sea.* — **curvis carinis,** *in the crooked ships :* abl. of means.

180. quod, *whereas* (i.e. as to the fact that): a *quod* clause of fact, used as acc. of specification; A. 572, *a* ; D. 824; B. 299, 2 ; G. 525, 2.

181. remenso : in a passive sense here.

182. omina : i.e. those referred to in *vv.* 171–175.

183. pro Palladio, *in lieu of the Palladium.* — **pro numine,** *in propitiation of the offended divinity.* The goddess is, however, identified with her image the Palladium, hence *pro* can be used with both, though not in precisely the same sense.

184. triste, *gloomy* (in its effect).

185. immensam molem : the gist of the idea is in these words. They were to make the horse huge so as to keep it outside, where it would protect them and not the enemy. — **tamen :** i.e. though it was in lieu of the Palladium, yet it was to be of no service to the Trojans.

186. roboribus : see n. on *v.* 112. — **caelo :** dat. of place to which.

187. recipi and **duci** are branches of the same general idea ; *neu* introduces a different one. Sinon accounts for the size of the horse, and at the same time suggests that disposal of it which he desires.

188. populum : obj. of *tueri.* — **populum . . . tueri,** *to protect the people under* [the guardianship of] *their ancient religion :* i.e. just as they had been protected by the Palladium, whose place the horse was to supply.

189. violasset : indir. disc. for fut. perf. — **Minervae :** obj. gen.

190. quod di . . . convertant, *may the gods turn the omen against himself* (Calchas): optative subjunctive; A. 441 ; D. 681, 1 ; B. 279, 1 ; G. 260. The anger of the gods had to be satisfied, but might by prayers be diverted from its original object to another person.

191. futurum [*esse*]: indir. disc. following the verb of saying implied in *iussit.*

193. ultro . . . venturam, *would come, though unassailed :* i.e. would make an offensive war, beyond the defensive warfare they were now waging. — **Asiam** = *Troiam.* — **Pelopea moenia** = *Graeciam :* Pelops was an ancestor of Agamemnon and Menelaus.

194. ea : i.e. the fates implied in *exitium.*

195. periuri Sinonis : Sinon's name was long a by-word in literature for an arch-traitor.

196. res, *his story.* — **capti** [*sunt*], *those were caught* : as antecedent of *quos* supply *ei*.

197. Larissaeus, *Thessalian.* Achilles did not come from Larissa, but from Phthia, another town in Thessaly.

199. aliud : by this prodigy the fall of Troy is shown to have been due to fate, and not merely to the wiles and valor of the Greeks. — **miseris,** [*to us*] *ill-fated.*

200. obicitur : for the long first syllable see A. 603, N.³; D. 968, N.; B. 362, 4; G. 703, 2, N. — **improvida :** *blinded,* not knowing the future.

201. Neptuno : dative of reference. — **ductus sorte :** a Roman custom transferred to Troy (cf. note on *v.* 178).

203. alta, *the deep.*

204. orbibus : abl. of manner with *incumbunt.*

205. incumbunt pelago, *lie heavily upon the sea* : they are, as it were, a burden to the sea on account of their huge size. — **pariter,** *side by side*

207, 208. pontum pone legit, *trails behind over the sea.* The verb *lego* seems literally to mean *pick,* hence used of the course of a vessel, and so here of the monster. — **sinuatque . . . terga,** *and winds their huge bodies in coils* (lit. *in a coil*). — **volumine** (abl. of manner): the plural would be more natural, but the singular is occasioned by the metre.

209. spumante salo : abl. absolute.

210. oculos : with *suffecti* (Introd. § 42).

212. visu : abl. of cause. — **agmine certo,** *with steady march* (like an army), not roaming about aimlessly as they might be expected to do if not divinely sent.

213. Laocoönta : acc. (Introd. § 92).

216. post (adv.), *next* or *then.* — **auxilio,** *to their help* : dat. of purpose (Introd. § 33).

218. collo, *about his neck* : dat. (Introd. § 27). — **circum . . . dati :** tmesis.

219. terga : obj. of *circum dati* (Introd. § 43). — **capite :** abl. of degree of difference ; sing. because the plur. *căpĭtĭbŭs* could not be used in hexameter. Cf. *volumine* in *v.* 208.

220. tendit, *strives.* — **divellere :** complementary inf. (Introd. § 77).

221. vittas : cf. *oculos* in *v.* 210 and *terga* in *v.* 219.

223. quales mugitus, cum, for *tales mugitus* (in apposition with *clamores*), *quales tolluntur,* etc., *such roarings as are raised when,* etc. So Dante, *Inferno,* ii. 22–24 :

> Like to a bull, that with impetuous spring
> Darts, at the moment when the fatal blow
> Hath struck him, but, unable to proceed,
> Plunges on either side.

224. incertam, *ill-aimed.* — **securim :** for form see A. 75, *b* ; D. 102, *e* ; B. 38, 1 ; G. 57, 1.

225. lapsu, *gliding* (as if it were a participle): abl. of manner. — **delubra summa :** the chief shrines of an ancient city were regularly in the stronghold (cf. the Capitol at Rome and the Parthenon at Athens).

226. saevae, *cruel*, in withdrawing her protection from Troy.

227. clipei : many statues of Minerva show a shield resting on the ground, the upper edge held by her hand. — **teguntur :** *hide themselves* : Introd. § 94.

228. tum vero : see note, *v.* 105. — **novus :** the former fear was mere terror at the serpents; the new is a religious awe. — **cunctis :** dat. of reference.

229. scelus expendisse merentem, *has expiated his guilt, as he deserves.*

230. robur : one of the many terms Virgil uses for the horse.

231. laeserit, intorserit : relative clauses of cause ; A. 535, *e* ; D. 730, I ; B. 288, 3 ; G. 633.

234. dividimus, etc., *we break down the walls, and* [thus] *lay open the defences of the city.* — **moenia :** more general in meaning than *muros.*

235. accingunt : sc. *se* ; see note on i. 210. — **rotarum lapsūs,** *rolling wheels* (lit. *the rollings of wheels*): a bold form of expression, common in poetry ; the quality or property of a person or thing, which would naturally be expressed by an adj., is embodied in an abstract noun, and the person or thing itself follows in the gen. This emphasizes the quality. Cf. *minae murorum*, 'menacing walls' (lit. 'menaces of walls'), iv. 88 ; cf. also iv. 132.

236. collo : dative (Introd. § 27).

238. feta armis, *teeming with arms*, i.e. with armed men : *metonymy* (Introd. § 100). — **pueri,** etc. : again a Roman custom. Many such customs of Virgil's time alluded to in the Æneid were supposed to have been imported direct from Troy. — **circum :** adv.

239. gaudent : because it was a sacred service.

240. illa subit : as Menelaus tells the story in the Odyssey (iv. 274-289 ; Bry. 355), Helen went thrice about the horse, calling the several chiefs by name, imitating by her voice the wife of each ; and they were only kept from betraying themselves by the strong hand of Ulysses laid upon their mouths. — **minans,** *towering high.*

243. substitit, *stopped* : stumbling, as it were, on the threshold, always a bad omen with the Romans. — **utero :** abl. of place from which.

244. immemores : they had forgotten Laocoön's warning (*v.* 45), and they heeded neither the omen of the stumbling of the horse nor the sound of arms from within.

245. monstrum infelix, *the inauspicious* (i.e. *fatal*) *prodigy.* — **arce :** abl. of place where.

246. tunc etiam, *then too* (besides the other warnings which she had given in vain). — **fatis . . . futuris,** *in prophecy of the fates* (lit. *in future fates*): abl. of manner. — **Cassandra :** daughter of Priam. She had been endowed by Apollo with the gift of prophecy ; but, as she rejected his love, the gift was accompanied with the curse that no one should believe her inspired words.

247. non credita : agrees with *ora.* — **Teucris :** dat. of agent (Introd. § 30).

248. quibus esset : THOUGH *that day was our last* (contrasting the signs of joy with their real fate); rel. clause of characteristic expressing concession ; A. 535, *e* ; D. 730, II ; B. 283, 3 ; G. 634. Notice how this idea is brought out by the position of *miseri* before *quibus*, etc.

249. velamus : decking temples with garlands (*fronde* is collective) had a religious as well as a festival meaning.

250. vertitur, *revolves.* — **ruit Oceano :** night, like day, was conceived as rising from the vast Ocean that encircles the earth.

251. involvens : notice the grave effect of the spondees.

252. Myrmidonum : soldiers of Achilles (*v.* 7), here used for all the Greeks. — **fusi per moenia,** *lying carelessly at rest throughout the city.* Cf. i. 214.

254. iam ibat, *was on its way already*, anticipating Sinon's success.

255. per . . . lunae, *by the friendly silence of the moon.*

256. flammas, *the signal light*, as a sign to Sinon : cf. vi. 518, where Helen is said to have held forth a lighted torch as a signal. — **cum . . . extulerat :** a temporal clause of the "*cum* inverse" type. Logically this should be the main clause and the preceding clause should be temporal, but the present arrangement adds emphasis : A. 546, *a* ; D. 751 ; B. 288, 2 ; G. 581. — **regia puppis :** Agamemnon's ship.

257. fatis deum iniquis, *by the hostile decrees* (lit. *fates*) *of the gods* — hostile, that is, to Troy. Usually the gods are made subject to the fates and act in a manner as their agents, but this distinction is not always observed. See also vi. 376.

258. utero : abl. of place where. — **Danaos . . . claustra,** *lets loose the Greeks from their pine-wood prison.* As the verb *laxat* can apply in slightly different senses to both *Danaos* and *claustra*, the zeugma, always a favorite form of expression (cf. notes on i. 356, ii. 54), is preferred to the ablative of separation (*claustris*). — **pinea :** see n. on *v.* 112.

259. laxat is in the same construction as *extulerat*, but the action of the latter verb precedes and that of the former is brought forward to present time (hist. pres.); hence the great difference of tense. — **auras,** *open air.*

260. cavo se robore promunt : see Fig. 19 (from a gem).

262. demissum lapsi per funem, *descending by a rope let down.*

263. Neoptolemus: in appos. with *Pelides.* — **primus Machaon:** Machaon, son of Æsculapius, was famous both as a surgeon and as a warrior; *primus* here means either *noble*, *peerless*, or *among the first*.

264. doli: i.e. the horse. Notice the variety of words Virgil uses to refer to the horse (cf. note on *v.* 230 and Introd. § 98).

266. portis patentibus: *through the open gates*; abl. of way by which (Introd. § 55).

267. conscia, *allied*, knowing each other's plans.

268. tempus erat: this, with *nox erat*, is a favorite form of transition with Virgil.

269. dono divum: cf. Milton, *Paradise Lost*, iv. 735: "And when we seek, as now, thy [i.e. God's] gift of sleep"; and *Psalm* cxxvii: "He giveth his beloved sleep."

271. adesse mihi, *to appear before me.*

272. raptatus bigis: i.e. by the chariot of Achilles; cf. i. 483.

Fig. 19

273. per ... tumentis, *with thongs drawn through his swollen feet.* — **lora:** acc. with the passive participle *traiectus*; see A. 395, N.[3]

274. ei mihi, *ah me !* — **mihi:** dat. of reference with *ei.* — **qualis erat,** *how he looked !* — **quantum mutatus,** *how changed.*

275. redit: i.e. as I seem to see him returning. The tense is used like the historical present for vividness. — **exuvias indutus Achilli:** *clad in the spoils of Achilles.* Hector killed Patroclus, who was wearing the armor of Achilles (Il. xvii. 188; Bry. 232). For case of *exuvias* see Introd. § 43.

276. puppibus: dat. of place to which.

278. volnera: apparently honorable wounds received in battle; not the hurts and bruises from being dragged at the car of Achilles. — **gerens,** *having* or *with.* — **quae plurima,** *of which he had received so many.* — **plurima:** emphasized by being put into the relative clause.

281. O lux, etc.: in his dream Æneas forgets that Hector has been slain, and the manner of his death and the cause of his disfigurement.

282. tenuere: sc. *te.*

283. exspectate: voc., with *Hector.* — **ut,** *how,* i.e. in how sad a plight.

287. ille nihil: sc. *respondet.* — **moratur,** *heed* (lit. *stay for*).

289. his: with a gesture.

290. alto a culmine, *from her lofty height,* i.e. her position of power.

291. sat . . . datum : a legal phrase; your debt to your country and king has been fully paid. — **si . . . possent . . . fuissent,** *if Troy could be saved* (at all) *by human hand, it would have been saved* (before) *by mine.*

293. penatis : i.e. the household gods of Troy. The *penates* that Æneas actually took with him in his flight (*v.* 717) were those of his own household, but these were regarded as representing the *penates* of the city, since the latter were thus entrusted to him in his dream. See n. on i. 68.

294. his : dative of reference.

295. quae : i.e. *moenia.* — **pererrato ponto :** abl. abs.

296. vittas Vestamque : hendiadys; see i. 61, note. An image of filleted Vesta is entrusted to Æneas in his dream.

297. ignem : the sacred fire, which was carried from the hearth of Vesta, in the mother city, to kindle that of the new community. The gods and fire here referred to were supposed to be preserved in the temple of Vesta at Rome.

298. diverso, etc., *the city is disturbed by many mingled sounds of grief.*— **miscentur :** the regular word for any confusion.

299. secreta . . . recessit, *stood in a retired spot, apart* [from others], *and concealed by trees.* Note that the participles *secreta* and *obtecta* are used as pred. nom. after *recessit.* — **secreta :** has its literal sense of *separated* (i.e. apart from other dwellings).

301. horror, *the dread din* of arms.

302. somno : abl. of separation. — **summi fastigia tecti,** *the summit of the roof of the house* (lit. *the top of the highest* [*part of the*] *house*).

303. ascensu supero, *I mount to* (lit. *by a climb I mount*). — **adsto,** etc., *I stand listening* [to the roar of battle] *just as, when the blaze driven by furious southern blasts falls upon the plenteous crops, or the hurrying torrent of a mountain flood overwhelms the fields,* etc., *the shepherd, ignorant of the cause, from the lofty summit of a rock, bewildered, hears* (**stupet accipiens**) *the roar.* Cf. Il. xi. 492–497 (Bry. 599).

306. boum labores : i.e. the fruits of their toil.

309. manifesta fides [sc. *est*], *the truth is clear* (belief is forced upon me of what would otherwise seem impossible).

310. Deiphobi : Deiphobus, the next of the sons of Priam after Hector and Paris, had married Helen after Paris' death ; his house was therefore the first destroyed. — **dedit ruinam,** *has fallen in ruins.*— **ruinam :** expresses both the crashing fall and the consequences of it (the ruins).

311. Volcano, *the fire,* but with a suggestion that Vulcan, the Fire God, is present in person to assist his mother Juno in destroying the city.

312. Ucalegon (i.e. his house): one of the counsellors of Priam.— **Sigea freta,** *the waters of Sigeum :* i.e. off Sigeum, a promontory near Troy.

313. exorĭtur : third conjugation here.

314. nec sat rationis, *and yet there is no reason.*

315. bello: dat. of purpose (Introd. § 33).

316. animi: notice the common use of the plural *animi* in the sense of *passion*, while *mentem* is the intellect or judgment.

317. succurrit, *it comes [to my thought] that it is noble to die under arms*; *mori* is subject of *esse* understood. Cf. the familiar line from Horace, *dulce et decorum est pro patria mori.*

318. Achivum: gen. plur. (Introd. § 91).

319. Panthus: another aged counsellor. — **arcis Phoebique,** *of Apollo in the citadel*: hendiadys.

321. ipse: i. e. he alone without attendants to bear the sacred burden. — **trahit:** translate by *carries* with *deos* and *drags* with *nepotem* (zeugma). — **cursu:** abl. of manner. — **amens tendit,** *comes running wildly.*

322. quo . . . loco, *where is the main struggle?* — **quam . . . arcem,** *what stronghold shall we occupy?* supposing the citadel to be already taken. This seems the best rendering of this much-vexed passage. Another meaning of the first question is, *In what condition is the state?* Panthus replies that all is lost; and Æneas accordingly rushes out in the general direction of the noise (*v.* 337). — **Panthu:** vocative. — **prendimus,** in poetry the present indic. is often used for the future; A. 468; D. 657; G. 228.

324. summa, *last.* — **ineluctabile,** *inevitable* (lit. *that cannot be wrestled away from*).

325. fuimus Troes, etc. " It was a common phrase with the Romans," says Appian, " to say, *Antiochus the Great has been* " : see A. 474; D. 659; G. 236, 1.

326. ferus: not a general epithet, but indicating his present state of feeling. — **Argos:** i. e. to Greece; acc. of place to which.

327. transtulit: according to the Greek legend, " the gods departed in a body from Troy on the night of its capture, bearing their own images with them." — **incensa . . . urbe,** *in the blazing city*: i. e. they have set fire to the city, and are masters in it.

328. mediis in moenibus: i. e. in the very citadel. — **adstans,** *standing there,* a vivid way of indicating its presence.

329. victor, *in his success* (lit. *as victor*): in app. with *Sinon.*

330. bipatentibus, *wide open* (lit. *with both folding-doors open*): abl. of the way by which (Introd. § 55).

331. milia quot, *as many thousands as,* etc.: sc. *tot milia* in appos. with *alii.*

332. angusta viarum, *the narrow ways.*

333. ferri acies, *the edge of the sword*: poetical for *the sharp-edged sword.*

334. parata neci, *ready for slaughter* (of the foe). — **primi vigiles,** *the foremost of the guards* (there is scarcely a show of resistance).

335. caeco: i. e. having no orders or plans, they fight wildly.

336. numine : the idea is that this, like all his actions, is under the divine direction.

337. Erinys, *the Fury,* i.e. the demon of battle.

340. oblati per lunam, *appearing in the moonlight.*

341. adglomerant : sc. *se.* — **Coroebus :** Cassandra's lover, lately (*illis diebus*) come to Troy, who was slain by Peneleus (*vv.* 424–425).

342. forte, *as it happened.*

343. insano : his love is mad because untimely. — **Cassandrae :** obj. gen.

344. gener, *as a son-in-law* (by betrothal).

345. furentis, *inspired*; but suggesting also the fact that Cassandra's prophecies were regarded as the ravings of a *distracted* person.

346. audierit : rel. clause of cause; cf. *laeserit, v.* 231.

347. confertos, *in close array* (as we say, shoulder to shoulder), indicating unity of purpose and readiness for any fate. — **audere in,** *to be bold for battle.*

348. super (adv.), *besides* (though already they were brave). — **his :** sc. *verbis*; abl. of means.

349. vobis : dat. of possession. — **extrema,** *the worst.*

350. sequi : complementary infin. depending on the phrase *certa cupido,* which is equivalent to a verb of wishing (in prose, *sequendi*; cf. *v.* 10): Introd. § 77. — **rebus,** *of affairs*: dat. of possession.

352. quibus : abl. of means.

353. incensae (emphatic), *you are hastening to defend a city already in flames.* — **moriamur et ruamus :** the first idea is the more important and really includes the second — as if we had " let us seek death by rushing into the thick of the fight." Hence this is not an instance of that reversal in the order of ideas called *hysteron proteron.*

354. una . . . salutem, *the vanquished have one safety only,* to hope *for no safety.* For *sperare* see Introd. § 74.

355. animis, *courage,* i.e. they had determination before, but now they are roused to madness.

356. improba . . . rabies, *ravening hunger has driven out* [*to prowl*] *in blind fury.* — **caecos :** in app. with *quos*; A. 282, *b*, D. 496, *b*; G. 325.

360. urbis : gen. of possession : translate, *the way through the middle of the city.* — **nox . . . umbra :** it is moonlight, but the streets are dark ; besides, such expressions are not to be taken too strictly.

361. quis . . . explicet, *who can tell in speech?* deliberative subjunctive ; A. 444 ; D. 678 ; B. 277 ; G. 259. The expression is a prelude to the account not of his own exploits, but of the scene of slaughter which they now witnessed in the streets.

364. inertia, *lifeless.*

365. religiosa, *venerable.*

366. dant : cf. note on *sumite, v.* 103.

367. victis : dative of reference.

368. crudelis luctus, *cruel anguish.* By a not uncommon figure the cruelty is transferred from the author or cause to the effect.

369. pavŏr : see Introd. § 110. — **plurima** (singular), *many a.* — **imago,** *form.*

371. socia agmina, *that we were a friendly band* : sc. *nos esse.*

372. ultro, *first,* i.e. without being spoken to (cf. *v.* 279).

373. sera segnities, *tardy,* or, imitating the alliteratior., *sluggish sloth.*

374. rapiunt, etc., *plunder and bear away* [*the spoil of*] *burning Troy.*

375. vos, etc., *are you* (emphatic) *now just* (lit. *first*) *coming ?*

376. neque fida satis, *not very trustworthy,* i.e. dubious, suspicious.

377. sensit delapsus = *se esse delapsum* : a Greek construction; A. 581, N.[3]; G. 527, N.[2] — **delapsus,** *fallen* (without knowing it).

378. retro . . . repressit, *shrinking back, he checked.*

379. aspris = *asperis.* — **veluti qui,** *like one who.*

380. pressit nitens, *has set foot on.* — **refūgit :** transitive. The perf. is used to express the moment when the man has just recoiled in sudden fear.

381. colla : acc. of specification (Introd. § 42).

382. haud secus : litotes; A. 326, *c* ; D. 947; B. 375, 1 ; G. 700. — **abibat,** *was about to flee* : inceptive imperf.; A. 471, *c* ; D. 653; B. 260, 3 ; G. 233.

383. densis . . . armis, *we plunge into their close array* (lit. *surround ourselves with*) : the verb is used in a middle sense.

384. passim : i.e. in all parts of the scene of battle.

385. adspirat, *favors,* lit. *breathes upon* (as a favorable wind) : in English we use a different figure, *smiles upon.*

386. successu animisque (abl. of cause), *exultant with the courage of success* (hendiadys).

387. salutis : obj. gen. with *iter.*

388. dextra, *auspicious* : we should expect *dextram,* but the word is made more lively by agreeing with the subject.

389. insignia, *equipments* : helmets, shields, etc., by which their wearers may be distinguished.

390. dolus, etc., *treachery or courage — who would ask which it is ?* A double or alternative question with *an* [sc. *sit*]. A. 335, *d* ; D. 627; B. 162, 4 ; G. 458. — **in hoste,** *in dealing with an enemy* (lit. *in the case of an enemy*).

392. clipei insigne decorum, *the gorgeous blazonry of his shield.* The expression is somewhat like *lapsus rotarum* (*v.* 235), though more complicated; it is, however, natural enough in poetry.

394. ipse Dymas, *Dymas too.*

396. Danais : dat. with *immixti* (Introd. § 28). — **haud numine nostro,** *with no favoring divinities* (abl. of manner) : i.e. the plan was destined to be fatal, as the sequel showed. Possibly, however, the idea that, as they were wearing Greek armor, they were not under their own divinities, was in Virgil's mind; for it is a privilege of poetry to mean two things at once. — **nostro**: A. 302, *b*; G. 312, R.[1]

397. congressi, *in hand-to-hand fight.*

398. Orco, *to Orcus.* Orcus is, properly, the god of Death, and Dis is god of the Lower World; but they are often confounded. *Orcus* is also used for the Lower World itself.

400. fida: because their ships were there.

401. conduntur, *hide themselves.*

402. heu nihil, etc., *alas, it is right for no man.* — **nihil:** cognate acc. with *fidere.* — **invitis divis:** dative with *fidere* (Introd. § 26). Throughout this book the gods are represented as bent on the destruction of Troy.

403. trahebatur: i.e. by Ajax Oileus, who dragged with her the statue of Pallas to which she clung. For his punishment, see i. 41-45. — **passis ... crinibus,** *with dishevelled hair.* — **Priameia virgo,** *Priam's maiden daughter.* Cassandra was said to have been the most beautiful of Priam's daughters.

404. templo: Æneas has now reached the citadel. Cf. *v.* 410. — **adytis:** the inner shrine of the temple.

406. lumina, *her eyes, I say.*

407. non tulit, *could not bear.*

408. periturus, *to die* (purpose; see n. on *v.* 47).

409. densis armis, *into the thick of the fight*: dative with the compound *incurro.*

410. primum: i.e. this was our first disaster. — **delubri:** i.e. the temple of Pallas, where the whole scene seems to take place.

411. obruimūr: Introd. § 110. — **miserrima:** because slain by their own fellow citizens.

412. facie: abl. of cause.

413. tum, etc.: a new element in their peril. — **gemitu ... ira,** *in grief and rage at the rescue of the maiden.*

415. gemini, *the two.*

416. adversi, *face to face* (pred.). — **rupto turbine,** *when a storm has burst forth.* — **quondam,** *sometimes.*

417. confligunt: the fitful blasts of a veering storm are often conceived as a conflict of the different winds. Cf. the storm, i. 81. — **laetus equis:** by a common and very old metaphor he is represented as driving his steeds like a warrior to battle.

419. Nereus: a sea god; his wife was Doris, daughter of Oceanus; their daughters were the Nereids.

420. si quos fudimus, *whomever* (i.e. *all whom*) *we have routed.*

421. insidiis, *by the trick* (see *vv.* 389-395).

422. mentita tela, *the lying* (not *counterfeited*) *weapons.*

423. ora . . . signant, *they mark our tongues, discordant from their own* : for the Trojans spoke a different dialect from the Greeks, though probably not a different language.

424. ilicet, *instantly* : see derivation in Vocabulary.

425. divae armipotentis : Minerva.

426. iustissimus unus, *most upright of all* ; *unus* merely emphasizes the superlative.

427. aequi : Introd. § 16.

Fig. 20 R. H. FRANKENBERG

428. dis aliter visum, *the gods judged otherwise* (lit. *it seemed otherwise to the gods*), i.e. if one draws an inference from his fate, for, though innocent, he suffered death like the guilty.

429. Panthu : voc.; see Introd. § 93.

430. infula : a broad woolen band worn by priests and others engaged in sacred offices ; even this badge of sanctity was no defence. Fig. 20 (from an ancient relief) represents a woman decorating a statue of Hermes with a fillet.

431–434. Nobly rendered in the old version by the Earl of Surrey :

> Ye Troyan ashes ! and last flames of mine !
> I call in witness, that at your last fall
> I fled no stroke of any Greekish sword,
> And if the fates would I had fallen in fight,
> That with my hand I did deserve it well.

431. cineres, flamma : voc. — **flamma extrema,** *last flames* : i.e. the blazing city is regarded as their funeral pile.

432. testor : sc. *vos.*

433. vitavisse : sc. *me*, as subject. — **vices Danaum,** *perils in combat with the Greeks.* — **vices,** literally *changes*, expresses the vicissitudes or varying fortunes of the combat.

434. ut caderem : purpose clause after *si fata fuissent*, which is equivalent to a verb of determining; A. 563, *d* ; D. 720, I, and *d* ; B. 295, 4 ; G. 546. — **manu,** *by my deeds*, such a death being regarded as the reward of valor.

436. gravior, *burdened.* — **Ulixi,** *given by Ulysses* : genitive; Introd. § 93.

437. protinus, (farther) *on.* — **vocati,** *being summoned* ; referring to himself and his two companions, Iphitus and Pelias.

438. hic vero : cf. *tum vero*, *v.* 105 and note. — **pugnam :** obj. of *cernimus.* — **ceu . . . forent,** *as if there were no fights elsewhere* : i.e. compared with this the others were not fights at all; A. 524; D. 803; cf. B. 307, I ; G. 602.

440. sic Martem indomitum : translate parenthetically, *so fierce the strife.* The construction is poetically loose; *Martem* may be taken as in apposition with *pugnam.*

441. acta testudine (abl. abs.) : the regular way of assault on a fortified place. Here there are two distinct attacks, one to scale the walls and one to burst in the gates; *ruentis* refers to the scaling party, *testudine* to the other. The defence to the former is in *v.* 445, etc., to the latter in *v.* 449.

442. haerent, *cling*, by hooks (crows) at the end : an anachronism, for scaling ladders were really a later invention. — **parietibus :** dative with *haerent* ; A. 368, 3, N. ; G. 346, N.[6] — **postis sub ipsos,** *close at the very gateway,* — so much advantage have they gained.

443. nituntur gradibus, *they* (the Greeks) *climb up the rounds* (or steps) of the ladders ; abl. of place where.

444. protecti, *protecting themselves.* — **fastigia,** *battlements*, or (more accurately) the projecting top of the wall.

445. contra : adverb.

446. his telis, *with these as missiles.* — **quando :** they saw that the end (*ultima*) was near, and therefore there was no use in sparing the house.

449. alii : opposed to those in *v.* 445. — **imas,** *below.*

450. fores : the great doors, opening inward.

451. instaurati animi, *our courage was refreshed* (at the sight of this resistance). — **succurrere :** depending on the idea of admonition or suggestion in *instaurati*, etc. (Introd. § 78).

453. limen erat, *there was an entrance, and,* etc. — **pervius . . . Priami,** *a much-used passage between the parts of Priam's palace.* — **inter se :** i.e. connecting them with each other.

454. postes a tergo, *a postern gate.* — **relicti :** i. e. when the palace was built.

455. infelix : because of Hector's death.

457. soceros : Priam and Hecuba. — **avo :** dat. of place to which. — **trahebat,** *used to lead* by the hand, as he followed, *non passibus aequis* (cf. *v.* 724).

458. evado, *I pass up and out* (by means of this passageway).

460. turrim : obj. of *convellimus.* — **in praecipiti,** *on the very edge.* — **summis tectis,** *from the top of the roof.* We may imagine it rising above the wall, and flush with the front, as in the machico-lated tower of the Palazzo Vecchio at Florence (see Fig. 21).

463. adgressi ferro : i. e. with crow-bars and other tools of iron. In this and the following verses, to *v.* 467, the spon-dees and dactyls may well represent, first, the slow effort, then the sudden toppling over and swift fall of the turret. — **quā summa tabulata,** *where the upper floor-ing* (i. e. the planking of the roof where the tower and roof join) *afforded weak fastenings* in which to apply the leverage.

465. ruinam trahit, *falls in ruins :* properly, carries with it a mass of ruins.

469. Pyrrhus : called Neoptolemus in *v.* 263 ; son of Achilles, who was sent for after his father's death. The *Scyria pubes* (*v.* 477) are the youth of Scyros, an island in the Ægean, where was the kingdom of his grandfather Lycomedes.

Fig. 21

Here begins the detailed account of the attack on the door, though it is interrupted by the action of Periphas and others told in *vv.* 476–478.

470. telis, etc. : *flashing with the gleam of brazen arms :* hendiadys.

471. in lucem : construed with *convolvit terga.* — **mala,** *poisonous.*

472. tumidum : i. e. with venom.

473. positis exuviis, *having shed his old skin :* an image of renewing one's youth which often suggested itself to ancient fancy.

475. arduus ad solem, *raising his head to the sunshine.* — **linguis :** abl. of means : translate as if the obj. of *darts.*

478. succedunt tecto, *come up to the house* and try to set it on fire, while Pyrrhus attacks the door.

480. perrumpit, vellit, *is trying to burst and wrench,* by repeated efforts (descriptive). — **postis,** *the frame* of the door. — **cardine :** a pivot-hinge let into the upper and lower casing (see Fig. 22).

481. cavavit, dedit (perf. definite, taking a new point of view as the narrative moves on), *has cut through the beams and made a vast breach.*

482. robora, *the wood* of the door itself. An entrance, however, is not yet effected, but only an aperture made. — **lato ore :** abl. of quality (Introd. § 61).

483. atria, etc. : the general arrangements of a Roman house are apparently kept in view.

485. vident : i.e. the invaders can now see the defenders (*armatos*). — **in limine primo :** i.e. those nearest the outside.

486. domus interior, *the house within.*

487. cavae aedes, *the spacious rooms* : i.e. the interior, where were apartments, apparently for the women, ranged like cloisters about an open court.

490. postis, *pillars.* — **oscula :** i.e. of farewell.

491. patria, *of his father* (Achilles). — **claustra,** *bolts and bars.*

492. sufferre [sc. *eum*], *stop him.* — **ariete :** three syllables (Introd. § 112). — **crebro :** not many battering-rams, but repeated blows of one.

493. cardine : cf. *v.* 480, note. — **postes,** *doorposts.*

Fig. 22

494. fit via : i.e. the door yields. — **rumpunt,** *they force.*

495. milite, *soldiery* : cf. *v.* 20.

496. non sic : i.e. not so violently : translate with *fertur furens* in *v.* 498.

497. moles : i.e. dykes, etc.

498. cumulo : abl. of manner.

500. caede : abl. of manner.

501. centum nurus : used to include Priam's own daughters and the wives of his fifty sons. — **Priamum :** his death is here only stated in general terms : details are given in *vv.* 506–558. — **per,** *amid.*

504. barbarico : i.e. of the East. Æneas here speaks from a Roman point of view. Cf. " barbaric pearl and gold," *Paradise Lost,* ii. 4.

506. forsitan (= *fors sit an*), *perhaps* (lit. *it would be a chance whether*). — **forsitan requiras,** *perhaps you may ask* : indir. quest. ; A. 447, *a,* N. ; D. 819 ; G. 457, 2, N. — **fuerint quae :** indir. quest. after *requiras.*

506–558. Cf. the account of the murder of Priam given in *Hamlet,* ii. 2. 474 ff. :

> The rugged Pyrrhus, he whose sable arms,
> Black as his purpose, did the night resemble, etc.

508. limina, *doors.* — **medium :** more lively than *mediis,* as agreeing with *hostem,* but it is required also by the metre. — **penetralibus :** i. e. the inner part of the house, given up to the uses of family life.

509. diu : modifies *desueta.*

510. circumdat umeris, *binds upon his shoulders* : dative. — **ferrum cingitur :** Introd. § 43.

511. fertur, *starts to rush.*

512. nudo sub aetheris axe : in a Roman house the penates were kept by the family hearth and altar, in the *atrium,* or principal hall, but not in the open air ; here, however, is apparently meant the peristyle, or court, which had a larger opening than the atrium, and contained a garden, or at least a tree or two.

515. nequiquam : for it afforded them no asylum.

516. praecipites, *driven headlong.* — **tempestate :** abl. of means depending on the idea of *driven* contained in *praecipites.*

519. mens tam dira, *so dreadful a thought.*

520. impulit : sc. *te.* — **cingi** (reflexive), *to gird yourself.* For the use of the infinitive see Introd. § 78.

521. non tali auxilio : i. e. prayers, not arms, must help us. — **nec defensoribus istis,** *nor such defenders* (i. e. armed defenders): *istis,* as " demonstrative of the second person," refers to Priam, as if she had said " defenders like you " (i. e. wielding arms, as you would try to do). For case see A. 356 and N. ; D. 349, 350 ; B. 212, I, and *a* ; G. 405 and N.[2]

522. non si, *no, not if,* etc. : sc. *egeret* ; see A. 517 ; D. 786 ; B. 304, I ; G. 597.

523. tandem, *pray* : a word of entreaty or impatience, used here as in questions ; A. 333, *a.* — **omnis,** *us all.*

524. simul, *with us* (lit. *at the same time*).

526. Pyrrhi de caede, *from slaughter at the hands of Pyrrhus.*

528. porticibus, *through the colonnades* : abl. of way by which (Introd. § 55). Polites has escaped from the *mêlée* at the door and is fleeing towards the back of the house along the colonnade between the pillars supporting the roof of the peristyle and the wall of the peristyle itself.

530. iam iamque tenet, *and now he is just about to grasp him, and closes on him* (lit. *presses him*) *with the spear* : the repetition of *iam* pictures the scene, and so makes the impression more lively.

531. evasit, *he came out* (from the colonnade).

533. in media morte, *in the jaws of death.*

534. voci iraeque, *angry words* : hendiadys ; see i. 61, note.

535. at : i. e. though you now triumph. The word is often thus used in entreaties, introducing a suggestion as opposed to some thought of the speaker which is itself unexpressed. — **pro talibus ausis,** *for such reckless deeds.*

536. caelo: dat. of possession. — **pietas,** *justice* (i.e. regard for piety and hatred of impiety). — **curet:** rel. clause of characteristic; A. 535, *a*; D. 726; B. 283, 2; G. 631, 2.

537. persolvant, reddant: opt. subjunc.; A. 441; D. 681, I; B. 279, 1; G. 260.

538. qui: the antecedent is *tibi* in *v.* 535. — **cernere:** inf. used instead of a substantive clause of result.

539. patrios . . . voltus, *hast defiled a father's sight,* i.e. made him ceremonially impure by making him see such a deed.

540. satum . . . mentiris, *whom you falsely call your father* (lit. *from whom you falsely claim that you are descended*), — for this deed " belies " his lineage. — **quo:** abl. of source (Introd. § 50).

541. in, *in the case of,* hence equal to *towards* (cf. note, *v.* 390). — **fidem,** *the faith* due to a suppliant.

542. erubuit, *respected,* i.e. blushed to disregard. — **sepulcro,** *for burial:* dat. of purpose (Introd. § 33).

544. sine ictu, *without force* enough to inflict a wound; lit. *without a blow.*

546. summo umbone, *the top of the boss* or knob in the centre of the shield (without piercing it).

547. referes: with an imperative force.

549. degenerem: referring to Priam's taunt in *v.* 540.

550. trementem: from the feebleness of age.

553. lateri = *in latus:* dat. with a verb of motion. — **capulo tenus,** *up to the hilt:* A. 221, 26; D. 277, *c*; B. 142, 3; G. 413, R.[1]

554. haec finis: *finis* is usually masculine.

555. sorte, *by fate;* strictly, the *lot* of an individual.

556. tot populis, *over so many tribes:* dative of reference.

557. Asiae: i.e. Asia Minor. — **iacet litore:** as if the body were still lying on the shore, where it had been thrown. Virgil seems to be thinking of the fate of Pompey.

558. sine nomine: i.e. unrecognizable.

560. subiit, *came to my mind.* — **imago,** *the vision,* i.e. the thought.

561. aequaevum: i.e. to Anchises.

563. direpta, casus: i.e. the probable pillaging of his house, and death of his son. — **domūs,** nominative. For quantity see Introd. § 110.

564. copia, *forces:* usually plural in this sense.

565. corpora . . . dedere, *in despair, have thrown themselves to the ground or into the fire.* — **aegra,** *sick at heart, in despair,* agrees with *corpora.*

567. iamque, etc., *and just at this moment I alone was left.* — **super . . . eram:** tmesis. — **limina Vestae servantem,** *keeping close to the threshold of Vesta,* i.e. of her shrine or temple, for the sake of sanctuary.

569. Tyndarida, *Helen,* called *daughter of Tyndareus* (the husband of her mother Leda), though Jupiter was her father. — **dant,** etc. : explains why he happened to see her.

570. erranti [sc. *mihi*]: he is still in the palace or the citadel ; at *v.* 632 he descends to the streets.

571. illa : Helen.

572. poenas Danaum, *punishment from the Greeks* : subjective gen. — **coniugis:** Menelaus hesitated at first whether to kill Helen with his own hand; but her old fascination prevailed, and later she appears in the Odyssey in full honor as his queen. See Landor's poem, *Menelaus and Helen at Troy.*

573. Erinys, *Fury* (as being the cause of strife and death).

574. aris invisa sedebat, *was crouching, hated woman, at the altar.*

575. ira, *a wrathful impulse.*

576. ulcisci : complementary inf. depending on *ira subit,* which is equivalent to a verb of wishing (Introd. § 78). — **sceleratas poenas,** *vengeance on the guilty.* — **sumere,** *inflict.*

577. scilicet : giving an ironical turn to the thought. — **Mycenas :** used for Greece in general. Helen came from Sparta.

580. turbā comitată, *attended by a throng.*

581. occiderit (fut. perf.): i. e. shall she return to Greece in triumph when Priam has perished?

585. exstinxisse nefas laudabor, *I shall be praised for having destroyed an impious creature.* — **laudabor :** equivalent to a verb of saying, "I shall be said with praise to have," etc. This extension of the personal use of *dicor, videor,* etc., with the inf. is peculiar to poetry ; A. 582, N.; D. 840 and *a* ; G. 528, N.[4] — **merentīs,** *deserved,* agrees with *poenas*: cf. *sceleratas, v.* 576.

587. flammae, *to have satisfied my heart with the fire of vengeance* : for gen. see Introd. § 22. — **cineres satiasse :** vengeance is imagined to be a satisfaction to the spirits of the dead — a very old idea. — **meorum,** *of my kinsmen.*

588. ferebar, *was swept on* or *carried away* (by avenging wrath).

589. se videndam obtulit, *presented herself in visible form* (lit. *to be seen*): A. 500, 4 ; D. 869 ; B. 337, 7, *a,* 2 ; G. 430.

590. pura in luce : i. e. not in that cloud or mist which usually shrouds a divinity.

591. confessa deam (for *se deam esse*), *revealing herself as a goddess.* — **qualis :** sc. *talem.*

592. caelicolis : dative. — **quanta :** the gods are represented as larger than men ; so Tennyson describes Helen as "a daughter of the gods, divinely tall" (*Dream of Fair Women*). Cf. Keats, *Hyperion,* i. 26–28 :

> She was a goddess of the infant world :
> By her in stature the tall Amazon
> Had stood a pigmy's height.

— **dextra,** *by the hand.* — **prehensum** [*me*] **continuit:** translate by two coördinate verbs, *grasped me and held me back.*

594. quis . . . tantus, *what great . . . is this which*: a common Latin form of expression. — **dolor,** *indignation* (felt as a sudden pang).

595. quonam: notice the force of *nam*; A. 333, *a*; D. 197, *d*; B. 90, 2, *d*; G. 106. The emphasis conveyed by *nam* gives the question the tone of a reproof. — **nostri,** *for me*: objective gen. — **tibi:** dat. of reference.

596. non = *nonne.*

597. liqueris, superet: indirect questions.

599. ni resistat, *did not my care withstand them.* The condition is cont. to fact with pres. subj. for imperf. in protasis, and perf. for pluperf. in apodosis (*tulerint*, etc.), by an old construction preserved in poetry: A. 517, *e*; D. 799; G. 596, R.[1]

600. hauserit, *would have drunk their blood.*

601. tibi (dat. of reference): it is not Helen that you should hate, or Paris that you should blame. Not that they are guiltless, but their guilt only fulfils the divine decree.—**facies invisa:** sc. *culpata est.*

604. obducta tuenti [*tibi*], *drawn over you as you look.*

605. umida circum caligat, *enwraps you with its damp shadows.*

Fig. 23

606. ne . . . time: i. e. do not fear to look at anything I show you, or hesitate to do (by my direction) what is still in your power. For construction see Introd. § 87.

608. moles: i. e. of the burned and ruined buildings.

609. mixto pulvere, *mingled with dust*: abl. abs.

610. Neptunus: Neptune, the builder of Troy for Laomedon, now takes the main part in its destruction.

612. Scaeas portas: the most important gate of Troy.

613. prima, *the foremost.* — **socium agmen:** i. e. the Greeks, who are still pouring from the ships.

616. nimbo effulgens, etc., *gleaming with divine effulgence and* [the light of] *the fierce Gorgon.* Probably referring to the divine effulgence surrounding the gods when they appeared to mortals, which is the origin of the technical *nimbus*, or *aureole*, of later times (see Figs. 23, 24). — **effulgens,** *gleaming*, a not uncommon conception of the divinities. — **Gorgone:** i. e. on her shield or her aegis, or both (see Fig. 24).

That snaky-headed Gorgon shield
That wise Minerva wore, unconquer'd virgin,
Wherewith she freez'd her foes to congeal'd stone.

Comus, vv. 447 ff.

617. pater : Jupiter.

619. eripe fugam : a stronger form for *cape fugam*; hinting also at escape from peril.

620. limine : abl. of place where.

624. tum vero, *then at length,* my eyes being opened.

625. Neptunia : cf. *v.* 610, note.

626. ac veluti . . . cum, *even as when.*

627. ferro . . . bipennibus: *cut by many a blow of the iron axe* (lit. *by the iron and by repeated axes*): hendiadys.

628. usque, *ever* (lit. *all the way,* to a place or time).

629. tremefacta comam, *its foliage quivering:* acc. of specification. — **vertice :** abl. of specification.

630. supremum : cognate acc. (Introd. § 37).

631. traxit ruinam, *has fallen with a crash:* cf. *v.* 465 and note. — **iugis :** abl. of separation with *avolsa*.

632. descendo : i.e. from the palace and citadel to the streets. — **deo :** i.e. Venus.

633. expedior, *I make my way out:* middle voice.

Fig. 24

634. iam, *at length.* — **perventum** [*est*]: impersonal, the regular construction when mere sequence of time and progress of action are to be indicated without personal reference.

635. tollere, *to carry,* belongs only with *optabam.* The crippled condition of Anchises is explained in *vv.* 648–649.

636. optabam primum, *it was my first wish :* the imperfect hints at the non-fulfilment of the wish.

637. excisa Troia : abl. abs. — **producere :** the indir. disc. would be *se producturum,* but here Virgil follows the analogy of verbs of refusing, which may take the complem. inf.

638. vos (emphatic): i.e. without me. — **quibus** [*est*]: dat. of possession. — **integer aevi :** *vigorous with youth* (lit. *sound in respect to age*): gen. of specification.

639. solidae : pred. adjective. — **suo :** i.e. without help from others. — **robore,** *might,* the strength of resistance; so here of the unimpaired vigor of manhood: abl. of means. — **vires :** the active powers, hence here of the ability to do and dare

642. una excidia, *it is enough and more that I have seen one destruction*, namely, that by Hercules and Telamon. Laomedon, father of Priam, had incensed the hero Hercules by withholding the sacred horses, the promised reward for the rescue of his daughter, and was slain by Telamon. A fuller form of expression would be *satis superque est quod vidimus*.

643. urbi: dat., as if with *supersum* (Introd. § 27).

644. sic positum, *lying thus* (helpless). Anchises has apparently composed himself on his couch, to meet death with dignity, and his friends are to leave him as already dead. — **adfati:** i.e. with the words of greeting, *salve, vale, ave*, uttered by the relatives when they parted from the body at the funeral pile.

645. ipse: i.e. without your staying to defend me or die with me. — **manu,** *by the sword* (lit. *hand*). Various views have been taken of this word, *by my own hand* (either by suicide or vain resistance to the enemy) or, better, in a general sense, *by the hand of man.* — **miserebitur,** etc.: i.e. both pity and desire for spoil will combine as motives to lead the enemy to kill me. I shall not die a lingering death by starvation. Leave me without hesitation, as if I were dead already.

646. facilis iactura sepulcri, *the loss of burial is easy to bear*: the expression of a sentiment so contradictory to all the ideas of the ancients brings out all the more strongly the old man's unselfish devotion.

648. demoror, *have I lingered out*: A. 466; D. 650; B. 259, 4; G. 230. — **ex quo** [*tempore*], *ever since*.

649. fulminis ventis, *by the blasts of the thunderbolt.* This had been his punishment for divulging the love of Venus for him. — **igni:** ablative.

651. nos = *ego.* — **effusi** [*sumus*] **lacrimis,** *were dissolved in tears.* — **lacrimis:** abl. of manner.

652. ne . . . vellet: depending on the idea of entreaty contained in *effusi* [*sumus*] *lacrimis.* — **vertere:** equal to the common *evertere*, as in i. 20, ii. 625.

653. incumbere, *add to the burden of overwhelming fate.* — **fato:** dat. (Introd. § 27).

654. haeret, etc., *clings firmly to his purpose and to the* (same) *spot*; zeugma.

655. feror, *start to rush*: cf. *v.* 511.

656. consilium refers to human means of safety. — **fortuna** refers to divine means. — **iam,** *any longer*.

657. mene . . . sperasti, *what! did you hope that* I *could depart* (i.e. that you could induce me to go)? *Me* is emphasized by its position and by the enclitic. — **te relicto:** abl. abs.

658. tantum nefas, etc., *can such an impiety fall from a father's lips?*

660. sedet animo, *is fixed in your mind* (abl. of place where). — **hoc:** i.e. his purpose.

661. patet ianua: alluding to Anchises' words in *v.* 645, etc. — **isti leto**, *that death you desire.*

662. iam, *straightway* (of an immediate future). — **multo de sanguine**, *reeking with the blood* (lit. *from*).

663. qui obtruncat, etc.: descriptive. Both acts indicate impiety as well as cruelty. The first syllable of *patris, patrem* being " common," the poet makes it short in the former, long in the latter.

664. hoc erat quod eripis, etc., *was it for this that you snatch me, that I should see*, etc.? — **hoc**: pred. nominative. — **quod ... eripis**: substantive clause, subject of *erat*; A. 572; D. 822; B. 299, 1; G. 525, 2. — **parens**: in his despair he reproaches Venus for saving him, and prepares to return to the fight, whence she had conducted him.

665. ut cernam: clause of purpose in appos. with *hoc.*

668. vocat, etc.: i.e. death, the only refuge of the conquered, calls us.

669. sinite revisam, *let me return to.* — **revisam**: substantive clause without *ut*, obj. of *sinite* (A. 565, *a*; D. 720, I, *d*; B. 295, 8; G. 546, R.²); *viso* is an old desiderative, meaning *go to see.*

670. numquam, *never*, expressing merely an emphatic negative.

671. hinc, *hereupon.* — **accingor rursus**, *I begin to gird on my sword again* (which had been laid aside on his return). — **clipeo ... aptans**: the left hand was thrust under one of the two straps on the back of the shield and grasped the other.

674. patri: i.e. to me. — **tendebat**: this appeal is imitated from the meeting of Hector and Andromache (Il. vi. 394-485; Bry. 515 ff.).

675. et nos, *us too.*

676. expertus, *after the trial you have made* (i.e. of arms).

678. quondam, *once* (but now no longer, since you desert me).

680. cum ... oritur: a "*cum* inverse " clause; A. 546, *a*; D. 751; B. 288; G. 581. — **dictu**: supine with *mirabile*; A. 510; D. 882, II; B. 340, 2; G. 436.

681. manus: i.e. as she held him out to his father; cf. *v.* 674.

682. levis apex, *a light tip* (of flame). As in the case of Servius Tullius, it signifies his future royalty. See Fig. 25 (from the Vatican MS.) for a curious picture of this scene.

683. tactu innoxia, *harmless to the touch*: abl. of specification. — **mollis**: with *comas.*

684. pasci, *stray*, as if it were an animal grazing.

685. trepidare, excutere, restinguere: histor. inf.; the construction, as usual, marks the haste and excitement of the occasion.

686. excutere, *snatch away*: properly, striking it off with the hand. — **sanctos**: because it was a divine omen.

688. caelo, *towards heaven*: dat. of place to which.

690. hoc tantum, *this only do I ask*: supply *precor.*

691. deinde, *then,* i.e. after having looked upon us and judged our case. —**firma :** i.e. by some fresh omen. In augury it was customary to wait for a second omen. This, if of similar meaning, confirmed the first; if of contrary meaning, it neutralized it.

692. -que, *when* (lit. *and*): we should expect *cum* in the inverse construction (see n. on *v.* 680). This use of two coördinate clauses instead of a main clause and a subordinate clause is called *parataxis:* A. 268, par. 4; G. 472, 2.

Fig. 25

693. intonuit laevum, *it thundered on the left* (a favorable sign in Roman augury: see *v.* 54, note); cognate acc. (Introd. § 37).

694. stella : i.e. a shooting-star or meteor, a phenomenon always regarded with superstition by the ancients.— **facem ducens,** *drawing a trail* of light, like a firebrand (*fax*) waved in the hand.

695. illam, *the star:* notice how the Latin, by the skilful use of pronouns, avoids repetition; in English we cannot secure the emphasis here by using a pronoun, as the Latin does.

696. Idaea silva : marking the place of gathering, on Mount Ida, southeast of Troy. The light, says the old commentator Servius, signified the future glory of the house; the fiery trail, that some would stay behind; the length of the path, their long voyage; the furrow (*sulcus*), that it must be by sea; and the sulphur smoke, the death of Æneas, or the war in Italy. Probably the Trojans did not see so much in the omen.— **claram,** *still bright.*

697. limite : abl. of manner (Introd. § 58).

699. victus, *giving way* (lit. *overcome*, i. e. by the omen). — se tollit ad auras, *rises up*, i. e. from the couch (see *v.* 644, note).

701. iam iam, etc.: Anchises' words. — mora : i. e. on my part. — adsum, *I am with you.*

702. nepotem : Ascanius.

703. numine, *divine protection.*—Troia : i. e. the new Troy that is to be.

704. cedo, *I resist no more.* — equidem only emphasizes the words.

705. clarior : translate by an adverb.

706. aestus, etc., *the surging flames roll the conflagration nearer*: it seems best to take *aestus* as subject rather than *incendia.*

707. ergo age : observe the haste marked by the abruptness and rapid movement of the verse. — imponere, *place yourself*: imperative pass. in middle sense.

708. subibo umeris, *I will take you upon my shoulders.* — umeris : abl. of means.

709. quo . . . cumque (tmesis), *however* (lit. *whithersoever*).

710. salus, *means of safety.*

711. longe, *at a distance*, apparently on account of the greater security of going in small parties; in charge, perhaps, of the servants. — servet vestigia, *follow in my footsteps.*

713. urbe egressis, *as you go out of the city* (lit. *for those having gone out*): dative of reference.

714. desertae, *lonely*: the adj. is poetically attached to *Cereris* instead of to *templum.*

715. religione, *reverence*: abl. of cause.

717. sacra, *sacred objects*: perhaps the gods (*penates*) themselves.

718. me, *for me* (emphatic).

719. attrectare, with subj. acc. *me*, is subj. of *est* understood. — donec abluero : similar purifying rites are common in all religions. — flumine vivo, *running water.*

722. insternor, *I spread*: see *vv.* 633 (note), 671, 707. — veste, pelle, *a tawny lion-skin as a robe*: hendiadys. — super : adverb. Fig. 26 is from an antique gem. Cf. Shakspere, *Julius Cæsar*, i. 2. 112–115 :

> Ay, as Æneas, our great ancestor,
> Did from the flames of Troy upon his shoulder
> The old Anchises bear, so from the waves of Tiber
> Did I the tired Cæsar.

725. opaca locorum, *dark places*: cf. *strata viarum*, i. 422.

726. movebant, *could alarm.*

729. suspensum, timentem : participles expressing cause.—comiti : i.e. Iulus; A. 367, *c*; G. 346, n.²

730. portis: A. 363; D. 373; B. 358, 2, *a*; G. 346, R.²

731. evasisse, *to have passed safely over.* — **creber** = *of many*, as if it agreed with *pedum*.

734. aera: probably helmets, etc., or it may be a case of hendiadys.

735. mihi: dat. of separation (Introd. § 32). — **male amicum**, *unfriendly.* — **nescio quod**, *some*: equivalent to a weak *aliquod*.

736. confusam eripuit mentem, *robbed me of my presence of mind in my confusion*: lit. *took away my confused senses*, i.e. took them away by confusing them.

Fig. 26

737. To avoid capture he had to follow by-paths (*avia*).

738, 739. heu, etc., *alas! my wife Creüsa either stayed behind, torn from me by unkind fate, or strayed from the path, or, tired out, sat down to rest, — it is uncertain which.* The doubt in Æneas' mind is whether she stopped without any human agency, as she might well do, being *misero fato erepta*, or whether the gods used some ordinary human means.

741. nec prius . . . quam, *nor did I look back . . . until.* This want of care, though strange to us, agrees with the manners of the ancients, according to which Æneas' chief care would be for Iulus. Of course in following the legend Virgil must get rid of Creüsa.

742. tumulum, sedem: place to which without a preposition (Introd. § 47).

743. collectis omnibus: abl. absolute. — **una**, *she alone.*

744. fefellit, *was missed by* (lit. *deceived*).

745. amens, *in my madness.* — **deorumque**: the enclitic *-que* is elided by *synapheia* (Introd. § 114).

746. in eversa urbe, *in the destruction of the city.*

749. fulgentibus armis: no longer seeking to avoid notice. His armor would have been brought along by some one of the servants.

750. stat, *my purpose is fixed.* — **renovare, reverti, obiectare**: infin. used as subjects of impersonal *stat* (Introd. § 73).

751. caput, *life.*

752. obscura limina: i.e. the archways or the like.

753. vestigia . . . lustro, *tracing back our footsteps, I follow them through the darkness. and scan them with my eyes.*

755. horror: i.e. scenes that make him shudder.— **animo:** sc. *est.*

756. si forte . . . tulisset, *if haply by any chance she had turned her steps thither*: indirect question. The repetition of *si forte* emphasizes the hopelessness of the search as well as its diligence.

761. asylo: selecting the temple of Juno, their patroness, for protection from their own forces (hence *asylo,* see Vocabulary); the Greek chiefs were here guarding their spoil in the vacant colonnades.

762. Phoenix: the aged instructor of Achilles.

764. adytis: dative of separation.

765. auro: abl. of material (Introd. § 51).

766. pueri, matres: the women and children are to be sold as slaves, an important part of the booty.

768. voces iactare, *to utter cries* [at random] *in the darkness.*

771. tectis, *among the houses*: abl. of place where.— **quaerenti . . . furenti,** *to me, as I sought and as I roamed wildly*: dat. agreeing with *mihi* in *v.* 773.

772. infelix: Creüsa just below assures him of her own felicity (*v.* 788); but she is " sad " from Æneas' point of view, as being cut off in her prime.

773. notā maior, *larger than the well-known form.* The spirits or shades of the dead were often regarded as larger than mortals. Apparently, too, Creüsa has become a minor divinity attendant on Cybele (*v.* 788).

774. stetĕrunt: for the short penult (systole), see Introd. § 111.

775. adfari, demere: histor. inf.

779. fas, *the divine will*: sc. *est.*— **ille,** *the great.*

780. longa tibi exsilia, *distant exile is your fate.*— **tibi:** dat. of possession with *exsilia* [*sunt*].

781. Lydius Thybris, *the Etruscan Tiber.* The Lydians were said to have colonized Etruria (Tuscany).

783. regia coniunx: Lavinia.

784. parta, *won,* though not yet possessed (cf. iii. 495).— **Creüsae** (obj. gen.), *for the loved Creüsa.*

785. non ego: emphatic.

786. servitum: supine, used with a verb of motion to express purpose; A. 509; D. 882, I; B. 340, 1; G. 435.

788. deum genetrix: Cybele, the chief divinity of this region. See n. on *v.* 773. Cf. iii. 111.

790. lacrimantem: sc. *me.*

792. conatus: sc. *sum.*— **dare . . . circum:** tmesis.

793. comprensa = *comprehensa.*

795. sic: i.e. bereft of her.

798. pubem (poetic for *iuventus*): a general expression for all who have outgrown their boyhood.— **exsilio,** *for exile,* and not for defence: dat. of purpose.

799. animis, opibus : abl. of specification. — **parati :** supply *deduci*, understood from *deducere*.

800. velim, *I should wish to lead* : subjunctive of integral part ; A. 593 ; D. 907 ; B. 324, 1 ; G. 629. — **pelago,** *over the sea* : Introd. § 55. — **deducere :** regularly used for leading forth a Roman colony.

801. iugis : abl. of place where.

803. spes opis, *hope of help* (i. e. of giving or receiving assistance).

804. cessi, *I gave way* (i. e. I yielded to fate).

BOOK III

1. Asiae : i. e. Asia Minor. — **evertere :** subj. of *visum* [*est*] ; Introd. § 73.

2. immeritam, *unoffending* ; Paris alone had done wrong. — **visum** [*est*], *it seemed best.*

3. humo, *from the ground*, showing its utter demolition. — **fumat :** the present, though historical, here denotes continued action ; the perfect (*visum* [*est*] and *cecidit*), a momentary act. — **Neptunia :** cf. ii. 625.

4. diversa exsilia, *exile in various places* (first one and then another). — **desertas,** *desolate,* i. e. remote and uninhabited.

5. sub ipsa, *hard by.*

6. Antandro : Antandros was a town at the foot of Mt. Ida, southeast of Troy.

8. prima aestas, *early summer.* The Trojan fugitives lived near Antandros during the winter following the capture of the city.

9. fatis : a variation upon the usual *ventis dare vela,* to indicate as well the divine guidance (which is emphasized throughout the poem) as their own helplessness.

10. cum . . . relinquo : this, logically the main clause, has become the temporal clause ; while *vix inceperat et iubebat,* the logical temporal clause, has become the main clause (see i. 36, note). This form of expression here gives a stronger suggestion of haste.

12. magnis dis : a spondaic verse (Introd. § 104). He carried, as it were, the protection of the greater gods of his country, as well as the *penates,* or household deities, whose actual images he took with him.

13. procul, *at some distance,* not necessarily very far : in reality, across a narrow strait. — **vastis campis :** abl. of quality. — **Mavortia :** Virgil makes the fierce tribes of Thrace know no god but Mars.

14. Lycurgo : dat. of agent. Lycurgus attacked the nurses of Bacchus with an ox-goad, and was blinded and afterwards destroyed by Jupiter (Il. vi. 130–140 ; Bry. 165).

15. hospitium antiquum, *an ancient friend.* — **socii penates,** *with household gods allied with ours* (a symbol of hospitality and friendship) ; *hospitium* and *penates* are in apposition with *terra.*

16. fuit, *lasted.*

17. fatis ingressus iniquis, *beginning* [the work] *with the fates unkind* (abl. abs.).

18. Aeneadas: there was a town Ænea on the west coast of Thrace, with whose name Virgil thus connects his story; also an earlier Ænos, at the mouth of the Hebrus, where was said to be a tomb of Polydorus. Here the two are identified in order to associate this region with Æneas.

19. Dionaeae matri, *to my mother, daughter of Dione.*

20. auspicibus, *protectors :* i. e. the sacrifices were intended to win their protection.— **supero :** modifies *regi.*— **nitentem taurum :** a white bullock was the usual Roman offering to Jupiter.

21. caelicolum : gen. plur.

22. quo summo [sc. *erant*], *on whose summit were :* A. 293; D. 510; B. 241, 1; G. 291, R.[2]

23. hastilibus : both the cornel and the myrtle have shoots suitable for spear-shafts.— **myrtus :** myrtle is sacred to Venus, and " loves the sea."

24. silvam, *thicket.*

25. ramis : cf. ii. 249 and note.

26. dictu : supine with *mirabile* ; see note on i. 434.

28. huic, *from that tree which,* etc.; *arbos* is attracted into the relative clause, and *huic* is dat. of reference (Introd. § 31).— **sanguine:** abl. of material (Introd. § 51). The prodigy of blood-drops from a tree is a widespread piece of folklore. A famous instance is in Spenser's *Faery Queen,* i. 2. 30–33.

29. mihi : dat. of reference. Translate, *my limbs.*

31. alterius, *of a second.*

32. temptare, *to try* or *explore :* cf. ii. 691 and note. He regards the prodigy as an omen.

34. nymphas agrestis : the hamadryads or nymphs of the grove, making their abode in trees ; the hamadryad was the spirit of the tree itself, born and perishing with it. First Æneas worships the divinities of the immediate place, then the greater divinity of all Thrace. — **venerabar,** *I prayed with reverence* (the request follows in *v.* 36).

35. Geticis, *Thracian.*

36. secundarent: the omen, though alarming as far as observed, was not understood, and might be a good one ; it had to be interpreted by further occurrences (see note on ii. 691). The subjunctive stands for the imperative (*secundate*) used in the prayer as directly expressed : A. 588; D. 887, III ; B. 316 ; G. 652.— **levarent,** *lighten the weight of the omen* (by making it favorable).

37. sed, *but* (instead of the result hoped for).

38. genibus, abl. of manner.— **harenae :** dat. with *obluctor.*

39. eloquar : deliberative subjunctive. The occurrence seems to him too frightful to relate.

40. vox reddita, *a voice in reply.*

41. quid⸳ . . . sepulto, *why do you mangle a victim of misfortune ? Spare him at length in the grave !* Though referring to himself, Polydorus does not use the first person until later. To supply *me* with *miserum* and *mihi* with *sepulto* weakens the effect.

42. parce, *forbear*: § 450, N.¹; G. 271, 2, N.² — **non . . . tulit,** *Troy did not bear me* (to be) *alien to you.*

43. aut . . . manat, *and it is from no tree-stock this gore flows.* The negative force is continued by *aut* and so another negative is not needed.

45. confixum: sc. *me.* — **ferrea seges,** *an iron crop*: i. e. the spears thrust into him have taken root, and grown up through the sand-mound that has heaped itself above his body.

46. iaculis . . . acutis, *has grown up with sharp javelins.*

47. tum vero (regularly used of the most important moment in a narrative), *ah ! then indeed*: before, his horror had been slight in comparison. — **ancipiti formidine,** *double terror*, from the sight and the voice. — **mentem:** acc. of specification.

48. stetĕrunt: as in ii. 774.

50. infelix: i. e. in all his later fortunes. Æneas tells the story as related to him by the ghost of Polydorus. — **alendum:** with *mandarat* to express purpose; A. 500, 4; D. 869; B. 337, 8, *b*, 2; G. 430.

51. regi: Polymestor. — **iam diffideret:** the imperfect with *iam* regularly denotes the beginning of an action.

53. ille: introduced to change the subject and refer to Polymestor. — **fractae:** sc. *sunt.*

54. res, *fortunes.* — **secutus,** *siding with.*

56. potĭtur is here of the third conjugation. — **quid:** cognate acc.

57. auri sacra fames, *accursed craving for gold* (cf. i. 349); *sacer* was anciently applied to things set apart for sacrifice to some deity, and hence doomed to perish. — **auri:** obj. gen. (Introd. § 14).

58. primum parentem, *to my father first*, as first in rank and age. The Trojan chiefs are consulted in turn, like the Roman senators, respecting the prodigy, and Anchises, as *princeps*, speaks first.

59. refero: the regular word for laying a matter before the Roman senate. — **sententia,** *view* (properly, official opinion, or vote).

60. excedere, linqui, dare: in apposition with *animus.*

61. linqui: the construction changes to the passive, but it need not change in translation. — **dare classibus austros,** *call the winds to the* [waiting] *ships.*

62. instauramus: the technical word for a renewal of any imperfect ceremonies. *The funeral rites* (*funus*) had, of course, been cut short, if not omitted altogether, by the murderer. Their due performance was thought to lay the ghost. See the long description of the funeral of Misenus in vi. 177–235, with the notes.

63. tumulo, *on* (lit. *to*) *the mound.* — **Manibus,** *to the dead*: dat. of reference. The *Manes* are the spirits of the dead considered as inhabiting the Lower World. When conceived as ghosts hovering about their old homes or haunting the living, they are *lemŭres* or *larvae*.

64. atra cupresso, *funereal cypress.*

65. Iliades : sc. *stant.*

66. inferimus, *we offer*: a sacrificial term. — **lacte :** abl. of material. Wine, oil, and honey might also be used in offerings to the dead.

67, 68. animam . . . condimus, etc., *we lay the* [perturbed] *spirit*: as we say " to lay a ghost." From the expression here it would seem that the soul was supposed to remain with the body after death ; but compare iv. 705, v. 517, which imply a different idea. The first view is doubtless the more primitive and less philosophical, and was retained and confused with the later one. — **supremum** (cognate acc.) **ciemus,** *we call upon him for the last time*: cf. ii. 644.

69. ubi . . . pelago, *as soon as the sea may be trusted*: *fides* [*est*] here takes the dat. as if it were a form of the verb *fido.* — **placata dant,** *render calm.* The sea is conceived as a person, and so is *appeased.*

70. lenis, *gently,* as if an adv. (*leniter*) modifying *crepitans.*

71. deducunt, *launch*: their ships were regularly beached while in port, and this word is the technical term for drawing them into the water.

73. sacra tellus : Delos. — **mari medio,** *in mid-sea.*

75. pius, *in filial love,* i.e. for his mother Latona, to whom Delos had given refuge at the time of his and his sister Diana's birth. Both Apollo and Diana are always represented as devoted to their mother.

76. errantem : it is possible that the little island of Delos from its position had often eluded the early mariners, and that thus the story arose that it was adrift, until its place was fixed by Myconus and Gyarus, to which Apollo was then supposed to have " moored " it. — **celsa :** Myconus is not high except as any island would be *celsa* compared to the sea.

77. immotam . . . ventos, *and he granted that it should be inhabited and immovable and should scorn the winds*: lit. *he gave* [it] *to be inhabited unmoved,* etc.; *immotam* is a pred. adj. and the infinitives are objects of *dedit.* So long as Delos was a wandering island it was unfit for habitation.

78. haec : sc. *tellus.*

79. egressi, *landing,* the regular word.

80. Anius : various legends connect him with Anchises and with Æneas. — **rex,** etc.: the two offices were no doubt regularly united in the most ancient times ; compare the functions of the early Roman kings.

81. vittis : these he wore as being a priest. — **tempora :** Introd. § 43. — **lauro :** sacred to Apollo.

83. hospitio, *in hospitality,* i.e. as hereditary friends (cf. *v.* 15).

84. templa : translate as if singular. A short time has elapsed between the arrival at Delos and the visit to the temple. — **saxo :** abl. of material.

85. propriam, *permanent.* — **Thymbraee :** Apollo is so called because he had a famous temple at Thymbra, near Troy.

86. mansuram, *that shall abide.*

87. Pergama, *citadel.* — **reliquias,** etc.: cf. i. 30.

88. quem sequimur : i.e. who shall be our guide? The present tense has a future meaning here : A. 468 ; D. 657 ; G. 228.

89. inlabere, *inspire :* Apollo, as the god of prophecy, is supposed to inspire his worshippers with knowledge, as well as his priest.

90. visa : sc. *sunt.*

91. limina, laurus : in many ancient representations of Delphi an altar appears in front of the temple ; there is a laurel near-by. — **-quē :** cf. *pulvīs,* i. 478; *domūs,* ii. 563.

92. mons : Mt. Cynthus. — **adytis reclusis,** *when the [doors of the] shrine were opened.* — **cortina** (lit. *vat* or *caldron*) is strictly the vessel which formed the body of the tripod; it was provided with a cover, on which the priestess sat.

93. submissi petimus terram, *we fall upon our knees on the ground.*

94. Dardanidae : the Trojans are fitly addressed as Dardanidae because their ancestor Dardanus came from Italy, the land which the oracle is about to mention. — **duri,** *hardy* (suggesting the toils they had undergone).

95. prima : translate as if an adv. — **tellus :** the antecedent, attracted into the relative clause. — **ubere laeto,** *in her fruitful bosom,* i.e. nourishing (alluding to *matrem,* below).

97. hic, *here :* i.e. in the land mentioned in *vv.* 94–96. — **oris :** abl. of place where.

99. mixto tumultu : abl. absolute.

100. moenia, *city.*

102. volvens monumenta, *unrolling the records* (like a scroll: cf. i. 262).

104. Iovis insula : Jupiter was said to have been born in Crete.

105. gentis cunabula : the existence of a Mt. Ida in Crete is evidence to Anchises that the Trojans came originally from that island.

106. habitant : i.e. the Cretans.

107. maximus pater, *our eldest ancestor,* i.e. the first founder of our race. — **audita,** *what I have heard.*

108. Rhoeteas, *Trojan :* Rhoeteum was a small town and promontory just north of Troy.

109. regno : dat. of purpose (Introd. § 33).

110. steterant, *had been built.*

111. hinc, *hence,* i.e. from this colony of Teucer. The translation may follow the Latin in leaving the verb unexpressed. — **cultrix,** *patroness.* —

Cybelae: obj. gen. with *cultrix*. Cybele was a mountain in Phrygia sacred to Cybĕle or Cybēbe, "mother of the gods," a Phrygian divinity worshipped in and about the Troad. — **Corybantia aera,** *the Corybantian cymbals.* The rites of Cybele were performed by the Corybantes, her votaries, with the clashing of cymbals, etc. She wears a turreted crown. Her car is pictured as drawn by lions. Her worship was introduced into Rome 204 B.C. and became very popular in the later republic. Her journey to Rome is quaintly represented in Fig. 27, from an ancient relief.

Fig. 27

112. Idaeum nemus: *the grove on Mt. Ida.* Anchises supposes that the name of the mountain near Troy was taken from Mt. Ida of Crete, and that from the same source came the worship of Cybele in the grove. The last syllable of *nemus* is long (Introd. § 110). — **fida silentia sacris,** *faithful secrecy for the mysteries,* i. e. those associated with her worship. The initiated were bound by an oath of secrecy.

115. Gnosia: Gnosus was the city of Minos, king of Crete.

116. nec longo cursu: about one hundred and fifty miles; abl. of degree of difference. — **Iuppiter:** as god of the sky and of storms. — **adsit:** proviso; A. 528; D. 811; B. 310, II; G. 573.

118. meritos, *due,* i. e. by custom.

120. nigram . . . albam: a black victim to the power whose wrath is deprecated; a white one to the friendly deity. — **felicibus,** *favoring.*

121. regnis: abl. of place from which.

122. Idomenea: acc. (Introd. § 93). According to the story, Idomeneus, leader of the Cretans in the Trojan War, overtaken by a storm on his return, had vowed to sacrifice to the sea-god the first living thing that should meet him on his safe arrival home. This proved to be his son, who was accordingly sacrificed; but a pestilence followed, and Idomeneus was driven from Crete and settled in Italy (*v.* 400). — **deserta:** sc. *esse.*

123. hoste : abl. of separation. — **adstare,** *stand ready* (for occupancy).

124. Ortygiae : Delos. — **pelago :** *over the sea :* abl. of the way by which (Introd. § 55).

125. bacchatam iugis, *whose heights are visited in the orgies,* i.e. in the rites of Bacchus : literally, *sought-in-revels on its heights* ; **bacchatam,** though participle of a deponent verb, is here used in a passive sense. *Iugis* is abl. of place where. — **Naxon :** object of *legimus* (*v.* 127).

126. niveam : on account of its much-prized white marble.

127. Cycladas : the islands just named belong to the Cyclades. — **freta . . . terris :** *the narrow seas broken up by frequent islands.*

128. vario certamine, *in varied contest ;* the vessels are racing each other.

129. petamus : direct discourse (hortatory subjunctive).

130. prosequitur, *attends.* This word is regularly used of human escort, and so here in a manner personifies the favoring wind. — **euntis** [sc. *nos*], *us as we go.*

131. Curetum : priests of Jupiter in Crete, where his worship was conducted with orgies and noisy rites, like that of Cybele. His infancy was passed there in concealment, and his cries were drowned by the clashing of the arms of the Curetes. See Fig. 28, from an ancient relief.

133. Pergameam : an historical Cretan town *Pergamum* is thus connected by Virgil with the wanderings of Æneas. — **laetam cognomine :** because Pergamum was also the name of the citadel of Troy.

134. amare : infinitive, in place of a substantive clause (Introd. § 78). — **tectis,** *for their habitations :* dat. of reference.

135. fere qualifies not merely *subductae* but the whole situation of affairs : the colony was well-nigh established. — **subductae :** the technical term for beaching the ancient ships, which were usually kept on land and only launched on occasion of a voyage (cf. n. on *v.* 71).

136. cōnūbiis (trisyllable ; Introd. § 115) : abl. of means, *match-making* (with Cretan women apparently).

137. tabida goes with *lues* (*v.* 139). — **membris,** *upon their limbs ;* dat. of reference with *venit.*

138. corrupto . . . tractu, *from an infected quarter of the sky ;* abl. of cause. This was until recent times the usual explanation of an epidemic. Cf. Thomson's description of plague and famine, *The Seasons, Summer,* *vv.* 1092–1134 ; especially *vv.* 1122–1125 :

> The circling sky,
> The wide enlivening air is full of fate ;
> And, struck by turns, in solitary pangs
> They fall, unblest, untended, and unmourn'd.

139. satis, *crops :* from *sero ;* here subst. in the same constr. as *membris.*

140. linquebant dulcis animas, *they laid down their dear lives.*

141. sterilĭs (acc. plural), etc., *burned the fields barren*, i.e. so that they became barren: A. 393, N.; D. 417, *a*; B. 177, 2; G. 340. — **Sirius:** at the period when the popular astronomy began, the Dog Star rose with the sun about the middle of July. Hence it is traditionally associated with extremely hot weather. — **exurere:** historical inf. (Introd. § 82).

142. negabat, *refused.*

143. remenso . . . mari (abl. abs.), *retracing [our course over] the sea.*

Fig. 28

144. veniam, *a gracious answer.* The question is in the indirect form in the next line.

145. finem: usually masculine (cf. ii. 554).

147. nox erat: cf. ii. 268 (note).

148. effigies, *images* (not *apparitions*): it was "a mixture of dream and vision."

150. ante oculos iacentis, *before my eyes as I lay* (lit. *of* [*me*] *lying*).

152. insertas, *set in the walls.*

154. delato, *when arrived,* i. e. if you should go. — **dicturus est,** *would say,* equivalent to *dicat;* a fut. apodosis, the protasis being implied in *delato:* A. 521, *a*; D. 802; B. 305, 1; G. 593, 2.

155. hic, *here.* — **ultro,** *unasked,* i. e. without your going to him. — **ad limina :** i. e. of your chamber.

157. sub te = *te duce.*

158. īdem (nom. plur. contracted) . . . **nepotes,** *we will also exalt,* etc.: A. 298, *b*; D. 547; B. 248, 1; G. 310; said rather of the general glories of the race than of the apotheosis of special heroes.

159. magnis, *for great things,* i. e. a mighty destiny.

160. ne linque : see Introd. § 87.

161. non haec, etc., *not this shore did,* etc.

162. Cretae : locative (Introd. § 72).

163-166. Repeated from i. 530-533, which see.

167. propriae, *permanent* (as in *v.* 85).

168. Iasius : a brother of Dardanus; he married a daughter of Teucer and thus became one of the founders of the Trojan race. — **pater :** merely an honorary epithet. — **principe,** *as founder :* not, of course, to the exclusion of Dardanus, just mentioned.

170. haud dubitanda, *no doubtful tidings.* — **Corythum** (afterwards Cortona): a very ancient city in Etruria. There were many traditions of its connection with Greeks and Pelasgians. — **requirat :** for imperative of dir. disc.

171. Dictaea, *Cretan :* Dicte was a mountain in Crete.

173-175. Cf. the vision of Eliphaz in Job, iv. 13-17.

175. corpore : abl. of separation.

176. supinas manus : see note on i. 93.

177. munera : i. e. a libation of wine.

178. focis : dat. of place to which. The hearth was the altar of the penates. — **laetus :** his cheerfulness, when he has fulfilled the sacrifice, comes from the assurance of divine direction.

179. ordine, *in full* with all the details.

180. prolem, *race.* — **ambiguam :** in its literal sense, *twofold.* — **geminos parentes :** the Cretan Teucer and the Italian Dardanus.

181. novo errore : perhaps a mere verbal antithesis to *veterum locorum,* i. e. the ancient homes of the race; *by a new mistake as to ancient places.* — **locorum :** obj. gen.

182. exercite, *driven on, pursued* or *harassed.* — **fatis :** abl. of instrument.

183. casus . . . canebat : Virgil is fond of alliteration, though not so much so as the earlier poets. See ii. 246-247 for Cassandra's prophecies.

184. nunc repeto, *now* (though before forgetful) *I recall.* — **portendere** [sc. *eam*]: the present inf. is here used to express a repeated action in past time (the so-called imperfect infinitive); in direct discourse, —*portendebat*, *vocabat*. See A. 584, *a*, N.; D. 830; G. 281, N. — **debita,** *as due.*

187. crederet, *would have believed*: deliberative subjunctive referring to past time; A. 444 and N.; D. 678; B. 277; G. 466. — **quem . . . moveret :** see ii. 247.

188. Phoebo : the god of prophecy, who, as he thought, must have commissioned the penates (cf. *vv.* 154–155). — **meliora,** *a higher destiny.*

189. ovantes : because they at length know their true destiny.

190. quoque : i.e. as well as Thrace. — **paucis relictis :** to account for the existence of the Cretan *Pergamum* in historical times (*v.* 133).

191. aequor : depending on *currimus*, in the sense of *navigare*, which is often used as transitive; but the construction of all such words resembles that of the cognate acc.

192. altum tenuere, *gained the deep.*

193. caelum, pontus, sc. *est.*

194. imber, *rain-cloud.*

195. hiemem, *storm.* — **inhorruit,** *roughened*, with a hint at the dread (*horror*) of the storm. — **tenebris :** abl. of manner. The allusion is doubtless to the common appearance of the darkening of the sea under a wind.

199. abstulit, *shut out*, but the figure is livelier in Latin. — **ignes,** *flashes.* — **nubibus :** abl. of place where; cf. *Paradise Regained*, iv. 410–413 :

> The clouds,
> From many a horrid rift, abortive pour'd
> Fierce rain with lightning mix'd, water with fire
> In ruin reconcil'd.

201. ipse : emphatic because Palinurus is the skilful pilot, and ought to know if anybody on board could. — **discernere,** *distinguish* : sc. *se* as subject.

202. viae : Introd. § 18.

203. tris adeo . . . soles, *for three full days*; acc. of duration of time; *adeo* grammatically modifies *tris.* — **caligine** (abl. of cause): to be taken with *incertos.*

206. aperire, volvere : depending on *visa* [*est*]. The land discloses the peaks and rolls up the smoke. — **fumum :** the sign of an inhabited country.

207. vela : it would seem that in all difficult places, as when nearing the coast, the ancients used only their oars. — **insurgimus :** we say *bend to the oars*; but the ancients used larger oars, so that the corresponding expression in Latin is *rise*, as here. — **mora :** sc. *est.*

208. caerula, *the dark blue sea.*

209. Strophadum : two islands of the Ionian Sea, west of Peloponnesus. They were said to be so called from the Greek verb meaning " to turn," because there Zetes and Calais, sons of Boreas, turned from pursuing the Harpies.

210. Graio: because the name has a Greek derivation. — **stant,** *lie.*

211. insulae Ionio: semi-hiatus (Introd. § 109). With *Ionio* sc. *mari.*

212. Harpyiae: perhaps originally personified storm-winds, but worked up by the mythographers into the monsters described in the text. They infested the house of Phineus, a king of Thrace, sent by the gods to punish him for his cruelty to his sons, but were driven away by the Argonauts, Zetes and Calais, as here described; hence *metu* (abl. of cause). There are countless references and allusions to the Harpies in ancient and modern literature. See Fig. 29. — **Phineia:** *of Phineus.*

Fig. 29

213. mensas: the Harpies snatched away the food from the table of Phineus before he could eat.

215. ira, *scourge,* the wrath is put for its instrument. — **Stygiis:** such monsters regularly had their home in the World Below. So in Milton, *Comus, vv.* 603–605:

> All the grisly legions that troop
> Under the sooty flag of Acheron,
> Harpies and Hydras.

216. voltus: sc. *sunt.*

218. famē: the *e* in the abl. of *fames* is long, as if of the fifth declension.

219. delati, *sailing in* (literally, *down*).

220. laeta, *thriving*: a common word for any luxuriant growth; here possibly only of numbers, *countless.*

221. custode: abl. of manner, or perhaps abl. absolute.

222. ferro: abl. of instrument. — **ipsum:** the emphasis is either to give a stronger indication of their honesty of purpose, or else to show a still greater folly on their part in calling on Jupiter, the protecting divinity of strangers, in their acts of violence.

223. in partem, etc., *to a share of the prey* (hendiadys, see n. on i. 61).

224. toros: i.e. for reclining. — **dapibus:** abl. of means; cf. the construction with *vescor* (Introd. § 56).

226. clangoribus: i.e. the noise of their flapping wings.

227. diripiunt, etc. Hence in Shakspere's *Tempest* (iii. 3) Ariel enters in the shape of a harpy, "claps his wings upon the table, and with a quaint device the banquet vanishes."

228. vox: their *cry* as birds of prey.

230. horrentibus, *darkening.*

232. ex diverso caeli, *from a different quarter of the sky.*

233. pedibus: abl. of instrument.

234. capessant: A. 588; D. 887, III; B. 316; G. 652. His words in dir. disc. would be, *capessite . . . gerendum est.*

236, 237. ac, *than.*—tectos . . . condunt, *they hide their swords here and there in the grass* (lit. *they place them here and there hidden*) *and secrete their shields* (lit. *hide them lying concealed*): tectos and latentia are proleptic; see n. on i. 69.

240. nova proelia, *strange warfare.*

241. foedare: in apposition with *proelia.*

242. plumis, tergo: abl. of place where.

243. sub, *up toward,* a common meaning of the word.

245. una, *one only,* with emphasis as usual.

246. infelix, *ill-omened.* — rumpit, *hurls forth.*

247. bellum: notice the emphasis on this word from its position as well as its repetition. — pro, *in return for*: i.e. to defend and continue the outrage already committed.

248. Laomedontiadae: spoken tauntingly, to remind the Trojans of their descent from one who was famous for breaking his word. Laomedon had refused to pay Apollo and Neptune the wages agreed upon for building the walls of Troy; and later, when his daughter Hesione was rescued from a sea-monster by Hercules, he had again withheld the promised reward.

252. Furiarum: apparently a mere confusion of the two sets of divinities. Such creatures were not very exactly defined in the minds of the ancients, and the two might easily be identified with each other, especially as these Harpies, as well as the Furies, were ministers of divine vengeance. Cf. *Paradise Lost,* ii. 596, " harpy-footed Furies." In *Lycidas, v.* 75, Milton calls Atropos, one of the Fates, " the blind Fury."

253. cursu: abl. of manner. — vocatis: the ordinary invocation of the winds, but here with the idea that they will surely be favorable.

255. non ante . . . quam, *never . . . until.* —datam, *granted you by fate.*

256. fames: an appropriate vengeance (cf. *v.* 217). — nostrae iniuria caedis, *the outrage of your murderous attack upon us* (lit. *of our slaughter*); nostrae is equivalent to an objective gen.; A. 348, *a*; D. 355; B. 243, 2; G. 364, N.²

257. subigat: A. 551, *c*; D. 758, *b*, N.; B. 292; G. 577.—mālis: from māla; notice the long penult. Celæno's prophecy was fulfilled in this manner: after their arrival in Italy, the Trojans, at a meal on the shore, used broad thin cakes as platters (*mensae*) and then ate the cakes (vii. 107 ff.).

259. sociis: dative of reference.

260. animi, *their spirits.*

261. exposcere: belonging properly with *votis precibusque* alone, but (by the common *zeugma*) used also with *armis.*

262. sint: subjunc. of integral part; A. 593; D. 907; B. 324, 1; G. 663, 1.

263. passis: i.e. in the ordinary attitude of prayer; cf. i. 93 and note.

264. meritos, i.e. *due* by custom to the higher (*magna*) gods.

266. placidi, *be propitious and,* etc.

267. rudentis: the clew-lines that held the sail furled (as seen in Fig. 30, Ulysses and the Sirens, from an antique gem).

268. undis: abl. of the way by which.

271-274. See map. All these places are off the coast of Greece and between the island of *Zacynthos* (now *Zante*) and the promontory of Actium. *Dulichium* is an unknown island; *Neritos,* a mountain in Ithaca. *Same* was an older name for Cephallenia (now Cephalonia).

271. saxis: abl. of cause.

273. Ulixi: objective genitive.

275. nautis: dat. of agent. — **aperitur,** *shows itself:* the temple of Apollo at Actium appears above the horizon as they approach.

276. urbi: i.e. Actium.

279. lustramur, *make an expiatory sacrifice.* —**votis,** etc.: i.e. by offering the vowed sacrifices they kindle the fire on the altars.

280. Actia: an ancient festival was held on the promontory of Actium in honor of Apollo, whose temple there, said to have been founded by the Argonauts, was renewed by Augustus in honor of the battle of Actium. This festival is made more distinguished by being here connected with Æneas. — **celebramus,** *we crowd,* the literal meaning of the word. — **ludis:** abl. of means.

Fig. 30

281. oleo labente, [*anointed*] *with slippery oil:* really abl. of manner. In their gymnastic games the ancients anointed their bodies with oil, apparently to prevent the muscles from becoming stiff from exposure. The regular emblem of the gymnast is a bottle of oil and strigils (see Fig. 31, objects found at Pompeii). — **palaestras:** properly, the place for wrestling, but often used, as here, for the exercise itself.

282. nudati: the games were all practised without any clothing; hence the term *gymnasium* (Gr. γυμνάσιον, from γυμνός, *naked*).

284. magnum . . . annum, *the sun revolves round the great circle of the year* (lit. *is rolled round the great year*): i.e. the sun is finishing its annual circuit and winter comes. *Annum* is the obj. of *circum* in *circumvolvitur*; A. 395, N.[2]; D. 412, *b*; B. 179, 3; G. 331, R.[1]

286. aere cavo, *of hollow* (i.e. concave) *bronze;* abl. of material. — **Abantis:** Abas, a mythical king of Argos, had a famous shield sacred to Juno. Virgil implies that this was taken to Troy by some Greek and there captured by the Trojans — perhaps by Æneas himself in the last battle.

287. postibus adversis (locative abl.), *on the doorposts in front* (i.e. as one enters the temple of Apollo). — **rem**, *act.* — **carmine:** such inscriptions were often in verse.

288. Aeneas: sc. *dedicat* (often omitted, as here).

289. tum: in the following spring. The winter has been spent at Actium.

291. aërias Phaeacum arces, *the lofty heights of the Phæacians*; i.e. Corcyra (now Corfu).

292. portu: dative.

293. Chaonio: Chaonia was a region in Epirus. — **celsam:** a stock epithet (cf. " Towered cities please us then." *L'Allegro*). The real Buthrotum was a low-lying coast town. For case, see Introd. § 47.

294. occupat, *meets*, with the additional idea of seizing them, as it were, with surprise.

295. regnare: indir. disc. in apposition with *fama.*

296. coniugio (= *coniuge*), *wife*: abl. with *potitum* (Introd. § 56). Andromache, the widow of Hector, had fallen in the distribution of booty to the lot of Pyrrhus, son of Achilles and great-grandson of Æacus (*Aeacidae*). The rest of the story is told in *vv.* 325 ff. — **sceptris:** for plur. see Introd. § 96.

297. cessisse, *had fallen* (passed over). — **patrio,** *of her own people*: her father, the king of the Cilicians, had been an ally of Troy.

298. amore, *desire*: abl. of means.

299. compellare: depends on *incensum* [*est*] *pectus*; cf. *amor cognoscere*, ii. 10.

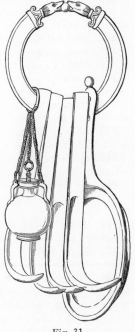

Fig. 31

301. sollemnis dapes, *the annual sacrifice of food*: such as was regularly made at the graves of the dead; it consisted of wine, milk, oil, honey, with more solid food, such as eggs and beans, while the graves were decorated with wreaths. — **cum . . . libabat,** *just at the time, as it chanced, when she was offering* (lit. *pouring*): A. 545; D. 750; B. 288, 1, A; G. 580.

302. falsi, *pretended*, i.e. named for the original (and so itself not " real "), a natural memorial of the old familiar places.

303. cineri: i.e. of Hector. — **Manis:** the spirit in its semi-deified condition would visit, like any divinity, the monument erected to it, and receive the offering.

304. Hectoreum ad tumulum, *to a mound consecrated to Hector,* i.e. a cenotaph erected to his memory. — **quem inanem,** *an empty tomb, which*: the ashes of Hector had been buried in Troy. — **caespite:** abl. of material.

305. geminas: the number is common. — **lacrimis,** *for tears*: A. 366, *b*; in prose it would be genitive.

307. monstris: the sudden appearance of Æneas seems to her a prodigy; she takes him at first for a spirit.

308. deriguit visu in medio, *even while gazing at me she swooned.*

309. longo tempore, *after a long time*; A. 424, *f.*

310. vera . . . adfers, *do you present yourself, a real form ?*

311. recessit: if *he* is a spirit from below, then Hector might be expected to appear in bodily form as well as he; cf. *v.* 303.

313. clamore, *wailing.* — **pauca** [*ei*] **furenti subicio,** *I throw in a few words amid her ravings.*

314. raris . . . hisco (incept.), *agitated, I open my lips in broken utterance*: lit. *in words here and there.* — **vocibus:** abl. of manner.

315. equidem, *'tis true* (with a hint that it is barely life, after all). — **extrema,** *dangers, sufferings.*

317. deiectam, *deprived* (with violence).

318. digna, *equal to her worth.* — **revisit,** *returns to.* Two questions are compressed into one: "What fate is hers, and is it worthy of her ? "

319. Hectoris Andromachen, *Hector's Andromache.* — **Pyrrhin'** = *Pyrrhine*: the omission of the *e* is colloquial and antiquated.

320. deiecit voltum, *she cast down her eyes* (lit. *countenance*): for the mention of Pyrrhus reminds her of her slavery and humiliation.

321. felix, etc., *the one most happy woman beyond all others.* — **Priameïa virgo:** Polyxena, promised in marriage, under a truce, to Achilles. It was at an interview with her that Achilles was treacherously shot in the heel by Paris. After the fall of Troy Pyrrhus, son of Achilles, sacrificed her at his father's tomb; see the *Hecuba* of Euripides; cf. Landor's poem, *The Espousals of Polyxena.*

323. sortitus: the *allotment* of captives among the victors.

325. nos = *ego*: opposed to Polyxena.

326. stirpis Achilleae: Pyrrhus.

327. servitio enixae, *having borne offspring to him in slavery* (a son named Molossus). — **secutus,** *following* (Introd. § 95).

328. Hermionen: the one child of Menelaus and Helen, daughter of Leda.

329. me famulo, etc.: i.e. I was his slave, and so he made me over to Helenus, a slave as well. A kind of apology for her present position. — **habendam,** *to be held as a servant*: the gerundive expresses purpose; A. 500, 4; D. 869; B. 337, 8, *b*, 2; G. 430.

331. coniugis: Hermione had been betrothed to Orestes. — **scelerum Furiis,** *the furies that avenged his crimes.* Cf. the speech of the First Fury in Shelley, *Prometheus Unbound,* act i:

> We are the ministers of pain, and fear,
> And disappointment, and mistrust, and hate,
> And clinging crime.

— **Orestes:** son of Agamemnon and Clytemestra. Agamemnon, on return-ing from Troy, had been murdered by Clytemestra. In vengeance, Orestes killed Clytemestra, and for this crime he was driven mad by the Furies.

332. patrias ad aras: but the altar where Pyrrhus was slain was usually said to be at Delphi.

333. reddita cessit, *has come by succession* (i.e. in the natural order, as if Helenus were his son).

334. cognomine: abl. of specification.

335. Chaoniam omnem dixit, *called the whole region Chaonia.* — **Chaone:** according to one story a brother of Helenus, accidentally killed by him.

336. iugis: dative.

338. aut: the alternative is between an accidental arrival (*venti*) and divine direction (*deus*).

339. quid: sc. *agit*; a common form of inquiry for one's health.

340. Troia (abl.): left unfinished by Virgil. The line completed would perhaps mean "whom, after the siege of Troy was already begun, Creüsa bore you."

341. ecqua cura? *ecqua* emphasizes the question, and expresses emotion: *has the boy — tell me — any regard?* — **tamen,** *though* she is dead, yet, etc. Virgil does not tell how Andromache had heard of the death of Creüsa.

342. ecquid, *at all:* cognate acc. as adv. — **antiquam,** *ancestral.*

343. avunculus: Creüsa was a daughter of Priam (cf. *patruus,* uncle on the father's side). — **excitat:** i.e. does their fame arouse him to emulate them?

348. multum lacrimas fundit, *sheds a flood of tears:* *multum* is adv. acc. (Introd. § 41). — **verba inter singula,** *with every word.*

349. Troiam: see note, *v.* 302. — **magnis:** dative, depending on *simu-lata* in its original sense of *made like.*

350. arentem rivum, *dry brook:* a picturesque way of contrasting it with the formidable Xanthus, the river of Troy. — **Xanthi:** appositional genitive depending on *cognomine* or *rivum* (Introd. § 10). — **cognomine:** abl. of specification, if *Xanthi* depends on *rivum*; otherwise abl. of quality.

351. amplector: cf. ii. 490. — **Scaeae:** cf. ii. 612.

353. porticibus: in imitation of the manners of heroic times the attend-ants are entertained in open galleries, of which there were many in the ancient houses; see Tabula Iliaca, p. 105, above. — **accipiebat**: the imperfect denotes the repetition, day after day, of the feast.

354. aulaï: Introd. § 91, *a*. The great courtyard of the palace is here referred to, where stood the altar of Jupiter. — **libabant**: the libation was a regular accompaniment to the feast (cf. i. 736). — **Bacchi**: cf. i. 177, 215.

355. impositis auro dapibus, *when the feast was served in golden dishes*.

356. dies alterque processit, *day after day went by*. Chronology of the poem seems to require that another winter should have been passed in Epirus; the lapse of time is given as Æneas' reason for addressing Helenus. Helenus is represented as possessing all powers of divination, being a *vates* (as priest of Apollo), an *auspex* (or augur), and an astrologer.

357. vocant, etc.: i. e. the weather again becomes favorable.

358. quaeso: the old form of *quaero*.

359. numina, *purposes*.

360. Clarii: Apollo is so called from Claros in Asia Minor, where he had a temple and an oracle. — **sentis**, *understand*: since he was a " seer," things future and unseen were to him objects of direct perception. — **sidera**, *the stars* in the astrological meaning, as " lords of life."

361. linguas, pinnae: the two forms of augury, from the voices of birds or their flight.

362. namque: the thought is, " I do not ask about my voyage or my destination; but, since one ill-boding prophet has sung of perils, how may I avoid or overcome these best? " — **prospera**: an epithet logically belonging to *cursum*, is here poetically made to agree with *religio*, *favoring prophecy* or *omens*.

364. petere, temptare: Introd. § 78. — **temptare**, *try to reach*. — **repostas** = *repositas* (Introd. § 91, *n*).

365. nefas (in appos. with *prodigium*), *a horror to tell*, probably on account of the bad luck of mentioning such a thing. We have something similar in our " Oh! don't speak of it."

367. famem: cf. iii. 255-257. — **vito**: cf. n. to iii. 88.

368. quid sequens, [*by*] *following what course?* — **possim**: apodosis of fut. less vivid condition; the protasis is implied in *sequens*.

370. resolvit: he removes the fillets because the sacrifice is ended and he now appears in his character as *vates*, or prophetic seer.

372. multo . . . numine, *awed by the mighty presence of the god*.

373. divino, *inspired*.

374. nam: introducing the reason of *pauca expediam* below. — **maioribus**: greater than Helenus; to wit, under the protection of Jove. — **ire**: indirect discourse dependent on the idea of *thinking* implied in *fides*.

375. manifesta fides, *the assurance is clear*.

376. sortitur, *decides* (lit. *draws by lot*). —**volvit vices,** *rules* (lit. *revolves*) *the changes* (*of human life*). — **is vertitur ordo,** *so moves on the succession of events* (as if in a great circle).

377. hospita (neut. plur.): not here "hospitable," but "which you shall traverse as a *hospes*," or stranger, i.e. *strange, foreign.* — **lustres :** subj. of purpose with *quo* (= *ut eo*); A. 531, *a*; D. 718; B. 282, 1, *a*; G. 545, 2.

380. scire . . . fari : i.e. he is not permitted by the Fates to know, nor by Juno to tell if he did know; A. 563, *a*; D. 720, I, *a*; B. 331, II; G. 423, N.[6]

381. Italiam : obj. of *dividit.* — **iam,** *now.* — **propinquam :** Italy was, in fact, not far from Buthrotum (see map), but it was not in that part of Italy that Æneas was to settle.

382. vicinos (pred. adj.), *as if near at hand.* — **paras :** sc. *cuius*, corresponding to *quam*; this omission of the relative when it would be in another case is not uncommon in Latin.

383. via dividit invia : observe the alliteration. — **terris,** *stretches of land*, i.e. the coasts along which he must sail.

384. ante : connect with *quam* in *v.* 387. — **Trinacria :** i.e. around Sicily. — **lentandus :** sc. *est.*

385. Ausonii : the Tuscan sea as opposed to the Ionian. — **lustrandum** [sc. *est*], *must be traversed.*

386. inferni lacus, *the lakes of the Lower World* : the marshy regions of Avernus in Campania were supposed to be an entrance to the infernal regions. See vi. 237. — **Aeaeae insula Circae :** the promontory of Circeii on the coast of Latium, once an island according to tradition. Circe, a sorceress who changed her guests into beasts, was said to have fled from Æa in Colchis to this region.

387. possis : A. 551, *c*; D. 758, *b*, N.; B. 292; G. 577.

389. tibi : dat. of agent with *inventa.* — **sollicito** (with *tibi*), *in your anxiety.* — **secreti fluminis :** the Tiber.

390. litoreis, *that grow on the bank.*

391. triginta capitum fetūs, *a litter of thirty young.*

392. nati : in the same construction as *sus*, with a verb to be supplied from *iacebit*; but we may translate *with her white*, etc.

393. is, ea : we should expect *tum* corresponding to *cum, v.* 389.

395. vocatus : i.e. in answer to prayer.

396. has : i.e. toward Epirus (Helenus' land).

398. Grais : dative of agent. Southern Italy was called *Magna Graecia.* It was colonized very early from Greece; so early that traditions were invented which, like that of Æneas, referred the settlements to heroes of the Trojan War.

399. Narycii Locri : Locrians of Narycium (on the mainland of Greece opposite Eubœa) were said to have been driven by storms to Southern Italy when on their way home from the Trojan War, and there to have founded the city of Locri, a little north of the extreme southern point.

400. Sallentinos: the Sallentini were a people of Calabria. — **milite:** abl. of means.

401. Lyctius Idomeneus: cf. n. on *v.* 122. Lyctos was a city of Crete. — **ducis Meliboei:** i. e. Philoctetes, a native of Melibœa in Thessaly.

402. subnixa muro, *resting on its wall*: referring to the desperate siege it stood from Hannibal. — **Petelia:** an old city of Bruttium, said to have been founded by Philoctetes, who was wrecked there on his return from the Trojan War. *Philoctetae* goes with *Petelia*.

403. steterint, *shall have come to anchor.*

405. velare (imperat. pass. in "middle" sense), *wrap your head close in a purple mantle.*

407. hostilis facies: this would be of evil omen.

408. hunc morem: Virgil ascribes an early origin to the Roman custom of covering the head while sacrificing. See Fig. 32 (veiled Roman sacrificing, from an ancient statue). — **teneto:** fut. imperative.

409. religione, *sacred observance* or *ritual.*

410. digressum, *on your departure* (from Italy, where Helenus assumes that the Trojans will land).

411. claustra, *the headlands* of the Strait of Messina, which are about four miles apart, and from a distance seem to close the passage. These seem wider apart (*rariores*) as ships approach them.

Fig. 32

412. laeva: i. e. along the eastern and southern shores of Sicily. Æneas is directed to sail south and west round the island. — **tibi:** dat. of agent.

414. haec loca . . . dissiluisse, *these shores, they say, sprang apart,* the strait being formed, as was thought, by some earthquake shock, connected, perhaps, with an eruption of Ætna. — **ruina,** *convulsion.*

415. tantum . . . vetustas, *so powerful to change is long lapse of time.*

416. cum . . . foret: concessive clause; A. 549; D. 755; B. 309, 3; G. 587. — **protinus una,** *continuously one.*

417. medio = *in medium.* — **undis:** abl. of means.

419. litore: *along the shore.* — **diductas,** *now separated.* — **angusto:** with *aestu* (abl. of manner).

420. dextrum latus: the Italian side of the strait. — **Scylla, Charybdis:** Scylla is a monster (cf. *vv.* 424–428); Charybdis is a whirlpool (cf. *vv.* 420–423). In Homer (Od. xii. 73–110; Bry. 100) Scylla is a monster with six

heads, each of which snatches a man from the deck (235-259; Bry. 293),
and Charybdis, dwelling below the flood, swallows the ship, which is afterwards cast forth, Ulysses clinging meanwhile to a wild fig-tree (428-441).

421. imo barathri gurgite, *in the depths of her abyss.* — **ter:** thrice
a day.

422. sorbet: the subject is *Charybdis.* — **sub auras,** *upward into the air.*

423. alternos, *in turn.* — **sidera:** hyperbole; cf. i. 103.

426. prima facies: *the upper part of her body*; sc. *est* with *facies.* —
pectore: abl. of quality.

427. postrema, *the lower part.*

428. caudas (Gr. acc.; Introd. § 42) **commissa,** *having the tails of dolphins fastened to the bellies of wolves.* The rock which stands for Scylla
is no longer formidable; but Charybdis still exists as a whirlpool or eddy
near the Sicilian coast, much dreaded by the native boatmen in some states
of the weather. Milton's description of Sin, in the famous allegory of Sin
and Death, owes some features to Virgil's Scylla:

> The one seem'd woman to the waist, and fair,
> But ended foul in many a scaly fold
> Voluminous and vast, a serpent arm'd
> With mortal sting: about her middle round
> A cry of hell-hounds never ceasing bark'd
> With wide Cerberean mouths full loud.
>
> *Paradise Lost,* ii. 650-655 (cf. 659-661).

429. lustrare, *to skirt along:* subject of *praestat* (Introd. § 73). —
metas: the Roman circus was divided lengthwise in the middle by a wall,
round which the race took place, and at each end of this were three conical
pillars called *metae,* round which the racers must turn: to these the promontory, which the ship must double, is compared (see Fig. 33). — **Pachyni:**
the southernmost point of Sicily.

430. cessantem, *lingering,* i.e. taking a less direct course. The word
belongs to the unexpressed subj. of *lustrare.*

432. caeruleis: the regular color of everything belonging to the sea. —
canibus resonantia: cf. Milton, *Comus, vv.* 257-258:

> Scylla wept,
> And chid her barking waves into attention.

433. prudentia, *foresight.*

435. illud, *this* (which follows). — **pro:** i.e. this is so important as to
take the place of all the rest. — **unum:** repeated for emphasis, but with a
slightly different shade of meaning, as contrasted with *omnibus.*

438. Iunoni: notice the force of the repetition. — **cane vota,** *chant
prayers:* all religious formulæ were in verse.

439. sic denique, *so at length,* i.e. so and only thus.

440. finis : Introd. § 47. — **mittĕre,** *you shall be suffered to go.*

441. huc delatus, *when you have come to land there, and,* etc. — **Cumaeam,** *of Cumae,* on the coast of Campania.

442. divinos : Lake Avernus was supposed to be the entrance to the infernal regions, and so, like everything connected with the life and functions of the gods, was in a manner *divinus.* — **Averna sonantia silvis,** *Avernus with its rustling forests :* *Averna* is neuter plur. and refers to the neighborhood of the lake. — **silvis :** abl. of instrument.

443. insanam, *frenzied,* i.e. possessed with prophetic inspiration. The reference is to the Cumæan Sibyl.

Fig. 33

444. notas et nomina, *signs and words :* i.e. the signs which express words.

445. carmina, *prophecies* (as being given in verse).

446. digerit in numerum, *arranges in* (lit. *into*) *due order.*

448. eadem (sc. *folia*), *these same leaves ;* object of *prendere* (*v.* 450). — **verso cardine,** *from the turning of the hinge,* i.e. the mere movement of the door is enough to disturb them (abl. abs.).

450. saxo (locative abl.), *in the cave.*

452. inconsulti abeunt, *men depart unadvised,* i.e. having received no response from the Sibyl, whom they had come to consult.

453. ne . . . tanti, etc., *let not any cost of delay be of such account to you as to prevent* (*quin*), etc. — **fuerint :** the perfect subjunctive is rarely used in exhortations (except in prohibitions). — **tanti :** genitive of indefinite value (Introd. § 15).

454. increpitent : concessive subjunctive; so also *vocet* and *possis :* A. 527, *a* ; D. 809; B. 309, 1; G. 606. — **vi,** *urgently.*

455. sinus : the hollow of the sail, best translated by the *sail* itself. — **secundos :** i.e. *with favorable winds.*

456. quin : referring back to *tanti, v.* 453. — **adeas, poscas :** subjunctive with a negatived expression of preventing; A. 558; D. 720, III ; B. 298; G. 554. — **oracula :** obj. of *canat.*

457. canat, resolvat : substantive clauses dependent on *poscas ; ut* is omitted: A. 565, *a* ; D. 720, *d* ; B. 295, 8; G. 546, R.² — **volens :** a standing religious word ; translate, *be pleased to,* etc.

459. fugias . . . feras (indir. quest.): i.e. avoid, if that is possible, or bear, if they are unavoidable.

460. expediet, *shall disclose :* in fact, she guides Æneas to Anchises, who himself gives the necessary instruction ; see Book vi. — **venerata,** *being duly reverenced :* passive.

461. quae, *of which*: object of *moneri.* — **liceat**: relative clause of characteristic; A. 535; D. 726; B. 283, 1; G. 631. — **te**: subj. of *moneri.*

464. dona: gifts at parting (as at meeting, cf. i. 647) were a common mark of respect, and such as are here spoken of were the usual form of wealth in

Fig. 34 **R. H. FRANKENBERG**

heroic times. — **auro**: abl. of means. — **gravia**: the final *a* is long (Introd. § 110). — **secto elephanto**: ivory was chiefly used in thin plates, for inlaying.

466. Dodonaeos: according to one story, Helenus had settled first at Dodona. The bronze vessels (*lebetas*) made there were famous, and were said to ring like a bell at the touch, being wrought or cast, probably, in a single piece. — **lebetas**: Greek acc. plur. (Introd. § 92).

467. consertam trilicem, *woven three-ply.* For chain mail see Fig. 34. — **hamis auroque,** *links of gold*: hendiadys.

468. conum, *the crest* (or *peak*) *and waving* (lit. *hairy, made of hair*) *plume of a shining helmet,* i.e. a helmet with gleaming crest, etc. The *conus* was the ridge or projection on the top of the helmet, upon which the crest was fastened; it was probably at first only a spike, whence the name (see Fig. 35).

Fig. 35

469. sua, *appropriate*: cf. n. to i. 461.

471. remigium, *outfit of oars*, or perhaps *oarsmen.* — **socios**: inserted to indicate that these presents of armor, etc. (*armis*), in contradistinction to the general supplies, were made to Æneas' companions individually and therefore conferred honor on them.

473. mora ne qua, *that no delay might be made while the wind blew fair* (lit. *to the wind*, etc., i.e. that the fair wind might not be hindered). — **vento**: dative of reference.

475. coniugio . . . superbo, *deemed worthy of proud marriage with Venus* (obj. genitive). For case of *coniugio* see n. on i. 335.

477. ecce tibi, *lo !* As ethical dat. with the interjection, *tibi* may be left untranslated (Introd. § 31).

478. tamen : i. e. though you are hasting towards it. — **praeterlabare :** subjunc. in a substantive clause of result subject of *necesse est* (A. 569, 2 ; D. 722 ; B. 295, 6 ; G. 553, 4) ; *ut* is omitted, cf. *canat* in *v.* 457.

479. pars illa : i. e. Latium.

480. pietate : abl. of cause. — **quid demoror austros :** i. e. why do I detain you from sailing with them ?

482. digressu (abl. of cause), *parting,* each to go his own way (*dis-*).

484. nec cedit honore, *she does not fall behind* (her husband) *in respect :* *honore* is abl. of specification.

487. sint : in relative clause of purpose. — **longum,** *enduring.*

489. mihi super, *remaining to me :* the dative is used as if *quae sola superes* were expressed, instead of the vocative with *super* ; the adv. *super* (= *remaining*) is itself equivalent to an adjective. — **Astyanactis :** Astyanax (son of Hector and Andromache) was hurled from the walls of Troy by Ulysses.

490. sic . . . ferebat, *so were his eyes,* etc.

491. pubesceret, *would be growing into youth* from boyhood, i. e. had he lived (the condition is implied in *nunc*). — **aevo :** abl. of quality.

493. vivite : notice that the words contain a farewell ; hence the imperative, instead of an optative subjunctive. — **quibus :** dat. of agent. — **fortuna peracta :** i. e. they have had their share of adverse fate, and are at length securely happy.

494. sua : used in its ordinary sense, but with emphasis, contrasted with *nos* ; *vestra* would be expected. — **alia . . . in fata,** *from one fate to another.*

495. parta, *secured.* — **aequor,** *expanse.*

496. semper cedentia retro, *ever receding in the distance :* in allusion to the instructions just given by Helenus (cf. especially *vv.* 381–383, 477–479).

498. melioribus auspiciis (abl. of manner), *under better auspices :* i. e. than those of Troy itself.

499. fuerit (fut. perf.), *will prove to be.*

500. Thybridis : the gen. (instead of the dat.) with *vicinus* is rare.

502. urbes : direct obj. of *faciemus,* the predicate acc. is *Troiam* (Introd. § 39). — **olim :** *hereafter.*

503. Epiro, Hesperia : abl. of place where. — **quibus :** dat. of possessor (sc. *est*).

504. unam faciemus Troiam : the allusion is probably to the town of Nicopolis, then lately established by Augustus in Epirus. In the charter of this town, it is said, the Epirotes were spoken of as "kinsmen of the Romans."—**utramque**: really belonging to *urbes*, but attracted by *Troiam*.

505. animis : abl. of specification.

506. pelago : abl. of the way by which.

507. Italiam : acc. of end of motion with *iter* (sc. *est*), which is equivalent to a verb of motion. — **brevissimus :** the Adriatic is about forty miles wide here. — **undis :** cf. *v.* 506, note.

508. ruit, *hastens to its setting.* — **opaci** (proleptic): they become dark by being in shadow.

509. sternimur (reflexive or "middle" use), *we stretch our limbs.*

510. sortiti remos, *casting lots for the oars,* i.e. having assigned each man to his "watch." Apparently not all were on duty at the oar at once.

511. curamus, *refresh* (a standing expression for eating and drinking). — **inrigat,** *steals over* (lit. *bedews*).

512. acta, *borne along* in her car. — **horis :** abl. of means; as the poets can personify, making the means the agent (cf. *v.* 533), so they can make the agent the means, and use the simple ablative.

513. surgit, *when,* etc. — **strato :** abl. of separation.

514. explorat, etc.: i.e. observes the heavens for clouds betokening wind and listens to catch the first sound of a breeze.

515. sidera notat : apparently to determine his course.

516. pluvias : rains were supposed to attend their rising with the sun.

517. Spondaic line: see Introd. § 104. — **auro :** the golden belt and sword of the hunter are represented by several very bright stars of the constellation. — **Oriōna :** *i* long, from the Greek.

518. cuncta constare, *all is settled* or *steady*: i.e. there are no signs of bad weather.

519. castra movemus : a military expression, suggested by the later customs of naval expeditions.

522. humilem : of the shore, as opposed to the hills in the background.

523. Italiam : a kind of indirect discourse; the cry is *Italia, Italia.* Observe the effect of the repetition and elision, expressing the glad, hurried, and repeated cry of the men.

524. clamore : abl. of manner.

525. corona : see i. 724.

528. maris, terrae, tempestatum : objective genitives.

529. ferte viam facilem, *grant us an easy passage*; *ferte* also hints at their *bearing* the vessels on their course.

530. crebrescunt, patescit (notice the effect of these inceptives): [as] *the winds freshen, the port widens as it comes nearer into view.* — **optatae :** stronger than *desired*; almost *prayed for.* — **portus :** the *Portus Veneris,* south of Hydruntum, in Calabria.

532. legunt, *furl* (gather in).

533. curvatus, *hollowed.* — **fluctu :** the wave is in a manner personified, hence the ablative of agent (Introd. § 53).

534. obiectae, *that protect it* (lit. *thrown in the way* [of the sea], i.e. like a breakwater).

535. gemino muro (abl. of manner), *like a double wall.*

536. refugit, *recedes :* i.e. it now shows its true position back at the bottom of the bay.

537. primum : i.e. in connection with Italy. — **omen :** the first sight that strikes their eyes is as usual taken as an omen.

538. candore : abl. of quality.

539. bellum : notice the repetition of this word, and each time in an emphatic position. — **hospita :** *strange,* as in *v.* 377.

540. bello, *for war* ; dat. of purpose.

541. idem : plur. — **olim,** *at times.* — **curru :** dative. — **succedere :** infinitive with *sueti* [*sunt*].

542. concordia, *peaceful,* as opposed to the trappings of war just referred to. — **iugo** (abl. of manner), *with the yoke.*

543. spes et pacis, *there is hope of peace as well.*

544. quae . . . accepit : i.e. by the warlike omen as well as by the sight of her temple, *v.* 531, near which they now land.

545. capita : Gr. acc. with *velamur,* which is used in the middle sense.

546. maxima, *as most important.*

547. Argivae : Juno was especially venerated in Argos.

548. ordine : i.e. with all the details.

549. A spondaic verse. — **cornua antemnarum,** *the tips of the yards.* The yards are adjusted to the wind (see Fig. 30).

550. Graiugenum : see note, *v.* 398.

551. hinc, *on this side.* — **Herculei :** many legends connected Hercules with this coast, but that respecting the founding of Tarentum has been lost. — **si vera,** etc.: these words belong only to *Herculei* (founded by him if, etc.).

552. diva Lacinia : a temple of Juno on the headland of Lacinium, on the east coast of Bruttium. — **contra,** *opposite* (on the other side of the bay).

553. Caulonis, Scylaceum : see map. — **navifragum :** though not rugged, the coast is in an exposed situation.

554. e fluctu, *rising from the waves.*

555. gemitum, *moaning* of the distant whirlpool. Cf. Spenser, *Faery Queen,* ii. 12. 2 :

> An hidous roaring far away they heard,
> That all their sences filled with affright ;
> And streight they saw the raging surges reard
> Up to the skyes.

556. fractas ... voces : *the sound of breakers dashing on the shore.*

558. haec illa, *this is that.*

559. hos : emphatic ; translate, *these are the cliffs which Helenus,* etc.

560. eripite, *save yourselves.* — **pariter,** *with even stroke.* — **insurgite :** see note to *v.* 207.

561. rudentem, *roaring* (of the noise of the water at the bow, as the helm is suddenly put to starboard to turn their course southward).

564. et idem (plur., agreeing with subject), *and again* (lit. *the same*).

565. subducta unda : abl. abs. expressing cause. — **Manis :** often thus used of the World Below in general. — **desedimus,** *we find ourselves sunk* (lit. *we have settled,* therefore are down).

566. ter : cf. i. 116. — **scopuli,** *the reefs* at the bottom. — **dedere :** i. e. as we descended to them.

567. rorantia, *wet with spray* : which, high as we were, was tossed still higher, seeming to reach the sky.

568. cum sole : at sunset.

569. Cyclopum oris : the east coast of Sicily, near Ætna.

570. portus ... immotus, *a haven undisturbed, and far from* (*ab*) *approach of winds.* — **ingens ipse,** *ample in itself* (and safe enough), but for the thunders of neighboring Ætna.

571. ruinis, *crashing sounds* (of falling bodies within).

572. prorumpit, *belches forth.* — **nubem :** i. e. the mountain sometimes throws smoke and ashes, sometimes a real eruption of lava.

573. turbine piceo, *with pitch-black* (i. e. thick like the smoke of pitch) *smoke-wreaths.* Milton's imitation of this description (*Paradise Lost,* i. 232–237) is famous.

575. viscera : i. e. liquid lava.

577. glomerat, *hurls in balls of fire.* — **fundo :** abl. of separation.

578. Enceladi : one of the giants who warred against the gods.

579. urgueri : indicates the oppressive weight of the mountain.

580. exspirare, etc., *breathes out through broken craters* (i. e. those broken by the outburst of the fire). Enceladus has been pierced by a thunderbolt and keeps breathing fire through the wounds.

581. mutet, *shifts.*

582. subtexere fumo, *lines with wreaths of smoke.*

583. tecti : it will be remembered that they usually went on shore at night. — **immania monstra,** *prodigious horrors.*

585. aethra (abl. of cause), *with the light.*

586. polus : sc. *erat.*

587. nox intempesta : *the dead of night.*

588. primo Eoo : i. e. at the earliest dawn. The adjective suggests the early hour, though the noun refers here to the quarter of the sky.

591. nova, *strange.* — **cultu,** *in plight, condition* (as resulting from care, food, etc.). Cf. Tennyson, *Enoch Arden:*

> Downward from his mountain-gorge
> Stept the long-hair'd, long-bearded solitary,
> Brown, looking hardly human, strangely clad,
> Muttering and mumbling.

593. respicimus : i. e. as we are returning to our ships.

594. consertum : supply *erat ei.* — **cetera** (Gr. accusative), *in other respects.*

597. paulum : opposed to *mox* below.

599. testor : sc. *vos.*

600. spirabile lumen, *the air we breathe.* Open air and daylight are often confused in ancient poetry ; so *ferre in auras, to bring to light.*

601. tollite, *take me on board* (strictly, *take me away*). — **quascumque :** *any whatsoever.* — **terras :** acc. of limit of motion.

602. scio : final *o* is shortened. — **me :** sc. *esse.*

603. petiisse : sc. *me* as subject.

605. spargite, *tear me in pieces and cast me* (lit. *scatter me*).

606. si pereo : pres. for fut.; A. 468; D. 657; B. 261; G. 228. Observe the hiatus between *pereo* and *hominum.*

607. genibus volutans haerebat, *grovelling on his knees he clung to us.*

608. qui : here = *quis.* — **fari :** poetical inf. instead of a subjunc. clause (Introd. § 78).

609. deinde, *since :* i. e. after the city was taken.

610. multa, *much :* cognate acc.

611. praesenti, *for the moment :* i. e. until we have heard his story.

613. infelicis : so called on account of his long wanderings.

614. genitore . . . paupere : abl. abs. expressing cause with *profectus.*

615. fortuna : i. e. my condition of poverty. — **mansisset :** i. e. would that I had been content to remain poor; A. 442; D. 681, II, 2; B. 279, 2; G. 261.

616. dum trepidi linquunt, *while, in trembling haste, they were leaving :* A. 556; D. 763; B. 293, I; G. 570.

618. sanie, etc. : these descriptive ablatives are equivalent to an adjective phrase qualifying *domus ; sanie* is used without a modifier, contrary to the rule, because it is coupled with *dapibus,* which has an adjective (Introd. § 61).

619. ipse, *the master* (opposed to *domus*).

621. nec visu facilis : i. e. one on whom no one can look without terror ; see A. 510; D. 882, II ; B. 340, 2 ; G. 436. — **ulli :** dat. of reference.

622. visceribus : abl. with *vescor* (Introd. § 56).

623. egomet : emphatic, *I, with my own eyes ;* the story is repeated from Od. ix. 289–293 ; Bry. 325.

628. quidem, *to be sure.*

629. oblitusve . . . Ithacus, *nor was the Ithacan forgetful of himself,* i. e. of his natural skill in stratagems.

630. simul = *simul ac, as soon as.*

634. vices : acc., *our places* or *posts.* — **circum :** adv.

635. terebramus : in Homer, Ulysses twirls the stake "as a ship-carpenter bores with an auger," while his companions hold it (Od. ix. 384; Bry. 446).

636. latebat, *was hidden* under the projecting brow.

637. Argolici : the shields of the Greeks were round while those of the Romans were long. — **clipei :** a large shield of brass, glittering as well as round. — **Phoebeae lampadis,** *the torch of Phœbus,* i. e. the sun. — **instar :** properly a noun in apposition with *quod,* but it may be translated by *like* (see ii. 15, note).

638. umbras : the vengeance for their death is looked upon as an offering to their departed spirits (cf. note to *v.* 321).

641. qualis, etc., *for as hideous and huge as Polyphemus, who,* etc.: the antecedent words would be *tales* and *tanti* agreeing with *Cyclopes, v.* 644.

643. volgo, *everywhere.*

645. tertia : i. e. is filling her horns *a third time.* Such formal ways of indicating lapse of time became a poetical convention. See, for example, *Hamlet,* iii. 2. 165–168 :

> Full thirty times hath Phœbus' cart gone round
> Neptune's salt wash and Tellus' orbèd ground,
> And thirty dozen moons with borrowed sheen
> About the world have times twelve thirties been.

646. cum traho, *since I have been dragging out,* etc. The present is used because he is still dragging out this miserable existence : A. 466; cf. D. 650; B. 259, 4; G. 580, R.[3]

647. ab rupe : the rock where he was on the lookout for ships (*v.* 651).

650. volsis radicibus : abl. of means. — **pascunt :** sc. *me.*

652. quaecumque fuisset, *whatever it should be :* subj. in informal indir. disc. standing for fut. perf. of the direct; A. 592, 2; D. 889; B. 323; G. 508, 3.

653. addixi, *surrendered :* a Roman law-term for giving anybody or anything completely into one's possession. — **satis :** i. e. I shall be satisfied whatever the result.

654. potius : i. e. rather than fall into their hands.

656. ipsum emphasizes the difference between a mere account of him (such as they had just heard) and the sight of the monster himself. — **vasta . . . moventem,** *moving along with his vast bulk,* i. e. with a clumsy, lumbering gait befitting his monstrous size; *mole* is abl. of manner.

657. nota : hence he could find his way thither.

658. This verse is a good example of *onomatopœia* or the fitting of sound to sense. The hesitating movement of the blinded giant is suggested by the series of spondees. — **cui :** dat. of separation.

659. manu : abl. of place where.

660. ea, *this* : referring to the sheep, but attracted into the gender of its predicate noun *voluptas*; A. 296, *a*; D. 532, *a*; B. 246, 5; G. 211, R.[5]

662. aequora, *the open sea* ; and even then the water was only up to his waist (*v.* 665).

663. inde : lit. *thence, from it* (i. e. from the sea). Translate, *with the salt water he washed,* etc.

664. dentibus infrendens, *gnashing his teeth* : abl. of instrument. — **gemitu :** abl. of manner.

665. iam, etc.: i. e. he has got so far into deep water (*medium,* cf. *v.* 73, note) without wetting his body.

666. celerare, incidere : historical infinitives.

667. sic merito, *as he deserved* (lit. *so having deserved* : i. e. *ut recipe-retur*).

668. remis : abl. of means.

669. ad sonitum vocis, *toward the sound* : *vox* is here poetically used for the *voice* (i. e. the splash and rattle) of the oars. Cf. *v.* 556, where it is used of the sound of the waves.

671. nec potis, etc., *and cannot keep above the waves in his pursuit* : i. e. he is out of his depth in the open sea (*Ionios fluctus*); *potis est,* older form of *potest,* often omits *est,* as here.

672. quo, *at which* : abl. of cause.

673. penitus : i. e. far from the sea.

676. ruit, complent : for change of number see ii. 64, note.

677. adstantis . . . torvo, *standing there to no purpose with fierce and angry looks* (lit. *with fierce eye*); *lumine* is abl. of manner, like *mole* in *v.* 656. — **nequiquam :** i. e. harmless in the distance.

678. caelo, *to the sky* : dat. of place to which.

679. quales cum, *as when* (lit., supplying *tales, such as when,* etc.).

681. constitĕrunt, *stand.* For the short penult see Introd. § 111. — **Iovis :** the oak is sacred to Jupiter. — **Dianae :** the cypress, a funereal tree, is sacred to Diana in her character of *Hecate,* or goddess of the Lower World.

682. rudentis excutere, *to shake out our sails* (properly, the ropes that held them to the yards when furled; see *v.* 267, note). — **quocumque,** *for any course.*

683. ventis : abl. of instrument. — **secundis :** i. e. to take advantage of the wind, and sail before it, though it would take them north (see below).

684. contra . . . cursus : this passage is of doubtful meaning. It may be rendered, *on the other hand the commands,* etc., *warn us* (lit. the ships)

*not to hold our course between Scylla and Charybdis, with little chance
of escape from death either way* (i. e. towards whichever side of the passage
we steer). *Viam* is in apposition with *Scyllam* and *Charybdim*; *discrimine
parvo* is abl. of quality; and *ni* is to be taken in the sense of *ne* by an
antiquated usage. The wind is evidently southerly, so that to follow their
first thought (*metus acer agit*) and run before the wind (*secundis*) would
bring them into the Straits of Messina between Scylla and Charybdis.
Apparently they could not go south on account of the wind, for their ships
could not lie so close to the wind as our modern craft.

686. retro, *directly back* whence they came, as their only other course
with a southerly wind was eastward again.

687. ecce autem, *but lo !* just at this crisis the wind changed fair and
gave them a southerly course. — **angusta,** etc. : because it came from the
strait where the promontory of Pelorus was.

688. vivo saxo : abl. of material.

690. talia, *such places as these* are pointed out by Achæmenides as they
pass. — **relegens errata litora,** *retracing his wanderings along the shore.*

692. Sicanio praetenta sinu, *stretched in front of a Sicilian bay*, i.e.
of the Great Harbor of Syracuse ; *sinu* is dat. with *praetenta*. The island
(Ortygia) lies east of the northern part of the harbor and north of the promontory of Plemmyrium.

693. priores, *the ancients.*

694. Alpheum : the river god Alphēus pursued the nymph Arethusa
from Elis under the sea to Sicily. The story is associated with the fountain
named Arethusa in the island of Ortygia. See Shelley's poem *Arethusa.*

696. ore : abl. of means. — **undis :** Introd. § 28 ; the prose construction
would be *cum* with the abl.

697. iussi, *as bidden* (by Helenus). — **numina magna :** probably Diana
and her brother Apollo.

698. stagnantis : i. e. the river Helorus overflowed the banks, rendering
the soil very fertile (*praepingue*).

699. hinc, *next.*

700. fatis . . . moveri, *by fate never permitted to be removed.* The
people of Camerina had been warned by an oracle not to drain a marsh (of
the same name) near their town. They disobeyed, and the enemy, entering
that way, captured the city.

702. immanis . . . dicta, *Gela, so called from the name of its impetuous stream.* — **Gelā** (nom.) : *a* long as in Greek. — **fluvii :** the double *i* in
gen. of nouns in *-ius* occurs in only one other place in Virgil, ix. 151.

704. magnanimum (gen. plur.), *high-spirited.*

705. datis ventis : i. e. probably, now sailing with the wind, as just here
the coast turns much more to the northward, and we must suppose another
favorable change of wind, as in *v.* 687.

706. dura saxis, *rough with rocks* (instrumental ablative).

707. inlaetabilis : on account of the death of Anchises.

711. nequiquam : because he did not live to reach Italy. — **periclis :** dat. of separation (Introd. § 32).

712. Helenus : see *vv.* 381–432. — **moneret :** after *cum* concessive.

713. Celaeno : see *vv.* 253–257.

714. hic, haec : both refer to the passage to Drepanum. For the gender see note on *ea, v.* 660.

716. unus : i.e. he alone spoke while the rest listened (*intentis*).

717. renarrabat, *recounted* (not telling them a second time, but going through them again by thus relating them).

718. hic : at this point. — **quievit,** *went to rest.*

BOOK IV

In the episode of Dido, one of the most famous stories in all literature, Virgil has not only come nearer than any ancient writer to the tone of modern romantic feeling, but he has delineated, with remarkable truth and delicacy of portraiture, the character at once of a fond woman and an oriental queen. Doubtless the poet owes something to the history of Antony and Cleopatra. The defeat at Actium, the death of Mark Antony, and the death of Cleopatra had produced a powerful effect on the Roman imagination and were fresh in all men's minds when this part of the Æneid was written. The story of the Egyptian queen may well have suggested to Virgil some traits in the character of the imperious Dido, and, in particular, the passion of barbaric wrath, pride, and despair which closes her life. Shakspere's Cleopatra may be compared with profit.

The episode of Dido has exercised a powerful effect on modern literature. Of English versions of the story one of the most interesting is that in Chaucer's *Legend of Good Women*, where the old tale is retold in the spirit of mediæval romance.

1. at : contrasting Dido's restlessness with *quievit*, end of Book iii. — **cura :** a regular word for the pangs of love.

2. venis, *with her blood* (lit. *with her veins*). — **carpitur,** *is consumed* : the image is that of a flame, which *catches* successively upon the objects within its reach.

3. multa, *great* : the four points are moral character (*virtus*), nobility (*gentis honos*), personal beauty (*voltus*), eloquence (*verba*). — **animo :** dative of place to which.

6. postera : belongs to *Aurora*. — **Phoebea lampade :** cf. iii. 637. Apollo is constantly identified with the sun.

8. male sana : see ii. 23, note.

9. suspensam, *in my anxiety* : cf. *cura*, above.

10. quis, etc., *who is this strange guest who*, etc.: as often happens in Latin, there are here two clauses compressed into one.

11. quem . . . armis, *how noble his mien ! how brave his heart and deeds of arms !* **quem** is in predicate apposition with *sese*; *forti pectore et armis* is abl. of quality. The literal translation is *bearing himself what [a man] in countenance, with what a brave heart and arms.*

12. equidem, *I'm sure.* — **vana,** *idle*, i. e. groundless.

13. degeneres: the emphasis on *degeneres* gives the passage a meaning different from the apparent sense of the words and is best reproduced in English by changing to the passive : "*ignoble souls are betrayed by fear* "; the implication is that Æneas' soul is NOT *degener*, since he is brave.

14. exhausta, *that he had endured.*

15. animo: abl. of place where.

16. ne . . . vellem, *not to wish*, etc.: substantive clause, subject of *sederet*; A. 563, *d*; D. 723; B. 295, 4; G. 546. — **cui,** *to any one.* — **vinclo:** abl. of manner.

17. deceptam morte fefellit, *deceived and disappointed me by his death.*

18. pertaesum fuisset (sc. *me*), *if I were not utterly weary*: impers. —**thalami taedaeque,** *of marriage and the bridal torch*: Introd. § 21. Torches were borne before the bridal pair in the marriage procession, and Hymenæus, the god of marriage, is represented with a torch (see *vv.* 167 (note), 338–339). Cf.

> They light the nuptial torch, and bid invoke
> Hymen, then first to marriage rites invoked.
> > *Paradise Lost,* xi. 590–591.

19. potui, *I might perhaps have*: A. 517, *c*; D. 797, *a*; B. 304, 3, *a*; G. 597, R.[3] — **culpae,** *fault*, i. e. proving false to the memory of Sychæus by loving another.

20, 21. miseri . . . penatis, *since poor Sychæus met his fate and our household gods were stained by a brother's murder* (lit. *since the fates of poor Sychæus and the penates bespattered*, etc.). For the murder of Dido's husband by her brother Pygmalion see i. 343–356.

22. animum . . . impulit, *has moved my heart to waver.* — **labantem:** proleptic; cf. *submersas*, i. 69 and note.

24. ima, *to its lowest depths.* — **optem:** potential subjunctive; A. 447, 1; D. 684; B. 280; G. 257. — **dehiscat, adigat:** subjunctive in substantive clauses of purpose, *ut* being omitted.

27. ante repeats *prius* (*v.* 24).

29. abstulit, *has borne away with him.* — **habeat, servet:** hortatory.

31. luce . . . sorori, *more loved* (voc.) *by your sister than light = sister, dearer to me than light.* — **luce:** abl. of comparison. — **sorori:** dat. of agent.

32. perpetua iuventa, *all your youth long*: abl. of duration of time; A. 424, *b*; D. 423; B. 231, 1; G. 393, R.² — **carpere** (passive), *will you waste away?* Cf. *carpitur*, *v.* 2.

33. noris: syncopated form of *noveris* (Introd. § 91, *n.*).

34. id . . . curare, *care for that*, i.e. whether you marry again or not. — **cinerem aut Manīs:** a reply to Dido's protestation above, *vv.* 28–29; the ashes and the shade of Sychæus can have no interest in her actions now.

35. esto, *and if they did* (lit. *let it be* [*so*]), referring to the preceding: even in that case, you have done all that could be expected. — **mariti,** *suitors.* — **aegram,** *in your grief*: sc. *te.*

36. Libyae, *of Libya.* — **Tyro:** a comparatively rare use of the ablative of place whence with a noun (but very common in English). — **despectus:** sc. *est.*

37. Africa: adj. — **triumphis dives:** i.e. warlike and victorious.

38. placito, *pleasing to you.* — **amori:** dative; an extension of the dat. with verbs of *resisting* or *contending* (Introd. § 28).

39. quorum consederis: indir. quest.

40. hinc . . . hinc: as usual, of the two sides.

41. infreni, *riding without bridles*, alluding to a well-known habit of the Numidians, who were famous as horsemen; but perhaps meant also to suggest the sense *unbridled, fierce.* — **inhospita:** i.e. on account of the marauding tribes on the shore.

42. deserta siti, *deserted because of drought*, and hence affording no retreat or assistance.

43. Barcaei: the wild tribes of the desert — like the modern Bedouins — would alarm the imagination still more than a regular force. — **Tyro:** ablative of place from which.

44. germani: i.e. Pygmalion; see i. 361.

45. dis auspicibus, *under the guidance of the gods*: abl. absolute. — **equidem,** *in fact.* — **Iunone secunda** (abl. abs.): Juno is mentioned both as tutelary divinity of Carthage and as goddess of marriage.

46. hunc cursum: i.e. their course hither.

47. quam = *qualem.* — **urbem:** pred. apposition.

48. coniugio tali: abl. of cause or means. The learner will have seen by this time that the ablative cannot accurately be divided off into its various categories, because an author himself often did not know which one he was using, any more than we determine exactly the shade of meaning in which we use a common preposition.

49. quantis rebus, *to what a height*: dative.

50. deos veniam: objects of a verb of *asking* (Introd. § 40). — **sacris litatis:** i.e. having propitiated the gods by fit offerings.

51. indulge, *give way to.*

52. desaevit, *until winter has spent its rage* (lit. *while it is spending*). — **aquosus:** cf. i. 535, note.

53. quassatae: sc. *sunt.* — **tractabile:** sc. *est.* — **caelum:** here, as often, put for the weather.

55. pudorem, *her scruples: pudor* is that feeling of shame which rises from self-respect.

56. per aras, *from altar to altar.*

57. This sacrifice was a kind of sin-offering.

58. Cereri: Ceres is called " the lawgiver " on account of the influence of agriculture on the institutions of nomadic tribes. She, together with Apollo and Bacchus, as well as Juno, has to do with marriage rites.

59. Iunoni: Juno was the special guardian of women, each woman having her own Juno, as every man his *genius.* She presided over marriage and (in her character of Lucina) over childbirth. — **ante omnis,** *above all* the other gods. — **cui . . . curae:** double dative (Introd. § 33); sc. *sunt.*

61. vaccae: here sacrificed, it seems, to Juno alone. — **media inter cornua,** *between the horns.*

62. ora: i. e. of the statues. — **spatiatur:** before a sacrifice the Roman performed a slow measured movement before the altar, holding a lighted torch. — **pinguis:** the portion laid upon the altar consisted principally of bones and fat.

63. instaurat diem donis, *renews the offerings the next day* (lit. *renews the day with gifts,* i. e. makes a new day of sacrifice by means of the offerings). This shows her anxiety to secure divine favor. Possibly the omens continued unfavorable. — **reclusis** (*opened*) **pectoribus:** dat. This ceremony represents the *extispicium,* the most important form of augury ; the heart, liver, etc., were the organs observed. The final syllable of *pectoribus* is here long : Introd. § 110.

65. ignarae: i. e. in thinking these rites can avail. — **furentem,** *one madly in love.*

66. ēst: A. 201; D. 257; B. 128 ; G. 172. — **mollis:** better taken with *flamma* than with *medullas.*

69. coniectā sagittā, *when the arrow has reached its mark.* Virgil avoids the repetition of *sagitta* by using *telis* and *ferrum* (*v.* 71) and *harundo* (*v.* 73).

70. Cresia: the Cretans were famous archers.

71. pastor agens: the figure is of a chance shot by a shepherd, which has taken effect without his knowledge.

75. paratam: emphatic; he need not go on, seeking a city yet to be built.

77. eadem, *she, again:* A. 298, *b*; D. 547; B. 248, 1 ; G. 310. Or *eadem* may agree with *convivia:* i. e. *a banquet, as on the night before.* — **labente die,** *at the close of day,* the usual time for the principal meal.

78. demens, *reckless,* since this would only inflame her unhappy passion.

79. pendet ab ore, *hangs on his words.*

80. digressi [*sunt*], *when the guests are gone.* — **lumen . . . premit,** *the moon in her turn hides her light.*

82. stratis relictis, *the couch* [in the banquet-hall] *which he has left.*

83. absens, absentem: a favorite collocation of words with the ancients, bringing the same or kindred words together.

84. Ascanium: the real Ascanius, who has of course been brought back by Venus. Cupid's masquerade is over (see i. 683–694). — **genitoris imagine capta,** *charmed by his likeness to his father* (*the image of his father* in him).

Fig. 36

85. infandum: used in its literal sense. — **si possit,** [*to try*] *if she can:* indirect question; A. 576, *a*; D. 814, *c*; B. 300, 3; G. 460, *b*.

87. portus, etc.: notice that the sentence falls into two parts connected by *-ve*; the second part is again subdivided by *aut.* — **propugnacula bello,** *ramparts for war.*

88. minae murorum, *menacing walls:* cf. *rotarum lapsus*, ii. 235, and n.

89. machina: a general word: prob. here the crane or *derrick* standing useless at the top of the unfinished walls (see Fig. 36).

90. quam, *that she* (Dido): subject of *teneri*, *was possessed.* — **peste,** *plague* (the madness of love).

91. famam, *regard for her reputation:* a common form of expression in Latin, where we with more exactness require two words instead of one. The Latin, with its small vocabulary and brevity of expression, often makes one word mean more than we do.

92. adgreditur, *accosts:* used of one who begins a dialogue.

93. vero: ironical. — **refertis,** *you carry off:* used of carrying away the booty won in battle.

94. puer tuus: Cupid.

96. nec . . . fallit, *nor does it at all escape me that,* etc.; *adeo* merely gives emphasis to the whole statement. — **fallit:** the subject is *te habuisse* (indir. disc.).

98. quo, etc., *to what end (with) all this strife ?* We must suppose an original ellipsis of *tendis,* or some such word, taking the noun (*certamine*) as abl. of means.

99. quin potius exercemus: *why do we not rather bring about ?* A. 449, *b*; B. 281, 3; G. 273.

101. per ossa, *throughout her frame:* cf. i. 660.

102. communem, *in common,* i. e. with joint authority.

103. auspiciis: since only the highest magistrates could " take the auspices," this word came to mean *authority.* — **liceat:** *let her:* sc. *ei,* i. e. Dido. — **marito:** dative with *servire.*

104. dotalis Tyrios, *the Tyrians as a dowry:* i. e. the portion brought by the wife to her husband (*dos*), not a marriage-portion settled upon the wife. The gift is spoken of as given to Venus, as if she too, as the mother of Æneas, were to become a tutelary deity of Carthage.

105. olli: Introd. § 91, *f.* — **enim:** giving the reason for her answering deceitfully, i. e. she matches craft with craft. — **simulata mente,** *with deceitful purpose.*

106. regnum Italiae: the kingdom which Æneas was to establish in Italy. — **averteret,** *turn aside:* sometimes, as here, a clause of purpose that does not contain a comparative is introduced by *quo, in order that:* A. 531, *a,* N.; D. 718, N.[2]; B. 282, 1, *a*; G. 545, R.[1] — **oras:** acc. of place to which.

107. quis . . . abnuat, *who so foolish as to refuse such an offer ?* deliberative subjunctive: A. 444; D. 678; B. 277; G. 265.

109. si . . . sequatur: the apodosis is contained in *quis talia,* etc., which is equivalent to a statement that Venus would assent in case, etc. — **quod memoras,** *which you suggest.*

110, 111. sed . . . feror, *but I am led by the fates, uncertain whether,* i. e. I have no will of my own, and it may be that this course is not fated. — **si . . . velit:** see note on *possit, v.* 85. — **si . . . profectis,** *whether Jupiter wishes that there should be one and the same city for the Tyrians and the wanderers from Troy:* dat. of possession.

115. qua ratione, *in what way.* — **quod instat,** *that which is urgent:* the marriage.

116. confieri (*conficio*): A. 204, *c*; D. 261, *c*; B. 131, N.; G. 173, N.[2] — **possit:** indir. quest.; the subject is the omitted antecedent of *quod.* — **paucis:** sc. *verbis.*

117. venatum: supine with *ire* to show purpose; A. 509; D. 882, I; B. 340, 1; G. 435.

119. Titan = *Sol.* Hyperion, the father of the Sun and Moon was a Titan.— **retexerit,** *shall disclose.*

120. his : dat. after *infundam.*— **grandine :** abl. abs.

121. dum trepidant alae, *while the huntsmen hurry hither and thither*: the *alae* are properly the outriders or "beaters" who drive the game towards the grand *battue*, as cavalry (the usual meaning of the word) serve as skirmishers in battle.— **indagine,** *with their closing lines* (of beaters), properly the driving in, i. e. the process by which the game are hemmed in at the skirts of the wood.

Fig. 37

125. si mihi certa : i. e. if I can rely on it.

126. This line is supposed to be wrongly inserted here from i. 73.

127. hic hymenaeus erit, *here shall be their marriage-rite.* — **non adversata petenti,** *not refusing her request*: sc. *ei* with *petenti.*

128. dolis repertis : abl. abs., but translate as if object of *risit.*

130. portis : abl. of place from which. — **iubare exorto :** abl. abs.

131. retia, plagae, venabula : the verb is *ruunt,* which with these subjects is equivalent to *are quickly brought,* but with *equites* etc. has its proper sense of *rush on, hasten forth.* Such a use of a verb in two senses is called *zeugma.* — **rara :** i. e. with large meshes.

132. Massyli : i. e. her African attendants. — **odora canum vis,** *the keen-scented pack of hounds.*

133. limina : the palace door. The picture is that of a distinguished Roman whose clients and friends wait at his door to escort him to the forum.— **primi,** *the noblest.*

137. chlamydem circumdata limbo, *wearing a Tyrian cloak with an embroidered border.* See Fig. 37. For acc. and middle voice see Introd. §§ 43, 94.

138. cui pharetra [est], *she has a quiver*: dat. of possessor.— **nodantur in aurum,** *is gathered into a knot with gold*; i. e. a gold band of some sort confined it.

139. fibula : apparently a gold buckle to her girdle.

142. infert se socium, *advances as her companion.* — **agmina iungit :** i. e. his own band with Dido's.

143. qualis . . . Apollo, *like Apollo, when,* etc.— **hibernam Lyciam,** *his winter home in Lycia.*

144. maternam : he was born in Delos.

145. instaurat, *renews* (after the interruption caused by his absence).

146. picti, *painted* (cf. the ancient Britons and other savage peoples). — **Agathyrsi :** Scythian tribe. The worshippers of Apollo came even " from the ends of the earth."

147. molli . . . fingens, *shaping his loose locks, he confines them with the soft garland.* — **fluentem :** Apollo is represented with long hair (cf. Milton's " unshorn Apollo ").

150. tantum decus, *an equal glory* (with Apollo).

151. ventum [*est*]: impersonal; A. 208, *d*; D. 266, *b*; B. 138, IV; G. 208, 2.

154. transmittunt (sc. *se*) **campos,** *course the open fields* : campos is obj. of *trans-.*

157. equo : abl. of cause.

158. pecora, *tame herds* (as he calls them with contempt). — **votis,** *in answer to his prayers* : indir. obj. of *dari.*

159. fulvum : a mere ornamental epithet.

164. tecta, *shelter.* — **amnes,** *broad rivers,* a descriptive exaggeration.

166–168. prima, *eldest* (of deities). — **Tellus, Iuno :** the ceremonies of a Roman marriage are, as it were, imitated by the powers of nature. The flashes of lightning (*ignes*) were the marriage-torches (see *vv.* 18, 338–339); the howling (*ulularunt*) of the nymphs in the tree-tops (*summo vertice*), i. e., apparently, the roaring of the wind, stood for the festal cries and the hymeneal song, while the word chosen suggests an evil omen. Tellus and Juno, deities of earth and sky, attended, apparently, as *auspices nuptiarum.* These were persons whose duty it was, originally, to take the auspices at a wedding (cf. i. 345, note), but who, in historical times, had merely a ceremonial function, repeating, doubtless, some set form of words, though no omens were actually taken. In this capacity Tellus and Juno *dant signum,* i. e. for the marriage to proceed.

To the names of these two deities are added the ceremonies belonging to each, — the flashes in the air, and the effects of the storm on the earth (*ulularunt,* etc.), in chiastic order : A. 597, *f*; D. 934, *f*; B. 350, 11, *c*; G. 682. The *pronuba* was a matron who conducted the bride to the bridal chamber, a duty which Juno here performs. The word was also one of her epithets as goddess of marriage. The sky is *conscius conubiis, witness of the wedlock.* — **conubiis :** dative; A. 377; D. 385; B. 188, 1; G. 344.

169. ille dies primus, *that day first was,* etc.

173. Fama : a celebrated personification. Cf. Bacon, *Fragment of an Essay of Fame* : " The poets make Fame a monster. They describe her in part finely and elegantly, and in part gravely and sententiously. They say, look how many feathers she hath, so many eyes she hath underneath ; so many tongues ; so many voices ; she pricks up so many ears. This is a flourish ; there follow excellent parables ; as that she gathereth strength in going; that she goeth upon the ground, and yet hideth her head in the clouds; that in the day-time she sitteth in a watch-tower, and flieth most by night; that she mingleth things done with things not done; and that she is a terror to great cities."

176. parva metu primo, *small at first because of fear.*

178. ira deorum, *in wrath at the gods*: objective genitive. The Titans who scaled Olympus were sons of Earth; and when they were cast down to Tartarus, Earth in anger produced the new brood of Giants. Cœus was of the former brood, Enceladus of the latter.

179. extremam sororem *her last* [*child*], *sister to Cœus*, etc.

181. monstrum: cf. iii. 658. — **cui,** etc., *who has as many watchful eyes beneath as there are feathers on her body, as many tongues, as many prating mouths, as many listening ears* (lit. *so many mouths sound, she pricks up so many ears*).

184. caeli medio terrae, *midway between heaven and earth*; *medio* is here a noun.

185. stridens, *whizzing* from the swiftness of her flight. The reference is to the buzz of rumor.

186. custos, *keeping watch.*

187. territat: i.e. by the consciousness that she is watching them.

188. tam, etc., *as often persistent in lying and falsehood as* [*she is*] *a messenger of truth.* — **ficti:** Introd. § 16. Cf. Shakspere, *Henry IV*, Part II, Induction:

> Upon my tongues continual slanders ride,
> The which in every language I pronounce,
> Stuffing the ears of men with false reports.

189. populos replebat, *was filling the ears of the people.*

190. facta, etc., *truth and falsehood* (lit. *things done*, etc.).

191, 192. venisse, dignetur: indir. disc. — **iungere:** complem. inf.

193. hiemem . . . quam longa fovere, *are making the whole winter long a time of wantonness.* To fondle or pamper the winter is a poetic way of saying to pass the winter in luxury. In fact, the winter is interrupted by the divine message (*v.* 222). — **quam longa** [sc. *tam longam*], *as long as it lasts.*

195. virum = *virorum.*

198. Hammone: Ammon, the great god of Thebes in Egypt (see Fig. 38), identified by the Romans with Jupiter ("whom gentiles Ammon call and Libyan Jove," *Paradise Lost*, iv. 277). Iarbas is here represented as having introduced his worship into Libya. — **rapta . . . nympha:** abl. abs.; translate as if abl. of source with *satus.*

200. vigilem ignem: the fire was never suffered to go out on the altar of Ammon.

201. excubias (appos. with *ignem*): the fires are poetically called *sentinels*.

202. solum, limina : either nominative (sc. *erat* and *erant*), or in the same construction as *ignem*. — **pingue** indicates frequent sacrifices and *florentia sertis* frequent festivals (cf. i. 417).

203. amens animi, *distracted in mind*; A. 358; D. 488; B. 204, 4; G. 374, N.[7]

204. dicitur orasse : personal constr.; A. 582; D. 840; B. 332, *c*; G. 528, 1. — **inter numina :** i. e. with their visible forms (statues) about him.

205. multa Iovem : two objects of a verb of *asking* (Introd. § 40).

206. nunc : opposed to the doubt he raises in *v.* 208 that their sacrifices are useless. — **Lenaeum libat honorem,** *pours out a libation of wine* (lit. *a Bacchic honor*).

208. an te . . . horremus, *or is it without reason that we stand in awe of thee?* The alternative is either that Jupiter does not see what is going on, or that he cares not for mortal affairs at all (which is conceived as unlikely); in the latter case the fear of the gods is idle.

Fig. 38

209, 210. caecique . . . miscent : *and are the fires in the clouds that terrify our hearts purposeless, and are the mutterings of the thunder without a meaning?* Literally, *Do blind fires in the clouds* (i. e. lightnings that strike blindly, without any definite purpose) *terrify our hearts and mingle empty* (i. e. meaningless) *murmurs?* These phenomena were regarded as the avenging action of Jupiter. — **miscent :** the word means to produce any confused effect; here used of the wild thunder. See Vocabulary.

212. pretio, *at a price* : i. e. on land she had purchased (see i. 367–368), not being strong enough to take it by force ; hence her conduct now is the more arrogant.

213. loci leges, *authority over the region.*

214. dominum, *as her lord* : said scornfully.

215. ille Paris : so called as being both vain and luxurious, and as being the successful suitor of another's wife. — **semiviro :** an epithet applied to Phrygians partly on account of their dress, but not appropriate to the Trojans of the heroic age.

216. mitra : a Phrygian cap, having lapels which covered ears and sometimes chin (see Fig. 39, head of Paris, from an antique bust). — **madentem :** i. e. with perfumed ointments.

217. subnixus, *supporting his chin.* Anything worn on the head, except for defence in battle, was regarded as a mark of effeminacy. The Emperor Hadrian " marched on foot and bare-headed over the snows of Caledonia and the sultry plains of Upper Egypt " (Gibbon). — **rapto,** *the spoil,* i. e. her and her kingdom. — **potĭtur :** here third conjugation.

218. quippe, *while we, forsooth* (with sarcasm). — **famam,** *story,* i. e. the belief that the gods help mankind ; cf. n. on *v.* 208. That is, we foolishly worship thee as a righteous divinity.

219. aras tenentem, *grasping the altar* : as appealing more urgently for protection. Cf. 1 Kings, i. 50 : "And Adonijah feared because of Solomon, and arose and went and caught hold on the horns of the altar."

221. oblitos famae : gen. with a verb of *forgetting* (Introd. § 18).

222. Mercurium : Mercury, the Italian god of merchandise (*merx*), was identified because of this function with the Grecian *Hermes,* the messenger of the gods, protector of heralds, and divinity of persuasion and intercourse between man and man. — **adloquitur :** the last syllable is lengthened before the cæsura.

223. vade age : cf. iii. 462. — **pinnis :** the wings of Mercury are here on his sandals ; sometimes they are also on his cap or on his staff.

224. ducem : object of *adloquere.*

225. non respicit, *pays no regard to.*

226. celeris per auras : i. e. swiftly through the air. The idea is something like " on the wings of the wind."

Fig. 39

227. non talem, *not such a man as this.*

228. -que ideo, *or for this.* — **bis :** once from Diomed (Il. v. 311–317; Bry. 378), and once from the flames of Troy (Æn. ii. 589–633). — **armis :** abl. of separation.

229. sed fore, *but* [she promised] *that he should be one who,* etc. Her promise included the warlike story of after ages, as implied in *v.* 231. — **qui regeret :** rel. clause of purpose or of characteristic.

232, 233. si . . . laborem, *if the glory of such great exploits fires him not at all, and he does not undertake the labor for the sake of his own renown.* — **nulla :** agrees with *gloria.* — **ipse** emphasizes *sua* but may be left untranslated.

234. Ascanio, arces : A. 369; cf. B. 187, II, *a* ; G. 346, N.²

235. spe : notice the hiatus at the cæsura (Introd. § 108). — **inimica :** so called in anticipation of later history (the Punic Wars), in which the very existence of Rome was threatened by the Carthaginians.

237. naviget : i. e. this one word of command contains the substance of the whole matter (*summa :* noun). — **haec, hic,** *this :* referring to the

command preceding, but agreeing as usual with the predicate (cf. iii. 714).
— **nostri :** we should expect *noster*, instead of the genitive of the personal
pronoun used possessively.

238–258. The descent of Mercury has been often imitated. Cf. the long
description of the descent of Raphael, *Paradise Lost*, v. 246 ff. :

> So spake th' Eternal Father, and fulfill'd
> All justice : nor delay'd the winged saint
> After his charge receiv'd.
>
> .   .   .   .
>
> At once on th' eastern cliff of Paradise
> He lights.
>
> .   .   .   .
>
> Like Maia's son he stood.

Of more recent poets Shelley has the most famous passage of this kind :

> But see, where thro' the azure chasm
>   Of yon forked and snowy hill
> Trampling the slant winds on high
>   With golden-sandalled feet, that glow
> Under plumes of purple dye,
> Like rose-ensanguined ivory,
>   A Shape comes now,
> Stretching on high from his right hand
> A serpent-cinctured wand.
>
> *Prometheus Unbound*, act i.

241. pariter cum, *as swiftly as* (lit. *equally with*).

242. virgam, *the rod* (*caduceus*) twined with two serpents ; often seen
as the emblem of commerce, on account of Mercury's function as god of
trade, but properly the herald's staff, and hence used by Mercury in the
manner described here. — **Orco, Tartara :** both words are used for the
Lower World.

244. morte resignat, *frees* (lit. *unseals*) *from death* : the thought of
v. 242 is repeated.

245. The narrative is resumed after the description. — **illa fretus,** *by
means of this* : Introd. § 66. — **agit,** *sets in motion.* — **trānat** = *transnat.*

247. Atlantis duri, *of much-enduring Atlas.* Maia, Mercury's mother,
was the daughter of Atlas. This mountain, the limit of the world to the
ancients, on which the heaven was supposed to rest, was made a mystical
demigod with human attributes (hence *senis, v.* 251).

248. cinctum . . . caput, *whose pine-grown head is ever girt,* etc.

251. senis, *the aged sire* : cf. our "old as the hills." — **horrida,** *unkempt.*

252. paribus nitens alis, *poised on even wing,* like a sailing bird :
A. 431 ; D. 469, *c* ; B. 218, 3 ; G. 401, N.[6] — **Cyllenius :** Mt. Cyllene in
Arcadia was the birthplace of Mercury.

256. terras, etc.: i.e. skimming near the water.

257. ad: regularly this preposition would precede *litus.*

258. avo: see note, *v.* 247.

260. novantem: i.e. planting new buildings to replace the *magalia.*

261. stellatus iaspide: i.e. on the hilt.

262. laena: a thick woolen cloak, much used under the empire instead of the *toga,* and of a "warm" purple (*ardebat murice*).

264. discreverat: i.e. had separated the thread of the warp with different color, gold-thread on purple.

265. invadit, *attacks* (like *adgreditur, v.* 92, but stronger). — **altae:** a hint at the future grandeur and hostility of Carthage.

266. uxorius, *in doting fondness for your wife.*

271. struis, *aim at,* but used with special reference to the city he is building. — **teris otia,** *waste your time* (lit. *wear away idleness,* i.e. make the time idle instead of laborious, and thus wear it away).

274. spes . . . Iuli (obj. gen.): i.e. the hope connected with Iulus as your heir. As thus used, in connection with *heredis,* the name suggests the Julian house, which claimed descent from Iulus (i. 288, vi. 789).

278. in tenuem, etc.: cf. *Tempest,* iv. 1. 148–150:

> These our actors,
> As I foretold you, were all spirits and
> Are melted into air, into thin air.

283. quid agat: the thought of Æneas *quid agam* (dubitative subj.), etc., in a sort of indir. disc. — **quo . . . adfatu,** *with what form of address?* — **ambire,** *to entreat.*

285. Imitated by Tennyson, *Passing of Arthur,* "This way and that dividing the swift mind."

286. versat, *turns rapidly:* an intensive verb.

287. alternanti, *to him, thus hesitating* whether to inform Dido or not.

289. aptent, cogant, parent, dissimulent: subj. in indir. disc. for imperat. in direct; a verb of ordering is implied in *vocat; summoning them he directs them to,* etc.

290. arma, *arms* (for defence in case of interference) or perhaps *equipments* for the ships. — **rebus novandis:** *for the new course of action.* — **sit:** indir. quest.

291. optima, *best of women:* a mere ornamental epithet.

292. nesciat: subjunc. in a dependent clause in indir. disc. — **speret,** *expect:* used of ill as well as of good expectation. — **rumpi:** A. 580, *c*; B. 331, I; G. 423, N.[5]

293. temptaturum [sc. *esse*]: depending on the idea of saying implied in *vocat.* — **aditus** (acc.), *ways of approach.* — **quae** [sc. *sint*], **quis** [sc. *sit*]: indirect questions, objects of *temptaturum* [*esse*]. — **mollissima fandi**

tempora, *the most pliant moments for speaking*: i. e. those when she will be most compliant. But Dido anticipates him and speaks first.

294. rebus, *for the business.* — **dexter,** *best fitted.*

296. quis possit: deliberative subjunctive.

298. tuta, *however safe*: modifies *omnia.* — **impia,** *cruel.*

300. inops animi: gen. of specification (Introd. § 17).

301. qualis Thyias, *like a Bacchant*: *Thy̆i̯ăs* is dissyllabic here. — **commotis sacris,** *at the revealing of the sacred emblems.* The orgies

Fig. 40

of Bacchus were accompanied by the brandishing of the thyrsus, the clashing of cymbals, and the carrying of the mystic cista containing sacred emblems, the bringing-out of which began the orgy. Cf. Wordsworth, *Duddon Sonnets,* xx:

> Dance, like a Bacchanal, from rock to rock,
> Tossing her frantic thyrsus wide and high.

Fig. 40 (from a vase painting) shows a Bacchic procession. The first Bacchanal has a double tibia, the second a torch and a thyrsus, the third a tambourine, the fourth a thyrsus.

302. audito Baccho, *hearing the cry to Bacchus,* i. e. *Euoë Bacche,* the customary cry of the Bacchants. — **trieterica orgia:** at Thebes; Cithæron, where the night orgies took place, is the mountain range south of the city.

304. ultro, *first,* i. e. before he has found heart to speak.

305. dissimulare posse, *that you could also conceal so great an outrage*: i. e. not only desert me but conceal your going.

306. tacitus: nom. instead of acc. with *te,* the omitted subject of *posse.*

307. The three motives appealed to are love, honor, and pity.

308. moritura Dido, *the thought of Dido, who will die.*

311. quid, *tell me.* — **non arva . . . ignotas,** *fields that were not strange and homes that were not unknown*; i.e. if you had a home to go to instead of being a wanderer in search of lands to settle in, even then you would wait for better weather.

313. peteretur : the apodosis of the two conditions contrary to fact.

314. mene fugis, *is it from me you fly ?* — **te :** obj. of *oro* (*v.* 319); in such appeals some words usually separate *per* and the words it governs.

315. aliud . . . nihil, *nothing else* (but prayers and appeals to your pity and honor).

316. conubia, *our union,* in its civil aspect. — **hymenaeos :** the formal rites of *marriage,* not fully completed, however (*inceptos*); cf. *v.* 172.

317. quicquam meum, *anything in me.*

318. domus : for genitive see Introd. § 20. — **istam mentem,** *that purpose of yours.*

320. propter : Introd. § 89, *d.*

321. odere : sc. *me.* — **infensi Tyrii** [sc. *sunt*]: i.e. my own people are indignant. — **eundem,** *too.*

322. qua sola, etc., *that fame* (as a faithful widow) *by which alone I was on my way to the skies :* she is thinking vaguely of deification.

323. cui, *to what ?* — **moribundam :** more vivid than *morientem.*

324. hoc nomen : i.e. of guest. It is said that this passage was recited by Virgil himself with peculiar pathos ; for, unlike most poets, he had great power of recitation. — **de coniuge,** *from that of husband.*

325. quid moror, *why do I delay* (to die)? — **an dum . . . destruat,** *is it that* [lit. *until*] *my brother Pygmalion may destroy,* etc. For *an* see A. 335, *b*; D. 627, *b*; B. 162, 4, *a*; G. 457, 1; for *destruat*, A. 553; D. 765; B. 293, III, 2; G. 572.

327. si qua, etc., *if any child by you had been born to me :* many heroes of ancient story had children by their forsaken brides ; and Dido, throughout, regards her own union with Æneas as a true marriage (*vv.* 172, 316). — **suscepta :** refers to the *taking up* of the child by its father, who thereby acknowledged it as his own.

328. ante fugam : still in the tone of reproach.

329. tamen, *after all :* implying a preceding concession (*although I had you no longer*). — **referret :** clause of purpose ; but it would in any case be subjunctive of integral part ; A. 593 ; D. 907 ; B. 324, 1 ; G. 663, 1.

331. monitis : abl. of cause, modifying the whole idea.

332. obnixus, *with a struggle.* — **premebat :** i.e. he did not let it appear in his face or in his words.

333. te : subject of *promeritam* [*esse*], but put next to *ego* on account of the fondness of the Latin for putting two pronouns together. — **quae**

plurima, *all*, *much as it is*, *which*; *plurima* is the object of *promeritam* [*esse*], but is attracted into the relative clause.

335. promeritam: see *v.* 317. — **nec me pigebit,** *nor shall I regret*: A. 354, *b*, *c*; D. 363, 364; B. 209, I and *a*; G. 377, R.³

336. ipse: sc. *sum.*

337. pro re, *as the case demands.* The two clauses *neque . . . nec* are a justification of his good faith: " I have concealed nothing and failed in no promise."

338. ne finge: Introd. § 87.

339. taedas: see note on *v.* 18.

340. me, *for myself, if the fates*, etc.: *me* is emphatic from its position — **meis . . . auspiciis,** *by my own guidance.*

342. primum: i.e. that would be my first choice.

343. colerem, *I should be cherishing.*

344. posuissem, *I should have established Pergamum, rebuilt by my hand*: i.e. I should not be here at all, but should have restored Troy and should now be there.

345. sed nunc, *but now* [as it is]. — **Gryneus, Lyciae:** names referring to Asiatic oracles of Apollo at Gryneum and Patara.

346. sortes: properly the word for the Italian form of oracle, which consisted in drawing from an urn a billet of wood with a verse upon it.

347. hic, haec: i.e. Italy; the pronoun has the gender of its predicate noun; see n. on iii. 660.

348. Observe the antithesis: *Phoenissam* is opposed to *Teucros*, as *Karthaginis* is to *Ausonia.*

349. quae tandem invidia, *pray why are you jealous that*, etc. — **considere:** depending on *invidia est = invidetis.*

350. et nos, *us too*, i.e. as well as you. — **fas:** sc. *est.* — **quaerere:** subject of *est* understood.

351. Anchisae: with *imago*, *v.* 353.

353. turbida, *troubled*, i.e. lest Æneas should fail to reach Italy.

354. puer, *the thought of the boy Ascanius.* — **capitis,** etc. (obj. gen.), *the wrong done to that dear life*; supply *admonet* from preceding line.

355. fatalibus, *destined* (by the fates).

357. utrumque caput: i.e. both yours and mine; *caput* is used as in *v.* 354.

361. sponte: sc. *meā.*

362. iamdudum tuetur, *had long been eyeing askance.* The present here is used like the historical present instead of the imperfect, but is modified by *iamdudum*, so that it is equal to the pluperfect in English upon the principle often cited.

363. totum, *from head to foot.*

364. tacitis, *silently* (lit. *with silent eyes*).

365. nec, etc.: i.e. all your pretended origin is false; such a heart could only come of a barbarian origin.

366. cautibus: ablative of place where.

367. Hyrcanae tigres: this comparison for hard-heartedness in love was long a literary convention. — **admorunt:** sc. *tibi.*

368. quae . . . reservo, *for what greater occasion do I keep my passion reserved?* i.e. why should I restrain myself?

369. num, etc.: Dido turns Æneas' self-command into a reproach. — **fletu:** abl. of cause. — **lumina:** i.e. did his glance waver so as to show any emotion?

370. amantem: *miseror,* unlike *misereor,* takes the accusative; A. 354, *a,* N.; G. 377, N.[2]

371. quae quibus (both interrog.), *what shall I say first, and what next?* (lit. *what shall I prefer to what?*) — **iam iam nec,** *no longer now.*

372. haec, *my affairs,* as *hic* often refers to what belongs to the first person. — **aequis,** *impartial:* i.e. the very gods are unjust.

373. fides: since one whose life I saved under such circumstances has broken faith, confidence can be secure nowhere.

376. nunc (emphatic): opposed to the time when she rescued him.

379. scilicet, etc. (ironical), *doubtless this is a task for the heavenly powers, a care to vex them in their repose.*

381. sequere: cf. *v.* 361. — **ventis, undas:** hinting at the perils which she hopes he may not escape.

382. equidem, *but:* i.e. go, but I hope it will be your destruction.

383. hausurum [*esse*]: the figure is harsh in English, "swallow your doom," i.e. meet your just doom, drowning among the rocks. For constr. see note on *rumpi, v.* 292; *te,* subject of the inf., is omitted. — **Dido:** acc., obj. of *vocaturum;* i.e. in his remorse, seeing that his fate is a just punishment.

384. atris ignibus, *with smoky torches,* such as the Furies bear. — **absens:** i.e. my memory shall haunt you like an avenging Fury. Closely imitated by Tasso, *Jerusalem Delivered,* xvi. 59, 60:

> Go, cruel man, and take with thee that peace
> Thou leav'st with me; I do not bid thee stay.
> But I will follow — hope for no release —
> My angry shade shall haunt thee on thy way;
> Like a new Fury I will dog thy path,
> With torch and serpents armed, to wreak my wrath.

386. umbra adero, *my ghost shall haunt you.*

387. veniet fama: the shades below were thought to receive news from earth through those newly dead (cf. ii. 547–549).

388. sermonem : i.e. the interview, not her own words merely, which have already come to a climax. — **auras :** the free air of heaven.

390. multa : the word repeated can hardly be used in two senses. Hence it must mean *preparing to say much, and at the same time hesitating to say it.* — **metu** (abl. of cause): i.e. of adding to her distress.

391. suscipiunt : apparently she falls fainting as she turns away.

392. thalamo, *into her chamber* : dat. of place to which. — **stratis :** abl. of place where with a verb of *placing.*

393. pius : although this is a stock epithet, yet Virgil seems to have purposely put it in here to remind us that Æneas is acting under divine direction, and to counteract our sympathy with the betrayed woman.

395. multa : cognate accusative. — **gemens :** concessive. — **animum :** accusative of specification.

397. tum vero : i.e. then more than ever. — **incumbunt,** *bend to* [*their task*]. — **litore :** locative ablative.

398. deducunt : the technical term.

399. frondentis, *still untrimmed* : cf. i. 552.

400. studio, *in their eagerness* : abl. of cause.

401. cernas, *you might discern them* (potential subjunctive). In prose the verb would be imperfect, but the present is used here just as the historical present is for past tenses : A. 447, 2 ; D. 686, *b* ; B. 280, 3 ; G. 258.

402. ac velut, *even as.*

403. reponunt, *lay away* : a common force of *re-* in composition.

405. calle angusto, *on their narrow track,* as the manner of ants is.

406. frumenta, *grains.*

407. moras, *the laggards* (lit. *the delays*): the fault put for the offenders by metonymy (Introd. § 100).

408. sensus : sc. *erat.*

409. fervĕre : an earlier form for *fervēre.*

410. arce ex summa, *from the top of the citadel,* where her palace appears to be, as were Priam's (see ii. 437 ff.) and other such palaces.

411. misceri, *disturbed,* filled confusedly.

412. quid : cognate accusative.

413. temptare : sc. *eum* (i.e. Æneas).

414. animos, *her proud heart.*

415. frustra moritura, *doomed to die in vain.*

416. vides properari, *you see men hastening* (lit. impersonal, *haste is being made*).

418. coronas : as offerings to the gods on setting sail.

419. si (= *siquidem*), etc., *if* (i.e. since) *I have been able to look forward to this great sorrow, I shall also be able to endure it.*

420. tamen, etc., *yet* (though I can bear it), *do me this one favor.*

422. colere, *was wont to regard* : hist. inf.

423. tempora, *moods.* — **noras :** cf. *noris* (*v.* 33).

424. hostem, *stranger.* On the meanings of *hostis,* see Vocabulary.

425. non ego, etc.: i.e. I am not an enemy, to be looked upon with suspicion.

426. Aulide : see note, ii. 116.

427. revelli, etc. There was a story that Anchises' bones were taken from the tomb by Diomedes, but afterwards restored to Æneas. The whole means, in general : I have not committed any inexpiable wrong against him; why should he not be placable?

428. cur negat, etc., *why does he refuse to admit ?*

429, 430. det, exspectet : hortatory.

432. pulchro : with a sarcastic emphasis; abl. of separation.

433. tempus inane, *mere time,* with perhaps the special idea of its being useless to him. — **requiem spatiumque,** *time for rest for my passion* (hendiadys), i.e. time for her madness to subside.

434. victam, *subdued* (as I shall then be). — **dolere,** *how to grieve.*

436. quam . . . remittam : for centuries an insoluble riddle. The old interpretation is the most intelligible : *When he shall have granted the favor* (i.e. the short delay), *I will repay it manifold* or *in ample measure* (*cumulatam*) *by my death.* Her death (which she has already spoken of, *v.* 385) would be the best solution of the difficulty for Æneas, and so a boon.

437. talis fletūs, *such tearful prayers.*

438. fertque refertque, *carries again and again.*

439. aut, *nor.* — **tractabilis,** *yielding.*

440. placidas, *kindly.* — **deus,** *some god.*

441. ac velut cum, as in *v.* 402. — **annoso robore :** abl. of quality (Introd. § 61).

443. inter se, *with each other.* — **it stridor,** *a creaking sound is heard* (lit. *a creaking goes* [*forth*]).

444. concusso stipite : abl. abs.

445. quantum, *as far as.*

447. vocibus, *appeals.*

449. mens, *his purpose,* as opposed to his feelings (*pectus*). — **volvuntur,** *are shed* (by Æneas). — **inanes :** because they are mere expressions of feeling and do not affect his action. Thus translated by Waller :

> And down his cheeks though fruitless tears do roll,
> Unmoved remains the purpose of his soul.

451. taedet : sc. *eam.* — **caeli convexa,** *the canopy of heaven.* — **tueri :** subject of *taedet* ; see n. on *v.* 335.

452. quo magis peragat, etc., *that she may the more surely,* etc.: clause of purpose dependent on *vidit,* with the underlying idea that the fates send these omens to drive her on to death; A. 531, *a*; D. 718; B. 282, 1, *a*; G. 545, 2. The sequence is irregular.

455. obscenum, *ill-omened.*

456. effata : sc. *est.*

457. templum, *a shrine* (for the adoration of the *Manes* of Sychæus).

458. coniugis antiqui, *dedicated to her former husband.*

459. festa : such garlands were usual upon solemn occasions (*v.* 202).

461. viri, *of her husband.*

462. culminibus, *on the housetops.* — **bubo :** here (only) feminine; sc. *visa est.* The owl has always been regarded as a bird of ill omen.

463. queri : cf. Gray's *Elegy* : "The moping owl does to the moon complain." — **longas . . . voces,** *draw out her note into a long wail.*

464. praedicta : i. e. old mysterious prophecies recurring to her mind at this time of anxiety.

465. agit, etc.: dreams also come to alarm her. Cf. Dryden, *Annus Mirabilis*, stanza 71 :

> In dreams they fearful precipices tread,
> Or shipwracked labor to some distant shore,
> Or in dark churches walk among the dead ;
> They wake with horror and dare sleep no more.

468. viam : cognate accusative. — **Tyrios :** her own people.

469. Eumenidum : a name for the Furies. It means literally "the Well-Wishers," and was apparently used to avoid the bad luck of calling them by their right name. — **Pentheus :** king of Thebes, who watched in conceal-ment the mysteries of Bacchus, and was torn in pieces by the Bacchanals. In his madness he is represented by Euripides as seeing all objects double. These scenes were familiar to the Romans on the stage, and were favorite subjects in works of art.

471. scaenis, *on the stage.* — **agitatus,** *pursued* (in the *Eumenides* of Æschylus). — **Orestes :** subject of *fugit, v.* 473.

472. matrem : as he had killed his mother Clytemestra, she is supposed to appear to him as a Fury. It was by these avenging deities that the ancients represented the stings of a guilty conscience driving the guilty man insane. See n. on iii. 331.

473. in limine : the Furies sit on the threshold that their victim may not escape.

474. concepit furias, *became possessed by madness.*

476. exigit : strictly, *weighs* ; here, *considers.*

477. spem fronte serenat, *smooths her brow with hope* (properly, ex-presses a hope by smoothing her brow): *spem* may be regarded as cognate accusative.

478. sorori : dative with a verb of *congratulating.*

479. reddat: purpose clause. — **eo,** *from him,* i.e. my love for him. — **amantem,** *your lovelorn sister.*

480. Oceani: the stream of Oceanus, surrounding the earth.

481. ultimus, *remotest of lands.* — **Atlas:** see *v.* 247 and note.

482. aptum: in its proper sense of *fitted,* i.e. studded.

483. hinc: *from there,* i.e. from that region. — **monstrata** [*est*], *has been brought to my knowledge.* — **sacerdos:** this African priestess is visiting Carthage.

484. Hesperidum: the Hesperides, daughters of Atlas, guarded the golden apples.

485. dabat, *used to give.*

486. mella, papaver: honey and poppy-seeds were a favorite seasoning among the Romans, sprinkled on more solid food (*spargens*); *soporiferum* is merely descriptive of the plant.

487. se promittit solvere, *professes to deliver* (from their griefs).

489. sistere, vertere: the ordinary feats of magic. — **fluviis:** dat. of reference.

490. nocturnos, *by night.* — **movet,** *calls forth* (lit. *disturbs*).

492. testor, etc.: cf. *v.* 357.

493. accingier (old form of inf.; Introd. § 91, *k*), *that I have recourse to* (the subject *me* is omitted); lit. *gird myself*: the figure is from the girding on of arms. — **artes:** obj. of the middle voice (Introd. § 43).

494. secreta: translate as an adverb. — **sub auras:** i.e. in the open interior court.

496. impius: perhaps alluding to his usual epithet *pius.*

497. superimponas: equivalent to an imperative; A. 439, *a*; D. 674, *a*; B. 275, 2; G. 263, 2.

500. tamen: though her sister's request and sudden pallor might make her suspicious. — **novis . . . sacris,** *is concealing, under the pretext of strange rites, her purpose to die.*

501. mente concipit, *can she imagine* (cf. *animo concipere,* with the same meaning): the abl. is locative.

502. morte: abl. of time when.

504. pyrā erectā, etc., *when she* (Anna) *had built a funeral-pile.* — **penetrali,** etc.: i.e. in the inner court; see n. on ii. 512.

505. ingenti taedis, *heaped high with pine,* such as was used for torches (abl. of means).

506. intendit, *wreathes.*

507. super: adverb. — **exuvias:** cf. *abolere, v.* 497. By destroying in this ceremonial manner every relic of the false lover, it was supposed that the unhappy love would be eradicated.

508. effigiem: apparently the effigy of Æneas is to be burned on the pile. She is well aware (*haud ignara*) herself of her purpose, but she conceals it.

509. crinis effusa: dishevelled hair is especially associated with magic rites.

510. ter centum : only a vague exaggeration, but *three hundred* and *six hundred* are often used vaguely in Latin like our *thousand.* — **tonat,** *calls aloud upon.* — **deos:** cognate acc. — **Erebum,** etc.: these gods of the Lower World are especially associated with magic rites.

511. tergeminam: Hecate, goddess of the Lower World and an especial patroness of magic, was known as Diana (Artemis) among the immortals, and as Luna (the Moon) to the dwellers on earth. — **ora:** in apposition with *Hecaten.*

512. sparserat : the lustration formed a part of almost all sacred rites. — **Averni :** near Cumæ, in Italy, and supposedly an entrance to the Lower World.

513. messae ad lunam, *cut by moonlight.* — **aënis :** these details all had a magic significance. The bronze was a relic of earlier times when this was the common metal.

514. nigri veneni : the association of dark color with poison is old and quite natural.

515. equi de fronte: the ancients believed that on the forehead of a colt at birth there was a piece of flesh of a dark color, called *hippomanes,* which was immediately devoured by the mother. If snatched away beforehand (*praereptus*), this was thought to be a powerful love-charm.

516. matri : dat. of separation (Introd. § 32). — **amor,** *love-charm.*

517. ipsa : Dido. — **mola,** etc. (abl. of manner), *sprinkling the bruised grain with holy hands* (i. e. ceremonially pure).

518. unum pedem, *with one foot loosed from the sandal* : certain rites were performed with one foot bare. — **recincta,** *ungirded* : the loose garments were associated with magic rites.

519. conscia : an allusion to astrology; of course if the stars revealed the fates they must be supposed to know them.

520. si quod numen, etc., *she prays to whatsoever deity has in charge those who love with unrequited affection* (*non aequo foedere*).

521. curae : dat. of purpose (Introd. § 33).

522. nox erat, etc.: cf. Dryden, *Annus Mirabilis,* stanza 216:

> The diligence of trades, and noiseful gain,
> And luxury, more late, asleep were laid;
> All was the Night's and in her silent reign
> No sound the rest of Nature did invade.

523. saeva, *raging.* — **quierant :** syncopated form of *quieverant.*

525. pictae, *many-colored*; cf. " spread their painted wings," *Paradise Lost,* vii. 434.

526. quae-que, *both those which . . . and.* — **dumis :** abl. of manner.

527. tenent, *inhabit.*

528. lenibant =*leniebant*: Introd. § 91, *m*.

529. Phoenissa: the verb is not strictly any one of the preceding, but these are all fused into one general idea of rest, to which *non* belongs (not to *infelix*). Render, *but not so the Phœnician queen*.

530. solvitur in somnos, *is relaxed in sleep.* — **oculis:** locative ablative. — **noctem:** i.e. the influence of night.

532. fluctuat, *her love ebbs and flows:* i.e. her love and wrath succeed each other in her mind in an ebbing and a flowing tide.

533. sic adeo insistit, *then thus she begins.*

534. en, quid ago? *ah! what shall I do?* i.e. how shall I try to find a way of escape? The present is used in place of the future, as in ii. 322, iii. 88. — **inrisa,** *mocked and derided,* i.e. by Æneas, who had cast her off.

535. Nomadum: a general term for the barbarous African tribes.

536. quos sim dedignata, *whom I have disdained:* subj. of characteristic; A. 535; D. 726; B. 283, 1; G. 631, 1.

537. ultima ... sequar: i.e. shall I humble myself to the most degrading exactions of the Trojans in order to be allowed to accompany them? The verb is used in a slightly different sense with the two objects.

538. quiane ... levatos, *shall I do so because they are glad (iuvat,* impers.) *of the relief they had by my help and because memory of former kindness remains in grateful hearts* (lit. *gratitude ... remains in the mindful*)? The interrogative -*ne* really belongs to an omitted *sequar.* — **levatos** = *eos levatos esse:* A. 486, *f*; D. 364; G. 533.

539. bene belongs with *facti*.

540. fac velle, *suppose I should wish it:* the subject *me* is omitted.

541. perdita: Dido addresses herself.

542. Laomedonteae: for the perjury of Laomedon see n. to iii. 248. — **sentis,** *have experienced.*

543. sola: i.e. shall I go alone with the Trojans as a mere camp-follower or shall I emigrate once more with my whole people?

545. inferar: i.e. to follow him to Italy with all my people.

546. agam pelago, *force upon the sea:* sc. *eos* as object of *agam* and antecedent of *quos*.

547. quin, *nay rather.*

548. prima: see Anna's arguments, *vv.* 31–53.

549. oneras, obicis: histor. present.

550. non licuit (exclamatory) = *why was it not!* etc. — **thalami expertem,** *unmarried.*

551. more ferae: i.e. like a wild creature, solitary in the woods; so the life of Camilla (xi. 568). — **curas:** i.e. of love; cf. *v.* 5.

552. Sychaeo: either an adj., or in a sort of appos. with *cineri.* — **servata** [*est*] (in the same construction as *v.* 550) = *why was it not,* etc. The incoherency of the whole speech pictures Dido's state of mind. From this verse Dante, who puts Dido in the second circle of Hell, speaks of her as " she who broke her faith to the ashes of Sychæus " (*Inferno*, v. 62).

553. tantos, *such wild.* — **rumpebat:** cf. note on ii. 129. Shakspere takes some liberties with the story in the famous passage in his *Merchant of Venice*, v. 1. 9–12:

> In such a night
> Stood Dido, with a willow in her hand,
> Upon the wild sea-banks and waft her love
> To come again to Carthage.

554. certus eundi, *determined to go* : *eundi* (gerund) is objective genitive with *certus*; A. 504; D. 874; B. 338, 1, *b*; G. 428.

556. forma : a phantom in the form of the god. — **eodem :** i.e. as in *vv.* 238 ff.

558. omnia : acc. of specification. — **coloremque :** a hypermetric verse (Introd. § 114).

559. iuventa : abl. of manner.

560. hoc sub casu, *just at this emergency.*

561. deinde, *next.*

563. illa : Dido.

564. certa mori, *bent on death,* and accordingly reckless. The infinitive is here used with an adjective, a poetical construction (Introd. § 81). — **vario,** *changing*: cf. *v.* 532.

565. non fugis, *will you not fly ?* The present is used for the future as in ii. 322, iii. 88, iv. 534. — **potestas :** sc. *est.*

566. iam, *presently.* — **trabibus :** i.e. the Carthaginian fleet.

567. fervĕre : as in *v.* 409.

568. attigerit : future perfect.

569. varium : A. 289, *c*; D. 504; B. 234, 2; G. 211, R.[4]

570. nocti : Introd. § 28.

571. umbris, *apparition.*

575. festinare : sc. *me* or *nos.*

576. sancte deorum, *holy deity*: A. 346, *b*; G. 372, N.[1]

578. sidera . . . feras, *grant us propitious stars* (weather).

581. rapiuntque ruuntque, *they hasten their departure* (lit. *they lay hold and rush*).

582. litora deseruere : i.e. and now they have left the shore (taking a new point of view to indicate the haste of the action).

585. Tithoni : husband of the dawn-goddess, Aurora; see Vocabulary. For the myth, see Tennyson's poem *Tithonus.*

587. aequatis, *even,* i.e. the ships were sailing right before the wind.

589. percussa, abscissa : middle use of the participles.

590. flaventis : the color universally ascribed to the hair of heroic persons by the ancients.

591. inluserit : i.e. laugh my power to scorn; the fut. perf. looks forward to the completion of the act, as if she said, "shall he succeed in doing so?"— **advena,** *an adventurer.*

592. non [= *nonne*] **expedient,** *will not my men,* etc. ?

593. A peculiar abruptness is given by the pause at the end of the fifth foot. Notice also the hurried movement of *v.* 594. Cf. n. on iii. 658.

594. flammas, *torches.*

595. mentem : i.e. her purpose of death.

596. nunc : emphatic.— **facta impia :** i.e. toward Sychæus.

597. tum decuit (emphatic), *then they ought* [*to have come home to you*]. — **cum . . . dabas,** *when you offered him the sceptre,* i.e. before you put the power in his hand: A. 471, *c*; D. 653; B. 260, 3; G. 233.— **en dextra :** i.e. the right hand given in making a pledge, as with us; spoken with scorn, i.e. this then is the honor of this most pious hero.

598. quem : i.e. *eius quem, of him who, they say,* etc.

600. non potui . . . divellere, *could I not have seized and torn?* Medea treated her brother Absyrtus in this way when she was fleeing from her home; A. 486, *a*; D. 829; B. 270, 2; G. 254, R.[1]

602. epulandum ponere, *served him up as a feast.* Atreus served up to his brother Thyestes the flesh of the two sons of Thyestes.

603. fuerat, *might have been:* A. 517, *b*; D. 797; B. 304, 3; G. 254, R.[3] — **fuisset,** *suppose it had been:* A. 440; D. 677; B. 278; G. 264.

604. faces, etc.: i.e. set the ships on fire. The Romans drew their ships on land and fortified them.— **tulissem,** *I ought to have,* etc.: A. 439, *b*; D. 672; G. 272, 3.

605. implessem : syncopated form of *implevissem* (Introd. § 91, *n*).

606. exstinxem : for *exstinxissem.* — **dedissem,** *and have thrown myself* [*into the flames*] *last of all*; *super* is an adverb meaning literally *on top.*

607. terrarum opera omnia, *all deeds of mortals.*

608. interpres . . . et conscia, *conscious witness :* properly agent, or even cause, as the goddess of marriage.

609. nocturnis, *by night.*— **triviis :** Hecate was worshipped at cross-roads (places where three roads met) and was hence called Trivia.— **ululata,** *invoked with shrieks.*

610. Dirae : see *v.* 473. — **di :** the special or tutelary divinity, but why more than one is not clear. Perhaps it was conceived as twofold; hence the expression *Manes,* and the custom of erecting two altars to the shade (cf. iii. 63). The idea of divinities in pairs was a common Roman notion.

611. accipite, *hear.* — **haec,** *these my words.* — **meritum,** *as I have deserved* (agreeing with *numen*). — **malis advertite numen,** *turn your power to* (avenge) *my sufferings.*

612. The language of the curses that follow depends upon the common belief in the prophetic power (" second sight ") of a person at the point of death and in the efficacy of a dying person's curse. — **audite**, *grant*.

613. caput, *creature*.

615–620. at, *at least*. These are the ominous lines which were opened by Charles I, when he consulted the *Sortes Vergilianae*, at Oxford. It will be noticed that they are so worded that they do not prevent the expedition of Æneas from being one of final glory and success. The curses are literally fulfilled in the later fortunes of Æneas (see the later books of the Æneid). — **bello**: Æneas fought against the Rutulians and the Latins in Italy.

616. Æneas left his companions and Ascanius in order to seek aid from Evander. — **finibus**: abl. of separation.

617. videat . . . funera: in the war in Italy.

619. optata: a general epithet of light; as we might say in English, " the boon of light."

620. cadat ante diem: Æneas reigned only three years. — **media . . . harena**: Æneas' body was swept away by the river Numicius.

622–629. tum vos . . . nepotes: an imprecation prophetic of the Punic Wars, which, strictly fulfilled, resulted in the greatest struggle, but also in the proudest military glory, of Rome.

623. exercete odiis, *pursue with hate*.

624. populis (dat. of possession): the Carthaginians and the Romans.

625. exoriare . . . ultor, *rise some avenger !* A. 439, *a*; D. 674, *a*; B. 275, 2; G. 263, 2. — **aliquis**: because referring to an indefinite person. No Roman, however, could hear it without thinking of Hannibal.

626. qui sequare, *to pursue*: relative clause of purpose.

628. contraria belongs with *undas* and *arma* as well as with *litora*.

629. ipsique nepotesque: i. e. may the warfare begin at once, and not cease. The *e* in *-que* is elided before the next verse (*synapheia*): Introd. § 114.

633. suam, *her own* (nurse). — **cinis**, *tomb* (lit. *ashes*).

634. mihi: with *huc siste, bring me hither Anna*.

635. corpus, *her body*, etc. : a very ancient rite of lustration. — **properet**: for constr., see *v.* 289, note.

636. pecudes: the black sheep, for a sacrifice to Pluto (*Iovi Stygio*). — **monstrata**, *appointed*.

637. sic veniat: i. e. after having made such preparations.

638. paravi: see *vv.* 504–508.

640. Dardanii capitis, *the Trojan*: *caput* is often used in the sense of *person* in such periphrases; cf. Eng. *soul*, and *body* in *everybody*, etc. Dido is really preparing her own pyre; but ostensibly the rite is to be a mock funeral, in which, to free her from her unhappy love, the *effigies* of Æneas and his *exuviae* are to be burned (see *vv.* 496, 507, 508).

641. studio anili : i. e. with the bustling zeal of an old woman. The old nurse is a stock figure in heroic story. Juliet's nurse is the most famous English example.

642. coeptis, *purpose* : abl. of cause. — **effera,** *maddened.*

643. aciem, *eyes.* — **trementis genas :** acc. of specification.

645. inrumpit : she rushes down from the tower (*v.* 586), where she has been hitherto, into the inner open court (*interiora limina*).

647. non hos in usus, *for no such service* : probably an ornamental sword or dagger given her by Æneas.

648. hic, *hereupon.*

649. paulum lacrimis, etc., *staying a little in tears and in thought* : abl. of manner.

650. que . . . que : correlative.

651. dum, etc. : limits *dulces, dear, so long as,* etc.

652. exsolvite : i. e. by my death.

654. magna : i. e. I shall go a famous woman. — **mei :** possess. gen., used instead of *mea* for metrical reasons.

656. ulta virum : i. e. in the way described in i. 360–364. — **poenas,** etc., *inflicted the due punishment.*

657. felix : a verb *fuissem* is implied, the apodosis of *tetigissent.* — **tantum,** *only* (lit. *so much* and no more).

659. os impressa toro, *pressing her lips to the couch.* — **os :** acc. with a participle used in the middle voice.

660. sic, sic : these words, though accompanying the fatal blows, refer not merely to those but to the whole situation ; though dying unavenged and by her own hand, still she prefers death to life.

661. hunc ignem : the blaze of the pile which is about to be kindled.

663. ferro : abl. of instrument.

664. comites, *her attendants.*

666. concussam, *startled.* — **bacchatur :** cf. *v.* 301.

667. femineo ululatu : hiatus.

669. ruat, *were falling in ruins* : A. 524 and N.²; D. 803 ; B. 307 ; G. 602.

672. trepido curso : i. e. running wildly (abl. of manner).

675. hoc illud, *was this what you meant ?* — **me fraude petebas,** *were you deceiving me* [all the while]?

676. hoc rogus, etc., *is this what the pyre,* etc., *were preparing,* etc. ? — **iste :** i. e. that *you* ordered me to build.

678. vocasses, *you should have called* : see note on *tulissem, v.* 604.

679. tulisset, *should have taken away.*

680. his . . . manibus, *even with these hands did I build* (the pyre)?

681. sic . . . abessem, *that I should thus be absent when you were laid out in death.* — **sic :** i. e. as I have been. — **ut abessem :** clause of purpose

683. date . . . abluam, *let me wash her wounds in water* (object clause without *ut*).

684. super: adv.

685. ore legam: a customary office of affection, like closing the eyes of the dying. — **sic fata,** etc., *as she spoke she had,* etc.

686. semianimem: the first *i* is read like *y*; Introd. § 112.

687. siccabat, *tried to stanch.*

689. stridit, *gurgles.*

690. cubito: A. 431; D. 469, *c*; B. 218, 3; G. 401, N.⁶—**adnixa,** *leaning.*

691. toro: dative, or possibly abl. of place.

692. quaesivit lucem: the ancients were strongly impressed with the thought that the last act of the dying was to gaze upon the light. — **reperta:** sc. *luce* (ablative absolute).

694. Irim: in the case of women, the thread of life was usually supposed to be cut by Proserpine (*v.* 698). Iris (the personified rainbow) was the messenger of Juno (see Fig. 41, from an ancient vase painting). Cf. Shakspere, *Tempest,* iv. 1. 76–82:

> Hail, many-color'd messenger, that ne'er
> Dost disobey the wife of Jupiter;
> Who with thy saffron wings upon my flowers
> Diffusest honey-drops, refreshing showers,
> And with each end of thy blue bow dost crown
> My bosky acres and my unshrubb'd down,
> Rich scarf to my proud earth.

695. quae . . . resolveret, *to disengage the struggling spirit from the close-locked limbs* (subj. of purpose).

Fig. 41

696. fato, i.e. by natural death. — **merita morte,** i.e. by death incurred by her own guilt.

698. illi: dat. of reference. — **crinem:** as a few hairs were plucked from the head of the victim before sacrifice, so the "fatal lock" had to be cut from the crown (*vertice*) of the dying person, who was regarded as an offering to the gods of the Lower World; cf. *sacrum, v.* 703.

699. Orco: poetical dat. after *damnaverat* (as if *addixerat*).

701. mille colores: i.e. the rainbow. — **trahens,** *drawing out* the long line of color. — **adverso sole,** *from the sun opposite:* abl. abs. expressing cause. Cf. Milton, *Comus, vv.* 992–995.

> Iris there with humid bow
> Waters the odorous banks, that blow
> Flowers of more mingled hue
> Than her purfled scarf can shew.

702. hunc: sc. *crinem.* — **Diti sacrum** (predicate), *as an offering to Pluto* (the god of the dead and of the World Below).

703. isto corpore, *from your body.*

704. una, *at the same time.*

705. in ventos : the breath was naturally identified with the life or soul ; cf. *animus, anima, exanimis*, etc. Dryden thus translates the passage :

> Thus while she spoke, she cut the fatal hair ;
> The struggling soul was loos'd, and life dissolv'd in air.

BOOK V

The games in this book in honor of Anchises make an agreeable interlude in the more serious action of the poem. Many of the incidents are taken from the account of the funeral games of Patroclus in the twenty-third book of the Iliad. The contest of ships, however, and the equestrian exhibition are wholly original. The burning of the fleet was a part of the old Trojan legend. It is interesting to observe that Milton, in his wish to follow the classical models of epic poetry, represents the fallen angels as engaging in athletic games to while away the time till the return of Satan from his scouting expedition (*Paradise Lost*, ii. 528 ff.).

1. interea : i.e. during the time of Dido's death. — **medium tenebat iter,** *was well on his way.*

2. certus : i.e. in his purpose (cf. iv. 554, 564). — **Aquilone,** *the wind.* Just as the names of various kinds of wood are used for *wood* in general in the description of the Horse, so the name of any wind may be put for *wind.* That Aquilo is not the North Wind here is clear from the direction in which the Trojans are sailing. The wind does not change until they are out of sight of land (*vv.* 8–10, 19).

3. iam conlucent : the pile built ostensibly to burn the effigy of Æneas now serves for her own cremation.

4. accenderit : indirect question.

5. duri, etc., *but the cruel pangs of a great love betrayed (polluto*, lit. *desecrated), and the knowledge of what a maddened woman can do, lead the hearts of the Trojans into sad forebodings.* Though they have no certain knowledge, yet they suspect the cause of the fire. — **amore polluto :** ablative absolute.

6. notum : *the knowledge* : neuter of participle used as substantive. — **quid possit :** an indirect question serving as a noun in apposition with *notum.*

11. inhorruit, *the waves grew rough with black shadows.* Virgil has in mind the dark appearance of the water produced by a squall ; cf. *atros, v.* 2, and see iii. 195.

12. ipse: even the pilot is at a loss.

13. quianam, *ah! why?*

14. paras, *have in store.*

15. colligere arma, *to secure the rigging*: i.e. to make all tight, and prepare for the gale. — **validis,** *vigorously* (lit. an adj. with *remis*).

16. obliquat sinus, *trims the sail*: they had been sailing with the wind astern (*aequatis velis,* iv. 587), probably from the southwest, and as the wind now comes from the west, they can no longer sail on the same course, so as to weather the Ægates islands (see map). The ancients could probably only sail within seven or eight points of the wind (nearly at right angles with it): see Fig. 30, for their rig.

17. auctor, *as surety.* — **spondeat:** future less vivid condition.

19. transversa, *athwart our course*: cognate acc.

20. aer, etc.: the ancients supposed clouds to be condensed air.

21. tantum, *merely* (so much as that even).

23. quōque, *and whither*: notice the quantity, — not *quŏque.* — **longe:** sc. *abesse.*

24. fraterna: see i. 570, note.

25. servata, *before observed*: i.e. in their former voyage.

27. iamdudum, qualifying *cerno, I have long since observed*: for tense see A. 466; D. 650; B. 259, 4; G. 230.

28. flecte viam velis, *turn the course of your voyage* (lit. *turn your course with your sails* (abl. of means), i.e. by setting them on that tack). — **an:** here introduces a single question. — **sit,** *could any land be,* etc.? Potential subjunctive.

29. quo optem: rel. clause of characteristic. — **demittere,** *bring into port.*

31. Anchisae ossa: cf. iii. 710.

32. secundi: the wind is now astern, for they have changed their course.

33. gurgite, *over the flood*: abl. of the way by which (Introd. § 55).

35. miratus, *having seen with wonder.*

36. adventum sociasque rates, *the arrival of the friendly ships*: hendiadys; cf. i. 61 (note). The figure is common in English poetry; see, e.g., *Paradise Lost,* x. 345: "with joy and tidings fraught."

37. pelle: Virgil here, as in many other places, preserves the remembrance of the earlier civilization, in which skins were the common clothing.

38. Troïa . . . genuit, *whom a Trojan mother bore to the river-god Crinisus.* — **Criniso flumine:** abl. of source. To punish the perfidy of Laomedon, Neptune sent to Troy a sea monster, to which (so an oracle commanded) maidens were to be thrown as prey. Egesta (or Segesta) was sent to Sicily by her father to avoid this doom. Acestes (Egestus) was her son by the river-god Crinisus.

39. parentum: i.e. through whom he was of kin to Æneas.

40. reduces: adj., *on their return.*

42. primo Oriente, *at early dawn*: cf. iii. 588 and note. — **fugarat:** poetical indicative for subjunctive.

45. genus . . . divum : Dardanus was a son of Jupiter.

46. completur : observe the incomplete tense.

47. ex quo [sc. *tempore*], *from the time when.*

49. nisi fallor : the Roman calendar was extremely confused till the reform of Julius Cæsar ; hence it is not unnatural that Virgil should attribute a doubt on the subject to Æneas.

51. Gaetulis, etc.: i. e. even in times of the utmost hardships and hazard. Notice the emphasis on *hunc*, = *on this day if I were passing it*, etc.

52. deprensus, *overtaken* by it. — **Mycenae:** appositional genitive with *urbe* (Introd. § 10). The singular of this noun is rare.

53. pompas exsequerer, etc., *I would perform the solemn procession* (hence the noun *exsequiae*, used of funeral rites).

54. suis, *appropriate*: as in iii. 469.

55. nunc, *but now* as it is, opposed to the supposition in *vv.* 51, 52. — **ultro,** *without our agency.*

56. haud equidem, *surely not.*

57. delati, *borne to land* (by favoring winds): cf. *demittere* in *v.* 29. — **intramus :** historical present.

58. laetum, *cheerful*, with more of gratitude than grief, assured as we are of divine favor.

59. poscamus ventos, *let us pray for favorable winds.* Some think the prayer is addressed to the winds themselves ; others, to the Manes of Anchises.

60. velit, *may he* [Anchises] *be pleased to grant that, when my city is established, I may offer him yearly these rites in temples consecrated to him.* Virgil may have in mind the *Parentalia*, a Roman festival held annually in February, at which offerings were made to the dead. — The construction is that of an object clause after *poscamus*, without *ut*.

61. Troia : abl. of source with *generatus*.

62. adhibete, *invite.*

64. si, *when.* — **nona Aurora :** the *novemdiale* was a festival on the ninth day after death, when the days of mourning were ended.

66. prima, *first of all.*

67. qui : the antecedents are the subjects of *adsint* (*v.* 70). — **viribus :** referring to wrestling.

68. incedit, *advances* proudly. — **iaculo :** javelin-throwing is not one of the games wihch actually follow.

69. fidit : here in the sense of *audet*.

71. ore favete, *keep silence* (lit. *favor with the mouth*): i. e. let only auspicious words be spoken ; the form regularly used for imposing silence when a religious ceremony is about to begin, because any quarrelling or ill-omened expressions would destroy the sanctity of the rites. — **ramis :** the wreath was a regular accompaniment of all religious ceremonies.

72. materna : i. e. sacred to Venus, his mother.

73. aevi maturus, genitive of specification; his age is contrasted with that of Helymus and Ascanius.

75. ille : Æneas.

76. tumulum : the tomb of Anchises.

77. carchesia, *bowls* : a vessel peculiar to Bacchus and Hercules. See Fig. 42. — **Baccho :** ablative of quality.

78. sanguine : of course of a slain victim.

79. purpureos, *gay* : the ancients applied the word to a wide range of colors on the purple side of red, and so often to any bright color.

80. recepti nequiquam : cf. iii. 711.

81. animae, umbrae : for the plural cf. the use of *Manes.*

82. non licuit : sc. *mihi.*

83. quicumque, *whatever,* but agreeing in gender with *Thybrim* : the expression implies a very human doubt as to his ever reaching the river, almost as if he said, " if there is any such."

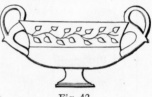

Fig. 42

84. adytis ab imis, *from the bottom of the tomb* : the tomb is a shrine, for Anchises is now a god. — **anguis :** the *genius* (*v.* 95, indwelling spirit, or tutelary divinity) of a place, especially of a tomb, is frequently typified by a serpent in ancient art. The worship of serpents is very ancient and wide-spread.

85. septem . . . tumulum, *formed seven rings, seven coils, quietly enfolding the tomb.*

87. cui : dative of reference. — **terga, squamam** (objs. of *incendebat*): translate, changing the construction, *whose skin flamed with dark-blue spots, his scales with gleaming specks, a thousand varied colors, such as the bow casts on clouds when over against the sun.* — **notae :** by a natural inversion of ideas the marks (*notae, fulgor*) are said to light up the material, as it were. Cf. Milton's gorgeous description of the serpent in Eden (*Paradise Lost,* ix. 498–504).

88. ceu, *as when.* — **nubibus :** locative ablative.

90. ille : the serpent; note this common use of the pronoun to change the subject. — **agmine longo,** *in trailing course.*

91. tandem : i. e. slowly. — **pateras :** the arrangements for libation here consisted of *pocula* (*carchesia,* so called) to hold the liquid, and a similar shallow vessel from which it was poured, *patera.* — **lēvia,** *polished* : notice the quantity. — **serpens :** participle.

92. dapes : described in *vv.* 77–78.

93. depasta, *with the offering consumed.*

94. hoc : abl. of cause. — **instaurat,** *renews,* i.e. continues with fresh zeal the sacrifice interrupted by the appearance of the snake.

95. genium loci : see note on *v.* 84. — **famulum :** as a deified person, Anchises might have a special attendant. — **-ne . . . -ne,** *whether . . . or :* as in i. 308.

96. putet : indirect question ; the direct question contained a deliberative subjunctive ; A. 575, *b* ; D. 816 ; B. 300, 2 ; G. 467. — **bidentis** (see iv. 57), etc. : a sacrifice of sheep, swine, and oxen was known as *suovetaurilia.*

Fig. 43

99. remissos, *returning* (allowed to return) to share in these solemnities : apparently the shade, like a divinity, came to receive the offering ; cf. iii. 303.

100. quae . . . copia = *eam copiam* (in appos. with *dona,* etc.) *quae cuique est, each according to his ability.* — **cuique :** dat. of possession.

102. ordine, *in long array :* all partake of the feast in companies ; each around its own kettle or fire. — **fusi :** cf. i. 212–214.

103. veribus : cf. i. 212. For cooking on spits see Fig. 43 (from a vase painting).

104. serena luce : abl. of quality with *Auroram.*

105. Phaethontis : here the sun-god, not (as usually) his son.

106. fama : the talk about the games.

108. visuri : future participle expressing purpose. A. 499, 2 ; D. 868 ; B. 337, 4 ; G. 670, 3. — **Aeneadas :** these famous exiles are more attractive even than the games. — **pars et,** *some also.* — **certare :** infinitive with *parati* to express purpose (Introd. § 81). — **parati :** plural with the collective noun *pars.*

109. circo: it may here be used of the place of gathering (*v.* 289) or of the circle of spectators (*coetu*, *v.* 107).

110. sacri: because used as offerings. — **tripodes:** the kettle with its tripod was a very common prize in games; the metals were comparatively rare, and even common utensils were works of art (see *v.* 266).

112. talenta, *masses.*

114. pares, *well-matched.* — **gravibus remis:** abl. of quality with *carinae.* The ancient galleys relied on oars for their manœuvres, but used sails for speed.

116. Pristim, etc.: these fabulous creatures were probably represented in the ships' figure-heads.

117. Memmi: it was a fancy of the Romans to derive their names and descent from these Trojan heroes.

119. urbis opus: *vast, like a city* or *a work worthy of a city.* — **versu,** *tier.* Triremes were not invented till some centuries later than

Fig. 44

the times which Virgil is describing (see Fig. 44, from an ancient relief).

120. terno ordine = *tribus ordinibus.*

123. caerulea: the regular color of the sea-divinities (iii. 432).

124. saxum: a rock evidently just at the surface.

125. olim, *sometimes.*

126. condunt: i.e. with clouds.

127. tranquillo, *in calm weather:* locative abl. of circumstance; A. 429, 3; cf. D. 485, N.; B. 228, 1; G. 385, N.[1]

129. frondenti: i.e. it is set up on the rock, leaves and all.

130. signum nautis, *as a sign for the sailors.* — **pater,** *with fatherly care.*

131. scirent: purpose, *unde* being equivalent to *ut inde.* — **circumflectere:** i.e. the tree on the rock marked the turning-point round which they were to sail, as the racers in the circus drove round the *meta* (see iii. 429, note).

134. pōpulea (notice the *ō*): because these were funeral games. When Hercules was returning from the Lower World, he gathered poplar leaves there for a garland; hence this tree was not only sacred to Hercules, the god of athletes, but was also an emblem of mourning.

136. intenta [sc. *sunt*], *are outstretched to the oars.*

137. intenti, *on the stretch* (i.e. with eager attention). Note the repetition : *intenta* (literal), *intenti* (figurative). — **haurit,** etc., *throbbing apprehension and eager desire for praise strain their beating hearts.*

139. finibus, *starting-places.*

140. prosiluere : said loosely of both ships and crew ; the perfect indicates the suddenness of the action.

141. versa : from *verto*, not *verro*.

142. pariter, *together*, no one being in advance.

143. tridentibus: the form usually given to a ship's beak, a reminiscence of which is still seen in the prow of the Venetian gondola. The *rostrum* was a massive projection of brass or iron, intended to sink or disable an enemy's ship, exactly like the modern " ram " (see Fig. 44).

144. biiugo certamine : the Homeric chariot-race is here brought in by way of comparison.

145. effusi carcere, *darting from the barriers* or starting-places ; properly, stalls in which the horses were confined until the word was given.

146. nec sic, etc., *nor so, over their teams in full career, do the drivers shake the waving reins.*

147. iugis : dat. of reference. — **proni :** the natural attitude for whipping the horses.

148. studiis : a regular word for expressions of approval which take sides. It includes both *plausu* and *fremitu*, which designate particular methods of showing favor. — **faventum,** *partisans :* archaic form of the genitive.

149. inclusa : i.e. by hills.

151. primis, *in the lead* (agreeing grammatically with *undis*).

152. turbam inter, *amid the confusion and noise* of his competitors.

154. aequo discrimine, *at an equal distance,* i.e. from Cloanthus : abl. of degree of difference.

155. locum . . . superare priorem (cogn. acc.): *to get the lead.*

156. habet, *has it* (i.e. the lead).

157. iunctis frontibus, *with prows abreast.*

159. tenebant, *were just reaching* the rock which was the half-way point (*metam*): see note on *v.* 131.

160. medio in gurgite, *at the middle of* [*the course over*] *the sea.*

161. compellat voce, *calls to.*

162. quo, *where* (lit. *whither*).— **tantum dexter,** *so far to the right :* *dexter* has the force of an adv.— **mihi :** ethical dat.; omit in translation (Introd. § 31). The construction was once common in English. Cf. Shakspere, *Comedy of Errors,* i. 2, 11 :

Villain, I say, knock me at this gate.

163. litus ama, *hug the shore* (i.e. of the rock).— **stringat sine :** *ut* omitted. — **palmula :** nominative. They leave the rock on the left.

165. pelagi, *the open sea.*

166. diversus, *so wide of the course* (i.e. so far from the rock).

167. revocabat : conative; A. 471, *c*; D. 653; B. 260, 3; G. 233.

168. tergo : dative with *instantem.* — **propiora tenentem,** *steering nearer the rocks.*

170. radit iter laevum interior, *skims along on the left, getting the inside track.* — **iter :** cogn. acc. — **priorem,** *his leader.*

171. tuta : i.e. because he has rounded the rock and is now inside on the straight and open course.

172. iuveni : dat. of reference.

174. decoris, *dignity.* — **socium** = *sociorum.* Observe the chiastic order.

176. rector, *as steersman.*

177. clavum torquet, *steers :* the Roman ship was steered with a long broad-bladed oar.

179. senior, fluens : explaining why he was *gravis.*

183. extremis duobus : dat. of reference.

184. Mnesthei : Greek dative; pronounced in two syllables.

185. ante, *ahead* (adv.).

186. totā praeeunte carinā, *by a whole length* (lit. *keel*): observe that the diphthong is here made short before the following vowel.

187. premit, *overlaps.*

188. media nave : a gangway ran down the ship between the rows of oarsmen.

190. sorte suprema = *on the last fatal day* (abl. of time).

192. usi : sc. *estis.*

193. Maleae : this headland, the extreme south of Greece, is proverbially dangerous to navigation.— **sequacibus undis,** *the pursuing waves,* from which it is hard to escape.

195. quamquam O, *and yet, O that* — : a half-expressed wish.

196. extremos, etc., *at least let us be ashamed to come off last.*— **hoc vincite,** *win this* at least : cognate acc.

199. subtrahitur solum (for *aequor*), *the course flies beneath them* (lit. passive). — **artus,** *frame.*

201. viris : i.e. Mnestheus' men, the crew of the Pristis.

202. animi : as in iv. 203.

203. iniquo, *dangerous,* between the rock and the ship of Mnestheus.

205. murice, *reef :* properly a rock jagged and rough, like the shellfish called *murex.*

206. obnixi crepuere, *crashed as they pulled against it.* — **inlisa pependit,** *struck upon the reef and hung there :* the stern was still afloat.

207. magno . . . morantur, *utter loud cries because of the delay* (lit. *delay with loud shouting*).

211. agmine . . . vocatis, *with the rapid driving of oars, and with an appeal to the winds.*

212. prona, *descending*: i.e. where he can run smoothly *down* to shore; cf. *devenere* (i. 365), *delato* (iii. 154), *demittere* (v. 29), *delati* (v. 57).

214. nidi, *nestlings.*

216. tecto, *from her home* (the rock): abl. of separation with *exterrita.*

217. radit, *skims*: notice the smooth, rapid movement of the verse.

218. secat ultima aequora, *cuts the waves on the home-stretch.*

221. brevibus vadis, *shallow reefs* (lit. *shoals*): the adjective really adds nothing, but expresses the idea from another point of view.

222. discentem : said with a touch of humor.

224. cedit, *she* (the Chimæra) *gives place.*

227. clamor, *the cheers* (from shore).

228. studiis : cf. *v.* 148, note.

229. hi : Cloanthus and his men.— **proprium,** *their deserved,* and so far *won* (*partum*).

230. ni teneant : for " are indignant at the disgrace (which will be theirs) if they do not," etc.; A. 592, 2; D. 905; B. 323; G. 508, 3.

231. hos : Mnestheus and his crew.

232. fors = *forsitan, perhaps.*

234. in vota : i.e. the gods are summoned to be witnesses *to his vows.*

235. aequora (cognate acc.): cf. iii. 191, v. 217, 862.

237. voti reus, *bound to my vow,* i.e. if my prayer is granted; A. 352, *a*; B. 208, 3; G. 374, N.[2]; cf. D. 337.—**exta :** the nobler entrails, heart, liver, etc.

240. chorus : many fanciful sea-monsters are supposed to attend the god. *Phorcus* was a son of Neptune and father of the Gorgons; *Panopea,* a sea-nymph; *Portunus,* the Italian god of harbors.

242. illa, *she* (the ship).

244. Anchisa : abl. of source.

247. in navis, *for each ship* (cf. *in dies*) that had shared in the race.— **optare, ferre :** A. 563, N.; D. 842; B. 295, 5, N.; G. 546, N.[3]

248. magnum talentum : a talent of silver was heavier than a talent of gold.

249. addit, *gives in addition.*

250. chlamydem : see Fig. 37.— **quam plurima,** etc., *round which a broad band of Melibœan purple ran.*

251. Meliboea, *of Melibœa,* a town in Thessaly, famous for the *murex.* Cf. *Paradise Lost,* xi. 240–244 :

> Over his lucid arms
> A military vest of purple flow'd
> Livelier than Melibœan, or the grain
> Of Sarra, worn by kings and heroes old
> In time of truce.

— **maeandro duplici,** *in a double meandering pattern,* so called from the winding course of the Mæander, a river of Asia Minor (see Fig. 45, from a Greek vase).

252. puer regius: Ganymede, who was taken up by an eagle to be cup-bearer of the gods (cf. i. 28); the hunting scene is *woven in (intextus)* the fabric of the *chlamys.* — **Ida :** locative abl.

253. iaculo: i.e. runs them down in the chase, pursuing them with the javelin.

254. quem praepes, etc.: another scene woven in the *chlamys.*

255. armiger : i.e. the eagle, often represented as bearing in his claws the thunderbolts of Jupiter.

256. tendunt : i.e. in the picture.

257. custodes : i.e. the old slaves (*paedagogi*) who, according to the practice of the ancients, would attend a youth of his consequence. — **saevit-que,** etc., *and the wild barking of dogs fills the air.*

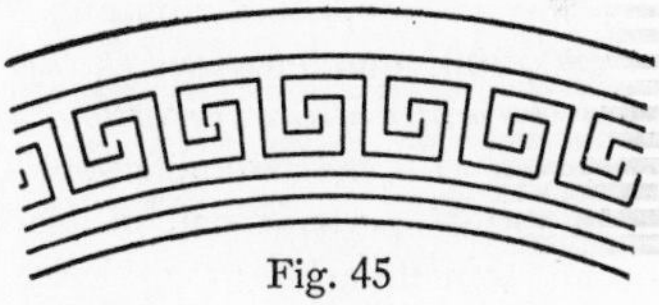

258. qui : the antecedent is *huic* in *v.* 259. — **virtute,** *in excellence.*

259. hamis auroque : hendiadys.

260. loricam : see Fig. 34. — **De-moleo :** dat. of separation.

Fig. 45

261. Ilio : the final *o* is shortened without elision before *alto.*

262. habere, *to keep* : infinitive of purpose (Introd. § 84). — **decus,** etc. : i.e. honorable and useful at the same time.

263. ferebant, *could bear.*

264. at, etc.: i.e. though two slaves could hardly carry it, yet it was once worn by a hero in ordinary use.

265. cursu, *in flight.* Notice that often in translating it is necessary to change the point of view. Thus here *cursu* refers to Demoleos; but in English we make it refer to the Trojans, although the other point of view is also possible.

266. dona : for construction see Introd. § 39. — **lebetas :** Gr. acc. plur. See *v.* 110, note.

269. taenis (= *taeniis*), *headbands* of ribbon, usually worn by athletes.

271. ordine: abl. of specification; one *row of oars* had been broken on the rocks (*vv.* 205–206).

272. agebat : A. 546, *a* ; D. 751 ; B. 288, B, 2 ; G. 581.

273. qualis : see *tali, v.* 280. — **aggere viae,** *roadway.* Roman roads were well crowned, and higher than the level of the land.

274. aerea rota : i.e. of a chariot. — **obliquum transiit,** *has run straight across.* — **gravis ictu** = *gravi ictu.*

276. fugiens, *trying to escape.*

279. in sua membra : i.e. one part of his body upon another.

281. tamen : i. e. though disabled in her oars.

283. servatam, reductos (emphatic), *on account of the saving, on account of the return.*

284. datur : the *ŭ* is lengthened before the cæsura. — **Minervae :** she was the goddess of all household arts, especially of spinning and weaving.

285. genus : acc. of specification. — **sub ubere,** *at her breast.*

286. tendit : sc. *iter.*

287. quem . . . silvae, *which forests surrounded on every side with circling hills :* a poetically inverted form of expression, but perfectly clear.

288. theatri circus, *the circuit of a theatre.* The word *theatrum* designates the place for the spectators on the hill-slopes that formed the *circus* or race-course in the valley between. The theatres and circuses of the ancients were ordinarily placed in similar natural valleys, sometimes with masonry to complete the outline.

289, 290. quo, etc., *and thither among many thousands the hero passed into the midst of the spectators, and took his seat on a raised mound.* — **consessu :** i. e. the assembled spectators (sitting together). The construction is doubtful; perhaps dat. of place to which (Introd. § 34). — **exstructo :** lit. *on* [something] *built up,* i. e. a mound or elevated seat of honor.

291. qui : the antecedent is *eorum,* to be supplied with *animos.* — **velint :** informal indir. disc.; A. 592, 2; D. 905; B. 323; G. 628. The account of the foot race is elaborately parodied by Pope, *Dunciad,* ii. 35 ff.

296. pio, *honest.* — **pueri :** Euryalus.

302. fama obscura, *unknown fame,* i. e. want of fame leaving them in obscurity; *oxymoron :* A. 641; D. 949; B. 375, 2; G. 694.

305. mihi : dat. of agent.

306. lēvato, *polished :* notice the quantity.

307. ferre : infin. of purpose.

308. unus = *idem.*

309. caput : acc. of specification. — **flava :** referring to the pallid green of the olive.

311. Amazoniam : the Amazons, as well as the Thracians, were allies of the Trojans and famous archers.

312. lato auro : *with a broad band of gold :* abl. of instrument. — **circum :** adv.

313. tereti gemma, *with its polished jewel :* abl. of instrument.

314. galea : abl. with *contentus* (Introd. § 66).

316. spatia, *the course.*

317. nimbo similes : i. e. in a confused crowd. — **ultima signant,** *they mark the goal* with their eye.

318. abit, *gets away.* — **corpora :** suggesting the notion of flying projectiles.

319. fulminis alis : the thunderbolt is represented on coins, and in poetry, as " winged."

320. A spondaic verse (Introd. § 104).

323. quo sub ipso, *at his very heels.*

325. incumbens umero, *all but touching* (lit. *leaning over*) *his shoulder.* — **supersint :** we should expect the imperfect contrary to fact, but the present makes the passage more lively by representing the condition as still possible.

326. ambiguumve relinquat, *or would leave the race in doubt.*

328. finem : fem. as in ii. 554. — **lēvi sanguine,** *in the slippery blood.*

329. ut forte, *as, by chance :* i.e. the course happened to lie across the spot of sacrifice ; *ut* is very loosely used in Latin so as to be equivalent to *when* or even *where* as here.

330. fusus : sc. *sanguis.* — **super :** adv.

331. presso, *as he strode* (more lit. *pressed the ground*).

334. ille : here emphasizes the distant subject, *Nisus.* — **amorum,** *of his friend.*

336. revolutus, *thrown backward* by the shock.

337. Euryalūs : the final syllable is long (Introd. § 110).

339. nunc, *now* (Nisus and Salius being out of the race). — **palma, victor :** in a sort of apposition with *Diores.*

340. caveae, *theatre :* properly *the concave rows of seats* ; cf. note, v. 288.

341. prima, *in front.* — **patrum :** the front seats were by Roman custom reserved for persons of rank and distinction, the senate occupying the orchestra, and the *equites* the first fourteen rows of the seats.

342. reddi : in prose, *ut reddatur* (Introd. § 78).

343. favor, *good will :* the word regularly used of enthusiasm among spectators of a play ; cf. *v.* 148.

344. veniens, *appearing.* Cf. *Paradise Lost*, iv. 448–450 :

> His grave rebuke,
> Severe in youthful beauty, added grace
> Invincible.

— **virtus,** *merit.*

345. proclamat, *appeals for him.*

346. subiit, *has come up* (in another's place). — **venit ad,** *has attained.*

347. reddantur : fut. less vivid condition, the apodosis being found in *frustra.*

349. palmam . . . nemo, *no one is going to disturb the order of the prizes* (lit. *move the prize from its order*): conative pres.; A. 467; D. 649; B. 259, 2; G. 227, N.[2]

350. me : i.e. personally, or unofficially. — **casus,** *misfortune :* acc. plur.

352. aureis: dissyllabic (Introd. § 112).

354. te lapsorum miseret: for case see Introd. § 21.

355. merui, *earned* [and should have had], *unless,* etc.: A. 517, *b*; D. 797, N.; B. 304, 3; G. 597, R.²—**laude,** *by merit* (as opposed to fortune or luck).

356. quae, *the same . . . as:* sc. *tulit.*—**tulisset,** *had put me out of the race* (lit. *had borne me [away]*).

357. dictis, *with these words:* abl. with *simul*; A. 432, *c*; D. 277, N.; B. 144, 2; G. 417, 12.

358. olli: not exactly *at him* (which would be accusative), but *in his face.*

359. artem, *the skilful work:* in apposition with *clipeum.*

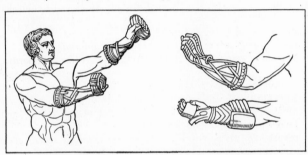

Fig. 46

360. Neptuni . . . refixum, *taken down from a sacred pillar of Neptune belonging to the Greeks* (i.e. as spoil of war); perhaps a gift from Helenus; see iii. 464 ff.—**Danais:** dat. of reference; in prose we should have the genitive; A. 377; D. 385; B. 188, 1, N.; G. 350, 1.

363. si cui [*est*], etc., *whoever has manliness and ready courage.*

364. adsit, *let him come forward:* hortatory.—**evinctis,** *bound* with the cestus (*caestus*), which was a sort of gauntlet (*v.* 405) like the brass knuckles of modern roughs (Fig. 46).

365. pugnae: genitive.

366. auro vittisque: i.e. gilded and wreathed horns, as was usual in such cases.

369. virum: gen. plur.

370. Paridem: Paris had great fame as a prize-fighter, though he was an indifferent warrior and worse patriot.

371. ad tumulum: i.e. at the funeral games at Hector's tomb.

372. victorem, *hitherto unconquered.*

373. se . . . veniens . . . ferebat, *boasted himself* (or *claimed*) *to be descended* (lit. *coming*): the participle agrees with the subject instead of with *se*; ci. *delapsus*, ii. 377. See A. 581, N.[3]; G. 527, N.[2] — **Amyci** : a famous mythical boxer in Asia Minor, defeated and slain by Pollux in the Argonautic expedition.

378. huic alius, *another boxer to match him.*

380. palma, *the contest.*

384. quo . . . usque : tmesis.

385. ducere . . . iube, *bid me lead off my prize.*

386. reddi : i.e. given him as his due. — **promissa,** *the promised prize.*

387. gravis, *sternly* (as if an adverb).

388. consederat : had seated himself, i.e. *was sitting.*

391. nobis, *of ours* (ethical dative, like *mihi* in *v.* 162). — **magister,** *teacher.*

392. nequiquam : i.e. his fame is now vain since a foreign boaster carries off the prize.

393. spolia : i.e. prizes (probably the cestus of the vanquished) won in former contests (called *spolia* because stripped, as it were, from his defeated opponents).

394. sub haec, *in reply.* — **gloria,** *ambi...*

395. sed enim, *but, you see.*

397. mihi : dat. of possession with *foret.* — **improbus,** *indecent boaster.*

399. haud equidem, *not, to be sure :* the real conclusion is obscured ; " I should have come, though not *pretio inductus.*"

400. moror, *care for.* — **deinde :** with *proiecit.*

403. ferre manum, *raise his hand :* as we might say, *bear a hand in fight.* — **intendere,** etc., *bind his arms with the stubborn hide.*

406. longe, *shrinking :* i.e. he retreats to some distance.

408. volumina, *the thongs of hide.* — **versat :** i.e. turns over as they lie on the ground.

409. senior : Entellus.

410. quid si vidisset : sc. *quid putasset*; the conclusion is designedly left to the imagination, as often also in English (" what if "). — **arma :** i.e. the cestus.

411. tristem : because Eryx was killed by Hercules.

412. tuus : Entellus addresses Æneas.

413. sanguine, etc.: i.e of those he had killed in his time.

414. his : dat. with *suetus* [*eram*].

415. aemula, *envious :* as if old age grudged what little strength might yet remain.

416. cānebat (from *caneo*) **sparsa,** *sprinkled gray on my two temples* (lit. *old age, sprinkled upon my two temples, was gray*).

418. sedet, *suits.* — **Aeneae :** dat. of reference. — **auctor,** strictly *a voucher :* here, one who confirms the view by his authority.

419. tibi, *for your sake* or *to please you :* dat. of reference.

421. duplicem: i.e. the *abolla*, or double-folded garment, worn by him on account of his age.

422. lacertosque: hypermetric verse (Introd. § 114).

423. exuit [sc. *vestibus*], *bared*.

426. in·digitos arrectus, *rising on his toes.*

430. ille, *the one*: Dares, as the first-named.

431. trementi: sc. *ei*; dat. of reference.

432. genua: dissyllable (Introd. § 112).

434. cavo lateri: dat. of indirect object. — **ingeminant,** *they strike thick and fast* (lit. *redouble*).

435. sonitus: i.e. their chests ring with the blows. — **auris:** what case? See the quantity.

436. crebra, *many times.*

437. gravis: lit. *solid, heavy*; translate *stood firm because of his weight* (cf. *v.* 447). — **nisu,** *position*: strictly referring to the bracing of the feet.

438. corpore modo, *by the movement of his body merely*: a technical expression; cf. Cic. Cat. i. 6, end. — **tela:** object of *exit* (here transitive).

439. molibus, *siege-works.*

440. sedet circum, *encamps about*, or *besieges.*

441. nunc . . . locum, *attempts now these approaches, now those, and examines the whole position with all his skill.* The verb *pererrat* has to be translated in two ways (so-called *zeugma*).

443. ostendit, *put forth.*

445. elapsus, *leaping aside.* — **cessit,** *dodged.*

446. effudit, *spent.* — **ultro,** *untouched*: i.e. without receiving a blow.

447. gravis graviterque, etc., *heavy man that he was, fell heavily.*

448. quondam, *sometimes.*

449. radicibus: abl. of separation; we say *by the roots.*

450. studiis, *in their excitement*: referring strictly to their *eager interest* in one side or the other.

451. caelo: dat. of place to which.

453. casu, *by his fall.*

454. ira: ablative.

455. tum, *now* (emphatic).

456. aequore toto, *over the whole field.*

457. ille: see note on *v.* 334.

458. quam multa, *with blows as thick as the hailstones that rattle on the roofs in a storm* (lit. *with how much hail storms rattle on the roofs, so with thick blows*, etc.): the proper correlative is supplied by the expression *sic densis.*

460. creber, *again and again*: cf. *v.* 436. — **versat,** *drives this way and that.* — **Dareta:** Introd. § 92.

462. saevire animis acerbis, *to rage in passionate fury.*

466. viris alias, *strength not his own* : i.e. some god's, alluding to the sudden change of the contest in *v.* 455. — **conversa numina,** *gods adverse* (lit. *turned,* as we speak of a *change* of luck or a *reversal* of fortune).

469. utroque, *from side to side.*

473. superans animis, *with towering pride.* — **tauro :** abl. of cause.

477. adversi, *so that it faced him.*

479. The feat here described was performed, it is said, by Cæsar Borgia.

480. effracto cerebro, *dashing out its brains.*

483. pro morte Daretis : a substitute, such as is found in many early religions, for human sacrifices, — puppets, some lower animal, or a symbolized act of sacrifice. — **meliorem :** spoken with some contempt of his antagonist, as well as because the substitute is more acceptable to the gods.

486. velint : as in *v.* 291. For shooting with the bow see Fig. 47 (from a vase painting).

487. ingenti manu, *with mighty hand,* as of heroic stature and strength. — **Seresti :** possibly the same with Sergestus, whose damaged ship might well furnish the mast and rigging necessary.

Fig. 47

488. traiecto in fune : fastened *by a cord passed over* or *through* the mast and tied to the bird's foot (cf. *v.* 511).

489. quo tendant ferrum : rel. clause of purpose.

490. deiectam sortem, *the lots thrown into it.* The lots were shaken in the helmet until one leaped out.

491. clamore secundo, *amid shouts of applause.*

494. oliva : perhaps an oversight, as Cloanthus (*v.* 246) is wreathed with laurel. Olive, palm, and laurel make the regular prizes of victory.

496. confundere foedus : at the bidding of Athene, Pandarus shot an arrow, wounded Menelaus, and thus broke the truce between the Trojans and the Greeks (Il. iv. 104; Bry. 115).

499. et ipse, *even he too.*

501. pro se quisque : in appos. with *viri.*

504. venit, *it reaches the goal* : i.e. the mast, though it misses the mark — the bird.

505. timuit pinnis, *showed its fright by its fluttering.*

506. omnia, *the whole place.*

508. alta petens, *aiming high,* because the other had aimed too low.

509. miserandus, *unlucky.*

511. quīs = *quibus.*

512. notos, *to the winds,* depending on *in.*

513. rapidus, *swiftly.* — **contenta,** *drawn.*

514. fratrem : Pandarus, regarded as a sort of patron saint of archery. — **in vota vocavit,** *called on in his prayers* (lit. *called to* [hear] *his vows*).

515. iam : with *laetam.*

517. astris aetheriis : according to a common view the soul was composed of fiery æther, from which also the stars were fed (cf. i. 608 and note, vi. 730–732). Hence the bird left its life in the natural home of spirit.

520. tamen : i.e. though he had lost the prize.

521. pater, *veteran that he was.* Note *patēr.* — **arcum :** i.e. its power.

522. futurum, *destined to be.*

523. augurio : abl. of quality. — **exitus ingens,** *the dread result* : sometimes understood of the burning of the ships. The prodigy, however, is probably a part of the old legend, and refers to later events in Sicily, perhaps her wars with Rome (*sera omina*).

524. terrifici : from their alarming words. — **cecinerunt,** *interpreted* : i.e. after the fulfilment.

528. crinem, *a trail of light* : cf. ii. 694.

529. haesere, *were transfixed.* The men were amazed, but the leaders at once interpreted the omen for good, and so removed any ill effects in their followers' minds.

534. exsortem . . . honores, *that you should receive a prize apart from the rest* (lit. *out of the lot,* i.e. out of course).

535. ipsĭus : a gift, as it were, bestowed by Anchises himself.

537. in magno munere, *as a great gift* (lit. *in the place of*) ; cf. the similar use of *pro.* — **Cisseus :** king of Thrace, father of Hecuba.

538. ferre : cf. *v.* 247. — **sui :** obj. gen. with *monumentum.*

541. Eurytion : who, we are to suppose, takes the second prize.

542. quamvis deiecit : the subjunctive is the regular prose construction with *quamvis* ; A. 527, *e* ; D. 809 ; B. 309, 6 ; G. 606, N.[1]

543. donis : abl. of specification with *proximus.*

545. nondum . . . misso : before the archery match was over, Æneas had given his directions for the show that was to follow, so that there might be no delay. A similar surprise for the spectators was frequent in the games at Rome ; and the introduction of it is here a special compliment to Augustus, who had revived this very *Troiae lusus.*

547. Epytiden : he seems to have acted the part of a *paedagogus,* a guardian who constantly attended youths of any distinction.

548. Ascanio: dat. with *dic, v.* 551.

550. ducat, ostendat: subjunctives in indirect for imperatives in direct discourse; cf. iv. 635. — **avo,** *in honor of his grandsire* (dat. of reference).

552. infusum: the multitude had poured in to watch the last sports, which did not require much space.

553. pariter, *well-matched.*

554. quos: obj. of *mirata.*

555. iuventus: i.e. the older youths; all able-bodied men fit for active service were *iuvenes* up to forty years of age.

556. tonsa corona, *with wreath close-trimmed*: probably confining the hair below the helmet. It has also been explained of the " circular tonsure," the hair cut round, in boyish fashion.

557. bina: the regular number (cf. i. 313).

558. lēvīs: cf. *lēvia* (*v.* 91), *lēvi* (*v.* 328). — **pectore summo,** *from the upper part of the chest.*

560. terni = *tres*: A. 137, *d*; D. 173, *e*; B. 81, 4, *d*; G. 97, N.[1] Cf. *v.* 85.

562. magistris: the *ductores.*

563. una acies: sc. *est.*

565. auctura Italos: a town called Politorium was fabled to have been colonized by Polites.

566. vestigia . . . ostentans: i.e. white on the front (*primi*) of his legs and on his forehead.

568. Atii: this fanciful ancestry for the Roman family of the Atii (the *gens Atia*) is, like the derivation of the Julian *gens* from Iulus (i. 288), a compliment to Augustus. He belonged to both families, for his mother (Atia) was the daughter of Julia (Cæsar's sister) and of M. Atius Balbus.

572. esse: cf. *vv.* 262 (note), 307.

575. excipiunt: referring back to *v.* 555.

576. veterum parentum, *of their forefathers.*

577. omnem . . . lustravere, *had paraded in front of the whole assembly and before the eyes of their friends.*

579. flagello: abl. of instrument, where the English idiom would suggest the accusative.

580–582. olli . . . tulere, *they* (i.e. the three *turmae* or *troops* of twelve each, *v.* 560) *rode apart in equal numbers* (**pares:** i.e. they formed in pairs, still keeping in three troops, and thus rode down the arena); *and then* (**atque**), *separating the divisions, the three troops* (**terni**) *broke up* (**agmina solvere:** i.e. each troop of twelve divided into two *chori* of six), *and again, at a signal* (**vocati**), *they wheeled and charged each other with hostile weapons* (i.e. each half-troop of six charged the corresponding half-troop which belonged to the same original troop of twelve). — Notice the long penult in *discurrēre.*

583. inde, etc., *then they enter upon other movements* (i.e. they ride apart again) *and counter-movements.*

584. adversi spatiis: in the opposite directions to those they had taken before; or, possibly, on opposite sides of the arena. — **alternos orbibus**, etc., *they interweave circles with circles in alternation*: i.e. they ride in circles, the different squads alternately inside and out.

587. pariter, *in even line*: i.e. together as one force.

588. 'Labyrinthus: the work of Dædalus, in which the Minotaur was kept. — **alta**: Crete is mountainous.

589. parietibus . . . iter, *to have had a way bordered* (lit. *woven*) *with blind walls*: i.e. without doors or windows to serve as guide. — **ancipitem- que . . . dolum**, *and to have been craftily laid out with a thousand paths to mislead*: lit. *to have had baffling craft* (i.e. a crafty plan of construction) *with a thousand paths.* — **mille viis**: abl. of quality with *dolum*.

590, 591. quā . . . error, *where the baffling maze that could not be retraced confused all signs of the course to be followed.* — **quā . . . falleret**: rel. clause of result. — **signa sequendi**: lit. *signs of following* (i.e. to be followed).

593. texunt, *they form in their winding course*: the whole seems like a richly woven web.

594. delphinum similes: the play of dolphins, in its life and brilliancy, relieves the architectural stiffness of the last comparison. For case see A. 385, *c*, 2; D. 351; B. 204, 3; G. 359, N.[4]

595. Carpathium, Libycum: sc. *mare.*

596. cursus (gen.), *manœuvres.* — **primus . . . rettulit**, *was the first to repeat.*

599. ipse, pubes: sc. *celebravit.*

600. porro, *in succession.*

601. patrium honorem, *its ancestral observance.*

602. Troia, Troianum: see note, *v.* 545. — **pueri**: sc. *dicuntur.*

603. hac . . . tenus: tmesis for *hactenus.* — **patri**: i.e. Anchises; cf. note on *avo, v.* 550, for construction.

605. tumulo: abl. of place where.

607. ventos adspirat: cf. iv. 223.

608. multa movens, *with many designs.*

609. per mille coloribus arcum, *along her bow of a thousand colors*: see iv. 694 and note.

613. secretae, *apart from the rest.*

616. superesse: exclamatory infinitive (Introd. § 83).

618. ergo, *thus*, prepared as they are already. — **haud ignara nocendi**, *skilled in mischief*: litotes; A. 326, *c*; D. 947; B. 375, 1; G. 700.

621. cui . . . fuissent, *as one who once had had a family, and name, and children*: a woman of dignity and of influence amongst the rest, and hence a suitable person for her scheme; A. 535, *e*; D. 730, I; B. 283, 3; G. 633.

624. traxerit : relative clause expressing cause.

627. cum ferimur, *while we are still borne on.* — **freta :** supply *omnia* with *freta.* — **saxa, sidera emensae :** the *stars* are put for the dangers of the sky, the *rocks* for those of the deep.

630. fraterni : cf. note on i. 570.

631. dare urbem : they are now a people without a city — a violent contradiction of terms to ancient notions.

633. nullane . . . moenia, *shall no walls any longer be called those of Troy ?*

635. infaustas puppis, *those ill-omened hulks.*

638. iam tempus agi [sc. *est*], *now is the time for deeds to be done.*

639. tantis prodigiis, *such prodigies admit no delay:* dat. of possession. — **quattuor arae :** erected perhaps to offer sacrifice for a prosperous voyage ; perhaps by the four ships' crews, or by Cloanthus, according to his vow (*v.* 237).

640. deus, etc.: i.e. his altars supply the means, and the dangers he threatens (those of the sea) the desire (*animum*).

642. sublata procul dextra, *lifting high her hand.*

645. tot : cf. ii. 501.

646. vobis : ethical dat. (see note on *v.* 162).

648. spiritus : sc. *est.*

651. quod careret, *because* [she said] *she alone was deprived of a share in such rites,* etc. — further explained by the next clause. Beroë's reason is indirectly quoted, hence the subjunctives ; A. 592, 3 ; D. 906 ; B. 323 ; G. 541.

655. ambiguae, etc., *gazed on the ships, vacillating between their unhappy clinging to the shore at hand and the kingdoms which summoned them by the fates.* — **spectare :** historical infinitive.

658. ingentem secuit arcum, *cut her path in a great bow* through the air, as a ship through the water ; the rainbow is her wake : cf. iv. 257, 700–701.

659. monstris : the bow suddenly appearing and the departure of Iris show the divine nature of the phenomenon.

660. focis penetralibus : probably their household fires in the interior of their huts or tents.

661. frondem : the branches with which the altars were decorated.

663. pictas : Homer describes ships as "scarlet-prowed." Figures of gods, etc., were also painted on the sterns. — **abiete** (trisyllable): abl. of material.

664. cuneos : the divisions of the seats of the theatres, so called from their shape (see Fig. 5).

665. perfert, *brings word.* — **ipsi,** *the spectators.*

666. respiciunt, *looking round behold.* — **in nimbo,** *in the cloud* of smoke.

668. sic, *just as he was.*

669. castra, *the encampment* (of huts, etc.) near the ships. — **magistri,** *masters* or *guardians* : the adult leaders (mentioned in *v.* 562) who had charge of the boys.

671. cives, *my countrywomen* : a name reminding them at once of their allegiance and their hopes.

677. sicubi . . . saxa : i. e. whatever hollow rocks (if there are any anywhere) may chance to be thereabout.

678. piget [sc. *eas*], *they loathe* (Introd. § 21).

679. mutatae, *coming to themselves.* — **Iuno,** *the influence of Juno.*

682. lentus . . . vapor, *the fire consumes slowly.*

683. est : from *edo*; cf. iv. 66. — **toto . . . pestis,** *the destruction sinks into the entire frame.*

685. abscindere : historical infinitive.

687. exosus : sc. *es.*

688. si quid, etc., *if thy ancient regard for piety pays any heed to mortal toils and troubles.*

691. vel tu, etc. : i. e. either let the fleet escape the flames, and thus rescue what little remains *(res tenuis)* to the Trojans, or — *the only thing left to do* in case you refuse — destroy it all suddenly.

696. turbidus imber aquā, *a wild drenching storm thick with the black south winds.* — **turbidus aqua :** expresses the *wildness* of the storm and the *drenching* of the rain ; the south winds are *black* because they bring such weather as this — *thick* and *dark* ; and the epithets, as often in poetry, are intentionally confused in their application. Cf. *vv.* 2, 11 : *atros Aquilone, inhorruit tenebris.*

697. super, *from above.*

702. nunc . . . versans, *turned his anxious thoughts* (lit. *shifted his great cares*) *now this way now that, pondering.* — **-ne . . . -ne,** *whether . . . or.* — **resideret :** the dir. quest. would be *residam* (deliberative).

704. Nautes : said to have been the priest of Pallas in Troy, and the preserver of the Palladium, which passed to his descendants, the *Nautii,* at Rome. — **unum,** *above all others.*

705. arte, *prophetic art.*

706. haec : i. e. the words of Nautes below. — **responsa :** so called because his words are. inspired and oracular. — **portenderet, posceret :** indir. quest.

711. est tibi, *you have* : i. e. he is ready to help you. — **divinae stirpis :** cf. *v.* 38.

712. volentem, *a willing adviser.*

713. trade : sc. *eos.* — **superant,** etc., *remain over from the lost ships,* after the serviceable ones are filled. — **quos pertaesum est,** etc.: Introd. § 21.

716. quidquid . . . est, *all who are*; lit. *whatever is* (neut. collective referring to persons). — **tecum,** *in your company.* — **pericli :** obj. genitive with *metuens* (adj.).

717. habeant sine, *allow them to have :* cf. *v.* 163 and note. — **fessi,** *since they are tired out.*

718. Acestam : see note, *v.* 38. Here Virgil follows the tradition. Cicero (Verr. v. 33) says : " Segesta is a very old town in Sicily, which is shown to have been founded by Æneas when he fled from Troy and came into these parts. The people of Segesta, accordingly, consider themselves to be bound to the Roman people, not only by constant alliance and friendship, but also by ties of blood (*cognatione*)." — **permisso nomine** (abl. abs.) = *by his permission,* which is thus courteously asked.

720. animo : abl. of place where. — **diducitur,** *is distracted by* (lit. *drawn apart into*), unwilling thus to divide his band and yet seeing the advantages of the course suggested by Nautes.

721. et, *and while he ponders thus.*

722. facies, etc. : not really the ghost of Anchises (who, when met in the Lower World, seems not to know of these occurrences ; see vi. 694 and note), but a vision sent from heaven and taking his shape. Cf. the human shape assumed by Iris (*v.* 620) and by Venus (i. 315). — **delapsa,** *gliding down* (from heaven, not up from the world of the dead).

725. nate . . . fatis : cf. iii. 182.

727. tandem, *in your extremity.*

730. gens dura : the Rutulians.

731. ante (adv.), *first.*

732. Averna : used in a general way of the Lower World.

733. meos, *with me.*

734. tristes umbrae : in apposition with *Tartara.*

735. colo. Huc : hiatus.

736. nigrarum : as customary in sacrificing to the gods below ; see vi. 243 ff. — **multo sanguine :** *after abundant sacrifice :* abl. of means.

737. genus : i. e. your descendants who are to live in Italy.

738. iamque vale : the vision speaks as a ghost might have spoken ; such spirits were thought to vanish at the approach of dawn. Cf. *Hamlet,* i. 5. 58 ff. :

> But soft! methinks I scent the morning air :
> Brief let me be.
> . . . Fare thee well at once :
> The glow-worm shows the matin to be near,
> And gins to pale his uneffectual fire.

— **torquet,** etc., *rolls on in the middle of her course.*

739. saevus: because it forces him to leave Æneas. — **Oriens** = *Aurora, dawn.*

743. cinerem: i. e. of his own hearth. The sacrifice of wheat and incense is offered to his own household deities.

744. Larem: the *Lares* were the special protectors of the household. They were the spirits of deceased ancestors or other deified persons, and were represented as youths in a short tunic, generally in the act of pouring a libation: see Fig. 48 (the trees are the olives before the house of Augustus).

The Lares were worshipped with flowers, fruit, wine, incense, and fine grain or cakes. — **penetralia:** i. e. the hearth.

745. farre pio: the salted meal regularly used in sacrifices; see ii. 133. — **acerra:** the box for holding incense; see Fig. 49, from an ancient wall painting.

748. constet, *is fixed*: indir. question.

749. consiliis: dat. of possession with *mora* [*est*], as in *v.* 639.

750. transcribunt, *they register*: i. e. for the new city. — **volentem,** *who wished it.*

751. deponunt, *they set aside.* — **animos:** in apposition with *matres* and *populum.* — **nil**

Fig. 48

egentis, *that feel no need of*; *nil* is adverbial acc. — **laudis:** Introd. § 22.

753. rudentisque: hypermetric (Introd. § 114).

754. bello: abl. of specification. — **virtus:** sc. *est.*

755. aratro: see i. 425.

756. Ilium, Troiam: these names here seem to be given to different quarters of the city, which was named Acesta.

758. indicit forum, *proclaims a court*: i. e. establishes courts of justice. — **patribus . . . vocatis** (abl. abs.): the senate (*patres*) are conceived as his council. — **iura:** here apparently equivalent to *leges.*

759. sedes: on Mt. Eryx in western Sicily stood in Virgil's time an ancient and much honored temple of Venus. He ascribes its foundation to Æneas.

761. sacer, *held in reverence.*

762. novem: the usual time for funeral rites; see *v.* 64 and note.

763. straverunt: see i. 66 and note.

766. morantur, etc., *they prolong the night and day.*

767. ipsi: see *v.* 716.

773. ex ordine, *one after another.*— **funem :** translate by a plural.

775. procul: *apart from the others.* — **pateram tenet :** i. e. makes a libation (see Fig. 48).— **exta . . . porricit :** cf. *vv.* 237–238 and note.

777, 778. Repeated from iii. 130 and iii. 290.

781. nec exsaturabile pectus, *and her insatiable heart.*

783. quam : the antecedent is *Junonis.*

784. infracta, *subdued.* Notice that the prefix *in-* has two meanings : one negative (in which it is compounded with the adjective), and the other inten- sive and the like (when it is compounded with the verb).

785. media . . . exedisse, *to have eaten the city of the Phrygians out of the vitals of the race* (eviscerating the nation, as it were, or, as we should say, destroying it root and branch).

Fig. 49

786. traxe : syncopated form of *traxisse* (Introd. § 91, *n*).

787. reliquias, etc., *the relics, the very ashes and bones of murdered Troy :* observe the emphasis.

788. sciat illa, *let* HER *tell* (for I can- not see any reason for such malignity).

790. caelo: i. e. has raised the waves to the stars, according to the common hyberbole (see i. 103, note).

794. classe amissa : exaggeration natural to strong feeling ; for the facts see *v.* 699.

795. terrae : a forced use of the dat. of indir. obj. ; in prose, *in terrā.*

796. quod superest, *this and this only I ask.* Juno has done us many injuries. These are irrevocable, — what's done is done and as to THAT we cannot pray for relief : there remains only THIS (*quod superest*) that you can do for us, and for this, then, we pray. — **liceat tibi** (hortatory), *allow yourself* (almost = *deign*).

798. ea moenia : i. e. the promised city near the Tiber.

799. Saturnius : Neptune was a son of Saturn.

801. genus : Venus was born from the sea near Cythera. — **merui,** *I have deserved it too.* — **furores,** etc. : the madness of the waves.

802. compressi : i. e. in Æneas' behalf.

803. Xanthum, Simoënta : in Homer the rescue of Æneas from Achilles by Neptune (*Poseidon*) took place before the struggle of Achilles with the rivers Xanthus and Simois. Here the two events seem to be brought together. Virgil probably follows a different tradition. See Iliad, Bks. xx, xxi.

804. mihi cura: sc. *est.*

809. congressum, etc., *who was encountering the son of Peleus, with the gods unfair* (not impartial, and therefore *unfavorable*) *and strength ill-matched* (zeugma).

810. cum cuperem (concessive): alluding to the treachery of Laomedon: see n. on iii. 248.

814. unus: i. e. Palinurus; see *v.* 859.

815. caput, *life.*

816. laeta, *till it was joyful* (proleptic).

817. auro: i. e. the golden harness.

818. effundit: *lets loose.*

820. tonanti: perhaps a general epithet of a chariot-wheel; or it may refer to the roaring of the waters below.

821. aquis: abl. of specification with *sternitur.*

822. facies: supply a verb (*appear* or *are seen*) in translation. — **cetē:** a Greek nominative plural, used for monsters of the deep in general.

823. chorus, *band* of sea-deities. — **Glauci:** a sea-divinity, said to be completely overgrown with "shellfish, seaweed, and stones." — **Inous Palaemon:** both Palæmon and his mother Ino were changed into sea-deities.

825. The sea nymphs mentioned in *vv.* 825, 826 were daughters of Nereus (Nereids). Thetis was mother of Achilles.

827. blanda gaudia, *flattering delights.* — **vicissim,** *in their turn.*

829. intendi velis, *to be hung with sails.*

830. fecere pedem, *made a tack:* a technical expression. The *pes* is the lower corner of the sail which is drawn in or out in the tacking. — **sinistros:** sc. *nunc.*

831. torquent, detorquent: of the different tacks.

832. cornua, *spars.* — **sua flamina,** *favoring gales.*

834. ad hunc contendere cursum, *to steer their course by him* (i. e. to follow his course).

835. metam: see note on iii. 429.

837. sub remis: every man close to his oar. — **fusi per sedilia:** cf. *fusi per herbam,* i. 214.

838. aetheriis: i. e. of the upper, fiery heaven.

840. tristia, *fatal.*

841. insonti: as it was against his will.

842. Phorbanti: one of the companions.

845. furare, *steal away* (like "stealing a nap"). — **labori:** a poetical extension of the dat. of separation (Introd. § 32).

848. me: emphatic here and in the following verse.

849. monstro: i. e. the terrible deep.

850. credam: deliberative subjunctive. — **quid enim:** as if he had answered the preceding questions by saying, *I cannot — for why*, etc.?

852. dabat, amittebat, tenebat: observe the force of these imperfects. Palinurus speaks without once losing his grasp of the helm, or letting his eyes wander from the stars.

853. amittebāt: for the long final syllable see Introd. § 110. — **oculos . . . tenebat,** *kept his eyes fixed on the stars.*

Fig. 50

854. Lethaeo: Lethe was the river of the World Below that gave forgetfulness (see vi. 714). — With 854–856 cf. Denham, *Song*:

> Come, I say, thou powerful god,
> And thy leaden charming-rod,
> Dipped in the Lethæan lake,
> O'er his wakeful temples shake.

So Spenser speaks of "sweet slumbering dew" (*Faery Queen*, i. 1. 36), Shakspere of "the honey-heavy dew of slumber" (*Julius Cæsar*, ii. 230), Milton of "the dewy-feather'd sleep" (*Il Penseroso, v.* 146) and of "the timely dew of sleep" (*Paradise Lost*, iv. 614).

855. vi soporatum Stygia, *sleep-drenched with Stygian moisture* (lit. *made sleepy with Stygian force*).

856. cunctanti [sc. *ei*], *although he resists*: dat. of reference. — **solvit,** *relaxes*, in contrast with *tenebat*, above.

857. primos : though agreeing with *artus*, goes in sense with *vix* ; no sooner had sleep relaxed his limbs than, etc.

858. et . . . proiecit, *than he hurled him.*

859. cum gubernaclo : Palinurus is thrown overboard with the *steering oar* and a part of the stern to which it was attached.

861. ales, *on his wings* (lit. *winged*, adj. agreeing with *ipse*).

862. iter : cognate accusative.

864. scopulos Sirenum : three rocky islands off the Bay of Naples. Cf. Spenser's beautiful stanzas, *Faery Queen*, ii. 12. 30–38.

865. quondam : after they were foiled by the wily Ulysses (Od. xii. 178–200), the Sirens cast themselves into the sea and perished. Fig. 50 (from an ancient vase painting) represents Ulysses and the Sirens ; cf. Fig. 30.

866. tum, etc. : the song of the Sirens is now replaced by the roar of the surf.

867. fluitantem [sc. *ratem*], *drifting* at random. Æneas is roused by the irregular movement of the ship and by the surge chafing against the cliffs.

869. multa : cognate acc.— **animum :** acc. of specification.

BOOK VI

2. Cumarum : Cumæ, a colony from Chalcis in Eubœa, was the oldest Greek settlement in Italy. It was situated on the coast, a few miles west of Naples.

3. obvertunt proras : contrary to our custom, the vessels were brought up to land stern on ; hence *praetexunt* of the line of sterns along the shore.

6. semina : i.e. as the fire is struck with flint and steel, the elements of fire seem to be in the flint.

8. silvas : in apposition with *tecta*.— **rapit,** *scour* for fuel or game.— **inventa,** etc., *find and show.*

9. arces, *heights* : the temple of Apollo was on a hill, its secret shrine (*adytum*) being the cave of the Sibyl. — **altus,** *on the height.*

10. horrendae : she is an object of awe as being inspired by Apollo.— **procul,** *at some distance* (from the shore).— **secreta,** *secret abode.*— **Sibyllae :** the Sibyls were inspired prophetesses of some god, usually Apollo. They were thought of as maidens dwelling in lonely places who uttered prophecies when under the influence of the god. The most famous of them was the Cumæan Sibyl.

11. cui, etc., *whose mind and soul the Delian prophet powerfully inspires, and to whom,* etc. (lit. *to whom the Delian prophet breathes a great mind and soul*).

12. Delius : Apollo, so called from his favorite abode at Delos.

13. Triviae : an epithet of Diana (iv. 511, 609).

14. Daedalus : his escape by flying is told by Ovid, Met. viii. 183–259; see pp. 291 ff. of the text.

17. Chalcidica arce, *the heights of Cumæ* : see n. on *v.* 2.

18. redditus : Dædalus first alighted at Cumæ.

20. letum Androgeo, etc.: Ægeus, king of Athens, had sent Androgeos, son of King Minos of Crete, to his death in an encounter with the wild bull of Marathon. As a punishment, the Athenians were forced to send every year seven youths and seven maidens to be devoured by the Minotaur, a monster, half man and half bull, whom Minos kept confined in the Labyrinth constructed for that purpose by Dædalus. Theseus, son of Ægeus, went to Crete and killed the Minotaur in the Labyrinth, with the help of Ariadne, daughter of Minos, who furnished him with a thread that he unrolled for guidance in retracing his path. — **tum,** *next*. The sculptures on the temple gates represent first two scenes in Attica : (1) the death of Androgeos and (2) the drawing of lots to determine the victims to be sent to Crete ; then two scenes in Crete : (3) Pasiphaë, (4) the Labyrinth, with Theseus and Ariadne.

21. Cecropidae : Cecrops was the fabulous founder of Athens.

22. ductis sortibus, *with the lots already drawn* : abl. abs.

23. contra : i. e. on the other door. — **mari :** abl. of separation.

24. tauri, obj. genitive. — **supposta furto,** *substituted by a trick*.

27. labor ille domus, *that house wondrously built* : the Labyrinth. The expression *labor domus* resembles *rotarum lapsus* (ii. 235) and *minae murorum* (iv. 88): see the notes. — **error,** *wanderings* (its original sense).

28. reginae, *the princess* : i.e. the daughter of Minos, Ariadne, who fell in love with Theseus. — **sed enim,** *but [the secret of the maze was revealed] for*. For the ellipsis see i. 19, ii. 164.

29. ipse resolvit : the builder of the Labyrinth taught the princess how to *unravel* its mystery by the guiding clue of thread. — **dolos ambagesque,** *deceitful windings* : hendiadys.

30. vestigia : i. e. of Theseus, who thus "threaded the maze."

31. sineret dolor, *had grief permitted* : hort. subj. expressing a past condition contrary to fact ; A. 521, *b* ; D. 774, footnote ; B. 305, 2 ; G. 598. — **haberes :** apodosis ; for tense see A. 517, *a* ; D. 798 ; B. 304, 2 ; G. 597 and R.[1]

32. casus effingere : i. e. to represent Icarus' flight and falling into the Icarian Sea, to which he gave his name. See the illustration (p. 267 of the text), from a wall painting at Pompeii.

33. omnia : two syllables. — **protinus . . . perlegerent,** *they would have continued to peruse* : for tense see n. on *haberes* in *v.* 31.

35. sacerdos : the Sibyl is priestess of Apollo, god of augury, and of Trivia (Hecate), goddess of the shades.

36. Glauci, *daughter of Glaucus*.

37. ista, *like those.*

38. intacto: i.e. by the yoke.

39. praestiterit, *it would be better*: potential subj.

40. morantur, *delay* [to execute] *the required rites.*

42. antrum: there is now shown at Cumæ, as the cave of the Sibyl, a series of passages cut in the rock (*aditus centum*). The real cave was destroyed by the Goths (A.D. 553).

43. aditus centum: apparently a hundred passages from the hall of the outer temple to the cave.

45. ventum erat, *they had come*: impersonal. — **virgo:** the Sibyl is already in the cavern. — **poscere,** etc., *it is time to seek the oracles* from Apollo: Introd. § 73.

47. unus, *the same*: predicate nom. with *mansere.*

48. non comptae, etc., *did not remain in its order.* Her hair had been loose and flowing, but not disordered. — **anhelum:** sc. *est.*

49. maior [*est*] **videri,** *she is taller to the sight* (lit. *to be seen*): for infinitive see Introd. § 81.

50. mortale: cognate accusative. — **quando** (causal), *for she is now inspired by the divine presence.* — **iam propiore,** *nearer and nearer.*

51. cessas, *do you hesitate?* Supply *ire.*

52. neque ante: i.e. not without vows and prayers.

53. attonitae: the cavern, too, is *awe-struck* or *inspired* by presence of the god. — **fata:** participle.

57. direxti = *direxisti.*

58. Aeacidae: Achilles was slain by the arrow of Paris, directed by Apollo. — **obeuntia,** *washing,* governing *terras.*

60. Massylum: cf. iv. 483. — **praetenta syrtibus** (dat.), *which line the syrtes*: the fields stretch along the shore of the syrtes.

62. hac . . . tenus: often thus found separate, a relic of the usage before they grew together. — **fuerit secuta,** *thus far* (and no farther) *may the fortune of Troy have pursued us*: hortatory subj.

63. iam, *now at last.*

64. obstitit, *were an offence.*

66. venturi, *of the future.* — **da considere,** *grant that the Trojans settle* (Introd. § 78). — **non indebita fatis,** *due to my destinies.*

68. deos: the penates.

69. templum: Virgil may be thinking of a temple of Apollo built by Augustus on the Palatine, containing the statue of that god between those of Latona and Diana.

70. festos dies: Virgil has in mind the *ludi Apollinares,* established 212 B.C.

71. te: the Sibyl. — **penetralia,** *shrine,* referring to the temple of Apollo at Rome in which the Sibylline books were kept.

73. lectos viros : the priests who had the care of the Sibylline books and consulted them in times of public emergency.

74. foliis ne manda : Introd. § 87. See iii. 445-452.

75. ludibria ventis, *as sport for the winds :* dat. of reference.

76. canas : equivalent to *ut canas,* but the subjunctive is really hortatory, expressing an imperative in indir. disc.; A. 565, *a* ; D. 887, III ; B. 316 ; G. 546, R.²

77. Phœbi . . . patiens, *not yet submissive to Phœbus :* the figure is that of an unruly horse. — **immanis,** *wildly.*

78. si, etc., *if perchance she may :* indir. quest.; cf. i. 181.

79. excussisse : the perf. inf. has the sense of the present, but is more emphatic; A. 486, *e* ; D. 829, N.; B. 270, 2, *a* ; G. 280, 2, *b.* — **tanto . . . fatigat,** *so much the more he plies the bit in.*

80. fingit premendo, *trains her by control.*

83. periclis : abl. with *defuncte* (Introd. § 56).

84. terrae graviora, *more dreadful perils of the land.* — **Lavini,** *of Lavinium,* their future kingdom (Introd. § 10).

86. non et venisse volent, *they shall not also be glad to have come.*

88. Simoïs, Xanthus : the former is held to stand for the Tiber, and the latter for the Numicius, where Æneas perished. — **non defuerint,** *shall not be wanting :* future perfect.

89. alius Achilles : i.e. Turnus, the young king of the Rutuli, whose heroic struggle against Æneas makes the subject of the remaining books. — **partus,** *sprung up* (ready) in Latium.

90. et ipse, *he too.* Achilles was son of the sea-goddess Thetis; Turnus, of the nymph Venilia. — **addita,** *a steadfast foe* (lit. *assigned,* i.e. as an enemy).

91. cum tu, etc., *while you, a supplicant, in your need shall entreat — and what tribes shall you not entreat ?* Æneas is made to go in search of aid to Evander, whose kingdom is on the Palatine, where was afterwards the site of Rome.

92. Italum = *Italorum.*

93. causa : sc. *erit.* — **coniunx :** Lavinia. — **iterum :** as was the case with Helen.

95. ito : the future imperative here denotes continuance. Cf. Tennyson, *Princess :*

> I hold
> That it becomes no man to nurse despair,
> But in the teeth of clench'd antagonisms
> To follow up the worthiest till he die.

96. qua, *by whatever way.*

97. quod = *id quod.* — **Graia :** Evander, whose help Æneas sought, was from Arcadia. He founded Pallanteum on the site of the later Rome. *Graia* is dissyllabic here. — **ab,** *from.*

99. antro: abl. of place from which.

100. ea frena, etc., *thus Apollo shakes the reins over her as she raves, and plies the spurs beneath her side,* continuing the figure of *v.* 77. — **ea** = *sic,* like the common use of adj. for adv.

104. mi: contraction of *mihi* (Introd. § 91, *h*).

105. praecepi: observe the force of *prae.*

107. dicitur, *is said to be.* — **Acheronte refuso,** *where Acheron overflows* (abl. abs.): it was the overflow of the river that was supposed to form Lake Avernus.

109. contingat, *be it my lot:* optative subjunctive; A. 441; D. 681, I; B. 279; G. 260. — **doceas:** A. 439, *a*; D. 674, *a*; B. 275, 2; G. 263, 2, *a*.

112. comitatus: Introd. § 95.

114. invalidus, *infirm though he was.*

115. ut peterem: subst. clause of purpose in appos. with *mandata.*

116. idem, *it was* HE *who.* — **gnati:** old form of *nati*; genitive with *miserere.*

117. omnia, *you can do all things:* cognate acc.

118. lucis Avernis, *the groves of Avernus.* This is a lake near Cumæ, of volcanic origin. In all this region there remain to this day the sulphurous exhalations and other signs of volcanic action, with which the ancients connected the entrance to the Lower World.

119. si: i.e. if they could do this, why not I, who am also of divine descent? — **Manis:** the spirits of the dead were conceived as dwelling beneath the earth. — **Orpheus:** a Thracian musician who descended into the Lower World to bring back his wife Eurydice. For the story, see Georg. iv. 454–527; Ovid, Met. x. 1–77.

120. cithara, fidibus: ablatives with *fretus*; notice the quantity of the first *i* in *fidibus.*

121. Pollux: Castor and Pollux were famous for their fraternal affection. The former was the son of Leda and Tyndareus; the latter was the son of Leda and Jupiter and so immortal. When Castor was slain Pollux was inconsolable. Jupiter finally consented to allow the two brothers to enjoy the gift of life alternately, each spending one day under the earth and the next among the gods.

122. viam: cognate accusative. — **Thesea:** his object in visiting the Lower World was to carry away Proserpina.

123. Alciden: Hercules, who brought up from Hades the three-headed dog Cerberus. — **mi:** see note, *v.* 104. — **ab Iove:** Venus, mother of Æneas, was a daughter of Jupiter.

126. Averno: used here for the Lower World as a whole; dative of place to which.

127. Ditis: Dis or Dis Pater was the king of the Lower World, corresponding to the Greek Hades, called also Pluto. His kingdom included the good as well as the bad, so that it does not answer to the modern phrase "infernal regions."

128. revocare gradum: not that the return is difficult in itself, but that it depends on conditions which not all can attain. Cf. *Paradise Lost*, ii. 432–433:

> Long is the way
> And hard, that out of hell leads up to light.

129. hoc, hic: agree in gender with the predicate nouns *opus* and *labor*; A. 296, *a*; cf. B. 246, 5; G. 211. — **pauci** (always with negative idea), *only a few.*

131. potuere [sc. *hoc*], *have been able to do this.*

132. Cocytus: the ancients imagined the Lower World as bounded by awful rivers: the Styx, river of hate, by which the gods sealed their oaths; the Acheron, river of woe, with its tributaries, the Phlegethon, river of fire, and the Cocytus, river of wailing.

133. amor: for Anchises.

134. innare: after *cupido est*, which = *cupis*; cf. ii. 10, note.

135. Tartara: that part of the Lower World to which evildoers were doomed.

136. peragenda: sc. *sint.*

137. foliis, vimine: abl. of specification with *aureus.*

138. Iunoni infernae: i.e. Proserpina, wife of Pluto and queen of the World Below. See n. on Ovid, x. 28.

140. non ante datur . . . quis, *it is not permitted to any one . . . until he has.* — **operta,** *the hidden regions.*

141. decerpserit: fut. perf.: A. 551, *c*; D. 758, *b*; B. 291, 1; G. 574.

142. hoc sibi suum, *this to be brought to her as her appropriate gift.*

145. ergo, *therefore,* since it is indispensable. — **alte,** *on high,* cf. *v.* 136.

148. vincere, *overcome* its resistance.

149. praeterea, *one thing more.* — **tibi:** ethical dative; may be left untranslated (Introd. § 31).

152. sedibus: dat. of place to which. — **ante,** *first.* — **sepulcro:** abl.

154. sic demum: as usual, with a negative implication, *only in this way.*

155. presso ore, *with fast-closed lips:* abl. abs.

156. defixus lumina, *with eyes cast down* (Introd. § 42).

157. caecos eventus: the Sibyl's predictions, the matter of the Golden Bough, and the death of one of his companions.

159. vestigia figit: i.e. walks slowly and thoughtfully. — **curis:** abl. of manner.

162. diceret: an indirect question depending on the idea of questioning implied in *serebant.*

164. Misenum: the death of a comrade named Misenus was part of the old legend. Cape Miseno, at one extremity of the Bay of Naples, still keeps his name. One account made him the pilot of the fleet; hence the apparent confusion between him and Palinurus.

165. ciere : see note on *videri*, *v.* 49.

166. Hectora circum, *by Hector's side.*

167. lituo : the *lituus* was a curved trumpet, for cavalry ; the *tuba*, a straight one, for infantry. Virgil uses the names indifferently (*v.* 233). So *concha* (*v.* 171), which is used for any wind instrument, hints at the rivalry with Triton (i. 144).

168. illum : *Hector.*

170. inferiora, *a less noble destiny.*

171. tum : at the time when he met his death.

173. aemulus Triton : in the spirit of the old mythology ; whoever excels in any art is said thereby to provoke the jealousy of some deity. — **exceptum immerserat,** *had seized and plunged.* — **credere :** poetical use of the infinitive with *dignus* (Introd. § 81).

175. circum : about the body of Misenus.

177. aram sepulcri, *the sepulchral mound*, or funeral pile.

178. arboribus : abl. of instrument. — **caelo :** dative.

179. itur, *they go* : impersonal ; cf. *v.* 45.

180. procumbunt, etc., *they lay low the pines* (lit. *the pines fall*).

181. fissile, *the riven* (lit. *cleavable*) *oak is split.*

182. montibus, *from the mountains.*

184. paribus armis, *with like tools.*

186. forte, *as it happened.* Since Æneas' purpose was the quest of the Golden Bough, the mention of it in the prayer is regarded as a fortunate chance.

187. si ostendat : the conclusion is omitted, as in English ; that is, it is never formulated even in the mind, but left vague, so that the whole equals a wish ; A. 442, *a*, N.[1] ; D. 683 ; G. 261, N.[1] — **arbore :** locative abl.

188. tanto, *this great.* — **quando :** gives the reason for the hope.

193. maternas aves : doves were sacred to Venus, and her chariot was drawn by them.

195. lucos, *that part of the grove.*

196. rebus, *fortunes* : dative.

199. tantum, *only so far.* — **prodire volando,** *flew in advance*, alighting here and there to feed ; *prodire* is hist. inf.; for the gerund see A. 507 ; D. 879 ; B. 338, 4, *a* ; G. 431.

200. quantum ... sequentum, *as the eyes of those who followed could keep them in sight* (lit. *could watch them by eyesight*). — **possent :** subjunc. in a relative clause of result.

201. grave olentis, *noisome.* — **grave :** cognate accusative.

203. sedibus optatis : abl. of place where. — **geminae,** *the pair.*

204. discolor, *of different hue,* i.e. from the rest. — **auri aura,** *the gleam of gold*: light and air (*aura*) are often confused in ancient poetry (cf. iii. 600 and note). Notice the alliteration.

206. fronde: abl. of manner. — **nova,** *strange.* — **non sua arbos,** *a tree not its own*: mistletoe is a parasitic plant, apparently without roots, which grows from seeds left by birds on the bark of trees.

211. cunctantem, *resisting*: so it seemed to Æneas in his eager haste, though in fact the branch made no resistance; cf. *v.* 146.

212. nec minus, *none the less* because of Æneas' absence.

213. ingrato, *thankless* (because unresponsive). — **suprema,** *last offices*: the funeral rites here described were those usual in Rome. It was not, however, till long after Æneas that cremation instead of burial became the ordinary practice.

214. pinguem: rich in resin. — **taedis:** abl. of means.

216. ante, *in front.* Cypress was apparently first used in the funeral pile for the sake of its aromatic odor. Boughs of it were also set in front of the door of the dead man's dwelling; here they seem to be set up for adornment in front of the pile.

217. armis: from an old and very general notion that these things went with the departed spirit, and were used by the dead in Hades.

219. frigentis, *cold in death*: more poetic than *mortui.*

221. purpureas vestes: a custom at great Roman funerals. — **nota,** *accustomed*: i.e. those he wore in his life.

222. subiere, *took up.*

223. ministerium: accusative, in appos. with the preceding clause; the usual construction in such cases. — **subiectam,** *beneath,* i.e. at the base of the pyre.

224. aversi, *turning away* their faces, as was the custom.

225. olivo: abl. of material. — **fuso:** i.e. these were poured on as a libation.

228. Corynaeus: apparently a priest.

229. socios, etc.: poetical for *undam circum socios tulit.*

231. lustravit: *purified* the company from the pollution of the presence of a corpse. — **novissima verba:** *salve, vale, ave* (cf. i. 219, ii. 644), with sometimes other words, like *sit tibi terra levis, ilicet,* or the like.

234. monte aerio: a promontory, several hundred feet high, on the Bay of Naples; it is called *Capo Miseno* to-day.

238. tuta, *sheltered*: part. of *tueor,* in a passive sense.

239. haud ullae volantes, *no flying creatures*: just in this neighborhood is situated the famous *grotta del cane,* in which dogs and other small animals are smothered by the carbonic acid accumulated along the bottom.

242. This verse is not in the best manuscripts. — **Aornon:** formerly supposed to be from ἄορνος (*aornos*), Greek for *birdless.* The Latin name corresponding to *Aornon* is *Avernum*; but the connection with the Greek word is impossible.

244. fronti invergit, *pours upon the forehead*: *vergere,* when used of pouring, signifies that the cup is completely turned upside down, as in offering to the infernal deities; while *fundere* is simply *to pour out,* the hand being held palm upwards.

245. saetas: the long hairs between the horns were plucked out and burnt as a first-offering (*libamina prima*), while certain prayers were said.

247. caelo: locative abl. Hecate, as the moon-goddess, was *caelo potens.*

248. supponunt: the action of placing the knife beneath belongs to the worship of the gods below.

249. suscipiunt: the blood is caught in bowls, and poured out with special solemnity, — not suffered to stream upon the ground.

250. matri Eumenidum: the mother of the Furies is Night, and her sister is Earth. Cf. iv. 469, note.

251. ense ferit: the sword no doubt had a magic power over the inhabitants of the world below.

252. Stygio regi: Pluto. — **nocturnas:** night was the regular time for sacrifices to the gods of the Lower World.

253. solida: the whole victim was burned in sacrifice to the gods below, since, after being devoted to them, no part could be eaten.

255. sub, *just at, just before.*

256. iuga silvarum, *the ridges covered with forests.* — **coepta** [*sunt*] **moveri:** A. 205, *a*; D. 263, *a*; B. 133, 1; G. 423, N.[3]

257. canes: these are the infernal hounds of Hecate.

258. dea: Hecate. — **procul,** etc.: the words regularly addressed to the uninitiated at the mysteries, but here addressed to the companions of Æneas, who were not like him entitled to visit the world below.

260. tu: opposed to *profani,* above.

261. animis, *courage* (Introd. § 57).

262. tantum, *so much,* and no more, as often. — **se immisit,** *plunged.*

263. ducem aequat, *keeps pace with his guide.*

264. umbrae (vocative), *ghosts,* as being only the "shadows" of persons.

265. Chaos: the Lower World. — **Phlegethon:** see note on *v.* 132. — **nocte:** abl. of manner or cause.

266. sit fas, *permit.* — **audita loqui,** *to tell what I have heard.* Virgil professes to follow the common tradition as to the World Below. — **sit:** sc. *fas.*

267. altā terrā, *deep in the earth.*

268. obscuri, *in the darkness.*

269. vacuas: i.e. destitute of real life and blood.

270. quale est iter, *even as one makes one's way* (lit. *as the way is*). — **maligna,** *niggardly.*

272. rebus : dat. with *abstulit*.

273. vestibulum : as in ii. 469. — **primis faucibus,** *in the very jaws* : at some distance underground from the place where Æneas and his companion entered the cave.

274. Luctus : these woes are at the door, as causing the death of men. — **Curae :** i. e. the stings of conscience personified.

> Man's feeble race what ills await,
> Labor and Penury, the racks of Pain,
> Disease, and Sorrow's weeping train,
> And Death, sad refuge from the storms of Fate.
>
> GRAY, *Progress of Poesy*, vv. 42-45.

Fig. 51

276. malesuada, *tempting to crime.* — **turpis,** *unsightly*.

277. Labos : archaic for *Labor*.

278. mala Gaudia, *sinful joys.* — **Leti :** in the Iliad Sleep and Death, the Sons of Night, are twin brothers (xiv. 231, xvi. 672). See Fig. 51 (from a vase painting), which represents the body of Memnon in the hands of the brothers Sleep and Death. The idea is a favorite one with modern poets. Of countless examples two typical ones may suffice :

> Care-charmer Sleep, son of the sable Night,
> Brother to Death, in silent darkness born.
>
> DANIEL, *Delia*, sonnet xlv.

> When in the down I sink my head,
> Sleep, Death's twin-brother, times my breath ;
> Sleep, Death's twin-brother, knows not Death,
> Nor can I dream of thee as dead.
>
> TENNYSON, *In Memoriam*, lxvii.

279. adverso in limine, *on the very threshold* (lit. *on the threshold in front*).

280. Eumenidum thalami: the Furies sleep at the threshold (iv. 473), but their avenging task is done in Tartarus (*v.* 570). — **ferrei** (dissyllabic here): from their implacable nature and inevitable power.

281. crinem: Introd. § 43.

282. in medio: sc. *vestibulo.*

283. quam . . . ferunt, *which, they say, vain dreams flocking everywhere* (*volgo*) *have for their abode.*

286. Scyllae biformes: see iii. 426.

287. Briareus: a hundred-handed giant. — **belua:** the Hydra, a nine-headed water-serpent, slain by Hercules as the second of his Twelve Labors.

288. horrendum: cognate acc. — **Chimaera:** a fire-breathing monster slain by Bellerophon. It had the head of a lion; a goat's head projected from the middle of its body ; and the hind part of its body was that of a dragon.

> All monstrous, all prodigious things,
> Abominable, inutterable, and worse
> Than fables yet have feign'd, or fear conceiv'd,
> Gorgons, and Hydras, and Chimæras dire.
>
> *Paradise Lost*, ii. 625–628.

289. Gorgones: the three daughters of the sea-god Phorcus. They had snaky hair, and their glance turned him who looked at them into stone. One of the Gorgons was Medusa, whom Perseus killed. — **Harpyiae:** see iii. 212. — **forma:** the Spanish giant Geryon, slain by Hercules, who carried off his famous herd of oxen.

294. admoneat: the pres. for the imperf. in a cond. contrary to fact makes the supposition vivid; A. 517, *e*; D. 799; G. 596, R.[1] Cf. i. 58, v. 325, and notes.

295. hinc: Æneas has now passed through the *vestibulum.* — **Acherontis:** Acheron, "the joyless," is the stream that embraces the whole of the Lower World. In Virgil's mind it is not kept distinct from the other infernal rivers, Cocytus ("Wailing Lamentation") and Styx ("Squalid Grief"), *v.* 323.

296. caeno: abl. of means. — **vasta voragine,** *of abysmal depth* (lit. *vast abyss*): abl. of quality.

297. Cocyto: dative of place to which.

299. squalore: Charon's squalid appearance agrees with the ancient ideas and habits of mourning (cf. i. 480, note). Dante (*Inferno*, iii. 82 ff.) imitates Virgil's description of Charon, making him the ferryman who conducts the souls of the damned over Acheron to Hell. — **cui mento,** *on whose chin* (lit. *to whom on the chin*): the relative *cui* is dat. of reference.

300. stant lumina flamma, *his eyes stand out in flame*: i.e. are like fixed balls of fire.

301. nodo (abl. of manner): another indication of neglect (and therefore a sign of mourning).

302. ipse: with his own hand, old as he is. — **velis** (abl.) **ministrat,** *tends the sails* (lit. *serves the boat with sails*).

304. deo [sc. *est*]: dat. of possession.

305. ad ripas effusa, *hurrying to the banks.*

306. defunctă vitā, *that had ended life*: for abl. see Introd. § 56.

307. magnanimum: gen. plur. (Introd. § 91, *c*).

309. quam multa, *as many as.* — **frigore:** abl. of time.

310. gurgite ab alto: i.e. as they reach land in their migrations.

313. orantes, etc.: the inf. with *oro* (instead of an obj. clause with *ut*) is poetical (Introd. § 78). — **primi** agrees (irregularly) with the subject. In *transmittere cursum, to make the passage across, cursum* is obj. of *trans* and *transmittere = se transmittere.*

315. navita: "that *grim ferryman* that poets write of" (*Richard III*, i. 4. 46).

318. quid volt, *what means?* So Fr. "Que veut dire?"

319. discrimine, *choice,* i.e. criterion.

320. hae: those whom Charon has rejected.

321. longaeva: the Sibyl, said the legend, had received the gift of as many years as the grains of sand which she held in her hand, but without the boon of youth.

322. certissima, *most surely.*

323. Cocyti stagna alta, Stygiam paludem: two expressions for the same sluggish river. Cf. Milton, *Paradise Lost,* ii. 577–580:

> Abhorred Styx, the flood of deadly hate;
> Sad Acheron, of sorrow, black and deep;
> Cocytus, nam'd of lamentation loud
> Heard on the rueful stream.

324. numen is poetically used as obj. of a verb of *swearing* (A. 388, *d*; cf. D. 408, N.; B. 176, 4, *a*; G. 333, 2, R.); cf. *v.* 351. It means literally *divinity* or *divine nature.* Virgil ascribes divinity to the Styx, just as every earthly river was thought to have its own god. — **fallere,** *to deceive,* is the regular expression for taking an oath with intent to break or evade it: — *by whose sacred stream even the gods fear to swear and break their oath.*

325. inops: perhaps this is an allusion to the piece of money with which the dead were furnished to pay their passage. (See figure, p. 205, above.) — **inhumata:** the unburied, it was believed, were not allowed to enter the Lower World.

327. ripas, *nor is it granted to convey them over the dread banks and hoarse flood, until,* etc.

328. sedibus quierunt, *have found rest in the tomb.*

332. animi, *in his heart* (locative); A. 358; D. 488; B. 232, 3; G. 374, N.[7]

333. mortis honore : i.e. burial.

334. Oronten : see i. 113. Leucaspis is not elsewhere mentioned by Virgil; he seems to have perished along with Orontes.

335. simul : i.e. with himself. — **vectos,** *sailing,* in the sense of a present participle.

337. sese agebat, *came walking.* — **Palinurus :** see v. 833 ff.

339. exciderat . . . effusus, *had fallen overboard headlong.*

343. mihi : dat. of agent with *repertus.*

344. hoc uno responso : some such oracle may have been in one of the legends, but it is not mentioned elsewhere by Virgil. Neptune had announced to Venus (v. 813) that the fleet would come safe, with the loss of only one man.

345. ponto incolumem, *safe on the sea* (loc. abl.). — **finis Ausonios :** acc. of place to which.

348. nec deus mersit : Palinurus does not know that it was the god of Sleep that threw him over (v. 859); nor did he perish by the sea (*v.* 358). It was by accident (*forte*), he thinks, that he fell overboard.

349. gubernaclum : obj. of *traxi* in *v.* 351.

350. cui, etc.: *to which I was clinging, having been assigned as its guardian, and [by which] I was guiding our course.* The relative *cui* serves as indir. obj. of both *datus* and *haerebam.*

351. maria : same construction as *numen* in *v.* 324.

352. timorem : subject of *cepisse* ; sc. *me* as object of *cepisse.*

353. quam tua . . . navis, *as that your ship, stripped of her equipment, and having cast off her pilot* (lit. *wrenched from her pilot*), *might swamp in those surging waves.* — **ne deficeret :** A. 564; D. 720, II ; B. 296, 2; G. 550. — **armis :** i.e. the tiller. — **magistro :** dative of separation.

355. tris noctes : so Ulysses floats two days and two nights (Od. v. 388; Bry. 465). The woodwork of the stern serves Palinurus as a sort of raft.

356. aqua : abl. of specification with *violentus.*

357. sublimis ab unda : i.e. raised high on a wave, from the crest of which, etc.

358. tuta tenebam, ni, *I was just reaching safety* [and should have been safe], *had not,* etc.: A. 517, *b* ; D. 797; G. 597, R.[2]

359. gravatum : sc. *me.*

360. capita montis : *the crags of the cliff* ; he was half out of water, grasping at the protuberances of the cliffs with hands bent and stiff (*uncis manibus*).

361. praedam, *a prize*: i.e. a shipwrecked man with some of his property about him.

362. fluctus habet: see v. 871.

363. quod te oro, *but I implore you* (see ii. 141 and note).

365. aut tu . . . aut tu: observe the emphasis and urgency expressed in the repetition of the pronoun, which is not itself emphatic. — **terram inice:** a mere formal burial was sufficient.

366. portus Velinos: on the coast of Lucania.

370. undas: i.e. of the Styx.

371. ut saltem quiescam: since I could not rest in life, having failed to reach the promised land with you.

373. tam dira cupido, *so wild a wish.*

377. cape, *take* to your heart for consolation. — **dicta,** *my words.*

379. prodigiis acti: it is said that the people of Lucania, suffering from pestilence, were commanded by an oracle to propitiate by sacrifice the shade of Palinurus.

381. Palinuri: a headland on the coast still bears the name *Punta di Palinuro.*

384. ergo: i.e. since they have quieted Palinurus.

385. iam inde ut prospexit, *at once when he espied.*

389. iam istinc, *right from where you are*: come no nearer.

392. euntem, *when he came* (lit. *going* on his journey to fetch Cerberus).

393. Pirithoum: he accompanied his friend Theseus to the Lower World to carry off Proserpine.

394. invicti viribus, *resistless in might*: my opposition to them would be vain. — **essent:** A. 527, *e*; D. 806, N.; cf. B. 309, 6; G. 605, N.

395. Tartareum custodem, *the watch-dog of Tartarus,* Cerberus. — **ille:** Hercules.

396. a solio regis, *from the monarch's very throne,* to which Cerberus is supposed to have fled, breaking his chain.

397. hi: Theseus and Pirithous. — **dominam:** Proserpine. — **Ditis:** limiting *thalamo.*

398. Amphrysia: Apollo, by whose gift the Sibyl was inspired, is called "the shepherd of Amphrysus," a river in the dominions of Admetus, whose flocks he kept. See Lowell's poem *The Shepherd of King Admetus.*

400. licet: i.e. for all we shall do to prevent. The subject of *licet* is the clause *ingens . . . umbras.*

401. aeternum latrans, *barking eternally*: *aeternum* is cognate acc.

402. casta, *chastely*: predicate adj. — **patrui:** Proserpine was the daughter of Jupiter, and Pluto was his brother.

404. imas ad umbras, *to the shades below.*

407. tumida: with *corda.*

408. nec plura his, *nor more than this she said.* — **donum:** for Proserpine; see *v.* 142.

409. tempore: A. 414, 424, *f*; D. 475, 477; B. 223, 357, 1; G. 403, N.⁴ — **visum:** not often did visitors come bearing this gift for Proserpine.

411. iuga, *benches* of the boat.

412. laxat foros, *clears the gangways.* — **alveo:** dissyllabic (Introd. § 115).

414. sutilis: the traditional notion of Charon's boat was got from Egypt, where light boats are made, like Moses' ark, of bulrushes or of the papyrus. — **paludem:** i. e. water from the marsh.

415. incolumīs: accusative.

416. glauca, *gray:* naturally no green thing could be found in the place of shades. — **in:** to be taken with both *limo* and *ulva*; such dislocations of words are common in poetry.

417. latratu trifauci, *with the barking from his three throats.* Cerberus had three heads, a dragon's tail, and snakes for hair on his neck.

418. adverso, *facing them.*

420. melle . . . offam, *a cake soporific with honey and medicinal plants:* see iv. 486.

421. famē: notice the long *e* (see iii. 218, note).

422. obiectam, *when thrown* (in his way).

424. sepulto, *buried* [*in sleep*]: cf. iii. 630.

425. inremeabilis, *not to be recrossed:* a usual epithet of the Styx, "from whose bourn no traveller returns."

427. in limine primo: following Virgil, Dante (*Inferno*, iv. 35) places just beyond the Styx the souls of pagans and unbaptized infants.

428. vitae: objective genitive with *exsortes.*

430. crimine, *accusation.* — **damnati mortis,** *condemned to death* (Introd. § 19).

431. nec sine sorte, sine iudice: a kind of hendiadys, as if it were "judges selected by lot." The unjustly slain have *now* an impartial trial.

432. quaesitor: the trial is represented as according to the usage of the Roman courts, not according to the Greek myth, which gave a bench consisting of three judges, Minos, Rhadamanthus, and Æacus. Here, Minos is the *quaesitor,* or President of the Court; the lots are drawn (*urnam movet*) to select the jurors (*iudice* includes both the *quaesitor* and the jury) who are to pass judgment on the person on trial; while the *concilium silentum* is the panel of jurors (*iudices*), when they have been selected from the shades themselves, the fellow citizens of the accused. — **urnam movet,** *shakes the urn* (i. e. to mix up the names). — **silentum:** old form for *silentium.*

433. discit: the investigation must not be thought of according to our proceedings, but as more like the French, in which the court is the agent of

the government to detect and punish. Hence, here, the judge himself conducts a preliminary investigation embracing the whole life and conduct of
the criminal, and not limited as with us to the particular offence.

435. insontes : i.e. having done nothing worthy of death. — **manu,** *by
their own hands.*

436. proiecere, *cast away.* — **quam vellent,** *how they would wish :*
subj. imperf. of a hopeless wish; A. 447, 1, N.; D. 685; cf. B. 280, 4;
G. 258, N.[1] In Od. xi. 489–491, Bry. 600, Achilles is made to say, "Would
I might rather be a bondman of the soil under a poor man without lot or
substance than lord of all the perished dead." Cf. Charles Lamb's essay,
New Year's Eve. — **aethere in alto :** i.e. on earth.

437. nunc (emphatic): as opposed to their feeling when alive. — **pauperiem, labores :** the hardships from which men have sought escape in
death. Suicide was a sort of epidemic among the later Romans; and it was
perhaps a part of Virgil's purpose to impress a wholesome horror of it.

438, 439. palus, Styx : two expressions for the same river, as in *v.* 323.
— **noviens :** cf. Milton, *Paradise Lost,* ii. 434–436:

> This huge convex of fire,
> Outrageous to devour, immures us round
> Ninefold.

440. fusi, *spread out* (in order to give room for solitude).

442. quos, *those whom :* its antecedent is the implied object of *celant.*

443. secreti, *retired.* — **myrtea,** because the myrtle was sacred to
Venus.

445. Phaedram, etc. These personages were: Phædra, who hanged
herself for love of her stepson Hippolytus; Procris, who was jealous of her
husband Cephalus and was accidentally shot by him with an arrow; Eriphyle,
who was bribed to send her husband Amphiaräus on the expedition against
Thebes, in which he was killed, and was slain by her son; Evadne, who
perished on the funeral pile of her husband Capäneus; Pasiphaë, mother
of the Minotaur; Laodamīa, wife of Protesiläus, who killed herself on
hearing of his death at Troy (see Wordsworth's *Laodamia*); Cænis, a
maiden, loved by Neptune: she was changed into the youth Cæneus and
then back again into a maiden.

446. nati volnera : the wounds inflicted by her son.

447. his : dat. of reference with *comes.*

450. recens a volnere, *her wound still fresh.*

451. quam : governed by *iuxta* and *agnovit.*

453. obscuram, *dim among the shadows.* — **qualem . . . lunam,** *as
when, in the early part of the month, one sees (or thinks he has seen) the
moon rise through the clouds.*

456. verus nuntius : perhaps the flame of her funeral pile (v. 3 ·7), from which they might infer the fact, or we may suppose the news to have come by ordinary channels. The emphasis is on *verus*.

457. exstinctam [*esse*]: sc. *te.* — **extrema secutam** [*esse*], *had tried 'he last resource* (i.e. death). Cf. *extrema pati*, i. 219.

458. funeris (emphatic), *was it death I brought on you?*

459. si qua fides, *and by whatever faith* : i.e. object which would sanction an oath.

462. senta situ, *rough with neglect.*

463. egere : notice the first *e* long, distinguishing the verb from *ĕgeo.* — **nec credere quivi,** *nor could I have believed.*

464. hunc tantum, *so great as this.*

466. extremum . . . hoc est, *these are* — *by fate* — *the last words that I can speak to you* : i.e. fate has decreed that I shall never have another opportunity. — **fato :** abl. of cause. — **quod :** cognate acc.

467. ardentem et torva tuentem animum, *the wrathful and fiercely gazing soul.* — **torva** is cognate acc. used adverbially.

468. lenibat = *leniebat* : conative imperf. — **lacrimas ciebat,** *shed tears.*

471. silex, cautes : pred. nom. with *stet* = *sit.* — **stet :** A. 524; D. 803; B. 307, I ; G. 602. — **Marpesia cautes :** Marpēsus was a mountain of Paros; so that the pale, unmoved figure of Dido is compared to Parian marble.

473. illi : dat. of reference.

474. respondet : i.e. shows loving sympathy for her sorrows ; " answers all her cares, and equals all her love " (Dryden).

477. datum molitur iter, *pursues the appointed way* (not *granted*).

478. ultima, *the last* before coming to the regions of blessedness and of torment. — **secreta,** *apart* (*se-cerno*).

479. Tydeus, Parthenopaeus, Adrastus : heroes of the legendary war of the Seven against Thebes, the chief event of the time immediately before the Trojan War.

481. ad superos, *among mortal men* (lit. *men above,* i.e. in this world).

484. Cereri sacrum : i.e. as a priest.

487. usque, *still.*

488. conferre gradum, *to walk by his side.*

492. petiere rates : the Grecian ships had been drawn up on the shore at Troy, and furnished a place of refuge. — **tollere vocem exiguam,** *raise their piping voice,* attempting the war-cry. So Homer speaks of the thin voice of the shades ; cf. Shakspere, *Hamlet,* i. 1. 115–116:

> The sheeted dead
> Did squeak and gibber in the Roman streets.

493. frustratur, *disappoints,* because they have no voice. — **hiantis,** *their open mouths.*

495. Deiphobum: see note, ii. 310. There were various legends of his death. The mutilation was merely savage revenge. The shade shows the wounds received by the body. — **ora, manus, tempora, nares:** acc. of specification with *lacerum* (Introd. § 42). So the ghost of Banquo appears to Macbeth with the "twenty trenched gashes on his head" (*Macbeth*. iii. 4. 27, 81).

498. vix adeo agnovit, *he could scarce so much as recognize.*

499. notis, *familiar.*

501. optavit sumere, *has chosen to inflict.*

502. cui, etc.: i. e. who has been permitted (by the gods) such outrages upon you? — **tantum:** subject of *licuit.*

503. tulit, *reported.*

505. tumulum, etc.: an empty tomb (*cenotaph*); such rites would allow the shade to cross the Styx; cf. iii. 62, note; vi. 327 f.

506. ter: see note, *v.* 231.

507. arma: cf. *v.* 233. — **te:** emphatic, as opposed to the tomb; hence not elided, but merely shortened before *amice* (Introd. § 109).

509. tibi relictum, *left undone by thee.*

510. Deiphobo, funeris umbris: i. e. both to the man himself (which would be friendship) and to the shade of the dead (which would be a religious duty).

511. Lacaenae, *the woman from Sparta* (Helen).

512. haec monumenta, *these memorials*, the ghastly mutilations.

513. ut, *how*: introduces an indirect question.

514. nimium, etc., *you must needs too well remember.*

515. venit: see ii. 237–238.

516. alvo: abl. of place.

517. illa: Helen. — **chorum,** *a festive dance.* — **euhantis orgia,** *shouting the wild cry of the [Bacchic] orgies.* — **orgia:** cogn. acc. with *euhantis.*

518. flammam tenebat: in ii. 256 it is said that the signal was given from Agamemnon's ship. In like manner cf. *v.* 525 with ii. 571–574. Virgil leaves us to settle the contradictions (if there are any) as we can.

523. coniunx: after the death of Paris, Helen was married to Deiphobus.

526. amanti, *to her fond husband* (Menelaus).

529. Aeolides: a name of insult for Ulysses, hinting that his real father was not Laertes, but the crafty Sisyphus, son of Æolus. — **talia,** *such sufferings.*

532. pelagi erroribus: Deiphobus was, of course, ignorant of Æneas' voyage or his settlement in Italy. The question is imitated from Homer, who places the world of shadows beyond the Ocean, whither only wandering could bring a man. The alternative is, whether Æneas has come hither by mere chance of travel or by divine direction.

534. adires: the imperf. is used because *fatigat* has also the sense of the perf., "has pursued and still pursues." — **turbida,** *gloomy:* the opposite of *liquida,* which means *bright* and *clear*; cf. Job, x. 21–22.

535. hac vice sermonum, *during this conversation* (lit. *interchange of speeches*).

536. medium axem: a night appears to have been spent in the preliminary sacrifices, and it is now past noon of the next day.

537. traherent, *they would have spent*; contrary to fact condition: for tense see A. 517, *a*; D. 798; B. 304, 2; G. 597, R.[1] The construction changes at *sed,* and so no formal protasis appears.

540. via findit, etc.: the two regions are the inner courts of the Underworld, the proper places of reward and punishment; but why the shades previously mentioned should be excluded does not appear.

541. dextera: sc. *est.*

542. Elysium: acc. of end of motion, after *iter* [*est*].

543. exercet poenas, *inflicts the doom*: i. e. by sending them to Tartarus (which is expressed in the coördinate clause *mittit,* etc.).

545. explebo numerum: i. e. of the shades (by returning to my place among them).

548. respicit, *looks off* (i. e. away from where he stands; not *looks back*).

549. moenia, *a fortress* or vast castle used as a dungeon, to which Phlegethon, the river "blazing with flame," serves as a moat. The image is drawn from a torrent of lava.

552. porta: sc. *est.*

553. bello: i. e. with the engines of war.

554. stat ad auras, *rises toward the sky*: i. e. (since this is the Lower World) *rises high.* — **ferrea turris,** *a tower* or "keep" of iron, rising high in the midst.

555. Tisiphone: one of the three Furies.

557. exaudiri, sonare: historical infinitives.

558. tractae catenae, *of clanking chains* (lit. *of a dragged chain*).

560. facies (plur.), *forms.*

566. Rhadamanthus: like Minos, he was a famous Cretan hero, said to have been made a judge in the world below. Here he appears in the character of a Roman *quaesitor parricidii,* trying greater offenders than those who come before Minos. The criminals are supposed to have contrived to conceal their guilt during life (*furto laetatus inani*).

567. castigat: this does not refer to punishment, but to the upbraiding, menacing language of the judge, which was perhaps accompanied with torture (*subigitque fateri*). There is therefore no real *hysteron proteron* (cf. n. on ii. 353). — **dolos,** *dark ways,* i. e. their secret crimes.

568, 569. quae quis, etc., *the crimes which any one, rejoicing in vain concealment, has committed on earth, and the atonement for which he has*

put off till death — too late. — **apud superos :** cf. *ad superos* in *v.* 481.
— **quae commissa piacula,** *the committed guilt, which,* equivalent to
commissa quorum piacula.

570. continuo : as soon as Rhadamanthus has passed judgment. —
sontis : obj. of *insultans.*

571. Tisiphone : the eldest of the Furies, who opens the awful doors
(*sacrae portae*) of Tartarus. — **quatit,** *scourges.*

572. anguis : acc. plural.

573. horrisono cardine : cf. Milton's celebrated imitation, *Paradise Lost,*
ii. 879–882 :

> On a sudden open fly,
> With impetuous recoil and jarring sound,
> Th' infernal doors, and on their hinges grate
> Harsh thunder.

574. custodia : Tisiphone ; within is the Hydra, fiercer than she ; and
still beyond, Tartarus itself, more dreadful than either.

575. facies quae, *what a shape.*

576. hiatibus : the gaping jaws of the several heads.

578. bis patet . . . quantus, *yawns straight downward and extends
into the darkness twice as far as is,* etc.

579. suspectus ad Olympum, *the upward look to Olympus.*

580. pubes : the Titans, sons of Earth, who warred with the gods and
were cast down into Tartarus.

581. fulmine : the thunderbolt of Jupiter.

582. Aloidas, sons of Aloeus, — Otus and Ephialtes, who in their war
against the gods tried to reach heaven by piling Ossa on Olympus and Pelion
on Ossa.

583. corpora : in apposition with *Aloidas.*

585. Salmonea : king of Elis, brother of Sisyphus, who contemptuously
imitated the thunder and lightning of Jupiter. — **dantem,** *who suffered.*

586. dum imitatur = *imitantem,* i. e. punished *for imitating* the thunders of Jupiter (so *qui . . . simularet* below).

588. per Elidis urbem : i. e. Olympia, built in especial honor of Zeus ;
thus the affront was increased.

591. aere, either a brazen chariot, as was that of Salmoneus, driven over
a bridge, or vessels of " sounding brass." — **simularet :** a relative clause
expressing cause. Cf. Dryden, *Astræa Redux, vv.* 197–198 :

> Which durst with horses' hoofs that beat the ground
> And martial brass belie the thunder's sound.

593. non ille faces, etc., *and it was no firebrand that* HE *threw, no
torch with smoky light* (lit. *not firebrands* HE, *nor lights smoky with
torches*) : *his* was no mere imitation of thunder and lightning.

594. immani turbine: i. e. the mighty whirling thunderbolt.

595. nec non et, *and likewise.* — **Tityon:** Tityos offered violence to Latona and was killed by Apollo and Diana.

596. cernere erat, *one might see,* by a common Greek construction. — **iugera,** the *iugerum* was about half an acre (240 feet by 120).

598. iecur: the liver, as the supposed seat of lust, is fitly the organ attacked. — **fecunda poenis,** *fertile for torture:* dat. of purpose.

599. rimatur epulis, *tears at his banquet:* dat. akin to end of motion.

600. renatis: as fast as they are devoured they grow again.

601. Lapithas: a tribe of Thessaly famous for their war with the Centaurs. — **Ixiona, Pirithoum:** Ixion was king of the Lapithæ, and Pirithous was his son. Ixion insulted Juno, and Pirithous (with Theseus) tried to carry off Proserpine.

602. iam, etc., *now, even now, tottering and seeming to fall* (lit. *about to slip and like [one] falling*). A hypermetric line (Introd. § 114).

603. genialibus toris, *banqueting couches,* especially those set for the birthday festival; dat. of reference.

604. fulcra, *props* or *supports* (gold-footed frames for couches).

605. maxima: sc. *natu.*

606. manibus: with *contingere.*

> Fill high the sparkling bowl,
> The rich repast prepare,
> Reft of a crown, he yet may share the feast:
> Close by the regal chair
> Fell Thirst and Famine scowl
> A baleful smile upon their baffled guest.
>
> GRAY, *The Bard, vv.* 77–82.

608. hic quibus, *here [are they] to whom,* etc.: the relative *quibus* (dat. with *invisi*) goes also with *pulsatus [est]* and *innexa [est],* with which it serves as dat. of agent. — **invisi [erant] fratres:** like Atreus and Thyestes

609. pulsatus parens: the act of striking a parent was regarded with peculiar horror. — **clienti:** the client had a certain sacred claim to the protection of his *patronus.*

610. qui . . . repertis: those who have found a treasure, and kept it all to their selfish use, — a type of all who are greedy of gain. — **incubuere,** *hoarded.*

612. arma impia: i. e. civil war.

613. dextras, *trust* (the pledge of the right hand), referring to servile insurrection; cf. *fallere numen, v.* 324.

615. poenam: sc. *exspectant* (in prose, *exspectent*): indirect question; so *mersit.* — **quae forma fortunave mersit,** *what form [of crime] or what fortune has overwhelmed them.*

616. saxum, etc.: this was the punishment of Sisyphus, — to roll a rock uphill, only to have it roll back when he reached the top. Cf. Thomson, *Castle of Indolence*, i. 12:

> Come, ye who still the cumbrous load of life
> Push hard up hill, but as the furthest steep
> You trust to gain, and put an end to strife,
> Down thunders back the stone with mighty sweep,
> And hurls your labors to the valley deep.

617. districti: fastened with their limbs strained apart, — the commonly reported punishment of Ixion.

618. Theseus: punished for his crime in attempting to carry off Proserpine. — **Phlegyas:** he burned the temple of Apollo at Delphi.

621. vendidit, imposuit: these were the special crimes of a period of civil war, such as Rome had just passed through.

622. fixit, refixit, *made and unmade* (lit. *set up and tore down*): laws were published by being posted up on brazen tablets, and when repealed were taken down again.

624. auso potiti, *gained what they had dared* (Introd. § 56).

625. sint: equivalent to a present condition contrary to fact.

629. susceptum munus: the task of hanging up the Golden Bough at the entrance to Pluto's palace as an offering to Proserpine (see *vv.* 142, 636).

630. Cyclopum educta caminis (abl. of separation): i.e. wrought at the forges of the Cyclops. The walls of Pluto were supposed to have been built of iron or steel.

631. adverso fornice, *with their arch in front of me*: abl. of quality.

632. praecepta, *the instructions* given by the gods.

634. medium, *intervening*.

635. corpus spargit: the water stands ready for ceremonial purification, as in the vestibule of a temple.

640. largior . . . purpureo, *here the atmosphere clothes the fields with freer air and with glowing light.* Cf. Milton, *Comus*, *vv.* 4–6:

> In regions mild of calm and serene air,
> Above the smoke and stir of this dim spot,
> Which men call earth.

— **largior,** *with freer air*, agrees with the subject but is practically adverbial and belongs in the predicate. — **et:** this connects the two ideas of freedom (*largior*) and brilliancy (*lumine purpureo*).

642–647. Imitated by Milton in his account of the fallen angels in hell, *Paradise Lost*, ii. 528 ff.:

Part on the plain, or in the air sublime
Upon the wing, or in swift race contend,
As at the Olympian games or Pythian fields;
Part curb their fiery steeds, or shun the goal
With rapid wheels, or fronted brigads form.

. . . .

. . . .

. . . . Others more mild,
Retreated in a silent valley, sing
With notes angelical to many a harp
Their own heroic deeds and hapless fall
By doom of battle.

644. pedibus plaudunt choreas, *dance a measure* (lit. *beat the dance with their feet*). — **choreas :** cogn. acc.

645. Threïcius sacerdos : Orpheus, "the Thracian bard" (*Paradise Lost*, vii. 34), the mythic father of song and institutor of the Orphic mysteries. — **longa :** as a priest.

646. obloquitur, etc., *accompanies their strains with the seven notes* (on his lyre). — **numeris :** dat. with *obloquitur*.

647. eadem : grammatically referring to *discrimina*, but really referring to the tune as a whole as both played and sung. — **pectine :** so called because inserted among the strings of the harp like the "comb" among the threads of the loom.

651. arma . . . inanis, *he* (Æneas) *gazes from afar upon the phantom arms and chariots of the heroes.*

653. quae gratia, etc., *the same fondness which they had for chariots and arms when living.* — **currum :** gen. pl.

657. vescentis, *feasting.* — **choro :** abl. of manner.

658. superne volvitur, *flows in the world above.* The Eridanus (Po) was held to have its rise in the infernal regions. In fact, near its source it flows underground for about two miles. — **plurimus amnis,** *mighty river.*

660. manus . . . passi, *the band* [of those] *who suffered*: A. 286, *b*; D. 501; B. 235, B, 2, *c*; G. 211, R.[1], exc. *a*. Cf. i. 212, v. 108.

662. vates, *poets.* — **Phoebo :** Apollo was the god of poetry.

663. vitam excoluere, etc., *adorned* or *ennobled human life by skilful inventions* (lit. *arts discovered*).

664. qui . . . merendo, *who by their deserts have made men* (lit. *some men*) *remember them*: i. e. the benefactors of mankind.

665. vitta : i. e. as if victors in the games.

667. Musaeum : selected as being the mythical father of poets. — **nam :** introducing the reason why the priestess addressed him particularly; the respect in which he is held indicates a corresponding distinction.

668. umeris : abl. of manner, not degree of difference.

670. illius ergo, *on account of him:* Introd. § 23.

672. atque, *and at once.*

675. fert ita, *so prompts.*

676. sistam: Musæus is to leave them when they have passed the ridge and the way is in sight.

677. ante (adv.), *ahead.*

678. dehinc: monosyllabic (Introd. § 115).

680. ituras, *destined to go:* the doctrine of *metempsychosis,* here hinted at, is further developed later.

681. lustrabat recolens, *surveyed thoughtfully.*

683. manus, *deeds,* i.e. martial exploits.

684. adversum, *toward him.*

690. ducebam animo, *I was considering.*

691. mea cura, *my fond hope.*

692. per: with *terras* as well as with *aequora.*

694. quam metui: and yet Anchises must have known that Æneas went to Africa by divine direction, and that his course to Italy was safe. The verse expresses, however, a father's natural anxiety. — **quid** (cognate acc.) **tibi nocerent,** *do you some injury.*

695. tua imago: the visions of Anchises, seen by Æneas in dreams; cf. iv. 351, v. 722.

697. stant sale, etc., *ride on the Tuscan wave:* the ships are still afloat, not hauled up on shore as at the end of a voyage.

698. amplexu: probably dative.

700-702. Repeated from ii. 792-794.

705. Lethaeum amnem: see *Hamlet,* i. 4. 32-34. Cf. the famous description in *Paradise Lost,* ii. 582-586.

706. volabant, *flitted:* the word expresses the noiseless and hurried movement of the spirits. The faint sound they make is compared to the humming of bees in summer.

710. horrescit, *starts.*

711. quae . . . porro, *what this river in the distance is.*

713. altera . . . debentur, *bodies are assigned by fate once more* (a second time). These souls are to live a second life on earth and are made to drink of Lethe in order to forget their former life.

718. quo . . . reperta, *that you may the more delight with me in Italy,* [*now*] *found* [*at last*]. For abl. see A. 431; D. 462; B. 219, 1; G. 408.

719. anne . . . animas, *what! are we to think that spirits go hence on high to* [the light of] *heaven?*

721. lucis . . . cupido, *so wild a desire of life.* Contempt of life, real or affected, was part of the old philosophic creed.

723. suscipit, *replies.*

724. principio, *in the first place.* — **terras :** i. e. the earth as a whole.

725. Titania astra : i. e. the sun.

726. spiritus intus alit, *a spirit within sustains* (i. e. keeps alive, vitalizes). Many ancient philosophers taught that the universe was permeated by a vital force (the *anima mundi*), which was the primary cause of all life and motion. — **infusa per artus mens,** *mind diffused through the members.*

727. mens : the *spiritus* just mentioned, but a more definite term, suggesting an intelligent soul. Cf. Thomson, *Castle of Indolence*, ii. 47 :

> Eternal, never-resting soul,
> Almighty power, and all-directing day,
> By whom each atom stirs and planets roll,
> Who fills, surrounds, informs, and agitates the whole.

— **agitat molem,** *gives motion to the whole mass.* — **magno corpore,** *with the vast frame* (of the universe).

728. inde genus, etc.: the mingling of spirit with a material body of the world is what causes organic or individual life. — **volantum** = *volantium.*

729. et . . . pontus, *and the strange shapes which the ocean brings forth.*

730. igneus . . . seminibus (dat. of possession), *these seeds* [of life] *have a fiery force and a heavenly origin.* — **seminibus :** this refers to the vital principle embodied in the various forms of living beings just mentioned, which is derived from the *spiritus* (or *mens*) that pervades and animates the universe. This *spiritus* is here identified with the heavenly *aether*, which is regarded as *pure flame.* Thus all creatures have a nature that consists essentially of this celestial fire, though (as Anchises goes on to explain) their gross bodies hinder its free action.

731. quantum, etc., *so far as their harmful bodies do not hamper them, and their earthy limbs and mortal frames do not make them dull* (or *sluggish*). The meaning is, that the gross nature of the body thwarts or impedes the free action of the spirit. Cf. Shakspere, *Merchant of Venice*, v. 1. 64, 65 :

> But whilst this muddy vesture of decay
> Doth grossly close it in.

Henry More, the English Platonist, in his poem on the *Præexistency of the Soul*, stanza 3, calls the soul

> A spark or ray of the Divinity
> Clouded in earthy fogs, yclad in clay.

733. hinc metuunt, etc., *hence* (i. e. from the hampering effect of the body) *it comes that they experience fear and desire, sorrow and delight.* These human emotions are here regarded as peculiar to *bodily* life and as inconsistent with the serene higher life of the spirit. — **neque auras dispi-ciunt,** *and they do not see the light,* because they are shut up in the prison-house of the body.

734. clausae : the fem. form shows that Virgil is thinking of *animae* (not *semina*) as the subject of the verbs in *v.* 733.

735. quin et supremo . . . reliquit, *nay, even when life has left them, with the last glimpse of light.*

736. miseris : dat. of separation.

737. penitus, etc., *it must of necessity be that many* [*evil qualities*], *clinging* [*to the soul*] *through a long period of growth, become strangely implanted therein* (lit. *it is utterly necessary that many things, long grown-together with the soul, become,* etc.). The figure is of parasitic growths, which become almost a part of the substance of what they grow on.

739. ergo : i. e. to cleanse the soul. The purification is by means of the three non-earthy elements — air, water, and fire. — **veterum malorum :** i. e. those of their earthly life. With this and the following lines cf. Shakspere, *Measure for Measure,* iii. 1. 122–126:

> To bathe in fiery floods, or to reside
> In thrilling region of thick-ribbed ice ;
> To be imprison'd in the viewless winds,
> And blown with restless violence about
> The pendent world.

743, 744. quisque . . . Manis, *we suffer, every man his own retribution.* By metonymy *Manes,* the soul that receives the penalty, is put for its destiny or life in the world below. — **per . . . Elysium,** etc.: after the purification by penance, the souls pass into Elysium, where a few (like Anchises) remain, freed from the necessity of returning to other bodies (*laeta arva tenemus*); the rest, after a further purification by time, go through another round of earthly life.

745. donec, etc., *until a long period* [of years], *when the cycle of time is completed, has removed the ingrained stain.*

746. purum, etc. (pred.), *has left pure the ethereal sense:* i. e. the *spiritus* (726) or *mens* (727) of which the soul is composed.

747. auraï simplicis ignem, *the flame of pure light* (the ether). — **auraï :** archaic form of genitive (Introd. § 91, *a*).

748. has omnis, *all these,* i. e. with the exception of the *pauci* mentioned in *v.* 744. — **rotam volvere,** *have completed the cycle.* See the myth in Plato's *Republic,* Book x.

750. immemores, etc. (pred.), *that without memory they may revisit the upper earth.* — **convexa :** i. e. under the arch of heaven.

754. possit : subjunctive in a relative clause of characteristic.

755. adversos legere, *scan those before them.*

756. quae deinde (= *dehinc*) **sequatur**, etc.: indir. quest. depending on *expediam*.

757. maneant : sc. *te* or *nos*.

758. animas : a direct object of *expediam* succeeds the two indirect questions. — **nostrum in nomen ituras,** *who are to succeed to our name.*

760. pura hasta : a "headless spear," given as a prize to young men after their first feat of arms.

761. proxima . . . loca, *holds by lot the place nearest to the light* (lit. *the nearest places of light*): i.e. will be the first to be born into the world of men.

762. Italo commixtus sanguine : he was son of Æneas and the Italian princess Lavinia.

763. postuma, *youngest.*

764. longaevo, *in your old age.* — **serum,** *last* or *your latest born* (adj. with *quem*).

766. Longa Alba : the "long white town," stretched along a ridge on the edge of Lake Albanus. It was supposed to be the old capital of the Latin league, from which rank it was dispossessed by Rome. Other Latin towns are mentioned below.

767. proximus, *close by.* — **Procas, Capys, Numitor, Silvius Aeneas :** kings of Alba.

768. Numitōr : the last syllable is here long (Introd. § 110).

770. si umquam acceperit : Æneas Silvius, it was said, was kept from his inheritance for 53 years. — **regnandam Albam,** *the throne of Alba :* A. 500, 4; D. 869; B. 337, 7, *b*, 2; G. 430.

772. umbrata quercu, *wreathed with oak.* The oak-wreath (*corona civilis*) was bestowed on him who had saved the life of a Roman citizen in battle. By vote of the Senate, such wreaths were hung before the door of Augustus as perpetual preserver of the people. Hence the allusion is a personal compliment.

773. Nomentum, etc.: old Latin towns near Rome.

776. tum . . . erunt, *these shall then be names,* i.e. places of note.

777. avo comitem, *a companion* (or champion) *to his grandfather.* The first exploit of Romulus was to restore his grandfather Numitor to the throne of Alba. — **Mavortius,** *son of Mars :* Romulus was the son of Mars and Rhea Silvia.

778. Ilia : Rhea Silvia.

779. vidĕn = *videsne.* — **geminae cristae :** the double plume was a distinguishing mark of Mars, though no representation of it appears in works of art; like him, Romulus is constantly represented with a helmet. It is by this sign that *his father* (Mars) *marks him by his own sign of honor as belonging to the world on high.* — **stant** and **signat :** indirect question with the poetical indicative instead of the subjunctive.

780. superum : pred. gen. (lit. *as being of the gods*).

781. huius auspiciis, *under his leadership*.

782. imperium aequabit : cf. i. 287.

783. una, *though but one city.* — **sibi :** dat. of reference. — **septem arces,** *the seven heights (septimontium)* : the name was first given to the Palatine, with its spurs and those of the adjoining Esquiline ; it was afterwards extended to the larger group of the famous " seven hills," with which at first it had nothing to do.

784. mater : Cybele, called *Berecyntia* from a mountain in Phrygia sacred to her. She was represented with the turreted crown (hence *turrita*) also worn by personified cities (see Fig. 28).

> The tow'red Cybele,
> Mother of an hundred gods.
>
> MILTON, *Arcades, vv.* 21–22.

786. partu : for case see Introd. § 66.

788. geminas acies, *your two eyes.* — **hanc gentem :** the Julian family.

789. Caesar : perhaps Julius Cæsar is meant, perhaps Augustus.

792. Divi : sc. *Caesaris.* Augustus was the adopted son of Julius Cæsar, who was deified after death and called *Divus.* — **aurea condet saecula rursus :** the first Golden Age, when all was peace and happiness, was during the reign of Saturn over Latium, of which he became king after Jupiter expelled him from heaven.

793. Latio : locative abl.

794. Saturno : dat. of agent. — **super Garamantas :** a tribe of interior Africa, which sent an embassy to Augustus. How this struck the Roman imagination is seen in the following verses. — **Indos :** the reference is to the East, generally. When Augustus was in Syria (20 B. C.), embassies from the Parthians and Indians restored the standards taken more than thirty years before from Crassus.

796. extra . . . vias : i. e. beyond the course of the sun along the zodiac. — **Atlas :** cf. iv. 247.

798. in adventum, *against his coming* (as we might say in English) : i. e. looking towards it.

799. responsis : i. e. oracles which are to be fulfilled by his coming. — **Maeotia tellus :** in southern Russia (Scythia).

800. turbant (intrans.), *are troubled.* — **septemgemini :** referring to the numerous mouths of the Delta of the Nile.

802. licet (= *though*) **fixerit :** A. 527, *b* ; D. 810 ; B. 309, 4 ; G. 607. — **Erymanthi pacarit nemora :** i. e. by killing the wild boar.

803. Lernam : referring to the Hydra (see *v.* 287). These exploits of Hercules were all within the limits of Arcadia, and so give no great notion of his wanderings. Atlas, Antæus, and Geryon might have suggested a wider range.

805. Liber: an old Italian god of fertility, identified with the Grecian Bacchus, god of wine, inspiration, and dramatic poetry. The triumphant march of Bacchus, in the fable, led him as far as India. His car was drawn by tigers or lynxes, guided by reins of vine-branch. — **Nysae :** somewhere in India.

806. dubitamus : *do we hesitate* (now that we behold the victories of Augustus)?

808. olivae : the symbol of peace.

809. menta : poetical plur. for singular.

810. regis : Numa, the second king, the reputed founder of most of the religious customs of Rome ; he was a native of the Sabine Cures.

812. imperium magnum : in fact a city of perhaps twenty or thirty thousand inhabitants, and a territory of about fifteen miles square. Anchises speaks in vision of the vast empire to follow.

814. Tullus : Tullus Hostilius, the third king.

815. iactantior, *too boastful*, as grandson of Numa. — **Ancus :** Ancus Marcius, the fourth king.

816. nunc: i. e. even before he begins his earthly career. — **nimium . . . auris,** *delighting too much in the breath of popular favor* (i. e. when intriguing for the kingdom): Ancus was said to be the founder of the *plebs* as an order in the state.

817. Tarquinios reges : Tarquinius Priscus, Servius Tullius, and Tarquinius Superbus, the fifth, sixth, and seventh kings.

818. fasces receptos, *the restored fasces.* The *fasces*, or bundles of rods and axe, were borne by the lictors before the highest officer, as the symbol of *imperium*, or military power. Brutus, it was said, wrested the *imperium* from the kings and restored it to the aristocracy.

819. consulis imperium : Brutus was consul 509 B. C.

820. natos . . . vocabit : Brutus sentenced to death his own sons for joining in a conspiracy to restore the exiled king. Hence *saevas secures.*

822. utcumque ferent minores, *however posterity shall report his deeds.* In these words Anchises admits the cruelty of the act, but immediately excuses it on the ground of patriotism.

824. Decios, etc.: the Decii, father, son, and grandson, solemnly devoted themselves to death, each to win a doubtful battle, in the war with the Latins, with the Samnites, and with Pyrrhus respectively ; Torquatus (T. Manlius) won his title, with a golden neck-chain, by slaying a gigantic Gaul ; later he put to death his own son for disobeying orders in war (hence *saevum securi*). Camillus, returning from banishment, drove back the victorious Gauls, winning back the standards captured by them in the battle of the Allia (*referentem signa*). The Drusi, a respectable but not eminent family, are here mentioned in compliment to Livia, wife of Augustus.

827. concordes animae : Pompey and Cæsar, in equal arms (*paribus in armis*), since their power was about equal.

830. socer: Cæsar, whose daughter Julia was the third and best beloved wife of Pompey. She died 54 B.C., while Cæsar was in Gaul. — **arce Monoeci,** *the rampart of Monœcus* (Monaco), on the coast just east of Nice. It is mentioned to signify Cæsar's march from Gaul into Italy.

831. Eois: the main reliance of Pompey was on the forces of the East.

832. ne . . . bella, *do not make such wars familiar to your hearts.* Virgil alludes to the naturally humane temper of both the rivals.

834. tu prior: Cæsar, as the more illustrious. Besides, the exploits of Cæsar, as a popular chief, were distasteful to the courtiers of Augustus, and it was fashionable to belittle them; hence the objurgatory tone. — **parce,** *forbear.* — **genus Olympo:** Cæsar, as a member of the *gens Iulia,* claimed descent from Venus and Anchises, and through Venus from Jupiter.

836. ille: L. Mummius, conqueror of Corinth, 146 B.C. — **triumphata:** here transitive in the sense of *triumph over.*

837. currum: alluding to the well-known triumphal procession from the Campus Martius past the Forum and up to the temple of Jupiter Capitolinus (*Capitolia ad alta*).

838. ille: L. Æmilius Paullus, conqueror of Perseus (*Aeaciden,* as descended from Achilles), 168 B.C. By Argos, etc., is meant all Greece, of which, in Anchises' time, this was the chief city.

840. templa Minervae: see ii. 163 ff.

841–844. Cato, etc. These heroes are Cato the Censor; Cossus, a hero of the early wars against the Gauls, who won the *spolia opima* by slaying the leader of the enemy with his own hand; the Gracchi, the celebrated tribunes of the people, one of whose ancestors had distinguished himself in Spain; the Scipios, Africanus elder and younger; Fabricius, "strong in poverty," who defeated Pyrrhus; Serranus (C. Atilius Regulus, consul 257 B.C.; not the famous Regulus), a general in the First Punic War. The name *Serranus* was said to have been given to Regulus from his being found sowing (*serentem*) in the field by the messengers who brought the news of his election as consul. — **te tacitum relinquat,** *pass you over in silence.*

843. cladem, *scourge.*

845. quo . . . Fabii, *whither, O Fabii, do you hurry me, wearied as I am ?* The meaning is that the exploits of the Fabii are too many for mention. — [*Fabius*] **Maximus:** the commander against Hannibal. The following verse (which is taken from Ennius) refers to his method of waging war, whence he was called Cunctator.

846. cunctando: i. e. by what are called dilatory tactics. — **rem,** *the state* (cf. *res publica*).

847. excudent alii mollius: Virgil has the Greeks in mind. — **spirantia:** as if the statues were alive.

848. ducent: *ducere* applies strictly to yielding materials, like metal, clay, or wax; its use here suggests that marble itself is pliable in the hands of a consummate artist.

849. orabunt melius: in forensic oratory, the names of Crassus, Hortensius, and Cicero stand as high as those of their Greek masters. But Anchises purposely disparages every other glory — art, oratory, science — in comparison with that of arms.

850. radio: *the rod* used to trace mathematical and astronomical diagrams (in sand originally).

854. mirantibus: sc. *eis* (Æneas and the Sibyl).

855. Marcellus: M. Claudius Marcellus, called the "Sword of Rome," one of the best generals against the Gauls, and afterwards against Hannibal. He won the *spolia opima* by slaying the Gallic chief Viridomarus. His name is mentioned last, to introduce that of his young namesake.

857. tumultu, *alarm:* strictly, the name for civil war.

858. sistet, *will support:* contrasted with *tumultu.* — **eques:** the most celebrated exploits of Marcellus were with cavalry.

859. tertia, *for the third time.* Before Marcellus the *spolia opima* had been won by Romulus and Cossus only (*v.* 841). — **Quirino:** the Sabine god of battles, identified by the Romans with the deified Romulus.

860. Aeneas: sc. *ait.* — **una:** with Marcellus.

861. iuvenem: the younger Marcellus, nephew of Augustus, who was adopted by him and recognized as his successor.

863. virum, *the hero* (the elder Marcellus). — **sic,** *thus.*

865. quantum instar in ipso: *what a noble bearing in the man himself!*

867. ingressus, *began to speak.*

868–886. See Introd., p. 6, for the anecdote of Virgil's recitation of these lines before Augustus.

869. ostendent tantum, *will only show him.* The younger Marcellus died in his twentieth year (23 B.C.).

871. propria . . . fuissent, *if this gift* (Marcellus) *were to be lasting:* subjunc. in a dependent clause in indir. disc. after *visa* [*est*], which is equivalent to a verb of *thinking.* The direct would be *fuerint* (fut. perf.).

872. quantos virum gemitus, *what lamentation of strong men!* — **ille campus:** the Campus Martius, in which Augustus had built a huge mausoleum in 27 B.C. — **Mavortis urbem:** i.e. Rome.

873. quae funera: in the funeral procession of young Marcellus, there were six hundred couches containing the images of his illustrious kindred. The funeral was on the *Campus Martius.*

874. tumulum: the ruins of the immense tomb are still to be seen near the Tiber.

876. in tantum spe, *so high in hope.* — **quondam,** *ever.*

877. se tantum iactabit, *boast itself so much.*

878. heu prisca fides, etc.: cf. Dryden, *Absalom and Achitophel,* i. 844–845:

> O, ancient honor! O, unconquered hand,
> Whom foes unpunished never could withstand!

879. illi: dat. with *obvius*; A. 370, *c*; D. 384; cf. B. 192, 1. Cf. i. 314.
— **tulisset:** i. e. if he had lived.

882. rumpas: A. 516, *b*, N.; B. 303, *b*; G. 596, 1.

885. inani: i. e. because the boy would never come to maturity.

887. aeris campis, *in the shadowy plains.*

890. gerenda: sc. *sint.*

893. geminae portae: this description of the horn and ivory gates is taken from the words of Penelope to Odysseus (Od. xix. 562–567; Bry. 678).
— **fertur,** *is reported to be.*

894. veris umbris, *true dreams.*

895. candenti elephanto: abl. of material.

896. mittunt: i. e. by this gate.

899. viam secat, *he takes his way* (lit. *cuts*).

900. Caietae: in the southern part of Latium. — **recto litore,** *straight along the coast*: abl. of the way by which (Introd. § 55).

901. Repeated from iii. 277.

II. SELECTIONS FROM OVID AND OTHER LATIN POETS

PYRAMUS AND THISBE

(OVID, *Metamorphoses,* iv. 55–166)

56. quas: the antecedent is *puellis.* — **praelata,** *surpassing* (lit. *preferred before*). — **puellis:** dat. after *prae-* (Introd. § 27).

57. tenuere, *lived in.*

58. coctilibus (from *coquo*), *made of burnt brick.* — **Semiramis** and her husband Ninus were the mythical founders of the ancient Assyrian kingdom of Nineveh. She was said to have become sole ruler after the death of Ninus, and Babylon (the city here referred to) was one of her mighty works.

59. primos gradus, *the first steps* (in their love).

60. taedae . . . coissent, *they would have been united by the rites of marriage also.* — **taedae,** lit. *torch*; often used for *marriage.* See Æneid, iv. 18, and note.

61. sed vetuere patres: this takes the place of the condition contrary to fact, of which *coissent* is the conclusion; A. 521, *a*; D. 802; B. 305, 1;

G. 600, 1. — **quod non**, etc., *but* THIS *they could not forbid* (i.e. that they should love each other).

62. ex aequo, *equally, alike.* — **captis . . . mentibus**, *in their passionate hearts* (lit. *caught*, i.e. by love: cf. Eng. *captivated*).

64. quo magis, etc., *the more it is covered, the more*, etc. — **quo :** abl. of degree with *magis* ; *eo* is omitted in the second clause. See A. 414, *a* ; D. 476; B. 223 ; G. 403.

65. quam duxerat, *which it* (the wall) *had happened to get.*

66. cum fieret, *when it was built.*

67. nulli : dat. of agent (Introd. § 30).

70. blanditiae, *soft words.*

71. hinc, *on this side.*

72. in vices, *in turn.*

73. invide, *envious, hateful.*

74. quantum erat, *how great a favor would it be* : the subject of *erat* is the substantive clause of result *ut sineres*, etc. — **erat :** A. 437, *a* ; D. 643, *b* ; B. 271, 1, *b* ; G. 254, R.[1] — **toto corpore iungi**, *to embrace.*

75. hoc si nimium [*est*], *if this is too much* (to ask). — **vel**, *even.* — **pateres**, *would open wide enough.*

79. parti, *side* (of the wall).

80. contra, *to the other side.*

84. multa : cognate accusative.

87. neve sit errandum, *and, that they might not lose their way* or *miss each other.* For the impersonal passive see A. 500, 3 ; D. 860, *a* ; B. 337, 8, *b*, 1 ; G. 251, 2. — **spatiantibus** [sc. *sibi*]: dat. of agent.

88. conveniant, lateant : in the same construction as *temptent* in *v.* 85. — **Nini :** the great tomb of Ninus was a landmark in the fields, at some distance from the city.

90. fonti : for case see Introd. § 35.

91. pacta placent, *the compact is agreed upon.*

92. aquis, *into the waters of the sea* (dat. for *in aquas*). Darkness was supposed to arise from the Western Sea as the sun sank into the waters.

93. callida, *slyly.*

94. fallit, *eludes.* — **suos**, *her family and servants.* — **vultum :** acc. of specification ("Greek accusative"); Introd. § 42.

96. audacem : sc. *eam.*

97. oblĭta (p.p. of *oblĭno*), *besmeared.* — **rictus**, *jaws :* for construction see *v.* 94 (*vultum*).

98. depositura, *to quench :* fut. participle expressing purpose; A. 499, 2 ; D. 868; B. 337, 4 ; G. 438, N.

99. ad, *by.*

101. velamina, *mantle.*

102. ut, *when.*

103. sine ipsa, *without its owner.*

105. serius egressus, *coming out* (to the rendezvous) *later* (than Thisbe).

110. nostra . . . est, *my life is stained with guilt.* — **miseranda** (voc.), *poor girl!*

111. metus, *of danger* (lit. *of fear*): gen. with *plena* (Introd. § 16). — **venires :** obj. of *iussi.* The subjunctive (without *ut*) expresses indirectly the imperative (*veni*) of direct speech. In prose the infinitive would be used.

112. nec, *and did not.* — **prior,** *first* (before you).

114. quicumque, etc., *whatever lions you are who,* etc.

115. timidi est, *it is a coward's part* (Introd. § 9). — **optare** (emphatic), *merely to pray for.* Suicide was often regarded by the ancients as an act of heroism.

117. notae : agrees with *vesti.*

119. quŏque : not the conjunction *quŏque,* but the relative *quō + que*; the antecedent is *ferrum.*

120. traxit : sc. *ferrum* as object.

122. non aliter quam, *just as.* The comparison is more vivid than poetical. — **vitiato . . . plumbo,** *by a flaw in the lead* (lit. abl. abs., *the lead being flawed*). — **fistula,** *a water-pipe.*

123. stridente, *hissing,* or *with a hissing sound.* — **tenui . . . foramine,** *through the narrow opening* : abl. of the way by which (Introd. § 55).

124. ictibus aëra rumpit, *pierces the air with its jets* (lit. *blows*).

125. arborei fetūs, *the fruit(s) of the* (mulberry) *tree.* — **caedis,** *of the blood.*

128. fallat, *disappoint* : clause of purpose.

130. quanta vitarit (= *vitaverit*) : indirect question.

131. ut . . . sic, *as . . . so* ; practically equivalent to *though . . . yet.* — **visa in arbore,** *in the tree which she saw.*

132. pomi, *of the fruit.* — **color :** before being stained with the blood of Pyramus, all mulberries (the story went) were snow-white (see *v.* 89). — **an haec sit,** *whether this is it* (the appointed tree): indirect question.

133. tremebunda, *quivering.*

134. retro pedem tulit, *shrank back.* — **buxo,** *than boxwood.*

135. gerens, *with* (lit. *bearing*). — **aequoris instar,** *like the sea* : Introd. § 23.

136. summum, *its surface* : really an adj. agreeing with *aequor* (cf. *summus mons*).

137. remorata, *after a moment's delay.* — **amores,** *lover.*

138. indignos, *blameless* (lit. *not deserving* such treatment). — **claro,** *loud.*

139. comas : for construction see *vv.* 94, 97.

140. cruori : dat. with *miscuit* ; A. 413, *a,* N. ; cf. D. 381 ; B. 358, 3 ; G. 348, and R.[1]

142. mihi : dat. of separation (Introd. § 32).

144. iacentes, *drooping.*

145. ad, *at.* — **a morte :** poetical use of abl. of agent instead of means; *mors* is personified.

146. visāque . . . illā, *closed them again when he had seen her*: abl. abs.

147. ense : abl. with *vacuum* (Introd. § 66).

149, 150. est et mihi, etc., *I too have a hand that is brave enough for this* [*deed*] *alone; I too have love* [*that is strong enough to do it*]. — **hic :** i. e. love.

151. exstinctum : sc. *te.*

152. quique, etc., *and you who could,* etc.

153. solā agrees with *morte.* — **nec,** *not even.*

154. hoc . . . estote rogati, *hear this prayer* (lit. *be asked for this one thing*). The expression (with the future imperative) is particularly formal and solemn; A. 449, 2; D. 690, *b*; B. 281, 1, *b*; G. 268, 2.

155. meus . . . parentes : A. 340, *a*; D. 323; B. 171, 2; G. 201, N.[2]

156. ut . . . non invideatis, *grant,* etc. : substantive clause of purpose in apposition with *hoc.* — **quos,** *those whom.*

159. duorum : sc. *corpora.*

160. pullos, *dark.*

161. gemini . . . cruoris, *as memorials of the death of us both.*

162, 163. aptato . . . ferro, *placing the point against her heart, she fell upon the sword.*

164. vota, *her prayers.*

166. quodque rogis superest, *what remains from their funeral pyres* (their ashes). — **rogis :** dat. with *superest* (Introd. § 27).

PERSEUS AND ANDROMEDA

(OVID, *Metamorphoses*, iv. 662–763)

662. Hippotades : Æolus, the wind god, was the son (or grandson) of Hippotes, a Trojan hero. For the cave or prison of the winds see Æneid, i. 50–91.

663. admonitor operum, *he who summons mortals to their daily tasks* (Introd. § 14).

664. ille : Perseus. He has already killed the Gorgon Medusa, and by means of her head has just turned the giant Atlas into the mountain of the same name. — **pennis :** he puts on the winged sandals (*talaria*) which the nymphs had given him to use in his travels and in his attack on the Gorgon.

665. parte ab utraque pedes = *utrumque pedem.* — **unco,** *curved.* The sword was provided with a curved hook as well as with a cutting edge. See Fig. 52. — **accingitur,** *girds himself* (the "middle" use): Introd. § 94.

668. Cephea (adj.), *of Cepheus,* the Æthiopian king. His wife, Cassiopeia, had striven

> To set her beauty's praise above
> The sea nymphs, and their power offended.
>
> MILTON

669. pendere, *to pay.* — **maternae . . . linguae,** *for her mother's* [*boastful*] *tongue.*

670. Hammon: the god whose oracle had ordered that Andromeda be given up to the monster. See Fig. 38.

671. simul = *simul ac, as soon as.* — **bracchia:** see note on iv. 94.

672. Abantiades: i. e. Perseus (grandson of Abas, king of Argos). — **nisi quod . . . moverat** = *nisi movisset.*

674. ratus esset, *he would have thought her.* — **inscius,** *unaware.* — **trahit ignes,** *is fired with love.*

675. correptus, *fascinated* (lit. *carried away*). — **formae,** *beauty.*

677. ut stetit, *when he had alighted* on the shore. — **catenis:** abl. with *digna* (Introd. § 66).

678. sed quibus, *but rather of those* [*chains*] *by which,* etc.

679. requirenti: sc. *mihi.*

680. cur . . . geras: indirect question.

681. virgo, *maiden as she was.*

683. quod potuit (parenthetical), *for this at least she could do:* she could veil her eyes, though she could not cover her face with her hands.

684. instanti: sc. *ei* (indir. obj. of *indicat*), *to him, when he urged her again and again.* — **sua delicta,** *faults of her own.*

686. quantaque . . . formae, *and what pride in beauty her mother had shown:* indir. question. — **formae:** obj. gen. (Introd. § 14).

688. immenso . . . imminet, *overhangs an immense space of sea* (like a huge jutting crag).

689. possidet, *covers.*

691. iustius: since the fault was the mother's.

694. hospes, *the stranger* (Perseus). — **lacrimarum,** *for tears.* — **manere,** *await:* i. e. you will have time enough to weep hereafter.

696. hanc ego si peterem, *if I* (emphatic) *were asking her in marriage.*

698, 699. superator, etc.: translate by a relative clause, — *I, Perseus, who overcame the snaky-haired Gorgon and who dared,* etc.

700. praeferrer, *I should be preferred.* — **gener,** *as a son-in-law.*

Fig. 52

701. dotibus, *marriage gifts* (from the suitor to the bride's parents). —
et meritum, *good service also.* — **modo,** *if only*: for subjunc. see A. 528;
D. 811; B. 310; G. 573.

702. servata, *if saved.* — **paciscor,** *I stipulate.*

703. legem, *the condition* (i. e. the terms offered). — **dubitaret :** deliberative subjunctive; A. 444; D. 678; B. 277; G. 265.

704. super, *besides* (over and above). — **dotale,** *as a dowry.*

705. concita, *at full speed* (lit. *urged on*).

707. dimotis undis, *parting the waves.*

708. tantum . . . quantum, *only so far . . . as.* — **Balearica :** the natives
of the Balearic Isles were famous for their skill with the sling.

709. medii . . . caeli, *through the air* (lit. a partitive gen. with *quantum*).
— **transmittere,** *carry* (as we speak of a gun's *carrying* a certain distance).

711. in aequore summo, *on the surface of the sea.*

712. in, *against.*

713. Iovis praepes, *the swift bird of Jove* (the eagle).

714. praebentem, etc.: i. e. sunning itself.

715. occupat aversum, *seizes upon it from behind* (lit. *turned away*).
— **neu,** *and, lest,* etc. — **ora,** *jaws.*

716. cervicibus : plural for singular (poetical).

717. missus praeceps volatu, *swooping down headlong*: abl. of manner.

718. pressit, *alighted on.*

719. Inachides : Perseus. — **curvo tenus hamo,** *up to the curved hook*:
A. 221, 26; D. 277, *c*; B. 142, 3; G. 417, 14.

720, 721. modo . . . modo, *now . . . now.* — **more,** *like* (lit. *in the
manner of*).

722. circumsona, *barking about him.*

723. ille : i. e. Perseus.

724. quāque patet, *and wherever he* (the dragon) *is exposed* (to attack).
— **obsita,** *covered.*

725. quā, *where.* — **tenuissima cauda,** *the slenderest part of his tail.*

726. desinit in piscem, *tapers into a fish's.*

728. pennae, *the wings* (on Perseus' sandals).

729. bibulis (from *bibo*), *soaked* (lit. *absorbent*). — **talaribus :** dat. with
credere.

732. nixus eo, *alighting on this.*

733. repetita, *piercing them again and again* (lit. passive, agreeing
with *ilia*).

735. implevēre : the verb is plural since *cum plausu clamor = clamor
et plausus*; A. 317, N.; D. 633; B. 254, 4; G. 211, R.[1] — **generum,** *him
as son-in-law.*

737. Cassiope : another form of the name *Cassiopeia* (Andromeda's
mother).

738. -que et = *et . . . et.*

740. anguiferum caput : the head of Medusa.

741. mollit humum foliis, *spreads a carpet of leaves on the ground* (lit. *softens the ground with leaves).* — **natas,** *that grow.*

742. Phorcynidos (gen.) : the sea god Phorcys (Phorcus), son of Neptune, was the father of the Gorgons.

743. virgă . . . medullā, *the branch* (of seaweed), *oeing newly plucked and still fresh, absorbed the strong poison of the monster in its porous pith.*

744. vim : i. e. the petrifying quality of Medusa's head.

745. percepit, *acquired.*

746. temptant, *try* (as an experiment).

747. idem contingere gaudent, *rejoice because the same thing happens*; A. 572, *b*; D. 839, *e*; B. 331, V; G. 533.

748. seminaque . . . undas, *and from them they propagate more seeds, which they toss through the waves.* The idea is that one lot of the petrified twigs has a similar effect on the next lot, and so on, as the seeds of a plant produce another crop.

750, 751. tacto ab aëre, *from contact with the air.* — **capiant . . . fiat :** both are introduced by *ut,* forming a substantive clause of result in apposition with *natura*; A. 570; D. 741; B. 297, 3; G. 557.

752. ille : Perseus.

753. Mercurio : Mercury had given Perseus winged sandals and the curved sword. — **bellica virgo,** i. e. Pallas (Minerva), who had given him his helmet, shield, and spear.

754. Iovis : Jupiter was Perseus' father.

755. alipedi, *to the god with winged feet* (Mercury).

756. et : the so-called epexegetical or explanatory *et* may be omitted in translating.

758. praecutiunt, *brandish* (at the head of the wedding procession).

763. Cepheni, *Æthiopian :* adj. (from *Cepheus).*

DÆDALUS AND ICARUS

(OVID, *Metamorphoses*, viii. 183–235)

183. Daedalus : a Greek name, meaning "the Skilful." He resembles Wayland, the smith of Germanic mythology (see Scott's *Kenilworth*).

184. loci natalis, *his native soil* (Athens): Introd. § 14.

185, 186. pelago, *from the sea.* — **licet . . . obstruat,** *though he* (Minos) *may shut off*; A. 527, *b*; D. 810; B. 309, 4; G. 607. — **illac,** *that way.*

187. possideat, *though he possess :* concession expressed by the hortatory subjunctive; A. 440; D. 677; B. 278; G. 264.

188. dimittit, *applies.*

189. naturam novat, *changes* [the fixed order of] *nature.*

191. ut . . . putes, *so that you would think they had grown on a slope.*

192. fistula, *Pan's pipe, shepherd's pipe* (Fig. 53). — **surgit,** *increases* (in length).

193. lino . . . imas, *he fastens them with thread in the middle and with bits of wax at the end.*

195. ut . . . imitetur, *so as to imitate :* clause of result. — **unā,** *near.*

196. se tractare, *that he is handling :* indir. disc. with *ignarus.*

197. renidenti, *glowing* (with eager interest). — **modo,** *now.*

199. lusu suo, *with his childish play.*

200. manus ultima, *the finishing touch* (lit. *the last hand*). — **coepto,** *to his work* (lit. *to the thing begun*).

201. libravit in, *balanced* (or *poised himself*) *on.*

Fig. 53

202. motaque pependit in aura, *and hovered in the air which was moved* (by his wings).

203. medio . . . limite, *in a middle course* (neither too high nor too low): abl. of the way by which; Introd. § 55.

204. demissior, *too low :* compar. of p.p. *demissus* as adj.; A. 291, *a* ; D. 154, N.; B. 240, 1 ; G. 297, 2.

205. gravet, adurat: with *ne, lest,* stating the purpose of *ut . . . curras,* which is a subst. clause, obj. of *moneo* (Introd. § 78).

Fig. 54

206. spectare, *to keep your eye on.* — **Boöten, Helicen, Orionis ensem :** various constellations. Icarus is to follow his father, not to direct his flight by observing the stars.

208. me duce : abl. absolute.

211. patriae (adj.), *the father's.*

212. non iterum repetenda, *never to be repeated.*

213. comiti, *for his companion.*

214. teneram prolem, *her young brood.*

215. damnosas, *harmful* (because destined to be his ruin).

217. hos: i. e. Dædalus and Icarus as they fly over the sea. The verb is *vidit* in *v.* 219. — **aliquis,** *some one.* — **captat ... pisces,** *was fishing.*

218. baculo ... innixus, *leaning on his staff.* See Fig. 54. — **stivā,** *on the handle of his plough.* Fig. 55 shows an ancient Greek plough.

219. qui: supply *eos* as antecedent. — **qui possent,** *since they could*; A. 535, *e*; D. 730, I; B. 283, 3; G. 634. — **aethera carpere,** *fly through the air.*

220, 221. Iunonia, *sacred to* (or *beloved by*) *Juno*: see Æneid, i. 15–16 and notes. — **laeva parte,** *on their left* (as they flew).

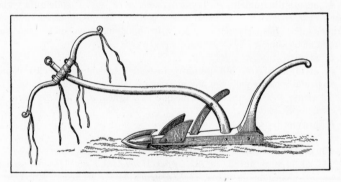

Fig. 55

224. caeli cupidine tactus, *prompted by eager desire to reach the sky*: objective genitive (Introd. § 14).

225. altius (adv.), *too high.* — **rapidi,** *fiercely burning* (i. e. with *devouring* heat: cf. *rapio*).

227. tabuerant: see *tabesco.* — **lacertos,** *arms.*

228. remigio carens, *lacking wings* (lit. *oarage*, i. e. rowing apparatus, oars). — **non ... percipit,** *does not catch.*

229. caeruleā: with *aquā.*

230. traxit, *derived, took.* The southeastern part of the Ægean Sea was called the Icarian Sea (*Mare Icarium*), and was thought to have been named after Icarus, who was drowned there.

231. nec iam, *no longer.*

233. dicebat, *kept saying.*

235. tellus: i. e. the island of *Icaria*, where a tomb supposed to be that of Icarus was shown to travellers.

ORPHEUS AND EURYDICE

(OVID, *Metamorphoses*, x. 1–77)

1. inde: i. e. from Crete, where Hymen had solemnized the marriage of Iphis and Ianthe. — **croceo . . . amictu:** cf. Milton, *L'Allegro*, 125–126:

> There let Hymen oft appear
> In saffron robe, with taper clear.

2. Ciconum: the Cicŏnes were a Thracian tribe.

3. Ŏrpheā (adj.), *of Orpheus*. — **nequiquam,** *in vain* (for the marriage was destined to come to a tragic end).

4. adfuit ille quidem, *he* (Hymen) *came, to be sure*. — **sollemnia verba,** *the accustomed words*. The marriage was ill-omened, as appeared — among other signs — from Hymen's silence when he should have spoken the usual words of blessing.

5. attulit, *brought with him*.

6. stridula, *hissing* and sputtering instead of burning with a clear flame : a particularly bad omen. For the marriage torch see note on Æneid, iv. 18.

7. usque, *always, ever*. — **nullosque . . . ignes,** *and did not blaze up when swung about*.

8. gravior [*erat*], *was even worse*.

9. nova : with *nupta*.

10. occidit, *fell dead*. — **talum,** *heel*.

11. ad superas auras, *in the Upper World* (*this* world, as opposed to Hades). — **Rhodopeïus vates,** *the Thracian bard* (Orpheus). Rhodope is a mountain range in Thrace.

12. ne non temptaret et umbras, *not to leave untried even the* (world of) *shades* : purpose. Cf. Æneid, vi. 119–120.

13. Taenaria . . . porta, *by the Tænarian portal*. On the promontory of Tænarus or Tænarum (now Cape Matapan) was a cavern supposed to be one of the entrances to the Lower World. For the abl. see n. on viii. 203.

14. simulacraque functa sepulcro, *the shades of the buried dead* (lit. *the shades having undergone burial*). Without due burial rites no soul could cross the Styx : see Æneid, vi. 305 ff. For abl. see Introd. § 56.

16. dominum : i. e. Pluto, the husband of Proserpine (Persephone). — **ad carmina,** *in accompaniment to his song*. — **nervis,** *the strings of his lyre*.

18. quicquid mortale creamur, *all we that are born of mortal race*.

19. falsi . . . oris, *without the subtle phrases of a deceitful tongue*. — **ambagibus** (abl. abs. with *positis*) : denotes any kind of ambiguous or evasive roundabout talk.

21. villosa, *shaggy*.

22. terna: A. 137, *d*; D. 173, *d*, *e*; B. 81, 4, *d*; G. 97, N.[1] — **Medusaei,** *snaky-haired* (like the Gorgon Medusa). — **vincirem:** subj. of purpose; he has not come to bind and carry away Cerberus, as Hercules had done.

23. calcata, *trodden upon.*

24. crescentes annos, *the years of her youth,* when she apparently had a long life ahead of her.

25. pati, *to suffer with patience.*

26. superā . . . in orā, *in the world above.*

27. an sit et hic, *whether he is also known here:* indir. question. —

Fig. 56

auguror, *I surmise.* — **esse,** *that he is* (known): indirect disc.; the subject (*eum*) is omitted.

28. veteris . . . rapinae: i.e. the carrying away of Proserpine by Pluto (as beautifully told in Metamorphoses, v. 385–408). See Fig. 56 (from an ancient relief).

31. properata, *untimely* (lit. *hastened*). — **retexite,** *reverse* (lit. *unweave*).

32. omnia debemus vobis, *all [that we have] we must render up to you:* literally, *we owe all things to you,* i.e. we possess our lives, and everything that we have, as a loan from you, which must be repaid sometime (by death).

35. humani generis regna, *rule over mankind.* Cf. Ecclesiastes, xii. 5: "Man goeth to his long home."

36. haec, *she* (Eurydice). — **iustos . . . annos,** *due [number of] years.*

37. iuris erit vestri, *will be under your sway* (i.e. will die and become one of your subjects): predicate genitive (Introd. § 9). — **pro munere poscimus usum,** *instead of a gift I ask [only] her dear companionship:* he implies that Eurydice will still belong to the gods below, and that she is to be *his* for a time only (i.e. until she has lived her life).

39. quod si, *but if.* — **veniam,** *this favor.* — **certum est mihi,** *it is my fixed resolve* (lit. *it has been decided by me*). — **mihi:** dat. of agent. — **nolle,** *to refuse.*

40. ad, *in harmony with.*

41–44. Even the tortures of the damned cease under the spell of the music of Orpheus. For Tantalus, Ixion, Sisyphus, and Tityos see Æneid, vi. 595–607. — **captavit,** *tried to catch.* — **iacuit,** *stood still.* — **iecur:** i. e. of Tityos. — **urnis vacarunt,** *were freed from their urns.* The Belides (granddaughters of Belus) were the Danaids (*Danaïdes*), the fifty daughters

Fig. 57

of Danaus. All of them except one (Hypermnestra) murdered their husbands and were condemned in Hades to draw water forever and pour it into a vessel full of holes. See Fig. 57 (from an ancient relief).

46. regia coniunx: Proserpine.

47. sustinet oranti . . . negare, *can bear to refuse his prayer* (lit. *him praying*). — **qui,** *he who:* i. e. Pluto. — **ima,** *the World Below.*

48. recentes, *new-come.*

50. legem, *the condition:* what the terms are, is defined in the substantive clause of purpose *ne flectat*; A. 561, *a*; D. 724; B. 294; G. 546, N.²

51. Avernas (adj.), *of Avernus* (the Lower World).

52. futura [esse]: indir. disc., dependent on the idea of *saying* implied in *legem.*

53. carpitur, *is traversed:* cf. *carpere viam,* an idiom for *to make one's way.*

55. telluris summae, *of the Upper World.*

56. ne deficeret, *that she might be missing:* the clause is obj. of *metuens;* A. 564; D. 720, II; B. 296, 2; G. 550. — **videndi:** Introd. § 16.

57. relapsa est, *vanished* (lit. *slipped back*).

58. captans, *seeking* (with inf.).

59. nil nisi, *nothing but.* — **cedentes,** *yielding* (i.e. unsubstantial).

60. iterum moriens, *she, dying a second time.*

61. quid . . . quereretur, *of what was she to complain?* Deliberative subjunctive; A. 444; D. 678; B. 277; G. 265. — **se . . . amatam** [*esse*]: indirect discourse.

62. supremum vale, *her last farewell*; A. 33; D. 68; B. 15, A, 3; G. 20, III.

63. acciperet, *could catch*: subjunc. clause of characteristic. — **eodem,** *to the same place* (where she had been *inter recentes umbras, v.* 48).

64. gemina, *twofold.*

65. qui, *he who.* — **timidus,** *in terror.* — **medio portante,** *the middle* [*neck*] *bearing chains.*

66. canis: i.e. Cerberus. Those who looked at Cerberus as he was led by Hercules in the Upper World are said to have been turned to stone.

67. per corpus oborto, *covering his body.*

68. qui: the antecedent is *Olenos.* — **in se traxit,** *took upon himself.* Lethæa, the wife of Olenos, boasted of her beauty as superior to that of some goddess; Olenos took the blame upon himself; both were turned to stone.

69. nocens, *guilty.* — **figurae,** *beauty*: dat. with *confisa* (Introd. § 26).

70. iunctissima, *most loving.*

72. [eum] orantem: i.e. Orpheus.

73. portitor, *ferryman* (Charon). See illustration at Æneid, vi. 322.

74. squalidus, *mourning,* lit. *dirty and neglected,* in accordance with the ancient custom of mourners: cf. "in sackcloth and ashes." — **Cereris sine munere:** i.e. without food.

77. Haemum: a mountain in Thrace.

ORPHEUS AND EURYDICE

(VIRGIL, *Georgics*, iv. 454–527)

454. Magna luis commissa, *you are atoning for a great crime.* The speaker is the sea-god Proteus, who has been asked by Aristæus to tell him why his bees are dying. After Eurydice became the wife of Orpheus, she was seen by Aristæus, a deity guarding herds and flocks and bees. He fell in love with her; indeed, it was while she was fleeing from Aristæus that Eurydice was fatally bitten by a snake. The nymphs, Proteus tells Aristæus, caused mortality among his bees to avenge the death of Eurydice, who was herself a nymph.

455. haudquaquam ad meritum, *not at all according to your deserts*; i.e. Aristæus is being punished far less than his offence deserves. — **ni fata resistant,** *unless the fates interpose.*

457. Illa : Eurydice. — **per flumina,** *along the banks of the river.*

458. puella : in apposition with **illa** ; *though but a girl.*

460. chorus aequalis Dryadum, *a band of mountain nymphs, her companions* (lit. *equals in age*). — **supremos montis** = *summos montis.*

461. Rhodopeïae arces, *the heights of Rhodope,* a mountain range in Thrace.

462. Pangaea : Pangæa was a mountain in Thrace.

463. Actias Orithyia : Orithyia, here spoken of as a nymph, was a daughter of Erechtheus, king of Athens. She had been carried off to Thrace by Boreas. *Acte* was an old name for Attica ; hence *Actias.*

464. Ipse : Orpheus. — **cava testudine :** Mercury is said to have made the lyre by fitting strings across the empty shell of a tortoise.

465. dulcis coniunx : vocative, but may be translated as an appositive to *te.* — **secum,** *by himself.*

467. fauces, *the jaws*; i. e. the cavern near Tænarum, which was supposed to be one of the entrances to the Lower World.

470. humanis precibus, *in response to human prayers.* — **mansuescere,** *to relent.*

472. luce carentum : i. e. of the dead.

473. quam multa . . . milia, *as the many thousands of birds which,* etc.

474. vesper . . . imber : when they go to roost at night or seek shelter from a storm.

475. defuncta vita, *who have finished life.*

476. magnanimum : a contraction of *magnanimorum.*

477. impositique . . . parentum : those who have died prematurely.

479. tardā : with *undā.*

480. noviens interfusa : the Styx flowed nine times round the region.

481, 482. ipsae . . . Tartara, *the very home of Death and the inmost regions of Tartarus.* — **caeruleos . . . anguis,** *having blue-black snakes entwined in their hair*: *anguis* is acc. of specification (Introd. § 42).

483. inhians, *with open jaws* (ready to bark).

484. rota orbis, *the whirling wheel.* The wind, stilled by the music of Orpheus, no longer moved Ixion's wheel.

485. pedem referens, *returning* from the Lower World. — **evaserat :** the subject is *Eurydice.*

487. legem, *condition*; Orpheus was not to look back at Eurydice until they had come into the Upper World.

490. Eurydicen : acc. — **iam . . . ipsa,** *when all but in the very light* (of this world).

491. victus animi, *overcome by his feelings*: *animi* is gen. of specification (Introd. § 17). — **Ibi,** *thereupon.*

492. effusus [sc. *est*], *was wasted.* — **tyranni,** *king,* i. e. Pluto.

493. foedera, *condition* ; cf. *legem* (*v.* 487). — **stagnis Avernis,** *from the pools of Avernus.*

496. condit, *is closing.*

499. fumus : sc. *fugit.*

500. diversa, *away* (in a different direction).

502. portitor Orci : Charon, who ferried souls across the Styx.

503. passus [est] transire : sc. *eum.*

505. numina : i. e. of the Lower World.

507. ex ordine, *in succession.*

508. deserti, *lonely.*

509. haec, *the story of his woes.*

510. tigris : the poet's fancy that there were tigers in Thrace need not be questioned.

515. integrat, *renews.*

516. Nulla Venus, *no wish for love.* — **hymenaei,** *thought of marriage.*

517. Hyperboreas : Virgil speaks of the Hyperboreans, the River Tanais, and the frosts of the Riphæan Mountains as if the places mentioned were in Thrace.

518. viduata, *free from.*

520. spretae quo munere, *slighted by this tribute of affection.* The women of Thrace felt themselves slighted by Orpheus as he mourned his lost wife. — **matres :** doubtless the unmarried women are meant. According to Ovid the Thracian women saw Orpheus while they were in the midst of their orgies, and, incensed at the scorn he had shown them, tore him to pieces.

523. Tum : i. e. after he had been torn in pieces.

524. gurgite medio, *in midstream.* — **Oeagrius :** Œagrus was the father of Orpheus.

526. anima fugiente, *with his dying* (lit. *fleeing*) *breath.*

527. toto flumine, *with all their flood.* — **referebant,** *echoed back.*

MIDAS AND THE GOLDEN TOUCH

(OVID, *Metamorphoses*, xi. 85–145)

85. hoc : this refers to the preceding story in Book xi. Orpheus has been torn to pieces by a band of raging Bacchantes, and Bacchus, in grief for the loss of his bard, has transformed them to trees : even *this* vengeance does not assuage his grief, and he retires to Mt. Timolus (Tmolus).

86. meliore, *better,* that is, than those who had murdered Orpheus. — **sui,** *his own* (i. e. sacred to him and one of his favorite resorts).

87. aureus : the River Pactolus in Lydia was famous for its golden sands. The story that follows accounts for these.

88. invidiosus, *enviable, an object of envy.* — **harenis :** abl. of cause.

89. cohors : in apposition with *Satyri Bacchaeque.*

90. Silenus: an aged Satyr, the foster father of Bacchus. — **abest,** *is missing.* — **titubantem,** *staggering, tottering.*

93. orgia, *the orgies* (the wild rites of Bacchic worship). — **tradiderat,** *had taught.* — **Cecropio Eumolpo :** hiatus (Introd. § 108). — **Eumolpo :** Eumolpus, here said to have joined Orpheus in teaching the Bacchic rites to Midas, was son of Neptune and priest of Ceres and Bacchus. He was thought to have brought the Eleusinian mysteries from Thrace to Eleusis in Attica. Hence he is called *Cecropian,* i.e. *Attic* (from Cecrops, an ancient fabulous king of that country).

94. sacrorum : i.e. the Bacchic rites, the *orgia.*

95. adventu : abl. of cause.

97. coegerat, *had gathered together.* The morning star is regarded as collecting the others at break of day and driving them off as a shepherd drives his sheep.

99. alumno, *foster son* (Bacchus).

100, 101. huic : i.e. Midas. — **optandi . . . muneris arbitrium,** *free choice in asking a reward*; A. 504; D. 874; B. 339, 1 ; G. 428. — **inutile :** i.e. as it turned out. — **gaudens . . . recepto,** *rejoicing at the recovery of his foster father.*

102. ille : i.e. Midas.

103. vertatur : subst. clause of result without *ut*; A. 568; D. 737; B. 279, 1 ; G. 553, 1.

104. solvit, *paid.*

105. indoluit : perf. of *indolesco.* — **petisset** (= *petiisset*): the subjunc. with *quod* expresses the thought of the god ; A. 540; D. 768; B. 286, 1 ; G. 541.

106. Berecyntius heros, *the Phrygian hero* (Midas): Berecyntus was a mountain in Phrygia.

107. fidem, *truth, good faith.*

108. non alta fronde virentem ilice virgam, *a twig from a low-growing leafy ilex* (holm oak), lit. *from an ilex a twig green with no high foliage.* — **fronde :** abl. of means.

112. Cereris, *of wheat.*

113. messis, *the grain* (lit. *the reaping*).

114. Hesperidas donasse putes, *you would think the Hesperides had given it*; i.e. that it was one of the golden apples from the garden of the Hesperides. — **putes :** potential subjunctive; A. 447, 2 ; D. 686, *b*; B. 280; G. 257.

117. Danaën eludere posset, *might have deceived Danaë.* Jupiter came to Danaë disguised in a shower of gold. See A. 446; D. 685; B. 280; G. 258.

118. vix . . . animo capit, *scarcely can he comprehend.* — **fingens,** *imagining.*

119. gaudenti [sc. *ei*], *for him, thus wild with joy.*

120. exstructas, *piled high.* — **tostae frugis,** *bread*: gen. with *egentes* (Introd. § 22).

121, 122. sive . . . contigerat, *whenever he touched*: pluperf. in a general condition; A. 518, *c*; D. 800; B. 302, 3; G. 567. — **Cerealia munera:** cf. *Cereris sine munere,* x. 74.

123. sive, *or if.* — **dapes,** *viands.*

124. lamina . . . premebat, *a yellow plate of metal covered the food as soon as his teeth touched it.*

125. auctorem muneris: a kind of pun; *the giver of the gift = Bacchus = wine.* Cf. Æneid, i. 215.

126. videres (potential subj.), *you might have seen.*

128. voverat, *had prayed for.*

130. meritus, *deservedly.* — **torquetur,** *he is tormented.* — **ab auro :** the gold is personified as voluntary agent; hence *ab* is used.

131. splendida, *gleaming* (with gold).

132. Lenaee : Lenæus (derived from the Greek word for *wine-press*) was a name of Bacchus.

133. eripe : supply *me.*

134. mite deum numen, *the kindly divinity*: *deum* (for *deorum*) is partitive genitive with *mite numen* ; it may be omitted in translation, or the phrase may be rendered, *the kindest divinity of* [*all*] *the gods.* — **peccasse :** sc. *se* as subject (indir. disc. with *fatentem*). — **fatentem :** sc. *eum.*

135. facti fide, *by faithful performance of the act* (of restitution). — **solvit,** *revoked.*

136. nēve, *and that you may not,* etc.: purpose. — **circumlĭtus** (*-lino*), *clothed* (or, more literally, *bedaubed*).

137. Sardibus : dat. with *vicinum* ; Sardis was one of the chief cities of Lydia. — **amnem :** the Pactolus (see *v.* 87).

138. per iugum ripae, *along the high bank* (lit. *the ridge of the bank*). — **labentibus obvius undis,** *upstream* (lit. *meeting the waves as they flow*); A. 370, *c* ; D. 384.

139. venias : A. 553 ; D. 765 ; B. 293, III, 2 ; G. 572.

140. fonti : dat. with *subde.* — **quā plurimus exit,** *where it issues in greatest volume.*

141. subde, *plunge.*

144. veteris . . . venae, *permeated with the seed of the ancient* (golden) *quality* (lit. *vein*).

145. arva . . . glaebis, *the fields are hard and yellow with gold in their moistened clods.*

THE DESTRUCTION OF CACUS

(VIRGIL, Æneid, viii. 190–267)

193. Hic: on the Aventine Mount. — **summota:** i.e. from sight.

203. Alcides: Hercules was the grandson of Alceus. — **hac,** *this way.*

207. stabulis, *pasture.*

209. pedibus rectis, *with their feet pointing ahead.*

214. Amphitryoniades: Hercules was supposed to be the son of Amphitryon.

226. paterna: i.e. of Vulcan, the god of smiths.

227. fultos: from *fulcio.*

228. Tirynthius: Hercules was brought up in Tiryns.

244. reseret, recludat: A. 524; D. 803; B. 307; G. 602.

248. insueta: cognate acc., equivalent to an adverb.

251. super: supply *erat.*

261. elisos oculos, *till his eyes started out.*

THE DESTRUCTION OF CACUS

(OVID, *Fasti*, i. 543–582)

543. illuc: to the vicinity of the River Tiber. — **Erytheïdas:** Geryon lived in the island of Erythea.

544. emensus . . . iter, *after wandering far and wide over the earth* (lit. *having measured a journey of the long world*).

545. domus Tegeaea, *the Arcadian house* (i.e. Evander's). Tegea was a town in Arcadia.

550. aversos: Cacus had dragged the cattle by their tails, so that their footprints appeared to lead away from the cave where he had hidden them.

553. facies: sc. *erat.* — **pro,** *in proportion to.*

554. Mulciber: a name given to Vulcan because of his ability to soften iron in the fire.

559. Servata male parte, *having lost* (lit. *having ill preserved*) *a part.* — **Iove natus:** Hercules.

560. furta, *the stolen cattle* (lit. *the stolen things*).

563. Ille: Cacus.

564. iuga, *yokes of oxen.* — **movissent,** *could have moved.*

565. caelum . . . illis: Hercules had borne the sky upon his shoulders in order that Atlas, who regularly bore this burden, might fetch for him the golden apples from the Garden of the Hesperides.

569. collatā dextrā, *hand to hand.*

571. Quis = *quibus.* — **nil agitur,** *naught is accomplished.* — **patrias,** *of his father* (Vulcan). — **male fortis,** *becoming frightened.*

573. Typhoëa (acc.): the giant Typhoeus was struck with a thunderbolt by Jupiter and buried under Mount Ætna. — **credas,** *you would think.*

575. adducta, *with force* (lit. *strained*).

576. sedit, *was planted, was dashed.*

581. Maxima: the so-called Ara Maxima of Hercules stood in the Forum Boarium in Rome.

ARION AND THE DOLPHIN

(OVID, *Fasti,* ii. 83–118)

85. a voce: abl. of agent (A. 405, N.[3]; D. 454; B. 216, 1; G. 401, R.[2]).

89. Palladis alite: the owl. The enmity between the owl and the crow arose because the owl supplanted the crow as the favorite bird of Minerva when the crow, as the bearer of unwelcome news, incurred the displeasure of the goddess.

91. Cynthia: Diana, so called because born on Mount Cynthus in Delos. — **tuis:** with *modis* (v. 92).

92. tamquam fraternis [*modis*], *as at her brother's* [*music*].

93-94. Siculas . . . urbes, Ausonis ora: Arion was returning from a professional tour in Sicily and Italy.

103. Ille: Arion.

108. suos sonos, *its proper notes.*

109. cānentia, *white*; modifies *tempora.*

110. tempora, *temples*: acc. of specification with *traiectus* (Introd. § 42). — **cantat olor:** the song of the dying swan was famed for its sweetness and pathos.

115. pretium vehendi: in apposition with the next verse.

117. Astris, etc.: thus is explained the constellation still known as the Dolphin.

THE PATRIOTISM OF THE FABII

(OVID, *Fasti,* ii. 195–242)

195. illa dies: the Ides of February. — **Veientibus armis,** *in the war against the people of Veii.*

198. gentiles, *all from the same gens.* — **arma professa manus,** *arms that promise deeds of might.* — **manus:** obj. of *professa.*

199. castris ab isdem, *from the same camp* as the leaders. *Camp* is figurative, not literal. The point is that the whole troop was of the same family.

200. quis = *quibus*.

201. Carmentis portae : a gate at Rome near the temple of Carmentis, and known as the *porta Carmentalis*. Carmentis was a goddess of prophecy and the mother of Evander, whom she had accompanied from Arcadia to Latium. — **dextro Iano**, *with the temple of Janus on the right*.

202. omen : an omen of ill fortune.

205. Cremeram : the Cremera, a small river in Etruria, famous as the site of the destruction of the Fabii.

214. parant, *they* (i. e. the enemy) *make ready*.

215. ultima, *the edges*.

216. occulere : translate after *apta*.

223. latis discursibus, *scattering widely* (lit. *with wide scatterings*).

224. nec . . . inest, *and they have no fear of any other foes* ; they do not suspect the ambuscade.

225. Male creditis, *it's ill trusting* (lit. *you trust ill*).

230. Quid . . . adest, *what help is left at the disastrous moment ?*

237. Herculeae gentis : the family of the Fabii was supposed to be descended from Hercules.

241. Maxime : Fabius Maximus, whose successful policy of delay against Hannibal gained for him the title of Cunctator.

THE DEIFICATION OF ROMULUS

(Ovid, *Fasti*, ii. 491–512)

491. Capreae paludem : the spot in the Campus Martius from which Romulus disappeared was known as the Goat's Pool.

495. missis, *darting*.

496. patriis equis : when Jupiter at length gave permission for Romulus to be taken up to heaven, Mars descended in his chariot and carried his son away.

497. crimine caedis : the Romans at first thought that Romulus had met with foul play.

503. humano maior, *larger than in life*.

505. Quirites, *the* [Roman] *citizens*. After the union of the Sabines with the Romans (so ran the legend), the name *Quirites* was adopted to designate the nation in its civil (in distinction from its military) capacity.

506. nec . . . suis, *and let them not profane my divinity by their tears*, i. e. by mourning for me as if I were merely a man.

507. Quirinum : after his deification Romulus was worshipped under the name Quirinus, and the Quirinal Hill was named after him.

512. referunt : when Ovid wrote, sacrifices were still offered to Quirinus on appointed days.

KING NUMA RECEIVES THE ANCILE

(OVID, *Fasti*, iii. 285–382)

285, 286. Ecce . . . spargit: in the previous lines Ovid has told of the peace that had come under the good King Numa. The dreadful storms now sent by Jupiter seem to threaten war or some other calamity. Fig. 58 represents Jupiter hurling thunderbolts at the giants.

287. Non alias, *never before or since* (lit. *not otherwise, at no other time*).

Fig. 58

288. Rex: Numa.

289. dea: the nymph Egeria, wife of Numa, gave him instruction in the religious rites he was supposed to have introduced among the Romans (*Illa Numae coniunx consiliumque fuit*). — **Ne terrere:** imper. passive (Introd. § 87).

290. flectitur, *may be turned aside.*

291. Picus Faunusque: Picus was an Italian prophetic divinity. He had been an Italian soothsayer, son of Saturnus and grandfather of King Latinus. He offended Circe and was changed by her into a woodpecker. The rustic deity Faunus (later identified with the Greek god Pan) was the patron of farmers and shepherds.

292. numen utrumque, *both of them deities* (in apposition with *Picus* and *Faunus*).

293. adhibeto: future imper. (A. 449; D. 690, *b*; B. 281, 1, *a*; G. 268, 2).

294. possint: sc. *ei* (Picus and Faunus) as subject.

295. Aventino suberat, *at the foot of the Aventine Mount there was.*

296. quo viso: abl. abs.

298. vena, *a streamlet* (lit. *a vein*).

308. fortius, *more strongly.*

316. in sua tela, *over his weapons*; with *arbitrium.*

322. Styx: an oath by the Styx could not be broken, even by Jupiter.

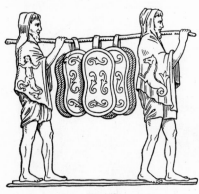

Fig. 59

325. Nobis . . . canentur: Ovid says that it is impious to inquire what spells were used to bring down Jupiter, and adds that he will tell only what a pious bard may reveal.

327. minores, *men of our time* (lit. *younger*).

328. Elicium: this name was applied to Jupiter because he was called down from the sky by incantations.

331. Corda: poetical plural for singular.

337. verum, *his real meaning.* — **ambage remota,** *in an obscure riddle* (lit. *ambiguity*).

339–342. Caede caput, etc.: "Cut off the head," said Jupiter; "of an onion," replied Numa. "A man's," said Jupiter; "hairs," replied Numa. "I demand the *life*," said Jupiter; "of a fish," was Numa's answer. Then Jupiter laughed, and admitted that he was beaten in the match of wits.

343. facito procures: equivalent to an imperative (A. 449, 2, *c*; G. 271, 1).

344. abigende: vocative of the gerundive.

345, 346. crastinus Cynthius, *to-morrow's sun.* The "Cynthian god," Phœbus Apollo, was born on Mount Cynthus in Delos.

347. motum: sc. *esse.*

352. crastina: sc. *verba.*

364. ille: i.e. Numa.

370. dicenti: sc. *mihi.* — **acta,** *what actually took place.*

378. quaque notes oculis, *wherever you look.*

379. consistere : *depends upon.*

382. insidiantis, *of anyone who plotted to steal it.* For the shields see Fig. 59.

TRIPTOLEMUS

(OVID, *Fasti*, iv. 507–562)

507. Cerealis, *sacred to Ceres* (because of the Eleusinian Mysteries).

509. glandes, mora : indicating the humble style in which Celeus lived.

516. subeat : *ut* is omitted. — **quantulacumque,** *small as it is.*

518. Instanti : sc. *ei* (i. e. to Celeus).

520. melior quanto, *how much better* : abl. of degree of difference.

521. ut, *as it were.* — **deorum,** *the nature of the gods.*

525. Sic : he adjures her, by her hopes of her daughter's safety, to enter his cottage.

527. qua, *how.*

530. invigiletque malis, *and lies awake and suffers* (lit. *lies awake over his sufferings*).

531. initura, *as she was about to enter.*

533. gustasse (= *gustavisse*) : sc. *papaver* as object.

534. imprudens, *unwittingly* Ceres broke her long fast. — **exsoluisse :** for *exsolvisse*, the *v* being treated as a vowel (*u*).

535. Quae, *she.*

536. mystae, *the initiates* (of the Eleusinian Mysteries). The ceremonies of the mysteries were in part a dramatization of the story of Ceres and her daughter. — **sidera visa,** *evening* (lit. *the seen stars*).

540. suo, *with her own* (mouth).

543. hoc est, *that is* ; equivalent to *id est* (i.e.).

545. liquefacta coagula lacte, *curdled milk* (lit. *rennet softened by milk*).

547. somni . . . causas : in apposition with *papavera.*

554. humanum . . . onus, *the dross of mortality.*

555. stulte pia, *foolishly fond*, because she did not understand the goddess's purpose.

557. Dum . . . fuisti : because of her love for her son she had spoiled his good fortune. The fire would have made him immortal. — **es :** sc. *scelerata.*

560. culta praemia, *the rewards of tillage.*

561. dracones : i.e. in her chariot drawn by dragons.

THE FOUNDING OF ROME AND THE DEATH OF REMUS

(OVID, *Fasti*, iv. 809–852)

809. frater Numitoris: Amulius.

810. gemino sub duce: under the control of the twin brothers, Romulus and Remus.

811, 812. utrique convenit (impersonal), *they both agree.*

814. magna . . . est, *great is the trust to be put in birds.* The Romans had firm faith in augury, i. e. in omens from birds' flight.

815. Alter . . . Palati: Romulus ascended the Palatine Hill, Remus the Aventine Hill.

817, 818. Pacto statur, *they stand by their agreement* (lit. *it is stood by the agreement*).

819. qua signet: relative clause of purpose.

820. Sacra Palis: the Palilia, a festival in honor of Pales, god of shepherds and cattle, was held on April 21. — **inde,** *then.*

821. Fossa: not a ditch, but *a pit.* — **ad solidum,** *to firm earth.*

822. vicino, *of the neighboring villages,* from which the *pastorum volgus* had come.

823. plenae: sc. *fossae.*

824. fungitur igne, *acts its part for the fire,* i. e. performs its function.

827. Condenti: sc. *mihi.*

828. mater: a title of honor, applied to goddesses in reference to their fostering care.

829. adhibere, *to call upon.*

831. Longa . . . terrae: i. e. *longa sit aetas potentiaque huic dominae terrae.* — **huic dominae terrae,** *to this land, the mistress* (of the world).

832. sub hac, *under her dominion.* — **dies** = *sol.*

833. Tonitru laevo: thunder on the left was a favorable sign.

834. polo, *from the sky.*

836. erat, *was finished* (lit. *was, existed*).

837. Celer: the leader of the *Celeres,* as the Roman knights were originally called. — **vocarat,** *had called by that name,* i. e. *Celer, swift.*

838. Sint curae tuae, *be in your care* (Introd. § 9).

842. His: sc. *muris.*

843. ausum: agrees with the obj. (*eum,* understood).

847. exemplaque fortia servat, *he ratifies the bold deed* (of Celer) *as an example* (lit. *preserves the bold example*).

848. Sic: i. e. with death to himself.

852. Invito: sc. *mihi* (dat. of separation).

FLORA'S DELIGHT IN THE SPRING

(OVID, *Fasti*, v. 207–220)

209. dotalibus, *given me as a dowry.*

210. fovet : sc. *eum* (i.e. *hortum*) as object. — **rigatur :** sc. *is* (i.e. *hortus*) as subject.

211. maritus : Zephyrus, the West Wind, was Flora's husband.

213. digestos, *in order* (lit. *set in order*).

IPHIGENIA AMONG THE TAURIANS

(OVID, *Ex Ponto*, iii. 2. 35–100)

35. Vos : the friend to whom the epistle is addressed and others who have remained faithful to the banished poet. — **seri nepotes,** *future generations.*

36. claraque . . . meis : Ovid tells the story to emphasize his regard for his faithful friends.

37. Sauromatae, Getae : Thracian tribes among whom Ovid was living. — **vos novere :** known through the accounts given his neighbors by Ovid (*v.* 39).

43. amicitiae nomen, *the term friendship.*

44. quos . . . habet : they are familiar with some of the finer things of civilization, even though living so far from Rome, the centre of the civilized world.

45. Tauros : a people living in what is now the Crimea. It was their custom to sacrifice strangers to Diana.

48. Consortem Phoebi deam : Diana.

49. Templa : the temple of Diana (plural for singular).

51. signum caeleste : the statue of Diana, stolen by Orestes and Iphigenia, as told below.

52. orba deā, *bereft of the statue of the goddess* : *dea* is ablative of separation.

54. cruore : the blood of human sacrifices.

55. taedae non nota iugali, *unmarried* (lit. *unknown to the marriage torch*). Torches were carried in Roman marriage rites. See Fig. 60.

59. Maeotide ora : Lake Mæotis, now the Sea of Azov.

62. nescio quam Iphigenian, *some woman named Iphigenia.*

65. ea : Iphigenia, made a priestess by Diana.

69. Orestes : a brother of Iphigenia. The friendship of Orestes and Pylades was famous.

71. Triviae: Diana, so called because she was worshipped at places where three roads met.

72. manūs: accusative of specification.

73. Graia sacerdos: Iphigenia.

74. ambiit, *encircled.* — **infula:** a red and white woolen band worn on the head by persons performing the priestly functions.

76. causas morae: Iphigenia acts as priestess *invita manu* (*v.*66).

77. ego: sc. *sum.*

Fig. 60

78. suo barbariora loco, *even more barbarous than the country* (where I am sacrificing).

82. consortes urbis suae, *fellow countrymen.*

85. periturus, *ready to die.*

86. in vices, *in turn.* — **pugnat uterque mori,** *each contends for the right to die.*

87. Exstitit . . . illis, *this was the one thing in which they did not agree.*

88. par, *the two friends* (lit. *the pair*).

90. ad fratrem: the letter is to be taken to Greece and given to her brother, Orestes, by whichever of the two captives returns to his native land.

93. Nec mora: as soon as Iphigenia learns that this is her brother, all three make their escape, taking the image with them.

96. nomen, *renown.*

97. volgaris, *well-known.*

99. hac: sc. *ora.*

PENELOPE TO ULYSSES

(OVID, *Heroides*, i. 25–84)

25. rediere : to Greece. The other Greek leaders have come back, but Ulysses is still on his wanderings.

26. ponitur : i.e. as a thank-offering. — **ad,** *before.* — **barbara praeda :** i.e. brought from Troy.

27. nymphae, *wives.*

28. illi : the husbands. — **suis :** sc. *fatis.*

31, 32. monstrat . . . mero : a plan of Troy and the positions of the armies in battle is drawn by the narrator in wine on the table.

35. Aeacides : Achilles.

36. missos, *galloping* (lit. *let go*).

37. te quaerere misso, *sent to seek you* ; poetical use of the infinitive to express purpose (Introd. § 84).

38. nato : Telemachus. — **Nestor :** son of Neleus and king of Pylos ; he was famed for his wisdom and eloquence and is said to have outlived three generations of men.

39. Rhesum : see note on Æneid, i. 469. — **Dolona** (acc.): see note on *Tristia*, iii. 4. 27.

40. ut, *how.*

42. tangere, *to visit.*

43. uno : Diomedes.

45. sinus : sc. *mei.*

46. Ismariis, *Thracian* ; Ismarus was a mountain in Thrace. — **equis :** the famous horses of Rhesus, which were captured by Ulysses and Diomedes in a night raid.

47. vestris lacertis : the arms of Ulysses and the other Greek leaders.

48. Ilios : nominative. — **et murus . . . esse solum,** *and that what was once a wall is levelled with the ground* (lit. *to be soil*).

50. dempto fine (abl. abs.), *forever.*

51. uni . . . restant : because Ulysses is still absent, as he was during the war.

52. incola victor, *the victorious settler.* Ovid is thinking of the Roman policy of colonizing captured towns and lands.

57. quae causa : sc. *sit.*

58. in quo orbe, *in what corner of the earth.*

60. mihi : dative of the agent with *rogatus.*

61. quam tibi reddat : relative clause of purpose. The antecedent is *charta.*

62. charta novata, *a new letter written* (lit. *a letter renewed*).

65. Misimus : i.e. for information about Ulysses.

66. ubi . . . abes, *where are you lingering away from* [home]?

67. moenia Phoebi : Apollo and Neptune built the walls of Troy.

68. votis : the prayers she had offered for the termination of the war.

69, 70. scirem, timerem, foret : subjunctive, because they are in the conclusion of a condition contrary to fact. The protasis (*si starent moenia*) is implied in what precedes.

72. patet area lata : there is a wider field for her anxiety about Ulysses than there was during the war.

75. quae vestra libido est, *such is the lustfulness of you men.*

77. narres, *you may be telling* [*your new wife*].

78. tantum, *only* ; who knows nothing but spinning and weaving.

79, 80. Fallar, vanescat, velis : optative subjunctives.

80. revertendi liber, *if free to return* (Introd. § 17).

81. Icarius : usually *Icarus*, father of Penelope. He is urging her to marry again.

82. cogit, *is trying to force.*

83. Increpet usque licet, *he may keep on chiding me. Increpet* is a subjunctive in a substantive clause with *licet* (so also *dicar* with *oportet*); A. 565 ; D. 722 ; B. 295, 6 ; G. 607.

DIDO TO ÆNEAS

(OVID, *Heroides*, vii. 181–194)

181. Aspicias utinam : optative subjunctive (A. 442 ; D. 681, II, 2 ; B. 279, 2 ; G. 261). — **quae . . . imago,** *how I look as I write.*

182. Troïcus ensis : Æneas, at the request of Dido, had given her a sword (see Æneid, iv. 646–647).

184. iam, *presently.*

185. munera : the sword.

189. male conscia = *non conscia.*

190. iam : as in *v.* 184.

191. Nec . . . inscribar, *nor shall my epitaph read.* — **Sychaei :** Dido's former husband (see Æneid, i. 343).

ARIADNE FALLS IN LOVE WITH THESEUS

(CATULLUS, lxiv. 76–102)

76. crudeli peste : a pestilence that came upon the Athenians while they were besieged by Minos forced them to surrender. — **coactam :** with *Cecropiam.*

78. decus innuptarum, *beautiful maidens.*

79. Cecropiam : Athens, so named from King Cecrops.

80. Quis = *quibus.* — **angusta moenia :** Athens was then a small city.

82, 83. potius . . . portarentur, *rather than that such victims from Athens — dead, yet not dead — should be carried to Crete. Funus* (lit. *funeral*) is sometimes used for *corpse.* These young men and maidens, though not yet killed, were doomed (and therefore as good as dead) as soon as they had been selected as victims. — **funera, nec funera :** oxymoron; A. 641 ; D. 949; B. 375, 2; G. 694.

84. nitens, *pressing on.*

86, 87. virgo regia : Ariadne.

87, 88. quam . . . alebat : the poet suggests that Ariadne was too innocent and too charming to suffer the fate that befell her at the hands of Theseus.

89. quales . . myrtos, *like the myrtles which,* etc.

90. colores = *flores.*

95. sancte puer : Cupid.

96. quaeque, *and thou who . . .,* i.e. Venus. — **Golgos** (nom. *Golgi*), **Idalium :** towns in Cyprus sacred to Venus.

98. in, *for* or *over.* — **hospite :** Theseus.

100. magis fulgore expalluit auri : vividly descriptive of the pallor of a person of dark complexion.

ARIADNE'S LAMENT

(CATULLUS, lxiv. 132-201)

132. Sicine (*sice,* old form of *sic,* + *-ne*), *is it thus that ?* The word is used in expressions of reproach.

133. Theseu : vocative.

134. neglecto numine divum, *scorning the power of the gods* (who might be expected to punish Theseus for his faithlessness).

135. devota periuria, *the curse of a broken oath* (lit. *accursed perjuries*). Theseus bears home the curse of Ariadne because of his broken vows.

138. immite pectus : that of Theseus. — **nostri,** *me :* genitive with *miserescere* (Introd. § 20).

140. miserae (sc. *mihi*) : dative with *sperare — to hope for myself, poor creature.*

143. Nunc . . . credat, *from henceforth let no woman believe.*

145. quis = *quibus :* dative of reference.

146. nil . . . iurare, *there is no oath that they fear to swear.*

148. nihil (adv. acc.), *not at all.*

149. in medio . . . leti : i.e. when Theseus was attacking the Minotaur. See Fig. 61 (from a vase painting). — **versantem** (from *versor*), *when you were.*

150. germanum : the Minotaur was a half-brother of Ariadne. — **crevi** (from *cerno*), *I resolved.*

151. quam . . . dēēssem, *than to fail you :* clause of result (A. 571, *a* ; D. 733 ; B. 284, 4 ; G. 299, 631, 3).

152, 153. pro quo, *in return for this.* — **dilaceranda praeda,** *prey to be torn in pieces.* — **iniecta . . . terra** (abl. abs.): the soul of the dead

Fig. 61

could not cross the Styx unless at least three handfuls of earth had been thrown upon the corpse.

155. conceptum : sc. *te.*

158. tibi non cordi fuerant, *had not been dear to you :* double dative (Introd. § 33).

159. prisci parentis, *your stern parent* ; Ægeus, who might refuse to receive Ariadne as his son's wife.

160. ducere : sc. *me* as object.

161. serva, *as your slave.*

162. permulcens, *gently bathing.* — **vestigia** = *pedes.*

164. ignaris, *senseless.*

165. nullis sensibus auctae, *void of understanding* (lit. *endowed with no senses*).

166. missas, *uttered.*

167. Ille : Theseus.

168. alga, *the weedy shore.*

169. extremo tempore, *at my last hour.*

170. invidit : used with dative (*auris*) and ablative (*nostris questibus*). The beach is so lonely that it seems as if chance intended that not even the winds should hear Ariadne's complaint.

173. tauro : the Minotaur.

174. religasset funem : the boat was moored to the shore, not left riding at anchor.

176. requiesset = *requievisset.*

178, 179. Idaeos montes : i.e. her home in Crete. — **ah ! . . . aequor,** *where* (*alas !*) *the raging sea* (lit. *surface of the sea*) *keeps* [*me*] *away, shutting* [*me*] *off by its wide waters.*

180. quemne reliqui, *seeing that I left him.*

182. memet : the enclitic -*met* emphasizes the pronoun.

183. quine, [*the very husband*] *who.*

184. nullo litus tecto (sc. *est*), *a houseless shore it is* : descriptive ablative. — **insula :** appos. with *litus.*

192. virum = *virorum.* — **vindice poena,** *with avenging punishment* ; *vindice,* in apposition with *poena,* is equivalent to an adjective.

194. exspirantis pectoris iras, *the wrath of your panting breasts.* The serpents that form the hair of the Furies show the rage that the Furies feel in their hearts.

196. vae miserae ! *woe to poor me !* — **extremis medullis,** *from my inmost soul.*

198. Quae . . . imo, *and since these* (my complaints) *are just* (*verae*) *and spring from the bottom of my heart.*

200, 201. quali mente, tali mente : Ariadne wishes that Theseus may return to Athens as forgetful as he was in leaving her. When Theseus set sail for Crete, his ship carried black sails. He promised his father to change these for white sails if he returned victorious. This he forgot to do, and his father Ægeus, from the cliff where he was watching for the vessel, saw the black sails and, supposing his son was dead, threw himself into the sea. Thus the curse of Ariadne was fulfilled.

OVID'S AUTOBIOGRAPHY

(OVID, *Tristia,* iv. 10. 1–58)

1. Ille lusor amorum, *that sportive writer of love poems.* Thus Ovid insists that his early verses should not be taken too seriously. — **qui fuerim :** indirect question, object of *noris* (*v.* 2).

2. noris = *noveris.* — **posteritas :** vocative.

3. gelidis undis : the water was that of cool mountain streams.

4. urbe : Rome.

6. cum . . . pari : 43 B.C., when both consuls, Aulus Hirtius and C. Vibius Pansa, fell in the war against Antony.

7. usque a proavis : his family belonged to the equestrian order and had belonged to it for several generations.

10. tribus ante quater mensibus, *twelve months before* (lit. *four times three*): ablative of degree of difference modifying *ante.*

12. liba : the *libum* was a kind of pancake, offered to the *genius* of a person on his birthday.

13, 14 : in these verses Ovid tells us that he was born on March 20. The five days' festival to Minerva, the so-called *Quinquatria*, began on March 19. The first day of the gladiatorial contests (*quae fieri pugnā cruenta solet*), which were a feature of the festival, was March 20. — **pugnā :** abl. with *cruenta.*

16. ab arte, *for professional skill.*

17. eloquium, *the life of the orator.*

19. caelestia sacra, *heavenly rites,* i. e. the composition of poetry (sacred to the Muses).

20. Musa : i. e. poetry.

22. Maeonides : Homer.

23. Helicone : Helicon was a mountain in Bœotia, sacred to Apollo and the Muses.

24. verba soluta modis, *words freed from metre,* i. e. prose.

25. numeros, *measures.* Compare what Pope says of himself:

> As yet a child, nor yet a fool to fame,
> I lisp'd in numbers, for the numbers came.
>
> *Prologue to the Satires,* 127–128.

28. liberior toga : in his sixteenth or seventeenth year the Roman boy laid aside his *toga praetexta* and assumed the *toga virilis,* the formal dress of the Roman citizen.

29. cum lato purpura clavo : a broad purple stripe running up and down the front of the tunic marked the Roman of senatorial rank. After the time of Augustus it was worn by certain of the wealthier families of the equestrian order.

30. studium, *interest* (in poetry).

33. primos honores : several minor offices might be held by a Roman before he offered himself for the quæstorship, the first in the series of higher offices (*cursus honorum*). The office mentioned by Ovid in the next line may have been that of police commissioner.

35. Curia restabat, *the senate house was ahead* (lit. *remained*). Ovid might have gone on into the senate, had he cared to pursue a political career. But he preferred a different sort of life, and exchanged the broad stripe of the senator for the narrower stripe of the equestrian order. — **coacta est,** *was narrowed.*

36. maius, *too great for.* — **illud onus:** i.e. the burden of a senatorship.

39. Aoniae sorores: the Muses. The region in Bœotia where Mount Helicon, sacred to the Muses, was situated, was called Aonia.

41. Temporis illius ... poetas: the poets contemporary with Ovid's early life, whom he mentions in the following verses.

44. Macer: the poem or poems referred to here have not survived; nor have the works of Ponticus and Bassus (*v.* 47).

45. ignes: Propertius wrote love poems (*ignes*).

46. sodalicii: Ovid and Propertius seem to have been members of a poetry club. Ponticus and Bassus may have belonged to the same circle.

47. heroo: sc. *versu.*

48. convictūs: noun.

51. vidi tantum, *I merely saw.* Virgil and Tibullus died in 19 B.C.

53. hic: Tibullus. — **Galle:** like Tibullus, an elegiac poet.

56. Thalia mea, *my sportive verse.* Thalia, the Muse of Comedy, is here mentioned as the patroness of light verse of any kind. Ovid is referring especially to his *Amores*, which he insists were not to be taken seriously.

57. legi: Roman authors frequently read their works to their friends before publication.

OVID'S LAST NIGHT IN ROME

(OVID, *Tristia,* i. 3. 1–62)

2. qua, *when.*

5. lux, *day.*

6. Ausoniae: Italy.

7. spatium, *time.* — **parandi:** depends upon *apta* (Introd. § 17).

8. longa mora: Ovid had been successful and happy so long that his mind was dull and slow when he had to make preparations for his departure.

9. servorum: sc. *parandorum*; gerundive construction dependent on *cura.* — **comites legendi:** gerund with object; used instead of the gerundive (*comitum legendorum*) for metrical reasons.

15. extremum (adv. acc.), *for the last time.*

16. modo de multis, *from the many I had a little while before.* Only a few friends remained to Ovid after he came under the displeasure of Augustus.

17. flentem: sc. *me.*

19. Nata : his daughter Perilla was married and living in Africa. — **sub,** *near.*

20. certior esse = *certior fieri.*

21. aspiceres : A. 518, *c*; D. 800; B. 302, 3; G. 597, R².

22. non taciti : litotes (A. 326, *c*; D. 947; B. 375; G. 700).

29. ab hac Capitolia cernens, *turning my eyes from her to the Capitol.*

30. quae . . . Lari : Ovid's house was near the Capitoline Hill. — **frustra :** being a neighbor to the Capitol, and to the gods of the Capitol, did not save Ovid from banishment.

31. Numina : Jupiter, Juno, and Minerva.

32. iam, *again.*

33. di relinquendi : in leaving Rome Ovid felt that he was leaving its gods as well. — **Quirini :** Romulus.

34. tempus in omne, *once for all.*

35. sero, *too late :* although it is too late to defend himself now that he has been wounded, still there is something he wishes to say in his own behalf.

36. odiis : abl. of separation.

37. caelesti viro : Augustus. — **deceperit,** *misled, betrayed.* — **error :** Ovid calls the offence for which he was banished *a mistake,* and he prays the gods, who know the truth, to tell Augustus that this offence, though a fault (*culpa*), was not a crime (*scelus*). See p. 237 above.

40. placato deo, *if this divinity* (Augustus) *be appeased.*

44. exstinctos focos : as the master of the house was banished, the hearth fire had been allowed to go out in evidence of the mourning of the whole household.

45. adversos, *in front of her.* The household gods were near the family hearth.

46. non valitura, *destined to be of no avail.*

48. Parrhasis, *Arcadian.* The maiden Callisto, daughter of the Arcadian king, was changed into a bear by Juno, and was then raised to the heavens by Jupiter, where she is now the constellation Ursa Maior.

51. aliquo properante, *when someone urged me to hurry.*

54. apta, *lucky.* He delayed, pretending that a lucky hour for his journey would come presently.

55. Ter limen tetigi : to stumble on the threshold when setting out from home was an unlucky sign, which could be obviated only by returning and crossing the threshold again. Ovid implies that he stumbled three times purposely, in order to gain delay. — **sum revocatus,** *I was called back* (by the evil omen).

57. 'Vale' dicto : abl. abs., as if *vale* were a noun.

62. Utraque, *for either reason.*

OVID'S SHIP

(OVID, *Tristia*, i. 10. 1–14)

1. **tutela :** *an object of care.*
3. **ad,** *at.*
6. **occupat,** *outstrips.* — **quamlibet ante,** *however long before.*
8. **fatiscit,** *springs a leak.*
9. **Cenchreis :** Cenchreæ was one of the harbors of Corinth.
12. **Palladio numine,** *by the divine help of Pallas.*

THAT YACHT OF MINE

(CATULLUS, iv)

For the metre, see p. 244 above.

1. **Phasellus :** a small boat, driven by a square sail. — **videtis :** the inscription is to be read by his guests as they look at the model.
2. **fuisse celerrimus** = *se fuisse celerrimum* (A. 581, N.[8]).
3. **trabis** = *navis.*
4, 5. **sive . . . linteo :** whether impelled by oars or by sail.
6. **hoc** (object of *negare*) : refers to the claim just made; the model declares that the places mentioned in the following verses *cannot deny* the good record (*hoc*) of the boat itself. The places are those visited by Catullus on his journey from Bithynia to Sirmio. — **minacis Hadriatici :** the Adriatic was often stormy.
7. **insulas Cycladas :** a dangerous region for ships.
8. **Rhodum nobilem :** once a place of commercial importance, Rhodes was famous among the Romans for its climate and its schools of rhetoric and philosophy.
9. **trucem Ponticum sinum :** of this region Ovid says (*Tristia*, iv. 4. 57–58):

> Neque iactantur moderatis aequora ventis,
> nec placidos portus hospita navis adit.

10. **post phasellus :** the adverb *post* is here used as an adjective qualifying *phasellus.* The boat was once a leafy tree on Cytorus.
11. **Cytorio in iugo :** Cytorus was a mountain in Paphlagonia, abounding in boxwood.
13. **Amastri :** Amastris was a city in Paphlagonia near Mount Cytorus.
16. **stetisse :** when it was a tree. Supply *se* as subject.
20, 21. **sive utrumque . . . in pedem,** *or if a favoring wind filled the sail* (lit. *fell upon both the sheets at the same time*). The *pedes* were

the two sheets, or ropes, attached to the lower corners of the square sail, by which the sail was fastened to the rail of the boat. The wind would strike the sheets at the same time when the boat was running before the wind.

22. litoralibus diis : sailors made their vows to Neptune and to lesser divinities of the sea to secure successful voyages.

23, 24. sibi : dat. of agent. — **esse facta :** sc *ait.* — **a mari novissimo,** *from the remotest sea.* — **ad limpidum lacum :** it is not to be supposed that the boat was itself actually fetched up rivers and over land to the Lacus Benacus, where his villa was located.

25. prius, *long ago.*

26. tibi = *vobis.* Sailors were accustomed to ask the twin gods, Castor and Pollux, to drive away storms.

A HOMESICK POET

(OVID, *Tristia*, iii. 8)

1. Triptolemi : Triptolemus was a god of agriculture, who first taught the sowing of seeds (p. 288 above). He was presented by Ceres with a chariot drawn by winged dragons. — **cuperem,** *I could desire. Vellem* (*v.* 3) and *optarem* (*v.* 5) are synonyms of *cuperem.*

2. ignotam : the earth did not know planted seeds before the coming of Triptolemus.

3. Medeae dracones : Medea escaped from Corinth in a chariot drawn by flying dragons after she had killed her children to punish Jason for his faithlessness.

5. iactandas sumere pinnas, *to put on wings and fly* (lit. *to put on wings to be flapped*).

6. Perseu, Daedale : Perseus flew with winged shoes on his way to slay the Gorgon Medusa; Dædalus made wings for himself and his son Icarus that he might escape from Crete, where he was imprisoned by Minos.

13. Si semel optandum est, *if you are to utter your prayer* [*for wings*] *once for all.* — **Augustum numen :** since he alone has power to give you wings to fly home.

20. rogandus erit [*mihi*]: *I shall have to ask him* (Augustus).

21. Quod . . . ampli, *meantime there is a smaller favor* [*that Augustus can grant*], *yet to me a great boon* (lit. *the likeness of a great gift*).

22 quolibet, *anywhere he will.*

23. faciunt [*me*], *agree* [*with me*].

24. Ei mihi, *woe is me!* — **corpora :** poetical plural for singular.

31. in tenet, *pervades.* — **nec . . . ullis,** *and I have not strength enough to rise.*

36 legenda, *before my eyes* (lit. *to be perceived*).

39. querar ut cum Caesaris ira, *that I complain to Cæsar's anger.* Note that *ira* is personified.

40. suas : equivalent to an objective gen.; A. 348, *a*; D. 355.

41. est usus : sc. *Augustus* as the subject. — **civiliter :** i. e. by not putting me to death.

42. loco : the place of my exile.

WINTER IN THRACE

(OVID, *Tristia*, iii. 10. 1–40)

1. istic, *there,* i. e. in Rome, whither the poem is to be sent. — **adempti,** *banished.*

3. suppositum, *beneath* (modifies *me*). — **stellis . . . aequor :** i. e. in a northern clime, where the constellations about the polestar do not set below the sea.

6. non digna=*indigna* : Ovid, a cultivated Roman, felt himself completely out of place in the midst of the rough tribes he mentions.

7. Dum . . . tepet : in the warm seasons, when the Danube was open, Ovid and his neighbors were defended from the northern tribes by the river. — **medio,** *that flows between.*

11. sub Arcto, *under the Bear,* i. e. in the North.

12. axe tremente, *the pole, quivering* (with the weight of the earth).

13. iactam (sc. *eam*), *where it has fallen* (lit. *thrown*).

15. prior, *the previous snowfall.*

Fig. 62

16. bima (sc. *nix*), *the snow of two years.*

19. arcent, *men keep out.* — **bracis :** trousers were used by the northern peoples, but not by the Romans. See Fig. 62 (old Dacian and boy).

20. ora, *face.*

23. Nuda, *by itself* (lit. *not covered*), i. e. without the jar.

24. frusta, *lumps* (of frozen wine).

25. ut, *how.*

27. Ipse: with *Hister* (*v*. 29). — **papyrifero amne:** the Nile.

28. multa ora: Ovid says the Danube had seven mouths (*Tristia*, ii. 189). — **freto:** the Black Sea.

37. glacie consistere, *freeze hard* (lit. *stand firm with ice*).

38. lubrica testa, *a covering of ice* (lit. *a slippery shell*).

UPON THE DEATH OF MY LADY'S SPARROW

(CATULLUS, iii)

1. Veneres Cupidinesque: the poet calls on all the divinities of beauty and love to mourn the fair Lesbia's loss. For the metre, see p. 243 above.

2. quantum . . . venustiorum, *all ye mortals of charm* (lit. *what of more charming men there is*).

4. deliciae, *the pet.*

5. oculis: abl. of comparison.

6. mellitus, *sweet as honey.* — **suam,** *his mistress.* — **norat** = *noverat.*

8. gremio, *lap.*

9. modo . . . modo, *now . . . now.*

10. pipiabat, *kept chirping.*

11. tenebricosum, *shadowy*, because it leads to Hades.

12. illuc unde, *to that place whence.* "The undiscover'd country from whose bourn no traveller returns."

13. vobis male sit, *may it go hard with you.*

14. bella: adjective.

16. miselle (voc.), *poor little.* This diminutive (of *miser*, *wretched*) and **turgiduli** (diminutive of *turgidus*, *swollen*) and **ocelli** (diminutive of *oculus*, *eye*) increase the pathos.

17. Tuā operā, *for your sake.*

AN INVITATION TO DINNER

(CATULLUS, xiii)

1. apud me, *with me, at my house.* The metre is the same as in iii.

4. candida puella: Fabullus must provide the entertainment as well as the food, and so must bring with him a pretty girl to play the lute during the meal.

5. sale, *wit.*

6. venuste noster, *my charming friend*; *noster* = *mi*.

8. plenus aranearum, *full of cobwebs*, i. e. empty.

9. contra, *in return.* — **meros amores,** *true affection.*

11. unguentum: choice perfumed ointment was an accompaniment of a fine dinner. — **puellae,** *sweetheart.*

HOME AGAIN!

(CATULLUS, xxxi)

1. Sirmio: a narrow peninsula in Lacus Benacus (the modern Lago di Garda). For the metre, see p. 244 above.

2. ocelle, *jewel, gem* (lit. *little eye*). — **liquentibus,** *clear*.

3. uterque: i.e. the waters of both lake and sea.

5. mi = *mihi*. — **Thyniam:** once a part of Bithynia, but used here for Bithynia as a whole.

6. liquisse = *reliquisse*.

7. solutis curis, *release from cares*.

8, 9. peregrino labore, *toil in foreign lands*. Catullus had been engaged for a year on the staff of the propraetor Memmius in Bithynia.

11. Hoc est quod unum est, *this in itself is reward enough*.

12. ero gaude, *rejoice at your master's return*.

14. quidquid . . . cachinnorum, *whatever there is in my home that can laugh* (lit. *whatever of laughs there is*).

FAREWELL TO BITHYNIA

(CATULLUS, xlvi)

6. ad . . . urbes: Catullus planned to visit cities in Asia Minor on his way back to Rome. The metre is the same as in iii.

11. diversae . . . viae: he and his companions came from Rome together, but are to return by different routes.

AT THE TOMB OF A BROTHER

(CATULLUS, ci)

2. advenio . . . inferias, *I come to be present at these sad funeral sacrifices*.

3. ut . . . mortis, *to offer you the last service for the dead* (lit. *of death*); the offerings are, as it were, his last gift to his brother.

5. tete: emphatic form of *te*.

7. haec: the offerings.

8. tradita, *offered*. — **ad inferias,** *as funeral gifts*.

10. ave atque vale: these words of farewell would have been spoken at the funeral, had any relative been present.

ODE TO AUGUSTUS

(Horace, *Odes*, i. 2)

For the metre, see p. 244 above.

1-24. Certain portents show the displeasure of the gods with the Romans for shedding the blood of their countrymen in civil war.

1, 2. terris : dative of place to which (Introd. § 34). — **nivis atque grandinis :** a heavy snowstorm or hailstorm was so rare in the warm climate of Rome that it was regarded as a sign of divine anger. — **dirae,** *ominous*. — **pater :** Jupiter (*pater deorum hominumque*). — **rubente :** his hand is *red* from the glow of the thunderbolt he wields.

3. sacras arcis : the two summits of the Capitoline Hill are meant. The northern summit was known as the Arx, because here was the first stronghold of the Romans. The southern summit bore the great temple of Jupiter Capitolinus. That these summits (and especially that on which Jupiter's own temple stood) had been struck was, Horace says, a clear indication of the gods' wrath. — **iaculatus,** *by striking* (lit. *having struck*).

5. terruit : observe the anaphora (A. 598, *f*; D. 939; B. 350, 11, *b*; G. 682). — **gentis** (acc.), *the nations, the whole world.* — **ne,** *with the fear that*; A. 564; D. 720, II; B. 296, 2; G. 550.

6. saeculum Pyrrhae : Pyrrha, daughter of Epimetheus and Pandora, and her husband Deucalion were the only human survivors of the Flood. — **nova monstra,** *strange prodigies.*

7. Proteus : a sea-god who used to come out from his home in the ocean now and then to pasture the sea-calves (seals) of Neptune along the shore. At such times he was sometimes caught and asked to make prophecies, for he was aged and very wise; but he could escape by his power of changing himself into other shapes (hence the word *protean*).

8. visere : infinitive of purpose (Introd. § 84).

10. sedes, *resting place.*

11. superiecto aequore, *the flooding sea.*

13, 14. flavum : the usual epithet of the muddy Tiber. — **retortis undis,** *his waters hurled back.* In time of flood the water appeared to be hurled back from the steeper bank on the Etruscan shore and to be driven out over the lower lands at the opposite bend of the river, as if to destroy whatever was in its way. In this low-lying district were the Regia, or Palace of Numa (*monumenta regis, v.* 15), and the Temple of Vesta (*v.* 16).

15. deiectum : supine expressing purpose (A. 509; D. 882, I; B. 340, 1; G. 435).

17. Iliae : the mother of Romulus and Remus, a mythical ancestress of the Julian family, of which Julius Cæsar and Augustus were members. After the birth of the twins she was thrown into the Tiber and became the wife of the river god. — **querenti:** Ilia is represented as complaining to her husband and urging him to avenge the assassination of Julius Cæsar.

18, 19. iactat: the river god is overfond of his wife (*uxorius*), and hence quite willing to listen to her complaints and wishes. — **sinistra . . . ripa,** *over the left bank,* i.e. the side on which are the lowlands. — **Iove non probante:** Jupiter had not appointed the Tiber to perform this act of vengeance.

21. Audiet: the subject is *iuventus* (*v.* 24). — **civis:** the war of citizens against citizens is emphasized as the cause of the portents.

22. quo . . . perirent, *by which it were better had the Parthians* (lit. *Persians*) *perished.* *Perirent* is subjunctive as the verb of a condition; the protasis is implied in *melius*.

24. rara, *thinned out* or *scanty.* The youth of the next generations that will hear about the civil wars will be less numerous because the population has been diminished by war and proscription.

25–40. The Romans, guilty of civil conflict, need some god as their mediator. Which god shall it be?

25, 26. vocet . . . ruentis imperi rebus, *call upon to aid the fortunes of our tottering empire.* — **Prece qua,** *with what prayer?* We need some new form of appeal, for Vesta, offended at the murder of Cæsar, her priest, no longer listens to the usual litanies (*carmina*).

27. virgines sanctae: the Vestal Virgins, who tended the never-dying fire in the Temple of Vesta, symbolical of the eternal power of Rome.

29. partis, *office, task.*

30. venias precamur, *come, we pray; venias* is hortatory subjunctive (A. 439, *a*; D. 674, *a*; B. 275, 2; G. 263, 2, *a*).

31. candentis umeros: acc. of specification with *amictus.*

32. augur Apollo: the god of Delphi and of oracles. Apollo, as the patron god of Augustus, might feel a special interest in the Roman people.

33. sive tu mavis: *or* [*do you come*], *if you prefer.* — **Erycina,** *Lady of Eryx,* i.e. Venus, who had a temple at Eryx at the western end of Sicily. She was the mythical ancestress of the Julian *gens.*

35, 36. sive . . . respicis, auctor, *or* [*do you*] *our founder* [*come*], *if you have regard for.* Appeal is made to Mars, the founder of the Roman race.

37. ludo: to Mars war was a sport.

38. leves: the first *e* is long.

39, 40. acer . . . voltus, *the fierce look.* — **Marsi peditis:** the Marsians were very brave soldiers.

41–52. A divine helper is already among the Romans — Mercury, who has assumed the form of Augustus. Long may Augustus live!

41. iuvenem: the *iuvenis* is Augustus, as is revealed in the later verses. Augustus was then thirty-five years old; but the term *iuvenis* included persons of military age between seventeen and forty-five.

43. filius Maiae : Mercury, son of Maia, daughter of Atlas. — **patiens,** *submitting, deigning.* — **vocari :** complementary to *patiens.*

45. serus . . . redeas, *may it be long ere you return.*

47. nostris vitiis iniquum, *estranged by our faults.*

48. ocior, *too swift.*

50. ames : the verb has an object acc. (*triumphos*) and a complementary inf. (*dici*). The reference in *triumphos* is probably to the triumphs of Augustus on his return from the East, 29 B.C. — **pater** = *pater patriae*: this term of respect was probably often applied to Augustus before it was formally conferred on him, 2 B.C. — **princeps** = *princeps senatus*: a title conferred on Augustus 28 B.C.

51. Medos : i.e. the Parthians, whom Horace called *Persae* in *v.* 22. — **equitare,** *to ride on their raids* in scorn of the heavier-armed Romans. — **inultos :** the defeat of Crassus by the Parthians had not yet been avenged.

52. te duce, *while thou art leader.* — **Caesar :** i.e. Augustus. Thus emphatically the ode closes with a distinct mention of the name of the divine man to whom it is addressed.

THE SHIP OF STATE

(HORACE, *Odes,* i. 14)

For the metre, see p. 245 above.

1. in mare, *out to sea.* Ancient vessels hugged the shore so far as possible. — **novi fluctus :** i.e. another civil war.

2. Fortiter occupa portum, *make an effort now, and gain the harbor* before the storm comes upon you.

3. ut, *how.*

4. nudum remigio, *stripped of oars.* — **latus :** sc. *sit.*

5. mālus : one of the subjects of *gemant.*

6. gemant, *groan,* strained by the last storm. — **sine funibus :** ancient ships, which were small, were undergirded by ropes in rough weather, to keep the planks from starting.

7, 8. durare, *withstand.* — **carinae :** poetical plural for singular. — **imperiosius aequor,** *the sea in its more lordly mood.*

10. di : the images of the gods placed in the stern of the vessel, so that they might be invoked by the sailors in time of danger, have been lost in the storm. — **iterum pressa malo,** *when again in distress.*

11. Pontica pinus: the forests of Pontus were noted for their ship-timber.

13. genus, *lineage.* — **inutile :** the reputation of Pontic timber would be no help in a storm.

14. pictis puppibus : the decorations on the after part of the vessel would also be of no avail.

15, 16. Tu nisi debes, *unless you are destined to be.* — **ludibrium,** *sport.*

17. Nuper, *lately,* i.e. during the civil wars. — **sollicitum taedium,** *a cause of anxiety and weariness.* — **quae:** sc. *eras.*

18. nunc: now that civil war threatens to come again. — **desiderium . . levis,** *an object of desire and no little care.*

19. nitentis, *glistening,* from the sun shining on the marble quarries.

20. Cycladas: storms often come up suddenly among these islands.

INTEGER VITAE

(HORACE, *Odes,* i. 22)

For the metre, see p. 244 above.

1. Integer vitae, *he who is blameless in his life*; *vitae* is genitive of specification (Introd. § 17), so also *sceleris* with *purus.*

3. gravida, *laden.*

4. Fusce: Aristius Fuscus, to whom this ode is addressed, was a friend who, Horace says, was almost his twin brother in taste and feelings.

5. Syrtis . . . aestuosas: a part of Libya near the coast, said to have been infested with dangerous animals and serpents.

6. facturus: sc. *est.*

7. quae loca = *per loca quae.* — **fabulosus,** *storied.* Various stories were doubtless told in Rome about this river in India, on the banks of which Alexander defeated Porus.

9. Namque: Horace goes on in a semi-serious way to prove that the just and innocent need no protection, by citing an adventure of his own.

10. meam Lalagen: cognate accusative with *canto.* — **ultra terminum,** *beyond my own boundaries* (i.e. those of his Sabine estate).

11. curis expeditis (abl. abs.) = *curis expeditus, care-free* (with no thought of danger).

13. quale portentum neque = *tale portentum quale neque, a monster such as neither.*

14. Daunias: Apulia, so called from a mythical king Daunus.

15. Iubae tellus: Mauretania, over which Juba was king in the time of Julius Caesar.

16. arida, *parched.*

17. pigris . . . campis, *lifeless plains,* i.e. the frigid zone.

19, 20. quod latus mundi, *that quarter of the world which.* — **malus Iuppiter,** *an unfriendly sky.* — **urget,** *lowers over.*

21, 22. sub curru, etc.: in the torrid zone. — **nimium propinqui solis,** *of the sun where he is much too near.* — **domibus negata,** *uninhabitable.*

23. dulce: cognate accusative (A. 390, *b*; D. 410; B. 176, *b*, N.; G. 333, 2, N.⁶). Use an adverb in translating.

DIVINE PROVIDENCE

(HORACE, *Odes*, i. 34)

For the metre, see p. 245 above.

1. cultor, *I, who was a worshipper.* The poet declares that he used seldom to go to the altars and that he gave scanty gifts to the gods. He will be more devout in future.

2, 3. insanientis . . . erro, *while I wandered [from the truth], well versed in my deluded wisdom*: oxymoron. — **sapientiae:** obj. gen. with *consultus.*

4. iterare, *to go over again.*

5. Diespiter: an archaic name of Jupiter.

6. nubila dividens plerumque, *who usually cleaves the clouds.*

7. per purum, *across a cloudless sky.*

9. quo, *[that chariot] by which.* — **bruta,** *dull* (lit. *heavy*); cf. Milton, *Comus,* 797, " the brute earth."

10. invisi Taenari, *of the hideous Lower World*; appositional genitive with *sedes* (Introd. § 10). Tænarum, here used of the whole Lower World, was a promontory at the southern end of the Peloponnesus, where was supposed to be one of the entrances to Hades.

11. Atlanteus finis, *Atlas, the utmost boundary of the earth.*

12, 13. Valet . . . deus: Horace recognizes not only the power of the god in the physical universe but also his ability to change human fortunes. — **ima summis mutare,** *to change the lowest with the highest* (A. 417, *b*; D. 472; B. 222 A; G. 404, N.[1]). — **insignem attenuat,** *makes the great man weak.*

14. obscura promens, *exalting the humble* (lit. *bringing forward obscure things*). — **Hinc,** *from one man* (lit. *hence*). — **apicem,** *the crown.*

15. Fortuna cum stridore acuto: Fortune is winged and comes unexpectedly to those whose lot she means to change.

16. hic, *upon another's head* (lit. *here*).

THE GOLDEN MEAN

(HORACE, *Odes*, ii. 10)

For the metre, see p. 244 above.

1, 2. Licini: the ode is addressed to Licinius Murena, a man of note in his time, and a colleague of Augustus in the consulship, 23 B.C. — **altum urgendo,** *by standing out to sea.*

3. nimium premendo, *by hugging too closely.*

4. iniquum, *unfriendly,* because of rocks or shoals.

5. Auream mediocritatem, *the golden mean.* For the term *golden* signifying the highest excellence, compare "the Golden Rule" and "Silence is golden."

6. tutus caret sordibus, *is safe from the squalor.* — **obsoleti,** *tumble down.*

8. sobrius, *in his moderation.* As the sailor avoids the dangers of the open sea and of the rocky shore, so the wise man will avoid both squalid poverty and wealth that excites envy. — **aula,** *palace.*

9. Saepius, *more frequently* than smaller pines.

13, 14. Sperat . . . sortem, *in adversity hopes for a change of fortune, in prosperity fears it*; i.e. the wise man will not lose hope in adversity or be over-confident in prosperity. — **praeparatum,** *trained* (by philosophy and experience).

15. reducit, *brings round.*

16. Iuppiter: as god of the atmosphere and weather.— **idem,** *but he also.*

17. si male nunc [sc. *est*], *if things are going badly now.* — **et,** *also.*

18. Quondam, *sometimes.*

22. appare, *show yourself.* — **sapienter idem,** *also, if you are wise.*

23, 24. contrahes . . . vela, *you will take in your swelling sail.* — **nimium secundo,** *too favorable.*

EVER THE GOLDEN MEAN

(Horace, *Odes*, ii. 18)

For the metre, see p. 246 above.

1, 2. Non . . . lacunar, *no ceiling adorned with ivory or gold,* etc. (lit. *neither ivory nor a golden ceiling*). The noun *ebur* is practically equivalent to the adj. *eburneum, of* (or *adorned with*) *ivory.* — **renidet,** *reflects the light.* — **lacunar :** Roman ceilings often had highly ornamental sunken panels which reflected the light.

3. trabes Hymettiae : Horace has in mind a Roman house of the more luxurious sort, in which the atrium was made splendid by the use of colored marbles. Here the architraves (*trabes, blocks,* lit. *beams*), of a white or light-bluish marble quarried on Mount Hymettus in Attica, were supported by columns of a yellowish marble that had been brought from Numidia.

4. premunt, *rest heavily upon.*

5, 6. neque . . . occupavi : i.e. nor have I become wealthy (and extravagant) all of a sudden. — **Attali . . . regiam,** *the palace of an Attalus.* The Attali, kings of Pergamos in Asia Minor, were famous for their wealth and splendor. — **ignotus heres,** *an unexpected heir.*

7, 8. Laconicas . . . purpuras : the shellfish from which purple (or scarlet) dye was made were especially numerous along the coast of Laconia. — **trahunt**, *spin* (lit. *draw* [the thread from the distaff]). — **honestae clientae**, *retainers* (feminine), *of gentle birth.* Only the very wealthy would have such persons among their retainers.

9–11. fides, *integrity.* — **ingeni benigna vena**, *a kindly vein of talent.* — **est :** sc. *mihi.* — **pauperemque . . . petit :** poor as he is, rich men are glad to be his friends.

12. Nihil . . . lacesso, *for nothing further do I importune the gods :* *lacesso* takes two objects, as a verb of asking. — **amicum :** his patron Mæcenas.

Fig. 63

14. beatus, *wealthy.* — **unicis Sabinis**, *in my one and only Sabine farm.* Horace had received this farm, situated about thirty miles from Rome, as a gift of Mæcenas. He spent much of his time there, gaining rest for mind and body from its seclusion and beautiful scenery.

15. Truditur dies die, *day crowds upon day* (lit. *is pushed on by day*). *Vv.* 15 and 16 join the thought of the preceding part of the ode to what follows : I am content with my lot because I remember that life is short, but you go on building because you do not recognize its brevity.

16. pergunt interire, *continue to wane.*

17. tu : the unidentified person whom Horace represents himself as addressing. — **secanda**, *to be hewn* into slabs for use in construction.

18. locas, *you are giving out contracts for.* — **sub ipsum funus**, *on the very brink of the grave.* — **sepulcri :** there is a contrast here between the house his body must occupy after death and the house he is now planning to occupy (*domos*).

20, 21. marisque Bais (dat.) **obstrepentis,** *of the sea that breaks upon Baiae.* Baiæ, about ten miles from Naples, was a favorite watering place. — **urges submovere litora,** *you work eagerly to push out the shore* (by extending your house out over the water, as if the land did not suffice).

22. parum locuples, *not rich enough* (lit. *too little rich*). — **continente ripa,** *so long as the shore confines you.*

Fig. 64

23, 24. Quid quod, *what of the fact that?* — **usque,** *one after another.* — **agri terminos:** the person addressed is so covetous of his neighbor's land that he does not hesitate to remove the stones set up at the corners to mark its extent — an act that brought on him the curse of the gods. Cf. Deuteronomy, xxvii. 17: "Cursed be he that removeth his neighbor's landmark."

25. clientium: his crime is the greater because he ought to defend the rights of his clients.

26, 27. avarus, *in your greed.* — **Pellitur:** translate by a plural; there are two subjects, *et uxor et vir.* The poor man is driven from home by the rich oppressor (see Fig. 63). — **paternos deos:** the *penates.*

28. sordidos: this emphasizes their poverty.

29–31. Nulla . . . aula . . . manet: no mansion more surely awaits the rich man than the mansion of death. — **certior,** *more certain,* or *more surely*; supply with *certior* an ablative of comparison (*aulā*). — **rapacis Orci fine,** *by the bounds of greedy death*; abl. with *destinata.* — **destinatā** (sc. *ei*): modifies *aulā* understood.

32. ultra : beyond the limits of life. — **Aequa,** *impartial.*

33. recluditur, *opens, opens itself.*

34. satelles Orci : Charon.

35. Promethea : even Prometheus, who stole fire from heaven to give life to his image of clay, was not crafty enough to escape from the world of the dead. See Fig. 64.

36. revexit, *ferry back.* — **captus,** *bribed.* — **Hic :** Orcus, i.e. Death.

37, 38. Tantalum, Tantali genus (Pelops and his line): persons of wealth and power.

38, 39. levare : *when summoned to relieve* (inf. of purpose). — **functum laboribus,** *whose toils and troubles are over* (lit. *having performed his toils*); Introd. § 56.

THE GOLDEN MEAN IN LIFE

(OVID, *Tristia*, iii. 4. 1–34)

1. tempore duro : Ovid has in mind the time since his banishment.

2. cognite, *known to be my friend.* — **res,** *fortunes.*

3. usibus, *by experience.*

4. nomina magna, *persons in high place.*

5. praelustria vita, *avoid worldly grandeur.*

6. saevum . . . venit : i.e. those in high place, as Ovid has learned from experience, have most power to injure one.

8. non prosit potius, si quis, *it were better, were there no one.*

11. ut, *how.* — **cortex :** the cork float holds up the top of the fishing net at the surface of the water, while the weights (*grave onus*) keep the lower edge submerged.

13. monitor, *your present adviser.*

14. in qua debebam, *where I ought still to be,* i.e. in Rome.

15. levis aura, *a gentle breeze.*

17. in plano, *on level ground.* — **vix . . . ipsum,** *yet that, indeed, is something that seldom* (lit. *hardly*) *happens.*

18. tacta humo : abl. abs.

19. Elpenor : a companion of Ulysses, who fell from a roof while drunk and broke his neck.

20. debilis umbra, *as a maimed ghost.*

21. Quid fuit ut, *what was the reason that?*

22. immensas aquas : the Icarian Sea, into which Icarus was said to have fallen.

25. bene qui latuit, *who has lived a retired life.*

27. Eumedes : a Trojan, whose son Dolon, induced to visit the Grecian camp as a spy by the promise that Hector would give him the horses of Achilles, was captured and killed.

29. natum : Phaëthon, who set fire to the world while attempting to drive the horses of Phœbus, the sun-god. His disastrous ride was stopped by Jupiter, who hurled a thunderbolt and struck the youth from the chariot. —**natas :** the sisters of Phaëthon wept at his fate and were changed into trees.

30. cepisset . . . Merops, *if Merops, as father, had taken Phaëthon* [*as his son*]. Merops was a king of Æthiopia, husband of Clymene and reputed father of Phaëthon. In order to prove himself the son of Phœbus, and not of Merops, Phaëthon sought the privilege of driving the chariot of Phœbus for a day.

32. propositi, *plan of life.*

TRUE MANLINESS

(HORACE, *Odes*, iii. 2)

For the metre, see p. 245 above.

1. amice, *cheerfully.* —**pauperiem,** *humble circumstances*; *angustam* (*narrow*) *pauperiem* means *privation*.

2. robustus acri militia, *grown hardy in stern military service.* — **puer,** *youth*: boys did not begin service until they were seventeen.

3. condiscat : hortatory subjunctive.

4. eques, *as a horseman*; in apposition with the subject of *vexet*.

5, 6. vitam . . . agat, *let him spend his life.* — **trepidis in rebus,** *in deeds of danger* (lit. *in perilous circumstances*). — **Illum :** obj. of *prospiciens* (*v.* 8), emphatic by position. Translate, *as they look out upon such a youth.* — **ex moenibus hosticis :** the wife and daughter of a king (*tyranni*) who is at war with the Romans look down from the walls of their town at a combat below, and are filled with fear lest the betrothed of the princess be slain by the Roman youth (*illum*).

9. suspiret : singular, though with two subjects (*matrona, virgo*). — **rudis agminum,** *unskilled in battles* (lit. *of battalions*); for the genitive see Introd. § 17.

10. sponsus . . . regius : the son of an allied king, betrothed to the princess, is fighting in the forces of her father. — **asperum leonem :** the young Roman warrior (*illum*).

11. tactu: supine with *asperum, dangerous to touch*; A. 510, N.²; D. 882, II; B. 340, 2; G. 436.

12. per medias . . . caedes, *through the thickest of the carnage.*

14. et, *as well.*

16. poplitibus: the back of the knee was a vulnerable spot.

17. Virtus, *true manlïness.* — **repulsae sordidae,** *shameful repulse.*

19. securis (acc.), *emblems of authority*: axes tied in bundles of rods made up the *fasces* borne by the lictors before the Roman magistrates.

20. arbitrio popularis aurae, *at the whim of popular favor.*

21, 22. recludens . . . caelum: it is manliness that raises great men and heroes to heaven (deifies them) after death. — **immeritis mori,** *to those who have not deserved to die.* — **negata . . . via:** manliness makes its way to heaven in the person of him who has it, along a path denied to those who have not exemplified manliness in their lives.

23, 24. udam . . . humum, *the damp ground,* suggesting the contrast between the meaner life of the earth and the better life of the gods.

25–27. Est . . . merces: *loyalty* (lit. *faithful silence*), too, has its reward. — **Cereris sacrum . . . arcanae,** *the sacred rites of mystic Ceres*; the mysteries celebrated at Eleusis in Attica in honor of Demeter (Ceres). — **Vetabo** [*eum*] **qui,** *I will forbid him who,* etc. In prose *veto* takes the acc. and inf. Horace uses the subjunctive (*sit, solvat*) instead, on the analogy of *cave* in prohibitions (A. 450; D. 676, *b*; B. 276, *c*; G. 271, 2). Translate by the infinitive.

28, 29. trabibus, *roof* (lit. *beams*). — **mecum solvat phaselon:** Horace would not put out to sea with such a person.

30. incesto addidit integrum, *joins the innocent man with the wicked* (in punishment). The perfect tense is here used to state a general truth.

31. raro: modifies *deseruit.*

32. deseruit, *gives up the pursuit of*; A. 475; B. 262, *B*, 1; G. 236, 2, N. — **pede claudo,** *though with halting foot*; to be taken with *Poena.* Retribution seldom fails to overtake the guilty, though it may come slowly. "The mills of the gods grind slow, but they grind fine."

REGULUS

(HORACE, *Odes*, iii. 5. 41–56)

For the metre, see p. 245 above.

41. Fertur: supply *Regulus* as subject.

42. ut capitis minor, *as one no longer a citizen.* The word *caput* was used to include all the legal rights of a Roman. *Capitis* is genitive of specification (Introd. § 17).

44. torvus, *sternly.* — **posuisse,** *to have fixed.*

46. auctor, *by his influence* (lit. *as an authority,* i.e. a person who influences others in making a decision). — **numquam alias,** *never before or since* (lit. *never on another occasion*).

51. obstantis propinquos : they urged him not to go back to Africa.

53, 54. quam si . . . relinqueret, *than if he were leaving* (for a holiday). — **longa negotia,** *the tedious business.*

55. Venafranos in agros, *for his estate at Venafrum.*

TO THE SPRING OF BANDUSIA

(Horace, *Odes,* iii. 13)

For the metre, see p. 245 above.

1. splendidior vitro, *clearer than crystal.*

2–5. digne mero, etc. : deserving of the wine Horace intends to pour into its waters as a libation, of the flowers he will throw on its surface, and of the kid he will to-morrow sacrifice in its honor. — **non sine floribus,** *and of the flowers too.* — **cui . . . destinat,** *whose forehead, swelling with young horns, promises a life of love and combat.*

8. suboles : in apposition with the subject of *inficiet.*

9. atrox hora, *the fierce season* (dogdays).

10. frigus amabile : during the midday rest for the cattle.

13. nobilium fontium, *one of the famous springs.* The promise has come true, and Bandusia is as famous as Castalia, Hippocrene, or Pirene.

14. me dicente, *when I tell of.* — **impositam,** *that stands upon.*

15. loquaces, *babbling.*

THE GOLDEN AGE

(Tibullus, i. 3. 35–50)

Albius Tibullus, an elegiac poet, was born about 54 B.C. and died probably in 19 B.C. We know very little about his life. His poems are characterized by tenderness of sentiment and grace of expression.

38. effusum . . . sinum, *its full sail, its spreading sails.*

40. presserat, *had loaded.*

43. non . . . habuit : there were no thieves in the Golden Age.

44. qui regeret : rel. clause of purpose.

46. obvia securis, *ready at hand for care-free* [*mortals*].

48. duxerat, *had fashioned.*

49. Iove : Jupiter succeeded his father, Saturn, in rule over the world. The Silver Age came in with him.

THE GOLDEN AGE

(OVID, *Metamorphoses*, i. 89–112)

91. verba minacia : i.e. laws defining various penalties.

101. rastro : see Fig. 65.

Fig. 65

106. Iovis arbore : the oak, especially the holm oak (*ilex*).

110. renovatus, *renewed* [*by tillage*]; in the Golden Age the soil never became exhausted and needed no fertilizing.— **cānebat :** note the quantity.

ABBREVIATIONS

abl. = ablative
abs. = absolutely, alone
acc. = accusative
adj. = adjective
adv. = adverb, adverbial
anteced. = antecedent
app., appos. = apposition
c. = common gender
cf. = compare
cogn. = cognate
comp. = comparative
compos. = composition
conj. = conjunction
dat. = dative
def., defect. = defective
dem. = demonstrative
dep. = deponent
desid. = desiderative
dim., dimin. = diminutive
distr., distrib. = distributive
esp. = especially
exc. = except
f. = feminine
fig. = figuratively
fr. = from
freq. = frequentative, frequently

gen. = genitive
ger. = gerund, gerundive
Gr. = Greek
imper. = imperative
imperf. = imperfect
impers. = impersonal
incep. = inceptive
inch. = inchoative
ind., indef. = indefinite
indecl. = indeclinable
inf. = infinitive
insep. = inseparable
intens. = intensive
interj. = interjection
interrog. = interrogative
intr., intrans. = intransitive
irr. = irregular
lit. = literally
m. = masculine
n. = neuter
neg. = negative
nom. = nominative
num. = numeral
obj. = object
opp. = opposed
orig. = originally
p. = present participle

pass. = passive
perf. = perfect
pers. = personal
pl. = plural
poss. = possessive
p.p. = perfect participle
prep. = preposition
pres. = present
prob. = probably
pron. = pronoun, pronominal
redupl. = reduplicated
reflex. = reflexive
rel. = relative
sc. = supply
sing. = singular
subj. = subjunctive
subst. = substantive
sup. = supine
superl. = superlative
trans. = transitive, transitively
v. = verb
v. a. = transitive verb
v. n. = intransitive verb
√ = root
† = form not found

VOCABULARY

ā, *see* **ab.**

ā, *see* **āh.**

ab (ā, abs), *prep. with abl.* away from. — *Used of place, time, and abstract ideas, with words of motion, separation, and the like,* from, off from. — *With words not implying motion,* on the side of, on. — *Of succession,* from, after, beginning with, since: **omnes a Belo.** — *With passives,* by, on the part of.

Abantiadēs, -ae, M. descendant of Abas (king of Argos), Perseus.

Abās, -antis, M. 1. A mythic king of Argos, grandson of Danaus, possessor of a famous shield which was sacred to Juno (iii. 286). — 2. A companion of Æneas (i. 121).

abdō, -dere, -didī, -ditum, *3. v. a.* put away, remove; hide, conceal, *with dat.* **lateri abdidit ensem,** *i.e.* plunged the sword deeply into his side. — *With reflexive,* conceal one's self by withdrawing, withdraw and hide, hide away.

abdūcō, -dūcere, -dūxī, -ductum, *3. v. a.* lead *or* conduct away *or* from; take with *(one)*; draw back *or* away: **capita ab ictu.**

abeō, -īre, -iī (-īvī), -itum, *v. n.* go from, go away, depart, withdraw, pass away, disappear, vanish.

abiēs, -ietis, F. fir *or* spruce.

abigō, -ere, -ēgī, -āctum [*ab* + *ago*]*, 3. v. a.* drive away.

abitus, -ūs [*abeo*]*,* M. departure.

abiūrō, -āre, -āvī, -ātum, *1. v. a.* swear off, deny on oath.

ablātus, -a, -um, *p.p. of* **auferō.**

abluō, -uere, -uī, -ūtum, *3. v. a.* wash off, wash away, cleanse, purify, wash.

abnegō, -āre, -āvī, -ātum, *1. v. a.* deny, refuse.

abnuō, -uere, -uī, *no sup., 3. v. a. and n.* make a sign with the head in token of refusal, refuse, deny, decline, forbid.

aboleō, -ēre, -ēvī, -itum, *2. v. a.* destroy, blot out, remove: **Sychaeum** *(from Dido's mind).*

abripiō, -ere, -ripuī, -reptum [*ab + rapio*]*, 3. v. a.* snatch from *or* away, drag off, carry off, tear away *or* from.

abrumpō, -rumpere, -rūpī, -ruptum, *3. v. a.* break off *or* away from, tear away, rend asunder, break away *(clouds).* — *Of discourse etc.,* break off: **sermonem.** — *Of law etc.,* violate, trample on: **fas.** — *Of life etc.,* tear *or* rend away, destroy, put an end to: **invisam lucem** (abandon). — **abruptus, -a, -um,** *p.p.* steep, precipitous. — **in abruptum,** precipitously.

abs, *fuller form of* **ab.**

abscēdō, -ere, -cessī, -cessum,
3. v. n. go away, retire; cease:
somnus (was over).

abscindō,-scindere,-scidī,-scis-
sum, *3. v. a.* cut *or* tear off *or*
away, tear, tear apart, sever.

abscondō, -dere, -dī *and* **-didī,**
-ditum, *3. v. a.* put away, put out
of sight, secrete, conceal, hide.
— *Of places as objects,* lose sight
of, lose (*below the horizon*), leave
behind.

absēns, -entis, *p. of* absum.

absistō, -sistere, -stitī, *no sup.,*
3. v. n. stand away *or* apart from;
withdraw, depart *or* go away, fly
from.— *Fig.* desist from, forbear,
refrain (*abs. or with inf.*): moveri.

abstineō, -tinēre, -tinuī, -ten-
tum [*abs + teneo*], *2. v. a. and n.*
hold *or* keep away from, hold *or*
keep off, abstain.

abstrahō, -ere, -trāxī, -trāctum
[*abs + traho*], *3. v. a.* drag away,
carry off.

abstrūdō, -ere, -ūsī, -ūsum, *3.*
v. a. thrust away, hide, conceal.

abstulī, *see* auferō.

absum, abesse, āfuī, āfutūrus,
irr. v. n. be away from, be absent
or distant, be missing. — **absēns,**
-sentis, *p. as adj.* absent, away;
with adv. force, in one's absence.

absūmō, -ere, -sūmpsī, -sūmp-
tum, *3. v. a.* take away; devour,
consume; kill, destroy.

abundō, -āre, -āvī, -ātum, *1. v.*
n. overflow, be in flood.

ac, *reduced form of* atque.

Acamās, -antis, M. son of Theseus
and Phædra, a hero in the Trojan
War (ii. 262).

acanthus, -ī, M. the plant acanthus, bear's-foot *or* brank-ursine.

Acarnān, -ānis, *adj.* of Acarnania,
a province of central Greece (now
Carnia). — M. *as subst.* an Acar-
nanian.

accēdō, -ere, -cessī, -cessum
(*perf. ind.* accestis *for* accessistis)
[*ad + cedo*], *3. v. n.* draw near, approach, come to, visit; be added.

accelerō (ad-), -āre, -āvī, -ātum
[*ad + celero*], *1. v. a. and n.* hasten, haste, make haste.

accendō, -ere, -cendī, -cēnsum
[*ad + † cando, cf. candeo*], *3. v. a.*
set on fire, kindle; inflame, fire,
excite, rouse.

accessus, -ūs [*accedo*], M. access,
approach.

accīdō, -ere, -cīdī, -cīsum [*ad +*
caedo], *3. v. a.* cut into, cut, hew,
fell.

accingō, -ere, -cīnxī, -cīnctum
(*inf. pass.* accingier) [*ad + cingo*],
3. v. a. gird on. — *Pass.* gird *or*
arm one's self with, gird on: **ac-**
cingier artes (have recourse to).
—*With abl. of means,* arm, equip,
provide. — *With reflexive or with-*
out, prepare one's self, make one's
self ready.

accipiō, -ere, -cēpī, -ceptum [*ad*
+ capio], *3. v. a.* take to (*one's*
self), take, receive; entertain (*as*
a guest); get, attain; take in, take
up; perceive, hear, observe, learn.

accipiter, -tris, M. a hawk.

accītus, -ūs [*accio*], M. (*only in*
abl. sing.), a summoning, summons, call.

acclīvis, -e [*ad + clivus*], *adj.* up-
sloping, ascending.

accolō, -ere, -coluī, *no sup.* [*ad + colo*], 3. *v. a.* dwell near.

accommodō, -āre, -āvī, -ātum [*ad + commodo*], 1. *v. a.* fit, adjust, adapt.

accubō, -āre, -uī, -itum [*ad + cubo*], 1. *v. n.* lie (lie down, *or* recline) at, by, *or* near.

accumbō, -ere, -cubuī, -cubitum [*ad + cumbo*], 3. *v. n.* lie on, recline (*at table*).

accumulō, -āre, -āvī, -ātum [*ad + cumulo*], 1. *v. a.* heap upon, heap up, load.

accurrō, -ere, -cucurrī *and* -currī, -cursum [*ad + curro*], 3. *v. n.* run to, run up, hasten up.

ācer, -cris, -cre, *adj.* sharp; violent, vehement, strong, passionate; bitter; subtle, sagacious, shrewd; active, ardent, spirited, zealous, brave; violent, fierce, severe, stern.

acerbus, -a, -um [*acer*], *adj.* harsh, biting, bitter; rough, morose, hostile; harsh, violent, grievous, sad, painful, distressing.

acernus, -a, -um [*acer*, maple], *adj.* made of maple, maple.

acerra, -ae, F. an incense-box.

acervus, -ī, M. a heap.

Acesta, -ae, F. a town of Sicily (v. 718).

Acestēs, -ae, M. a Sicilian king, son of the river god Crinisus by a Trojan woman Egesta or Segesta (i. 195, v. 36).

Achaemenidēs, -ae, M. a companion of Ulysses, left in Sicily (iii. 614).

Achāïcus, -a, -um, *adj.* Achæan, Grecian.

Achātēs, -ae, M. the trusty squire of Æneas.

Acherōn, -ontis, M. a river in Epirus, which flows through Lake Acherusia into the Ambracian Gulf; *hence*, a river in the infernal regions (vi. 295). — *Also*, the infernal regions, the World Below.

Achillēs, -is (-ī *or* -eī), M. the hero of the Iliad, son of Peleus and Thetis.

Achillēus, -a, -um, *adj.* of Achilles, Achilles'.

Achīvus, -a, -um, *adj.* Achæan, Grecian, Greek. — *Pl. as subst.* Achīvī, -ōrum, M. the Greeks.

Acīdalia, -ae, F. a name of Venus from a fountain (Acidalius) in Bœotia (i. 720).

aciēs, -ēī, F. point, edge, sharp edge; keen look, power of vision, the sight, the eye · line *or* order of battle, battle array (*of land or sea forces*), an army.

Acragās, -antis, M. a mountain and town in Sicily, called also Agrigentum, now Girgenti (iii. 703).

ācriter [*acer*], *adv.* sharply, fiercely, boldly: flens (bitterly).

acta, -ae, F. the seashore.

Actias, -adis, *adj.* F. of Acte (old name of Attica), Attic; Athenian.

Actius, -a, -um, *adj.* of Actium, a promontory and town of Epirus on the Ambracian Gulf, off which the victory of Octavius over Antony was gained, 31 B. C. (iii. 280).

āctor, -ōris [*ago*], M. a driver, herdsman.

acūmen, -minis [*acuo*], N. point, spear-point.

acuō, -ere, -uī, -ūtum, *3. v. a.* sharpen. — acūtus, -a, -um, *p.p. as adj.* sharpened, sharp; shrill.

acūtus, -a, -um, *p.p. of* acuō.

ad, *prep. with acc.* to, toward, against; before; near by, at, by: ad Troiam; ad superos (in the World Above); ad unum (to a man); ad meritum (according to your deserts). — *Of time,* at, by: ad lunam (by moonlight).

adamās, -antis, M. adamant (*the hardest of metals*), steel.

Adamastus, -ī, M. father of Achæmenides, an Ithacan (iii. 614).

adamō, -āre, -āvī, -ātum, *1. v. a.* love deeply; covet.

addīcō, -ere, -dīxī, -dictum, *3. v. a.* award, adjudge; deliver, make over, yield, surrender.

addō, -ere, -didī, -ditum, *3. v. a.* put near *or* to, add, attach, join: cognomen (give).

addūcō, -ere, -dūxī, -ductum, *3. v. a.* lead to, bring, draw (*to one's self*); draw *or* bend (*a bow*), strain.

adeō, -īre, -iī (-īvī), -itum, *irr. v. n. and a.* go to *or* toward, approach, accost; attack, set upon; enter on, attain, incur: labores; sidera.

adeō [*ad* + *eo*], *adv.* to that point, to that degree, so (*in space, time, or degree*); in fact, just, really, full (*with numbers*): iam adeo (just now); sic adeo (thus then).

adfābilis, -e [*adfor*], *adj.* to be spoken to, courteous: dictu (in speech).

adfātus, -ūs [*adfor*], M. address, mode of address.

adfectō, -āre, -āvī, -ātum [*adficio*], *1. v. a.* strive for, aim at, grasp at, catch, seize.

adferō, -ferre, attulī, adlātum, *irr. v. a.* bring to, bring. — *With reflexive,* come, arrive.

adficiō, -ere, -fēcī, -fectum [*ad* + *facio*], *3. v. a.* affect, be given to (*one*): vulnus.

adfīgō, -ere, -fīxī, -fīxum, *3. v. a.* fasten to, fix to *or* in, fasten. — adfīxus, -a, -um, *p.p.* keeping a firm hold: adfixus et haerens.

adflātus, -ūs [*adflo*], M. a breathing upon, breath.

adflīgō, -ere, -flīxī, -flīctum, *3. v. a.* (dash against), dash down, overthrow. — adflīctus, -a, -um, *p.p. as adj.* ruined, overwhelmed, wretched, miserable, distressful: vita; res.

adflō, -āre, -āvī, -ātum, *1. v. a. and n.* blow on, breathe on; inspire; breathe (*something on one*), bestow, impart: oculis adflarat honores.

adfluō, -ere, -flūxī, -flūxum, *3. v. n.* flow to, toward, *or* into; pour in, flock to, throng to.

adfor, -ārī, -ātus, *1. v. dep.* speak to, address, accost.

adforet, *see* adsum.

adfundō, -ere, -fūdī, -fūsum, *3. v. a.* pour upon.

adglomerō, -āre, -āvī, -ātum, *1. v. a. and n.* roll together, gather together; join, attach themselves to: lateri adglomerant nostro.

adgredior, -gredī, -gressus [*ad* + *gradior*], *3. v. dep.* go to, approach; attack, assault; accost; seize upon, lay hold of; undertake (*with inf.*).

adhaereō, -ēre, -haesī, -haesum, 2. *v. n.* cling to, cling.

adhibeō, -ēre, -buī, -bitum [ad + *habeo*], 2. *v. a.* have by or near, secure, apply, put on; summon, call; invite to a banquet, invite: **penatis.**

adhūc, *adv.* to this point (*of place, time, or degree*), still, yet, longer.

adiciō, -ere, -iēcī, -iectum [ad + *iacio*], 3. *v. a.* throw to or at; add.

adigō, -ere, -ēgī, -āctum [ad + *ago*], 3. *v. a.* drive to, force, send, hurl, plunge; *fig.* force, impel, compel, *with inf.*: **tendere.**

adimō, -ere, -ēmī, -ēmptum [ad + *emo*, take], take from or away: **lumen ademptum** (put out); **somnos** (deprive of); **ademptus Naso** (banished).

aditus, -ūs [*adeo***],** M. an entrance, approach, means of access, way of approach.

adiungō, -ere, -iūnxī, -iūnctum, 3. *v. a.* join to, add.

adiuvō, -āre, -iūvī, -iūtum, 1. *v. a. and n.* aid, assist, help.

adlābor, -lābī, -lāpsus, 3. *v. dep.* glide to or toward, approach, reach.

adlevō, -āre, -āvī, -ātum, 1. *v. a.* lift up.

adligō, *see* **alligō.**

adloquor, -loquī, -locūtus, 3. *v. dep.* speak to, address, accost, pray to.

admīror, -ārī, -ātus, 1. *v. dep.* wonder at, be surprised, admire, marvel at. — **admīrāns,** *p. as*

adj. with surprise, with admiration.

admittō, -ere, -mīsī, -missum, 3. *v. a.* let go to, admit, let in. — **admissus, -a, -um,** *p.p.* at full speed.

admoneō, -ēre, -uī, -itum, 2. *v. a.* admonish, warn, remind.

admonitor, -ōris [*admoneo***],** M. summoner, warner.

admoveō, -ēre, -mōvī, -mōtum, 2. *v. a.* move to, conduct, apply, bring to: **te ventus** (waft); **admorunt ubera tigres** (give suck).

adnītor, -nītī, -nīsus (-nīxus), 3. *v. dep.* struggle to, toward, or against; lean against, support one's self by, lean on; struggle for, strive, exert one's self.

adnō, -āre, -āvī, -ātum, 1. *v. a.* swim to, float to.

adnuō, -uere, -uī, *no sup.,* 3. *v. n. and a.* nod to, nod; nod assent, assent, agree; grant, promise (*by a nod*).

adoleō, -ēre, -uī, *no sup.,* 2. *v. a.* (add by growth); magnify (*in religious language*), sacrifice to; burn, kindle, light, sacrifice: **verbenas; honores; altaria taedis.**

adolēscō, -ere, -ēvī, -ultum, 3. *v. n.* grow up, mature. — **adultus, -a, -um,** *p.p.* mature, full grown, adult.

adoperiō, -īre, -eruī, -ertum, 4. *v. a.* cover over, cover.

adorior, -īrī, -ortus, 4. *v. dep.* rise up against, attack; enter upon, undertake, attempt (*with inf.*).

adōrō, -āre, -āvī, -ātum, 1. *v. a.* pray to, worship, adore.

adquiēscō, -ere, -ēvī, -ētum, 3.
v. n. come to rest, rest.

adquīrō, -ere, -sīvī, -sītum [ad
+ quaero], 3. v. a. get or procure
in addition, add to, acquire.

Adrastus, -ī, M. a king of Argos,
father-in-law of Tydeus (vi. 480).

adsciō, -īre, -īvī, no sup., 4. v. a.
take to one's self, receive.

adsēnsus, -ūs [adsentio], M. assent, agreement.

adsentiō, -īre, -sēnsī, -sēnsum,
4. v. n. assent, give assent, approve.

adservō, -āre, -āvī, -ātum, 1.
v. a. watch over, guard; keep in
custody.

adsiduē [adsiduus], adv. continually, constantly, incessantly.

adsiduus, -a, -um [adsideo], adj.
(sitting by), constant, perpetual,
incessant: sal; voces.

adsimilis, -e, adj. like, resembling,
similar.

adsimulō, -āre, -āvī, -ātum, 1.
v. a. imitate, counterfeit.

adspergō, see aspargō.

adspiciō, see aspiciō.

adspīrō, -āre, -āvī, -ātum, 1. v.
n. and a. breathe or blow to or
upon; be favorable, favor, assist,
smile on; breathe something upon:
ventos eunti; amaracus (breathe
its fragrance).

adstō, -stāre, -stitī, no sup., 1. v.
n. stand at or near, stand, stand
steady: adstitit oris (reached);
super adstitit arce (alighted).

adsuēscō, -ere, -ēvī, -ētum, 3.
v. a. accustom to: ne tanta animis adsuescite bella (become accustomed in your thoughts). —

Pass. be accustomed: adsueti
silvis.

adsuētus,-a,-um, p.p.of adsuēscō.

adsultus, -ūs [ad + saltus], M. an
attack, assault.

adsum, -esse, -fuī, -futūrus, irr.
v. n. be at, near, or by, be here, be
present: coram adsum (am here
before you).— Esp. (cf. "stand
by"), aid, help, assist, defend,
favor.— Also, come (and be present), approach.

adsurgō, -ere, -rēxī, -rēctum,
3. v. n. rise up, mount; rise in
height, stand (of high objects);
rise (in the heavens).

adulterium, -ī (-iī) [adulter], N.
adultery.

adultus, -a, -um, p.p. of adolēscō.

adūrō, -ere, -ussī, -ustum, 3. v.
a. scorch, singe.

advehō, -ere, -vexī, -vectum, 3.
v. a. carry to, convey, bear: advecta classis (by the winds).—
Pass. ride, sail; arrive, reach.

advēlō, -āre, -āvī, -ātum, 1. v. a.
wrap, encircle, surround, deck.

advena, -ae [cf. advenio], M. one
who arrives, a stranger, foreigner,
newcomer.

adveniō, -īre, -vēnī, -ventum, 4.
v. n. come to, arrive at, arrive,
reach.

adventō, -āre, -āvī, -ātum [ad-
venio], 1. v. n. come, arrive.

adventus, -ūs [advenio], M. arrival, approach, coming.

adversor, -ārī, -ātus [adversus],
1. v. dep. turn against, oppose, resist, withstand; refuse.

adversus, -a, -um, p.p. of advertō.

advertō, -ere, -vertī, -versum,
3. v. a. — *Act.* turn toward *or*
against: **puppim** (turn toward
the shore). — *Pass.* turn, direct
one's course. — *Fig.* turn, direct:
numen malis; mentes. — *With*
animum *or* **animo** (turn the mind
or turn with the mind), recognize,
attend to, give heed, heed, give
ear (*with or without object*):
animis advertite vestris. — *So*
without **animum: adverte** (give
heed). — **adversus, -a, -um,** *p.p.*
turned toward, facing, in front,
over against, toward: **obluctus**
adversae harenae (against the
sand); **sol adversus** (opposite).
— *Also*, opposing, unfavorable,
hostile, adverse: **venti adversi.**

advocō, -āre, -āvī, -ātum, *1. v. a.*
call to one, summon.

advolō, -āre, -āvī, -ātum, *1. v. n.*
run toward, run up.

advolvō, -ere, -volvī, -volūtus,
3. v. a. roll to *or* toward, roll up:
ornos.

adytum, -ī, N. the sanctuary of a
temple, inner shrine; a shrine,
also of a tomb as a temple of the
Manes: **ex imis adytis** (recesses).

Aeacidēs, -ae, M. son of Æacus
(Achilles and his son Pyrrhus,
and Perseus).

Aeaeus, -a, -um, *adj.* of Æa, an
island of the river Phasis, in
Colchis (iii. 386).

aedēs, -is, F. temple; *pl.* apartments, house.

aedificō, -āre, -āvī, -ātum [*aedes,*
facio], *1. v. a.* build, construct.

Aegaeus, -a, -um, *adj.* Ægean
(*i.e.* of the Ægean Sea).

aeger, -gra, -grum, *adj.* sick,
weak, sickly, suffering, weary,
worn, feeble; sick at heart, sad,
troubled.

aegrēscō, -ere, *no perf., no sup.*
[*aeger*], *3. v. n.* grow sick, grow
worse.

Aegyptius, -a, -um, *adj.* Egyptian
(viii. 688).

Aegyptus, -ī, F. Egypt (viii. 687).

aemulus, -a, -um, *adj.* vying with,
emulating, rivalling; envious,
jealous, grudging. — *Of things,*
grudging: **senectus.**

Aeneadēs, -ae, M. descendant of
Æneas. — *Pl.* the companions *or*
followers of Æneas.

Aenēās, -ae, M. the hero of the
Æneid. *See* **Silvius.**

Aenēis, -idos *or* **-idis,** F. the
Æneid.

aēnus, -a, -um [*aes*], *adj.* of copper *or* bronze, copper, bronze. —
N. *as subst.* **aēnum, -ī,** copper *or*
bronze kettle, kettle.

Aeolia [F. *of adj.* **Aeolius,** *fr.* **Ae-**
olus], F. a group of islands off the
Italian coast, now Lipari Islands
(i. 52).

Aeolidēs, -ae, M. son of Æolus;
Sisyphus; Ulysses (as the son
of Sisyphus) (vi. 529); surname
of Misenus (vi. 164).

Aeolus, -ī, M. the god of the winds.

aequaevus, -a, -um [*aequus, ae-*
vum], *adj.* of equal age.

aequālis, -e [*aequus*], *adj.* equal,
like; of same age. — M. *as subst.*
comrade.

aequē [*aequus*], *adv.* equally, alike.

aequinoctiālis, -e [*aequus, nox*],
adj. equinoctial.

aequō, -āre, -āvī, -ātum [aequus],
1. *v. a. and n.* make equal; equal;
make level; keep pace with:
laborem partibus iustis (divide);
caelo aequata machina (raised to);
lacrimis labores (do justice to).
— aequātus, -a, -um, *p.p.* level,
uniform, even, steady: aurae;
aequatis velis (before the wind).

aequor, -oris [cf. aequus], N. the
smooth sea; the sea, the waves,
the water; a level plain, a field.

aequoreus, -a, -um [aequor], *adj.*
of the sea.

aequus, -a, -um, *adj.* even, equal,
level; fair, just, impartial; favorable, kindly, calm, friendly:
oculi; aequo foedere amantes
(with requited love). — N. *as
subst.* aequum, -ī, justice, equity.
— ex aequō, equally.

āēr, -ĕris, M. the air; cloud, mist.

aerātus, -a, -um [aes], *adj.*
bronze-clad, bronze-plated.

aereus, -a, -um [aes], *adj.* brazen,
of bronze, bronze, copper.

aeripēs, -edis [aes, pes], *adj.*
bronze-footed.

āërius, -a, -um [aer], *adj.* belonging to the air, aërial, lofty, cloud-
capped: arces; mons; aurae,
venti (of heaven).

aes, aeris, N. copper, bronze. —
Things made of bronze, trumpet,
beak, cymbals, statues, plates,
arms, money.

aesculētum, -ī [aesculus], N. an
oak forest.

aestās, -ātis, F. summer, summer
air.

aestīvus, -a, -um [aestus], *adj.* of
summer, summer.

aestuō, -āre, -āvī, -ātum [aestus],
1. *v. n.* boil, seethe, roll in waves.

aestuōsus, -a, -um [aestus], *adj.*
torrid, hot, sweltering.

aestus, -ūs, M. heat, boiling; tide,
sea, waves, surge.

aetās, -ātis [aevum], F. age (young
or old), old age; time, lapse of time;
an age, a generation, a period.

aeternus, -a, -um [aevum], *adj.*
everlasting, eternal, enduring;
immortal, undying. — N. *as adv.*
aeternum, forever, eternally, un-
ceasingly.

aethēr, -eris, M. the upper air (conceived as a fiery element), the ether;
the sky, the heavens, heaven; the
atmosphere, the air, the open air.

aetherius, -a, -um [aether], *adj.*
belonging to the ether *or* upper
air, heavenly, celestial; of the air,
of the sky.

Aethiops, -opis, M. an Æthiopian.

aethra, -ae, F. clear weather, clear
sky.

Aetna, -ae, F. Mt. Ætna, the famous volcano in Sicily.

Aetnaeus, -a, -um, *adj.* belonging
to Mt. Ætna, of Ætna, Ætnean:
fratres (the Cyclopes) (iii. 678).

aevum, -ī, N. age (young or old),
life, time; old age: integer aevi
sanguis (fresh blood of youth);
aequum (the same age).

Āfrica, -ae, F. Africa.

Āfricus, -a, -um, *adj.* African. —
M. *as subst.* the southwest wind
(from that region).

Agamemnonius, -a, -um, *adj.* of
Agamemnon, Agamemnon's.

Agathyrsī, -ōrum, M. *pl.* a people
in Scythia (iv. 146).

Agēnor, -oris, M. a king of Phœnicia, father of Cadmus and ancestor of Dido (i. 338).

Agēnoridēs, -ae, M. Cadmus, son of Agenor.

ager, -rī, M. a field; land, soil.— *Pl.* farm, estate.

agger, -eris [*cf. aggero*], M. (what is heaped up), a mound, heap; dyke, rampart, wall, bed (*of a road*) : **tumuli** (summit).

aggerō, -āre, -āvī, -ātum [*agger*], *1. v. a.* heap up, pile up; gather, increase : **iras.**

aggerō, -ere, -gessī, -gestum [*ad +gero*], *3.v.a.* bear to, heap upon.

agitātor, -ōris [*agito*], M. a driver, charioteer.

agitō, -āre, -āvī, -ātum [*freq. of ago*], *1. v. a.* drive violently *or* frequently, hunt, pursue, drive, buffet; move: **mens agitat molem.** — *Fig.* trouble, vex, pursue, drive mad (*esp. of the Furies*), persecute. —*Of abstract things*, engage in, pursue, make haste in (**fugam**); pass, spend (**aevum**).

agmen, -inis [*ago*], N. a driving; a march, line of march; course, flow (*of a stream*), movement (*of oars*); band, army, battalion, throng, flock, herd : **agmine facto,** in column (*of attack*).

agna, -ae, F. a ewe lamb.

agnōscō, -ere, -nōvī, -nitum [*ad + gnosco*], *3. v. a.* recognize.

agnus, -ī, M. a lamb.

agō, -ere, ēgī, āctum, *3. v. a.* drive, lead, drive away; pursue, chase; urge *or* impel (*with inf.*); steer (**ratem**); do, act, perform, accomplish; *of time,*·pass, spend;

aliquem pelago (force upon); metus agit (inspires); vias (traverse); testudo acta (worked, formed); gemitum (raise, cause); gratias (give, return); vitam (spend); nullo discrimine agetur (shall be treated). —*With reflexive* (*or without*), proceed, move, go, come. — *Imp.* **age, agite,** come, come on.—*P.p.* N. *as subst.* **actum, -ī,** a deed, an act, one's action, a fact.

agrestis, -e [*ager*], *adj.* belonging to the country, rustic, rural, woodland. — *Pl. as subst.* countrymen, rustics.

agricola, -ae [*ager, colo*], M. cultivator of the land, husbandman, farmer.

Agrippa, -ae, M. M. Vipsanius Agrippa, son-in-law of Augustus, and his most distinguished general (viii. 682).

āh (ā), *interj.* ah!

Āiāx, -ācis, M. Ajax, name of two heroes of the Trojan War. 1. **Telamōnius,** son of Telamon and brother of Teucer. He contended with Ulysses for the arms of Achilles (ii. 414). — 2. **Oīleus,** son of Oileus. He offered violence to Cassandra, and was punished by Pallas (i. 41).

aiō, *v. defect., only pres. stem,* say, speak; affirm (*opp. to* **nego**).

āla, -ae, F. a wing; the wing of an army, cavalry (*which originally formed the wings*); riders in a hunt, huntsmen.

alacer (-cris), -cris, -cre, *adj.* active, lively, quick; eager; joyous, happy, cheerful.

ālātus, -a, -um [ala], adj. winged.

Alba, -ae [F. of albus, the white town], F. Alba Longa, the supposed mother city of Rome, built by Ascanius (i. 271).

Albānus, -a, -um, adj. Alban, belonging to Alba. — M. pl. as subst. the Albans (v. 600).

albeō, -ēre, no perf. or sup. [albus], 2. v. n. be white.

albēscō, -ere, no perf. or sup. [albeo], 3. v. n. grow white, gleam: lux (dawn).

albidus, -a, -um [albus], white.

albus, -a, -um, adj. pale white, white (opp. to ater, dull black, cf. candidus, shining white): pecus; scopuli ossibus.

Alcīdēs, -ae, M. descendant of Alceus (the father of Amphitryon); Hercules, his supposed grandson (v. 414).

āles, -itis [ala], adj. winged. — Subst. C. a bird: Iovis (the eagle).

Alētēs, -is, M. a companion of Æneas (i. 121).

alga, -ae, F. seaweed; the weedy shore.

aliās, adv. otherwise; on any other occasion, before or since.

aliēnus, -a, -um [alius], adj. belonging to another, of another, another's; strange, foreign.

ālifer, -era, -erum [ala, fero], adj. winged.

āliger, -era, -erum [ala, gero], adj. wing-bearing, winged: Amor; axis.

alimentum, -ī [alo], N. food (literal or figurative).

ālipēs, -pedis [ala, pes], adj. wing-footed. — As subst. M. Mercury.

aliquandō, adv. at some time, at length.

aliquī, see aliquis.

aliquis (aliquī), aliqua, aliquid (-quod), indef. adj. (and subst.), some, some one (indef. affirmative). — N. something. — With si and relative words, any, any one, anything.

aliter [alius], adv. otherwise: haud (non) aliter (just so).

alius, -a, -ud, pron. adj. other, another, some other (of several, cf. alter of two). — Esp.alius ... alius (one . . . another); alii . . . pars (some . . . another part; some . . . others).

alligō (adl-), -āre, -āvī, -ātum, 1. v. a. bind or tie to, fasten; moor; detain, confine, shut in.

almus, -a, -um [alo], adj. nourishing, fostering, cherishing, bountiful; propitious, kind, kindly; refreshing.

alō, -ere, aluī, altum (alitum), 3. v. a. nourish, feed; sustain, support; rear, bring up: Africa ductores (produce); volnus venis (of Dido, feeds, i.e. is consumed by).

Alōīdēs, -ae, M. descendant of Aloeus. — Pl. Otus and Ephialtes, giants (vi. 582).

Alphēnor, -oris, M. son of Niobe.

Alphēus, -ēī, M. a river of Elis which disappears under ground, and was fabled to reappear in Sicily (iii. 694).

Alpīnus, -a, -um, adj. of the Alps, Alpine.

altāria, -ium [altus], N. pl. an altar, altars.

altē [*altus*], *adv.* highly, on high, high; deeply, deep.

alter, -era, -erum, *pron. adj.* other (*of two, cf. alius, other of many*), the other. — alter ... alter, one ... the other. — alter ... alterius, one of another (*reciprocally*), of one another. — *In order*, the second, a second: primus ... alter. — *With negative:* nec alter (another, any other).

alternō, -āre, -āvī, -ātum [*alternus*], *1. v. n.* do by turns, alternate; waver, vacillate, hesitate.

alternus, -a, -um [*alter*], *adj.* belonging to the other, alternate, by turns, reciprocal. — *Pl.* man for man.

alteruter, -tra, -trum, *pron.* one or the other.

altor, -ōris [*alo*], M. foster father.

altrīx, -īcis [*alo*], F. a nurse. — *As adj.* nourishing, fostering: terra.

altus, -a, -um [*p.p. of alo* (grown up)], *adj.* high, lofty, great; deep. — N. *as subst.* altum, -ī, the heavens, heaven, the sky; the deep, the high sea, the main; *also in pl.*: tranquilla per alta. — ab alto, from on high.

alumnus, -ī, M., **-a, -ae,** F. [*alo*], foster child, nursling.

alveus, -ī [*alvus*], M. a hollow, cavity; a boat, skiff.

alvus, -ī [*alo*], F. the belly, the body (*inner or lower part*).

amābilis, -e [*amo*], *adj.* lovely, pleasant.

amāns, -antis, *see* amō.

amāracus, -ī, C. marjoram.

amārus, -a, -um, *adj.* bitter; unhappy, unwelcome, displeasing.

Amasēnus, -ī, M. a river in Latium (xi. 547).

Amastris, -is, F. a city in Paphlagonia.

Amāzonis, -idis, F. an Amazon (i. 490).

Amāzonius, -a, -um, *adj.* Amazonian, of the Amazons, a fabled nation of Scythia, composed only of women (v. 311).

amb- (am-, an-), *insep. prep. Only in composition,* around, on both sides, double.

ambāgēs, -is [*cf. ambigo*], F. a circuit, winding, circuitous way; a long story, details; obscurity, mystery, dark oracle, a riddle, evasion.

ambedō, -ere, -ēdī, -ēsum [*amb- + edo*], *3. v. a.* eat round, gnaw, eat; consume, devour.

ambigō, -ere, *no perf. or sup.,* *3. v. n.* hesitate, doubt. — *Impers.* ambigitur, it is in doubt.

ambiguus, -a, -um [*cf. ambigo*], *adj.* uncertain, doubtful, dark, mysterious, ambiguous: voces (dark hints).

ambiō, -īre, -iī (-īvī), -ītum [*amb- + eo*], *4. v. a. and n.* go round; encircle, surround; entreat, solicit: reginam.

ambitiō, -ōnis [*ambio*], F. ambition.

ambō, -ae, -ō [*cf. amb-*], *pron. adj.* both; two.

ambrosius, -a, -um, *adj.* divine, divinely beautiful.

āmēns, -entis [*a (ab) + mens*], *adj.* senseless, distracted, frenzied, frantic, raging, maddened, bewildered.

amīcē [*amicus*], *adv.* like a friend; cheerfully.

amiciō, -īre, -icuī (-ixī), -ictum [*amb-* + *iacio*], *4. v. a.* throw round, wrap round; wrap, conceal, cover.

amīcitia, -ae [*amicus*], F. friendship.

amictus, -ūs [*amicio*], M. an outer garment, robe, covering.

amīcus, -a, -um [*amo*], *adj.* loving, friendly; favoring, favorable. — M. *as subst.* a friend.

āmittō, -ere, -mīsī, -missum, *3. v. a.* let go, send off *or* away; abandon, lose.

Ammōn, *see* Hammōn.

amnis, -is, M. a river, a stream, a torrent.

amō, -āre, -āvī, -ātum, *1. v. a.* love, regard, delight in; keep close to: litus (hug). — amāns, -antis, *p. as subst.* C. a lover, loving man *or* woman.

amoenus, -a, -um, *adj.* picturesque, lovely, pleasant, charming.

amor, -ōris [*amo*], M. love, desire, longing; a love charm; an object of love, lover. — *Personified,* the god of love, Cupid, Love. — *Pl.* love poems.

āmoveō, -ēre, -mōvī, -mōtum, *2. v. a.* move away, remove, take away.

Amphīon, -onis, M. king of Thebes, husband of Niobe.

Amphitryōniadēs, -ae, M. son of Amphitryon (who was king of Thebes and husband of Alcmene); Hercules, reputed son of Amphitryon (viii. 103).

Amphrȳsius, -a, -um, *adj.* belonging to Amphrysus *or* Amphrysos, a river of Phthiotis, near which Apollo fed the flocks of King Admetus; Amphrysian, of Apollo: vates (*i. e.* the Sibyl, vi. 398).

amplē [*amplus*], *adv.* amply. — *Comp.* amplius, more, longer, again: non amplius unam (only one).

amplector, -ectī, -exus [*amb-* + *plecto*], *3. v. dep.* wind *or* twine round, surround, encompass, encircle; embrace, grasp: limina; tumulum (*of a snake*); ansas acantho (wreathe, *in carving*).

amplexus, -ūs [*amplector*], M. an embrace, caress.

amplius, *see* amplē.

amplus, -a, -um, *adj.* of large extent, great, ample, spacious, roomy; magnificent, splendid, glorious, superb.

Amycus, -ī, M. 1. A mythical king of the Bebrycians in Bithynia, a noted boxer; he invented the cestus (v. 373). — 2. A follower of Æneas (i. 221).

an, *conj. In disjunctive interrogations introducing the second part,* or, or rather, or on the other hand, or in fact. — *Often with the first part suppressed,* or, or indeed, or can it be that, why! tell me! — annon, or not. — anne (an + ne), *same as* an *alone.*

anceps, -cipitis [*amb-* + *caput*], *adj.* with two heads, doubleheaded; double, twofold; uncertain, doubtful, dubious, baffling; wavering, doubtful.

Anchīsēs, -ae, M. son of Capys and father of Æneas.

Anchīsēus, -a, -um, *adj.* belonging to Anchises, Anchisean.

Anchīsiadēs, -ae, M. son of Anchises, Æneas.

ancīle, -is, N. a shield said to have fallen from heaven in King Numa's reign.

ancora, -ae, F. an anchor.

Ancus, -ī, M. Ancus Marcius, fourth king of Rome (vi. 815).

Androgeōnēus, -a, -um, *adj.* of Androgeos.

Androgeōs (-eus), -ō(-ī), M. 1. A son of Minos, king of Crete, killed by the Athenians and Megarians (vi. 2). — 2. A Greek at the sack of Troy (ii. 371).

Andromachē, -ēs (-a, -ae), F. a daughter of King Eetion, and wife of Hector (ii. 456, iii. 303).

Andromeda, -ae, F. daughter of Cepheus and Cassiope, rescued by Perseus.

angō, -ere, *no perf. or sup., 3. v. a.* squeeze, compress.

anguicomus, -a, -um [*anguis, coma*], *adj.* snaky-haired.

anguifer, -fera, -ferum [*anguis, fero*], *adj.* snaky.

anguīnus, -a, -um [*anguis*], *adj.* snaky.

anguis, -is, M. *and* F. a snake, a serpent.

angulus, -ī, M. an angle, a corner.

angustus, -a, -um [*ango*], *adj.* close, narrow. — N. *with gen.* : angusta viarum (narrow ways); angustae res (adversity).

anhēlitus, -ūs [*anhelo*], M. panting; breath.

anhēlō, -āre, -āvī, -ātum [*anhelus*], *1. v. n.* breathe heavily, gasp, pant.

anhēlus, -a, -um [*cf. halo*], *adj.* panting, gasping : pectus (heaving).

anīlis, -e [*anus*], *adj.* of an old woman, an old woman's.

anima, -ae, F. breath, life: proicere (throw away life); purpurea (crimson stream of life). — *Of the departed,* shade, soul, spirit.

animal, -ālis [*anima*], N. living creature (*either man or beast*), animal.

animōsus, -a, -um [*animus*], *adj.* proud, undaunted.

animus, -ī, M. breath, life, soul, mind ; intention, purpose, will, desire, impulse. — *Also esp. in pl.* feeling(s), courage, heart, spirit, passions: successu animisque (the spirit of success). — *Instead of* mens, the mind, the intellect. — *Of the winds (personified),* wrath. — *In bad sense,* arrogance, pride, passion, wrath (*esp. in pl.*).

Anius, -ī (-iī), M. a king and priest of Apollo in Delos, who hospitably entertained Æneas (iii. 80).

Anna, -ae, F. Anna, the sister of Dido (iv. 9).

annālis, -e [*annus*], *adj.* yearly, annual. — M. (*sc.* liber), a record (*by years*), a chronicle, a report : laborum (details).

anne, *see* an.

annōsus, -a, -um [*annus*], *adj.* full of years, aged, old.

annus, -ī, M. a year ; a season. — *Adv.* quot annis (as many years as there are). yearly, every year.

annuus, -a, -um [*annus*], *adj.* that lasts a year ; yearly, annual.

Antandros (-us), -ī, F. a maritime town of Mysia, at the foot of Ida (iii. 6).

ante, *adv. and prep. Adv. of place*, before, in front, forward ; *of time*, before, sooner, first ; *as adj.* : **ante malorum** (of former trials). — *Prep.* before, in front of ; in preference to, above.

anteā [*ante* + *eă*], *adv.* before, formerly.

antecēdō, -ere, -cessī, -cessum, *3. v. n.* go before.

anteferō, -ferre, -tulī, -lātum, *irr. v. a.* bear before ; place before, prefer.

antemna, -ae, F. a sailyard.

Antēnor, -oris, M. a Trojan who was in favor of restoring Helen and making peace ; after the fall of Troy he went to Italy and founded Patavium (Padua) (i. 242).

Antēnoridēs, -ae, M. a son *or* descendant of Antenor (vi. 484).

antequam, *rel. adv.* sooner than, before, first before, ere.

Antheus, -eī (*acc.* **-ea**), M. a companion of Æneas (i. 181).

antīquus, -a, -um [*cf. ante*], *adj.* belonging to former times, former, old, ancient ; aged.

Antōnius, -ī, M. a Roman gentile name. — *Esp.* Mark Antony, the triumvir (viii. 685).

antrum, -ī, N. a cave, cavern, grotto.

Anūbis, -is *and* **-idis,** M. an Egyptian deity with a dog's head (viii. 698).

anus, -ūs, F. an old woman.

Āonius, -a, -um, *adj.* Aonian, of Aonia, the region of Mount Helicon in Bœotia : **sorores** (the Muses).

Aornos, -ī, M. Lake Avernus, now Lago d'Averno (vi. 242).

aper, aprī, M. a wild boar.

aperiō, -īre, -uī, -tum, *4. v. a.* uncover, lay bare, open ; show, reveal, disclose, make known, unfold : **futura.** — *Pass.* show itself, appear : **Apollo** (*i. e. his temple rising above the horizon*). — *Intrans.* appear : **montes.** — **apertus, -a, -um,** *p.p. as adj.* open, uncovered ; clear (*of the sky*).

apertē [*apertus*], *adv.* openly.

apertus, -a, -um, *p.p. of* aperiō.

apex, -icis, M. a tip, a point, a tongue (*of flame*) ; a crown.

apis, -is, F. a bee.

apīscor, -ī, aptus, *3. v. dep.* get, obtain.

Apollō, -inis, M. son of Jupiter and Latona, and twin brother of Diana ; god of the sun, of divination, of poetry and music, and president of the Muses ; also god of archery, of pestilence, and of medicine. — *Also,* his temple (identified with the god himself).

appāreō, -ēre, -uī, -itum [*ad* + *pareo*], *2. v. n.* appear, be visible, come into view, be disclosed, show one's self.

apparō, -āre, -āvī, -ātum [*ad* + *paro*], *1. v. a.* make ready, prepare.

appellō, -āre, -āvī, -ātum, *1. v. a.* address, speak to, accost ; name, call, hail.

appellō, -ere, -pulī, -pulsum [ad + pello], 3. v. a. drive, move, or bring to or toward.

appetō, -ere, -īvī (-iī), -ītum [ad + peto], 3. v. a. strive for, seek.

applicō, -āre, -āvī or -uī, -ātum or -itum [ad + plico], 1. v. a. drive, force, bring to (te oris); imprint, give: oscula.

aprīcus, -a, -um [aperio], adj. lying open; exposed to the sun, sunny; fond of sunshine, sunloving.

aptō, -āre, -āvī, -ātum [aptus], 1. v. a. fit, adapt, adjust, apply; accommodate; get ready, prepare, fit out, equip: classem velis.

aptus, -a, -um, adj. joined, fastened, attached; fit, proper; endowed, ornamented with: caelum stellis aptum (studded).

apud, prep. w. acc. with, by, near, at, in; at one's house.

aqua, -ae, F. water; a stream, a river.

aquilō, -ōnis, M. the north wind; a strong wind, wind (often in pl.); the North.

aquōsus, -a, -um [aqua], adj. rainy, watery, moist, humid.

ārā, -ae, F. an elevation or structure (of wood, stone, earth, etc.): ara sepulcri (a funeral pile). — Esp. an altar. — Ārae, pl. the Altars, dangerous rocks in the Mediterranean, between Sicily and Africa (i. 109).

Arabs, -abis, M. an Arab (viii. 706).

arānea, -ae, F. a spider; a cobweb.

arātor, -ōris [aro], M. ploughman.

arātrum, -ī [aro], N. a plough.

arbitrium, -ī (-iī) [arbiter], N. decision; free will, power; rule, control; whim.

arbor, -oris (old form arbōs), F. a tree; a tree trunk, a timber.

arboreus, -a, -um [arbor], adj. of a tree; treelike, branching: cornua.

arbōs, see arbor.

arbuteus, -a, -um [arbutus], adj. of the arbutus or wild strawberry-tree: fetus.

Arcadius, -a, -um, adj. Arcadian, of Arcadia, a mountainous district in the interior of Peloponnesus, which long retained its primitive simplicity and sylvan wildness (v. 299).

arcānus, -a, -um [arca], adj. secret, private, mystic. — N. as subst. arcānum, -ī, a secret.

Arcas, -adis, adj. Arcadian. — Pl. as noun, the Arcadians.

arceō, -ēre, -cuī, no sup. [akin to arca], 2. v. a. shut up, enclose, keep fast; shut off or out, keep off, ward off, keep at a distance; hinder, prevent: palmas (bind, prevent from raising).

accessō, -ere, -sīvī, -sītum, 3. v. a. call, summon, bring.

Arcitenēns (Arquitenēns),-entis [arcus, tenens], adj. holding a bow, bow-bearing. — M. the Bow-holder (Apollo), the archer god (iii. 75).

Arctos (-us), -ī, F. the Great and Little Bear (Ursa Major et Minor), a double constellation in the vicinity of the North Pole. — Pl. the Two Bears; the North Pole, the North.

Arctūrus, -ī, M. the brightest star in the constellation Boötes (i. 744).

arcus, -ūs, M. a bow; the rainbow; a curve, arch, bend.

ārdēns, *p. of* ārdeō.

ārdeō, -ēre, ārsī, (ārsūrus), 2. *v. n.* be on fire, burn, blaze; flash, glow, sparkle, shine: oculi; clipeus.— *Of color,* blaze, glisten, glitter: Tyrio ardebat murice laena.— *Of emotion,* burn, glow, rage, be wrathful; *and with inf.* burn, be eager: abire; scitari. —*Esp.* love, burn, be fired.— **ārdēns, -entis,** *as adj.* glowing, fiery, hot, blazing, sparkling, in fiery haste: Tyrii (eager); virtus (glowing).

ārdēsco, -ere, ārsī, *no sup.* [ardeo], 3. *v. n. inch.* take fire, kindle, become inflamed. — *Fig. of the passions,* burn, be inflamed, become more intense, increase in violence: tuendo.

ārdor, -ōris [*cf. ardeo*], M. burning, flame, fire, heat. — *Of the passions, etc.* heat, ardor, eagerness, enthusiasm, fire.

arduus, -a, -um, *adj.* steep; high, lofty, tall; erect, rising to his full height (*of a hero*): arduus ad solem (rearing himself, *of a snake*). — N. *pl.* ardua *as subst.* heights, high places.

ārea, -ae, F. a piece of ground. — *Fig.* a field: in curas.

ārēns, -entis, *p. of* āreō.

āreō, -ēre, *no perf. or sup.,* 2. *v. n.* be dry, be parched, dry up: herbae. — **ārēns, -entis,** *p. as adj.* dry, dried up: rivus.

Arethūsa, -ae, F. a fountain near Syracuse (iii. 696).

argentum, -ī, N. silver; silver plate, plate.

Argī, *see* Argos.

Argīvus, -a, -um, *adj.* of Argos, Argive; Greek, Grecian. — M. *pl.* Argīvī, -ōrum, the Greeks.

Argolicus, -a, -um, *adj.* of Argos, Argolic; Grecian.

Argos (*only nom. and acc.*), N., *more freq. pl.* Argī, -ōrum, M. the capital of the province Argolis in the Peloponnesus, sacred to Juno; Greece in general.

argumentum, -ī [*arguo*], N. proof, evidence.

arguō, -uere, -uī, -ūtum, 3. *v. a.* show, prove, make known, indicate: degeneres animos timor arguit (ignoble souls are known by fear).

āridus, -a, -um [*areo*], *adj.* dry, arid, parched, parching.

ariēs, -ietis, M. ram; battering ram, an engine, with a head like a ram's, for battering walls: ariete crebro (with frequent strokes of the battering ram).

Arīon, -onis, M. a famous Lesbian musician.

Arīonius, -a, -um, *adj.* of Arion.

arista, -ae, F. a head *or* ear of grain.

arma, -ōrum, N. *pl.* arms, weapons, armor; war, warfare, battle, contest; armed men, warriors, forces; implements, tools, utensils, instruments; equipment, tackle (*of a ship*).

armentum, -ī [*aro*], N. cattle for ploughing; a drove, herd, *of deer, horses, cattle, etc.*

armifer, -fera, -ferum [*arma, fero*], *adj.* arm-bearing, armed, warlike.

armiger, -era, -erum [*arma, gero*], *adj.* bearing arms, armed, warlike. — M. *as subst.* an armor-bearer: Iovis (*the eagle, bearing the thunderbolt*).

armipotēns, -entis [*arma, potens*], *adj.* powerful in arms, warlike, Lord of Arms.

armisonus, -a, -um [*arma, sono*], *adj.* resounding with arms, clad in ringing arms.

armō, -āre, -āvī, -ātum [*arma*], *1. v. a.* furnish with weapons, arm; fit out, equip, furnish. — armā-tus, -a, -um, *p.p. as adj.* armed. — M. *pl. as subst.* armed men, warriors.

armus, -ī, M. the shoulder; the upper arm; *of animals*, the shoulders, flanks.

arō, -āre, -āvī, -ātum, *1. v. a.* plough, cultivate; inhabit.

Arquitenēns, *see* Arcitenēns.

arrēctus, -a, -um, *p.p. of* ar-rigō.

arrigō, -ere, -rēxī, -rēctum [*ad + rego*], *3. v. a.* set up, raise, erect: aurīs (prick up); arrectis auribus (listening, attentive); arrecti oculi (staring). — *Fig.* rouse, excite: animum (encourage).

arripiō, -ere, -ripuī, -reptum [*ad + rapio*], *3. v. a.* snatch, catch, seize, grasp: hanc terram (make for).

Arrūns, -untis, M. an Etruscan (xi. 853).

ars, artis, F. art, skill, professional skill, knowledge, workmanship; a work of art; habit, practice; cunning, artifice, stratagem.

artifex, -icis [*ars, facio*], C. an artist, workman (*of skill*); a trickster, contriver.

artus, -a, -um [*cf. arceo*], *adj.* narrow, close, strait: compages (close-fitting).

artus, -ūs, M. a joint; a part (*of the body or of the world*); the body, the frame.

arvum, -ī [*aro*], N. land (*cultivated*), a field; a shore, a coast.

arx, arcis [*arceo*], F. a castle, citadel, stronghold; a height (caeli); peak, summit.

Ascanius, -ī, M. son of Æneas and Creüsa, called also Iulus.

ascendō, -ere, -scendī, -scēnsum [*ad + scando*], *3. v. n. and a.* ascend, mount, climb.

ascēnsus, -ūs [*ascendo*], M. ascending, ascent.

Asia, -ae, F. Asia.

aspargō (adspergō), -inis [*ad, spargo*], F. a sprinkling; drops, spray.

aspectō, -āre, -āvī, -ātum, *1. v. a. intens.* gaze at (*with some emotion*). — *Fig. of a place*, look toward, look out on, lie toward, lie opposite.

aspectus, -ūs [*aspicio*], M. a glance, look; the faculty *or* sense of seeing, sight; appearance, aspect, look.

asper, -era, -erum, *adj.* rough, uneven: rura aspera dumis; signis pocula (embossed): capita montis (craggy). — *Fig.* rough, harsh, hard, bitter, violent, cruel, fierce: Iuno; odia.

aspergō, -ere, -ersī, -ersum [*ad* + *spargo*], *3. v. a.* scatter; spatter, sprinkle, bedew.

asperō, -āre, -āvī, -ātum [*asper*], *1. v. a.* make rough, roughen.

aspiciō (adspiciō), -ere, -exī, -ectum [*ad* + *specio*], *3. v. a. and n.* look upon *or* at, behold, see; catch sight of, espy; look with respect, admiration, ·*or* regard : aspice nos (regard).— *Intr.* look, glance : aspice! (see!).

asportō, -āre, -āvī, -ātum [*abs- + porto*], *1. v. a.* carry away, carry off, take away.

Assaracus, -ī, M. Assaracus, a king of Phrygia, son of Tros, and grandfather of Anchises (i. 284).

assiliō, -īre, -siluī, -sultum [*ad + salio*], *4. v. n.* leap *or* dash against.

ast, *older form of* at.

astō, -āre, -stitī, *no sup.* [*ad + sto*], *1. v. n.* stand near, stand.

astrātus, -a, -um, *p.p. of* asternō, prostrate.

astrum, -ī, N. a star, a constellation : **Titania astra,** the sun.— *Pl.* heaven, the skies, on high : **sub astra** (up to the sky).

Astyanax, -actis (*acc.* -acta), M. son of Hector and Andromache; at the sack of Troy cast down by Ulysses from a tower (ii. 457, iii. 489).

asȳlum, -ī, N. a place of refuge, a sanctuary, asylum.

at (ast), *conj. adding a contrasted but not opposite idea,* but yet, and again, on the other hand, still.— *Of mere transition,* but, now.— *Adding a contrary or opposite idea.*

but, but on the other hand, on the contrary.— *After a negative idea,* but at least, but, yet still, at least.

āter, -tra, -trum, *adj.* black, dark; gloomy, dismal, sad, melancholy : **ignes; venenum** (deadly).

Athēnae, -ārum, F. *pl.* Athens.

Atīnās, -ātis, M. a Latin (xii. 661).

Atius, -ī, M. a Roman gentile name. — *Pl.* the members of this *gens* (v. 568).

Atlantēus, -a, -um, *adj.* of Atlas, Atlantean.

Atlās, -antis, M. king of Mauritania, son of Iapetus and Clymene, a lover of astronomy; changed by Perseus, with the aid of Medusa's head, into Mount Atlas, because he refused him a hospitable reception (i. 741).— The mountain itself in Northern Africa (iv. 247).

atque, ac [*ad + -que*], *conj. adding with emphasis, stronger than* et, and also, and besides, and even, and in fact, and.— *Adding something unexpected or important,* and lo, and then.— *In comparisons* (= quam), than, as : **haud secus ac** (just as); **haud minus ac** (not less than).

atquī [*at + qui, old abl. of* quis], *conj.* yet, and yet.

Atrīdēs, -ae, M. son of Atreus.— *Pl.* the sons of Atreus (Agamemnon and Menelaus, the leaders of the Greeks at Troy).

ātrium, -ī, N. the main court, the hall (*of a house*) ; *pl.* halls, rooms.

atrōx, -ōcis, *adj.* savage, fierce, wild, cruel, harsh.

Attalus, -ī, M. the name of several kings of Pergamos.

attamen, *conj.* still, yet, nevertheless.

attenuo, -āre, -āvī, -ātum [*ad* + *tenuo*, *cf. tenuis*], *1. v. a.* make thin; make weak, weaken.

attingō, -ere, -tigī, -tāctum [*ad* + *tango*], *3. v. a. and n.* touch; come to, approach, reach, arrive at: **te Aurora** (overtake, find).

attollō, -ere, *no perf., no sup.* [*ad* + *tollo*], *3. v. a.* lift up, raise up, throw up; erect, construct, raise; rouse: **iras.** — *Pass. or with reflexive,* lift one's self up, rise, appear, grow: **sese in auras; Punica se gloria.**

attonitus, -a, -um, *p.p. of* **attonō.**

attonō, -āre, -uī, -itum [*ad* + *tono*], *1. v. a.* (thunder at), seize (*with divine furor*), infuriate, frenzy. — **attonitus, -a, -um,** *p.p. as adj.* frenzied, frantic, confounded, awestruck, inspired.

attrectō, -āre, -āvī, -ātum [*ad* + *tracto*], *1. v. a.* handle, touch.

Atys, -yos, M. a young Trojan (v. 568).

auctor, -ōris [*augeo*], M. father, founder (*of a family or city*), progenitor, sire (*of animals*). — *Of buildings,* founder, builder, artist. — *Fig.* promoter, adviser, director, author. — *Of responsibility,* an authority, surety, guarantee.

audāx, -ācis [*cf. audeo*], *adj.* daring (*in good and bad sense*), bold, courageous, fearless, undaunted: **viribus audax** (presuming on his strength).

audēns, *p. of* **audeō.**

audeō, -ēre, ausus (*subj. perf.* **ausim**), *2. semi-dep.* venture, dare: **nefas; sperare; in proelia.** — **audēns, -entis,** *p. as adj.* daring, bold, fearless.

audiō, -īre, -īvī (-iī), -ītum, *4. v. a.* hear, hear of, listen, learn; hear (*as a judge*), inquire into: **dolos.**

auferō, auferre, abstulī, ablātum [*ab* (*abs*) + *fero*], *irreg. v. a.* bear away, carry off, remove, shut out; snatch away, steal. — *With reflexive,* withdraw, retire, depart.

augeō, -ēre, -xī, -ctum, *2. v. a.* increase, augment, add to; endow.

augur, -uris [*avis*], C. an augur (who foretold the future by observing the notes or flight of birds, the feeding of the sacred fowls, certain appearances of quadrupeds, and other unusual occurrences); a soothsayer, diviner, seer; prophetic (*in app. as adj.*): **augur Apollo.**

augurium, -ī (-iī) [*augur*], N. the observance and interpretation of omens, augury; prophecy, divination; a presentiment, foreboding; a sign, omen.

auguror, -ārī, -ātus [*augur*], *1. v. dep.* augur, prophesy, predict, surmise, suppose.

Augustus, -ī [*cf. augeo*], M. (magnified), august. — Title (used as name) of Octavius Cæsar as emperor (vi. 792).

Augustus, -a, -um, *adj.* of Augustus, Augustan.

aula, -ae (*gen.* aulāī), F. a court, courtyard, hall; a palace, royal court.

aulaeum, -ī, N. tapestry (*as covering for couches*); the curtain (*of a theatre*).

Aulis, -idis, F. a seaport of Bœotia, from which the Greeks set sail for Troy (iv. 426).

aura, -ae (*gen. sing.* aurāī), F. air (*in motion*), a breeze, wind, a blast; breath (*of favor*), favor (vi. 816); the air, the atmosphere. — *As inhaled*, air, vital air. — *Opposed to the earth or to the Lower World*, the heavens, the upper air, the Upper World: **ad auras** (to the sky; *also* to the open air, *esp. out of concealment*), on the breeze; **sub auras** (to light, into the air; in the open air); **fugit auras** (the open air, the light of day). — *Also*, a glittering, gleam: **auri**.

aurātus, -a, -um [*aurum*], *adj.* overlaid, plated, ornamented, *or* embroidered with gold, gilded, gilt.

aureus, -a, -um [*aurum*], *adj.* golden, of gold; adorned, set, *or* wrought with gold, gilded; glittering, gleaming.

auricomus, -a, -um [*aurum, coma*], *adj.* with golden hair; with golden leaves *or* foliage.

aurīga, -ae [*cf. aurea,* headstall, *ago*], C. a driver, a charioteer.

auris, -is, F. the ear.

aurōra, -ae, F. the morning, dawn, daybreak. — *Personified*, Aurora, the goddess of the morning, daughter of Hyperion, wife of Tithonus, and mother of Memnon (iv. 585).

aurum, -ī, N. gold. — *Of things of gold*, a goblet, a bit, a hair-band, gold plate, gold thread, gold coin, money.

ausim, *see* audeō.

Ausonia, -ae, F., a region in Italy; Italy (iii. 477).

Ausonis, -idis, *adj.* F. Ausonian, Italian.

Ausonius, -a, -um, *adj.* Ausonian, Italian, Latin. — M. *pl.* the Italians.

auspex, -icis [*avis, specio,* to look], C. an augur, diviner, soothsayer; *fig.* director, guide, leader, protector.

auspicium, -ī (-iī) [*auspex*], N. augury, auspices; sign, omen: **melioribus auspiciis.** — *Because only a commander could take the auspices*, command, authority, power, will: **meis auspiciis.**

auster, -trī, M. a south wind. — *For winds in general*: **furentes.**

ausum, -ī [N. *of ausus, p.p. of audeo*], N. an attempt, enterprise, daring deed.

aut, *conj. introducing an alternative.* — *Regularly exclusive*, or, or else: **obrue puppes aut age diversos.** — *Repeated*, either . . . or: **aut portum tenet aut subit ostia.** — *After negatives* (*expressed or implied*); *not exclusive, but distributing the negation*: **recusat prodere voce sua quemquam aut opponere morti.** — **nec . . . aut,** neither . . . nor: **nec revocare situs aut carmine iungere curat.** — *Without exclusion or negation*:

Anthea si quem videat aut Capyn.

autem, *conj. introducing an antithesis, or a mere transition, but always with some contrast,* but, on the contrary, on the other hand; also, too, again, now, but then, however, furthermore, then again.

Automedōn, -ontis, M. a son of Diores and charioteer of Achilles (ii. 477).

autumnus, -ī [*cf. augeo*], M. autumn (*the season of increase*).

auxilium, -ī (-iī) [*cf. augeo*], N. help, aid, assistance, succor.

avārus, -a, -um [*aveo,* to desire], *adj.* desirous, avaricious, covetous, greedy.

avē [*imper. of* †*aveo,* be well], hail!

āvehō, -ere, -xī, -ctum, *3. v. a.* bear *or* carry away.— *Pass.* be carried away, ride *or* sail away.

āvellō, -ere, -vellī *or* **-vulsī, -volsum (-vulsum),** *3. v. a.* tear *or* pull away *or* off, pluck out *or* off, carry off (*by violence*).

avēna, -ae, F. a stalk, straw, reed; a shepherd's pipe.

Aventīnus, -ī, M. ; **-um, -ī,** N. the Aventine, one of the seven hills of Rome (viii. 231).— *As adj.* **Aventīnus, -a, -um,** Aventine.

aveō, -ēre, *no perf. or sup., 2. v. a.* long for, be eager.

Avernus, -a, -um, of *or* belonging to Lake Avernus; of the Lower World (iv. 512).— N. *pl.* **Averna, -ōrum,** the neighborhood of Avernus, places near *or* about Avernus, the Lower World (iii. 442).

Avernus, -ī, M. Lake Avernus, in the neighborhood of Cumæ, Puteoli, and Baiæ, almost entirely enclosed by steep wooded hills (now Lago d'Averno). Its exhalations are said to have killed the birds flying over it; hence in fable it was placed near the entrance to the Lower World.— *Hence,* the Lower World (vi. 126).

āversus, -a, -um, *p.p. of* āvertō.

āvertō, -ere, -tī, -sum, *3. v. a.* turn away, avert, turn off, turn aside, keep off.— *With reflexive* (*sometimes without*), turn away, depart, retire, withdraw.— *Fig.* avert, ward off : casum; pestem (remove) ; curas (end).— **āversus, -a, -um,** *p.p. as adj.* turned *or* turning away, withdrawn, far (*from*) ; looking askance, unfriendly, hostile, estranged; backward.

avidus, -a, -um [*aveo,* to desire], *adj.* longing, desirous, eager; hungry.

avis, -is, F. a bird.

avītus, -a, -um [*avus*], *adj.* of one's grandfather.

āvius, -a, -um [*ab, via*], *adj.* at a distance from the way, untrodden, unfrequented.— N. *pl. as subst.* āvia, pathless, desolate regions, the wilderness.

avunculus, -ī [*cf. avus*], M. a mother's brother, maternal uncle.

avus, -ī, M. a grandfather, a grandsire, an ancestor.

axis, -is, M. an axle-tree ; a chariot; the axis of the heavens (*supposed to turn as spheres*) ; the pole; the heavens, the canopy (*of heaven*).

Babylōnius, -a, -um, *adj.* of Babylon, Babylonian.

bāca, -ae, F. a berry, small fruit (*esp. of the olive*).

bācātus, -a, -um [*baca*], *adj.* set *or* adorned with pearls : **monile** (pearl necklace).

Baccha, -ae, F. a female attendant of Bacchus, a Bacchante, a Mænad.

bacchor, -ārī, -ātus [*Bacchus*], 1. v. dep. celebrate the festival of Bacchus ; rave, rage, run madly about ; fly *or* run wildly : **fama.** — **bacchātus, -a, -um,** *p.p. in pass. sense,* sought in revels (iii. 125).

Bacchus, -ī, M. son of Jupiter and Semele, the god of wine and poets (i. 734).— *Fig.* wine (i. 215).

Bactra, -ōrum, N. Bactra, the chief city of Bactria (viii. 688).

baculum, -ī, N. (**-us, -ī,** M.), a staff.

Bāiae (*dissyllable*), **-ārum,** F. *pl.* a town in Campania.

Baleāricus, -a, -um, *adj.* Balearic, of the Balearic Isles, whose inhabitants were celebrated slingers.

balteus, -ī (*pl.* **baltea**), M. a baldric *or* shoulder-belt, a belt.

Bandusia, -ae, F. a spring celebrated by Horace.

barathrum, -ī, N. an abyss, chasm, gulf.

barba, -ae, F. the beard.

barbaricus, -a, -um, *adj.* foreign, barbaric.

barbariēs, *acc.* **-em,** F. an alien land ; a land of barbarians.

barbarus, -a, -um, *adj.* foreign, strange, barbarous.

Barcaeī, -ōrum, M. *pl.* Barcæans,

inhabitants of Barce, a town in Libya (iv. 43).

Barcē, -ēs, F. the nurse of Sychæus.

basis, -is (-eos), F. a pedestal.

Bassus, -ī, M. a Latin poet.

beātus, -a, -um [*p.p. of beo*], *adj.* happy, prosperous, blessed, fortunate : **sedes** (*Elysium*). — *Also* wealthy.

Bebrycius, -a, -um, *adj.* of Bebrycia (a province of Asia Minor, afterwards called Bithynia, the country of Amycus, a famous boxer), Bebrycian (v. 373).

Bēlīdēs, -ae, M. Palamedes, a Grecian hero, descendant of Belus (ii. 82).

Bēlides, -um, F. *pl.* the granddaughters of Belus, the Danaides, daughters of Danaus.

bellātor, -ōris [*bello*], M. a warrior.

bellātrīx, -īcis [*bello*], F. *adj.* that wages *or* carries on war, warlike ; warrior (*female*).

bellicus, -a, -um [*bellum*], *adj.* warlike.

bellipotēns, -entis [*bellum, potens*], *adj. as subst.* M. Lord of War (Mars).

bellō, -āre, -āvī, -ātum [*bellum*], *1. v. n.* wage *or* carry on war, war.

Bellōna, -ae [*bellum*], F. the goddess of war and sister of Mars (viii. 703).

bellum, -ī [*akin to duo*], N. war, warfare.— *Personified,* War.

bellus, -a, -um [*cf. bene*], *adj.* lovely, charming.

bēlua, -ae, F. a beast (*large or ferocious*), a monster : **Lernae** (*the Hydra*).

Bēlus, -ī, M. 1. Father of Dido (i. 621).— 2. Another ancestor of Dido's (i. 729).— 3. An ancestor of Palamedes (ii. 82).

bene [*bonus*] (melius, optimē), *adv.* well, beautifully; rightly, honorably; favorably, prosperously; fully, very.

benignus, -a, -um [*bonus, genus*], *adj.* good, kind, kindly, benignant, friendly.

Berecyntius, -a, -um, *adj.* of Berecyntus, a mountain in Phrygia, sacred to Cybele, on the river Sangarius, Berecyntian: **Berecyntia mater,** the Berecyntian goddess or mother, Cybele (vi. 784).

Beroē, -ēs, F. the wife of Doryclus of Epirus (v. 620).

Bessī, -ōrum, M. *pl.* a savage Thracian tribe.

bi- [*for dvi-, cf. bis*], *adv. prefix,* two, double.

bibō, -ere, bibī, *no sup., 3. v. a.* drink, drink of, drink in.

bibulus, -a, -um [*bibo*], *adj.* drinking freely; absorbent, thirsty: **favilla.**

bicolor, -ōris [*bi- + color*], *adj.* of two colors, two-colored: **equus** (dappled).

bidēns, -entis [*bi- + dens*], *adj.* with two teeth.— F. *as subst.* a sheep for sacrifice, victim.

bifōrmis, -e [*bi- + forma*], *adj.* two-formed, two-shaped.

bīgae, -ārum; *also* **-a, -ae** [*bi- + †agus (adj. akin to ago)*], F. a pair *of horses,* a span, double team; a two-horse car *or* chariot.

biiugus, -a, -um [*bi- + iugum*], *adj.* yoked two together: **certamen** (the contest with the bigæ, two-horse race, chariot race).

bilinguis, -e [*bi- + lingua*], *adj.* double-tongued, false, treacherous.

bīmus, -a, -um [*bis*], *adj.* of *or* for two years.

bīnī, -ae, -a [*bi-*], *distrib. adj.* two, two apiece *or* for each, two.

bipatēns, -entis [*bi- + patens*], *adj.* opening in two directions, swinging: **portae.**

bipennis, -e [*bi- + penna*], *adj.* two-edged.— *As subst.* **bipennis, -is** (*sc.* **securis**), F. an axe with two edges, battle-axe.

birēmis, -e [*bi- + remus*], *adj.* two-oared.— *As subst.* **birēmis, -is,** F. a vessel with two rows of benches *or* two banks of oars; *pl.* ships (*generally*).

bis [*for dvis, case-form of duo as adv.*], *adv. num.* twice: **bis tantum** (twice as much *or* far).

Bithȳnī, -ōrum, M. *pl.* the Bithynians (in Asia Minor).

Bitiās, -ae, M. a Carthaginian nobleman (i. 738).

bivium, -ī (-iī) [*bi- + via*], N. a place where two roads meet, a crossroad.

blanditia, -ae [*blandus*], F. caressing; *pl.* endearments.

blandus, -a, -um, *adj.* of smooth tongue, flattering, caressing, enticing, charming, alluring.

Boeōtius, -a, -um, *adj.* Bœotian, of Bœotia.

Bōla, -ae, F. a town of the Æqui, in Latium (vi. 775).

bonus, -a, -um (melior, optimus),
adj. good, beautiful, fit; skilful;
noble, virtuous, upright, honest;
favorable, favoring, propitious:
auspicia; Iuno.

Boōtēs, -ae, M. the constellation
Boötes (the ploughman).

Boreās, -ae, M. Boreas, the north
wind: **Boreae** (blasts from the
North). — *Personified,* Boreas,
the son of the river god Strymon,
and father of Calais and Zetes by
Orithyia, the daughter of Erechtheus, king of Attica.

bōs, bovis (*gen. pl.* **boum**), C. an
ox, a cow: **boves** (cattle).

brācae, -ārum, F. *pl.* breeches.

bracchium, -ī (-iī), N. an arm; a
branch; *pl.* the sailyards; natural walls of rock.

brattea, -ae, F. a thin plate, leaf
(*of metal*).

brevis, -e, *adj.* short; slight; shallow: **vada.** — N. *pl. as subst.* **brevia, -ium,** shallows, shoals.

breviter [*brevis*], *adv.* briefly, in
brief, with (*or* in) few words.

Briareus, -eī, M. a hundred-armed
giant, *also called* Ægæon (vi. 287).

brūma, -ae [*for* brevima (*old superlative of* brevis), *sc.* **dies**], F.
the shortest day *in the year,* the
winter solstice; winter time, winter.

brūmālis, -e [*bruma*], *adj.* wintry,
of winter.

brūtus, -a, -um, *adj.* heavy, dull,
solid.

Brūtus, -ī [*brutus*], M. a Roman
family name. — *Esp.* L. Junius
Brutus, who expelled Tarquinius
Superbus. He was saved by his

feigned stupidity, hence the surname (vi. 818).

būbō, -ōnis, M. (F. *only once*), an
owl, the horned owl.

bulla, -ae, F. a boss *or* knob.

bustum, -ī, N. the burned pyre; a
grave mound, tomb.

Būtēs, -ae, M. son of Amycus, king
of the Bebrycians, slain by Dares
at the tomb of Hector (v. 372).

Būthrōtum, -ī, N. a maritime town
of Epirus, now Butrinto (iii. 293).

buxifer, -era, -erum [*buxus, fero*],
boxwood-bearing, abounding in
boxwood.

buxus, -ī, F. boxwood.

Byrsa, -ae, F. the ancient citadel
of Carthage (i. 367).

cachinnus, -ī, M. a laugh, laughter.

cacūmen, -inis, N. the peak, top.

Cācus, -ī, M. son of Vulcan — a
fire-breathing monster, slain by
Hercules (viii. 194).

cadāver, -eris [*akin to* cado], N. a
dead body, a corpse.

Cadmēis, -idis, *adj.* F. of Cadmus.

Cadmus, -ī, M. son of Agenor and
founder of the citadel of Thebes
in Bœotia.

cadō, -ere, cecidī, cāsum, *3. v. n.*
fall down, sink down, fall: **folia;**
vela (are lowered). — *Of stars, etc.*
decline, set: **sidera.** — *In death,*
fall, perish, be slain. — *Fig.* happen, come to pass, befall one,
occur to one: **quocumque res
cadent.** — decrease, diminish, perish, decay, cease, subside, abate:
fragor; animi (sink). — *P. as adj.*
patria cadens (failing, going to
ruin).

cadŭcus, -a, -um [*cado*], *adj.* falling, fallen ; slain.

cadus, -ī, M. a large earthen vessel for liquids (*esp. wine*), a jar, vase ; a funeral urn.

caecus, -a, -um, *adj.* blind ; dark, invisible, concealed, secret, hidden : **caligo** ; **fores** ; **Mars** (blind warfare). — *Fig.* uncertain, dubious, blind, meaningless : **vestigia** ; **undae** (unknown) ; **parietes** (deceptive). — blind, heedless, reckless : **auri amor.**

caedēs, -is [*caedo*], F. a cutting *or* lopping off ; slaughter, murder, carnage ; blood, gore.

caedō, -ere, cecīdī, caesum [*causative of cado*], *3. v. a.* (cause to fall), cut, fell, cut down ; cut off ; slay, slaughter, sacrifice.

caelestis, -e (*sometimes gen. pl.* **caelestum**) [*caelum*], *adj.* heavenly, of heaven, celestial : **animi** (souls of the gods). — *Pl.* **caelestēs, -ium,** C. the inhabitants of heaven, the gods.

caelicola, -ae [*caelum, colo*], C. inhabitant of heaven, deity, god.

caelifer, -fera, -ferum [*caelum, fero*], *adj.* supporting the heavens, heaven-supporting : **Atlas.**

caelō, -āre, -āvī, -ātum [*caelum*, chisel], *1. v. a.* emboss, carve in relief, engrave, carve.

caelum, -ī, N. the sky, the heavens, Heaven ; the air, atmosphere, the weather.

Caeneus, -eī, M. a girl originally named Cænis, daughter of Elatus, changed by Neptune into a boy. According to Virgil, he again became a woman (vi. 448).

caenum, -ī, N. dirt, filth, mud, mire.

caeruleus (caerulus), -a, -um, *adj.* dark blue, blue-black, cerulean, sea-green, green : **colla ; canes.** — N. *pl.* **caerula,** the sea. — *Opposed to bright colors,* dark, gloomy, black : **imber ; vittae.**

Caesar, -aris, M. a family name in the gens Julia. — *Esp.:* 1. C. Julius Cæsar, the conqueror of Gaul. 2. C. Julius Cæsar Octavianus, surnamed Augustus (*originally* C. Octavius), the Roman emperor.

caesariēs, -ēī, F. the hair *of the head,* the locks.

caespes, -pitis, M. turf, sod.

caestus, -ūs, M. a cestus (a kind of glove for boxing, consisting of a thong loaded with lead or iron and wound round the hand), a gauntlet.

Caīcus, -ī, M. a companion of Æneas and commander of one of his ships (i. 183).

Cāiēta, -ae (-ē, -ēs), F. a town and its harbor in Latium (now Gaëta), supposed to have been named for Caieta, the old nurse of Æneas (vi. 900).

Calabrī, -ōrum, M. *pl.* the Calabrians, inhabitants of Calabria, a district in Lower Italy.

calathus, -ī, M. a wicker basket.

calcar, -āris [*calx*], N. a spur.

Calchās, -antis (*Greek acc.* **Calchanta**), M. a son of Thestor, the most distinguished seer among the Greeks at Troy (ii. 100).

calcō, -āre, -āvī, -ātum [*calx*], *1. v. a.* tread upon.

calefaciō, -ere, -fēcī, -factum [*caleo, facio*], 3. *v. a.*: *pass.* calefīō, -fierī, -factus sum [*caleo, facio*], make warm, heat, fire.

caleō, -ēre, -uī, *no sup.*, 2. *v. n.* be warm *or* hot, glow.

calidus, -a, -um [*cf. caleo*], *adj.* warm, hot.

cālīgō, -āre, *no perf.*, *no sup.*, 1. *v. n.* to be dark, misty, gloomy.

cālīgō, -inis, F. mist, fog, darkness.

calliditās, -tātis [*callidus*], F. cunning, craft, subtlety.

callidus, -a, -um, *adj.* crafty, sly.

callis, -is, M. a stony, narrow footway; a footpath, a path.

calor, -ōris [*cf. caleo*], M. warmth, heat, glow.

calx, calcis, F. the heel; the foot.

Calymnē, -ēs, F. an island in the Ægean Sea.

Camerīna, -ae, F. a town of Sicily, by a marsh of the same name (iii. 701).

Camilla, -ae, F. a Volscian heroine, an ally of Turnus.

Camillus, -ī, M. a name of several persons of the gens Furia, the most distinguished of whom was M. Furius Camillus, who conquered Veii, and delivered Rome from the Gauls, 390 B.C. (vi. 825).

camīnus, -ī, M. a smelting furnace, a forge *or* smithy; *pl.* chimneys (the crater of Ætna, where were supposed to be the forges of the Cyclopes).

campus, -ī, M. an even, flat place; a plain, field. *Esp.* the Campus Martius, a plain at Rome outside the walls, once belonging to the Tarquins. Afterwards it was dedicated to Mars, and became the meeting-place of the Roman people. In it was the tomb of Augustus and his family (vi. 872); a level surface (*of a rock*): immota attollitur unda campus.

candēns, *p. of* candeō.

candeō, -ēre, -uī, *no sup.* [*caneo*], 2. *v. n.* be white, shine, glisten; glow, be glowing hot: favilla. — candēns, -entis, *p.* glistening, shining, white: vacca.

candidus, -a, -um [*cf. candeo*], *adj.* glistening white, pure white, white; clear, bright: lilia; Dido (fair). — *Fig.* happy, prosperous.

candor, -ōris [*candeo*], M. a glossy whiteness; clearness, radiance, brightness, brilliancy, splendor.

cāneō, -ēre, -uī, *no sup.* [*canus*], 2. *v. n.* be white, gray, *or* hoary: senectus.

Canicula, -ae [*canis*], F. the Dog Star.

canis, -is, C. a dog.

canistra, -ōrum, N. *pl.* baskets woven from reeds.

cānitiēs, -em, -ē [*canus*], F. a gray color, hoariness; white *or* gray hair.

canō, -ere, cecinī, *no sup.*, 3. *v. a. and n.*, of either voice or instrument, sing, sound, play. — *With cogn. acc.* sing, recite, compose: carmina, paeana. — *Of the subject of song*, sing of, celebrate: bella exhausta (tell of). — *Of religious or inspired utterance*, repeat, recite, prophesy, foretell: vota Iunoni (chant).

canōrus, -a, -um [*cano*], *adj.* melodious, harmonious, sounding.

cantō, -āre, -āvī, -ātum [*cano*], *1. v. a.* sing, sing of.

cantus, -ūs [*cano*], M. tone, sound, melody; singing, song; blast (*of instruments*).

cānus, -a, -um, *adj.* gray, hoary, white.

capella, -ae [*caper*], F. a she-goat.

capessō, -ere, -essīvī *or* **-essiī, -essītum** [*capio*], *3. v. a. desid.* seize *or* catch at eagerly; lay hold of; *of place,* strive to reach, make for; take hold of anything with zeal, take upon one's self, undertake: **iussa; arma** (take up).

capillus, -ī, M. hair.

capiō, -ere, cēpī, captum, *3. v. a. In the widest sense,* take, lay hold of, seize: **sacra manu; praemia; hos comites** (take as companions); **cape dicta memor** (take them to heart).— *Of a position,* take possession of, seize, hold, occupy: **tumulum.**— *With* **ante,** anticipate.— *Of the mind,* win *or* gain, captivate, charm, ensnare, enchain; mislead, delude, deceive: **imagine** (deceive); **capta,** *of Dido* (betrayed).— *With the passions, etc., as subjects,* seize, lay hold of: **animum dementia cepit.**— **captus, -a, -um,** *p.p. as adj.* captured, captive, captivated: **auro captus** (bribed).— M. a prisoner, captive.

Capitōlium, -ī (-iī) [*caput*], N. the Capitol at Rome.— *Also pl.* (vi. 836).

capra, -ae, F. a she-goat.

caprea, -ae [*capra*], F. a wild she-goat.— **Capreae palus,** the Goat's Pool in the Campus Martius at Rome.

caprigenus, -a, -um [*caper,* √*gen* (*of gigno*)], *adj.* goat-born, of the goat kind: **pecus.**

captīvus, -a, -um [*captus*], *adj.* taken prisoner, captive.— M. a prisoner, captive.— F. *a female* prisoner *or* captive.— *Of things,* captured, plundered, taken as booty: **vestis.**

captō, -āre, -āvī, -ātum [*captus*], *1. v. a. intens.* strive to seize, lay hold of a thing with zeal, *etc.*; catch *or* snatch at; strive to catch, desire earnestly: **auribus aera** (listen to catch).

capulus, -ī [*capio*], M. the hilt, the handle.

caput, -itis, N. the head (*in every sense*). — *Of living creatures,* head, creature, person, life: **bina boum capita; carum** (Ascanius). — chief, principal, ruler, head; author, cause: **urbibus** (*of Rome*). — *Of things,* head, top, summit, point, peak.— *Esp.* **capitis minor,** having forfeited one's right (as a citizen).

Capys, -yos, M. 1. A companion of Æneas (i. 183), said to have founded Capua.— 2. The eighth king of Alba in Latium (vi. 768).

carbasus, -ī, F. Spanish flax; a sail.

carcer, -eris, M. a prison; *of a race-course,* the barrier *or* starting-place.

carchēsium, -ī (-iī), N. a cup, a goblet.

cardō, -inis, M. the pivot and socket (*by which doors were fixed, and made to open and shut*), a hinge; that about which every-thing revolves, the turning-point, crisis : **rerum.**

careō, -ēre, -uī, -itum, *2. v. n.* be without, lack, be free from; de-prive one's self of, do without, resign; be deprived of. — **carēns, -entis,** *p. as adj.* deprived of, without : **mortis honore** (funeral rites).— **carendus, -a, -um,** *ger. as adj.* to be lacked, to be missed.

carīna, -ae, F. the bottom of a ship, the keel; a vessel, boat, ship.

carmen, -inis, N. a song, lay, in-scription (*in verse*) ; a response of an oracle; a prophecy, predic-tion, *as being usually given in verse*; a magic formula, an incan-tation, a spell.— *Of birds,* song, note : **ferale carmen** (*of the owl*).

Carmentis, -is, F. a Roman god-dess.

Carpathius, -a, -um, *adj.* Carpa-thian, of Carpathus (an island in the Ægean, now Scarpanto) (v. 595).

carpō, -ere, -sī, -tum, *3. v. a.* pluck, pluck off, tear at: **ramum; saetas.**— *Fig. with the idea of* plucking, taking, *and* enjoying *extended in various ways* : **somnos** (enjoy) ; **vitalis auras** (breathe) ; **viam,** *etc.* (tread, pursue, *cf.* "*pick one's way*").— *Of the ef-fect of plucking,* wear away, con-sume, waste : **regina caeco car-pitur igni** (is wasted).

Carthāgō, *see* **Karthāgō.**

cārus, -a, -um, *adj.* dear, precious, beloved.

casa, -ae, F. a cottage.

Caspius, -a, -um, *adj.* of the Caspii (a nation of Media); Caspian : **regna** (vi. 798).

Cassandra, -ae, F. a daughter of Priam and Hecuba, priestess of Apollo. Endowed by him with prophetic powers, she continu-ally proclaimed the destruction of Troy, but, according to the terms of the gift, was believed by no one (ii. 246).

Cassiopē, -ēs, F. wife of Cepheus and mother of Andromeda; usu-ally called Cassiopeia.

cassis, -idis, F. a helmet.

cassus, -a, -um, *adj.* empty, void, hollow; wanting, devoid of, de-prived of, without (*with abl.*) ; vain, empty, useless, futile, fruit-less.—N. *acc.* in **cassum,** *see* **incas-sum.**

Castalius, -a, -um, *adj.* of Castalia (a fountain on Mount Parnassus, sacred to Apollo and the Muses), Castalian.

castellum, -ī [castrum], N. *dim.* a castle, fort, citadel, stronghold, fortress.

castīgō, -āre, -āvī, -ātum [castus, ago], *1. v. a.* chastise, punish; re-prove, chide, censure.

Castor, -oris, M. son of Leda and twin brother of Pollux.

castrum, -ī, N. *Sing.* a castle, fort, fortress : **Castrum Inui** (*a city of Latium*) (vi. 775).— *Pl.* **castra** (*several works together*), a fortified military *or* naval camp, an en-campment : **castra movere** (break up camp).

castus, -a, -um, *adj.* pure, unpol-luted, spotless, guiltless, chaste; pious, holy, sacred.

cāsus, -ūs [*cado*], M. a falling down, a fall, an overthrow ; what befalls, an event, accident, chance (**sub hoc casu**, at this crisis) ; *pl.* fate (*collectively*).— *Esp.* an adverse event, a misfortune, a calamity.

catēna, -ae, F. a chain, a fetter.

caterva, -ae, F. a crowd, troop, band, flock.

Catō, -ōnis [*catus*], M. (*lit.* the Shrewd), a family name in several Roman gentes. — *Esp.* M. Porcius Cato, the famous Censor, a rigid moralist (vi 841).

catulus, -ī, M. a whelp, a puppy ; a cub.

Catullus, -ī, M. a Latin poet.

Caucasus, -ī, M. a chain of mountains, inhabited by wild tribes, in Asia, between the Black and the Caspian Sea (iv. 367).

cauda, -ae, F. tail.

Caulōn, -ōnis, M. Caulon *or* Caulonia, a town founded by the Achæans on the east coast of Bruttium in the vicinity of the present Castel Vetere (iii. 553).

causa, -ae, F. a cause, reason, motive, occasion ; a feigned cause, a pretext, excuse (**morandi**) ; a case *or* cause (*in court*) : **orabunt causas.**

cautēs, -is, F. a rough pointed rock, a crag.

cautus, *see* caveō.

cavea, -ae [*cavus*], F. a hollow place, a cavity ; the theatre (*the circular part in which the spectators sat*), spectators' seats *or* benches : **consessus caveae** (the assembly in the theatre).

caveō, -ēre, cāvī, cautum, 2. *v. a. and n.* be on one's guard, beware. — *P.p. as adj.* cautus, -a, -um, cautious, wary.

caverna, -ae [*cavus*], F. a hollow, cavity, cave, cavern : **curvae cavernae.**

cavō, -āre, -āvī, -ātum [*cavus*], 1. *v. a.* make hollow, hollow out, dig *or* cut out. — **cavātus, -a, -um,** *p.p. as adj.* hollow, overhanging : **rupes.**

cavus, -a, -um, *adj.* concave, hollowed out, hollow, cavernous ; *of a vision*, without substance, hollow, empty ; *of a cloud*, hollow, enveloping : **nube cava amicti.**

Cecropia, -ae, F. Athens (*so called from King Cecrops*).

Cecropidēs, -ae, M. descendant of Cecrops. — M. *pl.* the Athenians (vi. 21), as the descendants of Cecrops, the most ancient king of Attica.

Cecropius, -a, -um, *adj.* of Cecrops, Attic.

cēdō, -ere, cessī, cessum, 3. *v. n.* retire, make way, depart, withdraw, recede ; pass away, vanish, forsake one ; yield, give place, submit : **cede deo; ne cede malis; nec cedit honore** (is behind in honor).

Celaenō, -ūs, F. one of the Harpies (iii. 211).

celeber, -bris, -bre, *adj.* numerous, thronging.

celebrō, -āre, -āvī, -ātum [*celeber*], 1. *v. a.* resort *or* go to in great numbers *or* often, frequent, throng ; celebrate, solemnize (**honorem**) ; honor, worship.

celer, -eris, -ere, *adj.* swift, quick, fleet, speedy.

Celer, -eris, M. the leader of the Roman Celeres (or Knights).

celerō, -āre, -āvī, -ātum [*celer***],** *1. v. a. and n.* quicken, hasten, hasten on.

Celeus, -eī, M. a native of Eleusis, the father of Triptolemus.

cella, -ae, F. a storehouse; a cell (*of bees*).

cēlō, -āre, -āvī, -ātum, *1. v. a.* hide, conceal, keep secret.

celsus, -a, -um [*p.p. of cello as adj.***],** raised high, high, lofty: **naves.**

cēna, -ae, F. a meal, a dinner.

Cenchreae, -ārum, F. one of the harbors of Corinth.

cēnō, -āre, -āvī, -ātum [*cena***],** *1. v. n.* dine.

Centaurus, -ī, M. a Centaur. The Centaurs were wild people in the mountains of Thessaly, who fought on horseback; according to fable, monsters of a double form (the upper parts human, the lower those of a horse), sons of Ixion and of a cloud in the form of Juno (vi. 286). — *Hence,* the name of a ship (*and so fem.*), the Centaur (v. 122).

centum, *indecl. num. adj.* a hundred; *often indef., as in Eng.*

centumgeminus, -a, -um [*centum + geminus***],** *adj.* hundredfold: **Briareus** (hundred-armed).

cēpa, -ae, F. an onion.

Cēphēnus, -a, -um, *adj.* of Cepheus, Æthiopian.

Cēphēus, -a, -um, *adj.* of Cepheus, Æthiopian.

Cēpheus, -eī, M. Cepheus, an Æthiopian king, the father of Andromeda.

Cēphīsus (-issus), -ī, M. a river of Phocis and Bœotia.

cēra, -ae, F. wax, piece of wax. — *Pl.* honeycomb.

Ceraunia, -ōrum, N. *pl.* the Ceraunian Mountains in Epirus (iii. 506).

Cerberus, -ī, M. the three-headed dog that guarded the entrance to the Lower World (vi. 417).

Cereālis, -e, *adj.* of Ceres, sacred to Ceres; wheaten: **arma** (utensils for bread-making).

cerebrum, -ī, N. the brain.

Cerēs, -eris, F. the goddess of grain, a daughter of Saturn and the mother of Proserpine; grain, flour, bread.

cernō, -ere, crēvī, crētum, *3. v. a.* sift, separate; distinguish, see, discern, turn the eyes toward, look at, perceive; decide, determine. — **certus, -a, -um,** *p.p.* decided, fixed, certain, sure, prescribed: **foedus.** — *Esp.* **certum est,** it is determined, one is resolved. — *Personally,* determined, resolved to: **eundi; mori.** — *From another point of view,* fixed, established, sure: **domus; mors; certissima proles** (undoubted); **cornus** (with unerring aim). — *So of persons,* steady, trustworthy, faithful. — *Of a mental state,* certain, sure: **certum facere** (inform, make known to one); **certior** (informed).

certāmen, -inis, N. contest, battle; struggle; match, rivalry.

certātim [*certo*], *adv.* earnestly, eagerly, in eager rivalry (*often translated by a verb*, vie with each other in, *etc.*).

certē [*certus*], *adv.* certainly, assuredly, surely.

certō, -āre, -āvī, -ātum [*certus*], *1. v. n. intens.* contend, fight, strive, struggle; emulate, vie with, rival: **remi**; **celeri sagitta**; **officio.** — *With infin.* strive, endeavor: **vincere.**

certus, -a, -um, *p.p. of* **cernō.**

cerva, -ae [*cervus*], F. a hind.

cervīx, -īcis, F. the neck, the back of the neck, back *or* shoulders.

cervus, -ī, M. a stag, a deer.

cessō, -āre, -āvī, -ātum [*cessum, p.p. of cedo*], *1. v. n. intens.* hang back, delay, linger, hesitate; be idle; cease.

cēterus (*not found*), **-a, -um,** *adj.* the other (*implying only two*), the rest, the remaining, the rest of: **rura.** — **cētera,** N. *pl. as subst.* everything else; *as adv.* in other respects, for the rest: **cetera Graius.**

cētus, -ī, M. (*pl.* N. **cētē**), a sea monster, whale, shark, *etc.*

ceu, *adv.* as, like, as if; as when, just as.

Chalcidicus, -a, -um, *adj.* of Chalcis (the chief city of Eubœa), Chalcidian; of Cumæ (a colony of Chalcis), Cumæan: **arx,** the heights of Cumæ (vi. 17).

chalybs, -ybis, M. steel.

Chāōn, -onis, M. a Trojan, the brother of Helenus (iii. 335).

Chāonius, -a, -um, *adj.* of Chaonia (a region of Epirus), Chaonian.

— **Chāonia,** F. (*sc.* **terra**), the country (iii. 335).

Chaos, *abl.* **Chaō,** N. (a yawning gulf), boundless, empty space, the kingdom of darkness; the Lower World (vi. 265). — *Personified,* Chaos (iv. 510).

Charites, -um, F. *pl.* the Graces, usually three (Aglaia, Euphrosyne, and Thalia).

Charōn, -ontis, M. the ferryman of the Styx (vi. 299).

charta, -ae, F. paper; a writing, a letter.

Charybdis, -is, F. a whirlpool in the Strait of Messina, between Sicily and Italy (iii. 420).

Chimaera, -ae, F. 1. A monster in Lycia, which vomited forth fire (in front a lion, in the hinder part a dragon, and in the middle a goat), slain by Bellerophon (vi. 288). — 2. One of the ships of Æneas (v. 118).

chlamys, -ydis, F. a woolen upper garment or cape, fastened by a clasp over the shoulder; a chlamys, cloak, military cloak.

chorda, -ae, F. a string (*of a lyre*).

chorēa (-ĕa), -ae, F. a dance in a ring, a dance.

chorus, -ī, M. a choral dance, a dance; a chorus, dancing band, choir; a multitude, band, troop.

cibus, -ī, M. food.

Cicones, -um, M. *pl.* the Cicones, a Thracian tribe.

cieō, ciēre, cīvī, citum, *2. v. a.* (*causative*), set in motion, move, stir, agitate: **aequora**; **tonitru caelum** (disturb); **aere viros** (rouse, stimulate). — *Less ex-*

actly, produce, call forth, cause, make : **gemitus ; lacrimas** (shed) ; **simulacra pugnae** (counterfeit) ; **stragem** (make havoc). — *Fig.* call upon : **animam**. — **citus, -a, -um,** *p.p. as adj.* hurried, swift, quick.

cīnctus, -ūs [*cingo*], M. a girding. — *Esp.* **cinctus Gabinus,** the Gabine girding, a manner of girding up the toga. Its corner was thrown over the left shoulder and brought under the right arm round to the breast. This fashion was customary in religious festivals (vii. 612).

cingō, -ere, cīnxī, cīnctum, *3. v. a.* surround. — *Of persons,* gird on, gird with ; *esp. in pass.* (*as middle*), gird one's self : **cingor armis ;** coil one's self (*of a serpent*). — **inutile ferrum cingitur** (girds on). — *Of parts of the body,* surround, bind on, encircle. — *Of things,* surround, encircle, enclose : **muris Albam ; urbem obsidione** (beset) ; **flamma** (encompass).

cingulum, -ī [*cingo*], N. a girdle, belt, sword-belt.

cinis, -eris, M. ashes, embers ; *of the dead,* ashes, tomb ; the spirit *or* shade.

circā, *adv.* round, around, about.

Circē, -ēs (-ae), F. a daughter of the Sun, said to have fled from Colchis to Circeii in Italy. She was famous for her sorceries, by which she changed her guests into beasts (iii. 386).

circuitus, -ūs [*circum + itus* (*cf. eo*)], M. a going round, a circuit.

circulus (circlus), -ī [*circus*], M. a circle, a ring, band ; a chain.

circum [*acc. of circus*], *adv.* around, round, about ; *prep. with acc.* near by, around, about.

circumdō, -dare, -dedī, -datum, *1. v. a.* put round, place round : **arma umeris** (buckle on) ; **collo bracchia ; chlamydem circumdata** (clad in). — *Also,* surround with, gird, encircle, enclose : **arces muro.**

circumferō, -ferre, -tulī, -lātum, *irr. v. a.* bear round, carry round ; encircle : **socios pura unda** (lustrate).

circumflectō, -ere, -xī, -xum, *3. v. a.* bend *or* turn about, wind round : **longos circumflectere cursus** (make a long circuit).

circumfluō, -ere, -flūxī, *no sup., 3. v. n.* flow round.

circumfundō, -ere, -fūdī, -fūsum, *3. v. a.* pour round : **nubes circumfusa** (enveloping). — *Fig. in passive,* gather, crowd round, flock together : **iuventus circumfusa.** — *Also,* surround : **gradientis circum dea fudit amictu** (envelope).

circumligō, -āre, -āvī, -ātum, *1. v. a.* bind round *or* to.

circumlinō, -ere, *no perf.,* **-litum,** *3. v. a.* surround, cover, clothe.

circumsiliō, -īre, *no perf. or sup.* [*circum + salio*], *4. v. n.* hop about.

circumsonus, -a, -um, *adj.* sounding around, barking about.

circumspiciō, -ere, -exī, -ectum [*circum + specio*], *3. v. a.* look round at, survey, espy, catch sight of, descry.

circumstō, -stāre, -stetī, *no sup.*, *1. v. n. and a.* stand around, be about, crowd round; surround, encompass, beset : **horror.**

circumtextus, -a, -um, *p.p. of* circumtexō, woven round.

circumveniō, -īre, -vēnī, -ventum, *4. v. a.* encompass, encircle, surround.

circumvolō, -āre, -āvī, -ātum, *1. v. a.* fly round; hover round, hover over.

circumvolvō, -ere, *no perf.*, -volūtum, *3. v. a.* roll *or* turn round. — *Pass.* revolve round.

circus, -ī, M. a circle, a ring; a circus, racecourse, course. — *Poetic, of a body of men gathered for sports,* the conclave.

Cisseus, -eī, M. a king of Thrace, father of Hecuba (v. 537).

Cithaerōn, -ōnis, M. a mountain in Bœotia, a favorite haunt of Bacchus (iv. 303).

cithara, -ae, F. a lyre, a cithara.

cito [*citus*], *adv.* quickly, soon.

citus, -a, -um, *p.p. of* cieō, *as adj.* hurried, swift, quick.

cīvīlis, -e [*civis*], *adj.* of a citizen, of citizens, *or* of the citizens, civil, civic : **quercus** (the civic crown, **corona civica,** a garland of oak leaves bestowed on a soldier who saved a citizen in war). — **bellum :** civil war.

cīvīliter [*civilis*], *adv.* courteously, kindly, mildly.

cīvis, -is, C. a citizen, a fellow-citizen, a fellow-countryman (*or* fellow-countrywoman).

clādēs, -is, F. disaster, loss, calamity; defeat, havoc, destruc-

tion. — *Of persons,* scourge, destroyer.

clam [*akin to celo*], *adv. and prep.* secretly, in secret, by surprise, unawares.

clāmō, -āre, -āvī, -ātum, *1. v. a.* call, call upon (*with a loud cry*) : **morientem.**

clāmor, -ōris [*clamo*], M. a loud cry, shriek, outcry, shout, shouting, clamor; noise, din, roar : **saxa dedere.**

clangor, -ōris [*clango*], M. a clang, clangor, blare, noise.

clārēscō, -ere, clāruī, *no sup.* [*clareo*], *3. v. n.* grow loud *or* bright : **sonitus** (increase).

Clarius, -a, -um, *adj.* of Claros (a town of Ionia, celebrated for a temple and oracle of Apollo), Clarian. — M. the Clarian god (Apollo) (iii. 360).

clārus, -a, -um, *adj.* loud, clear; bright, brilliant; distinct, manifest; renowned, famous, glorious, celebrated.

classis, -is, F. a fleet.

claudō, -ere, -sī, -sum, *3. v. a.* shut, close. — *Of the things enclosed,* shut up, confine, hem in, enclose, pen up, surround, encompass; shut off, cut off. — **clausus, -a, -um,** *p.p. as adj.* enclosed, confined, close, shut, pent up : **carcer.**

claudus, -a, -um, *adj.* lame, crippled, halting.

claustrum, -ī [*claudo*], N. fastening, lock, bolt, bar; door, gate, barrier : **Pelori** (*of the sides of a strait*).

clāva, -ae, F. a club.

clāviger, -gera, -gerum [*clava, gero*], *adj.* club-bearing, armed with a club.

clāvus, -ī, M. a nail, a peg; a tiller; a rudder, helm; a stripe (broad or narrow, on the tunic).

clēmentia, -ae [*clemens*], F. compassion, mercy.

cliēns, -entis [*p. of cluo*, hear, obey], C. a dependent, a client.

clienta, -ae [*cliens*], F. a female client *or* dependent.

clipeātus, -a, -um [*clipeus*], *adj.* armed with shields.

clipeus, M. (-um, N.), -ī, a shield (round, of the Greek pattern).

clīvus, -ī, M. a slope.

Cloanthus, -ī, M. a Trojan leader (i. 222).

Cluentius, -ī (-iī), M. a Roman gentile name, used collectively for the whole clan (v. 123).

Clūsīnus, -a, -um, *adj.* of Clusium, an Etruscan town (x. 655).

coāgulum, -ī [*co-, ago*], N. rennet.

coctilis, -e [*coctus, coquo*], *adj.* burned, of burnt bricks.

Cōcȳtus, -ī, M. a river of the World Below (vi. 323).

coeō, -īre, -īvī, -itum [*con-+eo*], *irr. v. n.* come together; curdle, congeal: sanguis formidine.

coepī, -isse, -tum [*co-+apio, cf. apiscor*], *v. a.* (take hold), begin, begin to speak. — coeptum, -ī, *p.p. as subst.* N. an undertaking, attempt, purpose.

coeptum, *see* coepī.

coerceō, -ēre, -uī, -itum [*con-+arceo*], 2. *v. a.* shut in together, surround; restrain, confine, curb.

coetus, -ūs [*con-+ itus, cf. coeo*], M. an assembling, meeting; an assemblage, an assembly, a crowd, throng, band, company, flock (*of birds*).

Coeus, -ī, M. a Titan, the father of Latona (iv. 179).

cognātus, -a, -um [*con- + (g)natus*], *adj.* akin, kindred, related.

cognōmen, -inis [*con-+(g)nomen*], N. family name, name.

cognōscō, -ere, -gnōvī, -gnitum [*con- + (g)nosco*], 3. *v. a.* examine, learn, listen to, hear, learn to know, recognize: haec cognoscite; casūs. — *In perf., etc.* have learned, know. — *P.p.* cognitus, -a, -um, known; *superl.* familiar.

cōgō, -ere, coēgī, coāctum [*con-+ago*], 3. *v. a.* drive together, collect, assemble (*of men, forces, etc.*): socios; agmina (keep in line, *of the rear guard, or officers*). — *Of size*, contract, reduce, narrow. — *Of consistency*, condense, congeal: in nubem cogitur aer. — *Fig.* force, compel, oblige (*with acc. and infin.*): quid (*cogn. acc.*) non mortalia pectora cogis? — coāctus, -a, -um, *p.p. as adj.* forced: lacrimae.

cohibeō, -ēre, -uī, -itum [*con- + habeo*], 2. *v. a.* hold together, contain, confine.

cohors, -ortis, F. a company (*of soldiery*), troop, squadron; *of other things*, band, crowd, multitude, line (*of ships*).

collābor, *see* conlābor.

Collātīnus, -a, -um, *adj.* of Collatia, a Sabine town (vi. 774).

colligō, -ere, -lēgī, -lēctum [*con-* + *lego*], 3. *v. a.* collect, bring together, assemble, gather; contract, reef; *pass.* come together, mass forces.

collis, -is, M. a hill.

colloquium, -ī (-iī) [*con-*, *loquor*], N. conference, conversation.

collum, -ī, N. the neck.

colō, -ere, coluī, cultum, 3. *v. a. and n.* cultivate, till, tend; inhabit, dwell in; cherish, regard, love, foster; reverence, worship, revere, honor : **penatis ; templum.** — **cultus, -a, -um,** *p.p.* cultivated, inhabited; elegant, highly finished : **culta praemia** (the rewards of tillage). — N. *pl. as subst.* **culta, -ōrum,** tilled fields, cultivated land.

colōnus, -ī [*colo*], M. a farmer, husbandman; a colonist.

color, -ōris, M. color, hue; complexion. — *Pl.* flowers.

coluber, -ubrī, M. a serpent, a snake.

columba, -ae, F. a dove, a pigeon.

columna, -ae, F. a pillar, a column, a support.

colus, -ī (-ūs), F. a distaff.

coma, -ae, F. the hair (*of the head*); leaves, foliage.

comāns, -antis [*p. of* † *como, -are, from coma*], *p. as adj.* long-haired, hairy, crested: **galea; cristae** (waving).

comātus, -a, -um [*p.p. of* † *como*], *adj.* long-haired; leafy.

comes, -itis [*con-, eo*], C. a companion, associate, follower, guide (*of the Sibyl*).

comitātus, -ūs [*comito*], M. a band of companions, an escort, a company, a retinue.

comitō, -āre, -āvī, -ātum [*comes*], 1. *v. a.* accompany, follow, attend.

comitor, -ārī, -ātus [*comito*], 1. *v. dep.* accompany, follow, escort, attend. — *P.p.* accompanying : **meum iter.**

commendō, -āre, -āvī, -ātum [*con-* + *mando*], 1. *v. a.* commit, entrust.

comminus [*con-* + *manus*], *adv.* hand to hand, in close combat.

commisceō, -ēre, -miscuī, -mixtum *or* **-mistum** [*con-* + *misceo*], 2. *v. a.* mix *or* mingle together, intermingle.

commissum, -ī [*p.p. of committo*], N. offence, fault, crime.

committō, -ere, -mīsī, -missum [*con-* + *mitto*], 3. *v. a.* combine, join, unite; join (*battle*), begin : **pugnam; commissos ludos** (have begun). — *With idea of a trust*, entrust, commit (*to*).—*Also,* commit, perpetrate.—**commissa,** *p.p.* N. *pl. as subst.* crimes, misdeeds; a crime.

commoveō, -ēre, -mōvī,-mōtum [*con-* + *moveo*], 2. *v. a.* move violently, agitate, move; reveal (iv. 301) ; rouse, excite, disturb, alarm, enrage, move (*with any emotion*).

commūnis, -e [*con-* + † *munis, cf. munus*], *adj.* belonging to two or more together, common: **periclum** (shared alike by both); **Troias et patriae communis Erinys** (alike, to both sides).

commūniter [*communis*], *adv.* in common.

cōmō, -ere, cōmpsī, cōmptum [con- + emo], 3. v. a. comb, arrange, braid.—cōmptus, -a, -um, p.p. as adj. plaited, in order: comae.

compāgēs, -is [com-, pango], F. a joining together, a connection, joint; structure.

compellō, -āre, -āvī, -ātum [cf. appello], 1. v. a. accost, address.

compellō, -ere, -pulī, -pulsum [con- + pello], 1. v. a. drive together; drive, force.

compendium, -ī (-iī) [con-, pendo], N. profit.

comperiō, -īre, -perī, -pertum [con + pario], 4. v. a. find out, discover, learn.

compēscō, -ere, -pēscuī, no sup. [com-, pes], 3. v. a. check, restrain; quench (thirst).

complector, -ī, -plexus [con- + plecto], 3. v. dep. clasp, encircle, embrace, hold, surround; seize, come upon or over, enfold: sopor artus.

compleō, -ēre, -ēvī, -ētum [con- + pleo], 2. v. a. fill up, fill full, fill; crowd, throng; complete: orbis.

complexus, -ūs [con- + plexus], M. an embrace.

compōnō, -ere, -posuī, -positum [con- + pono], 3. v. a. put together; found, build (urbem); dispose, lay, place: se (recline); diem (close); fluctus (calm); placida pace compostus (undisturbed in peaceful repose). — N. abl. of p.p. as adv. compositō, by arrangement, according to agreement.

compositō, see compōnō.

comprecor, -ārī, -ātus [con- + precor], 1. v. dep. implore.

comprehendō (-prēndō), -ere, -dī, -sum [con- + prehendo], 3. v. a. take hold of, grasp; embrace, comprise; recount, include, enumerate: formas scelerum.

comprimō, -ere, -pressī, -pressum [con- + premo], 3. v. a. press together, close; hold back, hold, check; curb, repress, stay: furores; impetus.

cōnāmen, -inis [conor], N. effort.

concavus, -a, -um, adj. hollow, concave, arched, vaulted: saxa (of caves).

concēdō, -ere, -cessī, -cessum, 3. v. n. and a. move away, retire, withdraw, come or go away; depart, cease: superis ab oris (by death); allow, permit. — concessus, -a, -um, p.p. as adj. permitted, allowed, permissible, lawful: concessa peto (things not forbidden).

concha, -ae, F. a shell, conch shell. — Also as an instrument, shell, conch, horn.

concidō, -ere, -cidī, no sup. [con- + cado], 3. v. n. fall (in a heap), fall to the ground; of death or fainting, fall, sink.

concieō, -iēre, -īvī, -itum, 2. (also conciō, 4.) v. a. stir up, rouse, swell.

conciliō, -āre, -āvī, -ātum [concilium], 1. v. a. gain over, secure, obtain.

concilium, -ī (-iī), N. an assembly (generally, cf. consilium, a deliberative body), gathering: piorum.

— *Also in sense of* consilium, a council : silentum (*as a jury*).

concio, -īre, -īvī, -ītum, *4. v. a., see* concieō.

concipiō, -ere, -cēpī, -ceptum [*con-* + *capio*], *3.v.a. and n.* conceive.— *With abstract objects,* admit, adopt, harbor, give way to : furias (be possessed by).— *Of ideas in words,* formulate, draw up, compose, make : foedus.— *Of the mind,* conceive, imagine : mente furores.

conclāmō, -āre, -āvī, -ātum, *1. v. n. and a.* cry aloud, shout.

conclūdō, -ere, -sī, -sum [*con-* + *claudo*], *3. v. a.* shut up, enclose ; surround, include : sulco (mark out).

concors, -rdis [*con-, cor*], *adj.* united in feeling, friendly, harmonious : animae ; frena (peaceful).

concrēdō, -ere, -didī, -ditum, *3. v. a.* entrust.

concrēscō, -ere, -crēvī, -crētum, *3. v. n.* grow together, harden, condense ; grow into.— concrētus, -a, -um, *p.p.* grown into, ingrained ; solidified.

concurrō, -ere, -currī (-cucurrī), -cursum, *3. v. n.* run with *or* together, flock together, assemble ; rush (*to a place*), rally ; meet, fight, contend : viris virgo.

concursus, -ūs, M. a rushing together ; a crowd, an assembly, a concourse.

concutiō, -ere, -cussī, -cussum [*con-* + *quatio*], *3. v. a.* shake violently ; agitate, alarm, trouble : urbs (panic-stricken) ; animum

concussus ; casu concussus acerbo (overwhelmed).

condēnsus, -a, -um, *adj.* crowded together.

condiscō, -ere, -didicī, *no sup., 3. v. a.* learn (thoroughly).

condō, -ere, -didī, -ditum, *3. v. a.* (put together) ; build, found, make, erect, establish, settle : urbem, moenia ; Romanam gentem ; aurea secula (bring in).— *With idea of preservation,* store, lay away : signa mente (treasure up).— *So also of concealment,* hide, secrete, conceal, withdraw (*one's self*) close : caput inter nubila ; se umbris ; sidera fluctibus.— *Esp. of the dead,* bury, lay to rest : ossa terra ; animam sepulcro.— *Of a sword,* bury, plunge to the hilt.

cōnferciō, -īre, *no perf.,* -fertum [*con-* + *farcio*], *4. v. a.* crowd together.— cōnfertus, -a, -um, *p.p. as adj.* in serried ranks, in close array.

cōnferō, -ferre, -tulī, -lātum (coll-), *irr. v. a.* bring together, bear together : gradum (walk by his side) ; collātā dextrā (hand to hand).

cōnfertus, -a, -um, *p.p. of* cōnferciō.

cōnfestim, *adv.* suddenly.

cōnficiō, -ficere, -fēcī, -fectum (*also* cōnfierī *as pass.*) [*con-* + *facio*], *3. v. a.* finish, complete, accomplish ; exhaust, waste, use up, destroy.— cōnfectus, -a, -um, *p.p. as adj.* wasted, worn out, exhausted, emaciated : macie ; curis.

cōnfīdō, -ere, -fīsus, *3. v. a. and
n.* trust in, rely on, trust to,
trust: rebus; huic monstro;
pelago sereno.

cōnfīgō, -ere, -fīxī, -fīxum,
3. v. a. pierce through, transfix,
strike down (*with a missile
weapon*).—cōnfīxus, -a, -um, *p.p.*
as *adj.* transfixed, struck down.

cōnfīō, -fierī, *pass. of* cōnficiō.

cōnfīsus, -a, -um, *p.p. of* cōnfīdō.

cōnfiteor, -fitērī, -fessus [*con- +
fateor*], *2. v. dep.* fully acknowledge, confess, avow; reveal, manifest.

cōnflīgō, -ere, -flīxī, -flīctum, *3.
v. n.* dash against (*each other*), be
in conflict, contend: venti (war
with each other).

cōnfugiō, -ere, -fūgī, no sup., *3.
v. n.* flee for refuge *or* succor, take
refuge.

cōnfundō, -ere, -fūdī, -fūsum,
3. v. a. pour together; confound,
confuse, disturb: foedus (break).
— *In pass.* mix itself, mingle,
blend. — cōnfūsus, -a, -um, *p.p.*
as *adj.* confounded, perplexed,
disordered: mentem.

congelō, -āre, -āvī, -ātum, *1. v. n.*
congeal, freeze; grow hard.

congemō, -ere, -gemuī, no sup.,
3. v. n. and a. sigh *or* groan deeply;
of a tree: congemuit supremum
(groaned its last).

congerō, -ere, -gessī, -gestum,
3. v. a. bear, bring, *or* carry together; heap up, gather; build,
construct, erect: aram. — con-
gestus, -a, -um, *p.p.* as *adj.*
gathered, heaped: turea dona.

congredior, -gredī, -gressus

[*con- + gradior*], *3. v. dep.* go,
come *or* meet together *or* with
one; fight, contend, engage.

congressus, -ūs, M. a meeting, encounter, interview.

coniciō, -ere, -iēcī, -iectum [*con-
+ iacio*], *3. v. a.* throw together
or at; hurl, cast, fling, shoot:
vestes; telum; coniecta sagitta.
— *With reflexive*, throw one's self,
rush, speed, hasten: Iris inter
medias sese (dashes).

cōnifer, -era, -erum [*conus, fero*],
adj. cone-bearing, coniferous.

cōnītor, -nītī, -nīsus *and* -nīxus
[*con- + nitor*], *3. v. dep.* lean
against; strain, struggle, make
an effort, strive; conīxus (with
mighty effort).

coniugium, -ī (-iī) [*cf. coniungo*],
N. a joining, union; marriage;
husband, wife.

coniungō, -ere, -iūnxī, -iūnc-
tum, *3. v. a.* join together, unite
attach, ally; moor (*a ship*).

coniūnx, -iugis [*cf. coniungo*], C. a
husband, a wife, a consort; a betrothed.

conlabefactō, -āre, *no perf. or
sup.* [*labo, facto*], *1. v. a.* to make
(anything) totter.

conlābor (coll-), -lābī, -lāpsus,
3. v. dep. fall together, collapse;
fall, sink, drop, faint. — conlāp-
sus, -a, -um, *p.p.* as *adj.* fainting, swooning, sinking, lifeless:
membra collapsa (fainting limbs);
ferro conlapsa (swooning from a
wound).

conlūceō, -ēre, *no perf., no sup.,*
2. v. n. shine brightly, blaze, glare,
gleam.

conlūstrō, -āre, -āvī, -ātum, *1.
v. a.* light up; examine, survey.

cōnor, -ārī, -ātus sum, *1. v. dep.*
undertake, attempt, try, venture,
endeavor.

conqueror, -ī, -questus, *3. v. dep.*
complain, lament.

cōnsanguineus, -a, -um [*con-,
sanguis*], *adj.* of kindred blood,
akin, related. — M. a kinsman:
Leti (brother).

cōnsanguinitās, -tātis [*con-, sanguis*], F. kindred, relationship,
consanguinity.

cōnscendō, -ere, -scendī, -scēn-
sum [*con-* + *scando*], *3. v. a. and
n.* mount, ascend; go on board,
embark, take ship: aequor (put
to sea).

cōnscius, -a, -um [*con-* + †*scius,
cf.* scio], *adj.* conscious, aware
of; allied (agmina); confeder-
ate, of accomplices (turba); conscious (*with one's self*), conscious
of guilt, self-conscious: virtus;
mens conscia recti. — *As subst.*
a witness.

cōnsequor, -sequī, -secūtus, *3.
v. dep.* attend, pursue, follow, follow closely.

cōnserō, -ere, -seruī, -sertum,
3. v. a. connect, entwine, tie, join,
fit, unite, fasten together: lorica
conserta hamis (woven); tegumen spinis. — *Esp. of hostilities,*
join (*in fight*), engage in: dextram; proelia.

cōnsessus, -ūs [*consido*], M. a
sitting together; an assembly:
caveae (spectators in the theatre).
— consessu exstructo, *see note
on* v. 290.

cōnsīderō, -āre, -āvī, -ātum, *1.
v. a.* gaze at, consider.

cōnsīdō, -ere, -sēdī (-sīdī),
-sessum, *3. v. n.* sit down, seat
one's self, alight (*of birds*): Ausonio portu (anchor). — *Esp.* settle down (*to dwell*), take up one's
abode: Cretae (*loc.*). — *Of inan-
imate subjects*, settle, sink down:
in ignis.

cōnsilium, -ī (-iī) [*cf.* consulo], N.
consultation, counsel; wise counsel, plan, purpose, course of conduct, course; advice.

cōnsistō, -ere, -stitī, -stitum, *3.
v. a. and n.* place one's self, take
one's stand, stand still, stand
firm, set foot on (terrā); take a
stand, make a halt, stand, halt,
remain, settle; rest: mens. —
consistit in, depends on.

cōnsōlor, -ārī, -ātus, *1. v. dep.* console, comfort.

cōnsonō, -āre, -uī, *no sup., 1. v. n.*
sound together *or* at the same
time, resound.

consors, -sortis, C. a sharer of
one's lot; a fellow-countryman;
a brother *or* sister.

cōnspectus, -ūs [*conspicio*], M.
sight, view, look, presence: e conspectu (out of one's sight); in conspectu; ire ad conspectum genitoris (to meet).

cōnspiciō, -ere, -spexī, -spec-
tum [*con-* + *specio*], *3. v. a.* gaze
upon, behold; get a sight of,
espy, descry, find.

cōnspīrō, -āre, -āvī, -ātum, *1. v.
n.* blow together, sound together.

cōnsternō, -ere, -strāvī, -strā-
tum, *3. v. a.* bestrew, cover.

cōnstituō, -ere, -uī, -ūtum [con- + statuo], 3. v. a. set up, place, put, set (metam); determine, resolve: quaerere.

cōnstō, -stāre, -stitī, (-stātūrus), 1. v. n. stand together; stand firm or immovable, be steadfast, be settled; animo sententia (is fixed). — Impers. constat, it is evident, it is certain.

cōnsul, -ulis, M. a consul, one of the two chief magistrates of the Roman state.

cōnsulō, -ere, -uī, -tum, 3. v. a. and n. consult (exta); take counsel. — consultus, -a, -um, p.p. as adj. skilled, well versed.

cōnsultum, -ī [N. p.p. of consulo], N. a thing deliberated or advised; usually pl. oracles, advice.

cōnsūmō, -ere, -sūmpsī, -sūmptum, 3. v. a. consume, devour, waste, destroy, use up: nocte consumpta (spent); sagitta consumpta (by fire).

cōnsurgō, -ere, -rēxī, -rēctum, 3. v. n. rise up, rise: nautae; venti; remi ordine (in ranks).

contāctus, -ūs [contingo], M. a touching, contact, touch.

contāgium, -ī (-iī) [con-, √tag of tango], N. contagion, infection.

contemnō, -ere, -psī, -ptum, 3. v. a. hold in contempt, despise, scorn: ventos (defy).

contendō, -ere, -dī, -tum, 3. v. a. and n. stretch, strain: contenta tela (on the stretch, aimed). — Fig. of straining the powers of mind or body, strive, exert one's self, struggle: petere. — With the idea of opposition, struggle, contend, strive for mastery: bello; cursu; ludo; contra Paridem (in boxing). — Of aim or direction, direct, aim, hold (a course); cursum (steer).

contentus, -a, -um, p.p. of contineō.

conterminus, -a, -um, adj. near, close by.

conterreō, -ēre, -uī, -itum, 2. v. a. terrify greatly, frighten, alarm.

contexō, -ere, -xuī, -xtum, 3. v. a. weave or twine together; put together, build, construct: equum trabibus acernis.

conticēscō, -ere, -ticuī, no sup. [con-, taceo], 3. v. n. inch. become still, hold one's peace: conticuere omnes (were hushed).

contiguus, -a, -um [cf. contingo], adj. adjacent, side by side.

contineō, -ēre, -tinuī, -tentum [con- + teneo], 2. v. a. and n. hold in, confine; hold back, restrain, check: gradum (halt). — contentus, -a, -um, p.p. as adj. content, satisfied: galeā.

contingō, -ere, -tigī, -tāctum [con- + tango], 3. v. a. and n. touch, seize, take hold of: funem manu; avem ferro (hit). — Less exactly, reach, arrive at, attain, gain, touch: Italiam; metam. Fig. (impersonal), be one's lot, happen, befall, be one's fate: oppetere.

continuō [abl. of continuus], adv. immediately, forthwith, without delay.

contorqueō, -ēre, -torsī, -tortum, 2. v. a. twist, turn, whirl; hurl.

contrā, *adv. and prep. Adv.* opposite, on the other side, on the opposite side; on the other hand, on the contrary, in return, in reply, in opposition. — *Prep.* over against, opposite, facing; against, in reply to, in opposition to: **Alciden contra; quae contra** (in reply to this).

contrahō, -ere, -trāxī, -trāctum, *3. v. a.* draw together, gather, collect, assemble; take in: **vela.**

contrārius, -a, -um [*contra*], *adj.* opposite, lying over against; opposed, contrary, adverse.

contremīscō, -ere, -tremuī, *no sup., 3. v. n. inch.* tremble, shake, shudder: **pontus.**

contundō, -ere, -tudī, -tūsum, *3. v. a.* bruise; crush, quell.

contus, -ī, M. a punt pole (*with pointed iron*), setting pole.

cōnūbium, -ī (-iī) [*con-, nubo*], N. marriage, wedlock.

cōnus, -ī, M. a cone; the peak (*of a helmet*); a crest.

convalēscō, -ere, -valuī, *no sup. 2. v. n.* grow strong, recover.

convallis, -is, F. a valley.

convectō, -āre, *no perf., no sup., 1. v. a.* bring together.

convellō, -ere, -vellī, -volsum (-vulsum), *3. v. a.* tear away, pluck up; cut away (**ferro**); tear apart, rend asunder, shatter (**naves**).

conveniō, -īre, -vēnī, -ventum, *4. v. n. and a.* come together, assemble, gather round, meet; accord, agree. — *Fig. impersonally,* it is agreed upon.

conventus, -ūs [*convenio*], M. a coming together; an assembly, conclave.

convertō, -ere, -tī, -sum, *3. v. a.* turn round, turn, invert, reverse, turn backward: **cuspis; omen in ipsum** (bring the disaster). — *Fig.* alter, change: **animi conversi; vias.** — **conversus, -a, -um,** *p.p. as adj.* inverted, reversed, adverse.

convexus, -a, -um [*p.p. of conveho*], *adj.* (brought together); vaulted, arched. — N. *as subst.* **convexum, -ī,** *also pl.* a vault, arch, recess, hollow (**nemorum**); **supera convexa** (the canopy of heaven, the Upper World); **convexa** (the rounded mass, *of mountains*).

convīcium, ī- (-iī), N. reproach, insult.

convictus, -ūs [*con-, vivo*], M. (a living together), intimacy; a circle (*of friends*).

convīvium, -ī (-iī) [*conviva*, guest; *con-, vivo*], N. a meal in company, a feast, banquet.

convocō, -āre, -āvī, -ātum, *1. v. a.* call together.

convolsus, -a, -um, *p.p. of convellō.*

convolvō, -ere, -volvī, -volūtum, *3. v. a.* roll together, writhe, coil.

coorior, -orīrī, -ortus [*con- + orior*], *3. and 4. v. dep.* arise, break out: **seditio.**

cōpia, -ae [*con- + ops*], F. plenty, abundance, a supply; ability, power, means, resources; opportunity, chance (*to do*): **fandi.** — *Concretely,* troops, forces (*in prose the pl.* **copiae**).

coquō, -ere, coxī, coctum, *3. v. a.* cook. — **coctus, -a, -um,** *p.p. as adj.* hardened (*in the fire*).

cor, cordis, N. the heart. — *Fig.* heart, soul (*of both moral and intellectual powers*). — *Of persons, as in English,* soul, heart : **iuvenes fortissima corda.** — *Phrase,* **cordi esse,** be dear, pleasing, desired.

Cora, -ae, F. a town of Latium, now Core (vi. 775).

cōram, *adv.* in presence, before the eyes, in person.

Corās, -ae, M. one of the founders of Tibur (vii. 672).

Corinthiacus, -a, -um, *adj.* Corinthian.

Corinthus, -ī, F. Corinth, a city of the Peloponnesus, famous for its bronze foundries and artistic skill; conquered by L. Mummius, 146 B.C. (vi. 836).

corneus, -a, -um [*cornu*], *adj.* of horn, horny, horn.

corneus, -a, -um [*cornus*], *adj.* of the cornel tree, of cornel wood.

cornipēs, -edis [*cornu, pes*], *adj.* horn-footed, horny-hoofed.

cornīx, -īcis, F. a crow.

cornū, -ūs, N. a horn, an antler; a hoof; a horn (*for blowing*); horn (*of the moon*); tip, yardarm; a bow (*with horn tips*).

cornum, -ī [*cornus*], N. the cornel cherry.

cornus, -ī, F. a cornel tree, a javelin (*of cornel wood*).

Coroebus, -ī, M. a Phrygian ally of Priam (ii. 341).

corōna, -ae, F. a garland, a wreath, a diadem, a crown; a circle *or* ring of defenders.

corōnō, -āre, -āvī, -ātum [*corona*], *1. v. a.* furnish with a garland *or* crown, crown; beset, encompass; **vina** (wreathe the bowl).

corporeus, -a, -um [*corpus*], *adj.* corporeal, of the body.

corpus, -oris, N. a body (*alive*); a corpse; the frame; form, figure; a person, an animal, a creature; bulk, mass. — *From association with burial,* the ghost, a shade, spirit. — *Phrases :* **corpore exire,** elude, dodge (by a movement of the body) : **toto corpore,** with all one's might.

corripiō, -ere, -ripuī, -reptum [*con- + rapio*], *3. v. a.* snatch up, seize, catch, lay violent hands on: **ferrum; offam; scuta correpta sub undis** (borne away). — *With* **corpus** *or a reflexive,* rise quickly, start up, tear one's self away, hurry off : **e stratis** (spring); **e somno.** — *Of sudden or rapid motion,* occupy, hurry over : **spatia; spatium medium ; viam** (speed on).

corrumpō, -ere, -rūpī, -ruptum [*con- + rumpo*], *3. v. a.* break up, spoil, ruin, damage; infect, poison, taint. — **corruptus, -a, -um,** *p.p. as adj.* tainted, infected : **tractus caeli.**

cortex, -icis, C. bark; cork.

cortīna, -ae, F. a kettle, a caldron; the tripod (*at Delphi*), the oracle (*see note on* iii. 92).

Cōrus (Caurus), -ī, M. the northwest wind.

coruscō, -āre, *no perf., no sup.* [*coruscus*], *1. v. a. and n.* shake, brandish, wave.

coruscus, -a, -um, *adj.* waving, quivering, tremulous (silvae); flashing, gleaming, coruscating: flammae; ensis; luce aëna.

Corybantius, -a, -um, *adj.* of the Corybantes (priests of Cybele who celebrated her worship with clanging cymbals), Corybantian (iii. 111).

Corynaeus, -ī, M. a priest of the Trojans (vi. 228).

Corythus, -ī, M. a town of Etruria, Cortona (iii. 170).

Cossus, -ī, M. a Roman family name in the Cornelian gens. — *Esp.* A. Cornelius Cossus, consul 428 B.C. (vi. 841).

costa, -ae, F. a rib; a side.

cothurnus, -ī, M. a hunting boot (covering the foot and lower part of the leg, and laced), a buskin.

crās, *adv.* to-morrow.

crassus, -a, -um, *adj.* thick, clotted: cruor.

crastinus, -a, -um [*cras*], *adj.* of the morrow, to-morrow's, next day's, next: ortus.

crātēra, -ae, F.; -ēr, -ēris, M. (*acc. Greek sing.* cratēra, *pl.* cratēras), a mixing vessel, a bowl, a jar (*of large size*); an oil jar.

creātrix, -īcis [*creo*], F. a mother.

crēber, -bra, -brum (-brior, -berrimus), *adj.* thick, close: Africus creber procellis (full of). — *Of closeness in time*, repeated, frequent, numerous, constant; anhelitus (quick, hurried); heros creber pulsat (*as adv.* again and again).

crēbrēscō, -ere, -bruī, *no sup.* [*creber*], *3. v. n. inch.* become frequent, increase, freshen (*of the wind*): aurae.

crēdibilis, -e [*credo*], *adj.* credible: credibile est (one may believe).

crēdō, -ere, -didī, -ditum, *3. v. n. and a.* put faith in, trust to, confide in, trust: equo; Austris. — *Trans.* entrust, confide to, commit: tibi sensus. — *With reflexive*, trust one's self to, venture on, hazard: se pugnae. — *With thing as object*, credit, believe, suppose, imagine: res credita; id Manis curare. — *With person as object*, trust, believe: Cassandra credita.

Cremera, -ae, F. a small river in Etruria.

cremō, -āre, -āvī, -ātum, *1. v. a.* burn, consume.

creō, -āre, -āvī, -ātum, *1. v. a.* create, produce, bring forth, beget.

crepīdō, -inis, F. a base, foundation.

crepitō, -āre, *no perf. or sup.* [*crepo*], *1. v. n.* crackle, rattle, rustle, clatter: malae (*with blows*); Auster (whistle).

crepō, -āre, -uī, -itum, *1. v. n.* crack, rattle, crash; break with a crash.

Crēs, -ētis, *adj.* Cretan. — M. *pl. as subst.* Crētes, -um, the Cretans (iv. 146).

crēscō, -ere, crēvī, crētum [*akin to* creo], *3. v. n.* grow up, be born, arise. — crētus, -a, -um, *p.p. as adj.* sprung from, descended from: Troiano sanguine.

Crēsius, -a, -um, *adj.* of Crete, Cretan (iv. 70).

Crēssus, -a, -um, *adj.* of Crete, Cretan (v. 285).

Crēta (Crētē), -ae, F. *of adj.* Crete, an island in the Mediterranean (iii. 104).

Crētaeus, -a, -um, *adj.* of Crete, Cretan (iii. 117).

Crētes, *see* **Crēs.**

Creūsa, -ae, F. a daughter of Priam, and wife of Æneas (ii. 562).

crīmen, -inis [*cerno*], N. a charge, accusation; a reproach, a crime, a fault.

crīnis, -is, M. the hair; the tail (*of a comet or shooting star*), a trail, a train.

Crīnīsus, -ī, M. a river on the southwest coast of Sicily; also, the river god (v. 38).

crīnītus, -a, -um [*crinis*], *adj.* long-haired.

crīspō, -āre, *no perf.*, **-ātum,** *1. v. a.* wave, brandish.

crista, -ae, F. a crest.

cristātus, -a, -um [*crista*], *adj.* crested (*as a famous warrior*).

croceus, -a, -um [*crocus*], *adj.* of saffron hue.

crūdēlis, -e [*crudus*], *adj.* harsh, cruel, unrelenting, ruthless; bitter, violent (**luctus; odium**); bloody, destructive, frightful: **funus; fata; arae; umbrae.**

crūdēliter [*crudelis*], *adv.* cruelly, barbarously.

crūdus, -a, -um [*akin to* **cruor**], *adj.* bloody, raw; made of rawhide (**caestus**); rough, rude, sturdy: **senectus.**

cruentō, -āre, -āvī, -ātum [*cruentus*], *1. v. a.* make bloody. — *P.p.*

as adj. **cruentātus, -a, -um,** bloodstained.

cruentus, -a, -um, *adj.* bloody, gory, bloodstained.

cruor, -ōris [√ *cru* (*in cruentus*)], M. blood, gore.

crūs, crūris, N. shank, shin, leg.

cubīle, -is [*cubo*], N. a bed, couch.

cubitum, -ī [*cubo*], N. the elbow.

culmen, -inis, N. top, summit, roof, housetop, height; *pl.* lofty abodes.

culpa, -ae, F. fault, crime, defect, guilt.

culpō, -āre, -āvī, -ātum [*culpa*], *1. v. a.* blame. — **culpātus, -a, -um,** *p.p. as adj.* blamable, blameworthy, to be blamed.

culter, -trī, M. a knife.

cultor, -ōris [*colo*], M. a worshipper.

cultrīx, -īcis [*colo*], F. a female inhabitant; protectress, patroness.

cultus, -a, -um, *p.p. of* **colō.**

cultus, -ūs [*colo*], M. cultivation, tillage; care; mode of life, manners, dress; care of the person, plight.

cum, *prep. with abl.* with.

cum, *adv. temporal,* when, since, while; *causal,* since; *concessive,* although, while.

Cūmae, -ārum, F. an ancient colony of the Chalcidians in Campania, the residence of the Sibyl (vi. 2).

Cūmaeus, -a, -um, *adj.* of Cumæ, Cumæan.

cumba (cymba), -ae, F. a boat, a skiff, a bark.

-cumbō, -ere, -cubuī, -cubitum [√ *cub*], *3. v. n.* lie, recline; *see* **accumbō.**

cumque (cunque), *adv. usually appended to relatives*, -soever.

cumulō, -āre, -āvī, -ātum [*cumulus*], *1. v. a.* heap up, pile up; heap up with, load with: **Acesten muneribus.**

cumulus, -ī, M. a mass, a heap, a pile.

cūnābula, -ōrum [*cunae*], N. *pl.* a cradle; *of a birthplace*, cradle, first home: **gentis nostrae.**

cūnae, -ārum, F. a cradle.

cūnctor, -ārī, -ātus, *1. v. dep.* linger, loiter; hesitate, delay, resist.

cūnctus, -a, -um [*con-* + *iunctus*], *adj. usually pl.* all (*together*), the whole.

cuneus, -ī, M. a wedge; a column (*of attack, in the form of a wedge*); *pl.* the rows of a theatre, benches of spectators.

cunque, *see* cumque.

cupīdō, -inis [*cupio*], F. *rarely* M. desire, longing, eagerness. —*Personified*, Love, Cupid.

cupidus, -a, -um [*cupio*], *adj.* desirous, eager.

cupiō, -ere, -īvī (-iī), -ītum, *3. v. a. and n.* long for, desire, be eager, covet, wish, be anxious, long, burn to.

cupressus, -ī, F. the cypress (a tall evergreen sacred to Pluto, and a sign of death and mourning).

cūr, *interrog. adv.* why? wherefore? for what purpose?

cūra, -ae, F. care, trouble, anxiety, concern, solicitude: **curae ingeminant.** — *Esp. of love*, distress (*of love*), love: **regina gravi saucia curā.** — *Concretely*, loved one, beloved, darling. — *With reference to an object*, solicitude, care, attention, pains, concern: **amantīs curae numen habet** (has in his care). — *In a weaker sense*, regard for, thought of, memory: **amissae parentis.** — *Concretely*, object of care, care, task, business: **quibus cura penum struere** (office). — *Personified in first sense*, Cares: **ultrices** (*pangs of conscience*).

cūrǎlium, -ī (-iī), N. coral.

Curēs, -ium, C. the chief town of the Sabines (vi. 811).

Cūrētes, -um, M. the most ancient inhabitants of Crete, priests of Jupiter (afterwards identified with the Corybantes) (iii. 131).

cūria, -ae, F. the senate house.

cūrō, -āre, -āvī, -ātum [*cura*], *1. v. a.* care for, take care of, be solicitous for, trouble one's self about: **corpora** (refresh). —*With inf.* care to, desire to.

currō, -ere, cucurrī, cursum, *3. v. n.* run, hasten; sail, flow, pass, skim, run, shoot, glide (*of a shooting star*): **stella; tremor; purpura; classis iter tutum** (speed); **aequor** (skim).

currus, -ūs [*curro*], M. a chariot, car; a team (*of horses*).

cursus, -ūs [*curro*], M. a running, course, passage, voyage, journey; pursuit, flight, race; gait, walk, haste; direction, way, course (*of ships, etc.*).

curvāmen, -minis [*curvo*], N. a bending, curve.

curvō, -āre, -āvī, -ātum [*curvus*], *1. v. a.* bend, bow, curve. — **cur-**

vătus, -a, -um, *p.p. as adj.* bent, arched, curved : **gurges** (swelling).

curvus, -a, -um, *adj.* crooked, bent, curved, winding : **puppes; colles; vallis; litus.**

cuspis, -idis, F. a point ; a spear, javelin, lance.

custōdia, -ae [*custos*], F. watch, guard, care, charge ; a guard *or* guardian.

custōdiō, -īre, -īvī *or* **-iī, -ītum** [*custos*], *4. v. a.* watch, guard.

custōs, -ōdis, C. a guard, watch, watchman, keeper, protector, attendant (*of Ascanius*) : **Fama sedet custos** (keeping watch).

-cutiō, -ere, -cussī, -cussum [*the form of* **quatio** *used in compos.*], *3. v. a.* strike.

cutis, -is, F. skin, hide.

Cybelē (-a), -ae, F. a mountain in Phrygia, sacred to Cybele (iii. 111) or Cybēbe, a Phrygian goddess worshipped as mother of the gods. Her worship was orgiastic, accompanied by drums and cymbals. Her effigies were crowned with towers, and her car was drawn by lions.

Cyclades, -um, F. *pl.* a group of islands around Delos in the Ægean Sea (iii. 127).

Cyclōpius, -a, -um, *adj.* of the Cyclopes : **saxa** (i. 201).

Cyclōps, -ōpis, M. a Cyclops. The Cyclopes were giants with one eye in the middle of the forehead. They served as the workmen of Vulcan (iii. 569, viii. 440).

cycnus, -ī, M. a swan.

Cyllēnius, -a, -um, *adj.* of Cyl-

lene, a mountain of Arcadia, the birthplace of Mercury : **Cyllenia proles,** the son born on Cyllene, Mercury (iv. 258).

cymba (cumba), -ae, F. a boat, a skiff, a bark.

cymbium, -ī (-iī), N. a cup, a bowl (*in form of a boat, cf.* **cymba**).

Cȳmodocē, -ēs; -ēa, -ēae, F. a sea nymph (v. 826, x. 225).

Cȳmothoē, -ēs, F. a sea nymph (i. 144).

Cynthia, -ae, F. the Cynthian goddess, Diana.

Cynthius, -ī (-iī), M. the Cynthian god, Apollo.

Cynthus, -ī, M. a mountain in Delos, the birthplace and favorite haunt of Apollo (i. 498).

cyparissus, -ī, F. the cypress (an evergreen tree used at funerals and planted by tombs).

Cyprus, -ī, F. an island in the Mediterranean (i. 622).

Cythēra, -ōrum, N. *pl.* the island south of Laconia (now Cerigo), where Venus landed from the sea (i. 680).

Cyth_ēus, -a, -um, *adj.* of Cythera. — F. *as subst.* **Cytherēa, -ae,** the goddess of Cythera, Venus.

Cytōrius, -a, -um, *adj.* of Cytorus.

Cytōrus, -ī, M. a mountain in Paphlagonia.

Daedalus, -ī [*daedalus,* skilful], M. a famous artisan of Athens who built the Labyrinth, and, escaping from Crete on artificial wings, landed at Cumæ (vi. 14).

Damasichthōn, -onis, M. a son of Niobe.

damma, -ae, F. a doe.

damnō, -āre, -āvī, -ātum [*damnum*], *1. v. a.* sentence, judge, doom, condemn.

damnōsus, -a, -um [*damnum*], *adj.* harmful, injurious.

damnum, -ī, N. harm, injury.

Danaē, -ēs, F. the mother of Perseus.

Danaus, -a, -um, *adj.* of Danaus, a mythic king of Egypt who settled in Argos, father of the Danaidæ, and king of Argos; *less exactly,* Grecian. — M. *pl. as subst.* **Danaī, -ōrum,** the Greeks.

†**daps, dapis,** F. a feast, a banquet, viands.

Dardania, -ae, F. the Trojan land, Troy.

Dardanidēs, -ae, M. son of Dardanus; *esp.* Æneas, descended from him. — *Pl.* the Trojans.

Dardanis, -idis, F. daughter of Dardanus; Trojan woman (Creüsa).

Dardanius, -a, -um, *adj.* of Dardanus; of Troy, Trojan. — F. *as subst.* **Dardania, -ae,** the Trojan land, Troy.

Dardanus, -a, -um, *adj.* of Dardanus, Dardanian; Trojan. — M. *pl. as subst.* **Dardanī, -ōrum,** the Trojans.

Dardanus, -ī, M. son of Jupiter and Electra, founder of the race of Priam and Æneas (iii. 167).

Darēs, -ētis, M. a Trojan boxer (v. 369).

dator, -ōris [√*da* (*in do*)], M. a giver.

Daunias, -adis, F. the realm of Daunus, Apulia.

Daunus, -ī, M. a king of Apulia, father of Turnus (xii. 22).

dē, *prep. with abl.* from, away from, down from, out of. — *Of part from a whole,* from, of, out of. — *Of cause, origin, and material,* from, of: **suo de nomine** (after); **de te suscepta** (begotten by). — *Fig.* of, in regard to, about, concerning, respecting, as to; in accordance with, by: **de more.**

dea, -ae [*deus*], F. a goddess.

dēbellō, -āre, -āvī, -ātum, *1. v. a.* subdue, vanquish, crush, quell.

dēbeō, -ēre, -uī, -itum [*de* + *habeo*], *3. v. a.* owe: **ludibrium** (are destined to be the sport). — *Pass.* be due, be destined, be appointed. — **dēbitus, -a, -um,** *p.p. as adj.* due, destined, appointed.

dēbilis, -e [*de* + *habilis*], *adj.* (unhandy); weak, maimed, powerless, crippled.

dēcēdō, -ere, -cessī, -cessum, *3. v. n.* withdraw, retire, depart.

decem, *indecl. num. adj.* ten.

dēcernō, -ere, -crēvī, -crētum, *3. v. a. and n.* decide, resolve, determine.

dēcerpō, -ere, -cerpsī, -cerptum [*de* + *carpo*], *3. v. a.* pluck off.

decet, decēre, decuit, *no sup.,* *2. v. a. and n.* it befits, behooves, is fitting, is proper. — *Past tenses,* ought.

dēcidō, -ere, -cidī, *no sup.* [*de* + *cado*], *3. v. n.* fall down, fall.

dēcīdō, -ere, -cīdī, -cīsum [*de* + *caedo*], *3. v. a.* cut off, lop.

dēcipiō, -ere, -cēpī, -ceptum [*de* + *capio*], *3. v. a.* deceive, mislead, betray.

Decius, -ī (-iī), M. a Roman gentile name. — *Esp.* two distinguished Romans, P. Decius Mus, who devoted themselves to death in battle for their country, one at Veseris (340 B.C.), the other at Sentinum (295 B.C.) (vi. 824).

dēclārō, -āre, -āvī, -ātum [*clarus*], *1. v. a.* make clear *or* plain; pronounce, proclaim, announce, declare.

dēclīnō, -āre, -āvī, -ātum, *1. v. a. and n.* bend down; lower, cast down; close: lumina somno.

dēcolor, -ōris, *adj.* discolored, stained.

decor, -ōris [*cf. decet*], M. beauty, comeliness, grace.

decorō, -āre, -āvī, -ātum [*decus*], *1. v. a.* make beautiful, adorn, embellish; honor.

decōrus, -a, -um [*cf. decet*], *adj.* decorated, adorned; beautiful, comely, lovely; glorious.

dēcurrō, -ere, -currī (-cucurrī), -cursum, *3. v. n.* run down; sail, fly, rush, march down *or* over; speed along.

decus, -oris [*cf. decet*], N. beauty, comeliness, grace; adornment, ornament; honor, glory, fame. — *Of persons concretely*, glory, pride: decus nostrum.

dēdicō, -āre, -āvī, -ātum, *1. v. a.* dedicate.

dēdignor, -ārī, -ātus, *1. v. dep.* disdain, scorn.

dēdō, -ere, -didī, -ditum, *3. v. a.* give, deliver.

dēdūcō, -ere, -dūxī, -ductum, *3. v. a.* lead down, draw *or* drag down; unfurl; launch; lead away, lead (*on an expedition*).

dēfendō, -ere, -dī, -fēnsum [*de* + †*fendo*, strike], *3. v. a.* ward off, keep off, avert: hunc furorem (defend me from). — *Also*, defend, guard, protect: se telis; defensus fatis.

dēfēnsor, -ōris [*defendo*], M. a defender, a protector, a champion.

dēferō, -ferre, -tulī, -lātum, *irr. v. a.* carry *or* bring down; drive, convey; land in; deliver, report, announce.

dēfessus, -a, -um, *adj.* tired out, worn out, fatigued.

dēficiō, -ere, -fēcī, -fectum (*pass.* defit) [*de* + *facio*], *3. v. a. and n.* give out, fail, be wanting to, cease: navis (sink, *in the sea*); quā deficit ignis (what the fire spares). — *Of persons*, faint, fail, sink, be exhausted.

dēfīgō, -ere, -fīxī, -fīxum, *3. v. a.* fasten down, plant in: hastae defixae (stuck in the ground). — *Fig.* fix, fasten, cast down: lumina; ora.

dēfleō, -ēre, -ēvī, -ētum, *2. v. a.* weep for, mourn for.

dēfluō, -ere, -flūxī, -flūxum, *3. v. n.* flow down, float down; fall, slide.

dēfōrmis, -e [*de, forma*], *adj.* misshapen, hideous.

dēfungor, -fungī, -fūnctus, *3. v. dep.* (perform to the end), finish, complete, have done with, pass through.

dēgener, -eris [de, genus], adj.
degenerate, ignoble.

dēgō, dēgere, no perf. or sup. [de
+ ago], 3. v. a. spend, lead, pass :
vitam.

dehinc [de + hinc], adv. from hence,
hence ; next (in time), hereupon,
then.

dehīscō, -ere, no perf. or sup., 3.
v. n. yawn, gape, open, fly open.

dēiciō, -ere, -iēcī, -iectum [de +
iacio], 3. v. a. throw down, hurl
down, drive down; in death, strike
down, bring down; cast down :
voltum. — dēiectus, -a, -um, p.p.
as adj. downcast, dejected ; deprived of.

deinde [de + inde], adv. from
thence, from here, thence, hence ;
from this or that time on, thereafter, hereafter ; then, thereupon,
next in succession : numquam deinde (never hereafter).

Dēiopēia (-ēa), -ae, F. a nymph
of Juno (i. 72).

Dēiphobē, -ēs, F. the Sibyl at Cumæ, daughter of Glaucus (vi. 36).

Dēiphobus, -ī, M. a son of Priam
(ii. 310).

dēlābor, -lābī, -lāpsus, 3. v. dep.
glide down, fall down; fall into
or upon.

dēliciae, -ārum, F. pl. the delight,
the pet.

dēlictum, -ī [p.p. of delinquo], N.
a fault, an offence.

dēligō, -ere, -lēgī, -lēctum [de +
lego], 3. v. a. pick out, choose, select.

dēliquēscō, -ere, -licuī, no sup.
[de + liquesco], 3. v. inch. melt.

dēlitēscō, -ere, -lituī, no sup. [de

+ latesco], 3. v. inch. hide away,
lie hidden, lurk, skulk.

Dēlius, -a, -um, adj. of Delos, Delian : Apollo (so called from his
birthplace) (iii. 162).

Dēlos, -ī, F. an island in the Ægean,
birthplace of Apollo and Diana
(iv. 144).

delphīn, -īnis, M. a dolphin.

dēlūbrum, -ī [cf. deluo], N. a temple, a shrine.

dēlūdō, -ere, -lūsī, -lūsum, 3. v.
a. mock, deceive, delude, cheat.

dēmēns, -entis [de + mens], adj.
(with the mind away), mad, insane, wild ; foolish, infatuated.

dēmentia, -ae [demens], F. madness, insanity, lunacy, frenzy ;
folly.

dēmergō, -ere, -mersī, -mersum,
3. v. a. sink, submerge.

dēmissē, adv. low.

dēmittō, -ere, -mīsī, -missum, 3.
v. a. send down, let down, let fall,
plunge ; throw out : multos Orco
(despatch) ; neci (consign) ; lacrimas (shed) ; navis (bring to
land). — Also, lower, sink, cast
down, hang down, suspend, droop.
— dēmissus, -a, -um, p.p. let
down, hanging (ex humeris laena) ; downcast ; low, subdued
(vox) ; descended, derived : nomen a magno Iulo.

dēmō, -ere, dēmpsī, dēmptum
[de + emo], 3. v. a. take away,
remove, dispel (curas) ; dempto
fine (without end, forever).

Dēmoleos, -ī, M. a Greek chieftain
in the Trojan War (v. 265).

dēmoror, -ārī, -ātus, 1. v. dep. delay, detain ; linger out : annos.

dēmum [*superl. of de*], adv. at last, at length, finally; at last (*and not before*), not till, only: tum demum (not till then).

dēnī, -ae, -a [*decem*], *distr. num. adj.* ten each, ten (*apiece*); ten.

dēnique, adv. finally, at length, at last.

dēns, dentis, M. a tooth; a fluke (*of an anchor*).

dēnseō, -ēre, *no perf.*,-ētum [*densus*], 2. v. a. make close, close up.

dēnsus, -a, -um, adj. thick, dense, close, crowded, serried: agmen; hostes; nubila; caligo. — *Also*, repeated, frequent: Austri; ictus.

dēnūntiō, -āre, -āvī, -ātum, 1. v. a. announce; threaten.

dēpāscō, -ere, -pāvī, -pāstum (*also pass. as dep.*), 3. v. a. crop, graze, feed upon, consume, tear, devour, waste: artus morsu (*of a serpent*).

dēpellō, -ere, -pulī, -pulsum, 3. v. a. drive off, drive down, drive away; repel, save from: classibus ignem.

dēpendeō, -ēre, *no perf., no sup.*, 2. v. n. hang down, hang from, hang on; depend on.

dēplōrō, -āre, -āvī, -ātum, 1. v. a. bewail, lament; give up for lost.

dēpōnō, -ere, -posuī, -positum, 3. v. a. put down, lay aside, lay down; get rid of, put off; abandon, leave behind.

dēprecor, -ārī, -ātus, 1. v. dep. pray to escape (*cf.* beg off).

dēprehendō (-prēndo), -ere, -prehendī -prehēnsum (-prēnsum), 3. v. a. overtake, catch, seize, find.

dēprēnsus, -a, -um, *p.p. of* dēprehendō.

dēprōmō, -ere, -prōmpsī, -prōmptum, 3. v. a. draw out (*for use*): tela pharetris.

Dercennus, -ī, M. an ancient king of the Latins (xi. 850).

dērigēscō, -ere, -riguī, *no sup.*, 3. v. inch. become stiff, swoon: sanguis (freeze). — *Also of the hair*, rise, bristle up.

dēripiō, -ere, -ripuī, -reptum [*de + rapio*], 3. v. a. snatch off, snatch down, tear away, tear off, drag down (*with speed*).

dēsaeviō, -īre, -iī, *no sup.*, 4. v. n. rage off *or* away, spend one's rage: pelago hiems.

dēscendō, -ere, -scendī, -scēnsum [*de + scando*], 3 v. n. climb down, come down, go down, descend, fall; sink down, sink in, penetrate (toto corpore pestis); descend to, give way to: preces in omnis.

dēscēnsus, -ūs [*descendo*], M. a descent.

dēscrībō, -ere, -scrīpsī, -scrīptum, 3. v. a. mark off, write off; write down, draw, map out, portray.

dēserō, -ere, -seruī, -sertum, 3. v. a. forsake, leave, abandon, quit, depart from: me; Lyciam; sedem. — dēsertus, -a, -um, *p.p. as adj.* abandoned, deserted, desolate, lonely, desert. — N. *pl.* solitudes, wilderness, desert, desert regions: Libyae.

dēserta, *see* dēserō.

dēsertor, -ōris [*desero*], M. a deserter, renegade, runaway.

dēsīderium, -ī (-iī) [*desidero*], N.
longing; an object of desire.

dēsīderō, -āre, -āvī, -ātum, *1. v.
a.* long for, desire.

dēsīdō, -ere, -sēdī, *no sup.*, *3. v.
n.* sink down.

dēsignō, -āre, -āvī, -ātum, *1. v. a.*
mark off, mark out.

dēsiliō, -īre, -siluī, -sultum [*de
+ salio*], *4. v. n.* leap down, leap,
spring.

dēsinō, -ere, -sīvī (-siī), -situm,
3. v. n. stop, close, end, cease.

dēsistō, -ere, -stitī, -stitum, *3.
v. n.* leave off, cease, forbear,
desist: incepto.

dēsōlō, -āre, -āvī, -ātum [*solus*],
1. v. a. lay waste.

dēspectō, -āre, *no perf.*, *no sup.*,
1. v. a. look down upon.

dēspiciō, -ere, -spexī, -spectum
[*de + specio*], *3. v. a.* look down
on: terras Iuppiter. — *Fig.* despise, scorn.

dēstinō, -āre, -āvī, -ātum, *1. v. a.*
set fast; doom, destine (me arae);
promise.

dēstituō, -ere, -stituī, -stitūtum
[*de + statuo*], *3. v. a.* leave.

dēstringō, -ere, -strīnxī, -stric-
tum, *3. v. a.* draw (*a sword*).

dēstruō, -ere, -ūxī, -ūctum, *3.
v. a.* tear down, demolish, destroy.

dēsuēscō, -ere, -suēvī, -suē-
tum, *3. v. a. and n.* disuse, lose a
custom. — dēsuētus, -a, -um,
p.p. as adj. disused, unused, unaccustomed: arma; agmina triumphis; corda.

dēsuētus, -a, -um, *p.p. of* dēsuēscō.

dēsum, -esse, -fuī, -futūrus, *irr.
v. n.* be away, be absent, be wanting, fail.

dēsuper, *adv.* from above.

dētegō, -ere, -tēxī, -tēctum, *3.
v. a.* uncover, disclose, unroof.

dētineō, -ēre, -tinuī, -tentum
[*de + teneo*], *2. v. a.* hold, detain.

dētorqueō, -ēre, -torsī, -tortum
(-torsum), *2. v. a.* turn off, turn
aside, turn, divert.

dētrahō, -ere, -trāxī, -trāctum,
3. v. a. drag off, drag away, draw
off, pull off; take away, steal.

dētrūdō, -ere, -trūsī, -trūsum,
3. v. a. thrust off, shove off: navis
scopulo. — *Also*, thrust down,
drive: Iovem regnis.

dēturbō, -āre, -āvī, -ātum, *1. v.
a.* hurl off, hurl down; drive off,
drive out: praecipitem a puppi;
animas.

deus, -ī (*pl.* deī, diī, dī), M. a god,
a deity. — *Sing. collectively*, the
divinity, the Deity. — *Without
distinction of sex*, a deity (*female*),
a goddess.

dēveniō, -īre, -vēnī, -ventum, *4.
v. n.* come down, descend. —
Esp. (*from the rising of the sea
towards the horizon*), arrive at,
come to, land at.

dēvolō, -āre, -āvī, -ātum, *1. v. n.*
fly down.

dēvolvō, -ere, -volvī, -volūtum,
3. v. a. roll down: trabes.

dēvorō, -āre, -āvī, -ātum, *1. v. a.*
devour, swallow up, engulf; repress: lacrimas.

dēvoveō, -ēre, -vōvī, -vōtum, *2.
v. a.* (vow away), devote, doom,
curse.

dexter, -tera, -terum (-tra, -trum), *adj.* the right (*opp. to* **laevus,** left), on the right side ; skilful, dexterous. — *From the custom of omens,* propitious. — F. *as subst.* (*sc.* **manus**) **dextra, -ae,** the right hand : **data** (*given as a pledge,* plighted faith).

dī, diī, *see* **deus.**

Dĭāna, -ae, F. the goddess of the moon, sister of Apollo, identified with Hecate.

diciō (*not found in nom. sing.*), **-ōnis** [*dico*], F. command, sway, power, control, dominion.

dicō, -āre, -āvī, -ātum, *1. v. a.* devote, assign, dedicate.

dīcō, -ere, dīxī, dictum, *3. v. a.* speak, say, tell ; command ; sing, celebrate (*in song or story*) ; name, call.

Dictaeus, -a, -um, *adj.* of Dicte (a mountain in Crete) ; Cretan, of Crete.

dictum, -ī [*p.p. of dico as subst.*], N. a word, a saying, speech, command : **dicto parere ; citius dicto.**

Dīdō, -ūs (-ōnis), F. the founder of Carthage, called also Elissa.

dīdūcō, -ere, -dūxī, -ductum [*dis- + duco*], *3. v. a.* draw apart, separate, divide ; distract.

Didymāōn, -onis, M. a famous artist in metal (v. 359).

diēs, -ēī, C. a day, daylight, day-time ; time, lapse of time ; proper time, fitting time, allotted time.

Diespiter, -tris, M. Jupiter.

ɗifferō, differre, distulī, dīlātum [*dis- + fero*], *irr. v. a.* put off, defer, delay.

difficilis, -e [*dis- + facilis*], *adj.* not easy, difficult, hard : **obitus** (painful, reluctant, *from stubborn resistance to death*) ; **scopuli** (dangerous).

diffīdō, -ere, -fīsus [*dis- + fido*], *3. v. n.* distrust, have no confidence in : **armis.**

diffugiō, -ere, -fūgī, *no sup.* [*dis- + fugio*], *3. v. n.* fly apart, scatter, disperse, flee (*in different directions*).

diffundō, -ere, -fūdī, -fūsum [*dis- + fundo*], *3. v. a.* pour away *or* forth ; scatter abroad, scatter, spread abroad : **haec in ora virum.**

dīgerō, -ere, -gessī, -gestum [*dis- + gero*], *3. v. a.* carry apart, separate ; arrange, dispose ; interpret, explain : **omina ; digestos colores** (in order).

digitus, -ī, M. a finger, a toe.

dignor, -ārī, -ātus [*dignus*], *1. v. dep.* deem worthy : me honore. — *With an action as obj.* deign, think fit : **sternere.** — **dignātus, -a, -um,** *p.p.* deemed worthy.

dignus, -a, -um, *adj.* worthy, deserving, suitable, fitting, fit, due.

dīgredior, -gredī, -gressus [*dis- + gradior*], *3. v. dep.* step aside, come away, depart : **e bello.**

dīgressus, -ūs [*digredior*], M. a departure, a parting.

diī, *see* **deus.**

dīiūdicō, -āre, -āvī, -ātum [*dis- + iudico*], *1. v. a.* decide (*judicially*).

dīlābor, -lābī, -lāpsus [*dis- + labor*], *3. v. dep.* glide away, depart : **calor** (leave the body).

dīlacerō, -āre, -āvī, -ātum [*dis- + lacero*], *1. v. a.* tear to pieces.

dīligō, -ere, -lēxī, -lēctum [*dis-* + *lego*], 3. *v. a.* (choose out); love, esteem; cherish. — dīlēctus, -a, -um, *p.p. as adj.* loved, beloved, dear.

dīmittō, -ere, -mīsī, -missum [*dis-* + *mitto*], 3. *v. a.* send away, let go, dismiss, send forth, send off.

dīmoveō, -ēre, -mōvī, -mōtum [*dis-* + *moveo*], 2. *v. a.* separate, move aside, part, cleave: aëra; polo umbram (disperse).

dīnumerō, -āre, -āvī, -ātum [*dis-* + *numero*], 1. *v. a.* reckon, calculate, count up.

Diomēdēs, -is, M. son of Tydeus, a famous Greek warrior at Troy (i. 752).

Diōnaeus, -a, -um, *adj.* of Dione (the mother of Venus), Dionæan: mater (*i. e.* Venus) (iii. 19).

Diōrēs, -is, M. a Trojan of the race of Priam (v. 297).

Dīrae, *see* dīrus.

dīrigō, -ere, -rēxī, -rēctum [*dis-* + *rego*] 3. *v. a.* dispose in line, arrange; aim, turn, direct: tela; cursum; gressum. — *P.p. as adj.*: dīrēctus, -a, -um, straight.

dīrimō, -ere, -ēmī, -ēmptum [*dis-* + *emo*, take], 3. *v. a.* take apart, separate, divide; end, put an end to: proelia.

dīripiō, -ere, -ripuī, -reptum [*dis-* + *rapio*], 3. *v. a.* tear away, tear asunder, snatch apart: tergora costis (strip). — *Of booty*, plunder, rifle, ravage, spoil: dapes (*of the Harpies*); direpta domus.

dīruō, -ere, -ruī, -rūtum [*dis-* + *ruo*], 3. *v. a.* destroy, ruin.

dīrus, -a, -um, *adj.* dire, dread, horrible, awful, frightful; ominous, ill-omened.— F. *pl. as subst.* Dīrae, -ārum, the Furies.

dīs, dītis, *see* dīves.

Dīs, Dītis [*akin to dives*], M. the god of the Lower World, Pluto.

dis- (dī-) [*akin to duo*], *insep. adv.* expressing *separation, distribution, opposition, and negation.*

discēdō, -ere, -cessī, -cessum, 3. *v. n.* go apart, go away, withdraw: bello (abandon).

discernō, -ere, -crēvī, -crētum, 3. *v. a.* put by, separate, divide; embroider; distinguish: diem noctemque (day from night).

discerpō, -ere, -cerpsī, -cerptum [*dis-+carpo*], 3. *v. a.* tear to pieces, mangle; scatter.

discessus, -ūs [*discedo*], M. a departure, a parting.

discō, -ere, didicī, *no sup.*, 3. *v. a.* learn, find out, come to know; learn how: currere.

discolor, -ōris, *adj.* of different color *or* colors, variegated.

discordia, -ae [*discors*], F. disagreement, discordance, discord. — *Personified*, Discord.

discors, -cordis [*dis-* + *cor*], *adj.* differing, varying, discordant: ora.

discrīmen, -inis [*cf.* discerno], N. a separation, a distinction; a division, a difference, an interval: vocum septem (notes of the scale); parvo leti (slight separation, narrow escape from death). — *Also*, a decision, a turning-point, a crisis, peril, hazard.

discumbō, -ere, -cubuī, -cubitum, 3. *v. n.* recline.

discurrō, -ere, -cucurrī (-currī), -cursum, *3. v. n.* run apart, separate, divide.

discursus, -ūs, M. a scattering.

discutiō, -ere, -cussī, -cussum [*dis-* + *quatio*], *3. v. a.* scatter, shake apart.

disertus, -a, -um, *p.p.* of disserō *as adj.* eloquent.

disiciō, -ere, -iēcī, -iectum [*dis-* + *iacio*], *3. v. a.* throw apart *or* aside, scatter, disperse, strew far and wide; demolish, shatter: rates. — disiectus, -a, -um, *p.p. as adj.* scattered, disordered, broken.

disiungō, -ere, -iūnxī, -iūnctum, *3. v. a.* disjoin, separate: Italis oris (drive from).

dispār, -paris, *adj.* unequal, of different lengths.

dispellō, -ere, -pulī, -pulsum, *3. v. a.* drive apart, force asunder; dissipate, dispel, scatter: umbras Somnus (cleave *by passing through*).

dispendium, -ī (-iī) [*dispendo*], N. (a paying out), expense, cost: morae.

dispēnsō, -āre, -āvī, -ātum, *1. v. a.* distribute.

dispergō, -ere, -spersī, -spersum [*dis-* + *spargo*], *3. v. a.* scatter, disperse.

dispiciō, -ere, -spexī, -spectum [*dis-* + *specio*], *3. v. a.* see, discern.

dispōnō, -ere, -posuī, -positum, *3. v. a.* (place here and there), arrange, set in order.

dissēnsus, -ūs [*dissentio*], M. dissension, discord.

dissiliō, -īre, -siluī, *no sup.* [*dis-* + *salio*], *4. v. n.* spring apart, leap apart, burst asunder.

dissimulō, -āre, -āvī, -ātum, *1. v. a. and n.* dissemble, conceal; hide one's feelings; remain hidden.

dissipō, -āre, -āvī, -ātum, *1. v. a.* scatter.

dissultō, -āre, *no perf. or sup.*, *1. v. n.* spring apart.

distendō, -ere, -tendī, -tentum (-tēnsum), *3. v. a.* stretch apart, distend, fill, store: nectare cellas.

distinguō, -ere, -tīnxī, -tīnctum, *3. v. a.* separate. — *P.p. as adj.* different, various, varied.

distō, distāre, *no perf., no sup.* [*dis-* + *sto*], *1. v. n.* stand off; be distant; differ.

distringō, -ere, -strīnxī, strictum [*dis-* + *stringo*], *3. v. a.* bind apart, stretch and bind; draw (*a sword*).

dītissimus, *see* dīves.

diū [*akin to dies*], *adv.* long, a long time.

dīvellō, -ere, -vellī, -volsum (-vulsum) [*dis-* + *vello*], *3. v. a.* tear asunder, tear to pieces, tear away.

dīverberō, -āre, -āvī, -ātum [*dis-* + *verbero*], *1. v. a.* cut asunder, cleave.

dīversus, -a, -um, *p.p.* of dīvertō.

dīvertō (-vortō), -ere, -vertī, -versum (-vorsum) [*dis-* + *verto*], *3. v. a. and n.* turn aside. —dīversus, -a, -um, *p.p as adj.* in different direction *or* directions, apart, separate, away; remote, far off; different, other, various, unlike: **ramus** (peculiar); **luctus** (different forms of); **ex diverso** (from a different quarter, from different directions).

dīves, dīvitis, *adj.* rich, abounding in, wealthy; precious: **ramus.** — *Collateral form,* **dīs, dītis (dītior, dītissimus).**

dīvidō, -ere, -vīsī, -vīsum, *3. v. a.* part, separate, divide, cut through, leave: **animum** (turn in different directions); **muros** (make a breach in).

dīvīnus, -a, -um [*divus*], *adj.* of a god, heavenly; prophetic; sacred, holy, godlike, divine: **parens; decor; ars.**

dīvitiae, -ārum [*dives*], F. *pl.* riches, wealth.

dīvortium, -ī (-iī) [*divorto*], N. a turning aside; a parting way, crossroads.

dīvus, -a, -um, *adj.* divine, godlike, heavenly. — M. **dīvus, -ī,** a god. — F. **dīva, -ae,** a goddess. — N. **dīvum, -ī,** the sky: **sub divo** (under the open sky).

dō, dare, dedī, datum, *1. v. a.* give (*in all senses, mixed with the idea of putting forth*), offer, present, bestow, grant, concede, permit, allow, afford, yield, supply: **aprum dari optat; fortuna dabatur; sceptra** (give away); **fata cursum** (ordain); **milia leto** (consign). — *Esp. of utterance,* say, tell, utter: **dicta; responsa.** — *With reflexive or* **corpora,** throw one's self, consign one's self, spring: **memet super ipsa dedissem; corpora ignibus.** — *In special phrases:* **poenas,** suffer,

cf. **solvo, luo, pendo** (*punishment being regarded by the ancients as a penalty paid*); **iura (leges),** administer. — *Also,* cause, give forth, display, make, form, produce, bring forth, *oftener with nouns as periphrasis for a verb:* **placata venti maria; prolem** (give birth to); **tabulata iuncturas** (offer, afford); **sonitum; gemitum; amplexus** (embrace); **dat corpore tortūs** (coils); **vela** (set, spread).

doceō, -ēre, docuī, doctum, *2. v. a.* show, teach, tell, explain, inform, recount. — **doctus, -a, -um,** *p.p. as adj.* skilled, skilful, experienced.

Dōdōnaeus, -a, -um, *adj.* of Dodona, a city of Epirus, famous for its oracle of Jupiter in an oak grove and for its manufacture of bronze (iii. 466).

doleō, -lēre, -luī, (-litūrus), *2. v. n. and a.* feel pain, suffer; grieve, grieve for, deplore, be sorry, sorrow.

Dolō, -ōnis, M. a Trojan scout.

Dolopes, -um, M. *pl.* a people of Thessaly who served under Achilles in the Trojan War, associated with the Myrmidons (ii. 7).

dolor, -ōris [*doleo*], M. a pain, a pang, suffering, sorrow, grief; resentment, indignation; a grievance.

dolus, -ī, M. a stratagem, a wile; deception, deceit, treachery (*esp. in pl.*).

domina, -ae [F. *of dominus*], F. a mistress, a lady, a queen (*used of mortals and of goddesses*).

dominor, -āri, -ātus [*dominus*], *1. v. dep.* lord it over, rule, govern, gain the mastery.

dominus, -ī, M. a lord, a ruler, a master.

domitor, -ōris [*domo*], M. a tamer, a subduer: maris (queller).

domō, -āre, -uī, -itum, *1. v. a.* tame, quell, subdue, vanquish, conquer, master.

domus, -ūs *or* **-ī,** F. a building, a house, a dwelling, a home, a habitation, home. — *Fig.* a house, a family, a race, a lineage. — *Acc.* domum, home. — *Locative,* domī, at home.

dōnārium, -ī (-iī) [*dono*], N. an offering.

dōnec, *adv.* until, till.

dōnō, -āre, -āvī, -ātum [*donum*], *1. v. a.* give, present (*with acc. and dat., something to somebody*). — *From another point of view,* present, endow, reward (*with acc. and abl., somebody with something*): Sergestum munere; donati omnes; donatus (honored with a present).

dōnum, -ī, N. a gift, a present, a reward.

Donūsa, -ae, F. a small island in the Ægean, famous for its green marble (iii. 125).

Dōricus, -a, -um, *adj.* of the Dorians (a division of the Greeks), Doric; of the Greeks, Grecian.

dorsum, -ī, N. a back; a ridge, a reef.

Doryclus, -ī, M. the husband of Beroe (v. 620).

dōs, dōtis [*do*], F. a marriage portion, dowry.

dōtālis, -e [*dos*], *adj.* of a marriage portion, as a dowry, given as a dowry.

dracō, -ōnis, M. a serpent, a dragon. — *Pl.* dragon chariot.

Drepanum, -ī, N. a town on the west coast of Sicily, now Trapani (iii. 707).

Drūsus, -ī, M. a name in the gens Livia and gens Claudia. — *Esp.* M. Livius Drusus, tribune 91 B. C. *and* Tib. Drusus Nero, a stepson of Augustus (vi. 824).

Dryades, -um, F. *pl.* Dryads, wood nymphs.

Dryopes, -um, M. *pl.* a Pelasgic tribe originally living near Parnassus (iv. 146).

dubitō, -āre -āvī, -ātum [*dubius*], *1. v. n. and a.* doubt, waver, question; hesitate (*with inf.*). — **dubitandus, -a, -um,** *ger. as adj.* to be doubted, questionable, doubtful.

dubius, -a, -um, *adj.* doubtful, wavering, in doubt, uncertain: res (critical). — *Fig.* unsteady: puppis.

dūcō, -ere, dūxī, ductum, *3. v. a.* guide, lead, conduct, escort, command: natum; Aenean; turmas; agmina. — *Fig. of a path,* lead, conduct: quā te ducit via. — *Of stars,* bring in, usher in: Lucifer diem. — *Of things,* draw: crinem sidera; facem stella; gemitus; pectora per augurium (lead); muros (extend). — *Esp. of lots,* draw, select (*by lot*): ductis sortibus; ductus sorte sacerdos. — *Of artistic work,* bring forth, draw, fashion: ensem;

vivos voltus. — *Of race or line of descent*, derive, draw: **genus; ducta series** (descending, coming down). — *Of time and condition*, lead, pass: **vitam** (drag out); **somnos** (enjoy). — *Also,* prolong, delay, draw out: **horas; voces.** — *From mercantile use*, reckon, consider, think, deem: **ducebam sic animo.**

ductor, -ōris [*duco*], M. a leader, a commander, a captain.

dūdum [*diu + dum*], *adv.* a while ago, just now; a long time ago, long ago.

dulcis, -e, *adj. of taste and smell*, sweet, fragrant; fresh (*of water*); pleasant, delightful, charming; dear, much loved. — N. *as cogn. acc.* sweetly.

Dūlichium, -ī (-iī), N. an island near Ithaca (iii. 271).

dum, *conj.* while, so long as; until.

dūmus, -ī, M. a bush, a briar, a bramble bush; thicket.

duo, duae, duo, *num. adj.* two.

duplex, -icis [*duo + †plex; cf. plico*], *adj.* twofold, double; **palmae** (both).

duplicō, -āre, -āvī, -ātum [*duplex*], *1. v. a.* double up, double: **duplicato poplite** (bent).

dūritia, -ae [*durus*], F. hardness.

dūrō, -āre, -āvī, -ātum [*durus*], *1. v. n. and a.* endure, persevere, hold out; hold out against, withstand; harden, congeal.

dūrus, -a, -um, *adj.* hard (*to the touch*), unyielding; hardy, toilworn; grievous, severe, difficult, toilsome, bitter (**casus; dolores**); harsh, cruel, fierce, savage, un-

feeling: **tempore duro** (time of misfortune).

dux, ducis [*duco*], C. a guide, a leader, a conductor; a driver (*of a chariot*); a chief, a leader, a king, a master; a pilot.

Dymās, -antis, M. a Trojan warrior (ii. 340).

ē, *see* ex.

ebur, -oris, N. ivory; a sheath.

eburnus, -a, -um [*ebur*], *adj.* of ivory, ivory; ivory-hilted.

ecce [*en + -ce*], *interj.* lo, see, behold.

Echīon, -ionis, M. one of the warriors sprung from the dragon's teeth sown by Cadmus.

ecquis (-quī), -qua, -quid (-quod) [*en + quis*], *pron. indef. interrog.* (whether) any? any at all? does (is) any?

edāx, -ācis [*edo*], *adj.* voracious; devouring, consuming: **ignis.**

ēdīcō, -ere, -dīxī, -dictum, *3. v. a.* (say publicly, publish), *properly of official announcement*, order, proclaim, charge, command.

ēdisserō, -ere, -seruī, -sertum, *3. v. a.* set forth (*in discourse*), declare, explain, relate.

edō, edere (ēsse), ēdī, ēsum, *3. v. a.* eat; consume, devour: **est flamma medullas; vapor carinas.**

ēdō, ēdere, ēdidī, ēditum, *3. v. a.* put forth, give forth; utter, set forth, speak. — *Pass.* spring, originate.

ēdoceō, -ēre, -docuī, -doctum, *2. v. a.* show forth, teach, declare, inform (*one*) of (*a thing, acc.*).

ēdūcō, -ere, -dūxī, -ductum, 3. *v. a.* lead forth, draw forth; raise up, build high: **turrim eductam**. — *Of a mother*, bring forth, bear. — *Of metals*, forge, work: **moenia educat caminis**.

efferō, efferre, extulī, ēlātum [*ex + fero*], *irr. v. a.* bring forth, carry out, bear away: **quos ex ignibus** (rescue); **ensem** (draw); **gressum** *or* **pedem** (go forth).— *With reflexive*, come forth, go forth. — *Of height*, raise, lift up, lift: **caput; bracchia ad auras; tellus elata mari**. — *With reflexive*, arise. — *Less exactly*, put forth, show forth, display: **puppis flammas; aurora diem; ortūs Titan**.

efferus, -a, -um [*ex + ferus*], *adj.* wild, maddened.

effētus, -a, -um [*ex + fetus*, *p.p.* of feo], *adj.* exhausted, worn out.

efficiō, -ere, -fēcī, -fectum [*ex + facio*], 3. *v. a.* make out, form, make.

effigiēs, -ēī [*effingo*], F. an image, a statue, a likeness, a resemblance, a copy.

effingō, -ere, -fīnxī, -fictum [*ex + fingo*], 3. *v. a.* form, mould, fashion; represent, imitate.

effluō, -ere, -flūxī, *no sup.* [*ex + fluo*], 3. *v. n.* flow forth; fall (*from one's hands*); escape.

effodiō, -ere, -fōdī, -fossum [*ex + fodio*], 3. *v. a.* dig out, dig up; make (*by digging*), dig; tear out, bore out: **lumen** (*of the Cyclops' eye*).

effor, -ārī, -ātus [*ex + for*], *1. v.* *dep.* speak out, say; tell, relate, disclose, divulge.

effringō, -ere, -frēgī, -frāctum [*ex + frango*], 3. *v. a.* break out, dash out.

effugiō, -ere, -fūgī, *no sup.* [*ex + fugio*], 3. *v. n. and a.* flee away, escape, fly from, speed away.

effugium, -ī (-iī) [*effugio*], N. an escape, a flight.

effulgeō, -ēre, -fulsī, *no sup.* [*ex + fulgeo*], 2. *v. n.* shine forth, gleam, glitter. (*Also* -ere, *3.*)

effundō, -ere, -fūdī, -fūsum [*ex + fundo*], 3. *v. a. and n.* pour out, pour forth, shed, breathe out: **lacrimas; fletus; questus; voces; halitus; animam** (sacrifice); **effusi imbres** (drenching rain). — *Also*, scatter, fling, let loose, waste: **crinis effusa sacerdos** (with dishevelled hair); **habenas; viris**. — *In pass.* rush headlong, pour forth, rush out: **turba effusa ruebat; effusi nimbo similes**. — *P.p.* effūsus, -a, -um, spread out, wide-spread; *of a sail*, full; *of rain*, in torrents.

ēgelidus, -a, -um, *adj.* (not cold), mild.

egēns, *p. of* egeō.

egēnus, -a, -um [*egeo*], *adj.* needy, destitute: **res** (humble, straitened).

egeō, -ēre, eguī, *no sup.*, 2. *v. n.* be in need, need, lack, be destitute, want; require, feel the need of, care for: **tali auxilio**. — egēns, -entis, *p. as adj.* poor, needy, destitute; desirous.

egestās, -tātis [*egeo*], F. poverty, want, need. — *Personified*, Want.

ego, meī, *pron.* I, myself.

egomet [*ego* + *-met*], *pron.* I myself.

ēgredior, -gredī, -gressus [*e* + *gradior*], *3. v. dep.* walk forth, come forth, set out, start; land, disembark.

ēgregius, -a, -um [*e-grege*], *adj.* (out of the herd), remarkable, excellent; famous, renowned, illustrious, noble.

ēgressus, -ūs [*egredior*], M. a way of escape.

eheu, *interj.* woe! alas

ei, *interj.* ah, alas: ei mihi (ah me!).

ēiaculor, -ārī, -ātus, *1. v. dep.* shoot forth, spout forth.

ēiciō, -ere, ēiēcī, ēiectum [*e* + *iacio*], *3. v. a.* throw out, cast out; cast up (*on shore from shipwreck*). — ēiectus, -a, -um, *p.p. as adj.* thrown on shore, shipwrecked.

ēiectō, -āre, -āvī, -ātum [*e* + *iacto*], *1. v. freq.* cast forth, vomit.

ēlābor, -lābī, -lāpsus, *3. v. dep.* glide out, dart forth, slip away.

ēlegāns, -antis, *adj.* fine, choice.

elephantus, -ī, M. an elephant; ivory.

Eleusīn, -īnis, F. Eleusis, a town in Attica, famous for the Eleusinian Mysteries.

ēliciō, -ere, -licuī (-lexī), -licitum [*e* + *lacio*], *3. v. a.* call forth, call down.

Ēlicius, -ī (-iī), M. a surname of Jupiter.

ēlīdō, -ere, -līsī, -līsum [*e* + *laedo*], *3. v. a.* dash out, force out. — ēlīsus, -a, -um, *p.p. as adj.* dashed up, dashing (*of spray*).

ēligō, -ere, -lēgī, -lēctum [*e* + *lego*], *3. v. a.* choose.

Ēlis, -idis, F. a district in western Peloponnesus, famous on account of its chief city, Olympia, where the Olympic games were held (iii. 694; vi. 588).

Elissa, -ae, F. a name of Dido (iv. 335).

ēloquium, -ī (-iī) [*eloquor*], N. eloquence, oratory.

ēloquor, -loquī, -locūtus, *3. v. dep.* speak out, relate, speak, tell.

Elpēnor, -oris, M. a companion of Ulysses.

ēlūdō, -ere, -sī, -sum, *3. v. a.* escape, deceive.

ēluō, -ere, -luī, -lūtum, *3. v. a.* wash out, wash off; wash away, atone for.

Ēlysium, -ī (-iī), N. Elysium, the abode of the blessed dead (vi. 542).

ēmētior, -īrī, -mēnsus, *4. v. dep.* measure out, measure off, measure; traverse, pass through: saxa sideraque.

ēmicō, -āre, -cuī, -cātum, *1. v. n.* spring out, leap out, leap up, spring up, spring forth, bound forward.

ēmineō, -ēre, -uī, *no sup.,* *2. v. n.* rise above (*the surface*).

ēminus [*e, manus*], *adv.* at *or* from a distance, from afar.

ēmittō, -ere, -mīsī, -missum, *3. v. a.* send forth, let go forth, let loose.

ēmoveō, -ēre, -mōvī, -mōtum, *2. v. a.* displace, remove: **cardine postis** (force); **emotae curae** (dispelled); **emota fundamenta** (upturned). — *Also*, move forth, display (sol orbem).

ēmūniō, -īre, -iī, -ītum, *4. v. a.* fortify, protect, secure.

ēn, *interj.* lo! behold! — *In question or exclamation with feeling of surprise, impatience, eagerness, or despair*, ah! pray!

Enceladus, -ī, M. one of the giants, son of Tartarus and the Earth. He was killed with the thunderbolt by Jupiter and buried under Ætna (iii. 578).

enim, *conj.* namely, for (*explaining a preceding assertion*), precisely.

ēniteō, -ēre, -uī, *no sup.*, *2. v. n.* shine forth, beam.

ēnītor, -nītī, -nīsus (-nīxus), *3. v. dep.* bring forth, bear children.

ēnō, -āre, -āvī, -ātum, *1. v. n.* swim out; float away, fly away.

ēnsis, -is, M. a sword.

Entellus, -ī, M. a Sicilian boxer (v. 387).

ēnumerō, -āre, -āvī, -ātum, *1. v. a.* count out; recount, enumerate, rehearse.

eō, īre, īvī (iī), itum [√i], *irr. v. n.* go (*in all senses*). — *Impers.* ītur, one goes.

eōdem, *adv.* to the same place.

Ēōus, -a, -um, *adj.* of the dawn, of the morning, Eastern. — M. *sing. as subst.* **Ēōus, -ī**, the dawn, the morning, the morning star; *pl.* the men of the East.

Epēos, -ī, M. the designer of the Trojan horse (ii. 264).

Ēpīrus, -ī, F. a district of Greece, on the Adriatic (iii. 292).

epulae, -ārum (-um, -ī), F. *pl.* a banquet, a feast; food, viands.

epulor, -ārī, -ātus [epulum], *1. v. dep.* feast, banquet: **dapibus** (feast on).

Ēpytidēs, -ae, M. son of Epytus (v. 547).

Ēpytus, -ī, M. a Trojan (ii. 340).

eques, -itis [equus], M. a rider, a horseman, a trooper; *pl.* cavalry, horsemen, horse. — *Esp.* a knight, a member of the equestrian order.

equester (equestris), -tris, -tre [eques], *adj.* of horsemen, equestrian.

equidem, *adv. of asseveration or concession*, surely, truly, by all means, no doubt, I am sure: **hoc equidem** (this at least); **haud equidem dignor** (I do not, to be sure); **atque equidem** (and in fact I do).

equitō, -āre, -āvī, -ātum [eques], *1. v. n.* ride, ride on raids.

equus, -ī, M. a horse.

Erebus, -ī, M. the god of darkness (iv. 510); the Lower World, Hades (iv. 26).

ergō, adv. As *prep. with genitive*, for the sake of, on account of: **illius ergo** (on his account). — As *illative particle*, therefore, consequently, then.

Ēridanus, -ī, M. the Greek name for the Po (vi. 659).

ērigō, -ere, -rēxī, -rēctum [e + rego], *3. v. a.* set up straight, raise, erect, set up, rear; build: **pyram; scopulos** (throw up).

Erīnys, -yos, F. a Fury (ii. 337); an evil genius, a curse (ii. 573).

Eriphȳlē, -ēs, F. the wife of Amphiaraus, who betrayed her husband for a golden necklace (vi. 445).

ēripiō, -ere, -ripuī, -reptum [*e* + *rapio*], *3. v. a.* snatch from *or* away, wrest, catch up, tear away, take away, steal, seize, rob one of (*a thing*): **vaginā ensem** (*i. e.* unsheathe); **mentem**; **nubes** (shut out). — *Esp. from danger, etc.* rescue, snatch: **me leto**; **fugam** (hasten one's flight); **eripite socii** (save yourselves).

errō, -āre, -āvī, -ātum, *1. v. n.* wander, rove, stray, roam; lose one's way; waver, wander (*of the eyes*); float, fly (**manus,** *of blows*), linger (**halitus**); wander from the truth. — **errātus, -a, -um,** *p.p.* wandered over. — N. *pl.* wanderings.

error, -ōris [*erro*], M. a wandering, turning, maze (*of the Labyrinth*); a mistake, an error, confusion; madness; deceit.

ērubēscō, -ere, -buī, *no sup., 3. v. n. and a.* redden, blush, be ashamed; respect, reverence.

ēructō, -āre, -āvī, -ātum, *1. v. n. and a.* belch forth.

ērudiō, -īre, -īvī (-iī), -ītum [*e, rudis*], *4. v. a.* (free from roughness), teach.

ērumpō, -ere, -rūpī, -ruptum, *3. v. a.* burst out from, break through: **nubem.**

ēruō, -ere, -ruī, -rutum, *3. v. a.* dig out, tear out, tear *or* pull up, undermine, overturn (*of walls, etc.*). destroy utterly: **opes.**

erus, -ī, M. a master, a lord.

Erycīna, -ae, F. Venus, the goddess of Eryx (a Sicilian town, famous for its temple of Venus).

Erycīnus, -a, -um, *adj.* of Eryx in Sicily (v. 759).

Erymanthus, -ī, M. a mountain in Arcadia, where Hercules killed the Erymanthian boar (v. 448).

Erythēïs, -idis, *adj.* F. of Erythea, an island off the coast of Spain.

Eryx, -ycis, M. 1. A mountain of Western Sicily, with a town of the same name (now San Giuliano) (i. 570). — 2. A son of Venus, killed by Hercules in a boxing match (v. 392 ff.).

ēst, *see* **edō.**

et, *conj.* and (*stronger than* -que *and weaker than* atque). — *With correlative conj.* **et . . . et,** both . . . and, and at the same time (*omitting the first*); **et . . . que,** both . . . and. — *With emphasis,* and that too, even, and also, and lo! and then; as well.

etiam [*et* + *iam*], *conj.* even now, still, yet; and now (*in addition to what has been stated before*), even, also, likewise.

etiamnum, *adv.* yet, still, even now.

Etrūria, -ae, F. a country of Central Italy (xii. 232).

Etrūscus, -a, -um, *adj.* Etruscan, of Etruria. — M. *pl.* the Etruscans.

etsī [*et* + *si*], *conj.* even if, although, though.

Euadnē, -ēs, F. Evadne, the wife of Capaneus (one of the Seven against Thebes), who burned herself on the funeral pile of her husband (vi. 447).

Euander (-drus), -drī, M. Evander, king of Pallanteum on the Tiber, who aided Æneas (viii. 119).

Euboicus, -a, -um, *adj.* of Eubœa (the island east of the coast of Bœotia and Attica), Eubœan (vi. 2).

euhāns, -antis, *p.* crying Euhan! (a name of Bacchus) *or* Euhoë! — **orgia** (shouting the cry of Bacchus in his orgies).

Eumēdēs, -is, M. a Trojan, father of Dolon.

Eumēlus, -ī, M. a Trojan (v. 665).

Eumenides, -um, F. *pl.* Wellwishers, the Furies (so called to propitiate them, or to avoid the omen of their name) (vi. 250).

Eumolpus, -ī, M. a fabulous Thracian bard.

Eurōpa, -ae, F. Europe, the continent.

Eurōtās, -ae, M. a river of Laconia, on which Sparta stood (now Vasiliko) (i. 498).

Eurōus, -a, -um, *adj.* of the east wind (Eurus); eastern.

Eurus, -ī, M. the southeast wind; wind.

Euryalus, -ī, M. a Trojan, the friend of Nisus, killed in an excursion through the Rutulian camp (v. 294 ff.; ix. 231 ff.).

Eurydicē, -ēs, F. the wife of Orpheus.

Eurypylus, -ī, M. a leader of the Greeks before Troy (ii. 114).

Eurytiōn, -ōnis, M. a companion of Æneas, son of Lycaon (v. 495).

Euxīnus, -a, -um, *adj.* Euxine, of the Euxine (Black Sea).

ēvādō, -ere, -vāsī, -vāsum, *3. v. n. and a.* go out, come out; escape from: **flammam; hostis.** — *With acc.* (*cognate*), pass over, pass through: **viam.** — *Also,* go up, mount up, ascend: **ad superas auras; gradūs.**

ēvānēscō, -ere, -nuī, *no sup., 3. v. n. incep.* vanish away, vanish.

ēvehō, -ere, -vexī, -vectum, *3. v. a.* carry away; bear up, bear aloft.

ēveniō, -īre, -vēnī, -ventum, *4. v. n.* come out; turn out, happen.

ēventus, -ūs [*evenio*], M. a result, an occurrence, an issue; fortune.

ēvertō, -ere, -vertī, -versum, *3. v. a.* turn upside down, upturn, overturn, overthrow; ruin, destroy.

ēvinciō, -īre, -vīnxī, -vīnctum, *4. v. a.* bind up, bind round; bind; crown (olivā).

ēvincō, -ere, -vīcī, -victum, *3. v. a.* vanquish, overcome.

ēvītābilis, -e [*evito*], *adj.* to be avoided.

ēvocō, -āre, -āvī, -ātum, *1. v. a.* call forth, call out, summon, conjure up (**animas**).

ēvolvō, -ere, -volvī, -volūtum, *3. v. a.* roll forth; pour forth, utter. — *With reflexive,* roll, roll down.

ēvomō, -ere, -uī, -itum, *3. v. a.* vomit forth, cast up.

ex (ec-, ē), *prep.* (*with abl.*). *Of space,* out of (*cf.* ab, away from), from: **patria ex Ithaca** (of). — *Of time,* from, after, since, ever since: **tempore ex illo.** — *Fig.* from, of: **ex ira corda residunt.** — *Partitively,* out of, from, of:

nihil ex tanta urbe; pauca e multis. — *Of material*, from, of, made of : pharetra ex auro. — *Also*, according to, in accordance with : ex more; ex ordine (in order). — *In composition (besides its literal meanings)*, fully, entirely, very much.

exaestuō, -āre, -āvī, -ātum, *1. v. n.* boil up, foam up.

exagitō, -āre, -āvī, -ātum, *1. v. a.* stir up, rouse.

exanimis, -e (-us, -a, -um) [*ex*, *anima*], *adj.* (out of breath), lifeless, dead; breathless (*with fear*), half dead with fear, terrified.

exanimō, -āre, -āvī, -ātum [*ex-animus*], *1. v. a.* frighten, terrify.

exanimus, *see* exanimis.

exārdēscō, -ere, -ārsī, *no sup.*, *3. v. n. incep.* blaze up; *of feelings*, blaze forth, burst forth, be fired, be inflamed : ignes animo; dolor.

exarō, -āre, -āvī, -ātum, *1. v. a.* write.

exaudiō, -īre, -īvī (-iī), -ītum, *4. v. a.* hear (*distinctly or from afar*) : voces.

excēdō, -ere, -cessī, -cessum, *3. v. n.* go out, depart, withdraw : scelerātā terrā; regione viarum (leave); palmā (give up); pestes (disappear).

excellēns, -entis [*p. of excello*], *adj.* noble.

excelsus, -a, -um [*ex + celsus*], *adj.* high, lofty.

excidium, -ī (-iī) [*exscindo*], N. overthrow, destruction.

excidō, -ere, -cidī, *no sup.* [*ex +* *cado*], *3. v. n.* fall out, fall off, fall down : Palinurus puppi; vox per auras (descend); ore nefas (fall). — *Also*, slip away, escape : dolores animo (*by forgetfulness*).

excīdō, -ere, -cīdī, -cīsum [*ex + caedo*], *3. v. a.* cut out, cut off, cut down, hew out; raze, lay waste.

exciō, -īre, -īvī (-iī), -cītum *and* -citum, *4. v. a.* call forth, summon; arouse, excite; produce, cause : undis molem (cause an uproar).

excipiō, -ere, -cēpī, -ceptum [*ex + capio*], *3. v. a.* take out, take up, take from *or* after : clipeum sorti. — *Esp.* take next, succeed (*to something*), follow, receive next : Romulus gentem; quis te casus (meets you). — *As a hunting term (transferred to war, etc.)*, catch, cut off, overtake, engage with : incautum (catch unawares); *fig. in same sense* : motus futuros (catch a hint of, learn). — *Of persons*, receive, greet, welcome : reduces gaza agresti (entertain); plausu pavidos. — *Of conversation*, take up the word, respond, answer, reply : sic regia Iuno.

excitō, -āre, -āvī, -ātum, *1. v. a.* call out, call forth; arouse, awaken, stimulate, excite, alarm.

exclāmō, -āre, -āvī, -ātum, *1. v. a. and n.* cry out.

excolō, -ere, -coluī, -cultum, *3. v. a.* cultivate, improve (*by tillage*); ameliorate, civilize, educate (*in polite arts*) : vitam per artis (adorn and improve).

excubiae, -ārum [*cf. excubo*], F. *pl.* (a lying out at night), a watch, guards; *of a fire*, sentinel, watch-fire.

excūdō, -ere, -cūdī, -cūsum, *3. v. a.* strike out, forge.

excutiō, -ere, -cussī, -cussum [*ex + quatio*], *3. v. a.* shake off, shake out, dash off, drive off, dislodge, dash from, drive out; rouse: **excutior somno** (rouse myself); **navis excussa magistro** (robbed of).

exedō, -ere, -ēdī, -ēsum, *3. v. a.* eat out; destroy.

exemplum, -ī, N. model, example; manner.

exeō, -īre, -īvī (-iī), -itum, *irr. v. n. and a.* go out, come forth: **amnis** (arise, overflow, empty). — *Trans. with acc.* escape from, escape, shun, avoid: **tela corpore** (elude, dodge).

exerceō, -ēre, -cuī, -citum [*ex + arceo*], *2. v. a.* keep busy, busy, drive (*to labor*), exercise, train: **labor apes; Diana choros** (lead the dance); **membra** (train). — *Of things,* employ, drive, work, manage. — *Of persons,* worry, drive, pursue, vex, harass, torment: **stirpem odiis; exercita curis Venus.**—*With employments as objects,* pursue, practise, occupy one's self with, ply: **palaestras; imperia** (hold sway).

exercitus, -ūs [*exerceo*], M. an army; a band, a flock.

exhālō, -āre, -āvī, -ātum, *1. v. a.* breathe out, exhale.

exhauriō, -īre, -hausī, -haus-tum, *4. v. a.* drain out, drain.

waste, wear out, exhaust. — *Fig. of trials and the like,* undergo, endure. — **exhaustus, -a, -um,** *p. p. as adj.* exhausted, worn out.

exhibeō, -ēre, -uī, -itum [*ex + habeo*], *2. v. a.* hold forth, show, display.

exhorrēscō, -ere, -horruī, *no sup., 3. v. n. incep.* shudder.

exigō, -ere, -ēgī, -āctum [*ex + ago*], *3. v. a.* drive out, drive, thrust: **exegit caecos rabies.** — *Also,* pass (*completely*), finish, end, fulfil: **exactis mensibus; annos.** — *With different meaning of* ago, weigh, ponder. — **exāctus, -a, -um,** *p.p. as adj.* discovered, found out. — N. *pl.* discoveries (*things found out*).

exiguus, -a, -um [*cf. exigo*], *adj.* weighed, exact; scanty, small, slight, little, short, feeble: **urbs; vox** (piping); **vires; exigui numero** (few, scanty).

eximō, -ere, -ēmī, -ēmptum [*ex + emo,* take], *3. v. a.* take away, remove, efface; satisfy: **fames exempta.**

exin, *adv.* = exinde, *which see.*

exinde, *adv.* (from thence), then, after that, afterwards.

exitiābilis, -e [*exitium*], *adj.* fatal.

exitiālis, -e [*exitium*], *adj.* destructive, deadly, ruinous; fatal: **donum Minervae.**

exitium, -ī, (-iī) [*exeo*], N. death; ruin, destruction, bane.

exitus, -ūs [*exeo*], M. a going out, a departure, an egress, an exit; death, end (*of life*); issue, event, result.

exonerō, -āre, -āvī, -ātum, *1. v. a.* disburden, free.

exoptō, -āre, -āvī, -ātum, *1. v. a.* long for, desire.

exōrdium, -ī (-iī) [*cf. exordior*], N. a beginning.

exorior, -orīrī, -ortus, *3. and 4. v. dep.* arise, rise.

exōrō, -āre, -āvī, -ātum, *1. v. a.* implore, beseech.

exōsus, -a, -um [*ex + osus (odi)*], *adj.* hating, abhorring.

expallēscō, -ere, -palluī, *no sup., 3. v. n.* turn very pale, turn pale.

expediō, -īre, -īvī (-iī), -ītum [*ex, pes*], *4. v. a. and n.* disentangle, set free; get out, bring forth, get ready, prepare; unfold, describe, explain; come through (*danger, etc.*). — *Pass.* make one's way (*through difficulties*). — curis expeditis, carefree.

expellō, -ere, -pulī, -pulsum, *3. v. a.* drive out, drive away, banish.

expendō, -ere, -pendī, -pēnsum, *3. v. a.* weigh out, weigh; pay (*acc. of penalty*), pay for (*acc. of crime*), suffer the penalty of, suffer (*as a penalty*).

experior, -īrī, -pertus, *4. v. dep.* try, attempt, make trial of: laborem (essay); expertus (having tried it).

expers, -ertis [*ex + pars*], *adj.* without a share; free from, without.

expiō, -āre, -āvī, -ātum, *1. v. a.* expiate, atone for.

expleō, -plēre, -plēvī, -plētum, *2. v. a.* fill up, fill; fill out, complete (**numerum**); satiate,

glut, satisfy: **expletus dapibus** (gorged); **animum ultricis flammae**.

explicō, -āre, -āvī (-uī), -ātum (-itum), *1. v. a.* unfold; describe, express: **cladem.**

explōrō, -āre, -āvī, -ātum, *1. v. a.* search out, explore, reconnoitre (**locos novos**); observe, try (**ventos**); ponder, meditate, consider: **quid optes.**

expōnō, -ere, -posuī, -positum, *3. v. a.* put forth, put out; unload, disembark, land.

exposcō, -ere, -poposcī, *no sup., 3. v. a.* beg earnestly.

exprōmō, -ere, -prōmpsī, -prōmptum, *3. v. a.* bring forth (*out of the storehouse*); speak out, utter: **voces.**

exquīrō, -ere, -quīsīvī, -quīsītum [*ex + quaero*], *3. v. a.* seek out, seek, search out; pray earnestly for: **pacem.**

exsanguis, -e, *adj.* bloodless, lifeless; pallid with fear.

exsaturābilis, -e [*exsaturo*], *adj.* satiable, to be satiated.

exscindō, -ere, -scidī, -scissum, *3. v. a.* cut down, tear down; overthrow, destroy.

exsecror, -ārī, -ātus [*ex + sacro*], *1. v. dep.* curse.

exsequiae, -ārum [*exsequor*], F. *pl.* a funeral procession, funeral rites.

exsequor, -sequī, -secūtus, *3. v. dep.* follow out; perform, execute; celebrate: **pompas.**

exserō, -ere, -seruī, -sertum, *3. v. a.* thrust out. — **exsertus, -a, -um,** *p.p. as adj.* bared, bare.

exsertō, -āre, *no perf., no sup.*
[*exsero*], *1. v. a.* stretch *or* thrust
out.

exsilium, ī (-iī) [*exsul*], N. exile;
pl. wanderings in exile, strange
lands.

exsistō, -ere, -stitī, -stitum, *3.
v. n.* stand forth, come to view,
appear.

exsolvō, -ere, -solvī, -solūtum,
3. v. a. unbind; set free, release,
relieve; pay: poenas.

exsomnis, -e [*ex, somnus*], *adj.*
sleepless, wakeful, watchful.

exsors, -rtis [*ex + sors*], *adj.*
without lot, without a share in,
deprived of; out of the lot (*i.e.
order of lots*), out of course.

exspectō, -āre, -āvī, -ātum, *1.
v. a. and n.* look out for, await, expect; hope for, long for; linger,
delay. — exspectātus, -a, -um,
p.p. as adj. expected, long looked
for: exspectate Hector.

exspīrō, -āre, -āvī, -ātum, *1. v.
a. and n.* breathe forth, breathe
out; breathe one's last, expire,
die. — *P.* panting.

exspuō, -ere, -spuī, -spūtum,
3. v. a. spit out, cast out.

exsternō, -āre, -āvī, -ātum, *1.
v. a.* drive mad, madden.

exstinguō, -uere, -stīnxī, -stīnc-
tum, *3. v. a.* put out, quench,
extinguish; destroy, kill, abolish:
exstinctus pudor (lost).

exstō, -stāre, *no perf., no sup.*, *1.
v. n.* stand out, overtop.

exstruō, -ere, -strūxī, -strūc-
tum, *3. v. a.* build up, pile up,
heap up. — exstrūctus, -a, -um,
p.p. as adj. high, raised, elevated.

exsul, -ulis [*ex, salio*], C. an exile,
a fugitive.

exsultō, -āre, -āvī, -ātum, *1. v. n.*
leap up, bound: corda (throb);
vada (dash up). — *Fig.* exult,
rejoice, triumph. — exsultāns,
-antis, *p. as adj.* exultant, proud,
triumphant.

exsuperō, -āre, -āvī, -ātum, *1.
v. n. and a.* tower above, overtop, mount up; surpass, overcome, prevail against; pass over,
pass by, pass beyond: solum.

exsurgō, -ere, -surrēxī, -sur-
rēctum, *3. v. n.* rise up.

exta, -ōrum, N. *pl.* entrails (*the
heart, liver, lungs, etc., observed for
auspices*).

extemplō [*ex-templo* (*abl. of templum*, place of observation), *an
augural word*], *adv.* forthwith, at
once, on the spot, immediately.

extendō, -ere, -tendī, -tēnsum
(-tentum), *3. v. a.* stretch out,
spread out, extend, lay (*one*)
prostrate: extenditur antro (is
stretched at full length); viris
(put forth).

externus, -a, -um [*exterus, extra*], *adj.* external, from abroad;
foreign, alien. — M. *as subst.* an
alien, a foreigner.

exterreō, -ēre, -terruī, -terri-
tum, *2. v. a.* affright, alarm,
frighten, confound.

exterus, -a, -um [*ex*], *adj.* external. — *Comp.* exterior. — *Superl.*
extrēmus, farthest, uttermost,
outmost; hindmost; last, final:
vocem (last words); extrema
in morte (in the extremity of
death). — N. *as adv.* extremum,

for the last time. — N. *pl. as
subst.* extrēma, -ōrum, extremi-
ties, last measures, dangers, sufferings, the last resort.

extorris, -is [*ex, terra*], C. an exile.

extrā [*exterus*], *prep.* outside,
without, beyond.

extrēmus, *see* exterus.

exuō, -uere, -uī, -ūtum, *3. v. a.*
put off, strip off, take off, put
away: alas; mentem. — *Also,*
strip, bare, free from: exuta
unum pedem (with one foot
bare).

exūrō, -ere, -ussī, -ustum, *3. v. a.*
burn up, consume, burn away,
purge away (scelus); scorch,
dry up, parch: agros Sirius.

exuviae, -ārum [*cf. exuo*], F. *pl.*
spoils, clothes (*stripped off*),
booty; remains, relics; a skin
(*stripped off*), slough (*of a
snake*).

faber, -brī, M. a smith.

Fabius, -ī (-iī), M. a Roman gentile
name borne by a long line of
distinguished citizens, *esp.* Q.
Fabius Maximus, commander
against Hannibal (vi. 845). —
As adj. Fabian.

fabricātor, -tōris [*fabrico*], M. a
framer, a contriver.

Fabricius, -ī (-iī) [*cf. fabrico*], M.
a Roman gentile name, *esp.* C.
Fabricius Luscinus, commander
against Pyrrhus (vi. 844).

fabricō, -āre, -āvī, -ātum [*fa-
brica*], *1. v. a.* fashion.

fābula, -ae [*for*], F. a tale, a story.

Fabullus, -ī, M. a friend of Catullus.

fābulōsus, -a, -um [*fabula*], *adj.*
famous in story, storied.

facessō, -ere, -cessī, -cessītum
[*facio*], *3. v. a. and n. intens.* do
(*eagerly*), perform, execute, hasten to do.

faciēs, -ēī [*facio*], F. make, form,
shape ; appearance, aspect, kind ;
face ; beauty ; a shape, an apparition, a spectre.

facilis, -e [*facio*], *adj.* easy (*both ac-
tively and passively*). — *Of mental
qualities,* ready, kindly, willing:
facilis te sequetur (willingly). —
Of things, passively, easy (*to do in
any manner*): descensus Averni ;
iactura sepulcri (easily borne) ;
exitus ; visu facilis (of gentle
aspect) ; fuga (ready).

faciō, -ere, fēcī, factum, *3. v. a.*
do, make; cause, execute, perform: iussa ; facta silentia (secure, enforce). — *Esp.* suit, agree
with. — *With double acc.* make:
te parentem. — *With inf.* cause,
force: me cernere. — *Phrases* :
fac, suppose; facio certum, inform; facio vela, make sail;
facio pedem, tack. — factus, -a,
-um, *p.p. as adj.* made, wrought,
formed. — N. *as subst.* factum,
-ī, a deed, an exploit, an act.

factum, N. *see* faciō.

falcātus, -a, -um [*falx*], *adj.*
scythe-shaped, hooked.

fallāx, -ācis [*fallo*], *adj.* deceitful,
treacherous, false.

fallō, -ere, fefellī, falsum, *3. v. a.*
deceive; elude, disappoint; be-
guile, delude, ensnare: dextras
(break a pledge). — virum (be
missed by). — *In pass.* be de-

ceived, be mistaken: **nisi fallor.**
— *With cogn. acc.* assume, counterfeit: **faciem.** — *Esp.* escape (notice of), be unknown to, be hidden from. — **falsus,** *p.p. as adj.* false, treacherous, deceitful, deceptive; groundless, delusive, counterfeit, fictitious, pretended, unreal, supposed, falsely suspected: **caedes.**

falsum, -ī, *p.p.* N. *as subst.* falsehood.

falsus, -a, -um, *p.p. of* **fallō.**

falx, falcis, F. a hooked knife, a sickle.

fāma, -ae [*for* **],** F. report, tidings; fame, tradition: **inanis** (belief). — *In a good sense,* fame, reputation, glory; *less commonly,* ill repute. — *Personified,* Rumor.

famēs, -is, F. hunger, famine, starvation; greed: **auri** (thirst). — *Personified,* Famine.

famula, -ae [F. *of* **famulus],** F. a maidservant, attendant, slave.

famulor, -ārī, -ātus [famulus], *1. v. dep.* serve, wait upon.

famulus, -ī, M. a house servant, manservant, attendant, slave.

fandum, *see* **for.**

far, farris, N. grain, spelt; meal (of the coarser kind, used as an offering, mixed with salt).

fās, *indel.* **[** *for* **],** N. right, (*divine*) law: **fas omne abrumpit** (violate all right). — *With* **est** (*expressed or implied*), allowed, permitted, just, lawful, fitting, right.

fascis, -is, M. a bundle, pack. — *Esp. pl.* the fasces (the bundle of rods with an axe, the emblem of

authority of a Roman magistrate).

fastīgium, -ī (-iī) [*cf. fastīgo*], N. the top, a summit, a roof, a peak; battlements, gable; a point (*of a narrative*): **summa sequar** (touch the principal points).

fastus, -ūs, M. pride, arrogance.

fātālis, -e [fatum], *adj.* fated, destined, appointed; fatal, ruinous, destructive.

fateor, -ērī, fassus, *2. v. dep.* confess, own, acknowledge, admit; consent, submit.

fātifer, -a, -um [fatum, fero], *adj.* fatal, deadly.

fatīgō, -āre, -āvī, -ātum, *1. v. a.* tire out, weary; worry, ply, vex, harass, pursue: **metu terras** (vex); **socios** (chide); **cervos cursu** (pursue in chase); **os** (ply).

fatīscō, -ere, *no perf., no sup., 3. v. n.* yawn, gape, crack; spring a leak.

fātum, -ī [N. *p.p. of* **for],** N. an oracle, a response, decree (*of fate*); fate, destiny; death.

faucēs, *see* **faux.**

Faunus, -ī, M. a son of Picus; he was honored as the patron god of shepherds and farmers.

faustus, -a, -um [faveo], *adj.* fortunate, auspicious: **parum fausta** (ill-omened).

fautrīx, -īcis [faveo], F. patroness, protecting goddess.

†**faux,** †**faucis,** F. (*only pl. and abl. sing.*), the throat, the jaws; a narrow pass, a defile; the channel of a river.

faveō, -ēre, fāvī, fautum, 2. *v. n.*
be favorable, favor, be propitious : **adsis favens** (kindly aid).
— *Religious expression with* (*or without*) **ore,** refrain from ill-omened expressions, keep religious silence. — **faventēs,** *p. as subst. in pl.* favorers, partisans : **clamor faventum.**

favilla, -ae, F. glowing ashes, embers ; cinders, sparks.

favor, -ōris [*faveo*], M. favor, partiality.

fax, facis, F. a torch, a brand, a firebrand : **face ferroque** (with sword and brand). — *Of a shooting star,* a trail (*of fire*).

fēcundus, -a, -um, *adj.* productive, fruitful, fertile, rich : **poenis** (fertile for torture).

fel, fellis, N. gall ; anger.

fēlīx, -īcis, *adj.* fruitful ; auspicious, favorable, gracious, favoring ; blest, happy, fortunate : **animae ; vivite felices.**

fēmina, -ae, F. a woman.

fēmineus, -a, -um [*femina*], *adj.* of a woman *or* women, female, feminine : **poena ; ululatus ; manus ; plangor.**

fenestra, -ae, F. a window ; an aperture, a breach.

fera, -ae [*ferus*], F. a wild beast.

fērālis, -e, *adj.* funereal ; mournful, ill-omened.

ferē, *adv.* almost, nearly, about, for the most part.

feretrum, -ī [*fero*], N. a bier.

ferīna, *see* ferīnus.

ferīnus, -a, -um [*ferus*], *adj.* of beasts, of a beast (*wild*). — **ferīna** (*sc.* **carō**), **-ae,** F. game, venison.

feriō, -īre, *no perf., no sup.,* 4. *v. a. and n.* strike, beat, lash ; wound, cut, sever ; kill, sacrifice ; play (*on the lyre*) : **carmina.**

ferō, ferre, tulī, lātum [√*fer*], *irr. v. a. and n.* bear.

1. *Simply,* bear, carry, support, wear : **vix illam famuli** (*of a weighty cuirass*) ; **flammas** (*torches*) ; **parmam hastamque.** — *Fig.* : **nostrae secum omina mortis.** — *Esp. of the body and its parts,* hold, carry : **se talem Dido** (appear such) ; **sic oculos** (such are the eyes). — *With idea of elevation,* bear, raise, rear, lift : **caelo capita alta** (*of Cyclopes*) ; **sublimem ad sidera Aenean.** — *Fig.* raise, extol, laud : **factis ad aethera Troiam ; Teucros insigni laude.**

2. *Of endurance,* bear, endure, suffer, submit to, brook : **laborem ; frena** (*of a horse*) ; **non tulit** (could not brook).

3. *With idea of motion,* bear, carry, convey, bring : **fertur equis** (is dragged). — *Fig.* bear, bring, carry, render, afford : **praemia digna** (bestow) ; **auxilium Priamo ; fama salutem ; vox fertur ad auris ; vim tela** (offer) ; **sidera caelo dextra** (set) ; **viam vento facilem** (grant) ; **omnia sub auras** (disclose). — *Esp. of religious offerings and acts,* bear, offer, render, perform : **sacra.** — *Esp. also of words, messages, etc.* : **haec Ascanio ; quae signa** (show, *of prophetic doves*) ; **quidve ferat** (what is his purpose). — *From the last use, absolutely,*

report, say, tell : **ferunt,** they say ; **fertur,** it is said. — *Also of destiny,* ordain, order, assign : **sic fata.**

4. *Of natural growth,* bear, generate, produce, yield, give birth to : **monstra pontus ; me Troia.**

5. *Less exactly, of any enforced motion,* drive, bear on, turn, lead, urge on : **flamina classem ; illam impetus** (send) ; **feror incensa furiis** (be driven madly on) ; **fatis incertis** (be urged on) ; **gressum** (hold, turn) ; **via fert ; pedem domum** (turn the steps). — *So in special phrases* : **manum,** join (*cf.* " *bear a hand*") ; **obvius** (meet). — *Esp. with a reflexive, or in pass. with middle sense,* be borne on, be driven, proceed, rush, go, advance, come : **me extra tecta** (come forth) ; **furiata mente ferebar ; sese obvia oculis** (offer, show) ; **sese halitus** (rise) ; **ferimur** (wander).

6. *Of motion from a place,* bear away, carry off (*both in bad and good sense*) : **praemia ferunt** (receive) ; **talentum ferre** (have). — *Esp.* : **rapio et fero,** pillage and plunder.

7. *Less common uses,* suggest, prompt : **ita corde voluntas.** — *Of continuance,* prolong, perpetuate : **vivus per ora feretur** (immortalize) ; **ludum in lucem ; fama nomen per annos.** — **ferēns, -entis,** *p. as adj.* favorable (*cf.* 5) : **ventus.**

ferōx, -ōcis [*ferus*], *adj.* fierce, wild, untamed, savage, spirited (*of a horse*), angry (*of a snake*) ; warlike, courageous ; proud, exultant.

ferrātus, -a, -um [*ferrum*], *adj.* iron-shod, iron-bound.

ferreus, -a, -um [*ferrum*], *adj.* of iron, iron : **seges** (*of spears*) ; **vox.** — *Fig.* hard-hearted.

ferrūgineus, -a, -um [*ferrugo,* rust], *adj.* rusty, dusky : **cymba** (*of Charon's boat*).

ferrum, -ī, N. iron ; a sword, an arrow, a knife, an axe, the iron (*of a spear or arrow*).

ferus, -a, -um, *adj.* wild, untamed ; rude, savage, fierce, cruel ; warlike, impetuous.

ferus, -ī, M. a wild beast, a monster ; a horse.

ferveō, -ēre, -vī (-buī), *no sup.* (*also* **fervō, -ĕre,** *3*), *2. v. n.* be hot, be warm ; be alive (*of busy action*), be in a turmoil : **litora flammis** (in seething flame) ; **opus** (be all alive) ; **opere semita** (teem with busy work).

fervidus, -a, -um [*ferveo*], *adj.* hot, glowing ; raging, in fury.

fessus, -a, -um, *adj.* weary, tired, worn out, spent, exhausted : **naves** (*personified*) ; **res** (shattered fortunes).

festīnō, -āre, -āvī, -ātum [*festinus*], *1. v. n.* make haste, hasten. — *With cognate accusative* : **fugam ; iussa.**

festīnus, -a, -um, *adj.* in haste.

fēstus, -a, -um, *adj.* festal, festive, sacred, holy : **frons ; dies** (festival). — N. *as subst.* **fēstum, -ī,** a festival.

fētus, -a, -um, *adj.* pregnant, breeding, teeming, delivered.

fētus, -ūs, M. bearing, breeding; offspring, brood, litter, young; fruit, growth.

fibra, -ae, F. a fibre, a filament; *pl.* the entrails.

fībula, -ae, F. a buckle, a clasp, a brooch.

fidēlis, -e [*fides*], *adj.* trustworthy, faithful.

Fĭdēna, -ae (*also pl.*), F. a town of Latium, about five miles north of Rome, now Castel Giubileo (vi. 773).

fidēs, -eī [*fido*], F. faith, good faith, loyalty, faithfulness, honor, honesty, integrity; credibility, trustworthiness, truth; a pledge, a promise; confidence, trust, reliance, belief, assurance, hopes.— *Personified,* Good Faith.

fidēs, -is, F. a string (*of the lyre*); *pl.* a lyre.

fīdō, -ere, fīsus, *3. v. n.* trust, confide in, have confidence: regnis; committere pugnam (venture).— **fīdēns, -entis,** *p. as adj.* trustful, confident, bold.

fīdūcia, -ae [*fido*], F. trust, confidence, reliance; presumption: generis (confidence in lineage).

fīdus, -a, -um [*fido*], *adj.* faithful, trusty; trustworthy: responsa; statio.

fīgō, -ere, fīxī, fīxum, *3. v. a.* fasten, fix (*esp. by piercing*), set up, hang up: leges (*hang up tablets,* make laws). — *Less exactly and fig.* fix, attach, fasten, plant, set firmly: oculos fixos tenebat; vestigia (plant); oscula (imprint); dicta animis (let sink deeply); fixum animo (a

deep-set purpose). — *Of the process,* pierce, transfix, shoot, hit, bring down: verubus viscera (stick on); harundine malum.— fīxus, -a, -um, *p.p. as adj.* firm, resolute, unmoved.

figūra, -ae [*cf. fingo*], F. form, figure.

fīlia, -ae, F. a daughter.

fīlius, ī (-iī), M. a son.

fīlum, -ī, N. a thread.

fimus, -ī (-um, -ī), M. (N.), filth, ordure, mud, dung.

findō, -ere, fidī, fissum, *3. v. a.* split, cleave; divide, separate.

fingō, -ere, fīnxī, fictum, *3. v. a.* fashion, make, mould, shape, form: crinem (arrange, *by stroking*).— *Fig.* train, subdue: corda (*of the Sibyl*).— *Of mental action,* frame, contrive, devise, invent, fancy, imagine. — fictus, *p.p. as adj.* false: pectus. — fictum, N. *as subst.* falsehood.

fīniō, -īre, -īvī (-iī), -ītum [*finis*], *4. v. a.* put an end to, end, finish; confine.

fīnis, -is, C. an end, a limit, a bound; *pl.* borders, region, country. — *Of the starting point of a race,* barriers; *and of the end,* the goal.

fīnitimus, -a, -um [*finis*], *adj.* bordering upon, neighboring.— M. *as subst.* a neighbor.

fīō, *see* faciō.

firmō, -āre, -āvī, -ātum [*firmus*], *1. v. a.* make strong, strengthen, fortify, steady (vestigia); confirm, ratify, reassure.

firmus, -a, -um, *adj.* steady, firm, solid, stable, strong; stout, resolute: pectus.

fissilis, -e [*fissus, findo*], *adj.*
cleavable, split, riven.

fistula, -ae, F. a water pipe; a
(*shepherd's*) pipe.

flagellō, -āre, -āvī, -ātum [*flagellum*], *1. v. a.* scourge, beat.

flagellum, -ī [*flagrum*], N. a whip,
a scourge, a lash.

flāgitō, -āre, -āvī, -ātum, *1. v. a.*
demand; solicit, call upon.

flagrō, -āre, -āvī, -ātum [√*flag*],
1. v. n. burn, blaze, glow, shine.
— **flagrāns, -antis,** *p. as adj.*
blazing, shining, bright, glowing,
beaming: **voltus.**

flāmen, -inis [*flo*], N. a blast, a
gale, a breeze.

flamma, -ae, F. a flame, a fire;
a fiery brand, a flaming torch;
a blazing pyre; fire *or* flame (*of
flashing eyes*); fire (*of Jove,* the
lightning); fire (*of love or passion*), love, passion, desire, fury.

flammō, -āre, -āvī, -ātum
[*flamma*], *1. v. a.* set on fire, inflame, fire. — **flammāns, -antis,**
p. as adj. fiery, blazing: **lumina.**
— **flammātus, -a, -um,** *p.p. as
adj.* inflamed, infuriated.

flātus, -ūs [*flo*], M. a breath, a
blast.

flāvēns, *p. of* **flāveō.**

flāveō, -ēre, *no perf., no sup.*
[*flavus*], *2. v. n.* be yellow.—
flāvēns, -entis, *p. as adj.* yellow,
golden, auburn.

flāvus, -a, -um, *adj.* golden, yellow; golden-haired; pale green:
oliva.

flēbilis, -e [*fleo*], *adj.* tearful,
mournful.

flectō, -ere, flexī, flexum, *3. v. a.*
bend, turn, guide, drive: **viam
velis; equos; iuga habenis.** —
Fig. bend, influence, persuade,
turn aside: **precibus; precando
fata** (turn). — **flexus, -a, -um,**
p.p. as adj. flexible, bent.

fleō, flēre, flēvī, flētum, *2. v. n.
and a.* weep, shed tears; mourn,
lament; *trans.* weep for, mourn,
bewail: **Anchisen.**

flētus, -ūs [*fleo*], M. a weeping, a
wail; tears, a flood of tears, a
tearful prayer.

flexilis, -e [*flexus, flecto*], *adj.*
flexible, pliant.

flō, flāre, flāvī, flātum, *1. v. n.*
blow.

flōreō, -ēre, -uī, *no sup.* [*flos*], *2.
v. n.* blossom, be in bloom, bloom;
be bright, gleam: **limina sertis**
(bloom).

flōreus, -a, -um [*flos*], *adj.* flowery,
blooming.

flōs, flōris, M. a flower, a blossom;
flowers.

fluctuō, -āre, -āvī, -ātum [*fluctus*], *1. v. n.* toss, ebb and flow;
waver, fluctuate: **amor irarum
aestu** (alternate with a tide).

fluctus, -ūs [*fluo*], M. a wave, a
tide; the sea, water. — *Fig., of
passion,* waves, a tide.

fluentum, -ī [*fluo*], N. a stream, a
river.

fluidus, -a, -um [*fluo*], *adj.* flowing, liquid.

fluitō, -āre, -āvī, -ātum [*fluo*], *1.
v. n.* flow; float, drift.

flūmen, -inis [*fluo*], N. a river, a
stream, water (*of a river*). —
*Less exactly, of the river god, of
tears* (flood), *of sweat, of blood.*

fluō, fluere, flūxī, flūxum, *3. v. n.*
flow, run, ebb; flow with, drip,
run with (**membra tabo**); fall
loosely; droop, fail: **spes.** —
fluēns, -entis, *p. as adj.* dripping; flowing, loose: **sinus; crinis.**

fluviālis, -e [*fluvius*], *adj.* of a
river.

fluvius, -ī (-iī) [*fluo*], M. a river, a
stream.

focus, -ī, M. a hearth, a fireplace, a
brazier; the hearth (*as emblem
of home*), the fireside, the household hearth; an altar.

fodiō, -ere, fōdī, fossum, *3. v. a.*
dig; prick, pierce.

foedē [*foedus*], *adv.* foully, basely,
shamefully.

foedō, -āre, -āvī, -ātum [*foedus*],
1. v. a. make hideous, befoul, disfigure, lacerate: **unguibus ora;
latebras ferro** (desecrate, *prob.
with reference to the sanctity of
the Horse*). — *Fig.* pollute, defile.

foedus, -a, -um, *adj.* foul, filthy;
horrible, base, vile.

foedus, -eris [√*fid in fides*], N. a
treaty, an alliance, a truce; a
bargain, an agreement, a contract, a pledge (*mutual*), a compact (*esp. of marriage*); a condition, terms: **certo foedere**
(by fixed laws); **aequo foedere
amantes** (on equal terms).

folium, -ī (-iī), N. a leaf, foliage.

follis, -is, M. a bag; *pl.* bellows.

fōmes, -itis, M. dry fuel.

fōns, fontis, M. a spring, a fountain; water, pure water; a lake.

†for, fārī, fātus, *1. v. dep.* speak,
say; tell, relate; foretell, predict. — **fandus, -a, -um,** *ger.* to
be spoken. — N. *as subst.* **fandum, -ī,** right (*opp. to* **nefandum**). — **fandō,** *ger.* in speaking;
by report. — **fātū,** *sup.* to be
spoken, to say.

forāmen, -inis [*cf. foris*], N. a hole,
fissure.

forceps, -cipis, C. tongs.

fore, forem, *see* **sum.**

foris, -is, F. a door; entrance,
opening.

fōrma, -ae, F. form, figure, shape,
appearance; fine form, beauty:
formā insignis. — *Concretely,* a
form, figure, vision, apparition,
phantom. — *Fig.* species, form,
kind, nature: **scelerum.**

formīca, -ae, F. an ant.

formīdō, -āre, -āvī, -ātum, *1. v. a.*
dread.

formīdō, -dinis, F. fear, dread,
terror, alarm: **formidine capti**
(seized with a panic).

fornāx, -ācis, F. a furnace, forge.

fornix, -icis, M. an arch.

fors, † fortis (*abl.* **forte**) [*fero*], F.
chance, hazard, fortune. — *Nom.*
(*sc.* **est** *or* **sit,** there is a chance),
equal to an adv. perhaps, per-
chance, possibly. — *Abl.* **forte,** by
chance, as it happened: **si forte**
(if by any chance); **quae forte
paratae** (happened to be, *etc.*);
forte fuit (there chanced to be).

forsan [*fors an,* a chance whether],
adv. perhaps, it may be.

forsitan [*fors sit an,* it may be a
chance whether], *adv.* perhaps,
possibly, mayhap.

forte, *see* **fors.**

fortis, -e, *adj.* strong, sturdy, stout, hardy, vigorous, stalwart; valiant, brave, steadfast, undaunted : Achates ; corda ; pectus.

fortiter [*fortis*], *adv.* strongly, firmly, boldly.

fortūna, -ae [*fors*], F. fortune, chance, hazard, destiny, fate; the goddess Fortune. — *In good sense,* good fortune, success, opportunity, chance : si modo sequatur ; fortuna fuit (glory) ; quae dabatur (chance of success). — *In bad sense,* fortune, fate, ill luck.

fortūnō, -āre, -āvī, -ātum [*fortuna*], *1. v. a.* make fortunate, bless.— fortūnātus, -a, -um, *p.p.* as *adj.* fortunate, blest, favored (*by fortune*), happy.

forum, -ī, N. a market-place, forum.

forus, -ī, M. a gangway (in a ship or boat, not apparently from one deck to another, but open spaces in the ship not occupied by the rowers) ; the hold.

fossa, -ae [*fodio*], F. a ditch, a pit.

foveō, -ēre, fōvī, fōtum, *2. v. a.* keep warm, brood ; embrace, fondle, caress : germanam amplexa sinu ; hiemem inter se (spend in dalliance). — *Fig.* cherish, foster, promote : Romanos ; hoc regnum gentibus esse (cherish the purpose, fondly hope) ; famam.

frāga, -ōrum, N. *pl.* strawberries.

fragilis, -e [*frango*], *adj.* that may be broken, fragile.

fragor, -ōris [*frango*], M. a break-

ing ; a crash, an uproar, a din ; applause (*by clapping of hands*) ; a loud report (*of thunder*).

fragrāns, *p. of* fragrō.

fragrō, -āre, -āvī, *no sup.,* *1. v. n.* smell sweet.— fragrāns, -antis, *p. as adj.* sweet-smelling, fragrant.

frangō, -ere, frēgī, frāctum [√*frag*], *3. v. a.* break, break up, break off ; shatter, crush, grind ; break down, wear out. — frāctus, -a, -um, *p.p.* as *adj.* broken, shattered, crushed : vires ; opes ; res ; voces.

frāter, -tris, M. a brother.

frāternus, -a, -um [*frater*], *adj.* of a brother, a brother's, brotherly.

fraudō, -āre, -āvī, -ātum [*fraus*], *1. v. a.* defraud, deprive of.

fraus, fraudis, F. deceit, wiles, a stratagem, deception, a trick, treachery.

fraxineus, -a, -um [*fraxinus*], *adj.* ashen, of ash.

fremitus, -ūs [*fremo*], M. a roaring, a roar ; uproar, shouting (*of applause*).

fremō, -ere, -uī, *no sup.,* *3. v. n. and a.* roar, shout, cry, howl ; resound, re-echo : ululatu tecta. — *Fig.* rage, rave, be wild, exult. —fremēns, -entis, *p.* as *adj.* fierce, wild.

frēnō, -āre, -āvī, -ātum [*frenum*], *1. v. a.* curb, restrain, bridle. — frēnātus, -a, -um, *p.p.* bridled, furnished with bridles.

frēnum, -ī (*pl. also* -ī, -ōrum), N. *and* M. a bridle, a bit, reins : ea frena furenti concutit (with such a powerful bit does he curb, *etc.*).

frequēns, -entis, *adj.* thronging, in great numbers.

frequenter [*frequens*], *adv.* frequently, often, in quick succession.

frequentō, -āre, -āvī, -ātum [*frequens*], *1. v. a.* crowd, people, inhabit, frequent.

fretum, -ī, N. a strait; the sea, waters.

frētus, -a, -um, *adj.* relying on, trusting to, confiding in; by means of.

frīgeō, -ēre, *no perf.*, *no sup.* *2. v. n.* be cold, be chilled: vires.— frīgēns, -entis, *p. as adj.* cold, stiff, lifeless.

frīgidus, -a, -um [*frigeo*], *adj.* cold, chill, cool, icy: horror; annus (season).

frīgus, -oris, N. cold, chill, frost, coolness; chill of fear *or* death.

frondēns, *p. of* frondeō.

frondeō, -ēre, *no perf.*, *no sup.* [*frons*], *2. v. n.* put forth leaves, be in leaf. — frondēns, -entis, *p. as adj.* leafy.

frondēscō, -ere, *no perf.*, *no sup.* [*frondeo*], *3. v. n.* put forth leaves.

frondeus, -a, -um [*frons*], *adj.* leafy.

frondōsus, -a, -um [*frons*], *adj.* leafy.

frōns, frondis, F. a leaf; leaves (*collectively*), foliage; a branch (*with leaves*); a garland.

frōns, frontis, F. the forehead, the brow; the face, the countenance; the prow; the face *or* brow of a cliff: sub adversa fronte.

frūgēs, *see* frūx.

frūmentum, -ī [*cf.* fruor], N. grain; *pl.* ears of grain.

fruor, fruī, frūctus [*cf.* frux], *3. v. dep.* enjoy: luce.

frūstrā, *adv.* in vain, to no purpose, uselessly, vainly.

frūstror, -ārī, -ātus [*frustra*], *1.v. dep.* disappoint, deceive: hiantīs clamor (fail).

frūstum, -ī, N. a piece, a bit, a morsel, a lump.

†frūx, frūgis, frūge, *and pl.* [*cf.* fruor], F. grain; meal (*ground coarse for sacrificing*); a cake: medicatae (*of the cake given to Cerberus*).

fūcus, -ī, M. a drone.

fuga, -ae, F. a flight, an escape; a running, speed, a course; exile.

fugāx, -ācis [*fuga*], *adj.* flying, fleet, fleeing; cowardly; prone to shun, eager to avoid.

fugiō, -ere, fūgī, (fugitūrus) [√*fug*], *3. v. a. and n.* flee, fly, escape, depart, recede; speed, rush; *trans.* flee from, fly from, escape, avoid, refuse.— *P.* fugiēns, fleeting.

fugō, -āre, -āvī, -ātum [*fuga*], *1. v. a.* put to flight, drive away, drive; chase, disperse, dispel.

fulciō, -īre, fulsī, fultum, *4. v. a.* prop up, support, sustain, secure.

fulcrum, -ī [*fulcio*], N. a support, a prop, a post, a pillar; a leg (*of a couch*).

fulgeō, -ēre, fulsī, *no sup.* (fulgō, -ere, *3.*), *2. v. n.* gleam, flash, shine, blaze, glare. — fulgēns, -entis, *p. as adj.* bright, gleaming, glittering.

fulgō, *see* fulgeō.

fulgor, -ōris [*cf. fulgeo*], M. a blaze, a flash, a glitter, a gleam; splendor, brightness.

fulgur, -uris [*cf. fulgeo*], N. lightning.

fulmen, -inis [*fulgeo*], N. a thunderbolt (*conceived as a missile*), lightning, a flash of lightning. — *Poetically, of persons,* thunderbolt (*destroying agency in war*).

fulmineus, -a, -um [*fulmen*], adj. like lightning, flashing; like a thunderbolt.

fulminō, -āre, -āvī, -ātum [*fulmen*], 1. v. n. lighten; flash and thunder (**armis**).

fulvus, -a, -um, adj. tawny, yellow.

fūmeus, -a, -um [*fumus*], adj. smoky.

fūmifer, -era, -erum [*fumus, fero*], adj. smoky.

fūmō, -āre, -āvī, -ātum [*fumus*], 1. v. n. smoke; steam, reek. — **fūmāns, -antis**, p. as adj. smoking, smoky.

fūmus, -ī, M. smoke.

fūnālis, -e [*funis*], adj. of a rope. — N. *as subst.* **fūnāle, -is**, a torch (*made on a cord*).

funda, -ae, F. a sling.

fundāmen, -inis [*fundo*], N. foundation.

fundāmentum, -ī [*fundo*], N. a foundation.

funditus [*fundus*], adv. from the bottom, from the foundation; utterly, entirely.

fundō, -āre, -āvī, -ātum [*fundus*], 1. v. a. (set on the bottom), secure, make fast; found, build, establish.

fundō, -ere, fūdī, fūsum [√*fud*], 3. v. a. pour, pour out, pour forth, shed; send forth (**armatos**); rout, put to flight; throw to the ground, lay low. — *With reflexive or in pass.* spread, extend, be spread; pour in, swarm round, press round.

fundus, -ī, M. the bottom, the foundation: **imo fundo** (the lowest depths).

fūnereus, -a, -um [*funus*], adj. of death, funereal, funeral: **frons** (dark, *in sign of mourning*).

fūnestō, -āre, -āvī, -ātum [*funestus*], 1. v. a. defile with murder; destroy.

fūnestus, -a, -um [*funus*], adj. deadly.

fungor, fungī, fūnctus, 3. v. dep. perform, discharge; receive (*burial*); act its part for: **igne focus**.

fūnis, -is, M. a rope, a cord, a cable.

fūnus, -eris, N. murder, slaughter, havoc; death; a corpse; a funeral, funeral rites: **sub funus** (on the brink of the grave).

furia, -ae [*furo*], F. *usually pl.* rage, madness, fury, frenzy; remorse: **scelerum; furiis incensa**. — *Personified,* a Fury (*goddess of divine vengeance*). — *Also of the* Harpies.

furibundus, -a, -um [*furo*], adj. mad, furious, frenzied.

furiō, -āre, -āvī, -ātum [*furia*], 1. v. a. drive mad, madden, infuriate. — **furiātus, -a, -um**, p.p. as adj. frenzied, frantic, infuriated.

furō, -ere, *no perf., no sup., 3. v. n.*
rage, rave, be crazed; do any-
thing wildly: **aestus ad auras**
(rise wildly). — **furēns, -entis,**
p. as adj. distracted, passion-
stricken, inspired, raging, furious, raving.

furor, -ōris [*furo*], M. fury, madness, rage, raving; *of love,* frenzy,
passion.— *Personified,* Rage.

fūror, -ārī, -ātus [*fur*], *1. v. dep.*
steal, get by stealth.— *Fig.* steal:
fessos oculos labori.

fūrtim [*fur*], *adv.* by stealth, secretly, stealthily.

fūrtīvus, -a, -um [*furtum*], *adj.*
stealthy; secret, hidden.

fūrtum, -ī [*fur*], N. theft, stealth;
deceit, craft, concealment; a
trick, a stratagem, an artifice;
furta, the stolen (cattle).

Fuscus, -ī, M. Aristius Fuscus, a
friend of Horace.

fūsilis, -e [*fundo*], *adj.* melted,
molten.

futūrus, -a, -um, *see* **sum.**

Gabiī, -ōrum, M. *pl.* a town of
Latium, early destroyed; famous
for the worship of Juno (vi. 773).

Gabīnus, -a, -um, *adj.* Gabine, of
Gabii (vii. 612). *See* **cīnctus.**

Gaetūlus, -a, -um, *adj.* Gætulian,
of the Gætuli (a nation of Africa,
now Morocco) (iv. 40).— M. *pl.*
the Gætuli.— *Less exactly,* African.

galea, -ae, F. a helmet.

Gallus, -a, -um, *adj.* of Gaul, Gallic.— M. *as subst.* a Gaul (vi. 858).

Gallus, -ī, M. C. Cornelius Gallus,
the poet, Virgil's friend.

Ganymēdēs, -is (-ī), M. Ganymede, a beautiful youth, son of
Laomedon, carried away by an
eagle to be the cupbearer of Jove
(i. 28).

Garamantes, -um, M. *pl.* a nation
in Africa (Fezzan) (vi. 794).

Garamantis, -idis, *adj.* of the
Garamantes; Libyan (iv. 198).

gaudeō, -ēre, gāvīsus, *2. v. n.*
feel joy, be delighted, rejoice;
delight in, take pleasure in. —
gaudēns, -entis, *p. as adj.* delighted, well pleased.

gaudium, -ī (-iī) [*cf. gaudeo*], N.
joy, delight, pleasure; a delight.
— *Personified*: **mala** (Criminal
Delights).

gaza, -ae, F. treasure, riches,
wealth.

Gela, -ae, F. a city of Sicily, on the
south coast, by a river of the
same name, now Terra Nuova
(iii. 702).

gelidus, -a, -um [*gelus*], *adj.* icy,
cold, cool; chill, clammy, shivering.

Gelōus, -a, -um, *adj.* of Gela,
Geloan (iii. 701).

gelus, -ūs, M. frost.

gemellus, -a, -um [*geminus*], *adj.*
twin-born.— M. *as subst.* a twin,
a twin brother.

geminō, -āre, -āvī, -ātum [*geminus*], *1. v. a.* double.

geminus, -a, -um, *adj.* twin-born,
twin; double, a pair of, both,
two; similar, corresponding. —
Pl. as subst. a pair, twins.

gemitus, -ūs [*gemo*], M. a groan-
ing, a groan, a sigh; wailing, lamentation; a roar, a hollow roar.

gemma, -ae, F. a gem, a jewel.

gemō, -ere, -uī, -itum, *3. v. n. and a.* groan, sigh, wail; bewail, lament; creak.

genae, -ārum (*rarely sing.*), F. cheeks.

gener, generī, M. a son-in-law; a daughter's suitor.

generātor, -ōris [*cf. genero*], M. a breeder.

generō, -āre, -āvī, -ātum [*genus*], *1. v. a.* beget; Anchisā generate (son of).

generōsus, -a, -um [*genus*], *adj.* high-born, noble; fine, excellent.

genetrīx, -īcis [√*gen* (*of gigno*)], F. a mother.

geniālis, -e [*genius*], *adj.* (of the Genius, *or relating to his worship*); cheerful, festival (*as the rites were of a jovial nature*), devoted to joy.

geniāliter [*genialis*], *adv.* joyously, jovially.

genitor, -ōris [√*gen* (*of gigno*)], M. a father, a sire.

genitus, -a, -um, *p.p. of* gignō.

genius, -ī (-iī), M. a tutelary divinity, a genius (a semi-divine personage attached to a person or place).

gēns, gentis [√*gen* (*of gigno*)], F. offspring; a race, a nation, a tribe: gentes (the nations, the whole world); gentibus (for all nations).

gentīlis, -e [*gens*], *adj.* (all) of one family (gens).

genū, -ūs, N. the knee: genua trahens (limbs).

genus, -eris [√*gen* (*of gigno*)], N. race, descent, family, lineage, birth; tribe, kind; offspring, progeny; a kind, a sort, a species.

germānus, -a, -um, *adj.* akin, of the same stock. — M. *as subst.* germānus, -ī, a brother. — F. germāna, -ae, a sister.

gerō, -ere, gessī, gestum [√*ges*], *3. v. a.* bear, carry, wield, wear; *also, poetically, of abstract ideas*: pacem; tempora umbrata quercu; vittas; tela; os habitumque; volnera (display); nomenque decusque (possess). — *Fig. of any action* (*esp. of war*), carry on, wage, manage: bellum.

Gēryon, -onis (Gēryonēs, -ae), M. a monster of Spain whose cattle were carried off by Hercules (viii. 202).

gestāmen, -inis [*gesto*], N. a thing borne; arms; an ornament, insignia.

gestiō, -īre, -īvī (-iī), -ītum, *4. v. n.* be eager.

gestō, -āre, -āvī, -ātum [*gero, gestus*], *1. v. a.* bear, carry, wear: pectora (possess).

Getae, -ārum, M. *pl.* a Thracian tribe on the Danube.

Geticē, *adv.* in the Getic language.

Geticus, -a, -um, *adj.* of the Getæ.

gignō, -ere, genuī, genitum [√*gen redupl.*], *3. v. a.* beget, bring forth, bear. — genitus, -a, -um, *p.p. as adj.* sprung, descended, son of.

glaciālis, -e [*glacies*], *adj.* icy, cold, frozen, frosty.

glaciēs, -ēī, F. ice, frost, cold.

gladius, -ī (-iī), M. a sword.

glaeba, -ae, F. a clod, a lump of earth; soil, land.

glāns, glandis, F. an acorn.

glaucus, -a, -um, *adj.* gray, sea-green.

Glaucus, -ī, M. 1. A fisherman of Anthedon, in Bœotia, who was changed into a sea-deity (v. 823). — 2. The father of Deiphobe, the priestess of Apollo at Cumæ, known as the Cumæan Sibyl (vi. 36). — 3. A grandson of Bellerophon, leader of the Lycians in the Trojan war (vi. 483).

glīscō, -ere, *no perf. or sup., 3. v. n.* increase.

globus, -ī, M. a ball, a sphere; a band, crowd.

glomerō, -āre, -āvī, -ātum, *1. v. a.* roll into a ball, roll up; gather, collect, mass: manum bello. — *In pass.* gather, assemble. — *Poetically*: saxa sub auras (throw forth balls of melted lava).

glōria, -ae, F. glory, fame, renown; vainglory, pride, ambition; the glory, the pride: Procas Troianae gentis.

glōrior, -ārī, -ātus [*gloria*], *1. v. dep.* glory, boast.

gnāscor, *see* nāscor.

gnātus, -a, -um, *p.p. of* (g)nāscor.

Gnōsius, -a, -um, *adj.* of Gnosus (the city of Minos, in Crete), Gnosian; Cretan (iii. 115).

Golgī, -ōrum, M. *pl.* a town in Cyprus.

Gorgō, -onis, F. a Gorgon (one of three mythical women of Libya, having some resemblance to the Furies).—*Esp.* Medusa, the chief of these sisters. She was slain by Perseus. Her head with serpent hair was placed in the shield or ægis of Jove and Pallas. — *Pl.* the three sisters, Gorgons (vi. 289). — *Also*, the Gorgon's head in the shield of Jove or Pallas (ii. 616).

Gracchus, -ī, M. a Roman family name in the Sempronian gens; *esp.* the two great reformers, Tiberius and Caius (Lat. Gaius) (vi. 842).

gradior, gradī, gressus, *3. v. dep.* walk, go, move, proceed, advance.

Gradīvus, -ī [*cf. gradior*], M. (the Strider), a name of Mars (iii. 35).

gradus, -ūs [*cf. gradior*], M. a step: conferre (*i.e.* walk together); continere; revocare; referre; sistere; celerare (pace). — *Also* a step (*of a temple or a funeral pile*), a round (*of a ladder*).

Grāiugena, -ae [*Graius*, √*gen* (*of gigno*)], M. a Grecian born, a Greek (iii. 550).

Grāius, -a, -um, *adj.* Greek. — M. a Greek; *pl.* the Greeks.

grāmen, -inis, N. grass, an herb; a grassy plain.

grāmineus, -a, -um [*gramen*], *adj.* grassy.

grandaevus, -a, -um [*grandis, aevum*], *adj.* aged, old.

grandis, -e, *adj.* large, great, huge: grandior aevo (older).

grandō, -dinis, F. hail.

grātēs (*abl.* -ibus) [*cf. gratus*], F. thanks: dicere (render); persolvere (pay a debt of gratitude).

grātia, -ae [*gratus*], F. regard, pleasure in, fondness for; gratitude, thankfulness.— *Pl.* thanks.

grātor, -ārī, -ātus [*gratus*], *1. v. dep.* congratulate.

grātus, -a, -um, *adj.* dear, pleasing, acceptable, beloved; grateful, thankful.

gravidus, -a, -um [*gravis*], *adj.* heavy; full, laden; teeming, big: imperiis Italiam; bellis urbem.

gravis, -e, *adj.* heavy, firm, solid; pregnant; grievous, hard, toilsome; burdened (*with years*); cruel, fierce; revered, of weight (*influence*). — N. *pl. as subst.* gravia, heavy toils, things hard to bear; serious events, results, *etc.* — N. *sing.* grave, *as adv.* ill, noisome: grave olens.

graviter [*gravis*], *adv.* heavily (*lit. and fig.*), violently, deeply, loudly.

gravō, -āre, -āvī, -ātum [*gravis*], *1. v. a.* weigh down, make heavy; trouble, annoy, burden.

gremium, -ī (-iī), N. the lap, the bosom, the breast: in vestris pono gremiis (lay at one's feet). — *Fig.* (*of a country, etc.*), bosom, lap, embrace: telluris.

gressus, -ūs [*gradior*], M. a step, a pace; gait, bearing; a way, course: efferre (proceed forth); comprimere (stay one's steps); ante ferre (go on before).

grex, gregis, M. (*rarely* F.), a herd, a flock.

Grȳnēus, -a, -um, *adj.* of Grynia (a town in Æolis where Apollo was worshipped), Grynean (iv. 345).

gubernāculum (-clum), -ī [*guberno*], N. a tiller, a helm.

gubernātor, -ōris [*guberno*], M. a helmsman, pilot.

gurges, -itis, M. a vortex, a whirlpool, an abyss, a gulf; a wave, a tide, waters, a stream; the sea, the ocean; a flood.

gustō, -āre, -āvī, -ātum [*gustus*], *1. v. a.* taste.

gutta, -ae, F. a drop; a tear.

guttur, -uris, N. the throat; the mouth.

Gyaros (-us), -ī, F. an island of the Ægean, now Calairo (iii. 76).

Gyās, -ae, M. a companion of Æneas (i. 222).

gȳrus, -ī, M. a circle; a coil, a fold (*of a serpent*).

habēna, -ae [*habeo*], F. a rein, a lash, a bridle: dare (immittere, effundere) habenas (give loose rein, *lit. and fig.*); premere habenas (tighten, pull in); immissis habenis (at full speed, without restraint).

habeō, -ēre, -uī, -itum, *2. v. a., lit. and fig.* hold, have, possess, keep; occupy, inhabit; wear. — *Also of the place where one is*: te pontus (cover); turba hunc (surround); me thalamus (be in, *changing point of view*). — *Of passions and the like*, possess, inspire: omnīs ardor. — *Also,* hold, consider, regard: domos suspectas; nullo discrimine (treat).

habilis, -e [*habeo*], *adj.* convenient, fit, suited; active.

habitō, -āre, -āvī, -ātum [*habeo*], *1. v. a. and n.* occupy, inhabit, dwell in; dwell, live.

habitus, -ūs [*habeo*], M. bearing, carriage, appearance; dress, garb.

hāc [*cf. hic*], *adv.* this way, here. — **hāc ... hāc,** here ... there.

hāctenus (*often separated*) [*hac + tenus*], *adv.* hitherto, to this point, thus far; to this day.

Hadriāticum (*sc. mare*), **-ī,** N. the Adriatic.

haedus, -ī, M. a kid.

Haemus, -ī, M. a mountain range in Thrace.

haereō, -ēre, haesī, haesum, 2. *v. n.* stick, cleave, adhere, cling, stick fast, hang, hold fast, be fastened; stand motionless, be rooted to the spot, remain fixed, stand fast; hesitate, pause, be in doubt, linger; hang upon (*of the gaze or of pursuit*): **hic terminus** (be fixed); **aspectu conterritus.**

hālitus, -ūs [*halo*], M. breath; an exhalation, a vapor.

hālō, -āre, -āvī, -ātum, 1. *v. n.* exhale; be fragrant.

Hammōn (Ammōn), -ōnis, M. an African divinity identified with Jupiter (iv. 198).

hāmus, -ī, M. a hook, a link, a barb.

harēna, -ae, F. sand, earth; the seashore, beach, strand.

harēnōsus, -a, -um [*harena*], *adj.* sandy.

Harpalycē, -ēs, F. a female warrior of Thrace (i. 317).

Harpȳia, -ae, F. Harpy, a monster with the body of a bird and a human face and voice (iii. 212).

harundō, -inis, F. a reed, a fishing rod, an arrow shaft, an arrow.

hasta, -ae, F. a spear shaft, a spear; a wand.

hastīle, -is [*hasta*], N. a spear shaft, a spear; a shoot, a sapling.

haud, *neg. adv.* (*commonly negativing some particular word*; *cf.* **non,** *general negative*), not, by no means: **haud mora** (there is no delay).

haudquāquam, *adv.* by no means, not at all.

hauriō, -īre, hausī, haustum, 4. *v. a.* drink, drain, exhaust; drink in, take in, draw in, receive: **vocem auribus; oculis monumenta** (feast the eyes upon, gaze upon); **corda pavor** (absorb, possess); **supplicia scopulis** (suffer death by drowning); **ensis inimicus** (*of persons*, drink their blood). — N. *pl. p.p. as subst.* **hausta,** draughts.

haustus, -ūs [*haurio*], M. a draught.

hebeō, -ēre, *no perf., no sup.* [*cf.* **hebes**], 2. *v. n.* be dull: **sanguis** (be chilled).

hebetō, -āre, -āvī, -ātum [*hebes*], 1. *v. a.* blunt, dull; dim, impair.

Hebrus, -ī, M. a river of Thrace, now Maritza (i. 317).

Hecatē, -ēs, F. a goddess associated with the Lower World. She was especially identified as a three-formed goddess with the Moon (in heaven), Diana (on earth), and Proserpine (in the World Below).

Hector, -oris, M. the eldest son of Priam, and the most famous warrior of the Trojans; slain by Achilles and dragged round the walls of Troy.

Hectoreus, -a, -um, *adj.* of Hector; of Troy, Trojan.

Hecuba, -ae, F. the wife of Priam (ii. 501).

hēia, *interj.* ho! what ho! come on! come! on!

Helena, -ae, F. Helen, the daughter of Jupiter and Leda, carried off by Paris (i. 650).

Helenus, -ī, M. a son of Priam (iii. 295 ff.).

Helicē, -ēs, F. the constellation of the Great Bear.

Helicōn, -ōnis, M. a mountain in Bœotia, sacred to Apollo and the Muses. — *Fig.* poetry.

Helōrus (-um), -ī, M. *and* N. a city on the east coast of Sicily. A wide, slow river of the same name flowed over the flat land in the vicinity (iii. 698).

Helymus, -ī, M. a companion of Æneas (v. 73).

herba, -ae, F. an herb, a weed, a plant; grass, herbage; sward.

Herculēs, -is, M. the famous demigod, renowned for his strength and services to mankind, represented with a club and lion's skin. The poplar was sacred to him.

Herculeus, -a, -um, *adj.* of Hercules: **Tarentum** (founded by Hercules, Herculean. iii. 551).

hērēs, -ēdis, C. an heir.

Hermionē, -ēs, F. daughter of Menelaus and Helen; wife of Orestes (iii. 328).

hērōs, -ōis (-ōos), M. a demigod, a hero.

hērōus, -a, -um [*heros*], *adj.* of a hero, heroic. — M. *as subst.* (*sc.*

versus), heroic (epic) verse, epic poetry.

Hesperia, *see* **Hesperius.**

Hesperis, -ides, F. *adj.* Western, Hesperian, Italian. — *Pl. subst.* the Hesperides, the daughters of Hesperus, keepers of a garden of golden apples in the far West (iv. 484).

Hesperius, -a, -um, *adj.* Western; Hesperian, Italian. — F. **Hesperia** (*sc.* **terra**), the Western land, Italy (as viewed from Greece), Hesperia (i. 530).

heu, *interj.* (*of grief or pain*), alas! ah! oh! ah me!

heus, *interj.* (*of calling*), ho! hallo! ho there!

hiātus, -ūs [*hio*], M. a gaping, an opening; a yawning mouth, a mouth.

hībernus, -a, -um [*cf. hiems*], *adj.* of (the) winter, wintry, winter's, stormy. — N. *pl. as subst.* **hīberna, -ōrum,** winters.

Hibērus, -a, -um, *adj.* Iberian, Spanish; western: **gurges.**

hic, haec, hoc, *dem. pron.* (*as subst. or adj., of something near in time, place, or thought*), this, he, she, it, such. — *Of indefinite persons*, this man, one. — *Often repeated, or correlative with another pron.* this . . . that, he . . . he, one ... another, the former ... the latter. — *Also,* the following, as follows. — *In abl. with comparative,* so much, the more.

hīc [*hic*], *adv.* here, there; hereupon.

hiems, hiemis, F. winter, storm, tempest. — *Personified,* the Storm.

hinc [cf. hic], adv. from here, hence, from there, from this, from these; here, on this side; then, thereupon, next, hereupon.— Often, repeated or opposed to another adv.: hinc ... hinc, hinc atque hinc (illinc), on this side ... on that, here ... there, on every side, around.

hiŏ, -āre, -āvī, -ātum, 1. v. n. gape, yawn.— hiāns, -antis, p. as adj. opening the mouth, gaping.

Hippocoōn, -ontis, M. a companion of Æneas (v. 492).

Hippotadēs, -ae, M. Æolus, son (or grandson) of Hippotes.

hirsūtus, -a, -um, adj. hairy, rough, shaggy.

hīscō, -ere, no perf., no sup. [hio], 3. v. n. gape, open the mouth.

Hister, -trī, M. the lower Danube.

hodiē [† hŏ- (stem) or hō (abl.) of pron. √hŏ (cf. hic) + diē (abl. of dies)], adv. to-day.— Weakened, with negatives, now, surely: numquam hodie moriemur (emphasizing the negative).

homō, -inis, C. a man (or woman), a mortal.

honestus, -a, -um [honos, old form of honor], adj. honorable, of gentle birth.

honor (-ōs), -ōris, M. honor, glory, fame, dignity; reward, prize, meed of praise; worship, sacrifice, reverence, an offering, an observance (patrius honor); beauty, grace, charm; adornment, decoration.

honōrō, -āre, -āvī, -ātum [honor] 1. v. a. honor, respect, observe with honor.

hōra, -ae, F. an hour; time, moment; season: in horas, from hour to hour.— Personified, Hōrae, -ārum, pl. the Hours (attendants of the Sun, Moon, etc.).

Horātius, -ī (-iī), M. Q. Horatius Flaccus the poet, Horace.

horrendus, see horreō.

horrēns, see horreō.

horreō, -ēre, horruī, no sup., 2. v. n. and a. stand erect, bristle, be rough: colla colubris.— From the tingling sensation of fear, shudder, shudder at, dread.— horrēns, -entis, p. as adj. bristling, rough, prickly, shaggy. — horrendus, -a, -um, ger. p. as adj. horrible, dreadful, awful, frightful, dread.— N. as adv. dreadfully. — N. pl. prodigies, horrors.

horrēscō, -ere, horruī, no sup. [horreo], 3. v. n. and a. tremble, shudder; dread: visu; morsus mensarum (shudder at).

horridus, -a, -um [horreo], adj. rough, shaggy, bristling: hastilibus myrtus.— Fig. dreadful, dread, horrid, frightful, awful.

horrificō, -āre, -āvī, -ātum [horrificus], 1. v. a. terrify, cause terror or horror, affright.

horrificus, -a, -um [horreo, facio], adj. terrible, frightful.

horrisonus, -a, -um [horreo, sonus], adj. dread-sounding, of awful sound.

horror, -ōris [horreo], M. a bristling; a shudder; dread, horror: armorum (dread sound).

hortātor, -ōris [hortor], M. an encourager, suggester, inciter.

hortor, -ārī, -ātus, *1. v. dep.* exhort, encourage, advise, urge, address (*with words of encouragement as a leader*).

hortus, -ī, M. a garden.

hospes, -itis, C. a host; a guest, a stranger. — *As an address*, stranger, friend. — *Also*, a friend (hereditary *or* family, *in the peculiar relation of antiquity*).

hospita, -ae [*hospes*], F. a stranger.

hospitium, -ī (-iī) [*hospes*], N. entertainment, hospitality; alliance, friendship; a retreat, shelter; a friend, an ally.

†**hospitus, -a, -um** (*only in* F. *and* N. *pl.*) [*hospes*], *adj.* strange, foreign.

hostia, -ae, F. a victim (*for sacrifice*).

hosticus, -a, -um [*hostis*], *adj.* hostile, of the enemy, the enemy's.

hostīlis, -e [*hostis*], *adj.* of an (the) enemy, the enemy's, hostile.

hostis, -is, C. a stranger; an enemy (*of the country, cf.* **inimicus,** one's own private enemy), a foe; the enemy.

hūc [*hic*], *adv.* hither, here (*of motion*): **includunt** (in this); **adde** (to this); **huc atque illuc** (this way and that).

hūmānus, -a, -um [*cf.* **homo**], *adj.* of man, human, mortal, of mortals.

humilis, -e [*humus*], *adj.* low: **humilis volat; Italia** (low-lying).

humō, -āre, -āvī, -ātum [*humus*], *1. v. a.* bury, inter.

humus, -ī, F. the ground, the earth, the soil. — **humī,** on the ground: **procumbit humi bos.**

Hyades, -um, F. *pl.* the Hyades, a group of seven stars in the head of Taurus (the Bull), whose rising with the sun was attended by storms (i. 744; iii. 516).

Hydaspes, -is, M. a river of India.

hydra, -ae, F. a hydra *or* water-serpent (in the infernal regions, acting, like monsters generally, as a minister of divine vengeance — perhaps the shade of the famous Hydra of Lerna, killed by Hercules: vi. 576. This had nine heads, which multiplied as fast as they were cut off).

hydrus (-os), -ī, M. a water-snake, a serpent.

Hymenaeus, -ī, M. Hymen, the marriage god; marriage, wedlock; nuptial rites, a wedding; a nuptial song.

Hymettius, -a, -um, *adj.* of *or* from Hymettus, a mountain in Attica; of marble from Hymettus.

Hypanis, -is, M. a Trojan (ii. 340).

Hyperboreus, -a, -um, *adj.* of the Hyperboreans, a race supposed to live in the far North; Hyperborean.

Hyrcānus, -a, -um, *adj.* of the Hyrcani, a nation on the Caspian Sea, comprehended under the general idea of the Parthians, with whom the Romans were long at war (iv. 367).

Hyrtacidēs, -ae, M. son of Hyrtacus (Hippocoön or Nisus) (v. 492; ix. 234).

iambus, -ī, M. an iambic foot *or* verse.

Iāpyx, -ygis, M. Iapyx, the northwesterly wind, blowing from Iapygia or Apulia into Greece (viii. 710).

Iarbās, -ae, M. a king of the Gætulians in Libya, son of Jupiter Ammon, and a suitor of Dido (iv. 36).

Iasidēs, -ae, M. descendant of Iasius (v. 843).

Iasius, -ī (-iī), M. the brother of Dardanus, son of Jupiter and Electra. He married a daughter of Teucer, and so was one of the founders of the Trojan race (iii. 168).

iaspis, -idis, F. jasper.

ibǐ [*cf. is*], *adv.* there; then, thereupon.

ibīdem [*ibi* + *-dem*], *adv.* in the same place, on the same spot; at the same time.

Īcarius, -ī (-iī), M. Penelope's father, usually called Icarus (-os).

Īcarus, -ī, M. the son of Dædalus, who fell accompanying his father's flight (vi. 31).

īcō, īcere, īcī, ictum, *3. v. a.* strike, hit.

ictus, -ūs [*ico*], M. a stroke, a blow, a jet (*of water*).

Īda, -ae (Īdē, -ēs), F. a mountain of Phrygia, near Troy (ii. 801).

Īdaeus, -a, -um, *adj.* Idæan, of Ida, a mountain in the centre of Crete, the seat of a famous worship of Jupiter. Here he was supposed to have been nursed in secret (iii. 105). — *Also,* Idæan, of (the Phrygian) Ida (ii. 696).

Īdaeus, -ī, M. Priam's herald and charioteer (vi. 485).

Īdalius, -a, -um, *adj.* of Idalium, Idalian (v. 760). — F. Idalia, a town and grove of Cyprus (i. 693). — N. Idalium, *another form of the same name* (i. 681).

idcircō [*id* (N. *acc. of is*) + *circo* (*dat. or abl. of circus*)], *adv.* for that reason, therefore, for this purpose. — *With negatives,* for all that, for that, on that account.

īdem, eadem, idem [*is* + *-dem*], *adj. pron.* the same, the very, the like. — *Often equivalent to a mere connective,* also, likewise, as well. *See* **eōdem.**

ideō [*id* (N. *acc. of is*) + *eo*], *adv.* for this reason, therefore, on this account.

Īdomeneus, -eī (*acc.* **-ea**), M. a hero of the Trojan war, leader of the Cretans (iii. 122).

igitur, *adv.* in that case; *as conj.* accordingly, therefore.

ignārus, -a, -um [*in-* + *gnarus* (√*gna*)], *adj.* not knowing, ignorant, senseless; unacquainted with; unaware, unsuspecting: **au-res** (deaf).

ignāvus, -a, -um [*in-* + *gnavus* (√*gna*)], *adj.* idle, slothful, without spirit.

igneus, -a, -um [*ignis*], *adj.* fiery, blazing, burning.

ignipotēns, -entis [*ignis, potens*], M. Lord of Fire (*Vulcan*).

ignis, -is, M. fire, flame, heat, brand, flash: **ignes** (lightnings); **aeterni** (*the stars*). — *Fig.* passion, love, fury, wrath, frenzy. — *Pl.* loves, love poems.

ignōbilis, -e [*in-* + (*g*)*nobilis*], *adj.* ignoble, inglorious, obscure.

ignōrō, -āre, -āvī, -ātum [*cf. ignarus*], *1. v. a.* not know, be unaware of, be ignorant of.

ignōscō, -ere, -nōvī, -nōtum [*in-* + (*g*)*nosco*], *3. v. n.* pardon, forgive.

ignōtus, -a, -um [*in-* + (*g*)*notus*], *adj.* unknown, obscure; strange; unobserved : **heres** (unexpected).

īlex, -icis, F. a holm oak.

īlia, -ōrum, N. *pl.* the entrails.

Īlia, -ae, F. a name for Rhea Silvia, the mother of Romulus and Remus (i. 274).

Īliacus, -a, -um, *adj.* of Ilium, Trojan.

Īlias, -adis, F. a Trojan woman. — *Also,* the Iliad of Homer.

īlicet [*i* (*imper. of eo*) + *licet*, go, you may], *adv.* (*orig. formula of dismissal for an assembled people,* it is over, you may depart). — *Transferred,* forthwith, immediately, at once.

Īlionē, -ēs, F. the oldest daughter of Priam, married to Polymestor, king of Thrace (i. 653).

Īlioneus, -eī (*acc.* -ea), M. 1. An aged Trojan, companion of Æneas (i. 120). — 2. A son of Niobe.

Īlios, -ī (-iī), F. Troy.

Īlium, -ī (-iī), N. a name of Troy, city of Ilus.

Īlius, -a, -um, *adj.* Ilian, Trojan, of Troy.

illāc [*ille*], *adv.* that way.

ille (ollus), illa, illud, *dem. pron.* (*conceived as more remote than* hic), that, these. — *Without noun,* he, she, that, it. — *Contrary to English usage, of what follows,* this, these, these things. — *Often repeated or opposed to another pron.* the other, that one, that, the former (*cf.* hic). — *Of a conspicuous person or object (as if pointed at),* the great, that. — *In comparisons (to make the comparison more vivid, as if it were actually in sight),* some, a. — *In imitation of Homeric* ὅ γε, *redundant, merely continuing the subject of discourse.* — **ex illo,** from that time.

illīc [*ille*], *adv.* there, in that place.

illinc [*ille*], *adv.* thence, from there; on that side, that side : **hinc illinc** (on this side and that).

illūc [*ille*], *adv.* thither, that way.

Illyricus, -a, -um, *adj.* of Illyria, a region east of the Adriatic, north of Greece proper.

Īlus, -ī, M. 1. the mythical founder of Ilium, grandfather of Priam (vi. 650); 2. a name of Iulus (i. 268).

imāgō, -inis, F. a representation, an imitation, a copy; appearance, shape : **genitoris** (a resemblance); **formae** (empty form). — *Esp.* a phantom, a shade, an apparition, a form : **magna mei** (I, a renowned shade); **pallentis Adrasti.** — *Of the mind,* a picture, a conception, a thought, an idea : **pietatis; pugnae; plurima mortis** (form).

imbellis, -e [*in-, bellum*], *adj.* unwarlike : **telum** (ineffective).

imber, -bris, M. rain, rainstorm, rain-cloud, storm; water (*of the sea*); a flood of tears.

imbuō, -ere, -uī, -ūtum, *3. v. a.*
dip, moisten.

imitābilis, -e [*imitor*], *adj.* imita-
ble : non imitabile fulmen (that
cannot be imitated).

imitor, -ārī, -ātus, *1. v. dep.* imitate, counterfeit, copy ; take the
form of.

immānis, -e, *adj.* huge, monstrous,
enormous ; inhuman, wild, fierce,
savage, cruel : nefas ; fluvius (impetuous) ; monstra (prodigious).

immemor, -oris [*in-* + *memor*],
adj. unmindful, forgetful ; regardless, heedless, unheeding ;
free from memory (*of the souls of
the dead drinking the waters of
Lethe*).

immēnsus, -a, -um [*in-* + *mensus*, *p.p.* of *metior*], *adj.* unmeasured, immeasurable, huge,
immense, unbounded, enormous,
boundless, vast ; tremendous, prodigious.

immergō, -ere, -mersī, -mersum
[*in* + *mergo*], *3. v. a.* plunge,
drown, overwhelm.

immeritus, -a, -um [*in-* + *meritus*], *adj.* undeserving, who deserves not ; undeserving of evil,
unoffending.

immineō, -ēre, *no perf., no sup.*
[*in* + *mineo*], *2. v. n.* overhang,
project over, threaten : silex
(hangs threatening).

immisceō, -ēre, -miscuī, -mis-
tum (-mixtum) [*in* + *misceo*],
2. v. a. mix in, mingle : maculae
igni ; manus manibus (mingle
fist with fist, *of boxers*) ; immixti
Danais (mingled with) ; nocti se
(vanish, be lost).

immītis, -e [*in-* + *mitis*], *adj.* cruel,
ruthless, ferocious.

immittō, -ere, -mīsī, -missum
[*in* + *mitto*], *3. v. a.* let go in,
send in, let in, send to : avīs
terris. — *Esp. in p.p.* : immissi
Danai (bursting in). — *Less exactly*, let loose, let fly, let go :
immissa barba (flowing). — *With
reflexive*, throw one's self, rush.
— *Esp. of driving*, let loose, let
go, spur on : immissis habenis
(without control, *of fire*). — *Fig.*
inspire, inflict : curas.

immō, *more or less contradicting
what precedes, often to assert something stronger*, no, nay, nay rather,
nay but.

immōbilis, -e [*in-* + *mobilis*], *adj.*
immovable, unmoved, unshaken.

immolō, -āre, -āvī, -ātum [*in*,
mola], *1. v. a.* sacrifice, slay.

immorior, -morī, -mortuus [*in* +
morior], *3. v. dep.* die upon.

immortālis, -e [*in* + *mortalis*],
adj. immortal, undying, eternal.

immōtus, -a, -um [*in-* + *motus*,
p.p. of moveo], *adj.* unmoved, undisturbed, immovable, unshaken,
secure, fixed : unda (tranquil) ;
immotum sederet animo (im-
movably fixed).

immūgiō, -īre, -īvī (-iī), *no sup.*
[*in* + *mugio*], *4. v. n.* bellow
within ; resound within.

immundus, -a, -um [*in-* + *mundus*], *adj.* unclean, foul, filthy.

immūnis, -e, *adj.* free from.

impār, -paris [*in-* + *par*], *adj.* unequal, uneven ; ill-matched : puer
congressus Achilli (on unequal
terms).

impavidus, -a, -um [in- + pavidus], adj. undaunted, fearless.

impediō, -īre, -īvī (-iī), -ītum [in, pes], 4. v. a. entangle, entwine, interweave; hinder, hamper.

impellō, -ere, -pulī, -pulsum [in + pello], 3. v. a. strike upon, strike, smite: cuspide montem. — Also, of the result, push over, overthrow, overturn: turrim. — Esp. urge on, urge, drive, force on: remos; manu euntem. — Fig. urge, impel, induce, force, compel; shake: animum labantem.

impēnsa, -ae [impensus], F. cost, expense.

impēnsē [impensus], adv. expensively, earnestly. — Comp. impēnsius.

imperiōsus, -a, -um [imperium], adj. powerful; imperious, lordly, violent.

imperium, -ī (-iī) [impero], N. command, authority, sway, rule; a command, an order; an empire.

imperō, -āre, -āvī, -ātum, 1. v. a. and n. command, order: ferri dona.

impete [in, peto], abl. M. with force.

impetus, -ūs [in, peto], M. a violent rush, an impulse; force, violence (of attack), momentum; speed.

impiger, -gra, -grum [in- + piger], adj. active, energetic: hausit pateram (nothing loth).

impingō, -ere, -pēgī, -pāctum [in + pango], 3. v. a. dash against: agmina muris (force to).

impius, -a, -um [in- + pius], adj. impious, sacrilegious, godless; accursed (of anything without divine qualities of mercy and justice). Furor; Fama. — Poetically: fata (of impiety); Tartara (impious, the abode of the impious). — M. impious wretch.

implācābilis, -e [in- + placabilis], adj. implacable, unappeasable.

implācātus, -a, -um [in- + placatus], adj. inexorable, insatiable.

implectō, -ere, -plexī, -plectum, 3. v. a. entwine.

impleō, -plēre, -plēvī, -plētum [in + †pleo], 2. v. a. fill in, fill up, fill; satiate, satisfy; inspire: sinus (swell); manum pinu (seize with full hand); animum veris (fill, inspire).

implicō, -āre, -āvī (-uī), -ātum (-itum) [in + †plico], 1. v. a. entwine, interweave, enfold, entangle: crinem auro; comam laeva (grasp); se dextrae (clasp); ossibus ignem (kindle).

implōrō, -āre, -āvī, -ātum [in + ploro], 1. v. a. and n. call upon, beseech, implore; beg for.

impōnō, -ere, -posuī, -positum [in + pono], 3. v. a. place upon, place, lay; serve up; impose, lay upon, fix, put, enjoin: finem pugnae; paci morem (ordain); dominum patriae. — P.p. impositus, -a, -um, standing upon.

impotēns, entis [in + potens], adj. violent, furious.

imprecor, -ārī, -ātus [in + precor], 1. v. dep. pray (for something against some one).

imprimō, -ere, -pressī, -pressum [in + premo], 3. v. a. impress. — impressus, -a, -um, p.p. chased (of ornament).

improbus, -a, -um [*in-* + *probus*], *adj.* wicked, bad, mischievous, malicious, cruel; shameless; ravenous: **fortuna** (malicious goddess); **rabies ventris** (ravening).

improperātus, -a, -um [*in-* + *properatus*, *p.p. of propero*], *adj.* not hastened, lingering.

imprōvidus, -a, -um [*in-* + *providus*], *adj.* unforeseeing.

imprōvīsus, -a, -um [*in-* + *provisus*], *adj.* unforeseen, unexpected, sudden. — **imprōvīsō**, *abl.* N. as *adv.* unexpectedly.

imprūdēns, -entis [*in-* + *prudens*], *adj.* not foreseeing, unknowing, without knowing it.

impūbēs, -is (*also* -eris) [*in-* + *pubes*], *adj.* beardless, youthful.

impulsus, -ūs [*impello*], M. impulse, shock, force.

impūne [N. *acc. of impunis; in-*, *poena*], *adv.* with impunity; without danger, safely, without harm.

īmus, -a, -um, *superl. of* **īnferus**.

in-, *negative prefix*, in-, un-, not.

in, *prep. With abl.* in, within, on, upon, among. — *Special phrases*: **in verbo**, at the word; **in primis (imprimis)**, among the first, especially. — *Often*, in the matter of, in case of, in regard to: **in hoste**; **in hoste Priamo**. — *With acc.* into, upon, among, to, towards, against, at, for: **nos in sceptra reponis** (restore to power); **in te committere** (upon); **quietum in Teucros animum** (towards). — *Esp. of distribution*, among: **in navis**;

spargere in volgum. — *Also of purpose, tendency, etc.*, for: **audere in proelia**. — *Often*, in, on: **considere in ignis**; **in puppim ferit**. — *Special phrases*: **in dies**, from day to day; **in vicem**, **invicem**, in turn.

inaccessus, -a, -um, *adj.* inaccessible.

Īnachidēs, -ae, M. descendant of Inachus, Perseus.

inamābilis, -e, *adj.* unlovely, hateful.

inamoenus, -a, -um, *adj.* cheerless, joyless.

inānis, -e, *adj.* empty, void, substanceless: **regna** (*of the shades*). — *Fig.* empty, idle, useless: **lacrimae**; **tempus** (mere). — N. as *subst.* **ināne**, empty air.

inarātus, -a, -um, *adj.* unploughed.

inausus, -a, -um, *adj.* undared, unattempted.

incānus, -a, -um, *adj.* covered with gray, gray, hoary.

incassum (in cassum), *adv.* in vain, vainly, to no purpose. *See* **cassus**.

incautus, -a, -um, *adj.* incautious, careless, off one's guard.

incēdō, -ere, -cessī, -cessum, 3. *v. n.* move on, proceed, move, advance.

incendium, -ī (-iī) [*incendo*], N. burning, a fire, fire, a conflagration.

incendō, -ere, -cendī, -censum [*in* + †*cando*], 3. *v. a.* set on fire, kindle, burn, light, light up; fire, excite, torment. — **incēnsus, -a, -um**, *p.p.* burning, on fire, fired.

inceptum, *see* incipiō.

incertus, -a, -um, *adj.* uncertain, doubtful, wavering; unsteady; irregular: **securis** (ill-aimed).

incessus, -ūs [*incedo*], M. walk, gait.

incestō, -āre, -āvī, -ātum [*incestus, in-* + *castus*], *1. v. a.* defile, pollute.

incestus, -a, -um [*in-* + *castus*], *adj.* impure, sinful, wicked.

incidō, -ere, -cidī, (-cāsūrus) [*in-* + *cado*], *3. v. n.* fall upon, fall.

incīdō, -ere, -cīdī, -cīsum [*in* + *caedo*], *3. v. a.* cut into, cut off, cut : **funem.**

incingō, -ere, -cīnxī, -cīnctum, *3. v. a.* gird.

incipiō, -ere, -cēpī, -ceptum [*in* + *capio*], *3. v. a. and n.* begin, undertake; begin (*to speak, etc.*). — **inceptus, -a, -um,** *p.p. as adj.* begun, attempted.— N. *as subst.* **inceptum, -ī,** an undertaking, an attempt, a purpose.

inclēmentia, -ae [*inclemens*], F. cruelty, rigor, harshness.

inclūdō, -ere, -clūsī, -clūsum [*in* + *claudo*], *3. v. a.* shut up, shut in, enclose. — **inclūsus, -a, -um,** *p.p. as adj.* shut up, in confinement, enclosed, confined.

inclutus, -a, -um [*in* + † *clutus, p.p. of* clueo], *adj.* famous, renowned, famed.

incognitus, -a, -um, *adj.* untried, unknown, uncertain.

incohō (inchoō), -āre, -āvī, -ātum, *1. v. a.* begin, undertake: **aras** (build).

incola, -ae, C. [*incolo*], an inhabitant, a settler.

incolō, -ere, -coluī, *no sup., 3. v. a.* dwell in, inhabit.

incolumis, -e, *adj.* safe, unharmed, uninjured.

incomitātus, -a, -um, *adj.* unattended, unaccompanied.

inconcessus, -a, -um, *adj.* unallowed, forbidden, unlawful.

incōnsultus, -a, -um, *adj.* unadvised, without advice.

incrēdibilis, -e, *adj.* incredible.

incrēmentum, -ī [*cf. cresco*], N. growth, increase; *pl.* seeds.

increpitō, -āre, -āvī, -ātum, *1. v. a.* (rattle); chide, rebuke, taunt, find fault with; challenge.

increpō, -āre, -āvī (-uī), -ātum (-itum), *1. v. a. and n.* rattle, clatter, sound; chide, rebuke.

incrēscō, -ere, -crēvī, -crētum, *3. v. n.* grow in, grow up.

incubō, -āre, -āvī (-uī), -ātum (-itum), *1. v. n.* lie down upon, lie upon; brood upon (**ponto nox**); lie upon (*to watch*), guard (*in secret*), hoard.

incultus, -a, -um, *adj.* uncultivated, untilled, wild; unkempt, uncared-for.— N. *pl. as subst.* **inculta, -ōrum,** wild regions, a wilderness.

incumbō, -ere, -cubuī, -cubitum, *3. v. n.* lie upon, lean upon, lean over, fall upon : **laurus arae** (overhang). — *Fig.* bend to (*of oars, etc.*), bend one's energies, exert one's self, strive. — *In proverbial expressions*: **fato urgenti,** lend one's weight to, urge on, hasten.

incurrō, -ere, -currī (-cucurrī), -cursum, *3. v. n.* rush on, rush in, rush.

incursus, -ūs, M. onrush, attack.

incurvō, -āre, -āvī, -ātum, *1. v. a.* bend, writhe.

incūs, -cūdis, F. an anvil.

incūsō, -āre, -āvī, -ātum [*in, causa*], *1. v. a.* accuse, blame, find fault with.

incustōdītus, -a, -um, *adj.* unguarded, untended.

incutiō, -ere, -cussī, -cussum [*in + quatio*], *3. v. a.* strike into; lend, inspire : vim.

indāgō, -inis, F. closing in (*of game*) ; toils, nets.

inde [*im (case of is) + de (cf. de-hinc)*], *adv.* from there, from this, from that place, thence; then, next, afterwards : iam inde ut, immediately when.

indēbitus, -a, -um, *adj.* not due; unpromised.

indecor (-decoris), -oris [*in-, decus*], *adj.* unhonored, inglorious, obscure.

indēlēbilis, -e [*in-, deleo*], *adj.* indestructible, imperishable.

indēprēnsus, -a, -um [*in- + deprehensus*], *adj.* undiscovered, unperceived; baffling, undiscoverable.

indicium, -ī (-iī) [*index*], N. an information; a charge, testimony; a mark, sign.

indīcō, -ere, -dīxī, -dictum, *3. v. a.* declare, proclaim, give orders for.

indignē [*indignus*], *adv.* undeservedly.

indignor, -ārī, -ātus [*indignus*], *1. v. dep.* deem unworthy, be indignant at, disdain, scorn; chafe, be indignant, be angry.

indignus, -a, -um, *adj.* unworthy, undeserving; undeserved, shameful, unjust; blameless (lacertos).

indolēscō, -ere, -doluī, *no sup.*, *3. v. n.* be sorry, grieve.

indomitus, -a, -um, *adj.* unsubdued, untamed; untamable, indomitable; fierce, invincible.

indōtātus, -a, -um [*in- + p.p. of doto, cf. dos*], *adj.* undowered, without a dowry.

indūcō, -ere, -dūxī, -ductum, *3. v. a.* lead on; draw on, draw over (caestus manibus); overlay: inducto gelu (that covers it). — *Fig.* induce: inductus pretio (bribed).

indulgeō, -ēre, -dulsī, -dultum, *2 v. n.* favor, indulge; indulge in, give way to: dolori.

induō, -uere, -uī, -ūtum, *3. v. a.* put on, assume, take on; clothe, deck with, adorn : cratera coronā. — *In pass.* put on, clothe one's self with: galeam; indutus exuvias (clad in).

indūrēscō, -ere, -dūruī, *no sup.*, *3. v. n.* grow hard, harden.

indūrō, -āre, -āvī, -ātum, *1. v. a.* harden.

Indus, -a, -um, *adj.* of India, Indian. — M. *pl. as subst.* Indī, -ōrum, the Indians.

inēluctābilis, -e [*cf. luctor*], *adj.* inevitable.

ineō, -īre, -īvī (-iī), -itum, *irr. v. a.* go into *or* to, enter ; enter upon, take up, take part in (certamina); form (consilium).

inermis, -e (-us, -a, -um) [*in-, arma*], *adj.* unarmed, defenceless.

iners, -ertis [*in-* + *ars*], *adj.* (without skill), helpless; inactive, idle, sluggish, cowardly, spiritless: **pecora**; **corpora** (lifeless, dead).

inexcītus, -a, -um, *adj.* unmoved, undisturbed.

inexpertus, -a, -um, *adj.* untried, unattempted.

inextrīcābilis, -e, *adj.* inextricable.

īnfabricātus, -a, -um, *adj.* unwrought, unformed.

īnfāmia, -ae [*in-*, *fama*], F. disgrace.

īnfandus, -a, -um [*in-* + *fandus*, *p. of for*], *adj.* unspeakable; horrible, dreadful, accursed. — N. O horror!

īnfāns, -antis [*in-* + *fans*, *p. of for*], *adj.* speechless. — *As subst.* C. an infant, a child.

īnfaustus, -a, -um, *adj.* ill-fated, ill-omened: **puppes**.

īnfectus, -a, -um [*in-* + *factus*], *adj.* not made, not done, undone, unfinished: **facta atque infecta** (things true and false). ·

īnfectus, -a, -um, *p.p. of* **īnficiō.**

īnfēlīx, -īcis, *adj.* unlucky, unfortunate; ill-omened, wretched, ill-fated.

īnfēnsus, -a, -um, *adj.* hostile, deadly: **ignis**.

īnferiae, -ārum [*inferus*], F. *pl.* offerings in honor of the dead, funeral sacrifices *or* gifts.

īnfernus, -a, -um [*inferus*], *adj.* of the Lower World, of the gods below, of Hades.

īnferō, īnferre, intulī, inlātum, *irr. v. a.* bring in, bring to, bear on, bring, introduce: **bellum** (make, *of offensive war*); **deos** (introduce). — *Esp.* offer, sacrifice: **honores.** — *With reflexive or in pass.* rush, advance, proceed.

īnferus, -a, -um, *adj.* (īnferior; īnfimus, īmus), low, below, beneath. — *Comp.* inferior, less: **inferiora secutus** (a lower destiny). — *Superl.* lowest, deepest, nethermost, the bottom of, the depths of, innermost: **ad pedes** (even to the very feet); **manes** (the lowest depths). — *Phrases:* **ab imo, ex imo,** from the bottom, utterly, from the foundations.

īnfēstus, -a, -um, *adj.* hostile, destructive, fatal: **tela** (levelled); **volnus** (deadly thrust). — N. *pl.* as subst. **īnfēsta, -ōrum,** adversity.

īnficiō, -ere, -fēcī, -fectum [*in* + *facio*], *3. v. a.* dye, stain; poison, taint. — **īnfectus, -a, -um,** *p.p.* as adj. stained; ingrown (*of the earthly taint of crime*): **scelus.**

īnfīgō, -ere, -fīxī, -fīxum, *3. v. a.* fix in *or* on, impale. — *Pass.* fix itself, become fixed. — **īnfīxus, -a, -um,** *p.p.* as adj. fixed, fastened: **volnus** (deep).

īnfindō, -ere, -fidī, -fissum, *3. v. a.* cleave.

īnfit [*in* + *fit, of fio*], *defect. v. n.* begins; begins to speak, *etc.*

īnflammō, -āre, -āvī, -ātum, *1. v. a.* set on fire; fire, excite, inflame.

īnflectō, -ere, -flexī, -flexum, *3. v. a.* bend; move, affect, touch.

īnflētus, -a, -um, *adj.* unwept.

īnflō, -āre, -āvī, -ātum, *1. v. a.*
blow into, fill (*with wind*), swell
(*of sails*).

īnfōrmis, -e [*in-* + *forma*], *adj.*
shapeless; unsightly, misshapen,
hideous, horrid.

īnfōrmō, -āre, -āvī, -ātum, *1. v.
a.* shape, form, fashion.

īnfrā, *adv.* beneath, below.

īnfrendeō, -ēre, *no perf., no sup.,*
2. v. n. gnash (*the teeth*).

īnfrēnus, -a, -um [*in-* + *frenum*],
unbridled: Numidae (with unbridled horses; *perhaps in a
double sense*).

īnfrequēns, -entis, *adj.* infre-
quent.

īnfringō, -ere, -frēgī, -frāctum
[*in* + *frango*], *3. v. a.* break off,
break, bruise, crush, shiver; break
down, shatter, vanquish. — īn-
frāctus, -a, -um, *p.p. as adj.*
shattered, broken, crushed, over-
borne.

īnfula, -ae, F. a fillet (a headband
of wool used in sacred rites).

īnfundō, -ere, -fūdī, -fūsum, *3.
v. a.* pour on, pour out, pour
down: populus (crowded); nix
infusa (fallen); mens infusa per
artus (permeating, diffused).

ingeminō, -āre, -āvī, -ātum, *1.
v. a. and n.* redouble, repeat, renew: ingeminans Creusam vocavi (with repeated cries). —
Without obj. redouble, increase,
be repeated: ignes (flash repeatedly).

ingemō, -ere, -gemuī, *no sup.,* 3
v. n. and a. groan, sigh, mourn,
lament.

ingenium, -ī (-iī) [*in,* √*gen* (*of*
gigno)], N. character, disposition,
nature, heart; genius, talent.

ingēns, -entis [*in-* + *gens,* out of
its kind], *adj.* enormous, huge,
vast, immense, great, mighty:
argentum (a vast amount of); gemitus (deep, loud); exitus (great,
important); manus (stout).

ingrātus, -a, -um, *adj.* unpleasing;
ungrateful, unheeding, thankless:
cinis.

ingredior, -gredī, -gressus [*in* +
gradior], *3. v. dep.* walk, proceed, gc; enter; land (*from a
vessel*); enter upon, begin, undertake.

ingruō, -uere, -uī, *no sup., 3. v. n.*
rush upon, assail; come on, fall
upon, burst forth: horror armorum (roll on).

inhaereō, -ēre, -haesī, -haesum,
2. v. n. cling to.

inhiō, -āre, -āvī, -ātum, *1. v. n.*
gape at, stand open-mouthed;
gaze open-mouthed, pry into,
gaze at. — *P.* inhiāns, with open
jaws.

inhonestus, -a, -um, *adj.* inglorious, dishonorable.

inhorreō, -ēre, -uī, *no sup., 2. v.
n.* bristle, grow rough, roughen:
unda.

inhospitālis, -e, *adj.* inhospitable,
perilous: Caucasus.

inhospitus, -a, -um, *adj.* inhospitable, dangerous.

inhumātus, -a, -um, *adj.* unburied.

iniciō, -icere, -iēcī, -iectum [*in-*
+ *iacio*], *3. v. a.* throw upon,
cast upon, hurl. — *With reflexive,*
throw one's self, rush.

inimīcus, -a, -um [*in-* + *amicus*], *adj.* unfriendly, hostile, of an enemy, of the foe, as an enemy. *Also as noun.*

inīquus, -a, -um [*in-* + *aequus*], *adj.* unequal, uneven; unfair, unjust; hostile, unfriendly, unfavorable, estranged, unfortunate: **sors** (unhappy).

iniūria, -ae [*in-*, *ius*], F. injustice, wrong, outrage, insult: **longa** (tale of wrong); **sceleris nostri** (guilt).

iniussus, -a, -um, *adj.* unbidden, unforced.

iniūstus, -a, -um, *adj.* unjust.

inlābor, -lābī, -lāpsus, 3. *v. dep.* glide in, move in; *of a divinity*, enter, fill, inspire.

inlaetābilis, -e, *adj.* joyless, mournful.

inlīdō, -ere, -līsī, -līsum [*in* + *laedo*], 3. *v. a.* dash in (*to something*), dash upon, crash upon; crush.

inlūdō, -ere, -lūsī, -lūsum, 3. *v. n. and a.* mock at, make sport of: **capto.**

inlūstris, -e, *adj.* famous, noble, illustrious.

inluviēs, -ēī [*in-*, *luo*], F. dirt, filth.

innātō, -āre, -āvī, -ātum, 1. *v. n.* swim *or* float in *or* on.

innectō, -ere, -nexuī, -nexum, 3. *v. a.* entwine, bind, enwrap; weave, devise, invent, plan: **fraus.**

innītor, -nītī, -nīsus (-nīxus), 3. *v. dep.* lean on, rest on, be supported by.

innō, -nāre, -nāvī, -nātum, 1. *v.* *n. and a.* swim in *or* into, float, swim, sail.

innoxius, -a, -um, *adj.* harmless, innocent.

innumerus, -a, -um, *adj.* without number, numberless, unnumbered.

†innūptus, -a, ¦-um, *adj.* unmarried (*of a woman*), maiden.

inoffēnsus, -a, -um [*offendo*], *adj.* unobstructed, unhindered: **pede** (without stumbling).

inolēscō, -ere, -lēvī, *no sup.*, 3. *v. n.* grow in (into), become implanted.

inopīnus, -a, -um [*in-*, *cf.* *opinor*], *adj.* unexpected.

inops, -opis, *adj.* without resources, helpless, poor, destitute: **inops animi** (bereft of sense, frenzied).

Īnōus, -a, -um, *adj.* of Ino (the daughter of Cadmus and wife of Athamas of Thebes. Flying from her husband, she threw herself into the sea and became a divinity); son of Ino (v. 823).

inplūmis, -e [*pluma*], *adj.* without feathers, unfledged.

inquam, *v. def.* say.

inremeābilis, -e [*meo*], *adj.* irretraceable.

inrīdeō, -ēre, -rīsī, -rīsum, 2. *v. a.* laugh at, scorn, ridicule. — inrīsus, -a, -um, *p.p.* mocked, scorned, insulted, with ridicule.

inrigō, -āre, -āvī, -ātum, 1. *v. a.* drop upon, pour down upon, shed; bedew with, bathe, refresh.

inrītō, -āre, -āvī, -ātum, 1. *v. a.* excite, anger, incense.

inritus, -a, -um [*in-* + *ratus*], adj.
invalid, annulled; useless, ineffective, idle, in vain.

inrumpō, -ere, -rūpī, -ruptum,
3. v. a. and n. break in, burst in,
break through, force.

inruō, -ruere, -ruī, *no sup., 3. v.
n. and a.* rush in, rush on, fall
down.

īnsalūtātus, -a, -um, *adj.* not sa-
luted, without a farewell.

īnsānia, -ae [*insanus*], F. madness, insanity, frenzy, delusion,
rage.

īnsāniō, -īre, -iī (-īvī), -ītum
[*insanus*], *4. v. n.* be mad, be deluded.

īnsānus, -a, -um, *adj.* unsound
(*of mind*), mad, wild, insane,
frantic, violent; inspired.

īnscius, -a, -um [*in-* + †*scius, cf.
scio*], *adj.* unconscious, ignorant;
unaware, bewildered.

īnscrībō, -ere, -scrīpsī, -scrīp-
tum, *3. v. a.* write upon, in-
scribe, mark: pulvis hastā. —
Esp. to designate in an inscription: nec inscribar (nor shall my
epitaph read).

īnsequor, -sequī, -secūtus, *3. v.
dep.* follow up, pursue; harass,
be close upon; *intrans.* follow,
come next, ensue; *with inf.* continue, proceed.

īnserō, -rere, -ruī, -rtum, *3. v. a.*
put *or* set in, insert.

īnsertō, -āre, -āvī, -ātum [*cf. in-
sero*], *1. v. a.* put in, thrust in,
insert. — *With reflexive*, meddle
with, interpose in.

īnsideō, -sidēre, -sēdī, -sessum
[*in* + *sedeo*], *2. v. n. and a.* sit

upon, sit down on; settle on,
settle, occupy.

īnsidiae, -ārum [*insideo*], F. *pl.* an
ambush, an ambuscade, a lying
in wait; treachery, a stratagem,
wiles, a trick, secret mischief.

īnsidior, -ārī, -ātus [*insidiae*], *1.
v. dep.* lie in wait for, plot to
steal.

īnsīdō, -ere, -sēdī, -sessum, *3.
v. a. and n.* settle on, sit on,
alight upon.

īnsigne, *see* īnsignis.

īnsignis, -e [*in, signum*], *adj.*
marked, conspicuous; adorned,
splendid, brilliant; famous, renowned, glorious, noble, distinguished. — N. *sing. and pl. as
subst.* īnsigne (īnsignia), a device, an ornament, a decoration;
trappings, insignia.

īnsinuō, -āre, -āvī, -ātum, *1. v.
n.* work in (*by winding*); steal
in; steal over: pavor per pectora.

īnsistō, -ere, -stitī, *no sup., 3. v. a.
and n.* stand upon, set foot upon,
tread; enter upon, begin.

īnsomnium, -ī (-iī) [*somnus*], N.
a dream, a vision.

īnsonō, -āre, -sonuī, *no sup., 1.
v. n.* sound, resound, roar: flagello (crack).

īnsōns, -sontis, *adj.* innocent, unoffending, guiltless.

īnspērātus, -a, -um, *adj.* un-
hoped-for, unlooked-for.

īnspiciō, -ere, -spexī, -spectum
[*in* + *specio*], *3. v. a.* look in
upon, overlook; spy out.

īnspīrō, -āre, -āvī, -ātum, *1. v. a.*
breathe in, breathe upon; inspire, infuse: ignem (enkindle).

inspoliātus, -a, -um, *adj.* undespoiled.

īnstabilis, -e, *adj.* unstable, unsteady.

īnstar [*akin to* **insto**], N. *indecl.* an image, a likeness.— *In appos. as adj.* like, equal: **montis equus** (huge as).

īnstaurō, -āre, -āvī, -ātum, *1. v. a.* (set up) ; renew, repeat, begin anew : **diem donis** (repeat another day) ; **talia Grais** (repeat, requite) ; **instaurati animi** (courage restored).

īnsternō, -ere, -strāvī, -strātum, *3. v. a.* spread over; cover, spread.

īnstīgō, -āre, -āvī, -ātum [*in +* †*stigo*], *1. v. a.* goad on; stimulate, incite, urge on.

īnstituō, -ere, -uī, -ūtum [*in +* **statuo**], *3. v. a.* set up, build, found ; establish, ordain, introduce (*a custom*).

īnstō, -stāre, -stitī, (-stātūrus), *1. v. n. and a.* stand on, stand over ; press on, pursue, assail, attack ; be busy, urge on, urge ; impend, be urgent, be at hand ; ply, be eager, strive.

īnstruō, -ere, -strūxī, -strūctum, *3. v. a.* pile up, spread (**mensas**) ; arrange, draw up, array, set in order ; provide (*with*), furnish, arm : **armis socios** ; **sepulcra** (build) ; **instructus Eois adversis** (in array with) ; **instructus dolis** (armed with).

īnsuētus, -a, -um, *adj.* unaccustomed, unusual, unwonted, unfamiliar.— N. *pl.* **īnsuēta,** *as adv.* beyond his wont.

īnsula, -ae, F. an island : **paene** (peninsula).

īnsultō, -āre, -āvī, -ātum [*in +* **salto**], *1. v. n.* leap upon; exult over, insult.

īnsum, inesse, īnfuī, *irr. v. n.* be in, be on, be there.

īnsuō, -ere, -suī, -sūtum, *3. v. a.* sew in, stitch in.

īnsuper, *adv.* above, over, over all ; moreover, besides.

īnsuperābilis, -e, *adj.* unconquerable, invincible.

īnsurgō, -ere, -surrēxī, -surrēctum, *3. v. n.* rise upon ; rise, arise : **campis tenebrae** (overspread).

intāctus, -a, -um, *adj.* untouched ; unbroken, ignorant of the yoke ; maiden, chaste, pure.

intāminātus, -a, -um [*cf.* **contamino**], *adj.* unstained, unsullied.

integer, -gra, -grum [*in-,* √*tag* (*of* **tango**)], *adj.* (untouched), unbroken, entire, whole ; fresh, vigorous, unimpaired; blameless, innocent, righteous.

integrō, -āre, -āvī, -ātum [*integer*], *1. v. a.* renew.

intemerātus, -a, -um, *adj.* unpolluted, untainted, pure, inviolate : **munera** (of unmixed wine).

intempestus, -a, -um [*in-,* **tempus**], *adj.* untimely, unseasonable; gloomy.

intendō, -ere, -tendī, -tentum (-tēnsum), *3. v. a.* stretch upon, stretch out *or* to, stretch, strain : **vela** (spread) ; **vela Zephyri** (swell). — *Also,* hang with, cover with : **bracchia tergo; locum**

sertis. — **intentus, -a, -um,** *p.p.*
as adj. strained, stretched; on
the stretch, intent, eager.

intentō, -āre, -āvī, -ātum [*inten-*
tus], *1. v. a.* stretch out: **anguīs**
(hold threateningly, brandish).
— *Fig.* threaten, menace: **mor-**
tem.

intentus, -a, -um, *p.p. of* **intendō.**

intepēsco, -ere, -tepuī, *no sup., 3.*
v. n. grow warm.

inter, *prep.* between, among, amid,
in among, into the midst of.
— *With reflexive* (*as reciprocal*),
with each other, on, from, by, to,
etc. in all reciprocal relations : **in-**
ter sese (with each other, alternately).

interclūdō, -ere, -clūsī, -clūsum
[*inter + claudo*], *3. v. a.* shut off,
cut off ; detain.

interdum, *adv.* sometimes.

intereā, *adv.* meanwhile, meantime.

intereō, -īre, -iī, -itum, *irr. v. n.*
perish ; wane.

interfor, -fārī, -fātus, *1. v. dep.*
interrupt.

interfundō, -ere, -fūdī, -fūsum,
3. v. a. pour between; suffuse,
stain, fleck ; *pass.* flow between
or among.

interior, -ius [*inter*], *comp. adj.*
inner, inside: **domus** (the interior of). — *Superl.* **intimus, -a,**
-um, inmost, farthest.

interlūceō, -ēre, -lūxī, *no sup.,*
2. v. n. shine *or* show light
through.

interluō, -ere, *no perf., no sup.,*
3. v. a. flow between, wash (*of*
rivers).

internectō, -ere, *no perf., no sup.,*
3. v. a. bind together, bind up :
fibula crinem.

internōdium,-ī (-iī)[*inter, nodus*],
N. the space between joints.

interpres,-etis, C. an agent, a messenger, an interpreter : **divum** (a
prophet) ; **harum curarum** (author, *of Juno as agent in the mar-*
riage relation).

interritus, -a, -um, *adj.* unterri-
fied, undaunted, fearless, undis-
mayed.

interrumpō, -ere, -rūpī, -ruptum,
3. v. a. break off, discontinue.

intersum, -esse, -fuī, *no sup.,*
irr. v. n. be among, dwell among,
remain with.

intervallum, -ī, N. (space between
stakes of the rampart), distance
(*between*), interval.

intexō, -ere, -texuī, -textum, *3.*
v. a. weave in, interweave, in-
terlace; surround, entwine (*with*
something) : **latera frondibus.**

intimus, *see* **interior.**

intonō, -āre, -uī, *no sup., 1. v. n.*
thunder.

intōnsus, -a, -um, *adj.* unshorn.

intorqueō, -ēre, -torsī, -tortum,
2. v. a. hurl, hurl against.

intrā [*cf. inter*], *prep.* within (*of po-*
sition or motion), inside ; within
the limits of.

intrāctābilis, -e, *adj.* unmanage-
able, fierce, violent.

intrāctātus, -a, -um, *adj.* untried,
unattempted.

intremō, -ere, -uī, *no sup., 3. v. n.*
tremble, quake, quiver.

intrō, -āre, -āvī, -ātum [*cf. intra*],
1. v. a. enter : **limen** (cross).

intrōgredior, -gredī, -gressus [*intro-* + *gradior*], 3. *v. dep.* enter, come in.

intrōrsus [*intro-* + *versus*], *adv.* within.

intus [*in*], *adv.* within, inside; indoors, in the house.

inultus, -a, -um, *adj.* unavenged; unpunished.

inūtilis, -e, *adj.* useless, worthless; unavailing, impotent.

Inuus, -ī, M. a god identified with Pan as the guardian of cattle: Castrum Inui, a town of Latium (vi. 775).

invādō, -ere, -vāsī, -vāsum, 3. *v. n. and a.* go into, go against; proceed, go on; begin; attack, invade, storm, rush into, rush in, force: thalamum (violate).

invalidus, -a, -um, *adj.* infirm, feeble, weak, powerless.

invehō, -ere, -vexī, -vectum, 3. *v. a.* bear on; *pass.* ride, sail, be borne.

inveniō, -īre, -vēnī, -ventum, 4. *v. a.* come upon, hit upon, find, discover, invent, devise; find (*learn*).

inventor, -ōris [*invenio*], M. a finder, a discoverer; a deviser, a contriver: scelerum.

invergō, -ere, *no perf., no sup.*, 3. *v. a.* turn downward, empty; pour down upon, pour.

invictus, -a, -um, *adj.* unconquered, unconquerable, invincible.

invideō, -ēre, -vīdī, -vīsum, 2. *v. n. and a.* (look askance at), envy, be jealous of; grudge, deny, refuse. — invīsus, -a, -um, *p.p. as*

adj. an object of hatred, hated, detested, hideous, odious: haud invisus caelestibus (not unfriended by). — invidendus, -a, -um, *ger. as adj.* that excites envy, enviable: aula.

invidia, -ae, F. envy, hatred, malice; grudging, jealousy: quae est? (why grudge ?).

invidiōsus, -a, -um [*invidia*], *adj.* enviable, exciting envy.

invidus, -a, -um, *adj.* envious, malicious, hateful.

invigilō, -āre, -āvī, -ātum, 1. *v. n.* lie *or* be kept awake.

inviolābilis, -e, *adj.* inviolable, sacred.

invīsō, -ere, -vīsī, -vīsum, 3. *v. a.* visit, go to see.

invīsus, -a, -um, *p.p. of* invideō.

invīsus, -a, -um, *adj.* unseen.

invītō, -āre, -āvī, -ātum, 1. *v. a.* invite, allure; persuade.

invītus, -a, -um, *adj.* unwilling, against one's will, with reluctance, reluctant.

invius, -a, -um [*in-* + *via*], *adj.* pathless, inaccessible, difficult of access *or* passage, dangerous: via invia; saxa.

invocō, -āre, -āvī, -ātum, 1. *v. a.* call upon, invoke, adore.

involvō, -ere, -volvī, -volūtum, 3. *v. a.* wrap up, enwrap, involve, surround, shut in; engulf.

Īonius, -a, -um, *adj.* Ionian (of the sea so called). — N. *as subst.* Īonium (*sc.* mare), the Ionian Sea (iii. 211).

Īopās, -ae, M. a Carthaginian bard (i. 740).

Īphigenīa, -ae, F. daughter of Agamemnon.

Īphitus, -ī, M. a Trojan (ii. 435).

ipse, -a, -um [*is* + -*pse*], *pron. intens.* self, very, even. — *Without other pronoun or noun,* himself, yourself, *etc.* — *In special phrases*: ipsi venient, of themselves, voluntarily; ipse, the chief, the leader; ipsi, the men themselves.

īra, -ae, F. anger, wrath, rage, ire, fury; angry impulse.

īrāscor, īrāscī, īrātus [*ira*], *3. v. dep.* be angry, become enraged.

Īris, -idis (*also* -is), F. the messenger of the gods (especially of Juno), the personified rainbow (iv. 694).

is, ea, id, *pron. dem.* he, she, it, they, this, that, these, those; such a (*with a correlative*), so great.

Ismarius, -a, -um, *adj.* Ismarian (of Ismarus, a Thracian mountain); Thracian.

Ismēnus, -ī, M. son of Amphion and Niobe.

iste, ista, istud [*is*], *pron. dem.* that (*esp. of the person addressed*), he, she, they; these, those.

istīc [*isti* + -*ce*], *adv.* there.

istinc [*cf. iste*], *adv.* from there (*where you are*), where you are.

ita, *adv.* so, in that way, thus.

Ītalia, -ae, F. Italy.

Italus, -a, -um, *adj.* Italian. — *Pl. as subst.* the Italians.

iter, itineris [√*i* (*of eo*)], N. a way, a course, a journey, a passage.

iterō, -āre, -āvī, -ātum, *1. v. a.* repeat, do again; go over again: cursus.

iterum, *adv.* a second time, again, once more, repeatedly.

Ithacus, -a, -um, *adj.* Ithacan, of Ithaca (the home of Ulysses in the Ionian Sea). — M. the Ithacan (Ulysses) (ii. 104). — F. Ithaca, the island itself, Ithaca.

Iūlus, -ī, M. a name of Ascanius, son of Æneas (i. 267).

Ixīōn, -onis, M. a king of the Lapithæ, who was bound to a wheel in the World Below as a punishment for his crimes (vi. 601).

Ixīonius, -a, -um, *adj.* of Ixion.

iaceō, -ēre, -uī, -itum, *2. v. n.* lie, lie down; lie asleep; lie dead, lie low; be situated; remain; cease to move, lie *or* stand still. — iacēns, -entis, *p. as adj.* prostrate, low-lying.

iaciō, -ere, iēcī, iactum, *3. v. a.* throw, cast, hurl, fling. — *Of foundations, walls, etc.* lay, throw, throw up: muros. — *Of flowers,* scatter. — *P.p.* iactus, -a, -um, fallen: nix.

iactō, -āre, -āvī, -ātum [*iacio, iactus*], *1. v. a.* throw, cast, hurl; scatter, strew; toss, shake, agitate, throw (*to and fro*), flap (*wings*), stir; drive, pursue; throw out, fling out, send forth, utter, pour forth; revolve: pectore curas. — *With reflexive,* boast, vaunt one's self, show one's pride. — iactāns, -antis, *p. as adj.* boastful, arrogant.

iactūra, -ae [*iacio*], F. a throwing away; loss.

iaculor, -ārī, -ātus [iaculum], *1. v. dep.* hurl a javelin; hurl, throw, cast (ignem); strike, smite.

iaculum, -ī [iacio], N. a javelin, a dart, a missile weapon.

iam, *adv.* already, now, at last, now at length; presently, soon, forthwith. — *Often with the pres. and the imperf.* begin to (*do anything*). — *Phrases*: **nec iam,** and now no more, and no longer (*so with other negatives, expressed or implied*); **iam inde,** immediately; **iam tum,** even then; **iam dūdum,** long ago, long since, at once; **iam prīdem,** long since; **iam iam,** at every moment, even now; **iam nunc,** even now. — *With comp.* still, even, now: **iam proprior;** **nec iam amplius** (and now no longer).

iamdūdum, *see* iam.

iamprīdem, *see* iam.

iānitor, -ōris [cf. Ianus, ianua], M. a doorkeeper, guardian (*of an entrance*).

iānua, -ae [akin to Ianus], F. a door, an entrance; an avenue, a means of access, a way.

Iānus, -ī, M. Janus, an Italian god, represented with two faces. He was the guardian and patron of doorways and beginnings. His temple was shut in time of peace.

iecur, iecoris (iecinoris), N. the liver.

ieiūnium, -ī (-iī), N. a fast.

iocus, -ī, M. a jest. — *Personified*, the god of jesting.

iuba, -ae, N. the mane; the crest (*of a helmet, made of hair*), the crest (*of a serpent*).

Iuba, -ae, M. the name of two famous Numidian kings.

iubar, -aris, N. rays of light, brightness; the dawn, the morning: iubare exorto.

iubeō, -ēre, iussī, iussum, *2. v. a.* bid, order, command, ordain. — **iussus, -a, -um,** *p.p. as adj.* bidden, presented, ordered, directed. — N. iussum, -ī, a command, an order, a mandate.

iūcundus, -a, -um [iocus], *adj.* joyful; pleasant: lumen.

iūdex, -icis [ius, dico], C. a judge, an arbitrator.

iūdicium, -ī (-iī) [iudex], N. a decision, a judgment.

iugālis, -e [iugum], *adj.* of the yoke; conjugal, of marriage; nuptial.

iūgerum, -ī [cf. iugum], N. an acre (*loosely; properly a little more than half an acre*).

iugō, -āre, -āvī, -ātum [iugum], *1. v. a.* unite (*in marriage*).

iugulum, -ī [iugum], N. the throat.

iugum, -ī [√iug (of iungo)], N. a yoke; a team, a pair of horses; a ridge; a thwart, a bench.

Iūlius, -a, -um, *adj.* Julian (the name of the gens at Rome to which Cæsar belonged). — M. the name of Cæsar, and his adopted son Augustus.

iūnctūra, -ae [iunctus, iungo], F. a joint, a fastening.

iungō, -ere, iūnxī, iūnctum [√iug], *3. v. a.* join, unite, clasp (*hand*), put together; fasten; harness, yoke; *of treaties*, make, celebrate. — *P.p.* iūnctus, -a, -um, joined, at peace with.

Iūnō, -ōnis, F. the queen of the gods, wife of Jupiter, patroness of the Greeks against the Trojans, identified with Astarte, the deity of the Phœnicians.— Of Proserpine, queen: Iuno inferna (vi. 138).

Iūnōnius, -a, -um, adj. of Juno, sacred to Juno: Iunonia hospitia (Juno's, prompted by Juno).

Iuppiter, Iovis [†Iovi- + pater], M. Jupiter, Jove, the supreme divinity of the Romans, identified with the Greek Zeus.—Also, oy personification, the sky, the air, the weather, the rain.— Of Pluto, as the king of the Lower World: Iuppiter Stygius (iv. 638).

iūrō, -āre, -āvī, -ātum [cf. ius], 1. v. n. and a. swear, swear by: per caput; numen.

iūs, iūris, N. right, justice, law (unwritten, cf. lex, statute); a right, a privilege, a claim; a tie (of right that one holds over another), an obligation.

iussum, -ī, see iubeō.

†iussus, -ūs (only in abl. sing.) [iubeo], M. a command, a mandate.

iūstē [iustus], adv. justly, rightly, fairly.

iūstitia, -ae [iustus], F. justice, right, uprightness.

iūstus, -a, -um [ius], adj. just, fitting, right, regular; upright; fair, proportional, equal.

Iūturna, -ae, F. a water nymph, sister of Turnus (xii. 244).

iuvenālis, -e [iuvenis], adj. of youth, of a youth, youthful: corpus; arma.

iuvenca, -ae [F. of iuvencus], F. a heifer.

iuvencus, -ī [iuvenis], M. a bullock, a steer, a bull.

iuvenis, -e, adj. young, youthful. — As subst. a young man (in the prime of life, up to forty-five years of age).

iuventa, -ae [iuvenis], F. youth.

iuventās, -tātis [iuvenis], F. youth.

iuventūs, -tūtis [iuvenis], F. youth; the youth, young men.

iuvō, -āre, iūvī, iūtum, 1. v. a. and n. help, aid, assist; profit, avail, be of use; please, give pleasure, delight.— Impers. with an inf. it delights, one is pleased, one is glad.

iūxtā [cf. iungo], adv. and prep. near by, near, closely, next to, next, by one's side.

Karthāgō, -inis, F. Carthage, the famous city in North Africa (near modern Tunis), once the rival of Rome.

labefaciō, -ere, -fēcī, -factum [labo, facio], 3. v. a. make totter, loosen; weaken, cause to waver.—labefactus, -a, -um, p.p. as adj. shaken, agitated, overcome.

lābēs, -is [cf. lābor], F. a fall, a slide, a giving way: prima mali (first stroke of misfortune).— Also, a taint, a spot, a stain; impurity.

labō, -āre, -āvī, -ātum, 1. v. n. totter, stagger; waver, vacillate. — labāns, -antis, p. tottering, wavering, yielding.

lābor, lābī, lāpsus [*cf. labo*], *3. v. dep.* slide, glide, fall, slip, waver; descend, sink, swoop (*of birds*); slip away, pass away, fail, decline.— **lābēns, -entis,** *p. as adj. with participial meanings; also,* slippery.

labor (labōs), -ōris, M. toil, labor; fruit of toil, workmanship, handicraft; task, business; sorrow, trial, trouble, misfortune; pangs, throes; *of the sun,* struggle, eclipse.— *Personified,* Toil.

labōrō, -āre, -āvī, -ātum [*labor*], *1. v. a. and n.* elaborate, work out; work, labor.— **labōrātus, -a, -um,** *p.p. as adj.* wrought, worked, embroidered.

Labyrinthus, -ī, M. the Labyrinth in Crete (v. 588).

lac, lactis, N. milk; milky juice.

Lacaenus, -a, -um, *adj.* Lacedæmonian, Laconian; *esp. in* F. the Spartan dame, Helen (vi. 511).

Lacedaemonius, -a, -um, *adj.* Spartan, Lacedæmonian (iii. 328).

lacer, -era, -erum, *adj.* torn, mangled, maimed, bruised, disfigured.

lacerō, -āre, -āvī, -ātum [*lacer*], *1. v. a.* tear, rend, tear in pieces, mangle.

lacertus, -ī, M. the upper arm, the arm.

lacessō, -ere, -sīvī, -sītum, *3. v. a.* provoke, challenge; attack; importune.

Lacīnius, -a, -um, *adj.* of Lacinium (a promontory of Southern Italy, on which was a temple of Juno, iii. 552). The name of the promontory is the N. of the adj.

Lacōnicus, -a, -um, *adj.* Laco-nian; of Laconia in the Peloponnesus.

lacrima, -ae, F. a tear, weeping.

lacrimābilis, -e [*lacrimo*], *adj.* tearful, mournful, dismal.

lacrimō, -āre, -āvī, -ātum [*lacrima*], *1. v. n. and a.* weep, shed tears; mourn, lament.

lacrimōsus, -a, -um [*lacrima*], *adj.* tearful, causing tears.

lacūnar, -āris, N. a panelled ceiling.

lacus, -ūs, M. a lake, a pond, a pool; a river, a stream.

laedō, -ere, laesī, laesum, *3. v. a.* strike, dash; hurt, pain, mar, wound; offend, thwart.

laena, -ae, F. a cloak, a mantle.

Lāertius, -a, -um, *adj.* of Laertes, the father of Ulysses (iii. 272).

laetitia, -ae [*laetus*], F. joy, gladness, cheerfulness, enjoyment.

laetor, -ārī, -ātus [*laetus*], *1. v. dep.* rejoice, be glad; sport.

laetus, -a, -um, *adj.* glad, joyous, cheerful, joyful, happy; delighting in, proud of, exultant with; fortunate (**res**); rich, fertile, plenteous; fruitful; rich in, abounding in: **laetissimus umbrae lucus.** — *Of animals,* thriving, fat, sleek: **armenta.**

laevus, -a, -um, *adj.* left, on the left hand. — *From inferior readiness of the left hand,* foolish. — *From science of auspices,* ominous, boding, unpropitious. — F. *as subst.* **laeva** (*sc.* **manus**), the left hand: **laevā** (with the left hand, on the left). — N. *pl.* **laeva,** the left hand, places on the left. — N. **laevum,** *as adv.* on the left.

Lalagē, -ēs, F. a girl celebrated by Horace.

lambō, -ere, *no perf., no sup., 3. v. a.* lick; *of fire and the like,* play round, lick; *of a river,* wash: **loca Hydaspes.**

lāmentābilis, -e [*lamentum*], *adj.* lamentable, pitiable.

lāmentum, -ī, N. a shriek, a groan, a cry, a lamentation, a wailing.

lāmina (lammina), -ae, F. a plate (*of metal*).

lampas, -adis, F. a light, a torch, a burning brand.

lāna, -ae, F. wool.

lancea, -ae, F. a lance, spear.

langueō, -ēre, -uī, *no sup., 2. v. n.* faint.

languēscō, -ere, languī, *no sup., 3. v. n.* languish, grow faint *or* dim.

languor, -ōris [*langueo*], M. languor, faintness, weakness.

lāniger, -era, -erum [*lana, gero*], *adj.* wool-bearing, fleecy; tufted (*with wool*).

laniō, -āre, -āvī, -ātum, *1. v. a.* tear, rend, mangle, mutilate, disfigure (*by tearing*).

Lāocoōn, -ontis, M. a priest of Apollo, killed by two serpents for his sacrilege in violating the Wooden Horse (ii. 41, 201).

Lāodamīa, -ae, F. wife of Protesilaus, who killed herself for love of him (vi. 447).

Lāomedontēus, -a, -um, *adj.* of Laomedon, descended from Laomedon; Trojan (iv. 542).

Lāomedontiadēs, -ae, M. son (descendant) of Laomedon. — *Pl.* the Trojans (descendants of him as founder of the race: iii. 248).

lapidōsus, -a, -um [*lapis*], *adj.* stony, hard as stone.

lapis, -idis, M. a stone, stone, a rock: **Parius** (marble).

Lapithae, -ārum, M. a tribe of Thessaly, famous for their battle with the Centaurs (vi. 601).

lāpsō, -āre, -āvī, -ātum [*lapsus, labor*], *1. v. n.* slip.

lāpsus, -ūs [*labor*], M. a falling, a fall, a slip; a gliding motion, a swoop (*of birds*), course (*of stars*): **rotarum** (rolling wheels).

laquear, -āris, N. a hollow (*in a ceiling; made by the crossing of beams*), a ceiling: **tecti** (fretted ceiling).

laqueus, -ī, M. a noose, a snare. — *Pl.* fetters, bonds.

Lār, Laris, M. a household god, a tutelary divinity (v. 744); one's home.

largus, -a, -um, *adj.* wide, spacious, free; copious, plenteous, abundant: **fletus** (flood of tears).

Lārissaeus, -a, -um, *adj.* of Larissa (a town of Thessaly, the supposed abode of Achilles), Larissæan (ii. 197).

lascīvus, -a, -um, *adj.* playful, sportive: **grex.**

lassus, -a, -um, *adj.* weary, worn, tired, fatigued.

lātē [*latus*], *adv.* broadly, widely, far and wide, afar, in all directions, far and near.

latebra, -ae [*lateo*], F. hiding place, lurking place, covert, retreat.

latebrōsus, -a, -um [*latebra*], *adj.* full of hiding places, crannied: **pumex.**

lateō, -ēre, -uī, *no sup.,* 2. *v. n. and a.* lie concealed, be hidden, skulk, hide, be covered, lurk; be unknown, be unknown to, lie hidden; live a retired life. — **latēns, -entis,** *p. as adj.* hidden, secret, unknown.

latex, -icis, M. a fluid, a liquid, water *or* wine.

Latīnus, -a, -um, *adj.* of Latium, Latin.— *As subst.* M. *sing.* Latinus, king of the region (vi. 891); *pl.* the Latins.

Latium, -ī (-iī), N. the plain of Italy south of the Tiber (i. 6).

Lātōna, -ae, F. the mother of Apollo and Diana (i. 502).

Lātōnius, -a, -um, *adj.* of Latona.

Lātōus, -a, -um, *adj.* of Latona.

lātrātor, -ōris [*latro*], M. barker.

lātrātus, -ūs [*latro*], M. a barking, a yelping, a cry (*of hounds*).

lātrō, -āre, -āvī, -ātum, 1. *v. n.* bark, yelp, roar.

latrō, -ōnis, M. a robber; a hunter.

lātus, -a, -um, *adj.* broad, wide.

latus, -eris, N. the side, the flank; quarter, region: **mundi.**

laudō, -āre, -āvī, -ātum [*laus*], 1. *v. a.* praise, commend, approve, speak well of, extol.

Laurēns, -entis, *adj.* Laurentian, of Laurentum, a town of Latium, occupied by Turnus as the chief seat of the war with Æneas (v. 797).

laurus, -ūs *and* **-ī,** F. the laurel, the bay; a laurel crown.

laus, laudis, F. praise, glory, fame, renown, credit; virtue, merit; a noble action.

Lăvīnia, *see* **Lăvīnius.**

Lăvīnius, -a, -um, *adj.* of Lavinium (the town built by Æneas in Latium and named in honor of Lavinia his wife), Lavinian. — F. **Lăvīnia,** the daughter of King Latinus, married to Æneas (vi. 764).— N. **Lăvīnium,** the town itself.

lavō, -āre (-ere), lavāvī (lāvī), lavātum (lautum, lōtum) [*akin to luo*], 1. *and* 3. *v. a.* wash, bathe, wash off; wet, moisten, bedew.

laxō, -āre, -āvī, -ātum [*laxus*], 1. *v. a.* loosen, relax, unbind, open: **rudentis** (let go); **foros** (clear). — *Fig.* relax, refresh.

laxus, -a, -um, *adj.* loose, slack, loosened.

lea, -ae [*leo*], F. a lioness.

leaena, -ae, F. a lioness.

lebēs, -ētis, M. a kettle, a caldron.

Lebinthos (-us), -ī, F. an island in the Ægean Sea.

lectulus, -ī [*dim. of lectus*], M. a little bed, a bed.

lectus, -ī, M. a bed, a couch.

Lēda, -ae, F. the mother of Helen and Castor and Pollux (i. 652).

Lēdaeus, -a, -um, *adj.* of Leda, descendant of Leda (iii. 328).

lēgifer, -era, -erum [*lex, fero*], *adj.* lawgiving, lawgiver.

legiō, -ōnis [*lego*], F. a legion, a troop.

legō, -ere, lēgī, lēctum, 3. *v. a.* gather, collect; take in (*sails*); pick, pick up, catch; choose, elect, select; review, contemplate, scan, perceive, behold; read; coast along, skim, pass over *or* by; trace, track, follow.

— lēctus, -a, -um, *p.p. as adj.*
gathered ; chosen, choice, picked,
select.

Lēnaeus, -a, -um, *adj.* of (to)
Bacchus, Lenæan ; of wine (iv.
207). — M. Lenæus, a name of
Bacchus.

lēniō, -īre, -īvī (-iī), -ītum [*lenis*],
4. v. a. mitigate, relieve, assuage,
soothe, moderate.

lēnis, -e, *adj.* moderate, gentle,
soothing.

lēniter [*lenis*], *adv.* gently.

lentē [*lentus*], *adv.* slowly.

lentō, -āre, -āvī, -ātum [*lentus*],
1. v. a. bend.

lentus, -a, -um, *adj.* clinging,
tough ; pliant, bending, twining ;
sluggish, slow, idle.

leō, -ōnis, M. a lion.

lepus, -oris, M. a hare.

Lerna, -ae, F. a lake and marsh
near Argos, where Hercules slew
the famous Hydra (vi. 287).

lētālis, -e [*letum*], *adj.* deadly, mortal, fatal, of death.

Lēthaea, -ae, F. wife of Olenos.

Lēthaeus, -a, -um, *adj.* of Lethe
(the river of forgetfulness in the
World Below), Lethæan ; soporific (v. 854).

lētifer, -era, -erum [*letum, fero*],
adj. mortal, deadly, fatal.

lētō, -āre, -āvī, -ātum [*letum*], *1.
v. a.* kill, slay.

lētum, -ī, N. death ; destruction,
ruin. — *Personified*, Death.

Leucaspis, -is, M. a Trojan (vi.
334).

Leucātēs, -ae, M. (-ē, -ēs, F.), a
promontory at the southern
extremity of Leucadia, off the
western coast of Acarnania (iii.
274).

levāmen, -inis [*levo*], N. means of
relief, solace, comfort, relief.

levis, -e, *adj.* light, swift, agile,
rapid ; slight, trivial, unimportant, of little weight ; mild, gentle ; fickle.

lēvis, -e, *adj.* smooth, polished.

levō, -āre, -āvī, -ātum [*levis*], *1.
v. a.* lighten ; lift up, lift, raise ; relieve, alleviate (laborem); loosen,
strike off (manicas); assist : auxilio viros.

lēvō, -āre, -āvī, -ātum [*lēvis*], *1.
v. a.* polish. — lēvātus, -a, -um,
p.p. as adj. polished.

lēx, lēgis, F. a law (*written, cf. ius,*
prescriptive right), a statute, a
decree, an ordinance ; a term, a
condition, terms ; *pl.* authority :
loci.

lībāmen, -inis [*libo*], N. a libation ;
a first sacrifice, an offering.

libēns, *see* libeō.

libenter [*libens*], *adv.* gladly.

libeō, -ēre, libuī (libitum est),
libitum, *2. v. n.* please, be pleasing. — *Esp. impers.* it pleases, is
one's pleasure. — libēns, -entis,
p. as adj. willing, ready, with a
free will, gladly.

liber, -brī, M. bark.

līber, -era, -erum, *adj.* free, at
liberty : liberior toga (*the toga
virilis*).

Līber, -erī, M. an Italian divinity
identified with Bacchus (vi. 805).

lībertās, -ātis [*liber*, free], F. liberty, freedom ; permission.

libīdō, -idinis [*libet*], F. desire,
lustfulness.

lībō, -āre, -āvī, -ātum, *1. v. a.*
pour (*a libation*), make a libation; offer, sacrifice. — *As the
libation was the beginning of
drinking,* drink, quaff; sip, taste:
oscula (gently kiss).

lībrō, -āre, -āvī, -ātum [*libra*], *1.
v. a.* balance, poise; swing, brandish; hurl.

lībum, -ī, N. a pancake (*used in
sacrifices*).

Liburnus, -a, -um, *adj.* of the
Liburni (a nation of Illyria, on
the eastern side of the Adriatic),
Liburnian. — *Pl.* the Liburni (i.
244).

Libya, -ae, F. a region of Africa
(i. 22).

Libycus, -a, -um, *adj.* Libyan, of
Libya; African.

Libystis, -idis, F. *adj.* Libyan, of
Libya; African (v. 37).

licet, -ēre, licuit (licitum est),
2. v. n. be allowed, be permitted.
— *Impers.* it is allowed, permitted, granted, it is lawful *or* possible, one may. — licet, although,
though.

Licinius, -ī (-iī), M. Licinius Murena, a friend of Horace.

lignum, -ī, N. wood, timber; a
structure of timber (*the Wooden
Horse*).

ligō, -āre, -āvī, -ātum, *1. v. a.*
bind, fasten.

līlium, -ī (-iī), N. a lily.

Lilybēius, -a, -um, *adj.* of Lily-
bæum, a promontory on the
southern coast of Sicily (iii. 706).

limbus, -ī, M. a fringe, a border.

līmen, -inis, N. a threshold; an
entrance, a passageway, a door,
a gate; a house, a palace, a
temple, a chamber, a home, a
habitation, an abode; the starting post (*of a race*), the beginning. — in limine, close at hand.

līmes, -itis, M. a cross-path, a road,
path; the track (*of a meteor,
etc.*); boundary, limit.

līmōsus, -a, -um [*limus*], *adj.*
muddy, miry, swampy.

limpidus, -a, -um, *adj.* limpid,
clear.

līmus, -ī, M. mud, mire, slime, clay,
soil.

līneus, -a, -um [*linum*], *adj.* of
flax.

lingua, -ae, F. a tongue; language; note, voice.

linquō, -ere, līquī, lictum [√*lic*],
3. v. a. leave, abandon, forsake,
quit, lose; cease, leave off, desist
from.

linteum, -ī [*linum*], N. canvas, a
sail.

līnum, -ī, N. flax; a thread.

liquefaciō, -ere, -fēcī, -factum
[*liqueo, facio*], *3. v. a.* melt, dissolve, liquefy, soften.

liquēns, *p.* of liqueō.

līquēns, *p.* of līquor.

liqueō, -ēre, licuī, *no sup.*, *2. v. n.*
flow, be clear, be limpid. — liquēns, -entis, *p. as adj.* clear,
liquid, limpid. — liquet, *impers.*
it is clear, evident.

liquēscō, -ere, licuī, *no sup.* [*liqueo*], *3. v. n.* begin to melt.

liquidus, -a, -um [*cf. liqueo*], *adj.*
liquid, flowing; clear, pure, limpid; serene.

līquor, -ī, *no perf.* [*cf. liquidus*], *3.
v. dep.* flow: guttae.

līs, lītis, F. strife, contention, dispute, lawsuit, case (*at law*).

litō, -āre, -āvī, -ātum, *1. v. a. and n.* sacrifice (*with favorable omens*); appease an offended divinity (*by sacrifice*); offer successfully, perform acceptably: litandum [est] (atonement must be made).

lītorālis, -e [*litus*], *adj.* of the shore.

lītoreus, -a, -um [*litus*], *adj.* of the shore, of the beach.

lītus, -oris, N. the shore, a beach, the strand, the coast.

lituus, -ī, M. a staff (curved at the end, used in augury); a trumpet, a horn.

līveō, -ēre, *no perf. or sup., 2. v. n.* be livid *or* dusky.— **līvēns, -entis,** *p. as adj.* dusky.

līvidus, -a, -um [*cf. liveo*], *adj.* dark blue, livid, black and blue, dusky, dark, leaden (*lead-colored*); bruised.

locō, -āre, -āvī, -ātum [*locus*], *1. v. a.* place, put, set; set up, build; fix, station; settle, dispose; give out contracts.

Locrī, -ōrum, M. *pl.* a race of Greece who settled in Southern Italy (iii. 399).

locuplēs, -plētis, *adj.* rich.

locus, -ī, M. (*also* N. *in pl.*), a place, space, a region, a site, a situation, a position, a spot (*of ground*), tract; room, opportunity, chance (**precibus**); condition, situation, state.—*Phrase:* dare locum (give way, make way).

longaevus, -a, -um [*longus, aevum*], *adj.* of great age, aged; in one's old age.

longē [*longus*], *adv.* afar, far off, far, at a distance, far away; far up, high up; from afar, from a distance; *of time,* long; **longe lateque** (far and wide).— *Comp.* **longius,** very far.

longinquus, -a, -um [*cf. longus*], *adj.* distant, remote, far off; ancient, long-continued.

longus, -a, -um, *adj.* long; spacious, wide, extensive; prolonged; distant; *of time,* long, continued, long-continued; lingering; tedious.

loquāx, -ācis [*loquor*], *adj.* talkative; noisy, chattering, babbling.

loquēla, -ae [*loquor*], F. speech, discourse, words (*in pl.*).

loquor, loquī, locūtus, *3. v. dep.* speak (*in any form of utterance*).

lōrīca, -ae [*lorum*], F. a coat of mail, a cuirass.

lōrum, -ī, N. a thong, a strap; a rein, a bridle.

lūbricus, -a, -um, *adj.* slippery, slimy. — N. *pl. as subst.* **lūbrica,** slippery ground.

lūceō, -ēre, lūxī, *no sup.* [*lux*], *2. v. n.* shine, gleam, be bright; be resplendent, be splendid. — *Fig.* appear, show itself.—**lūcēns,-entis,** *p. as adj.* bright, splendid, brilliant.

lūcidus, -a, -um [*lux*], *adj.* bright, shining, brilliant, glittering, radiant.

lūcifer, -era, -erum [*lux, fero*], *adj.* light-bringing. — M. *as subst.* Lucifer, the morning star (ii. 801).

luctor, -ārī, -ātus, *1. v. dep.* struggle, wrestle, strive.

lūctus, -ūs [lugeo], M. grief, sorrow, mourning, distress; wailing, mournful complaint. — Personified, Grief.

lūcus, -ī, M. a sacred grove; a wood, a grove.

lūdibrium, -ī (-iī) [ludo], N. mockery, sport; the sport (as, of the winds).

lūdō, -ere, lūsī, lūsum, 3. v. a. and n. play, sport, frolic; mock, deceive, delude, cheat, trick.

lūdus, -ī [ludo], M. sport, play, a game, a pastime; a festival game. — Pl. games (a set festival), sports.

luēs, -is, F. a plague, a pestilence, a blight.

lūgeō, -ēre, lūxī, no sup., 2. v. n. and a. mourn, lament: Lugentes Campi, the Fields of Mourning (vi. 441).

lūgubris, -e [lugeo], adj. mournful, grieving, full of grief.

lūmen, -inis [lux], N. light, a glare; the light of life; daylight, day, a day: lumine quarto. — Also, the eye. — Phrase: caeli spirabile lumen, light and air.

lūna, -ae [cf. lux], F. the moon, moonlight.

lūnātus, -a, -um [p.p. of luno, from luna], adj. half-moon shaped, crescent.

luō, -uere, -uī, no sup., 3. v. a. pay, pay or atone for; undergo.

lupa, -ae [F. of lupus], F. a she-wolf.

lupus, -ī, M. a wolf.

lūsor, -ōris [ludo], M. one who plays or sports; a sportive writer: amorum.

lūstrālis, -e [lustro], adj. lustral, of purification: aqua.

lūstrō, -āre, -āvī, -ātum [lustrum], 1. v. a. purify (by lustration), sprinkle (with holy water). — Pass. purify one's self, offer sacrifice for expiation.— From the regular process of lustration, traverse, pass over, pass round, parade in front of, pass through, sail over; examine, scan, reconnoitre; track, trace; observe, survey, review; of the sun, etc. encompass, illuminate.

lūstrum, -ī [luo], N. a purification. — From the periodic purification at Rome, a lustre (period of five years); pl. years, time.

lustrum, -ī, N. a den, a lair: ferarum; invia lustra (wilds).

lūsus, -ūs [ludo], M. sport, play, a game.

lūx, lūcis [√luc], F. light, daylight; dawn, daybreak; a day; the light of life, life; light (solace, stay); the upper light, the Upper World.

lūxuriō, -āre, -āvī, -ātum, 1. v. n. be luxuriant, bear huge crops.

lūxus, -ūs, M. luxury; dalliance, wantonness; splendor, magnificence, pomp.

Lyaeus, -a, -um, adj. of Bacchus (i. 686).

Lyaeus, -ī, M. a name of Bacchus (iv. 58).

lychnus, -ī, M. a lamp.

Lycius, -a, -um, adj. Lycian, of Lycia. — F. Lycia, a division of Asia Minor famous for its bowmen, and in alliance with Troy. — M. pl. the Lycians.

Lyctius, -a, -um, *adj.* of Lyctos
(a city of Crete), Lyctian; Cretan (iii. 401).

Lycūrgus, -ī, M. a Thracian king
who persecuted the worshippers
of Bacchus (iii. 14).

Lycus, -ī, M. a companion of Æneas
(i. 222).

Lȳdius, -a, -um, *adj.* Lydian, of
Lydia; Tuscan, Etrurian.

lympha, -ae, F. water.

lynx, -ncis, C. a lynx.

lyra, -ae, F. a lyre.

lyricus, -a, -um [*lyra*], *adj.* lyric,
of (one's) lyre.

Macer, -crī, M. Æmilius Macer, a
poet, and a friend of Virgil and
Ovid.

Machāōn, -onis, M. a famous surgeon and warrior of the Trojan
War (ii. 263).

māchina, -ae, F. a crane, an engine, a derrick.

maciēs, -ēī, F. leanness, emaciation.

mactō, -āre, -āvī, -ātum, *1. v. a.*
sacrifice, offer; slaughter, kill,
slay.

macula, -ae, F. a spot, a stain.

maculō, -āre, -āvī, -ātum [*macula*], *1. v. a.* spot, stain, defile,
sully.

maculōsus, -a, -um [*macula*], *adj.*
spotted, marked with spots.

madefaciō, -ere, -fēcī, -factum
[*madeo, facio*], *3. v. a.* wet, soak;
stain (*of blood*).

madeō, -ēre, -uī, *no sup., 2. v. n.*
be wet, flow, drip, be soaked. —
madēns, -entis, *p. as adj.* wet,
soaked, drenched; besmeared.

madēscō, -ere, maduī, *no sup.*
[*madeo*], *3. v. n.* become moist,
moisten.

madidus, -a, -um [*madeo*], *adj.*
moist, wet, dripping, soaking.

Maeander, -drī, M. a river of
Lydia famous for its windings;
fig. a winding border.

Maeonidēs, -ae, M. a native of
Mæonia in Lydia; Homer.

Maeonius, -a, -um, *adj.* Mæonian,
of Mæonia (in Lydia); Lydian
(iv. 216).

Maeōtis, -idos, *adj.* F. of Lake
Mæotis in Scythia (the Sea of
Azov).

Maeōtius, -a, -um, *adj.* of the
Mæotæ (a people of Scythia),
Mæotian (vi. 799).

maereō, -ēre, *no perf., no sup., 2.
v. n.* be sad, mourn, lament.

maestus, -a, -um [*cf. maereo*],
adj. sad, mournful, sorrowful,
anxious; gloomy, stern.

māgālia, -ium, N. *pl.* huts.

magicus, -a, -um, *adj.* magic.

magis (-e) [√*mag* (*cf. magnus*)],
adv. more, rather.

magister, -trī [*magis*], M. a chief,
a leader; an overseer; a captain, a steersman, a pilot; a master, a teacher.

magistra, -ae [F. *of magister*], F.
a mistress. — *As adj.* masterly:
ars.

magistrātus, -ūs [*magister*], M.
office, a magistracy; a magistrate.

magnanimus, -a, -um [*magnus,
animus*], *adj.* great-souled, generous, noble-minded; high-spirited,
spirited.

magnus, -a, -um [√*mag*], *comp.*
maior, *superl.* **maximus,** *adj.* vast,
great, spacious, huge ; powerful,
mighty; distinguished, illustrious.
— **magnō,** at a great price. —
maiōrēs, M. *pl. as subst.* one's
elders. — **maiōra,** N. *pl. as subst.*
worse sufferings.—**maximus** (*with
or without* **nātū**), oldest, eldest.
— M. **Maximus,** a name of several
Roman families, *esp.* Q. Fabius
Maximus, a hero of the Second
Punic War (vi. 845).

Māia, -ae, F. the daughter of Atlas and mother of Mercury (i.
297).

maior, *see* **magnus.**

māla, -ae, F. the cheekbone, the
jawbone, the jaw.

male [*malus*], *adv.* badly, ill; not
very, not well ; not much, hardly,
scarcely ; not, un- : **male amicus**
(unfriendly) ; **male fidus** (un-
trustworthy) ; **male sanus** (distracted).

Malea, -ae, F. a dangerous headland at the southeastern extremity of Peloponnesus (v. 193).

malesuādus, -a, -um [*male, sua-
deo*], *adj.* tempting to ill.

malignus, -a, -um [*malus,* √*gen*
(*of gigno*)], *adj.* spiteful, ill-
disposed, malign, malicious, envious, baleful: **oculi.** — *Fig.* (*from
idea of grudging*), scanty : **lux.**

mālō, mālle, māluī, *no sup.* [*mage
+ volo*], *irr. v. a.* wish more,
choose rather, choose, prefer,
would rather, wish rather.

malus, -a, -um, *comp.* **peior,**
superl. **pessimus,** *adj.* bad, evil,
wicked ; unfriendly ; injurious,
pernicious, fatal, noxious, poisonous. — M. a wicked person. —
Pl. the wicked. — N. an evil, a
disaster, a calamity, a misfortune ; mischief, a pest, a plague,
misery, suffering, hardship.

mālus, -ī, M. a mast.

mamma, -ae, F. a breast.

mandātum, *see* **mandō.**

mandō, -āre, -āvī, -ātum
[*manus, do*], *1. v. a.* entrust,
command, order, enjoin; consign, entrust, commit: **foliis
carmina.** — **mandātum, -ī,** *p.p.*
N. *as subst.* a command, an injunction, an order, an instruction.

mandō, -ere, mandī, mānsum, *3.
v. a.* chew, champ : **membra** (devour) ; **humum** (bite the dust).

māne, N. *defect.* morning; in the
morning (*abl.*), on the morrow.

maneō, -ēre, mānsī, mānsum, *2.
v. a. and n.* remain, continue,
linger, abide, remain unchanged ;
abide by, stand by ; await, wait
for.

Mānēs, -ium, M. *pl.* the gods below (*spirits of the departed*), the
blessed dead ; the Lower World ;
the spirits of the departed, a
ghost, a shade, a spirit : **quisque
suos patimur Manīs** (destiny in
the World Below).

manica, -ae [*manus*], F. a sleeve ;
pl. manacles, chains.

manifēstus, -a, -um [*manus +
†festus* (*p.p. of* †*fendo*)], *adj.*
(struck *or* seized with the hand,
hence caught in the act) ; clear,
plain, evident, made plain, clearly
visible.

mānō, -āre, -āvī, -ātum, *1. v. n.*
flow, run, drip.

mānsuēscō, -ere, -suēvī, -suē-
tum, *3. v. n.* grow mild, relent:
precibus.

mantēle, -is [*akin to manus*], N. a
towel, a napkin.

Mantua, -ae, F. a city in Northern Italy; also the district (*or*
municipality) of which the city
was the centre.

manus, -ūs, F. a hand. — *Fig. in
many special senses, as in English*,
might, force, force of arms, deeds
of might, valor, combat; art,
skill, labor, handiwork (artificum) : a band, a company, a
troop. — *Phrases*: inter manus
(in one's grasp) ; effugit imago
(grasp) ; manus ferre, enter on a
work, *also*, raise the hands (*in
boxing*).

Mārcellus, -ī, M. a family name
in the Claudian gens. — *Esp.* M.
Claudius Marcellus, who conquered the Insubrians (Gauls),
slew Viridomarus, their chief,
with his own hand, gaining the
spolia opima, and took Milan
(222 B.C.). He afterwards was
successful against Hannibal, and
captured Syracuse (vi. 855).—
Also, M. Marcellus, the nephew
of Augustus, who died young,
23 B.C. (vi. 883).

Mārcus, -ī, M. a Roman praeno-
men.— *Esp.* M. Tullius Cicero,
the orator.

mare, -is, N. a sea, the sea, the
waves.

margō, -inis, M. margin, edge;
bank (*of a stream*).

marītus, -ī, M. a husband, a bride-
groom; a suitor.

marmor, -oris, N. marble.

marmoreus, -a, -um [*marmor*],
adj. of *or* like marble; white as
marble; smooth, marble (*of the
sea*).

Marpēsius, -a, -um, *adj.* of Mar-
pesus (a mountain in the island of
Paros), Marpesian (vi. 471).

Mārs, Mārtis, M. the Latin god of
war ; war, battle, conflict, warfare : caeco Marte (*see note on* ii.
335).

Marsus, -a, -um, *adj.* Marsian, of
the Marsi (a tribe in Latium).

Mārtius, -a, -um, *adj.* of Mars,
sacred to Mars.

massa, -ae, F. a mass.

Massȳlus, -a, -um, *adj.* of the
Massyli (a nation of northern
Africa), Massylian.— M. *pl.* the
Massylians (vi. 60).

māter, -tris, F. a mother, a matron.
*Esp. as appellative of the goddess
Cybele.— Also of animals*, a dam.
— *Also of a country as the parent
of her children.*

māternus, -a, -um [*mater*], *adj.*,
of a (one's) mother, maternal.

mātrōna, -ae [*mater*], F. a matron,
a wife.

mātūrō, -āre, -āvī, -ātum [*maturus*], *1. v. a.* hasten.

mātūrus, -a, -um, *adj.* ripe (*lit.
and fig.*), mature, of full age.

Maurus, -a, -um, *adj.* Moorish.

Maurūsius, -a, -um, *adj.* of the
Mauri (a race of northern Africa),
Moorish; African, of Africa (iv.
206).

Māvors, -ortis, M. Mars.

Māvortius, -a, -um, *adj.* of Mars, martial, warlike; sacred to Mars; son of Mars.

maximus, *see* **magnus.**

Maximus, *see* **magnus.**

meātus, -ūs [*meo*], M. a movement, a revolution: caeli (courses of the heavenly bodies).

Mēdēa, -ae, F. daughter of Æetes, king of Colchis, a famous witch.

medeor, -ērī, *only pres. stem, 2. v. dep.* treat (*medically*), cure. — **medendō,** *ger.* by treatment.

Mēdī, -ōrum, M. *pl.* the Medes; the Parthians, a tribe with whom the Romans were long at war.

medicō, -āre, -āvī, -ātum [*medicus*], *1. v. a.* medicate.— **medicātus, -a, -um,** *p.p. as adj.* prepared (*with drugs*), drugged.

mediocritās, -tātis [*medius*], F. a middle state, the mean (*between two extremes*).

meditor, -ārī, -ātus, *1. v. dep.* intend, purpose, think of.

medius, -a, -um, *adj.* middle, the middle of, the midst of; between, mid, midway between, just between, intervening, right among; in the midst, in the middle, the thick *or* thickest of, the depth of: **medio in conspectu** (right in one's sight); **medios cursus torquet nox** (midway in her course). — N. *as subst.* middle: **in medium** (into the centre, into the midst); **medio** *or* **in medio,** in the middle, in the midst, midway.

Medōn, -ontis, M. a Trojan warrior or an ally of the Trojans (vi. 483).

medulla, -ae [*akin to medius*], F. the marrow; the inmost frame: **extremis medullis** (inmost heart).

Medūsa, -ae, F. the chief Gorgon, daughter of Phorcus.

Medūsaeus, -a, -um, *adj.* Medusalike.

Megarus, -a, -um, *adj.* of Megara (a city of Sicily, also known as Hybla), Megarian (iii. 689).

mel, mellis, N. honey.

Meliboeus, -a, -um, *adj.* of Meliboea (a town of Thessaly, whence came Philoctetes), Meliboean.

melior, *see* **bonus.**

Melitē, -ēs, F. a sea-nymph (v. 825).

melius, *see* **bene.**

mellītus, -a, -um [*mel*], *adj.* honeyed, sweet as honey, lovely.

membrum, -ī, N. a limb, a member; a member (*of a society*). — *Pl.* the frame, the body, the form.

meminī, -isse (*only perf. stem in sense of present*) [√*men,* cf. *mens*], *v. a.* remember, recollect, recall, call to mind; *with inf.* remember to, not forget to, take care to.

Memmius, -ī (-iī), M. a Roman gentile name (v. 117).

Memnōn, -onis, M. son of Aurora and king of the Æthiopians. His arms were fabled to have been made by Vulcan at the request of Aurora. In the Trojan war he fought on the Trojan side (i. 489).

memor, -oris, *adj.* remembering, mindful, with a good memory; faithful, loyal (**sodales**); thoughtful, careful, provident,

caring for: **ira** (ever-mindful);
dum memor ipse mei (so long as
I retain a remembrance of myself); **cape dicta memor** (heed-
fully).

memorābilis, -e [*memoro*], *adj.*
memorable, glorious.

memorō, -āre, -āvī, -ātum [*me-*
mor], *1. v. a.* call to mind, recall;
tell, say, speak; narrate, relate,
speak of, tell of, mention; call.
— **memorātus, -a, -um,** *p.p.* as
adj. renowned, much talked of.

mendāx, -ācis [*cf. mentior*], *adj.*
false, lying, untruthful, deceitful.

Menelāus, -ī, M. the husband of
Helen and brother of Agamemnon (ii. 264).

Menoetēs, -ae, M. a Trojan, companion of Æneas (v. 161).

mēns, mentis [√*men, cf. me-*
minī], F. the mind, the intellect;
the memory; thought; an idea,
a purpose, a resolution. — *Often*
not differing from animus, heart,
soul, feelings, desire.

mēnsa, -ae, F. a table; food, banquet, feast.

mēnsis, -is, M. a month.

mēnsūra, -ae [*metior, mensus*],
F. measure, size, width.

mentior, -īrī, -ītus, *4. v. a. and n.*
lie, pretend falsely: **mentita tela**
(counterfeit, lying).

mentum, -ī, N. the chin.

mercēs, -ēdis [*merx*], F. pay, reward.

mercor, -ārī, -ātus [*merx*], *1. v.*
dep. buy, purchase, pay a price
for: **magno mercentur** (pay a
great price for).

Mercurius, -ī (-iī) [*merx*], M.
Mercury, the Roman god of gain.
He was identified with the Greek
Hermes, and as such regarded
as the son of Jupiter and Maia,
grandson of Atlas, messenger of
the gods, and conductor of souls
to the infernal world, in which
last capacity he carried the rod
twined with serpents, or caduceus, identical with the herald's
staff.

mereō, -ēre, -uī, -itum, *2. v. a.*
earn, win, gain; deserve, deserve
well (*or* ill), merit. — *Pass. as*
dep. same senses. — **merēns, -en-**
tis, *p.* as *adj.* deserved, merited:
poenae. — **meritus, -a, -um,** *p.p.*
as *adj.* deserving; deserved, well
won, due, as one deserves, just.
—N. *as subst.* meritum, -ī, a service, a merit, desert; a favor.

mergō, -ere, mersī, mersum, *3.*
v. a. plunge; drown, overwhelm,
swallow up.

mergus, -ī [*mergo*], M. a sea-bird,
a diver.

meritum, *see* mereō.

meritus, -a, -um, *p.p.* of mereō
and mereor.

Merops, -opis, M. an Æthiopian
king, husband of Clymene and
supposed father of Phaëthon,
really a son of Phœbus.

merus, -a, -um, *adj.* pure, unmixed, unadulterated. — N. *as*
subst. merum (*sc.* vīnum), unmixed wine, pure wine.

merx, mercis, F. merchandise,
wares.

Messāpus, -ī, M. king of Messapia
in Southern Italy (ix. 523).

messis, -is [*meto*], F. a reaping, a crop; grain.

-met, *insep. intens. particle used with pronouns,* self: egomet; memet.

mēta, -ae [*akin to metior*], F. a goal, a limit, a boundary; the end: media (middle point).

Metabus, -ī, M. king of the Volsci, father of Camilla (xi. 564).

metallum, -ī, N. a mine; metal, ore.

Metanīra, -ae, F. the wife of Celeus.

mētior, -īrī, mēnsus, *4. v. dep.* measure.

metō, -ere, messuī, messum, *3. v. a.* mow.

metuō, -uere, -uī, -ūtum [*metus*], *3. v. a. and n.* fear, dread, be alarmed, be afraid of. — *Ger. as adj.* metuendus, -a, -um, terrible.

metus, -ūs, M. fear, dread, alarm, terror, consternation. — *Personified,* Fear.

meus, -a, -um [*cf. me*], *poss. adj.* my, mine, my own. — M. *pl.* my friends, followers, countrymen, subjects, kindred, *etc.*

Mezentius, -ī (-iī), M. an Etruscan tyrant, slain by Æneas (ix. 522).

mī, *dat. of* ego.

micō, -āre, -uī, *no sup., 1. v. n.* quiver, dart, move (*rapidly to and fro*); tremble; palpitate, throb, beat rapidly (**corda**); flash, sparkle, gleam.

Midas, -ae, M. a Phrygian king who had the gift of the golden touch.

migrō, -āre, -āvī, -ātum, *1. v. n.* move (*in a body*), migrate, depart.

mīles, -itis, M. a soldier; soldiery, soldiers, troops.

mīlitāris, -e [*miles*], *adj.* warlike.

mīlitia, -ae [*miles*], F. soldiership, warfare, military service.

mille, *pl.* **mīlia, -ium,** a thousand. — *Pl. also* miles.

minae, -ārum [*cf. mineo*], F. *pl.* threats, menaces, threatening perils: minae murorum, threatening walls.

mināx, -ācis [*minae*], *adj.* threatening.

Minerva, -ae, F. the Roman goddess of wisdom, partially identified with the Greek Pallas Athene. She was the daughter of Jupiter, the patroness of arts and sciences, especially the household arts, and the inventress of the olive.

minimē [*minimus*], *adv.* least.

minister, -trī [*minus*], M. a servant, an attendant. — *In apposition (as adj.),* aiding, abetting: Calchante ministro (by the aid of).

ministerium, -ī (-iī) [*minister*], N. a service, an office.

ministrō, -āre, -āvī, -ātum [*minister*], *1. v. a. and n.* attend, serve; supply, afford; tend.

Mīnōius, -a, -um, *adj.* of Minos (vi. 14).

minor, -ārī, -ātus [*minae*], *1. v. dep.,* threaten, menace; tower (*threateningly*); bode, portend; threaten to fall.

minor, *see* **parvus.**

Mīnōs, -ōis, M. a Cretan king, famous as a lawgiver and made a judge in the World Below (vi. 432).

Mīnōtaurus, -ī, M. the Minotaur, a monster, half man, half bull, killed by Theseus (vi. 26).

minus, *see* **parvus.**

mīrābilis, -e [miror], *adj.* wonderful, marvellous, admirable.

mīror, -ārī, -ātus [mirus], *1. v. dep.* wonder, marvel; marvel at, wonder at, admire; gaze at with wonder *or* admiration. — **mīrandus, -a, -um,** *ger. as adj.* wonderful, marvellous.

mīrus, -a, -um, *adj.* strange, marvellous, wondrous, surprising, extraordinary.

misceō, -ēre, miscuī, mixtum (mistum), *2. v. a.* mingle, mix, confuse, confound, unite, blend: **maria caelo; inter nemora** (disperse). — *Passive or with reflexive,* mingle, unite, be united, be joined: **se corpore mens** (*of the soul of the world,* permeate, be diffused). — *Of any confusion,* disturb, confound, embroil, trouble: **se maria** (are thrown into confusion). — *Of the effect,* cause (*confusedly*), stir, raise: **incendia** (spread). — **mixtus, -a, -um,** *p.p.* mingled, *often with change of point of view,* mingled with, with mingled, *etc.*: **mixto pulvere fumus** (smoke mingled with dust).

misellus, -a, -um [dim. of miser], *adj.* poor, wretched.

Mīsēnus, -ī, M. 1. The trumpeter of Æneas (vi. 162 ff.). — 2. (*sc.* **mōns**), Misenum, the promontory north of the Bay of Naples (now Miseno) (vi. 234).

miser, -era, -erum, *adj.* wretched, pitiable, unfortunate, ill-fated, unhappy. — *As subst.* a wretch, unhappy man, a wretched being. — N. a pity, a wretched thing. — *In a kind of apposition,* O misery! O pitiable fate!

miserābilis, -bile [miseror], *adj.* miserable, pitiable, wretched, unhappy, poor, lamentable.

miserē [miser], *adv.* lamentably.

misereō, -ēre, -uī, -itum [miser], *2. v. a. and n.* feel pity, take pity on, have compassion on. — *Impersonal (with person as object),* pity, feel compassion, commiserate: **te lapsorum** (you pity the fallen). — *Pass. as dep. in same sense.*

misereor, -ērī, -itus, *2. v. dep.,* see **misereō.**

miserēscō, -ere, *no perf., no sup.* **[misereo],** *3. v. n.* pity, have compassion on, take pity on.

miseror, -ārī, -ātus [miser], *1. v. dep.* pity, have compassion on, take pity on. — **miserandus, -a, -um,** *ger. as adj. and subst.* to be pitied, wretched, unfortunate; unhappy person, unlucky man, *etc.*

missile, -is [N. of **missilis,** *adj.*; *cf.* **mitto**], N. a missile, a weapon (*hurled*).

mītēscō, -ere, *no perf., no sup.* **[mitis],** *3. v. incept.* grow mild, soften, become gentle.

mītigō, -āre, -āvī, -ātum [mitis, ago], *1. v. a.* soften, appease.

mītis, -e, *adj.* mild, kindly.

mitra, -ae, F. a cap (of the Phrygian form, with lappets tied under the chin).

mittō, -ere, mīsī, missum, 3. v. a. let go, dismiss, suffer to go, send, despatch, consign, throw: sub leges orbem (subject to); timorem (dismiss *from one's mind*); certamen (dismiss); voces (utter); se (throw one's self, descend). — *Esp. of funeral offerings*, offer: sollemnia. — *P.p.* missus, -a, -um, darting (ignes); galloping: equi.

Mnestheus, -eī (-eos), M. a Trojan, companion of Æneas (v. 116).

mōbilitās, -tātis [*mobilis*], F. freedom of motion; swiftness, rapidity of motion.

moderor, -ārī, -ātus [*modus*], 1. v. dep. govern, manage.— *P.p. as adj.* moderate.

modestus, -a, -um [*modus*], adj. modest.

modo [*abl. of modus*], adv. (in a measure *or* minute portion, *of time or degree*), just now, lately, a little while ago.— modo . . . modo, now . . . now.— *Of degree*, only, merely: modo non (all but, almost).— *Esp. with the hortatory subj. or similar construction*, only, provided, so long as.

modulor, -ārī, -ātus [*modus*], 1. v. dep. set to measure; sing, play.

modus, -ī, M. limit, a bound, an end; manner, way, mode; metre, a measure.— *Pl.* strains, music.

moenia, -ium, N. *pl.* walls, fortifications; a city, a citadel.

mola, -ae [*molo*], F. meal (*used in sacrifices*).

molāris, -is [*mola*], M. a millstone; a huge stone.

mōlēs, -is, F. mass, bulk, size, weight; the mass (*of the universe*); a mass of rocks (*or other material*), a huge mass (*of Ætna*), a massive structure *or* pile (*of buildings*), a huge frame (*of the Horse*); mass of waves, turmoil; siege-works (*in pl.*); a wall, a dyke, a mole; trouble, labor, toil, difficulty.

mōlior, -īrī, -ītus [*moles*], 4. v. dep. pile up, heap, build (*with toil*), frame, construct: fugam (undertake); moram (cause); talia (undertake); iter (pursue); locum (fortify).

molliō, -īre, -īvī, -ītum [*mollis*], 4. v. a. soften, make soft; soothe, calm, appease.

mollis, -e, adj. soft, tender, delicate, pliant, flexible; easy, mild, gentle: aditus (gentle means of approach).

molliter [*mollis*], adv. softly, gently: excudent alii spirantia mollius aera (gracefully, softly-flowing, *of the lines in art*).

moneō, -ēre, monuī, monitum, 2. v. a. remind, warn, admonish, advise; teach, show, suggest, direct.

monīle, -is, N. a necklace.

monimentum, *see* monumentum.

monitor, -ōris [*moneo*], M. an admonisher, an adviser, a counsellor, a guide, a teacher.

monitum, -ī, N. [*p.p. of moneo*], N. a warning, a command.

monitus, -ūs [*moneo*], M. a warning; advice, counsel; a command, a mandate.

Monoecus, -ī, M. a name of Hercules: arx Monoeci, a town in Liguria (now Monaco), so called from a legend of Hercules (vi. 830).

mōns, montis, M. a mountain, a hill, a crag.

mōnstrō, -āre, -āvī, -ātum [*monstrum*], *1. v. a.* point out, show; appoint, direct, tell, teach, command.

mōnstrum, -ī, N. a prodigy, a wonder, a portent, a portentous sight; a hideous creature, a monster, a pest.

montānus, -a, -um [*mons*], *adj.* of the mountain, mountain.

monumentum (moni-), -ī [*moneo*], N. a memorial, a monument, a record, a relic, a reminder.

mora, -ae, F. delay, hesitation; reluctance, objection; loitering, stay; a pause, a respite; a hindrance, an obstacle; a cause for delay; a defence.

morbus, -ī, M. sickness, illness; a disease, a malady. — *Personified, pl.* Diseases.

mordeō, -ēre, momordī, morsum, *2. v. a.* bite, champ.

moribundus, -a, -um [*morior*], *adj.* dying, in the agony of death; doomed to die, mortal.

morior, morī (-īrī), mortuus (moritūrus) [*mors*], *3. v. dep.* die, be slain, fall (*in battle*), perish; wither, fade. — moriēns, -entis, *p. as adj.* dying, failing. — mortuus, -a, -um, *p.p. as adj.* dead.

moror, -ārī, -ātus [*mora*], *1. v. dep.* delay, linger, loiter; be detained, be delayed, be hindered, be held back; pause, wait, stay; cling to; *trans.* stay, retard, delay, hold back; *with negative,* care for, prize, desire, care: nil moror (I have no objection).

mors, mortis [√*mor* (*of morior*)], F. death: mortis honos (honors due to death, burial).

morsus, -ūs [*mordeo*], M. a bite; jaws, teeth, fangs; fluke.

mortālis, -e [*mors*], *adj.* mortal, human, of man, of a mortal man, of mortals. — M. a mortal. — N. *pl.* mortal affairs, affairs of men.

mortifer, -fera, -ferum [*mors, fero*], *adj.* deadly, fatal.

mōrum, -ī, N. a mulberry.

mōrus, -ī, F. a mulberry tree.

mōs, mōris, M. a manner, habit, custom, usage, rite: de (ex) more (according to custom).— *Pl.* habits, character. — *Also,* a law, a precept, a rule, restraint: sine more (without restraint, wildly); paci (terms).

mōtus, -ūs [*moveo*], M. motion, a movement: pedum (activity).

moveō, -ēre, mōvī, mōtum, *2. v. a. and n.* set in motion, move; agitate, shake. — *Esp.:* castra, break camp, march. — *With reflexive,* move, proceed. — *Also,* remove, change, disturb. — *Fig.* stir up, excite, rouse, disturb; revolve (*in the mind*), meditate; begin; disclose (arcana); influence, affect, attract.

mox, *adv.* presently, soon; hereafter.

mūcrō, -ōnis, M. the edge, the point (*of a sword, etc.*); a sword.

mūgiō, -īre, -iī (-īvī), *no sup., 4. v. n.* bellow, roar.

mūgītus, -ūs [*mugio*], M. a bellowing, a lowing.

mulceō, -ēre, mulsī, mulsum, 2. *v. a.* stroke, soften (*by stroking*); caress; soothe, allay, mollify, assuage, calm.

Mulciber, -berī [*mulceo*], M. Vulcan.

multa, -ae, F. a fine; penalty, punishment.

multiplex, -icis [*multus, plico*], *adj.* of many folds, manifold.

multō, -āre, -āvī, -ātum [*multa*, a fine], *1. v. a.* fine, punish, visit (*with a penalty*).

multus, -a, -um, *adj.* many, many a, much. — *Translated by numerous words of quantity, size, or degree,* great, full, numerous, plentiful, copious, thick, loud, a great deal of, heavy, constant. — M. *and* F. *pl.* many (persons), many men (women).— N. *sing. and pl.* much, many things; *adverbially,* much, greatly, loudly. — *Abl.* multō, *as adv.* much, a great deal, far.— *Comparative degree,* plūs, N. (plūrēs, plūra, *pl.*), more. — N. *as adv.* more, longer. — *Superlative* plūrimus, -a, -um, very much, very many, very large, very great, very many a, very high, very wide, very thick, *and the like.*

mundus, -ī, M. the world.

mūniō, -īre, -īvī (-iī), -ītum [*cf. moenia*], *4. v. a.* fortify, protect.

mūnus, -eris, N. office, duty, function; a rite, a sacrifice, an offering; a gift, a favor, a boon, a prize; a service; a tribute.

mūrex, -icis, M. a shellfish (*used for dyeing purple*); purple dye, purple; a jagged rock.

murmur, -uris, N. a murmur, a whisper, murmuring, a muttering (*of thunder*).

mūrus, -ī, M. a wall.

Mūsa, -ae, F. a Muse.

Mūsaeus, -ī, M. a mythical pre-Homeric Athenian bard and musician (vi. 667).

muscus, -ī, M. moss.

mussō, -āre, -āvī, -ātum, *1. v. n.* mutter; hesitate.

mūtābilis, -e [*muto*], *adj.* changeful, changeable, fickle, changing, inconstant.

mūtō, -āre, -āvī, -ātum, *1. v. a.* change, alter, transform; shift, exchange.

mūtus, -a, -um, *adj.* dumb, silent.

mūtuus, -a, -um, *adj.* mutual.

Mycēnē, -ēs (-ae, -ārum; -a, -ae), F. the city of Agamemnon in Greece; Greece (in general).

Myconos (-us), -ī, F. one of the Cyclades (iii. 76).

Mygdonidēs, -ae, M. Corœbus, son of Mygdon (ii. 342).

Myrmidones, -um, M. *pl.* a tribe of Thessaly, subjects of Achilles (ii. 7).

myrteus, -a, -um [*myrtus*], *adj.* of myrtle.

myrtus, -ī (*also,* -ūs), F. a myrtle tree, a myrtle; myrtle (*leaves*); a myrtle shaft; *collectively,* myrtles.

mysta, -ae, M. an initiate

Nāis, -idos, F. a Naiad, a water nymph.

nam, *conj.* for; *with interrogatives,* pray, now (*see* quisnam).

namque, *conj. stronger than* nam, for surely, for no doubt, for in fact.

nārēs, -ium, F. the nostrils, the nose.

nārrō, -āre, -āvī, -ātum, *1. v. a.* tell, relate, recount.

Nārycius, -a, -um, *adj.* of Narycium (a city of the Locri on the Eubœan Sea, the birthplace of Ajax Oileus; also another city of the same name in Bruttium), Narycian (iii. 399).

nāscor, nāscī, nātus (gnātus) [√*gna*], *3. v. n.* be born. — **nāscēns, -entis,** *p. as adj.* new-born, at birth. — **nātus (gnātus), -a, -um,** *p.p. as adj.* fitted by nature; *as subst.* son, daughter, offspring.

Nāsō, -ōnis [*nasus*], M. P. Ovidius Naso, Ovid.

nāsus, -ī, M. nose.

nātālis, -e [*natus*], *adj.* native, of one's birth. — M. *as subst.* (*sc.* dies), birthday.

natō, -āre, -āvī, -ātum [*no*], *1. v. n.* swim, float; be submerged, be flooded. — **natāns, -antis,** *p. as adj.* swimming: lumina.

nātū (*only in abl.*) [*nascor*], M. by birth. — *Regularly used to define* maior *and* maximus, older, eldest.

nātūra, -ae [*natus*], F. nature (*in all senses*).

nātus (gnā-), *see* nāscor.

nauta, -ae (*also* nāvita) [*cf. navis*], M. a sailor, a seaman, a mariner, a boatman, a ferryman.

Nautēs, -is, M. a Trojan, companion of Æneas (v. 704).

nauticus, -a, -um [*nauta*], *adj.* of sailors: clamor.

nāvālis, -e [*navis*], *adj.* of ships, naval, nautical: corona (*made in form of beaks of ships, the honor of a naval engagement*). — N. *pl.* nāvālia (*sc.* castra), shipyards, docks.

nāvifragus, -fraga, -fragum [*navis, frango*], *adj.* shipwrecking, fatal to ships.

nāvigium, -ī (-iī) [*see navigo*], N. a boat, a vessel, a ship.

nāvigō, -āre, -āvī, -ātum [*navis, ago*], *1. v. n.* sail, set sail, embark; *with acc.* sail upon, navigate, traverse.

nāvis, -is, F. a ship, a boat, a vessel, a fleet (*in plural*).

nāvita, *see* nauta.

Naxus (-os), -ī, F. one of the Cyclades (iii. 125).

nē, *adv.* (*only in special forms of speech*), no, not. — *In composition, cf.* neque, nemo, *etc.* — *In imperative and hortatory forms of speech:* tu ne cede malis. — *Conj. with subjunctive* (*orig. the adverb with hortatory forms*), that not, that no, *etc.,* lest, not to. — *With verbs of fearing,* lest, that.

-ne (-n'), *enclitic interrog.* whether (*usually omitted in Eng. in direct questions*); *in double questions in second place,* or.

nebula, -ae, F. a mist, a fog; a cloud.

nec (neque), *neg. conj.* and not, neither, nor, and yet not. — **nec (neque)** . . . **nec (neque),** neither

... nor. — **nec non (nec non et)**, and also, and likewise, nor less, so too, then too, as well.

necdum, *adv.* not yet, and not yet.

necesse, N. *adj. indecl.* (*nom. and acc.*) necessary, fated, required. — *With* **est**, it is necessary, it must be that, one cannot but.

necō, -āre, -āvī, -ātum [*nex*], *1. v. a.* kill, slay.

nectar, -aris, N. nectar (*the drink of the gods*). — *Less exactly, of other drinks.*

nectō, -ere, nexuī, nexum, *3. v. a.* bind, bind together, tie, twine; encircle, twine with. — **nexus, -a, -um**, *p.p. as adj.* close-twined: **artūs** (close-locked); **retia** (woven).

nefandus, -a, -um [*ne +fandus* (*for*)], *adj.* unspeakable, horrible, accursed, impious, godless: **odia** (unutterable). — N. *as subst.* **nefandum, -ī**, crime, wrong.

nefās [*ne +fas*], N. *indecl.* impiety, wrong, crime, sacrilege, a foul disgrace: **nefas dictu** (horrible to tell). — *With* **est** (*often omitted*), it is impious (a crime, wrong, *etc.*). — *Concretely*, an impious creature, a curse.

neglegō, -ere, -lēxī, -lēctum [*nec + lego*], *3. v. a.* disregard, neglect, slight, scorn, contemn. — *P. p.* **neglēctus, -a, -um**, uncared-for.

negō, -āre, -āvī, -ātum, *1. v. n. and a.* say no, say ... not, deny, say that no, *etc.*; refuse, deny (*one anything*), decline. — *P. p.* **negātus, -a, -um**, denied (*to*): **domibus** (uninhabitable).

negōtium, -ī (-iī) [*nec + otium*], N. business.

Nelēïus, -a, -um, *adj.* Nelean (from Neleus, the father of Nestor).

nēmō, -inis [*ne + homo*], M. no man, no one, nobody.

nemorōsus, -a, -um [*nemus*], *adj.* woody, well-wooded.

nempe, *adv.* certainly, assuredly, to be sure.

nemus, -oris, N. a grove, a forest.

Neoptolemus, -ī, M. a name of Pyrrhus, the son of Achilles (ii. 263).

nepōs, -ōtis, M. a grandson; *in pl.* descendants, progeny, offspring, posterity, future generations.

Neptūnius, -a, -um, *adj.* of Neptune, Neptune's: **Troia** (built by Neptune).

Neptūnus, -ī, M. the god of the sea (the Greek Poseidon), brother of Jove and Pluto; the sea.

neque, *see* **nec**.

nequeō, -quīre, -quīvī (-quiī), -quitum [*ne + queo*], *4. v. irr.* cannot, not be able, be unable.

nēquīquam, *adv.* (not in any manner), in vain, uselessly, to no purpose, without effect; without reason.

nē quis, *see* **nē** *and* **quis**.

Nērēis, -idis, F. a daughter of Nereus, a Nereid, a sea nymph.

Nēreus, -eī, M. a sea god, father of the Nereids (ii. 419).

Nēritos, -ī, F. a mountain in the island of Ithaca (iii. 271).

nervōsus, -a, -um [*nervus*], *adj.* sinewy.

nervus, -ī, M. a sinew, a tendon; a bowstring, a string (*of a lyre*).

nescio, -īre, -īvī (-iī), *no sup.* [*ne + scio*], *4. v. a.* not know, know not, be ignorant, be unaware, be unacquainted with: **nescio quis,** some one or other, some one I know not who, some one, some.

nescius, -a, -um [*ne, cf. scio*], *adj.* not knowing, ignorant, unaware, in ignorance; unable, that cannot.

Nestor, -oris, M. king of Pylos, famous for his age and experience. He fought in the Trojan War.

neu, *see* **nēve.**

nēve (neu) [*nē + ve*], *conj.* or not, and not.

nex, necis [*cf. neco*], F. death, murder, slaughter.

nexus, -ūs, M. a coil, a fold, clasp.

nī, *conj.* (*equal to* nisi), if not, unless.

Nīcaea, -ae, F. a city in Bithynia.

nīdus, -ī, M. a nest; a nestling, young (*birds in a nest*).

niger, -gra, -grum, *adj.* black, dark, dusky, swarthy, gloomy.

nigrāns, *p. of* **nigrō.**

nigrēscō, -ere, nigruī, *no sup.* [*nigreo*], *3. v. incept.* grow black, turn black.

nigrō, -āre, -āvī, -ātum [*niger*], *1. v. n.* be black. — **nigrāns, -antis,** *p. as adj.* black, dark.

nihil (nīl) [*ne + hilum*, a trifle], N. *indecl.* nothing; *as adv.* not at all, not in the least, not a whit, not.

nīl, *see* **nihil.**

Nīlus, -ī, M. the Nile (vi. 800).

nimbōsus, -a, -um [*nimbus*], *adj.* cloudy, cloud-capped; stormy.

nimbus, -ī, M. a storm-cloud, a cloud, a dark cloud; a storm, a tempest, rain; a bright cloud (*enclosing the gods*).

nīmīrum [*ne + mirum,* no wonder], *adv.* doubtless, no doubt, surely.

nimis, *adv.* too, too much.

nimium [N. *of nimius; cf. nimis*], *adv.* too, too much, all too; very, most indeed.

Ninus, -ī, M. an Assyrian king.

Niobē, -ēs, F. daughter of Tantalus, wife of Amphion, the king of Thebes.

Nīsaeē, -ēs, F. a sea nymph (v. 826).

nisi [*ne + sī*], *conj.* unless, if not, except.

nīsus, -ūs [*nitor*], M. an effort: rapidus (flight, plunge); idem (position, poise).

Nīsus, -ī, M. a Trojan who, with his companion Euryalus, was slain in attempting to pass the enemy's lines (v. 294 ff.; ix. 230 ff.).

niteō, -ēre, (nituī, *referred to* **nitēscō),** *no sup., 2. v. n.* shine, glisten, sparkle. — **nitēns, -entis,** *p. as adj.* shining, bright, sparkling, glistening; sleek.

nitēscō, -ere, nituī, *no sup.* [*niteo*], *3. v. n.* shine.

nitidus, -a, -um [*cf. niteo*], *adj.* bright, shining, blooming; sleek.

nītor, nītī, nīsus (nīxus), *3. v. dep.* lean against, push, lean on, press on, step on, climb, climb up, rely upon, rest upon: **paribus alis** (be poised on).

nivālis, -e [*nix*], *adj.* snowy; white as snow, snowy white.

niveus, -a, -um [*nix*], *adj.* snowy; snow-white, pure white.

nix, nivis, F. snow.

nīxor, -ārī, *no perf., no sup.* [*nixus*], *1. v. dep.* struggle.

nō, nāre, nāvī, *no sup., 1.v.n.* swim, float, sail.

nōbilis, -e [√*gno* (*cf.* (*g*)*nosco*)], *adj.* noble, famous.

nōbilitās, -tātis [*nobilis*], F. nobility, rank.

nocēns, *see* noceō.

noceō, -ēre, nocuī, nocitum [*cf. noxa, neco* (√*nec*)], *2.v.n.* do mischief, be hurtful, be injurious, injure, harm : **haud ignara nocendi** (of mischief). — **nocēns, -entis,** *p. as adj.* harmful, guilty.

nocturnus, -a, -um [*nox*], *adj.* of the night, nocturnal, nightly ; *as adv.* by night, in the night.

nōdō, -āre, -āvī, -ātum [*nodus*], *1. v. a.* knot, tie up, bind in a knot : **crines.**

nōdus, -ī, M. a knot, a coil (*of a serpent*).

nōlō, nōlle, nōluī [*ne + volo*], *irr. v.* be unwilling.

Nomas, -adis, M. a Nomad (one of a wandering, pastoral people) ; *pl.* the Numidians, an African people (iv. 320).

nōmen, -inis [√*gno cf.* (*nosco*)], N. a name ; a word ; a hero ; a family, a race ; name, renown, glory, distinction, reputation : **nomina magna** (persons in high place).

Nōmentum, -ī, N. a Sabine city (vi. 773).

nōminō, -āre, -āvī, -ātum [*nomen*], *1. v. a.* call by name.

nōn [*ne + unum*], *adv.* no, not.

nōndum [*non + dum*], *adv.* not yet.

nōnne [*non + -ne*], *interrog. adv.* (does one) not.

nōnus, -a, -um [*novem*], *num. adj.* ninth.

nōscō, -ere, nōvī, nōtum [√*gno*], *3. v. a.* learn, recognize ; *in perf., etc.* know, be acquainted with. — **nōtus, -a, -um,** *p.p. as adj.* well-known, familiar, wonted ; famous, renowned. — N. *as subst.* **nōtum, -ī,** knowledge.

noster, -tra, -trum [*nos*], *adj. pron.* our, ours, of us, my, mine, of me.

nota, -ae [√*gno, cf. nosco*], F. a mark, a sign ; a letter.

nōtitia, -ae [*notus*], F. acquaintance.

notō, -āre, -āvī, -ātum [*nota*], *1. v. a.* mark ; observe, notice.

nōtus, -a, -um, *p.p. of* nōscō.

Notus, -ī, M. the South Wind ; the wind.

novem, *num. adj. indecl.* nine.

noviēns (-iēs) [*novem*], *num. adv.* nine times.

noviēs, *see* noviēns.

novitās, -tātis [*novus*], F. newness, novelty, strangeness : **rerum; regni** (infancy).

novō, -āre, -āvī, -ātum [*novus*], *1. v. a.* renew, make new, refit, repair ; repeat : **tecta novantem** (building new houses) ; **charta novata** (newly written letter).—*Fig.* change : **fidem** (break).

novus, -a, -um, *adj.* new, fresh ; strange ; young : **aestas** (early). — **novissimus, -a, -um,** *superl.* latest, last.

nox, noctis, F. night, darkness. — *Personified,* Night.

noxa, -ae, F. a fault, guilt.

noxius, -a, -um [*noxa*], *adj.* harmful, guilty.

nūbēs, -is, F. a cloud; the region of clouds, the clouds, the sky, the heavens.

nūbila, -ōrum [nubes], N. pl. the clouds.

nūbilus, -a, -um [nubes], adj. lowering, cloudy, gloomy.

nūbō, -ere, nūpsī, nūptum, 3. v. a. and n. veil; marry (said of the wife). — nūpta, F. p.p. as noun, a bride.

nūdō, -āre, -āvī, -ātum [nudus], 1. v. a. strip, lay bare, bare, uncover: aras (reveal); terga (expose). — nūdātus, -a, -um, p.p. as adj. bared, naked.

nūdus, -a, -um, adj. naked, bare, uncovered, stripped; open: aetheris axis.

nūllus, -a, -um [ne + ullus], adj. no, none. — M. and F. none, no one, nobody.

num, conj. interrog. whether (often not expressed in Eng. but indicated by the order, is any? does any? etc.). — Regularly expecting the answer no.

Numa, -ae, M. Numa Pompilius, the second king of Rome.

nūmen, -inis [nuo], N. (a nod). — Esp. the divine will, power (of the gods), permission, purpose, approval, decree; inspiration, presence (of a god), divine nature, divine interposition or protection; oracle: perverso numine, by a fatal impulse. — Also, divinity, deity (with genitive): Iunonis. — Also concretely, a divinity, a divine being: numina magna deum (forms); media inter numina divum (images).

numerō, -āre, -āvī, -ātum [numerus], 1. v. a. count.

numerōsus, -a, -um [numerus], adj. tuneful.

numerus, -ī, M. a number; a large number, numbers; order; musical measure, metre, time, tune, the notes of the scale (pl.).

Numidae, -ārum, M. pl. the Numidians, a people of Northern Africa (iv. 41).

Numitor, -ōris, M. the grandfather of Romulus and Remus (vi. 768).

numquam [ne + umquam], adv. never; not at all, by no means.

nunc [num + -ce], adv. now: nunc ... nunc, now ... now, sometimes ... again.

nūntia, -ae [F. of nuntius], F. a messenger (female).

nūntiō, -āre, -āvī, -ātum [nuntius], 1. v. a. report, announce, bring tidings.

nūntius, -ī (-iī), M. a messenger, a reporter. — In appos. as adj. bringing news or tidings, reporting. — Also, news, message, tidings, report.

nūper [novus], adv. lately, just now, not long ago.

nurus, -ūs, F. a daughter-in-law; a young unmarried woman; a dame.

nūsquam [ne + usquam], adv. nowhere; never.

nūtō, -āre, -āvī, -ātum [nutus], 1. v. n. nod, totter.

nūtrīmentum, -ī [nutrio], N. food, nourishment; fuel.

nūtrīx, -īcis [nutrio], F. a nurse.

nūtus, -ūs [nuo], M. a nod; will.

nympha, -ae, F. a nymph; a bride, a wife.

Nȳsa, -ae, F. a city of India, said to have been built by Bacchus in his expedition to India. *Otherwise,* a mountain sacred to him (vi. 805).

Ō, *interj.* oh! O!

ob (obs), *prep.* on account of, for, for the sake of, through. — *In comp.* to, towards, against, before, over, *etc.*

obdūcō, -ere, -dūxī, -ductum, *3. v. a.* draw over, spread over.

obeō, -īre, -īvī (-iī), -itum, *irr. v. a.* go to, go over, visit; surround, encircle: **pugnas** (engage in); **terras maria** (wash, encompass); **mortem** (suffer, meet).

obex, -icis, C. a bar, a barrier.

obiciō, -ere, -iēcī, -iectum [ob + iacio], *3. v. a.* throw against, throw to; expose, offer: **clipeos ad tela** (oppose, present). — **obiectus, -a, -um,** *p.p. as adj.* thrown in the way, lying in the way, opposing.

obiectō, -āre, -āvī, -ātum [ob + iacto], *1. v. a.* throw against; expose, risk.

obiectus, -ūs [ob + iactus, cf. obicio], M. a throwing in the way, opposition, obstacle.

obitus, -ūs [obeo], M. death.

oblinō, -ere, -lēvī, -litum, *3. v. a.* daub, smear.

oblīquō, -āre, -āvī, -ātum [obliquus], *1. v. a.* turn obliquely; **sinus** (brace, swing).

oblīquus, -a, -um, *adj.* sidewise, across.

oblīvīscor, -ī, oblītus, *3. v. dep.* forget, think no more of. — **oblītus, -a, -um,** *p.p.* forgetting, forgetful; careless of, heedless of.

oblīvium, -ī (-iī) [cf. obliviscor], N. forgetfulness.

obloquor, -ī, -locūtus, *3. v. dep.* sing to *(with accompaniment of).*

obluctor, -ārī, -ātus, *1. v. dep.* struggle against, brace one's self against.

obmūtēscō, -ere, -mūtuī, *no sup.,* *3. v. n. incept.* hush, be silent, become speechless.

obnītor, -ī, -nīsus (-nīxus), *3. v. dep.* struggle against, lean *or* push against, lean on; struggle, strive. — **obnīxus, -a, -um,** *p.p.* with an effort: **obnixae umeris** (pushing); **remi** (striking on *or* against).

oborior, -orīrī, -ortus, *4. v. dep.* rise against, rise over. — **obortus, -a, -um,** *p.p. as adj.* rising, flowing *(of tears),* blinding.

obruō, -ere, -ruī, -rutum, *3. v. a.* overwhelm, bury.

obscēnus, -a, -um, *adj.* filthy, vile, foul; unsightly, ugly, hideous, horrible; ominous, ill-omened.

obscūrō, -āre, -āvī, -ātum [obscurus], *1. v. a.* darken, obscure.

obscūrus, -a, -um, *adj.* dark, dim, gloomy, dusky; obscured, obscure, humble, lowly, unknown, little known, in the dark, unseen: **fama** (doubtful, dimmed); **obscuris vera involvens** (wrapping up the truth in dark hints).

obserō, -ere, -sēvī, -situm, *3. v. a.* sow *(with),* cover.

observō, -āre, -āvī, -ātum, *1. v. a.* watch, mark, observe, notice, trace.

obsideō, -ēre, -sēdī, -sessum [*ob + sedeo*], *2. v. a.* blockade, beset, guard, besiege, occupy.

obsidiō, -ōnis [*obsideo*], F. a siege, a blockade.

obsolēscō, -ere, -ēvī, -ētum, *3. v. n.* wear out. — *P.p.* obsolētus, -a, -um, tumble-down, ruinous.

obstipēscō, -ere, -stipuī, *no sup.* [*ob + sti(stu)pesco*], *3. v. n.* be amazed, be dazed, be stunned, be struck dumb, stand amazed *or* aghast, be thunderstruck.

obstō, -stāre, -stitī, (-stātūrus), *1. v. n.* stand in the way of, hinder, withstand, retard: obstitit quibus Ilium (be obnoxious, be an offence).

obstrepō, -ere, -uī, -itum, *3. v. n.* roar against: mare (breaks upon).

obstruō, -ere, -strūxī, -strūctum, *3. v. a.* block up, seal (*of the ears*).

obsum, -esse, -fuī, *irr. v. n.* be in the way; harm, injure.

obtegō, -ere, -tēxī, -tēctum, *3. v. a.* cover, obscure, hide, conceal.

obtorqueō, -ēre, -torsī, -tortum, *2. v. a.* twist.

obtruncō, -āre, -āvī, -ātum, *1. v. a.* cut down, butcher, slay.

obtundō, -ere, -tudī, -tūsum (-tūnsum), *3. v. a.* dull (*orig. by beating*), blunt. — obtūsus, -a, -um, *p.p. as adj.* unfeeling.

obtūsus, -a, -um, *p.p. of* obtundō.

obtūtus, -ūs [*cf. obtueor*], M. a gaze, a fixed stare.

obumbrō, -āre, -āvī, -ātum, *1. v. a.* overshadow, darken.

obuncus, -a, -um, *adj.* hooked, curved.

obvertō, -ere, -vertī, -versum, *3. v. a.* turn towards, turn.

obvius, -a, -um [*ob, via*], *adj.* in the way, opposed, exposed, in front; ready, at hand; to meet.

occāsus, -ūs [*ob + casus*], M. a fall, ruin.

occidō, -ere, -cidī, -cāsum [*ob + cado*], *3. v. n.* fall, fall dead, perish, be slain.

occiduus, -a, -um [*occido*], *adj.* setting: dies (the West).

occubō, -āre, *no perf., no sup.* [*ob + cubo*], *1. v. n.* lie (*dead*), lie low in: umbris.

occulō, -ere, -culuī, -cultum, *3. v. a.* bury, cover, hide, conceal. — occultus, -a, -um, *p.p. as adj.* concealed, secret, hidden.

occultō, -āre, -āvī, -ātum [*occulo*], *1. v. a.* hide, conceal.

occultus, -a, -um, *p.p. of* occulō.

occumbō, -ere, -cubuī, -cubitum [*ob + cumbo*], *3. v. n.* fall, die, be slain: morti (fall a prey).

occupō, -āre, -āvī, -ātum [*ob + capio*], *1. v. a.* seize, take possession of, win, gain; attack, strike down; overtake, outstrip; overspread, fill; aurīs (meet).

occurrō, -ere, -currī (-cucurrī), -cursum [*ob + curro*], *3. v. n.* run to meet, rush to, rush in, come in the way, meet; appear, meet one's eyes: medius (come in to interrupt).

ōceanus, -ī, M. the ocean. — *Personified*, Ocean.

ocellus, -ī [*dim. of oculus*], M. a little eye, an eye. — *Fig.* the gem, the jewel.

ōcior, -ius, *adj.* swifter.— N. ōcius, *as adv.* more swiftly, quicker; quickly, forthwith, at once.

ōcius, *see* ōcior.

oculus, -ī, M. eye.

ōdī, ōdisse, ōsus, *v. a. defect.* hate: sedem (curse).

odium, -ī (-iī) [*odī*], N. hatred, hate.

odor, -ōris, M. an odor, a fragrance, a perfume.

odōrō, -āre, -āvī, -ātum [*odor*], *1. v. a.* perfume. — odōrātus, -a, -um, *p.p.* perfumed, fragrant.

odōrus, -a, -um [*odor*], *adj.* keen-scented.

Oeagrius, -a, -um, *adj.* of Œagrus (a king in Thrace, father of Orpheus); Thracian.

Oenōtrus, -a, -um, *adj.* of Œnotria (the southern part of Italy), Œnotrian (i. 532).

offa, -ae, F. a ball of dough, a cake.

offēnsa, -ae [*offendo*], F. an offence.

offerō, offerre, obtulī, oblātum [*ob + fero*], *irr. v. a.* bring to, present, hold out. — *With reflexive or in pass.* appear, present one's self, come in one's way, expose, offer one's self.

officium, -ī (-iī) [*ob, facio*], N. a service, a kind office.

Oīleus, -eī (-ēī, -eos), M. a king of Locris, father of Ajax. The name was added to that of Ajax either in the genitive or nominative, or as an adj., to distinguish him from Ajax son of Telamon (i. 41).

Ōlearos, -ī, F. one of the Cyclades, now Antiparos, an island in the Ægean Sea (iii. 126).

Ōlenos, -ī, M. a fabulous person, turned into stone, husband of Lethæa.

oleō, -ēre, oluī, *no sup.,* *2. v. n.* smell. — olēns, -entis, *p. as adj.* smelling (*good, bad, or indifferent*): grave olens (noisome).

oleum, -ī, N. oil.

olfaciō, -ere, -fēcī, -factum [*oleo, facio*], *3. v. a.* smell.

ōlim [*ollus*], *adv.* at that (*past*) time, formerly, once, just now. — *Of future time,* hereafter, by-and-by; at some time, at any time. — *Indefinitely,* sometimes, often.

olīva, -ae, F. the olive tree; an olive wreath, olive leaves.

olīvum, -ī, N. olive oil, oil.

ollus, -a, -um, *see* ille.

olor, -ōris, M. a swan.

Olympus, -ī, M. a mountain on the northern frontier of Thessaly, regarded as the home of the gods; the heavens, heaven, the sky.

ōmen, -inis, N. an omen, a portent, a prodigy: primis ominibus (first marriage); omina (auspices).

omnigenus, -a, -um [*omnis, genus*], *adj.* of all sorts *or* kinds, of every kind.

omnīnō [*omnis*], *adv.* altogether, entirely, utterly.

omniparēns, -entis [*omnis, parens*], *adj.* all-producing, parent of all.

omnipotēns, -entis [*omnis, potens*], *adj.* all-powerful, omnipotent, almighty.— M. *as subst.* the All-powerful (*Jupiter*).

omnis, -e, *adj.* all, every : **cura** (the utmost). — *Often like* **totus,** the whole, the entire. — N. *pl.* everything, all, all things.

onerō, -āre, -āvī, -ātum [*onus*], *1. v. a.* load, burden, fill, cover ; heap, pile ; overload, overwhelm ; load (in), put up : **vina cadis.**

onerōsus, -a, -um [*onus*], *adj.* burdensome, heavy, weighty.

onus, -eris, N. a burden, a weight, a load ; **onus mortale** (the dross of mortality).

onustus, -a, -um [*onus*], *adj.* burdened, laden, loaded.

opācō, -āre, -āvī, -ātum [*opacus*], *1. v. a.* darken, shade, throw a shadow on, overshadow.

opācus, -a, -um, *adj.* dark, shaded, shady, overshadowed ; overshadowing, shady : **ulmus.** — N. *pl.* **opaca locorum** (dark places) ; **opaca viarum** (dark ways).

opera, -ae [*opus*], F. service : **tuā operā** (for your sake).

operiō, -īre, operuī, opertum [*ob + pario*], *4. v. a.* cover, enshroud. — **opertus, -a, -um,** *p.p. as adj.* covered, secret, hidden. — N. *pl. as subst.* hidden regions, depths : **telluris operta.**

operor, -ārī, -ātus [*opus*], *1. v. dep.* be busied.

opertus, *p.p. of* **operiō.**

opifex, -ficis [*opus, facio*], M. a workman, artist.

opīmus, -a, -um [*cf. ops*], *adj.* fruitful, rich, fertile : **spolia** (princely, *the spoils taken by a commander-in-chief from a commander-in-chief in personal combat*).

Ōpis, -is, F. a nymph of Diana (xi. 836).

oportet, -ēre, -uit, *no sup. 2. v. impers.* it befits, it is fitting, it is right.

opperior, -īrī, -perītus (-pertus) [*ob + † perior*], *4. v. dep.* await, wait for.

oppetō, -ere, -petīvī (-iī), -petītum [*ob + peto*], *3. v. a.* meet (*sc.* mortem), fall, perish, be slain, meet death.

oppidum, -ī, N. a town.

oppōnō, -ere, -posuī, -positum [*ob + pono*], *3. v. a.* place towards, set against, array against ; expose (**quemquam morti**). — *In passive or with a reflexive,* turn against, oppose, stand in the way, face (*something*). — **oppositus, -a, -um,** *p.p.* opposing, in opposition.

opportūnus, -a, -um, *adj.* fit, meet, well-suited.

opprimō, -ere, -pressī, -pressum [*ob + premo*], *3. v. a.* press down *or* against ; overwhelm.

oppugnō, -āre, -āvī, -ātum [*ob + pugno*], *1. v. a. and n.* attack, assail, fight against, lay siege to.

†ops, opis, F. *sing.* (*exc. nom.*) wealth, means ; aid, help, assistance : **non opis est nostrae** (it is not in our power). — *Pl.* means, resources, riches, power : **has evertit opes** (this realm).

optimus, *see* **bonus.**

optō, -āre, -āvī, -ātum [*cf. ops*], *1. v. a.* wish, desire, long, long for ; pray, hope ; choose ; prefer.

opulentus, -a, -um [*ops*], *adj.* rich, wealthy.

opus, -eris, N. work, labor, toil; a task, an undertaking, an employment, a deed *or* action; a work.

opus, *indecl.* N. (*with* **esse**), there is need, one needs, one requires.

ōra, -ae, F. an edge, a border; a coast; a shore; a country, a region: **superis ab oris** (the Upper World; *this world, as opposed to the lower regions*).

ōrāculum, -ī [*oro*, speak], N. a response, an oracle, a prophecy. — *Less exactly,* an oracle (*place or source of prophetic words*).

orbis, -is, M. a circle, a circuit, a ring, a disc, a wheel; a coil; a region; the circle of the world, the world (*either* **orbis terrarum** *or* **orbis** *alone*); a world (**peregrinus**); the heavens.—*Fig.* a cycle (*of time*), a revolution (*of the heavenly bodies*).

orbus, -a, -um, *adj.* bereft; childless.

Orcus, -ī, M. a god of the Lower World identified with Pluto, Death; the World Below, Hades (iv. 242).

ōrdior, -īrī, ōrsus [*cf. ordo*], 4. *v. dep.* begin, begin (*to speak*).

ōrdō, -inis [*cf. ordior*], M. a row, a rank, a series, a line, a bank (*of oars*); rank, class (*in society*); order, array, arrangement: **omnīs uno habetis** (estimation); **fatorum** (fixed order); (**ex**) **ordine,** in regular order, regularly, in succession, in detail.

Orēades, -um, F. *pl.* mountain nymphs (i. 500).

Orestēs, -ae (-is), M. son of Agamemnon. He killed his mother Clytemestra, and was therefore driven mad by the Furies (iii. 331; iv. 471).

orgia, -ōrum, N. *pl.* the orgies, the festival of Bacchus (celebrated with wild revelry).

oriēns, *see* **orior.**

orīgō, -inis [*orior*], F. a beginning, an origin, a source; lineage, race, a stock.

Ŏriōn, -onis (-ōnis), M. a mythic hunter placed in the heavens as a constellation; Orion (the constellation) (i. 535).

orior, orīrī, ortus, 3. *and* 4. *v. dep.* rise, arise, begin, appear; be born, spring. — **oriēns, -entis,** *p.* rising. — M. *as subst.* the rising sun, the dawn, the East.— **ortus, -a, -um,** *p.p.* sprung (*of origin or birth*).

Orīthȳia, -ae, F. a daughter of Erechtheus, king of Athens.

ōrnātus, -ūs [*orno*], M. adornment, ornament, attire.

ōrnō, -āre, -āvī, -ātum, 1. *v. a.* adorn, furnish, equip, trick out.

ornus, -ī, F. an ash.

ōrō, -āre, -āvī, -ātum [*ōs*], 1. *v. a. and n.* pray, plead, beg, beseech, entreat, implore, beg for, supplicate.

Orontēs, -is (-ī), M. commander of Æneas' Lycian allies (i. 113).

Orphēus, -a, -um, *adj.* of Orpheus, Orphean.

Orphēūs, -eī (-eos), M. a mythic bard. He rescued his wife from the World Below by his music, but was afterwards torn in pieces by the Thracian women (vi. 119).

ōrsus, *p.p. of* **ōrdior.**

ortus, ūs [*orior*], M. a rising, the dawn; source.

Ortygia, -ae, F. 1. A name of Delos (iii. 124). — 2. An island in the harbor of Syracuse (iii. 694).

ōs, ōris, N. the mouth; the face, the countenance; the lips, the jaws; a head; language, words, speech, the voice; an entrance, an opening, mouth (*of a river*), an aperture, door : ante ora (before the eyes) ; ora discordia (language) ; manus inter -que ora (under the hands and before the face) ; ora exsertans (head) ; virum diffundit in ora (spread abroad in the mouths of men); tria Dianae (forms) ; summo ore (just with the lips).

os, ossis, N. a bone; *pl.* the bones, the frame, the inmost frame.

ōsculum, -ī [*dim. of* ōs], N. a lip, the mouth; a kiss.

Osīnius, -ī, M. king of Clusium (x. 655).

ostendō, -ere, -tendī, -tēnsum (-tentum) [*obs* + *tendo*], 3. *v. a.* stretch before, stretch out; exhibit, show, point out.— *With reflexive*, show one's self, appear.

ostentō, -āre, -āvī, -ātum [*obs* + *tento*], 1. *v. a.* show, display, point out.

ōstium, -ī (-iī), N. the mouth; a door, a gate, an entrance; *pl.* the mouth (*of a river*), a harbor.

ostrum, -ī, N. purple (*a color made from a shellfish*), purple fabrics.

Othryadēs, -ae, M. son of Othrys (ii. 319).

ōtium, -ī (-iī), N. rest, ease, idleness, quiet, leisure, repose.

ovis, -is, F. a sheep.

ovō, -āre, -āvī, -ātum, 1. *v. n.* rejoice, triumph, exult, express one's joy. — ovāns, -antis, *p. as adj.* exulting, rejoicing, delighted, glad.

pābulum, -ī [*cf. pasco*], N. food, fodder, pasturage, nourishment.

Pachȳnus (-um), -ī, M. *and* N. (F.) the southeastern extremity of Sicily (Capo di Passaro) (iii. 429).

pācifer, -era, -erum [*pax, fero*], *adj.* peaceful.

pacīscō, -ere, *no perf.*, pactum [√*pac*, bind], 3. *v. a.* agree, bargain, agree upon. — pactus, -a, -um, *p.p.* agreed upon, promised, appointed. — N. an agreement. — pacīscor, *pass. as dep.* barter, bargain.

pacīscor, *see* pacīscō.

pācō, -āre, -āvī, -ātum [*pax*], 1. *v. a.* reduce to peace, give peace to; subdue.

Pactōlus (-os), -ī, M. a river of Lydia, famous for its golden sands.

pactus, -a, -um, *p.p. of* pacīscō.

Padūsa, -ae, F. an artificial mouth of the Padus (Po), or canal, running into the Adriatic near Ravenna (xi. 457).

Paeān, -ānis, M. the physician of the gods; also used as a name of Apollo. — *Hence*, a hymn to Apollo, a hymn (*to any deity*), a song of triumph *or* of thanksgiving (vi. 657).

paene, *adv.* almost. — paene īnsula, a peninsula.

paenitet, -ēre, -uit, *no sup.* [*akin to poena*], 2. *v. a. impers.* it repents; one repents, regrets.

Palaemōn, -onis, M. a son of King Athamas and Ino, changed to a sea-god (v. 823).

palaestra, -ae, F. a palæstra *or* wrestling school, a place for wrestling, a ring; wrestling, games.

palam, *adv.* openly.

Palamēdēs, -is, M. a Grecian hero (ii. 82).

Palātīnus, -a, -um, *adj.* of the Palatine Mount, one of the seven hills of Rome (ix. 9).

Palātium, -ī (-iī), N. the Palatine Mount.

palātum, -ī, N. palate.

Pales, -is, F. the goddess of shepherds and cattle.

Palinūrus, -ī, M. the helmsman of Æneas, murdered on the coast of Italy after swimming to land (iii. 202, vi. 337).

palla, -ae, F. a robe (*esp. for women, prob. a mantle or shawl*).

Palladius, -a, -um, *adj.* of Pallas. — N. *as subst.* **Palladium, -ī (-iī),** the Palladium, or statue of Pallas in Troy, stolen by Ulysses and Diomede (ii. 166).

Pallantēus, -a, -um, *adj.* of Pallanteum. — N. *as subst.* **Pallantēum, -ēī,** Evander's city in Italy (named after the Arcadian city from which he came) (viii. 54).

Pallas, -adis, F. the Grecian divinity identified by the Romans with Minerva, a goddess of war and of household arts and of learning, the discoverer of the olive.

Pallās, -antis, M. 1. The son of Evander, killed by Turnus while fighting for Æneas (viii. 104). — 2. An ancient Arcadian chief, ancestor of Evander (viii. 54).

palleō, -ēre, palluī, *no sup.* [*cf. pallidus*], 2. *v. n.* be pale, be pallid. — **pallēns, -entis,** *p. as adj.* pale, pallid.

pallēscō, -ere, palluī, *no sup.* [*palleo*], 3. *v. n.* grow pale *or* yellow.

pallidus, -a, -um [*palleo*], *adj.* pale, pallid, wan.

pallor, -ōris [*palleo*], M. paleness, pallor.

palma, -ae, F. the palm (*of the hand*), the hand; the palm tree, the palm, a palm branch; victory; a prize; a victor.

palmōsus, -a, -um [*palma*], *adj.* abounding in palm trees, palmgrown, palmy.

palmula, -ae [*palma*], F. an oarblade.

pālor, -ārī, -ātus, 1. *v. dep.* wander, straggle. — **palāns, -antis,** *p. as adj.* straggling, in disorder.

palūs, -ūdis, F. a marsh, a pool, a lake, water (*stagnant*).

pampineus, -a, -um [*pampinus*], *adj.* of vine branches *or* vinewreathed : **habenae.**

Pandarus, -ī, M. a Lycian archer who shot an arrow among the Greeks, and thus broke the treaty between them and the Trojans (v. 496).

pandō, -ere, pandī, pānsum (passum), 3. *v. a.* spread out, extend, spread; expose, open, lay open; show, disclose, unfold, relate, pub-

lish, reveal. — **passus, -a, -um,**
p.p. as adj. spread, extended;
dishevelled (*of hair*).

Pangaeus, -a, -um, *adj.* of Pangæa, a mountain in Thrace.

**pangō, -ere, pānxī (pēgī, pepi-
gī), pāctum [√pag],** *3. v. a.* fasten, fix; agree upon.

Panopē, -ēs, F. a town in Phocis.

Panopēa, -ae, F. a sea nymph (v.
240).

Panopēs, -is, M. an attendant of
Acestes (v. 300).

Pantagiās, -ae, M. a river of Sicily
(iii. 689).

Panthūs, -ī, M. a Trojan priest of
Apollo (ii. 318).

papāver, -eris, N. poppy.

Paphos (-us), -ī, F. a city of Cyprus famous for an ancient temple
of Venus (i. 415).

papilla, -ae, F. breast.

**papȳrifer, -era, -erum [papyrus,
fero],** *adj.* that bears papyrus.

pār, paris, *adj.* equal, no less,
like, well-matched, corresponding, even : **sententia, aetas** (the
same); **discurrere pares** (ride
apart in equal numbers); **alae**
(even, balanced).

pār, paris, N. a pair, the two.

parātus, -ūs [paro], M. preparation; trappings, ornaments.

Parcae, -ārum, F. *pl.* the Fates,
goddesses of birth and death
(Nona, Decuma, and Morta), and
so the arbiters of human destiny;
identified with the Greek Μοῖραι
(Clotho, Lachesis, and Atropos)
(i. 22).

**parcō, -ere, pepercī (parsī), (par-
sūrus),** *3. v. n. and a.* spare (*re-*

frain from using or destroying);
refrain from, forbear, cease; preserve.

parcus, -a, -um, *adj.* sparing, niggardly.

parēns, -entis [p. of pario], C. a
parent, a father, a mother; an
ancestor, a forefather.

pārēns, *p. of* pāreō.

pāreō, -ēre, pāruī, pāritum, *2.
v. n.* appear; obey. — **pārēns,
-entis,** *p.* obedient.

pariēs, -ietis, M. a wall (*of a
house*).

**pariō, -ere, peperī, partum (pa-
ritūrus),** *3. v. a.* secure, procure,
win : **sibi letum** (find a means of,
etc.). — *Also,* bring forth, bear.
— *Pass.* be born. — **partus, -a,
-um,** *p.p.* acquired, gained, secured, won.

Paris, -idis, M. the son of Priam
and Hecuba. He awarded the
prize of beauty to Venus over
Juno (Hera) and Minerva (Pallas), and thus won Helen.

pariter [par], *adv.* equally, alike,
in like manner, as well . . . as, together, at the same time, side by
side, on equal terms.

Parius, -a, -um, *adj.* of Paros, Parian (i. 593).

parma, -ae, F. a shield (*small and
round*), a buckler.

parō, -āre, -āvī, -ātum, *1. v. a.* procure, provide; prepare, prepare
for; begin, attempt; be about to,
intend. — **parātus, -a, -um,** *p.p.*
prepared, ready.

Paros, -ī, F. one of the Cyclades,
famous for its white marble (iii.
126).

Parrhasis, -idis, *adj.* F. of Parrhasia, an Arcadian town; Arcadian.

pars, partis, F. a part, a portion, a share; a place, a region; a direction, a side. — *Repeated,* one part ... another, some ... some. — *Pl.* a part (*on the stage*), a rôle; office, task.

Parthenopaeus, -ī, M. the son of Atalanta and Meleager, who fought in the Theban and Trojan wars (vi. 480).

Parthenopē, -ēs, F. an ancient name of Naples.

Parthī, -ōrum, M. *pl.* the Parthians, a warlike people in Scythia.

partior, -īrī, -ītus [*pars*], *4. v. dep.* divide, share. — **partītus, -a, -um,** *p.p.* divided.

partus, -a, -um, *p.p.* of pariō.

partus, -ūs [*pario*], M. birth; offspring.

parum [*akin to parvus*], *adv.* little, too little, not much, not very: laetus (far from).

parumper [*parum*], *adv.* but a little while, for a moment.

parvulus, -a, -um [*parvus*], *adj.* little.

parvus, -a, -um, *adj.* small, little, slight, humble. — N. *subst.* a little, humble circumstances. — *Comp.* minor, minus. — minōrēs (*sc.* nātū), *pl. as subst.* the younger (ones), the men of our time, descendants, posterity. — minus, N. *as adv.* less, too little, not.

pāscō, -ere, pāvī, pāstum [√*pa*], *3. v. a. and n.* pasture, feed, tend; nourish, maintain, foster, support; breed: equos. — *Intrans.* browse, feed, graze. — *Pass.* as

dep. feed, graze, feed on, pluck. — *Fig.,* of flame, play round, stray about: circum tempora.

pāscor, *see* pāscō.

pāscuum, -ī [*pascor*], N. a pasture.

Pāsiphaē, -ēs, F. the wife of Minos king of Crete, the mother of the Minotaur (vi. 25).

passer, -eris, M. a sparrow.

passim [*pando*], *adv.* far and wide, everywhere, here and there, in all directions.

passus, -a, -um, *p.p.* of pandō.

passus, -a, -um, *p.p.* of patior.

passus, -ūs [*pando*], M. a step.

pāstor, -ōris [*cf. pasco*], M. a shepherd, a herdsman.

pāstōrālis, -e [*pastor*], *adj.* of shepherds.

pāstus, -a, -um, *p.p.* of pāscō *and* pāscor.

Patavium, -ī (-iī), N. a city near the Adriatic, founded by Antenor (Padua) (i. 247).

patefaciō, -ere, -fēcī, -factum [*pateo, facio*], *3. v. a.* lay open, open.

pateō, -ēre, patuī, *no sup.,* *2. v. n.* lie open, be open, extend, be exposed, gape, yawn; appear, be disclosed. — **patēns, -entis,** *p.* wide, open, free.

pater, -tris, M. a father, a sire, an ancestor, a forefather, a parent; *pl.* the nobles, chiefs, elders, senators.

patera, -ae [*akin to pateo*], F. a bowl (*flat like a saucer, for libations*); a cup.

paternus, -a, -um [*pater*], *adj.* of a father, paternal, hereditary, ancestral.

patēscō, -ere, -uī, *no sup.* [*pateo*], *3. v. n.* lie open ; be disclosed, become manifest, be revealed : **Danaum insidiae.**

patiēns, *p. of* patior.

patior, patī, passus, *3. v. dep.* suffer, endure, bear, undergo; tolerate, allow, permit, submit, deign; withstand. — **patiēns, -entis,** *p. as adj.* patient, submissive to : **Phoebi.**

patria, -ae [F. *of patrius, sc. terra*], F. one's country, a country (*of one's own*), home, native city, native land.

patrius, -a, -um [*pater*], *adj.* fatherly, of a father, a father's, of one's fathers *or* ancestors, ancestral, filial (*paid to a parent*): vis patria (like his father's). — *Also* (*as adj. of* patria), of one's country *or* native city, national, native : **palaestrae.**

Patrōn, -ōnis, M. an Arcadian in the company of Æneas (v. 298).

patrōnus, -ī [*pater*], a patron ; an advocate.

patruus, -ī [*pater*], M. an uncle (*on the father's side*).

patulus, -a, -um [*pateo*], *adj.* wide-spreading : **arbor.**

paucus, -a, -um, *adj.* (*mostly pl.*), a few (*only*), few. — M. *pl.* a few, few. — N. *pl.* **pauca,** a few things, a few words. — *Abl.* **paucīs,** in a few words, briefly.

paulātim [*paulus*], *adv.* little by little, gradually, slowly, by degrees.

paulisper [*paulus*], *adv.* a little while, for a while.

paulum, *see* paulus.

paulus, -a, -um [*akin to paucus*], *adj.* a little. — **paulum,** N. *acc. as adv.* a little, a while, a moment.

pauper, -eris, *adj.* poor, in poverty, lowly. — M. a poor man.

pauperiēs, -ēī [*pauper*], F. poverty, humble circumstances.

paveō, -ēre, pāvī, *no sup.*, *2. v. n.* fear, be terrified, tremble with fear, be in suspense.

pavidus, -a, -um [*paveo*], *adj.* trembling, frightened, in alarm, awe-struck.

pavitō, -āre, *no perf.*, *no sup.* [*paveo*], *1. v. n.* tremble (*with fear*).

pavor, -ōris [*paveo*], M. fear, terror, dread, anxiety : **pavor pulsans** (anxious throbbing).

pāx, pācis [√*pac* (*in paciscor*)], F. peace, pardon, favor.

peccō, -āre, -āvī, -ātum, *1. v. n.* err, sin.

pecten, -inis [*pecto*], M. a comb ; a quill *or* plectrum (with which the strings of the lyre were struck).

pectus, -oris, N. the breast, the chest ; the mind, wisdom ; the heart, the soul, courage.

pecus, -oris, N. cattle, a flock, a herd, a stud, sheep ; a swarm (*of bees*).

pecus, pecudis, F. a beast (*of any kind of cattle*), a sheep ; a victim (*for sacrifice*) ; *pl.* beasts, brutes, flocks, herds.

pedes, -itis [*pes*], M. *or adj.* on foot, a foot-soldier ; *collectively,* infantry, foot-soldiers.

pelagus, -ī, N. the sea, the deep.

Pelagus, -a, -um, *adj.* Grecian (from the supposed ancient inhabitants). — M. *pl.* the Greeks.

Peliās, -ae, M. a Trojan (ii. 435).

Pēlīdēs, -ae, M. son (descendant) of Peleus. — *Esp.* of Achilles his son, and Pyrrhus his grandson.

pellāx, -ācis [*pellicio*], *adj.* alluring, enticing, deceitful.

pellis, -is, F. a skin, a hide.

pellō, -ere, pepulī, pulsum, *3. v. a.* strike, thrust; drive away, drive out, expel, banish: **lacrimas** (dry).

Pelopēus, -a, -um, *adj.* of Pelops, the son of Tantalus and father of Atreus. He was served up as food for the gods by his father, restored to life by Jupiter, and furnished with an ivory shoulder in place of the one eaten. He gained control of the Peloponnesus, which was named for him. — **Pelopea moenia,** *i. e.* of Argos, the chief city of the Peloponnesus (ii. 193).

Pelōrus (-um), -ī, M. *and* N. a high promontory on the northeast coast of Sicily, now called Capo di Faro, one of the headlands of the Straits of Messina (iii. 411).

pelta, -ae, F. a shield (small, light, and curved, used by barbarians, *cf.* **clipeus,** the round shield of the Greeks, and **scutum,** the oblong shield of the Romans).

penātēs, -ium, M. *pl.* the penates, the household gods (gods of the household, or of the state considered as a household). — *Fig.* a home, a house, a habitation, an abode, a dwelling.

pendeō, -ēre, pependī, *no sup.,* *2. v. n.* hang, be suspended; overhang, lean forward; linger, be suspended (*of work*).

pendō, -ere, pependī, pēnsum, *3. v. a.* weigh; pay, suffer (*a penalty*).

Pēneleus, -eī (-eos), M. a leader of the Bœotians in the Trojan War (ii. 425).

Pēnelopē, -ēs, F. the faithful wife of Ulysses.

penetrālis, -e [*penetro*], *adj.* inner, interior, the inmost. — N. *pl. as subst.* penetrālia, -ium, the interior, the inmost apartments *or* recesses, the inner shrine, a sanctuary.

penetrō, -āre, -āvī, -ātum [*cf. penitus*], *1. v. a.* penetrate, enter, make one's way into.

penitus, *adv.* from within; within, far within, far down, deeply; far away, afar, far; utterly, wholly, entirely.

penna, -ae [*peto*], F. a feather, a wing.

Penthesilēa, -ae, F. queen of the Amazons (i. 491).

Pentheus, -eī (-eos), M. a king of Thebes who despised the rites of Bacchus, and was torn in pieces by his mother and sisters. He was driven mad by the Furies (iv. 469).

penus, -ūs (-ī), C. provisions, store.

peplum, -ī, N. a robe (for women, a large and splendid outer mantle). — *Esp.* the state robe carried in procession at Athens and offered to Pallas Athene every five years (i. 480).

per, *prep.* through, by, over, across, throughout, along; among; during: **per auris** (to); **per annos**

(for); **per augurium** (into). —
Fig. through, by means of, by,
on account of. — *In adjurations*,
by. — *As adv. in comp.* through,
thoroughly, over.

peragō, -ere, -ēgī, -āctum, *3. v. a.*
perform (*to the end*), finish, complete, accomplish; pass, spend
(*time*); continue; go over, consider.

peragrō, -āre, -āvī, -ātum [*per,
ager*], *1. v. a.* wander over, roam
over, traverse.

percellō, -ere, -culī, -culsum, *3.
v. a.* strike down, fell; move, affect, strike.— **perculsus, -a, -um,**
p.p. stricken, smitten; filled, inspired.

percipiō, -ere, -cēpī, -ceptum
[*per + capio*], *3. v. a.* take entirely. catch, receive, acquire:
rigorem.

**percurrō, -ere, -cucurrī (-currī),
-cursum,** *3. v. a.* run over *or*
through: **nomina.**

percutiō, -ere, -cussī, -cussum
[*per + quatio*], *3. v. a.* strike,
beat; move, affect.

perdō, -ere, -didī, -ditum, *3. v. a.*
destroy, ruin; lose. — **perditus,
-a, -um,** *p.p. as adj.* ruined, desperate, wretched.

perdūcō, -ere, -dūxī, -ductum,
3. v. a. lead, bring, force to come.

peredō, -ere, -ēdī, -ēsum, *3. v. a.*
devour, consume, waste away.

peregrīnus, -a, -um [*peregre*],
adj. foreign; in a foreign land:
labor.

perennis, -e [*per, annum*], *adj.*
everlasting, undying; unfailing,
never dry.

pereō, -īre, -īvī (-iī), -itum, *irr.
v. n.* go to ruin, perish, be ruined;
fall, die, be slain.

pererrō, -āre, -āvī, -ātum, *1. v. a.*
wander over, roam over; spread
through; scan, examine, search,
survey.

perferō, -ferre, -tulī, -lātum, *irr.
v. a.* carry through; bring, bring
news, bring word: **perfer te** (proceed, go on). — *Also,* bear (*to the
end*), endure, suffer, have to bear:
duros labores.

perficiō, -ere, -fēcī, -fectum [*per
+ facio*], *3. v. a.* perform, complete, finish, accomplish; make,
work, fashion.

perfidus, -a, -um, *adj.* false, per-
fidious, treacherous.

perflō, -āre, -āvī, -ātum, *1. v. a.*
blow over.

perfodiō, -ere, -fōdī, -fossum,
3. v. a. pierce.

perfringō, -ere, -frēgī, -frāctum
[*per + frango*], *3. v. a.* break
through, force through; accomplish (*by force*).

perfundō, -ere, -fūdī, -fūsum,
3. v. a. pour over; drench, wash;
anoint; dye.

Pergameus, -a, -um, *adj.* of
Pergamum, of Troy, Trojan. —
F. **Pergamea,** the name given by
Æneas to his city in Crete (iii.
133).

Pergamum, -ī (-a, -ōrum), N. the
citadel of Troy; Troy in general,
the whole city.

pergō, -ere, perrēxī, perrēctum
[*per + rego*], *3. v. n.* keep on, proceed, advance, go on, continue
(*in action or speech*).

perhibeō, -ēre, -hibuī, -hibitum [per + habeo], 2. v. a. hold out, bring forward; report, assert, declare, say, call.

perīculum (-clum), -ī [cf. experior], N. a trial; peril, hazard, risk, danger.

perimō, -ere, -ēmī, -ēmptum [per + emo], 3. v. a. destroy, kill, slay.

Periphās, -antis, M. a companion of Pyrrhus at the sack of Troy (ii. 476).

periūrium, -ī (-iī) [periurus], N. perjury.

periūrus, -a, -um [per, ius], adj. perjured.

perlābor, -lābī, -lāpsus, 3. v. dep. glide over, glide through.

perlegō, -ere, -lēgī, -lēctum, 3. v. a. survey, scan.

permātūrēscō, -ere, -mātūruī, no sup., 3. v. n. ripen thoroughly.

permētior, -īrī, -mēnsus, 4. v. dep. measure over; traverse.

permisceō, -ēre, -miscuī, -mixtum (-mistum), 2. v. a. mingle, mix (thoroughly). — permixtus, -a, -um, p.p. mingled; in the midst of.

permittō, -ere, -mīsī, -missum, 3. v. a. let go by or through; give up, give over; commit, consign; allow, permit, grant: permisso nomine (using the name by permission).

permulceō, -ēre, -mulsī, -mulsum (-ctum), 2. v. a. stroke; soothe; rub or bathe gently.

pernīx, -īcis, adj. active, agile, fleet, swift.

perōdī, -ōdisse, -ōsus, def. v. a. utterly hate, execrate, curse.

perpetuus, -a, -um [per, peto], adj. continuing, continuous, constant, perpetual, entire: perpetua iuventa (all your youth long); in perpetuum (forever).

perquīrō, -ere, -quīsīvī, -quīsītum [per + quaero], 3. v. a. seek diligently, search for thoroughly.

perrumpō, -ere, -rūpī, -ruptum, 3. v. a. break through.

Persae, -ārum, M. pl. the Persians; the Parthians.

persentiō, -īre, -sēnsī, -sēnsum, 4. v. a. feel (deeply), perceive.

Persephonē, -ēs, F. Proserpine, goddess of the Lower World.

persequor, -sequī, -secūtus, 3. v. dep. follow up, follow, pursue.

Perseus, -eī (-eos), M. Perseus, son of Jupiter and Danaë.

persolvō, -ere, -solvī, -solūtum, 3. v. a. pay in full, pay, render, give in payment.

personō, -āre, -uī, -itum, 1. v. n. and a. sound through or over, cause to resound, sound: citharā (play).

perstō, -stāre, -stitī, (-stātūrus), 1. v. n. stand firmly; persist, remain unmoved, remain fixed.

pertaedet, -ēre, -taesum est, 2. v. impers. it wearies thoroughly, one is thoroughly tired of (with obj. of feeling in the gen.).

pertaesum, see pertaedet.

pertemptō, -āre, -āvī, -ātum, 1. v. a. try (thoroughly); pervade, seize, fill, possess: gaudia pectus.

perveniō, -īre, -vēnī, -ventum, 4. v. n. come through, arrive, reach: perventum [est], impers. (I have reached).

pervertō, -ere, -vertī, -versum,
3. v. a. turn awry, pervert. —
perversus, -a, -um, *p.p. as adj.*
perverse, wrong-headed : **numine**
(fatal).

pervius, -a, -um [*per, via*], *adj.*
passable: **usus tectorum** (a much-
used passage, *etc.*).

pēs, pedis, M. the foot : **pedem tulisset,** turn the steps. — *Also,* the
rope at the lower corner of a sail,
the sheet : **facere pedem** (make
a tack).

pessimus, *see* **malus.**

pestifer, -era, -erum [*pestis,
fero*], *adj.* pestilential, venomous.

pestis, -is, F. a plague, a pest ; an
infection, a taint ; a calamity,
ruin, destruction, mischief.

Petēlia, -ae, F. a city on the Gulf
of Tarentum, founded by Idomeneus (iii. 402).

petō, -ere, petīvī (-iī), petītum,
3. v. a. go to ; assail, attack ;
make for, flee to ; aim at ; pursue : **peteretur Troia** (sail to
Troy) ; **terram** (fall to) ; **astra**
(mount to). — *From the idea of
aiming at,* seek, search for, look
for ; ask for, ask, beg, desire :
quidve petunt (what their purpose).

Phaeāces, -um, M. *pl.* the Phæacians, the mythic inhabitants of
Corcyra, famed for their luxury
(iii. 291).

Phaedimus, -ī, M. a son of Niobe.

Phaedra, -ae, F. the wife of Theseus and daughter of Minos. She
became enamored of her stepson
Hippolytus (vi. 445).

Phaëthōn, -ontis, M. (the bright
one), a name of the Sun (v. 105).

phalanx, -angis, F. a phalanx (a
body of Grecian troops) ; an
army, a force, a battalion.

phalerae, -ārum, F. *pl.* an ornament (of metal plates worn on
the breast), trappings (*of horses*) :
equus phaleris insignis.

pharetra, -ae, F. a quiver.

phaselus (-sellus), -ī, M. a ship,
a boat, a yacht.

Phēgeus, -eī (-eos), M. a slave of
Æneas (v. 263).

Philoctētēs, -ae, M. a celebrated
archer, son of Pæan, king of Melibœa. He received from Hercules the poisoned arrows on
which depended the destruction
of Troy. He came to Italy after
the Trojan War and founded
Petelia (iii. 402).

Philomēla, -ae, F. daughter of
Pandion, king of Athens. She
was changed into a nightingale.
— *Hence,* a nightingale.

Phīnēius, -a, -um, *adj.* of Phineus,
a king of Thrace, who was struck
blind, and was afterwards tormented by the Harpies (iii. 212).

Phlegethōn, -ontis, M. a river of
fire in Hades (vi. 265).

Phlegyās, -ae, M. a king of Orcho-
menus in Bœotia, father of Ixion. He burned the temple of
Apollo (vi. 618).

Phoebē, -ēs, F. Phœbe, Diana.

Phoebēus, -a, -um, *adj.* of
Phœbus.

Phoebus, -ī, M. a name of Apollo
as god of the sun (the Bright) ;
the Sun.

Phoenīces, -um, M. *pl.* the Phœnicians (the inhabitants of Phœnicia, the coast-land east of the Mediterranean).

Phoenïssa, -ae, F. *adj.* Phœnician. — *Subst.* a Phœnician woman.

Phoenīx, -īcis, M. the instructor of Achilles (ii. 762).

Pholoē, -ēs, F. a female slave (v. 285).

Phorbās, -antis, M. a sailor of Æneas' fleet (v. 842).

Phorcus, -ī, M. a sea-divinity, also called Phorcys (v. 240).

Phorcȳnis, -idis (-idos), F. the daughter of Phorcus (the seagod), Medusa.

Phrygius, -a, -um, *adj.* Phrygian, of Phrygia, the country of Asia Minor of which Troy was a district. — F. *pl. as subst.* **Phrygiae, -ārum**, the Phrygian (i.e. Trojan) women.

Phryx, Phrygis, M. a Phrygian; a Trojan.

Phthïa, -ae, F. a district of Thessaly, the home of Achilles (i. 284).

piābilis, -e [*pio*], *adj.* expiable.

piāculum, -ī [*pio*], N. an expiatory rite *or* offering, a purification: **commissa piacula** (atonement for guilt incurred).

piāmen, -inis [*pio*], N. means *or* rites of expiation.

picea, -ae [F. *of piceus*], F. a pitch pine, a pine tree.

piceus, -a, -um [*pix*], *adj.* of pitch, pitchy; dark (*like the smoke of pitch*), thick, lurid, smoky: **turbo** (pitch-black wreaths).

pictūra, -ae [*pictus, pingo*], F. a painting, a picture.

pictūrātus, -a, -um [*pictura*], *adj.* embroidered, wrought with designs: **vestes**.

Pīcus, -ī, M. a son of Saturn and grandfather of Latinus.

pietās, -tātis [*pius*], F. filial affection, dutiful love, filial piety; love (*for a kinsman*); reverence (*for the gods*); piety, devotion; justice (*recognition of piety*), regard.

piger, pigra, pigrum [*piget*], *adj.* sluggish, lifeless.

piget, -ēre, -uit (-itum est), 2. *v. impers.* it irks, one regrets, one is loth, one loathes, it is irksome: **piget [eas] incepti**.

pignus, -oris, N. a pledge; a security; a sign (*as by giving the hand*), a token (*as a gift*); *pl., of children*, pledges.

Pīlumnus, -ī, M. an Apulian deity or deified king, ancestor of Turnus (ix. 4).

pīneus, -a, -um [*pinus*], *adj.* of pine, of pines.

pingō, -ere, pīnxī, pictum [√*pig*], 3. *v. a.* paint, dye, color; embroider, ornament. — **pictus, -a, -um**, *p.p. as adj.* embroidered, painted, bright-colored, variegated, ornamented with varied plumage: **volucres**.

pinguis, -e, *adj.* fat, rich; resinous, pitchy, unctuous; fertile, rich: **ara** (rich in victims).

pīnifer, -era, -erum [*pinus, fero*], *adj.* pine-bearing, pine-clad.

pinna, -ae, F. a feather, a wing; an arrow.

pīnus, -ī (-ūs) [*akin to pix*], F. a pine tree, a pine; a ship.

piō, -āre, -āvī, -ātum [*pius*], *1. v. a.* purify; appease, propitiate; expiate, atone for.

pīpiō, -īre, *no perf. or sup.*, *4. v. n.* chirp.

Pīrithous, -ī, M. a son of Ixion who attempted to carry off Proserpine from the World Below (vi. 393, 601).

piscis, -is, M. a fish.

piscōsus, -a, -um [*piscis*], *adj.* full of fish, fish-haunted.

pistrix, -icis, F. a sea-monster.

pius, -a, -um, *adj.* filial, devoted (*to parents*), fond; pious, virtuous, just; pure, holy, sacred: amor (devoted); far (consecrated); piorum concilia (of the blest); numina (righteous); manus (pure).

placeō, -ēre, placuī, placitum, *2. v. n.* please, delight, give pleasure. — *Often to be translated by a change of construction*, approve, delight in. — *Also impersonally*, it is one's will, one determines, it is determined, it is thought best. — placitus, -a, -um, *p.p. in act. sense*, pleasing, agreeable, determined on, decided: sic placitum (so it is fated).

placidē [*placidus*], *adv.* gently, quietly, peacefully.

placidus, -a, -um [*placeo*], *adj.* calm, still, quiet, peaceful, gentle; steady; kindly, propitious: pax; aures; pectus; caput.

plācō, -āre, -āvī, -ātum, *1. v. a.* appease, pacify, soothe, calm, quiet: ventos.

plaga, -ae, F. a region.

plaga, -ae, F. a hunting net, a snare, a toil.

plāga, -ae, F. a blow, stroke, wound.

plangō, -ere, plānxī, plānctum, *3. v. a.* strike, beat.

plangor, -ōris [*plango*], M. an outcry, a shriek.

planta, -ae, F. the sole, the foot.

plānus, -a, -um, *adj.* level.

plaudō, -ere, plausī, plausum, *3. v. a. and n.* beat (*with the feet or the hands*), flap (*wings*): choreas (dance a measure).

plaustrum, -ī, N. a wagon.

plausus, -ūs [*plaudo*], M. clapping, flapping, fluttering; applause.

Plēïades, -dum, F. *pl.* the seven daughters of Atlas, changed into stars.

Plēmyrium, -ī (-iī), N. a promontory of Sicily, near Syracuse (iii. 693).

plēnus, -a, -um [*pleo*], *adj.* full, filled, well-filled.

plerumque [*plerus*], *adv.* for the most part, usually.

plicō, -āre, -āvī (-uī), -ātum (-itum), *1. v. a.* fold, roll up.

plūma, -ae, F. feathers.

plumbum, -ī, N. lead.

plūrimus, -a, -um, *see* multus.

plūs, plūris, *see* multus.

pluvia, -ae, F. rain.

pluviālis, -e [*pluvia*], *adj.* of rain, rainy.

pluvius, -a, -um [*pluo*], *adj.* rainy, showery, rain-bringing: Hyades.

pōculum, -ī [*cf. poto*], N. a drinking cup, a goblet, a bowl.

poena, -ae, F. a penalty, punishment; revenge, vengeance.

Poenus, -a, -um, *adj.* Carthaginian (*properly* Phœnician). — M. *pl.* the Carthaginians.

poēta, -ae, M. a poet.

Polītēs, -ae, M. a Trojan, son of Priam (ii. 526).

pollex, -icis [*polleo*], M. thumb.

polliceor, -ērī, pollicitus [*por-* (*akin to pro*) + *liceor*, bid], 2. *v. dep.* offer, promise.

polluō, -ere, -luī, -lūtum, 3. *v. a.* pollute, infect, defile; violate: pollutus amor (blighted).

Pollūx, -ūcis, M. son of Jupiter and Leda, brother of Castor, famed as a pugilist. On the death of Castor, Pollux obtained permission to relieve his brother in the World Below by alternately taking his place (vi. 121).

polus, -ī, M. the pole, the North Pole; the heavens.

Polyboetēs, -ae, M. a Trojan, a priest of Ceres (vi. 484).

Polydōrus, -ī, M. a son of Priam, sent to Thrace, and slain there by Polymestor (iii. 45 ff.).

Polyphēmus, -ī, M. the Cyclops whose one eye was put out by Ulysses (iii. 641).

Pōmetiī, -ōrum, M. *pl.* Suessa Pometia, an ancient Volscian city (vi. 775).

pompa, -ae, F. a religious procession, a sacred rite.

pōmum, -ī, N. a fruit, an apple.

pondus, -eris [*cf. pendo*], N. a weight, a burden, a load.

pōne, *adv.* behind.

pōnō, -ere, posuī, positum, 3. *v. a.* lay down, put down; lay aside, lose, abandon, drop, shed; yield (*of fruits*); place, set, pitch (*a camp*), found, lay; offer; set up, appoint (*a contest*); serve up, fix

(*a limit*), determine; lay to rest (*bury*), lay out (*a body*); fix: voltum.

pōns, pontis, M. a bridge, a gangway.

Ponticus, -a, -um, *adj.* 1. Pontic, of the Pontus Euxinus (Black Sea).— 2. Pontic, of Pontus, a country in Asia Minor.

Ponticus, -ī, M. a Latin poet.

pontus, -ī, M. the sea; a wave.— Pontus, -ī, M. the Pontus Euxinus, the Euxine Sea (Black Sea).

poples, -itis, M. the knee.

populāris, -e [*populus*], *adj.* popular, of the people.

pōpuleus, -a, -um [*populus*], *adj.* of the poplar, of poplar, poplar.

populō, -āre, -āvī, -ātum, 1. *v. a.* ravage, lay waste, devastate, pillage, plunder; despoil: auribus.

populus, -ī, M. a people, a state, a nation, a tribe; the common people, the populace, the crowd.

por-, *prep.* (*only in compos.*), to, toward.

porriciō, -ere, *no perf.*, -rectum [*prob. por-* + *iacio*], 3. *v. a.* cast forth (as an offering), scatter.

porrigō (porgō), -ere, -rēxī, -rēctum [*por-* + *rego*], 3. *v. a.* stretch out, extend.

porrō, *adv.* forward, afar off, beyond; hereafter, in later times, later.

porta, -ae, F. a gate, a passage, an outlet, a way (*in or out*).

portendō, -ere, -tendī, -tentum [*por-* + *tendo*], 3. *v. a.* portend, forebode, foretell, threaten.

portentum, -ī [*portendo*], N. a prodigy, a monster.

porticus, -ūs [*porta*], F. a colonnade, a gallery, an arcade.

portitor, -ōris [*portus*], M. a boatman, a ferryman ; *esp.* of Charon, ferryman of the Styx (vi. 298).

portō, -āre, -āvī, -ātum, *1. v. a.* convey, carry, bear, bring ; carry off, bear away : **bellum** (make *or* declare).

Portūnus, -ī [*portus*], M. the Italian god of harbors, the Greek Palæmon (v. 241).

portus, -ūs, M. a harbor, a haven, a port.

poscō, -ere, poposcī, *no sup., 3. v. a.* ask, beg, demand, claim, require, pray for : **numina** (supplicate).

possideō, -ēre, -sēdī, -sessum [*por-* + *sedeo*], *2.v.a.* possess, occupy ; cover.

possum, posse, potuī [*potis* + *sum*], *irr. v. n.* can, be able, have power ; *with acc. of pron. or adj.* have power, can do : **omnia ; si quid numina possunt.** — **potēns, -entis,** *p. as adj.* strong, powerful, mighty, ruling over, master of : **potentes terrae** (rulers of).

post, *adv.* behind, after ; later, afterwards, next, hereafter, in after times. — *Prep.* behind, after.

posteritās, -tātis [†*posterus*], F. posterity.

†posterus, -a, -um [*post*], *adj.* coming after, following, next. — *Comp.* **posterior, -ius,** later. — *Superl.* **postrēmus, -a, -um,** latest, last ; lowest. — **postumus,** late-born, youngest.

posthabeō, -ēre, -uī, -itum, *2. v. a.* hold in less esteem.

postis, -is [*post*], M. a doorpost, a door, an entrance.

postpōnō, -ere, -posuī, -positum, *3. v. a.* place behind, hold in less honor.

postquam, *adv.* (later than), after, when, as soon as, since, now that.

postrēmus, *see* posterus.

postulō, -āre, -āvī, -ātum, *1. v. a.* ask, demand.

postumus, *see* posterus.

potēns, -entis, *p. of* possum.

potentia, -ae [*potens*], F. power, might, sway, rule.

potestās, -tātis [*potis*], F. power, might, rule, sway ; opportunity, chance.

potior, -īrī, -ītus (potĭtur, *in* 3) [*potis*], *4. v. dep.* become master of, gain, gain possession of, seize : **auso** (succeed in) ; **tellure** (gain, arrive at).

potior, -ius, *see* potis.

potis, -e, *adj.* powerful, able. — *Comp.* **potior, -ius,** *adj.* preferable, better. — **potius,** N. *as adv.* rather, more.

pōtō, -āre, -āvī, -ātum, *1. v. a.* drink.

prae, *prep. with abl.* before, in front of.

praebeō, -ēre, -uī, -itum [*prae* + *habeo*], *2. v. a.* hold forth, show ; furnish, afford, provide.

praecelsus, -a, -um, *adj.* very high, lofty.

praeceps, -cipitis [*prae, caput*], *adj.* head foremost, headlong ; with headlong speed, in (one's) haste, flying, swift, driven headlong ; steep down, precipitous : **in praeceps** (straight downward).

praeceptum, -ī [*p.p. of praecipio*], N. an instruction, an injunction, an order, a command, a precept, a warning.

praecīdō, -ere, -cīdī, -cīsum [*prae + caedo*], *3. v. a.* cut off. — **praecīsus, -a, -um,** *p.p. as adj.* steep.

praecipiō, -ere, -cēpī, -ceptum [*prae + capio*], *3. v. a.* take beforehand; learn beforehand, anticipate; prescribe, enjoin, give instructions.

praecipitō,-āre,-āvī,-ātum [*praeceps*], *1. v. a. and n.* drive headlong, hurry on, hurl headlong; fall headlong, hasten : **flumina mento** (pour). — *P.p.* hurrying on : **nox.**

praecipuē [*praecipuus*], *adv.* especially, particularly.

praecipuus, -a, -um [*prae, capio*], *adj.* (taken before), especial : **honores.**

praeclārus, -a, -um, *adj.* very bright; famous, glorious, splendid, magnificent.

praecō, -ōnis, M. a herald.

praecordia, -ōrum [*prae, cor*], N. *pl.* the breast, the heart.

praecutiō, -ere, -cussī, -cussum [*prae + quatio*], *3. v. a.* shake, wave, *or* brandish before.

praeda, -ae, F. booty, a prize, plunder, spoil, prey; game.

praedīcō, -ere, -dīxī, -dictum, *3. v. a.* foretell, prophesy, give warning; warn, inform.

praedictum, -ī [N. *p.p. of praedico*], N. a prediction, a prophecy.

praeeō, -īre, -īvī (-iī), -itum, *irr. v. n.* go before, be in advance.

praeferō, -ferre, -tulī, -lātum, *irr. v. a.* carry in front (*before one*), offer : **frons hominem** (represent). — *Also,* prefer, choose rather, choose in preference.

praeficiō, -ere, -fēcī, -fectum [*prae + facio*], *3. v. a.* set over, put in charge.

praefīgō, -ere, -fīxī, -fīxum, *3. v. a.* fix in front. — **praefīxus, -a, -um,** *p.p.* pointed, headed.

praegestiō, -īre, *no perf. or sup.,* *4. v. a.* desire eagerly.

praelūstris, -tre [*cf. lux*], *adj.* very brilliant, magnificent. — N. *pl. as subst.* worldly grandeur.

praemetuō, -ere, *no perf., no sup.,* *3. v. n.* fear beforehand, be anxious.

praemittō, -ere, -mīsī, -missum, *3. v. a.* send before, send in advance, send forward.

praemium, -ī (-iī) [*prae, emo*], N. a prize, a reward, a recompense (*good or bad*).

praenatō, -āre, -āvī, -ātum, *1. v. a.* swim by, float by; flow by (*of a river*).

praeparō, -āre, -āvī, -ātum, *1. v. a.* prepare. — *P.p.* trained.

praepes, -etis [*prae + √pet, cf. peto*], *adj.* swiftly-flying, swift. — M. *as subst.* a bird.

praepinguis, -e, *adj.* very fat, very rich, fertile, teeming.

praepōnō, -ere, -posuī, -positum, *3. v. a.* prefer, honor more (*than*).

praeportō, -āre, -āvī, -ātum, *1. v. a.* bear before, show, portend.

praeripiō, -ere, -ripuī, -reptum [*prae + rapio*], *3. v. a.* snatch away from (*in advance*).

praeruptus, -a, -um [*p.p. of prae-rumpo*], *as adj.* (broken off in front), precipitous, steep, broken: **aquae mons.**

praesaepe, -saepis [*prae + saepe* (*akin to saepio*)], N. a stall, a stable; a hive.

praesāgium, -ī (-iī) [*prae-sagio*, feel beforehand], N. a presage *or* a presentiment, a prophetic instinct.

praescius, -a, -um [*prae + scius*, *cf. scio*], *adj.* foreknowing, divining, prescient, presaging.

praesēns, -entis [*prae + †sens*, *p. of sum*], *adj.* present, before one; immediate, imminent, instant; powerful: **animus** (stout heart).

praesentiō, -īre, -sēnsī, -sēnsum, *4. v. a.* feel beforehand, foresee, divine.

praesideō, -ēre, -sēdī, *no sup.* [*prae + sedeo*], *2. v. n.* preside over.

praesignis, -e [*prae, signum*], *adj.* conspicuous, brilliant.

praestō, -stāre, -stitī, -stitum, *1. v. n. and a.* stand before, excel, surpass. — *Impers.* **praestat,** it is better.— **praestāns, -antis,** *p.* surpassing, splendid, magnificent.

praestō, *adv.* present, at hand: **clementia** (in your heart).

praestruō, -ere, -strūxī, -strūctum, *3. v. a.* build in front of, block up.

praesum, -esse, -fuī, *no sup.*, *irr. v. n.* be in charge of.

praesūmō, -ere, -sūmpsī, -sūmptum, *3. v. a.* take before, anticipate.

praetendō, -ere, -tendī, -tentum, *3. v. a.* stretch before, hold out; pretend, make a pretence of. — **praetentus, -a, -um,** *p.p. as adj.* stretched before, lying along, opposite.

praeter, *prep.* beyond; except.

praettereā, *adv.* further, moreover, besides; afterwards, again, hereafter, henceforth.

praetereō, -īre, -īvī (-iī), -itum, *irr. v. a. and n.* pass beyond, pass by; omit, pass over; go by, pass.

praeterlābor, -lābī, -lāpsus, *3. v. dep.* glide by, flow by, sail by.

praetervehor, -vehī, -vectus, *3. v. dep.* ride by, sail by.

praetexō, -ere, -texuī, -textum, *3. v. a.* (weave in front of); cover (*with something*), fringe, line; conceal, disguise.

praetrepidāns, -antis, *p. as adj.* throbbing, eager.

praevertō, -ere, -vertī, -versum, *3. v. a.* turn aside.— *Pass.* (*as dep.*) outstrip.

praevideō, -ēre, -vīdī, -vīsum, *2. v. a.* foresee, see (*in advance*).

prātum, -ī, N. a meadow.

prāvus, -a, -um, *adj.* crooked; false. — N. *as subst.* falsehood.

precor, -ārī, -ātus [*prex*], *1. v. dep.* pray, supplicate, pray for, beg: **precando** (by prayers).

prehendō, -ere, prehendī, prehēnsum (prēndō, -ere, prēndī, prēnsum), *3. v. a.* seize, grasp, grasp at.

premō, -ere, pressī, pressum, *3. v. a.* press, rest heavily upon, load, press down: **oculos** (close); **fronde crinem** (confine, adorn):

vestigia (plant, set); **partem rostro** (overlap); **litus** (hug); **humum** (lie prostrate upon); **solo presso** (on the ground which one presses). — *Also*, repress, confine, hold in check, control, rule, overwhelm: **vestigia** (check, stay); **placida aequora pontus** (calm); **animae premuntur nocte** (are plunged, hidden); **quies iacentem** (overcome); **corde dolorem** (suppress, conceal); **luna lumen** (hide); **presso ore** (closed lips); **habenas** (hold in, tighten); **mentem pressus formidine** (overwhelmed, weighed down). — *Also*, press hard, pursue, attack, assail, chase.

prēndō, *see* **prehendō.**

prēnsō (prehēnsō), -āre, -āvī, -ātum [*prendo*], *1. v. a.* grasp, catch at, catch, seize.

pressō, -āre, -āvī, -ātum [*pressus, premo*], *1. v. a.* press.

pretium, -ī (-iī), N. a price, a reward, a bribe, a prize.

†**prex,** †**-cis,** F. a prayer.

Priamēius, -a, -um, *adj.* of Priam, son (daughter) of Priam.

Priamidēs, -ae, M. son of Priam.

Priamus, -ī, M. 1. The aged king of Troy (ii. 506). — 2. The son of Polites (v. 564).

prīdem [*prae* + *-dem*], *adv.* some time ago, for some time.

prīmitiae, -ārum [*primus*], F. *pl.* the first fruits.

prīmō, *see* **prior.**

prīmum, *see* **prior.**

prīmus, *see* **prior.**

prīnceps, -ipis [*primus, capio*], *adj.* first, foremost, at the head.

— M. *as subst.* a chief, a leader; a founder (*of a family*).

prīncipium, -ī (-iī) [*princeps*], N. the beginning. — *Abl.* **prīncipiō,** *as adv.* in the beginning, in the first place, first, first of all.

prior, -ōris, *adj.* former, first, ancient, ahead. — *Of degree*, superior. — M. *pl. as subst.* **priōrēs, -um,** the ancients, men of former times, ancestors. — N. **prius** *as adv.* before, earlier, first, sooner, rather, long ago. — **prīmus, -a, -um,** *superl.* first, foremost, earliest; the outer, the edge, the front, in front; fore (**pes**); rising (*of the sun, etc.*); most ancient. — *Of degree*, first, highest, chief, best, noblest. — *As subst. in pl.* the first, the best, the chief, the noblest. — N. *pl.* the first place, the van. — **prīmō,** N. *abl. as adv.* first, at first. — **prīmum,** N. *acc. as adv.* first, in the first place, for the first time, immediately. — **ut (cum) primum,** when first, as soon as; **quam primum,** as soon as possible; **in primis,** especially.

prīscus, -a, -um [*prius*], *adj.* ancient, early, venerable; stern: **parens.**

prīstinus, -a, -um [*prius*], *adj.* former, old, original.

Pristis, -is, F. a sea-monster; the name of a ship (v. 116).

prius, *see* **prior.**

priusquam (*often separated*), *adv.* sooner than, rather than, before.

prō (prōd-), *prep.* before, in front of; in defence of, on behalf of, for, for the sake of; in return for, instead of, in proportion to: **pro re**

(under the circumstances, for the occasion, as the case demands); **pro se** (according to one's ability). —*In compos.* **prō-, prōd-**, before, in front, forward, down, forth, for, in favor of.

prō, *interj.* oh! (*of surprise, grief, or indignation*).

proavus, -ī, M. a great-grandfather; an ancestor.

probitās, -tātis [*probus*], F. goodness.

probō, -āre, -āvī, -ātum [*probus*], *1. v. a.* test, approve, permit.

Procās, -ae, M. a king of Alba (vi. 767).

procāx, -ācis, *adj.* insolent (*in demand*); boisterous.

prōcēdō, -ere, -cessī, -cessum, *3. v. n.* go *or* come forward, advance, go on, go, come forth, proceed; glide on, pass: **dies**; **irae**.

procella, -ae, F. a storm, a blast, a squall, a tempest.

procerēs, -um, M. *pl.* the chiefs, the leaders, the nobles.

prōclāmō, -āre, -āvī, -ātum, *1. v. a.* cry aloud, cry out.

Procris, -is (-idis), F. the wife of Cephalus, who was accidentally shot by her husband (vi. 445).

procul, *adv.* at a distance, afar, far, far away, apart: **procul este** (withdraw, come not near).

Proculus, -ī, M. Julius Proculus, a Roman senator.

prōcumbō, -ere, -cubuī, -cubitum, *3. v. n.* lie prostrate, sink down; fall, be slain; be overthrown, fall in ruins.

prōcūrō, -āre, -āvī, -ātum, *1. v. a.* take care of, attend to.

prōcurrō, -ere, -currī (-cucurrī), -cursum, *3. v. n.* run forward; *of a reef*, run out, project.

prōcurvus, -a, -um, *adj.* curved, bent, winding.

procus, -ī, M. a suitor.

prōdeō, -īre, -īvī (-iī), -itum [*prod- + eo*], *irr. v. n.* go forward, go *or* come forth, advance; run out: **rupes**.

prōdigium, -ī (-iī), N. a portent, a sign, a prodigy, an omen, an evil prophecy.

prōditiō, -ōnis [*prodo*], F. treachery.

prōdō, -ere, -didī, -ditum, *3. v. a.* give forth; propagate, found (*a race*); betray, treacherously destroy.

prōdūcō, -ere, -dūxī, -ductum, *3. v. a.* lead forth, prolong.

proelium, -ī (-iī), N. a battle, a fight, a combat, fighting.

profānus, -a, -um [*pro, fanum*], *adj.* unholy, profane. — *Esp.* uninitiated.

prōferō, -ferre, -tulī, -lātum, *irr. v. a.* carry forward, bring forward; display, reveal; extend; utter.

prōficiō, -ere, -fēcī, -fectum [*pro + facio*], *3. v. n.* profit, avail.

proficīscor, -ficīscī, -fectus, *3. v. dep.* set out, proceed, come from; *of descent*, proceed from, originate with.

profiteor, -ērī, -fessus [*pro + fateor*], *2. v. dep.* promise, offer.

proflō, -āre, -āvī, -ātum, *1. v. a.* breathe out, belch forth.

profor (*not found*), **-fārī, -fātus**, *1. v. dep.* speak out, speak.

profugus, -a, -um [*pro, fugio*], *adj.* fugitive, exiled. — M. *as subst.* a fugitive, an exile.

profundus, -a, -um, *adj.* deep, profound, the depths of (**caelum**); *of darkness,* deepest.

prōgeniēs, -ēī [*pro,* √*gen* (*of gigno*)], F. offspring, progeny, a line, a race; a son.

prōgignō, -ere, -genuī, -genitum, *3. v. a.* beget, bring forth.

prōgredior, -gredī, -gressus [*pro* + *gradior*], *3. v. dep.* proceed, go forth, advance, come forth.

prohibeō, -ēre, -hibuī, -hibitum [*pro* + *habeo*], *2. v. a.* hold off, drive off, ward off, avert; forbid, prevent, restrain, keep from.

prōiciō, -ere, -iēcī, -iectum [*pro* + *iacio*], *3. v. a.* throw forth *or* out, throw away, cast away, expose; offer (**corpus**); throw forward, cast, throw down, throw, put forward, let drop. — prōiectus, -a, -um, *p.p. as adj.* projecting: **saxa.**

prōlābor, -lābī, -lāpsus, *3. v. dep.* slide forward *or* down; fall in ruins, fall.

prōlēs, -is, F. progeny, offspring, a line, a family, a race; a son, a descendant.

prōluō, -ere, -luī, -lūtum, *3. v. a.* wash: **proluit se** (drains a mighty draught).

prōluviēs, -ēī [*proluo*], F. excrement.

prōmereor, -ērī, -meritus, *2. v. dep.* deserve (*well or ill of one*), serve one: **plurima te promeritam** (the very many favors I owe you).

Promētheūs, -eī (-eos), M. son of Iapetus. He moulded clay images of men and gave them life by means of fire stolen from heaven.

prōmissum, -ī [*p.p. of promitto*], N. a promise, what one has promised.

prōmittō, -ere, -mīsī, -missum, *3. v. a.* let go forth; give out, promise: **me ultorem.**

prōmō, -ere, prōmpsī, prōmptum [*pro* + *emo*], *3. v. a.* take out; put forth, employ; raise to notice, exalt: **obscura.** — *With reflexive,* come forth. — prōmptus, -a, -um, *p.p. as adj.* at hand, ready; manifest.

prōnuba, -ae [*pro, nubo*], F. the matron attending the bride at a marriage; *as an epithet of Juno,* Pronuba, the goddess of marriage (iv. 166).

prōnus, -a, -um [*pro*], *adj.* bending forward; headlong, rapid, swift-flowing: **prona maria** (unobstructed).

prŏpāgō, -inis, F. offspring, progeny, descendants, line.

prope, *adv. and prep.* near.

properē [*properus*], *adv.* quickly.

properō, -āre, -āvī, -ātum [*properus*], *1. v. a. and n.* haste, hasten, make haste, hasten forth: **properata fata** (untimely).

Propertius, -ī (-iī), M. Sextus Propertius, the Latin poet.

propinquō, -āre, -āvī, -ātum [*propinquus*], *1. v. n.* approach, come near, draw near.

propinquus, -a, -um [*prope*], *adj.* near, neighboring, near by; akin, kindred. — M. *as subst.* a kinsman.

propior, -ius [*prope*], *compar. adj.* nearer. — N. *pl.* propiōra, the nearer space. — N. *sing.* propius, *as adv.* nearer, more closely. — proximus, -a, -um, *superl.* next, nearest, close by.

propius, *see* propior.

prōpōnō, -ere, -posuī, -positum, 3. *v. a.* set forth, propose, offer. — N. *p.p. as subst.* prōpositum, -ī, plan *or* course of life.

Propontis, -idis, F. the Propontis (Sea of Marmora).

proprius, -a, -um, *adj.* one's own, appropriate; lasting, permanent, perpetual, one's own forever.

propter, *prep.* on account of, for the sake of.

prōpugnāculum, -ī [*propugno*], N. a bulwark, a rampart.

prōra, -ae, F. the prow.

prōripiō, -ere, -ripuī, -reptum [*pro + rapio*], 3. *v. a. and n.* drag forth; hasten, hurry away.

prōrumpō, -ere, -rūpī, -ruptum, 3. *v. a.* belch forth.— *Pass.* break forth: proruptum mare (a raging sea).

prōsequor, -sequī, -secūtus, 3. *v. dep.* follow after, attend, speed on one's way, follow, escort; proceed, go on; dismiss, take leave of.

Prōserpina, -ae, F. the wife of Pluto and the daughter of Ceres. She was stolen by Pluto (iv. 698).

prōsiliō, -īre, -siluī (-īvī, -iī), *no sup.* [*pro + salio*], 4. *v. n.* leap forth, dart forth.

prōspectō, -āre, -āvī, -ātum, 1. *v. a.* look out upon, gaze at *or* upon.

prōspectus, -ūs [*prospicio*], M. an outlook, a prospect, a view.

prōsper, -era, -erum [*pro, spero*], *adj.* according to one's hopes, favorable, propitious.

prōspiciō, -ere, -spexī, -spectum [*pro + specio*], 3. *v. a. and n.* look out upon, behold, gaze at, see; look out, look forth, gaze.

prōsum, prōdesse, prōfuī, *irr. v. n.* profit, be of advantage, avail.

prōtegō, -ere, -tēxī, -tēctum, 3. *v. a.* cover, protect, defend.

prōtendō, -ere, -tendī, -tentum (-tēnsum), 3. *v. a.* stretch out.

Prōteūs, -eī (-eos), M. a sea-god who could take many shapes.

prōtinus [*pro + tenus*], *adv.* forward; next, then, afterwards; immediately, forthwith.

prōtrahō, -ere, -trāxī, -tractum, 3. *v. a.* drag forth.

prōturbō, -āre, -āvī, -ātum, 1. *v. a.* overthrow.

prōvehō, -ere, -vexī, -vectum, 3. *v. a.* carry forward, bear on. — *Pass.* sail, proceed, go on.

proximus, *see* propior.

prūdentia, -ae [*prudens*], F. foresight, wisdom, skill.

pruīna, -ae, F. frost.

pruīnōsus, -a, -um [*pruina*], *adj.* frosty, rimy, white with frost.

prūna, -ae, F. a live coal.

pūbēns, -entis [*pubes*], *adj.* full-grown, juicy (*of herbs at maturity*).

pūbēs, -is, F. the groin; youth, young men; a band; offspring: Titania.

pūbēscō, -ere, pūbuī, *no sup.* [*cf. pubes*], 3. *v. n.* grow up, come to manhood; ripen.

pudeō, -ēre, -uī (puditum est), -itum, 2. v. a. and n. shame, be ashamed; as impers. with acc. it shames one, one is ashamed, one disdains.

pudicus, -a, -um [pudeo], adj. modest, chaste.

pudor, -ōris [pudeo], M. shame, modesty, chastity, honor, decency.

puella, -ae [puer], F. a girl; sweetheart.

puer, -erī, M. a boy, a lad, a youth, a child.

puerīlis, -e [puer], adj. of a boy or boys; childish.

pugna, -ae [√pug (of pugno)], F. a fight, a combat, a battle, a contest.

pugnō, -āre, -āvī, -ātum [pugna], 1. v. n. fight, wage war, contend; resist, fight against; struggle.

pugnus, -ī [√pug (of pugno)], M. the fist.

pulcher, -chra, -chrum, adj. beautiful, fair, comely; glorious, noble, excellent, famous.

pullus, -a, -um, adj. dark-colored.

pulmō, -ōnis, M. lung.

pulsō, -āre, -āvī, -ātum [pulsus, pello], 1. v. a. and n. beat, batter, strike, strike on or against; throb; sound (on the lyre): pulsans pavor (anxious throbbing). — pulsātus, -a, -um, p.p. as adj. wave-beaten, reëchoing: saxa.

pulsus, -ūs [pello], M. a beating, a trampling.

pulverulentus, -a, -um [pulvis], adj. dusty, in a cloud of dust.

pulvis, -eris, C. dust.

pūmex, -icis, M. pumice stone, porous rock.

pūniceus, -a, -um [Punicus], adj. red (made from Tyrian dye), crimson, purple.

Pūnicus, -a, -um [Poenus], adj. Punic, Carthaginian, of Carthage.

puppis, -is, F. the stern; a ship. — a puppi, astern.

pūrgō, -āre, -āvī, -ātum [purus, ago], 1. v. a. clean, clear, purge away: se nubes (clears away).

purpura, -ae, F. purple, crimson, red; a purple robe.

purpureus, -a, -um [purpura], adj. purple, red, crimson; rosy, ruddy; bright, brilliant.

pūrus, -a, -um, adj. clean, pure, clear, bright, limpid; unstained, innocent: hasta (headless). — N. as subst. pūrum, -ī, a clear or cloudless sky.

putō, -āre, -āvī, -ātum [putus, clean], 1. v. a. clean; clear up; reckon, account, consider; think, suppose, revolve, ponder.

Pygmaliōn, -ōnis, M. Dido's brother (i. 347).

Pyladēs, -is, M. the friend and companion of Orestes.

Pylos (-us), -ī, F. a city in Elis; it was the home of Nestor.

pyra, -ae, F. a funeral pile, a pyre.

Pȳramus, -ī, M. the youthful lover of Thisbe.

Pyrgō, -ūs, F. the nurse of Priam's children (v. 645).

Pyrrha, -ae, F. the wife of Deucalion.

Pyrrhus, -ī, M. the son of Achilles (called also Neoptolemus). After the Trojan War, he founded a kingdom in Epirus. He was slain by Orestes (ii. 469; iii. 296).

quā [*abl. of qui, quis*], *rel. adv.* by which way, whereby; where, wherever; by which, as. — *Interr. adv.* how ? in what way ?

quadrīgae, -ārum, F. *pl.* a four-horse team; a four-horse chariot.

quadrupēs, -pedis [*quattuor, pes*], *adj.* going on four feet.—*As subst.* a quadruped, a horse.

quaerō, -ere, quaesīvī, quaesītum [*originally quaeso*], *3. v. a.* seek, search for, look for, seek out; desire; acquire (**munus**) ; ask for, ask, enquire, miss, look for (*and not find*).— quaesō, enquire: talia (make such enquiries).

quaesītor, -ōris [*quaeso*], M. an investigator, a judge.

quaesō, *see* quaerō.

quālis, -e, *pron. adj. interr.* of what sort, what, what a man (*or the like*) : qualis erat (how he looked!). — *Rel.* as, such (*implied in what precedes*) . . . as. — *Equal to an adv.* just as, as.

quam [*qui*], *adv. interr.* how, how much. — *Rel.* as much as, than. — *With anteced. omitted*, as many as, so . . . as.

quamlibet [*quam + libet*], *adv.* however much, however long.

quamquam, *adv.* although, though ; and yet, still.

quamvīs [*quam + vis*], *adv.* as you wish, however much, however; although, though.

quandō, *adv. and conj. Indef.* at any time, ever : si quando.— *Rel.* when, now that; *causal*, since, inasmuch as, seeing that.

quandōquidem (*rarely* quandŏ-), *adv.* since, inasmuch as.

quantuluscumque, -ulacumque, -ulumcumque [*dim. of quantus + cumque*], *adj.* however small, small though it was.

quantus, -a, -um, *pron. adj. interr.* how great ? how much ? what a, what. — *Rel.* as. — *With omitted antecedent*, as great as, as much as, not less than. — *Acc. as adv.* how much, how; as much, as, as (so) far as.

quārē [*quā + rē*], *adv. interr.* on what account ? why ? — *Rel.* on which account, wherefore ; therefore.

quārtus, -a, -um [*quattuor*], *num. adj.* fourth.

quasi [*quam + si*], *conj.* as if.

quassō, -āre, -āvī, -ātum [*quatio*], *1. v. a.* shake, brandish; shatter, batter.

quater [*quattuor*], *num. adv.* four times.

quatiō, -ere, *no perf.*, quassum, *3. v. a.* shake, flap (*the wings*), agitate, cause to tremble, threaten ; shatter, demolish, rend : fundamenta.

quattuor, *num. adj. indecl.* four.

-que, *enclitic conj.* and. — -que . . . -que, both . . . and, as well . . . as, and (*omitting the first*). — *Equal to* cum, when: vix fatus erat, subitoque intonuit.

queō, quīre, quīvī (-iī), quitum, *4. v. n.* can, be able.

quercus, -ūs, F. an oak (*sacred to Jove*) ; oak leaves : civilis (the civic crown of oak leaves, given for saving the life of a fellow-citizen).

querēla (-ella), -ae [*queror*], F. a complaint.

queror, querī, questus, *3. v. n. and
a.* complain; bewail, complain of:
plura querens (uttering further
complaints); **bubo** (wail, cry).

querulus, -a, -um [*queror*], *adj.*
complaining, grievous.

questus, -ūs [*queror*], M. a complaint, a lament.

quī, quae, quod, *rel. pron.* who,
which, that; these (those) who,
what, whoever, whatever.—**quod,**
N. as to which: **quod te oro** (and
so I pray). — *Also,* a thing which:
quod superest (the only thing remaining). — **ex quo,** from the
time when, since, after.

quia, *conj.* because: **quiane** (is it
because?).

quianam (*or separate*) [*quia + nam*],
adv. why, pray?

quīcumque, quae-, quod- (*also
separate*), *indef. rel. pron.* whoever,
whatever, all who, any whatever,
every possible: **quocumque leto**
(by any death, no matter what).
—N. *with partitive gen.*: **quodcumque regni** (this realm such as it is).

quīdam, quaedam, quoddam
(*subst.* quiddam), *indef. pron.* a
certain; a certain one, one.

quidem, *adv.* truly; but, however:
haud impune quidem.

quiēs, -ētis, F. rest, repose, sleep,
slumber, leisure, ease, quiet, lull.

quiēscō, -ere, quiēvī, quiētum
[*cf. quies*], *3. v. n.* rest, be laid to
rest (ossa), repose; cease, be
stilled, become silent; lie idle;
die down: **flamma.** — **quiētus,**
-a, -um, *p.p. as adj.* quiet, calm,
peaceful, undisturbed: **quietos
cura sollicitat** (their tranquil rest).

quiētus, -a, -um, *p.p. of* quiēscō.

quīlibet, quae-, quid-, *indef. pron.*
whom you please, any and every
one.

quīn [*quī* (*abl. of quis*) + *-ne*], *adv.
interr.* why not? (*in commands
and exhortations*), now, nay, even,
nay even, nay more, rather. —
Rel. conj. so that not, but that,
that not.— **quin etiam,** nay even,
moreover.

quīnam, *see* quisnam.

quīnī, -ae, -a [*quinque*], *num. adj.
pl.* five each, five at a time; five.

quīnquāgintā [*quinque*], *num. adj.
indecl.* fifty.

quīnque, *num. adj. indecl.* five.

quippe, *adv.* truly, no doubt, in
fact, doubtless. — *Ironical,* forsooth.

Quirīnālis, -e, *adj.* of Quirinus
(Romulus) (vii. 612).

Quirīnus, -ī, M. the name given to
Romulus as the divinity of Rome
(i. 292).

Quirītēs, -ium, M. *pl.* the Roman
citizens, the Romans — an ancient name supposed to have
come down from the time of
Romulus.

quis (quī), quae (qua, *indef.*),
quid (quod), *interr. pron.* who,
what, what sort of. — **quid,** N.
why, what; (*interr. and exclam.*)
how is it with? what about? what
of?— *Indef.* any, any one (*sometimes equal to* each one), anything,
some one, something.

quisnam (quī-), quae-, quid-
(quod-) (*also separate*), *interr.
and indef.* who pray, what pray,
who, what (*emphatic*).

quisquam, quae-, quid- (quic-), *indef. pron.* any one, any man, anything.

quisque, quae-, quid- (quic-), *indef. pron.* each one (*of several*), each, every, every one, every man, everything, all.

quisquis, quidquid (quicquid), *indef. rel. pron.* whoever, whatever.

quīvīs, quaevīs, quodvīs [*qui+vis*], *indef. pron. as adj.* any.

quō [*qui*], *adv.* whither (*interr. and rel.*); to what end, for what purpose, of what use.

quō [*qui*], *conj.* (*adv.*) (by which), in order that, that.

quōcircā, *adv.* wherefore.

quōcumque, *rel. adv.* whithersoever, in whatever way, for any course.

quod [*qui*], *conj.* because, in that, as to, as to the fact that; *in Eng. sometimes expressed by* therefore. — quod si, but if, now if.

quōlibet [*quo + libet*], *adv.* whither one pleases, anywhere.

quōmodo (quō modo), *adv.* in what way, how, in the way in which, as.

quōnam, *adv.* whither pray, oh whither, whither, where.

quondam [*quom (cum) + -dam*], *adv.* (at a certain time), once, formerly, before, just now, a while ago; one day, hereafter, by and by; sometime, sometimes.

quoniam [*quom + iam*], *adv.* (*conj.*) now that, seeing that, since, inasmuch as.

quoque, *conj.* also, too, as well, not less, even.

quot, *adj. indecl. rel.* how many, as many as, as.

quotannīs [*quot, annus*], *adv.* yearly, every year.

quotiēns [*quot*], *adv.* how many times, how often; as often as.

quousque, *adv.* how far; how long.

rabidus, -a, -um [*cf. rabies*], *adj.* raving, raging; ravenous.

rabiēs, -em, -ē [*rabio*], F. madness, rage, raving (*inspiration*), fury (*of storms, etc.*): ventris (ravening hunger).

radiō, -āre, -āvī, -ātum [*radius*], 1. v. n. to emit rays, gleam.

radius, -ī (-iī), M. a staff, a rod; a spoke; a ray.

rādīx, -īcis, F. a root.

rādō, -ere, rāsī, rāsum, 3. v. a. scrape, rub, shave; graze; pass closely, coast along. — *With cogn. acc.* (iter), cleave, skim.

rāmus, -ī, M. a bough, a branch, a twig.

rapāx, -ācis [*rapio*], *adj.* eager for prey, devouring, greedy, fierce, cruel; rushing (*of a river in flood*).

rapidus, -a, -um [*cf. rapio*], *adj.* fierce, consuming, blazing; hurrying, swift, rapid, quick: ungula (flying); vortex (whirling).

rapīna, -ae [*rapio*], F. robbery; plunder, booty.

rapiō, -ere, rapuī, raptum, 3. v. a. snatch, snatch away, seize, sweep away, carry off; tear from or off; plunder, steal, ravish, capture, sack; rescue; sweep along, scour; kindle; hurry on (*intrans.*). — raptum, -ī, N. *p.p. as subst.* plunder, booty, spoil.

raptō, -āre, -āvī, -ātum [*raptus, rapio*], 1. v. a. drag.

raptor, -ōris [*rapio*], M. a plunderer.— *In app. as adj.* plundering, prowling.

rārēscō, -ere, *no perf., no sup.* [*rarus*], *3. v. n. incept.* grow thin: claustra Pelori (widen, grow wider).

rārō [*rarus*], *adv.* seldom.

rārus, -a, -um, *adj.* loose, wide apart, thin, scattered, few, thinned out; here and there: retia (large-meshed, coarse); voces (broken).

rāstrum, -ī [*rado*], N. a hoe *or* mattock, a stub-hoe.

ratiō, -ōnis [*reor*], F. a reckoning, a plan, a way, means; intelligence: sat rationis (any sense).

ratis, -is, F. a raft; a boat, a ship, a vessel.

ratus, -a, -um, *p.p. of* reor.

raucus, -a, -um, *adj.* hoarse, roaring, screaming, clanging, ringing.

re- (red-), *prep. in comp.* back, again, un- (*reversing the action*), forth.

rebellis, -e [*re-* + *bellum*], *adj.* renewing a war, insurgent, rising (*in arms, after conquest*).

recaleō, -ēre, *no perf. or sup.*, *2. v. n.* be warmed, run warm.

recēdō, -ere, -cessī, -cessum, *3. v. n.* move back, withdraw, retire, retreat, recede, draw back; depart, pass away.

recēns, -entis, *adj.* fresh, new, recent, new-made, new-come: prata rivis (kept fresh).

recēnseō, -ēre, -cēnsuī, -cēnsum (-cēnsītum), *2. v. a.* reckon up, recount.

recessus, -ūs [*recedo*], M. a recess.

recidīvus, -a, -um [*recido*], *adj.* recurring; renewed, restored.

recidō (reccidō), -ere, reccidī, *no sup.* [*re-* + *cado*], *3. v. n.* fall back, return, light upon.

recīdō, -ere, -cīdī, -cīsum [*re-* + *caedo*], *3. v. a.* hew out, quarry; cut off, clip. — *P.p.* rounded.

recingō, -ere, *no perf.*, -cīnctum, *3. v. a.* unbind, ungird, unloose, loosen: recincta veste (in flowing robe).

recipiō, -ere, -cēpī, -ceptum [*re-* +*capio*], *3.v.a.* take back, recover, rescue, receive (*of something due*), exact; receive (*generally*), admit: ad se (receive by one's side).— *With reflexive,* retire.

recitō, -āre, -āvī, -ātum, *1. v. a.* read aloud, recite.

reclūdō, -ere, -clūsī, -clūsum [*re-* + *claudo*], *3. v. a.* unclose, open, lay bare, disclose; unsheathe.

recognōscō, -ere, -gnōvī, -gnitum, *3. v. a.* review, examine.

recolō, -ere, -coluī, -cultum, *3. v. a.* retill; consider, survey.

recondō, -ere, -condidī, -conditum, *3. v. a.* hide away, conceal, deposit; close again.

recordor, -ārī, -ātus [*re-, cor*], *1. v. dep.* recall to mind, recall.

recreō, -āre, -āvī, -ātum, *1. v. a.* revive, refresh.

rēctē [*rectus*], *adv.* rightly, suitably, successfully, well.

rēctor, -ōris [*rego*], M. a ruler, a pilot, a steersman.

rēctum, *see* rego.

recubō, -āre, *no perf., no sup.*, *1. v. n.* lie on the back, recline, lie at length, lie.

recursō, -āre, -āvī, -ātum, *1. v. n.* run back; recur, be renewed.

recursus, -ūs, M. a returning course, counter-movement.

recurvus, -a, -um, *adj.* bent back, crooked.

recūsō, -āre, -āvī, -ātum [*re-* + †*causo*], *1. v. a. and n.* be reluctant, refuse, reject, object, decline: **longe** (shrink back afar).

recutiō, -ere, *no perf.,* **-cussum** [*re-* + *quatio*], *3. v. a.* strike back. — **recussus, -a, -um,** *p.p. as adj.* reëchoing.

reddō, -ere, -didī, -ditum [*red-* + *do*], *3. v. a.* give back, restore, return, repay, render, bestow, give forth, yield; utter, reply; render, make, imitate: **te nomine** (recall, call to mind). — *With reflexive or in pass.* return, go back: **redditus** (returning); **reddita cessit,** came by succession.

redeō, -īre, -iī (-īvī), -itum [*red-* + *eo*], *irr. v. n.* go back, return, come back, come in (*in a race*).

redigō, -ere, -ēgī, -āctum [*red-* + *ago*], *3. v. a.* reduce; drive down *or* back.

redimiō, -īre, -iī, -ītum, *4. v. a.* bind round, encircle, wreathe.

redimō, -ere, -ēmī, -ēmptum [*red-* + *emo,* buy], *3. v. a.* buy back, ransom, redeem.

reditus, -ūs [*redeo*], M. a return.

redoleō, -ēre, -oluī, *no sup.* [*red-* + *oleo*], *2. v. a. and n.* smell of, be fragrant with.

redūcō, -ere, -dūxī, -ductum, *3. v. a.* lead back, bring back, draw back, restore; rescue: **reducti remi** (plied with vigor).— **reductus, -a, -um,** *p.p. as adj.* retired, secluded: **vallis.**

redux, -ucis, *adj.* returned, returning, restored.

refellō, -ere, -fellī, *no sup.* [*re-* + *fallo*], *3. v. a.* refute, disprove.

referō, -ferre, rētulī (rett-), relātum, *irr. v. a.* bring back, bear back, bring again: **pedem, gradus** (start back) ; echo back. — *With reflexive or in pass.* return, come back, go back, betake one's self, turn: **relatam classem nuntio** (returned) ; **referri spes** (decline, fail). — *Also,* repeat, renew, restore, resemble; bring forth, utter (**voces**) ; rehearse, sing; report, relate, answer ; pay, render, perform (**sollemnia**) ; consign (**hunc sedibus**) ; carry off (**laudem**) ; turn (**oculos**) ; change (**consilia**).

reficiō, -ere, -fēcī, -fectum [*re-* + *facio*], *3. v. a.* remake, renew, give anew.

refīgō, -ere, -fīxī, -fīxum, *3. v. a.* unfix, tear down.

reflectō, -ere, -flexī, -flexum, *3. v. a.* bend back, bend: **animum** (turn one's attention).

refluō, -ere, *no perf. or sup.,* *3. v. n.* flow back.

refringō, -ere, -frēgī, -frāctum [*re-* + *frango*], *3. v. a.* break off.

refugiō, -ere, -fūgī, *no sup.,* *3. v. a. and n.* fly back, shrink back from, flee away, recede, recoil from ; shrink, be reluctant, refuse, shrink from: **animus meminisse** (shrinks from the recollection).

refugus, -a, -um [*fugio*], *adj.* ever-fleeing.

refulgeō, -ēre, -fulsī, *no sup.,* *2. v. n.* shine forth, gleam, shine.

refundō, -ere, -fūdī, -fūsum, *3. v. a.*
pour back, pour forth, throw back.
— refūsus, -a, -um, *p.p.* thrown
up, poured forth, overflowing.

refūtō, -āre, -āvī, -ātum, *1. v. a.*
refute, prove false.

rēgālis, -e [*rex*], *adj.* kingly, royal,
regal.

rēgia, *see* rēgius.

rēgificus, -a, -um [*rex, facio*], *adj.*
regal.

rēgīna, -ae [*rex*], F. a queen, a princess. — *In app. as adj.* royal.

regiō, -ōnis [*rego*], F. a direction,
a course; a region, a quarter; climate.

rēgius, -a, -um [*rex*], *adj.* of a king,
royal; princely, queenly, magnificent. — rēgia, -ae, F. *as subst.* (*sc.*
domus), royal abode, palace, royal
city.

rēgnātor, -ōris [*regno*], M. a ruler,
a sovereign.

rēgnō, -āre, -āvī, -ātum [*regnum*], *1. v. n. and a.* reign, rule,
bear sway; rule over: regnandam Albam (the throne of Alba).
— *Impers.*: regnabitur (the rule
shall be).

rēgnum, -ī [*rego*], N. a realm, a kingdom; regal power, throne, reign;
seat of empire.

regō, -ere, rēxī, rēctum, *3. v. a.*
direct, guide, steer; govern, rule,
sway, control. — rēctus, -a, -um,
p.p. as adj. straight, direct, right:
recto litore (straight along the
shore). — N. *as subst.* rēctum, -ī,
right, virtue.

rēiciō, -ere, -iēcī, -iectum [*re-* +
iacio], *3. v. a.* throw back, throw
off, hurl back.

relābor, -lābī, -lāpsus, *3. v. dep.*
slip back, vanish.

relanguēscō, -ere, -languī, *no
sup.*, *3. v. n.* faint, fall lifeless.

relegō, -ere, -lēgī, -lēctum, *3. v.
a.* coast by again, sail by *or* along
again, retrace.

relevō, -āre, -āvī, -ātum, *1. v. a.*
lighten, relieve, refresh.

rěligiō, -ōnis, F. reverence for the
gods, piety, devotion, religion,
veneration; a ceremony, an observance, a rite; sanctity, holi-
ness; a divinity (*a thing sacred*):
prospera (omens).

rěligiōsus, -a, -um [*religio*], *adj.*
sacred, venerable.

religō, -āre, -āvī, -ātum, *1. v. a.*
bind back, bind fast.

relinquō, -ere, -līquī, -lictum, *3.
v. a.* leave behind, leave, abandon, depart from, forsake, give
up, relinquish, desert.

rěliquiae, -ārum [*reliquus*], F. *pl.*
remnants, relics, remains: Danaum (remnants left by).

relūceō, -ēre, -lūxī, *no sup.*, *2. v.
n.* shine back; shine out, shine,
glare, gleam.

remaneō, -ēre, -mānsī, *no sup.*,
2. v. n. remain.

remeō, -āre, -āvī, *no sup.*, *1. v. n.*
return.

remētior, -īrī, -mēnsus, *4. v. dep.*
measure back, retrace.

rēmex, -igis, M. a rower, an oars-
man; *collectively*, oarsmen.

rēmigium, -ī (-iī) [*remex*], N.
rowing; oars (*collectively*), oarsmen; oarage: alarum.

reminīscor, -ī, *no p.p.*, *3. v. dep.*
remember.

remittō, -ere, -mīsī, -missum, 3.
v. a. send back, return, repay;
give up, yield, relax; abate.

remordeō, -ēre, *no perf.*, -mor-
sum, 2.*v. a.* gnaw; vex, trouble.

remoror, -ārī, -ātus, *1. v. dep.* delay, pause.

removeō, -ēre, -mōvī, -mōtum,
2. *v. a.* move away, remove, put
away; hide, shroud, veil: caelum.
— *P.p.* obscure (ambages).

remūgiō, -īre, *no perf., no sup.*,
4. *v. n.* bellow forth, resound, bellow, roar.

Remus, -ī, M. the brother of Romulus (i. 292).

rēmus, -ī, M. an oar.

renārrō, -āre, -āvī, -ātum, *1. v. a.*
relate, tell, recount.

renāscor, -ī, -nātus, *3. v. dep.* grow
or spring again.

renīdeō, -ēre, *no perf. or sup.*, 2.*v. n.*
shine, reflect the light.—renīdēns,
-entis, *p. as adj.* beaming, glad.

renovō, -āre, -āvī, -ātum, *1. v. a.*
renew; renew by tillage.

reor, rērī, ratus [*res*], 2. *v. dep.*
reckon; think, suppose, judge. —
P.p. as adj. ratus, -a, -um, firm,
sure, certain.

repellō, -ere, reppulī, repulsum,
3. *v. a.* drive back, dash back,
spurn, repel, thwart, reject.

rependō, -ere, -pendī, -pēnsum,
3. *v. a.* weigh back; pay back,
requite: magna (fully requite);
fata fatis (balance).

repente [*repens*], *adv.* suddenly, unexpectedly, quickly.

reperiō, -īre, repperī, repertum
[*re- + pario*], *4. v. a.* find, detect,
discover.

repetō, -ere, -petiī (-īvī), -petī-
tum, *3. v. a.* seek again, go back
to, return to; seek; trace back;
repeat; remember.

repleō, -ēre, -plēvī, -plētum
[*re- + †pleo*], 2. *v. a.* fill up, fill,
swell.

repōnō, -ere, -posuī, -positum,
3. v. a. put back, replace, restore,
renew; lay *or* put down, lay aside,
abandon; lay away, store away,
store up, bury: haec imis sensibus (let sink deep). — repositus
(repostus), -a, -um, *p.p. as adj.*
far away, remote; buried.

reportō, -āre, -āvī, -ātum, *1. v. a.*
bring back, carry back; report,
announce.

reposcō, -ere, *no perf., no sup.*, 3.
v. a. demand back, demand (*as
due*), claim, call for.

repostus, -a, -um, *see* repōnō.

reprimō, -ere, -pressī, -pressum
[*re- + premo*], 3. *v. a.* hold back,
check, restrain, stop.

repulsa, -ae [*repello*], F. a repulse.

requiēs, -ētis (-ēī), F. rest, cessa-
tion, repose, respite.

requiēscō, -ere, -quiēvī, -quiē-
tum, *3. v. n.* rest, come to rest.

requīrō, -ere, -quīsīvī, -quīsītum
[*re- + quaero*], *3. v. a.* seek out,
search for, seek, call for, miss;
ask, enquire.

rēs, reī, F. a thing, a matter; an
event, an affair, a circumstance;
an exploit, an enterprise, an undertaking; a state of things; a
conflict. — *Pl.* nature, the world,
the universe; fortune(s), circumstances; power, the State, empire,

government (*also sing.*); property, estate: **fessi rerum** (weary of toil); **pro re** (under the circumstances, as the case demands).

rescindō, -ere, -scidī, -scissum, *3. v. a.* cut away; tear down, destroy.

resecō, -āre, -secuī, -sectum, *1. v. a.* cut off, trim; reap.

reserō, -āre, -āvī, -ātum, *1. v. a.* unclose, lay open.

reservō, -āre, -āvī, -ātum, *1. v. a.* keep back, reserve, hold in reserve, save.

†**reses, -idis** [*cf. resideo*], *adj.* idle, inactive, dormant, peaceful, at rest.

resīdō, -ere, -sēdī, *no sup., 3. v. n.* sit down, sink down, settle, fall back; subside, become calm.

resignō, -āre, -āvī, -ātum, *1. v. a.* unseal, open.

resistō, -ere, -stitī, *no sup., 3. v. n.* stop, make a stand, stand firm; resist, oppose, withstand, interpose; stand forth.

resolvō, -ere, -solvī, -solūtum, *3. v. a.* unloose, unbind, disentangle, disengage; melt; break through, relax, scatter: **ambages** (unravel); **iura** (violate).

resonō, -āre, -āvī, *no sup., 1. v. n.* resound.

respectō, -āre, *no perf., no sup., 1. v. a.* regard.

respergō, -ere, -spersī, -spersum [*re- + spargo*], *3. v. a.* besprinkle, stain.

respiciō, -ere, -spexī, -spectum, *3. v. a. and n.* look back, look round, look up; look back at *or* for, see behind one; look round, see; notice; consider, regard, have regard for.

respīrō, -āre, -āvī, -ātum, *1. v. n.* breathe, take breath.

respondeō, -ēre, -spondī, -spōnsum, *2. v. n.* answer, reply, correspond to, respond, match, reciprocate.

respōnsum, -ī [N. *p. p. of* respondeo], N. an answer, a reply; a response, an oracle.

restinguō, -ere, -stīnxī, -stīnctum, *3. v. a.* quench, extinguish.

restituō, -ere, -stituī, -stitūtum [*re- + statuo*], *3. v. a.* set up again, restore.

restō, -stāre, -stitī, *no sup., 1. v. n.* remain, be left, be in store.

resultō, -āre, *no perf.,* -ātum [*re- + salto*], *1. v. n.* spring back; reecho.

resūmō, -ere, -sūmpsī, -sūmptum, *3. v. a.* take again, resume.

resupīnus, -a, -um, *adj.* on the back; with head thrown back; haughty.

resurgō, -ere, -surrēxī, -surrēctum, *3. v. n.* rise again: **amor** (return).

retardō, -āre, -āvī, -ātum, *1. v. a.* check, keep back.

rēte, -is, N. a net.

retegō, -ere, -tēxī, -tēctum, *3. v. a.* uncover, lay bare, disclose, expose.

retentō, -āre, -āvī, -ātum, *1. v. a.* hold back, detain, retard.

retexō, -ere, -uī, -textum, *3. v. a.* unweave, reverse, cancel.

retināculum, -ī [*retinco*], N. a cable, a rope.

retineō, -ēre, -tinuī, -tentum
[re- + teneo], 2. v. a. hold back,
detain, stop, restrain.

retorqueō, -ēre, -torsī, -tortum,
2. v. a. twist or bend back; hurl
back.

retrāctō, -āre, -āvī, -ātum, 1. v. a.
handle again, withdraw, retract.

retrahō, -ere, -trāxī, -trāctum,
3. v. a. draw back, drag back:
trahunt retrahunt (drag to and
fro).

retrō, adv. back, backward: arva
cedentia retro (receding in the
distance).

retrōrsum [retro + vorsus, p.p. of
verto], adv. back.

retrōrsus [retro + vorsus], adv.
back.

reus, -ī [res], M. a defendant; a
debtor: voti (bound by one's
vow).

revehō, -ere, -vexī, -vectum, 3.
v. a. carry back, ferry back.

revellō, -ere, -vellī, -vulsum
(vols-), 3. v. a. wrench away, tear
away or up, drag from; dig up,
disturb.

revertor, -ī, -versus (also act. re-
vertī), 3. v. dep. turn back, return.

revinciō, -īre, -vīnxī, -vīnctum,
4. v. a. bind back, bind fast,
wreathe.

revīsō, -ere, no perf., no sup., 3. v.
a. and n. revisit, return to.

revocābilis, -e [revoco], adj. to be
called back.

revocāmen, -inis [revoco], N. a recall.

revocō, -āre, -āvī, -ātum, 1. v. a.
call back, restore, renew, revive;

rescue; retrace (gradum); detain, dissuade.

revolvō, -ere, -volvī, -volūtum,
3. v. a. roll back, throw back;
throw over; go round again,
repeat, renew. — revolūtus, -a,
-um, p.p. in special senses: ille
iacuit (rolling over); revoluta toro
est (fell back); in veterem figuram (restored); revoluta, returned.

revomō, -ere, -vomuī, no sup., 3.
v. a. throw up.

rēx, rēgis [√reg (of rego)], M. a
king. — As adj. in app. ruling.

Rhadamanthus, -ī, M. a brother
of Minos, and son of Jupiter; a
judge in the World Below (vi.
566).

Rhēsus, -ī, M. a king of Thrace.

Rhīphaeus, -a, -um, adj. of the
Rhiphæan mountains in Scythia.

Rhodopē, -ēs, F. a mountain range
in Thrace.

Rhodopēius, -a, -um, adj. of
Rhodope, Thracian.

Rhodos, -ī, F. Rhodes, an island
off the coast of Asia Minor.

Rhoetēius, -a, -um, adj. Rhœ-
tean, of Rhœteum (a promontory
of the Troad); Trojan (v. 646).

rictus, -ūs, M. the open mouth;
pl. jaws.

rīdeō, -ēre, rīsī, rīsum, 2. v. a.
and n. laugh at, smile at, smile
upon; laugh, smile.

rigeō, -ēre, riguī, no sup., 2. v. n.
be stiff; of the hair, stand on end.

rigidus, -a, -um [cf. rigeo], adj.
stiff, rigid, hard.

rigō, -āre, -āvī, -ātum, 1. v. a.
wash, bathe, water.

rigor, -ōris, M. hardness.

rīma, -ae, F. a crack, a chink, a seam, a cleft.

rīmor, -ārī, -ātus [*rima*], *1. v. dep.* pry into, search, tear at.

rīmōsus, -a, -um [*rima*], *adj.* full cf chinks, leaky.

rīpa, -ae, F. a bank (*of a river*).

Rīpheus, -eī (-eos), M. a Trojan warrior (ii. 339).

rīte [*ritus*], *adv.* with due ceremony, in due form, duly; rightly, fitly.

rītus, -ūs, M. a rite, a religious custom *or* ceremony.

rīvus, -ī, M. a stream, a brook, a river.

rōbur, -oris, N. hard wood, timber, wood; a beam, a log; a trunk; an oak tree, oak; strength, force, vigor, courage.

rōbustus, -a, -um [*robus*, *old form of robur*], *adj.* hard; hardy, sturdy.

rogitō, -āre, -āvī, *no sup.* [*rogo*], *1. v. a.* ask, enquire.

rogō, -āre, -āvī, -ātum, *1. v. a.* ask, beg, sue for, ask for, beseech.

rogus, -ī, M. a funeral pile, a pyre.

Rōma, -ae, F. Rome.

Rōmānus, -a, -um, *adj.* Roman, of Rome. — M. a Roman.

Rōmulus, -a, -um, *adj.* of Romulus.

Rōmulus, -ī, M. the mythical founder of Rome (i. 276).

rōrō, -āre, -āvī, -ātum [*ros*], *1. v. n. and a.* drop dew, drip; bedew, sprinkle.

rōs, rōris, M. dew; water, moisture.

rōscidus, -a, -um [*ros*], *adj.* wet with dew, dewy.

roseus, -a, -um [*rosa*], *adj.* of roses; rose-colored, rosy.

rōstrātus, -a, -um [*rostrum*], *adj.* adorned with ships' beaks.

rōstrum, -ī [*rodo*], N. a beak; a beak (*of a ship*), ram.

rota, -ae, F. a wheel; a chariot: **volvere rotam** (run a course, complete a cycle, *of years*).

rubeō, -ēre, *no perf. or sup.*, *2. v. n.* be red.

ruber, -bra, -brum, *adj.* red, ruddy: litus (of the Red Sea).

rubēscō, -ere, -rubuī, *no sup.* [*rubeo*], *3. v. n.* redden, be reddened.

rubēta, -ae [*rubus*], F. a thicket.

rudēns, -entis, M. a rope, a hawser, a line, a sheet, clewline, cordage.

rudis, -e, *adj.* raw, rough, crude, unworked, rude; ignorant, untrained, unskilled; strange.

rudō, -ere, -īvī, *no sup.*, *3. v. n.* roar.

ruīna, -ae [*ruo*], F. a fall, a crash, a convulsion, wreck; downfall, ruin, disaster, calamity, destruction; a falling mass; *pl.* ruins: **trahere ruinam** (fall in ruins, fall with a crash).

ruīnōsus, -a, -um [*ruina*], *adj.* ruined, ruinous.

rūmor, -ōris, M. rumor, report.

rumpō, -ere, rūpī, ruptum [√ *rup*], *3. v. a. and n.*, *lit.* break, burst, break down, break through, burst open; break off, sever, tear; force (**aditūs**); throw out, let loose, hurl forth, utter: **questūs**; **vocem** (break one's silence). — *With reflex. or in pass.* break forth, burst forth.—*Fig.* break, break through,

violate: **moras** (break through);
fata (escape).

ruō, -ere, ruī, rutum, *3. v. a. and
n.* overthrow, destroy, lay waste;
throw up, dash up, upturn; fall
(*violently*), fall *or* flow in torrents,
fall in ruins, totter, set (*of the
sun*, hasten to its setting); run
blindly, dash, rush, rush on, rush
forth, hurry: **nox Oceano** (burst
forth); **voces** (pour forth).

rūpēs, -is [√*rup* (*of rumpo*)], F. a
rock (*broken or precipitous*), a cliff.

rūricola, -ae [*rus, colo*], M. a rustic, a countryman.

rūrsum (rūrsus) [*re- + vorsum
(-us)*], *adv.* back, again; anew,
once more, a second time.

rūs, rūris, N. the country (*opposed
to the city*); a field.

rūsticus, -a, -um [*rus*], *adj.* rustic,
rural.

rutilus, -a, -um, *adj.* red.

rūtrum, -ī, N. a spade.

Rutulus, -a, -um, *adj.* of the Rutuli, a people of Latium whose
chief city was Ardea. Under the
lead of Turnus they resisted the
settlement of the Trojans in Italy.
— M. *pl.* the people.

Sabaeus, -a, -um, *adj.* of Saba (a
town in Arabia famous for its
myrrh and frankincense), Sabæan
(i. 416). — M. *pl. subst.* the Sa-
bæans (viii. 706).

Sabīnus, -a, -um, *adj.* Sabine. The
Sabines were ancient neighbors
of the Latins. — N. *pl. as subst.*
a Sabine farm *or* estate.

sacculus, -ī [*dim. of saccus*], M. a
little bag *or* sack.

sacer, -cra, -crum [√*sac* (*in san-
cio*)], *adj.* consecrated, sacred,
holy, devoted, dedicated: **sacra
sedes** (*as devoted to sacrifice*); accursed. — N. *as subst.* **sacrum, -ī,**
the sacred mysteries. — N. *pl. as
subst.* **sacra, -ōrum,** sacred utensils, holy emblems, sacred images,
sacrifices, ceremonies, offerings,
sacred rites, mysteries.

sacerdōs, -dōtis [*sacer*], C. a
priest, a priestess.

Sacēs, -ae, M. a Rutulian (xii. 651).

sacrificium, -ī (iī) [*sacer, facio*], N.
a sacrifice.

sacrilegus, -a, -um [*sacer, lego*],
adj. stealing sacred things, sacrilegious, impious.

sacrō, -āre, -āvī, -ātum [*sacer*],
1. v. a. consecrate, dedicate, make
sacred. — **sacrātus, -a, -um,** *p.p.
as adj.* consecrated, sacred, holy.

saeculum (saeclum), -ī, N. a generation, a race of men, an age; *pl.*
ages, an age: **per saecula** (forever).

saepe, *adv.* oftentimes, often. —
saepius, *compar.* often, again and
again.

saepes, -is, F. a hedge.

saepiō, -īre, saepsī, saeptum
[*saepes*], *4. v. a.* enclose, hedge
about, surround, shut up.

saeta, -ae, F. a bristle, shaggy hair.

saeviō, -īre, -īvī (-iī), -ītum
[*saevus*], *4. v. n.* rage, rave, be
angry, become furious.

saevus, -a, -um, *adj.* raging, furious, roused to fury, fierce, savage, relentless, cruel, bitter. — *In
good sense,* fierce in conflict.

Sagaris, -is, M. a Trojan (v. 263).

sagitta, -ae, F. an arrow.

sāl, salis, M. *and* N. salt ; salt water, the salt sea, the sea. — *Fig.* wit.

saliō, -īre, -uī, saltum, *4. v. n.* leap.

Salius, -ī (-iī), M. a Trojan (v. 298).

Sallentīnus, -a, -um, *adj.* of the Sallentini (a people of Calabria), Sallentine (iii. 400).

Salmōneus, -eos, M. a son of Æolus. He ruled in ᾿Elis, and in his pride imitated the thunder and lightning of Jupiter, for which impiety he was hurled to the World Below by a thunderbolt (vi. 585).

salsus, -a, -um [*p.p. of salo* (*fr. sal*)], *adj.* salted, salt, briny.

saltem, *adv.* at least, at any rate.

saltus, -ūs [*salio*], M. a bound, a leap, a spring.

saltus, -ūs, M. an opening (*in the woods*), a pasture, a glade ; open woods, a grove, woodland.

salum, -ī [*sal*], N. the sea, the deep.

salūs, -ūtis [*akin to salvus*], F. health, welfare, safety, preservation ; hope of safety, means of safety.

salūtō, -āre, -āvī, -ātum [*salus*], *1. v. a.* (wish health to), greet, salute, hail, welcome.

salvē, *see* salveo.

salveō, -ēre, *no perf., no sup.* [*salvus*], *2. v. n.* be well. — salvē (-ēte), *imper.* hail! welcome!

salvus, -a, -um, *adj.* in safety, safe.

Samē, -ēs, F. an island (later Cephalonia) in the Ionian Sea (iii. 271).

Samos (-us), -ī, F. a large island off the coast of the Ionian part of Asia Minor, famous for its temple of Juno (i. 16).

sanciō, -īre, sānxī, sānctum [√*sac, in sacer*], *4. v. a.* make sacred. — **sānctus, -a, -um,** *p.p. as adj.* sacred, holy, inviolable ; reverend, venerable, venerated.

sānctus, -a, -um, *p.p. of* sanciō.

sanguineus, -a, -um [*sanguis*], *adj.* bloody, blood-stained, bloodshot, blood-red.

sanguinulentus, -a, -um [*sanguis*], *adj.* covered with blood.

sanguis, -inis, M. blood, gore. — *Also,* race, stock, family ; progeny.

saniēs, -ēī, F. matter, foul gore, froth (*of a serpent*).

sānus, -a, -um, *adj.* sound, well, healthy ; rational, sane : male sana (distracted).

sapienter [*sapiens*], *adv.* wisely.

sapientia, -ae [*sapiens*], F. wisdom.

sarcina, -ae, F. burden.

Sardīs (-ēs), -ium, F. Sardis, the capital of Lydia.

Sarmaticē, *adv.* in the Sarmatian language.

Sarmaticus, -a, -um, *adj.* of the Sarmatians, a tribe north of the Black Sea.

Sarpēdōn, -onis, M. a king of Lycia killed before Troy (i. 100).

sat, *see* satis.

sata, *see* serō.

satelles, -itis, C. an attendant.

satiō, -āre, -āvī, -ātum [*satis*], *1. v. a.* satisfy, glut, feed abundantly ; appease, avenge.

satis (sat), *adj. and adv.* enough, sufficient. — *With negatives,* not very. — *As subst.* N. enough.

sator, -ōris [*sero*], M. planter ; a progenitor, a father.

Sāturnius, -a, -um, *adj.* Saturnian, of Saturn. — M. *as subst.* son of Saturn. — F. *as subst.* daughter of Saturn, Juno.

Sāturnus, -ī [*fr.* √ *of sero*], M. an ancient divinity of Italy, presiding over agriculture. His supremacy was supposed to mark the golden age of primitive virtue and simplicity. In later times he was identified with the Greek Cronos, and to him were attached the myths of that ancient divinity. Hence, he was son of Uranus, and father of Jupiter, Juno, Neptune, and other gods (vi. 794).

saturō, -āre, -āvī, -ātum [*satur*], *1. v. a.* fill, satiate, satisfy, feed full.

Satyrus, -ī, M. a Satyr.

saucius, -a, -um, *adj.* wounded, stricken.

Sauromatae, -ārum, M. *pl.* a Slavic tribe.

saxeus, -a, -um [*saxum*], *adj.* rocky, of rock.

saxum, -ī, N. a rock, a stone.

Scaea, -ae (Scaeae, -ārum), *adj.* F. (*with* **porta**), Scæan, the western (left) gate of Troy, the principal and most famous entrance (ii. 612).

scaena, -ae, F. a scene (the arched back of the stage, in front of which the action took place), a canopy (*of woods like the scene*); the stage.

scālae, -ārum [*scando*], F. *pl.* a scaling ladder *or* ladders, a ladder.

scandō, -ere, *no perf., no sup., 3. v. a. and n.* climb, scale, ascend, mount.

scelerō, -āre, *no perf.,* **-ātum** [*scelus*], *1. v. a.* pollute, defile. — **scelerātus, -a, -um,** *p.p. as adj.* wicked, guilty, impious, infamous, accursed; of the accursed, of guilt: **poenae** (inflicted on the guilty).

scelestus, -a, -um [*scelus*], *adj.* wicked, evil.

scelus, -eris, N. villainy, wickedness; a crime, an evil deed: **scelus infectum** (taint of guilt).

scēptrum, -ī, N. a sceptre; rule, power, dominion; a kingdom, a realm, the throne.

scīlicet [*sci* (*imper. of scio*) + licet, know, you may], *adv.* certainly; *ironically,* forsooth, truly, doubtless.

scindō, -ere, scidī, scissum [√*scid*], *3. v. a.* split, cleave, rive; tear, rend; divide; *with reflexive* (*or in pass.*), divide, separate: **volgus** (is rent, *into factions*).

scintilla, -ae, F. a spark.

sciō, scīre, scīvī, scītum, *4. v. a.* know, know how to; learn.

Scīpiadēs, -ae, M. a son of the Scipios. — *Pl.* the Scipios, the famous family of leaders and statesmen at Rome (vi. 843).

scītor, -ārī, -ātus [*scitus, scio*], *1. v. dep.* enquire, learn, search into: **oracula** (consult).

scopulus, -ī, M. a crag, a cliff, a rock, a reef.

scrībō, -ere, scrīpsī, scrīptum, *3. v. a.* write. — *P.p. pl. as subst.,* **scrīpta, -ōrum,** writings.

scrīptor, -ōris [*scribo*], M. a writer.

scrūpeus, -a, -um, *adj.* of sharp stones, stony, flinty: **spelunca** (of jagged rocks).

scūtātus, -a, -um [*scutum*], *adj.*
armed with a shield.

scūtum, -ī, N. a shield (of the
Roman pattern, oblong and bent
round the body).

Scylacēum, -ī, N. a town of Southern Italy on the coast of Bruttium, near a promontory thought
dangerous for ships (iii. 553).

Scylla, -ae, F. 1. A sea monster
supposed to inhabit some rocks
in the Strait of Messina, on the
coast of Bruttium (iii. 420). — 2.
Pl. Scyllas, including a number
of monsters of the kind first mentioned (vi. 286). — 3. The name
of a ship (v. 122).

Scyllaeus, -a, -um, *adj.* of Scylla
(i. 200).

Scȳrius, -a, -um, *adj.* of Scyros
(the island off the coast of Eubœa where Achilles was concealed,
disguised as a girl), Scyrian (ii.
477).

Scythia, -ae, F. a country north of
the Black Sea.

Scythicus, -a, -um, *adj.* Scythian.

sē, *see* suī.

sē- (sēd-), *prep. only in compos.*
apart, without, away.

sēcēdō, -ere, -cessī, -cessum
[*se-* + *cedo*], *3. v. n.* depart.

sēcernō, -ere, -crēvī, -crētum
[*se-* + *cerno*], *3. v. a.* separate,
set apart. — sēcrētus, -a, -um,
p.p. as adj. separate, apart, retired, remote; obscure, concealed, hidden. — N. *pl. as subst.*
sēcrēta, secret abode.

sēcessus, -ūs [*secedo*], M. a retire-
ment; a retreat, a recess.

secius, *see* secus.

sēclūdō, -ere, -clūsī, -clūsum
[*se-* + *claudo*], *3. v. a.* shut off,
shut up; put aside, banish. —
sēclūsus, -a, -um, *p.p. as adj.* secluded, retired.

secō, -āre, -uī, sectum, *1. v. a.*
cut, carve, hew; sever, cut off;
skim over; *of passing through,*
cleave, cut, plough (*the sea*), divide: viam (take one's way).

sēcrētus, -a, -um, *p.p. of* sēcernō.

secundō, -āre, *no perf., no sup.*
[*secundus*], *1. v. a.* favor, prosper.

secundus, -a, -um [*sequor*], *adj.*
(following), second; prosperous,
favorable, propitious, auspicious,
fair (*of winds*): vires secundae
(victorious strength); secundo
clamore (joyous, auspicious); sinus implere secundos (fill the bellying sail with favoring winds);
currus (smoothly gliding, flying).
—*With* res, prosperity, good fortune, success. — N. *pl. as subst.*
secunda, -ōrum, prosperity.

secūris, -is [*seco*], F. an axe. —
Pl. the axes (of the lictors), as
emblems of authority.

sēcūrus, -a, -um [*se-* + *cura*], *adj.*
free from care; regardless, heedless: amorum; latices (that free
from care).

secus [√*sec* (*of sequor*)], *adv.*
otherwise. — *With negatives,* not
otherwise, not less, no more, just
so, even so; *with* atque (quam),
just like, even as. — *Compar.* secius, *with negatives,* no less, none
the less, nevertheless.

sed, *conj.* but, yet.

sedeō, -ēre, sēdī, sessum [√*sed*],
2. v. n. sit, sit down; alight (*of*

birds) ; encamp; sink in (*of a weapon or wound*) ; be settled, fixed, determined, please (be one's pleasure) : id Aeneae sedet.

sēdēs, -is [√*sed* (*of sedeo*)], F. a seat, a throne, a resting place; *sing. or pl.* a house, a dwelling place, a home, a settlement; a foundation, a position ; a region, a place ; a temple ; a city ; a last resting place, a tomb : imae sedes (the lowest depths) ; sacra sedes (*of the steps of an altar*) ; penetralis sedes (the inner court).

sedīle, -is [*sedes*], N. a seat, a bench, a thwart.

sēditiō, -ōnis [*sed-* + *itio* (*cf. eo*)], F. a civil dissension, a mutiny, an outbreak, a riot, an uprising.

sēdō, -āre, -āvī, -ātum [√*sed*], 1. *v. a.* settle down ; quiet. — **sēdātus, -a, -um**, *p.p. as adj.* calm, quiet.

sēdūcō, -ere, -dūxī, -ductum [*se-* + *duco*], 3. *v. a.* draw apart, separate, part asunder.

seges, -etis, F. growing grain, a field of grain ; a crop, a growth, a thicket : telorum seges.

sēgnis, -e, *adj.* slow, sluggish, laggard. — *Compar.* sēgnior, -ius, slower, less active : haud segnior (not less vigorous).

sēgnitiēs, -ēī [*segnis*], F. sloth, tardiness.

Selīnūs, -ūntis, F. a town on the southern coast of Sicily, famous for palms (iii. 705).

semel, *adv.* once, once for all.

sēmen, -inis [*sero*], N. a seed ; *pl.* elements, vital principles, seeds of life, germs (*of life, of fire*).

sēmēsus, -a, -um [*semi-* + *esus*], *adj.* half-eaten.

sēmianimis, -e [*semi-, animus*], *adj.* half alive, expiring, dying.

sēmifer, -era, -erum [*semi-* + *ferus*], *adj.* half-brute, monstrous.

sēmihomō, -inis [*semi-* + *homo*], *adj.* half-man.

sēminex, -necis [*semi-* + *nex*], *adj.* half dead, dying.

sēminō, -āre, -āvī, -ātum [*semen*], 1. *v. a.* sow, plant ; produce.

Semīramis, -idis, F. a queen of Assyria.

sēmisepultus, -a, -um [*semi-* + *sepultus*], *adj.* half buried.

sēmita, -ae [*se-*, *meo*, go], F. a by-path, a path, a way.

sēmivir, -virī, *adj.* half-man, effeminate, unmanly.

semper, *adv.* always, forever, ever, constantly.

sēmustus, -a, -um [*semi-* + *ustus* (*uro*)], *adj.* half burned, half consumed, charred.

senātus, -ūs [*senex*], M. the elders ; the Senate.

senecta, -ae [*senex*], F. age, old age.

senectūs, -tūtis [*senex*], F. age, old age.

seneō, -ēre, *no perf. or sup.* [*cf. senex*], 2. *v. n.* be old, spend one's last years.

senex, senis, *adj.* old, aged, venerable. — *Usually as subst.* M. an old man (*over forty-five*), an aged sire. — **senior, -ōris,** *compar.* older ; old, elderly, aged, venerable ; *as subst.* an elder, an old man.

sēnī, -ae, -a [*sex*], *distrib. adj. pl.* six each, six at a time.

senīlis, -e [*senex*], adj. old man's, aged.

sēnsus, -ūs [*sentio*], M. feeling, perception; a feeling; the mind, intelligence; the passions; the senses, the sense.

sententia, -ae [*sentio*], F. a way of thinking, a judgment; a purpose, a resolution, a determination; an opinion, a view of things; counsel (*a plan of action*).

sentiō, -īre, sēnsī, sēnsum, 4. *v. a.* perceive (*by the senses or mind*), hear, feel, see, observe; become aware; know, learn; learn to know, find out, understand.

sentis, -is, M. a thorn bush, a briar, a bramble.

sentus, -a, -um [*akin to sentis*], adj. rough, overgrown.

sēparō, -āre, -āvī, -ātum [*se-* + *paro*], 1. *v. a.* separate, divide; disjoin.

sepeliō, -īre, -īvī (-iī), sepultum, 4. *v. a.* bury, inter. — sepultus, -a, -um, *p.p. as adj. and subst.* buried; *also of wine and sleep*, overcome, buried: parce sepulto (spare one in his grave); custode sepulto (asleep).

septem, *indecl. num. adj.* seven.

septemgeminus, -a, -um, *adj.* sevenfold, seven-mouthed: Nilus.

septēnī, -ae, -a [*septem*], *num. adj. pl.* seven each, seven at a time; seven.

septimus, -a, -um [*septem*], *num. adj.* seventh.

sepulcrum, -ī [*sepelio*], N. a tomb, a burial place; burial.

sequāx, -ācis [*sequor*], adj. following, pursuing.

sequor, sequī, secūtus, 3. *v. dep.* follow (*lit. and fig.*), chase, pursue: iussa (obey); sequetur facilis (come away, *of plucking a branch*). — *Also*, accompany, side with: factum fortuna (prosper). — *Also*, follow after, aim at, seek: Italiam. — *Also of a route*, follow out, pursue, trace, pass through, go over, undergo: avia; fastigia; meliora (a higher destiny); fata (accomplish); quid sequens (following what course); extrema ferro (seek a desperate remedy). — sequēns, -entis, *p. as adj.* pursuing; *as subst.* a pursuer, the next.

serēnō, -āre, -āvī, -ātum [*serenus*], 1. *v. a.* clear, calm, smooth.

serēnus, -a, -um, *adj.* clear, fair, cloudless; calm, placid: nubes (light, dry). — N. *as subst.* serēnum, -ī, fair weather.

Serestus, -ī, M. one of the followers of Æneas (i. 611).

Sergestus, -ī, M. one of the followers of Æneas (i. 510).

Sergius, -a, -um, *adj.* a Roman gentile name: domus, the Sergian house (v. 121).

seriēs, -ēī [1. *sero*], F. a row, a line; a succession, a chain, a train.

sermō, -ōnis [1. *sero*], M. talk, conversation, speech, discourse, words; rumor.

1. serō, -ere, *no perf.*, sertum, 3. *v. a.* join, weave: multa serebant (talked much).

2. serō, -ere, sēvī, satum, 3. *v. a.* sow, plant; beget. — satus, -a, -um, *p.p. as adj.* sown; sprung from, born, descended from. — M.

as subst. son of, descendant of. — N. *pl.* sown fields, growing crops.

sērō [*abl. of* serus], *adv.* late; too late. — *Comp.* sērius.

serpēns, -entis [*p. of serpo*], c. a serpent, a snake.

serpō, -ere, serpsī, *no sup.*, *3. v. n.* crawl, creep; *of sleep*, steal over one.

Serrānus, -ī, M. C. Atilius Regulus Serranus, a famous Roman whose election to the consulship was announced to him while plough-ing (vi. 844).

sertum, -ī [*p.p. of* 1. *sero*], N. a gar-land, a wreath.

sērus, -a, -um, *adj.* late, too late, tardy; latest.

serva, -ae [F. *of servus*], F. a maid-servant.

servātor, -ōris [*servo*], M. a pre-server.

serviō, -īre, -īvī (-iī), -ītum [*servus*], *4. v. n.* be a slave, serve; obey, be subject to.

servitium, -ī (-iī) [*servus*], N. slav-ery, servitude.

servō, -āre, -āvī, -ātum [*servus*], *1.v.a.* watch over, guard, protect; save, preserve, keep alive; ratify; keep, maintain, hold, continue in, remain close to, live in (on); ob-serve, watch, note: fidem (keep one's word *or* faith). — servāns, -antis (*superl.* servantissimus), *p. as adj.* observant.

servus, -ī, M. a slave, a servant.

seu, *see* sīve.

sevērus, -a, -um, *adj.* grave, stern; dreadful: amnis.

sex. *num. adj. indecl.* six.

sī, *conj.* if, in case, *in conditions.* — *Also, where the condition is a mere form,* if (*it is true that*), since, as, when, whenever. — *In wishes,* if only, O if, O that, would that. — *With indef. pron. and adverbs:* si quis, *etc.,* if any one, *etc.,* whoever, whenever, *etc.* — *In a proviso,* if, in case, provided. — *Esp.* si modo, if only, provided that. — *Also* quam si, *in comparisons,* than if, than when, as if, as when. — *In indirect questions,* in case, if, whether. — *Concessive,* even if, though. — *In asseverations,* if, as sure as.

sībila, -ōrum, N. *pl.* a hissing, hisses.

sībilus, -a, -um, *adj.* hissing.

sībilus, -ī, M. a rustling.

Sibylla, -ae, F. a Sibyl, a female seer. One of the most famous was the Cumæan, by whom Æneas was conducted to the World Below (iii. 452; vi. 10 ff.).

sīc [*si* + -*ce*], *adv.* so, thus, in this way, in this wise, in this guise.

Sicānius, -a, -um, *adj.* of the Si-cani, Sicanian; Sicilian, of Sicily. — F. Sicānia, -ae, Sicily.

Sicānus, -a, -um, *adj.* of the Si-cani (a race of Italy, supposed to have colonized Sicily), Sicanian; Sicilian. — M. *pl.* the Sicani.

siccō, -āre, -āvī, -ātum [*siccus*], *1. v. a.* dry, dry up: cruores (stanch).

siccus, -a, -um, *adj.* dry, dried up, thirsty, parched.

sīcine [*sice, old form of sic,* + -*ne*], *interrog. adv.* thus, so (*in a ques-tion*); is it thus that . . . ?

sīcubĭ. *adv.* if anywhere, wherever.

Siculus, -a, -um, *adj.* Sicilian.

sīdereus, -a, -um [*sidus*], *adj.* star-like, starry.

sīdō, -ere, sīdī, *no sup.* [√*sed (of sedeo)*], *3. v. n.* sit down; alight.

Sīdōn, -ōnis, F. an ancient city of Phœnicia, from which Tyre was colonized (i. 619).

Sīdŏnius, -a, -um, *adj.* of Sidon, Sidonian; Tyrian, Phœnician.

sīdus, -eris, N. a constellation, a quarter of the sky; a heavenly orb (*including sun and moon*), a star: **sidera emensae** (starry regions). — *Also, mostly in pl.*, the heavens, Heaven, the stars of heaven, the skies, the sky; a season: **hiberno sidere.**

Sīgē(i)us, -a, -um, *adj.* of Sigeum, a promontory of the Troad.

signō, -āre, -āvī, -ātum [*signum*], *1. v. a.* mark, mark out (**viam**); discern, mark, notice, fix the eye on (**ultima; ora**); honor, distinguish, mark.

signum, -ī, N. a mark, a sign; a track; a signal, a watchword; an image, a figure, a carving, a relief; embroidery; a constellation, a star, a sign (*of the Zodiac*); *in pl.* the standards (*of an army*).

silēns, *p. of* sileō.

silentium, -ī (-iī) [*silens*], N. stillness, silence, quiet; secrecy.

Sīlēnus, -ī, M. an old Satyr, chief attendant of Bacchus.

sileō, -ēre, -uī, *no sup.*, *2. v. n. and a.* be silent, keep silence, be dumb, be still, be quiet, be noiseless; leave unsung. — **silēns, -entis,** *p. as adj.* silent, still. — M. *pl. as subst.* the silent shades.

silēscō, -ere, *no perf. or sup.* [*sileo*], *3. v. n.* become silent, be hushed, become calm.

silex, -icis, C. flint; a rock, a cliff.

silva, -ae, F. a wood, a forest, woodland, the woods; a thicket, a thick growth: **iuga silvarum,** wooded heights.

silvestris, -tre [*silva*], *adj.* woodland.

Silvius, -ī (-iī) [*silva*], M. a name of several kings of Alba, *esp.* the son of Æneas and founder of the line, and Silvius Æneas, a later offshoot of the stock (vi. 763).

similis, -e [*cf. simul*], *adj.* like, of the same kind, similar.

Simoīs, -entis, M. a river of the Troad (i. 100); also a river in Epirus named after it (iii. 302).

simplex, -icis [*sim-* (*as in simul, similis*) + *-plex* (*cf. plico*)], *adj.* single, simple; pure, untainted; unsuspecting.

simul [*cf. similis*], *adv.* at the same time, at once, together; immediately. — *With participle*, while: **simul memorans.** — **simul ... simul,** at once ... and, and at the same time, both ... and also. — **simul (ac),** as soon as.

simulācrum, -ī [*simulo*], N. an image, a statue; a spectre, a ghost, a phantom; a mimicry, an imitation.

simulō, -āre, -āvī, -ātum [*similis*], *1. v. a.* make like, counterfeit, imitate; pretend, feign: **simulans multa** (making many pretences). — **simulātus, -a, -um,** *p.p.* made like, counterfeit, pretended, false: **simulata mente** (with deceitful purpose); verba (assumed); magnis Pergama (imitating, *etc.*).

sīn [*si* + *ne*, if not], *conj.* but if, if however, if on the other hand.

sine, *prep.* without : sine fine furens (ungovernably).

singulī, -ae, -a [*cf. simul*], *adj. pl.* one at a time, one by one, each in detail, singly (*in adv. force*) : inter singula verba (with every word). — N. *as subst.* each thing, everything, every object, every point *or* detail.

singultus, -ūs, M. sobbing, sobs.

sinister, -tra, -trum, *adj.* left-hand, left, on the left. — F. *as subst.* sinistra (*sc.* manus), the left hand.

sinō, -ere, sīvī, situm, 3. *v. a.* permit, allow, let, suffer.

Sinōn, -ōnis, M. the spy who induced the Trojans to admit the Wooden Horse (ii. 79).

sinuō, -āre, -āvī, -ātum [*sinus*], 1. *v. a.* bend, fold, twist.

sinus, -ūs, M. a bend, a hollow surface; a fold (*of a garment*); a curve; a bay, a gulf, a cove; a bellying (i. e. *swelling*) sail; the bosom (*where the folds of the garment cross*), the lap, the breast; an embrace : Cocytus sinu labens (in its winding course).

Sipylus, -ī, M. son of Niobe.

sīqua, sīquando, sīquis, *see* sī, quis, *etc.*

Sīrēn, -ēnis, F. *mostly pl.* the Sirens, monsters with women's heads and the bodies of birds, who enticed mariners to the shore. Their abode was upon three islands off the Bay of Naples, which were called Sirenum scopuli (v. 864).

Sīrius, -ī (-iī), M. Sirius, the Dog Star, which rose with the sun (at the period when the popular astronomy began) about the middle of July; hence associated with extreme heat (iii. 141).

Sirmiō, -ōnis, M. an Italian peninsula (now Sermione), the home of Catullus.

sistō, -ere, stitī (stetī), statum [√*sta* (*of* sto) *reduplicated*], 3. *v. a. and n.* Trans. (*causative*) (cause to stand), set, place; bring; stop, stay, check (gradum); set up, restore, be the stay of. — *Intrans.* stand still, settle, stop, stay.

sistrum, -ī, N. a sistrum, a musical instrument of rods moving in a frame, used by the Egyptians in the worship of Isis and perhaps in war.

Sīsyphus, -ī, M. a king of Corinth, son of Æolus.

sitis, -is, F. thirst, drought.

situs, -ūs [*sino*], M. a position, a place; neglect, want of care.

sīve (seu) [*si* + *-ve*], *conj.* or if. — *Repeated*, if either . . . or, whether . . . or, if . . . or if, if . . . or if on the other hand, either . . . or.

sobrius, -a, -um, *adj.* sober, temperate, in (one's) moderation.

socer, -erī, M. a father-in-law; *pl.* parents-in-law.

sociō, -āre, -āvī, -ātum [*socius*], 1. *v. a.* ally, attach, unite, join, associate : urbe domo nos (adopt us, share with us).

socius, -a, -um [√*sec* (*in* sequor)], *adj.* accompanying, allied, associated, friendly : agmina (allied, of friends); **arma** (alliance in arms); **agmen** (band of allies); **rates** (allied, of his countrymen); **penates** (kindred). — M. *and* F. *as subst.* a companion, a follower, a friend, an associate, a comrade.

sodālicium, -ī (-iī) [*sodalis*], N. comradeship, intimate friendship.

sodālis, -is, C. a companion, a comrade.

sōl, sōlis, M. the sun; sunshine, the heat *or* light of the sun: **sol cadens** (the west, the setting sun, the region of sunset). — *Pl.* days.

sōlācium, -ī (-iī) [*solor*], N. solace, consolation.

sōlāmen, -inis [*solor*], N. solace, comfort.

soleō, -ēre, solitus, 2. *v. semidep.* be wont, be accustomed, use.

solidus, -a, -um [*solum*], adj. solid, firm, stout, strong; entire; unimpaired, vigorous.— N. *as subst.* **solidum, -ī,** the solid ground, the firm earth.

solium, -ī (-iī), N. a seat, a throne.

sollemnis, -e, *adj.* yearly, annual, stated, appointed; solemn, sacred, festival; customary, time-honored. — N. *pl. as subst.* **sollemnia,** sacred rites, funeral ceremonies.

sollicitō, -āre, -āvī, -ātum [*sollicitus*], 1. *v. a.* stir up, agitate; disturb, trouble, worry.

sollicitus, -a, -um, *adj.* agitated, troubled, anxious, in anxiety.

sōlor, -ārī, -ātus, 1. *v. dep.* console, relieve, comfort, cheer, encourage; alleviate, lighten, relieve: **casum** (find comfort for); **solando lenire** (relieve by consolation).

solum, -ī, N. the ground, the land, the earth, the soil, earth, land; a site; the surface: **subtrahitur solum** (the surface of the sea flies beneath them).

sōlus, -a, -um, *gen.* **-ius,** *adj.* alone, single, only, the only; lonely, solitary, deserted, in loneliness, in solitude.

solvō, -ere, solvī, solūtum, 3. *v. a. Of a bond* (*lit. and fig.*), unbind, loosen, relax, cast off, dismiss: **funem; corde metum; pudorem.** — *Of the person or thing bound,* release, set free, deliver, loosen, break up, dissolve, relax, unfurl: **te corpore; se luctu** (shake off); **phaselum** (unmoor); **solutae Iliades crinem** (with hair unbound, flowing hair); **lumina** (relax); **solvitur in somnos** (sinks); **vela** (unfurl); **solutae curae** (release from cares).— *Also,* pay (*unbind an obligation*), discharge, perform: **vota; omnia** (all your duties).

somnium, -ī (-iī) [†*somnus*], N. a dream.

somnus, -ī [√*sop* (*of sopio*)], M. sleep, slumber; a dream, a vision; night. — *Personified,* Sleep.

sonipēs, -edis [*sonus, pes*], M. the horse with ringing hoof, the prancing steed.

sonitus, -ūs [*sono*], M. a sound, a noise, a din, a rattle, a crash, a clang: **pedum** (tramp).

sonō, -āre, -uī, -itum [*sonus*], 1. *v. n.* give forth a sound, sound, resound, ring, roar; rattle; twang (*of a bow, etc.*); thunder. — *With cognate acc.* sound, speak: **neç**

mortale sonans (with no mortal voice); **nec vox hominem sonat** (sound human). — **sonāns, -antis,** *p. as adj.* sounding, resounding, roaring, murmuring, rattling, twanging, noisy, screaming : **pelagus; scopuli; arcus; turba.**

sonōrus, -a, -um [*cf. sono*], *adj.* sounding, noisy, roaring.

sōns, sontis, *adj.* guilty. — M. *pl. as subst.* the guilty.

sonus, -ī, M. a sound, a ring, a murmur, a din, an uproar ; voice. — *Pl.* speech, story.

sōpiō, -īre, -īvī (-iī), -ītum, *4. v. a.* lull to sleep. — **sōpitus, -a, -um,** *p.p. as adj.* put to sleep : **sopitus somno** (buried in sleep); **ignes** (half extinguished).

sopor, -ōris [*cf. sopio*], M. sleep. — *Personified,* Sleep.

sopōrifer, -era, -erum [*sopor, fero*], *adj.* sleep-inducing, drowsy.

sopōrō, -āre, *no perf.,* **-ātum** [*sopor*], *1. v. a.* put to sleep. — **sopōrātus, -a, -um,** *p.p. as adj.* soporific, endued with sleep, sleep-drenched.

sopōrus, -a, -um [*sopor*], *adj.* drowsy.

sorbeō, -ēre, -uī, *no sup., 2. v. a.* suck in, swallow up.

sordēs, -is, F. dirt, filth, squalor.

sordidus, -a, -um [*sordes*], *adj.* foul, filthy, squalid ; base, shameful.

soror, -ōris, F. a sister.

sors, sortis, F. a lot, a division, a part ; a lot (*cast*), fate, destiny, fortune ; an allotment : **ultra sortem senectae** (beyond the common lot); **sorte** (by lot, by fate, by allotment). — *Also (from divination by lots), generally pl.,* an oracle, oracles, prophetic words.

sortior, -īrī, -ītus [*sors*], *4. v. dep.* allot, choose by lot, obtain ; divide by lot, decide.

sortītus, -ūs [*sortior*], M. an assignment, an allotment.

sospes, -itis, *adj.* happy and prosperous.

spargō, -ere, sparsī, sparsum, *3. v. a.* strew, scatter, spread, diffuse ; sprinkle ; bestrew, besprinkle, bespatter ; stain, spot. — *P.p.* dishevelled : **capilli.**

Sparta, -ae, F. also called Lacedæmon, the capital of Laconia (ii. 577).

Spartānus, -a, -um, *adj.* Spartan (i. 316).

Spartē, -ēs, F. Sparta.

spatior, -ārī, -ātus [*spatium*], *1. v. dep.* walk to and fro.

spatiōsus, -a, -um [*spatium*], *adj.* huge.

spatium, -ī (-iī), N. (*often pl.*), a space, a distance, an interval, room, place, a course, size ; **spatio extremo** (at the end of the course); **corripiunt spatia** (they fly over the course). — *Fig.* time, room : **furori.**

speciēs, -ēī [*specio*], F. appearance, a sight : **specie movetur** (by appearances).

speciōsus, -a, -um [*species*], *adj.* beautiful, splendid.

spectābilis, -e [*specto*], *adj.* visible, conspicuous, notable, splendid.

spectāculum, -ī [*specto*], N. a spectacle, a sight.

spectō, -āre, -āvī, -ātum [*cf. specio*], *1. v. a.* gaze upon, gaze at; view, consider, regard. — spectātus, -a, -um, *p.p.* tried, tested, proved.

specula, -ae [*cf. specio*], F. a watchtower, a lookout.

speculor, -ārī, -ātus [*specula*], *1. v. dep.* watch, watch to see, take sight at, aim at, espy.

specus, -ūs, M., F., N. a cave.

spēlunca, -ae, F. a chasm, a cavern, a cave, a cleft (*in a rock*), a grotto.

spernō, -ere, sprēvī, sprētum, *3. v. a.* spurn; scorn, reject, despise, disdain, slight.

spērō, -āre, -āvī, -ātum [*spes*], *1. v. a. and n.* hope, hope for; expect, wait for; fear.

spēs, speī, F. hope, expectation.

spīculum, -ī [*spica*], N. a dart (*a light missile weapon*), a javelin.

spīna, -ae, F. a thorn; the spine.

Spīō, -ūs, F. a sea-nymph (v. 826).

spīra, -ae, F. a coil, a fold.

spīrābilis, -e [*spiro*], *adj.* respirable: spirabile lumen (light and air).

spīritus, -ūs [*spiro*], M. the breath, the breath of life; life; spirit *or* soul; high spirit, courage; a celestial soul (*the divine ether*).

spīrō, -āre, -āvī, -ātum, *1. v. n. and a.* breathe, blow.—*With cogn. acc.* breathe forth, breathe, shed. — spīrāns, -antis, *p.*: aera (breathing, *as if alive*); exta (palpitating).

spissus, -a, -um, *adj.* thick, close, close-packed: arena.

splendeō, -ēre, *no perf., no sup.*, *2. v. n.* shine, gleam.

splendidus, -a, -um [*splendeo*], *adj.* bright, clear; magnificent, stately.

spoliō, -āre, -āvī, -ātum [*spolium*], *1. v. a.* strip, despoil, spoil; deprive, bereave, rob.

spolium, -ī (-iī), N. spoil, spoils, trophy.

sponda, -ae, F. a couch.

spondeō, -ēre, spopondī, spōnsum [√*spond*, pour (*libations*)], *2. v. a. and n.* promise, promise one's self, be assured of. — spōnsus, *p.p. as subst.* M. a betrothed husband. — spōnsa, *p.p. as subst.* F. a betrothed bride, one's betrothed.

spōnsa, spōnsus, *see* spondeō.

sponte [*abl. of lost spons*], F. of one's own accord, voluntarily, by one's own wishes *or* will: sponte sua (spontaneously, of itself, of themselves); sponte mea componere curas (in my own way, by my own will).

spūma, -ae [*spuo*], F. foam, spray.

spūmeus, -a, -um [*spuma*], *adj.* foamy, foaming, foam-covered.

spūmiger, -era, -erum [*spuma, gero*], *adj.* foaming.

spūmō, -āre, -āvī, -ātum [*spuma*], *1. v. n.* foam, be covered with foam *or* spray. — spūmāns, -antis, *p. as adj.* foaming: ensis cruore (reeking).

spūmōsus, -a, -um [*spuma*], *adj.* foamy, foaming.

squāleō, -ēre, -uī, *no sup.*, *2. v. n.* be rough. — squālēns, -entis, *p. as adj.* rough, unkempt.

squālidus, -a, -um, *adj.* squalid, in mourning guise, mourning; filthy.

squālor,-ōris [*squaleo*], M. foulness, filthiness.

squāma, -ae, F. a scale (*of a serpent*).

squāmeus, -a, -um [*squama*], adj. scaly.

squāmiger, -era, -erum [*squama, gero*], adj. scaly.

squāmōsus, -a, -um [*squama*], adj. scaly.

stabilis, -e [*sto*], adj. stable, firm; lasting.

stabulō, -āre, *no perf., no sup.* [*stabulum*], 1. *v. n.* have a stable, be kept; dwell, have their stalls.

stabulum, -ī [*sto*], N. a stall, a stable; an abode (*of wild beasts*); a pasture.

stāgnō, -āre, -āvī, -ātum [*stagnum*], 1. *v. n.* stagnate. — stāgnāns, -antis, *p. as adj.* stagnant.

stāgnum, -ī, N. a pool, standing water; a lake. — *In pl.* deep waters, the depths (*of the sea where the water is still*), a sluggish stream, sluggish waters.

statiō, -ōnis [*sto*], F. a standing; a station, a resting place; a harbor, a roadstead.

statuō, -uere, -uī, -ūtum [*status*], 3. *v. a.* set up, place; build, found; throw up (*a mound*); resolve, decide.

stella, -ae, F. a star, a planet; a shooting star, a meteor.

stellātus, -a, -um [*stella*], adj. studded (*as with stars*).

sterilis, -e, adj. barren, sterile, unfruitful.

sternō, -ere, strāvī, strātum, 3. *v. a.* spread out, lay flat, strew; lay low, fell, bring down, slay, slaughter; lay waste, sweep away, overwhelm, overthrow; level, smooth; bestrew, cover. — *Pass.* fall, lie strewn, throw one's self down. — strātus, -a, -um, *p.p. as adj.* outspread; slain: stratum ostrum (a purple couch). — N. *sing. and pl.* strātum, strāta, a bed, a couch; a pavement.

Sthenelus, -ī, M. a Grecian warrior, the charioteer of Diomede (ii. 261).

stillō, -āre, -āvī, -ātum, 1. *v. n.* drop, trickle.

stimulō, -āre, -āvī, -ātum [*stimulus*], 1. *v. a.* spur on, goad; *fig.* goad to frenzy, excite, urge, incite.

stimulus, -ī, M. a goad, a spur.

stīpendium, -ī (-iī) [*stips, pendo*], N. tribute.

stīpes, -itis [*akin to stipo*], M. a trunk, a tree trunk.

stīpō, -āre, -āvī, -ātum [*cf. stipes*], 1. *v. a.* cram, crowd, pack; stow, load; accompany, escort, attend upon.— stīpātus, -a, -um, *p.p.* dense, escorted.

stirps, stirpis, C. a stock, a stem, a root (*with the stock*); a race, a lineage, a family. — *Of individuals*, a scion, the progeny.

stīva, -ae, F. a plough handle.

stō, stāre, stetī, (statūrus) [√*sta*], 1. *v. n., lit. and fig., of persons and things*, stand, stand there, lie, be (*in descriptions*); stand erect, stand on end (comae); rise (*of a tower, etc.*), be built; stand out (lumina flammā). — *Esp., lit. and fig.*, stand fast *or* firm, take one's stand, remain; lie at anchor; rest *or* depend on : stat gravis Entellus ; ferri acies ; vires solidae ; res Ilia ; puppes, classes ; spes (rest on) ; cura (centre in). — *Impers.* stat, it is fixed *or* determined, one is resolved : stat casūs renovare. —*Impers. pass.* statur, they stand *or* abide by : pacto.

strāgēs, -is [*cf. sterno*], F. slaughter, havoc, carnage : confusae stragis acervus (a confused heap of slain).

strātum, *see* sternō.

strepitus, -ūs [*strepo*], M. a noise, a din, a roar ; a busy hum (*of a city*).

strepō, -ere, -uī, *no sup.*, 3. *v. n.* ring, sound : strepit murmure (is alive with).

strīdeō, -ēre, strīdī, *no sup.*, 2. *v. n.* grate, creak ; roar, howl (*of the blast*) ; twang ; flap (*of wings*) ; gurgle (*of a wound*) ; hiss, whiz.

strīdō, -ere, strīdī, *no sup.*, 3. *v. n. same senses as* strīdeō.

strīdor, -ōris [*strido*], M. a creaking, a clanking, a whizzing ; a flapping of wings, whistling wings.

strīdulus, -a, -um [*strido*], *adj.* whizzing, hissing.

stringō, -ere, strīnxī, strictum, 3. *v. a.* bind, compress ; draw, unsheathe ; touch, graze ; strip, trim ; wear away *or* wash (*of a river*).

Strophades, -um, F. *pl.* two islands of the Ionian Sea south of Zacynthus (iii. 209).

struō, -ere, strūxī, strūctum, 3. *v. a.* pile, heap up ; build, erect, raise ; dispose, arrange, prepare, set forth (penum) ; plot, design, aim at, accomplish ; load with.

Strȳmōn, -ōnis, M. a river in Thrace.

studium, -ī (-iī) [*cf. studeo*], N. zeal, eagerness ; diligence, care, earnestness ; eager interest, desire ; favor, enthusiasm, applause ; a pursuit, a study, an interest : studia contraria (different parties).

stultē [*stultus*], *adv.* foolishly, ignorantly.

stultus, -a, -um, *adj.* foolish.

stupefaciō, -ere, -fēcī, -factum [*stupeo, facio*], 3. *v. a.* stun, daze, stupefy, astonish, overwhelm.

stupeō, -ēre, -uī, *no sup.*, 2. *v. n. and a.* be amazed, be thunderstruck, be astonished, wonder, marvel ; marvel at.

stuppa, -ae, F. tow, hemp (*used for calking*).

stuppeus, -a, -um [*stuppa*], *adj.* of tow, hempen.

Stygius, -a, -um, *adj.* of the Styx, Stygian ; of the Lower World, of Hades : Iuppiter, rex (Pluto).

Styx, -ygis, F. the river that surrounded the World Below.

suādeō, -ēre, suāsī, suāsum, 2. *v. n. and a.* advise, counsel, persuade, invite, suggest, prompt, impel : tibi haec litora Delius (warned you to seek).

suādus, *see* malesuāda.

suāvis, -e, *adj.* sweet.

sub, *prep. with abl.* under, below, beneath ; near (*a high object*), at the foot of, close to, just at, just behind, in (*a lower place, or of light and night conceived as above*) : sub pectore (in one's breast) ; sub sole (in the sun, in the sunlight, under the light of the sun; **sub antris** (in). — *With acc.* under, beneath, toward, up to (*up under*); about: **sub ora** (before the face); **sub auras** (to the light of day, up, forth); **sub noctem** (toward night). — *In comp., as adv.* under; up; in place of; slightly; by stealth; toward; after.

subdō, -dere, -didī, -ditum, *3. v. a.* place under; plunge: **se subdit,** plunges, dives.

subdūcō, -ere, -dūxī, -ductum, *3. v. a.* draw up, beach (*ships*); take from under, take away, withdraw, remove, steal: **subducta unda** (slipping from beneath).

subeō, -īre, -īvī (-iī), -itum, *irr. v. n. and a.* go under; take up, support, bear; be harnessed to, draw (**currum**); come up, succeed, take the place of, come next, follow; approach, enter, come into *or* to; take (*the helm*); occur, come to one's mind, suggest itself: **subit ira** (the angry desire comes over, anger prompts). — **subitus, -a, -um,** *p.p. as adj.* (coming stealthily,) sudden, unexpected. — *Abl.* **subitō,** *as adv.* suddenly, unexpectedly.

subiciō, -ere, -iēcī, -iectum [*sub + iacio*], *3. v. a.* throw under, place under; set (*of fire*), kindle; throw in. — **subiectus, -a, -um,** *p.p. as adj.* placed *or* applied beneath, beneath. — M. *pl. as subst.* **subiectī,** subjects, the conquered.

subigō, -igere, -ēgī, -āctum [*sub + ago*], *3. v. a.* impel, shove; subdue, conquer; compel, force, constrain.

subitō [*subitus*], *adv.* suddenly.

subitus, -a, -um. *p.p. of* subeō.

sublābor, -lābī, -lāpsus, *3. v. dep.* fall back, fail.

sublātus, -a, -um, *p.p. of* sufferō *and* tollō.

subligō, -āre, -āvī, -ātum, *1. v. a.* bind beneath, bind on.

sublīmis, -e, *adj.* high, lofty; on high, raised high, borne aloft.

sublūstris, -e [*cf.* **lux**], *adj.* dimly lighted, glimmering.

submergō, -ere, -mersī, -mersum, *3. v. a.* drown, overwhelm, sink.

submittō, -ere, -mīsī, -missum, *3. v. a.* let down, sink; cast down (*the eyes*); subdue, subject (**animos amori**).

submoveō, -ēre, -mōvī, -mōtum, *2. v. a.* remove, clear away, drive away; push out: **litora.** — **submōtus, -a, -um,** *p.p.* hollowed out.

subnectō, -ere, -nexuī, -nexum, *3. v. a.* bind beneath; bind round, fasten, bind, confine.

subnexus, -a, -um, *p.p. of* subnectō.

subnīxus, -a, -um, *p.p. as adj.* supported by, resting on, sitting.

subolēs, -is, F. offspring; a child, an infant.

subrēmigō, -āre, *no perf. or sup.,* *1. v. n.* row quietly along.

subrīdeō, -ēre, -rīsī, *no sup.,* *2. v. n.* smile.

subrigō, *see* surgō.

subs-, *form of* sub *in composition.*

subsequor, -sequī, -secūtus, *3. v. dep.* follow closely.

subsīdō, -ere, -sēdī, -sessum, *3. v. n.* sink down, sink; subside, abate : Acestes galea (remain at the bottom).

subsistō, -ere, -stitī, *no sup.*, *3. v. n.* stay behind, lag behind, stop, halt ; hold out.

subsum, -esse, -fuī, *irr. v. n.* be under *or* at the foot of.

subtēmen, -inis [*cf. subtexo*], N. the woof, thread.

subter [*sub*], *adv.* beneath, below, underneath. — *Prep.* (*with acc. or abl.*), under, beneath.

subtexō, -ere, -texuī, -textum, *3. v. a.* line ; cover with a veil, veil.

subtrahō, -ere, -trāxī, -trāctum, *3. v. a.* withdraw : subtrahitur solum (the sea flies beneath them).

suburgeō, -ēre, *no perf.*, *no sup.*, *2. v. a.* force up to, force towards, drive close to.

subvectō, -āre, -āvī, -ātum [*cf. subveho*], *1. v. a.* transport, ferry over.

subvehō, -ere, -vexī, -vectum, *3. v. a.* carry up.—*Pass.* be borne up, ride, drive : nox bigis subvecta (driving her two-horse chariot).

subvolvō, -ere, *no perf.*, *no sup.*, *3. v. a.* roll up.

succēdō, -ere, -cessī, -cessum [*sub + cedo*], *3. v. n.* go beneath ; go down ; take up (*a burden*), bear, draw (*of a chariot drawn by a yoke*) ; come to, repair to, go into, approach ; enter.

successor, -ōris [*succedo*], M. a successor.

successus, -ūs [*succedo*], M. success.

succingō, -ere, -cīnxī, -cīnctum [*sub + cingo*], *3. v. a.* bind under, gird about.

succumbō, -ere, -cubuī, -cubitum [*sub + cumbo*], *3. v. n.* fall under ; yield to, give way to.

succurrō, -ere, -currī, -cursum [*sub + curro*], *3. v. n.* run to aid, come to the rescue of, rescue, save, help, relieve, succor ; occur (*to one's mind*) : succurrit (the thought occurs to me).

sūcus, -ī, M. juice ; dye.

sūdō, -āre, -āvī, -ātum, *1. v. n. and a.* sweat ; reek with : sanguine.

sūdor, -ōris [*sudo*], M. sweat, perspiration.

suēscō, -ere, suēvī, suētum, *3. v. n. and a.* be wont, be accustomed, be used. — suētus, -a, -um, *p.p.* accustomed, used, wont.

sufferō, -ferre, sustulī, sublātum [*sub* (*subs-*) + *fero*], *irr.v. a.* bear up ; withstand, hold out, resist.

sufficiō, -ere, -fēcī, -fectum [*sub + facio*], *3. v. a. and n.* dip in, dye ; supply, furnish ; be sufficient, hold out, be able. — suffectus, -a, -um, *p.p.* suffused.

suffundō, -ere, -fūdī, -fūsum [*sub + fundo*], *3. v. a.* pour in, fill. — suffūsus, -a, -um, *p.p.* suffused, filled, overflowing.

suī, *gen.* (*nom. wanting*), *reflex. pron. 3d pers. referring to the subject*, himself, herself, itself, themselves ; *reciprocal*, one another, each other, one the other. — *Redupl.*, sēsē, *in same senses*.

sulcō, -āre, -āvī, -ātum [*sulcus*], *1. v. a.* plough.

sulcus, -ī, M. a furrow ; a train (*of meteor*).

Sulmō, -ōnis, M. an Italian town, Ovid's birthplace.

sulpur, -uris, N. sulphur.

sum, esse, fuī, futūrus [√*es and* √*bhu*], *irr. v. n.* be, exist, live. —*Impers.* it is possible, it is allowed, one can, one may. — **forem,** *etc., equivalent to* essem. — **fore,** *equivalent to* futūrus, *etc.,* esse. — futūrus, -a, -um, *p.p. as adj.* future, coming. — N. futūrum *and pl.* futūra, *as subst.* the future.

summa, -ae [F. *of summus*], F. the main thing, the chief point.

summus, *see* superus.

sūmō, -ere, sūmpsī, sūmptum [*sub + emo,* take], *3. v. a.* take, accept, assume, put on, wear, bear (*arms*); take up, adopt. — *Esp.* with **poenas,** exact (*the penalty*), inflict, satisfy (*the debt of vengeance due*).

suō, -ere, suī, sūtum, *3. v. a.* sew.

super, *adv. and prep. Adv.* above, over, over all, up on *or* above, on the top; over and above, remaining, left, besides, further, furthermore, and then: **satis superque** (enough and more than enough). — *Also,* from above. — *Prep.* (*with acc.*), upon (*oftener of motion to*), on the top of, above, over, besides, beyond; (*with abl.*) upon, on (*of rest*); on (*fig.*), concerning, about, for the sake of, for.

superātor, -ōris [*supero*], M. conqueror.

superbia, -ae [*superbus*], F. pride, arrogance, insolence.

superbus, -a, -um [*super*], *adj.* overweening, proud, haughty, arrogant, insolent; lawless, fierce,

ferocious; splendid, magnificent, superb, glorious, high, stately: **aulaea; coniugium** (high alliance). — *Also, in a good sense,* proud, lofty, high-minded: **anima Bruti.**

superēmineō, -ēre, *no perf., no sup., 2. v. a.* tower above.

superiaciō, -ere, -iēcī, -iectum, *3. v. a.* throw over. — *P.p.* superiectus, -a, -um, spread over, all-covering, flooding.

superimpōnō, -ere, *no perf.,* **-positum,** *3. v. a.* to place *or* lay (*anything*) upon.

supernĕ [*supernus*], *adv.* above, in the World Above (*on earth*).

superō, -āre, -āvī, -ātum [*superus*], *1. v. a. and n.* rise above, surmount; ascend; overcome, conquer, vanquish, prevail upon, overpower; surpass; gain the mastery, win (*a race*); gain (**locum priorem**); go over, pass beyond, pass, pass by (**Gyan**); be over and above, remain, survive; be lofty *or* elated (**animis**).

superstes, -stitis [*supersto*], *adj.* remaining, surviving.

supersum, -esse, -fuī, *irr. v. n.* (be over and above), remain, survive, still remain, be left, continue: **quod superest,** what alone remains, as to the rest, furthermore.

superus, -a, -um [*cf. super*], *adj.* (*mostly pl.*), above, upper, above; on high, high: **regna** (*of heaven*), **orae** (the Upper World). — M. *pl. as subst.* superī, -ōrum, the gods above; the World Above, men on earth; mortal men: **apud superos** (in the Upper World, on earth). — N. *pl. as subst.* **supera,** **-ōrum,** the World Above, the heavens, the sky, Heaven. — *Compar.* superior, -ōris. — *Superl.* suprēmus, -a, -um, last, supreme, extreme: **macies; salus** (last hope of safety) ; **supremo in tempore** (last crisis, utmost need) ; **montes** (highest, mountain heights). — N. *pl. as subst.* suprēma, -ōrum, the last offices, last sad rites, funeral rites. — N. *sing. as subst. or adv.* suprēmum, the last time, for the last time : **supremum gemuit** (groaned his last). — **summus, -a, -um,** highest, the top of, uppermost, topmost, the highest part of, upper, the surface of, the end of, the head of, the tip of : **summo in fluctu** (the crest). — *Fig.* highest, supreme, most important, chief, main, utmost, greatest, extreme ; last, final, supreme : **fastigia rerum** (principal points) ; **summa res** (the main struggle) ; **dies** (final, supreme moment). — N. *pl. as subst.* the top, the summit.

supīnus, -a, -um [*sub*], *adj.* lying on the back ; *of the hands,* upturned, suppliant.

suppleō, -ēre, -plēvī, -plētum [*sub* + *pleo*], 2. *v. a.* supply, fill up.

supplex, -plicis [*sub* + *-plex* (*cf. plico*)], *adj.* (kneeling), suppliant, as a suppliant, entreating, on one's knees (*fig.*), in supplication, in suppliant guise ; *as subst.* a suppliant.

suppliciter [*supplex*], *adv.* as a suppliant, in suppliant guise.

supplicium, -ī (-iī) [*supplex*], N. punishment, a penalty : **dira supplicia** (traces of punishment, wounds).

suppōnō, -ere, -posuī, -positum (-postum) [*sub* + *pono*], 3. *v. a.* place beneath, put under, apply ; substitute. — *P.p.* suppositus, -a, -um, lying beneath, beneath.

suprā, *prep. with acc.* above, over.

suprēmus, -a, -um, *see* superus.

sūra, -ae, F. the calf of the leg, the ankle ; the leg.

surgō (*rarely* subrigō), -ere, surrēxī, surrēctum [*sub* + *rego*], 3. *v. n.* raise one's self, rise, arise ; grow, increase : **animo sententia** (occur to) ; **limina gradibus** (stand high, crown).

sūs, suis, C. a swine, a boar, a sow, a pig.

suscipiō, -ere, -cēpī, -ceptum [*subs-* + *capio*], 3. *v. a.* take up, raise up, catch ; take upon one's self ; bear, beget ; begin, take up, reply.

suscitō, -āre, -āvī, -ātum [*subs-* + *cito*], 1. *v. a.* shake up, stir up ; rouse, stir, provoke, awake.

suspectus, -ūs [*suspicio*], M. a look upward, height, distance (*up*).

suspendō, -ere, -pendī, -pēnsum [*subs-* + *pendo*], 3. *v. a.* hang up, hang, suspend ; dedicate (**arma**) ; check, hold back : **fletum.** — suspēnsus, -a, -um, *p.p.* hung up, suspended ; floating ; anxious, in suspense, in alarm : **multo suspensum numine** (awed).

suspiciō, -ere, -spexī, -spectum [*subs-* + *specio*], 3. *v. a. and n.* look up at ; gaze at, observe. —

suspectus, -a, -um, *p.p. as adj.* suspected, an object of suspicion, distrusted.

suspicor, -ārī, -ātus, *1. v. dep.* suspect.

suspīrō, -āre, -āvī, -ātum [*sub- + spiro*], *1. v. n.* sigh.

sustentō, -āre, -āvī, -ātum [*subs- + tento*], *1. v. a.* hold up, hold, support.

sustineō, -ēre, -uī, -tentum [*subs- + teneo*], *2. v. a.* hold up, hold out, hold, withstand; bear, be strong enough.

sustulī, *see* tollō.

sūtilis, -e [*sutus, suo*], *adj.* sewn, sewed: cymba (patched, *either of hides, rushes, or papyrus*).

suus, -a, -um [*cf. se*], *poss. pron.* (*of 3d pers. reflex.*), his, her, its, their; his own, *etc.*; one's own, favoring, propitious, favorable, suitable, appropriate, fitting. — M. *pl.* his, *etc.*, friends, followers, companions, fellow-citizens, men, race, *etc.* — N. his, *etc.* affairs, property, interests, *etc.*

Sy̆chaeus, -a, -um, *adj.* of Sy-chæus: cinis (iv. 552).

Sy̆chaeus, -ī, M. the husband of Dido (i. 343).

syrtis, -is, F. a sandbank, a shoal. — Two shallow bays on the coast of Africa were called respectively Syrtis Maior (now Gulf of Sidra) and Minor (Gulf of Cabes). — *Pl.* the Syrtes; the sandbanks, bars and coast of all that region.

tābeō, -ēre, *no perf., no sup.* [*ta-bes*], *2. v. n.* waste away, melt away: tabentes artus (dripping).

tābēs, -is, F. a wasting, pining; pestilence.

tābēscō, -ere, tābuī, *no sup.* [*ta-beo*], *3. v. n.* begin to melt, melt.

tābidus, -a, -um [*tabes*], *adj.* wasting.

tabula, -ae, F. a plank, a board.

tabulātus, -a, -um [*tabula*], *adj.* boarded, floored. — N. *as subst.* tabulātum, -ī, a floor, a story, an upper story.

tābum, -ī [*cf. tabes*], N. matter (*of putrefaction*), gore.

taceō, -ēre, -uī, -itum, *2. v. n.* be silent, keep silence; be noiseless, be still. — tacitus, -a, -um, *p.p. as adj.* silent (*often equal to adv.* silently); still, noiseless, quiet; secret, in secret, unseen, unnoticed; unmentioned, unsung: quis te tacitum relinquat?

taciturnus, -a, -um [*tacitus*], *adj.* silent, without speaking.

tacitus, -a, -um [*taceo*], *adj.* still, silent, secret.

tāctus, -ūs [*tango*], M. touch.

taeda, -ae, F. a pine tree, pine wood; a pine torch, a torch; the marriage torch, marriage.

taedet, -ēre, -uit (taesum, per-taesum est), *2. v. impers.* it wearies, it disgusts, one is weary (disgusted), one loathes.

taedium, ī (-iī) [*taedet*], N. weariness, loathing; a cause of weariness.

Taenarius, -a, -um, *adj.* of Tæn-arum.

Taenarum, -ī, N. a promontory in Laconia, near which was a cavern thought to lead to Hades.

taenia, -ae, F. a ribbon, a fillet.

taeter, -tra, -trum, *adj.* foul, disgusting, loathsome.

tālāris, -e [*talus*], *adj.* of the heel. — N. *pl.* the talaria, the winged sandals of Mercury.

talentum, -ī, N. a talent, a Greek weight varying from about sixty to about one hundred pounds; weight, mass.

tālis, -e, *pron. adj.* such, in such guise, so; like this, this: **non Achilles talis** (not thus cruel).

tālus, -ī, M. the heel.

tam, *adv.* so, so much, as, as much, to such a degree: **tam dira cupido** (such dread desire). — **tam . . . quam, tamquam,** as much as, as if, as well . . . as, no less . . . than.

tamen, *adv.* yet, still, however, nevertheless, none the less, after all.

tamquam, *see* tam.

Tanais, -is, M. the River Tanais (the Don).

tandem [*tam + -dem*], *adv.* at last, at length, finally. — *With interrog. and imper. clauses indicating eagerness,* pray, I pray, tell me: **huc tandem concede** (I entreat).

tangō, -ere, tetigī, tāctum [√*tag*], *3. v. a.* touch, take hold of, grasp; reach, attain; go *or* come to, visit; stumble at (limen); have to do with, be involved in; move, affect, come home to (*one*): **mentem mortalia.**

Tantalis, -idis, F. daughter of Tantalus, Niobe.

Tantalus, -ī, M. 1. King of Phrygia, son of Jupiter and father of Niobe. — 2. A son of Niobe.

tantummodo, *adv.* only.

tantus, -a, -um, *pronom. adj.* so great, so much, such (*in size, degree, etc.*), as great, such great. — **tantō** (*abl.*) **magis,** so much the more, all the more. — **tantī,** *gen.* of such account. — **tantum,** *acc. as adv.* so much, in such a degree, as much . . . (as), no more . . . (than), thus far, so long; *also,* so much (*and no more*), only, merely.

tardē [*tardus*], *adv.* slowly.

tardō, -āre, -āvī, -ātum [*tardus*], *1. v. a.* retard, keep back, impede, hamper, check, make sluggish. — **tardāns, -antis,** *p. as adj.* sluggish: **senectus.**

tardus, -a, -um, *adj.* slow, sluggish, tardy, slow-moving.

Tarentum, -ī, N. a city of Apulia at the northeast corner of the great gulf which indents the southern extremity of Italy (iii. 551).

Tarquinius, -a, -um, *adj.* a Roman gentile name. — *Esp.* Tarquinius Superbus, Tarquin, the last king of Rome. — *Pl.* the Tarquins, the dynasty who were supposed to have come from Tarquinii, and reigned many years at Rome; *as adj.* Tarquinian (vi. 817).

Tartareus, -a, -um, *adj.* of Tartarus, Tartarean, infernal.

Tartarus, -ī (*pl.* **-a, -ōrum**), M. (N.), Tartarus, the abode of the damned; the Lower World.

Taurī, -ōrum, M. *pl.* the Taurians, a Scythian tribe.

taurīnus, -a, -um [*taurus*], *adj.* of a bull.

taurus, -ī, M. a bull.

-te, *emphatic enclitic, see* tūte.

tēctum, *see* tegō.

Tegeaeus, -a, -um, *adj.* of Tegea, a town of Arcadia (v. 299); Arcadian.

tegmen (tegumen), -inis [*tego*], N. a covering; garb, clothing.

tegō, -ere, tēxī, tēctum, *3. v. a.* cover; protect, shelter; clothe, deck, adorn, veil; bury (*the dead*); hide, conceal. — tēctus, -a, -um, *p.p.* covered, concealed, hidden; keeping silence, dissimulating (*in mid. sense*, concealing one's self). — N. (*sing. and pl.*) *as subst.* tēctum, -ī; tēcta, -ōrum, a roof, a ceiling; a house, a hall, an abode, a home, a palace; a hiding place.

tegumen, *see* tegmen.

tēla, -ae [*texo*], F. a web (*in the loom*), the warp, weaving, a loom.

tellūs, -ūris, F. the earth; the soil, land, the ground, earth (*as material*); a land, a region, a country. — *Personified*, Earth.

tēlum, -ī, N. a weapon (*missile*), a missile, a javelin, a dart, an arrow, a shaft; a weapon (*of any kind*, the cestus, the stake *with which Ulysses bored out the Cyclops' eye*).

temerē, *adv.* heedlessly. — haud temere, not without a meaning, no mere accident.

temerō, -āre, -āvī, -ātum, *1. v. a.* profane, pollute, desecrate.

temnō, -ere, *perf. and sup. not found* [√*tem*, cut], *3.v .a.* despise, scorn, defy, treat with contempt.

temperō, -āre, -āvī, -ātum [*tempus*], *1. v. a. and n.* temper, calm, appease; restrain one's self, refrain: a lacrimis.

tempestās, -ātis [*tempus*], F. a space of time, a season; the weather; a storm, a tempest, a gale. — *In pl. personified* (*as obj. of worship*), the Storms.

templum, -ī, N. a consecrated spot; a temple, a tomb (*as shrine of the Manes*).

temptō, -āre, -āvī, -ātum, *1. v. a.* try (*the strength of, lit. and fig.*), attempt, try (*experimentally*), test, venture on; tempt, solicit; search, explore, examine: proelia (risk, try the issue of); auxilium (seek); terras (try to reach). — *With inf.* try, endeavor, attempt.

tempus, -oris, N. a time, a point of time, an interval, a season (*of the year*), a period; time (*as continuous*); the (*right*) time, the best time, high time, an occasion, an opportunity; circumstances: tempore extremo (last hour). — *Also,* the temple, the temples (*of the head*).

tenāx,-ācis [*teneo*], *adj.* tenacious, clinging.

tendō,-ere, tetendī, tentum (tēnsum) [*cf.* teneo], *3. v. a. and n.* stretch, stretch out, extend, hold out; distend, fill (*sails*); pitch (*a tent*), encamp; raise (*the eyes*); tend, be inclined; aim, aim at, direct: quo tendant ferrum. — *With* gressum, iter (*or intrans. without*), make one's way, hold one's course, turn one's steps, proceed, advance, come. — *With inf.* intend, strive; struggle.

tenebrae, -ārum, F. *pl.* darkness, night, gloom; the Shades, the World Below.

tenebricōsus, -a, -um [*tenebrae*], *adj.* shadowy, gloomy, dark.

tenebrōsus, -a, -um [*tenebrae*], *adj.* dark, darkened, dim, gloomy: aër.

Tenedos, -ī, F. an island in the Ægean, off the Troad (ii. 21).

teneō, -ēre, tenuī, tentum [√*ten* (*in tendo*)], *2. v. a. and n.* hold, cling to, grasp; have, possess; cover (polum); pervade (**membra**) ; occupy, inhabit, be in *or* on (altum) ; control, guard, rule ; reach (tuta), gain (metam); keep, maintain, retain, hold (*fast*); hold (*back*), bind, detain, delay, hold (*bound*), restrain; hide (lunam) ; keep (*this way or that*), direct, turn: solo fixos oculos; immota lumina. — *Also, of a course,* keep, hold : iter ; fugam (pursue one's flight). —*Absolutely* (*with implied object*) : tenent Danai qua deficit ignis (possess whatever, *etc.*; hold possession *or* sway wherever).

tener, -era, -erum, *adj.* delicate, tender, soft; of tender years *or* age, young.

tenor, -ōris [*teneo*], M. (*steady*) course.

tentōrium, -ī (-iī) [*tentus, p.p.* of *tendo*], N. a tent.

tenuis, -e [√*ten* (*of tendo*)], *adj.* thin (*of texture or consistency*), fine, slight, delicate, slender, fragile, light, airy, substanceless : ventus; aurae ; fumus ; vitae (without substance) ; aurum (thread of) ; rima (narrow). — *Fig.* humble, feeble : res Teucrum.

tenus [√*ten* (*of teneo*)], *prep.* as far as, up to.

tepeō, -ēre, *no perf. or sup., 2. v. n.* be warm, reek.

tepidus, -a,-um [*tepeo*], *adj.* warm, still warm (*of a body*), not yet cold.

tepor, -ōris [*tepeo*], M. warmth, warm weather.

ter [*tres*], *adv.* three times, thrice.

tercentum, *adj. indecl.* thrice a hundred, three hundred.

terebrō, -āre, -āvī, -ātum [*terebra*], *1. v. a.* bore, bore into, bore out, pierce.

teres, -etis [*tero*], *adj.* smooth and round (*cylindrical*), round, smooth, polished.

tergeminus, -a, -um, *adj.* having three bodies, threefold, triple.

tergum, -ī, N. the back, the body (*of Cerberus*) ; a skin, a hide, *esp.* a bull's hide. — **a tergo,** from behind, in the rear, behind. — **in tergum,** backward.

tergus, -oris, N. the back ; a hide.

terminō, -āre, -āvī, -ātum [*terminus*], *1. v. a.* fix bounds to, limit.

terminus, -ī, M. a bound, a boundary, a boundary stone, a limit ; a fixed bound, destined end.

ternus, -a, -um [*ter*], *usually pl., adj.* threefold, three at a time, three each ; three.

terō, -ere, trīvī, trītum, *3. v. a.* rub, chafe : calcem calce Diores (tread on the heels). — *Also,* wear away (*of time*), waste, pass : otia (waste the time in idleness).

terra, -ae, F. dry land, the earth, the lar d; soil, the ground; a land, a country, stretch of country : orbis terrarum, the circle of the lands, the whole world, the world. — *Personified,* Terra, the Earth.

terrēnus, -a, -um [*terra*], *adj.* of earth, earthy.

terreō, -ēre, -uī, -itum, 2. *v. a.* frighten, alarm, affright, terrify, scare, frighten away, scare away; drive in terror, hunt, pursue: me patris imago (haunt).

terribilis, -e [*terreo*], *adj.* dreadful, dread, terrible.

terrificō, -āre, *no perf., no sup.* [*terrificus*], *1. v. a.* frighten, terrify, alarm.

terrificus, -a, -um [*terreo, facio*], *adj.* awe-inspiring, dread.

terrigena, -ae, M. *as adj.* [*terra*, √*gen* (*of gigno*)], earth-born.

territō, -āre, *no perf., no sup.* [*freq. of terreo*], *1. v. a.* alarm, frighten, affright; pursue, menace.

terror, -ōris [*terreo*], M. fright, terror.

tertius, -a, -um [*ter*], *adj.* third.

testa, -ae, F. a shell; a jar (*of earthenware*).

testis, -is, C. a witness.

testor, -ārī, -ātus [*testis*], *1. v. dep.* call to witness, swear by, protest before; declare (*calling something to witness*), swear, protest, bear witness; give warning, exhort, bear witness to a thing, testify to (*as a souvenir*); entreat (*calling something to witness*), adjure.

testūdō, -inis [*testa*], F. a tortoise; the testudo, a column of attack in which the shields overlapped, forming a continuous roof like the plates of the tortoise; vaulted *or* arched roof: templi.—*Esp.* a lyre.

Teucer (-crus), -crī, M. 1. A son of Telamon (king of Salamis), and half-brother of Ajax. He settled in Crete, founding a new Salamis (i. 619). — 2. A son of Scamander (said to be a Cretan) and the nymph Idæa. He figures as the great founder of the Trojan line through his daughter Batea, who married Dardanus (i. 235).

Teucria, -ae, F. the land of Teucer, the Trojan land, Troy (ii. 26).

Teucrus, -a, -um, *adj.* Trojan. — *Pl.* Teucrī, -ōrum, the Trojans.

texō, -ere, texuī, textum, 3. *v. a.* weave, plait; build, frame.

textilis, -e [*textus, texo*], *adj.* woven, of woven stuffs.

thalamus, -ī, M. a chamber, a room, a bedchamber; (*also pl.*) marriage, wedlock.

Thalīa, -ae, F. 1. The Muse of comedy and light verse. — 2. A sea-nymph (v. 826).

Thapsus, -ī, F. a city on a promontory of the same name, on the eastern coast of Sicily (iii. 689).

Thaumantias, -adis, F. daughter of Thaumas, Iris (ix. 5).

theātrum, -ī, N. a theatre; a place for games.

Thēbae, -ārum, F. Thebes, a city of Bœotia (iv. 470).

Thersilochus, -ī, M. a Trojan (vi. 483).

thēsaurus, -ī, M. a hoard, a treasure.

Thēseus, -eī (-eos), M. a king of Athens, slayer of the Minotaur. He assisted Pirithous in carrying off Proserpine from the infernal regions, for which impiety he was forced to sit upon a rock forever. He was honored as a special divinity by the Athenians, and is sometimes treated as the founder of their race (vi. 122).

Thessandrus, -ī, M. a Greek hero (ii. 261).

Thetis, -idis, F. a sea-nymph, one of the Nereids, mother of Achilles by Peleus (v. 825).

Thisbē, -ēs, F. a maiden of Babylon, beloved by Pyramus.

Thoāns, -antis, M. Thoans or Thoas, a king of the Tauri.

Thoās, -antis, M. a Greek in the Wooden Horse (ii. 262).

thōrāx, -ācis, M. a breastplate.

Thrācia, -ae, F. Thrace.

Thrācius, -a, -um, *adj.* Thracian.

Thrāx, -ācis, M. a Thracian.

Thrēicius, -a, -um, *adj.* of Thrace, Thracian.

Thrēissa, -ae, F. a Thracian (woman), Thracian.

Thȳbrīnus, -a, -um, *see* Tiberīnus.

Thȳbris, -idis, M. the Tiber (Tiberis), the great river of Rome.

Thȳias, -adis, F. a Bacchante, a Mænad, one of the women who joined in the frenzied rites of Bacchus (iv. 302).

Thymbraeus, -a, -um, *adj.* Thymbræan, of Thymbra, a city near Troy famous for its temple of Apollo. — M. *as subst.* the god of Thymbra (Apollo) (iii. 85).

Thymoetēs, -ae, M. a Trojan at the siege of Troy (ii. 32).

thymum, -ī, N. thyme.

Thȳnia, -ae, F. a region in Bithynia; Bithynia (*as a whole*).

Tiberīnus (Thȳ-), -a, -um, *adj.* of the Tiber. — M. *as subst.* the Tiber (*half personified*).

Tiberis, -is (-idos), M. the Tiber.

tībia, -ae, F. a pipe (*for music*).

Tibullus, -ī, M. Albius Tibullus, the poet.

tigris, -is (-idis), C. a tiger, a tigress.

Timāvus, -ī, M. a river between Istria and Venetia, which, flowing from seven rocky sources, makes a short course into the Adriatic (i. 244).

timeō, -ēre, -uī, *no sup., 2. v. a. and n.* fear, dread; be in fear; show one's fear.

timidus, -a, -um [timeo], *adj.* fearful, timid, frightened, cowardly.

Timōlus (Tmōlus), -ī, M. a mountain of Lydia, famous for wines.

timor, -ōris [timeo], M. fear, dread, alarm; terror (object of fear).

tingō (tinguō), -ere, tīnxī, tīnctum [√ting], *3. v. a.* wet, bathe, dip; dye, stain.

tinnītus, -ūs [tinnio], M. a ringing (*sound*).

Tīrynthius, -a, -um, *adj.* of Tiryns, an ancient town of Argolis, where Hercules was educated. — M. *as subst.* the Tirynthian, Hercules (viii. 228).

Tīsiphonē, -ēs, F. one of the Furies (vi. 555).

Tītān, -ānis, M. a name of the Sun God (iv. 119).

Tītānis, -idos, *adj.* F. descended from the Titans.

Tītānius, -a, -um, *adj.* of the Titans (a mysterious race of giants, sons of Heaven and Earth, who warred against Zeus), Titanian. One of the Titans was Hyperion, father of the Sun and the Moon, and these are called Titans also:

— Titania pubes; Titania astra
(the sun).

Tīthōnus, -ī, M. a son of Laomedon who married Aurora and became the father of Memnon. He
was changed into a locust (ci-
cada) at his wife's request, since,
endowed with immortality, he
had not received eternal youth
(iv. 585).

titubō, -āre, -āvī, -ātum, *1. v. n.
and a.* stumble, reel, totter. —
titubātus, -a, -um, *p.p.* tottering,
stumbling.

Tityus (-os), -ī, M. a giant of
Eubœa who offered violence to
Latona (or to Diana). He was
punished in Tartarus, stretched
out on the ground and having his
liver torn by vultures (vi. 595).

Tmarius, -a, -um, *adj.* of Tmaros
(a mountain in Epirus). — *Hence,*
of Epirus (v. 620).

toga, -ae, F. the toga.

togātus, -a, -um [*toga*], *adj.* clad in
the toga, of the toga (*wearing it*).

tolerābilis, -e [*tolero*], *adj.* tolera-
ble, endurable: non (unendur-
able).

tollō, -ere, sustulī, sublātum
[√*tol*, *perf. and sup. from suf-
fero*], *3. v. a.* lift, raise (*in all
Eng. senses*); take up and carry
off, take away, carry off; put an
end to; lay aside; forbear: in astra nepotes (raise to heaven, *as
gods*); fluctus (throw up, toss up);
sublato pectore (with lofty neck);
sublata dextra (uplifted); vocem
(send up, send forth); clamores
(raise); in tantum spe (raise
their hopes so high). — *With re-*

flexive, raise one's self, rise, spring
up, mount up.

Tolumnius, -ī (-iī), M. a Rutulian
augur (xii. 258).

tondeō, -ēre, totondī, tōnsum, *2.
v. a.* shear, clip, trim; crop, graze
on, feed on. — tōnsus, -a, -um,
p.p. as adj. trimmed, clipped,
sheared: tonsa oliva (olive leaves,
stripped off); tonsa corona (leafy
garland).

tonitrus, -ūs [*tono*], M. thunder, a
clap of thunder.

tonō, -āre, -uī, -itum (*in comp.*),
1. v. n. thunder: Aetna; axis (*of
a chariot*); tonat ter centum deos
(calls with loud voice upon, thunders the names of).

torpēscō, -ere, torpuī, *no sup.* [*tor-
peo*], *3. v. n.* grow numb *or* dull.

Torquātus, -ī [*torques*], M. name of
Titus Manlius Torquatus, given
him for slaying a Gaul in single
combat (vi. 825).

torqueō, -ēre, torsī, tortum, *2.
v. a.* whirl, twist, twirl, turn, haul
round (*yards*); torture, torment;
from the spinning motion of a dart,
hurl, throw, fling; roll; toss up
(*spray*); rule, sway, control: torquet medios nox cursus (is passing the midpoint of her circling
course). — tortus, -a, -um, *p.p. as
adj.* twisted.

torrēns, *see* torreō.

torreō, -ēre, -uī, tostum, *2. v. a.*
roast, parch. — torrēns, -entis, *p.
as adj.* roaring, raging. — M. *as
subst.* a torrent.

tortor, -ōris [*torqueo*], M. a torturer.

tortus, -ūs [*torqueo*], M. a coil, a
writhing coil (*of a snake*).

torus, -ī, M. a bed, a couch : **viridans** (green couch of turf) ; **riparum** (grassy couches). — *Pl.* the muscles (*esp. of the neck*), the neck.

torvus, -a, -um, *adj.* piercing (*of eyes*), grim, glaring, savage, stern, frowning. — N. *pl. as adv.* fiercely.

tot, *indecl. adj.* so many, as many, thus many.

totidem [*tot*], *indecl. adj.* just so many, just as many, as many, the same number, a like number.

totiēns (-ēs) [*tot*], *adv.* so many times, as many times, so often, as often.

tōtus, -a, -um, *adj.* the whole of (*a thing taken collectively*), all, the whole, entire. — *Often equal to an adv.* entirely, completely, wholly, all over, all.

trabea, -ae, F. a trabea, a robe (woven in stripes, worn by Roman magistrates).

trabs (trabēs), -is, F. a beam, a timber ; a block (*of marble*) ; a ship. — *Pl.* a roof.

trāctābilis, -e [*tracto*], *adj.* manageable ; *of the weather,* fit for navigation ; *of persons,* yielding, tractable.

trāctō, -āre, -āvī, -ātum [*tractus, traho*], *1. v. a.* handle.

trāctus, -ūs [*traho*], M. a tract, a quarter, a region.

trādō, -ere, -didī, -ditum [*trans + do*], *3. v. a.* hand over, give over, give in charge, surrender, bestow ; offer ; tell, recite.

trahō, -ere, trāxī, trāctum, *3. v. a.* drag, drag on *or* along, drag away, bear on (*of rivers, etc.*), carry with it (*of something falling,*

etc.) ; carry off (*as captive*), carry away ; draw, lead (*of children, etc.*) ; draw (*lots*) ; spin ; draw out, derive, trace ; utter with difficulty (**vocem**) ; drag out, while away, waste (**vitam; noctem**) ; absorb, draw in : **per ossa furorem.**

trāiciō, -ere, -iēcī, -iectum [*trans + iacio*], *3. v. a. and n.* throw across ; pass (*anything*) through ; pierce, transfix. — *Intrans.* pass across, pass.

trāmes, -itis [*trans, meo*], M. a crosspath, a byway ; a path, a course.

trānō (trāns-), -āre, -āvī, -ātum [*trans + no*], *1. v. a.* swim across, cross (*of rivers*), sail through *or* across (*of birds, etc.*).

tranquillus, -a, -um, *adj.* still, calm, quiet, tranquil. — N. *as subst., abl.* **tranquillō,** in calm weather.

trāns, *prep.* across, through, over.

trānscrībō, -ere, -scrīpsī, -scrīptum [*trans + scribo*], *3. v. a.* register, enroll ; transfer.

trānscurrō, -ere, -cucurrī (-currī), no sup., 3. v. n. run across, shoot across.

trānseō, -īre, -iī (-īvī), -itum, *irr. v. n. and a.* pass over, cross ; pass by, pass.

trānsferō, -ferre, -tulī, -lātum, *irr. v. a.* carry over, transfer.

trānsfīgō, -ere, -fīxī, -fīxum, *3. v. a.* thrust through ; transfix, pierce.

trānsiliō, -īre, -uī (-īvī), no sup. [*trans + salio*], *4. v. a.* leap across, spring over.

trānsitus, -ūs [*transeo*], M. a passage (*across*).

trānsmittō, -ere, -mīsī, -missum
3. v. a. and n. send across; assign
over, hand over, assign. — *With
acc. depending on* trans, pass over:
campos; cursum.

trānsportō, -āre, -āvī, -ātum, *1.
v. a.* bear across, carry across.

trānstrum, -ī [*trans*], N. a cross-
beam; a thwart, a bench (*for
rowers*).

trānsvertō, -ere, -vertī, -versum,
3. v. a. turn athwart.—trānsversa,
p.p. N. *pl. as adv.* athwart one's
course.

trāxe *for* trāxisse, *from* trahō.

trecentī, -ae, -a [*tres, centum*],
num. adj. pl. three hundred.

tremebundus, -a, -um [*tremo*],
adj. trembling, quivering.

tremefaciō, - ere, -fēcī, -factum
[*tremo, facio*], 3. v. a. make
tremble, shake. — tremefactus,
-a, -um, *p.p.* shaken; trembling,
quivering, shuddering.

tremendus, *see* tremō.

tremēscō, -ere, *no perf., no sup.*
[*tremo*], 3. v. n. and a. incept.
tremble; tremble at, shudder at.

tremō, -ere, -uī, *no sup.*, 3. v. a.
and n. tremble, quake, quake with
fear, shake, quiver; tremble at,
shudder at. — tremēns, -entis,
p. as adj. trembling, quivering, frightened. — tremendus, -a,
-um, *p. ger.* dreadful, awful, dread.

tremor, -ōris [*tremo*], M. a trembling.

tremulus, -a, -um [*tremo*], *adj.*
trembling, quivering.

trepidō, -āre, -āvī, -ātum [*trepidus*], *1. v. n.* tremble, quake with
fear; hurry to and fro, bustle.

trepidus, -a, -um, *adj.* trembling,
agitated, shuddering, quaking;
bustling, hurrying, confused, in
confusion, in agitation; frightened, anxious, alarmed; perilous,
of danger.

trēs, tria, *num. adj. pl.* three.

tricorpor, -oris [*tres, corpus*], *adj.*
three-bodied.

tridēns, -dentis [*tres, dens*], *adj.*
three-toothed, three-pronged. —
M. *as subst.* a trident, the attribute of Neptune.

trietēricus, -a, -um, *adj.* biennial
(once in three years according to
the ancients, who counted both
termini of a period).

trifaux, -faucis [*tres, faux*], *adj.*
three-throated, triple-jawed.

trīgintā, *indecl. num. adj.* thirty.

trilīx, -līcis [*tres, licium*], *adj.*
three-ply, threefold (*of three thick-
nesses*).

Trīnacrius, -a, -um, *adj.* of Sicily
(called Trinacria from its three
promontories), Sicilian. — F. *as
subst.* Trīnacria, -ae, Sicily (v.
555).

trinōdis,-e [*tres, nodus*], *adj.* three-
knotted, knotty.

Triōnēs, -um, M. *pl.* the Great and
Little Bears, Ursa Major and Minor (i. 744).

triplex,-icis [*tres,-plex* (*cf. plico*)],
adj. threefold, triple.

Triptolemus, -ī, M. son of Celeus
(*see Fasti*, iv. 509–562).

tripūs, -odis, M. a tripod, a three-
legged stand used for cooking
and for sacred rites; the Tripod,
or cauldron on a tripod, at Delphi, on which the priestess sat

when delivering the oracle; *pl.* oracles.

trīstis, -e, *adj.* mournful, wretched, sad, sorrowful; grim, gloomy, sullen, stern; bitter, dreary, mournful, melancholy; ill-omened, fatal, dreadful, cruel, baneful.

trisulcus, -a, -um [*tres, sulcus*], *adj.* three-forked.

Trītōn, -ōnis, M. a sea-god, son of Neptune, represented as blowing a conch-shell (i. 144). — *Pl.* sea-gods (v. 824).

Trītōnia, -ae, *adj. and subst.* F. a name of Pallas (Minerva) of uncertain origin (ii. 171).

Trītōnis, -idis, F. same as **Trītōnia.**

triumphō, -āre, -āvī, -ātum [*triumphus*], *1. v. n. and a.* triumph; lead in triumph, triumph over, conquer, subdue.

triumphus, -ī, M. a triumph (in the Roman sense, where the general with his army went in procession to the Capitol to offer a sacrifice); a triumph (*generally*), a victory.

trivium, -ī (-iī) [N. *of trivius*], N. a square, *where three ways met,* corners, crossroads.

Trivius, -a, -um [*tres, via*], *adj.* of three ways. — M. *and* F. of gods whose temples were built at the junction of three ways. — F. **Trivia,** *as subst.* Hecate or Diana (vi. 13).

Trōas, -adis, F. *adj.* Trojan, a Trojan woman.

Trōia [F. *of Troius*], F. 1. Troy. — 2. A city of the same name in Epirus (iii. 349). — 3. The game of the Trojan youths in honor of Anchises (v. 602).

Trōiānus, -a, -um, *adj.* Trojan. — *As subst.* a Trojan.

Trōicus, -a, -um, *adj.* Trojan.

Trōilus, -ī, M. a son of Priam killed in the Trojan War (i. 474).

Trōiugena, -ae [*Troia,* √*gen (of gigno*)], C. born in Troy, Trojan. — *As subst.* a Trojan.

Trōius, -a, -um, *adj.* of Troy, Trojan.

tropaeum, -ī, N. a trophy (regularly a tree-trunk arrayed in arms and left standing on the field).

Trōs, -ōis, M. a king of Phrygia (*see* **Dardanus**). — *As adj.* Trojan. — *As subst.* a Trojan. — *Pl.* the Trojans, said to be named for him.

trucīdō, -āre, -āvī, -ātum, *1. v. a.* cut down, slaughter.

truculentus, -a, -um [*trux*], *adj.* fierce, cruel; stormy.

trudis, -is [*trudo*], F. a boathook, a pole.

trūdō, -ere, trūsī, trūsum, *3. v. a.* push, push on, shove.

truncus, -a, -um, *adj.* lopped, stripped (*of branches*); maimed, mutilated, broken.

truncus, -ī [*from the adj.*], M. a trunk (*of a tree*), a stock; a headless trunk (*of a man*).

trux, trucis, *adj.* wild, grim.

tū, tuī, *pers. pron.* thou, you.

tuba, -ae, F. a trumpet (*straight, cf.* **cornu,** a curved horn).

tueor, tuērī, tuitus (tūtus), 2. v. dep. look at, gaze at, gaze upon, look, behold; protect, defend. — **tūtus, -a, -um,** *p.p.* protected, safe, secure, without danger, in safety, undisturbed, unharmed:

dare tuta vela (sail safely); **fides** (secure, trustworthy). — N. *sing.* or *pl.* **tūtum, tūta**, a safe place, safe retreat, a safe position; security, safety.

Tullius, -ī (-iī), M. M. Tullius Cicero, the orator.

Tullus, -ī, M. Tullus Hostilius, the third king of Rome (vi. 814).

tum, *adv.* then, at that time; thereupon, next; then again, then too, besides: **iam tum**, even then, then already; **tum vero**, *emphatic, introducing the most important point of a narrative.*

tumeō, -ēre, *no perf., no sup.*, 2. *v. n.* swell, be swollen.

tumidus, -a, -um [*tumeo*], *adj.* swelling (*lit. and fig.*), swollen, rising, huge: **coluber; fluctūs; ira; auster.**

tumulō, -āre, -āvī, -ātum [*tumulus*], *1. v. a.* entomb, bury.

tumultus, -ūs [*cf. tumeo*], M. an uproar, a tumult, a noise, a disturbance, a commotion, disorder, confusion, alarm; *of the mind*, anxiety, agitation, excitement: **laetitia mixto tumultu.**

tumulus, -ī [*tumeo*], M. a mound, a hill; a tomb.

tunc [*tum + -ce*], *adv.* at that time, then.

tundō, -ere, tutudī, tūnsum (tūsum *in comp.*) [√*tud*], *3. v. a.* strike, beat; assail (*by words*).

turba, -ae, F. a disturbance, a tumult, confusion; a throng, crowd, a multitude, a gang, a crew; a herd, a flock.

turbidus, -a, -um [*turba*], *adj.* confused, wild; turbid, roily, stormy,

whirling (*of rain*); *of persons*, agitated, troubled: **imago.**

turbō, -āre, -āvī, -ātum [*turba*], *1. v. a.* agitate, disturb, stir up; throw into confusion, drive in a panic, chase, scatter; alarm, disturb, trouble; break off (*a truce*), spread alarm (among). — **turbātus, -a, -um**, *p.p. as adj.* agitated, disordered, panic-stricken, in confusion, frightened, alarmed; angry, troubled; confused, excited.

turbō, -inis [*turba*], M. a whirling, a whirling eddy; a whirlwind, a hurricane.

tūreus, -a, -um [*tus*], *adj.* of incense.

turgidulus, -a, -um [*dim. of turgidus*], *adj.* swollen a little.

turgidus, -a, -um [*turgeo*], *adj.* swollen, swelling.

tūricremus, -a, -um [*tus, cremo*], *adj.* incense-burning, smoking with incense.

turma, -ae, F. a troop (*of horse*), a squadron.

Turnus, -ī, M. the young Rutulian king who resisted the settlement of Æneas.

turpis, -e, *adj.* foul, unseemly, filthy, soiled, squalid; base, dishonorable, vile, disgraceful.

turris, -is, F. a tower, a turret.

turrītus, -a, -um [*turris*], *adj.* crowned with towers (*of Cybele*); towering, pinnacled.

tūs, tūris, N. frankincense, incense

Tuscus, -a, -um, *adj.* Tuscan, Etruscan.

tūtāmen, -inis [*tutor*], N. a protection, a defence.

tūte [tu + -te], *pron.* thou, you (*emphatic*), you yourself.

tūtēla, -ae [*tutus*], F. a charge, an object of care.

tūtor, -ārī, -ātus [*tutus*], *1. v. dep.* protect, defend, support.

tūtus, -a, -um, *p.p. of* tueor.

tuus, -a, -um [*tu*], *poss. pron.* thy, your, thine, yours. — *Pl. as subst.* your (friends, men, *etc.*; affairs, interests, *etc.*).

Tȳdeus, -eī (-eos), M. the father of Diomedes. He fought in the Theban war (vi. 479).

Tȳdīdēs, -ae, M. son of Tydeus, Diomedes (i. 471).

Tyndaris, -idis, F. daughter of Tyndareus; Helen, as daughter of Leda, his wife (ii. 601).

Typhōeūs, -eos, M. a giant (also called Typhon), struck by lightning and buried under Ætna by Jupiter.

Typhōius, -a, -um, *adj.* of Typhon (or Typhoeus). — tela Typhoia (the bolts of Typhon, by which he was slain) (i. 665).

tyrannus, -ī, M. a king; a tyrant, a despot.

Tyrius, -a, -um, *adj.* of Tyre, Tyrian; of Carthage, Carthaginian. — M. a Tyrian; a Carthaginian.

Tyros (-us), -ī, F. Tyre, the great city of Phœnicia, from which came the colony of Dido. It was most famous for its purple dye (i. 346).

Tyrrhēnus, -a, -um, *adj.* Etruscan, Etrurian, Tuscan.

ūber, -eris [*uber*], *adj.* fertile, productive, rich, abundant, abounding.

ūber, -eris, N. (*oftener pl.*), an udder, the breast; the bosom (*of the earth*), fertility: (tellus) vos ubere laeto accipiet (in her fertile bosom); ubere glebae (fertility of the soil).

ubĭ, *adv. interrog.* where; *rel.* where; when, whenever, after, as soon as.

ubīque [*ubi + -que*], *adv.* everywhere, on all sides, all around.

Ūcalegōn, -ontis, M. a Trojan (ii. 312).

ūdus, -a, -um, *adj.* damp, wet, moist.

ulcīscor, ulcīscī, ultus, *3. v. dep.* avenge.

Ulixēs, -ī (-eī, -is), M. Ulysses (Odysseus), Greek hero of the Trojan War famed for his cunning. His wanderings are the theme of the Odyssey (ii. 7).

ūllus, -a, -um [*unus*], *pron. adj.* any, any one.

ulmus, -ī, F. an elm.

ulterior, -us, *adj. comp.* the farther. — N. ulterius, *as adv.* farther. — *Superl.* ultimus, -a, -um, farthest, extreme, uttermost, at the end, very first: origo. — *Of time*, last, final. — *Of degree*, last, extreme: iussa (most degrading, most arrogant). — N. *pl.* the end, the farthest point, the last struggle.

ulterius, *see* ulterior.

ultimus, -a, -um, *see* ulterior.

ultor, -ōris [*ulciscor*], M. avenger.

ultrā, *adv.* farther, beyond; further, more, besides; *prep.* beyond.

ultrīx, -īcis [*ulciscor*], F. an avenger (*female*); *as adj.* avenging.

ultrō, *adv.* beyond, furthermore, in

addition, besides; voluntarily, of one's own accord; unprovoked, unaddressed, first (*without being spoken to*).

ultus, -a, -um, *p.p. of* ulcīscor.

ululātus, -ūs [*ululo*], M. a wailing, a shrieking.

ululō, -āre, -āvī, -ātum, *1. v. n. and a.* howl, wail, cry, shriek; *of a place,* resound with wails, *etc.* — ululātus, -a, -um, *p.p. in pass. sense,* worshipped with cries.

ulva, -ae, F. sedge, coarse grass.

umbō, -ōnis, M. a boss (*of a shield*); a shield.

umbra, -ae, F. a shade, a shadow; darkness, gloom; a ghost, an apparition, a shade; *pl.* the realm of shades, the shades, the World Below.

umbrifer, -fera, -ferum [*umbra, fero*], *adj.* shady.

umbrō, -āre, -āvī, -ātum [*umbra*], *1. v. a.* shade, overshadow.

umbrōsus, -a, -um [*umbra*], *adj.* shady, dark, gloomy.

ūmectō, -āre, -āvī, -ātum [*umeo*], *1. v. a.* moisten, bedew, bathe.

ūmeō, -ēre, *no perf., no sup., 2. v. n.* be moist, be wet. — ūmēns, -entis, *p. as adj.* moist, damp, dewy.

umerus, -ī, M. the shoulder.

ūmidus, -a, -um [*umeo*], *adj.* moist, damp, dewy; liquid.

umquam, *adv.* ever, at any time.

ūnā [*abl. of unus*], *adv.* together, at the same time, along with, at once.

ūnanimus, -a, -um [*unus, animus*], *adj.* of one mind, sympathizing.

ūnctus, -a, -um, *p.p. of* ungō.

uncus, -a, -um, *adj.* bent, hooked, crooked: manus (clenched).

unda, -ae, F. a wave, a billow, sea; water, the waters, a stream.

unde, *adv.* 1. *Interrog.* whence, from whence, from what source. — 2. *Rel.* from whence, whence; from whom, from which.

ūndecimus, -a, -um [*undecim*], *num. adj.* eleventh.

undique [*unde + -que*], *adv.* from all sides, from every quarter; on all sides, everywhere, all around.

undō, -āre, -āvī, -ātum [*unda*], *1. v. n.* wave, flow in waves, roll in waves. — undāns, -antis, *p. as adj.* rolling up; surging, seething, waving.

undōsus, -a, -um [*unda*], *adj.* billowy, boisterous, wave-washed.

ungō (unguō), -ere, ūnxī, ūnctum, *3. v. a.* smear, anoint, besmear. — ūnctus, -a, -um, *p.p. as adj.* smeared: carina (well-pitched).

unguentum, -ī [*unguo*], N. an unguent, a perfume.

unguis, -is, M. a nail (*of the finger or toe*); a claw, a talon.

ungula, -ae, F. a hoof.

ūnicus, -a, -um [*unus*], *adj.* one and only, one, single.

ūnus, -a, -um, *num. adj.* one, the same, a like, a single, alone, only, only one, the sole. — *Esp.* haud unus, more than one, not the same; ad unum, to a man. — *Emphatic,* the one, the very (*with superlatives*), especially, more than all others.

urbs, urbis, F. a city.

urgeō, -ēre, ursī, *no sup.,* 2. *v. a.*
press hard, press close; drive,
drive on, force, urge on, hasten
(*a task*), work eagerly; pursue,
press close upon, attack; stand
out to (altum, sea); weigh down,
lower *or* brood over, overwhelm:
urgens fatum (overwhelming);
poenis urgentur (are tormented).

urna, -ae, F. a jar, an urn.

ūrō, ūrere, ussī, ustum [√*us*],
3. *v. a.* burn (*lit. and fig.*); fire,
set on fire; worry, disturb.

ursa, -ae, F. a she-bear.

usquam, *adv.* anywhere.

usque, *adv.* all the way, even (to);
all the time, constantly, ever; one
after another: **quo usque** (how
far, how long).

ūsus, -ūs [*utor*], M. use, employment; experience; purpose; custom, what is customary: **pervius
usus tectorum** (a much-used passage). — *With* **esse,** there is need
of.

ut (utī), *adv.* (*and conj.*). 1. *Interrog.*
how. — 2. *Rel.* as, just as; when,
as soon as, no sooner than, *sometimes practically* where (v. 329,
388); *with subj.* that, in order
that, so that, to; although, even if.

utcumque [*ut + cumque, cf. quicumque*], *adv.* however, in whatever way.

uter, utra, utrum, *interrog. pron.*
which of the two?

uterque, utraque, utrumque
[*uter + -que*], *pron. adj.* each (*of
two*), both, either.

uterus, -ī, M. the womb; the belly;
offspring.

utī, *see* **ut.**

ūtilis, -e [*utor*], *adj.* useful, of use,
fit.

ūtiliter [*utilis*], *adv.* profitably, better.

utinam [*uti + nam*], *conj.* O that,
would that.

ūtor, ūtī, ūsus, 3. *v. dep.* use, employ; enjoy, take advantage of;
show: **his vocibus usa est** (made
use of).

utrimque, *adv.* on either side.

utrōque [*uterque*], *adv.* to either
side.

uxor, -ōris, F. wife.

uxōrius, -a, -um [*uxor*], *adj.* uxori-
ous, devoted to one's wife (*to ex-
cess*).

vacca, -ae, F. a cow, heifer.

vacō, -āre, -āvī, -ātum, 1. *v. n.* be
empty, free from, unoccupied:
vacare domos hoste (the dwellings are vacant, deserted by the
enemy). — *Impersonal,* there is
(one has) time *or* leisure (*for a
thing*).

vacuus, -a, -um [*vaco*], *adj.* vacant, open, empty, deserted; unobstructed, clear: **aurae; caelum**
(free); **metu** (free from, without;
fearless, undaunted).

vādō, -ere, *no perf., no sup.,* 3. *v. n.*
go, walk, proceed, go on: **ille
ducem vadentem aequat** (as she
walked, moved); **vade age,** come
go, go on now, *of command, encouragement, or farewell.*

vadum, -ī [*cf. vado*], N. a ford, a
shoal, a shallow, a sandbank; the
bottom of the sea, the depths;
the sea, the waters, a wave.

vae, *interj.* woe! alas!

vāgīna, -ae, F. a sheath, a scabbard.

vāgītus, -ūs [*vagio*], M. a crying.

vagor, -ārī, -ātus [*vagus*], *1. v. dep.* move to and fro, roam, rove, wander, stray; spread abroad.

vagus, -a, -um, *adj.* wandering, roving, unsteady.

valēns, *p. of* valeō.

valeō, -ēre, -uī, (-itūrus), *2. v. n.* be strong, be stout, be sturdy; be well; have power, have force, avail, be good (*in anything*), be able, can; *imper.* be well, farewell, adieu. — valēns, -entis, *p. as adj.* strong, stout, sturdy.

validus, -a, -um [*valeo*], *adj.* vigorous, strong, stout, sturdy, stalwart, powerful.

vallis (-ēs), -is, F. a valley.

vallō, -āre, -āvī, -ātum [*vallum*], *1. v. a.* to fortify with a rampart, intrench.

vallum, -ī, N. a rampart.

valva, -ae, F. a door.

vānescō,-ere, *no perf. or sup.*[*vanus*], *3. v. n.* vanish, come to naught.

vānus, -a, -um, *adj.* empty, bodiless, idle; baseless, vain, groundless; fruitless; false, deceitful. — N. *pl.* vāna, *as adv.* vainly.

vapor, -ōris, M. steam, vapor; heat, fire.

varius, -a, -um, *adj.* diverse, different, various; varying, changeable, variable, changeful, inconstant; motley, variegated, of varied hue: irarum aestus (ebbing and flowing, fluctuating).

vāstō, -āre, -āvī, -ātum [*vastus*], *1. v. a.* devastate, lay waste, make desolate, ravage.

vāstus, -a, -um, *adj.* desolate, laid waste, desert; huge, enormous, immense, far-stretching, vast, unfathomable, measureless, boundless (*of the sea and sky*); mighty, frightful, tremendous; deafening.

vātēs, -is, C. a soothsayer, a diviner, a seer, a prophet, a prophetess; an inspired bard, a bard, a poet.

-ve, *conj. enclitic* or. — *Repeated,* -ve . . . -ve, either . . . or.

vectis, -is, M. a bar, a bolt.

vectō, -āre, -āvī, -ātum [*vectus, veho*], *1. v. a.* carry, transport.

vehō, -ere, vexī, vectum, *3. v. a.* carry; *of sailing and riding,* convey, bear, carry, bring, bring in; draw, lead, conduct, drive. — *Pass.* (*almost as dep.*), be borne, ride, sail, journey.

Vēiēns, -entis, *adj.* of Veii, an ancient Etruscan city.

vel [*volo*], *conj.* or (*not exclusive, cf.* aut); *repeated* (*or in other combinations*), either . . . or.—*Also,* even.

vēlāmen, -inis [*velo*], N. a veil, a covering, a garment, clothing.

vēlifer, -fera, -ferum [*velum, fero*], *adj.* sail-bearing.

Velīnus, -a, -um, *adj.* of Velia, a town of Lucania near which Palinurus met his death (vi. 366).

vēlivolus, -a, -um [*velum, volo*], *adj.* winged with sails: mare (i. e. *covered with sails like wings*).

vellō, -ere, vellī (vollī), vulsum (volsum), *3. v. a.* pull, pluck; pull up, pull out, tear out, tear up, tear away.

vellus, -eris, N. a fleece; a lock of wool (*used as a festoon*).

vēlō, -āre, -āvī, -ātum [*velum*], *1. v. a.* cover (*esp. of the head*), veil, crown, adorn, clothe. —*Pass.* (*as middle*) cover *etc.* one's self. — vēlātus, -a, -um, *p.p.* veiled, covered; sail-clad.

vēlōx, -ōcis, *adj.* swift, fleet.

vēlum, -ī, N. a cloth, a covering; a sail; dare vela (set sail).

velut (-utī), *adv.* just as, as, as if, as when, like, as it were.

vēna, -ae, F. a vein: aquae (a streamlet).

vēnābulum, -ī [*venor*], N. a hunting spear.

Venāfrānus, -a, -um, *adj.* of *or* at Venafrum, a Samnite town.

vēnātrīx, -īcis [*venor*], F. a huntress.

vēnātus, -ūs [*venor*], M. hunting, the chase.

vēndō, -ere, -didī, -ditum [*venum + do*], *3. v. a.* sell; betray.

venēnifer, -fera, -ferum [*venenum, fero*], *adj.* venomous.

venēnō, -āre, -āvī, -ātum [*venenum*], *1. v. a.* poison.

venēnum, -ī, N. poison, venom.

venerābilis, -e [*veneror*], *adj.* venerable, venerated, revered, held in reverence.

venerō, -āre, -āvī, -ātum, *1. v. a.* worship, reverence, adore; pray, supplicate, offer prayers to *or* at. — *Pass.* veneror as *dep.* in same senses. — venerātus, -a, -um, *p.p.* being duly reverenced.

venia, -ae, F. favor, pardon, indulgence; a boon: veniam precari (a gracious answer).

veniō, -īre, vēnī, ventum, *4. v. n.* come. — veniēns, -entis, *p. as adj.* coming, future. — ventūrus, -a, -um, *fut. p. as adj.* to come, future; N. *as subst.* the future.

vēnor, -ārī, -ātus, *1. v. dep.* hunt.

venter, -tris, M. the belly: ventris rabies (rage of hunger).

ventōsus, -a, -um [*ventus*], *adj.* windy, stormy, boisterous.

ventus, -ī, M. wind.

Venus, -eris, F. Venus, the goddess of love and beauty; love.

venustus, -a, -um [*Venus*], *adj.* charming, lovely.

vēr, vēris, N. the spring.

†verber, -eris, N. (*mostly pl.*), a lash, a whip; scourging, a blow.

verberō, -āre, -āvī, -ātum [*verber*], *1. v. a.* lash, beat, strike: sidera verberat unda.

verbōsus, -a, -um [*verbum*], *adj.* wordy.

verbum, -ī, N. a word: verba inter singula (with every word). — *Pl.* words, language, discourse.

vērē [*verus*], *adv.* truly, with truth.

vereor, -ērī, veritus, *2. v. dep.* fear, dread; *with ind. quest.* be anxious, be concerned; *with inf.* be afraid (*to do anything*), shrink (*from doing*).

Vergilius, -ī (-iī), M. a Roman gentile name. — *Esp.* Publius Vergilius Maro, Virgil (*the established Eng. word*), the poet.

vērnus, -a, -um [*ver*], *adj.* spring, of spring.

vērō [*abl. of verus*], *adv.* truly, in truth, doubtless, assuredly, certainly, forsooth (*ironical*); however, but.

verrō, -ere, verrī, versum, *3. v. a. and n.* sweep, sweep over, skim.

verso, -āre, -āvī, -ātum [*verto*], *1. v. a.* turn (*esp. repeatedly or with violence*), roll, toss about, wheel, wind; drive about, drive this way and that; turn over, revolve, ponder, meditate (**consilia; curas**); practise: **dolos.**

versor, -ārī, -ātus, *1. v. dep.* dwell, abide, be.

versus, -ūs [*verto*], M. a turn, a turning; a line, a row; verse.

vertex (vortex), -icis [*verto*], M. a whirl, an eddy, a whirlpool, a vortex. — *From the peculiar growth of hair*, the crown (*of the head*), the head; the top, the summit: **saxi; caeli** (the heights); **a vertice,** from above.

vertō, -ere, vertī, versum, *3. v. a. and n.* turn (*lit. and fig.*); turn round, reverse, invert; turn towards, direct; turn away, drive off, divert, transfer; upturn, turn over, overturn, overthrow; destroy, ruin; change, alter; ponder; turn (*one's mind*), change (*one's purpose*): **spicula infensi** (present, level); **praedas** (drive off); **stimulos** (ply); **in viscera viris** (turn against); **arces** (overthrow). — *With reflexive and in passive*, turn one's self, turn; change, be changed; revolve, roll; tend: **se in cruorem vina; aestas septima** (is rolling on); **caelum** (revolve); **quo se vertant hospitia.**

verū, -ūs, N. a spit.

vērum, *see* vērus.

vērus, -a, -um, *adj.* true, real; just. —N. *sing. and pl. as subst.* vērum, vēra, the truth, things true. — N.

as adv. vērum, truly, in truth; but, however, yet, still.

vēscor, vēscī, *no p.p.,* 3. *v. dep.* feed on, eat, subsist on, feast on: **aurā** (breathe the vital air).

vesper, -erī *and* -eris, M. the evening; the evening star; the West.

Vesta, -ae, F. the goddess of household fire. She is the emblem of household purity and family life. Her fire was kept constantly burning in her temple as the hearth of the State considered as a family (i. 292).

vester, -tra, -trum [*vos*], *pron. adj.* your, yours.

vestibulum, -ī, N. a porch, a portico, a vestibule, an entrance.

vestīgium, -ī (-iī) [*vestigo*], N. a track, a trace, a footprint; a sign, a token; a step, a footstep; the feet, a course; the fetlocks (*of a horse*).

vestīgō, -āre, -āvī, -ātum, *1. v. a.* track, trace; examine, search for.

vestiō, -īre, -īvī (-iī), -ītum [*vestis*], *4. v. a.* clothe, cover.

vestis, -is, F. a garment, a robe, a covering, clothing, vesture; a fabric, stuffs, hangings, cloth, drapery.

vetō, -āre, -uī, -itum, *1. v. a.* forbid, prohibit. — vetitus, -a, -um, *p.p. as adj.* forbidden, unlawful.

vetus, -eris, *adj.* old, aged, ancient, former.

vetustās, -ātis [*vetus*], F. age, antiquity, lapse of time.

vetustus, -a, -um [*vetus*], *adj.* ancient.

vexō, -āre, -āvī, -ātum [*veho*], *1. v. a.* shake; harass, torment.

via, -ae, F. a road, a way, a path, a street; a passage, a course; a journey *or* voyage; *fig.* a way, a means. — *Pl.* journeys, journeyings, wanderings.

viātor, -ōris [*via*], M. a wayfarer, a traveller.

vibrō, -āre, -āvī, -ātum, 1. v. n. vibrate, quiver.

vice, *see* vicis.

vīcīnia, -ae [*vicinus*], F. neighborhood.

vīcīnus, -a, -um [*vicus*], adj. near, neighboring, in the vicinity, close by.

vicis (*gen.; no nom. sing. found*), **F.** change, interchange; *pl.* changes, chances, fortune; perils: **in vices** (in turn).

vicissim [*vicis*], adv. alternately, in turn.

victor, -ōris [√*vic* (*of vinco*)], M. a victor, a conqueror; *as adj.* victorious, triumphant.

victōria, -ae [*victor*], F. victory, triumph.

victrīx, -īcis [√*vic* (*of vinco*)], F. a conqueror (*female*). — *Also, as adj. in* F. *and* N. victorious, conquering, successful.

vīctus, -ūs [*vivo*], M. a living, a sustenance, support (*of life*), food.

viden, *see* video.

videō, -ēre, vīdī, vīsum, 2. v. a. and n. see (*with the eye or mind*), behold, witness, experience: **viden** (= videsne), do you see? — *Pass.* be seen, seem, appear; seem best, seem good, be determined.

viduō, -āre, -āvī, -ātum [*viduus*], 1. v. a. bereave. — *P.p.* deprived of, free from.

viduus, -a, -um, adj. bereft of wife *or* husband; widowed.

vigeō, -ēre, no perf., no sup., 2. v. n. thrive, flourish, be in vigor; be powerful, gain strength.

vigēscō, -ere, viguī, no sup. [*vigeo*], 3. v. n. grow vigorous.

vigil, -ilis [*vigeo*], adj. wakeful, awake, watchful, sleepless, unsleeping: **ignis** (undying). — **M.** *as subst.* a watchman, a sentinel, a guard.

vigilō, -āre, -āvī, -ātum [*vigil*], 1. v. n. be awake, wake, awake, wake up, rouse, watch. — **vigilāns, -antis,** *p. as adj.* watchful.

vīgintī, indecl. adj. twenty.

vigor, -ōris [*vigeo*], M. vigor, activity, strength, force.

vīlis, -e, adj. cheap, worthless, paltry, mean.

villōsus, -a, -um [*villus*], adj. shaggy.

villus, -ī, M. a coarse hair; the nap (*of cloth*).

vīmen, -inis, N. a twig, a shoot.

vinciō, -īre, vīnxī, vīnctum, 4. v. a. bind, tie up; *esp. of garlands,* twine, encircle.

vinclum, *see* vinculum.

vincō, -ere, vīcī, victum [√*vic*], 3. v. a. and n. defeat, overpower; surpass, outvie, excel; prevail against, overcome; win, conquer, prevail: **hoc vincite** (gain this victory). — *Esp.* melt (*snow*).

vinculum (vinclum), -ī [*vincio*], N. a bond, a fetter; a band, a strap (*of the sandals*), a thong (*of the cestus*); a rope, a cord, a mooring, a cable; *fig.* a bond, a tie (*esp. of marriage*).

vindex, -icis, c. an avenger: vindice poena (with avenging punishment).

vindico, -āre, -āvī, -ātum [vindex], 1. v. a. set free, release, punish.

vīnētum, -ī [vinum], N. a vineyard.

vīnum, -ī, wine.

violābilis, -e [violo], adj. to be violated: non violabile numen (inviolable).

violenter [violens], adv. violently.

violentia, -ae [violentus], F. violence, fury.

violentus, -a, -um [cf. vis], adj. violent, boisterous.

violō, -āre, -āvī, -ātum [cf. vis], 1. v. a. do violence to, injure, mar; profane, sully, stain (fig.), violate.

vīpera, -ae, F. a viper, a serpent.

vīpereus, -a, -um [vipera], adj. of snakes, snaky, of the serpent.

vir, virī, M. a hero, a man, a husband.

virectum, -ī [vireo], N. a grassy spot, a green thicket.

vireō, -ēre, no perf., no sup., 2. v. n. be green, flourish, put forth leaves.

virga, -ae [cf. vireo], F. a shoot, a twig, a sapling; a rod, a wand.

virgineus, -a, -um [virgo], adj. of a maiden, maiden, maidenly.

virgō, -inis, F. a maiden, a maiden daughter.

virgultum, -ī [virga], N. a thicket.

viridāns, -antis [p. of virido], adj. green.

viridis, -e [vireo], adj. green, grassy; mossy (antrum); fresh, vigorous; tender: aevum.

virīlis, -e [vir], adj. manly, heroic.

virtūs, -ūtis [vir], F. manliness, manhood, bravery, courage, heroism; virtue, excellence; pl. valorous deeds.

vīs, vīs, F. sing. power, strength, might; force, violence, injury; a pack (of hounds). — Pl. vīrēs, -ium, strength, power, force, energy, vigor; powers, forces.

vīscera, see vīscus.

viscum, -ī, N. mistletoe.

vīscus, -eris (generally pl.), N. the flesh (or soft parts inside the skin); the viscera (the lungs, liver, etc. used for divination), the entrails; fig. the bowels (of a mountain), the vitals (of one's country).

vīsō, -ere, vīsī, vīsum [video], 3. v. a. go to see, visit; examine, look at, see.

vīsum, -ī [N. p.p. of video], N. a sight, a spectacle; a portent.

vīsus, -ūs [video], M. the sight, vision, the gaze, a look; a sight, an omen; appearance, aspect.

vīta, -ae [cf. vivo], F. life (existence, also the conditions of life, nature), life (i. e. the vital principle), the breath of life, the vital spark; the soul, the shade, a spirit; a mode of life, life (course of life).

vītālis, -e [vita], adj. of life, vital.

vitiō, -āre, -āvī, -ātum [vitium], 1. v. a. taint, poison, flaw.

vitium, -ī (-iī), N. fault, flaw, defect.

vitō, -āre, -āvī, -ātum, 1. v. a. avoid, shun.

vitrum, -ī, N. glass, crystal.

vitta, -ae, F. a fillet, a band.

vitulus, -ī, M. a bullock.

vīvidus, -a, -um [*vivus*], *adj.* active, lively, vigorous.

vīvō, -ere, vīxī, vīctum, 3. *v. n.* live, be alive, pass one's life; remain, keep alive : sub pectore volnus; stuppa (*as being on fire*). — *Esp. in imper.* may you live, farewell, adieu.

vīvus, -a, -um [*vivo*], *adj.* alive, living, lifelike; growing; natural; flowing, perennial; solid (*of rock*). — *Pl. as subst.* the living, living creatures.

vix, *adv.* with difficulty, hardly, scarcely, barely. — *Also, of time,* hardly, just, no sooner.

vocālis, -e [*voco*], *adj.* singing, sweet-voiced.

vōciferor, -ārī, -ātus [*vox, fero*], 1. *v. dep.* cry out, shout, cry, exclaim.

vocō, -āre, -āvī, -ātum [*vox*], 1. *v. a. and n.* call (*in every shade of invitation and of command*); call for, pray for; call upon, invoke, pray to; invite, summon; call together; call by name, name; direct : ad poenam (bring to justice); me ad fata (ask to share); lux ultima (summon); aurae vela (invite); cursus vela (direct); cursum ventus (guide).

volātilis, -e [*volatus, p.p. of volo*], *adj.* flying, winged.

volātus, -ūs [*volo*], M. flight.

Volcānus, -ī, M. Vulcan, the god of fire in its destructive and mechanical forms. He was fabled to have a forge beneath the Lipari Islands, where he wrought the thunderbolts of Jupiter. — *Fig.* fire (ii. 311).

volgāris, -e [*volgus*], *adj.* popular, of the folk; common, base, vulgar; well-known.

volgō, -āre, -āvī, -ātum [*volgus*], 1. *v. a.* spread abroad, publish, make known.

volgō [*abl. of volgus*], *adv.* generally, commonly, everywhere.

volgus, -ī, N. (*sometimes* M.), the populace, the crowd, the people; *of animals,* the mass, the herd.

volitō, -āre, -āvī, -ātum [*volo*], 1. *v. n.* flit about, fly to and fro, flit, fly abroad, fly about.

volnerō (vulnerō), -āre, -āvī, -ātum [*volnus*], 1. *v. a.* wound.

volnificus, -a, -um [*volnus, facio*], *adj.* wounding, destructive.

volnus (vulnus), -eris, N. a hurt, a wound, a stroke, a blow; a weapon; a pang, a pain.

volō, -āre, -āvī, -ātum, 1. *v. n.* fly, fly about, flit; whirl along, skim, rush, speed; be hurled; shoot (*of stars*) : fama volat (rumor reports). — volāns, -antis, *p. as subst.* winged creature, flying creature, bird.

volō, velle, voluī, *no sup., irr. v. a.* (*often with obj. implied*), wish, will, be willing, consent, allow, choose, design: hunc laetum diem esse velis (graciously make). — *Also,* intend, purpose, have in view, mean. — *With acc. and inf.* claim, will have it that. — volēns, -entis, *p. as adj.* willing, propitious, gracious.

Volscēns, -entis, M. a Latin hero (ix. 370).

Volscus, -a, -um, *adj.* Volscian, of the Volsci, a people of Latium who waged stubborn war against the Romans, but were finally conquered about 325 B.C. — *Pl. as subst.* the Volscians (ix. 505).

voltur, -uris, M. a vulture.

voltus (vultus), -ūs, M. expression (*of the face*), the countenance, the aspect; appearance, look.

volūbilis, -e [*volvo*], *adj.* winding, twisting.

volucer (-cris), -cris, -cre [*volo*], *adj.* flying, winged; rapid, fleet, swift; fleeting: **somnus.** — F. *as subst.* a winged creature, a bird.

volūmen, -inis [*volvo*], N. a roll, a coil, a fold, a band.

voluntās, -ātis [*volens* (*volo*)], F. wish, will, desire, good pleasure.

voluptās, -ātis [*cf. volo*], F. pleasure, delight, enjoyment.

Volusus, -ī, M. a Rutulian chief (xi. 463).

volūtō, -āre, -āvī, -ātum [*volutus, volvo*], *1. v. a. and n.* roll; roll back, send echoing, make echo, echo; writhe, grovel. — *Fig.* revolve, ponder, meditate: **secum corde.**

volvō, -ere, volvī, volūtum, *3. v. a.* roll (*of motion in any direction*): **huc illuc volvens oculos.** — 1. roll (*on*): **propius aestus incendia volvunt; ad litora fluctūs.** — 2. roll down *or* over, throw headlong: **Simois corpora; magister volvitur.** — 3. roll up, roll uphill, toss; **fumum; saxum; venti mare; volvimur undis.** — 4. unroll (*of a scroll*), disclose, reveal, relate: **volvens fatorum arcana movebo; monumenta.** —

5. *Of regular revolution, etc.*, revolve, run round, roll round, run the round of, spin (*the thread of destiny*): **tot volvere casus** (run the round of); **sic volvere Parcas.** — 6. *Fig.* turn over *or* revolve (*in the mind*), ponder: **plurima per noctem.**

Pass. (*as middle*), roll, flow, glide, lie wallowing: **Eridanus; fundo volvuntur in imo.** — roll down, fall: **lacrimae.** — roll up, sweep: **flamma per culmina.** — roll round, revolve, run round: **volvendis mensibus; medio volvuntur sidera lapsu** (are gliding on).

Intrans. roll, revolve, roll by: **volventibus annis.**

vōmer, -eris, M. a ploughshare; ploughing.

vomō, -ere, -uī, -itum, *3. v. a. and n.* vomit, belch forth, send forth: **fumum.**

vorāgō, -inis [*voro*], F. an abyss, a whirlpool, a yawning chasm.

vorō, -āre, -āvī, -ātum, *1. v. a.* devour; swallow up, engulf.

vortex, *see* **vertex.**

vōsmet [*vos* + *emphatic particle -met*], *pron.* yourselves.

vōtum, *see* **voveō.**

voveō, -ēre, vōvī, vōtum, *2. v. a.* vow, devote, dedicate; pray for. — **vōtus, -a, -um,** *p.p. as adj.* vowed, votive. — N. *as subst.* **vōtum, -ī,** a vow; a prayer; a votive offering.

vōx, vōcis [*cf. voco*], F. a voice, the voice; a cry; a note, a tone, a sound; word *or* words, language, speech: **vox excidit ore** (these words, *etc.*) ; **prodere voce sua** (by his words) ; **rumpit vocem** (utter a voice, break silence) ; **compellat voce Menoeten** (aloud) ; **sic voce precatur** (with these words) ; **nostra voce** (from my lips).

vulnerō, *see* **volnerō.**

vulnus, *see* **volnus.**

vultus, *see* **voltus.**

Xanthus, -ī, M. 1. A river of the Troad (i. 473). — 2. A stream in Epirus (iii. 350). — 3. A river in Lycia, a favorite haunt of Apollo (iv. 143).

Zacynthos, -ī, F. an island in the Ionian sea, now Zante (iii. 270).

Zephyrus, -ī, M. Zephyrus (the west wind) ; wind.

LATIN WORD LIST

The words prescribed by the College Entrance
Examination Board for the third and fourth years
in Latin are given below

THIRD YEAR

1. abhorreō
2. accūsō
3. acerbus
4. adflīgō
5. adhūc
6. adimō
7. adipīscor
8. admoneō
9. adsequor
10. adsiduus
11. aedēs
12. aerārium
13. aeternus
14. agitō
15. agrestis
16. aiō
17. aliquandō
18. aliquot
19. āmēns
20. amō
21. anima
22. antequam

23. appetō
24. aptus
25. āra
26. ārdeō
27. argentum
28. argūmentum
29. ars
30. arx
31. atrōx
32. attendō
33. auferō
34. auris
35. auspicium
36. avāritia
37. avidus
38. avus
39. beātus
40. benevolentia
41. caelum
42. carcer
43. careō

44. cārus
45. caveō
46. celeber
47. celebrō
48. cēnsor
49. certāmen
50. certō, -āre
51. cervīx
52. cīvīlis
53. clārus
54. clēmēns
55. collēga
56. colō
57. colōnus
58. comes
59. comitātus
60. comitia
61. commendō
62. complector
63. conciliō
64. concitō
65. concordia

ENGLISH WORD LIST

The words prescribed by the College Entrance
Examination Board for the third and fourth years
in Latin are given below

THIRD YEAR

1. (shudder) shrink from
2. charge, accuse
3. bitter
4. strike down
5. up to here, so far, hitherto
6. take away, deprive
7. attain, obtain
8. remind, warn
9. attain
10. uninterrupted
11. temple; *plur.* house
12. treasury
13. everlasting
14. drive, pursue
15. rustic, boorish
16. say
17. at some time, at length
18. some
19. without mind, mad
20. love
21. breath, life, soul
22. (sooner than) before
23. strive after
24. fit, suitable
25. altar
26. blaze, glow
27. silver, money
28. proof
29. skill, art, theory
30. citadel
31. cruel, horrible
32. turn attention to, listen to
33. bear off
34. ear
35. auspices, omen
36. greed
37. eager, desirous
38. grandfather
39. blessed, happy, wealthy
40. good will, friendship
41. sky, heaven
42. prison
43. be without, do without
44. dear, beloved
45. beware
46. crowded, frequent, famous
47. crowd, make famous, celebrate
48. censor
49. contest
50. struggle
51. neck, head
52. belonging to a citizen
53. bright, illustrious
54. mild, merciful
55. colleague
56. cherish, worship
57. husbandman, settler
58. companion
59. retinue
60. elections
61. intrust
62. embrace
63. win over
64. arouse, excite
65. harmony, agreement

66. condō
67. coniūnx
68. cōnscientia
69. cōnsīderō
70. cōnstantia
71. cōnsulāris
72. cōnsulātus
73. cōnsultum
74. contentus
75. contingit
76. cōntiō
77. convīvium
78. corrumpō
79. creō
80. crēscō
81. crīmen
82. crūdēlis
83. cruentus
84. culpa
85. cūnctus
86. cūria
87. damnō
88. dēbilitō
89. decet
90. dēclārō
91. dēdecus
92. dēlectō
93. dēlictum
94. dēlūbrum
95. dēmēns
96. dēnique
97. dēnūntiō
98. dēprecor
99. dēsignō
100. dēsinō
101. dictitō

102. dīlēctus (dēlēctus)
103. dīligō
104. discō
105. discrīmen
106. dissimulō
107. diūturnus
108. dīvīnus
109. dīvitiae
110. doctrīna
111. domicilium
112. dominus
113. dōnō
114. dubius
115. dulcis
116. ecquis
117. egeō
118. equidem
119. ergā
120. ergō
121. errō
122. ērudiō
123. etenim
124. ēvertō
125. excelsus
126. exemplum
127. exigō
128. eximius
129. exitium
130. exsilium
131. exsistō
132. exstinguō
133. externus
134. exterus
135. facinus
136. fānum
137. fās

138. fateor
139. fātum
140. faveō
141. fax
142. fēlīx
143. fidēlis
144. fingō
145. flāgitium
146. flāgitō
147. flagrō
148. flamma
149. flectō
150. flōreō
151. foedus, -eris
152. formīdō, -inis
153. fortasse
154. forum
155. frequēns
156. frētus
157. frīgus
158. frūctus
159. fruor
160. furō
161. fūrtum
162. gaudeō
163. gradus
164. grātulātiō
165. grex
166. habitō
167. haereō
168. haud
169. hesternus
170. hīc (adv.)
171. hinc
172. hodiē
173. hodiernus
174. honestus
175. hūmānus
176. iaceō
177. idcircō

66. put together, found, hide
67. spouse, husband, wife
68. consciousness, conscience
69. consider
70. consistency, firmness
71. belonging to a consul, ex-consul
72. consulship
73. decree
74. satisfied
75. it happens
76. assembly
77. banquet
78. break, corrupt, bribe
79. make, elect
80. grow larger
81. decision, charge
82. cruel
83. bloodstained
84. blame, guilt
85. all together, entire
86. senate-house
87. condemn
88. weaken
89. it becomes, behooves
90. make clear
91. disgrace
92. give joy, delight
93. fault, crime
94. sacred place, shrine
95. without mind, unreasonable
96. finally, at last
97. announce, give warning
98. beg off
99. mark out, choose
100. cease, desist
101. keep saying

102. conscription, levy
103. pick, choose, love
104. learn
105. turning point, crisis, peril
106. dissemble
107. lasting, long-continued
108. of god, divine
109. riches, wealth
110. teaching, learning
111. residence
112. master
113. make a gift, present
114. doubtful
115. sweet, pleasant
116. any one at all
117. be in need, want
118. indeed
119. toward
120. therefore
121. wander, make a mistake
122. educate
123. and indeed, for
124. overturn
125. high, distinguished
126. sample, example
127. drive out, exact, collect
128. taken out, outstanding
129. destruction, ruin
130. banishment
131. come out, come into being
132. put out, quench
133. outside, foreign
134. outside, foreign
135. deed, crime
136. shrine
137. divine right, law

138. confess, admit
139. destiny, oracle
140. favor
141. torch, firebrand
142. lucky
143. faithful
144. mold, invent
145. outrage
146. demand
147. burn, flare
148. flame, fire
149. bend, turn
150. flourish
151. treaty
152. fear, panic
153. perchance, perhaps
154. market place
155. crowded
156. trusting, relying
157. cold, chill
158. produce, fruit, grain
159. enjoy
160. rave, rage
161. theft
162. rejoice
163. step, rank
164. congratulation
165. herd, crowd
166. occupy, dwell in
167. stick
168. not
169. of yesterday
170. here, at this point
171. hence
172. today
173. of today
174. honorable, respected
175. of man, kindly, cultured
176. lie (on the ground)
177. therefore

178. Īdūs
179. igitur
180. ignōminia

181. ignōscō
182. imāgō

183. immānis
184. immō
185. impendeō
186. improbus
187. inānis
188. index
189. indicō, -āre

190. industria
191. inertia
192. īnferī
193. īnfestus
194. ingenium
195. inlūstris
196. innocēns
197. īnsidior
198. intendō
199. interdum
200. intueor
201. invideō
202. invidia

203. īra
204. īrāscor
205. iterum
206. iūcundus
207. iūdex
208. iuventūs
209. Kalendae

210. lābor, lābī
211. lacrima
212. laetor
213. laetus
214. largior

215. lateō
216. latrō, -ōnis
217. latrōcinium

218. lēgō, -āre

219. legō, -ere
220. levō
221. libenter
222. liber, -brī
223. libīdō
224. locuplēs
225. longinquus
226. lūdus

227. lūgeō
228. lūmen
229. lūxuria
230. maeror
231. magister

232. manifestus

233. mānsuētūdō
234. meminī
235. -met
236. mīlitia
237. minae
238. minor, -ārī
239. misceō
240. misericordia

241. moenia
242. molestus

243. mōlior
244. monumentum

245. morbus
246. morior
247. mūnicipium
248. nauta
249. necessārius

250. necessitūdō
251. nefārius

252. nēquitia

253. nesciō

254. nex
255. nimis
256. nimius

257. Nōnae
258. notō
259. nūmen
260. nūper
261. nusquam
262. nūtus
263. obeō

264. oblīvīscor
265. obscūrus
266. obsecrō
267. occīdō
268. ōdī
269. ōmen
270. omittō
271. opīnor
272. optō
273. ōra
274. orbis
275. ōrnō
276. ōs, ōris
277. ōtium
278. pactum
279. paenitet

280. palam
281. parēns
282. pariēs
283. pariō

284. parricīda

178. Ides
179. therefore, thus
180. disgrace, degradation
181. not know, pardon
182. likeness, picture, portrait
183. huge
184. on the contrary
185. overhang, threaten
186. not upright, wicked
187. empty
188. witness, informer
189. point out, betray, reveal
190. application
191. idleness
192. the dead
193. hostile
194. inborn gift, talent
195. illustrious
196. guiltless, upright
197. lie in ambush, plot
198. stretch, strain
199. sometimes
200. gaze upon, admire
201. look upon, envy
202. envy, hatred, unpopularity
203. wrath
204. become (be) angry
205. again
206. pleasant, agreeable
207. judge, juror
208. youth
209. first day of the month
210. glide, slip
211. tear
212. rejoice
213. joyful
214. give abundantly, lavish, bribe

215. be hidden
216. highwayman, thief
217. robbery, band of robbers
218. appoint formally, send as envoy
219. pick, choose, read
220. make light, relieve
221. gladly
222. book
223. lust
224. wealthy
225. far off, at a distance
226. play, school; *plur.* games
227. mourn
228. light
229. extravagance
230. grief, mourning
231. master, teacher, helmsman
232. plain, visible, manifest
233. gentleness
234. remember, recall
235. self, own
236. military service
237. threats
238. threaten
239. mix, mingle, confuse
240. kindheartedness, clemency, pity
241. fortifications, walls
242. troublesome, annoying
243. put up, plot
244. (means of recalling) monument
245. sickness
246. die
247. free town
248. sailor
249. necessary

250. close relationship
251. unspeakable, criminal
252. worthlessness, shiftlessness
253. know not, be unaware
254. slaughter, murder
255. too much
256. exceedingly, excessive
257. Nones
258. mark
259. nod, divine will
260. newly, recently
261. nowhere
262. nod, command
263. go against, meet attend
264. forget
265. dark, concealed
266. implore
267. cut down, slay
268. hate
269. omen
270. leave out, pass by
271. believe, think
272. wish for, pray for
273. shore, district
274. circle
275. equip, adorn
276. mouth, face
277. leisure, peace
278. agreement
279. (it repents one) repent
280. openly
281. parent
282. wall (of a house)
283. bring forth, bear, gain
284. murderer (of a parent), traitor

285. parum
286. patefaciō
287. patientia

288. patria
289. peccō
290. penitus
291. perdō
292. perniciēs
293. pertimēscō
294. pestis

295. pius
296. plācō

297. plānus
298. plēnus
299. possideō
300. potius, potissimum

301. prae
302. praecipuus
303. praeclārus
304. praeditus
305. praedō
306. praetereō
307. praetermittō
308. praetor
309. praetūra
310. pretium
311. prīdem
312. prīvō
313. profectō
314. profiteor

315. proinde
316. proprius

317. prōsum

318. pudet

319. pudor

320. pulcher
321. pūniō
322. quaesō
323. quaestiō
324. quaestus
325. quālis
326. quamquam
327. quamvīs

328. quandō
329. quasi
330. querēla
331. quia
332. quiēscō

333. quisnam
334. quisquis
335. quīvīs

336. quoad

337. quondam

338. quot
339. quotiēns
340. recitō
341. recordor
342. rēctē
343. rēgnō
344. repetō

345. reprehendō
346. repudiō
347. requīrō
348. restō
349. reus
350. rōbur
351. ruō
352. sacer

353. sacerdōs
354. salvus
355. sānctus

356. sanguis
357. sānē
358. sānō
359. sapiēns
360. scelerātus
361. scelus
362. scīlicet

363. sēcernō
364. sedeō
365. sēdēs
366. sēmen
367. senectūs
368. senex
369. sepeliō
370. sermō
371. serviō
372. sevērus
373. sīca
374. sīn
375. sinō
376. societās
377. soleō

378. solvō

379. somnus
380. soror
381. sors
382. spīritus
383. splendor
384. spoliō
385. spolium
386. stabilis
387. strepitus
388. stultus
389. stuprum
390. suādeō
391. suffrāgium
392. sūmptus
393. supplex
394. supplicātiō
395. tabella

285. (too) little
286. make open, reveal
287. endurance, patience
288. one's country
289. injure, do wrong
290. deep within
291. ruin, destroy
292. destruction, ruin
293. become (be) afraid
294. plague, pestilence, ruin
295. dutiful, devoted
296. make pleasant, appease
297. level, plain
298. full
299. possess, acquire
300. rather, preferably; chiefly, especially
301. in front of
302. special, excellent
303. very bright, famous
304. equipped, endowed
305. pirate
306. pass by
307. pass by
308. prætor
309. prætorship
310. price
311. long ago
312. deprive
313. truly, in truth
314. say openly, profess, register
315. therefore
316. belonging to, characteristic
317. be advantageous, benefit
318. (it shames one) be ashamed
319. shame, modesty
320. beautiful
321. punish
322. beg, beseech
323. inquiry, trial, court
324. gain, profit
325. of what kind
326. although, and yet
327. however much, although
328. when
329. as if
330. complaint
331. because
332. come to rest, keep quiet
333. who indeed
334. whoever
335. anyone (you please)
336. (up to where) as long as
337. at some time, at last
338. how many
339. how often
340. read aloud
341. recall
342. rightly
343. be king, rule
344. seek back, demand, recollect
345. censure, blame
346. spurn, reject
347. demand
348. remain, be left
349. defendant
350. oak, strength
351. rush, dig
352. set apart, holy, cursed
353. priest
354. safe
355. sacred, holy
356. blood
357. truly, indeed
358. make healthy, cure
359. wise
360. criminal
361. crime
362. you may know, of course
363. set aside, separate
364. sit
365. seat
366. seed
367. old age
368. old man
369. bury
370. talk, conversation
371. serve
372. strict
373. dagger
374. but if
375. let, permit
376. fellowship, alliance
377. be wont, accustomed
378. untie, release, perform, pay
379. sleep
380. sister
381. lot, fate
382. breath, pride
383. brilliance
384. despoil
385. spoil
386. steadfast
387. noise, uproar
388. foolish
389. debauch
390. advise
391. ballot, vote
392. outlay, expense
393. bending, suppliant
394. thanksgiving
395. tablet, letters

396. tabula	412. testor	430. verbum
397. taceō	413. togātus	431. versus, -ūs
398. tālis		432. vērum (*conj.*)
399. tametsī	414. tolerō	433. vestīgium
400. tamquam	415. totiēns	434. vetō
401. tandem	416. tractō	435. vexō
402. tantum	417. triumphus	436. vidēlicet
403. tēctum	418. tunc	
404. temeritās	419. ulcīscor	437. vigilō
405. temperantia	420. urgeō	438. vīlla
406. templum	421. ūsitatus	439. vinculum
	422. usquam	440. vindicō
407. tenebrae	423. utinam	441. vīnum
408. tenuis	424. utrum	442. violō
409. terminus	425. varius	443. virgō
	426. vectīgal	444. vitium
410. testāmentum	427. vēndō	445. voluptās
411. testimōnium	428. venēnum	446. voveō
	429. venia	447. vultus

FOURTH YEAR

1. accendō	22. aptō	42. bibō
2. acuō	23. arceō	43. bōs
3. aēnus	24. arcus	44. bracchium
4. aequor	25. arduus	45. caecus
5. āēr	26. armentum	46. caeruleus
6. aethēr	27. arō	47. caleō
7. aevum	28. arrigō	48. candeō
8. agnōscō	29. artus, -ūs	49. canis
9. āla	30. arvum	50. canō
10. albus	31. asper	51. cānus
11. āles	32. astō	52. capillus
12. almus	33. astrum	53. carīna
13. altāria	34. āter	54. carmen
14. alternus	35. attonō	55. carpō
15. ambō	36. augurium	56. castus
16. amictus		57. caterva
17. amnis	37. aura	58. cavus
18. amplector	38. aurōra	59. celerō
19. anguis	39. aurum	60. celsus
20. antrum	40. avis	61. cervus
21. appāreō	41. axis	62. cessō

396. board, archive
397. keep still
398. of such kind
399. as if, although
400. as if, so to say
401. at length
402. so much, only
403. roof, building
404. rashness
405. self-control
406. sacred precinct, temple
407. darkness
408. thin, humble
409. boundary line, limit
410. last will
411. evidence, testimony

412. call to witness
413. dressed in the toga, civilian
414. bear, endure
415. so often
416. handle
417. a triumph
418. then, at that time
419. avenge, punish
420. press on, urge
421. common, customary
422. anywhere
423. would that
424. whether
425. different, diverse
426. tax, tribute
427. sell
428. poison
429. pardon, permission

430. word
431. line, verse
432. truly, but
433. track, trace
434. forbid
435. harass, plunder
436. you may see, of course
437. watch
438. farmhouse
439. bond, fetter
440. claim, punish
441. wine
442. ravish
443. maiden
444. fault, vice
445. pleasure
446. vow
447. face, countenance

FOURTH YEAR

1. kindle
2. sharpen
3. of copper, bronze
4. sea
5. air
6. upper air, sky
7. lifetime, age
8. recognize
9. wing
10. white
11. winged, bird
12. nourishing, kindly
13. altar
14. alternating, by turns
15. both
16. cloak
17. river
18. embrace
19. snake
20. cave, grotto
21. appear

22. fit to
23. confine, keep off
24. bow, arch
25. high, steep
26. cattle, herd
27. plough
28. raise up
29. joint, limbs
30. field
31. rough, harsh
32. stand near
33. star
34. black
35. thunder at
36. knowledge of augury
37. air, breeze
38. dawn
39. gold
40. bird
41. axle, axis

42. drink
43. ox, cow
44. arm (of body)
45. blind, dark, hidden
46. dark blue, green
47. be warm, glow
48. be white, glow
49. dog
50. sing
51. white, hoary
52. hair
53. keel
54. song
55. pluck
56. pure
57. crowd
58. hollow
59. hasten
60. high
61. stag
62. delay

63. ceu
64. chorus
65. cieō
66. cingō
67. cinis
68. citus
69. clipeus
70. cognōmen
71. collum
72. coma
73. comitor
74. compellō, -āre
75. cōnscius
76. cōnūbium
77. cor
78. corōna
79. coruscus
80. crātēr
81. crepō
82. crīnis
83. crista
84. cruor
85. crūs
86. culmen
87. -cumbō
88. cūnctor
89. cupīdō
90. currus
91. curvus
92. cuspis
93. -cutiō
94. daps
95. decōrus
96. decus
97. dēmum
98. dēns
99. dēnsus
100. digitus
101. dignor
102. dīrus
103. dīves
104. dīvus
105. dolus

106. domō
107. dōnec
108. dōnum
109. dūdum

110. duplex
111. ebur
112. ecce
113. edō, ēsse
114. ēn
115. ēnsis
116. epulae
117. ērigō
118. ēvādō
119. exsultō
120. extemplō
121. exuō
122. exuviae

123. faciēs

124. famulus
125. fatīgō
126. faux
127. fēmina
128. feriō
129. ferōx
130. ferveō
131. fīdus
132. flāvus
133. flō
134. flōs
135. fluctus
136. fluvius
137. fodiō
138. foedus, -a, -um
139. folium
140. fōns
141. for
142. foris
143. foveō
144. fraus
145. fremō

146. frēnum
147. fretum
148. frōns, -ndis
149. fulgeō
150. fulmen

151. fulvus
152. fūmus
153. fūnis
154. fūnus
155. furia
156. galea
157. gelidus
158. geminus
159. gemō
160. gener
161. genitor
162. genū
163. germānus
164. gignō
165. glomerō
166. gradior
167. grāmen
168. gremium
169. gurges
170. habēna
171. harēna
172. harundō
173. hasta
174. hauriō
175. herba
176. hērōs
177. heu
178. hiō
179. horreō
180. hospes
181. humus
182. hymenaeus
183. iaculum
184. ictus
185. ignārus
186. ignōtus
187. īlex

63. as, as if
64. dance, troop
65. move, stir up
66. gird, surround
67. ashes
68. swift
69. shield
70. surname
71. neck
72. hair, foliage
73. accompany
74. hail, address
75. conscious
76. marriage
77. heart
78. wreath
79. waving, flashing
80. mixing bowl
81. creak, rattle
82. hair
83. crest
84. gore
85. thigh, leg, shin
86. top
87. lie, lean
88. delay
89. desire
90. chariot
91. bent
92. spear point
93. shake
94. feast, banquet
95. becoming
96. beauty, ornament
97. at last
98. tooth
99. thick
100. finger, toe
101. deem worthy
102. fearful, cursed
103. rich
104. godlike, god
105. deceit, trickery

106. vanquish, subdue
107. until
108. gift
109. lately, for a long time
110. twofold
111. ivory
112. lo!
113. eat
114. lo!
115. sword
116. banquet
117. raise up
118. go out, escape
119. leap up, exult
120. forthwith
121. put off, lay aside
122. garment, armor, spoils
123. form, appearance, face
124. servant
125. wear out, tire
126. jaws, defile
127. woman
128. strike
129. wild, fierce
130. boil, glow
131. faithful
132. yellow
133. blow
134. flower, bloom
135. flood, billow
136. river
137. dig
138. foul
139. leaf
140. spring
141. speak
142. door
143. warm, cherish
144. fraud, deceit
145. mutter. roar

146. bit, bridle
147. strait
148. leaf, foliage
149. gleam, flash
150. lightning, thunderbolt
151. tawny
152. smoke
153. rope
154. funeral, death
155. rage
156. helmet
157. ice-cold
158. twin
159. groan, lament
160. son-in-law
161. begetter, parent
162. knee
163. own brother
164. beget
165. collect
166. step, walk
167. grass
168. lap, bosom
169. whirlpool
170. rein
171. sand
172. reed, arrow
173. spear
174. drink, drain
175. herb, grass
176. hero
177. alas
178. yawn, gape
179. bristle, shudder
180. guest, stranger
181. ground
182. wedding song
183. javelin
184. blow
185. not knowing
186. unknown
187. oak

188. imber
189. immineō
190. immittō
191. implicō
192. induō
193. ingēns
194. īnsignis

195. intrō, -āre
196. intus
197. iuvencus
198. iuvenis
199. iuventa
200. iūxtā
201. lacertus
202. lacus
203. laedō
204. laevus
205. latebra
206. laurus
207. laxō
208. lentus
209. leō
210. lētum
211. lēvis
212. lībō

213. līmen
214. lingua
215. liquidus
216. lōrīca
217. lūceō
218. luctor
219. lūcus
220. lūdō
221. lūna
222. lupus
223. lūstrō
224. mactō

225. macula
226. madeō
227. maestus

228. mānēs
229. marmor
230. membrum
231. memor

232. mēnsa
233. mergō
234. mēta

235. metior

236. micō
237. misereor
238. miseror
239. mītis
240. mōlēs
241. mollis
242. mōnstrum
243. morsus

244. mox
245. mūcrō
246. mūgiō
247. mulceō
248. nectō
249. nefās
250. nemus
251. nepōs

252. nēquīquam
253. nervus
254. nī
255. niger
256. nimbus
257. niteō
258. nītor, nītī
259. nix
260. nō
261. nōdus
262. nūbēs
263. nūbila
264. nympha
265. obstipēscō

266. obvius
267. ōcior
268. ōlim
269. opācus
270. ōrdior
271. orīgō
272. os, ossis
273. ōsculum
274. ovō
275. palleō
276. palma

277. pandō
278. pāscō
279. passim
280. pāstor
281. patera
282. paveō
283. pectus
284. pecus, -udis
285. pelagus
286. pellis
287. pendeō
288. penetrālis
289. penna (pinna)
290. pharetra
291. pignus
292. pingō
293. pinguis
294. pīnus
295. plausus
296. polus
297. pondus
298. pontus
299. porrigō
300. postis
301. praeceps
302. precor
303. prīncipium
304. prōgeniēs
305. prōlēs
306. prōnus
307. properō

188. rainstorm
189. threaten
190. send at, let go
191. enfold
192. put on
193. huge
194. marked, distinguished
195. enter
196. inside
197. bullock
198. young, young man
199. youth
200. close by
201. upper arm
202. lake
203. hurt, injure
204. left
205. hiding place
206. laurel
207. loosen
208. slow, pliant
209. lion
210. death
211. smooth
212. taste, sip, offer a libation
213. threshold
214. tongue, language
215. liquid, clear
216. corselet
217. gleam, shine
218. struggle, wrestle
219. grove
220. play
221. moon
222. wolf
223. purify, illumine
224. magnify, honor, sacrifice
225. spot, stain, disgrace
226. be dripping
227. sad

228. shades
229. marble
230. limb
231. mindful, remembering
232. table, dish
233. immerse, sink
234. boundary mark, limit, goal
235. measure out, distribute
236. dart, flash, gleam
237. pity
238. pity
239. kind
240. mass, pile, dike
241. soft, kind
242. warning, portent
243. bite, fluke (of anchor)
244. presently
245. sword point
246. low, bellow
247. stroke, soothe
248. bind
249. impiety
250. forest
251. grandson, descendant
252. in vain
253. sinew, string
254. if not
255. black
256. storm cloud
257. gleam
258. strive
259. snow
260. swim
261. knot
262. cloud
263. the clouds
264. nymph
265. be amazed

266. in the way of
267. swifter
268. formerly
269. shaded, dark
270. begin
271. origin, source
272. bone
273. kiss
274. rejoice
275. be pale
276. palm (tree and hand)
277. spread out
278. feed
279. here and there
280. herdsman
281. bowl
282. tremble with fear
283. breast
284. cattle
285. sea
286. skin, hide
287. hang, be suspended
288. innermost
289. feather
290. quiver
291. pledge, token
292. paint
293. fat, rich
294. pine tree
295. applause
296. pole, sky
297. weight
298. sea
299. reach forth, extend
300. doorpost
301. headlong
302. pray
303. beginning
304. lineage, offspring
305. offspring
306. stretched out
307. hasten

308. prōra
309. pūbēs
310. pulsō
311. pulvis
312. puppis
313. purpura
314. quatiō
315. rabiēs
316. radius
317. rādīx
318. rāmus
319. ratis
320. raucus
321. rēgīna
322. reor
323. retrō
324. rīdeō
325. rigeō
326. rīte
327. rōstrum
328. rota
329. rubeō
330. ruīna

331. rūpēs
332. sacrō
333. saeculum

334. saeviō
335. saevus
336. sal
337. saliō
338. saucius
339. scēptrum
340. scindō
341. scopulus
342. secō
343. secūris
344. secus (*adv.*)
345. sēgnis
346. sepulcrum
347. serēnus

348. serō; satus
349. serpō
350. sertum
351. sērus
352. siccus
353. sīdō
354. sīdus
355. signō
356. sileō
357. simulācrum
358. sinus
359. sistō

360. socer
361. solidus
362. sōlor
363. solum, -ī
364. sonō
365. sopor
366. spargō
367. spēlunca
368. spernō
369. spīculum
370. spīrō
371. spūma
372. stabulum
373. stāgnum
374. stella
375. sternō
376. stimulus
377. stirps
378. strīdeō
379. stringō
380. struō
381. stupeō
382. subitus
383. sublīmis
384. suēscō
385. sulcus
386. super
387. superbus
388. superī

389. surgō
390. suspendō
391. suspiciō, -ere

392. taeda
393. taurus
394. tellūs
395. tepeō
396. ter
397. texō
398. thalamus
399. tingō
400. tondeō
401. tonō
402. torqueō
403. torreō
404. torus
405. torvus
406. tremō
407. trepidus
408. trīstis
409. truncus
410. tumeō
411. tundō
412. turba
413. turbō, -inis
414. ūber (*subst.*)
415. ultor
416. ululō
417. umbra
418. umerus
419. umidus
420. uncus, -a, -um
421. unda
422. unguis
423. ūrō
424. vādō
425. vānus
426. vāstus
427. vātēs
428. -ve
429. vellō
430. vēlō

308. prow
309. youth
310. beat
311. dust
312. poop, stern
313. purple
314. shake
315. madness, frenzy
316. staff, ray
317. root
318. bough
319. raft, ship
320. roaring
321. queen
322. think
323. back, again
324. laugh
325. be stiff
326. duly
327. beak
328. wheel
329. be red
330. downfall, destruction
331. rock, cliff
332. make holy
333. generation, century, time
334. rage
335. fierce, savage
336. salt, sea
337. leap
338. wounded
339. staff
340. split, tear down
341. crag
342. cut
343. axe
344. otherwise
345. sluggish
346. tomb
347. bright, clear, peaceful

348. sow; born
349. creep
350. wreath
351. late, tardy
352. dry
353. settle
354. star, constellation
355. seal, mark
356. be silent
357. image, statue
358. bosom, bay, fold
359. make stand, stand still
360. father-in-law
361. whole, solid
362. comfort
363. soil, ground
364. make a sound
365. slumber
366. spatter, sprinkle
367. cave
368. reject
369. javelin
370. breathe
371. foam
372. stall, stable
373. pool
374. star
375. spread, lay low
376. goad, spur
377. root, trunk
378. shrill, hiss
379. draw tight, graze
380. pile up, build, plan
381. be dazed
382. sudden
383. lofty
384. become accustomed
385. furrow, track
386. over, above
387. overbearing
388. those above, the gods

389. rise up
390. hang
391. look from below, suspect
392. torch
393. bull
394. earth
395. be warm
396. thrice
397. weave, construct
398. bridal chamber
399. wet, dip
400. shear
401. thunder
402. twist, turn
403. roast
404. couch
405. grim
406. tremble
407. trembling
408. sad
409. stock, trunk
410. swell
411. lash, assail
412. crowd
413. whirlwind
414. udder, fertility
415. avenger
416. yell
417. shade
418. shoulder
419. moist
420. crooked, curved
421. wave
422. nail, claw
423. burn
424. walk, go
425. vain
426. huge, vast
427. seer, prophet
428. or
429. pluck
430. veil, cover

431. vēlōx
432. vēlum
433. velut
434. veneror
435. vēnor
436. verber

437. vertex
438. vicis
439. vinciō
440. virga
441. viridis
442. vīscus

443. vīsō
444. vitta
445. volō, -āre
446. volucer
447. volvō

The words prescribed by the New York State Syllabus in Latin for the third and fourth years, and not found in the College Entrance Examination Board list, are given below

THIRD YEAR

1. adulēscentia
2. āmentia
3. audācia
4. bellō
5. certē
6. colōnia
7. cōnfiteor
8. coniūrātiō
9. contingō
10. cūstōdia

11. dēcēdō
12. dēprehendō
13. dēsignātus
14. dīligentia
15. dissentiō
16. dolor
17. domesticus

18. exaudiō
19. excellō
20. expetō
21. exsultō
22. falsus
23. faucēs
24. fēlīcitās
25. furor
26. gravitās

27. iactō
28. illūstrō
29. immineō
30. immortālis
31. imperātor
32. incendium
33. incrēdibilis
34. īnferus
35. ingredior
36. innocentia
37. īnsignis

38. interitus
39. intersum

40. iūdicium
41. iussū
42. laetitia
43. līberālis

44. macula
45. mītis
46. nāvālis
47. nervus
48. nōminō
49. odium
50. ōrnāmentum

51. patrius

52. percipiō
53. perīculōsus
54. populāris

55. praeferō
56. prūdentia
57. quō (conj.)
58. redimō
59. rēgius
60. reprimō
61. retardō
62. scientia
63. secūris
64. sēnsus
65. sevēritās
66. stimulus
67. subiciō

68. trānsmittō
69. triumphō
70. turpitūdō
71. ūtilitās
72. varietās
73. veneror
74. verber
75. vīsō

431. swift
432. veil, sail
433. just as
434. revere
435. hunt
436. lash, stripes

437. top, whirl
438. turn
439. bind
440. twig, wand
441. green
442. entrails, vitals

443. look at, visit
444. ribbon, fillet
445. fly
446. winged
447. roll

The words prescribed by the New York State Syllabus in Latin for the third and fourth years, and not found in the College Entrance Examination Board list, are given below

THIRD YEAR

1. youth
2. insanity, madness
3. boldness
4. make war
5. surely, at least
6. colony
7. confess
8. conspiracy
9. happen
10. protection, custody, garrison
11. go away, die
12. seize, surprise
13. marked out, elect
14. carefulness
15. disagree
16. pain, grief
17. belonging to the house, inner
18. hear from a distance
19. surpass
20. ask for
21. leap up, exult
22. deceptive, false
23. jaws, defile
24. luck
25. rage, madness
26. weight, seriousness

27. throw about, boast
28. light up, honor
29. threaten
30. immortal
31. commander
32. conflagration
33. unbelievable
34. below
35. step into, begin
36. uprightness, honesty
37. marked, distinguished
38. destruction, death
39. be between, be of importance
40. judgment, trial
41. by order of
42. joyfulness, joy
43. of a freeman, gentlemanly
44. spot, stain, disgrace
45. kind
46. of a ship, naval
47. sinew, string
48. name
49. hate, hatred
50. adornment, equipment

51. belonging to a father, inherited
52. notice
53. dangerous, risky
54. of the people, popular, democratic
55. bear before, prefer
56. foresight, wisdom
57. that
58. ransom, redeem
59. of a king, royal
60. repress, check
61. keep back, delay
62. knowledge
63. axe
64. feeling
65. strictness
66. goad, spur
67. throw under, conquer
68. send across, cross
69. celebrate a triumph
70. baseness
71. usefulness
72. variety
73. revere
74. lash, stripes
75. look at, visit

FOURTH YEAR

1. aequō
2. agitō
3. amēns
4. anima
5. antequam
6. āra
7. arx
8. attonitus
9. auferō
10. aureus
11. certāmen
12. cervīx
13. complector
14. compōnō

15. concutiō
16. coniugium
17. corripiō
18. crīmen
19. cruentus
20. dēmittō
21. doleō
22. dominor
23. dūrus
24. equidem
25. ēruō
26. exanimus
27. excutiō
28. exsequor
29. fās
30. fātālis

31. fēlīx
32. ferreus
33. fessus
34. fīgō
35. flectō
36. fleō
37. flētus
38. fluō

39. fōrma
40. frangō
41. fundō
42. fūnis
43. gaudeō
44. gaudium
45. gemitus
46. grātus
47. gressus
48. haereō
49. haud
50. horridus
51. hospitium

52. immānis
53. immēnsus
54. inānis
55. incēdō
56. incumbō
57. īnferī
58. ingeminō
59. īnscius
60. intendō
61. invādō
62. īra
63. iuventūs
64. lābor
65. lacrimō
66. laetus
67. lateō
68. linquō
69. locō
70. longaevus
71. lūctus
72. lūgeō
73. magnanimus
74. memorō
75. minae
76. minor
77. mīrābilis

78. mōnstrō
79. namque
80. nefandus

81. nūbilus
82. nūmen
83. nūsquam
84. obruō
85. ōcius
86. ōmen
87. ostentō
88. pallēns
89. parcō
90. peragō

91. pergō
92. pietās
93. pius
94. placidus
95. prehendō
96. prōcumbō

97. prōmittō
98. prōtinus
99. rapidus
100. rapiō
101. reliquiae
102. rēmus
103. resīdō
104. resolvō
105. respiciō
106. rumpō
107. ruō
108. sacer

109. sacerdōs
110. sonitus
111. spolium
112. succurrō
113. tendō

FOURTH YEAR

1. make equal
2. drive, pursue
3. without mind, mad
4. breath, life, soul
5. (sooner than) before
6. altar
7. citadel
8. thunderstruck
9. bear off
10. golden
11. contest
12. neck, head
13. embrace
14. put together, put to rest
15. shake up, shatter
16. wedlock
17. snatch up, press on
18. decision, charge
19. bloodstained
20. let go down, depress
21. grieve
22. be master
23. hard, harsh
24. indeed
25. cast out, overthrow
26. breathless, lifeless
27. shake out
28. follow out, perform
29. divine right, law
30. death-dealing, destined
31. lucky
32. of iron
33. tired out
34. fasten
35. bend, turn
36. weep
37. weeping
38. flow
39. shape, beauty
40. break
41. pour out
42. rope
43. rejoice
44. joy
45. groan
46. pleasing, grateful
47. step, walk
48. stick
49. not
50. bristling, terrible
51. guest friendship, shelter
52. huge
53. unmeasured
54. empty
55. walk on
56. lean on, bend to
57. the dead
58. redouble
59. not knowing
60. stretch, strain
61. attack
62. wrath
63. youth
64. glide, slip
65. shed tears
66. joyful
67. be hidden
68. leave
69. place
70. long-lived
71. grief, mourning
72. mourn
73. high-spirited
74. recall, recount
75. threats
76. threaten
77. wonderful
78. point out
79. for indeed, for
80. unutterable, ac-cursed
81. cloudy
82. nod, divine will
83. nowhere
84. overwhelm
85. more swiftly
86. omen
87. display
88. pale
89. spare
90. drive through, ac-complish
91. continue
92. devotion
93. dutiful, devoted
94. quiet, serene
95. seize
96. fall forward, lie down
97. promise
98. at once
99. swift
100. seize
101. remnant
102. oar
103. settle back
104. untie
105. look back, regard
106. break
107. rush, dig
108. set apart, holy, cursed
109. priest
110. sound
111. spoil
112. run up, assist
113. stretch

114. terreō
115. testor
116. trabs
117. tumidus
118. turbidus

119. turbō
120. urgeō
121. ūsquam
122. validus
123. vehō
124. vestis

125. vetō
126. vīctus
127. vīsus
128. voveō

114. frighten
115. call to witness
116. beam
117. swelling, swollen
118. disturbed, turbulent

119. disturb
120. press on, urge
121. anywhere
122. strong
123. carry
124. cloth, garment

125. forbid
126. livelihood, food
127. sight
128. vow

𝕿𝖍𝖊 𝕬𝖙𝖍𝖊𝖓𝖆𝖚𝖒 𝕻𝖗𝖊𝖘𝖘

GINN AND COMPANY · PRO-
PRIETORS · BOSTON · U.S.A.

DATE DUE